OXFORD WORLD'S CLASSICS

PENDENNIS

WILLIAM MAKEPEACE THACKERAY was born in 1811 in Calcutta. In 1817 he was sent to England to be educated as a gentleman. From Charterhouse school, he went to Cambridge in 1829. His career at university was undistinguished, and led into an unsettled young-manhood. After false starts in the law, in art (which he studied in Paris) and journalism he compounded his misfortunes with an imprudent marriage in 1835. Tragically, his wife went mad five years later, leaving Thackeray with two young daughters to provide for. His first successes in authorship came with publications (of a largely satirical nature) in *Fraser's Magazine* and *Punch*. Triumph came with the publication of *Vanity Fair* (1847–8). This serialized novel promoted Thackeray to the rank of Dickens's principal rival in fiction. It was followed by the more autobiographical *Pendennis* (1848–50) and the historical *Henry Esmond* (1852), works which consolidated Thackeray's reputation without equalling the runaway popularity of his first full-length novel. Thackeray's energies flagged somewhat in the second half of his writing life. He lectured in America in 1852 and 1855; stood unsuccessfully for parliament as an Independent Liberal in 1857. His stature as a leading man of letters was confirmed in 1859, when he took over the editorship of the new *Cornhill Magazine* (a post he held until 1862). Thackeray's last years were his most prosperous. But since 1850 his health had never been good, and his writing suffered correspondingly. He died suddenly in December 1863.

JOHN SUTHERLAND is Lord Northcliffe Professor of Modern English Literature at University College London, and is the author of a number of books, including *Thackeray at Work*, *Victorian Novelists and Publishers*, and *Mrs Humphry Ward*. He has also edited *Vanity Fair*, *The Woman in White*, Trollope's *Early Short Stories*, *Late Short Stories*, and *The Way We Live Now* and written *Is Heathcliff a Murderer?* and *Can Jane Eyre Be Happy?* in Oxford World's Classics.

OXFORD WORLD'S CLASSICS

For almost 100 years Oxford World's Classics have brought readers closer to the world's great literature. Now with over 700 titles—from the 4,000-year-old myths of Mesopotamia to the twentieth century's greatest novels—the series makes available lesser-known as well as celebrated writing.

The pocket-sized hardbacks of the early years contained introductions by Virginia Woolf, T. S. Eliot, Graham Greene, and other literary figures which enriched the experience of reading. Today the series is recognized for its fine scholarship and reliability in texts that span world literature, drama and poetry, religion, philosophy and politics. Each edition includes perceptive commentary and essential background information to meet the changing needs of readers.

OXFORD WORLD'S CLASSICS

WILLIAM MAKEPEACE
THACKERAY

The History of Pendennis

His Fortunes and Misfortunes
His Friends and His Greatest Enemy

With Illustrations by the Author

Edited with an Introduction and Notes by
JOHN SUTHERLAND

Oxford New York
OXFORD UNIVERSITY PRESS

Oxford University Press, Great Clarendon Street, Oxford OX2 6DP

Oxford New York
Athens Auckland Bangkok Bogotá Buenos Aires Calcutta
Cape Town Chennai Dar es Salaam Delhi Florence Hong Kong Istanbul
Karachi Kuala Lumpur Madrid Melbourne Mexico City Mumbai
Nairobi Paris São Paulo Singapore Taipei Tokyo Toronto Warsaw
and associated companies in Berlin Ibadan

Oxford is a registered trade mark of Oxford University Press

First published as a World's Classics paperback 1994
Reissued as an Oxford World's Classics paperback 1999

British Library Cataloguing in Publication Data
Data available

Library of Congress Cataloging in Publication Data
Thackeray, William Makepeace, 1811–1863. Pendennis
The history of Pendennis: his fortunes and misfortunes, his friends and his greatest enemy / William Makepeace Thackeray; edited with an introduction by John Sutherland; with illustrations by the author.
p. cm.—(Oxford world's classics)
Includes bibliographical references (p.).
I. Sutherland, John, 1938– . II. Title. III. Series.
823'.8—dc20 PR5616.A2S87 1994 93–29775

ISBN 0–19–283959–4

1 3 5 7 9 10 8 6 4 2

Printed in Great Britain by
Cox & Wyman, Reading, Berkshire

CONTENTS

INTRODUCTION

WOULD success spoil Thackeray? It was a question much asked among the novelist's friends and admirers as he embarked on his new serial novel in November 1848. Edward FitzGerald was sure that now he was a literary lion 'Thack' would forget his comrades and his art would suffer. 'Success, coming late, has turned his head,' Thomas Babington Macaulay concluded as the early numbers of *Pendennis* emerged.[1] Carlyle—who had always had doubts about Thackeray's fibre—also feared that he was too 'weak' to resist the blandishments of the upper classes, whose darling he suddenly was. Carlyle (himself notoriously dyspeptic) was particularly apprehensive about the great dinners Thackeray was eating: satirists, like hunting dogs, should be kept hungry. The author of *Vanity Fair* was indeed dining well and riding high in 1848. He was, as he jubilantly told his mother, at the top of the tree with Dickens.[2] 'I reel from dinner party to dinner party—I wallow in turtle and swim in claret and Shampang' (*Letters*, ii. 535), he informed his new friend, Lady Blessington, at the same heady period.

Success had not come easily. Few writers have served as arduous an apprenticeship. Like Pendennis, his 'greatest enemy' over the hard years had been himself. Born with a decent-sized silver spoon in his mouth and a respectable pedigree, Thackeray idled away his educational advantages at public school and university. He squandered his second chance—a career in law. He was too easily distracted to succeed in that drudging line. His family supported him for a while as an art student, but although gifted Thackeray was not quite talented enough to make his way in the world as anything more than a witty car-

[1] Quoted by Gordon Ray, *Thackeray: The Age of Wisdom* (London, 1958), 48. Hereafter referred to as *AW*.

[2] *The Letters and Private Papers of William Makepeace Thackeray*, ed. G. N. Ray, 4 vols. (Cambridge, Mass., 1945–6), ii. 333. Hereafter referred to as *Letters*.

toonist. And even in this department, as he ruefully noted, he could not compete with his idol Cruikshank or his young protégé John Leech.

Thackeray lost much of his patrimony (originally around £20,000) through his fatal addiction to gambling and by speculation in unprofitable newspapers. Impoverished at 25, he wasted the remaining asset of the Thackeray name by marrying imprudently a wife with no dowry and an Irish background. The marriage progressed from imprudence to disaster when Isabella, having borne two surviving daughters, lost her reason. She was diagnosed as incurably mad and had to be incarcerated in 1845. In her asylum—entirely unconscious of the world—she survived her husband by thirty years.

Thackeray slaved for most of the 1830s in the anonymous ranks of journalism, 'writing for his life', earning himself a formidable reputation for literary savagery. It was here he met the originals of Shandon, Bludyer, Finucane, Wagg, and Warrington—the rogues, hacks, and occasional gentleman who made up the literary underworld, 'Bohemia' (as he was the first to call it). By 1840, Thackeray was a star in this dubious firmament. But money was always short and there was no guarantee that he might ever be anything more than the best of the hacks.

Around 1846, however, things began to go right for Thackeray. His connection with the new journal *Punch* was instrumental in this upward turn in his fortune. The magazine uniquely employed Thackeray's diverse abilities: cartoonist, journalist, raconteur, clubman, man of the world. He made a great hit with his serial, *The Snobs of England* (by 'one of themselves'—an endearing Thackerayan touch) which ran from February 1846 to February 1847 and reportedly raised circulation by 5,000. Thackeray gave the word 'snob' its complex modern meaning. English society was enabled to see itself in an entertaining, but by no means flattering, mirror. Bradbury and Evans, the publishers of *Punch* (and printers of Dickens), were encouraged to propose that Thackeray write a novel for them, provisionally conceived as 'Pen and Pencil Sketches of English Society'. It should be in the new Dickensian serial style of twenty monthly 'numbers', illustrated by Thackeray him-

self, and issued from the *Punch* office as a sister publication of the comic magazine. It was the first novel that Bradbury and Evans had published, and Thackeray's first full-size work. It would also be the first significant piece of writing to come out under Thackeray's own name, rather than a pseudonym. The result of this many-fronted experiment was *Vanity Fair* (January 1847–July 1848). After a slowish start, the serial attained sales that Thackeray (rather over-optimistically) claimed were equal to those of the Inimitable himself.[3]

In Dantean middle age Thackeray had made it, against all the odds. He was profoundly grateful and proclaimed himself a reformed character, resolving to forgo his bachelor clubman's life, and be a paterfamilias to his two motherless girls. On the strength of *Vanity Fair*'s popularity Bradbury and Evans went on to offer the magnificent sum of £2,000, sight unseen, for a new novel to run on from *Vanity Fair* almost without a break. Trained by his years on the magazines Thackeray was undaunted. He accepted the challenge and the money.

The Snobs of England and *Vanity Fair* had flayed national hypocrisy, the class system, the marriage market, and the 'ready money society'. Thackeray was, as Charlotte Brontë put it (to his great embarrassment), an 'eagle' in the power of his satire.[4] Over the centuries, Britain has developed a strategy for dealing with eagles. Rather than crush them—as tyrannies do—British society embraces its critics, makes much of them, co-opts them into the establishment. After writing the kind of plays that would have got him shot in Russia, Bernard Shaw discovered, to his astonishment, that England had installed him as a kind of unofficial bishop (and paid his satires as much attention as they did the sermons of their lords spiritual, GBS ruefully added).

Would Thackeray be co-opted by the world whose values

[3] Thackeray's sales as a serialist never amounted to even half of Dickens's. The subject is dealt with in Robert Patten, *Charles Dickens and his Publishers* (London, 1978), 229–30, and Peter Shillingsburg, *Pegasus in Harness* (Charlottesville, Va., 1992), 75–7.

[4] Charlotte Brontë delivered her eulogy of Thackeray as a Daniel come to judgement over Victorian society in the 2nd edn. of *Jane Eyre* (1847).

he satirized? He was conscious of the risk. Indeed, he accepted it as a challenge, and made it the theme of his new novel. *Pendennis*'s massive bulk pivots on a recurrent dilemma, depicted on the illustration for the cover. This cover exists in two published forms: that for the frontispiece of the two-volume book *Pendennis* (see pp. xliv–xlv of this edition) and that for the cover of the monthly serial (see p. xliii). The design is rich in its allusion. The origin is Reynolds's well-known painting, *Garrick between Tragedy and Comedy*. It has a clear reference to Thackeray's dilemma in November 1848. Was he to remain a 'serious' writer or let himself become a mere crowd pleaser?

What is prominent in Thackeray's reworking of this conventional topos is the eroticism he injects into it. On the one side of the Pen/Thackeray figure is the 'world' (mermaids, sexuality, Blanche, the major's selfish philosophy). On the other side is the home (wife, children, the church, Laura). The salient feature of the frontispiece version is that the young man at the centre is fascinatedly eyeing the siren's breasts, which clearly exert a stronger pull than her traditionally bewitching song. And he is clearly trying to break free from his mute, dull-looking wife (or fiancée). There are no children, only a glum little Victorian *putto*. The young rogue has, one feels, already committed the act of sexual betrayal in his mind. In the serial-cover version, the Pen/Thackeray figure is older by some years and now made of stronger stuff. He flinches away from the (less voluptuous) temptress, with a look of stern disgust on his face, and two children clamping his leg. Both he and his wife (no doubt now of her relationship) look worn down by life.

Vanity Fair had been panoramic in method, a sweeping picture of a whole society, seething like Frith's painting *Derby Day*. Ask who the hero(ine) is, and you come up with at least four candidates. *Pendennis* was to be narrower in its perspective. Thackeray intended his new novel to follow the moral and sentimental education of an *homme sensuel moyen* (as George Saintsbury puts it)—an average young man of normal sensibility. A new genre was to hand, called (though not by him) the *Bildungsroman*. Gordon Ray—Thackeray's partisan biographer—goes so far as to call *Pendennis* 'the first true *Bildungsroman* in English fiction'

(*AW* 110). Ray's claim is almost but not quite true. As its borrowed name implies, the genre originated in Europe with Goethe's 1774 bestseller *The Sorrows of Young Werther*. Following Goethe, the *Bildungsroman* typically depicted the growth, through suffering, love, experience of the world, and moral crisis, of a literary young man. Suicide or death from sheer hypersensitivity was a standard climax.

In Britain, the *Bildungsroman* was pioneered by two notable Germanophiles: Edward Bulwer-Lytton with *Ernest Maltravers* (1837) and G. H. Lewes, with *Ranthorpe* (1847). Thackeray detested Bulwer-Lytton (who was immensely regarded in his day) and had conducted a twelve-year-long satirical feud against him. By 1848 he had largely made his peace with the dandy 'barnet' although there are still some spiteful hits to be found in *Pendennis* (baronets—e.g. Sir Francis Clavering and Sir Derby Oaks—make a notably poor showing). On the other hand, Thackeray was very admiring of the author of *Ranthorpe*. Lewes was one of England's leading intellectuals and, more importantly, as a reviewer had hailed the author of *Vanity Fair* as 'the best writer in England'. Thackeray returned the compliment by reading *Ranthorpe* with respect. *Pendennis* has distinct resemblances to Lewes's novel. *Ranthorpe* narrates the growth of the young hero's literary mind as, like Pen, he makes the ingenuous errors of youth. Like Pen, Percy Ranthorpe makes a false professional start as a lawyer and goes on to write a best-selling work of literature. Like Pen again, Percy is torn between two women—the 'good' Isola (with whom he was brought up) and the worldly flirt, Florence. In his struggles, Percy is sustained by a manly friend, Wynton, who anticipates Warrington's role in *Pendennis*.[5]

Jerome Buckley, who has written a monograph on the *Bildungsroman*, claims that *Pendennis* does not belong to the genre, which properly got going in England only with *David Copperfield*[6] which started its serial run six months after *Pendennis*. It too has a young hero growing up, mak-

[5] For summaries of the novels mentioned here, and other Victorian *Bildungsromanen*, see J. Sutherland, *The Longman Companion to Victorian Fiction* (London, 1988).

[6] Jerome Buckley, *Season of Youth: The Bildungsroman from Dickens to Golding* (Cambridge, Mass., 1974), 29.

ing false starts in life, torn between two women, and finally succeeding with his pen. The main difference is that Dickens, always more egotistical than Thackeray, dispenses with the manly friend and replaces him with a false mentor, Steerforth. Buckley's objection to *Pendennis* is that, unlike Copperfield, Thackeray's hero does not develop organically, from inside—there is no real *Entwicklung*. Pen's maturity is gained mainly from the external accidents of fortune and illness. Buckley's objection is, I think, unfair, although it is hardly worth arguing the point as to whether *Pendennis* is a *Bildungsroman*, or merely the genre's principal precursor.

The *Bildungsroman* drifts naturally into autobiographical confession, the novelist's book of himself. On coming across *Pendennis* in later life Thackeray was heard to murmur, 'Yes, it is very like—it is certainly very like.' But how like? how much of his inner life, his 'secrets', *himself*, was Thackeray prepared to divulge to the Victorian reading public for 1*s*. an instalment? Reading *Pendennis* with some awareness of the author's personal background is to embark on a fascinating game of hide and seek. In broad outline, the lives of William Makepeace Thackeray and Arthur Pendennis run parallel. They have the same birthdate (1811). 'Grey Friars'—the school in which we first encounter the hero—is transparently Charterhouse, which Thackeray attended. 'Fairoaks', in the town of 'Clavering' is clearly identifiable as Larkbeare, Ottery St Mary, young Thackeray's family home in Devon from 1825. In addition to blissful summer holidays, adolescent William spent a year there (like Pen) being coached before going up to university in 1829. At St Boniface's College, 'Oxbridge', Arthur makes the same mistakes as did his exact contemporary at Trinity College, Cambridge. The two undergraduates slack at their studies, gamble away a large part of their small patrimonies, fall in with 'fast friends', and are ignominiously 'plucked'. Both are set by their disappointed guardians to read for the bar in London. Both drift more or less aimlessly into Bohemian journalism. Both eventually make their mark in the world with a hit novel.

In passing Thackeray introduced a host of his friends

and family into the novel, more or less recognizably. It was never unconscious. As for Helen Pendennis, 'she is my mother', he uncompromisingly declared (*Letters*, ii. 457). He did not mean his mother as she now was, in 1848–50, a crotchety lady in her late fifties, but the beautiful woman he recalled from his childhood. Significantly, Helen Pendennis is not allowed to grow old; she dies of an obscure heart complaint at 39, still sexually desirable and with the appearance of a 25-year-old (as the faded Madame Fribsby enviously notes). The Helen Pendennis character delves deep into Thackeray's feelings for his mother, and her background. The unhappy romance when Helen was 17 (narrated in the third number) alludes to a love catastrophe Thackeray's mother experienced at the same age. The young Anne Becher fell in love imprudently, and was falsely told by her family, who opposed the match, that her lover had died. The young man, persuaded it was for the best, went along with the deception. Anne dutifully married a man ten years older than herself and decently well-off. Later, as a married woman in India, she met at a party the young lover for whom she had mourned. After the fortuitous death of Thackeray's father three years later she at last married Henry Carmichael-Smyth, who was now rich enough to claim her hand. Although Thackeray got on very well with his stepfather he evidently felt that his mother had betrayed his father (and his father's son) by getting married again so soon to a man she had always loved better. In the novel he duly bestowed on her the name of the most famous adultress in literature.

It is not hard (indeed, Thackeray makes it all too easy) to identify other originals in the cast of *Pendennis*. Pen's adoptive 'sister' Laura is clearly modelled on the novelist's orphaned cousin, Mary Graham, who was taken into Mrs Carmichael-Smyth's house and brought up as William's adoptive sister. Originals can be found for many other relatives.[7] Beyond the family a whole gallery of the author's college, club, literary, and social acquaintance were decanted into the populous world of the novel. Some of Thackeray's depictions got him into hot water. Predict-

[7] See Gordon Ray, *The Buried Life* (London, 1952).

ably, for instance, the unkind depiction of 'Captain' Shandon (i.e. William Maginn, an early patron of Thackeray's) roused Hibernian ire. The affectionate, but cruelly condescending, portrait of Henry Foker went down badly with its original, and allegedly got Thackeray blackballed from the Traveller's Club. One cannot imagine that Alexis Soyer put too much care into dishes for Thackeray at the Reform Club, after reading the hilarious version of himself as 'Mirobolant'.

Pendennis is certainly 'very like' in all sorts of ways. But Thackeray took precautions against too exact a Pen-portrait—particularly where he himself was concerned. Pen is physically unlike his author: small ('dumpy' as his enemies say), soft-skinned, dandyish, exquisite. The author of *Pendennis* was described (only too aptly) as a 'mountain of blubber' (*AW* 77) and looked much older than his 37 years. As a young man, he was hairy, massive, short-sighted, shambling, and broken-nosed. There were other, more complex, factors clouding the self-portrait. Thackeray did not really believe that novels (particularly Victorian novels) could, or should, tell the whole truth about a man's growing up. Thackeray outlines his reservations playfully in the digressive Chapter 41 ('Contains a Novel Incident'), where Pendennis and Warrington have a 'philosophical conversation' on the publishability of the younger man's autobiographical romance, 'Leaves from the Lifebook of Walter Lorraine'. It is significant that although Pen is quite prepared to take his adolescent love experiences to market in the form of a fashionable novel, Warrington would never do such a thing with his more Zolaesque marital history. 'Bluebeard' only divulges his past *in extremis*, to a select company gathered round the deathbed of Helen Pendennis. Nothing less would drag the story from him. He never mentions it again thereafter, even to his *fidus Achates*, Pen.

Famously, Thackeray prefaces his novel with a statement which stakes out in the most forthright fashion the limitations of the Victorian novel:

> Since the author of Tom Jones was buried, no writer of fiction among us has been permitted to depict to his utmost power a MAN. We must drape him, and give him a certain conventional

simper. Society will not tolerate the Natural in our Art. Many ladies have remonstrated and subscribers left me because, in the course of the story, I described a young man resisting and affected by temptation.

Thackeray protests so feelingly about the restraint imposed on the Victorian novelist in matters of sex that one hesitates to contradict him. This preface is routinely cited as the authoritative description of the hobbled condition of the mid-Victorian novelist. As such, it is familiar to many who have never read *Pendennis*. But one should beware of taking Thackeray at his word when he lays down the law like this. The preface contains some very dubious protestations (such as the 'very precise plan' which he alleges himself to have had when he started). While nodding agreement with Thackeray's prefatorial complaint ('Tom Jones, quite right, impossible in 1848, skirts round piano legs') one can forget that this novel displays on its cover the picture of a man ogling a woman's breast. It is not a cover one could have got away with on a paperback until quite recently and taken with the mock servility of the preface it is an astonishing piece of effrontery. The attentive reader will find plenty more sexual 'frankness' lurking in the edges and crevices of Thackeray's narrative.

Rather than being decoyed by Thackeray's general complaints about inhibition one should, I think, register the remark 'Many ladies have remonstrated' which rings much truer. Who were these 'ladies' and why might they have been offended? Three, at least, can be guessed at: Thackeray's mother, his best friend's wife Jane Brookfield, and his 'sister', Mary Graham. How might they have read the novel, in which they were made—unwillingly—to play parts? Close reading suggests that for all his remarks about the impossibility of 'frankness' Thackeray, if we attend to his artful hints and coded language, penetrated much further into Arthur Pendennis's sexual privacies than did Fielding into Tom Jones's.

Foremost among the remonstrating ladies must have been the novelist's mother, 'Mrs Pendennis'. Despite the novel's studied genuflection to the 'sainted' Helen there was constant friction between her real-life original and William Thackeray. By the 1840s, he found his mother

('Mater Dolorosa' as he called her) humourless and tyrannically religious. Thackeray introduces tellingly subversive touches into his ostensibly adulatory depiction of Helen. In the early chapters, for instance, he makes it clear by a deft parenthesis (see p. 993) that she is well aware of the Reverend Smirke's passion for her, and is indeed encouraging it. As a fanatic evangelical, Mrs Carmichael-Smyth would have been appalled by the implication that she could lead a clergyman into sexual temptation.

Then there is Thackeray's much quoted aside on the attentiveness with which Helen broods over her son's affairs of the heart. 'I have no doubt', the narrator observes, 'there is a sexual jealousy on the mother's part, and a secret pang' (p. 298). This insight into the illicit desires of mothers is taken up again in number 17, when Helen comes to take up her rightful place by her son's sickbed, evicting Fanny in the process. She is convinced, of course, that the little trollop has slept with her son and murderously flings the first stone with all the force that a good woman's arm can muster. We infer, however, that Helen's punitiveness is inspired less by moral affront than the secret desire to possess her son sexually herself. Having exiled the poor servant girl (who saved Pen's life) to the gutter outside the house, Helen posts herself by Arthur's bed, less a nurse than a virtuous dragon, 'with her Bible in her lap, without which she never travelled' (p. 658). The holy book is significant, but so is the part of the body it is covering.

As it happened, servants were very much to the point where Thackeray's relations with his mother were concerned. There had been friction between Mrs Carmichael-Smyth and her son on the question of the governesses whom he employed for his daughters after he set up as a paterfamilias in Kensington, in 1846. Educational questions aside, Mrs Carmichael-Smyth could not be persuaded that her son did not have sexual designs on these ladies—even when they had been deliberately chosen (as Victorian servants were often chosen) for their unaphrodisiac plainness. By an odd coincidence, a reckless review of *Jane Eyre* exacerbated Mrs Carmichael-Smyth's suspicions. In the *Quarterly Review* for December 1848

Elizabeth Rigby put into general circulation the rumour that the pseudonymous 'Currer Bell' (a name with a meaningful echo of 'Laura Bell') was once herself a governess in Thackeray's household and had conceived the character of Mr Rochester as revenge against her employer and seducer (it was implied). A 'surreptitious family' was invented to embellish the rumour—which, in the usual way of things, swept round London like wild-fire. Preposterous as it was, the *Quarterly*'s canard touched a very sensitive area of his private life. For, like the gothic master of Thornfield Hall, Thackeray did indeed have a mad wife locked away. Not, it should be said, in the attic of his house in Young Street, but in a nursing home at Camberwell.

Thackeray felt immensely guilty at having committed his wife. This guilt surfaces time and again in *Pendennis*, with its recurrent allusion to the Bluebeard fable. Perrault's fairy story had a bitter relevance for Thackeray. Bluebeard, it will be recalled, is the oversexed domestic ogre who kills his wives when he tires of them, and locks their bodies in a secret chamber of his house. In the person of Warrington (nicknamed 'Bluebeard'—ostensibly for his facial stubble) Thackeray elaborates the wife-killer allusion in complex ways. What Pen's manly friend discloses in the dusk of Helen's dying moments is that he has a wife whom he has disposed of—not by murder, or incarceration in the attic, but by bribery and the surrender of his prospects in life. It is something none of them, not even Pen who lives with Warrington, knew. And because of the shameful fact of having a wife who must be kept from the world's eye 'stunning Warrington' can never use his talents. He is doomed, forever, to be a 'hack'.

When Thackeray said *Pendennis* was very like, there was more than one version of himself that he was thinking of. No more than Warrington did he want to remain a mere 'writer' all his life—his contempt for the profession is expressed in the creation of parasitic vermin like Wagg, bruisers like Bludyer (who slashes a book he has barely read, then sells the review copy for his supper), alcoholic impostors like Shandon with his preposterous *Pall Mall Gazette* ('written by gentlemen for gentlemen') composed

in debtors' prison. Thackeray's distaste for the writing 'trade' is expressed in George Warrington's haughty conviction that, as a gentleman (he is the third son of a baronet), he has descended to sewer level. 'I don't tell the world . . . that George Warrington writes for bread' he declares, with a blush (p. 394). Thackeray's own contempt for the writing trade was recklessly uttered in the narrator's remark at the end of Chapter 34 of *Pendennis*: 'there are no race of people who talk about books, or, perhaps, who read books, so little as literary men'. This slander sparked off a bitter feud with Dickens and his followers.

Thackeray later conceded that he had gone too far, but the 'no race of people' passage none the less expressed his own career frustration. In the novel 'literature' is merely a stepping-stone for Pen who, we guess, is clearly destined for a career in parliament. Warrington, shackled to Mrs Bluebeard, can never enter public life—not even to the extent of signing his brilliant articles. How, Thackeray must have wondered, could he, similarly shackled, rise in the world and expose himself to the brutality of the election crowd?[8] 'Warrington's the man' wrote one reviewer, demanding more of Bluebeard's story. Thackeray did not, however, make Warrington the hero of a sequel (although his ancestors figure as the heroes of *Henry Esmond* and *The Virginians*). Nor, if one calculates, does Bluebeard make much of a presence in *Pendennis* itself, appearing centrally as he does in only three or four chapters and two of the novel's full-page illustrations. None the less, Warrington dominates *Pendennis*. It is his cruel dilemma that lingers in the reader's mind. He is a cleverer writer than Pen and more 'honest' (the point is made at Oxbridge that Pen is not above telling lies). Warrington's morals are less flexible (he would never sell himself to Blanche for a seat in Parliament). Above all, he is more sexually potent (the bristly blue beard, in conjunction with the silky locks of the prematurely balding Pen make the point clearly enough). Warrington is the bigger man—but he can never have the woman he loves, the novel's great

[8] Thackeray did, in 1857, stand as MP for Oxford, unsuccessfully (he lost because the Nonconformist vote went against him).

sexual prize. Laura goes to a lesser, and unworthy, fellow.

In order to understand how Thackeray came to create Warrington and his predicament, one should turn to the second of our supposedly offended ladies, Jane Brookfield. Thackeray's involvement with Mrs Brookfield became a major emotional crisis (and potentially a scandal) during the composition of *Pendennis*. This intimate department of Thackeray's life, although it was freely gossiped about, was only officially disclosed (and then with tantalizing gaps) in 1958, with the second part of G. N. Ray's pioneering biography of the novelist. Thackeray had known William Brookfield, Jane's husband, since their university days together. In the early years of their friendship Brookfield (two years older) was more dominant. Thackeray did not cut quite the dash at Cambridge that 'Pendennis of Boniface' may suggest and Brookfield was reckoned to be the more brilliant of the two. Brookfield was also 'faster' than Thackeray—with the moral dangers the term hints at in *Pendennis*. One of the things one knows about Brookfield, for instance, is that he had an opium habit which worried his college friends. Tennyson wrote him a stern letter while they were undergraduates together, urging him to give up the drug. When they left Cambridge (Brookfield with more distinction than Thackeray) the young men remained bosom friends. Sexual morals were notoriously lax at university, where prostitution was regarded as a necessary and controllable evil by the authorities. They were even laxer in London. As bachelors around town Brookfield and Thackeray evidently continued their roistering. There is a record, in 1833, of the two young men going off to 'a divan [i.e. smoking room] where a female—of course naked—danced for them'.[9] It is in 1833 in the novel that Pen and Warrington undertake their 'wild nights of carouse'. But Thackeray—protesting too much, we may think—insists that these 'nights were not so wicked as such nights sometimes are' (p. 378). Elsewhere the narrator reiterates that these 'bachelor nights' (whose pleasures are never exactly described) were passed 'in joviality, not vice' (p. 370). The line may have been a fine one. We know that Thackeray contracted venereal disease at some point in his early

[9] Peter Levi, *Tennyson* (London, 1993), 103.

life—perhaps at Cambridge, perhaps in Paris, probably in London.

Having sown their wild oats as profusely as even Major Pendennis would have allowed, Brookfield and Thackeray settled down to the business of life. Brookfield took orders in 1834, and served in a succession of low-paying curacies round the country. Both men married early. Thackeray's main motive for doing so, as his correspondence and diaries make clear, was to find a morally acceptable outlet for his exuberant sexual desires. Blinded by this need, he chose badly. Presumably Brookfield had the same prophylactic motive. He proposed to Jane Elton and they married in 1841. Brookfield was now a curate at St James's, Piccadilly, with a meagre £190 a year. Now that he was in London, he and Thackeray again saw much of each other. Brookfield had clearly drawn a better ticket in the marriage stakes. Jane Elton was beautiful, high-born, and twelve years younger than her husband. She was well-educated (unlike Thackeray's Isabella), emotionally stable, and socially assured. (In later life, Jane Brookfield ran a famous literary salon, and herself wrote novels.) From the first, Jane was a wife to be proud of and the ornament of her husband's household.

Despite this advantage, Brookfield did not prosper. He failed to get preferments (a lingering taint of 'looseness' hung about him). At a period of fanaticism in the Church of England, he had no powerful religious sentiments. There were no children, which was distressing and unmanning. Brookfield finally became an Inspector of Schools in early 1848. It was a step in life, but by no means a great one. The original relationship of the friends was reversed. Thackeray was now the swell, dining at Holland House and hobnobbing with grandees. Thackeray had always admired Jane. In early 1848 admiration became passion. He was, as he had been in his pre-marital days, denied a decent outlet for his carnal needs and turned, irresistibly, to his best friend's wife. But Thackeray, of course, was not free to love, even a woman free (as Jane was not) to reciprocate. When Isabella first showed suicidal tendencies, Thackeray was obliged to sleep with a cord tied round their waists, so that she would not wake and try to

kill herself (as she once did in 1840). That cord was an emblem of his bondage, even now that they would for ever sleep in separate beds. The key sentence in *Pendennis* is uttered by Foker: '[A man] may marry, and find he likes somebody else better' (p. 583). Thackeray had certainly found someone that he liked better than his poor Isabella, locked up in her padded room in Camberwell.

In the last days of October 1848, while he was working on the opening of *Pendennis*, Thackeray and Jane spent a few nights together at Clevedon Court, her family's stately home. Brookfield was away on business. As Catherine Peters reconstructs the episode, 'Jane seems to have encouraged Thackeray's devotion to her by cautiously hinting that her marriage was unhappy . . . and something occurred—probably no more than an intimate conversation and a chaste embrace—which was a turning-point in Thackeray's feeling for her.'[10] As a result of this 'something' they reached what Ray calls 'the Clevedon understanding'—the essence of which was that Thackeray might be free to adore Jane but he must never touch her. It was a recipe for trouble. Liberated by the agreement, Thackeray wrote Jane long love letters in French (they have a distinct flavour of Blanche's *Mes soupirs* about them). William Brookfield was apparently kept informed of everything.

As Thackeray later recalled, the first part of the book was written in the after-glow of 'Clevedon in '48'. On 18 December 1848 (while he was writing the third number) he told Jane 'we will love each other', and that he thinks about her 'always'. He apparently sublimated his sexual desire by eliding it with filial and paternal love—an extraordinarily dangerous thing to do, emotionally. 'When I think about you or my mother or my children (I ought to think more about those 2 dear little women) a natural Grace follows and I say God pardon me and make me pure' (*Letters*, ii. 471). Injudiciously Thackeray confided his passion to Mrs Carmichael-Smyth. 'My mother, dear good woman that she is, loves you', he told Jane a few days after the 'Clevedon understanding' (*Letters*, ii. 453). One may doubt this. Mrs Carmichael-Smyth was too

[10] Catherine Peters, *Thackeray's Universe* (London, 1987), 184.

steeped in evangelicalism to approve such dangerous meddling with marriage vows (Thackeray's no less than the Brookfields'—he was still a married man in the eyes of God and his mother). But the confession to his mother explains the illustrated ('Poor Pen') episode in Chapter 8 where Pen throws himself on to his mother's breast with the agonized exclamation 'O mother! I love her, I love her!' In the novel Helen is melted and gives up her opposition to the disastrous match with Emily Fotheringay. Did Thackeray hope that his mother would sanction his near-adulterous affair with Jane?

Not everyone at Clevedon was understanding. On 2 January 1849 Harry Hallam, Jane's young cousin, bluntly told Thackeray to keep away from Jane. Thackeray protested to Jane: 'I see no shame in owning that I love you. I have William's permission, your's, that of my own heart . . . Who has a right to forbid me my great happiness?' (*Letters*, ii. 493). In late June there was a further shock, when Thackeray learnt that Jane was pregnant. He had apparently suppressed any thought of continuing sexual relations between the Brookfields. Since Jane was only a few weeks pregnant in June, the information may well have been intended as another warning.

On learning of Jane's condition, Thackeray flung off to France (the 'Incontinent', as he once called it). He had begun the novel in excellent health, but stress was beginning to tell on him. In mid-September, he contracted a fever, which almost killed him. Publication of the novel had to be suspended for three months. In *Pendennis* the hero also suffers a fever in late summer which almost kills him. Thackeray's ailment (though there was never a certain diagnosis) was probably cholera which was then at epidemic levels in London. It is slightly different in the novel. Pendennis, we are told, falls into his fever from his superhuman efforts to conquer his lust for Fanny Bolton—a struggle which brings him to death's door. Thackeray, one guesses, suspected that his own fever was at least partly the consequence of the emotional strain of the last nine months.

The confinement was difficult for Thackeray, who for long periods was exiled from Jane's presence and excluded

from her thoughts. When a daughter was born in February 1850 Brookfield, with incredible insensitivity, chose to call her 'Magdalene'. It may have been a tribute to the prostitute rescue missions that were springing up all over London. It may also have been an oblique rebuke to his 'unfaithful' wife. As Catherine Peters deduces, the shock of the pregnancy 'forced Thackeray to face the sexual content of his love for Jane. From this point the eventual explosion became inevitable' (p. 185). The final rupture between Thackeray and the Brookfields did not, in the event, take place until 1851, well after the end of *Pendennis*. The whole novel, however, was conceived in a state of what Gordon Ray aptly calls 'longing passion unfulfilled'.

The third lady who might well have been offended by *Pendennis* was Thackeray's 'sister', Mary Graham (later Mrs Charles Carmichael). Mary's early background is exactly reflected in Laura Bell's. Mary (Thackeray's cousin, on his mother's side) was left an orphan aged 5 and brought up as Thackeray's sister at Larkbeare. It was a sexually confused relationship (cousins may marry, siblings may not). We are told in Chapter 3 that Helen 'had made up her mind that he was to marry little Laura, who would be eighteen when Pen was twenty-six' (p. 36). Perhaps Mrs Carmichael-Smyth had nursed some such scheme. The relationship between the young people during their formative years is sketchy, but seems to have been fond. They fell out badly, however, after Thackeray's marriage. None the less, Mary helped Thackeray nurse his wife in her pregnancies and looked after the children in the early years of Isabella's illness. She also helped out Thackeray in his financial difficulties, standing bond for him in 1839 and giving him £500 in 1841 (a generosity directly echoed in *Pendennis*). Mary married in 1841, and as a married woman acted as Thackeray's housekeeper in 1842. As Ray tells us, this 'gave rise to much friction'. In 1846 the Carmichaels were in dispute with Thackeray's parents over money. Thereafter—although she lived until 1871—Mary does not figure in the biographical account.

One thing is clear, Thackeray fell out with Mary in the 1840s. Why? Like Laura, Mary may have taken a censorious line on her 'brother's' profligacy. At points in

Pendennis, Laura's sisterly advice takes on a distinctly shrewish tone which seems strangely out of character (e.g. 'Go and work; go and mend, dear Arthur, for I see your faults', pp. 347–8). In these circumstances, why put Mary (a married woman in 1848) so recognizably at the centre of his novel as the purest, most desirable of maidens? Why lavish so much eulogy on her as his 'sainted heroine'. Above all, why call her 'Laura Bell' when this was the working name of a well-known courtesan famous as 'the Queen of London whoredom'. It was equivalent to calling a character in a novel of 1963 'Mandy Rice Davies'. Richard Altick suggests an unconscious motive.[11] But Thackeray was a man of the world, and no one was better at the 'science of names' (as Henry James called it). Almost any page of *Pendennis* will turn up a gem: the Marquis of Steyne (corrupt nobleman), the Reverend Otto Rose (scented clergyman), the Reverend Felix Rabbits (a clergyman with a bundle of children), Miss Kewsy (the betrothed of a barrister who hopes to rise in the world). Even principal characters have loaded names: Pen redeems himself by the pen ('Arthur' also implies quest); Blanche Amory is 'amoral' (and empty, or blank); Helen, as we have said, is rather tepid towards her Menelaus. It boggles the mind to think that Thackeray didn't know what he was doing when he applied the name Laura Bell to his sainted heroine. But what, one asks again, *was* he doing? Probably one has to accept that biographical explanation—for all the exhilarating sense of secret doors being opened—can only take us so far.

As he wrote *Pendennis* Thackeray was acutely aware of a split between his private and public selves. Privately, over 1848–50, he was racked with sexual and moral crises, the details of which he had to keep to himself. Publicly he was, as he said (ironically relishing the Carlylean terminology), 'a great man'. He had two selves, apparently incompatible, could he combine them in his new work? There is a remark in the last double number which seems to me crucial

[11] Richard Altick, *The Presence of the Present* (Columbus, Ohio, 1991), 540.

in understanding the novel: 'could we know the man's feelings as well as the author's thoughts—how interesting most books would be!' (p. 911). *Pendennis* is interesting for just that double revelation. Beneath the authorial design—the 'literature'—the man's feelings are constantly erupting. Sometimes they boil over into excesses of emotionalism, sentimentalism, apparently irrelevant savagery, and—it must be admitted—bad writing. But for most of its immense length *Pendennis* sustains a fascinating tension between the private sources of fiction and its public forms.

John Carey, in his stimulating study *Thackeray: Prodigal Genius*, entitles his chapter on *Pendennis* 'What Went Wrong?' A lot, according to Carey; most of it originating in Thackeray's disastrous willingness, after *Vanity Fair*, to make his books 'more complaisant'. In other words, he sold out, as his friends feared he would. No one (least of all Thackeray) would deny that *Pendennis* has its structural weaknesses, its *longueurs*, and (his word) 'stupidity'. But Carey draws too firm a line under Thackeray's first major novel for many readers and is too willing to discard everything that followed. It seems more useful to ask the question 'What went right?' A lot, loyal Thackerayans would maintain, and a lot of different things. More than *Vanity Fair*, *Pendennis* reverts to the condition of the Victorian miscellany and one could select a hundred incidental felicities to recommend. But two qualities above all mark an advance in Thackeray's art: his control of comic effect, and his subtle, but pervasive, responsiveness to history.

One encounters a new vein of Thackerayan humour in this novel—mellower, less forced—which the author was to cultivate over the rest of his writing career. *Pendennis* is the first of his novels which can truly be called a conversation ('a sort of confidential talk between writer and reader', as the preface puts it). At times, as in the happiest of conversations, things got heated (in the 'Dignity of Literature' or the 'No Irish Need Apply' spats, for example). Thackeray has a harsh edge to his tongue and a caricaturist's sharpness which can draw blood. At other times, Thackeray's conversation modulated into 'philosophic' meditation, a kind of abstracted talking to himself, or thinking aloud. The author was later to refine

the practice into that most characteristic Thackerayan genre, the 'Roundabout Papers' (see, for instance, the much-quoted 'How lonely we are in the world' meditation, pp. 183–4).

Pendennis is, above all, a deliciously funny book. Take, as one example among hundreds, the scene in which Pen—in the pit of Wertherian despair—informs his uncle, on whom he has made an unexpected morning call, that he has been 'plucked':

> The major had heard of plucking, but in a very vague and cursory way, and concluded that it was a ceremony performed corporally upon rebellious University youth. 'I wonder you can look me in the face after such a disgrace, sir,' he said; 'I wonder you submitted to it as a gentleman.'
>
> 'I couldn't help it, sir. I did my classical papers well enough: it was those infernal mathematics, which I have always neglected.'
>
> 'Was it—was it done in public, sir?' the major said.
>
> 'What?'
>
> 'The—the plucking?' asked the guardian, looking Pen anxiously in the face.
>
> Pen perceived the error under which his guardian was labouring, and in the midst of his misery the blunder caused the poor wretch a faint smile, and served to bring the conversation down from the tragedy-key. (pp. 244–5)

Pen's response reflects the Thackerayan tone of the novel. He smiles ruefully, he does not sneer at the old snob's ignorance.

The other department in which *Pendennis* marks a significant advance is in the complexity off its historical resonance. The narrative's twenty-year sweep covers the period in which Hanoverian England modulated into Victorianism. It was a slow and intricate process of cultural change involving the rise to power of the middle classes, imperialism, industrialization, and introjection on a massive scale of the values of the evangelical revival. In the first chapter of the novel, Major Pendennis, simulacrum of the Great Duke and Regency dandy, is very much at home in England. By number 22, history has moved him well to the side-lines. Where have all the *gentlemen* gone he wonders? 'The breed is gone—there's no use for 'em; they're replaced by a parcel of damned cotton-spinners

and utilitarians, and young sprigs of parsons with their hair combed down their backs. I'm getting old: they're getting past me' (p. 872). The major's first trip down to Fairoaks from London in Chapter 7 is by stage-coach (the misnamed 'Alacrity'). The major's final trip down to Fairoaks is by courtesy of the Great Western Railway. Between the two journeys a world has slipped away. With the passage of chapters and years we observe the gradual transformation of Pen's Byronism into mid-Victorian 'manliness'. The taciturn ethic of muscular Christianity is fully formed in Pen and Warrington's meeting, after long separation, in the penultimate number (set around 1847):

> The pair greeted each other with the rough cordiality which young Englishmen use one to another: and which carries a great deal of warmth and kindness under its rude exterior. Warrington smiled and took his pipe out of his mouth, and said, 'Well, young one!' Pen advanced and held out his hand, and said, 'How are you, old boy?' And so this greeting passed between two friends who had not seen each other for months. (p. 895)

Thackeray is lovingly attentive to ephemeral detail and the flux of fashion. Heads—once covered with the romantic mane—are slicked with bear's grease; moustaches and different styles of beard come and go; frock-coats replace tails. Even Mirobolant's *pantalon Écossais* have their historical date-stamp. *Pendennis* marks with chronometric precision such things as the fashionability of Pen's Cuban cigar and Warrington's 'manly' working-man's pipe. *Pendennis* has its anachronisms (Thackeray helpfully points some out to us) but the novel charts with great sensitivity what it felt like to be in a momentously changing age. If for nothing else, *Pendennis* may be read as a corrective to the modern habit of seeing 'Victorian', or 'nineteenth-century England' as all of a lump. And while recalling the past decades in which most of his readers had come of age (Thackeray, incidentally, always assumes his reader is middle-aged and middle-class) *Pendennis* reverberates to the seething political world around them all as he wrote. We tend to forget how turbulent the late 1840s were and that *Pendennis* was begun, and to a large extent formed, by the events of 1848. This 'year of revolutions' saw an

abortive uprising in Ireland (in the wake of the famine) and a bloody insurrection in France with repercussions which swept across Europe. The embattled middle-European with his gun who looks out from the vignette of Chapter 42 had immediate resonance, recalling conflicts about which the reader could learn in that month's *Times*.

Closer to home there was very nearly a revolution in England, in the form of the Chartist uprising. Thackeray covered the great Kennington rally of March 1848 for the *Morning Chronicle*.[12] It was a period of high alarm for the middle classes—the class that subscribed to *Pendennis*. The Church of England was also in upheaval, with the defection of Newman. Thackeray rarely alludes directly to these cataclysms in *Pendennis*, but employs knowing asides to the reader of his day that later readers can easily miss. Much of *Pendennis* only makes full sense if we re-insert it back into the nervous middle-class mood of 1848–50. The French and Irish uprisings inspired in Thackeray a reactive chauvinism which grates on modern ears, unless we contextualize it as an 1848 reflex. The English were profoundly grateful that they were not as other nations. *Punch* in January 1849 carried a huge cartoon of a massively serene John Bull, surrounded by his happy family, while around the bubble foreigners of all kinds battle and slaughter each other in the name of 'liberty', 'Socialism', 'les droits des femmes'. 'There is no place like home', the caption declares. English (whether grilled mutton chops, manly inarticulacy, or demure English maidens) is best. So Mr Punch thought, so Thackeray thought, so most of his readers thought.

Thackeray's chauvinism expresses itself in many different ways in *Pendennis*. A flagrant example is the (apparently) gratuitous mockery of Mirobolant, hero of the July 1830 Revolution ('they present arms to him in his own country', Strong tells Pen). This absurd frog cook—the narrative intimates—has the temerity to appear in his revolutionary decorations and his ludicrous finery at an English ball. It adds to the *cuisinier*'s Gallic effrontery that

[12] See G. N. Ray (ed.), *Thackeray's Contributions to the Morning Chronicle* (Urbana, Ill., 1955), 192–201.

the ball takes place in 1833, the period immediately following the English Reform Bill (the admirably English Pynsent is canvassing votes among the newly enfranchised county voters). The great Bill was a revolution by due course of law, and couldn't the French learn a thing or two from it!—or so the novel comfortingly implies to a reader of 1849. On the face of it, the comic Mirobolant subplot looks like the worst kind of nationalistic jeering. In context, it falls into place as a horrified reaction to the 10,000 victims of the 1848 French Revolution. Thackeray, we should remember, was no Podsnap. He was a lover of France, and a frequent visitor to the country (he wrote some informed sketches of his visits to Paris for *Punch* while *Pendennis* was running). French was his second language. He took a French refugee into his house in 1849–50 (the artist Louis Marvy, who probably helped him with the illustrations to *Pendennis*). What Thackeray was responding to in the insulting depiction of Mirobolant was not France, but France in 1848.

Thackeray's depiction of the Irish in *Pendennis* is even more chauvinistic and somewhat less defensible—even if one reconstructs what it was like to be an Englishman in 1848. He had personal reasons for hating the race (notably his Irish mother-in-law, who had made his early married life wretched). The Irishmen in *Pendennis* are universally drunken, combative, frequently charming, and always, above all things, 'improvident'. Costigan, the sometime soldier of fortune and duellist, is presented in the novel as a tipsy old fool, who gets tipsier, senile, and more foolish as the novel goes on. If he is given money, he spends it that same night on drink. Shandon—for all his great journalistic gifts—can only be kept out of debtors' prison by the heroic efforts of his wife and friends. The 'Captain' is incorrigibly spendthrift. Any money he gets he straightaway spends on drink and the cards.

Like many Englishmen Thackeray was profoundly disturbed by the condition of Ireland, which he knew at first hand. But he evidently could not bring himself to believe that the Irish were not themselves responsible for their squalor. Give them money, and the Irish will only spend it on booze (and steal your booze into the bargain, like the

tipsy housemaid Mrs Flanagan). Thackeray's depiction of the Irish in *Pendennis* got him into at least three rows during the course of the novel's publication, and provoked uncomfortably convincing death threats.

Thackeray's attitude to English revolution was more complex. There is, for instance, Warrington's rather forced encomium on the virtues of the working class and public-bar society in Chapter 30:

> there's character here. I like to talk with the strongest man in England, or the man who can drink the most beer in England, or with that tremendous republican of a hatter, who thinks Thistlewood [the political assassin] was the greatest character in history. I like gin-and-water better than claret. I like a sanded floor in Carnaby Market better than a chalked one in May Fair. I prefer Snobs, I own it. (p. 376)[13]

This theoretical praise should be set against the funniest subplot in the closing numbers of the novel, James Morgan's uprising against the tyrannical regime of Major Pendennis. Morgan is Major Pendennis's 'man'. For most of the novel he pads along 'velvet-footed' in the background, one of the thousands of servants who keep middle-class society going. Morgan knows how to curl the major's wig, wax his shoes, prepare the mysteries of his toilette, and grill his chop just as he likes it. But over the years, as it emerges in the last numbers, Morgan has been making himself a 'capitalist'. Having drunk too much one night, and the major being particularly 'aughty to him, Morgan rebels. He orders his astonished master out of 'his' (Morgan's) house. 'Mr' Morgan, as he tells the major, intends to be a gentleman—perhaps, even, to go into Parliament. There ensues the final comic episode in which the major again shows his military pluck, as he did at Clavering fifteen years before. The revolutionary butler is outwitted, and cowed by the major's pistol. It is, symbolically, a weapon which the major was given by his 'old patron' the Duke of Wellington. Even more symbolically, the pistol is empty. All the middle classes had in 1848 with which to put down the threatened revolution was bluff

[13] It being 1834, Warrington is using the term 'snob' in its pre-Thackerayan sense of 'low fellow'.

and backbone. They succeeded. The comedy of Morgan's rebellion is as fine as anything Thackeray wrote. But the episode gains extra savour from the alarms fresh in the minds of the novel's first readers. And it sustains to the end the high achievements of a novel which, for all its occasional unevenness, has traditionally been the favourite with Thackerayans.

NOTE ON THE TEXT

THACKERAY made the contract for *Pendennis* in June 1848, as *Vanity Fair* was drawing to its triumphant close. The payment offered by Bradbury and Evans reflected the earlier novel's success: £2,000 (as opposed to the £1,200 he had received for *Vanity Fair*). This worked out at £100 a monthly number, spread out over 20 months. For this payment Thackeray engaged to provide monthly copy for 32 pages of printed text, designs for two engravings on steel, and for a variable number of woodcuts. At the contract stage, and for the first ten numbers, the idea was to run the new novel the same length as *Vanity Fair*. But in August 1849 the narrative was rescheduled to a 'Homeric' 24 numbers, with a proportionate increase in payment. At this stage in the text, Pen had just embarked on his literary career and Thackeray had hit a good vein. Evidently sales had not been affected by Dickens's *David Copperfield*, which began monthly publication (also under the imprint of Bradbury and Evans) in May 1849.

Trained by years of journalism, Thackeray was the most fluent of writers. But he often (as with *Vanity Fair*) had most difficulty with openings. *Pendennis* was no exception. His childhood memories, particularly his relationship with his formidable mother, released emotions which were hard to control. One should not, of course, be taken in by the facetious claim made in the preface (i.e. afterword): 'Perhaps the lovers of "excitement" may care to know that this book began with a very precise plan, which was entirely put aside.' Thackeray evidently began with a foundational idea, expressed in the verbose title, and depicted in the allegorical illustration for the number cover. Loosely, this idea is 'Pen's dilemma' in the key decisions of his life. Will he follow the urgings of his bad angels (the major, Blanche) or his good angels (Laura, Warrington)?

Thackeray made a false start on composition in August 1848 and quickly rejected what he had written as too 'sentimental'. (Peter Shillingsburg surmises this material may have resurfaced later in the book.) He made another

start in October, and again rejected what he had written. Later in the same month, he made a third start. He credited this last, successful, attempt to a story which he heard from a young lady friend. It concerned a young man, determined to marry beneath him, outwitted by a ruthless father.[1] This gave him the 'comical business' that he wanted. It seems that Thackeray got his first number in shape around 18 October for publication on 1 November 1848. Thereafter, composition was a monthly race with the calendar. Thackeray's letters of the period are regularly punctuated with complaints of how he has just managed to finish his 'work' on the monthly number—sometimes as late as the 30th. But, as Peter Shillingsburg reminds us, 'work' meant more than just dashing words on to paper. Thackeray was thoroughly professional, however pressed he might be. He had to prepare his two large illustrations early in the month, so they could be engraved on steel; so too his designs for woodcuts had to be done early—although the engraving process was less time-consuming. As the month progressed he had to read and correct proof (which might come piecemeal, as he supplied copy to the printer). As the month drew to an end, it was necessary to measure the printed material exactly to the 32-page length, placing the woodcuts strategically in the text. Desperately hurried as he was, Thackeray only missed three deadlines in his whole career as a serialist, as Shillingsburg calculates.

It was a stressful mode of work (more so as Thackeray was writing and drawing for *Punch* on the side). The novelist underwent violent mood swings, fluctuating between despondency at the 'stupidity' of what he was writing, and jubilation at how good it was. Towards the end of the month, as he told his mother, 'I get so nervous that I don't speak to anybody scarcely, and once actually got up in the middle of the night and wrote in my night-shimee' (*Letters*, ii. 311). One of the principal debates in Thackeray studies over recent years is, writing as he did on his reflexes in this

[1] The authoritative account of the early composition of the novel is given by Peter Shillingsburg, in his edn. of *Pendennis* (New York, 1991), 375–6.

way, how much of his novel did he foresee? It is not easy to be definite. And Thackeray makes judgement harder, by mocking his own 'carelessness', playing up his reputation as a feckless *improvisatore*. 'What a shame the Author dont write a complete good story' (*Letters*, ii. 686), he observed on re-reading what he took to be an egregiously 'stupid part' of *Pendennis*.

Without falling into Thackeray's trap, it is safe to say that over two years and a bit he was sometimes in better charge of his material than at other times. The first sequence (Pen's infatuation with Emily Costigan) could be extracted as a perfect novella in its own right. Moving closer, the first number is a brilliant example of Thackeray's regressive narrative technique—his ability to hook his readers, then prime them with necessary antecedent information. It opens with the delightful scene of Major Pendennis in his club. With the surprising letter, and its repercussions, we double back to Pen's pathetic-comic falling in love with La Fotheringay. We then double further back in time to Helen's wholly pathetic courtship and unsatisfactory marriage.

After the story leaves Devon, things are much less sure. Pen's university career is abbreviated to an unsatisfactory interlude. Thackeray evidently lost his nerve faced with this section of his hero's growing up. Perhaps the episode brought back too many memories of his early relationship with William Brookfield. More likely, the 'university snobs' chapters of *The Snobs of England* had provoked anger. The arrival of the Claverings into the novel's action imports a host of new faces, but seems not to have been extensively thought through. The bridge to Pen's apprenticeship in London is similarly rickety. He seems never himself to have considered a career in law; it is a bright idea of the 15-year-old (if we care to be precise) Laura. Nor is it clear why and how Pen drifts into journalism, other than his accidental meeting with Warrington.

It is true that at times one can see Thackeray laying the ground for future plot developments. Peter Shillingsburg, for instance, notes how the communicating windows by which Altamont makes his final escape are mentioned as early as Chapter 42. But equally one can cite other places

where Thackeray was leaving future development of plot to his extraordinarily sure powers of invention. It is not clear on p. 685, for instance, that even two months before the scene of Helen Pendennis's death the novelist had decided that Warrington should be already married. (Bluebeard has some distinctly bigamous thoughts at the end of Chapter 53.) It seems doubtful that when protracting the joke about Fribsby's 'French carabineer' lover in the eighth number Thackeray foresaw that her spouse was to be John Armstrong, alias Jack Amory, alias Colonel Altamont. This revelation in the last pages is so hurried that we don't notice the flagrant improbabilities: how, for example, the drunken Altamont avoided being seen at the Clavering ball by *two* of his former wives; or how Armstrong-Amory-Altamont, a servant of the East India Company, managed to change his identity twice in India (Major Pendennis, who has not seen him for thirty years, recognizes him on the spot, despite his wig).

The month-to-month composition of *Pendennis* was distracted on many fronts. The novel was begun in haste, while *Vanity Fair* was completing. The author's emotional life was in turmoil. Thackeray—like other serialists—was responsive to his 'gentle reader' and afflicted by more than his share of very ungentle readers. (See, for instance, the vignette of himself being cudgelled on p. 670.) The four principal controversies that he became involved in during the serialization of *Pendennis* are recorded in the 'Explanatory Notes'. Most dramatically, Thackeray nearly died during the composition of his twelfth number, in September 1849. Publication was suspended for three months. And when he returned to the novel, it was with a distinctly different mood.

The serial divisions in *Pendennis* occurred after the following chapters: November, 1848, 1–3; December, 4–6; January, 1849, 7–10; February, 11–14; March, 15–16 (in later editions, Thackeray dropped a chapter's worth of material from this number; from this point on, the first edition's chapter numbering is one more than in the edition printed here); April, 17–19; May, 20–2; June, 23–5; July, 26–8; August, 29–31; September, 32–5 (after this number, publication was suspended for three months due

to Thackeray's illness); January, 1850, 36–8; February, 39–41; March, 42–4; April, 45–7; May, 48–51; June, 52–4; July, 55–7; August, 58–60; September, 61–3; October, 64–6; November, 67–70; December, 71–5 (the last number was a 'double'; it cost 2*s*. and contained 64 pages and prefatory material). The division between the volumes in the first (1849/50) two-volume edition occurred between Chapters 38 and 39 (as numbered here).

Only fragments of the manuscript of *Pendennis* survive.[2] The history of subsequent textual changes is complicated. Unusually, Thackeray (or a trusted delegate) made a large number of changes in later editions of the novel. This text photographically reproduces the 'Oxford' edition of 1908, which reset the 1864 edition which the editor, George Saintsbury, assumed to have been the last supervised by the author (who died in 1863). Saintsbury carefully annotated revisions and changes (mainly excisions of dated material) which Thackeray, or an editorial delegate, made. They will be found here as an appendix, pp. 979–1004. Saintsbury's 1908 text is recognized as the best available at anything like an affordable price. Uniquely for an affordable text it also has all Thackeray's illustrations more or less where he wanted them. Reading *Pendennis* without the illustrations is to get only half the novel. Serious students of the novel should, of course, consult Peter Shillingsburg's 1991 'Garland' edition. In addition to an authoritative account of the history of the text, this edition contains Nicholas Pickwoad's expert description of Thackeray's work as an illustrator.

Pendennis sold more than *Vanity Fair* in its first versions, although over the next few years the earlier novel sold more as a reprint. (Peter Shillingsburg estimates something over 8,000 copies were sold of *Pendennis* in its original parts.) Over the century, *Pendennis* was level with *Henry Esmond* as Thackeray's second-most-popular work. From the first reviews of the early numbers, *Pendennis* was well received. On its completion, G. H. Lewes declared in the

[2] For a description of the surviving MS evidence, see Peter Shillingsburg (ed.), *Pendennis* (New York, 1991), 380–1, 436–8, and John Sutherland, *Thackeray at Work* (London, 1974), 45–55.

Leader 'We gravely assert that England has at no time produced a writer of fiction with whom Thackeray may not stand in honourable comparison.' Lewes particularly liked the new mellowness in Thackeray: 'In *Vanity Fair* we felt the scoundrelism and pretence oppressive. In *Pendennis* this is no longer the case.' None the less, there was the undercurrent of uneasiness about Thackeray's 'cynicism' that always worried his contemporaries. The *Athenaeum*, for instance, objected to 'such a ruthless insistence on the blemishes, incompletenesses, and disappointments which canker every human good and happiness'. And a number of reviewers chorused the complaint that, as Lewes put it, Thackeray showed in his writing 'a want of respect for his art, a want of respect for his public'. One of the most illuminating of contemporary reviews was that by David Masson in the *North British Review* (May 1851), comparing *Pendennis* and its great serial rival, *David Copperfield*.[3]

In the longer term, few novels have been more influential than *Pendennis*. Two aspects stand out as having left an enduring mark on literature and its practitioners. The character of Warrington pioneered the 'manly' English hero—later boosted by the cult of 'muscular' Christianity and the public school ethos set up by Dr Arnold at Rugby in the 1840s. Warrington is the procreator of the taciturn, inscrutable, physically powerful, hairy, philistine, chauvinist, 'Tom Brown' ideal of English masculinity on which the Empire was built. Read in this light the 'manly' exchanges between Warrington ('Old Fellow') and Pendennis (the 'Young 'un') in the later chapters are among the most effective propaganda ever penned.

More directly the Lamb Court chapters inspired, among young readers, a cult of London literary bohemia. An army of would-be Pendennises was recruited. As Nigel Cross records (in *The Common Writer*, Cambridge, 1985): 'it was *Pendennis* that gave definition to Victorian bohemianism by refashioning the often sordid world of Maginn and Hook [i.e. "Mr Wagg" in the novel] into a romantic

[3] Contemporary reviews, and an analysis of contemporary reactions to *Pendennis* will be found in Geoffrey Tillotson and Donald Hawes (eds.), *Thackeray: The Critical Heritage* (London, 1968).

Corporation of the Goosequill'. The teenage Edmund Yates read *Pendennis* in monthly parts and could not wait 'to get admitted to the ranks of literary men, among whom I might possibly, by industry and perseverance, rise to some position'. A generation later Andrew Lang testified to the novel's potency, 'Marryat never made us wish to run away to sea . . . But the story of Pen made one wish to run away to literature' (p. 110).

SELECT BIBLIOGRAPHY

Two surveys of Thackeray criticism are valuable: Dudley Flamm, *Thackeray's Critics: An Annotated Bibliography of British and American Criticism, 1836–1901* (Chapel Hill, NC, 1966); John C. Olmsted, *Thackeray and his Twentieth Century Critics* (New York, 1977). The authoritative biography is by Gordon N. Ray, in two volumes: *Thackeray: The Uses of Adversity* (London, 1955); *Thackeray: The Age of Wisdom* (London, 1958). Ray is editor of the four volumes of *Letters and Private Papers of William Makepeace Thackeray* (London, 1945–6) and is also author of the study in biographical criticism, *The Buried Life* (Cambridge, Mass., 1952).

The following book-length studies of Thackeray are recommended, though not all agree with each other on the question of how to read Thackeray:

Lionel Stevenson, *The Showman of Vanity Fair* (London, 1947)
J. Y. T. Greig, *Thackeray: A Reconsideration* (London, 1950)
Geoffrey Tillotson, *Thackeray the Novelist* (Cambridge, 1954)
John Loofbourow, *Thackeray and the Form of Fiction* (Princeton, NJ, 1963)
Juliet McMaster, *Thackeray: The Major Novels* (Manchester, 1971)
Barbara Hardy, *The Exposure of Luxury: Radical Themes in Thackeray's Fiction* (London, 1972)
John Sutherland, *Thackeray at Work* (London, 1974)
John Carey, *Thackeray: Prodigal Genius* (London, 1977)
Robert A. Colby, *Thackeray's Canvass of Humanity* (Columbus, Ohio, 1979)
Edgar F. Harden, *The Emergence of Thackeray's Serial Fiction* (Athens, Ga., 1979)
Catherine Peters, *Thackeray's Universe* (London, 1987)
Michael Lund, *Reading Thackeray* (Detroit, 1988)

A valuable introduction to Thackeray's working methods and the production of his fiction is given in: Peter Shillingsburg, *Pegasus in Harness* (Charlottesville, Va., 1992). The socio-literary background to *Pendennis* is dealt with in Nigel Cross, *The Common Writer* (Cambridge, 1985). The reception of *Pendennis* (and Thackeray's other major works) is valuably described (with extensive citation) in: Geoffrey Tillotson and Donald Hawes, *Thackeray: The Critical Heritage* (London, 1968). Donald Hawes has also co-edited *Pendennis* with J. I. M. Stewart for the 'Penguin Classics' series (Harmondsworth, 1986). Peter

Shillingsburg has edited *Pendennis* with a full textual critical apparatus and a commentary on the illustrations by Nicholas Pickwoad (New York, 1991). Accompanying this edition, Edgar Harden has prepared a full explanatory annotation to the novel in his two-volume *Annotations for the Selected Works of William Makepeace Thackeray* (New York, 1990). The *Pendennis* notes are to be found in voume i.

Two essays in the journal *Costerus*, NS 2 (1974; Rodolphi N.V., Amsterdam, and J. Faust & Co., South Carolina) are useful to a reading of *Pendennis*: Joan Stevens, 'Thackeray's Pictorial Capitals' (pp. 113–40) and Peter L. Shillingsburg, 'Thackeray Texts' (pp. 287–314). See also J. W. Dodds, *The Age of Paradox* (London, 1953), and Richard Altick, *The Presence of the Present* (Columbus, Ohio, 1991).

A CHRONOLOGY OF THACKERAY'S LIFE AND WORKS

1811	18 July: Born in Calcutta, India
1817	Sent by his parents to England
1822–8	At Charterhouse School
1829–30	At Trinity College, Cambridge; leaves without a degree
1830–1	July–Mar.: In Weimar
1831	June: Enters Middle Temple, with view to a career in law
1832–6	From July 1832 largely resident in Paris; studies art and contributes to various journals
1834	May: First identified contribution to *Fraser's Magazine*
1835	Meets Isabella Shawe, whom he marries in Aug. 1836
1837	Settles in London (18 Albion Street); with the *Yellowplush Correspondence* (*Fraser's*, Nov. 1837–Aug. 1838) enjoys his first notable literary success
1839	*Catherine* (*Fraser's*, May 1839–Feb. 1840)
1840	*A Shabby-Genteel Story* (*Fraser's*, June–Oct.); *Paris Sketch Book*, Thackeray's first book, published; beginning of his wife's madness
1841	*The Second Funeral of Napoleon*; *The Great Hoggarty Diamond* (*Fraser's*, Sept.–Dec.)
1843	*The Irish Sketch Book*
1844	*Barry Lyndon* (*Fraser's*, Jan.–Dec.); undertakes a trip to the East (22 Aug.–26 Nov.)
1845	Wife, now incurably insane, placed in care
1846	*Notes of a Journey from Cornhill to Grand Cairo*; *The Snobs of England* (*Punch*, Mar. 1846–Feb. 1847); moves with his daughters to 13 Young Street, Kensington; publishes his first Christmas book, *Mrs. Perkins's Ball*
1847–8	*Vanity Fair* published in monthly numbers (Jan. 1847–June 1848)
1848–50	*Pendennis* published in 23 monthly numbers (the last being a double instalment) from Nov. 1848–Nov. 1850, interrupted by severe illness Sept.–Nov. 1849

1851	Lectures on the English Humourists in London (May–July); resigns from *Punch*
1852	*Esmond* published in 3 volumes
1852–3	Lectures in America on the English Humourists (Nov.–April)
1853–5	*The Newcomes* published in 24 (as 23) monthly numbers (Oct.–Aug.)
1854	*The Rose and the Ring*
1855–6	Lecturing in America on *The Four Georges* (Oct.–April), not published in England until 1860
1856–7	Lectures in Britain (Nov.–May)
1857	July: Stands unsuccessfully as Independent Liberal for the city of Oxford
1857–9	*The Virginians* published in 24 (as 23) monthly numbers (Nov.–Oct.)
1858	The 'Garrick Club Affair', provoked by a malicious article by Edmund Yates in *Town Talk*, sets Thackeray against Dickens
1859	August: Accepts editorship of the *Cornhill Magazine*; the first issue put out Jan. 1860; Thackeray holds the post until Mar. 1862, when he resigns
1860	*Lovel the Widower* (*Cornhill*, Jan.–June); *The Four Georges* (*Cornhill*, July–Oct.); *Roundabout Papers* (*Cornhill*, Jan. 1860–Nov. 1863)
1861–2	*Philip* published in *Cornhill* (Jan. 1861–Aug. 1862)
1862	March: Moves to 2 Palace Green, Kensington
1863	May: Begins writing *Denis Duval*, published posthumously and incomplete, *Cornhill*, Mar.–June 1864
	24 Dec.: Dies; buried Kensal Green Cemetery

More detailed chronologies may be found in *Letters* (vol. i), and in Colby, *Thackeray's Canvass of Humanity* (see Select Bibliography). The fullest chronological bibliography of Thackeray's works is to be found in Lewis Melville, *William Makepeace Thackeray* (vol. ii), London, 1910. This last, however, should be supplemented by reference to the *Cambridge Bibliography of English Literature* and the *Wellesley Index* for publications of Thackeray's identified by subsequent scholarship.

[May.]

No. VII. Price 1s.

THE HISTORY

OF

PENDENNIS.

HIS FORTUNES AND MISFORTUNES,

HIS FRIENDS AND HIS GREATEST ENEMY.

BY

W. M. THACKERAY,

Author of "Vanity Fair," the "Snob Papers" in Punch, &c. &c.

LONDON. BRADBURY & EVANS, 11, BOUVERIE STREET.

J. MENZIES, EDINBURGH; T. MURRAY, GLASGOW; AND J. M'GLASHAN, DUBLIN.

Bradbury & Evans,] 1849. [Printers, Whitefriars.

[*Facsimile of wrapper to one of the original monthly numbers.*]

THE HISTORY
OF
PENDENNIS
VOL. I

BY W M THACKERAY

LONDON.
BRADBURY & EVANS. BOUVERIE STREET.
1850

[*Facsimile of title-page to vol. i, first edition.*]

THE HISTORY

OF

PENDENNIS

VOL. II.

BY

W M THACKERAY

LONDON

BRADBURY & EVANS BOUVERIE STREET

1850.

[*Facsimile of title-page to vol. ii, first edition.*]

CONTENTS

LIST OF PLATES

TO DR. JOHN ELLIOTSON

MY DEAR DOCTOR,

Thirteen months ago, when it seemed likely that this story had come to a close, a kind friend brought you to my bedside, whence, in all probability, I never should have risen but for your constant watchfulness and skill. I like to recall your great goodness and kindness (as well as many acts of others, showing quite a surprising friendship and sympathy) at that time, when kindness and friendship were most needed and welcome.

And as you would take no other fee but thanks, let me record them here in behalf of me and mine, and subscribe myself,

Yours most sincerely and gratefully,

W. M. THACKERAY.

PREFACE

If this kind of composition, of which the two years' product is now laid before the public, fail in art, as it constantly does and must, it at least has the advantage of a certain truth and honesty, which a work more elaborate might lose. In his constant communication with the reader, the writer is forced into frankness of expression, and to speak out his own mind and feelings as they urge him. Many a slip of the pen and the printer, many a word spoken in haste, he sees and would recall as he looks over his volume. It is a sort of confidential talk between writer and reader, which must often be dull, must often flag. In the course of his volubility, the perpetual speaker must of necessity lay bare his own weaknesses, vanities, peculiarities. And as we judge of a man's character, after long frequenting his society, not by one speech, or by one mood or opinion, or by one day's talk, but by the tenor of his general bearing and conversation; so of a writer, who delivers himself up to you perforce unreservedly, you say, Is he honest? Does he tell the truth in the main? Does he seem actuated by a desire to find out and speak it? Is he a quack, who shams sentiment, or mouths for effect? Does he seek popularity by claptraps or other arts? I can no more ignore good fortune than any other chance which has befallen me. I have found many thousands more readers than I ever looked for. I have no right to say to these,

You shall not find fault with my art, or fall asleep over my pages ; but I ask you to believe that this person writing strives to tell the truth. If there is not that, there is nothing.

Perhaps the lovers of 'excitement' may care to know that this book began with a very precise plan, which was entirely put aside. Ladies and gentlemen, you were to have been treated, and the writer's and the publishers' pocket benefited, by the recital of the most active horrors. What more exciting than a ruffian (with many admirable virtues) in St. Giles's, visited constantly by a young lady from Belgravia ?* What more stirring than the contrasts of society ? the mixture of slang and fashionable language ? the escapes, the battles, the murders ? Nay, up to nine o'clock this very morning, my poor friend, Colonel Altamont, was doomed to execution, and the author only relented when his victim was actually at the window.

The 'exciting' plan was laid aside (with a very honourable forbearance on the part of the publishers) because, on attempting it, I found that I failed from want of experience of my subject ; and never having been intimate with any convict in my life, and the manners of ruffians and jail-birds being quite unfamiliar to me, the idea of entering into competition with M. Eugène Sue* was abandoned. To describe a real rascal, you must make him so horrible that he would be too hideous to show ; and unless the painter paints him fairly, I hold he has no right to show him at all.

Even the gentlemen of our age—this is an attempt to describe one of them, no better nor worse than most educated men—even these we cannot show as they are, with the notorious foibles and selfishness of their lives and their education. Since the author of *Tom Jones* was buried,* no writer of fiction among us has been permitted to depict to his utmost power a MAN. We must drape him, and give him a certain conventional simper. Society will not tolerate the Natural in our Art. Many ladies have

remonstrated and subscribers left me because, in the course of the story, I described a young man resisting and affected by temptation. My object was to say that he had the passions to feel, and the manliness and generosity to overcome them. You will not hear—it is best to know it—what moves in the real world, what passes in society, in the clubs, colleges, mess-rooms,—what is the life and talk of your sons. A little more frankness than is customary has been attempted in this story; with no bad desire on the writer's part, it is hoped, and with no ill consequence to any reader. If truth is not always pleasant, at any rate truth is best, from whatever chair—from those whence graver writers or thinkers argue, as from that at which the story-teller sits as he concludes his labour, and bids his kind reader farewell.

KENSINGTON,
November 26th, 1850.

PENDENNIS

CHAPTER I

SHOWS HOW FIRST LOVE MAY INTERRUPT BREAKFAST

NE fine morning in the full London season, Major Arthur Pendennis came over from his lodgings, according to his custom, to breakfast at a certain club in Pall Mall,* of which he was a chief ornament.[1] At a quarter-past ten the major invariably made his appearance in the best blacked boots in all London, with a checked morning cravat that never was rumpled until dinner-time, a buff waistcoat which bore the crown of his sovereign on the buttons, and linen so spotless that Mr. Brummell* himself asked the name of his laundress, and would probably have employed her had not misfortunes compelled that great man to fly the country. Pendennis's coat, his white gloves, his whiskers, his very cane, were perfect of their kind as specimens of the costume of a military man *en retraite*. At a distance, or seeing his back merely, you would have taken him to be not more than thirty years old : it was only by a nearer inspection that you saw the factitious nature of his rich brown hair, and that there were a few crow's-feet round about the somewhat faded eyes of his handsome mottled face. His nose was of the Wellington pattern.* His hands and wristbands were

[1] These numerals in the text refer to words or passages in the first edition, subsequently omitted or altered, which will be found restored in the Appendix.

beautifully long and white. On the latter he wore handsome gold buttons given to him by his Royal Highness the Duke of York,* and on the others more than one elegant ring, the chief and largest of them being emblazoned with the famous arms of Pendennis.

He always took possession of the same table in the same corner of the room, from which nobody ever now thought of ousting him. One or two mad wags and wild fellows had, in former days, endeavoured[2] to deprive him of this place; but there was a quiet dignity in the major's manner as he took his seat at the next table, and surveyed the interlopers, which rendered it impossible for any man to sit and breakfast under his eye; and that table—by the fire, and yet near the window—became his own. His letters were laid out there in expectation of his arrival, and many was the young fellow about town who looked with wonder at the number of those notes, and at the seals and franks which they bore. If there was any question about etiquette, society, who was married to whom, of what age such and such a duke was, Pendennis was the man to whom every one appealed. Marchionesses used to drive up to the Club and leave notes for him, or fetch him out. He was perfectly affable. The young men liked to walk with him in the Park or down Pall Mall; for he touched his hat to everybody, and every other man he met was a lord.

The major sat down at his accustomed table then, and while the waiters went to bring him his toast and his hot newspaper, he surveyed his letters through his gold double eyeglass,[3] and examined one pretty note after another, and laid them by in order. There were large solemn dinner cards, suggestive of three courses and heavy conversation; there were neat little confidential notes, conveying female entreaties; there was a note on thick official paper from the Marquis of Steyne,* telling him to come to Richmond to a little party at the 'Star and Garter';[4] and another from the Bishop of Ealing and Mrs. Trail, requesting the honour of Major Pendennis's company at Ealing House, all of which letters Pendennis read gracefully, and with the more satisfaction, because Glowry, the Scotch surgeon, breakfasting opposite to him, was looking on, and hating him for having so many invitations, which nobody ever sent to Glowry.

These perused, the major took out his pocket-book to

see on what days he was disengaged, and which of these many hospitable calls he could afford to accept or decline.

He threw over Cutler, the East India Director, in Baker Street, in order to dine with Lord Steyne and the little French party at the 'Star and Garter'; the bishop he accepted because, though the dinner was slow, he liked to dine with bishops ; and so went through his list and disposed of them according to his fancy or interest. Then he took his breakfast and looked over the paper, the Gazette, the births and deaths, and the fashionable intelligence, to see that his name was down among the guests at my Lord So-and-so's fête, and in the intervals of these occupations carried on cheerful conversation with his acquaintances about the room.

Among the letters which formed Major Pendennis's budget for that morning there was only one unread, and which lay solitary and apart from all the fashionable London letters, with a country post-mark and a homely seal. The superscription was in a pretty delicate female hand, marked 'Immediate' by the fair writer[5]; yet the major had, for reasons of his own, neglected up to the present moment his humble rural petitioner, who to be sure could hardly hope to get a hearing among so many grand folks who attended his levee. The fact was, this was a letter from a female relative of Pendennis, and while the grandees of her brother's acquaintance were received and got their interview, and drove off, as it were, the patient country letter remained for a long time waiting for an audience in the ante-chamber, under the slop-basin.

At last it came to be this letter's turn, and the major broke a seal with 'Fairoaks' engraved upon it, and 'Clavering St. Mary's' for a post-mark. It was a double letter, and the major commenced perusing the envelope before he attacked the inner epistle.

'Is it a letter from another *jook?*' growled Mr. Glowry inwardly. 'Pendennis would not be leaving that to the last, I'm thinking.'

'My dear Major Pendennis,' the letter ran, 'I beg and implore you to come to me *immediately*' ('Very likely,' thought Pendennis, 'and Steyne's dinner to-day')—'I am in the very greatest grief and perplexity. My dearest boy, who has been hitherto everything the fondest mother could wish, is grieving me *dreadfully*. He has formed—I can hardly write it—a passion, an infatuation,'—the major

grinned—'for an actress who has been performing here. She is at least twelve years older than Arthur—who will not be eighteen till next February—and the wretched boy insists upon marrying her.'

'Hey! What's making Pendennis swear now?' Mr. Glowry asked of himself, for rage and wonder were concentrated in the major's open mouth, as he read this astounding announcement.

'Do, my dear friend,' the grief-stricken lady went on, 'come to me instantly on the receipt of this; and, as Arthur's guardian, entreat, command, the wretched child to give up this most deplorable resolution.' And, after more entreaties to the above effect, the writer concluded by signing herself the major's 'unhappy affectionate sister, Helen Pendennis.'

'Fairoaks, Tuesday,' the major concluded, reading the last words of the letter—'A d——d pretty business at Fairoaks, Tuesday; now let us see what the boy has to say;' and he took the other letter, which was written in a great floundering boy's hand, and sealed with the large signet of the Pendennises, even larger than the major's own, and with supplementary wax sputtered all round the seal, in token of the writer's tremulousness and agitation.

The epistle ran thus—

FAIROAKS, Monday, Midnight.

MY DEAR UNCLE,—In informing you of my engagement with Miss Costigan, daughter of J. Chesterfield Costigan, Esq., of Costiganstown, but, perhaps, better known to you under her professional name of Miss Fotheringay, of the Theatres Royal Drury Lane and Crow Street,* and of the Norwich and Welsh Circuit, I am aware that I make an announcement which cannot, according to the present prejudices of society at least, be welcome to my family. My dearest mother, on whom, God knows, I would wish to inflict no needless pain, is deeply moved and grieved, I am sorry to say, by the intelligence which I have this night conveyed to her. I beseech you, my dear sir, to come down and reason with her and console her. Although obliged by poverty to earn an honourable maintenance by the exercise of her splendid talents, Miss Costigan's family is as ancient and noble as our own. When our ancestor, Ralph Pendennis, landed with Richard II. in Ireland,* my Emily's forefathers were kings of that country. I have the information from Mr. Costigan, who, like yourself, is a military man.

It is in vain I have attempted to argue with my dear mother, and prove to her that a young lady of irreproachable character and lineage, endowed with the most splendid gifts of beauty and genius,

who devotes herself to the exercise of one of the noblest professions, for the sacred purpose of maintaining her family, is a being whom we should all love and reverence, rather than avoid;—my poor mother has prejudices which it is impossible for my logic to overcome, and refuses to welcome to her arms one who is disposed to be her most affectionate daughter through life.

Although Miss Costigan is some years older than myself, that circumstance does not operate as a barrier to my affection, and I am sure will not influence its duration. A love like mine, sir, I feel, is contracted once and for ever. As I never had dreamed of love until I saw her—I feel now that I shall die without ever knowing another passion. It is the fate of my life;[6] and having loved once, I should despise myself, and be unworthy of my name as a gentleman, if I hesitated to abide by my passion: if I did not give all where I felt all, and endow the woman who loves me fondly with my whole heart and my whole fortune.

I press for a speedy marriage with my Emily—for why, in truth, should it be delayed? A delay implies a doubt, which I cast from me as unworthy. It is impossible that my sentiments can change towards Emily—that at any age she can be anything but the sole object of my love. Why, then, wait? I entreat you, my dear uncle, to come down and reconcile my dear mother to our union, and I address you as a man of the world, *qui mores hominum multorum vidit et urbes*,* who will not feel any of the weak scruples and fears which agitate a lady who has scarcely ever left her village.

Pray, come down to us immediately. I am quite confident that —apart from considerations of fortune—you will admire and approve of my Emily.

Your affectionate nephew,
Arthur Pendennis, Jr.

When the major had concluded the perusal of this letter, his countenance assumed an expression of such rage and horror that Glowry, the surgeon, felt in his pocket for his lancet, which he always carried in his card-case, and thought his respected friend was going into a fit. The intelligence was indeed sufficient to agitate Pendennis. The head of the Pendennises going to marry an actress ten years his senior,—a headstrong boy about to plunge into matrimony. 'The mother has spoiled the young rascal,' groaned the major inwardly, 'with her cursed sentimentality and romantic rubbish. My nephew marry a tragedy queen! Gracious mercy, people will laugh at me so that I shall not dare show my head!' And he thought with an inexpressible pang that he must give up Lord Steyne's dinner at Richmond, and must lose his rest and pass the night in an abominable tight mail-coach, instead of taking pleasure,

as he had promised himself, in some of the most agreeable and select society in England.[7]

He quitted his breakfast-table for the adjoining writing-room, and there ruefully wrote off refusals to the marquis, the earl, the bishop, and all his entertainers; and he ordered his servant to take places in the mail-coach for that evening, of course charging the sum which he disbursed for the seats to the account of the widow and the young scapegrace of whom he was guardian.

CHAPTER II

A PEDIGREE AND OTHER FAMILY MATTERS

EARLY in the Regency of George the Magnificent* there lived in a small town in the west of England, called Clavering, a gentleman whose name was Pendennis. There were those alive who remembered having seen his name painted on a board, which was surmounted by a gilt pestle and mortar over the door of a very humble little shop in the city of Bath, where Mr. Pendennis exercised the profession of apothecary and surgeon; and where he not only attended gentlemen in their sick-rooms, and ladies at the most interesting periods of their lives, but would condescend to sell a brown-paper plaster to a farmer's wife across the counter,—or to vend tooth-brushes, hair-powder, and London perfumery.[1]

And yet that little apothecary who sold a stray customer a pennyworth of salts, or a more fragrant cake of Windsor soap, was a gentleman of good education, and of as old a family as any in the whole county of Somerset. He had a Cornish pedigree which carried the Pendennises up to the time of the Druids,—and who knows how much further back? They had intermarried with the Normans at a very

late period of their family existence, and they were related to all the great families of Wales and Brittany. Pendennis had had a piece of University education too, and might have pursued that career with honour, but in his second year at Oxbridge* his father died insolvent, and poor Pen was obliged to betake himself to the pestle and apron. He always detested the trade, and it was only necessity, and the offer of his mother's brother, a London apothecary of low family, into which Pendennis's father had demeaned himself by marrying, that forced John Pendennis into so odious a calling.

He quickly after his apprenticeship parted from the coarse-minded practitioner his relative, and set up for himself at Bath with his modest medical ensign. He had for some time a hard struggle with poverty; and it was all he could do to keep the shop[2] in decent repair, and his bedridden mother in comfort: but Lady Ribstone happening to be passing to the Rooms with an intoxicated Irish chairman who bumped her ladyship up against Pen's very door-post, and drove his chair-pole through the handsomest pink bottle in the surgeon's window, alighted screaming from her vehicle, and was accommodated with a chair in Mr. Pendennis's shop, where she was brought round with cinnamon and sal volatile.

Mr. Pendennis's manners were so uncommonly gentlemanlike and soothing, that her ladyship, the wife of Sir Pepin Ribstone, of Codlingbury, in the county of Somerset, Bart., appointed her preserver, as she called him, apothecary to her person and family, which was very large. Master Ribstone coming home for the Christmas holidays from Eton, over-ate himself and had a fever, in which Mr. Pendennis treated him with the greatest skill and tenderness. In a word, he got the good graces of the Codlingbury family, and from that day began to prosper. The good company of Bath patronized him, and amongst the ladies especially he was beloved and admired. First his humble little shop became a smart one: then he discarded the selling of tooth-brushes and perfumery[3]: then he shut up the shop altogether, and only had a little surgery attended by a genteel young man: then he had a gig with a man to drive him; and, before her exit from this world, his poor old mother had the happiness of seeing from her bedroom window to which her chair was rolled, her beloved John step

into a close carriage of his own, a one-horse carriage it is true, but with the arms of the family of Pendennis handsomely emblazoned on the panels. 'What would Arthur say now ?' she asked, speaking of a younger son of hers—'who never so much as once came to see my dearest Johnny through all the time of his poverty and struggles !'

'Captain Pendennis is with his regiment in India, mother,' Mr. Pendennis remarked, 'and, if you please, I wish you would not call me Johnny before the young man—before Mr. Parkins.'

Presently the day came when she ceased to call her son by any title of endearment or affection ; and his house was very lonely without that kind though querulous voice. He had his night-bell altered and placed in the room in which the good old lady had grumbled for many a long year, and he slept in the great large bed there. He was upwards of forty years old when these events befell ; before the war was over ; before George the Magnificent came to the throne ;* before this history indeed : but what is a gentleman without his pedigree ? Pendennis, by this time, had his handsomely framed and glazed, and hanging up in his drawing-room between the pictures of Codlingbury House in Somersetshire, and St. Boniface's College, Oxbridge, where he had passed the brief and happy days of his early manhood. As for the pedigree, he had taken it out of a trunk, as Sterne's officer called for his sword,* now that he was a gentleman and could show it.

About the time of Mrs. Pendennis's demise, another of her son's patients likewise died at Bath ; that virtuous old woman, old Lady Pontypool, daughter of Reginald twelfth Earl of Bareacres, and by consequence great-grand-aunt to the present earl, and widow of John second Lord Pontypool, and likewise of the Reverend Jonas Wales, of the Armageddon Chapel, Clifton. For the last five years of her life her ladyship had been attended by Miss Helen Thistlewood, a very distant relative of the noble house of Bareacres, before mentioned, and daughter of Lieutenant R. Thistlewood, R.N., killed at the battle of Copenhagen.* Under Lady Pontypool's roof Miss Thistlewood found a shelter[4]; the doctor, who paid his visits to my Lady Pontypool at least twice a day, could not but remark the angelical sweetness and kindness with which the young lady bore her elderly relative's ill-temper ; and it was, as they were

going in the fourth mourning coach to attend her ladyship's venerated remains to Bath Abbey, where they now repose, that he looked at her sweet pale face and resolved upon putting a certain question to her, the very nature of which made his pulse beat ninety, at least.

He was older than she by more than twenty years, and at no time the most ardent of men. Perhaps he had had a love affair in early life which he had to strangle—perhaps all early love affairs ought to be strangled or drowned, like

so many blind kittens: well, at three-and-forty he was a collected quiet little gentleman in black stockings with a bald head, and a few days after the ceremony he called to see her, and, as he felt her pulse, he kept hold of her hand in his, and asked her where she was going to live now that the Pontypool family had come down upon the property, which was being nailed into boxes, and packed into hampers, and swaddled up with haybands, and buried in straw, and locked under three keys in green-baize

plate-chests, and carted away under the eyes of poor Miss Helen,—he asked her where she was going to live finally.

Her eyes filled with tears, and she said she did not know. She had a little money. The old lady had left her a thousand pounds, indeed; and she would go into a boarding-house or into a school: in fine, she did not know where.

Then Pendennis, looking into her pale face, and keeping hold of her cold little hand, asked her if she would come and live with him? He was old compared to—to so blooming a young lady as Miss Thistlewood (Pendennis was of the grave old complimentary school of gentlemen and apothecaries), but he was of good birth, and, he flattered himself, of good principles and temper. His prospects were good, and daily mending. He was alone in the world, and had need of a kind and constant companion, whom it would be the study of his life to make happy; in a word, he recited to her a little speech, which he had composed that morning in bed, and rehearsed and perfected in his carriage, as he was coming to wait upon the young lady.

Perhaps if he had had an early love-passage, she too had one day hoped for a different lot than to be wedded to a little gentleman who rapped his teeth and smiled artificially, who was laboriously polite to the butler as he slid upstairs into the drawing-room, and profusely civil to the lady's-maid, who waited at the bedroom door; for whom her old patroness used to ring as for a servant, and who came with even more eagerness;[5] perhaps she would have chosen a different man—but she knew, on the other hand, how worthy Pendennis was, how prudent, how honourable; how good he had been to his mother, and constant in his care of her; and the upshot of this interview was, that she, blushing very much, made Pendennis an extremely low curtsy, and asked leave to—to consider his very kind proposal.

They were married in the dull Bath season, which was the height of the season in London. And Pendennis having previously, through a professional friend, M.R.C.S.,* secured lodgings in Holles Street, Cavendish Square, took his wife thither in a chaise and pair; conducted her to the theatres, the Parks, and the Chapel Royal; showed her the folks going to a Drawing-room, and, in a word, gave her all the pleasures of the town. He likewise left cards upon Lord Pontypool, upon the Right Honourable the Earl of Bare-

acres, and upon Sir Pepin and Lady Ribstone, his earliest and kindest patrons. Bareacres took no notice of the cards. Pontypool called, admired Mrs. Pendennis, and said Lady Pontypool would come and see her, which her ladyship did, per proxy of John her footman, who brought her card, and an invitation to a concert five weeks off. Pendennis was back in his little one-horse carriage, dispensing draughts and pills at that time: but the Ribstones asked him and Mrs. Pendennis to an entertainment, of which Mr. Pendennis talked to the last day of his life.

The secret ambition of Mr. Pendennis had always been to be a gentleman. It takes much time and careful saving for a provincial doctor, whose gains are not very large, to lay by enough money wherewith to purchase a house and land: but besides our friend's own frugality and prudence, fortune aided him considerably in his endeavour, and brought him to the point which he so panted to attain. He laid out some money very advantageously in the purchase of a house and small estate close upon the village of Clavering before mentioned.[6] A lucky purchase which he had made of shares in a copper-mine added very considerably to his wealth, and he realized with great prudence while this mine was still at its full vogue. Finally, he sold his business, at Bath, to Mr. Parkins, for a handsome sum of ready money, and for an annuity to be paid to him during a certain number of years after he had for ever retired from the handling of the mortar and pestle.

Arthur Pendennis, his son, was eight years old at the time of this event, so that it is no wonder that the lad, who left Bath and the surgery so young, should forget the existence of such a place almost entirely, and that his father's hands had ever been dirtied by the compounding of odious pills, or the preparation of filthy plasters. The old man never spoke about the shop himself, never alluded to it; called in the medical practitioner of Clavering to attend his family; sunk the black breeches and stockings altogether; attended market and sessions, and wore a bottle-green coat and brass buttons with drab gaiters, just as if he had been an English gentleman all his life. He used to stand at his lodge-gate, and see the coaches come in, and bow gravely to the guards and coachmen as they touched their hats and drove by. It was he who founded

the Clavering Book Club : and set up the Samaritan Soup and Blanket Society. It was he who brought the mail, which used to run through Cacklefield before, away from that village and through Clavering. At church he was equally active as a vestryman and a worshipper. At market every Thursday, he went from pen to stall ; looked at samples of oats, and munched corn ; felt beasts, punched geese in the breast, and weighed them with a knowing air ; and did business with the farmers at the 'Clavering Arms,' as well as the oldest frequenter of that house of call. It was now his shame, as it formerly was his pride, to be called doctor, and those who wished to please him always gave him the title of squire.

Heaven knows where they came from, but a whole range of Pendennis portraits presently hung round the doctor's oak dining-room ; Lelys and Vandykes he vowed all the portraits to be, and when questioned as to the history of the originals, would vaguely say they were 'ancestors of his.'[7] His little boy believed them to their fullest extent, and Roger Pendennis of Agincourt, Arthur Pendennis of Crécy, General Pendennis of Blenheim and Oudenarde, were as real and actual beings for this young gentleman as —whom shall we say ?—as Robinson Crusoe, or Peter Wilkins, or the Seven Champions of Christendom,* whose histories were in his library.

Pendennis's fortune, which was not above eight hundred pounds a year, did not, with the best economy and management, permit of his living with the great folks of the county ; but he had a decent comfortable society of the second best sort. If they were not the roses, they lived near the roses, as it were, and had a good deal of the odour of genteel life. They had out their plate, and dined each other round in the moonlight nights twice a year, coming a dozen miles to these festivals ; and besides the county, the Pendennises had the society of the town of Clavering, as much as, nay, more than, they liked : for Mrs. Pybus was always poking about Helen's conservatories, and intercepting the operation of her soup-tickets and coal-clubs : Captain Glanders (H.P., 50th Dragoon Guards) was for ever swaggering about the squire's stables and gardens, and endeavouring to enlist him in his quarrels with the vicar, with the postmaster, with the Reverend F. Wapshot of Clavering Grammar School, for over-flogging his son, Angle-

sea Glanders—with all the village in fine. And Pendennis and his wife often blessed themselves that their house of Fairoaks* was nearly a mile out of Clavering, or their premises would never have been free from the prying eyes and prattle of one or other of the male and female inhabitants there.

Fairoaks lawn comes down to the little river Brawl, and on the other side were the plantations and woods (as much as were left of them) of Clavering Park, Sir Francis Clavering, Bart. The park was let out in pasture and fed down by sheep and cattle when the Pendennises came first to live at Fairoaks. Shutters were up in the house: a splendid freestone palace, with great stairs, statues, and porticoes, whereof you may see a picture in the *Beauties of England and Wales*. Sir Richard Clavering, Sir Francis's grandfather, had commenced the ruin of the family by the building of this palace: his successor had achieved the ruin by living in it. The present Sir Francis was abroad somewhere; nor could anybody be found rich enough to rent that enormous mansion, through the deserted rooms, mouldy clanking halls, and dismal galleries of which Arthur Pendennis many a time walked trembling when he was a boy. At sunset, from the lawn of Fairoaks, there was a pretty sight: it and the opposite park of Clavering were in the habit of putting on a rich golden tinge, which became them both wonderfully. The upper windows of the great house flamed so as to make your eyes wink; the little river ran off noisily westward, and was lost in a sombre wood, behind which the towers of the old abbey church of Clavering (whereby that town is called Clavering St. Mary's to the present day) rose up in purple splendour. Little Arthur's figure and his mother's cast long blue shadows over the grass; and he would repeat in a low voice (for a scene of great natural beauty always moved the boy, who inherited this sensibility from his mother) certain lines beginning, 'These are thy glorious works, Parent of Good; Almighty! thine this universal frame,'* greatly to Mrs. Pendennis's delight. Such walks and conversation generally ended in a profusion of filial and maternal embraces; for to love and to pray were the main occupations of this dear woman's life; and I have often heard Pendennis say, in his wild way, that he felt that he was sure of going to heaven, for his mother never could be happy there without him.

As for John Pendennis, as the father of the family, and that sort of thing, everybody had the greatest respect for him : and his orders were obeyed like those of the Medes and Persians. His hat was as well brushed, perhaps, as that of any man in this empire. His meals were served at the same minute every day, and woe to those who came late, as little Pen, a disorderly little rascal, sometimes did. Prayers were recited, his letters were read, his business dispatched, his stables and garden inspected, his hen-houses and kennel, his barn and pigsty visited, always at regular hours. After dinner he always had a nap with the *Globe* newspaper on his knee, and his yellow bandanna handkerchief on his face (Major Pendennis sent the yellow handkerchiefs from India, and his brother had helped in the purchase of his majority, so that they were good friends now). And so, as his dinner took place at six o'clock to a minute, and the sunset business alluded to may be supposed to have occurred at about half-past seven, it is probable that he did not much care for the view in front of his lawn windows, or take any share in the poetry and caresses which were taking place there.

They seldom occurred in his presence. However frisky they were before, mother and child were hushed and quiet when Mr. Pendennis walked into the drawing-room, his newspaper under his arm. . . . And here, while little Pen, buried in a great chair, read all the books of which he could lay hold, the squire perused his own articles in the *Gardener's Gazette*, or took a solemn hand at piquet with Mrs. Pendennis or an occasional friend from the village.

Pendennis usually took care that at least one of his grand dinners should take place when his brother, the major, who, on the return of his regiment from India and New South Wales, had sold out and gone upon half-pay, came to pay his biennial visit to Fairoaks. 'My brother, Major Pendennis,' was a constant theme of the retired doctor's conversation. All the family delighted in my brother the major. He was the link which bound them to the great world of London, and the fashion. He always brought down the last news of the nobility, and[8] spoke of such with soldier-like respect and decorum. He would say, 'My Lord Bareacres has been good enough to invite me to Bareacres for the pheasant shooting,' or, 'My Lord

CALM SUMMER EVENINGS

Steyne is so kind as to wish for my presence at Stillbrook for the Easter holidays ;' and you may be sure the whereabouts of my brother the major was carefully made known by worthy Mr. Pendennis to his friends at the Clavering Reading-room, at justice-meetings, or at the county-town. Their carriages would come from ten miles round to call upon Major Pendennis in his visits to Fairoaks ; the fame of his fashion as a man about town was established throughout the county. There was a talk of his marrying Miss Hunkle, of Lilybank, old Hunkle the attorney's daughter, with at least fifteen hundred a year to her fortune; but, my brother the major declined.[9] 'As a bachelor,' he said, 'nobody cares how poor I am. I have the happiness to live with people who are so highly placed in the world, that a few hundreds or thousands a year more or less can make no difference in the estimation in which they are pleased to hold me. Miss Hunkle, though a most respectable lady, is not in possession of either the birth or the manners, which would entitle her to be received into the sphere in which I have the honour to move. I shall live and die an old bachelor, John : and your worthy friend, Miss Hunkle, I have no doubt, will find some more worthy object of her affection than a worn-out old soldier on half pay.' Time showed the correctness of the surmise ; Miss Hunkle married a young French nobleman, and is now at this moment living at Lilybank, under the title of Baroness de Carambole, having been separated from her wild young scapegrace of a baron very shortly after their union.

The major[10] had a sincere liking and regard for his sister-in-law, whom he pronounced, and with perfect truth, to be as fine a lady as any in England.[11] Indeed, Mrs. Pendennis's tranquil beauty, her natural sweetness and kindness, and that simplicity and dignity which a perfect purity and innocence are sure to bestow upon a handsome woman, rendered her quite worthy of her brother's praises. I think it is not national prejudice which makes me believe that a high-bred English lady is the most complete of all Heaven's subjects in this world. In whom else do you see so much grace, and so much virtue ; so much faith, and so much tenderness ; with such a perfect refinement and chastity ? And by high-bred ladies I don't mean duchesses and countesses. Be they ever so high in station, they can

be but ladies, and no more. But almost every man who lives in the world has the happiness, let us hope, of counting a few such persons amongst his circle of acquaintance—women in whose angelcial natures there is something awful, as well as beautiful, to contemplate; at whose feet the wildest and fiercest of us must fall down and humble ourselves, in admiration of that adorable purity which never seems to do or to think wrong.

Arthur Pendennis had the good fortune to have such a mother. During his childhood and youth, the boy thought of her as little less than an angel—a supernatural being, all wisdom, love, and beauty. When her husband drove her into the county town, to the assize balls or concerts, he would step into the assembly with his wife on his arm, and look the great folks in the face, as much as to say, 'Look at that, my lord; can any of you show me a woman like *that?*' She enraged some country ladies with three times her money, by a sort of desperate perfection which they found in her. Miss Pybus said she was cold and haughty; Miss Pierce, that she was too proud for her station; Mrs. Wapshot, as a doctor of divinity's lady, would have the *pas* of her, who was only the wife of a medical practitioner. In the meanwhile, this lady moved through the world quite regardless of all the comments that were made in her praise or disfavour. She did not seem to know that she was admired or hated for being so perfect; but carried on calmly through life, saying her prayers, loving her family, helping her neighbours, and doing her duty.

That even a woman should be faultless, however, is an arrangement not permitted by nature, which assigns to us mental defects, as it awards to us headaches, illnesses, or death: without which the scheme of the world could not be carried on,—nay, some of the best qualities of mankind could not be brought into exercise. As pain produces or elicits fortitude and endurance; difficulty, perseverance; poverty, industry and ingenuity; danger, courage and what not; so the very virtues, on the other hand, will generate some vices; and, in fine, Mrs. Pendennis had that vice which Miss Pybus and Miss Pierce discovered in her, namely, that of pride; which did not vest itself so much in her own person, as in that of her family. She spoke about Mr. Pendennis (a worthy little

gentleman enough, but there are others as good as he) with an awful reverence, as if he had been the Pope of Rome on his throne, and she a cardinal kneeling at his feet, and giving him incense. The major she held to be a sort of Bayard among majors: and as for her son Arthur, she worshipped that youth with an ardour which the young scapegrace accepted almost as coolly as the statue of the saint in St. Peter's receives the rapturous osculations which the faithful deliver on his toe.

This unfortunate superstition and idol-worship of this good woman was the cause of a great deal of the misfortune which befell the young gentleman who is the hero of this history, and deserves therefore to be mentioned at the outset of his story.

Arthur Pendennis's schoolfellows at the Grey Friars School* state that, as a boy, he was in no ways remarkable either as a dunce or as a scholar.[12] He never read to improve himself out of school hours, but, on the contrary, devoured all the novels, plays, and poetry, on which he could lay his hands. He never was flogged, but it was a wonder how he escaped the whipping-post. When he had money he spent it royally in tarts for himself and his friends; he has been known to disburse nine-and-sixpence out of ten shillings awarded to him in a single day. When he had no funds he went on tick. When he could get no credit he went without, and was almost as happy. He has been known to take a thrashing for a crony without saying a word; but a blow, ever so slight, from a friend would make him roar. To fighting he was averse from his earliest youth, as indeed to physic, the Greek grammar, or any other exertion, and would engage in none of them, except at the last extremity. He seldom if ever told lies, and never bullied little boys. Those masters or seniors who were kind to him, he loved with boyish ardour. And though the doctor, when he did not know his Horace, or could not construe his Greek play, said that that boy Pendennis was a disgrace to the school, a candidate for ruin in this world, and perdition in the next; a profligate who would most likely bring his venerable father to ruin and his mother to a dishonoured grave, and the like—yet as the doctor made use of these compliments to most of the boys in the place (which has not turned out an unusual number of felons and pick-pockets), little Pen, at first uneasy and terrified by these

charges, became gradually accustomed to hear them; and he has not, in fact, either murdered his parents, or committed any act worthy of transportation or hanging up to the present day.

There were many of the upper boys, among the Cistercians with whom Pendennis was educated, who assumed all the privileges of men long before they quitted that seminary. Many of them, for example, smoked cigars—and some had already begun the practice of inebriation. One had fought a duel with an ensign in a marching regiment in consequence of a row at the theatre—another actually kept a buggy and horse at a livery stable in Covent Garden, and might be seen driving any Sunday in Hyde Park with a groom with squared arms and armorial buttons by his side. Many of the seniors were in love, and showed each other in confidence poems addressed to, or letters and locks of hair received from, young ladies—but Pen, a modest and timid youth, rather envied these than imitated them as yet. He had not got beyond the theory as yet—the practice of life was all to come. And by the way, ye tender mothers and sober fathers of Christian families, a prodigious thing that theory of life is, as orally learned at a great public school. Why, if you could hear those boys of fourteen who blush before mothers and sneak off in silence in the presence of their daughters, talking among each other—it would be the women's turn to blush then. Before he was twelve years old[13] little Pen had heard talk enough to make him quite awfully wise upon certain points—and so, madam, has your pretty little rosy-cheeked son, who is coming home from school for the ensuing holidays. I don't say that the boy is lost, or that the innocence has left him which he had from 'Heaven, which is our home,' but that the shades of the prison-house are closing very fast over him, and that we are helping as much as possible to corrupt him.

Well—Pen had just made his public appearance in a coat with a tail, or *cauda virilis*, and was looking most anxiously in his little study glass to see if his whiskers were growing, like those of more fortunate youths his companions; and, instead of the treble voice with which he used to speak and sing (for his singing voice was a very sweet one, and he used when little to be made to perform 'Home, sweet Home,' 'My Pretty Page,' and a French song or two

which his mother had taught him, and other ballads for the delectation of the senior boys), had suddenly plunged into a deep bass diversified by a squeak, which[14] set master and scholars laughing—he was about sixteen years old in a word, when he was suddenly called away from his academic studies.

It was at the close of the forenoon school, and Pen had been unnoticed all the previous part of the morning till now, when the doctor put him on to construe in a Greek play. He did not know a word of it, though little Timmins, his form-fellow, was prompting him with all his might. Pen had made a sad blunder or two—when the awful chief broke out upon him.

'Pendennis, sir,' he said, 'your idleness is incorrigible and your stupidity beyond example. You are a disgrace to your school, and to your family, and I have no doubt will prove so in after-life to your country. If that vice, sir, which is described to us as the root of all evil be really what moralists have represented (and I have no doubt of the correctness of their opinion), for what a prodigious quantity of future crime and wickedness are you, unhappy boy, laying the seed! Miserable trifler! A boy who construes δε *and*, instead of δε *but*, at sixteen years of age, is guilty not merely of folly, and ignorance, and dullness inconceivable, but of crime, of deadly crime, of filial ingratitude, which I tremble to contemplate. A boy, sir, who does not learn his Greek play cheats the parent who spends money for his education. A boy who cheats his parent is not very far from robbing or forging upon his neighbour. A man who forges on his neighbour pays the penalty of his crime at the gallows. And it is not such a one that I pity (for he will be deservedly cut off); but his maddened and heart-broken parents, who are driven to a premature grave by his crimes, or, if they live, drag on a wretched and dishonoured old age. Go on, sir, and I warn you that the very next mistake that you make shall subject you to the punishment of the rod. Who's that laughing? What ill-conditioned boy is there that dares to laugh?' shouted the doctor.

Indeed, while the master was making this oration, there was a general titter behind him in the schoolroom. The orator had his back to the door of this ancient apartment, which was open, and a gentleman who was quite familiar

with the place, for both Major Arthur and Mr. John Pendennis had been at the school, was asking the fifth-form boy who sat by the door for Pendennis. The lad grinning pointed to the culprit against whom the doctor was pouring out the thunders of his just wrath—Major Pendennis could not help laughing. He remembered having stood under that very pillar where Pen the younger now stood, and having been assaulted by the doctor's predecessor years and years ago. The intelligence was 'passed round' that it was Pendennis's uncle in an instant, and a hundred young faces wondering and giggling, between

terror and laughter, turned now to the new-comer and then to the awful doctor.

The major asked the fifth-form boy to carry his card up to the doctor, which the lad did with an arch look. Major Pendennis had written on the card, 'I must take A. P. home; his father is very ill.'

As the doctor received the card, and stopped his harangue with rather a scared look, the laughter of the boys, half constrained until then, burst out in a general shout. 'Silence !' roared out the doctor, stamping with his foot. Pen looked up and saw who was his deliverer; the major beckoned to him gravely, and tumbling down his books Pen went across.

The doctor took out his watch. It was two minutes to one. 'We will take the Juvenal at afternoon school,' he said, nodding to the captain, and all the boys understanding the signal gathered up their books and poured out of the hall.

Young Pen saw by his uncle's face that something had happened at home. 'Is there anything the matter with—my mother?' he said. He could hardly speak, though, for emotion, and the tears which were ready to start.

'No,' said the major, 'but your father's very ill. Go and pack your trunk directly; I have got a post-chaise at the gate.'

Pen went off quickly to his boarding-house to do as his uncle bade him; and the doctor, now left alone in the schoolroom, came out to shake hands with his old schoolfellow. You would not have thought it was the same man. As Cinderella at a particular hour became, from a blazing and magnificent princess, quite an ordinary little maid in a grey petticoat, so, as the clock struck one, all the thundering majesty and awful wrath of the schoolmaster disappeared.

'There is nothing serious, I hope,' said the doctor. 'It is a pity to take the boy otherwise. He is a good boy, rather idle and unenergetic, but an honest gentlemanlike little fellow, though I can't get him to construe as I wish. Won't you come in and have some luncheon? My wife will be very happy to see you."

But Major Pendennis declined the luncheon. He said his brother was very ill, had had a fit the day before, and it was a great question if they should see him alive.

'There's no other son, is there?' said the doctor. The major answered, 'No.'

'And there's a good eh—a good eh—property, I believe?' asked the other, in an off-hand way.

'H'm—so so,' said the major. Whereupon this colloquy came to an end. And Arthur Pendennis got into a post-chaise with his uncle, never to come back to school any more.

As the chaise drove through Clavering, the ostler standing whistling under the archway of the 'Clavering Arms' winked the postilion ominously, as much as to say all was over. The gardener's wife came and opened the lodge-gates, and let the travellers through with a silent shake of the head. All the blinds were down at Fairoaks—the face of the old

footman was as blank when he let them in. Arthur's face was white too, with terror more than with grief. Whatever of warmth and love the deceased man might have had, and he adored his wife and loved and admired his son with all his heart, he had shut them up within himself; nor had the boy been ever able to penetrate that frigid outward barrier. But Arthur had been his father's pride and glory through life, and his name the last which John Pendennis had tried to articulate whilst he lay with his wife's hand clasping his own cold and clammy palm, as the flickering spirit went out into the darkness of death, and life and the world passed away from him.

The little girl, whose face had peered for a moment under the blinds as the chaise came up, opened the door from the stairs into the hall, and taking Arthur's hand silently as he stooped down to kiss her, led him upstairs to his mother. Old John opened the dining-room for the major. The room was darkened with the blinds down, and surrounded by all the gloomy pictures of the Pendennises. He drank a glass of wine. The bottle had been opened for the Squire four days before. His hat was brushed, and laid on the hall table: his newspapers, and his letter-bag, with 'John Pendennis, Esq., Fairoaks,' engraved upon the brass plate, were there in waiting. The doctor and the lawyer from Clavering, who had seen the chaise pass through, came up in a gig half an hour after the major's arrival, and entered by the back door. The former gave a detailed account of the seizure and demise of Mr. Pendennis, enlarged on his virtues and the estimation in which the neighbourhood held him; on what a loss he would be to the magistrates' bench, the County Hospital, etc. Mrs. Pendennis bore up wonderfully, he said, especially since Master Arthur's arrival. The lawyer stayed and dined with Major Pendennis, and they talked business all the evening. The major was his brother's executor, and joint guardian to the boy with Mrs. Pendennis. Everything was left unreservedly to her, except in case of a second marriage,—an occasion which might offer itself in the case of so young and handsome a woman, Mr. Tatham gallantly said, when different provisions were enacted by the deceased. The major would of course take entire superintendence of everything under this most impressive and melancholy occasion. Aware of this authority, old John the footman

when he brought Major Pendennis the candle to go to bed, followed afterwards with the plate-basket; and the next morning brought him the key of the hall clock—the squire always used to wind it up of a Thursday, John said. Mrs. Pendennis's maid brought him messages from her mistress. She confirmed the doctor's report, of the comfort which Master Arthur's arrival had caused to his mother.

What passed between that lady and the boy is not of import. A veil should be thrown over those sacred emotions of love and grief. The maternal passion is a sacred mystery to me. What one sees symbolized in the Roman churches in the image of the Virgin Mother with a bosom bleeding with love, I think one may witness (and admire the Almighty bounty for) every day. I saw a Jewish lady, only yesterday, with a child at her knee, and from whose face towards the child there shone a sweetness so angelical, that it seemed to form a sort of glory round both. I protest I could have knelt before her too, and adored in her the Divine beneficence in endowing us with the maternal *storgè*,* which began with our race and sanctifies the history of mankind.[15]

As for Arthur Pendennis, after that awful shock which the sight of his dead father must have produced on him, and the pity and feeling which such an event no doubt occasioned, I am not sure that in the very moment of the grief, and as he embraced his mother and tenderly consoled her, and promised to love her for ever, there was not springing up in his breast a sort of secret triumph and exultation. He was the chief now and lord. He was Pendennis; and all round about him were his servants and handmaids. 'You'll never send me away,' little Laura said, tripping by him, and holding his hand. 'You won't send me to school, will you, Arthur?'

Arthur kissed her and patted her head. No, she shouldn't go to school. As for going himself, that was quite out of the question. He had determined that that part of his life should not be renewed. In the midst of the general grief, and the corpse still lying above, he had

leisure to conclude that he would have it *all* holidays for the future, that he wouldn't get up till he liked, or stand the bullying of the doctor any more, and had made a hundred of such day-dreams and resolves for the future. How one's thoughts will travel! and how quickly our wishes beget them! When he with Laura in his hand went into the kitchen on his way to the dog-kennel, the fowl-houses, and other his favourite haunts, all the servants were assembled in great silence with their friends, and the labouring men and their wives, and Sally Potter who went with the post-bag to Clavering, and the baker's man from Clavering—all there assembled and drinking beer on the melancholy occasion—rose up on his entrance and bowed or curtsied to him. They never used to do so last holidays, he felt at once and with indescribable pleasure. The cook cried out, 'O Lord,' and whispered, 'How Master Arthur do grow!' Thomas, the groom, in the act of drinking, put down the jug alarmed before his master. Thomas's master felt the honour keenly. He went through and looked at the pointers. As Flora put her nose up to his waistcoat, and Ponto, yelling with pleasure, hurtled at his chain, Pen patronized the dogs, and said, 'Poo Ponto, poo Flora,' in his most condescending manner. And then he went and looked at Laura's hens, and at the pigs, and at the orchard, and at the dairy; perhaps he blushed to think that it was only last holidays he had in a manner robbed the great apple-tree, and been scolded by the dairymaid for taking cream.

They buried John Pendennis, Esq., 'formerly an eminent medical practitioner at Bath, and subsequently an able magistrate, a benevolent landlord, and a benefactor to many charities and public institutions in this neighbourhood and county,' with one of the most handsome funerals that had been seen since Sir Roger Clavering was buried here, the clerk said, in the abbey church of Clavering St. Mary's. A fair marble slab, from which the above inscription is copied, was erected over the Fairoaks pew in the church. On it you may see the Pendennis coat of arms, and crest, an eagle looking towards the sun, with the motto, '*Nec tenui penna*,'* to the present day. Doctor Portman alluded to the deceased most handsomely and affectingly, as 'our dear departed friend,' in his sermon next Sunday; and Arthur Pendennis reigned in his stead.

CHAPTER III

IN WHICH PENDENNIS APPEARS AS A VERY YOUNG MAN INDEED

ARTHUR was about sixteen years old, we have said, when he began to reign; in person (for I see that the artist who is to illustrate this book, and who makes sad work of the likeness, will never be able to take my friend off), he had what his friends would call a dumpy, but his mamma styled a neat little figure. His hair was of a healthy brown colour, which looks like gold in the sunshine; his face was round, rosy, freckled, and good-humoured; his whiskers[1] were decidedly of a reddish hue;* in fact, without being a beauty, he had such a frank, good-natured kind face, and laughed so merrily at you out of his honest blue eyes, that no wonder Mrs. Pendennis thought him the pride of the whole county. Between the ages of sixteen and eighteen he rose from five feet six to five feet eight inches in height, at which altitude he paused. But his mother wondered at it. He was three inches taller than his father. Was it possible that any man could grow to be three inches taller than Mr. Pendennis?

You may be certain he never went back to school; the discipline of the establishment did not suit him, and he liked being at home much better. The question of his return was debated, and his uncle was for his going back. The doctor wrote his opinion that it was most important for Arthur's success in after-life that he should know a Greek play thoroughly, but Pen adroitly managed to hint to his mother what a dangerous place Greyfriars was, and what sad wild fellows some of the chaps there were, and the timid soul, taking alarm at once, acceded to his desire to stay at home.

Then Pen's uncle offered to use his influence with His Royal Highness the Commander-in-Chief, who was pleased to be very kind to him, and proposed to get Pen a com-

mission in the Foot Guards. Pen's heart leaped at this: he had been to hear the band at St. James's play on a Sunday, when he went out to his uncle. He had seen Tom Ricketts, of the fourth form, who used to wear a jacket and trousers so ludicrously tight, that the elder boys could not forbear using him in the quality of a butt or 'cockshy'—he had seen this very Ricketts arrayed in crimson and gold, with an immense bearskin cap on his head, staggering under the colours of the regiment. Tom had recognized him and gave him a patronizing nod. Tom, a little wretch whom he had cut over the back with a hockey-stick last quarter—and there he was in the centre of the square, rallying round the flag of his country, surrounded by bayonets, crossbelts, and scarlet, the band blowing trumpets and banging cymbals—talking familiarly to immense warriors with tufts to their chins and Waterloo medals. What would not Pen have given to [2] enter such a service?

But Helen Pendennis, when this point was proposed to her by her son, put on a face full of terror and alarm. She said, 'She did not quarrel with others who thought differently, but that in her opinion a Christian had no right to make the army a profession. Mr. Pendennis never, never would have permitted his son to be a soldier. Finally, she should be very unhappy if he thought of it.' Now Pen would have as soon cut off his nose and ears as deliberately, and of aforethought malice, made his mother unhappy; and, as he was of such a generous disposition that he would give away anything to anyone, he instantly made a present of his visionary red coat and epaulettes [3] to his mother.

She thought him the noblest creature in the world. But Major Pendennis, when the offer of the commission was acknowledged and refused, wrote back a curt and somewhat angry letter to the widow, and thought his nephew was rather a spoony.

He was contented, however, when he saw the boy's performances out hunting at Christmas, when the major came down as usual to Fairoaks. Pen had a very good mare, and rode her with uncommon pluck and grace. He took his fences with great coolness and judgement. He wrote to the chaps at school about his top-boots, and his feats across country. He began to think seriously of a scarlet coat: and his mother must own that she thought

it would become him remarkably well; though, of course, she passed hours of anguish during his absence, and daily expected to see him brought home on a shutter.

With these amusements, in rather too great plenty, it must not be assumed that Pen neglected his studies altogether. He had a natural taste for reading every possible kind of book which did not fall into his school-course. It was only when they forced his head into the waters of knowledge that he refused to drink. He devoured all the books at home from Inchbald's *Theatre* to White's *Farriery;* he ransacked the neighbouring book-cases. He found at Clavering an old cargo of French novels, which he read with all his might; and he would sit for hours perched upon the topmost bar of Doctor Portman's library steps with a folio on his knees, whether it were Hakluyt's *Travels*, Hobbes's *Leviathan*, *Augustini Opera*, or Chaucer's *Poems*. He and the vicar were very good friends, and from his reverence Pen learned that honest taste for port wine which distinguished him through life. And as for Mrs. Portman, who was not in the least jealous, though her doctor avowed himself in love with Mrs. Pendennis, whom he pronounced to be by far the finest lady in the county—all her grief was, as she looked up fondly at Pen perched on the book-ladder, that her daughter, Minny, was too old for him—as indeed she was—Miss Mira Portman being at that period only two years younger than Pen's mother, and weighing as much as Pen and Mrs. Pendennis together.

Are these details insipid? Look back, good friend, at your own youth, and ask how was that? I like to think of a well-nurtured boy, brave and gentle, warm-hearted and loving, and looking the world in the face with kind honest eyes. What bright colours it wore then, and how you enjoyed it! A man has not many years of such time. He does not know them whilst they are with him. It is only when they are passed long away that he remembers how dear and happy they were.[4]

Mr. Smirke, Dr. Portman's curate, was engaged, at a liberal salary, to walk or ride over from Clavering and pass several hours daily with the young gentleman. Smirke was a man perfectly faultless at a tea-table, wore a curl on his fair forehead, and tied his neckcloth with a melancholy grace. He was a decent scholar and mathematician,

and taught Pen as much as the lad was ever disposed to learn, which was not much. For Pen had soon taken the measure of his tutor, who, when he came riding into the courtyard at Fairoaks on his pony, turned out his toes so absurdly, and left such a gap between his knees and the saddle, that it was impossible for any lad endowed with a sense of humour to respect such an equestrian. He nearly killed Smirke with terror by putting him on his mare, and taking him a ride over a common, where the county fox-hounds (then hunted by that stanch old sportsman, Mr. Hardhead, of Dumplingbeare), happened to meet. Mr. Smirke, on Pen's mare, Rebecca* (she was named after Pen's favourite heroine, the daughter of Isaac of York), astounded the hounds as much as he disgusted the huntsman, laming one of the former by persisting in riding amongst the pack, and receiving a speech from the latter, more remarkable for energy of language, than any oration he had ever heard since he left the bargemen on the banks of Isis.

Smirke and his pupil[5] read the ancient poets together, and rattled through them at a pleasant rate, very different from that steady grubbing pace with which the Cistercians used to go over the classic ground, scenting out each word as they went, and digging up every root in the way. Pen never liked to halt, but made his tutor construe when he was at fault, and thus galloped through the Iliad and the Odyssey, the tragic play-writers, and the charming wicked Aristophanes (whom he vowed to be the greatest poet of all). But he went so fast that, though he certainly galloped through a considerable extent of the ancient country, he clean forgot it in after-life, and had only such a vague remembrance of his early classic course as a man has in the House of Commons, let us say, who still keeps up two or three quotations; or a reviewer who, just for decency's sake, hints at a little Greek.[6]

Besides the ancient poets, you may be sure Pen read the English with great gusto. Smirke sighed and shook his head sadly both about Byron and Moore. But Pen was a sworn fire-worshipper and a Corsair; he had them by heart, and used to take little Laura into the window and say, 'Zuleika, I am not thy brother,'* in tones so tragic that they caused the solemn little maid to open her great eyes still wider. She sat, until the proper hour for retirement, sewing at Mrs. Pendennis's knee, and listening to Pen

reading out to her of nights without comprehending one word of what he read.

He read Shakespere to his mother (which she said she liked, but didn't), and Byron, and Pope, and his favourite *Lalla Rookh*, which pleased her indifferently. But as for Bishop Heber, and Mrs. Hemans above all, this lady used to melt right away, and be absorbed into her pocket-handkerchief, when Pen read those authors to her in his kind boyish voice. The *Christian Year**was a book which appeared about that time. The son and the mother whispered it to each other with awe—faint, very faint, and seldom in after-life Pendennis heard that solemn church-music : but he always loved the remembrance of it, and of the times when it struck on his heart, and he walked over the fields full of hope and void of doubt, as the church-bells rang on Sunday morning.

It was at this period of his existence, that Pen broke out in the 'Poet's Corner' of the *County Chronicle*, with some verses with which he was perfectly well satisfied. His are the verses signed 'NEP.' addressed 'To a Tear'; 'On the Anniversary of the Battle of Waterloo'; 'To Madame Caradori singing at the Assize Meetings'; 'On St. Bartholomew's Day' (a tremendous denunciation of Popery, and a solemn warning to the people of England to rally against emancipating the Roman Catholics),* etc., etc.—all which masterpieces poor Mrs. Pendennis kept along with his first socks, the first cutting of his hair, his bottle, and other interesting relics of his infancy. He used to gallop Rebecca over the neighbouring Dumpling Downs, or into the county town, which, if you please, we shall call Chatteris, spouting his own poems, and filled with quite a Byronic afflatus as he thought.

His genius at this time was of a decidedly gloomy cast. He brought his mother a tragedy, at which, though he killed sixteen people before the second act, Helen laughed so, that he thrust the masterpiece into the fire in a pet. He projected an epic poem in blank verse, *Cortez, or the Conqueror of Mexico, and the Inca's Daughter*. He wrote part of *Seneca, or the Fatal Bath*, and *Ariadne in Naxos*; classical pieces, with choruses and strophes and anti-strophes, which sadly puzzled Mrs. Pendennis; and began a *History of the Jesuits*, in which he lashed that Order with tremendous severity. His loyalty did his mother's heart

good to witness. He was a stanch, unflinching Church-and-King man in those days; and at the election, when Sir Giles Beanfield stood on the Blue interest, against Lord Trehawk, Lord Eyrie's son, a Whig and a friend of Popery, Arthur Pendennis, with an immense bow for himself, which his mother made, and with a blue ribbon for Rebecca, rode alongside of the Reverend Doctor Portman, on his grey mare Dowdy, and at the head of the Clavering voters, whom the doctor brought up to plump for the Protestant Champion.

On that day Pen made his first speech at the Blue hotel: and also, it appears, for the first time in his life—took a little more wine than was good for him. Mercy! what a scene it was at Fairoaks, when he rode back at ever so much o'clock at night. What moving about of lanterns in the courtyard and stables, though the moon was shining out; what a gathering of servants, as Pen came home, clattering over the bridge and up the stable-yard, with half a score of the Clavering voters yelling after him the Blue song of the election.

He wanted them all to come in and have some wine—some very good madeira—some capital madeira—John, go and get some madeira,—and there is no knowing what the farmers would have done, had not Madam Pendennis made her appearance in a white wrapper, with a candle—and scared those zealous Blues so by the sight of her pale handsome face, that they touched their hats and rode off.

Besides these occupations and amusements in which Mr. Pen indulged, there was one which forms the main business and pleasure of youth, if the poets tell us aright, whom Pen was always studying;[7] and which, ladies, you have rightly guessed to be that of Love. Pen sighed for it first in secret, and, like the lovesick swain in Ovid, opened his breast and said, 'Aura, veni.' What generous youth is there that has not courted some such windy mistress in his time?

Yes, Pen began to feel the necessity of a first love—of a consuming passion—of an object on which he could concentrate all those vague floating fancies under which he sweetly suffered—of a young lady to whom he could really make verses, and whom he could set up and adore, in place of those unsubstantial Ianthes and Zuleikas to whom he addressed the outpourings of his gushing muse. He read

his favourite poems over and over again, he called upon Alma Venus the delight of gods and men, he translated Anacreon's odes, and picked out passages suitable to his complaint from Waller, Dryden, Prior, and the like. Smirke and he were never weary, in their interviews, of discoursing about love. The faithless tutor entertained him with sentimental conversations in place of lectures on algebra and Greek; for Smirke was in love too. Who could help it, being in daily intercourse with such a woman? Smirke was madly in love (as far as such a mild flame as Mr. Smirke's may be called madness) with Mrs. Pendennis. That honest lady, sitting down below stairs teaching little Laura to play the piano, or devising flannel petticoats for the poor round about her, or otherwise busied with the calm routine of her modest and spotless Christian life, was little aware what storms were brewing in two bosoms upstairs in the study—in Pen's as he sat in his shooting-jacket, with his elbows on the green study-table, and his hands clutching his curly brown hair, Homer under his nose, —and in worthy Mr. Smirke's, with whom he was reading. Here they would talk about Helen and Andromache. 'Andromache's like my mother,' Pen used to avouch; 'but I say, Smirke, by Jove I'd cut off my nose to see Helen'; and he would spout certain favourite lines which the reader will find in their proper place in the third book. He drew portraits of her—they are extant still—with straight noses and enormous eyes, and 'Arthur Pendennis delineavit et pinxit' gallantly written underneath.

As for Mr. Smirke, he naturally preferred Andromache. And in consequence he was uncommonly kind to Pen. He gave him his Elzevir Horace, of which the boy was fond, and his little Greek Testament which his own mamma at Clapham had purchased and presented to him. He bought him a silver pencil-case; and in the matter of learning let him do just as much or as little as ever he pleased. He always seemed to be on the point of unbosoming himself to Pen: nay, he confessed to the latter that he had a—an attachment, an ardently cherished attachment, about which Pendennis longed to hear, and said, 'Tell us, old chap, is she handsome? has she got blue eyes or black?' But Doctor Portman's curate, heaving a gentle sigh, cast up his eyes to the ceiling, and begged Pen faintly to change the conversation. Poor Smirke! He invited

Pen to dine at his lodgings over Madame Fribsby's, the milliner's, in Clavering, and once when it was raining, and Mrs. Pendennis, who had driven in her pony-chaise into Clavering with respect to some arrangements, about leaving off mourning probably, was prevailed upon to enter the curate's apartments, he sent for pound-cakes instantly. The sofa on which she sat became sacred to him from that day: and he kept flowers in the glass which she drank from ever after.

As Mrs. Pendennis was never tired of hearing the praises of her son, we may be certain that this rogue of a tutor neglected no opportunity of conversing with her upon the subject. It might be a little tedious to him to hear the stories about Pen's generosity, about his bravery in fighting the big naughty boy, about his fun and jokes, about his prodigious skill in Latin, music, riding, etc.—but what price would he not pay to be in her company? and the widow after these conversations, thought Mr. Smirke a very pleasing and well-informed man. As for her son, she had not settled in her mind whether he was to be Senior Wrangler and Archbishop of Canterbury, or Double First Class at Oxford and Lord Chancellor. That all England did not possess his peer was a fact about which there was, in her mind, no manner of question.

A simple person, of inexpensive habits, she began forthwith to save, and, perhaps, to be a little parsimonious, in favour of her boy. There were no entertainments, of course, at Fairoaks, during the year of her weeds. Nor, indeed, did the doctor's silver dish-covers, of which he was so proud, and which were flourished all over with the arms of the Pendennises, and surmounted with their crest, come out of the plate-chest again for long, long years. The household was diminished, and its expenses curtailed. There was a very blank anchorite repast when Pen dined from home: and he himself headed the remonstrance from the kitchen regarding the deteriorated quality of the Fairoaks beer. She was becoming miserly for Pen. Indeed, who ever accused women of being just? They are always sacrificing themselves or somebody for somebody else's sake.

There happened to be no young woman in the small circle of friends who were in the widow's intimacy whom Pendennis could by any possibility gratify by endowing her with the inestimable treasure of a heart which he was

longing to give away. Some young fellows in this predicament bestow their young affections upon Dolly, the dairymaid, or cast the eyes of tenderness upon Molly, the blacksmith's daughter. Pen thought a Pendennis much too grand a personage to stoop so low. He was too high-minded for a vulgar intrigue, and at the idea of a seduction, had he ever entertained it, his heart would have revolted as from the notion of any act of baseness or dishonour. Miss Minny Portman was too old, too large, and too fond of reading Rollin's *Ancient History*. The Miss Boardbacks, Admiral Boardback's daughters (of St. Vincent's, or Fourth of June House,* as it was called), disgusted Pen with the London airs which they brought into the country.[8] Captain Glanders's (H.P., 50th Dragoon Guards) three girls were in brown-holland pinafores as yet, with the ends of their hair-plaits tied up in dirty pink ribbon. Not having acquired the art of dancing, the youth avoided such chances as he might have had of meeting with the fair sex at the Chatteris Assemblies; in fine, he was not in love, because there was nobody at hand to fall in love with. And the young monkey used to ride out, day after day, in quest of Dulcinea; and peep into the pony-chaises and gentlefolks' carriages, as they drove along the broad turnpike roads, with a heart beating within him, and a secret tremor and hope that *she* might be in that yellow post-chaise coming swinging up the hill, or one of those three girls in beaver bonnets in the back seat of the double gig, which the fat old gentleman in black was driving at four miles an hour. The post-chaise contained a snuffy old dowager of seventy, with a maid, her contemporary. The three girls in the beaver bonnets were no handsomer than the turnips that skirted the roadside. Do as he might, and ride where he would, the fairy princess whom he was to rescue and win had not yet appeared to honest Pen.

Upon these points he did not discourse to his mother. He had a world of his own. What ardent, imaginative soul has not a secret pleasure-place in which it disports? Let no clumsy prying or dull meddling of ours try to disturb it in our children. Actaeon was a brute for wanting to push in where Diana was bathing. Leave him occasionally alone, my good madam, if you have a poet for a child. Even your admirable advice may be a bore sometimes.[9] Yonder little child may have thoughts too

deep even for your great mind, and fancies so coy and timid that they will not bare themselves when your ladyship sits by.

Helen Pendennis by the force of sheer love divined a great number of her son's secrets. But she kept these things in her heart (if we may so speak), and did not speak of them. Besides, she had made up her mind that he was to marry little Laura: she would be eighteen when Pen was six-and-twenty, and had finished his college career; and had made his grand tour; and was settled either in London, astonishing all the metropolis by his learning and eloquence at the bar, or better still in a sweet country parsonage surrounded with hollyhocks and roses, close to a delightful romantic ivy-covered church, from the pulpit of which Pen would utter the most beautiful sermons ever preached.

While these natural sentiments were waging war and trouble in honest Pen's bosom, it chanced one day that he rode into Chatteris, for the purpose of carrying to the *County Chronicle* a tremendous and thrilling poem for the next week's paper; and putting up his horse, according to custom, at the stables of the 'George Hotel' there, he fell in with an old acquaintance. A grand black tandem, with scarlet wheels, came rattling into the inn yard, as Pen stood there in converse with the ostler about Rebecca; and the voice of the driver called out, 'Hallo, Pendennis, is that you?' in a loud patronizing manner. Pen had some difficulty in recognizing under the broad-brimmed hat and the vast great-coats and neckcloths, with which the newcomer was habited, the person and figure of his quondam schoolfellow, Mr. Foker.*

A year's absence had made no small difference in that gentleman. A youth who had been deservedly whipped a few months previously, and who spent his pocket-money on tarts and hardbake, now appeared before Pen in one of those costumes to which the public consent, which I take to be quite as influential in this respect as Johnson's Dictionary, has awarded the title of 'swell.' He had a bulldog between his legs, and in his scarlet shawl neckcloth was a pin representing another bulldog in gold: he wore a fur waistcoat laced over with gold chains; a green cut-away coat with basket buttons, and a white upper-

coat ornamented with cheese-plate buttons, on each of which was engraved some stirring incident of the road or the chase; all of which ornaments set off this young fellow's figure to such advantage, that you would hesitate to say which character in life he most resembled, and whether he was a boxer *en goguette*, or a coachman in his gala suit.

'Left that place for good, Pendennis?' Mr. Foker said, descending from his landau and giving Pendennis a finger.

'Yes, this year or more,' Pen said.

'Beastly old hole,' Mr. Foker remarked. 'Hate it. Hate the doctor; hate Towzer, the second master; hate everybody there. Not a fit place for a gentleman.'

'Not at all,' said Pen, with an air of the utmost consequence.

'By gad, sir, I sometimes dream, now, that the doctor's walking into me,' Foker continued (and Pen smiled as he thought that he himself had likewise fearful dreams* of this nature). 'When I think of the diet there, by gad, sir, I wonder how I stood it. Mangy mutton, brutal beef, pudding on Thursdays and Sundays, and that fit to poison you. Just look at my leader—did you ever see a prettier animal? Drove over from Baymouth. Came the nine mile in two-and-forty minutes. Not bad going, sir.'

'Are you stopping at Baymouth, Foker?' Pendennis asked.

'I'm coaching there,' said the other, with a nod.

'*What?*' asked Pen, and in a tone of such wonder that Foker burst out laughing, and said, 'He was blowed if he didn't think Pen was such a flat as not to know what coaching meant.'

'I'm come down with a coach from Oxbridge. A tutor, don't you see, old boy? He's coaching me, and some other men, for the Little-go. Me and Spavin have the drag between us. And I thought I'd just tool over, and go to the play. Did you ever see Rowkins do the hornpipe?' and Mr. Foker began to perform some steps of that popular dance in the inn yard, looking round for the sympathy of his groom and the stable men.

Pen thought he would like to go to the play too: and could ride home afterwards, as there was a moonlight. So he accepted Foker's invitation to dinner, and the young men entered the inn together, where Mr. Foker stopped at the bar, and called upon Miss Rummer, the landlady's

fair daughter, who presided there, to give him a glass of 'his mixture.'

Pen and his family had been known at the 'George' ever since they came into the country; and Mr. Pendennis's carriage and horses always put up there when he paid a visit to the county town. The landlady dropped the heir of Fairoaks a very respectful curtsy, and complimented him upon his growth and manly appearance, and asked news of the family at Fairoaks, and of Doctor Portman and the Clavering people, to all of which questions the young gentleman answered with much affability. But he spoke to Mr. and Mrs. Rummer with that sort of good nature with which a young prince addresses his father's subjects; never dreaming that those *bonnes gens* were his equals in life.

Mr. Foker's behaviour was quite different. He inquired for Rummer and the cold in his nose, told Mrs. Rummer a riddle, asked Miss Rummer when she would be ready to marry him, and paid his compliments to Miss Brett, the other young lady in the bar, all in a minute of time, and with a liveliness and facetiousness which set all these ladies in a giggle; and he gave a cluck, expressive of great satisfaction, as he tossed off his mixture which Miss Rummer prepared and handed to him.

'Have a drop,' said he to Pen.[10] 'Give the young one a glass, R., and score it up to yours truly.'

Poor Pen took a glass, and everybody laughed at the face which he made as he put it down—gin, bitters, and some other cordial, was the compound with which Mr. Foker was so delighted as to call it by the name of Foker's own. As Pen choked, sputtered, and made faces, the other took occasion to remark to Mr. Rummer that the young fellow was green, very green, but that he would soon form him; and then they proceeded to order dinner—which Mr. Foker determined should consist of turtle and venison; cautioning the landlady to be very particular about icing the wine.

Then Messrs. Foker and Pen strolled down the High Street together—the former having a cigar in his mouth, which he had drawn out of a case almost as big as a portmanteau. He went in to replenish it at Mr. Lewis's, and talked to that gentleman for a while, sitting down on the counter: he then looked in at the fruiterer's, to see the

pretty girl there: [11] then they passed the *County Chronicle* office, for which Pen had his packet ready, in the shape of 'Lines to Thyrza,' but poor Pen did not like to put the letter into the editor's box while walking in company with such a fine gentleman as Mr. Foker. They met heavy Dragoons of the regiment always quartered at Chatteris; and stopped and talked about the Baymouth balls, and what a pretty girl was Miss Brown, and what a dem fine woman Mrs. Jones was. It was in vain that Pen recalled to his own mind how stupid Foker used to be at school—how he could scarcely read, how he was not cleanly in his person, and notorious for his blunders and dullness. Mr. Foker was not much more refined now than in his school-days: and yet Pen felt a secret pride in strutting down High Street with a young fellow who owned tandems, talked to officers, and ordered turtle and champagne for dinner. He listened, and with respect too, to Mr. Foker's accounts of what the men did at the University of which Mr. F. was an ornament, and encountered a long series of stories about boat-racing, bumping, college grass-plats, and milk-punch—and began to wish to go up himself to college to a place where there were such manly pleasures and enjoyments. Farmer Gurnett, who lives close by Fairoaks, riding by at this minute and touching his hat to Pen, the latter stopped him, and sent a message to his mother to say that he had met with an old schoolfellow, and should dine in Chatteris.

The two young gentlemen continued their walk, and were passing round the Cathedral Yard, where they could hear the music of the afternoon service (a music which always exceedingly affected Pen), but whither Mr. Foker came for the purpose of inspecting the nursery-maids who frequent the Elms Walk there,[12] and here they strolled until with a final burst of music the small congregation was played out.

Old Doctor Portman was one of the few who came from the venerable gate. Spying Pen, he came and shook him by the hand, and eyed with wonder Pen's friend, from whose mouth and cigar clouds of fragrance issued, which curled round the doctor's honest face and shovel hat.

'An old schoolfellow of mine, Mr. Foker,' said Pen. The doctor said 'H'm': and scowled at the cigar. He did not mind a pipe in his study, but the cigar was an abomination to the worthy gentleman.

'I came on bishop's business,' the doctor said. 'We'll ride home, Arthur, if you like ?'

'I—I'm engaged to my friend here,' Pen answered.

'You had better come home with me,' said the doctor.

'His mother knows he's out, sir,' Mr. Foker remarked: 'don't she, Pendennis ?'

'But that does not prove that he had not better come home with me,' the doctor growled, and he walked off with great dignity.

'Old boy don't like the weed, I suppose,' Foker said. 'Ha! who's here ?—here's the general, and Bingley, the manager. How do, Cos ? How do, Bingley ?'

'How does my worthy and gallant young Foker ?' said the gentleman addressed as the general; and who wore a shabby military cape with a mangy collar, and a hat cocked very much over one eye.

'Trust you are very well, my very dear sir,' said the other gentleman, 'and that the Theatre Royal will have the honour of your patronage to-night. We perform *The Stranger*,* in which your humble servant will——'

'Can't stand you in tights and Hessians, Bingley,' young Mr. Foker said. On which the general, with the Irish accent, said, 'But I think ye'll like Miss Fotheringay, in Mrs. Haller, or me name's not Jack Costigan.'

Pen looked at these individuals with the greatest interest. He had never seen an actor before; and he saw Dr. Portman's red face looking over the doctor's shoulder, as he retreated from the Cathedral Yard, evidently quite dissatisfied with the acquaintances into whose hands Pen had fallen.

Perhaps it would have been much better for him had he taken the parson's advice and company home. But which of us knows his fate ?

YOUTH BETWEEN PLEASURE AND DUTY

CHAPTER IV

MRS. HALLER

HAVING returned to the 'George,' Mr. Foker and his guest sat down to a handsome repast in the coffee-room; where Mr. Rummer brought in the first dish, and bowed as gravely as if he was waiting upon the Lord-Lieutenant of the county.[1] Pen could not but respect his connoisseurship as he pronounced the champagne to be condemned gooseberry, and winked at the port with one eye. The latter he declared to be of the right sort; and told the waiters there was no way of humbugging *him*.

All these attendants he knew by their Christian names, and showed a great interest in their families; and as the London coaches drove up, which in those early days used to set off from the 'George,' Mr. Foker flung the coffee-room window open, and called the guards and coachmen by their Christian names, too, asking about their respective families, and imitating with great liveliness and accuracy the tooting of the horns as Jem the ostler whipped the horses' cloths off, and the carriages drove gaily away.

'A bottle of sherry, a bottle of sham, a bottle of port and a shass caffy, it ain't so bad, hey, Pen?' Foker said, and pronounced, after all these delicacies and a quantity of nuts and fruit had been dispatched, that it was time to 'toddle.' Pen sprang up with very bright eyes, and a flushed face; and they moved off towards the theatre, where they paid their money to the wheezy old lady slumbering in the money-taker's box. 'Mrs. Dropsicum, Bingley's mother-in-law, great in Lady Macbeth,' Foker said to his companion. Foker knew her too.

They had almost their choice of places in the boxes of the theatre, which was no better filled than country theatres usually are, in spite of the 'universal burst of attraction and galvanic thrills of delight' advertised by

Bingley in the playbills. A score or so of people dotted the pit-benches, a few more kept a-kicking and whistling in the galleries, and a dozen others who came in with free admissions were in the boxes where our young gentlemen sat. Lieutenants Rodgers and Podgers and young Cornet Tidmus of the Dragoons occupied a private box. The performers acted to them, and these gentlemen seemed to hold conversations with the players when not engaged in the dialogue, and applauded them by name loudly.

Bingley the manager, who assumed all the chief tragic and comic parts except when he modestly retreated to make way for the London stars, who came down occasionally to Chatteris, was great in the character of the Stranger. He was attired in the tight pantaloons and Hessian boots which the stage legend has given to that injured man, with a large cloak and beaver and a hearse-feather in it drooping over his raddled old face, and only partially concealing his great buckled brown wig. He had the stage jewellery on too, of which he selected the largest and most shiny rings for himself, and allowed his little finger to quiver out of his cloak with a sham diamond ring covering the first joint of the finger and twiddling in the faces of the pit. Bingley made it a favour to the young men of his company to go on in light comedy parts with that ring. They flattered him by asking its history. The stage has its traditional jewels as the Crown and all great families have. This had belonged to George Frederick Cooke, who had had it from Mr. Quin,* who may have bought it for a shilling. Bingley fancied the world was fascinated by its glitter.

He was reading out of the stage-book—that wonderful stage-book—which is not bound like any other book in the world, but is rouged and tawdry like the hero or heroine who holds it; and who holds it as people never do hold books: and points with his finger to a passage, and wags his head ominously at the audience, and then lifts up eyes and finger to the ceiling, professing to derive some intense consolation from the work between which and heaven there is a strong affinity.[2]

As soon as the Stranger saw the young men, he acted at them; eyeing them solemnly over his gilt volume as he lay on the stage-bank showing his hand, his ring, and his Hessians. He calculated the effect that every one of these ornaments would produce upon his victims: he was deter-

mined to fascinate them, for he knew they had paid their money; and he saw their families coming in from the country and filling the cane chairs in his boxes.

As he lay on the bank reading, his servant, Francis, made remarks upon his master.

'Again reading,' said Francis; 'thus it is, from morn to night. To him nature has no beauty—life no charm. For three years I have never seen him smile' (the gloom of Bingley's face was fearful to witness during these comments of the faithful domestic). 'Nothing diverts him. Oh, if he would but attach himself to any living thing, were it an animal—for something man must love.'

[*Enter Tobias* (*Goll*) *from the hut.*] He cries, 'Oh, how refreshing, after seven long weeks, to feel these warm sunbeams once again. Thanks, bounteous Heaven, for the joy I taste!' He presses his cap between his hands, looks up and prays. The Stranger eyes him attentively.

Francis to the Stranger. 'This old man's share of earthly happiness can be but little. Yet mark how grateful he is for his portion of it.'

Bingley. 'Because, though old, he is but a child in the leading-string of hope.' (He looks steadily at Foker, who, however, continues to suck the top of his stick in an unconcerned manner.)

Francis. 'Hope is the nurse of life.'

Bingley. 'And her cradle—is the grave.'

The Stranger uttered this with the moan of a bassoon in agony, and fixed his glance on Pendennis so steadily that the poor lad was quite put out of countenance. He thought the whole house must be looking at him; and cast his eyes down. As soon as ever he raised them Bingley's were at him again. All through the scene the manager played at him.[3] How relieved the lad was when the scene ended, and Foker, tapping with his cane, cried out, 'Bravo, Bingley!'

'Give him a hand, Pendennis; you know every chap likes a hand,' Mr. Foker said; and the good-natured young gentleman, and Pendennis laughing, and the Dragoons in the opposite box, began clapping hands to the best of their power.

A chamber in Wintersen Castle closed over Tobias's hut and the Stranger and his boots; and servants appeared bustling about with chairs and tables. 'That's Hicks and Miss Thackthwaite,' whispered Foker. 'Pretty girl, ain't

she, Pendennis ? But stop—hurray—bravo ! here's the Fotheringay.'

The pit thrilled and thumped its umbrellas ; a volley of applause was fired from the gallery : the Dragoon officers and Foker clapped their hands furiously : you would have thought the house was full, so loud were their plaudits. The red face and ragged whiskers of Mr. Costigan were seen peering from the side-scene. Pen's eyes opened wide and bright, as Mrs. Haller entered with a downcast look, then rallying at the sound of the applause, swept the house with a grateful glance, and, folding her hands across her breast, sank down in a magnificent curtsy. More applause, more umbrellas ; Pen this time, flaming with wine and enthusiasm, clapped hands and sang ' Bravo ' louder than all. Mrs. Haller saw him, and everybody else, and old Mr. Bows, the little first fiddler of the orchestra (which was this night increased by a detachment of the band of the Dragoons, by the kind permission of Colonel Swallowtail), looked up from the desk where he was perched, with his crutch beside him, and smiled at the enthusiasm of the lad.

Those who have only seen Miss Fotheringay in later days, since her marriage and introduction into London life, have little idea how beautiful a creature she was at the time when our friend Pen first set eyes on her, and I warn my reader, as beforehand, that the pencil which illustrates this work (and can draw an ugly face tolerably well, but is sadly put out when it tries to delineate a beauty) can give no sort of notion of her. She was of the tallest of women, and at her then age of six-and-twenty—for six-and-twenty she was, though she vows she was only nineteen—in the prime and fullness of her beauty. Her forehead was vast, and her black hair waved over it with a natural ripple,[4] and was confined in shining and voluminous braids at the back of a neck such as you see on the shoulders of the Louvre Venus—that delight of gods and men. Her eyes, when she lifted them up to gaze on you, and ere she dropped their purple deep-fringed lids, shone with tenderness and mystery unfathomable. Love and Genius seemed to look out from them and then retire coyly, as if ashamed to have been seen at the lattice. Who could have had such a commanding brow but a woman of high intellect ? She never laughed (indeed, her teeth were not good), but a smile of endless tenderness and sweetness played round her beauti-

ful lips, and in the dimples of her cheeks and her lovely chin. Her nose defied description in those days. Her ears were like two little pearl shells, which the ear-rings she wore (though the handsomest properties of the theatre) only insulted. She was dressed in long flowing robes of black, which she managed and swept to and fro with wonderful grace, and out of the folds of which you only saw her sandals occasionally; they were of rather a large size; but Pen thought them as ravishing as the slippers of Cinderella. But it was her hand and arm that this magnificent creature most excelled in, and somehow you could never see her but through them. They surrounded her. When she folded them over her bosom in resignation; when she dropped them in mute agony, or raised them in superb command; when in sportive gaiety her hands fluttered and waved before her, like—what shall we say?—like the snowy doves before the chariot of Venus—it was with these arms and hands that she beckoned, repelled, entreated, embraced her admirers—no single one, for she was armed with her own virtue, and with her father's valour, whose sword would have leapt from its scabbard at any insult offered to his child—but the whole house, which rose to her, as the phrase was, as she curtsied and bowed and charmed it.

Thus she stood for a minute—complete and beautiful—as Pen stared at her. 'I say, Pen, isn't she a stunner?' asked Mr. Foker.

'Hush!' Pen said. 'She's speaking.'

She began her business in a deep sweet voice. Those who know the play of *The Stranger* are aware that the remarks made by the various characters are not valuable in themselves, either for their sound sense, their novelty of observation, or their poetic fancy.[5]

Nobody ever talked so. If we meet idiots in life, as will happen, it is a great mercy that they do not use such absurdly fine words. The Stranger's talk is sham, like the book he reads, and the hair he wears, and the bank he sits on, and the diamond ring he makes play with—but, in the midst of the balderdash, there runs that reality of love, children, and forgiveness of wrong, which will be listened to wherever it is preached, and sets all the world sympathizing.

With what smothered sorrow, with what gushing pathos, Mrs. Haller delivered her part! At first, when as Count Wintersen's housekeeper, and preparing for his Excellency's

arrival, she has to give orders about the beds and furniture, and the dinner, etc., to be got ready, she did so with the calm agony of despair. But when she could get rid of the stupid servants, and give vent to her feelings to the pit and the house, she overflowed to each individual as if he were her particular confidant, and she was crying out her griefs on his shoulder : the little fiddler in the orchestra (whom she did not seem to watch, though he followed her ceaselessly) twitched, twisted, nodded, pointed about, and when she came to the favourite passage, 'I have a William, too, if he be still alive—Ah, yes, if he be still alive. His little sisters, too. Why, Fancy, dost thou rack me so ? Why dost thou image my poor children fainting in sickness, and crying to—to—their mum-um-*other* '—when she came to this passage little Bows buried his face in his blue cotton handkerchief, after crying out 'Bravo.'

All the house was affected. Foker, for his part, taking out a large yellow bandanna, wept piteously. As for Pen, he was gone too far for that. He followed the woman about and about—when she was off the stage, it and the house were blank ; the lights and the red officers reeled wildly before his sight. He watched her at the side-scene—where she stood waiting to come on the stage, and where her father took off her shawl : when the reconciliation arrived, and she flung herself down on Mr. Bingley's shoulders, whilst the children clung to their knees, and the Countess (Mrs. Bingley) and Baron Steinforth (performed with great liveliness and spirit by Garbetts)—while the rest of the characters formed a group round them, Pen's hot eyes only saw Fotheringay, Fotheringay. The curtain fell upon him like a pall. He did not hear a word of what Bingley said, who came forward to announce the play for the next evening, and who took the tumultuous applause, as usual, for himself. Pen was not even distinctly aware that the house was calling for Miss Fotheringay, nor did the manager seem to comprehend that anybody else but himself had caused the success of the play. At last he understood it, stepped back with a grin, and presently appeared with Mrs. Haller on his arm. How beautiful she looked ! Her hair had fallen down, the officers threw her flowers. She clutched them to her heart. She put back her hair, and smiled all round. Her eyes met Pen's. Down went the curtain again : and she was gone. Not one note could he hear of the overture

which the brass band of the Dragoons blew by kind permission of Colonel Swallowtail.

'She *is* a crusher, ain't she now ?' Mr. Foker asked of his companion.

Pen did not know exactly what Foker said, and answered vaguely. He could not tell the other what he felt ; he could not have spoken, just then, to any mortal. Besides, Pendennis did not quite know what he felt yet ; it was something overwhelming, maddening, delicious ; a fever of wild joy and undefined longing.

And now Rowkins and Miss Thackthwaite came on to dance the favourite double hornpipe, and Foker abandoned himself to the delights of this ballet, just as he had to the tears of the tragedy, a few minutes before. Pen did not care for it, or indeed think about the dance, except to remember that that woman was acting with her in the scene where she first came in. It was a mist before his eyes. At the end of the dance he looked at his watch and said it was time for him to go.

'Hang it, stay to see *The Bravo of the Battle-Axe*,'*Foker said. 'Bingley's splendid in it ; he wears red tights, and has to carry Mrs. B. over the Pine-bridge of the Cataract, only she's too heavy. It's great fun, do stop.'

Pen looked at the bill with one lingering fond hope that Miss Fotheringay's name might be hidden, somewhere, in the list of the actors of the after-piece, but there was no such name. Go he must. He had a long ride home. He squeezed Foker's hand. He was choking to speak, but he couldn't. He quitted the theatre, and walked frantically about the town, he knew not how long ; then he mounted at the 'George' and rode homewards, and Clavering clock sang out one as he came into the yard at Fairoaks. The lady of the house might have been awake, but she only heard him from the passage outside his room as he dashed into bed and pulled the clothes over his head.

Pen had not been in the habit of passing wakeful nights, so he at once fell off into a sound sleep. Even in later days and with a great deal of care and other thoughtful matter to keep him awake, a man from long practice or fatigue or resolution *begins* by going to sleep as usual, and gets a nap in advance of Anxiety. But she soon comes up with him and jogs his shoulder, and says : 'Come, my man, no more of this laziness ; you must wake up and have a talk with me.'

Then they fall-to together in the midnight. Well, whatever might afterwards happen to him, poor little Pen was not come to this state yet; he tumbled into a sound sleep—did not wake until an early hour in the morning, when the rooks began to caw from the little wood beyond his bedroom windows; and—at that very instant and as his eyes started open, the beloved image was in his mind. 'My dear boy,' he heard her say, 'you were in a sound sleep, and I would not disturb you: but I have been close by your pillow all this while: and I don't intend that you shall leave me. I am Love! I bring with me fever and passion: wild longing, maddening desire; restless craving and seeking. Many a long day ere this I heard you calling out for me; and behold now I am come.'

Was Pen frightened at the summons? Not he. He did not know what was coming: it was all wild pleasure and delight as yet. And as, when three years previously, and on entering the fifth form at the Cistercians, his father had made him a present of a gold watch, which the boy took from under his pillow and examined on the instant of waking: for ever rubbing and polishing it up in private and retiring into corners to listen to its ticking: so the young man exulted over his new delight; felt in his waistcoat pocket to see that it was safe; wound it up at nights, and at the very first moment of waking hugged it and looked at it.—By the way, that first watch of Pen's was a showy ill-manufactured piece: it never went well from the beginning, and was always getting out of order. And after putting it aside into a drawer and forgetting it for some time, he swapped it finally away for a more useful time-keeper.

Pen felt himself to be ever so many years older since yesterday. There was no mistake about it now. He was as much in love as the best hero in the best romance he ever read. He told John to bring his shaving-water with the utmost confidence. He dressed himself in some of his finest clothes that morning: and came splendidly down to breakfast, patronizing his mother and little Laura, who had been strumming her music lesson for hours before; and who after he had read the prayers (of which he did not heed one single syllable), wondered at his grand appearance, and asked him to tell her what the play was about?

Pen laughed and declined to tell Laura what the play was about. In fact it was quite as well that she should not know.

THE CURATE COME TO GRIEF

Then she asked him why he had got on his fine pin and beautiful new waistcoat ?

Pen blushed and told his mother that the old schoolfellow with whom he had dined at Chatteris was reading with a tutor at Baymouth, a very learned man ; and as he was himself to go to College, and as there were several young men pursuing their studies at Baymouth—he was anxious to ride over—and—and just see what the course of their reading was.

Laura made a long face. Helen Pendennis looked hard at her son, troubled more than ever with the vague doubt and terror which had been haunting her ever since the last night, when Farmer Gurnett brought back the news that Pen would not return home to dinner. Arthur's eyes defied her. She tried to console herself, and drive off her fears. The boy had never told her an untruth. Pen conducted himself during breakfast in a very haughty and supercilious manner ; and, taking leave of the elder and younger lady, was presently heard riding out of the stable-court. He went gently at first, but galloped like a madman as soon as he thought that he was out of hearing.

Smirke, thinking of his own affairs, and softly riding with his toes out, to give Pen his three hours' reading at Fairoaks, met his pupil, who shot by him like the wind. Smirke's pony shied, as the other thundered past him ; the gentle curate went over his head among the stinging-nettles in the hedge. Pen laughed as they met, pointed towards the Baymouth road, and was gone half a mile in that direction before poor Smirke had picked himself up.

Pen had resolved in his mind that he *must* see Foker that morning ; he must hear about her ; know about her ; be with somebody who knew her ; and honest Smirke, for his part, sitting up among the stinging-nettles, as his pony cropped quietly in the hedge, thought dismally to himself, ought he to go to Fairoaks now that his pupil was evidently gone away for the day ? Yes, he thought he might go, too. He might go and ask Mrs. Pendennis when Arthur would be back ; and hear Miss Laura her Watts's Catechism. He got up on the little pony—both were used to his slipping off—and advanced upon the house from which his scholar had just rushed away in a whirlwind.

Thus love makes fools of all of us, big and little ; and the curate had tumbled over head and heels in pursuit of it, and Pen had started in the first heat of the mad race.

CHAPTER V

MRS. HALLER AT HOME

PEN galloped on to Baymouth, put up[1] at the inn stables, and ran straightway to Mr. Foker's lodgings, of whom he had taken the direction on the previous day. On reaching these apartments, which were over a chemist's shop whose stock of cigars and soda-water went off rapidly by the kind patronage of his young inmates, Pen only found Mr. Spavin, Foker's friend, and part owner of the tandem which the latter had driven into Chatteris, who was smoking, and teaching a little dog, a friend of his, tricks with a bit of biscuit.

Pen's healthy red face, fresh from the gallop, compared oddly with the waxy debauched little features of Foker's chum. Mr. Spavin remarked the circumstance. 'Who's that man?' he thought; 'he looks as fresh as a bean. *His* hand don't shake of a morning, I'd bet five to one.'

Foker had not come home at all. Here was a disappointment!—Mr. Spavin could not say when his friend would return. Sometimes he stopped a day, sometimes a week. Of what college was Pen? Would he have anything? There was a very fair tap of ale. Mr. Spavin was enabled to know Pendennis's name, on the card which the latter took out and laid down (perhaps Pen in these days was rather proud of having a card)—and so the young men took leave.

Then Pen went down the rock, and walked about on the sand, biting his nails by the shore of the much-sounding sea. It stretched before him bright and immeasurable. The blue waters came rolling into the bay, foaming and roaring hoarsely: Pen looked them in the face with blank eyes.

hardly regarding them. What a tide there was pouring into the lad's own mind at the time, and what a little power had he to check it! Pen flung stones into the sea, but it still kept coming on. He was in a rage at not seeing Foker. He wanted to see Foker. He must see Foker. 'Suppose I go on—on the Chatteris road, just to see if I can meet him,' Pen thought. Rebecca was saddled in another half-hour, and galloping on the grass by the Chatteris road. About four miles from Baymouth, the Clavering road branches off, as everybody knows, and the mare naturally was for taking that turn, but, cutting her over the shoulder, Pen passed the turning, and rode on to the turnpike without seeing any sign of the black tandem and red wheels.

As he was at the turnpike, he might as well go on: that was quite clear. So Pen rode to the 'George,' and the ostler told him that Mr. Foker was there sure enough, and that 'he'd been a-makin' a tremendous row the night afore, a-drinkin' and a-singin', and wanting to fight Tom the post-boy: which I'm thinking he'd have had the worst of it,' the man added, with a grin. 'Have you carried up your master's 'ot water to shave with?' he added, in a very satirical manner, to Mr. Foker's domestic, who here came down the yard bearing his master's clothes, most beautifully brushed and arranged. 'Show Mr. Pendennis up to 'un,' and Pen followed the man at last to the apartment where, in the midst of an immense bed, Mr. Harry Foker lay reposing.

The feather-bed and bolsters swelled up all round Mr. Foker, so that you could hardly see his little sallow face and red silk nightcap.

'Hullo!' said Pen.

'Who goes there? brother, quickly tell,' sang out the voice from the bed. 'What! Pendennis again? Is your mamma acquainted with your absence? Did you sup with us last night? No—stop—who supped with us last night, Stoopid?'

'There was the three officers, sir, and Mr. Bingley, sir, and Mr. Costigan, sir,' the man answered, who received all Mr. Foker's remarks with perfect gravity.

'Ah, yes: the cup and merry jest went round. We chanted: and I remember I wanted to fight a postboy. Did I thrash him, Stoopid?'

'No, sir. Fight didn't come off, sir,' said Stoopid, still

with perfect gravity. He was arranging Mr. Foker's dressing-case—a trunk, the gift of a fond mother, without which the young fellow never travelled. It contained a prodigious apparatus in plate; a silver dish, a silver mug, silver boxes and bottles for all sorts of essences, and a choice of razors ready against the time when Mr. Foker's beard should come.

'Do it some other day,' said the young fellow, yawning and throwing up his little lean arms over his head. 'No, there was no fight; but there was chanting. Bingley chanted, I chanted, the general chanted—Costigan, I mean.—Did you ever hear him sing "The Little Pig under the Bed," Pen?'

'The man we met yesterday,' said Pen, all in a tremor, 'the father of——'

'Of the Fotheringay—the very man. Ain't she a Venus, Pen?'

'Please, sir, Mr. Costigan's in the sittin'-room, sir, and says, sir, you asked him to breakfast, sir. Called five times, sir; but wouldn't wake you on no account; and has been year since eleven o'clock, sir——'

'How much is it now?'

'One, sir.'

'What would the best of mothers say,' cried the little sluggard, 'if she saw me in bed at this hour? She sent me down here with a grinder. She wants me to cultivate my neglected genius—he, he! I say, Pen, this isn't quite like seven o'clock school, is it, old boy?' and the young fellow burst out into a boyish laugh of enjoyment. Then he added: 'Go in and talk to the general whilst I dress. And I say, Pendennis, ask him to sing you "The Little Pig under the Bed"; it's capital.' Pen went off in great perturbation, to meet Mr. Costigan, and Mr. Foker commenced his toilet.

Of Mr. Foker's two grandfathers, the one from whom he inherited a fortune was a brewer; the other was an earl, who endowed him with the most doting mother in the world. The Fokers had been at the Cistercian school from father to son; at which place, our friend, whose name could be seen over the playground wall, on a public-house sign, under which 'Foker's Entire' was painted, had been dreadfully bullied on account of his trade, his uncomely countenance, his inaptitude for learning and cleanliness, his gluttony

and other weak points. But those who know how a susceptible youth, under the tyranny of his schoolfellows, becomes silent and a sneak, may understand how in a very few months after his liberation from bondage he developed himself as he had done ; and became the humorous, the sarcastic, the brilliant Foker, with whom we have made acquaintance. A dunce he always was, it is true ; for learning cannot be acquired by leaving school and entering at college as a fellow-commoner ; but he was now (in his own peculiar manner) as great a dandy as he before had been a slattern, and when he entered his sitting-room to join his two guests, arrived scented and arrayed in fine linen, and perfectly splendid in appearance.

General or Captain Costigan—for the latter was the rank which he preferred to assume—was seated in the window with the newspaper held before him at arm's length. The captain's eyes were somewhat dim ; and he was spelling the paper, with the help of his lips, as well as of those bloodshot eyes of his, as you see gentlemen do to whom reading is a rare and difficult occupation. His hat was cocked very much on one ear ; and as one of his feet lay up in the window-seat, the observer of such matters might remark, by the size and shabbiness of the boots which the captain wore, that times did not go very well with him. Poverty seems as if it were disposed, before it takes possession of a man entirely, to attack his extremities first : the coverings of his head, feet, and hands, are its first prey. All these parts of the captain's person were particularly rakish and shabby. As soon as he saw Pen he descended from the window-seat and saluted the new-comer, first in a military manner, by conveying a couple of his fingers (covered with a broken black glove) to his hat, and then removing that ornament altogether. The captain was inclined to be bald, but he brought a quantity of lank iron-grey hair over his pate, and had a couple of wisps of the same falling down on each side of his face. Much whisky had spoiled what complexion Mr. Costigan may have possessed in his youth. His once handsome face had now a copper tinge. He wore a very high stock, scarred and stained in many places ; and a dress-coat tightly buttoned up in those parts where the buttons had not parted company from the garment.

'The young gentleman to whom I had the honour to be introjuiced yesterday in the Cathedral Yard,' said the

captain, with a splendid bow and wave of his hat. 'I hope I see you well, sir. I marked ye in the thayater last night during me daughter's perfawrumance ; and missed ye on my return. I did but conduct her home, sir, for Jack Costigan, though poor, is a gentleman ; and when I reintered the house to pay me respects to me joyous young friend, Mr. Foker—ye were gone. We had a jolly night of ut, sir—Mr. Foker, the three gallant young Dragoons, and your 'umble servant. Gad, sir, it put me in mind of one of our old nights when I bore His Majesty's commission in the Foighting Hundtherd and Third.' And he pulled out an old snuff-box, which he presented with a stately air to his new acquaintance.

Arthur was a great deal too much flurried to speak. This shabby-looking buck was—was her father.[2] 'I hope Miss F——, Miss Costigan is well, sir,' Pen said, flushing up. 'She—she gave me greater pleasure, than—than I—I—I ever enjoyed at a play. I think, sir—I think she's the finest actress in the world,' he gasped out.

'Your hand, young man ! for ye speak from your heart,' cried the captain. 'Thank ye, sir ; an old soldier and a fond father thanks ye. She *is* the finest actress in the world. I've seen the Siddons, sir, and the O'Nale*—they were great, but what were they compared to Miss Fotheringay ? I do not wish she should ashume her own name while on the stage. Me family, sir, are proud people ; and the Costigans of Costiganstown think that an honest man, who has borne Her Majesty's colours in the Hundtherd and Third, would demean himself by permitting his daughter to earn her old father's bread.'

'There cannot be a more honourable duty, surely,' Pen said.

'Honourable ! Bedad, sir, I'd like to see the man who said Jack Costigan would consent to anything dishonourable. I have a heart, sir, though I am poor ; I like a man who has a heart. You have : I read it in your honest face and steady eye. And would you believe it ?' he added, after a pause, and with a pathetic whisper, 'that that Bingley who has made his fortune by me child, gives her but two guineas a week : out of which she finds herself in dresses, and which, added to me own small means, makes our all ?'

Now the captain's means were so small as to be, it may be said, quite invisible. But nobody knows how the wind

is tempered to shorn Irish lambs, and in what marvellous places they find pasture. If Captain Costigan, whom I had the honour to know, would but have told his history, it would have been a great moral story. But he neither would have told it if he could, nor could if he would; for the captain was not only unaccustomed to tell the truth—he was unable even to think it—and fact and fiction reeled together in his muzzy, whiskified brain.

He began life rather brilliantly with a pair of colours, a fine person and legs, and one of the most beautiful voices in the world. To his latest day he sang, with admirable pathos and humour, those wonderful Irish ballads which are so mirthful and so melancholy: and was always the first himself to cry at their pathos. Poor Cos! he was at once brave and maudlin, humorous and an idiot; always good-natured, and sometimes almost trustworthy. Up to the last day of his life he would drink with any man, and back any man's bill: and his end was in a spunging-house, where the sheriff's officer, who took him, was fond of him.

In his brief morning of life, Cos formed the delight of regimental messes, and had the honour of singing his songs, bacchanalian and sentimental, at the tables of the most illustrious generals and commanders-in-chief, in the course of which period he drank three times as much claret as was good for him, and spent his doubtful patrimony. What became of him subsequently to his retirement from the army, is no affair of ours. I take it, no foreigner understands the life of an Irish gentleman without money, the way in which he manages to keep afloat—the wind-raising conspiracies, in which he engages with heroes as unfortunate as himself—the means by which he contrives, during most days of the week, to get his portion of whisky-and-water: all these are mysteries to us inconceivable: but suffice it to say, that through all the storms of life Jack had floated somehow, and the lamp of his nose had never gone out.

Before he and Pen had had a half-hour's conversation, the captain managed to extract a couple of sovereigns from the young gentleman for tickets for his daughter's benefit, which was to take place speedily; and was not a *bona-fide* transaction such as that of the last year, when poor Miss Fotheringay had lost fifteen shillings by her venture; but was an arrangement with the manager, by which the lady was to have the sale of a certain number of tickets, keeping

for herself a large portion of the sum for which they were sold.

Pen had but two pounds in his purse, and he handed them over to the captain for the tickets; he would have been afraid to offer more lest he should offend the latter's delicacy. Costigan scrawled him an order for a box, lightly slipped the sovereigns into his waistcoat, and slapped his hand over the place where they lay. They seemed to warm his old sides.

'Faith, sir,' said he, 'the bullion's scarcer with me than it used to be, as is the case with many a good fellow. I won six hundtherd of 'em in a single night, sir, when me kind friend, His Royal Highness the Duke of Kent,* was in Gibralthar.'[3]

Then it was good to see the captain's behaviour at breakfast, before the devilled turkey and the mutton chops! His stories poured forth unceasingly, and his spirits rose as he chatted to the young men. When he got a bit of sunshine, the old lazzarone basked in it; he prated about his own affairs and past splendour, and all the lords, generals, and lord-lieutenants he had ever known. He described the death of his darling Bessie, the late Mrs. Costigan, and the challenge he had sent to Captain Shanty Clancy, of the Slashers, for looking rude at Miss Fotheringay as she was on her kyar in the Phaynix; and then he described how the captain apologized, gave a dinner at the Kildare Street, where six of them drank twinty-one bottles of claret, etc. He announced that to sit with two such noble and generous young fellows was the happiness and pride of an old soldier's existence; and having had a second glass of curaçao, was so happy that he began to cry. Altogether we should say that the captain was not a man of much strength of mind, or a very eligible companion for youth; but there are worse men, holding much better places in life, and more dishonest, who have never committed half so many rogueries as he. They walked out, the captain holding an arm of each of his dear young friends, and in a maudlin state of contentment. He winked at one or two tradesmen's shops where, possibly, he owed a bill, as much as to say, 'See the company I'm in—sure I'll pay you, my boy,' and they parted finally with Mr. Foker at a billiard-room, where the latter had a particular engagement with some gentlemen of Colonel Swallowtail's regiment.

Pen and the shabby captain still walked the street together ; the captain, in his sly way, making inquiries about Mr. Foker's fortune and station in life. Pen told him how Foker's father was a celebrated brewer, and his mother was Lady Agnes Milton, Lord Rosherville's daughter. The captain broke out into a strain of exaggerated compliment and panegyric about Mr. Foker, whose 'native aristocracie' he said, 'could be seen with the twinkling of an oi—and only served to adawrun other qualities which he possessed, a foine intellect and a generous heart.'[4]

Pen walked on, listening to his companion's prate, wondering, amused, and puzzled. It had not as yet entered into the boy's head to disbelieve any statement that was made to him ; and being of a candid nature himself, he took naturally for truth what other people told him. Costigan had never had a better listener, and was highly flattered by the attentiveness and modest bearing of the young man.

So much pleased was he with the young gentleman, so artless, honest, and cheerful did Pen seem to be, that the captain finally made him an invitation, which he very seldom accorded to young men, and asked Pen if he would do him the fevour to enter his humble abode, which was near at hand, where the captain would have the honour of inthrojuicing his young friend to his daughter, Miss Fotheringay ?

Pen was so delightfully shocked at this invitation that he thought he should have dropped from the captain's arm at first, and trembled lest the other should discover his emotion. He gasped out a few incoherent words, indicative of the high gratification he should have in being presented to the lady for whose—for whose talents he had conceived such an admiration—such an extreme admiration ; and followed the captain, scarcely knowing whither that gentleman led him. He was going to see her ! He was going to see her ! In her was the centre of the universe. She was the kernel of the world for Pen. Yesterday, before he knew her, seemed a period ever so long ago—a revolution was between him and that time, and a new world about to begin.

The captain conducted his young friend to that quiet little street in Chatteris, called Prior's Lane, which lies close by Dean's Green and the canons' houses, and is overlooked by the enormous towers of the cathedral ; there the captain dwelt modestly in the first floor of a low-gabled house, on

the door of which was the brass plate of 'Creed, Tailor and Robe-maker.' Creed was dead, however. His widow was a pew-opener in the cathedral hard by; his eldest son was a little scamp of a choir-boy, who played toss-halfpenny, led his little brothers into mischief, and had a voice as sweet as an angel. A couple of the latter were sitting on the door-step,[5] and they jumped up with great alacrity to meet their lodger, and plunged wildly, and rather to Pen's surprise, at the swallow-tails of the captain's dress-coat; for the truth is, that the good-natured gentleman, when he was in cash, generally brought home an apple or a piece of gingerbread for these children. 'Whereby the widdy never pressed me for rint when not convanient,' as he remarked afterwards to Pen, winking knowingly, and laying a finger on his nose.

As Pen[6] followed his companion up the creaking old stair, his knees trembled under him. He could hardly see when he entered, following the captain, and stood in the room—in her room. He saw something black before him, and waving as if making a curtsy, and heard, but quite indistinctly, Costigan making a speech over him, in which the captain, with his usual magniloquence, expressed to 'me child' his wish to make her known to 'his dear and admirable young friend, Mr. Awther Pindinnis, a young gentleman of property in the neighbourhood, a person of refoined moind and emiable manners, a sincare lover of poethry, and a man possest of a feeling and affectionate heart.'

'It is very fine weather,' Miss Fotheringay said, in an Irish accent, and with a deep rich melancholy voice.

'Very,' said Mr. Pendennis. In this romantic way their conversation began; and he found himself seated on a chair, and having leisure to look at the young lady.

She looked still handsomer off the stage than before the lamps. All her attitudes were naturally grand and majestical. If she went and stood up against the mantel-piece her robe draped itself classically round her; her chin supported itself on her hand, the other lines of her form arranged themselves in full harmonious undulations—she looked like a Muse in contemplation. If she sat down on a cane-bottomed chair, her arm rounded itself over the back of the seat, her hand seemed as if it ought to have a sceptre put into it, the folds of her dress fell naturally round her in order;[7] all her movements were graceful and imperial. In the morning you could see her hair was blue-black, her com-

plexion of dazzling fairness, with the faintest possible blush flickering, as it were, in her cheek. Her eyes were grey, with prodigious long lashes; and as for her mouth, Mr. Pendennis has given me subsequently to understand, that it was of a staring red colour, with which the most brilliant geranium, sealing-wax, or Guardsman's coat, could not vie.

'And very warm,' continued this empress and Queen of Sheba.

Mr. Pen again assented, and the conversation rolled on in this manner. She asked Costigan whether he had had a pleasant evening at the 'George,' and he recounted the supper and the tumblers of punch. Then the father asked her how she had been employing the morning.

'Bows came,' said she, 'at ten, and we studied Ophalia. It's for the twenty-fourth, when I hope, sir, we shall have the honour of seeing ye.'

'Indeed, indeed, you will,' Mr. Pendennis cried; wondering that she should say 'Ophalia,' and speak with an Irish inflection of voice naturally, who had not the least Hibernian accent on the stage.

'I've secured 'um for your benefit, dear,' said the captain, tapping his waistcoat pocket, wherein lay Pen's sovereigns, and winking at Pen, with one eye, at which the boy blushed.

'Mr.——the gentleman's very obleging,' said Mrs. Haller.

'My name is Pendennis,' said Pen, blushing. 'I—I—hope you'll—you'll remember it.' His heart thumped so as he made this audacious declaration, that he almost choked in uttering it.

'Pendennis'—she answered slowly, and looking him full in the eyes, with a glance, so straight, so clear, so bright, so killing, with a voice so sweet, so round, so low, that the word and the glance shot Pen through and through, and perfectly transfixed him with pleasure.

'I never knew the name was so pretty before,' Pen said.

''Tis a very pretty name,' Ophelia said. 'Pentweazle's not a pretty name. Remember, papa, when we were on the Norwich Circuit, young Pentweazle, who used to play second old men, and married Miss Rancy, the Columbine;* they're both engaged in London now, at the Queen's, and get five pounds a week. Pentweazle wasn't his real name. 'Twas Judkin gave it him, I don't know why. His name

was Harrington ; that is, his real name was Potts ; fawther a clergyman, very respectable. Harrington was in London, and got in debt. Ye remember, he came out in Falkland, to Mrs. Bunce's Julia.'

'And a pretty Julia she was,' the captain interposed ; 'a woman of fifty, and a mother of ten children. 'Tis you who ought to have been Julia, or my name's not Jack Costigan.'

'I didn't take the leading business then,' Miss Fotheringay said modestly ; 'I wasn't fit for't till Bows taught me.'

'True for you, my dear,' said the captain : and bending to Pendennis, he added, 'Rejuiced in circumstances, sir, I was for some time a fencing-master in Dublin (there's only three men in the empire could touch me with the foil once, but Jack Costigan's getting old and stiff now, sir), and my daughter had an engagement at the thayater there ; and 'twas there that my friend, Mr. Bows,[8] gave her lessons and made her what ye see. What have ye done since Bows went, Emily ?'

'Sure, I've made a pie,' Emily said, with perfect simplicity. She pronounced it 'poy.'

'If ye'll try it at four o'clock, sir, say the word,' said Costigan gallantly. 'That girl, sir, makes the best veal-and-ham pie in England, and I think I can promise ye a glass of punch of the right flavour.'

Pen had promised to be at home to dinner at six o'clock, but the rascal thought he could accommodate pleasure and duty in this point, and was only too eager to accept this invitation. He looked on with delight and wonder whilst Ophelia busied herself about the room, and prepared for the dinner. She arranged the glasses, and laid and smoothed the little cloth, all which duties she performed with a quiet grace and good humour, which enchanted her guest more and more. The 'poy' arrived from the baker's in the hands of one of the little choir-boy's brothers at the proper hour : and at four o'clock, Pen found himself at dinner—actually at dinner with the handsomest woman in all creation—with his first and only love, whom he had adored ever since when? —ever since yesterday, ever since for ever. He ate a crust of her making, he poured her out a glass of beer, he saw her drink a glass of punch—just one wine-glass full—out of the tumbler which she mixed for her papa. She was perfectly good-natured, and offered to mix one for Pendennis too.

It was prodigiously strong ; Pen had never in his life drunk so much spirits-and-water. Was it the punch or the punch-maker who intoxicated him ?

Pen tried to engage her[9] in conversation about poetry and about her profession. He asked her what she thought of Ophelia's madness, and whether she was in love with Hamlet or not ? 'In love with such a little ojous wretch as that stunted manager of a Bingley ?' She bristled with indignation at the thought. Pen explained it was not of her he spoke, but of Ophelia of the play . 'Oh, indeed ; if no offence was meant, none was taken : but as for Bingley, indeed, she did not value him—not that glass of punch.' Pen next tried her on Kotzebue. 'Kotzebue ? who is he ?' —'The author of the play in which she had been performing so admirably.' 'She did not know that—the man's name at the beginning of the book was Thompson,' she said. Pen laughed at her adorable simplicity. He told her of the melancholy fate of the author of the play, and how Sand had killed him. It was for the first time in her life that Miss Costigan had ever heard of Mr. Kotzebue's existence, but she looked as if she was very much interested, and her sympathy sufficed for honest Pen.

And in the midst of this simple conversation, the hour and a quarter which poor Pen could afford to allow himself passed away only too quickly ; and he had taken leave, he was gone, and away on his rapid road homewards on the back of Rebecca. She was called upon to show her mettle in the three journeys which she made that day.

'What was that he was talking about, the madness of Hamlet, and the theory of the great German critic on the subject ?' Emily asked of her father.

''Deed then I don't know, Milly dear,' answered the captain. 'We'll ask Bows when he comes.'

'Anyhow he's a nice, fair-spoken pretty young man,' the lady said : 'how many tickets did he take of you ?'

'Faith, then, he took six, and gev me two guineas, Milly,' the captain said. 'I suppose them young chaps is not too flush of coin.'

'He's full of book-learning,' Miss Fotheringay continued. 'Kotzebue ! He, he, what a droll name indeed, now ; and the poor fellow killed by Sand, too !* Did ye ever hear such a thing ? I'll ask Bows about it, papa dear.'

'A queer death, sure enough,' ejaculated the captain, and

changed the painful theme. ''Tis an elegant mare the young gentleman rides,' Costigan went on to say; 'and a grand breakfast, intirely, that young Mister Foker gave us.'

'He's good for two private boxes, and at leest twenty tickets, I should say,' cried the daughter, a prudent lass, who always kept her fine eyes on the main chance.

'I'll go bail of that,' answered the papa; and so their conversation continued awhile, until the tumbler of punch was finished; and their hour of departure soon came, too; for at half-past six Miss Fotheringay was to appear at the theatre

again, whither her father always accompanied her; and stood, as we have seen, in the side-scene watching her, and drank spirits-and-water in the green-room with the company there.

'How beautiful she is,' thought Pen, cantering homewards. 'How simple and how tender! How charming it is to see a woman of her genius busying herself with the humble offices of domestic life, cooking dishes to make her old father comfortable, and brewing him drink! How rude it was of me to begin to talk about professional matters, and

how well she turned the conversation! By the way, she talked about professional matters herself; but then with what fun and humour she told the story of her comrade, Pentweazle, as he was called! There is no humour like Irish humour. Her father is rather tedious, but thoroughly amiable; and how fine of him, giving lessons in fencing after he quitted the army, where he was the pet of the Duke of Kent! Fencing! I should like to continue my fencing, or I shall forget what Angelo taught me. Uncle Arthur always liked me to fence—he says it is the exercise of a gentleman. Hang it! I'll take some lessons of Captain Costigan. Go along, Rebecca—up the hill, old lady. Pendennis, Pendennis—how she spoke the word! Emily, Emily! how good, how noble, how beautiful, how perfect, she is!'

Now the reader, who has had the benefit of overhearing the entire conversation which Pen had with Miss Fotheringay, can judge for himself about the powers of her mind, and may perhaps be disposed to think that she has not said anything astonishingly humorous or intellectual in the course of the above interview.[10]

But what did our Pen care? He saw a pair of bright eyes, and he believed in them—a beautiful image, and he fell down and worshipped it. He supplied the meaning which her words wanted; and created the divinity which he loved. Was Titania the first who fell in love with an ass, or Pygmalion the only artist who has gone crazy about a stone? He had found her; he had found what his soul thirsted after. He flung himself into the stream and drank with all his might. Let those who have been thirsty own how delicious that first draught is. As he rode down the avenue towards home—Pen shrieked with laughter as he saw the Reverend Mr. Smirke once more coming demurely away from Fairoaks on his pony. Smirke had dawdled and stayed at the cottages on the way, and then dawdled with Laura over her lessons—and then looked at Mrs. Pendennis's gardens and improvements until he had perfectly bored out that lady; and he had taken his leave at the very last minute without that invitation to dinner which he fondly expected.

Pen was full of kindness and triumph. 'What, picked up and sound?' he cried out, laughing. 'Come along back, old fellow, and eat my dinner—I have had mine: but we will have a bottle of the old wine and drink her health, Smirke.'

Poor Smirke turned the pony's head round, and jogged along with Arthur. His mother was charmed to see him in such high spirits, and welcomed Mr. Smirke for his sake, when Arthur said he had forced the curate back to dine. He gave a most ludicrous account of the play of the night before, and of the acting of Bingley the manager, in his rickety Hessians, and the enormous Mrs. Bingley as the countess, in rumpled green satin and a Polish cap : he mimicked them, and delighted his mother and little Laura, who clapped her hands with pleasure.

'And Mrs. Haller ?' said Mrs. Pendennis.

'She's a stunner, ma'am,' Pen said, laughing, and using the words of his revered friend, Mr. Foker.

'A *what*, Arthur ?' asked the lady.

'What *is* a stunner, Arthur ?' cried Laura, in the same voice.

So he gave them a queer account of Mr. Foker, and how he used to be called Vats-and-Grains, and by other contumelious names at school : and how he was now exceedingly rich, and a fellow-commoner at St. Boniface. But gay and communicative as he was, Mr. Pen did not say one syllable about his ride to Chatteris that day, or about the new friends whom he had made there.

When the two ladies retired, Pen, with flashing eyes, filled up two great bumpers of madeira, and looking Smirke full in the face, said, 'Here's to her !'

'Here's to her !' said the curate, with a sigh, lifting the glass : and emptying it, so that his face was a little pink when he put it down.

Pen had even less sleep that night than on the night before. In the morning, and almost before dawn, he went out and saddled that unfortunate Rebecca himself, and rode her on the Downs like mad. Again Love had roused him—and said, 'Awake, Pendennis, I am here.' That charming fever—that delicious longing—and fire, and uncertainty ; he hugged them to him—he would not have lost them for all the world.

CHAPTER VI

CONTAINS BOTH LOVE AND WAR

For some time after this,[1] honest Mr. Smirke had a very easy time with his pupil. Rebecca was the animal who suffered most in the present state of Pen's mind, for, besides those days when he could publicly announce his intention of going to Chatteris to take a fencing-lesson, and went thither with the knowledge of his mother, whenever he saw three hours clear before him, the young rascal made a rush for the city, and found his way to Prior's Lane. He was as frantic with vexation when Rebecca went lame, as Richard at Bosworth, when his horse was killed under him : and got deeply into the books of the man who kept the hunting stables at Chatteris for the doctoring of his own, and the hire of another animal.

Then, and perhaps once in a week, under pretence of going to read a Greek play with Smirke, this young reprobate set off so as to be in time for the 'Competitor' down coach, stayed a couple of hours in Chatteris, and returned on the 'Rival,' which left for London at ten at night. Once his secret was nearly lost by Smirke's simplicity, of whom Mrs. Pendennis asked whether they had read a great deal the night before, or a question to that effect. Smirke was about to tell the truth, that he had never seen Mr. Pen at all, when the latter's boot-heel came grinding down on Mr. Smirke's toe under the table, and warned the curate not to betray him.

They had had conversations on the tender subject, of course.[2] There must be a confidant and depositary somewhere. When informed, under the most solemn vows of secrecy, of Pen's condition of mind, the curate said, with no small tremor, 'that he hoped it was no unworthy object—no unlawful attachment, which Pen had formed'—for if so, the poor fellow felt it would be his duty to break his vow and inform Pen's mother, and then there would be a quarrel, he

felt, with sickening apprehension, and he would never again have a chance of seeing what he most liked in the world.

'Unlawful, unworthy!' Pen bounced out at the curate's question. 'She is as pure as she is beautiful; I would give my heart to no other woman. I keep the matter a secret in my family, because—because—there are reasons of a weighty nature which I am not at liberty to disclose. But any man who breathes a word against her purity insults both her honour and mine, and—and dammy, I won't stand it.'

Smirke, with a faint laugh, only said, 'Well, well, don't call me out, Arthur, for you know I can't fight:' but by this compromise the wretched curate was put more than ever into the power of his pupil, and the Greek and mathematics suffered correspondingly.

If the reverend gentleman had had much discernment, and looked into the 'Poets' Corner' of the *County Chronicle*, as it arrived in the Wednesday's bag, he might have seen 'Mrs. Haller,' 'Passion and Genius,' 'Lines to Miss Fotheringay of the Theatre Royal,' appearing every week; and other verses of the most gloomy, thrilling, and passionate cast. But as these poems were no longer signed 'NEP' by their artful composer, but subscribed 'EROS,' neither the tutor nor Helen, the good soul, who cut all her son's verses out of the paper, knew that Nep was no other than that flaming Eros, who sang so vehemently the charms of the new actress.

'Who is the lady,' at last asked Mrs. Pendennis, 'whom your rival is always singing in the *County Chronicle?* He writes something like you, dear Pen, but yours is much the best. Have you seen Miss Fotheringay?'

Pen said yes, he had; that night he went to see *The Stranger*, she acted Mrs. Haller. By the way, she was going to have a benefit, and was to appear in Ophelia—suppose we were to go—Shakespere you know, mother—we can get horses from the 'Clavering Arms.' Little Laura sprang up with delight; she longed for a play.

Pen introduced 'Shakespere you know,' because the deceased Pendennis, as became a man of his character, professed an uncommon respect for the bard of Avon, in whose works he safely said there was more poetry than in all Johnson's *Poets* put together. And though Mr. Pendennis did not much read the works in question, yet he enjoined

Pen to peruse them, and often said what pleasure he should have, when the boy was of a proper age, in taking him and mother to see some good plays of the immortal poet.

The ready tears welled up in the kind mother's eyes as she remembered these speeches of the man who was gone. She kissed her son fondly, and said she would go. Laura jumped for joy. Was Pen happy ?—was he ashamed ? As he held his mother to him, he longed to tell her all, but he kept his counsel. He would see how his mother liked her ; the play should be the thing, and he would try his mother like Hamlet's.

Helen, in her good humour, asked Mr. Smirke to be of the party. That ecclesiastic had been bred up by a fond parent at Clapham, who had an objection to dramatic entertainments, and he had never yet seen a play. But, Shakespere !—but to go with Mrs. Pendennis in her carriage, and sit a whole night by her side !—he could not resist the idea of so much pleasure, and made a feeble speech, in which he spoke of temptation and gratitude, and finally accepted Mrs. Pendennis's most kind offer. As he spoke he gave her a look, which made her exceedingly uncomfortable. She had seen that look more than once, of late, pursuing her. He became more positively odious every day in the widow's eyes.

We are not going to say a great deal about Pen's courtship of Miss Fotheringay, for the reader has already had a specimen of her conversation, much of which need surely not be reported. Pen sat with her hour after hour, and poured forth all his honest boyish soul to her. Everything he knew, or hoped, or felt, or had read, or fancied, he told to her. He never tired of talking and longing. One after another, as his thoughts rose in his hot eager brain, he clothed them in words, and told them to her. Her part of the *tête-à-tête* was not to talk, but to appear as if she understood what Pen talked,[3] and to look exceedingly handsome and sympathizing. The fact is, whilst he was making one of his tirades [4] the lovely Emily, who could not comprehend a tenth part of his talk, had leisure to think about her own affairs, and would arrange in her own mind how they should dress the cold mutton, or how she would turn the black satin, or make herself out of her scarf a bonnet like Miss Thackthwaite's new one, and so forth. Pen spouted Byron

and Moore; passion and poetry: her business was to throw up her eyes, or fixing them for a moment on his face, to cry, 'Oh, 'tis beautiful! Ah, how exquisite! Repeat those lines again.' And off the boy went, and she returned to her own simple thoughts about the turned gown, or the hashed mutton.

In fact Pen's passion was not long a secret from the lovely Emily or her father. Upon his second visit, his admiration was quite evident to both of them, and on his departure the old gentleman said to his daughter, as he winked at her over his glass of grog, 'Faith, Milly darling, I think ye've hooked that chap.'

'Pooh, 'tis only a boy, papa dear,' Milly remarked. 'Sure he's but a child.'[5]

'Ye've hooked 'um, anyhow,' said the captain, 'and let me tell ye he's not a bad fish. I asked Tom at the 'George,' and Flint, the grocer, where his mother dales—fine fortune—drives in her chariot—splendid park and grounds—Fairoaks Park—only son—property all his own at twenty-one—ye might go further and not fare so well, Miss Fotheringay.'

'Them boys are mostly talk,' said Milly seriously. 'Ye know at Dublin how ye went on about young Poldoody, and I've a whole desk full of verses he wrote me when he was in Trinity College; but he went abroad, and his mother married him to an Englishwoman.'

'Lord Poldoody was a young nobleman; and in them it's natural: and ye weren't in the position in which ye are now, Milly dear. But ye mustn't encourage this young chap too much, for, bedad, Jack Costigan won't have any thrifling with his daughter.'

'No more will his daughter, papa, you may be sure of *that*,' Milly said. 'A little sip more of the punch—sure, 'tis beautiful. Ye needn't be afraid about the young chap—I think I'm old enough to take care of myself, Captain Costigan.'

So Pen used to come day after day, rushing in and galloping away, and growing more wild about the girl with every visit. Sometimes the captain was present at their meetings; but having a perfect confidence in his daughter, he was more often inclined to leave the young couple to themselves, and cocked his hat over his eye, and strutted off on some errand when Pen entered. How delightful those

interviews were! The captain's drawing-room was a low wainscoted room, with a large window looking into the dean's garden. There Pen sat and talked—and talked to Emily, looking beautiful as she sat at her work—looking beautiful and calm, and the sunshine came streaming in at the great windows, and lighted up her superb face and form. In the midst of the conversation, the great bell would begin to boom, and he would pause smiling, and be silent until the sound of the vast music died away—or the rooks in the cathedral elms would make a great noise towards sunset—or the sound of the organ and the choristers would come over the quiet air, and gently hush Pen's talking.

By the way, it must be said, that Miss Fotheringay, in a plain shawl and a close bonnet and veil, went to church every Sunday of her life, accompanied by her indefatigable father, who gave the responses in a very rich and fine brogue, joined in the psalms and chanting, and behaved in the most exemplary manner.

Little Bows, the house-friend of the family, was exceedingly wroth at the notion of Miss Fotheringay's marriage with a stripling seven or eight years her junior. Bows, who was a cripple, and owned that he was a little more deformed even than Bingley the manager, so that he could not appear on the stage, was a singular wild man of no small talents and humour. Attracted first by Miss Fotheringay's beauty, he began to teach her how to act.* He shrieked out in his cracked voice the parts, and his pupil learned them from his lips by rote, and repeated them in her full rich tones. He indicated the attitudes, and set and moved those beautiful arms of hers. Those who remember this grand actress on the stage can recall how she used always precisely the same gestures, looks, and tones; how she stood on the same plank of the stage in the same position, rolled her eyes at the same instant and to the same degree, and wept with precisely the same heart-rending pathos and over the same pathetic syllable. And after she had come out trembling with emotion before the audience, and looking so exhausted and tearful that you fancied she would faint with sensibility, she would gather up her hair the instant she was behind the curtain, and go home to a mutton-chop and a glass of brown stout; and the harrowing labours of the day over, she went to bed and snored as resolutely and as regularly as a porter.

Bows then was indignant at the notion that his pupil should throw her chances away in life by bestowing her hand upon a little country squire. As soon as a London manager saw her he prophesied that she would get a London engagement, and a great success. The misfortune was that the London managers had seen her. She had played in London three years before, and failed from utter stupidity. Since then it was that Bows had taken her in hand and taught her part after part. How he worked and screamed, and twisted, and repeated lines over and over again, and with what indomitable patience and dullness she followed him! She knew that he made her: and let herself be made. She was not grateful, or ungrateful, or unkind, or ill-humoured. She was only stupid; and Pen was madly in love with her.

The post-horses from the 'Clavering Arms' arrived in due time, and carried the party to the theatre at Chatteris, where Pen was gratified in perceiving that a tolerably large audience was assembled. The young gentlemen from Baymouth had a box, in the front of which sat Mr. Foker and his friend Mr. Spavin, splendidly attired in the most full-blown evening costume. They saluted Pen in a cordial manner, and examined his party, of which they approved, for little Laura was a pretty little red-cheeked girl with a quantity of shining brown ringlets, and Mrs. Pendennis, dressed in black velvet with the diamond cross which she sported on great occasions, looked uncommonly handsome and majestic. Behind these sat Mr. Arthur, and the gentle Smirke with the curl reposing on his fair forehead, and his white tie in perfect order. He blushed to find himself in such a place—but how happy was he to be there. He and Mrs. Pendennis brought books of *Hamlet* with them to follow the tragedy, as is the custom of honest country-folks who go to a play in state. Samuel, coachman, groom, and gardener to Mr. Pendennis, took his place in the pit, where Mr. Foker's man was also visible. It was dotted with non-commissioned officers of the Dragoons, whose band, by kind permission of Colonel Swallowtail, were, as usual, in the orchestra; and that corpulent and distinguished warrior himself, with his Waterloo medal and a number of his young men, made a handsome show in the boxes.

'Who is that odd-looking person bowing to you, Arthur?' Mrs. Pendennis asked of her son.

Pen blushed a great deal. 'His name is Captain Costigan, ma'am,' he said—'a Peninsular officer.' In fact it was the captain in a new shoot of clothes, as he called them, and with a large pair of white kid gloves, one of which he waved to Pendennis, whilst he laid the other sprawling over his heart and coat-buttons. Pen did not say any more. And how was Mrs. Pendennis to know that Mr. Costigan was the father of Miss Fotheringay?

Mr. Hornbull, from London, was the Hamlet of the night, Mr. Bingley modestly contenting himself with the part of Horatio, and reserving his chief strength for William in *Black-Eyed Susan*,* which was the second piece.

We have nothing to do with the play: except to say, that Ophelia looked lovely, and performed with admirable wild pathos: laughing, weeping, gazing wildly, waving her beautiful white arms, and flinging about her snatches of flowers and songs with the most charming madness. What an opportunity her splendid black hair had of tossing over her shoulders! She made the most charming corpse ever seen; and while Hamlet and Laertes were battling in her grave, she was looking out from the back scenes with some curiosity towards Pen's box, and the family party assembled in it.

There was but one voice in her praise there. Mrs. Pendennis was in ecstasies with her beauty. Little Laura was bewildered by the piece, and the Ghost, and the play within the play (during which, as Hamlet lay at Ophelia's knee, Pen felt that he would have liked to strangle Mr. Hornbull), but cried out great praises of that beautiful young creature. Pen was charmed with the effect which she produced on his mother—and the clergyman, for his part, was exceedingly enthusiastic.

When the curtain fell upon that group of slaughtered personages, who are dispatched so suddenly at the end of *Hamlet*, and whose demise astonished poor little Laura not a little, there was an immense shouting and applause from all quarters of the house; the intrepid Smirke, violently excited, clapped his hands, and cried out 'Bravo! Bravo!' as loud as the Dragoon officers themselves. These were greatly moved—*ils s'agitaient sur leurs bancs*, to borrow a phrase from our neighbours. They were led cheering into action by the portly Swallowtail, who waved his cap—the non-commissioned officers in the pit, of course, gallantly

following their chiefs. There was a roar of bravos rang through the house; Pen bellowing with the loudest, 'Fotheringay! Fotheringay!' Messrs. Spavin and Foker giving the view halloo from their box. Even Mrs. Pendennis began to wave about her pocket-handkerchief, and little Laura danced, laughed, clapped, and looked up at Pen with wonder.

Hornbull led the *bénéficiaire* forward, amidst bursts of enthusiasm—and she looked so handsome and radiant, with her hair still over her shoulders, that Pen hardly could contain himself for rapture: and he leaned over his mother's chair, and shouted, and hurrayed, and waved his hat. It was all he could do to keep his secret from Helen, and not say, "Look! That's the woman! Isn't she peerless? I tell you I love her.' But he disguised these feelings under an enormous bellowing and hurraying.

As for Miss Fotheringay and her behaviour, the reader is referred to a former page for an account of that. She went through precisely the same business. She surveyed the house all round with glances of gratitude; and trembled, and almost sank with emotion, over her favourite trap-door. She seized the flowers (Foker discharged a prodigious bouquet at her, and even Smirke made a feeble shy with a rose, and blushed dreadfully when it fell into the pit)—she seized the flowers and pressed them to her swelling heart—etc. etc.—in a word—we refer the reader to page 48. Twinkling in her breast poor old Pen saw a locket which he had bought of Mr. Nathan in High Street, with the last shilling he was worth, and a sovereign borrowed from Smirke.

Black-Eyed Susan followed, at which sweet story our

gentle-hearted friends were exceedingly charmed and affected : and in which Susan, with a russet gown and a pink ribbon in her cap, looked to the full as lovely as Ophelia. Bingley was great in William. Goll, as the Admiral, looked like the figure-head of a seventy-four ; and Garbetts, as Captain Boldweather, a miscreant who forms a plan for carrying off Black-Eyed Susan,* and waving an immense cocked hat, says, 'Come what may, he *will* be the ruin of her'—all these performed their parts with their accustomed talent ; and it was with a sincere regret that all our friends saw the curtain drop down and end that pretty and tender story.

If Pen had been alone with his mother in the carriage as they went home, he would have told her all that night ; but he sat on the box in the moonshine smoking a cigar by the side of Smirke, who warmed himself with a comforter. Mr. Foker's tandem and lamps whirled by the sober old Clavering posters, as they were a couple of miles on their road home, and Mr. Spavin saluted Mrs. Pendennis's carriage with some considerable variations of 'Rule, Britannia,' on the key-bugle.

It happened two days after the above gaieties that Mr. Dean of Chatteris entertained a few select clerical friends at dinner at his Deanery House. That they drank uncommonly good port wine, and abused the bishop over their dessert, are very likely matters : but with such we have nothing at present to do. Our friend Doctor Portman, of Clavering, was one of the dean's guests, and being a gallant man, and seeing from his place at the mahogany, the dean's lady walking up and down the grass, with her children sporting around her, and her pink parasol over her lovely head—the doctor stepped out of the French windows of the dining-room into the lawn, which skirts that apartment, and left the other white neckcloths to gird at my lord bishop. Then the doctor went up and offered Mrs. Dean his arm, and they sauntered over the ancient velvet lawn, which had been mowed and rolled for immemorial deans, in that easy, quiet, comfortable manner, in which people of middle age and good temper walk after a good dinner, in a calm golden summer evening, when the sun has but just sunk behind the enormous cathedral-towers, and the sickle-shaped moon is growing every instant brighter in the heavens.

Now at the end of the Dean's garden, there is, as we have stated, Mrs. Creed's house, and the windows of the first-floor room were open to admit the pleasant summer air. A young lady of six-and-twenty, whose eyes were perfectly wide open, and a luckless boy of eighteen, blind with love and infatuation, were in that chamber together; in which persons, as we have before seen them in the same place, the reader will have no difficulty in recognizing Mr. Arthur Pendennis and Miss Costigan.

The poor boy had taken the plunge. Trembling with passionate emotion, his heart beating and throbbing fiercely, tears rushing forth in spite of him, his voice almost choking with feeling, poor Pen had said those words which he could withhold no more, and flung himself and his whole store of love, and admiration, and ardour, at the feet of this mature beauty. Is he the first who has done so? Have none before or after him staked all their treasure of life, as a savage does his land and possessions against a draught of the fair-skins' fire-water, or a couple of bauble eyes?

'Does your mother know of this, *Arthur?*' said Miss Fotheringay slowly. He seized her hand madly and kissed it a thousand times. She did not withdraw it. '*Does* the old lady know it?' Miss Costigan thought to herself, 'Well, perhaps she may,' and then she remembered what a handsome diamond cross Mrs. Pendennis had on the night of the play, and thought, 'Sure 'twill go in the family.'

'Calm yourself, dear Arthur,' she said, in her low rich voice, and smiled sweetly and gravely upon him. Then with her disengaged hand, she put the hair lightly off his throbbing forehead. He was in such a rapture and whirl of happiness that he could hardly speak. At last he gasped out, 'My mother has seen you and admires you beyond measure. She will learn to love you soon: who can do otherwise? She will love you because I do.'

''Deed then, I think you do,' said Miss Costigan, perhaps with a sort of pity for Pen.

Think he did! Of course here Mr. Pen went off into a rhapsody which, as we have perfect command over our own feelings,[6] we have no right to overhear. Let the poor boy fling out his simple heart at the woman's feet, and deal gently with him. It is best to love wisely, no doubt: but to love foolishly is better than not to be able to love at all. Some of us can't: and are proud of our impotence too.

At the end of his speech Pen again kissed the imperial hand with rapture—and I believe it was at this very moment, and while Mrs. Dean and Doctor Portman were engaged in conversation, that young Master Ridley Roset, her son, pulled his mother by the back of her capacious dress and said, 'I say, ma! look up there'—and he waggled his innocent head.

That was, indeed, a view from the dean's garden such as seldom is seen by deans—or is written in chapters.* There was poor Pen performing a salute upon the rosy fingers of his charmer, who received the embrace with perfect calmness and good humour. Master Ridley looked up and grinned, little Miss Rosa looked at her brother, and opened the mouth of astonishment. Mrs. Dean's countenance defied expression, and as for Dr. Portman, when he beheld the scene, and saw his prime favourite and dear pupil Pen, he stood mute with rage and wonder.

Mrs. Haller spied the party below at the same moment, and gave a start and a laugh. 'Sure, there's somebody in the dean's garden,' she cried out; and withdrew with perfect calmness, whilst Pen darted away with his face glowing like coals. The garden party had re-entered the house when he ventured to look out again. The sickle moon was blazing bright in the heavens then, the stars were glittering, the bell of the cathedral tolling nine, the Dean's guests (all save one, who had called for his horse Dumpling, and ridden off early) were partaking of tea and buttered cakes in Mrs. Dean's drawing-room—when Pen took leave of Miss Costigan.

Pen arrived at home in due time afterwards, and was going to slip off to bed, for the poor lad was greatly worn and agitated, and his high-strung nerves had been at almost a maddening pitch—when a summons came to him by John the old footman, whose countenance bore a very ominous look, that his mother must see him below.

On this he tied on his neckcloth again, and went downstairs to the drawing-room. There sat not only his mother but her friend, the Reverend Doctor Portman. Helen's face looked very pale by the light of the lamp—the doctor's was flushed, on the contrary, and quivering with anger and emotion.

Pen saw at once that there was a crisis, and that there had been a discovery. 'Now for it,' he thought.

'Where have you been, Arthur?' Helen said, in a trembling voice.

'How can you look that—that dear lady, and a Christian clergyman in the face, sir?' bounced out the doctor, in spite of Helen's pale, appealing looks. 'Where has he been? Where his mother's son should have been ashamed to go. For your mother's an angel, sir, an angel. How dare you bring pollution into her house and make that spotless creature wretched with the thoughts of your crime?'

'Sir!' said Pen.

'Don't deny it, sir,' roared the doctor. 'Don't add lies, sir, to your other infamy. I saw you myself, sir. I saw you from the dean's garden. I saw you kissing the hand of that infernal painted——'

'Stop,' Pen said, clapping his fist on the table, till the lamp flickered up and shook. 'I am a very young man, but you will please to remember that I am a gentleman—I will hear no abuse of that lady.'

'Lady, sir!' cried the doctor, '*that* a lady—you—you—you stand in your mother's presence and call that—that woman a lady——'

'In anybody's presence,' shouted out Pen. 'She is worthy of any place. She is as pure as any woman. She is as good as she is beautiful. If any man but you insulted her, I would tell him what I thought; but as you are my oldest friend, I suppose you have the privilege to doubt of my honour.'

'No, no, Pen, dearest Pen,' cried out Helen, in an excess of joy. 'I told, I told you, doctor, he was not—not what you thought:' and the tender creature coming trembling forward flung herself on Pen's shoulder.

Pen felt himself a man, and a match for all the doctors in Doctordom. He was glad this explanation had come. 'You saw how beautiful she was,' he said to his mother, with a soothing, protecting air, like Hamlet with Gertrude in the play. 'I tell you, dear mother, she is as good. When you know her you will say so. She is of all, except you, the simplest, the kindest, the most affectionate of women. Why should she not be on the stage?—She maintains her father by her labour.'

'Drunken old reprobate,' growled the doctor, but Pen did not hear or heed.

A VIEW FROM THE DEAN'S GARDEN

'If you could see, as I have, how orderly her life is, how pure and pious her whole conduct, you would—as I do—yes, as I do'—(with a savage look at the doctor)—'spurn the slanderer who dared to do her wrong. Her father was an officer, and distinguished himself in Spain. He was a friend of His Royal Highness the Duke of Kent, and is intimately known to the Duke of Wellington, and some of the first officers of our army. He has met my uncle Arthur at Lord Hill's,* he thinks. His own family is one of the most ancient and respectable in Ireland, and indeed is as good as our own. The—the Costigans were kings of Ireland.'

'Why, God bless my soul,' shrieked out the doctor, hardly knowing whether to burst with rage or laughter, 'you don't mean to say you want to *marry* her?'

Pen put on his most princely air. 'What else, Dr. Portman,' he said, 'do you suppose would be my desire?'

Utterly foiled in his attack, and knocked down by this sudden lunge of Pen's, the doctor could only gasp out, 'Mrs. Pendennis, ma'am, send for the major.'

'Send for the major? with all my heart,' said Arthur, Prince of Pendennis and Grand Duke of Fairoaks, with a most superb wave of the hand. And the colloquy terminated by the writing of those two letters which were laid on Major Pendennis's breakfast-table, in London, at the commencement of Prince Arthur's most veracious history.

CHAPTER VII

IN WHICH THE MAJOR MAKES HIS APPEARANCE

UR acquaintance, Major Arthur Pendennis, arrived in due time at Fairoaks, after a dreary night passed in the mail-coach, where a stout fellow-passenger, swelling preternaturally with great-coats, had crowded him into a corner, and kept him awake by snoring indecently; where a widow lady, opposite, had not only shut out the fresh air by closing all the windows of the vehicle, but had filled the interior with fumes of Jamaica rum-and-water, which she sucked

perpetually from a bottle in her reticule; where, whenever he caught a brief moment of sleep, the twanging of the horn at the turnpike gates, or the scuffling of his huge neighbour wedging him closer and closer, or the play of the widow's feet on his own tender toes, speedily woke up the poor gentleman to the horrors and realities of life—a life which has passed away now, and become impossible, and only lives in fond memories. Eight miles an hour, for twenty or five-and-twenty hours, a tight mail-coach, a hard seat, a gouty tendency, a perpetual change of coachmen grumbling because you did not fee them enough, a fellow passenger partial to spirits-and-water—who has not borne these evils in the jolly old times? and how could people travel under such difficulties? And yet they did.[1] Night and morning passed, and the major, with a yellow face, a bristly beard, a wig out of curl, and strong rheumatic griefs shooting through various limbs of his uneasy body, descended at the little lodge-gate at Fairoaks, where the portress and gardener's wife reverentially greeted him; and, still more respectfully, Mr. Morgan, his man.

Helen was on the look-out for this expected guest, and saw him from her window. But she did not come forward immediately to greet him. She knew the major did not like to be seen at a surprise, and required a little preparation before he cared to be visible. Pen, when a boy, had incurred sad disgrace, by carrying off from the major's dressing-table a little morocco box, which it must be confessed contained the major's back teeth, which he naturally would leave out of his jaws in a jolting mail-coach, and without which he would not choose to appear. Morgan, his man, made a mystery of mystery of his wigs: curling them in private places: introducing them privily to his master's room; nor without his head of hair would the major care to show himself to any member of his family, or any acquaintance. He went to his apartment then and supplied these deficiencies; he groaned, and moaned, and wheezed, and cursed Morgan through his toilet, as an old buck will, who has been up all night with a rheumatism, and has a long duty to perform. And finally, being belted, curled, and set straight, he descended upon the drawing-room, with a grave majestic air, such as befitted one who was at once a man of business and a man of fashion.

Pen was not there, however; only Helen, and little Laura

sewing at her knees; and to whom he never presented more than a forefinger, as he did on this occasion after saluting his sister-in-law. Laura took the finger trembling and dropped it—and then fled out of the room. Major Pendennis did not want to keep her, or indeed to have her in the house at all, and had his private reason for disapproving of her; which we may mention on some future occasion. Meanwhile Laura disappeared, and wandered about the premises seeking for Pen: whom she presently found in the orchard, pacing up and down a walk there in earnest conversation with Mr. Smirke. He was so occupied that he did not hear Laura's clear voice singing out, until Smirke pulled him by the coat, and pointed towards her as she came running.

She ran up and put her hand into his. 'Come in, Pen,' she said; 'there's somebody come: Uncle Arthur's come.'

'He is, is he?' said Pen, and she felt him grasp her little hand. He looked round at Smirke with uncommon fierceness, as much as to say, I am ready for him or any man. Mr. Smirke cast up his eyes as usual, and heaved a gentle sigh.

'Lead on, Laura,' Pen said, with a half-fierce, half-comic air—'lead on, and say I wait upon my uncle.' But he was laughing in order to hide a great anxiety: and was screwing his courage inwardly to face the ordeal which he knew was now before him.

Pen had taken Smirke into his confidence in the last two days, and after the outbreak attendant on the discovery of Doctor Portman, and during every one of those forty-eight hours which he had passed in Mr. Smirke's society, had done nothing but talk to his tutor about Miss Fotheringay—Miss Emily Fotheringay—Emily, etc., to all which talk Smirke listened without difficulty, for he was in love himself, most anxious in all things to propitiate Pen, and indeed very much himself enraptured by the personal charms of this goddess, whose like, never having been before at a theatrical representation, he had not beheld until now. Pen's fire and volubility, his hot eloquence and rich poetical tropes and figures, his manly heart, kind, ardent, and hopeful, refusing to see any defects in the person he loved, any difficulties in their position that he might not overcome, had half convinced Mr. Smirke that the arrangement proposed by Mr. Pen was a very feasible and prudent one, and that it

would be a great comfort to have Emily settled at Fairoaks, Captain Costigan in the yellow room, established for life there, and Pen married at eighteen.

And it is a fact that in these two days, the boy had almost talked over his mother, too; had parried all her objections one after another with that indignant good sense which is often the perfection of absurdity; and had brought her almost to acquiesce in the belief that if the marriage was doomed in heaven, why doomed it was—that if the young woman was a good person, it was all that she for her part had to ask; and rather to dread the arrival of the guardian uncle who she foresaw would regard Mr. Pen's marriage in a manner very different to that simple, romantic, honest, and utterly absurd way, in which the widow was already disposed to look at questions of this sort.[2] Helen Pendennis was a country-bred woman, and the book of life, as she interpreted it, told her a different story to that page which is read in cities.[3] It pleased her (with that dismal pleasure which the idea of sacrificing themselves gives to certain women) to think of the day when she would give up all to Pen, and he should bring his wife home, and she would surrender the keys and the best bedroom, and go and sit at the side of the table, and see him happy. What did she want in life, but to see the lad prosper? As an empress certainly was not too good for him, and would be honoured by becoming Mrs. Pen; so if he selected humble Esther instead of Queen Vashti, she would be content with his lordship's choice. Never mind how lowly or poor the person might be who was to enjoy that prodigious honour, Mrs. Pendennis was willing to bow before her and welcome her, and yield her up the first place. But an actress—a mature woman, who had long ceased blushing except with rouge, as she stood under the eager glances of thousands of eyes—an illiterate and ill-bred person, very likely, who must have lived with light associates, and have heard doubtful conversation—oh! it was hard that such a one should be chosen, and that the matron should be deposed to give place to such a Sultana.

All these doubts the widow laid before Pen during the two days which had of necessity to elapse ere the uncle came down; but he met them with that happy frankness and ease which a young gentleman exhibits at his time of life, and routed his mother's objections with infinite satis-

faction to himself. Miss Costigan was a paragon of virtue and delicacy; she was as sensitive as the most timid maiden; she was as pure as the unsullied snow; she had the finest manners, the most graceful wit and genius, the most charming refinement, and justness of appreciation in all matters of taste; she had the most admirable temper and devotion to her father, a good old gentleman of high family and fallen fortunes, who had lived, however, with the best society in Europe: he was in no hurry, and could afford to wait any time—till he was one-and-twenty. But he felt (and here his face assumed an awful and harrowing solemnity) that he was engaged in the one only passion of his life, and that DEATH alone could close it.

Helen told him, with a sad smile and shake of the head, that people survived these passions, and as for long engagements contracted between very young men and old women—she knew an instance in her own family—Laura's poor father was an instance—how fatal they were.

Mr. Pen, however, was resolved that death must be his doom in case of disappointment, and rather than this—rather than balk him in fact—this lady would have submitted to any sacrifice or personal pain, and would have gone down on her knees and have kissed the feet of a Hottentot daughter-in-law.

Arthur knew his power over the widow, and the young tyrant was touched whilst he exercised it. In those two days he brought her almost into submission, and patronized her very kindly; and he passed one evening with the lovely pie-maker at Chatteris, in which he bragged of his influence over his mother; and he spent the other night in composing a most flaming and conceited copy of verses to his divinity, in which he vowed, like Montrose,* that he would make her famous with his sword and glorious by his pen, and that he would love her as no mortal woman had been adored since the creation of womankind.

It was on that night, long after midnight, that wakeful Helen, passing stealthily by her son's door, saw a light streaming through the chink of the door into the dark passage, and heard Pen tossing and tumbling and mumbling verses in his bed. She waited outside for a while, anxiously listening to him. In infantile fevers and early boyish illnesses, many a night before, the kind soul had so kept watch. She turned the lock very softly now, and went in

so gently, that Pen for a moment did not see her. His face was turned from her. His papers on his desk were scattered about, and more were lying on the bed round him. He was biting a pencil and thinking of rhymes and all sorts of follies and passions. He was Hamlet jumping into Ophelia's grave : he was the Stranger taking Mrs. Haller to his arms, beautiful Mrs. Haller, with the raven ringlets falling over her shoulders. Despair and Byron, Thomas Moore and all the Loves of the Angels, Waller and Herrick, Béranger* and all the love-songs he had ever read, were working and seething in this young gentleman's mind, and he was at the very height and paroxysm of the imaginative frenzy, when his mother found him.

'Arthur,' said the mother's soft silver voice : and he started up and turned round. He clutched some of the papers and pushed them under the pillow.

'Why don't you go to sleep, my dear ?' she said, with a sweet tender smile, and sat down on the bed and took one of his hot hands.

Pen looked at her wildly for an instant. 'I couldn't sleep,' he said—'I—I was—I was writing.'—And hereupon he flung his arms round her neck and said, 'Oh, mother, I love her, I love her !'—How could such a kind soul as that help soothing and pitying him ? The gentle creature did her best : and thought with a strange wonderment and tenderness, that it was only yesterday that he was a child in that bed : and how she used to come and say her prayers over it before he woke upon holiday mornings.

They were very grand verses, no doubt, although Miss Fotheringay did not understand them ; but old Cos, with a wink and a knowing finger on his nose, said, 'Put them up with th' other letthers, Milly darling. Poldoody's pomes was nothing to this.' So Milly locked up the manuscripts.

When then, the major being dressed and presentable, presented himself to Mrs. Pendennis, he found in the course of ten minutes' colloquy that the poor widow was not merely distressed at the idea of the marriage contemplated by Pen, but actually more distressed at thinking that the boy himself was unhappy about it, and that his uncle and he should have any violent altercation on the subject. She besought Major Pendennis to be very gentle with Arthur : 'He has a very high spirit, and will not brook unkind words,' she hinted. 'Doctor Portman spoke to him rather roughly—

POOR PEN

and I must own unjustly, the other night—for my dearest boy's honour is as high as any mother can desire—but Pen's answer quite frightened me, it was so indignant. Recollect he is a man now; and be very—very cautious,' said the widow, laying a fair long hand on the major's sleeve.

He took it up, kissed it gallantly, and looked in her alarmed face with wonder, and a scorn which he was too polite to show. '*Bon Dieu!*' thought the old negotiator, 'the boy has actually talked the woman round, and she'd get him a wife as she would a toy if master cried for it. Why are there no such things as *lettres de cachet*—and a Bastille for young fellows of family?' The major lived in such good company that he might be excused for feeling like an earl.—He kissed the widow's timid hand, pressed it in both his, and laid it down on the table with one of his own over it, as he smiled and looked her in the face.

'Confess,' said he, 'now, that you are thinking how you possibly can make it up to your conscience to let the boy have his own way.'

She blushed and was moved in the usual manner of females. 'I am thinking that he is very unhappy—and I am too——'

'To contradict him or to let him have his own wish?' asked the other; and added, with great comfort to his inward self, 'I'm d—d if he shall.'

'To think that he should have formed so foolish and cruel and fatal an attachment,' the widow said, 'which can but end in pain whatever be the issue.'

'The issue shan't be marriage, my dear sister,' the major said resolutely. 'We're not going to have a Pendennis, the head of the house, marry a strolling mountebank from a booth. No, no, we won't marry into Greenwich Fair, ma'am.'

'If the match is broken suddenly off,' the widow interposed, 'I don't know what may be the consequence. I know Arthur's ardent temper, the intensity of his affections, the agony of his pleasures and disappointments, and I tremble at this one if it must be. Indeed, indeed, it must not come on him too suddenly.'

'My dear madam,' the major said, with an air of the deepest commiseration, 'I've no doubt Arthur will have to suffer confoundedly before he gets over the little

disappointment. But is he, think you, the only person who has been so rendered miserable?'

'No, indeed,' said Helen, holding down her eyes. She was thinking of her own case, and was at that moment seventeen again, and most miserable.

'I, myself,' whispered her brother-in-law, 'have undergone a disappointment in early life. A young woman with fifteen thousand pounds, niece to an earl—most accomplished creature—a third of her money would have run up my promotion in no time, and I should have been a lieutenant-colonel at thirty: but it might not be. I was but a penniless lieutenant: her parents interfered: and I embarked for India, where I had the honour of being secretary to Lord Buckley, when commander-in-chief*—without her. What happened? We returned our letters, sent back our locks of hair!' (the major here passed his fingers through his wig), 'we suffered—but we recovered. She is now a baronet's wife with thirteen grown-up children; altered, it is true, in person; but her daughters remind me of what she was, and the third is to be presented early next week.'

Helen did not answer. She was still thinking of old times. I suppose if one lives to be a hundred, there are certain passages of one's early life whereof the recollection will always carry us back to youth again, and that Helen was thinking of one of these.

'Look at my own brother, my dear creature,' the major continued gallantly: 'he himself, you know, had a little disappointment when he started in the—the medical profession—an eligible opportunity presented itself. Miss Balls, I remember the name, was daughter of an apoth—a practitioner in very large practice; my brother had very nearly succeeded in his suit.—But difficulties arose: disappointments supervened, and—and I am sure he had no reason to regret the disappointment, which gave him this hand,' said the major, and he once more politely pressed Helen's fingers.

'Those marriages between people of such different rank and age,' said Helen, 'are sad things. I have known them produce a great deal of unhappiness.—Laura's father, my cousin, who—who was brought up with me'—she added, in a low voice, 'was an instance of that.'

'Most injudicious,' cut in the major. 'I don't know

anything more painful than for a man to marry his superior in age or his inferior in station. Fancy marrying a woman of a low rank of life, and having your house filled with her confounded tag-rag-and-bobtail relations! Fancy your wife attached to a mother who dropped her *h*'s, or called Maria Marire! How are you to introduce her into society? My dear Mrs. Pendennis, I will name no names, but in the very best circles of London society I have seen men suffering the most excruciating agony, I have known them to be cut, to be lost utterly, from the vulgarity of their wives' connexions. What did Lady Snapperton do last year at her *déjeuner dansant* after the Bohemian Ball? She told Lord Brouncker that he might bring his daughters or send them with a proper chaperon, but that she would not receive Lady Brouncker: who was a druggist's daughter, or some such thing, and as Tom Wagg remarked of her, never wanted medicine certainly, for she never had an *h* in her life. Good Ged, what would have been the trifling pang of a separation in the first instance to the enduring affliction of a constant misalliance and intercourse with low people?'

'What, indeed!' said Helen, dimly disposed towards laughter, but yet checking the inclination, because she remembered in what prodigious respect her deceased husband held Major Pendennis and his stoiies of the great world.

'Then this fatal woman is ten years older than that silly young scapegrace of an Arthur. What happens in such cases, my dear creature? I don't mind telling *you*, now we are alone: that in the highest state of society, misery, undeviating misery, is the result. Look at Lord Clodworthy come into a room with his wife—why, good Ged, she looks like Clodworthy's mother. What's the case between Lord and Lady Willowbank, whose love match was notorious? He has already cut her down twice when she has hanged herself out of jealousy for Mademoiselle de Sainte-Cunegonde, the dancer; and mark my words, good Ged, one day he'll *not* cut the old woman down. No, my dear madam, you are not in the world, but I am: you are a little romantic and sentimental (you know you are—women with those large beautiful eyes always are); you must leave this matter to my experience. Marry this woman! Marry at eighteen an actress of thirty—bah! bah!—I would as soon he sent into the kitchen and married the cook.'

'I know the evils of premature engagements,' sighed out Helen : and as she has made this allusion no less than thrice in the course of the above conversation, and seems to be so oppressed with the notion of long engagements and unequal marriages, and as the circumstance we have to relate will explain what perhaps some persons are anxious to know, namely who little Laura is, who has appeared more than once before us, it will be as well to clear up these points in another chapter.

CHAPTER VIII

IN WHICH PEN IS KEPT WAITING AT THE DOOR, WHILE THE READER IS INFORMED WHO LITTLE LAURA WAS

NCE upon a time, then, there was a young gentleman of Cambridge University who came to pass the long vacation at the village where young Helen Thistlewood was living with her mother, the widow of the lieutenant slain at Copenhagen. This gentleman, whose name was the Reverend Francis Bell, was nephew to Mrs. Thistlewood, and by consequence, own cousin to Miss Helen, so that it was very right that he should take lodgings in his aunt's house, who lived in a very small way ; and there he passed the long vacation, reading with three or four pupils who accompanied him to the village. Mr. Bell was a fellow of a college, and famous in the University for his learning and skill as a tutor.

His two kinswomen understood pretty early that the reverend gentleman was engaged to be married, and was only waiting for a college living to enable him to fulfil his engagement. His intended bride was the daughter of another parson, who had acted as Mr. Bell's own private tutor in Bell's early life, and it was whilst under Mr. Coacher's roof, indeed, and when only a boy of seventeen

or eighteen years of age, that the impetuous young Bell had flung himself at the feet of Miss Martha Coacher, whom he was helping to pick peas in the garden. On his knees, before those peas and her, he pledged himself to an endless affection.

Miss Coacher was by many years the young fellow's senior: and her own heart had been lacerated by many previous disappointments in the matrimonial line. No less than three pupils of her father had trifled with those young affections. The apothecary of the village had despicably jilted her. The Dragoon officer, with whom she had danced so many, many times during that happy season which she passed at Bath with her gouty grandmamma, one day gaily shook his bridle-rein and galloped away, never to return. Wounded by the shafts of repeated ingratitude, can it be wondered at that the heart of Martha Coacher should pant to find rest somewhere? She listened to the proposals of the gawky gallant honest boy, with great kindness and good humour; at the end of his speech she said, 'Law, Bell, I'm sure you are too young to think of such things'; but intimated that she too would revolve them in her own virgin bosom. She could not refer Mr. Bell to her mamma, for Mr. Coacher was a widower, and being immersed in his books, was of course unable to take the direction of so frail and wondrous an article as a lady's heart, which Miss Martha had to manage for herself.

A lock of her hair, tied up in a piece of blue ribbon, conveyed to the happy Bell the result of the Vestal's conference with herself. Thrice before had she snipped off one of her auburn ringlets, and given them away. The possessors were faithless, but the hair had grown again: and Martha had indeed occasion to say that men were deceivers, when she handed over this token of love to the simple boy.

Number 6, however, was an exception to former passions—Francis Bell was the most faithful of lovers. When his time arrived to go to college, and it became necessary to acquaint Mr. Coacher of the arrangements that had been made, the latter cried, 'God bless my soul, I hadn't the least idea what was going on'; as was indeed very likely, for he had been taken in three times before in precisely a similar manner; and Francis went to the University resolved to conquer honours, so as to be able to lay them at the feet of his beloved Martha.

This prize in view made him labour prodigiously. News came, term after term, of the honours he won. He sent the prize-books for his college essays to old Coacher, and his silver declamation cup to Miss Martha. In due season he was high among the Wranglers, and a fellow of his college; and during all the time of these transactions a constant tender correspondence was kept up with Miss Coacher, to whose influence, and perhaps with justice, he attributed the successes which he had won.

By the time, however, when the Rev. Francis Bell, M.A., and Fellow and Tutor of his College, was twenty-six years of age, it happened that Miss Coacher was thirty-four, nor had her charms, her manners, or her temper improved since that sunny day in the spring-time of life when he found her picking peas in the garden. Having achieved his honours, he relaxed in the ardour of his studies, and his judgement and tastes also perhaps became cooler. The sunshine of the pea-garden faded away from Miss Martha, and poor Bell found himself engaged—and his hand pledged to that bond in a thousand letters—to a coarse, ill-tempered, ill-favoured, ill-mannered, middle-aged woman.

It was in consequence of one of many altercations (in which Martha's eloquence shone, and in which therefore she was frequently pleased to indulge) that Francis refused to take his pupils to Bearleader's Green, where Mr. Coacher's living was, and where Bell was in the habit of spending the summer: and he bethought him that he would pass the vacation at his aunt's village, which he had not seen for many years—not since little Helen was a girl, and used to sit on his knee. Down, then, he came and lived with them. Helen was grown a beautiful young woman now. The cousins were nearly four months together, from June to October. They walked in the summer evenings: they met in the early morn. They read out of the same book when the old lady dozed at night over the candles. What little Helen knew, Frank taught her. She sang to him: she gave her artless heart to him. She was aware of all his story. Had he made any secret?—had he not shown the picture of the woman to whom he was engaged, and with a blush—her letters, hard, eager, and cruel? The days went on and on, happier and closer, with more kindness, more confidence, and more pity. At last one morning in October came when Francis went back to college, and

the poor girl felt that her tender heart was gone with him.

Frank too wakened up from the delightful midsummer-dream to the horrible reality of his own pain. He gnashed and tore at the chain which bound him. He was frantic to break it and be free. Should he confess ?—give his savings to the woman to whom he was bound, and beg his release ?—there was time yet—he temporized. No living might fall in for years to come. The cousins went on corresponding sadly and fondly : the betrothed woman, hard, jealous, and dissatisfied, complaining bitterly, and with reason, of her Francis's altered tone.

At last things came to a crisis, and the new attachment was discovered. Francis owned it, cared not to disguise it, rebuked Martha with her violent temper and angry imperiousness, and, worst of all, with her inferiority and her age.

Her reply was, that if he did not keep his promise she would carry his letters into every court in the kingdom —letters in which his love was pledged to her ten thousand times ; and, after exposing him to the world as the perjurer and traitor he was, she would kill herself.

Frank had one more interview with Helen, whose mother was dead then, and who was living companion with old Lady Pontypool—one more interview, where it was resolved that he was to do his duty ; that is, to redeem his vow ; that is, to pay a debt cozened from him by a sharper ; that is, to make two honest people miserable. So the two judged their duty to be, and they parted.

The living fell in only too soon ; but yet Frank Bell was quite a gray and worn-out man when he was inducted into it. Helen wrote him a letter on his marriage, beginning 'My dear cousin,' and ending 'always truly yours.' She sent him back the other letters, and the lock of his hair—all but a small piece. She had it in her desk when she was talking to the major.

Bell lived for three or four years in his living, at the end of which time, the chaplainship of Coventry Island falling vacant, Frank applied for it privately, and having procured it, announced the appointment to his wife. She objected, as she did to everything. He told her bitterly that he did not want *her* to come : so she went. Bell went out in Governor Crawley's time,* and was very intimate

with that gentleman in his later years. And it was in Coventry Island, years after his own marriage, and five years after he had heard of the birth of Helen's boy, that his own daughter was born.

She was not the daughter of the first Mrs. Bell, who died of island fever very soon after Helen Pendennis and her husband, to whom Helen had told everything, wrote to inform Bell of the birth of their child. 'I was old, was I ?' said Mrs. Bell the first ; 'I was old, and her inferior, was I ? but I married you, Mr. Bell, and kept you from marrying her !' and hereupon she died. Bell married a colonial lady, whom he loved fondly. But he was not doomed to prosper in love ; and, this lady dying in childbirth, Bell gave up too : sending his little girl home to Helen Pendennis* and her husband, with a parting prayer that they would befriend her.

The little thing came to Fairoaks from Bristol, which is not very far off, dressed in black, and in company of a soldier's wife, her nurse, at the parting from whom she wept bitterly. But she soon dried up her grief under Helen's motherly care.

Round her neck she had a locket with hair, which Helen had given—ah ! how many years ago—to poor Francis, dead and buried. This child was all that was left of him, and she cherished, as so tender a creature would, the legacy which he had bequeathed to her. The girl's name, as his dying letter stated, was Helen Laura. But John Pendennis, though he accepted the trust, was always rather jealous of the orphan ; and gloomily ordered that she should be called by her own mother's name ; and not by that first one which her father had given her. She was afraid of Mr. Pendennis, to the last moment of his life. And it was only when her husband was gone that Helen dared openly to indulge in the tenderness which she felt for the little girl.

Thus it was that Laura Bell became Mrs. Pendennis's daughter. Neither her husband nor that gentleman's brother, the major, viewed her with very favourable eyes. She reminded the first of circumstances in his wife's life which he was forced to accept, but would have forgotten much more willingly : and as for the second, how could he regard her ? She was neither related to his own family of Pendennis, nor to any nobleman in this empire,

and she had but a couple of thousand pounds for her fortune.

And now let Mr. Pen come in, who has been waiting all this while.

Having strung up his nerves, and prepared himself, without at the door, for the meeting, he came to it determined to face the awful uncle. He had settled in his mind that the encounter was to be a fierce one, and was resolved on bearing it through with all the courage and dignity of the famous family which he represented. And he flung open the door and entered with the most severe and warlike expression, armed cap-à-pie, as it were, with lance couched and plumes displayed, and glançing at his adversary, as if to say, 'Come on, I'm ready.'

The old man of the world, as he surveyed the boy's demeanour, could hardly help a grin at his admirable pompous simplicity. Major Pendennis too had examined his ground; and finding that the widow was already half won over to the enemy, and having a shrewd notion that threats and tragic exhortations would have no effect upon the boy, who was inclined to be perfectly stubborn and awfully serious, the major laid aside the authoritative manner at once, and with the most good-humoured natural smile in the world, held out his hands to Pen, shook the lad's passive fingers gaily, and said, 'Well, Pen, my boy, tell us all about it.'

Helen was delighted with the generosity of the major's good humour. On the contrary, it quite took aback and disappointed poor Pen, whose nerves were strung up for a tragedy, and who felt that his grand entrée was altogether balked and ludicrous. He blushed and winced with mortified vanity and bewilderment. He felt immensely inclined to begin to cry—'I—I—I didn't know that you were come till just now,' he said: 'is—is—town very full, I suppose?'

If Pen could hardly gulp his tears down, it was all the Major could do to keep from laughter. He turned round and shot a comical glance at Mrs. Pendennis, who too felt that the scene was at once ridiculous and sentimental. And so, having nothing to say, she went up and kissed Mr. Pen: as he thought of her tenderness and soft obedience to his wishes, it is very possible too the boy was melted.

('What a couple of fools they are,' thought the old

guardian. ‘If I hadn't come down, she would have driven over in state to pay a visit and give her blessing to the young lady's family.’)

‘Come, come,’ said he, still grinning at the couple, ‘let us have as little sentiment as possible, and Pen, my good fellow, tell us the whole story.’

Pen got back at once to his tragic and heroical air. ‘The story is, sir,’ said he, ‘as I have written it to you before. I have made the acquaintance of a most beautiful and most virtuous lady; of a high family, although in reduced circumstances: I have found the woman in whom I know that the happiness of my life is centred; I feel that I never, never can think about any woman but her. I am aware of the difference of our ages and other difficulties in my way. But my affection was so great that I felt I could surmount all these; that we both could: and she has consented to unite her lot with mine, and to accept my heart and my fortune.’

‘How much is that, my boy?’ said the major. ‘Has anybody left you some money? I don't know that you are worth a shilling in the world.’

‘You know what I have is his,’ cried out Mrs. Pendennis.

‘Good heavens, madam, hold your tongue!’ was what the guardian was disposed to say; but he kept his temper, not without a struggle. ‘No doubt, no doubt,’ he said. ‘You would sacrifice anything for him. Everybody knows that. But it is, after all then, your fortune which Pen is offering to the young lady; and of which he wishes to take possession at eighteen.’

‘I know my mother will give me anything,’ Pen said, looking rather disturbed.

‘Yes, my good fellow, but there is reason in all things. If your mother keeps the house, it is but fair that she should select her company. When you give her house over her head, and transfer her banker's account to yourself for the benefit of Miss What-d'you-call-'em—Miss Costigan—don't you think you should at least have consulted my sister as one of the principal parties in the transaction? I am speaking to you, you see, without the least anger or assumption of authority, such as the law and your father's will give me over you for three years to come—but as one man of the world to another—and I ask you, if you think that, because you can do what you like with your mother,

therefore you have a right to do so? As you are her dependent, would it not have been more generous to wait before you took this step, and at least to have paid her the courtesy to ask her leave?'

Pen held down his head, and began dimly to perceive that the action on which he had prided himself as a most romantic, generous instance of disinterested affection, was perhaps a very selfish and headstrong piece of folly.

'I did it in a moment of passion,' said Pen, floundering; 'I was not aware what I was going to say or to do' (and in this he spoke with perfect sincerity). 'But now it is said, and I stand to it. No; I neither can nor will recall it. I'll die rather than do so. And I—I don't want to burthen my mother,' he continued. 'I'll work for myself. I'll go on the stage, and act with her. She—she says I should do well there.'

'But will she take you on those terms?' the major interposed. 'Mind, I do not say that Miss Costigan is not the most disinterested of women: but, don't you suppose now, fairly, that your position as a young gentleman of ancient birth and decent expectations forms a part of the cause why she finds your addresses welcome?'

'I'll die, I say, rather than forfeit my pledge to her,' said Pen, doubling his fists and turning red.

'Who asks you, my dear friend?' answered the imperturbable guardian. 'No gentleman breaks his word, of course, when it has been given freely. But after all, you can wait. You owe something to your mother, something to your family—something to me as your father's representative.'

'Oh, of course,' Pen said, feeling rather relieved.

'Well, as you have pledged your word to her, give us another, will you, Arthur?'

'What is it?' Arthur asked.

'That you will make no private marriage—that you won't be taking a trip to Scotland, you understand.'

'That would be a falsehood. Pen never told his mother a falsehood,' Helen said.

Pen hung down his head again, and his eyes filled with tears of shame. Had not this whole intrigue been a falsehood to that tender and confiding creature who was ready to give up all for his sake? He gave his uncle his hand.

'No, sir—on my word of honour, as a gentleman,' he said, 'I will never marry without my mother's consent!'

and giving Helen a bright parting look of confidence and affection unchangeable, the boy went out of the drawing-room into his own study.

'He's an angel—he's an angel,' the mother cried out, in one of her usual raptures.

'He comes of a good stock, ma'am,' said her brother-in-law—'of a good stock on both sides.' The major was greatly pleased with the result of his diplomacy—so much so, that he once more saluted the tips of Mrs. Pendennis's glove, and dropping the curt, manly, and straightforward tone in which he had conducted the conversation with the lad, assumed a certain drawl, which he always adopted when he was most conceited and fine.

'My dear creature,' said he, in that his politest tone, 'I think it certainly as well that I came down, and I flatter myself that last *botte* was a successful one. I tell you how I came to think of it. Three years ago my kind friend Lady Ferrybridge sent for me in the greatest state of alarm about her son Gretna, whose affair you remember, and implored me to use my influence with the young gentleman, who was engaged in an *affaire de cœur* with a Scotch clergyman's daughter, Miss MacToddy. I implored, I entreated gentle measures. But Lord Ferrybridge was furious, and tried the high hand. Gretna was sulky and silent, and his parents thought they had conquered. But what was the fact, my dear creature? The young people had been married for three months before Lord Ferrybridge knew anything about it. And that was why I extracted the promise from Master Pen.'

'Arthur would never have done so,' Mrs. Pendennis said.

'He hasn't—that is one comfort,' answered the brother-in-law.

Like a wary and patient man of the world, Major Pendennis did not press poor Pen any farther for the moment, but hoped the best from time, and that the young fellow's eyes would be opened before long to see the absurdity of which he was guilty. And having found out how keen the boy's point of honour was, he worked upon that kindly feeling with great skill, discoursing him over their wine after dinner, and pointing out to Pen the necessity of a perfect uprightness and openness in all his dealings, and entreating that his communications with his interesting young friend (as the major politely called Miss Fotheringay)

should be carried on with the knowledge, if not approbation, of Mrs. Pendennis. 'After all, Pen,' the major said, with a convenient frankness that did not displease the boy, whilst it advanced the interests of the negotiator, 'you must bear in mind that you are throwing yourself away. Your mother may submit to your marriage as she would to anything else you desired, if you did but cry long enough for it: but be sure of this, that it can never please her. You take a young woman off the boards of a country theatre and prefer her, for such is the case, to one of the finest ladies in England. And your mother will submit to your choice, but you can't suppose that she will be happy under it. I have often fancied, *entre nous*, that my sister had it in her eye to make a marriage between you and that little ward of hers—Flora, Laura—what's her name? And I always determined to do my small endeavour to prevent any such match. The child has but two thousand pounds, I am given to understand. It is only with the utmost economy and care that my sister can provide for the decent maintenance of her house, and for your appearance and education as a gentleman; and I don't care to own to you that I had other and much higher views for you. With your name and birth, sir—with your talents, which I suppose are respectable, with the friends whom I have the honour to possess, I could have placed you in an excellent position—a remarkable position for a young man of such exceeding small means, and had hoped to see you, at least, try to restore the honours of our name. Your mother's softness stopped one prospect, or you might have been a general, like our gallant ancestor who fought at Ramillies and Malplaquet. I had another plan in view: my excellent and kind friend, Lord Bagwig, who is very well disposed towards me, would, I have little doubt, have attached you to his mission at Pumpernickel,* and you might have advanced in the diplomatic service. But, pardon me for recurring to the subject; how is a man to serve a young gentleman of eighteen, who proposes to marry a lady of thirty, whom he has selected from a booth in a fair?—well, not a fair—a barn. That profession at once is closed to you. The public service is closed to you. Society is closed to you. You see, my good friend, to what you bring yourself. You may get on at the bar, to be sure, where I am given to understand that gentlemen of merit occasionally marry out of their kitchens; but in no other

profession. Or you may come and live down here—down here, *mon Dieu!* for ever' (said the major, with a dreary shrug, as he thought with inexpressible fondness of Pall Mall), 'where your mother will receive the Mrs. Arthur that is to be, with perfect kindness; where the good people of the county won't visit you; and where, by Gad, sir, I shall be shy of visiting you myself, for I'm a plain-spoken man, and I own to you that I like to live with gentlemen for my companions; where you will have to live, with rum-and-water-drinking gentlemen-farmers, and drag through your life the young husband of an old woman, who, if she doesn't quarrel with your mother, will at least cost that lady her position in society, and drag her down into that dubious caste into which you must inevitably fall. It is no affair of mine, my good sir. I am not angry. Your downfall will not hurt me further than that it will extinguish the hopes I had of seeing my family once more taking its place in the world. It is only your mother and yourself that will be ruined. And I pity you both from my soul. Pass the claret: it is some I sent to your poor father; I remember I bought it at poor Lord Levant's sale. But of course,' added the major, smacking the wine, 'having engaged yourself, you will do what becomes you as a man of honour, however fatal your promise may be. However, promise us on your side, my boy, what I set out by entreating you to grant—that there shall be nothing clandestine, that you will pursue your studies, that you will only visit your interesting friend at proper intervals. Do you write to her much?'

Pen blushed and said, 'Why, yes, he had written.'

'I suppose verses, eh! as well as prose? I was a dab at verses myself. I recollect when I first joined, I used to write verses for the fellows in the regiment; and did some pretty things in that way. I was talking to my old friend General Hobbler about some lines I dashed off for him in the year 1806, when we were at the Cape, and, Gad, he remembered every line of them still; for he'd used 'em so often, the old rogue, and had actually tried 'em on Mrs. Hobbler, sir—who brought him sixty thousand pounds. I suppose you've tried verses, eh, Pen?'

Pen blushed again, and said, 'Why, yes, he had written verses.'

'And does the fair one respond in poetry or prose?' asked

the major, eyeing his nephew with the queerest expression, as much as to say, 'O Moses and Green Spectacles!*what a fool the boy is.'

Pen blushed again. She had written, but not in verse, the young lover owned, and he gave his breast-pocket the benefit of a squeeze with his left arm, which the major remarked, according to his wont.

'You have got the letters there, I see,' said the old campaigner, nodding at Pen and pointing to his own chest (which was manfully wadded with cotton by Mr. Stultz).* 'You know you have. I would give twopence to see 'em.'

'Why,' said Pen, twiddling the stalks of the strawberries, 'I—I——' but this sentence never finished; for Pen's face was so comical and embarrassed, as the major watched it, that the elder could contain his gravity no longer, and burst into a fit of laughter, in which chorus Pen himself was obliged to join after a minute: when he broke out fairly into a guffaw.

It sent them with great good humour into Mrs. Pendennis's drawing-room. She was pleased to hear them laughing in the hall as they crossed it.

'You sly rascal!' said the major, putting his arm gaily on Pen's shoulder, and giving a playful push at the boy's breast-pocket. He felt the papers crackling there sure enough. The young fellow was delighted—conceited—triumphant—and in one word, a spoony.

The pair came to the tea-table in the highest spirits. The major's politeness was beyond expression. He had never tasted such good tea, and such bread was only to be had in the country. He asked Mrs. Pendennis for one of her charming songs. He then made Pen sing, and was delighted and astonished at the beauty of the boy's voice: he made his nephew fetch his maps and drawings, and praised them as really remarkable works of talent in a young fellow: he complimented him on his French pronunciation: he flattered the simple boy as adroitly as ever lover flattered a mistress: and when bed-time came, mother and son went to their several rooms perfectly enchanted with the kind major.

When they had reached those apartments, I suppose Helen took to her knees as usual: and Pen read over his letters before going to bed: just as if he didn't know every

word of them by heart already. In truth there were but three of those documents: and to learn their contents required no great effort of memory.

In No. 1—

Miss Fotheringay presents grateful compliments to Mr. Pendennis, and in her papa's name and her own begs to thank him for his *most beautiful presents.* They will always be *kept carefully;* and Miss F. and Captain C. will never forget the *delightful evening* which they passed on *Tuesday last.*

No. 2 said:—

Dear Sir, we shall have a small quiet party of *social friends* at our *humble board,* next Tuesday evening, at an *early tea,* when I shall wear the *beautiful scarf* which, with its *accompanying delightful verses,* I shall *ever, ever cherish:* and papa bids me say how happy he will be if you will join '*the feast of reason and the flow of soul*' in our *festive little party,* as I am sure will be your *truly grateful*—EMILY FOTHERINGAY.

No. 3 was somewhat more confidential, and showed that matters had proceeded rather far.

You were *odious* yesterday night (the letter said). Why did you not come to the stage-door? Papa could not escort me on account of his eye; he had an accident, and fell down over a loose carpet on the stair on Sunday night. I saw you looking at Miss Diggle all night; and you were *so enchanted* with Lydia Languish you scarcely once looked at Julia. I could have *crushed* Bingley, I was so *angry.* I play *Ella Rosenberg** on Friday: will you come then? *Miss Diggle performs*—ever your—E. F.

These three letters Mr. Pen used to read at intervals, during the day and night, and embrace with that delight and fervour which such beautiful compositions surely warranted. A thousand times at least he had kissed fondly the musky satin paper, made sacred to him by the hand of Emily Fotheringay. This was all he had in return for his passion and flames, his vows and protests, his rhymes and similes, his wakeful nights and endless thoughts, his fondness, fears, and folly. The young wiseacre had pledged away his all for this: signed his name to endless promissory notes, conferring his heart upon the bearer: bound himself for life, and got back twopence as an equivalent. For Miss Costigan was a young lady of such perfect good conduct and self-command, that she never would have thought of giving

more, and reserved the treasures of her affection until she could transfer them lawfully at church.

Howbeit, Mr. Pen was content with what tokens of regard he had got, and mumbled over his three letters in a rapture of high spirits, and went to sleep delighted with his kind old uncle from London, who must evidently yield to his wishes in time ; and, in a word, a preposterous state of contentment with himself and all the world.

CHAPTER IX

IN WHICH THE MAJOR OPENS THE CAMPAIGN

ALL persons who have the blessed[1] privilege of an entrée into the most select circles must admit that Major Pendennis was a man of no ordinary generosity and affection, in the sacrifice which he now made. He gave up London in May—his newspapers and his mornings—his afternoons from club to club, his little confidential visits to my ladies—his rides in Rotten Row, his dinners, and his stall at the Opera, his rapid escapades to Fulham or Richmond on Saturdays and Sundays, his bow from my lord duke or my lord marquis at the great London entertainments, and his name in the *Morning Post** of the succeeding day—his quieter little festivals, more select, secret, and delightful—all these he resigned to lock himself into a lone little country house, with a simple widow and a greenhorn of a son, a mawkish curate, and a little girl of ten years of age.

He made the sacrifice, and it was the greater that few knew the extent of it. His letters came down franked from town, and he showed the invitations to Helen with a sigh. It was beautiful and tragical to see him refuse one party after another—at least to those who could understand, as Helen didn't, the melancholy grandeur of his self-denial.

Helen did not, or only smiled at the awful pathos with which the major spoke of the Court Guide in general : but young Pen looked with great respect at the great names upon the superscriptions of his uncle's letters, and listened to the major's stories about the fashionable world with constant interest and sympathy.

The elder Pendennis's rich memory was stored with thousands of these delightful tales, and he poured them into Pen's willing ear.[2] He knew the name and pedigree of everybody in the *Peerage*, and everybody's relations. 'My dear boy,' he would say, with a mournful earnestness and veracity, 'you cannot begin your genealogical studies too early ; I wish to Heavens you would read in Debrett every day. Not so much the historical part (for the pedigrees, between ourselves, are many of them very fabulous, and there are few families that can show such a clear descent as our own) as the account of family alliances, and who is related to whom. I have known a man's career in life blasted by ignorance on this all-important subject. Why, only last month, at dinner at my Lord Hobanob's, a young man, who has lately been received amongst us, young Mr. Suckling (author of a work, I believe), began to speak lightly of Admiral Bowser's conduct for ratting*to Ministers, in what I must own is the most audacions manner. But who do you think sat next and opposite to this Mr. Suckling ? Why—why, next to him was Lady Grampound, Bowser's daughter, and opposite to him was Lord Grampound, Bowser's son-in-law. The infatuated young man went on cutting his jokes at the admiral's expense, fancying that all the world was laughing with him, and I leave you to imagine Lady Hobanob's feelings—Hobanob's !—those of every well-bred man, as the wretched *intru* was so exposing himself. *He* will never dine again in South Street. I promise you *that*.'

With such discourses the major entertained his nephew, as he paced the terrace in front of the house for his two hours' constitutional walk, or as they sat together after dinner over their wine. He grieved that Sir Francis Clavering had not come down to the Park, to live in it since his marriage, and to make a society for the neighbourhood. He mourned that Lord Eyrie was not in the country, that he might take Pen and present him to his lordship. 'He has daughters,' the major said. 'Who

knows ? you might have married Lady Emily or Lady Barbara Trehawk ; but all those dreams are over ; my poor fellow, you must lie on the bed which you have made for yourself.'

These things to hear did young Pendennis seriously incline. They are not so interesting in print as when delivered orally ; but the major's anecdotes of the great George, of the Royal Dukes, of the statesmen, beauties, and fashionable ladies of the day, filled young Pen's soul with longing and wonder ; and he found the conversations with his guardian, which sadly bored and perplexed poor Mrs. Pendennis, for his own part never tedious.

It can't be said that Mr. Pen's new guide, philosopher, and friend discoursed him on the most elevated subjects, or treated the subjects which he chose in the most elevated manner. But his morality, such as it was, was consistent. It might not, perhaps, tend to a man's progress in another world, but it was pretty well calculated to advance his interests in this ; and then it must be remembered that the major never for one instant doubted that his views were the only views practicable, and that his conduct was perfectly virtuous and respectable. He was a man of honour, in a word : and had his eyes, what he called, open. He took pity on this young greenhorn of a nephew, and wanted to open his eyes too.

No man, for instance, went more regularly to church when in the country than the old bachelor. 'It don't matter so much in town, Pen,' he said, 'for there the women go and the men are not missed. But when a gentleman is *sur ses terres*, he must give an example to the country people : and if I could turn a tune, I even think I should sing. The Duke of St. David's, whom I have the honour of knowing, always sings in the country, and let me tell you, it has a doosed fine effect from the family pew. And you are somebody down here. As long as the Claverings are away you are the first man in the parish : or as good as any. You might represent the town if you played your cards well. Your poor dear father would have done so had he lived ; so might you. Not if you marry a lady, however amiable, whom the country people won't meet. Well, well : it's a painful subject. Let us change it, my boy.' But if Major Pendennis changed the subject once, he recurred to it a score of times in the day : and the

moral of his discourse always was, that Pen was throwing himself away. Now it does not require much coaxing or wheedling to make a simple boy believe that he is a very fine fellow.

Pen[3] was glad enough, we have said, to listen to his elder's talk. The conversation of Captain Costigan became by no means pleasant to him, and the idea of that tipsy old father-in-law haunted him with terror. He couldn't bring that man, unshaven and reeking of punch, to associate with his mother. Even about Emily—he faltered when the pitiless guardian began to question him. 'Was she accomplished ?' He was obliged to own, no. 'Was she clever ?' Well, she had a very good average intellect : but he could not absolutely say she was clever. 'Come, let us see some of her letters.' So Pen confessed that he had but those three of which we have made mention—and that they were but trivial invitations or answers.

'*She* is cautious enough,' the major said drily. 'She is older than you, my poor boy ;' and then he apologized with the utmost frankness and humility, and flung himself upon Pen's good feelings, begging the lad to excuse a fond old uncle, who had only his family's honour in view—for Arthur was ready to flame up in indignation whenever Miss Costigan's honesty was doubted, and swore that he would never have her name mentioned lightly, and never, never would part from her.

He repeated this to his uncle and his friends at home, and also, it must be confessed, to Miss Fotheringay and the amiable family at Chatteris, with whom he still continued to spend some portion of his time. Miss Emily was alarmed when she heard of the arrival of Pen's guardian, and rightly conceived that the major came down with hostile intentions to herself. 'I suppose ye intend to leave me, now your grand relation has come down from town. He'll carry ye off, and you'll forget your poor Emily, Mr. Arthur !'

Forget her ! In her presence, in that of Miss Rouncy, the Columbine and Milly's confidential friend of the company, in the presence of the captain himself, Pen swore he never could think of any other woman but his beloved Miss Fotheringay ; and the captain, looking up at his foils, which were hung as a trophy on the wall of the room where Pen and he used to fence, grimly said, he would not advoise

any man to meddle rashly with the affections of *his* darling child ; and would never believe his gallant young Arthur, whom he treated as a son, whom he called his son, would ever be guilty of conduct so revolting to every idaya of honour and humanitee.

He went up and embraced Pen after speaking. He cried, and wiped his eye with one large dirty hand as he clasped Pen with the other. Arthur shuddered in that grasp, and thought of his uncle at home. His father-in-law looked unusually dirty and shabby ; the odour of whisky-and-water was even more decided than in common. How was he to bring that man and his mother together ? He trembled when he thought that he had absolutely written to Costigan (enclosing to him a sovereign, the loan of which the worthy gentleman needed), and saying that one day he hoped to sign himself his affectionate son, Arthur Pendennis. He was glad to get away from Chatteris that day ; from Miss Rouncy the confidante ; from the old toping father-in-law ; from the divine Emily herself. 'O Emily, Emily,' he cried inwardly, as he rattled homewards on Rebecca, 'you little know what sacrifices I am making for you !—for you who are always so cold, so cautious, so mistrustful !' [4]

Pen never rode over to Chatteris but the major found out on what errand the boy had been. Faithful to his plan, Major Pendennis gave his nephew no let or hindrance ; but somehow the constant feeling that the senior's eye was upon him ; an uneasy shame attendant upon that inevitable confession which the evening's conversation would be sure to elicit in the most natural simple manner, made Pen go less frequently to sigh away his soul at the feet of his charmer than he had been wont to do previous to his uncle's arrival. There was no use trying to deceive *him ;* there was no pretext of dining with Smirke, or reading Greek plays with Foker ; Pen felt, when he returned from one of his flying visits, that everybody knew whence he came, and appeared quite guilty before his mother and guardian, over their books or their game at piquet.

Once having walked out half a mile, to the 'Fairoaks Inn,' beyond the Lodge gates, to be in readiness for the 'Competitor' coach, which changed horses there, to take a run for Chatteris, a man on the roof touched his hat to the young gentleman : it was his uncle's man, Mr. Morgan, who

was going on a message for his master, and had been took up at the Lodge, as he said. And Mr. Morgan came back by the 'Rival,' too; so that Pen had the pleasure of that domestic's company both ways. Nothing was said at home. The lad seemed to have every decent liberty; and yet he felt himself dimly watched and guarded, and that there were eyes upon him even in the presence of his Dulcinea.

In fact, Pen's suspicions were not unfounded, and his guardian had sent forth to gather all possible information regarding the lad and his interesting young friend. The discreet and ingenious Mr. Morgan, a London confidential valet, whose fidelity could be trusted, had been to Chatteris more than once, and made every inquiry regarding the past history and present habits of the captain and his daughter. He delicately cross-examined the waiters, the ostlers, and all the inmates of the bar at the 'George,' and got from them what little they knew respecting the worthy captain. He was not held in very great regard there, as it appeared. The waiters never saw the colour of his money, and were warned not to furnish the poor gentleman with any liquor for which some other party was not responsible. He swaggered sadly about the coffee-room there, consumed a toothpick, and looked over the paper, and if any friend asked him to dinner he stayed.[5]

From the servants of the officers at the barracks Mr. Morgan found that the captain had so frequently and outrageously inebriated himself there, that Colonel Swallowtail had forbidden him the mess-room. The indefatigable Morgan then put himself in communication with some of the inferior actors of the theatre, and pumped them over their cigars and punch, and all agreed that Costigan was poor, shabby, and given to debt and to drink. But there was not a breath upon the reputation of Miss Fotheringay: her father's courage was reported to have displayed itself on more than one occasion towards persons disposed to treat his daughter with freedom. She never came to the theatre but with her father: in his most inebriated moments that gentleman kept a watch over her; finally Mr. Morgan, from his own experience, added that he had been to see her hact, and was uncommon delighted with the performance, besides thinking her a most splendid woman.

Mrs. Creed, the pew-opener, confirmed these statements

to Doctor Portman, who examined her personally.[6] Mrs. Creed had nothing unfavourable to her lodger to divulge. She saw nobody; only one or two ladies of the theatre. The captain did intoxicate himself sometimes, and did not always pay his rent regularly, but he did when he had money, or rather Miss Fotheringay did. Since the young gentleman from Clavering had been and took lessons in fencing, one or two more had come from the barracks; Sir Derby Oaks, and his young friend, Mr. Foker, which was often together; and which was always driving over from Baymouth in the tandem. But on the occasions of the lessons, Miss F. was very seldom present, and generally came downstairs to Mrs. Creed's own room.

The doctor and the major, consulting together as they often did, groaned in spirit over that information. Major Pendennis openly expressed his disappointment; and, I believe, the divine himself was ill pleased at not being able to pick a hole in poor Miss Fotheringay's reputation.

Even about Pen himself, Mrs. Creed's reports were desperately favourable. 'Whenever he come,' Mrs. Creed said, 'she always have me or one of the children with her. And Mrs. Creed, marm, says she, if you please, marm, you'll on no account leave the room when that young gentleman's here. And many's the time I've seen him a-lookin' as if he wished I was away, poor young man: and he took to coming in service-time, when I wasn't at home, of course: but she always had one of the boys up if her pa wasn't at home, or old Mr. Bows with her a-teaching of her her lesson, or one of the young ladies of the theaytre.'

It was all true: whatever encouragements might have been given him before he avowed his passion, the prudence of Miss Emily was prodigious after Pen had declared himself: and the poor fellow chafed against her hopeless reserve.[7]

The major surveyed the state of things with a sigh. 'If it were but a temporary liaison,' the excellent man said, 'one could bear it. A young fellow must sow his wild oats, and that sort of thing. But a virtuous attachment is the deuce. It comes of the d—d romantic notions boys get from being brought up by women.'

'Allow me to say, major, that you speak a little too like a man of the world,' replied the doctor. 'Nothing can

be more desirable for Pen than a virtuous attachment for a young lady of his own rank and with a corresponding fortune—this present infatuation, of course, I must deplore as sincerely as you do. If I were his guardian, I should command him to give it up.'

'The very means, I tell you, to make him marry to-morrow. We have got time from him, that is all, and we must do our best with that.'

'I say, major,' said the doctor, at the end of the conversation in which the above subject was discussed, 'I am not, of course, a playgoing man—but suppose, I say, we go and see her.'

The major laughed—he had been a fortnight at Fairoaks, and strange to say, had not thought of that. 'Well,' he said, 'why not? After all, it is not my niece, but Miss Fotheringay the actress, and we have as good a right as any other of the public to see her if we pay our money.' So upon a day when it was arranged that Pen was to dine at home, and pass the evening with his mother, the two elderly gentlemen drove over to Chatteris in the doctor's chaise, and there, like a couple of jolly bachelors, dined at the 'George Inn,' before proceeding to the play.

Only two other guests were in the room—an officer of the regiment quartered at Chatteris, and a young gentleman whom the doctor thought he had somewhere seen. They left them at their meal, however, and hastened to the theatre. It was *Hamlet* over again. Shakespere was Article XL* of stout old Doctor Portman's creed, to which he always made a point of testifying publicly at least once in a year.

We have described the play before, and how those who saw Miss Fotheringay perform in Ophelia saw precisely the same thing on one night as on another. Both the elderly gentlemen looked at her with extraordinary interest, thinking how very much young Pen was charmed with her.

'Gad,' said the major between his teeth, as he surveyed her when she was called forward as usual, and swept curtsies to the scanty audience, 'the young rascal has not made a bad choice.'

The doctor applauded her loudly and loyally. 'Upon my word,' said he, 'she is a very clever actress; and I must say, major, she is endowed with very considerable personal attractions.'

'So that young officer thinks in the stage-box,' Major Pendennis answered, and he pointed out to Doctor Portman's attention the young Dragoon of the 'George' coffee-room, who sat in the box in question, and applauded with immense enthusiasm. She looked extremely sweet upon him too, thought the major: but that's their way—and he shut up his natty opera-glass and pocketed it, as if he wished to see no more that night. Nor did the doctor, of course, propose to stay for the after-piece, so they rose and left the theatre; the doctor returning to Mrs. Portman, who was on a visit at the Deanery, and the major walking home full of thought towards the 'George,' where he had bespoken a bed.

CHAPTER X

FACING THE ENEMY

MAJOR PENDENNIS[1] reached the hotel presently, and found Mr. Morgan, his faithful valet, awaiting him at the door, who stopped his master as he was about to take a candle to go to bed, and said, with his usual air of knowing deference, 'I think, sir, if you would go into the coffee-room, there's a young gentleman there as you would like to see.'

'What, is Mr. Arthur here?' the major said, in great anger.

'No, sir—but his great friend, Mr. Foker, sir. Lady Hagnes Foker's son is here, sir. He's been asleep in the coffee-room, since he took his dinner, and has just rung for his coffee, sir. And I think, p'raps, you might like to git into conversation with him,' the valet said, opening the coffee-room door.

The major entered; and there indeed was Mr. Foker, the only occupant of the place.[2] He had intended to go to the play too, but sleep had overtaken him after a copious meal, and he had flung up his legs on the bench, and indulged in a nap instead of the dramatic amusement. The major was meditating how to address the young man, but the latter prevented him that trouble.

'Like to look at the evening paper, sir?' said Mr. Foker, who was always communicative and affable; and he took up the *Globe* from his table, and offered it to the new-comer.

'I am very much obliged to you,' said the major, with a grateful bow and smile. 'If I don't mistake the family likeness, I have the pleasure of speaking to Mr. Henry Foker, Lady Agnes Foker's son. I have the happiness to name her ladyship among my acquaintances—and you bear, sir, a Rosherville face.'

'Hullo! I beg your pardon,' Mr. Foker said; 'I took you,'—he was going to say—'I took you for a commercial gent.' But he stopped that phrase. 'To whom have I the pleasure of speaking?' he added.

'To a relative of a friend and schoolfellow of yours—Arthur Pendennis, my nephew, who has often spoken to me about you in terms of great regard. I am Major Pendennis, of whom you may have heard him speak. May I take my soda-water at your table? I have had the pleasure of sitting at your grandfather's.'

'Sir, you do me proud,' said Mr. Foker, with much courtesy. 'And so you are Arthur Pendennis's uncle, are you?'

'And guardian,' added the major.

'He's as good a fellow as ever stepped, sir,' said Mr. Foker.

'I am glad you think so.'

'And clever, too—I was always a stupid chap, I was—but you see, sir, I know 'em when they are clever, and like 'em of that sort.'

'You show your taste and your modesty, too,' said the major. 'I have heard Arthur repeatedly speak of you, and he said your talents were very good.'

'I am not good at the books,' Mr. Foker said, wagging his head—'never could manage that—Pendennis could—he used to do half the chaps' verses—and yet you are his guardian; and I hope you will pardon me for saying that I think he's what *we* call a flat,' the candid young gentleman said.

The major found himself on the instant in the midst of a most interesting and confidential conversation. 'And how is Arthur a flat?' he asked, with a smile.

'You know,' Foker answered, winking at him—he

would have winked at the Duke of Wellington with just as little scruple[3]—'You know Arthur's a flat—about women, I mean.'

'He is not the first of us, my dear Mr. Harry,' answered the major. 'I have heard something of this—but pray tell me more.'

'Why, sir, you see—it's partly my fault. We went to the play one night,[4] and Pen was struck all of a heap with Miss Fotheringay—Costigan her real name is—an uncommon fine gal she is too; and the next morning I introduced him to the general, as we call her father—a regular old scamp—and *such* a boy for whisky-and-water!—and he's gone on being intimate there. And he's fallen in love with her—and I'm blessed if he hasn't proposed to her,' Foker said, slapping his hand on the table, until all the dessert began to jingle.

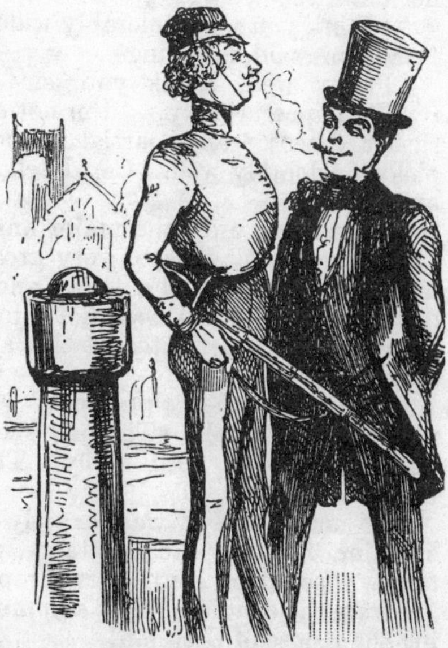

'What! you know it too?' asked the major.

'Know it! don't I? and many more too. We were talking about it at mess, yesterday, and chaffing Derby Oaks—until he was as mad as a hatter. Know Sir Derby Oaks? We dined together, and he went to the play: we were standing at the door smoking, I remember, when you passed in to dinner.'

'I remember Sir Thomas Oaks, his father, before he was a baronet or a knight; he lived in Cavendish Square, and was Physician to Queen Charlotte.'

'The young one is making the money spin, I can tell you,' Mr. Foker said.

'And is Sir Derby Oaks,' the major said, with great delight and anxiety, 'another *soupirant?*'

'Another *what?*' inquired Mr. Foker.

'Another admirer of Miss Fotheringay?'

'Lord bless you! we call him Mondays, Wednesdays, and Fridays, and Pen Tuesdays, Thursdays, and Saturdays. But mind you, nothing wrong! No, no! Miss F. is a deal too wideawake for that, Major Pendennis. She plays one off against the other. What you call two strings to her bow.'

'I think you seem tolerably wideawake, too, Mr. Foker,' Pendennis said, laughing.

'Pretty well, thank you, sir—how are you?' Foker replied imperturbably. 'I'm not clever, p'raps: but I *am* rather downy;* and partial friends say I know what's o'clock tolerably well. Can I tell you the time of day in any way?'

'Upon my word,' the major answered, quite delighted, 'I think you may be of very great service to me. You are a young man of the world, and with such one likes to deal. And as such I need not inform you that our family is by no means delighted at this absurd intrigue in which Arthur is engaged.'

'I should rather think not,' said Mr. Foker. 'Connection not eligible. Too much beer drunk on the premises. No Irish need apply.* That I take to be your meaning.'

The major said it was, exactly:[5] and he proceeded to examine his new acquaintance regarding the amiable family into which his nephew proposed to enter, and soon got from the candid witness a number of particulars regarding the House of Costigan.

We must do Mr. Foker the justice to say that he spoke most favourably of Mr. and Miss Costigan's moral character. 'You see,' said he, 'I think the general is fond of the jovial bowl, and if I wanted to be very certain of my money, it isn't in his pocket I'd invest it—but he has always kept a watchful eye on his daughter, and neither he nor she will stand anything but what's honourable. Pen's attentions to her are talked about in the whole company, and I hear all about them from a young lady who used to be very intimate with her, and with whose family I sometimes take tea in a friendly way. Miss Rouncy says, Sir Derby Oaks

has been hanging about Miss Fotheringay ever since his regiment has been down here ; but Pen has come in and cut him out lately, which has made the baronet so mad, that he has been very near on the point of proposing too. Wish he would : and you'd see which of the two Miss Fotheringay would jump at.'

'I thought as much,' the major said. 'You give me a great deal of pleasure, Mr. Foker. I wish I could have seen you before.'

'Didn't like to put in my oar,' replied the other. 'Don't speak till I'm asked, when, if there's no objections, I speak pretty freely. Heard your man had been hankering about my servant—didn't know myself what was going on until Miss Fotheringay and Miss Rouncy had the row about the ostrich feathers, when Miss R. told me everything.'

'Miss Rouncy, I gather, was the confidante of the other.'

'Confidant ? I believe you. Why, she's twice as clever a girl as Fotheringay, and literary and that, while Miss Foth. can't do much more than read.'

'She can write,' said the major, remembering Pen's breast-pocket.

Foker broke out into a sardonic 'He, he ! Rouncy writes her letters,' he said : 'every one of 'em ; and since they've quarrelled, she don't know how the deuce to get on. Miss Rouncy is an uncommon pretty hand, whereas the other one makes dreadful work of the writing and spelling when Bows ain't by. Rouncy's been settin' her copies lately—she writes a beautiful hand, Rouncy does.'

'I suppose you know it pretty well,' said the major archly : upon which Mr. Foker winked at him again.

'I would give a great deal to have a specimen of her handwriting,' continued Major Pendennis. 'I dare say you could give me one.'

'That would be too bad,' Foker replied. 'Miss[6] F.'s writin' ain't so *very* bad, I dare say ; only she got Miss R. to write the first letter, and has gone on ever since. But you mark my word, that till they are friends again the letters will stop.'

'I hope they will never be reconciled,' the major said, with great sincerity. 'You[7] must feel, my dear sir, as a man of the world, how fatal to my nephew's prospects in life is this step which he contemplates, and how eager we all must be to free him from this absurd engagement.'

'He has come out uncommon strong,' said Mr. Foker. 'I have seen his verses; Rouncy copied 'em. And I said to myself when I saw 'em, "Catch *me* writin' verses to a woman—that's all."'

'He has made a fool of himself, as many a good fellow has before him. How can we make him see his folly, and cure it? I am sure you will give us what aid you can in extricating a generous young man from such a pair of schemers as this father and daughter seem to be. Love on the lady's side is out of the question.'

'Love, indeed!' Foker said. 'If Pen hadn't two thousand a year when he came of age——'

'If Pen hadn't *what?*' cried out the major, in astonishment.

'Two thousand a year: hasn't he got two thousand a year?—the general says he has.'

'My dear friend,' shrieked out the major, with an eagerness which this gentleman rarely showed, 'thank you!—thank you!—I begin to see now. Two thousand a year! Why, his mother has but five hundred a year in the world. She is likely to live to eighty, and Arthur has not a shilling but what she can allow him.'

'What! he ain't rich then?' Foker asked.

'Upon my honour he has no more than what I say.'

'And you ain't going to leave him anything?'

The major had sunk every shilling he could scrape together on annuity, and of course was going to leave Pen nothing; but he did not tell Foker this. 'How much do you think a major on half-pay can save?' he asked. 'If these people have been looking at him as a fortune, they are utterly mistaken—and—and you have made me the happiest man in the world.'

'Sir to YOU,' said Mr. Foker politely, and when they parted for the night they shook hands with the greatest cordiality; the younger gentleman promising the elder not to leave Chatteris without a further conversation in the morning. And as the major went up to his room, and Mr. Foker smoked his cigar against the door pillars of the 'George,' Pen, very likely ten miles off, was lying in bed kissing the letter from his Emily.

The next morning, before Mr. Foker drove off in his drag, the insinuating major had actually got a letter of Miss Rouncy's in his own pocket-book. Let it be a lesson

THE GENERAL'S SALUTATION OF THE MAJOR

to women how they write. And in very high spirits Major Pendennis went to call upon Doctor Portman at the Deanery, and told him what happy discoveries he had made on the previous night. As they sat in confidential conversation in the dean's oak breakfast parlour they could look across the lawn and see Captain Costigan's window, at which poor Pen had been only too visible some three weeks since. The doctor was most indignant against Mrs. Creed, the landlady, for her duplicity in concealing Sir Derby Oaks's constant visits to her lodgers, and threatened to excommunicate her out of the cathedral. But the wary major thought that all things were for the best; and, having taken counsel with himself overnight, felt himself quite strong enough to go and face Captain Costigan.

'I'm going to fight the dragon,' he said, with a laugh, to Doctor Portman.

'And I shrive you, sir, and bid good fortune go with you,' answered the doctor. Perhaps he and Mrs. Portman and Miss Mira, as they sat with their friend, the dean's lady, in her drawing-room, looked up more than once at the enemy's window to see if they could perceive any signs of the combat.

The major walked round, according to the directions given him, and soon found Mrs. Creed's little door. He passed it, and as he ascended to Captain Costigan's apartment, he could hear a stamping of feet, and a great shouting of 'Ha, ha!' within.

'It's Sir Derby Oaks taking his fencing lesson,' said the child who piloted Major Pendennis. 'He takes it Mondays, Wednesdays, and Fridays.'

The major knocked, and at length a tall gentleman came forth, with a foil and mask in one hand, and a fencing glove on the other.

Pendennis made him a deferential bow. 'I believe I have the honour of speaking to Captain Costigan—my name is Major Pendennis.'

The captain brought his weapon up to the salute, and said, 'Major, the honer is moine; I'm deloighted to see ye.'

CHAPTER XI

NEGOTIATION

THE major and Captain Costigan were old soldiers and accustomed to face the enemy, so we may presume that they retained their presence of mind perfectly : but the rest of the party assembled in Cos's sitting-room were, perhaps, a little flurried at Pendennis's apparition. Miss Fotheringay's slow heart began to beat, no doubt, for her cheek flushed up with a great healthy blush, as Lieutenant Sir Derby Oaks looked at her with a scowl. The little crooked old man in the window-seat, who had been witnessing the fencing match between the two gentlemen (whose stamping and jumping had been such as to cause him to give up all attempts to continue writing the theatre music, in the copying of which he had been engaged) looked up eagerly towards the new-comer as the major of the well-blacked boots entered the apartment distributing the most graceful bows to everybody present.

'Me daughter—me friend, Mr. Bows—me gallant young pupil and friend, I may call 'um, Sir Derby Oaks,' said Costigan, splendidly waving his hand, and pointing each of these individuals to the major's attention. 'In one moment, meejor, I'm your humble servant,' and to dash into the little adjoining chamber where he slept, to give a twist to his lank hair with his hair-brush (a wonderful and ancient piece), to tear off his old stock and put on a new one which Emily had constructed for him, and to assume a handsome clean collar, and the new coat which had been ordered upon the occasion of Miss Fotheringay's benefit, was with the still active Costigan the work of a minute.

After him Sir Derby entered, and presently emerged from the same apartment, where he also cased himself in his little shell-jacket, which fitted tightly upon the young officer's big person ; and which he, and Miss Fotheringay, and poor Pen too, perhaps, admired prodigiously.

Meanwhile conversation was engaged in between the actress and the new-comer; and the usual remarks about the weather had been interchanged before Costigan re-entered in his new 'shoot,' as he called it.

'I needn't apologoize to ye, meejor,' he said, in his richest and most courteous manner, 'for receiving ye in me shirt-sleeves.'

'An old soldier can't be better employed than in teaching a young one the use of his sword,' answered the major gallantly. 'I remember in old times hearing that you could use yours pretty well, Captain Costigan.'

'What, ye've heard of Jack Costigan, major,' said the other greatly.

The major had, indeed; he had pumped his nephew concerning his new friend, the Irish officer;[1] and said that he perfectly well recollected meeting Mr. Costigan, and hearing him sing at Sir Richard Strachan's table at Walcheren.*

At this information, and the bland and cordial manner in which it was conveyed, Bows looked up, entirely puzzled. 'But we will talk of these matters another time,' the major continued, perhaps not wishing to commit himself; 'it is to Miss Fotheringay that I came to pay my respects to-day:' and he performed another bow for her, so courtly and gracious, that if she had been a duchess he could not have made it more handsome.

'I had heard of your performances from my nephew, madam,' the major said, 'who raves about you, as I believe you know pretty well. But Arthur is but a boy, and a wild enthusiastic young fellow, whose opinions one must not take *au pied de la lettre*; and I confess I was anxious to judge for myself. Permit me to say your performance delighted and astonished me. I have seen our best actresses, and, on my word, I think you surpass them all. You are as majestic as Mrs. Siddons.'

'Faith, I always said so,' Costigan said, winking at his daughter. 'Major, take a chair.' Milly rose at this hint, took an unripped satin garment off the only vacant seat, and brought the latter to Major Pendennis with one of her finest curtsies.

'You are as pathetic as Miss O'Neill,' he continued, bowing and seating himself; 'your snatches of song reminded me of Mrs. Jordan in her best time, when we

were young men, Captain Costigan; and your manner reminded me of Mars.* Did you ever see the Mars, Miss Fotheringay?'

'There was two Mahers in Crow Street,' remarked Miss Emily. 'Fanny was well enough, but Biddy was no great things.'

'Sure, the major means the god of war, Milly, my dear,' interposed the parent.

'It is not that Mars I meant, though Venus, I suppose, may be pardoned for thinking about him,' the major replied, with a smile directed in full to Sir Derby Oaks, who now re-entered in his shell-jacket, but the lady did not understand the words of which he made use, nor did the compliment at all pacify Sir Derby, who, probably, did not understand it either, and at any rate received it with great sulkiness and stiffness; scowling uneasily at Miss Fotheringay, with an expression which seemed to ask what the deuce does this man here?

Major Pendennis was not in the least annoyed by the gentleman's ill-humour. On the contrary, it delighted him. 'So,' thought he, 'a rival is in the field;' and he offered up vows that Sir Derby might be, not only a rival, but a winner too, in this love-match in which he and Pen were engaged.

'I fear I interrupted your fencing lesson; but my stay in Chatteris is very short, and I was anxious to make myself known to my old fellow-campaigner Captain Costigan, and to see a lady nearer who had charmed me so much from the stage. I was not the only man *épris* last night, Miss Fotheringay (if I must call you so, though your own family name is a very ancient and noble one). There was a reverend friend of mine, who went home in raptures with Ophelia; and I saw Sir Derby Oaks fling a bouquet which no actress ever merited better. I should have brought one myself, had I known what I was going to see. Are not those the very flowers in a glass of water on the mantelpiece yonder?'

'I am very fond of flowers,' said Miss Fotheringay, with a languishing ogle at Sir Derby Oaks—but the baronet still scowled sulkily.

'Sweets to the sweet—isn't that the expression of the play?' Mr. Pendennis asked, bent upon being good-humoured.

‘ ’Pon my life, I don’t know. Very likely it is. I ain’t much of a literary man,’ answered Sir Derby.

‘ Is it possible ?’ the major continued, with an air of surprise. ‘You don’t inherit your father’s love of letters, then, Sir Derby ? He was a remarkably fine scholar, and I had the honour of knowing him very well.’

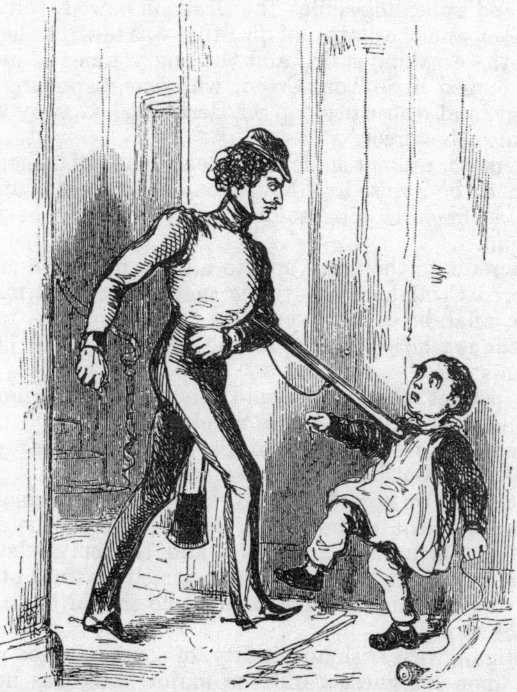

‘ Indeed,’ said the other, and gave a sulky wag of his head.

‘ He saved my life,’ continued Pendennis.

‘ Did he now ?’ cried Miss Fotheringay, rolling her eyes first upon the major with surprise, then towards Sir Derby with gratitude—but the latter was proof against those glances ; and far from appearing to be pleased that the apothecary, his father, should have saved Major Pendennis’s

life, the young man actually looked as if he wished the event had turned the other way.

'My father, I believe, was a very good doctor,' the young gentleman said, by way of reply. 'I'm not in that line myself. I wish you good morning, sir. I've got an appointment — Cos, bye-bye — Miss Fotheringay, good morning.' And, in spite of the young lady's imploring looks and appealing smiles, the Dragoon bowed stiffly out of the room, and the clatter of his sabre was heard as he strode down the creaking stair; and the angry tones of his voice as he cursed little Tom Creed, who was disporting in the passage, and whose peg-top Sir Derby kicked away with an oath into the street.

The major did not smile in the least, though he had every reason to be amused. 'Monstrous handsome young man that—as fine a looking soldier as ever I saw,' he said to Costigan.

'A credit to the army and to human nature in general,' answered Costigan. 'A young man of refoined manners, polite affabilitee, and princely fortune. His table is sumptuous: he's adawr'd in the regiment; and he rides sixteen stone.'

'A perfect champion,' said the major, laughing. 'I have no doubt all the ladies admire him.'

'He's very well, in spite of his weight, now he's young,' said Milly; 'but he's no conversation.'

'He's best on horseback,' Mr. Bows said; on which Milly replied, that the baronet had ridden third in the steeplechase on his horse Tareaways, and the major began to comprehend that the young lady herself was not of a particular genius, and to wonder how she should be so stupid and act so well.

Costigan, with Irish hospitality, of course pressed refreshment upon his guest: and the major, who was no more hungry than you are after a lord mayor's dinner, declared that he should like a biscuit and a glass of wine above all things, as he felt quite faint from long fasting—but he knew that to receive small kindnesses flatters the donors very much, and that people must needs grow well disposed towards you as they give you their hospitality.

'Some of the old madara, Milly love,' Costigan said, winking to his child—and that lady, turning to her father a glance of intelligence, went out of the room, and down the

stair, where she softly summoned her little emissary Master Tommy Creed: and giving him a piece of money, ordered him to go buy a pint of madara wine at the 'Grapes,' and sixpennyworth of sorted biscuits at the baker's, and to return in a hurry, when he might have two biscuits for himself.

Whilst Tommy Creed was gone on this errand, Miss Costigan sat below with Mrs. Creed, telling her landlady how Mr. Arthur Pendennis's uncle, the major, was above stairs; a nice, soft-spoken old gentleman; that butter wouldn't melt in his mouth: and how Sir Derby had gone out of the room in a rage of jealousy, and thinking what must be done to pacify both of them.

'She keeps the keys of the cellar, major,' said Mr. Costigan, as the girl left the room.

'Upon my word, you have a very beautiful butler,' answered Pendennis gallantly, 'and I don't wonder at the young fellows raving about her. When we were of their age, Captain Costigan, I think plainer women would have done our business.'

'Faith, and ye may say that, sir—and lucky is the man who gets her. Ask me friend Bob Bows here whether Miss Fotheringay's moind is not even shuparior to her person, and whether she does not possess a cultiveated intellect, a refoined understanding, and an emiable disposition?'

'Oh, of course,' said Mr. Bows rather drily. 'Here comes Hebe blushing from the cellar. Don't you think it is time to go to rehearsal, Miss Hebe? You will be fined if you are late'—and he gave the young lady a look, which intimated that they had much better leave the room and the two elders together.

At this order Miss Hebe took up her bonnet and shawl, looking uncommonly pretty, good-humoured, and smiling: and Bows gathered up his roll of papers, and hobbled across the room for his hat and cane.

'Must you go?' said the major. 'Can't you give us a few minutes more, Miss Fotheringay? Before you leave us, permit an old fellow to shake you by the hand, and believe that I am proud to have had the honour of making your acquaintance, and am most sincerely anxious to be your friend.'

Miss Fotheringay made a low curtsy at the conclusion of this gallant speech, and the major followed her retreating steps to the door, where he squeezed her hand with the

kindest and most paternal pressure. Bows was puzzled with this exhibition of cordiality. 'The lad's relatives can't be really wanting to marry him to her,' he thought—and so they departed.

'Now for it,' thought Major Pendennis; and as for Mr. Costigan, he profited instantaneously by his daughter's absence to drink up the rest of the wine; and tossed off one bumper after another of the madeira from the 'Grapes,' with an eager shaking hand. The major came up to the table, and took up his glass and drained it with a jovial smack. If it had been Lord Steyne's particular, and not public-house Cape, he could not have appeared to relish it more.

'Capital madeira, Captain Costigan,' he said. 'Where do you get it? I drink the health of that charming creature in a bumper. Faith, captain, I don't wonder that the men are wild about her. I never saw such eyes in my life, or such a grand manner. I am sure she is as intellectual as she is beautiful; and I have no doubt she's as good as she is clever.'

'A good girl, sir—a good girl, sir,' said the delighted father; 'and I pledge a toast to her with all my heart. Shall I send to the—to the cellar for another pint? It's handy by. No? Well, indeed, sir, ye may say she is a good girl, and the pride and glory of her father—honest old Jack Costigan. The man who gets her will have a jew'l to a wife, sir; and I drink his health, sir, and ye know who I mean, major.'

'I am not surprised at young or old falling in love with her,' said the major, 'and frankly must tell you, that though I was very angry with my poor nephew Arthur, when I heard of the boy's passion—now I have seen the lady I can pardon him any extent of it. By George, I should like to enter for the race myself, if I weren't an old fellow and a poor one.'

'And no better man, major, I'm sure,' cried Jack, enraptured. 'Your friendship, sir, delights me. Your admiration for my girl brings tears to me eyes—tears, sir—manlee tears—and when she leaves me humble home for your own more splendid mansion, I hope she'll keep a place for her poor old father, poor old Jack Costigan.'—The captain suited the action to the word, and his bloodshot eyes were suffused with water, as he addressed the major.

'Your sentiments do you honour,' the other said. 'But,

Captain Costigan, I can't help smiling at one thing you have just said.'

'And what's that, sir ?' asked Jack, who was at a too heroic and sentimental pitch to descend from it.

'You were speaking about our splendid mansion—my sister's house, I mean.'

'I mane the park and mansion of Arthur Pendennis, Esq., of Fairoaks Park, whom I hope to see a mimber of Parliament for his native town of Clavering, when he is of ege to take that responsible stetion,' cried the captain, with much dignity.

The major smiled.[2] 'Fairoaks Park, my dear sir !' he said. 'Do you know our history ? We are of excessively ancient family certainly, but I began life with scarce enough money to purchase my commission, and my eldest brother was a country apothecary, who made every shilling he died possessed of out of his pestle and mortar.'

'I have consented to waive that objection, sir,' said Costigan majestically, 'in consideration of the known respectability of your family.'

'Curse your impudence !' thought the major ; but he only smiled and bowed.

'The Costigans, too, have met with misfortunes ; and our house of Castle Costigan is by no manes what it was. I have known very honest men apothecaries, sir, and there's some in Dublin that has had the honour of dining at the Lord Leftenant's teeble.'

'You are very kind to give us the benefit of your charity,' the major continued : 'but permit me to say that is not the question. You spoke just now of my little nephew as heir of Fairoaks Park, and I don't know what besides.'

'Funded property, I've no doubt, meejor, and something handsome eventually from yourself.'

'My good sir, I tell you the boy is the son of a country apothecary,' cried out Major Pendennis ; 'and that when he comes of age he won't have a shilling.'

'Pooh, major, you're laughing at me,' said Mr. Costigan ; 'me young friend, I make no doubt, is heir to two thousand pounds a year.'

'Two thousand fiddlesticks ! I beg your pardon, my dear sir, but has the boy been humbugging you ? it is not his habit. Upon my word and honour, as a gentleman and an

executor to my brother's will too, he left little more than five hundred a year behind him.'

'And with aconomy, a handsome sum of money too, sir,' the captain answered. 'Faith, I've known a man drink his clar't, and drive his coach-and-four on five hundred a year and strict aconomy, in Ireland, sir. We'll manage on it, sir—trust Jack Costigan for that.'

'My dear Captain Costigan—I give you my word that my brother did not leave a shilling to his son Arthur.'

'Are ye joking with me, Meejor Pendennis?' cried Jack Costigan. 'Are ye thrifling with the feelings of a father and a gentleman?'

'I am telling you the honest truth,' said Major Pendennis. 'Every shilling my brother had, he left to his widow: with a partial reversion, it is true, to the boy. But she is a young woman, and may marry if he offends her—or she may outlive him, for she comes of an uncommonly long-lived family. And I ask you, as a gentleman and a man of the world, what allowance can my sister, Mrs. Pendennis, make to her son out of five hundred a year, which is all her fortune—that shall enable him to maintain himself and your daughter in the rank befitting such an accomplished young lady?'

'Am I to understand, sir, that the young gentleman, your nephew, and whom I have fosthered and cherished as the son of me bosom, is an imposther who has been thrifling with the affections of me beloved child?' exclaimed the general, with an outbreak of wrath. 'Have[3] a care, sir, how you thrifle with the honour of John Costigan. If I thought any mortal man meant to do so, be heavens I'd have his blood, sir—were he old or young.'

'Mr. Costigan!' cried out the major.

'Mr. Costigan can protect his own and his daughter's honour, and will, sir,' said the other. 'Look at that chest of dthrawers, it contains heaps of letthers that that viper has addressed to that innocent child. There's promises there, sir, enough to fill a bandbox with; and when I have dragged the scoundthrel before the courts of law, and shown up his perjury and his dishonour, I have another remedy in yondther mahogany case, sir, which shall set me right, sir, with any individual—ye mark me words, Major Pendennis—with any individual who has counselled your nephew to insult a soldier and a gentleman. What? Me daughter to be jilted, and me grey hairs dishonoured by an

apothecary's son! By the laws of Heaven, sir, I should like to see the man that shall do it.'

'I am to understand then that you threaten in the first place to publish the letters of a boy of eighteen to a woman of eight-and-twenty: and afterwards to do me the honour of calling me out,' the major said, still with perfect coolness.

'You have described my intentions with perfect accuracy, Meejor Pendennis,' answered the captain, as he pulled his ragged whiskers over his chin.

'Well, well; these shall be the subjects of future arrangements, but before we come to powder and ball, my good sir, do have the kindness to think with yourself in what earthly way I have injured you? I have told you that my nephew is dependent upon his mother, who has scarcely more than five hundred a year.'

'I have my own opinion of the correctness of that assertion,' said the captain.

'Will you go to my sister's lawyers, Messrs. Tatham here, and satisfy yourself?'

'I decline to meet those gentlemen,' said the captain, with rather a disturbed air. 'If it be as you say, I have been athrociously deceived by someone, and on that person I'll be revenged.'

'Is it my nephew?' cried the major, starting up and putting on his hat. 'Did he ever tell you that his property was two thousand a year? If he did, I'm mistaken in the boy. To tell lies has not been a habit in our family, Mr. Costigan, and I don't think my brother's son has learned it as yet. Try and consider whether you have not deceived yourself; or adopted extravagant reports from hearsay. As for me, sir, you are at liberty to understand that I am not afraid of all the Costigans in Ireland, and know quite well how to defend myself against any threats from any quarter. I come here as the boy's guardian to protest against a marriage, most absurd and unequal, that cannot but bring poverty and misery with it: and in preventing it I conceive I am quite as much your daughter's friend (who I have no doubt is an honourable young lady), as the friend of my own family: and prevent the marriage I will, sir, by every means in my power. There, I have said my say, sir.'

'But I have not said mine, Major Pendennis—and ye shall hear more from me,' Mr. Costigan said, with a look of tremendous severity.

''Sdeath, sir, what do you mean ?' the major asked, turning round on the threshold of the door, and looking the intrepid Costigan in the face.

'Ye said, in the course of conversation, that ye were at the "George Hotel," I think,' Mr. Costigan said, in a stately manner. 'A friend shall wait upon ye there before ye leave town, sir.'

'Let him make haste, Mr. Costigan,' cried out the major, almost beside himself with rage. 'I wish you a good-morning, sir.' And Captain Costigan bowed a magnificent bow of defiance to Major Pendennis over the landing-place as the latter retreated down the stairs.

CHAPTER XII

IN WHICH A SHOOTING MATCH IS PROPOSED

ARLY mention has been made in this history of Mr. Garbetts, Principal Tragedian, a promising and athletic young actor, of jovial habits and irregular inclinations, with whom and Mr. Costigan there was a considerable intimacy. They were the chief ornaments of the convivial club held at the 'Magpie Hotel'; they helped each other in various bill transactions in which they had been engaged, with the mutual loan of each other's valuable signatures. They were friends, in fine ;[1] and Mr. Garbetts was called in by Captain Costigan immediately after his daughter and Mr. Bows had quitted the house, as a friend proper to be consulted at the actual juncture. He was a large man, with a loud voice and fierce aspect, who had the finest legs of the whole company, and could break a poker in mere sport across his stalwart arm.

'Run, Tommy,' said Mr. Costigan to the little messenger, 'and fetch Mr. Garbetts from his lodgings over the tripe-

shop, ye know, and tell 'em to send two glasses of whisky-and-water, hot, from the "Grapes."' So Tommy went his way; and presently Mr. Garbetts and the whisky came.

Captain Costigan did not disclose to him the whole of the previous events, of which the reader is in possession; but, with the aid of the spirits-and-water, he composed a letter of a threatening nature to Major Pendennis's address, in which he called upon that gentleman to offer no hindrance to the marriage projected between Mr. Arthur Pendennis and his daughter, Miss Fotheringay, and to fix an early day for its celebration: or, in any other case, to give him the satisfaction which was usual between gentlemen of honour. And should Major Pendennis be disinclined to this alternative, the captain hinted that he would force him to accept by the use of a horsewhip, which he should employ upon the major's person. The precise terms of this letter we cannot give, for reasons which shall be specified presently; but it was, no doubt, couched in the captain's finest style, and sealed elaborately with the great silver seal of the Costigans—the only bit of the family plate which the captain possessed.

Garbetts was dispatched, then, with this message and letter; and bidding Heaven bless 'um, the general squeezed his ambassador's hand, and saw him depart. Then he took down his venerable and murderous duelling-pistols, with flint locks, that had done the business of many a pretty fellow in Dublin: and having examined these, and seen that they were in a satisfactory condition, he brought from the drawer all Pen's letters and poems which he kept there, and which he always read before he permitted his Emily to enjoy their perusal.

In a score of minutes Garbetts came back with an anxious and crestfallen countenance.

'Ye've seen 'um?' the captain said.

'Why, yes,' said Garbetts.

'And when is it for?' asked Costigan, trying the lock of one of the ancient pistols, and bringing it to a level with his oi—as he called that bloodshot orb.

'When is what for?' asked Mr. Garbetts.

'The meeting, my dear fellow?'

'You don't mean to say you mean mortal combat, captain?' Garbetts said, aghast.

'What the devil else do I mean, Garbetts?—I want to

shoot that man that has trajuiced me honor, or meself dthrop a victim on the sod.'

'D—— if I carry challenges,' Mr. Garbetts replied. 'I'm a family man, captain, and will have nothing to do with pistols—take back your letter;' and, to the surprise and indignation of Captain Costigan, his emissary flung the letter down, with its great sprawling superscription and blotched seal.

'Ye don't mean to say ye saw 'um and didn't give 'um the letter?' cried out the captain, in a fury.

'I saw him, but I could not have speech with him, captain,' said Mr. Garbetts.

'And why the devil not?' asked the other.

'There was one there I cared not to meet, nor would you,' the tragedian answered, in a sepulchral voice. 'The minion Tatham was there, captain.'

'The cowardly scoundthrel!' roared Costigan. 'He's frightened, and already going to swear the peace against me.'

'I'll have nothing to do with the fighting, mark that,' the tragedian doggedly said, 'and I wish I'd not seen Tatham, neither, nor that bit of——'

'Hold your tongue, Bob Acres. It's my belief ye're no better than a coward,' said Captain Costigan, quoting Sir Lucius O'Trigger,* which character he had performed with credit, both off and on the stage, and after some more parley between the couple they separated in not very good humour.

Their colloquy has been here condensed, as the reader knows the main point upon which it turned. But the latter will now see how it is impossible to give a correct account of the letter which the captain wrote to Major Pendennis, as it was never opened at all by that gentleman.

When Miss Costigan came home from rehearsal, which she did in the company of the faithful Mr. Bows, she found her father pacing up and down their apartment in a great state of agitation, and in the midst of a powerful odour of spirits-and-water, which, as it appeared, had not succeeded in pacifying his disordered mind. The Pendennis papers were on the table surrounding the empty goblets and now useless teaspoon, which had served to hold and mix the captain's liquor and his friend's. As Emily entered he seized her in his arms, and cried out: 'Prepare yourself, me child,

me blessed child,' in a voice of agony, and with eyes brimful of tears.

'Ye're tipsy again, papa,' Miss Fotheringay said, pushing back her sire. 'Ye promised me ye wouldn't take spirits before dinner.'

'It's to forget me sorrows, me poor girl, that I've taken just a drop,' cried the bereaved father—'it's to drown me care that I drain the bowl.'

'Your care takes a deal of drowning, captain dear,' said Bows, mimicking his friend's accent; 'what has happened? Has that soft-spoken gentleman in the wig been vexing you?'

'The oily miscreant! I'll have his blood!' roared Cos. Miss Milly, it must be premised, had fled to her room out of his embrace, and was taking off her bonnet and shawl there.

'I thought he meant mischief. He was so uncommon civil,' the other said. 'What has he come to say?'

'Oh, Bows, he has overwhellum'd me,' the captain said. 'There's a hellish conspiracy on foot against me poor girl; and it's me opinion that both them Pendennises, nephew and uncle, is two infernal thrators and scoundthrels, who should be conshumed from off the face of the earth.'

'What is it? What has happened?' said Mr. Bows, growing rather excited.

Costigan then told him the major's statement, that the young Pendennis had not two thousand nor two hundred pounds a year; and expressed his fury that he should have permitted such an impostor to coax and wheedle his innocent girl, and that he should have nourished such a viper in his own personal bosom. 'I have shaken the reptile from me, however,' said Costigan; 'and as for his uncle, I'll have such a revenge on that old man, as shall make 'um rue the day he ever insulted a Costigan.'

'What do you mean, general?' said Bows.

'I mean to have his life, Bows—his villanous, skulking life, my boy;' and he rapped upon the battered old pistol-case in an ominous and savage manner. Bows had often heard him appeal to that box of death, with which he proposed to sacrifice his enemies; but the captain did not tell him that he had actually written and sent a challenge to Major Pendennis, and Mr. Bows therefore rather disregarded the pistols in the present instance.

At this juncture Miss Fotheringay returned to the common sitting-room from her private apartment, looking perfectly healthy, happy, and unconcerned, a striking and wholesome contrast to her father, who was in a delirious tremor of grief, anger, and other agitation. She brought in a pair of ex-white satin shoes with her, which she proposed to rub as clean as might be with bread-crumb; intending to go mad with them upon next Tuesday evening in Ophelia, in which character she was to reappear on that night.

She looked at the papers on the table; stopped as if she was going to ask a question, but thought better of it, and going to the cupboard, selected an eligible piece of bread wherewith she might operate on the satin slippers: and afterwards, coming back to the table, seated herself there commodiously with the shoes, and then asked her father, in her honest Irish brogue, 'What have ye got them letthers, and pothry, and stuff, of Master Arthur's out for, pa? Sure ye don't want to be reading over that nonsense.'

'Oh, Emilee!' cried the captain, 'that boy whom I loved as the boy of mee bosom is only a scoundthrel, and a deceiver, mee poor girl:' and he looked in the most tragical way at Mr. Bows opposite; who, in his turn, gazed somewhat anxiously at Miss Costigan.

'He! pooh! Sure the poor lad's as simple as a schoolboy,' she said. 'All them children write verses and nonsense.'

'He's been acting the part of a viper to this fireside, and a traitor in this familee,' cried the captain. 'I tell ye he's no better than an impostor.'

'What has the poor fellow done, papa?' asked Emily.

'Done? He has deceived us in the most athrocious manner,' Miss Emily's papa said. 'He has thrifled with your affections, and outraged my own fine feelings. He has represented himself as a man of property, and it turruns out that he's no betther than a beggar. Haven't I often told ye he had two thousand a year? He's a pauper, I tell ye, Miss Costigan; a depindant upon the bountee of his mother; a good woman, who may marry again, who's likely to live for ever, and who has but five hundred a year. How dar he ask ye to marry into a family which has not the means of providing for ye? Ye've been grossly

deceived and put upon, Milly, and it's my belief his old ruffian of an uncle in a wig is in the plot against us.'

'That soft old gentleman? What has he been doing, papa?' continued Emily, still imperturbable.

Costigan informed Milly that when she was gone, Major Pendennis told her in his double-faced Pall Mall polite manner, that young Arthur had no fortune at all, that the major had asked him (Costigan) to go to the lawyers ('wherein he knew the scoundthrels have a bill of mine, and I can't meet them,' the captain parenthetically remarked), and see the lad's father's will: and finally, that an infernal swindle had been practised upon him by the pair, and that he was resolved either on a marriage, or on the blood of both of them.

Milly looked very grave and thoughtful, rubbing the white satin shoes. 'Sure, if he's no money, there's no use marrying him, papa,' she said sententiously.

'Why did the villain say he was a man of prawpertee?' asked Costigan.

'The poor fellow always said he was poor,' answered the girl. ''Twas you would have it he was rich, papa—and made me agree to take him.'

'He should have been explicit and told us his income, Milly,' answered the father. 'A young fellow who rides a blood mare, and makes presents of shawls and bracelets, is an impostor if he has no money;—and as for his uncle, bedad I'll pull off his wig whenever I see 'um. Bows, here, shall take a message to him and tell him so. Either it's a marriage, or he meets me in the field like a man, or I tweak 'um on the nose in front of his hotel or in the gravel walks of Fairoaks Park before all the county, bedad.'

'Bedad, you may send somebody else with the message,' said Bows, laughing. 'I'm a fiddler, not a fighting man, captain.'

'Pooh, you've no spirit, sir,' roared the general. 'I'll be my own second, if no one will stand by and see me injured. And I'll take my case of pistols and shoot 'um in the coffee-room of the "George."'

'And so poor Arthur has no money?' sighed out Miss Costigan rather plaintively. 'Poor lad, he was a good lad, too: wild and talking nonsense, with his verses and pothry and that, but a brave, generous boy, and indeed I liked

him—and he liked me too,' she added rather softly, and rubbing away at the shoe.

'Why don't you marry him if you like him so?' Mr. Bows said rather savagely. 'He is not more than ten years younger than you are. His mother may relent, and you might go and live and have enough at Fairoaks Park. Why not go and be a lady? I could go on with the fiddle, and the general live on his half-pay. Why don't you marry him? You know he likes you.'

'There's others that likes me as well, Bows, that has no money and that's old enough,' Miss Milly said sententiously.

'Yes, d—— it,' said Bows, with a bitter curse—'that are old enough and poor enough and fools enough for anything.'

'There's old fools, and young fools too. You've often said so, you silly man,' the imperious beauty said, with a conscious glance at the old gentleman. 'If Pendennis has not enough money to live upon, it's folly to talk about marrying him: and that's the long and short of it.'

'And the boy?' said Mr. Bows. 'By Jove! you throw a man away like an old glove, Miss Costigan.'

'I don't know what you mean, Bows,' said Miss Fotheringay placidly, rubbing the second shoe. 'If he had had half of the two thousand a year that papa gave him, or the half of that, I would marry him. But what is the good of taking on with a beggar? We're poor enough already. There's no use in my going to live with an old lady that's testy and cross, maybe, and would grudge me every morsel of meat. (Sure, it's near dinner time, and Suky not laid the cloth yet), and then,' added Miss Costigan, quite simply, 'suppose there was a family?—why, papa, we shouldn't be as well off as we are now.'

''Deed then, you would not, Milly dear,' answered the father.

'And there's an end to all the fine talk about Mrs. Arthur Pendennis of Fairoaks Park—the member of Parliament's lady,' said Milly, with a laugh. 'Pretty carriages and horses we should have to ride!—that you were always talking about, papa. But it's always the same. If a man looked at me, you fancied he was going to marry me; and if he had a good coat, you fancied he was as rich as Crazes.'

'—As Crœsus,' said Mr. Bows.

'Well, call 'um what ye like. But it's a fact now that papa has married me these eight years a score of times. Wasn't I to be my Lady Poldoody of Oystherstown Castle? Then there was the navy captain at Portsmouth, and the old surgeon at Norwich, and the Methodist preacher here last year, and who knows how many more? Well, I bet a penny, with all your scheming, I shall die Milly Costigan at last. So poor little Arthur has no money? Stop and take dinner, Bows: we've a beautiful beefsteak pudding.'

'I wonder whether she is on with Sir Derby Oaks,' thought Bows, whose eyes and thoughts were always watching her. 'The dodges of women beat all comprehension; and I am sure she wouldn't let the lad off so easily, if she had not some other scheme on hand.'

It will have been perceived that Miss Fotheringay, though silent in general, and by no means brilliant as a conversationist, where poetry, literature, or the fine arts were concerned, could talk freely, and with good sense, too, in her own family circle. She cannot justly be called a romantic person: nor were her literary acquirements great: she never opened a Shakespeare from the day she left the stage, nor, indeed, understood it during all the time she adorned the boards: but about a pudding, a piece of needlework, or her own domestic affairs, she was as good a judge as could be found; and not being misled by a strong imagination or a passionate temper, was better enabled to keep her judgement cool. When, over their dinner, Costigan tried to convince himself and the company that the major's statement regarding Pen's finances was unworthy of credit, and a mere ruse upon the old hypocrite's part so as to induce them, on their side, to break off the match, Miss Milly would not, for a moment, admit the possibility of deceit on the side of the adversary: and pointed out clearly that it was her father who had deceived himself, and not poor little Pen who had tried to take them in. As for that poor lad, she said she pitied him with all her heart. And she ate an exceedingly good dinner: to the admiration of Mr. Bows, who had a remarkable regard and contempt for this woman, during, and after which repast, the party devised upon the best means of bringing this love-matter to a close. As for Costigan, his idea of tweaking the major's nose vanished with his supply of after-dinner whisky-and-water; and he was submissive to his daughter, and ready

for any plan on which she might decide, in order to meet the crisis which she saw was at hand.

The captain, who, as long as he had a notion that he was wronged, was eager to face and demolish both Pen and his uncle, perhaps shrank from the idea of meeting the former, and asked, 'What the juice they were to say to the lad if he remained steady to his engagement, and they broke from theirs ?' 'What ? don't you know how to throw a man over ?' said Bows ; 'ask a woman to tell you ?' and Miss Fotheringay showed how this feat was to be done simply enough—nothing was more easy. 'Papa writes to Arthur to know what settlements he proposes to make in event of a marriage ; and asks what his means are. Arthur writes back and says what he's got, and you'll find it's as the major says, I'll go bail. Then papa writes, and says it's not enough, and the match had best be at an end.'

'And, of course, you enclose a parting line, in which you say you will always regard him as a brother,' said Mr. Bows, eyeing her in his scornful way.

'Of course, and so I shall,' answered Miss Fotheringay. 'He's a most worthy young man, I'm sure. I'll thank ye hand me the salt. Them filberts is beautiful.'

'And there will be no noses pulled, Cos, my boy ? I'm sorry you're balked,' said Mr. Bows.

''Dad, I suppose not,' said Cos, rubbing his own.—'What'll ye do about them letters, and verses, and pomes, Milly darling ? Ye must send 'em back.'

'Wigsby would give a hundred pound for 'em,' Bows said, with a sneer.

''Deed, then, he would,' said Captain Costigan, who was easily led.

'Papa !' said Miss Milly. 'Ye wouldn't be for not sending the poor boy his letters back ? Them letters and pomes is mine. They were very long, and full of all sorts of nonsense, and Latin, and things I couldn't understand the half of—indeed, I've not read 'em all ; but we'll send 'em back to him when the proper time comes.' And going to a drawer, Miss Fotheringay took out from it a number of the *County Chronicle and Chatteris Champion*, in which Pen had written a copy of flaming verses celebrating her appearance in the character of Imogen, and putting by the leaf upon which the poem appeared (for, like ladies of her profession, she kept the favourable printed notices of her

performances), she wrapped up Pen's letters, poems, passions, and fancies, and tied them with a piece of string neatly, as she would a parcel of sugar.

Nor was she in the least moved while performing this act. What hours the boy had passed over those papers! What love and longing: what generous faith and manly devotion—what watchful nights and lonely fevers might they tell of! She tied them up like so much grocery, and sat down and made tea afterwards with a perfectly placid and contented heart: while Pen was yearning after her ten miles off: and hugging her image to his soul.

CHAPTER XIII

A CRISIS

THE[1] major came away from his interview with Captain Costigan in a state of such concentrated fury as rendered him terrible to approach! 'The impudent bog-trotting scamp,' he thought, 'dare to threaten *me!* Dare to talk of permitting his damned Costigans to marry with the Pendennises! Send me a challenge! If the fellow can get anything in the shape of a gentleman to carry it, I have the greatest mind in life not to balk him. Psha! what would people say if I were to go out with a tipsy mountebank, about a row with an actress in a barn!' So when the major saw Dr. Portman, who asked anxiously regarding the issue of his battle with the dragon, Mr. Pendennis did not care to inform the divine of the general's insolent behaviour, but stated that the affair was a very ugly and disagreeable one, and that it was by no means over yet.

He enjoined Doctor and Mrs. Portman to say nothing about the business at Fairoaks[2]; and then he returned to his hotel, where he vented his wrath upon Mr. Morgan his

valet, 'dammin and cussin upstairs and downstairs,' as that gentleman observed to Mr. Foker's man, in whose company he partook of dinner in the servants' room of the 'George.'

The servant carried the news to his master; and Mr. Foker having finished his breakfast about this time, it being two o'clock in the afternoon, remembered that he was anxious to know the result of the interview between his two friends, and having inquired the number of the major's sitting-room, went over in his brocade dressing-gown, and knocked for admission.

Major Pendennis had some business, as he had stated, respecting a lease of the widow's, about which he was desirous of consulting old Mr. Tatham, the lawyer, who had been his brother's man of business, and who had a branch office at Clavering, where he and his son attended market and other days three or four in the week. This gentleman and his client were now in consultation when Mr. Foker showed his grand dressing-gown and embroidered skull-cap at Major Pendennis's door.

Seeing the major engaged with papers and red-tape, and an old man with a white head, the modest youth was for drawing back—and said, 'Oh, you're busy—call again another time.' But Mr. Pendennis wanted to see him, and begged him, with a smile, to enter: whereupon Mr. Foker took off the embroidered tarboosh or fez (it had been worked by the fondest of mothers) and advanced, bowing to the gentlemen and smiling on them graciously. Mr. Tatham had never seen so splendid an apparition before as this brocaded youth, who seated himself in an arm-chair, spreading out his crimson skirts, and looking with exceeding kindness and frankness on the other two tenants of the room. 'You seem to like my dressing-gown, sir,' he said to Mr. Tatham. 'A pretty thing, isn't it? Neat, but not in the least gaudy. And how do *you* do, Major Pendennis, sir, and how does the world treat you?'

There was that in Foker's manner and appearance which would have put an Inquisitor into good humour, and it smoothed the wrinkles under Pendennis's head of hair.

'I have had an interview with that Irishman (you may speak before my friend, Mr. Tatham here, who knows all the affairs of the family), and it has not, I own, been very satisfactory. He won't believe that my nephew is poor: he says

we are both liars : he did me the honour to hint that I was a coward, as I took leave. And I thought when you knocked at the door, that you might be the gentleman whom I expect with a challenge from Mr. Costigan—that is how the world treats me, Mr. Foker.'

'You don't mean that Irishman, the actress's father ?' cried Mr. Tatham, who was a Dissenter himself, and did not patronize the drama.

'That Irishman, the actress's father—the very man. Have not you heard what a fool my nephew has made of himself about the girl ?' [3]—and Major Pendennis had to recount the story of his nephew's loves to the lawyer, Mr. Foker coming in with appropriate comments in his usual familiar language.

Tatham was lost in wonder at the narrative. Why had not Mrs. Pendennis married a serious man, he thought—Mr. Tatham was a widower—and kept this unfortunate boy from perdition ? As for Mr. Costigan's daughter, he would say nothing : her profession was sufficient to characterize *her*. Mr. Foker here interposed to say he had known some uncommon good people in the booths, as he called the Temple of the Muses. Well, it might be so, Mr. Tatham hoped so—but the father, Tatham knew personally—a man of the worst character, a wine-bibber and an idler in taverns and billiard-rooms, and a notorious insolvent. 'I can understand the reason, major,' he said, 'why the fellow would not come to my office to ascertain the truth of the statements which you made him.—We have a writ out against him and another disreputable fellow, one of the play-actors, for a bill given to Mr. Skinner of this city, a most respectable grocer and wine and spirit merchant, and a member of the Society of Friends. This Costigan came crying to Mr. Skinner—crying in the shop, sir—and we have not proceeded against him or the other, as neither were worth powder and shot.'

It was whilst Mr. Tatham was engaged in telling this story that a third knock came to the door, and there entered an athletic gentleman in a shabby braided frock, bearing in his hand a letter with a large blotched red seal.

'Can I have the honour of speaking with Major Pendennis in private ?' he began—'I have a few words for your ear, sir. I am the bearer of a mission from my friend, Captain Costigan '—but here the man with the bass voice paused,

faltered, and turned pale—he caught sight of the red and well-remembered face of Mr. Tatham.

'Hullo, Garbetts, speak up!' cried Mr. Foker, delighted.

'Why, bless my soul, it is the other party to the bill!' said Mr. Tatham. 'I say, sir; stop, I say.' But Garbetts, with a face as blank as Macbeth's when Banquo's ghost appears upon him, gasped some inarticulate words, and fled out of the room.

The major's gravity was also entirely upset, and he burst out laughing. So did Mr. Foker, who said, 'By Jove, it was a good 'un.' So did the attorney, although by profession a serious man.

'I don't think there'll be any fight, major,' young Foker said; and began mimicking the tragedian. 'If there is, the old gentleman—your name Tatham?—very happy to make your acquaintance, Mr. Tatham—may send the bailiffs to separate the men;' and Mr. Tatham promised to do so. The major was by no means sorry at the ludicrous issue of the quarrel. 'It seems to me, sir,' he said to Mr. Foker, 'that you always arrive to put me into good humour.'

Nor was this the only occasion on which Mr. Foker this day was destined to be of service to the Pendennis family. We have said that he had the entrée of Captain Costigan's lodgings, and in the course of the afternoon he thought he would pay the general a visit, and hear from his own lips what had occurred in the conversation, in the morning, with Mr. Pendennis. Captain Costigan was not at home. He had received permission, nay, encouragement from his daughter, to go to the convivial club at the 'Magpie Hotel,' where no doubt he was bragging at that moment of his desire to murder a certain ruffian; for he was not only brave, but he knew it too, and liked to take out his courage, and, as it were, give it an airing in company.

Costigan then was absent, but Miss Fotheringay was at home washing the tea-cups whilst Mr. Bows sat opposite to her.

'Just done breakfast, I see—how do?' said Mr. Foker, popping in his little funny head.

'Get out, you funny little man,' cried Miss Fotheringay.

'You mean come in,' answered the other. 'Here we are!' and entering the room he folded his arms and began twirling his head round and round with immense rapidity, like Harlequin in the pantomime when he first issues from

his cocoon or envelope. Miss Fotheringay laughed with all her heart: a wink of Foker's would set her off laughing, when the bitterest joke Bows ever made could not get a smile from her, or the finest of poor Pen's speeches would only puzzle her. At the end of the harlequinade he sank down on one knee and kissed her hand. 'You're the drollest little man,' she said, and gave him a great good-humoured slap. Pen used to tremble as he kissed her hand. Pen would have died of a slap.

These preliminaries over, the three began to talk; Mr. Foker amused his companions by recounting to them the scene which he had just witnessed of the discomfiture of Mr. Garbetts, by which they learned, for the first time, how far the general had carried his wrath against Major Pendennis. Foker spoke strongly in favour of the major's character for veracity and honour, and described him as a tip-top swell, moving in the upper circle of society, who would never submit to any deceit—much more to deceive such a charming young woman as Miss Foth.

He touched delicately upon the delicate marriage question, though he couldn't help showing that he held Pen rather cheap. In fact, he had a perhaps just contempt for Mr. Pen's high-flown sentimentality; his own weakness, as he thought, not lying that way. 'I knew it wouldn't do, Miss Foth,' said he, nodding his little head. 'Couldn't do. Didn't like to put *my* hand into the bag, but knew it couldn't do. He's too young for you: too green: a deal too green: and he turns out to be poor as Job. Can't have him at no price, can she, Mr. Bo?'

'Indeed he's a nice poor boy,' said the Fotheringay rather sadly.

'Poor little beggar,' said Bows, with his hands in his pockets, and stealing up a queer look at Miss Fotheringay. Perhaps he thought and wondered at the way in which women play with men, and coax them and win them and drop them.

But Mr. Bows had not the least objection to acknowledge that he thought Miss Fotheringay was perfectly right in giving up Mr. Arthur Pendennis, and that in his idea the match was always an absurd one: and Miss Costigan owned that she thought so herself, only she couldn't send away two thousand a year. 'It all comes of believing papa's silly stories,' she said; 'faith, I'll choose for meself another

time'—and very likely the large image of Lieutenant Sir Derby Oaks entered into her mind at that instant.

After praising Major Pendennis, whom Miss Costigan declared to be a proper gentleman entirely, smelling of lavender, and as neat as a pin—and who was pronounced by Mr. Bows to be the right sort of fellow, though rather too much of an old buck, Mr. Foker suddenly bethought him to ask the pair to come and meet the major that very evening at dinner at his apartment at the 'George.' 'He agreed to dine with me, and I think after the—after the little shindy this morning, in which I must say the general was wrong, it would look kind, you know.—I know the major fell in love with you, Miss Foth. : he said so.'

'So she may be Mrs. Pendennis still,' Bows said, with a sneer,—'No, thank you, Mr. F.—I've dined.'

'Sure, that was at three o'clock,' said Miss Costigan, who had an honest appetite, 'and I can't go without you.'

'We'll have lobster-salad and champagne,' said the little monster, who could not construe a line of Latin, or do a sum beyond the rule of three. Now, for lobster-salad and champagne in an honourable manner, Miss Costigan would have gone anywhere—and Major Pendennis actually found himself at seven o'clock, seated at a dinner-table in company with Mr. Bows, a professional fiddler, and Miss Costigan, whose father had wanted to blow his brains out a few hours before.

To make the happy meeting complete, Mr. Foker, who knew Costigan's haunts, dispatched Stoopid to the club at the 'Magpie,' where the general was in the act of singing a pathetic song, and brought him off to supper. To find his daughter and Bows seated at the board was a surprise indeed—Major Pendennis laughed, and cordially held out his hand, which the general officer grasped *avec effusion*, as the French say. In fact he was considerably inebriated, and had already been crying over his own song before he joined the little party at the 'George.' He burst into tears more than once, during the entertainment, and called the major his dearest friend. Stoopid and Mr. Foker walked home with him : the major gallantly giving his arm to Miss Costigan. He was received with great friendliness when he called the next day, when many civilities passed between the gentlemen. On taking leave he expressed his anxious desire to serve Miss Costigan on any occasion in which he could be

useful to her, and he shook hands with Mr. Foker most cordially and gratefully, and said that gentleman had done him the very greatest service.

'All right,' said Mr. Foker: and they parted with mutual esteem.

On his return to Fairoaks the next day, Major Pendennis did not say what had happened to him on the previous night, or allude to the company in which he had passed it. But he engaged Mr. Smirke to stop to dinner; and any person accustomed to watch his manner might have remarked that there was something constrained in his hilarity and talkativeness, and that he was unusually gracious and watchful in his communications with his nephew. He gave Pen an emphatic God bless you when the lad went to bed; and as they were about to part for the night, he seemed as if he was going to say something to Mrs. Pendennis, but he bethought him that if he spoke he might spoil her night's rest, and allowed her to sleep in peace.

The next morning he was down in the breakfast-room earlier than was his custom, and saluted everybody there with great cordiality. The post used to arrive commonly about the end of this meal. When John, the old servant, entered, and discharged the bag of its letters and papers, the major looked hard at Pen as the lad got his—Arthur blushed, and put his letter down. He knew the hand, it was that of old Costigan, and he did not care to read it in public. Major Pendennis knew the letter, too. He had put it into the post himself in Chatteris the day before.

He told little Laura to go away, which the child did, having a thorough dislike to him; and as the door closed on her, he took Mrs. Pendennis's hand, and giving her a look full of meaning, pointed to the letter under the newspaper which Pen was pretending to read. 'Will you come into the drawing-room?' he said. 'I want to speak to you.' And she followed him, wondering, into the hall.

'What is it?' she said nervously.

'The affair is at an end,' Major Pendennis said. 'He has a letter there giving him his dismissal. I dictated it myself yesterday. There are a few lines from the lady, too, bidding him farewell. It is all over.'

Helen ran back to the dining-room, her brother following. Pen had jumped at his letter the instant they were gone.

He was reading it with a stupefied face. It stated what the major had said, that Mr. Costigan was most gratified for the kindness with which Arthur had treated his daughter, but that he was only now made aware of Mr. Pendennis's pecuniary circumstances. They were such that marriage was at present out of the question, and considering the great disparity in the age of the two, a future union was impossible. Under these circumstances, and with the deepest regret and esteem for him, Mr. Costigan bade Arthur farewell, and suggested that he should cease visiting, for some time at least, at his house.

A few lines from Miss Costigan were enclosed. She asquiesced in the decision of her papa. She pointed out that she was many years older than Arthur, and that an engagement was not to be thought of. She would always be grateful for his kindness to her, and hoped to keep his friendship. But at present, and until the pain of the separation should be over, she entreated they should not meet.

Pen read Costigan's letter and its enclosure mechanically, hardly knowing what was before his eyes. He looked up wildly, and saw his mother and uncle regarding him with sad faces. Helen's, indeed, was full of tender maternal anxiety.

'What—what is this ?' Pen said. 'It's some joke. This is not her writing. This is some servant's writing. Who's playing these tricks upon me ?'

'It comes under her father's envelope,' the major said. 'Those letters you had before were not in her hand : that is hers.'

'How do you know ?' said Pen very fiercely.

'I saw her write it,' the uncle answered, as the boy started up ; and his mother, coming forward, took his hand. He put her away.

'How came you to see her ? How came you between me and her ? What have I ever done to you that you should—oh, it's not true ; it's not true !'—Pen broke out with a wild execration. 'She can't have done it of her own accord. She can't mean it. She's pledged to me. Who has told her lies to break her from me ?'

'Lies are not told in the family, Arthur,' Major Pendennis replied. 'I told her the truth, which was, that you had no money to maintain her, for her foolish father had represented you to be rich. And when she knew how poor you were, she withdrew at once, and without any persuasion of mine.

She was quite right. She is ten years older than you are. She is perfectly unfitted to be your wife, and knows it. Look at that handwriting, and ask yourself, is such a woman fitted to be the companion of your mother ?'

'I will know from herself if it is true,' Arthur said, crumpling up the paper.

'Won't you take my word of honour ? Her letters were written by a confidante of hers, who writes better than she can—look here. Here's one from the lady to your friend, Mr. Foker. You have seen her with Miss Costigan, as whose amanuensis she acted '—the major said, with ever so little of a sneer, and laid down a certain billet which Mr. Foker had given to him.

'It's not that,' said Pen, burning with shame and rage. 'I suppose what you say is true, sir, but I'll hear it from herself.'

'Arthur !' appealed his mother.

'I *will* see her,' said Arthur. 'I'll ask her to marry me, once more. I will. No one shall prevent me.'

'What, a woman who spells affection with one *f* ? Nonsense, sir. Be a man, and remember that your mother is a lady. She was never made to associate with that tipsy old swindler or his daughter. Be a man and forget her, as she does you.'

'Be a man and comfort your mother, my Arthur,' Helen said, going and embracing him : and seeing that the pair were greatly moved, Major Pendennis went out of the room and shut the door upon them, wisely judging that they were best alone.

He had won a complete victory. He actually had brought away Pen's letters in his portmanteau from Chatteris : having complimented Mr. Costigan, when he returned them, by giving him the little promissory note which had disquieted himself and Mr. Garbetts : and for which the major settled with Mr. Tatham.

Pen rushed wildly off to Chatteris that day, but in vain attempted to see Miss Fotheringay, for whom he left a letter, enclosed to her father. The enclosure was returned by Mr. Costigan, who begged that all correspondence might end ; and after one or two further attempts of the lad's, the indignant general desired that their acquaintance might cease. He cut Pen in the street. As Arthur and Foker were pacing the Castle walk, one day, they came upon

Emily on her father's arm. She passed without any nod of recognition. Foker felt poor Pen trembling on his arm.

His uncle wanted him to travel, to quit the country for a while, and his mother urged him too : for he was growing very ill, and suffered severely. But he refused, and said point-blank he would not go. He would not obey in this instance : and his mother was too fond, and his uncle too wise to force him. Whenever Miss Fotheringay acted he rode over to the Chatteris theatre and saw her. One night there were so few people in the house that the manager returned the money. Pen came home and went to bed at eight o'clock, and had a fever. If this continues, his mother will be going over and fetching the girl, the major thought, in despair. As for Pen, he thought he should die. We are not going to describe his feelings, or give a dreary journal of his despair and passion. Have not other gentlemen been balked in love besides Mr. Pen ? Yes, indeed : but few die of the malady.

CHAPTER XIV

IN WHICH MISS FOTHERINGAY MAKES A NEW ENGAGEMENT

WITHIN a short period of the events above narrated, Mr. Manager Bingley was performing his famous character of Rolla, in *Pizarro*, to a house so exceedingly thin, that it would appear as if the part of Rolla was by no means such a favourite with the people of Chatteris as it was with the accomplished actor himself. Scarce anybody was in the theatre. Poor Pen had the boxes almost all to himself, and sat there lonely, with bloodshot eyes, leaning over the ledge, and gazing haggardly towards the scene, when Cora* came in. When she was not on the stage he saw nothing. Spaniards and Peruvians, processions and battles, priests and virgins of the sun, went in and out,

A CUT DIRECT

and had their talk, but Arthur took no note of any one of them; and only saw Cora whom his soul longed after. He said afterwards that he wondered he had not taken a pistol to shoot her, so mad was he with love, and rage, and despair; and had it not been for his mother at home, to whom he did not speak about his luckless condition, but whose silent sympathy and watchfulness greatly comforted the simple half heart-broken fellow, who knows but he might have done something desperate, and have ended his days prematurely in front of Chatteris jail? There he sat then, miserable, and gazing at her. And she took no more notice of him than he did of the rest of the house.

The Fotheringay was uncommonly handsome, in a white raiment and leopard-skin, with a sun upon her breast, and fine tawdry bracelets on her beautiful glancing arms. She spouted to admiration the few words of her part, and looked it still better. The eyes, which had overthrown Pen's soul, rolled and gleamed as lustrous as ever; but it was not to him that they were directed that night. He did not know to whom, or remark a couple of gentlemen, in the box next to him, upon whom Miss Fotheringay's glances were perpetually shining.

Nor had Pen noticed the extraordinary change which had taken place on the stage a short time after the entry of these two gentlemen into the theatre. There were so few people in the house, that the first act of the play languished entirely, and there had been some question of returning the money, as upon that other unfortunate night when poor Pen had been driven away. The actors were perfectly careless about their parts, and yawned through the dialogue, and talked loud to each other in the intervals. Even Bingley was listless, and Mrs. B. in Elvira spoke under her breath.

How came it that all of a sudden Mrs. Bingley began to raise her voice and bellow like a bull of Bashan? Whence was it that Bingley, flinging off his apathy, darted about the stage and yelled like Kean? Why did Garbetts and Rowkins and Miss Rouncy try, each of them, the force of their charms or graces, and act and swagger and scowl and spout their very loudest at the two gentlemen in box No. 3?

One was a quiet little man in black, with a grey head and

a jolly, shrewd face—the other was in all respects a splendid and remarkable individual. He was a tall and portly gentleman with a hooked nose and a profusion of curling brown hair and whiskers; his coat was covered with the richest frogs, braiding, and velvet. He had under-waistcoats, many splendid rings, jewelled pins and neck-chains. When he took out his yellow pocket-handkerchief with his hand that was cased in white kids, a delightful odour of musk and bergamot was shaken through the house. He was evidently a personage of rank, and it was at him that the little Chatteris company was acting.

He was, in a word, no other than Mr. Dolphin, the great manager from London, accompanied by his faithful friend and secretary Mr. William Minns: without whom he never travelled. He had not been ten minutes in the theatre before his august presence there was perceived by Bingley and the rest: and they all began to act their best and try to engage his attention. Even Miss Fotheringay's dull heart, which was disturbed at nothing, felt perhaps a flutter, when she came in presence of the famous London impresario. She had not much to do in her part, but to look handsome, and stand in picturesque attitudes encircling her child: and she did this work to admiration. In vain the various actors tried to win the favour of the great stage sultan. Pizarro never got a hand from him. Bingley yelled, and Mrs. Bingley bellowed, and the manager only took snuff out of his great gold box. It was only in the last scene, when Rolla comes in staggering with the infant (Bingley is not so strong as he was, and his fourth son, Master Talma Bingley, is a monstrous large child for his age)—when Rolla comes staggering with the child to Cora, who rushes forward with a shriek, and says, 'O God, there's blood upon him!'—that the London manager clapped his hands, and broke out with an enthusiastic bravo.

Then having concluded his applause, Mr. Dolphin gave his secretary a slap on the shoulder, and said, 'By Jove, Billy, she'll do!'

'Who taught her that dodge?' said old Billy, who was a sardonic old gentleman. 'I remember her at the Olympic, and hang me if she could say Bo to a goose.'

It was little Mr. Bows in the orchestra who had taught her the 'dodge' in question. All the company heard the

THE MANAGER FROM LONDON

applause, and, as the curtain went down, came round her and congratulated and hated Miss Fotheringay.

Now, Mr. Dolphin's appearance in the remote little Chatteris theatre may be accounted for in this manner. In spite of all his exertions, and the perpetual blazes of triumph, coruscations of talent, victories of good old English comedy, which his play-bills advertised, his theatre (which, if you please, and to injure no present susceptibilities and vested interests, we shall call the Museum Theatre) by no means prospered, and the famous impresario found himself on the verge of ruin. The great Hubbard had acted legitimate drama for twenty nights, and failed to remunerate anybody but himself: the celebrated Mr. and Mrs. Cawdor had come out in Mr. Rawhead's tragedy, and in their favourite round of pieces, and had not attracted the public. Herr Garbage's lions and tigers had drawn for a little time, until one of the animals had bitten a piece out of the Herr's shoulder; when the Lord Chamberlain interfered, and put a stop to this species of performance: and the grand Lyrical Drama, though brought out with unexampled splendour and success, with Monsieur Poumons as first tenor, and an enormous orchestra, had almost crushed poor Dolphin in its triumphant progress: so that great as his genius and resources were, they seemed to be at an end. He was dragging on his season wretchedly with half salaries, small operas, feeble old comedies, and his ballet company; and everybody was looking out for the day when he should appear in the *Gazette*.*

One of the illustrious patrons of the Museum Theatre, and occupant of the great proscenium-box, was a gentleman whose name has been mentioned in a previous history; that refined patron of the arts, and enlightened lover of music and the drama, the Most Noble the Marquis of Steyne. His lordship's avocations as a statesman prevented him from attending the playhouse very often, or coming very early. But he occasionally appeared at the theatre in time for the ballet, and was always received with the greatest respect by the manager, from whom he sometimes condescended to receive a visit in his box. It communicated with the stage, and when anything occurred there which particularly pleased him, when a new face made its appearance among the coryphées, or a fair dancer executed a *pas* with especial grace or agility, Mr. Wenham, Mr. Wagg,* or

some other aide de camp of the noble marquis, would be commissioned to go behind the scenes, and express the great man's approbation, or make the inquiries which were prompted by his lordship's curiosity, or his interest in the dramatic art. He could not be seen by the audience, for Lord Steyne sat modestly behind a curtain, and looked only towards the stage—but you could know he was in the house, by the glances which all the *corps de ballet*, and all the principal dancers, cast towards his box. I have seen many scores of pairs of eyes (as in the Palm Dance in the ballet of *Cook at Otaheite*, where no less than a hundred and twenty lovely female savages, in palm-leaves and feather aprons, were made to dance round Floridor as Captain Cook) ogling that box as they performed before it, and have often wondered to remark the presence of mind of Mademoiselle Sauterelle, or Mademoiselle de Bondi (known as la petite Caoutchouc), who, when actually up in the air quivering like so many shuttlecocks, always kept their lovely eyes winking at that box in which the great Steyne sat. Now and then you would hear a harsh voice from behind the curtain cry, 'Brava, brava,' or a pair of white gloves wave from it, and begin to applaud. Bondi, or Sauterelle, when they came down to earth, curtsied and smiled, especially to those hands, before they walked up the stage again, panting and happy.

One night this great prince, surrounded by a few choice friends, was in his box at the Museum, and they were making such a noise and laughter that the pit was scandalized, and many indignant voices were bawling out silence so loudly, that Wagg wondered the police did not interfere to take the rascals out. Wenham was amusing the party in the box with extracts from a private letter which he had received from Major Pendennis, whose absence in the country at the full London season had been remarked, and of course deplored by his friends.

'The secret is out,' said Mr. Wenham; 'there's a woman in the case.'

'Why, d—— it, Wenham, he's your age,' said the gentleman behind the curtain.

'*Pour les âmes bien nées, l'amour ne compte pas le nombre des années*,' said Mr. Wenham, with a gallant air. 'For my part, I hope to be a victim till I die, and to break my heart every year of my life.' The meaning of which

sentence was, 'My lord, you need not talk; I'm three years younger than you, and twice as well *conservé*.'

'Wenham, you affect me,' said the great man, with one of his usual oaths. 'By —— you do. I like to see a fellow preserving all the illusions of youth up to our time of life—and keeping his heart warm as yours is. Hang it, sir, it's a comfort to meet with such a generous, candid creature. Who's that gal in the second row, with blue ribbons, third from the stage—fine gal. Yes, you and I are sentimentalists. Wagg I don't think so much cares—it's the stomach rather more than the heart with you, eh, Wagg, my boy?'

'I like everything that's good,' said Mr. Wagg generously. 'Beauty and burgundy, Venus and venison. I don't say that Venus's turtles are to be despised, because they don't cook them at the "London Tavern": but—but tell us about old Pendennis, Mr. Wenham,' he abruptly concluded—for his joke flagged just then, as he saw that his patron was not listening. In fact, Steyne's glasses were up, and he was examining some object on the stage.

'Yes, I've heard that joke about Venus's turtle and the "London Tavern" before—you begin to fail, my poor Wagg. If you don't mind I shall be obliged to have a new jester,' Lord Steyne said, laying down his glass. 'Go on, Wenham, about old Pendennis.'

'Dear Wenham, he begins,'—Mr. Wenham read,—'As you have had my character in your hands for the last three weeks, and no doubt have torn me to shreds, according to your custom, I think you can afford to be good-humoured by way of variety, and to do me a service. It is a delicate matter, *entre nous, une affaire de cœur*. There is a young friend of mine who is gone wild about a certain Miss Fotheringay, an actress at the theatre here, and I must own to you, as handsome a woman, and, as it appears to me, as good an actress as ever put on rouge. She does Ophelia, Lady Teazle, Mrs. Haller—that sort of thing. Upon my word, she is as splendid as Georges in her best days,* and, as far as I know, utterly superior to anything we have on our scene. *I want a London engagement for her.* Can't you get your friend Dolphin to come and see her—to engage her—to take her out of this place? A word from a noble friend of ours (you understand) would be invaluable, and if you could get the Gaunt House interest for me—I will promise *anything* I can in return for your service—which I shall consider one of the greatest *that can be done to me.* Do, do this now as a good fellow, which *I always said you were*: and in return, command yours truly,—A. Pendennis.'

'It's a clear case,' said Mr. Wenham, having read this letter; 'old Pendennis is in love.'

'And wants to get the woman up to London—evidently,' continued Mr. Wagg.

'I should like to see Pendennis on his knees, with the rheumatism,' said Mr. Wenham.

'Or accommodating the beloved object with a lock of his hair,' said Wagg.

'Stuff,' said the great man. 'He has relations in the county, hasn't he? He said something about a nephew whose interest could return a member. It is the nephew's affair, depend on it. The young one is in a scrape. I was myself—when I was in the fifth form at Eton—a market-gardener's daughter—and swore I'd marry her. I was mad about her—poor Polly!' Here he made a pause, and perhaps the past rose up to Lord Steyne, and George Gaunt was a boy again not altogether lost. 'But I say, she must be a fine woman from Pendennis's account. Have in Dolphin, and let us hear if he knows anything of her.'

At this Wenham sprang out of the box, passed the servitor who waited at the door communicating with the stage, and who saluted Mr. Wenham with profound respect; and the latter emissary, pushing on and familiar with the place, had no difficulty in finding out the manager, who was employed, as he not unfrequently was, in swearing and cursing* the ladies of the *corps de ballet* for not doing their duty.

The oaths died away on Mr. Dolphin's lips, as soon as he saw Mr. Wenham; and he drew off the hand which was clenched in the face of one of the offending coryphées, to grasp that of the new-comer. 'How do, Mr. Wenham? How's his lordship to-night? Looks uncommonly well,' said the manager, smiling, as if he had never been out of temper in his life; and he was only too delighted to follow Lord Steyne's ambassador, and pay his personal respects to that great man.

The visit to Chatteris was the result of their conversation: and Mr. Dolphin wrote to his lordship from that place, and did himself the honour to inform the Marquis of Steyne that he had seen the lady about whom his lordship had spoken, that he was as much struck by her talents as he was by her personal appearance, and that he had made

an engagement with Miss Fotheringay, who would soon have the honour of appearing before a London audience, and his noble and enlightened patron the Marquis of Steyne.

Pen read the announcement of Miss Fotheringay's

engagement in the Chatteris paper, where he had so often praised her charms. The editor made very handsome mention of her talent and beauty, and prophesied her success in the metropolis. Bingley, the manager, began to advertise 'The last night of Miss Fotheringay's engage-

ment.' Poor Pen and Sir Derby Oaks were very constant at the play: Sir Derby in the stage-box, throwing bouquets and getting glances—Pen in the almost deserted boxes, haggard, wretched, and lonely. Nobody cared whether Miss Fotheringay was going or staying except those two—and perhaps one more, which was Mr. Bows of the orchestra.

He came out of his place one night, and went into the house to the box where Pen was; and he held out his hand to him, and asked him to come and walk. They walked down the street together; and went and sat upon Chatteris bridge in the moonlight, and talked about *Her*. 'We may sit on the same bridge,' said he: 'we have been in the same boat for a long time. You are not the only man who has made a fool of himself about that woman. And I have less excuse than you, because I'm older and know her better. She has no more heart than the stone you are leaning on; and it or you or I might fall into the water, and never come up again, and she wouldn't care. Yes—she would care for me, because she wants me to teach her: and she won't be able to get on without me, and will be forced to send for me from London. But she wouldn't if she didn't want me. She has no heart and no head, and no sense, and no feelings, and no griefs or cares whatever. I was going to say no pleasures—but the fact is, she does like her dinner, and she is pleased when people admire her.'

'And you do?' said Pen, interested out of himself, and wondering at the crabbed homely little old man.

'It's a habit, like taking snuff, or drinking drams,' said the other. 'I've been taking her these five years, and can't do without her. It was I made her. If she doesn't send for me, I shall follow her: but I know she'll send for me. She wants me. Some day she'll marry, and fling me over, as I do the end of this cigar.'

The little flaming spark dropped into the water below, and disappeared; and Pen, as he rode home that night, actually thought about somebody but himself.

CHAPTER XV

THE HAPPY VILLAGE

UNTIL the enemy had retired altogether from before the place, Major Pendennis was resolved to keep his garrison in Fairoaks. He did not appear to watch Pen's behaviour, or to put any restraint on his nephew's actions, but he managed, nevertheless, to keep the lad constantly under his eye or those of his agents, and young Arthur's comings and goings were quite well known to his vigilant guardian.

I suppose there is scarcely any man who reads this or any other novel but has been balked in love some time or the other, by fate and circumstance, by falsehood of women, or his own fault. Let that worthy friend recall his own sensations under the circumstances, and apply them as illustrative of Mr. Pen's anguish. Ah, what weary nights and sickening fevers! Ah, what mad desires dashing up against some rock of obstruction or indifference, and flung back again from the unimpressionable granite! If a list could be made this very night in London of the groans, thoughts, imprecations of tossing lovers, what a catalogue it would be! I wonder what a percentage of the male population of the metropolis will be lying awake at two or three o'clock to-morrow morning, counting the hours as they go by, knelling drearily, and rolling from left to right, restless, yearning, and heart-sick? What a pang it is! I never knew a man die of love, certainly, but I have known a twelve-stone man go down to nine stone five under a disappointed passion, so that pretty nearly a quarter of him may be said to have perished: and that is no small portion. He has come back to his old size subsequently—perhaps is bigger than ever: very likely some new affection has closed round his heart and ribs and made them comfortable, and young Pen is a man who will console himself like the rest of us. We say this lest the ladies should be disposed to deplore him prematurely, or be seriously uneasy with regard to his complaint. His mother was, but

what will not a maternal fondness fear or invent? 'Depend on it, my dear creature,' Major Pendennis would say gallantly to her, 'the boy will recover. As soon as we get her out of the country we will take him somewhere, and show him a little life. Meantime make yourself easy about him. Half a fellow's pangs at losing a woman result from vanity more than affection. To be left by a woman is the deuce and all, to be sure; but look how easily we leave 'em.'

Mrs. Pendennis did not know. This sort of knowledge had by no means come within the simple lady's scope. Indeed, she did not like the subject, or to talk of it: her heart had had its own little private misadventure, and she had borne up against it, and cured it: and perhaps she had not much patience with other folks' passions, except, of course, Arthur's, whose sufferings she made her own, feeling indeed very likely, in many of the boy's illnesses and pains, a great deal more than Pen himself endured. And she watched him through this present grief with a jealous silent sympathy; although, as we have said, he did not talk to her of his unfortunate condition.

The major must be allowed to have had not a little merit and forbearance, and to have exhibited a highly creditable degree of family affection. The life at Fairoaks was uncommonly dull to a man who had the entrée of half the houses in London, and was in the habit of making his bow in three or four drawing-rooms of a night. A dinner with Doctor Portman or a neighbouring squire now and then; a dreary rubber at backgammon with the widow, who did her utmost to amuse him—these were the chief of his pleasures. He used to long for the arrival of the bag with the letters, and he read every word of the evening paper. He doctored himself too, assiduously—a course of quiet living would suit him well, he thought, after the London banquets. He dressed himself laboriously every morning and afternoon: he took regular exercise up and down the terrace walk. Thus, with his cane, his toilet, his medicine chest, his backgammon-box, and his newspaper, this worthy and worldly philosopher fenced himself against ennui; and if he did not improve each shining hour, like the bees by the widow's garden-wall, Major Pendennis made one hour after another pass as he could; and rendered his captivity just tolerable.[1]

Pen sometimes took the box at backgammon of a night, or would listen to his mother's simple music of summer evenings—but he was very restless and wretched in spite of all : and has been known to be up before the early daylight even, and down at a carp-pond in Clavering Park, a dreary pool with innumerable whispering rushes and green alders, where a milkmaid drowned herself in the baronet's grandfather's time, and her ghost was said to walk still. But Pen did not drown himself, as perhaps his mother fancied might be his intention. He liked to go and fish there, and think and think at leisure, as the float quivered in the little eddies of the pond, and the fish flapped about him. If he got a bite he was excited enough : and in this way occasionally brought home carps, tenches, and eels, which the major cooked in the Continental fashion.

By this pond, and under a tree, which was his favourite resort, Pen composed a number of poems suitable to his circumstances—over which verses he blushed in after-days, wondering how he could ever have invented such rubbish. And, as for the tree, why, it is in a hollow of this very tree, where he used to put his tin box of ground-bait, and other fishing commodities, that he afterwards—but we are advancing matters. Suffice it to say, he wrote poems and relieved himself very much. When a man's grief or passion is at this point, it may be loud, but it is not very severe. When a gentleman is cudgelling his brain to find any rhyme for sorrow, besides borrow and to-morrow, his woes are nearer at an end than he thinks for. So were Pen's. He had his hot and cold fits, his days of sullenness and peevishness, and of blank resignation and despondency, and occasional mad paroxysms of rage and longing, in which fits Rebecca would be saddled and galloped fiercely about the country, or into Chatteris, her rider gesticulating wildly on her back, and astonishing carters and turnpikemen as he passed, crying out the name of the false one.

Mr. Foker became a very frequent and welcome visitor at Fairoaks during this period, where his good spirits and oddities always amused the major and Pendennis, while they astonished the widow and little Laura not a little. His tandem made a great sensation in Clavering market-place, where he upset a market-stall, and cut Mrs. Pybus's poodle over the shaven quarters, and drank a glass of raspberry bitters at the 'Clavering Arms.' All the society in

the little place heard who he was, and looked out his name in their *Peerages*. He was so young, and their books so old, that his name did not appear in many of their volumes ; and his mamma, now quite an antiquated lady, figured amongst the progeny of the Earl of Rosherville, as Lady Agnes Milton still. But his name, wealth, and honourable lineage were speedily known about Clavering, where you may be sure that poor Pen's little transaction with the Chatteris actress was also pretty freely discussed.

Looking at the little old town of Clavering St. Mary from the London road as it runs by the lodge at Fairoaks, and seeing the rapid and shining Brawl winding down from the town and skirting the woods of Clavering Park, and the ancient church tower and peaked roofs of the houses rising up amongst the trees and old walls, behind which swells a fair background of sunshiny hills that stretch from Clavering westwards towards the sea—the place appears to be so cheery and comfortable that many a traveller's heart must have yearned towards it from the coach-top, and he must have thought that it was in such a calm friendly nook he would like to shelter at the end of life's struggle. Tom Smith, who used to drive the 'Alacrity' coach, would often point to a tree near the river, from which a fine view of the church and town was commanded, and inform his companion on the box that 'artises come and take hoff the church from that there tree. It was a habbey once, sir'—and, indeed, a pretty view it is, which I recommend to Mr. Stanfield or Mr. Roberts, for their next tour.*

Like Constantinople seen from the Bosphorus ; like Mrs. Rougemont viewed in her box from the opposite side of the house ; like many an object which we pursue in life, and admire before we have attained it ; Clavering is rather prettier at a distance than it is on a closer acquaintance. The town, so cheerful of aspect a few furlongs off, looks very blank and dreary. Except on market days there is nobody in the streets. The clack of a pair of pattens echoes through half the place, and you may hear the creaking of the rusty old ensign at the 'Clavering Arms,' without being disturbed by any other noise. There has not been a ball in the Assembly Rooms since the Clavering volunteers gave one to their colonel, the old Sir Francis

Clavering; and the stables which once held a great part of that brilliant but defunct regiment, are now cheerless and empty, except on Thursdays, when the farmers put up there, and their tilted carts and gigs make a feeble show of liveliness in the place, or on Petty Sessions, when the magistrates attend in what used to be the old card-room.

On the south side of the market rises up the church, with its great grey towers, of which the sun illuminates the delicate carving; deepening the shadows of the huge buttresses, and gilding the glittering windows and flaming vanes. The image of the patroness of the church was wrenched out of the porch many centuries ago: such of the statues of saints as were within reach of stones and hammer at that period of pious demolition are maimed and headless, and of those who were out of fire, only Dr. Portman knows the names and history, for his curate, Smirke, is not much of an antiquarian, and Mr. Simcoe (husband of the Honourable Mrs. Simcoe), incumbent and architect of the chapel of ease in the lower town, thinks them the abomination of desolation.

The Rectory is a stout, broad-shouldered brick house, of the reign of Anne. It communicates with the church and market by different gates, and stands at the opening of Yew-tree Lane, where the Grammar School (Rev. —— Wapshot) is; Yew-tree Cottage (Miss Flather); the butcher's slaughtering-house, an old barn or brew-house of the abbey times, and the Misses Finucane's establishment for young ladies. The two schools had their pews in the loft on each side of the organ, until the Abbey Church getting rather empty, through the falling off of the congregation, who were inveigled to the heresy-shop in the lower town, the doctor induced the Misses Finucane to bring their pretty little flock downstairs; and the young ladies' bonnets make a tolerable show in the rather vacant aisles. Nobody is in the great pew of the Clavering family, except the statues of defunct baronets and their ladies: there is Sir Poyntz Clavering, knight and baronet, kneeling in a square beard opposite his wife in a ruff: a very fat lady, the Dame Rebecca Clavering, in alto-rilievo, is borne up to heaven by two little blue-veined angels, who seem to have a severe task—and so forth. How well in after-life Pen remembered those effigies, and how often in youth he scanned them as the doctor was grumbling the sermon

from the pulpit, and Smirke's mild head and forehead curl peered over the great Prayer-book in the desk!

The Fairoaks folks were constant at the old church; their servants had a pew, so had the doctor's, so had Wapshot's, and those of Misses Finucane's establishment, three maids and a very nice-looking young man in a livery. The Wapshot family were numerous and faithful. Glanders and his children regularly came to church: so did one of the apothecaries. Mrs. Pybus went, turn and turn about, to the Low Town Church, and to the Abbey: the Charity School and their families of course came; Wapshot's boys made a good cheerful noise, scuffling with their feet as they marched into the church and up the organ-loft stair, and blowing their noses a good deal during the service. To be brief, the congregation looked as decent as might be in these bad times. The Abbey Church was furnished with a magnificent screen, and many hatchments and heraldic tombstones. The doctor spent a great part of his income in beautifying his darling place; he had endowed it with a superb painted window, bought in the Netherlands, and an organ grand enough for a cathedral.

But in spite of organ and window, in consequence of the latter very likely, which had come out of a Papistical place of worship and was blazoned all over with idolatry, Clavering New Church prospered scandalously in the teeth of orthodoxy; and many of the doctor's congregation deserted to Mr. Simcoe and the honourable woman his wife. Their efforts had thinned the very Ebenezer hard by them, which building before Simcoe's advent used to be so full, that you could see the backs of the congregation squeezing out of the arched windows thereof. Mr. Simcoe's tracts fluttered into the doors of all the doctor's cottages, and were taken as greedily as honest Mrs. Portman's soup, with the quality of which the graceless people found fault. With the folks at the ribbon factory situated by the weir on the Brawl side, and round which the Low Town had grown, orthodoxy could make no way at all. Quiet Miss Mira was put out of court by impetuous Mrs. Simcoe and her female aides de camp. Ah, it was a hard burthen for the doctor's lady to bear, to behold her husband's congregation dwindling away; to give the precedence on the few occasions when they met to a notorious Low Churchman's wife who was the daughter of an Irish peer; to know that

there was a party in Clavering, their own town of Clavering, on which her doctor spent a great deal more than his professional income, who held him up to odium because he played a rubber at whist; and pronounced him to be a heathen because he went to the play. In her grief she besought him to give up the play and the rubber—indeed, they could scarcely get a table now, so dreadful was the outcry against the sport—but the doctor declared that he would do what he thought right, and what the great and good George III did (whose chaplain he had been): and as for giving up whist because those silly folks cried out against it, he would play dummy to the end of his days with his wife and Mira, rather than yield to their despicable persecutions.

Of the two families, owners of the factory (which had spoiled the Brawl as a trout-stream and brought all the mischief into the town), the senior partner, Mr. Rolt, went to Ebenezer; the junior, Mr. Barker, to the New Church. In a word, people quarrelled in this little place a great deal more than neighbours do in London; and in the Book Club, which the prudent and conciliating Pendennis had set up, and which ought to have been a neutral territory, they bickered so much that nobody scarcely was ever seen in the reading-room, except Smirke, who, though he kept up a faint amity with the Simcoe faction, had still a taste for magazines and light worldly literature; and old Glanders, whose white head and grizzly moustache might be seen at the window; and, of course, little Mrs. Pybus, who looked at everybody's letters as the post brought them (for the Clavering reading-room, as everyone knows, used to be held at Baker's Library, London Street, formerly Hog Lane), and read every advertisement in the paper.

It may be imagined how great a sensation was created in this amiable little community when the news reached it of Mr. Pen's love-passages at Chatteris. It was carried from house to house, and formed the subject of talk at high-church, low-church, and no-church tables; it was canvassed by the Misses Finucane and their teachers, and very likely debated by the young ladies in the dormitories, for what we know; Wapshot's big boys had their version of the story, and eyed Pen curiously as he sat in his pew at church, or raised the finger of scorn at him as he passed through Chatteris. They always hated him and called

him Lord Pendennis, because he did not wear corduroys as they did, and rode a horse, and gave himself the airs of a buck.

And, if the truth must be told, it was Mrs. Portman herself who was the chief narrator of the story of Pen's loves. Whatever tales this candid woman heard, she was sure to impart them to her neighbours; and after she had been put into possession of Pen's secret by the little scandal at Chatteris, poor Doctor Portman knew that it would next day be about the parish of which he was the rector. And so indeed it was; the whole society there had the legend—at the news-room, at the milliner's, at the shoe-shop, and the general warehouse at the corner of the market; at Mrs. Pybus's, at the Glanders', at the Honourable Mrs. Simcoe's soirée, at the factory; nay, through the mill itself the tale was current in a few hours, and young Arthur Pendennis's madness was in every mouth.

All Doctor Portman's acquaintances barked out upon him when he walked the street the next day. The poor divine knew that his Betsy was the author of the rumour, and groaned in spirit. Well, well, it must have come in a day or two, and it was as well that the town should have the real story. What the Clavering folks thought of Mrs. Pendennis for spoiling her son, and of that precocious young rascal of an Arthur, for daring to propose to a play-actress, need not be told here. If pride exists amongst any folks in our country, and assuredly we have enough of it, there is no pride more deep-seated than that of twopenny old gentlewomen in small towns. 'Gracious goodness,' the cry was, 'how infatuated the mother is about that pert and headstrong boy who gives himself the airs of a *lord* on his *blood-horse*, and for whom *our* society is not good enough, and who would marry an odious painted actress off a booth, where very likely he wants to rant himself. If dear good Mr. Pendennis had been alive this scandal would never have happened.'

No more it would, very likely, nor should we have been occupied in narrating Pen's history. It was true that he gave himself airs to the Clavering folks. Naturally haughty and frank, their cackle and small talk and small dignities bored him, and he showed a contempt which he could not conceal. The doctor and the curate were the only people Pen cared for in the place—even Mrs. Portman shared in the

general distrust of him, and of his mother, the widow, who kept herself aloof from the village society, and was sneered at accordingly, because she tried, forsooth, to keep her head up with the great county families. She, indeed! Mrs. Barker at the factory has four times the butcher's meat that goes up to Fairoaks, with all their fine airs.

Etc. etc. etc.: let the reader fill up these details according to his liking and experience of village scandal. They will suffice to show how it was that a good woman, occupied solely in doing her duty to her neighbour and her children, and an honest, brave lad, impetuous, and full of good, and wishing well to every mortal alive, found enemies and detractors amongst people to whom they were superior, and to whom they had never done anything like harm. The Clavering curs were yelping all round the house of Fairoaks, and delighted to pull Pen down.

Doctor Portman and Smirke were both cautious of informing the widow of the constant outbreak of calumny which was pursuing poor Pen, though Glanders, who was a friend of the house, kept him *au courant*. It may be imagined what his indignation was: was there any man in the village whom he could call to account? Presently some wags began to chalk up 'Fotheringay for ever!' and other sarcastic allusions to late transactions at Fairoaks' gate. Another brought a large playbill from Chatteris, and wafered it there one night. On one occasion Pen, riding through the Lower Town, fancied he heard the factory boys jeer him; and finally, going through the doctor's gate into the churchyard, where some of Wapshot's boys were lounging, the biggest of them, a young gentleman about twenty years of age, son of a neighbouring small squire, who lived in the doubtful capacity of parlour-boarder with Mr. Wapshot, flung himself into a theatrical attitude near a newly-made grave, and began repeating Hamlet's verses over Ophelia, with a hideous leer at Pen.

The young fellow was so enraged that he rushed at Hobnell major with a shriek very much resembling an oath, cut him furiously across the face with the riding-whip which he carried, flung it away, calling upon the cowardly villain to defend himself, and in another minute knocked the bewildered young ruffian into the grave which was just waiting for a different lodger.

Then, with his fists clenched, and his face quivering with

passion and indignation, he roared out to Mr. Hobnell's gaping companions, to know if any of the blackguards would come on? But they held back with a growl, and retreated, as Doctor Portman came up to his wicket, and Mr. Hobnell, with his nose and lip bleeding piteously, emerged from the grave.

Pen, looking death and defiance at the lads who retreated towards their side of the churchyard, walked back again through the doctor's wicket, and was interrogated by that gentleman. The young fellow was so agitated he could scarcely speak. His voice broke into a sob as he answered, 'The —— coward insulted me, sir,' he said; and the doctor passed over the oath, and respected the emotion of the honest suffering young heart.

Pendennis the elder, who, like a real man of the world, had a proper and constant dread of the opinion of his neighbour, was prodigiously annoyed by the absurd little tempest which was blowing in Chatteris, and tossing about Master Pen's reputation. Doctor Portman and Captain Glanders had to support the charges of the whole Chatteris society against the young reprobate, who was looked upon as a monster of crime. Pen did not say anything about the churchyard scuffle at home; but went over to Baymouth, and took counsel with his friend Harry Foker, Esq., who drove over his drag presently to the 'Clavering Arms,' whence he sent Stoopid with a note to Thomas Hobnell, Esq., at the Rev. J. Wapshot's, and a civil message to ask when he should wait upon that gentleman.

Stoopid brought back word that the note had been opened by Mr. Hobnell, and read to half a dozen of the big boys, on whom it seemed to make a great impression; and that, after consulting together, and laughing, Mr. Hobnell said he would send an answer 'arter arternoon school, which the bell was a-ringing: and Mr. Wapshot, he came out in his master's gownd.' Stoopid was learned in academical costume, having attended Mr. Foker at St. Boniface.

Mr. Foker went out to see the curiosities of Clavering meanwhile; but not having a taste for architecture, Doctor Portman's fine church did not engage his attention much, and he pronounced the tower to be as mouldy as an old Stilton cheese. He walked down the street and looked at

'DOES ANYBODY WANT MORE?'

[illegible] window of the [illegible] at that gentleman [illegible] [illegible] Madame [illegible]

workwoman in her [illegible] [illegible] very long [illegible] the town and [illegible]

the few shops there; he saw Captain Glanders at the window of the reading-room, and having taken a good stare at that gentleman, he wagged his head at him in token of satisfaction; he inquired the price of meat at the butcher's with an air of the greatest interest, and asked 'when was next killing day?' he flattened his little nose against Madame Fribsby's window to see if haply there was a pretty

workwoman in her premises; but there was no face more comely than the doll's or dummy's wearing the French cap in the window, only that of Madame Fribsby herself, dimly visible in the parlour, reading a novel. That object was not of sufficient interest to keep Mr. Foker very long in contemplation, and so, having exhausted the town and the inn stables, in which there were no cattle, save the single old pair of posters that earned a scanty livelihood

by transporting the gentry round about to the county dinners, Mr. Foker was giving himself up to ennui entirely when a messenger from Mr. Hobnell was at length announced.

It was no other than Mr. Wapshot himself, who came with an air of great indignation, and, holding Pen's missive in his hand, asked Mr. Foker 'how dared he bring such an unchristian message as a challenge to a boy of his school?'

In fact, Pen had written a note to his adversary of the day before, telling him that if after the chastisement which his insolence richly deserved, he felt inclined to ask the reparation which was usually given amongst gentlemen, Mr. Arthur Pendennis's friend, Mr. Henry Foker, was empowered to make any arrangements for the satisfaction of Mr. Hobnell.

'And so he sent *you* with the answer—did he, sir?' Mr. Foker said, surveying the schoolmaster in his black coat and clerical costume.

'If he had accepted this wicked challenge, I should have flogged him,' Mr. Wapshot said, and gave Mr. Foker a glance which seemed to say, 'and I should like very much to flog you too.'

'Uncommon kind of you, sir, I'm sure,' said Pen's emissary. 'I told my principal that I didn't think the other man would fight,' he continued, with a great air of dignity. 'He prefers being flogged to fighting, sir, I dare say. May I offer you any refreshment, Mr. —— ? I haven't the advantage of your name.'

'My name is Wapshot, sir, and I am master of the Grammar School of this town, sir,' cried the other: 'and I want no refreshment, sir, I thank you, and have no desire to make your acquaintance, sir.'

'I didn't seek yours, sir, I'm sure,' replied Mr. Foker. 'In affairs of this sort, you see, I think it is a pity that the clergy should be called in, but there's no accounting for tastes, sir.'

'I think it's a pity that boys should talk about committing murder, sir, as lightly as you do,' roared the schoolmaster; 'and if I had you in my school——'

'I dare say you would teach me better, sir,' Mr. Foker said, with a bow. 'Thank you, sir. I've finished my education, sir, and ain't a-going back to school, sir—when

I do, I'll remember your kind offer, sir. John, show this gentleman downstairs—and, of course, as Mr. Hobnell likes being thrashed, we can have no objection, sir, and we shall be very happy to accommodate him, whenever he comes our way.'

And with this, the young fellow bowed the elder gentleman out of the room, and sat down and wrote a note off to Pen, in which he informed the latter, that Mr. Hobnell was not disposed to fight, and proposed to put up with the caning which Pen had administered to him.

CHAPTER XVI

WHICH CONCLUDES THE FIRST PART OF THIS HISTORY

PEN'S conduct in this business of course was soon made public, and angered his friend Doctor Portman not a little; while it only amused Major Pendennis. As for the good Mrs. Pendennis, she was almost distracted when she heard of the squabble, and of Pen's unchristian behaviour. All sorts of wretchedness, discomfort, crime, annoyance, seemed to come out of this transaction in which the luckless boy had engaged: and she longed more than ever to see him out of Chatteris for a while—anywhere removed from the woman who had brought him into so much trouble.

Pen, when remonstrated with by this fond parent, and angrily rebuked by the doctor for his violence and ferocious intentions, took the matter *au grand sérieux*, with the happy conceit and gravity of youth: said[1] that he would permit no man to insult him upon this head without vindicating his own honour, and appealing,[2] asked whether he could have acted otherwise as a gentleman, than as he did in resenting the outrage offered to him, and in offering satisfaction to the person chastised?

'*Vous allez trop vite*, my good sir,' said the uncle, rather puzzled, for he had been indoctrinating his nephew with

some of his own notions upon the point of honour—old-world notions savouring of the camp and pistol a great deal more than our soberer opinions of the present day—'between men of the world I don't say; but between two schoolboys, this sort of thing is ridiculous, my dear boy—perfectly ridiculous.'

'It is extremely wicked, and unlike my son,' said Mrs. Pendennis, with tears in her eyes; and bewildered with the obstinacy of the boy.

Pen kissed her, and said with great pomposity, 'Women, dear mother, don't understand these matters—I put myself into Foker's hands—I had no other course to pursue.'

Major Pendennis grinned and shrugged his shoulders. The young ones were certainly making great progress, he thought. Mrs. Pendennis declared that that Foker was a wicked horrid little wretch, and was sure that he would lead her dear boy into mischief, if Pen went to the same college with him. 'I have a great mind not to let him go at all,' she said: and only that she remembered that the lad's father had always destined him for the college in which he had had his own brief education, very likely the fond mother would have put a veto upon his going to the University.

That he was to go, and at the next October term, had been arranged between all the authorities who presided over the lad's welfare. Foker had promised to introduce him to the right set; and Major Pendennis laid great store upon Pen's introduction into college life and society by this admirable young gentleman. 'Mr. Foker knows the very best young men now at the University,' the major said, 'and Pen will form acquaintances there who will be of the greatest advantage through life to him. The young Marquis of Plinlimmon is there, eldest son of the Duke of St. David's—Lord Magnus Charters is there, Lord Runnymede's son; and a first cousin of Mr. Foker (Lady Runnymede, my dear, was Lady Agatha Milton, you of course remember), Lady Agnes will certainly invite him to Logwood; and far from being alarmed at his intimacy with her son, who is a singular and humorous, but most prudent and amiable young man, to whom, I am sure, we are under every obligation for his admirable conduct in the affair of the Fotheringay marriage, I look upon it as one of the very luckiest things which could have happened to Pen, that he

should have formed an intimacy with this most amusing young gentleman.'

Helen sighed; she supposed the major knew best. Mr. Foker had been very kind in the wretched business with Miss Costigan, certainly, and she was grateful to him. But she could not feel otherwise than a dim presentiment of evil; and all these quarrels, and riots, and worldliness, scared her about the fate of her boy.

Doctor Portman was decidedly of opinion that Pen should go to college. He hoped the lad would read, and have a moderate indulgence of the best society too. He was of opinion that Pen would distinguish himself: Smirke spoke very highly of his proficiency: the doctor himself had heard him construe, and thought he acquitted himself remarkably well. That he should go out of Chatteris was a great point, at any rate; and Pen, who was distracted from his private grief by the various rows and troubles which had risen round about him, gloomily said he would obey.

There were assizes, races, and the entertainments and the flux of company consequent upon them, at Chatteris, during a part of the months of August and September, and Miss Fotheringay still continued to act, and take farewell of the audiences at the Chatteris theatre during that time. Nobody seemed to be particularly affected by her presence, or her announced departure, except those persons whom we have named; nor could the polite county folks, who had houses in London, and very likely admired the Fotheringay prodigiously in the capital, when they had been taught to do so by the fashion which set in in her favour, find anything remarkable in the actress performing on the little Chatteris boards. Many a genius and many a quack, for that matter, has met with a similar fate before and since Miss Costigan's time. This honest woman meanwhile bore up against the public neglect, and any other crosses or vexations which she might have in life, with her usual equanimity; and ate, drank, acted, slept, with that regularity and comfort which belongs to people of her temperament. What a deal of grief, care, and other harmful excitement, does a healthy dullness and cheerful insensibility avoid! Nor do I mean to say that Virtue is not Virtue because it is never tempted to go astray; only that dullness is a much finer gift than we give it credit for

being, and that some people are very lucky whom Nature has endowed with a good store of that great anodyne.

Pen used to go drearily in and out from the play at Chatteris during this season, and pretty much according to his fancy. His proceedings tortured his mother not a little, and her anxiety would have led her often to interfere, had not the major constantly checked, and at the same time encouraged her; for the wily man of the world fancied he saw that a favourable turn had occurred in Pen's malady. It was the violent efflux of versification, among other symptoms, which gave Pen's guardian and physician satisfaction. He might be heard spouting verses in the shrubbery walks, or muttering them between his teeth as he sat with the home party of evenings. One day prowling about the house in Pen's absence, the major found a great book full of verses in the lad's study. They were in English, and in Latin; quotations from the classic authors were given in the scholastic manner in the foot-notes. He can't be very bad, wisely thought the Pall-Mall philosopher: and he made Pen's mother remark (not, perhaps, without a secret feeling of disappointment, for she loved romance like other soft women), that the young gentleman during the last fortnight came home quite hungry to dinner at night, and also showed a very decent appetite at the breakfast-table in the morning. 'Gad, I wish I could,' said the major, thinking ruefully of his dinner pills. 'The boy begins to sleep well, depend upon that.' It was cruel, but it was true.

Having no other soul to confide in[3]—the lad's friendship for the curate redoubled, or rather, he was never tired of having Smirke for a listener on that one subject. What is a lover without a confidant? Pen employed Mr. Smirke, as Corydon does the elm-tree, to cut out his mistress's name upon. He made him echo with the name of the beautiful Amaryllis. When men have left off playing the tune, they do not care much for the pipe; but Pen thought he had a great friendship for Smirke, because he could sigh out his loves and griefs into his tutor's ears; and Smirke had his own reasons for always being ready at the lad's call.[4]

The poor curate was naturally very much dismayed at the contemplated departure of his pupil. When Arthur should go, Smirke's occupation and delight would go too.

What pretext could he find for a daily visit to Fairoaks, and that kind word or glance from the lady there, which was as necessary to the curate as the frugal dinner which Madame Fribsby served him? Arthur gone, he would only be allowed to make visits like any other acquaintance: little Laura could not accommodate him by learning the Catechism more than once a week: he had curled himself like ivy round Fairoaks: he pined at the thought that he must lose his hold of the place. Should he speak his mind and go down on his knees to the widow? He thought over any indications in her behaviour which flattered his hopes. She had praised his sermon three weeks before: she had thanked him exceedingly for his present of a melon, for a small dinner-party which Mrs. Pendennis gave: she said she should always be grateful to him for his kindness to Arthur: and when he declared that there were no bounds to his love and affection for that dear boy, she had certainly replied in a romantic manner, indicating her own strong gratitude and regard to all her son's friends. Should he speak out?—or should he delay? If he spoke and she refused him, it was awful to think that the gate of Fairoaks might be shut upon him for ever—and within that door lay all the world for Mr. Smirke.

Thus, O friendly readers, we see how every man in the world has his own private griefs and business, by which he is more cast down or occupied than by the affairs or sorrows of any other person. While Mrs. Pendennis is disquieting herself about losing her son, and that anxious hold she has had of him, as long as he has remained in the mother's nest, whence he is about to take flight into the great world beyond—while the major's great soul chafes and frets, inwardly vexed as he thinks what great parties are going on in London, and that he might be sunning himself in the glances of dukes and duchesses, but for those cursed affairs which keep him in a wretched little country hole—while Pen is tossing between his passion and a more agreeable sensation, unacknowledged yet, but swaying him considerably, namely, his longing to see the world—Mr. Smirke has a private care watching at his bedside, and sitting behind him on his pony; and is no more satisfied than the rest of us. How lonely we are in the world! how selfish and secret, everybody! You and your wife have pressed the same pillow for forty years and fancy your-

selves united.—Psha, does she cry out when you have the gout, or do you lie awake when she has the toothache? Your artless daughter, seemingly all innocence and devoted to her mamma and her piano-lesson, is thinking of neither, but of the young lieutenant with whom she danced at the last ball—the honest frank boy just returned from school is secretly speculating upon the money you will give him, and the debts he owes the tart-man. The old grandmother crooning in the corner and bound to another world within a few months, has some business or cares which are quite private and her own—very likely she is thinking of fifty years back, and that night when she made such an impression, and danced a cotillon with the captain before your father proposed for her: or, what a silly little overrated creature your wife is, and how absurdly you are infatuated about her—and, as for your wife—O philosophic reader, answer and say—Do you tell *her* all? Ah, sir—a distinct universe walks about under your hat and under mine—all things in nature are different to each—the woman we look at has not the same features, the dish we eat from has not the same taste to the one and the other—you and I are but a pair of infinite isolations, with some fellow-islands a little more or less near to us.* Let us return, however, to the solitary Smirke.

Smirke had one confidante for his passion—that most injudicious woman, Madame Fribsby. How she became Madame Fribsby, nobody knows: she had left Clavering to go to a milliner's in London as Miss Fribsby—she pretended that she had got the rank in Paris during her residence in that city. But how could the French king, were he ever so much disposed, give her any such title? We shall not inquire into this mystery, however. Suffice to say, she went away from home a bouncing young lass; she returned a rather elderly character, with a Madonna front and a melancholy countenance—bought the late Mrs. Harbottle's business for a song—took her elderly mother to live with her; was very good to the poor, was constant at church, and had the best of characters. But there was no one in all Clavering, not Mrs. Portman herself, who read so many novels as Madame Fribsby. She had plenty of time for this amusement, for, in truth, very few people besides the folks at the Rectory and Fairoaks employed her; and by a perpetual perusal of such works (which were by no

THE CURATE'S CONFIDANTE

means so moral or edifying in the days of which we write as they are at present), she had got to be so absurdly sentimental, that in her eyes life was nothing but an immense love-match ; and she never could see two people together, but she fancied they were dying for one another.

On the day after Mrs. Pendennis's visit to the curate, which we have recorded many pages back, Madame Fribsby settled in her mind that Mr. Smirke must be in love with the widow, and did everything in her power to encourage this passion on both sides. Mrs. Pendennis she very seldom saw, indeed, except in public, and in her pew at church. That lady had very little need of millinery, or made most of her own dresses and caps ; but on the rare occasions when Madame Fribsby received visits from Mrs. Pendennis, or paid her respects at Fairoaks, she never failed to entertain the widow with praises of the curate, pointing out what an angelical man he was, how gentle, how studious, how lonely ; and she would wonder that no lady would take pity upon him.

Helen laughed at these sentimental remarks, and wondered that madame herself did not compassionate her lodger, and console him. Madame Fribsby shook her Madonna front. '*Mong cure a boco souffare,*' she said, laying her hand on the part she designated as her *cure.* '*Il est more en Espang,** *madame,*' she said, with a sigh. She was proud of her intimacy with the French language, and spoke it with more volubility than correctness. Mrs. Pendennis did not care to penetrate the secrets of this wounded heart : except to her few intimates she was a reserved and it may be a very proud woman ; she looked upon her son's tutor merely as an attendant on that young prince, to be treated with respect as a clergyman certainly, but with proper dignity as a dependent on the house of Pendennis. Nor were madame's constant allusions to the curate particularly agreeable to her. It required a very ingenious sentimental turn indeed to find out that the widow had a secret regard for Mr. Smirke, to which pernicious error, however, Madame Fribsby persisted in holding.

Her lodger was very much more willing to talk on this subject with his soft-hearted landlady. Every time after that she praised the curate to Mrs. Pendennis, she came away from the latter with the notion that the widow herself had been praising him. '*Être soul au monde est bien*

ouneeyong,' she would say, glancing up at a print of a French carbineer in a green coat and brass cuirasse which decorated her apartment—' Depend upon it, when Master Pendennis goes to college his ma will find herself very lonely. She is quite young yet.—You wouldn't suppose her to be five-and-twenty. *Monsieur le Cury, song cure est touchy—j'ong suis sure—Je conny cela biang—Ally, Monsieur Smirke.*'

He softly blushed; he sighed; he hoped; he feared; he doubted; he sometimes yielded to the delightful idea—his pleasure was to sit in Madame Fribsby's apartment, and talk upon the subject, where, as the greater part of the conversation was carried on in French by the milliner, and her old mother was deaf, that retired old individual (who had once been a housekeeper, wife and widow of a butler in the Clavering family) could understand scarce one syllable of their talk.

When Major Pendennis announced to his nephew's tutor that the young fellow would go to college in October, and that Mr. Smirke's valuable services would no longer be needful to his pupil, for which services the major, who spoke as grandly as a lord, professed himself exceedingly grateful, and besought Mr. Smirke to command his interests in any way—[5] the curate felt that the critical moment was come for him, and was racked and tortured by those severe pangs which the occasion warranted.[6]

And now that Arthur was going away[7] Helen's heart was rather softened towards the curate, from whom, perhaps divining his intentions, she had shrunk hitherto: she bethought her how very polite Mr. Smirke had been; how he had gone on messages for her; how he had brought books and copied music; how he had taught Laura so many things, and given her so many kind presents, her heart smote her on account of her ingratitude towards the curate; —so much so, that one afternoon when he came down from study with Pen, and was hankering about the hall previous to his departure, she went out and shook hands with him with rather a blushing face, and begged him to come into her drawing-room, where she said they now never saw him. And as there was to be rather a good dinner that day, she invited Mr. Smirke to partake of it; and we may be sure that he was too happy to accept such a delightful summons.

Helen [8] was exceedingly kind and gracious to Mr. Smirke

during dinner, redoubling her attentions, perhaps because Major Pendennis was very high and reserved with his nephew's tutor. When Pendennis asked Smirke to drink wine, he addressed him as if he was a Sovereign speaking to a petty retainer, in a manner so condescending, that even Pen laughed at it, although quite ready, for his part, to be as conceited as most young men are.

But Smirke did not care for the impertinences of the major so long as he had his hostess's kind behaviour; and he passed a delightful time by her side at table, exerting all his powers of conversation to please her, talking in a manner both clerical and worldly, about the Fancy Bazaar, and the Great Missionary Meeting, about the last new novel, and the bishop's excellent sermon—about the fashionable parties in London, an account of which he read in the newspapers—in fine, he neglected no art, by which a college divine who has both sprightly and serious talents, a taste for the genteel, an irreproachable conduct, and a susceptible heart, will try and make himself agreeable to the person on whom he has fixed his affections.

Major Pendennis came yawning out of the dining-room very soon after his sister and little Laura had left the apartment.[9]

Now Arthur, flushed with a good deal of pride at the privilege of having the keys of the cellar, and remembering that a very few more dinners would probably take place which he and his dear friend Smirke could share, had brought up a liberal supply of claret for the company's drinking, and when the elders with little Laura left him, he and the curate began to pass the wine very freely.

One bottle speedily yielded up the ghost, another shed more than half its blood, before the two topers had been much more than half an hour together—Pen, with a hollow laugh and voice, had drunk off one bumper to the falsehood of women, and had said sardonically, that wine at any rate was a mistress who never deceived, and was sure to give a man a welcome.

Smirke gently said that he knew for his part some women who were all truth and tenderness; and casting up his eyes towards the ceiling, and heaving a sigh as if evoking some being dear and unmentionable, he took up his glass and drained it, and the rosy liquor began to suffuse his face.

Pen trolled over some verses he had been making that morning, in which he informed himself that the woman who had slighted his passion could not be worthy to win it: that he was awaking from love's mad fever, and, of course, under these circumstances, proceeded to leave her, and to quit a heartless deceiver: that a name which had one day been famous in the land, might again be heard in it: and, that though he never should be the happy and careless boy he was but a few months since, or his heart be what it had been ere passion had filled it and grief had wellnigh killed it; that though to him personally death was as welcome as life, and that he would not hesitate to part with the latter, but for the love of one kind being whose happiness depended on his own,—yet he hoped to show he was a man worthy of his race, and that one day the false one should be brought to know how great was the treasure and noble the heart which she had flung away. Pen, we say, who was a very excitable person, rolled out these verses in his rich sweet voice, which trembled with emotion whilst our young poet spoke. He had a trick of blushing when in this excited state, and his large and honest grey eyes also exhibited proofs of a sensibility so genuine, hearty, and manly, that Miss Costigan, if she had a heart, must needs have softened towards him; and very likely she was, as he said, altogether unworthy of the affection which he lavished upon her.

The sentimental Smirke was caught by the emotion which agitated his young friend. He grasped Pen's hand over the dessert dishes and wine-glasses. He said the verses were beautiful: that Pen was a poet, a great poet, and likely by Heaven's permission to run a great career in the world. 'Go on and prosper, dear Arthur,' he cried: 'the wounds under which at present you suffer are only temporary, and the very grief you endure will cleanse and strengthen your heart. I have always prophesied the greatest and brightest things of you, as soon as you have corrected some failings and weaknesses of character, which at present belong to you. But you will get over these, my boy, you will get over these; and when you are famous and celebrated, as I know you will be, will you remember your old tutor and the happy early days of your youth?'

Pen swore he would: with another shake of the hand

across the glasses and apricots. 'I shall never forget how kind you have been to me, Smirke,' he said. 'I don't know what I should have done without you. You are my best friend.'

'Am I *really*, Arthur ?' said Smirke, looking through his spectacles ; and his heart began to beat so that he thought Pen must almost hear it throbbing.

'My best friend, my friend *for ever*,' Pen said. 'God bless you, old boy,' and he drank up the last glass of the second bottle of the famous wine which his father had laid in, which his uncle had bought, which Lord Levant had imported, and which now, like a slave indifferent, was ministering pleasure to its present owner, and giving its young master delectation.

'We'll have another bottle, old boy,' Pen said, 'by Jove we will. Hurray !—claret goes for nothing. My uncle was telling me that he saw Sheridan drink five bottles at Brookes's,* besides a bottle of maraschino. This is some of the finest wine in England, he says. So it is, by Jove. There's nothing like it. *Nunc vino** *pellite curas—cras ingens iterabimus æquor*,—fill your glass, old Smirke, a hogshead of it won't do you any harm.' And Mr. Pen began to sing the drinking song out of *Der Freischütz*.* The dining-room windows were open, and his mother was softly pacing on the lawn outside, while little Laura was looking at the sunset. The sweet fresh notes of the boy's voice came to the widow. It cheered her kind heart to hear him sing.

'You—you are taking too much wine, Arthur,' Mr. Smirke said softly—'you are exciting yourself.'

'No,' said Pen, 'women give headaches, but this don't. Fill your glass, old fellow, and let's drink—I say, Smirke, my boy—let's drink to her—*your* her, I mean, not mine, for whom I swear I'll care no more—no, not a penny—no, not a fig—no, not a glass of wine. Tell us about the lady, Smirke ; I've often seen you sighing about her.'

'Oh !' said Smirke—and his beautiful cambric shirt-front and glistening studs heaved with the emotion which agitated his gentle and suffering bosom.

'Oh—what a sigh !' Pen cried, growing very hilarious : 'fill, my boy, and drink the toast ; you can't refuse a toast, no gentleman refuses a toast. Here's her health, and good luck to you, and may she soon be Mrs. Smirke.'

'*Do* you say so?' Smirke said, all of a tremble. 'Do you really say so, Arthur?'

'Say so; of course, I say so. Down with it. Here's Mrs. Smirke's good health: Hip, hip, hurray!'

Smirke convulsively gulped down his glass of wine, and Pen waved his over his head, cheering so as to make his mother and Laura wonder on the lawn, and his uncle, who was dozing over the paper in the drawing-room, start, and say to himself, 'That boy's drinking too much.' Smirke put down the glass.

'I accept the omen,' gasped out the blushing curate. 'Oh, my dear Arthur, you—you know her——'

'What—Mira Portman? I wish you joy: she's got a dev'lish large waist; but I wish you joy, old fellow.'

'Oh, Arthur!' groaned the curate again, and nodded his head, speechless.

'Beg your pardon—sorry I offended you—but she *has* got a large waist, you know—devilish large waist,' Pen continued—the third bottle evidently beginning to act upon the young gentleman.

'It's not Miss Portman,' the other said, in a voice of agony.

'Is it anybody at Chatteris or at Clapham? Somebody here? No—it ain't old Pybus? it can't be Miss Rolt at the factory—she's only fourteen.'

'It's somebody rather older than I am, Pen,' the curate cried, looking up at his friend, and then guiltily casting his eyes down into his plate.

Pen burst out laughing. 'It's Madame Fribsby, by Jove, it's Madame Fribsby. Madame Frib, by the immortal gods!'

The curate could contain no more. 'Oh, Pen,' he cried, 'how can you suppose that any of those—of those more than ordinary beings you have named—could have an influence upon this heart, when I have been daily in the habit of contemplating perfection! I may be insane, I may be madly ambitious, I may be presumptuous—but for two years my heart has been filled by one image, and has known no other idol. Haven't I loved you as a son, Arthur?—say, hasn't Charles Smirke loved you as a son?'

'Yes, old boy, you've been very good to me,' Pen said, whose liking, however, for his tutor was not by any means of the filial kind.

'My means,' rushed on Smirke, 'are at present limited, I own, and my mother is not so liberal as might be desired; but what she has will be mine at her death. Were she to hear of my marrying a lady of rank and good fortune, my mother would be liberal; I am sure she would be liberal. Whatever I have or subsequently inherit—and it's five hundred a year at the very least—would be settled upon her, and—and—and you at my death—that is——'

'What the deuce do you mean?—and what have I to do with your money?' cried out Pen, in a puzzle.

'Arthur, Arthur!' exclaimed the other wildly. 'You say I am your dearest friend—let me be more. Oh, can't you see that the angelic being I love—the purest, the best of women—is no other than your dear, dear angel of a—mother?'

'My mother!' cried out Arthur, jumping up and sober in a minute. 'Pooh! damn it, Smirke, you must be mad—she's seven or eight years older than you are.'

'Did *you* find that any objection?' cried Smirke piteously, and alluding, of course, to the elderly subject of Pen's own passion.

The lad felt the hint, and blushed quite red. 'The cases are not similar, Smirke,' he said, 'and the allusion might have been spared. A man may forget his own rank and elevate any woman to it; but allow me to say our positions are very different.'

'How do you mean, dear Arthur?' the curate interposed sadly, cowering as he felt that his sentence was about to be read.

'Mean?' said Arthur. 'I mean what I say. My tutor, I say *my tutor*, has no right to ask a lady of my mother's rank of life to marry him. It's a breach of confidence. I say it's a liberty you take, Smirke—it's a liberty. Mean, indeed!'

'Oh, Arthur!' the curate began to cry with clasped hands and a scared face, but Arthur gave another stamp with his foot, and began to pull at the bell. 'Don't let's have any more of this. We'll have some coffee, if you please,' he said, with a majestic air: and the old butler entering at the summons, Arthur bade him to serve that refreshment.

John said he had just carried coffee into the drawing-room, where his uncle was asking for Master Arthur, and the old man gave a glance of wonder at the three empty

claret-bottles. Smirke said he thought he'd—he'd rather not go into the drawing-room, on which Arthur haughtily said, 'As you please,' and called for Mr. Smirke's horse to be brought round. The poor fellow said he knew the way to the stable and would get his pony himself, and he went into the hall and sadly put on his coat and hat.

Pen followed him out uncovered. Helen was still walking up and down the soft lawn as the sun was setting, and the curate took off his hat and bowed by way of farewell, and passed on to the door leading to the stable court by which the pair disappeared. Smirke knew the way to the stable, as he said, well enough. He fumbled at the girths of the saddle, which Pen fastened for him, and put on the bridle and led the pony into the yard. The boy was touched by the grief which appeared in the other's face as he mounted. Pen held out his hand and Smirke wrung it silently.

'I say, Smirke,' he said, in an agitated voice, 'forgive me if I have said anything harsh—for you have always been very, very kind to me. But it can't be, old fellow, it can't be. Be a man. God bless you.'

Smirke nodded his head silently, and rode out of the lodge gate: and Pen looked after him for a couple of minutes, until he disappeared down the road, and the clatter of the pony's hoofs died away. Helen was still lingering on the lawn waiting until the boy came back—she put his hair off his forehead and kissed it fondly. She was afraid he had been drinking too much wine. Why had Mr. Smirke gone away without any tea?

He looked at her with a kind humour beaming in his eyes; 'Smirke is unwell,' he said, with a laugh. For a long while Helen had not seen the boy looking so cheerful. He put his arm round her waist, and walked her up and down the walk in front of the house. Laura began to drub on the drawing-room window and nod and laugh from it. 'Come along, you two people,' cried out Major Pendennis; 'your coffee is getting quite cold.'

When Laura was gone to bed, Pen, who was big with his secret, burst out with it, and described the dismal but ludicrous scene which had occurred. Helen heard of it with many blushes, which became her pale face very well, and a perplexity which Arthur roguishly enjoyed.

'Confound the fellow's impudence,' Major Pendennis said

as he took his candle, ‘where will the assurance of these people stop ?’ Pen and his mother had a long talk that night, full of love, confidence, and laughter, and the boy somehow slept more soundly and woke up more easily than he had done for many months before.

Before the great Mr. Dolphin quitted Chatteris, he not only made an advantageous engagement with Miss Fotheringay, but he liberally left with her a sum of money to pay off any debts which the little family might have contracted during their stay in the place, and which, mainly through the lady's own economy and management, were not considerable. The small account with the spirit merchant, which Major Pendennis had settled, was the chief of Captain Costigan's debts, and though the captain at one time talked about repaying every farthing of the money, it never appears that he executed his menace, nor did the laws of honour in the least call upon him to accomplish that threat.

When Miss Costigan had seen all the outstanding bills paid to the uttermost shilling, she handed over the balance to her father, who broke out into hospitalities to all his friends, gave the little Creeds more apples and gingerbread than he had ever bestowed upon them, so that the widow Creed ever after held the memory of her lodger in veneration, and the young ones wept bitterly when he went away; and in a word managed the money so cleverly that it was entirely expended before many days, and that he was compelled to draw upon Mr. Dolphin for a sum to pay for travelling expenses when the time of their departure arrived.

There was held at an inn in that county town a weekly meeting of a festive, almost a riotous character, of a society of gentlemen who called themselves the Buccaneers. Some of the choice spirits of Chatteris belonged to this cheerful club. Graves, the apothecary (than whom a better fellow never put a pipe in his mouth and smoked it), Smart, the talented and humorous portrait-painter of High Street, Croker, an excellent auctioneer, and the uncompromising Hicks, the able editor for twenty-three years of the *County Chronicle and Chatteris Champion*, were amongst the crew of the Buccaneers, whom also Bingley, the manager, liked to join of a Saturday evening, whenever he received permission from his lady.

Costigan had been also an occasional Buccaneer. But a

want of punctuality of payments had of late somewhat excluded him from the society, where he was subject to disagreeable remarks from the landlord, who said that a Buccaneer who didn't pay his shot was utterly unworthy to be a Marine Bandit. But when it became known to the 'Ears, as the Clubbists called themselves familiarly, that Miss Fotheringay had made a splendid engagement, a great revolution of feeling took place in the club regarding Captain Costigan. Solly, mine host of the 'Grapes,' [10] told the gents in the Buccaneers' room one night how noble the captain had beayved; having been round and paid off all his ticks in Chatteris, including his score of three pound fourteen here—and pronounced that Cos was a good feller, a gentleman at bottom, and he, Solly, had always said so, and finally worked upon the feelings of the Buccaneers to give the captain a dinner.

The banquet took place on the last night of Costigan's stay at Chatteris, and was served in Solly's accustomed manner. As good a plain dinner of old English fare as ever smoked on a table was prepared by Mrs. Solly; and about eighteen gentlemen sat down to the festive board. Mr. Jubber (the eminent draper of High Street) was in the chair, having this distinguished guest of the club on his right. The able and consistent Hicks officiated as croupier on the occasion; most of the gentlemen of the club were present, and H. Foker, Esq., and —— Spavin, Esq., friends of Captain Costigan, were also participators in the entertainment. The cloth having been drawn, the chairman said, 'Costigan, there is wine, if you like,' but the captain preferring punch, that liquor was voted by acclamation: and 'Non Nobis' having been sung in admirable style by Messrs. Bingley, Hicks, and Bullby (of the Cathedral choir, than whom a more jovial spirit 'ne'er tossed off a bumper or emptied a bowl'), the chairman gave the health of the 'King,' which was drunk with the loyalty of Chatteris men, and then, without further circumlocution, proposed their friend, 'Captain Costigan.'

After the enthusiastic cheering, which rang through old Chatteris, had subsided, Captain Costigan rose in reply, and made a speech of twenty minutes, in which he was repeatedly overcome by his emotions.

The gallant captain said he must be pardoned for incoherence, if his heart was too full to speak. He was quitting

a city celebrated for its antiquitee, its hospitalitee, the beautee of its women, the manly fidelitee, generositee, and jovialitee of its men. (Cheers.) He was going from that ancient and venerable city, of which, while Mimoree held her sayt, he should never think without the fondest emotion, to a methrawpolis where the talents of his daughter were

about to have full play, and where he would watch over her like a guardian angel. He should never forget that it was at Chatteris she had acquired the skill which she was about to exercise in another sphere, and in her name and his own, Jack Costigan thanked and blessed them. The gallant officer's speech was received with tremendous cheers.

Mr. Hicks, croupier, in a brilliant and energetic manner, proposed Miss Fotheringay's health.

Captain Costigan returned thanks in a speech full of feeling and eloquence.

Mr. Jubber proposed the Drama and the Chatteris theatre, and Mr. Bingley was about to rise, but was prevented by Captain Costigan, who, as long connected with the Chatteris theatre, and on behalf of his daughter, thanked the company. He informed them that he had been in garrison, at Gibraltar, and at Malta, and had been at the taking of Flushing.* The Duke of York was a patron of the Drama;* he had the honour of dining with His Royal Highness and the Duke of Kent many times; and the former had justly been named the friend of the soldier. (Cheers.)

The Army was then proposed, and Captain Costigan returned thanks. In the course of the night he sang his well-known songs, 'The Deserter,' 'The Shan Van Voght,'* 'The Little Pig under the Bed,' and 'The Vale of Avoca.' The evening was a great triumph for him—it ended. All triumphs and all evenings end. And the next day, Miss Costigan having taken leave of all her friends, having been reconciled to Miss Rouncy, to whom she left a necklace and a white satin gown—the next day, he and Miss Costigan had places in the 'Competitor' coach rolling by the gates of Fairoaks Lodge—and Pendennis never saw them.

Tom Smith, the coachman, pointed out Fairoaks to Mr. Costigan, who sat on the box smelling of rum-and-water—and the captain said it was a poor place—and added, 'Ye should see Castle Costigan, County Mayo, me boy,' which Tom said he should like very much to see.

They were gone, and Pen had never seen them! He only knew of their departure by its announcement in the county paper the next day: and straight galloped over to Chatteris to hear the truth of this news. They were gone indeed. A card of 'Lodgings to let' was placed in the dear little familiar window. He rushed up into the room and viewed it over. He sat ever so long in the old window-seat looking into the dean's garden: whence he and Emily had so often looked out together. He walked, with a sort of terror, into her little empty bedroom. It was swept out and prepared for new-comers. The glass which had reflected her fair face was shining ready for her successor. The curtains lay

square folded on the little bed : he flung himself down and buried his head on the vacant pillow.

Laura had netted a purse into which his mother had put some sovereigns, and Pen had found it on his dressing-table that very morning. He gave one to the little servant who had been used to wait upon the Costigans, and another to the children, because they said they were very fond of her. It was but a few months back, yet what years ago it seemed since he had first entered that room ! He felt that it was all done. The very missing her at the coach had something fatal in it. Blank, weary, utterly wretched and lonely the poor lad felt.

His mother saw She was gone by his look when he came home. He was eager to fly too now, as were other folks round about Chatteris. Poor Smirke wanted to go away from the sight of the siren widow. Foker began to think he had had enough of Baymouth, and that a few supper parties at St. Boniface would not be unpleasant. And Major Pendennis longed to be off, and have a little pheasant-shooting at Stillbrook, and get rid of all annoyances and *tracasseries** of the village. The widow and Laura nervously set about the preparation for Pen's kit, and filled trunks with his books and linen. Helen wrote cards with the name of Arthur Pendennis, Esq., which were duly nailed on the boxes ; and at which both she and Laura looked with tearful, wistful eyes. It was not until long, long after he was gone, that Pen remembered how constant and tender the affection of these women had been, and how selfish his own conduct was.

A night soon comes, when the mail, with echoing horn and blazing lamps, stops at the lodge-gate of Fairoaks, and Pen's trunks and his uncle's are placed on the roof of the carriage, into which the pair presently afterwards enter. Helen and Laura are standing by the evergreens of the shrubbery, their figures lighted up by the coach lamps ; the guard cries, 'All right': in another instant the carriage whirls onward ; the lights disappear, and Helen's heart and prayers go with them. Her sainted benedictions follow the departing boy. He has left the home-nest in which he has been chafing, and whither, after his very first flight, he returned bleeding and wounded ; he is eager to go forth again, and try his restless wings.

How lonely the house looks without him! The corded trunks and book-boxes are there in his empty study. Laura asks leave to come and sleep in Helen's room: and when she has cried herself to sleep there, the mother goes softly into Pen's vacant chamber, and kneels down by the bed on which the moon is shining, and there prays for her boy, as mothers only know how to plead. He knows that her pure blessings are following him, as he is carried miles away.

CHAPTER XVII

ALMA MATER

EVERY man, however brief or inglorious may have been his academical career, must remember with kindness and tenderness the old University comrades and days. The young man's life is just beginning: the boy's leading-strings are cut, and he has all the novel delights and dignities of freedom. He has no idea of cares yet, or of bad health, or of roguery, or poverty, or to-morrow's disappointment. The play has not been acted so often as to make him tired. Though the after-drink, as we mechanically go on repeating it, is stale and bitter, how pure and brilliant was that first sparkling draught of pleasure!—How the boy rushes at the cup, and with what a wild eagerness he drains it! But old epicures who are cut off from the delights of the table, and are restricted to a poached egg and a glass of water, like to see people with good appetites; and, as the next best thing to being amused at a pantomime oneself is to see one's children enjoy it, I hope there may be no degree of age or experience to which mortal may attain, when he shall become such a glum philosopher, as not to be pleased by the sight of happy youth. Coming back a few weeks since from a brief visit to the old University of Oxbridge,* where my friend Mr. Arthur Pendennis passed some period

of his life, I made the journey in the railroad by the side of a young fellow at present a student of St. Boniface. He had got an exeat somehow, and was bent on a day's lark in London: he never stopped rattling and talking from the commencement of the journey until its close (which was a great deal too soon for me, for I never was tired of listening to the honest young fellow's jokes and cheery laughter); and when we arrived at the terminus nothing would satisfy him but a hansom cab,* so that he might get into town the quicker, and plunge into the pleasures awaiting him there. Away the young lad went whirling, with joy lighting up his honest face; and as for the reader's humble servant, having but a small carpet-bag, I got up on the outside of the omnibus, and sat there very contentedly between a Jew pedlar smoking bad cigars, and a gentleman's servant taking care of a poodle-dog, until we got our fated complement of passengers and boxes, when the coachman drove leisurely away. *We* weren't in a hurry to get to town. Neither one of us was particularly eager about rushing into that near smoking Babylon, or thought of dining at the Club that night, or dancing at the Casino. Yet a few years more, and my young friend of the railroad will be not a whit more eager.

There were no railroads made when Arthur Pendennis went to the famous University of Oxbridge; but he drove thither in a well-appointed coach, filled inside and out with dons, gownsmen, young freshmen about to enter, and their guardians, who were conducting them to the University. A fat old gentleman, in grey stockings, from the City, who sat by Major Pendennis inside the coach, having his pale-faced son opposite, was frightened beyond measure, when he heard that the coach had been driven for a couple of stages by young Mr. Foker, of St. Boniface College, who was the friend of all men, including coachmen, and could drive as well as Tom Hicks himself. Pen sat on the roof, examining coach, passengers, and country, with great delight and curiosity. His heart jumped with pleasure as the famous University came in view, and the magnificent prospect of venerable towers and pinnacles, tall elms and shining river, spread before him.

Pen had passed a few days with his uncle at the major's lodgings, in Bury Street, before they set out for Oxbridge. Major Pendennis thought that the lad's wardrobe wanted

renewal ; and Arthur was by no means averse to any plan which was to bring him new coats and waistcoats. There was no end to the sacrifices which the self-denying uncle made in the youth's behalf. London was awfully lonely. The Pall Mall pavement was deserted ; the very red-jackets had gone out of town. There was scarce a face to be seen in the bow-windows of the clubs. The major conducted his nephew into one or two of those desert mansions, and wrote down the lad's name on the candidate list of one of them ; and Arthur's pleasure at this compliment on his guardian's part was excessive. He read in the parchment volume his name and titles, as 'Arthur Pendennis, Esq., of Fairoaks Lodge, ——shire, and St. Boniface College, Oxbridge ; proposed by Major Pendennis, and seconded by Viscount Colchicum,' with a thrill of intense gratification. 'You will come in for ballot in about three years, by which time you will have taken your degree,' the guardian said. Pen longed for the three years to be over, and surveyed the stucco-halls, and vast libraries, and drawing-rooms, as already his own property. The major laughed slyly to see the pompous airs of the simple young fellow, as he strutted out of the building. He and Foker drove down in the latter's cab one day to the Grey Friars, and renewed the acquaintance with some of their old comrades there. The boys came crowding up to the cab as it stood by the Grey Friars gates, where they were entering, and admired the chestnut horse, and the tights and livery and gravity of Stoopid, the tiger. The bell for afternoon school rang as they were swaggering about the playground talking to their old cronies. The awful doctor passed into school with his grammar in his hand. Foker slunk away uneasily at his presence, but Pen went up blushing, and shook the dignitary by the hand. He laughed as he thought that well-remembered Latin Grammar had boxed his ears many a time. He was generous, good-natured, and, in a word, perfectly conceited and satisfied with himself.

Then they drove to the parental brew-house. Foker's Entire* is composed in an enormous pile of buildings, not far from the Grey Friars, and the name of that well-known firm is gilded upon innumerable public-house signs, tenanted by its vassals in the neighbourhood : the venerable junior partner and manager did honour to the young lord of the vats and his friend, and served them

with silver flagons of brown stout, so strong that you would have thought, not only the young men, but the very horse Mr. Harry Foker drove, was affected by the potency of the drink, for he rushed home to the west-end of the town at a rapid pace, which endangered the pie-stalls and the women on the crossings, and brought the cab-steps into collision with the posts at the street corners, and caused Stoopid to swing fearfully on his board behind.

The major was quite pleased when Pen was with his young acquaintance; listened to Mr. Foker's artless stories with the greatest interest; gave the two boys a fine dinner at a Covent Garden coffee-house, whence they proceeded to the play; but was above all happy when Mr. and Lady Agnes Foker, who happened to be in London, requested the pleasure of Major Pendennis and Mr. Arthur Pendennis's company at dinner in Grosvenor Street. 'Having obtained the entrée into Lady Agnes Foker's house,' he said to Pen, with an affectionate solemnity which befitted the importance of the occasion, 'it behoves you, my dear boy, to keep it. You must mind and *never* neglect to call in Grosvenor Street when you come to London. I recommend you to read up carefully, in Debrett, the alliances and genealogy of the Earls of Rosherville, and if you can, to make some trifling allusions to the family, something historical, neat, and complimentary, and that sort of thing, which you, who have a poetic fancy, can do pretty well. Mr. Foker himself is a worthy man, though not of high extraction or indeed much education. He always makes a point of having some of the family porter served round after dinner, which you will on no account refuse, and which I shall drink myself, though *all* beer disagrees with me confoundedly.' And the heroic martyr did actually sacrifice himself, as he said he would, on the day when the dinner took place, and old Mr. Foker, at the head of his table, made his usual joke about Foker's Entire. We should all of us, I am sure, have liked to see the major's grin, when the worthy old gentleman made his time-honoured joke.

Lady Agnes, who, wrapped up in Harry, was the fondest of mothers, and one of the most good-natured though not the wisest of women, received her son's friend with great cordiality; and astonished Pen by accounts of the severe course of studies which her darling boy was pursuing, and

which she feared might injure his dear health. Foker the elder burst into a horse-laugh at some of these speeches, and the heir of the house winked his eye very knowingly at his friend. And Lady Agnes then going through her son's history from the earliest time, and recounting his miraculous sufferings in the measles and whooping-cough, his escape from drowning, the shocking tyrannies practised upon him at that horrid school, whither Mr. Foker would send him because he had been brought up there himself, and she never would forgive that disagreeable doctor, no, never—Lady Agnes, we say, having prattled away for an hour incessantly about her son, voted the two Messieurs Pendennis most agreeable men ; and when the pheasants came with the second course, which the major praised as the very finest birds he ever saw, her ladyship said they came from Logwood (as the major knew perfectly well) and hoped that they would both pay her a visit there—at Christmas, or when dear Harry was at home for the vacations.

'God bless you, my dear boy,' Pendennis said to Arthur, as they were lighting their candles in Bury Street afterwards to go to bed. 'You made that little allusion to Agincourt, where one of the Roshervilles distinguished himself, very neatly and well, although Lady Agnes did not quite understand it : but it was exceedingly well for a beginner—though you oughtn't to blush so, by the way—and I beseech you, my dear Arthur, to remember through life, that with an entrée—with a good entrée, mind—it is just as easy for you to have good society as bad, and that it costs a man, when properly introduced, no more trouble or *soins* to keep a good footing in the best houses in London than to dine with a lawyer in Bedford Square. Mind this when you are at Oxbridge pursuing your studies, and for Heaven's sake be *very* particular in the acquaintances which you make. The *premier pas* in life is the most important of all—did you write to your mother to-day ?—No ?—well, do, before you go, and call and ask Mr. Foker for a frank—They like it—Good night. God bless you.'

Pen wrote a droll account of his doings in London, and the play, and the visit to the old Friars, and the brewery, and the party at Mr. Foker's, to his dearest mother, who was saying her prayers at home in the lonely house at Fairoaks, her heart full of love and tenderness unutterable for

the boy: and she and Laura read that letter and those which followed, many, many times, and brooded over them as women do. It was the first step in life that Pen was making—Ah! what a dangerous journey it is, and how the bravest may stumble and the strongest fail. Brother wayfarer! may you have a kind arm to support yours on the path, and a friendly hand to succour those who fall beside you. May truth guide, mercy forgive at the end, and love accompany always. Without that lamp how blind the traveller would be, and how black and cheerless the journey!

So the coach drove up to that ancient and comfortable inn the 'Trencher,' which stands in Main Street, Oxbridge, and Pen with delight and eagerness remarked, for the first time, gownsmen going about, chapel bells clinking (bells in Oxbridge are ringing from morning-tide till evensong)—towers and pinnacles rising calm and stately over the gables and antique house-roofs of the city. Previous communications had taken place between Dr. Portman on Pen's part, and Mr. Buck, Tutor of Boniface, on whose side Pen was entered; and as soon as Major Pendennis had arranged his personal appearance, so that it should make a satisfactory impression upon Pen's tutor, the pair walked down Main Street, and passed the great gate and belfry-tower of St. George's College, and so came, as they were directed, to St. Boniface, where again Pen's heart began to beat as they entered at the wicket of the venerable ivy-mantled gate of the college. It is surmounted with an ancient dome almost covered with creepers, and adorned with the effigy of the saint from whom the House takes its name, and many coats-of-arms of its royal and noble benefactors.

The porter pointed out a queer old tower at the corner of the quadrangle, by which Mr. Buck's rooms were approached, and the two gentlemen walked across the square, the main features of which were at once and for ever stamped in Pen's mind—the pretty fountain playing in the centre of the fair grass-plats; the tall chapel windows and buttresses rising to the right; the hall, with its tapering lantern and oriel window; the lodge, from the doors of which the master issued awfully in rustling silks: the lines of the surrounding rooms pleasantly broken by carved chimneys, grey turrets, and quaint gables—all these Mr. Pen's eyes drank in with an eagerness which belongs to first impressions; and Major Pendennis surveyed with that

calmness which belongs to a gentleman who does not care for the picturesque, and whose eyes have been somewhat dimmed by the constant glare of the pavement of Pall Mall.

St. George's is the great college of the University of Oxbridge, with its four vast quadrangles, and its beautiful hall and gardens, and the Georgians, as the men are called, wear gowns of a peculiar cut, and give themselves no small airs of superiority over all other young men. Little St. Boniface is but a petty hermitage in comparison of the huge consecrated pile alongside of which it lies. But considering its size it has always kept an excellent name in the University. Its *ton* is very good: the best families of certain counties have time out of mind sent up their young men to St. Boniface: the college livings are remarkably good, the fellowships easy; the Boniface men had had more than their fair share of University honours; their boat was third upon the river; their chapel choir is not inferior to St. George's itself; and the Boniface ale the best in Oxbridge. In the comfortable old wainscoted college hall, and round about Roubilliac's statue* of St. Boniface (who stands in an attitude of seraphic benediction over the uncommonly good cheer of the fellows' table) there are portraits of many most eminent Bonifacians. There is the learned Dr. Griddle, who suffered in Henry VIII's time, and Archbishop Bush who roasted him—there is Lord Chief Justice Hicks—the Duke of St. David's, K.G., Chancellor of the University and member of this college—Sprott the poet, of whose fame the college is justly proud—Doctor Blogg, the late master, and friend of Doctor Johnson, who visited him at St. Boniface—and other lawyers, scholars, and divines, whose portraitures look from the walls, or whose coats-of-arms shine in emerald and ruby, gold and azure, in the tall windows of the refectory. The venerable cook of the college is one of the best artists in Oxbridge,[1] and the wine in the fellows' room has long been famed for its excellence and abundance.

Into this certainly not the least snugly sheltered arbour amongst the groves of Academe, Pen now found his way, leaning on his uncle's arm, and they speedily reached Mr. Buck's rooms, and were conducted into the apartment of that courteous gentleman.

He had received previous information from Dr. Portman regarding Pen, with respect to whose family, fortune, and personal merits the honest doctor had spoken with no small

enthusiasm. Indeed, Portman had described Arthur to the tutor as 'a young gentleman of some fortune and landed estate, of one of the most ancient families in the kingdom, and possessing such a character and genius as were sure, under the proper guidance, to make him a credit to the college and the University.' Under such recommendations, the tutor was, of course, most cordial to the young freshman and his guardian, invited the latter to dine in hall, where he would have the satisfaction of seeing his nephew wear his gown and eat his dinner for the first time, and requested the pair to take wine at his rooms after hall, and in consequence of the highly favourable report he had received of Mr. Arthur Pendennis, said, he should be happy to give him the best set of rooms to be had in college—a gentleman-pensioner's set,* indeed, which were just luckily vacant.[2] When a college magnate takes the trouble to be polite, there is no man more splendidly courteous. Immersed in their books, and excluded from the world by the gravity of their occupations, these reverend men assume a solemn magnificence of compliment in which they rustle and swell as in their grand robes of state. Those silks and brocades are not put on for all comers or every day.

When the two gentlemen had taken leave of the tutor in his study, and had returned to Mr. Buck's ante-room, or lecture-room, a very handsome apartment, turkey-carpeted, and hung with excellent prints and richly framed pictures, they found the tutor's servant already in waiting there, accompanied by a man with a bag full of caps and a number of gowns, from which Pen might select a cap and gown for himself, and the servant, no doubt, would get a commission proportionable to the service done by him. Mr. Pen was all in a tremor of pleasure as the bustling tailor tried on a gown, and pronounced that it was an excellent fit; and then he put the pretty college cap on, in rather a dandified manner, and somewhat on one side, as he had seen Fiddicombe, the youngest master at Grey Friars, wear it. And he inspected the entire costume with a great deal of satisfaction in one of the great gilt mirrors which ornamented Mr. Buck's lecture-room: for some of these college divines are no more above looking-glasses than a lady is, and look to the set of their gowns and caps quite as anxiously as folks do of the lovelier sex.[3]

Then Davis, the skip or attendant, led the way, keys in

hand, across the quadrangle, the major and Pen following him, the latter blushing, and pleased with his new academical habiliments, across the quadrangle to the rooms which were destined for the freshman; and which were vacated by the retreat of the gentleman-pensioner, Mr. Spicer. The rooms were very comfortable, with large cross-beams, high wainscots, and small windows in deep embra-

sures. Mr. Spicer's furniture was there, and to be sold at a valuation, and Major Pendennis agreed on his nephew's behalf to take the available part of it, laughingly, however, declining (as, indeed, Pen did for his own part) six sporting prints, and four groups of opera-dancers with gauze draperies, which formed the late occupant's pictorial collection.

Then they went to hall, where Pen sat down and ate his commons with his brother freshmen, and the major took his place at the high-table along with the college dignitaries and other fathers or guardians of youth, who had come up

with their sons to Oxbridge; and after hall they went to Mr. Buck's to take wine; and after wine to chapel, where the major sat with great gravity in the upper place, having a fine view of the master in his carved throne or stall under the organ-loft, where that gentleman, the learned Doctor Donne,* sate magnificent, with his great Prayer-book before him, an image of statuesque piety and rigid devotion. All the young freshmen behaved with gravity and decorum, but Pen was shocked to see that atrocious little Foker, who came in very late, and half a dozen of his comrades in the gentlemen-pensioners' seats, giggling and talking as if they had been in so many stalls at the opera.[4]

Pen could hardly sleep at night in his bedroom at the 'Trencher'; so anxious was he to begin his college life, and to get into his own apartments. What did he think about, as he lay tossing and awake? Was it about his mother at home; the pious soul whose life was bound up in his? Yes, let us hope he thought of her a little. Was it about Miss Fotheringay, and his eternal passion, which had kept him awake so many nights, and created such wretchedness and such longing? He had a trick of blushing, and if you had been in the room, and the candle had not been out, you might have seen the youth's countenance redden more than once, as he broke out into passionate incoherent exclamations regarding that luckless event of his life. His uncle's lessons had not been thrown away upon him; the mist of passion had passed from his eyes now, and he saw her as she was. To think that he, Pendennis, had been enslaved by such a woman, and then jilted by her! that he should have stooped so low, to be trampled on in the mire! that there was a time in his life, and that but a few months back, when he was willing to take Costigan for his father-in-law!——

'Poor old Smirke!' Pen presently laughed out—'well, I'll write and try and console the poor old boy. He won't die of his passion, ha, ha!' The major, had he been awake, might have heard a score of such ejaculations uttered by Pen as he lay awake and restless through the first night of his residence at Oxbridge.

It would, perhaps, have been better for a youth, the battle of whose life*was going to begin on the morrow, to have passed the eve in a different sort of vigil: but the world had got hold of Pen in the shape of his selfish old

Mentor: and those who have any interest in his character must have perceived ere now, that this lad was very weak as well as very impetuous, very vain as well as very frank, and if of a generous disposition, not a little selfish in the midst of his profuseness, and also rather fickle, as all eager pursuers of self-gratification are.

The six months' passion had aged him very considerably. There was an immense gulf between Pen the victim of love, and Pen the innocent boy of eighteen, sighing after it: and so Arthur Pendennis had all the experience and superiority, besides that command which afterwards conceit and imperiousness of disposition gave him over the young men with whom he now began to live.

He and his uncle passed the morning with great satisfaction in making purchases for the better comfort of the apartments which the lad was about to occupy. Mr. Spicer's china and glass was in a dreadfully dismantled condition, his lamps smashed, and his bookcases by no means so spacious as those shelves which would be requisite to receive the contents of the boxes which were lying in the hall at Fairoaks, and which were addressed to Arthur in the hand of poor Helen.

The boxes arrived in a few days, that his mother had packed with so much care. Pen was touched as he read the superscriptions in the dear well-known hand, and he arranged in their proper places all the books, his old friends, and all the linen and table-cloths which Helen had selected from the family stock, and all the jam-pots which little Laura had bound in straw, and the hundred simple gifts of home.[5]

CHAPTER XVIII

PENDENNIS OF BONIFACE

UR friend Pen was not sorry when his Mentor took leave of the young gentleman on the second day after the arrival of the pair in Oxbridge, and we may be sure that the major on his part was very glad to have discharged his duty, and to have the duty over. More than three months of precious time had that martyr of a major given up to his nephew. Was ever selfish man called upon to make a greater sacrifice ? Do you know many men or majors who would do as much ? A man will lay down his head, or peril his life for his honour, but let us be shy how we ask him to give up his ease or his heart's desire. Very few of us can bear that trial. Let us give the major due credit for his conduct [1] during the past quarter, and own that he has quite a right to be pleased at getting a holiday. Foker and Pen saw him off in the coach, and the former youth gave particular orders to the coachman to take care of that gentleman inside. It pleased the elder Pendennis to have his nephew in the company of a young fellow who would introduce him to the best set of the University. The major rushed off to London and thence to Cheltenham, from which watering-place he descended upon some neighbouring great houses, whereof the families were not gone abroad, and where good shooting and company was to be had.[2]

We are not about to go through[3] Pen's young academical career very minutely. Alas, the life of such boys does not bear telling altogether. I wish it did. I ask you, does yours ? As long as what we call our honour is clear, I suppose your mind is pretty easy. Women are pure, but not men. Women are unselfish, but not men. And I would not wish to say of poor Arthur Pendennis that he was worse than his neighbours, only that his neighbours

are bad for the most part. Let us have the candour to own as much at least. Can you point out ten spotless men of your acquaintance? Mine is pretty large, but I can't find ten saints in the list.

During the first term of Mr. Pen's University life, he attended classical and mathematical lectures with tolerable assiduity; but discovering before very long time that he had little taste or genius for the pursuing of the exact sciences, and being perhaps rather annoyed that one or two very vulgar young men, who did not even use straps to their trousers* so as to cover the abominably thick and coarse shoes and stockings which they wore, beat him completely in the lecture-room, he gave up his attendance at that course, and announced to his fond parent that he proposed to devote himself exclusively to the cultivation of Greek and Roman Literature.

Mrs. Pendennis was, for her part, quite satisfied that her darling boy should pursue that branch of learning for which he had the greatest inclination; and only besought him not to ruin his health by too much study, for she had heard the most melancholy stories of young students who, by over fatigue, had brought on brain-fevers and perished untimely in the midst of their University career. And Pen's health, which was always delicate, was to be regarded, as she justly said, beyond all considerations or vain honours. Pen, although not aware of any lurking disease which was likely to endanger his life, yet kindly promised his mamma not to sit up reading too late of nights, and stuck to his word in this respect with a great deal more tenacity of resolution than he exhibited upon some other occasions, when perhaps he was a little remiss.

Presently he began too to find that he learned little good in the classical lecture. His fellow-students there were too dull, as in mathematics they were too learned for him. Mr. Buck, the tutor, was no better a scholar than many a fifth-form boy at Grey Friars; might have some stupid humdrum notions about the metre and grammatical construction of a passage of Æschylus or Aristophanes, but had no more notion of the poetry than Mrs. Binge, his bed-maker; and Pen grew weary of hearing the dull students and tutor blunder through a few lines of a play, which he could read in a tenth part of the time which they gave to it. After all, private reading, as he began to perceive,

was the only study which was really profitable to a man ; and he announced to his mamma that he should read by himself a great deal more, and in public a great deal less. That excellent woman knew no more about Homer than she did about Algebra, but she was quite contented with Pen's arrangements regarding his course of studies, and felt perfectly confident that her dear boy would get the place which he merited.

Pen did not come home until after Christmas, a little to the fond mother's disappointment, and Laura's, who was longing for him to make a fine snow fortification, such as he had made three winters before. But he was invited to Logwood, Lady Agnes Foker's, where there were private theatricals, and a gay Christmas party of very fine folks, some of them whom Major Pendennis would on no account have his nephew neglect. However, he stayed at home for the last three weeks of the vacation, and Laura had the opportunity of remarking what a quantity of fine new clothes he brought with him, and his mother admired his improved appearance and manly and decided tone.

He did not come home at Easter ; but when he arrived for the long vacation, he brought more smart clothes ; appearing in the morning in wonderful shooting-jackets, with remarkable buttons ; and in the evening in gorgeous velvet waistcoats, with richly-embroidered cravats, and curious linen. And as she pried about his room, she saw, oh, such a beautiful dressing-case, with silver mountings, and a quantity of lovely rings and jewellery. And he had a new French watch and gold chain, in place of the big old chronometer, with its bunch of jingling seals, which had hung from the fob of John Pendennis, and by the second-hand of which the defunct doctor had felt many a patient's pulse in his time. It was but a few months back Pen had longed for this watch, which he thought the most splendid and august timepiece in the world ; and just before he went to college, Helen had taken it out of her trinket-box (where it had remained unwound since the death of her husband) and given it to Pen with a solemn and appropriate little speech respecting his father's virtues and the proper use of time. This portly and valuable chronometer Pen now pronounced to be out of date, and, indeed, made some comparisons between it and a warming-pan, which Laura thought disrespectful, and he left the watch in a drawer,

in the company of soiled primrose gloves, cravats which had gone out of favour, and of that other school watch which has once before been mentioned in this history. Our old friend, Rebecca, Pen pronounced to be no longer up to his weight, and swapped her away for another and more powerful horse, for which he had to pay rather a heavy figure. Mrs. Pendennis gave the boy the money for the new horse; and Laura cried when Rebecca was fetched away.

Also Pen brought a large box of cigars branded 'Colorados,' 'Afrancesados,' 'Telescopios,' Fudson,* Oxford Street, or by some such strange titles, and began to consume these not only about the stables and green-houses, where they were very good for Helen's plants, but in his own study,—which practice his mother did not at first approve. But he was at work upon a prize-poem, he said, and could not compose without his cigar, and quoted the late lamented Lord Byron's lines in favour of the custom of smoking. As he was smoking to such good purpose, his mother could not of course refuse permission: in fact, the good soul coming into the room one day in the midst of Pen's labours (he was consulting a novel which had recently appeared, for the cultivation of the light literature of his own country as well as of foreign nations became every student)—Helen, we say, coming into the room and finding Pen on the sofa at this work, rather than disturb him went for a light-box and his cigar-case to his bedroom, which was adjacent, and actually put the cigar into his mouth and lighted the match at which he kindled it. Pen laughed, and kissed his mother's hand as it hung fondly over the back of the sofa. 'Dear old mother,' he said, 'if I were to tell you to burn the house down, I think you would do it!' And it is very likely that Mr. Pen was right, and that the foolish woman would have done almost as much for him as he said.

Besides the works of English 'light literature' which this diligent student devoured, he brought down boxes of the light literature of the neighbouring country of France: into the leaves of which when Helen dipped, she read such things as caused her to open her eyes with wonder. But Pen showed her that it was not he who made the books, though it was absolutely necessary that he should keep up his French by an acquaintance with the most celebrated

writers of the day, and that it was as clearly his duty to read the eminent Paul de Kock,* as to study Swift or Molière. And Mrs. Pendennis yielded with a sigh of perplexity. But Miss Laura was warned off the books, both by his anxious mother, and that rigid moralist Mr. Arthur Pendennis himself, who, however *he* might be called upon to study every branch of literature in order to form his mind and to perfect his style, would by no means prescribe such a course of reading to a young lady whose business in life was very different.

In the course of this long vacation Mr. Pen drank up the bin of claret which his father had laid in, and of which we have heard the son remark that there was not a headache in a hogshead; and this wine being exhausted, he wrote for a further supply to 'his wine merchants,' Messrs. Binney and Latham, of Mark Lane, London: from whom, indeed, old Doctor Portman had recommended Pen to get a supply of port and sherry on going to college. 'You will have, no doubt, to entertain your young friends at Boniface with wine parties,' the honest rector had remarked to the lad. 'They used to be customary at college in my time, and I would advise you to employ an honest and respectable house in London for your small stock of wine, rather than to have recourse to the Oxbridge tradesmen, whose liquor, if I remember rightly, was both deleterious in quality and exorbitant in price.' And the obedient young gentleman took the doctor's advice, and patronized Messrs. Binney and Latham at the rector's suggestion.

So when he wrote orders for a stock of wine to be sent down to the cellars at Fairoaks, he hinted that Messrs. B. and L. might send in his University account for wine at the same time with the Fairoaks bill. The poor widow was frightened at the amount. But Pen laughed at her old-fashioned views, said that the bill was moderate, that everybody drank claret and champagne now, and, finally, the widow paid, feeling dimly that the expenses of her household were increasing considerably, and that her narrow income would scarce suffice to meet them. But they were only occasional. Pen merely came home for a few weeks at the vacation. Laura and she might pinch when he was gone. In the brief time he was with them ought they not to make him happy?

Arthur's own allowances were liberal all this time;

indeed, much more so than those of the sons of far more wealthy men. Years before, the thrifty and affectionate John Pendennis, whose darling project it had ever been to give his son a University education, and those advantages of which his own father's extravagance had deprived him, had begun laying by a store of money which he called Arthur's Education Fund. Year after year in his book his executors found entries of sums vested as A. E. F., and during the period subsequent to her husband's decease, and before Pen's entry at college, the widow had added sundry sums to this fund, so that when Arthur went up to Oxbridge it reached no inconsiderable amount. Let him be liberally allowanced, was Major Pendennis's maxim. Let him make his first entrée into the world as a gentleman, and take his place with men of good rank and station; after giving it to him, it will be his own duty to hold it. There is no such bad policy as stinting a boy—or putting him on a lower allowance than his fellows. Arthur will have to face the world and fight for himself presently. Meanwhile we shall have procured for him good friends, gentlemanly habits, and have him well backed and well trained against the time when the real struggle comes. And these liberal opinions the major probably advanced both because they were just, and because he was not dealing with his own money.

Thus young Pen, the only son of an estated country gentleman, with a good allowance, and a gentlemanlike bearing and person, looked to be a lad of much more consequence than he was really; and was held by the Oxbridge authorities, tradesmen, and undergraduates, as quite a young buck and member of the aristocracy. His manner was frank, brave, and perhaps a little impertinent, as becomes a high-spirited youth. He was perfectly generous and free-handed with his money, which seemed pretty plentiful. He loved joviality, and had a good voice for a song. Boat-racing had not risen in Pen's time to the *fureur* which, as we are given to understand, it has since attained in the University; and riding and tandem-driving were the fashions of the ingenuous youth. Pen rode well to hounds, appeared in pink, as became a young buck, and not particularly extravagant in equestrian or any other amusement, yet managed to run up a fine bill at Nile's, the livery-stable keeper, and in a number of other quarters.

In fact, this lucky young gentleman had almost every taste to a considerable degree. He was very fond of books of all sorts: Doctor Portman had taught him to like rare editions, and his own taste led him to like beautiful bindings. It was marvellous what tall copies, and gilding, and marbling, and blind-tooling, the booksellers and binders put upon Pen's bookshelves. He had a very fair taste in matters of art, and a keen relish for prints of a high school—none of your French opera dancers, or tawdry racing prints, such as had delighted the simple eyes of Mr. Spicer, his predecessor — but your Stranges, and Rembrandt etchings, and Wilkies* before the letter, with which his apartments were furnished presently in the most perfect good taste, as was allowed in the University, where this young fellow got no small reputation. We have mentioned that he exhibited a certain partiality for rings, jewellery, and fine raiment of all sorts; and it must be owned that Mr. Pen, during his time at the University, was rather a dressy man, and loved to array himself in splendour. He and his polite friends would dress themselves out with as much care in order to go and dine at each other's rooms, as other folks would who were going to enslave a mistress. They said he used to wear rings over his kid gloves, which he always denies; but what follies will not youth perpetrate with its own admirable gravity and simplicity? That he took perfumed baths is a truth; and he used to say that he took them after meeting certain men of a very low set in hall.

In Pen's second year, when Miss Fotheringay made her chief hit in London, and scores of prints were published of her, Pen had one of these hung in his bedroom, and confided to the men of his set how awfully, how wildly, how madly, how passionately, he had loved that woman. He showed them in confidence the verses that he had written to her, and his brow would darken, his eyes roll, his chest heave with emotion as he recalled that fatal period of his life, and described the woes and agonies which he had suffered. The verses were copied out, handed about, sneered at, admired, passed from coterie to coterie. There are few things which elevate a lad in the estimation of his brother boys, more than to have a character for a great and romantic passion. Perhaps there is something noble in it at all times—among very young men, it is considered heroic

—Pen was pronounced a tremendous fellow. They said he had almost committed suicide : that he had fought a duel with a baronet about her. Freshmen pointed him out to each other. As at the promenade time at two o'clock he swaggered out of college, surrounded by his cronies, he was famous to behold. He was elaborately attired. He would ogle the ladies who came to lionize the University, and passed before him on the arms of happy gownsmen, and give his opinion upon their personal charms, or their

toilettes, with the gravity of a critic whose experience entitled him to speak with authority. Men used to say that they had been walking with Pendennis, and were as pleased to be seen in his company as some of us would be if we walked with a duke down Pall Mall. He and the proctor capped each other as they met, as if they were rival powers, and the men hardly knew which was the greater.

In fact, in the course of his second year, Arthur Pendennis had become one of the men of fashion in the University. It is curious to watch that facile admiration, and simple fidelity of youth. They hang round a leader : and wonder

at him, and love him, and imitate him. No generous boy ever lived, I suppose, that has not had some wonderment of admiration for another boy ; and Monsieur Pen at Oxbridge had his school, his faithful band of friends, and his rivals. When the young men heard at the haberdashers' shops that Mr. Pendennis, of Boniface, had just ordered a crimson satin cravat, you would see a couple of dozen crimson satin cravats in Main Street in the course of the week—and Simon, the jeweller, was known to sell no less than two gross of Pendennis pins, from a pattern which the young gentleman had selected in his shop.

Now if any person with an arithmetical turn of mind will take the trouble to calculate what a sum of money it would cost a young man to indulge freely in all the above propensities which we have said Mr. Pen possessed, it will be seen that a young fellow, with such liberal tastes and amusements, must needs in the course of two or three years spend or owe a very handsome sum of money. We have said our friend Pen had not a calculating turn. No one propensity of his was outrageously extravagant ; and it is certain that Paddington's tailor's account ; Guttlebury's cook's bill for dinners ; Dilley[4] Tandy's bill with Finn, the printseller, for Raphael-Morghens, and Landseer proofs, and Wormall's dealings with Parkton, the great bookseller, for Aldine editions, black-letter folios, and richly illuminated Missals of the sixteenth century ;* and Snaffle's or Foker's score with Nile the horse-dealer, were, each and all of them, incomparably greater than any little bills which Mr. Pen might run up with the above-mentioned tradesmen. But Pendennis of Boniface had the advantage over all these young gentlemen, his friends and associates, of a universality of taste : and whereas young Lord Paddington did not care twopence for the most beautiful print, or to look into any gilt frame that had not a mirror within it ; and Guttlebury did not mind in the least how he was dressed, and had an aversion for horse exercise, nay a terror of it ; and Snaffle never read any printed works but the *Racing Calendar* or *Bell's Life*,* or cared for any manuscript except his greasy little scrawl of a betting-book :—our catholic-minded young friend occupied himself in every one of the branches of science or pleasure above mentioned, and distinguished himself tolerably in each.

Hence young Pen got a prodigious reputation in the

University, and was hailed as a sort of Crichton; and as for the English verse prize, in competition for which we have seen him busily engaged at Fairoaks, Jones of Jesus carried it that year certainly, but the undergraduates thought Pen's a much finer poem, and he had his verses printed at his own expense, and distributed in gilt morocco covers amongst his acquaintance. I found a copy of it lately in a dusty corner of Mr. Pen's bookcases, and have it before me this minute, bound up in a collection of old Oxbridge tracts, University statutes, prize-poems by successful and unsuccessful candidates, declamations recited in the college chapel, speeches delivered at the Union Debating Society, and inscribed by Arthur with his name and college, 'Pendennis—Boniface'; or presented to him by his affectionate friend Thompson or Jackson, the author. How strange the epigraphs look in those half-boyish hands, and what a thrill the sight of the documents gives one after the lapse of a few lustres!* How Fate, since that time, has removed some, estranged others, dealt awfully with all! Many a hand is cold that wrote those kindly memorials, and that we pressed in the confident and generous grasp of youthful friendship. What passions our friendships were in those old days, how artless and void of doubt! How the arm you were never tired of having linked in yours under the fair college avenues or by the river-side, where it washes Magdalen Gardens, or Christ Church Meadows, or winds by Trinity and King's, was withdrawn of necessity, when you entered presently the world, and each parted to push and struggle for himself through the great mob on the way through life! Are we the same men now that wrote those inscriptions—that read those poems? that delivered or heard those essays and speeches so simple, so pompous, so ludicrously solemn; parodied so artlessly from books, and spoken with smug chubby faces, and such an admirable aping of wisdom and gravity? Here is the book before me: it is scarcely fifteen years old. Here is Jack moaning with despair and Byronic misanthropy, whose career at the University was one of unmixed milk-punch. Here is Tom's daring Essay in defence of suicide and of republicanism in general, à propos of the death of Roland and the Girondins—Tom's, who wears the starchiest tie in all the diocese, and would go to Smithfield rather than eat a beefsteak on a Friday in Lent. Here is Bob of the

—— Circuit, who has made a fortune in Railroad Committees[5]—bellowing out with Tancred and Godfrey,* 'On to the breach, ye soldiers of the cross, Scale the red wall and swim the choking foss. Ye dauntless archers, twang your cross-bows well; On, bill and battle-axe and mangonel! Ply battering-ram and hurtling catapult, Jerusalem is ours —*id Deus vult*.' After which comes a mellifluous description of the gardens of Sharon and the maids of Salem, and a prophecy that roses shall deck the entire country of Syria, and a speedy reign of peace be established—all in undeniably decasyllabic lines, and the queerest aping of sense and sentiment and poetry. And there are Essays and Poems along with these grave parodies, and boyish exercises (which are at once frank and false, and so mirthful, yet, somehow, so mournful), by youthful hands, that shall never write more. Fate has interposed darkly, and the young voices are silent, and the eager brains have ceased to work. This one had genius and a great descent, and seemed to be destined for honours which now are of little worth to him: that had virtue, learning, genius—every faculty and endowment which might secure love, admiration, and worldly fame: an obscure and solitary churchyard contains the grave of many fond hopes, and the pathetic stone which bids them farewell—I saw the sun shining on it in the fall of last year, and heard the sweet village choir raising anthems round about. What boots whether it be Westminster or a little country spire which covers your ashes, or if, a few days sooner or later, the world forgets you?

Amidst these friends then, and a host more, Pen passed more than two brilliant and happy years of his life. He had his fill of pleasure and popularity. No dinner or supper party was complete without him; and Pen's jovial wit, and Pen's songs, and dashing courage, and frank and manly bearing, charmed all the undergraduates.[6] Though he became the favourite and leader of young men who were much his superiors in wealth and station, he was much too generous to endeavour to propitiate them by any meanness or cringing on his own part, and would not neglect the humblest man of his acquaintance in order to curry favour with the richest young grandee in the University. His name is still remembered at the Union Debating Club, as one of the brilliant orators of his day.* By the way, from

having been an ardent Tory in his freshman's year, his principles took a sudden turn afterwards, and he became a Liberal of the most violent order. He avowed himself a Dantonist, and asserted that Louis XVI was served right. And as for Charles I, he vowed that he would chop off that monarch's head with his own right hand were he then in the room at the Union Debating Club, and had Cromwell no other executioner for the traitor. He and Lord Magnus Charters, the Marquis of Runnymede's son, before mentioned, were the most truculent republicans of their day.

There are reputations of this sort made quite independent of the collegiate hierarchy, in the republic of gownsmen. A man may be famous in the Honour-lists and entirely unknown to the undergraduates: who elect kings and chieftains of their own, whom they admire and obey, as negro-gangs have private black sovereigns in their own body, to whom they pay an occult obedience, besides that which they publicly profess for their owners and drivers. Among the young ones Pen became famous and popular: not that he did much, but there was a general determination that he could do a great deal if he chose. 'Ah, if Pendennis of Boniface would but try,' the men said, 'he might do anything.' He was backed for the Greek Ode won by Smith of Trinity; everybody was sure he would have the Latin hexameter prize which Brown of St. John's, however, carried off, and in this way one University honour after another was lost by him, until, after two or three failures, Mr. Pen ceased to compete. But he got a declamation prize in his own college, and brought home to his mother and Laura at Fairoaks a set of prize-books begilt with the college arms, and so big, well-bound, and magnificent, that these ladies thought there had been no such prize ever given in a college before as this of Pen's, and that he had won the very largest honour which Oxbridge was capable of awarding.

As vacation after vacation and term after term passed away without the desired news that Pen had sat for any scholarship or won any honour, Doctor Portman grew mightily gloomy in his behaviour towards Arthur, and adopted a sulky grandeur of deportment towards him, which the lad returned by a similar haughtiness. One vacation he did not call upon the doctor at all, much to his mother's annoyance, who thought that it was a privilege

to enter the Rectory-house at Clavering, and listened to Dr. Portman's antique jokes and stories, though ever so often repeated, with unfailing veneration. 'I cannot stand the doctor's patronizing air,' Pen said. 'He's too kind to me, a great deal too fatherly. I have seen in the world better men than him, and I am not going to bore myself by listening to his dull old stories.'[7] The tacit feud between Pen and the doctor made the widow nervous, so that she too avoided Portman, and was afraid to go to the Rectory when Arthur was at home.

One Sunday in the last long vacation, the wretched boy pushed his rebellious spirit so far as not to go to church, and he was seen at the gate of the 'Clavering Arms' smoking a cigar, in the face of the congregation as it issued from St. Mary's. There was an awful sensation in the village society; Portman prophesied Pen's ruin after that, and groaned in spirit over the rebellious young prodigal.

So did Helen tremble in her heart, and little Laura—Laura had grown to be a fine young stripling by this time, graceful and fair, clinging round Helen and worshipping her, with a passionate affection. Both of these women felt that their boy was changed. He was no longer the artless Pen of old days, so brave, so artless, so impetuous, and tender. His face looked careworn and haggard, his voice had a deeper sound, and tones more sarcastic. Care seemed to be pursuing him; but he only laughed when his mother questioned him, and parried her anxious queries with some scornful jest. Nor did he spend much of his vacations at home; he went on visits to one great friend or another, and scared the quiet pair at Fairoaks by stories of great houses whither he had been invited, and by talking of lords without their titles.

Honest Harry Foker, who had been the means of introducing Arthur Pendennis to that set of young men at the University, from whose society and connexions Arthur's uncle expected that the lad would get so much benefit; who had called for Arthur's first song at his first supper-party; and who had presented him at the Barmecide Club, where none but the very best men of Oxbridge were admitted (it consisted in Pen's time of six noblemen, eight gentlemen-pensioners, and twelve of the most select commoners of the University), soon found himself left far behind by the young freshman in the fashionable world of

Oxbridge, and being a generous and worthy fellow, without a spark of envy in his composition, was exceedingly pleased at the success of his young protégé, and admired Pen quite as much as any of the other youth did. It was he who followed Pen now, and quoted his sayings; learned his songs, and retailed them at minor supper-parties, and was never weary of hearing them from the gifted young poet's own mouth—for a good deal of the time which Mr. Pen might have employed much more advantageously in the pursuit of the regular scholastic studies was given up to the composition of secular ballads, which he sang about at parties according to University wont.

It had been as well for Arthur if the honest Foker had remained for some time at college, for, with all his vivacity, he was a prudent young man, and often curbed Pen's propensity to extravagance: but Foker's collegiate career did not last very long after Arthur's entrance at Boniface. Repeated differences with the University authorities caused Mr. Foker to quit Oxbridge in an untimely manner. He would persist in attending races on the neighbouring Hungerford Heath, in spite of the injunctions of his academic superiors. He never could be got to frequent the chapel of the college with that regularity of piety which Alma Mater demands from her children; tandems, which are abominations in the eyes of the heads and tutors, were Foker's greatest delight, and so reckless was his driving and frequent the accidents and upsets out of his drag, that Pen called taking a drive with him taking the 'Diversions of Purley';* finally, having a dinner-party at his rooms to entertain some friends from London, nothing would satisfy Mr. Foker but painting Mr. Buck's door vermilion, in which freak he was caught by the proctors; and although young Black Strap, the celebrated negro-fighter, who was one of Mr. Foker's distinguished guests, and was holding the can of paint while the young artist operated on the door, knocked down two of the proctor's attendants and performed prodigies of valour, yet these feats rather injured than served Foker, whom the proctor knew very well, and who was taken with the brush in his hand, summarily convened, and sent down from the University.

The tutor wrote a very kind and feeling letter to Lady Agnes on the subject, stating that everybody was fond of the youth; that he never meant harm to any mortal

creature; that he for his own part would have been delighted to pardon the harmless little boyish frolic, had not its unhappy publicity rendered it impossible to look the freak over, and breathing the most fervent wishes for the young fellow's welfare—wishes no doubt sincere, for Foker, as we know, came of a noble family on his mother's side, and on the other was heir to a great number of thousand pounds a year.

'It don't matter,' said Foker, talking over the matter with Pen—'a little sooner or a little later, what is the odds? I should have been plucked for my Little-go again, I know I should—that Latin I cannot screw into my head, and my mamma's anguish would have broke out next term. The governor will blow like an old grampus, I know he will, —well, we must stop till he gets his wind again. I shall probably go abroad and improve my mind with foreign travel. Yes, *parly-voo*'s the ticket. It'ly, and that sort of thing. I'll go to Paris, and learn to dance and complete my education. But it's not me I'm anxious about, Pen. As long as people drink beer I don't care—it's about you I'm doubtful, my boy. You're going too fast, and can't keep up the pace, I tell you. It's not the fifty you owe me—pay it or not when you like—but it's the everyday pace, and I tell you it will kill you. You're livin' as if there was no end to the money in the stockin' at home. You oughtn't to give dinners, you ought to eat 'em. Fellows are glad to have you. You oughtn't to owe horse bills, you ought to ride other chaps' nags. You know no more about betting than I do about Algebra: the chaps will win your money as sure as you sport it. Hang me if you are not trying at everything. I saw you sit down to écarté last week at Trumpington's, and taking your turn with the bones after Ringwood's supper. They'll beat you at it, Pen, my boy, even if they play on the square, which I don't say they don't, nor which I don't say they do, mind. But *I* won't play with 'em. You're no match for 'em. You ain't up to their weight. It's like little Black Strap standing up to Tom Spring—the Black's a pretty fighter, but, Law bless you, his arm ain't long enough to touch Tom—and I tell you, you're going it with fellers beyond your weight. Look here—if you'll promise me never to bet nor touch a box nor a card, I'll let you off the two ponies.'*

But Pen laughingly said, 'that though it wasn't convenient to him to pay the two ponies at that moment, he by no means wished to be let off any just debts he owed;' and he and Foker parted, not without many dark forebodings on the latter's part with regard to his friend, who Harry thought was travelling speedily on the road to ruin.

'One must do at Rome as Rome does,' Pen said, in a dandified manner, jingling some sovereigns in his waistcoat-pocket. 'A little quiet play at écarté can't hurt a man who plays pretty well—I came away fourteen sovereigns richer from Ringwood's supper, and, gad! I wanted the money.'—And he walked off, after having taken leave of poor Foker, who went away without any beat of drum, or offer to drive the coach out of Oxbridge, to superintend a little dinner which he was going to give at his own rooms in Boniface, about which dinners, the cook of the college, who had a great respect for Mr. Pendennis, always took especial pains for his young favourite.

CHAPTER XIX

RAKE'S PROGRESS

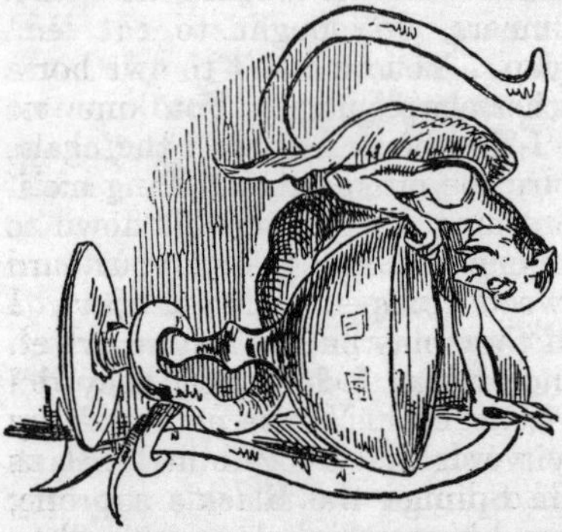

IN[1] Pen's second year Major Pendennis paid a brief visit to his nephew, and was introduced to several of Pen's University friends—the gentle and polite Lord Plinlimmon, the gallant and open-hearted Magnus Charters, the sly and witty Harland; the intrepid Ringwood, who was called Rupert in the Union Debating Club, from his opinions and the bravery of his blunders; Broadbent, styled Barebones Broadbent from the republican nature of his opinions (he was of a Dissenting family from Bristol, and a perfect Boanerges of debate); and

Bloundell-Bloundell,* whom Mr. Pen entertained at a dinner whereof his uncle was the chief guest.[2]

The major said, 'Pen, my boy, your dinner went off *à merveillè ;* you did the honours very nicely—you carved well—I am glad you learned to carve—it is done on the sideboard now in most good houses, but is still an important point, and may aid you in middle life—young Lord Plinlimmon is a very amiable young man, quite the image of his dear mother (whom I knew as Lady Aquila Brownbill) ; and Lord Magnus's republicanism will wear off—it sits prettily enough on a young patrician in early life, though nothing is so loathsome among persons of our rank—Mr. Broadbent seems to have much eloquence and considerable reading ; your friend Foker is always delightful ; but your acquaintance, Mr. Bloundell, struck me as in all respects a most ineligible young man.'

'Bless my soul, sir, Bloundell-Bloundell !' cried Pen, laughing ; 'why, sir, he's the most popular man of the University. He was in the — Dragoons before he came up.[3] We elected him of the Barmecides the first week he came up—had a special meeting on purpose—he's of an excellent family—Suffolk Bloundells, descended from Richard's Blondel, bear a harp in chief—and motto "O Mong Roy." '

'A man may have a very good coat of arms, and be a tiger, my boy,' the major said, chipping his egg ; 'that man is a tiger, mark my word—a low man. I will lay a wager that he left his regiment, which was a good one (for a more respectable man than my friend, Lord Martingale, never sat in a saddle),* in bad odour. There is the unmistakable look of slang and bad habits about this Mr. Bloundell. He frequents low gambling-houses and billiard hells, sir—he haunts third-rate clubs—I know he does. I know by his style. I never was mistaken in my man yet. Did you remark the quantity of rings and jewellery he wore ? That person has Scamp written on his countenance, if any man ever had. Mark my words and avoid him. Let us turn the conversation. The dinner was a *leetle* too fine, but I don't object to your making a few extra *frais* when you receive friends. Of course you don't do it often, and only those whom it is your interest to *fêter*. The cutlets were excellent, and the *soufflé* uncommonly light and good. The third bottle of champagne was not necessary ; but you

have a good income, and as long as you keep within it, I shall not quarrel with you, my dear boy.'

Poor Pen! the worthy uncle little knew how often those dinners took place, while the reckless young Amphitryon delighted to show his hospitality and skill in *gourmandise*. There is no art[4] about which boys are more anxious to have an air of knowingness. A taste and knowledge of wines and cookery appears to them to be the sign of an accomplished *roué* and manly gentleman.[5] Pen, in his character of Admirable Crichton, thought it necessary to be a great judge and practitioner of dinners; we have just said how the college cook respected him, and shall soon have to deplore that that worthy man so blindly trusted our Pen. In the third year of the lad's residence at Oxbridge, his staircase was by no means encumbered with dish-covers and desserts, and waiters carrying in dishes, and skips opening iced champagne; crowds of different sorts of attendants, with faces sulky or piteous, hung about the outer oak, and assailed the unfortunate lad as he issued out of his den.

Nor did his guardian's advice take any effect, or induce Mr. Pen to avoid the society of the disreputable Mr. Bloundell.[6]

The young magnates of the neighbouring great college of St. George's, who regarded Pen, and in whose society he lived, were not taken in by Bloundell's flashy graces and rakish airs of fashion. Broadbent called him Captain Macheath, and said he would live to be hanged. Foker, during his brief stay at the University with Macheath, with characteristic caution, declined to say anything in the captain's disfavour, but hinted to Pen that he had better have him for a partner at whist than play against him, and better back him at écarté than bet on the other side. 'You see, he plays better than you do, Pen,' was the astute young gentleman's remark: 'he plays uncommon well, the captain does;—and Pen, I wouldn't take the odds too freely from him, if I was you. I don't think he's too flush of money, the captain ain't.' But beyond these dark suggestions and generalities, the cautious Foker could not be got to speak.

Not that his advice would have had more weight with a headstrong young man, than advice commonly has with a lad who is determined on pursuing his own way. Pen's

PEN'S STAIRCASE—I. A LITTLE DINNER

appetite for pleasure was insatiable, and he rushed at it wherever it presented itself, with an eagerness which bespoke his fiery constitution and youthful health. He called taking pleasure 'seeing life,' and quoted well-known maxims from Terence, from Horace, from Shakespeare, to show that one should do all that might become a man. He bade fair to be utterly used up and a *roué*, in a few years, if he were to continue at the pace at which he was going.

One night after a supper-party in college, at which Pen and Macheath had been present, and at which a little quiet vingt-et-un had been played,[7] as the men had taken their caps and were going away, after no great losses or winnings on any side, Mr. Bloundell playfully took up a green wine-glass from the supper-table, which had been destined to contain iced cup, but into which he inserted something still more pernicious, namely a pair of dice, which the gentleman took out of his waistcoat-pocket, and put into the glass. Then giving the glass a graceful wave which showed that his hand was quite experienced in the throwing of dice, he called, 'Seven's the main,' and whisking the ivory cubes gently on the table, swept them up lightly again from the cloth, and repeated this process two or three times. The other men looked on, Pen, of course, among the number, who had never used the dice as yet, except to play a humdrum game of backgammon at home.

Mr. Bloundell, who had a good voice, began to troll out the chorus from *Robert the Devil*,* an opera then in great vogue, in which chorus many of the men joined, especially Pen, who was in very high spirits, having won a good number of shillings and half-crowns at the vingt-et-un—and presently, instead of going home, most of the party were seated round the table playing at dice, the green glass going round from hand to hand until Pen finally shivered it, after throwing six mains.

From that night Pen plunged into the delights of the game of hazard as eagerly as it was his custom to pursue any new pleasure. Dice can be played of mornings as well as after dinner or supper. Bloundell would come into Pen's rooms after breakfast, and it was astonishing how quick the time passed as the bones were rattling. They had little quiet parties with closed doors, and Bloundell devised a box lined with felt, so that the dice should make

no noise, and their tell-tale rattle not bring the sharp-eared tutors up to the rooms. Bloundell, Ringwood, and Pen were once very nearly caught by Mr. Buck, who, passing in the quadrangle, thought he heard the words, 'Two to one on the caster,' through Pen's open window; but when the tutor got into Arthur's rooms he found the lads with three Homers before them, and Pen said he was trying to coach the two other men, and asked Mr. Buck with great gravity what was the present condition of the River Scamander, and whether it was navigable or no?

Mr. Arthur Pendennis did not win much money in these transactions with Mr. Bloundell, or indeed gain good of any kind except a knowledge of the odds at hazard, which he might have learned out of books.[8]

One Easter vacation, when Pen had announced to his mother and uncle his intention not to go down, but stay at Oxbridge and read, Mr. Pen was nevertheless induced to take a brief visit to London in company with his friend Mr. Bloundell. They put up at a hotel in Covent Garden, where Bloundell had a tick, as he called it, and took the pleasures of the town very freely after the wont of young University men. Bloundell still belonged to a military club, whither he took Pen to dine once or twice (the young men would drive thither in a cab, trembling lest they should meet Major Pendennis on his beat in Pall Mall), and here Pen was introduced to a number of gallant young fellows with spurs and moustachios, with whom he drank pale ale of mornings and beat the town of a night. Here he saw a deal of life, indeed: nor in his career about the theatres and singing-houses which these roaring young blades frequented, was he very likely to meet his guardian. One night, nevertheless, they were very near to each other: a plank only separating Pen, who was in the boxes of the Museum Theatre, from the major, who was in Lord Steyne's box, along with that venerated nobleman. The Fotheringay was in the pride of her glory. She had made a hit: that is, she had drawn very good houses for nearly a year, had starred the provinces with great éclat, had come back to shine in London with somewhat diminished lustre, and now was acting with 'ever increasing attraction,' etc., 'triumph of the good old British drama,' as the playbills avowed, to houses in which there was plenty of room for anybody who wanted to see her.

It was not the first time Pen had seen her, since that memorable day when the two had parted in Chatteris. In the previous year, when the town was making much of her, and the press lauded her beauty, Pen had found a pretext for coming to London in term-time, and had rushed off to the theatre to see his old flame. He recollected it rather than renewed it. He remembered how ardently he used to be on the look-out at Chatteris, when the speech before Ophelia's or Mrs. Haller's entrance on the stage was made by the proper actor. Now, as the actor spoke, he had a sort of feeble thrill: as the house began to thunder with applause, and Ophelia entered with her old bow and sweeping curtsy, Pen felt a slight shock and blushed very much as he looked at her, and could not help thinking that all the house was regarding him. He hardly heard her for the first part of the play: and he thought with such rage of the humiliation to which she had subjected him, that he began to fancy he was jealous and in love with her still. But that illusion did not last very long. He ran round to the stage door of the theatre to see her if possible, but he did not succeed. She passed indeed under his nose with a female companion, but he did not know her—nor did she recognize him. The next night he came in late, and stayed very quietly for the after-piece, and on the third and last night of his stay in London—why, Taglioni was going to dance at the Opera—Taglioni! and there was to be *Don Giovanni*, which he admired of all things in the world: so Mr. Pen went to *Don Giovanni* and Taglioni.*

This time the illusion about her was quite gone. She was not less handsome, but she was not the same, somehow. The light was gone out of her eyes which used to flash there, or Pen's no longer were dazzled by it. The rich voice spoke as of old, yet it did not make Pen's bosom thrill as formerly. He thought he could recognize the brogue underneath: the accents seemed to him coarse and false. It annoyed him to hear the same emphasis on the same words only uttered a little louder: worse than this, it annoyed him to think that he should ever have mistaken that loud imitation for genius, or melted at those mechanical sobs and sighs. He felt that it was in another life almost, that it was another man who had so madly loved her. He was ashamed and bitterly humiliated, and very lonely.

Ah, poor Pen! the delusion is better than the truth sometimes, and fine dreams than dismal waking.

They went and had an uproarious supper that night, and Mr. Pen had a fine headache the next morning, with which he went back to Oxbridge, having spent all his ready money.

As all this narrative is taken from Pen's own confessions, so that the reader may be assured of the truth of every word of it, and as Pen himself never had any accurate notion of the manner in which he spent his money, and plunged himself in much deeper pecuniary difficulties, during his luckless residence at Oxbridge University, it is, of course, impossible for me to give any accurate account of his involvements, beyond that general notion of his way of life, which we have[9] sketched a few pages back. He does not speak too hardly of the roguery of the University tradesmen, or of those in London whom he honoured with his patronage at the outset of his career. Even Finch, the money-lender, to whom Bloundell introduced him, and with whom he had various transactions, in which the young rascal's signature appeared upon stamped paper, treated him, according to Pen's own account, with forbearance, and never mulcted him of more than a hundred per cent. The old college cook, his fervent admirer, made him a private bill, offered to send him in dinners up to the very last, and never would have pressed his account to his dying day. There was that kindness and frankness about Arthur Pendennis, which won most people who came in contact with him, and which, if it rendered him an easy prey to rogues, got him, perhaps, more goodwill than he merited from many honest men. It was impossible to resist his good nature, or, in his worst moments, not to hope for his rescue from utter ruin.

At the time of his full career of University pleasure, he would leave the gayest party to go and sit with a sick friend. He never knew the difference between small and great in the treatment of his acquaintances, however much the unlucky lad's tastes, which were of the sumptuous order, led him to prefer good society; he was only too ready to share his guinea with a poor friend, and when he got money had an irresistible propensity for paying, which he never could conquer through life.

In his third year at college, the duns began to gather awfully round about him, and there was a levee at his oak

PEN'S STAIRCASE—2. A FEW LITTLE BILLS

which scandalized the tutors, and would have scared many a stouter heart. With some of these he used to battle, some he would bully (under Mr. Bloundell's directions, who was a master in this art, though he took a degree in no other), and some deprecate. And it is reported of him that little Mary Frodsham, the daughter of a certain poor gilder and frame-maker, whom Mr. Pen had thought fit to employ, and who had made a number of beautiful frames for his fine prints, coming to Pendennis with a piteous tale that her father was ill with ague, and that there was an execution in their house, Pen in an anguish of remorse rushed away, pawned his grand watch and every single article of jewellery except two old gold sleeve-buttons, which had belonged to his father, and rushed with the proceeds to Frodsham's shop, where, with tears in his eyes, and the deepest repentance and humility, he asked the poor tradesman's pardon.

This, young gentlemen, is not told as an instance of Pen's virtue, but rather of his weakness. It would have been much more virtuous to have had no prints at all. He still owed for the baubles which he sold in order to pay Frodsham's bill, and his mother had cruelly to pinch herself in order to discharge the jeweller's account, so that she was in the end the sufferer by the lad's impertinent fancies and follies. We are not presenting Pen to you as a hero or a model, only as a lad, who, in the midst of a thousand vanities and weaknesses, has as yet some generous impulses, and is not altogether dishonest.

We have said it was to the scandal of Mr. Buck the tutor that Pen's extravagances became known : from the manner in which he entered college, the associates he kept, and the introductions of Doctor Portman and the major, Buck for a long time thought that his pupil was a man of large property, and wondered rather that he only wore a plain gown. Once on going up to London to the Levée with an address from His Majesty's Loyal University of Oxbridge, Buck had seen Major Pendennis at St. James's in conversation with two Knights of the Garter, in the carriage of one of whom the dazzled tutor saw the major whisked away after the Levée. He asked Pen to wine the instant he came back, let him off from chapels and lectures more than ever, and felt perfectly sure that he was a young gentleman of large estate.

Thus, he was thunderstruck when he heard the truth, and received a dismal confession from Pen. His University debts were large, and the tutor had nothing to do, and of course Pen did not acquaint him, with his London debts. What man ever does tell all when pressed by his friends about his liabilities? The tutor learned enough to know that Pen was poor, that he had spent a handsome, almost a magnificent allowance, and had raised around him such a fine crop of debts, as it would be very hard work for any man to mow down; for there is no plant that grows so rapidly when once it has taken root.

Perhaps it was because she was so tender and good that Pen was terrified lest his mother should know of his sins. 'I can't bear to break it to her,' he said to the tutor in an agony of grief, 'Oh, sir, I've been a villain to her'—and he repented, and he wished he had the time to come over again, and he asked himself, 'Why, why did his uncle insist upon the necessity of living with great people, and in how much did all his grand acquaintance profit him?'

They were not shy, but Pen thought they were, and slunk from them during his last terms at college. He was as gloomy as a death's-head at parties, which he avoided of his own part, or to which his young friends soon ceased to invite him. Everybody knew that Pendennis was 'hard up.' That man Bloundell, who could pay nobody, and who was obliged to go down after three terms, was his ruin, the men said. His melancholy figure might be seen shirking about the lonely quadrangles in his battered old cap and torn gown, and he who had been the pride of the University but a year before, the man whom all the young ones loved to look at, was now the object of conversation at freshmen's wine parties, and they spoke of him with wonder and awe.

At last came the Degree Examinations. Many a young man of his year whose hob-nailed shoes Pen had derided, and whose face or coat he had caricatured—many a man whom he had treated with scorn in the lecture-room or crushed with his eloquence in the debating club—many of his own set who had not half his brains, but a little regularity and constancy of occupation, took high places in the honours or passed with decent credit. And where in the list was Pen the superb, Pen the wit and dandy, Pen the poet and orator? Ah, where was Pen the widow's darling

and sole pride? Let us hide our heads, and shut up the page. The lists came out; and a dreadful rumour rushed through the University, that Pendennis of Boniface was plucked.

CHAPTER XX

FLIGHT AFTER DEFEAT

DURING[1] the latter part of Pen's residence at the University of Oxbridge, his uncle's partiality had greatly increased for the lad. The major was proud of Arthur, who had high spirits, frank manners, a good person, and high gentlemanlike bearing. It pleased the old London bachelor to see Pen walking with the young patricians of his University, and he (who was never known to entertain his friends, and whose stinginess had passed into a sort of byword among some wags at the club, who envied his many engagements, and did not choose to consider his poverty) was charmed to give his nephew and the young lords snug little dinners at his lodgings, and to regale them with good claret, and his very best bons mots and stories: some of which would be injured by the repetition, for the major's manner of telling them was incomparably neat and careful; and others, whereof the repetition would do good to nobody. He paid his court to their parents through the young men, and to himself as it were by their company. He made more than one visit to Oxbridge, where the young fellows were amused by entertaining the old gentleman, and gave parties and breakfasts, and fêtes, partly to joke him and partly to do him honour. He plied them with his stories. He made himself juvenile and hilarious in the company of the young lords. He went to hear Pen at a grand debate at the Union, crowed and cheered, and rapped his stick in chorus with the cheers of the men, and was astounded at the boy's eloquence and fire. He thought he had got a young Pitt

for a nephew. He had an almost paternal fondness for Pen. He wrote to the lad letters with playful advice and the news of the town. He bragged about Arthur at his clubs, and introduced him with pleasure into his conversation; saying, that Egad, the young fellows were putting the old ones to the wall; that the lads who were coming up, young Lord Plinlimmon, a friend of my boy, young Lord Magnus Charters, a chum of my scapegrace, etc., would make a greater figure in the world than ever their fathers had done before them. He asked permission to bring Arthur to a grand fête at Gaunt House; saw him with ineffable satisfaction dancing with the sisters of the young noblemen before mentioned; and gave himself as much trouble to procure cards of invitation for the lad to some good houses, as if he had been a mamma with a daughter to marry, and not an old half-pay officer in a wig. And he boasted everywhere of the boy's great talents, and remarkable oratorical powers; and of the brilliant degree he was going to take. Lord Runnymede would take him on his embassy, or the duke would bring him in for one of his boroughs, he wrote over and over again to Helen; who, for her part, was too ready to believe anything that anybody chose to say in favour of her son.

And all this pride and affection of uncle and mother had been trampled down by Pen's wicked extravagance and idleness! I don't envy Pen's feelings (as the phrase is), as he thought of what he had done. He had slept, and the tortoise had won the race. He had marred at its outset what might have been a brilliant career. He had dipped ungenerously into a generous mother's purse; basely and recklessly spilt her little cruse. Oh, it was a coward hand that could strike and rob a creature so tender! And if Pen felt the wrong which he had done to others, are we to suppose that a young gentleman of his vanity did not feel still more keenly the shame he had brought upon himself? Let us be assured that there is no more cruel remorse than that; and no groans more piteous than those of wounded self-love. Like Joe Miller's friend,* the senior wrangler, who bowed to the audience from his box at the play, because he and the king happened to enter the theatre at the same time, only with a fatuity by no means so agreeable to himself, poor Arthur Pendennis felt perfectly convinced that all England would remark the absence of his name

from the examination-lists, and talk about his misfortune. His wounded tutor, his many duns, the skip and bed-maker who waited upon him, the undergraduates of his own time and the years below him, whom he had patronized or scorned—how could he bear to look any of them in the face now ? He rushed to his rooms, into which he shut himself, and there he penned a letter to his tutor, full of thanks, regards, remorse, and despair, requesting that his name might be taken off the college books, and intimating a wish and expectation that death would speedily end the woes of the disgraced Arthur Pendennis.

Then he slunk out, scarcely knowing whither he went, but mechanically taking the unfrequented little lanes by the backs of the colleges, until he cleared the University precincts, and got down to the banks of the Camisis* River, now deserted, but so often alive with the boat-races, and the crowds of cheering gownsmen, he wandered on and on, until he found himself at some miles' distance from Oxbridge, or rather was found by some acquaintances leaving that city.

As Pen went up a hill, a drizzling January rain beating in his face, and his ragged gown flying behind him—for he had not divested himself of his academical garments since the morning—a post-chaise came rattling up the road, on the box of which a servant was seated, whilst within, or rather half out of the carriage window, sat a young gentleman smoking a cigar, and loudly encouraging the postboy. It was our young acquaintance of Baymouth, Mr. Spavin, who had got his degree, and was driving homewards in triumph in his yellow post-chaise. He caught a sight of the figure, madly gesticulating as he worked up the hill, and of poor Pen's pale and ghastly face as the chaise whirled by him.

'Wo !' roared Mr. Spavin to the postboy, and the horses stopped in their mad career, and the carriage pulled up some fifty yards before Pen. He presently heard his own name shouted, and beheld the upper half of the body of Mr. Spavin thrust out of the side-window of the vehicle, and beckoning Pen vehemently towards it.

Pen stopped, hesitated—nodded his head fiercely, and pointed onwards, as if desirous that the postilion should proceed. He did not speak ; but his countenance must have looked very desperate, for young Spavin, having stared

at him with an expression of blank alarm, jumped out of the carriage presently, ran towards Pen holding out his hand, and grasping Pen's said, 'I say—hullo, old boy, where are you going, and what's the row now ?'

'I'm going where I deserve to go,' said Pen, with an imprecation.

'This ain't the way,' said Mr. Spavin, smiling. 'This is the Fenbury road. I say, Pen, don't take on because you are plucked. It's nothing when you are used to it. I've been plucked three times, old boy—and after the first time I didn't care. Glad it's over, though. You'll have better luck next time.'

Pen looked at his early acquaintance,—who had been plucked, who had been rusticated, who had only, after repeated failures, learned to read and write correctly, and who, in spite of all these drawbacks, had attained the honour of a degree. 'This man has passed,' he thought, 'and I have failed !' It was almost too much for him to bear.

'Good-bye, Spavin,' said he ; 'I'm very glad you are through. Don't let me keep you ; I'm in a hurry—I'm going to town to-night.'

'Gammon,' said Mr. Spavin. 'This ain't the way to town ; this is the Fenbury road, I tell you.'

'I was just going to turn back,' Pen said.

'All the coaches are full with the men going down,' Spavin said. Pen winced. 'You'd not get a place for a ten-pound note. Get into my yellow ; I'll drop you at Mudford, where you have a chance of the Fenbury mail. I'll lend you a hat and a coat ; I've got lots. Come along ; jump in, old boy—go it, leathers !'—and in this way Pen found himself in Mr. Spavin's post-chaise, and rode with that gentleman as far as the 'Ram Inn' at Mudford, fifteen miles from Oxbridge ; where the Fenbury mail changed horses, and where Pen got a place on to London.

The next day there was an immense excitement in Boniface College, Oxbridge, where, for some time, a rumour prevailed, to the terror of Pen's tutor and tradesmen, that Pendennis, maddened at losing his degree, had made away with himself—a battered cap, in which his name was almost discernible, together with a seal bearing his crest of an eagle looking at a now extinct sun, had been found three miles on the Fenbury road, near a mill-stream ; and, for four-and-twenty hours, it was supposed that poor Pen had

flung himself into the stream, until letters arrived from him, bearing the London post-mark.

The mail reached London at the dreary hour of five ; and he hastened to the inn at Covent Garden, at which he was accustomed to put up, where the ever-wakeful porter admitted him, and showed him to a bed. Pen looked hard at the man, and wondered whether Boots knew he was plucked ? When in bed he could not sleep there. He

tossed about until the appearance of the dismal London daylight, when he sprang up desperately, and walked off to his uncle's lodgings in Bury Street ; where the maid, who was scouring the steps, looked up suspiciously at him, as he came with an unshaven face, and yesterday's linen. He thought she knew of his mishap, too.

'Good 'evens, Mr. Harthur, what *'as* 'appened, sir ?' Mr. Morgan, the valet, asked, who had just arranged the well

brushed clothes and shiny boots at the door of his master's bedroom, and was carrying in his wig to the major.

'I want to see my uncle,' he cried, in a ghastly voice, and flung himself down on a chair.

Morgan backed before the pale and desperate-looking young man, with terrified and wondering glances, and disappeared into his master's apartment.

The major put his head out of the bedroom door as soon as he had his wig on.

'What? examination over? Senior Wrangler, double First Class, hey?' said the old gentleman—'I'll come directly;' and the head disappeared.

'They don't know what has happened,' groaned Pen; 'what will they say when they know all?'

Pen had been standing with his back to the window, and to such a dubious light as Bury Street enjoys of a foggy January morning, so that his uncle could not see the expression of the young man's countenance, or the looks of gloom and despair which even Mr. Morgan had remarked.

But when the major came out of his dressing-room neat and radiant, and preceded by faint odours from Delcroix's shop,* from which emporium Major Pendennis's wig and his pocket-handkerchief got their perfume, he held out one of his hands to Pen, and was about addressing him in his cheery, high-toned voice, when he caught sight of the boy's face at length, and dropping his hand, said, 'Good God! Pen, what's the matter?'

'You'll see it in the papers at breakfast, sir,' Pen said.

'See what?'

'My name isn't there, sir.'

'Hang it, why *should* it be?' asked the major, more perplexed.

'I have lost everything, sir,' Pen groaned out; 'my honour's gone; I'm ruined irretrievably; I can't go back to Oxbridge.'

'Lost your honour?' screamed out the major. 'Heaven alive! you don't mean to say you have shown the white feather?'

Pen laughed bitterly at the word feather, and repeated it. 'No, it isn't that, sir. I'm not afraid of being shot; I wish to God anybody would. I have not got my degree. I—I'm plucked, sir.'

The major had heard of plucking, but in a very vague and

cursory way, and concluded that it was some ceremony performed corporally upon rebellious University youth. 'I wonder you can look me in the face after such a disgrace, sir,' he said; 'I wonder you submitted to it as a gentleman.'

'I couldn't help it, sir. I did my classical papers well enough: it was those infernal mathematics, which I have always neglected.'

'Was it—was it done in public, sir?' the major said.

'What?'

'The—the plucking?' asked the guardian, looking Pen anxiously in the face.

Pen perceived the error under which his guardian was labouring, and in the midst of his misery the blunder caused the poor wretch a faint smile, and served to bring down the conversation from the tragedy-key, in which Pen had been disposed to carry it on. He explained to his uncle that he had gone in to pass his examination, and failed. On which the major said, that though he had expected far better things of his nephew, there was no great misfortune in this, and no dishonour as far as he saw, and that Pen must try again.

'*Me* again at Oxbridge,' Pen thought, 'after such a humiliation as that!' He felt that, except he went down to burn the place, he could not enter it.

But it was when he came to tell his uncle of his debts that the other felt surprise and anger most keenly, and broke out into speeches most severe upon Pen, which the lad bore, as best he might, without flinching. He had determined to make a clean breast, and had formed a full, true, and complete list of all his bills and liabilities at the University, and in London. They consisted of various items, such as

London Tailor.	Oxbridge do.
Oxbridge do.	Bill for horses.
Haberdasher, for shirts and gloves.	Printseller.
Jeweller.	Books.
College Cook.	Binding.
Crump, for desserts.	Hairdresser and Perfumery.
Bootmaker.	Hotel Bill in London.
Wine Merchant in London.	Sundries.

All which items the reader may fill in at his pleasure—such accounts have been inspected by the parents of many University youth—and it appeared that Mr. Pen's bills in all

amounted to about seven hundred pounds; and, furthermore, it was calculated that he had had more than twice that sum of ready money during his stay at Oxbridge. This sum he had spent, and for it had to show—what ?'

'You need not press a man who is down, sir,' Pen said to his uncle gloomily. 'I know very well how wicked and idle I have been. My mother won't like to see me dishonoured, sir,' he continued, with his voice failing; 'and I know she will pay these accounts. But I shall ask her for no more money.'

'As you like, sir,' the major said. 'You are of age, and my hands are washed of your affairs. But you can't live without money, and have no means of making it that I see, though you have a fine talent in spending it, and it is my belief that you will proceed as you have begun, and ruin your mother before you are five years older.—Good morning; it is time for me to go to breakfast. My engagements won't permit me to see you much during the time that you stay in London. I presume that you will acquaint your mother with the news which you have just conveyed to me.'

And pulling on his hat, and trembling in his limbs somewhat, Major Pendennis walked out of his lodgings before his nephew, and went ruefully off to take his accustomed corner at the club. He saw the Oxbridge examination-lists in the morning papers, and read over the names, not understanding the business, with mournful accuracy. He consulted various old fogies of his acquaintance, in the course of the day, at his clubs; Wenham, a dean, various civilians; and, as it is called, 'took their opinion,' showing to some of them the amount of his nephew's debts, which he had dotted down on the back of a card, and asking what was to be done, and whether such debts were not monstrous, preposterous? What was to be done?—There was nothing for it but to pay. Wenham and the others told the major of young men who owed twice as much—five times as much—as Arthur, and with no means at all to pay. The consultations, and calculations, and opinions comforted the major somewhat. After all, *he* was not to pay.

But he thought bitterly of the many plans he had formed to make a man of his nephew, of the sacrifices which he had made, and of the manner in which he was disappointed. And he wrote off a letter to Doctor Portman, informing him of the direful events which had taken place, and begging the

doctor to break them to Helen. For the orthodox old gentleman preserved the regular routine in all things, and was of opinion that it was more correct to ' break ' a piece of bad news to a person by means of a (possibly maladroit and unfeeling) messenger, than to convey it simply to its destination by a note. So the major wrote to Doctor Portman, and then went out to dinner, one of the saddest men in any London dining-room that day.

Pen, too, wrote his letter, and skulked about London streets for the rest of the day, fancying that everybody was looking at him and whispering to his neighbour, 'That is Pendennis of Boniface, who was plucked yesterday.' His letter to his mother was full of tenderness and remorse : he wept the bitterest tears over it—and the repentance and passion soothed him to some degree.

He saw a party of roaring young blades from Oxbridge in the coffee-room of his hotel, and slunk away from them, and paced the streets. He remembers, he says, the prints which he saw hanging up at Ackermann's window in the rain, and a book which he read at a stall near the Temple : at night he went to the pit of the play, and saw Miss Fotheringay, but he doesn't in the least recollect in what piece.

On the second day there came a kind letter from his tutor, containing many grave and appropriate remarks upon the event which had befallen him, but strongly urging Pen not to take his name off the University books, and to retrieve a disaster which, everybody knew, was owing to his own carelessness alone, and which he might repair by a month's application. He said he had ordered Pen's skip to pack up some trunks of the young gentleman's wardrobe, which duly arrived with fresh copies of all Pen's bills laid on the top.

On the third day there arrived a letter from home ; which Pen read in his bedroom, and the result of which was that he fell down on his knees, with his head in the bed-clothes, and there prayed out his heart, and humbled himself ; and having gone downstairs and eaten an immense breakfast, he sallied forth and took his place at the 'Bull and Mouth,' Piccadilly, by the Chatteris coach for that evening.

CHAPTER XXI

PRODIGAL'S RETURN

UCH a letter as the major wrote of course sent Doctor Portman to Fairoaks, and he went off with that alacrity which a good man shows when he has disagreeable news to communicate. He wished the deed done, and done quickly. He is sorry, but *que voulez-vous ?* the tooth must be taken out, and he has you into the chair, and it is surprising with what courage and vigour of wrist he applies the forceps. Perhaps he would not be quite so active or eager if it were *his* tooth ; but, in fine, it is your duty to have it out. So the doctor, having read the epistle out to Mira and Mrs. Portman, with many damnatory comments upon the young scapegrace who was going deeper and deeper into perdition, left those ladies to spread the news through the Clavering society, which they did with their accustomed accuracy and dispatch, and strode over to Fairoaks to break the intelligence to the widow.

She had the news already. She had read Pen's letter, and it had relieved her somehow. A gloomy presentiment of evil had been hanging over her for many, many months past. She knew the worst now, and her darling boy was come back to her repentant and tender-hearted. Did she want more ? All that the rector could say (and his remarks were both dictated by common sense, and made respectable by antiquity) could not bring Helen to feel any indignation or particular unhappiness, except that the boy should be unhappy. What was this degree that they made such an outcry about, and what good would it do Pen ? Why did Doctor Portman and his uncle insist upon sending the boy to a place where there was so much temptation to be risked, and so little good to be won ? Why didn't they leave him at home with his mother ? As for his debts, of course they must be paid ;—his debts !—wasn't his father's money all his, and hadn't he a right to spend it ? In this

way the widow met the virtuous doctor, and all the arrows of his indignation somehow took no effect upon her gentle bosom.

For some time past, an agreeable practice, known since times ever so ancient, by which brothers and sisters are wont to exhibit their affection towards one another, and in which Pen and his little sister Laura had been accustomed to indulge pretty frequently in their childish days, had been given up by the mutual consent of those two individuals. Coming back from college after an absence from home of some months, in place of the simple girl whom he had left behind him, Mr. Arthur found a tall, slim, handsome young lady, to whom he could not somehow proffer the kiss which he had been in the habit of administering previously, and who received him with a gracious curtsy and a proffered hand, and with a great blush which rose up to the cheek, just upon the very spot which young Pen had been used to salute.

I am not good at descriptions of female beauty ; and, indeed, do not care for it in the least (thinking that goodness and virtue are, of course, far more advantageous to a young lady than any mere fleeting charms of person and face), and so shall not attempt any particular delineation of Miss Laura Bell at the age of sixteen years.* At that age she had attained her present altitude of five feet four inches, so that she was called tall and gawky by some, and a Maypole by others, of her own sex, who prefer littler women. But if she was a Maypole, she had beautiful roses about her head, and it is a fact that many swains were disposed to dance round her. She was ordinarily pale, with a faint rose tinge in her cheeks ; but they flushed up in a minute when occasion called, and continued so blushing ever so long, the roses remaining after the emotion had passed away which had summoned those pretty flowers into existence. Her eyes have been described as very large from her earliest childhood, and retained that characteristic in later life. Good-natured critics (always females) said that she was in the habit of making play with those eyes, and ogling the gentlemen and ladies in her company ; but the fact is, that Nature had made them so to shine and to look, and they could no more help so looking and shining than one star can help being brighter than another. It was doubtless to mitigate their brightness that Miss Laura's eyes were provided with two pairs of veils in the shape of the longest and finest black

eyelashes, so that, when she closed her eyes, the same people who found fault with those orbs, said that she wanted to show her eyelashes off ; and, indeed, I dare say that to see her asleep would have been a pretty sight.

As for her complexion, that was nearly as brilliant as Lady Mantrap's, and without the powder which her ladyship uses. Her nose must be left to the reader's imagination : if her mouth was rather large (as Miss Piminy avers, who, but for her known appetite, one would think could not swallow anything larger than a button), everybody allowed that her smile was charming, and showed off a set of pearly teeth, whilst her voice was so low and sweet, that to hear it was like listening to sweet music. Because she is in the habit of wearing very long dresses, people of course say that her feet are not small : but it may be, that they are of the size becoming her figure, and it does not follow, because Mrs. Pincher is always putting *her* foot out, that all other ladies should be perpetually bringing theirs on the tapis. In fine, Miss Laura Bell, at the age of sixteen, was a sweet young lady. Many thousands of such are to be found, let us hope, in this country, where there is no lack of goodness, and modesty, and purity, and beauty.

Now, Miss Laura, since she had learned to think for herself (and in the past two years her mind and her person had both developed themselves considerably), had only been half pleased with Pen's general conduct and bearing. His letters to his mother at home had become of late very rare and short. It was in vain that the fond widow urged how constant Arthur's occupations and studies were, and how many his engagements. ' It is better that he should lose a prize,' Laura said, ' than forget his mother : and indeed, mamma, I don't see that he gets many prizes. Why doesn't he come home and stay with you, instead of passing his vacations at his great friends' fine houses ? There is nobody there will love him half so much as—as you do.' ' As *I* do only, Laura,' sighed out Mrs. Pendennis. Laura declared stoutly that she did not love Pen a bit, when he did not do his duty to his mother : nor would she be convinced by any of Helen's fond arguments, that the boy must make his way in the world ; that his uncle was most desirous that Pen should cultivate the acquaintance of persons who were likely to befriend him in life ; that men had a thousand ties and calls which women could not understand, and so forth. Perhaps

Helen no more believed in these excuses than her adopted daughter did; but she tried to believe that she believed them, and comforted herself with the maternal infatuation. And that is a point whereon I suppose many a gentleman has reflected, that, do what we will, we are pretty sure of the woman's love that once has been ours; and that that untiring tenderness and forgiveness never fail us.

Also, there had been that freedom, not to say audacity, in Arthur's latter talk and ways, which had shocked and displeased Laura. Not that he ever offended her by rudeness, or addressed to her a word which she ought not to hear, for Mr. Pen was a gentleman, and by nature and education polite to every woman, high and low; but he spoke lightly and laxly of women in general; was less courteous in his actions than in his words—neglectful in sundry ways, and in many of the little offices of life. It offended Miss Laura that he should smoke his horrid pipes in the house; that he should refuse to go to church with his mother, or on walks or visits with her, and be found yawning over his novel in his dressing-gown, when the gentle widow returned from those duties. The hero of Laura's early infancy, about whom she had passed so many, many nights talking with Helen (who recited endless stories of the boy's virtues, and love, and bravery, when he was away at school), was a very different person from the young man whom now she knew; bold and brilliant, sarcastic and defiant, seeming to scorn the simple occupations or pleasures, or even devotions, of the women with whom he lived, and whom he quitted on such light pretexts.

The Fotheringay affair, too, when Laura came to hear of it (which she did first by some sarcastic allusions of Major Pendennis, when on a visit to Fairoaks, and then from their neighbours at Clavering, who had plenty of information to give her on this head), vastly shocked and outraged Miss Laura. A Pendennis fling himself away on such a woman as that! Helen's boy galloping away from home, day after day, to fall on his knees to an actress, and drink with her horrid father! A good son want to bring such a man and such a woman into his house, and set her over his mother! 'I would have run away, mamma; I would, if I had had to walk barefoot through the snow,' Laura said.

'And *you* would have left me too, then?' Helen answered; on which, of course, Laura withdrew her previous

observation, and the two women rushed into each other's embraces with that warmth which belonged to both their natures, and which characterizes not a few of their sex. Whence came all this indignation of Miss Laura about Arthur's passion ? Perhaps she did not know that, if men throw themselves away upon women, women throw themselves away upon men, too ; and that there is no more accounting for love, than for any other physical liking or antipathy : perhaps she had been misinformed by the Clavering people and old Mrs. Portman, who was vastly bitter against Pen, especially since his impertinent behaviour to the doctor, and since the wretch had smoked cigars in church-time : perhaps, finally, she was jealous ; but this is a vice in which it is said the ladies very seldom indulge.

Albeit she was angry with Pen ; against his mother she had no such feeling ; but devoted herself to Helen with the utmost force of her girlish affection—such affection as women, whose hearts are disengaged, are apt to bestow upon the near female friend. It was devotion—it was passion—it was all sorts of fondness and folly ; it was a profusion of caresses, tender epithets and endearments, such as it does not become sober historians with beards to narrate. Do not let us men despise these instincts because we cannot feel them. These women were made for our comfort and delectation, gentlemen—with all the rest of the minor animals.

But as soon as Miss Laura heard that Pen was unfortunate and unhappy, all her wrath against him straightway vanished, and gave place to the most tender and unreasonable compassion. He was the Pen of old days once more restored to her, the frank and affectionate, the generous and tender-hearted. She at once took side with Helen against Doctor Portman, when he outcried at the enormity of Pen's transgressions. Debts ? what were his debts ? they were a trifle; he had been thrown into expensive society by his uncle's order, and of course was obliged to live in the same manner as the young gentlemen whose company he frequented. Disgraced by not getting his degree ? the poor boy was ill when he went in for the examinations : he couldn't think of his mathematics and stuff on account of those very debts which oppressed him ; very likely some of the odious tutors and masters were jealous of him, and had favourites of their own whom they wanted to put over his head. *Other* people

disliked him, and were cruel to him, and were unfair to him, she was very sure. And so, with flushing cheeks and eyes bright with anger, this young creature reasoned ; and she went up and seized Helen's hand, and kissed her in the doctor's presence, and her looks braved the doctor, and seemed to ask how he dared to say a word against her darling mother's Pen ?

When that divine took his leave, not a little discomfited and amazed at the pertinacious obstinacy of the women, Laura repeated her embraces and arguments with tenfold fervour to Helen, who felt that there was a great deal of cogency in most of the latter. There must be some jealousy against Pen. She felt quite sure that he had offended some of the examiners, who had taken a mean revenge of him—nothing more likely. Altogether, the announcement of the misfortune vexed these two ladies very little indeed. Pen, who was plunged in his shame and grief in London, and torn with great remorse for thinking of his mother's sorrow, would have wondered, had he seen how easily she bore the calamity. Indeed, calamity is welcome to women if they think it will bring truant affection home again : and if you have reduced your mistress to a crust, depend upon it that she won't repine, and only take a very little bit of it for herself, provided you will eat the remainder in her company.

And directly the doctor was gone, Laura ordered fires to be lighted in Mr. Arthur's rooms, and his bedding to be aired ; and had these preparations completed by the time Helen had finished a most tender and affectionate letter to Pen : when the girl, smiling fondly, took her mamma by the hand, and led her into those apartments where the fires were blazing so cheerfully, and there the two kind creatures sat down on the bed, and talked about Pen ever so long. Laura added a postscript to Helen's letter, in which she called him her dearest Pen, and bade him come home *instantly*, with two of the handsomest dashes under the word, and be happy with his mother and his affectionate sister Laura.

In the middle of the night—as these two ladies, after reading their Bibles a great deal during the evening, and after taking just a look into Pen's room as they passed to their own—in the middle of the night, I say, Laura, whose head not unfrequently chose to occupy that pillow which

the nightcap of the late Pendennis had been accustomed to press, cried out suddenly, 'Mamma, are you awake ?'

Helen stirred and said, 'Yes, I'm awake.' The truth is, though she had been lying quite still and silent, she had not been asleep one instant, but had been looking at the night-lamp in the chimney, and had been thinking of Pen for hours and hours.

Then Miss Laura (who had been acting with similar hypocrisy, and lying, occupied with her own thoughts, as motionless as Helen's brooch, with Pen's and Laura's hair in it, on the frilled white pincushion on the dressing-table) began to tell Mrs. Pendennis of a notable plan which she had been forming in her busy little brains ; and by which all Pen's embarrassments would be made to vanish in a moment, and without the least trouble to anybody.

'You know, mamma,' this young lady said, 'that I have been living with you for ten years, during which time you have never taken any of my money, and have been treating me just as if I was a charity girl. Now, this obligation has offended me very much, because I am proud and do not like to be beholden to people. And as, if I had gone to school—only I wouldn't—it must have cost me at least fifty pounds a year, it is clear that I owe you fifty times ten pounds, which I know you have put into the bank at Chatteris for me, and which doesn't belong to me a bit. Now, to-morrow we will go to Chatteris, and see that nice old Mr. Rowdy, with the bald head, and ask him for it—not for his head, but for the five hundred pounds : and I dare say he will lend you two more, which we will save and pay back ; and we will send the money to Pen, who can pay all his debts without hurting anybody, and then we will live happy ever after.'

What Helen replied to this speech need not be repeated, as the widow's answer was made up of a great number of incoherent ejaculations, embraces, and other irrelative matter. But the two women slept well after that talk ; and when the night-lamp went out with a splutter, and the sun rose gloriously over the purple hills, and the birds began to sing and pipe cheerfully amidst the leafless trees and glistening evergreens on Fairoaks lawn, Helen woke too, and as she looked at the sweet face of the girl sleeping beside her, her lips parted with a smile, blushes on her cheeks, her spotless bosom heaving and falling with gentle

undulations, as if happy dreams were sweeping over it—Pen's mother felt happy and grateful beyond all power of words, save such as pious women offer up to the Beneficent Dispenser of love and mercy—in whose honour a chorus of such praises is constantly rising up all round the world.

Although it was January and rather cold weather, so sincere was Mr. Pen's remorse, and so determined his plans of economy, that he would not take an inside place in the coach, but sat up behind with his friend the guard, who remembered his former liberality, and lent him plenty of great-coats. Perhaps it was the cold that made his knees tremble as he got down at the lodge gate, or it may be that he was agitated at the notion of seeing the kind creature for whose love he had made so selfish a return. Old John was in waiting to receive his master's baggage, but he appeared in a fustian jacket, and no longer wore his livery of drab and blue. 'I'se garner and stable-man, and lives in the ladge now,' this worthy man remarked, with a grin of welcome to Pen, and something of a blush; but instantly as Pen turned the corner of the shrubbery and was out of eye-shot of the coach, Helen made her appearance, her face beaming with love and forgiveness—for forgiving is what some women love best of all.

We may be sure that the widow, having a certain other object in view, had lost no time in writing off to Pen an account of the noble, the magnanimous, the magnificent offer of Laura, filling up her letter with a profusion of benedictions upon both her children. It was probably the knowledge of this money-obligation which caused Pen to blush very much when he saw Laura, who was in waiting in the hall, and who this time, and for this time only, broke through the little arrangement of which we have spoken, as having subsisted between her and Arthur for the last few years; but the truth is, there has been a great deal too much said about kissing in the present chapter.

So the Prodigal came home, and the fatted calf was killed for him, and he was made as happy as two simple women could make him. No allusions were made to the Oxbridge mishap, or questions asked as to his farther proceedings, for some time. But Pen debated these anxiously in his own mind, and up in his own room, where he passed much time in cogitation.

A few days after he came home, he rode to Chatteris on his horse, and came back on the top of the coach. He then informed his mother that he had left the horse to be sold; and when that operation was effected, he handed her over the cheque, which she, and possibly Pen himself, thought was an act of uncommon virtue and self-denial, but which Laura pronounced to be only strict justice.

He rarely mentioned the loan which she had made, and which, indeed, had been accepted by the widow with certain modifications; but once or twice, and with great hesitation and stammering, he alluded to it, and thanked her. It evidently pained his vanity to be beholden to the orphan for succour. He was wild to find some means of repaying her.

He left off drinking wine, and betook himself, but with great moderation, to the refreshment of whisky-and-water. He gave up cigar-smoking; but it must be confessed that of late years he had liked pipes and tobacco as well or even better, so that this sacrifice was not a very severe one.

He fell asleep a great deal after dinner when he joined the ladies in the drawing-room, and was certainly very moody and melancholy. He watched the coaches with great interest, walked in to read the papers at Clavering assiduously, dined with anybody who would ask him (and the widow was glad that he should have any entertainment in their solitary place), and played a good deal at cribbage with Captain Glanders.

He avoided Dr. Portman, who, in his turn, whenever Pen passed, gave him very severe looks from under his shovel-hat. He went to church with his mother, however, very regularly, and read prayers for her at home to the little household. Always humble, it was greatly diminished now: a couple of maids did the work of the house of Fairoaks: the silver dish-covers never saw the light at all. John put on his livery to go to church and assert his dignity on Sundays, but it was only for form's sake. He was gardener and outdoor man, vice Upton, resigned. There was but little fire in Fairoaks kitchen, and John and the maids drank their evening beer there by the light of a single candle. All this was Mr. Pen's doing, and the state of things did not increase his cheerfulness.

For some time Pen said no power on earth could induce him to go back to Oxbridge again, after his failure there;

but one day, Laura said to him, with many blushes, that she thought, as some sort of reparation, of punishment on himself for his—for his idleness, he ought to go back and get his degree, if he could fetch it by doing so ; and so back Mr. Pen went.

A plucked man is a dismal being in a University ; belonging to no set of men there, and owned by no one. Pen felt himself plucked indeed of all the fine feathers which he had won during his brilliant years, and rarely appeared out of his college ; regularly going to morning chapel, and shutting himself up in his rooms of nights, away from the noise and suppers of the undergraduates. There were no duns about his door, they were all paid—scarcely any cards were left there. The men of his year had taken their degrees, and were gone. He went into a second examination, and passed with perfect ease. He was somewhat more easy in his mind when he appeared in his bachelor's gown.

On his way back from Oxbridge he paid a visit to his uncle in London ; but the old gentleman received him with very cold looks, and would scarcely give him his forefinger to shake. He called a second time, but Morgan, the valet, said his master was from home.

Pen came back to Fairoaks, and to his books and to his idleness, and loneliness and despair. He commenced several tragedies, and wrote many copies of verses of a gloomy cast. He formed plans of reading and broke them. He thought about enlisting—about the Spanish legion*—about a profession. He chafed against his captivity, and cursed the idleness which had caused it. Helen said he was breaking his heart, and was sad to see his prostration. As soon as they could afford it, he should go abroad—he should go to London—he should be freed from the dull society of two poor women. It *was* dull—very, certainly. The tender widow's habitual melancholy seemed to deepen into a sadder gloom ; and Laura saw with alarm that the dear friend became every year more languid and weary, and that her pale cheek grew more wan.

CHAPTER XXII

NEW FACES

THE inmates of Fairoaks were drowsily pursuing this humdrum existence, while the great house upon the hill, on the other side of the River Brawl, was shaking off the slumber in which it had lain during the lives of two generations of masters, and giving extraordinary signs of renewed liveliness.

Just about the time of Pen's little mishap, and when he was so absorbed in the grief occasioned by that calamity as to take no notice of events which befell persons less interesting to himself than Arthur Pendennis, an announcement appeared in the provincial journals which caused no small sensation in the county at least, and in all the towns, villages, halls and mansions, and parsonages for many miles round Clavering Park. At Clavering Market; at Cackleby Fair; at Chatteris Sessions; on Gooseberry Green, as the squire's carriage met the vicar's one-horse contrivance, and the inmates of both vehicles stopped on the road to talk; at Tinkleton Church gate, as the bell was tolling in the sunshine, and the white smocks and scarlet cloaks came trooping over the green common, to Sunday worship; in a hundred societies round about—the word was, that Clavering Park was to be inhabited again.

Some five years before, the county papers had advertised the marriage at Florence, at the British Legation, of Francis Clavering, Esq., only son of Sir Francis Clavering, Bart., of Clavering Park, with Jemima Augusta, daughter of Samuel Snell, of Calcutta, Esq., and widow of the late J. Amory, Esq. At that time the legend in the county was that Clavering, who had been ruined for many a year, had married a widow from India with some money. Some of the county folks caught a sight of the newly-married pair. The Kickleburys, travelling in Italy, had seen them.

Clavering occupied the Poggi Palace at Florence, gave parties, and lived comfortably—but could never come to England. Another year—young Peregrine, of Cackleby, making a Long Vacation tour, had fallen in with the Claverings occupying Schloss Schinkenstein, on the Mummel See. At Rome, at Lucca, at Nice, at the baths and gambling-places of the Rhine and Belgium, this worthy couple might occasionally be heard of by the curious, and rumours of them came, as it were by gusts, to Clavering's ancestral place.

Their last place of abode was Paris, where they appear to have lived in great fashion and splendour after the news of the death of Samuel Snell, Esq., of Calcutta, reached his orphan daughter in Europe.

Of Sir Francis Clavering's antecedents little can be said that would be advantageous to that respected baronet. The son of an outlaw, living in a dismal old château near Bruges, this gentleman had made a feeble attempt to start in life with a commission in a Dragoon regiment, and had broken down almost at the outset. Transactions at the gambling-table had speedily effected his ruin; after a couple of years in the army he had been forced to sell out, had passed some time in Her Majesty's prison of the Fleet, and had then shipped over to Ostend to join the gouty exile, his father. And in Belgium, France, and Germany, for some years, this decayed and abortive prodigal might be seen lurking about billiard-rooms and watering-places, punting at gambling-houses, dancing at boarding-house balls, and riding steeplechases on other folks' horses.

It was at a boarding-house at Lausanne, that Francis Clavering made what he called the lucky *coup* of marrying the widow Amory, very lately returned from Calcutta. His father died soon after, by consequence of whose demise his wife became Lady Clavering. The title so delighted Mr. Snell of Calcutta, that he doubled his daughter's allowance; and, dying himself soon after, left a fortune to her and her children, the amount of which was, if not magnified by rumour, something very splendid indeed.

Before this time there had been, not rumours unfavourable to Lady Clavering's reputation, but unpleasant impressions regarding her ladyship. The best English people abroad were shy of making her acquaintance; her manners were not the most refined; her origin was lamentably low

and doubtful. The retired East Indians, who are to be found in considerable force in most of the Continental towns frequented by English, spoke with much scorn of the disreputable old lawyer and indigo-smuggler her father, and of Amory, her first husband, who had been mate of the Indiaman in which Miss Snell came out to join her father at Calcutta. Neither father nor daughter were in society at Calcutta, or had ever been heard of at Government House. Old Sir Jasper Rogers, who had been Chief Justice of Calcutta, had once said to his wife, that he could tell a queer story about Lady Clavering's first husband; but greatly to Lady Rogers's disappointment, and that of the young ladies his daughters, the old judge could never be got to reveal that mystery.

They were all, however, glad enough to go to Lady Clavering's parties, when her ladyship took the Hôtel Bouilli in the Rue Grenelle at Paris, and blazed out in the polite world there in the winter of 183—. The Faubourg St. Germain took her up. Viscount Bagwig, our excellent ambassador, paid her marked attention. The princes of the family frequented her salons. The most rigid and noted of the English ladies resident in the French capital acknowledged and countenanced her; the virtuous Lady Elderbury, the severe Lady Rockminster, the venerable Countess of Southdown—people, in a word, renowned for austerity, and of quite a dazzling moral purity:—so great and beneficent an influence had the possession of ten (some said twenty) thousand a year exercised upon Lady Clavering's character and reputation. And her munificence and goodwill were unbounded. Anybody (in society) who had a scheme of charity was sure to find her purse open. The French ladies of piety got money from her to support their schools and convents; she subscribed indifferently for the Armenian patriarch; for Father Barbarossa, who came to Europe to collect funds for his monastery on Mount Athos; for the Baptist Mission to Quashyboo, and the Orthodox Settlement in Feefawfoo, the largest and most savage of the Cannibal Islands. And it is on record of her, that, on the same day on which Madame de Cricri got five napoleons from her in support of the poor persecuted Jesuits,* who were at that time in very bad odour in France, Lady Budelight put her down in her subscription-list for the Rev. J. Ramshorn, who had had a vision which ordered him to

convert the Pope of Rome. And more than this, and for the benefit of the worldly, her ladyship gave the best dinners, and the grandest balls and suppers, which were known at Paris during that season.

And it was during this time, that the good-natured lady must have arranged matters with her husband's creditors in England, for Sir Francis reappeared in his native country, without fear of arrest; was announced in the *Morning Post*, and the county paper, as having taken up his residence at Mivart's Hotel; and one day the anxious old housekeeper at Clavering House beheld a carriage and four horses drive up the long avenue, and stop before the moss-grown steps in front of the vast melancholy portico.

Three gentlemen were in the carriage—an open one. On the back seat was our old acquaintance, Mr. Tatham of Chatteris, whilst in the places of honour sat a handsome and portly gentleman enveloped in moustachios, whiskers, fur collars, and braiding, and by him a pale languid man, who descended feebly from the carriage, when the little lawyer, and the gentleman in fur, had nimbly jumped out of it.

They walked up the great moss-grown steps to the hall-door, and a foreign attendant, with ear-rings and a gold-laced cap, pulled strenuously at the great bell-handle at the cracked and sculptured gate. The bell was heard clanging loudly through the vast gloomy mansion. Steps resounded presently upon the marble pavement of the hall within; and the doors opened, and finally, Mrs. Blenkinsop, the housekeeper, Polly, her aide de camp, and Smart, the keeper, appeared bowing humbly.

Smart, the keeper, pulled the wisp of hay-coloured hair which adorned his sunburnt forehead, kicked out his left heel, as if there were a dog biting at his calves, and brought down his head to a bow. Old Mrs. Blenkinsop dropped a curtsy. Little Polly, her aide de camp, made a curtsy, and several rapid bows likewise: and Mrs. Blenkinsop, with a great deal of emotion, quavered out, 'Welcome to Clavering, Sir Francis. It du my poor eyes good to see one of the family once more.'

The speech and the greetings were all addressed to the grand gentleman in fur and braiding, who wore his hat so magnificently on one side, and twirled his moustachios so royally. But he burst out laughing, and said, 'You've

saddled the wrong horse, old lady—I'm not Sir Francis Clavering what's come to revisit the halls of my ancestors. Friends and vassals ! behold your rightful lord !'

And he pointed his hand towards the pale, languid gentleman, who said, 'Don't be an ass, Ned.

'Yes, Mrs. Blenkinsop, I'm Sir Francis Clavering ; I recollect you quite well. Forgot me, I suppose ?—How dy do ?' and he took the old lady's trembling hand ; and nodded in her astonished face, in a not unkind manner.

Mrs. Blenkinsop declared upon her conscience that she would have known Sir Francis anywhere ; that he was the very image of Sir Francis his father, and of Sir John who had gone before.

'Oh yes—thanky—of course—very much obliged—and that sort of thing,' Sir Francis said, looking vacantly about the hall. 'Dismal old place, ain't it, Ned ? Never saw it but once, when my governor quarrelled with my gwandfather, in the year twenty-thwee.'

'Dismal ?—beautiful !—the Castle of Otranto !—the Mysteries of Udolpho,* by Jove !' said the individual addressed as Ned. 'What a fire-place ! You might roast an elephant in it. Splendid carved gallery ! Inigo Jones, by Jove ! I'd lay five to two it's Inigo Jones.'

'The upper part by Inigo Jones ; the lower was altered by the eminent Dutch architect, Vanderputty, in George the First his time, by Sir Richard, fourth baronet,' said the housekeeper.

'Oh, indeed,' said the baronet. 'Gad, Ned, you know everything.'

'I know a few things, Frank,' Ned answered. 'I know that's not a Snyders over the mantelpiece—bet you three to one it's a copy. We'll restore it, my boy. A lick of varnish, and it will come out wonderfully, sir. That old fellow in the red gown, I suppose, is Sir Richard.'

'Sheriff of the county, and sat in Parliament in the reign of Queen Anne,' said the housekeeper, wondering at the stranger's knowledge ; 'that on the right is Theodosia, wife of Harbottle, second baronet, by Lely,* represented in the character of Venus, the Goddess of Beauty — her son Gregory, the third baronet, by her side, as Cupid, God of Love, with a bow and arrows ; that on the next panel is Sir Rupert, made a knight banneret by Charles the First, and whose property was confuscated by Oliver Cromwell.'

'Thank you—needn't go on, Mrs. Blenkinsop,' said the baronet. 'We'll walk about the place ourselves. Frosch, give me a cigar. Have a cigar, Mr. Tatham ?'

Little Mr. Tatham tried a cigar which Sir Francis's courier handed to him, and over which the lawyer spluttered fearfully. 'Needn't come with us, Mrs. Blenkinsop. What's-his-name—you—Smart—feed the horses and wash their mouths. Shan't stay long. Come along, Strong—I know the way : I was here in twenty-thwee,* at the end of my gwandfather's time.' And Sir Francis and Captain Strong, for such was the style and title of Sir Francis's friend, passed out of the hall into the reception-rooms, leaving the discomfited Mrs. Blenkinsop to disappear by a side-door which led to her apartments, now the only habitable rooms in the long-uninhabited mansion.

It was a place so big that no tenant could afford to live in it ; and Sir Francis and his friend walked through room after room, admiring their vastness and dreary and deserted grandeur. On the right of the hall door were the saloons and drawing-rooms, and on the other side the oak room, the parlour, the grand dining-room, the library, where Pen had found books in old days. Round three sides of the hall ran a gallery, by which, and corresponding passages, the chief bedrooms were approached, and of which many were of stately proportions and exhibited marks of splendour. On the second story was a labyrinth of little discomfortable garrets, destined for the attendants of the great folks who inhabited the mansion in the days when it was first built : and I do not know any more cheering mark of the increased philanthropy of our own times, than to contrast our domestic architecture with that of our ancestors, and to see how much better servants and poor are cared for at present, than in times when my lord and lady slept under gold canopies, and their servants lay above them in quarters not so airy or so clean as stables are now.

Up and down the house the two gentlemen wandered, the owner of the mansion being very silent and resigned about the pleasure of possessing it ; whereas the captain, his friend, examined the premises with so much interest and eagerness that you would have thought he was the master, and the other the indifferent spectator of the place. 'I see capabilities* in it—capabilities in it, sir,' cried the captain. 'Gad, sir, leave it to me, and I'll make it the

pride of the country, at a small expense. What a theatre we can have in the library here, the curtains between the columns which divide the room! What a famous room for a galop!—it will hold the whole shire. We'll hang the morning parlour with the tapestry in your second salon in the Rue de Grenelle, and furnish the oak room with the Moyen-age cabinets and the armour. Armour looks splendid against black oak, and there's a Venice glass in the Quai Voltaire, which will suit that high mantelpiece to an inch, sir. The long saloon, white and crimson of course; the drawing-room yellow satin; and the little drawing-room light blue, with lace over—hey?'

'I recollect my old governor caning me in that little room,' Sir Francis said sententiously; 'he always hated me, my old governor.'

'Chintz is the dodge, I suppose, for my lady's rooms—the suite in the landing, to the south, the bedroom, the sitting-room, and the dressing-room. We'll throw a conservatory out, over the balcony. Where will you have your rooms?'

'Put mine in the north wing,' said the baronet, with a yawn, 'and out of the reach of Miss Amory's confounded piano. I can't bear it. She's scweeching from morning till night.'

The captain burst out laughing. He settled the whole further arrangements of the house in the course of their walk through it; and, the promenade ended, they went into the steward's room, now inhabited by Mrs. Blenkinsop, and where Mr. Tatham was sitting poring over a plan of the estate, and the old housekeeper had prepared a collation in honour of her lord and master.

Then they inspected the kitchen and stables, about both of which Sir Francis was rather interested, and Captain Strong was for examining the gardens; but the baronet said, 'D—— the gardens, and that sort of thing!' and finally he drove away from the house as unconcernedly as he had entered it; and that night the people of Clavering learned that Sir Francis Clavering had paid a visit to the Park, and was coming to live in the county.

When this fact came to be known at Chatteris, all the folks in the place were set in commotion: High Church and Low Church, half-pay captains and old maids and dowagers, sporting squireens of the vicinage, farmers, tradesmen, and

factory people—all the population in and round about the little place. The news was brought to Fairoaks, and received by the ladies there, and by Mr. Pen, with some excitement. 'Mrs. Pybus says there is a very pretty girl in the family, Arthur,' Laura said, who was as kind and thoughtful upon this point as women generally are: 'a Miss Amory, Lady Clavering's daughter by her first marriage. Of course, you will fall in love with her as soon as she arrives.'

Helen cried out, 'Don't talk nonsense, Laura.' Pen laughed, and said, 'Well, there is the young Sir Francis for you.'

'He is but four years old,' Miss Laura replied. 'But I shall console myself with that handsome officer, Sir Francis's friend. He was at church last Sunday, in the Clavering pew, and his moustachios were beautiful.'

Indeed the number of Sir Francis's family (whereof the members have all been mentioned in the above paragraphs) was pretty soon known in his town, and everything else, as nearly as human industry and ingenuity could calculate, regarding his household. The Park avenue and grounds were dotted now with town folks of the summer evenings, who made their way up to the great house, peered about the premises, and criticized the improvements which were taking place there. Loads upon loads of furniture arrived in numberless vans from Chatteris and London; and numerous as the vans were, there was not one but Captain Glanders knew what it contained, and escorted the baggage up to the Park House.

He and Captain Edward Strong had formed an intimate acquaintance by this time. The younger captain occupied those very lodgings at Clavering which the peaceful Smirke had previously tenanted, and was deep in the good graces of Madame Fribsby, his landlady; and of the whole town, indeed. The captain was splendid in person and raiment; fresh-coloured, blue-eyed, black-whiskered, broad-chested, athletic—a slight tendency to fullness did not take away from the comeliness of his jolly figure—a braver soldier never presented a broader chest to the enemy. As he strode down Clavering High Street, his hat on one side, his cane clanking on the pavement, or waving round him in the execution of military cuts and soldatesque manœuvres—his jolly laughter ringing through the otherwise silent street

—he was as welcome as sunshine to the place, and a comfort to every inhabitant in it.

On the first market-day he knew every pretty girl in the market: he joked with all the women; had a word with the farmers about their stock, and dined at the Agricultural Ordinary at the 'Clavering Arms,' where he set them all dying with laughter by his fun and jokes. 'Tu be sure he be a vine feller, tu be sure that he be,' was the universal opinion of the gentlemen in top-boots. He shook hands with a score of them, as they rode out of the inn-yard on their old nags, waving his hat to them splendidly as he smoked his cigar in the inn-gate. In the course of the evening he was free of the landlady's bar, knew what rent the landlord paid, how many acres he farmed, how much malt he put in his strong beer; and whether he ever run in a little brandy unexcised by kings from Baymouth, or the fishing villages along the coast.

He had tried to live at the great house first; but it was so dull he couldn't stand it. 'I am a creature born for society,' he told Captain Glanders. 'I'm down here to see Clavering's house set in order; for between ourselves, Frank has no energy, sir, no energy; he's not the chest for it, sir' (and he threw out his own trunk as he spoke); 'but I must have social intercourse. Old Mrs. Blenkinsop goes to bed at seven, and takes Polly with her. There was nobody but me and the Ghost for the first two nights at the great house, and I own it, sir, I like company. Most old soldiers do.'

Glanders asked Strong where he had served? Captain Strong curled his moustache, and said, with a laugh, that the other might almost ask where he had *not* served. 'I began, sir, as cadet of Hungarian Uhlans, and when the war of Greek independence broke out, quitted that service in consequence of a quarrel with my governor, and was one of seven who escaped from Missolonghi, and was blown up in one of Botzaris's fireships, at the age of seventeen. I'll show you my Cross of the Redeemer, if you'll come over to my lodgings and take a glass of grog with me, captain, this evening. I've a few of those baubles in my desk. I've the White Eagle of Poland; Skrzynecki gave it me' (he pronounced Skrzynecki's name with wonderful accuracy and gusto) 'upon the field of Ostrolenko. I was a lieutenant of the fourth regiment, sir, and we marched through

Diebitsch's lines—bang thro' 'em into Prussia, sir, without firing a shot. Ah, captain, that was a mismanaged business. I received this wound by the side of the King before Oporto—where he would have pounded the stock-jobbing Pedroites, had Bourmont followed my advice ; and I served in Spain with the King's troops, until the death of my dear friend, Zumalacarreguy,* when I saw the game was over, and hung up my toasting-iron, captain. Alava offered me a regiment[1] ; but I couldn't—damme, I couldn't—and now, sir, you know Ned Strong—the Chevalier Strong they call me abroad—as well as he knows himself.'

In this way almost everybody in Clavering came to know Ned Strong. He told Madame Fribsby, he told the landlord of the 'George,' he told Baker at the reading-rooms, he told Mrs. Glanders, and the young ones, at dinner : and, finally, he told Mr. Arthur Pendennis, who, yawning into Clavering one day, found the Chevalier Strong in company with Captain Glanders ; and who was delighted with his new acquaintance.

Before many days were over, Captain Strong was as much at home in Helen's drawing-room as he was in Madame Fribsby's first floor ; and made the lonely house very gay with his good humour and ceaseless flow of talk. The two women had never before seen such a man. He had a thousand stories about battles and dangers to interest them —about Greek captives, Polish beauties, and Spanish nuns. He could sing scores of songs, in half a dozen languages, and would sit down to the piano and troll them off in a rich, manly voice. Both the ladies pronounced him to be delightful—and so he was : though, indeed, they had not had much choice of man's society as yet, having seen in the course of their lives but few persons, except old Portman and the major, and Mr. Pen, who was a genius, to be sure ; but then your geniuses are somewhat flat and moody at home.

And Captain Strong acquainted his new friends at Fairoaks, not only with his own biography, but with the whole history of the family now coming to Clavering. It was he who had made the marriage between his friend Frank and the widow Amory. She wanted rank, and he wanted money. What match could be more suitable ? He organized it ; he made those two people happy. There was no particular romantic attachment between them ; the widow

was not of an age or a person for romance, and Sir Francis, if he had his game of billiards, and his dinner, cared for little besides. But they were as happy as people could be. Clavering would return to his native place and country, his wife's fortune would pay his encumbrances off, and his son and heir would be one of the first men in the county.

'And Miss Amory?' Laura asked. Laura was uncommonly curious about Miss Amory.

Strong laughed. 'Oh, Miss Amory is a muse—Miss Amory is a mystery—Miss Amory is a *femme incomprise.*' 'What is that?' asked simple Mrs. Pendennis—but the chevalier gave her no answer; perhaps could not give her one. 'Miss Amory paints, Miss Amory writes poems, Miss Amory composes music, Miss Amory rides like Diana Vernon.* Miss Amory is a paragon, in a word.'

'I hate clever women,' said Pen.

'Thank you,' said Laura. For her part she was sure she should be charmed with Miss Amory, and quite longed to have such a friend. And with this she looked Pen full in the face, as if every word the little hypocrite said was Gospel truth.

Thus an intimacy was arranged and prepared beforehand between the Fairoaks family and their wealthy neighbours at the Park; and Pen and Laura were to the full as eager for their arrival, as even the most curious of the Clavering folks. A Londoner, who sees fresh faces and yawns at them every day, may smile at the eagerness with which country people expect a visitor. A Cockney comes amongst them, and is remembered by his rural entertainers for years after he has left them, and forgotten them very likely—floated far away from them on the vast London sea. But the islanders remember long after the mariner has sailed away, and can tell you what he said and what he wore, and how he looked and how he laughed. In fine, a new arrival is an event in the country not to be understood by us, who don't, and had rather not, know who lives next door.

When the painters and upholsterers had done their work in the house, and so beautified it, under Captain Strong's superintendence, that he might well be proud of his taste, that gentleman announced that he should go to London, where the whole family had arrived by this time, and should speedily return to establish them in their renovated mansion.

Detachments of domestics preceded them. Carriages came down by sea, and were brought over from Baymouth by horses which had previously arrived under the care of grooms and coachmen. One day the 'Alacrity' coach brought down on its roof two large and melancholy men, who were dropped at the Park lodge with their trunks, and who were Messieurs Frederick and James, metropolitan foot-

men, who had no objection to the country, and brought with them state and other suits of the Clavering uniform.

On another day, the mail deposited at the gate a foreign gentleman, adorned with many ringlets and chains. He made a great riot at the lodge gate to the keeper's wife (who, being a West-country woman, did not understand his English or his Gascon French), because there was no carriage in waiting to drive him to the house, a mile off, and

because he could not walk entire leagues in his fatigued state and varnished boots. This was Monsieur Alcide Mirobolant, formerly chef of His Highness the Duc de Borodino, of His Eminence Cardinal Beccafico, and at present chef of the *bouche* of Sir Clavering, Baronet: Monsieur Mirobolant's library, pictures, and piano had arrived previously in charge of the intelligent young Englishman, his aide de camp. He was, moreover, aided by a professed female cook, likewise from London, who had inferior females under her orders.

He did not dine in the steward's room, but took his nutriment in solitude in his own apartments, where a female servant was affected to his private use. It was a grand sight to behold him in his dressing-gown composing a menu. He always sat down and played the piano for some time before.[2] If interrupted he remonstrated pathetically.[3] Every great artist, he said, had need of solitude to perfectionate his works.

But we are advancing matters in the fullness of our love and respect for Monsieur Mirobolant,* and bringing him prematurely on the stage.

The Chevalier Strong had a hand in the engagement of all the London domestics, and, indeed, seemed to be the master of the house. There were those among them who said he was the house-steward, only he dined with the family. Howbeit, he knew how to make himself respected, and two of by no means the least comfortable rooms of the house were assigned to his particular use.

He was walking upon the terrace finally upon the eventful day, when, amidst an immense jangling of bells from Clavering Church, where the flag was flying, an open carriage and one of those travelling chariots or family arks, which only English philoprogenitiveness could invent, drove rapidly with foaming horses through the Park gates, and up to the steps of the Hall. The two *battants* of the sculptured door flew open. Two superior officers in black, the large and melancholy gentlemen, now in livery with their hair in powder, the country menials engaged to aid them, were in waiting in the hall, and bowed like tall elms when autumn winds wail in the park. Through this avenue passed Sir Francis Clavering with a most unmoved face: Lady Clavering, with a pair of bright black eyes, and a good-humoured countenance, which waggled and nodded very

graciously: Master Francis Clavering, who was holding his mamma's skirt (and who stopped the procession to look at the largest footman, whose appearance seemed to strike the young gentleman), and Miss Blandy, governess to Master Francis, and Miss Amory, her ladyship's daughter, giving her arm to Captain Strong. It was summer, but fires of welcome were crackling in the great hall chimney, and in the rooms which the family were to occupy.

Monsieur Mirobolant had looked at the procession from one of the lime-trees in the avenue. '*Elle est là,*' he said, laying his jewelled hand on his richly-embroidered velvet waistcoat with glass buttons; '*je t'ai vue; je te bénis, ô ma sylphide, ô mon ange!*' and he dived into the thicket, and made his way back to his furnaces and saucepans.

The next Sunday the same party which had just made its appearance at Clavering Park, came and publicly took possession of the ancient pew in the church, where so many of the baronet's ancestors had prayed, and were now kneeling in effigy. There was such a run to see the new folks, that the Low Church was deserted, to the disgust of its pastor; and as the state barouche, with the greys and coachmen in silver wig, and solemn footmen, drew up at the old churchyard gate, there was such a crowd assembled there as had not been seen for many a long day. Captain Strong knew everybody, and saluted for all the company. The country people vowed my lady was not handsome, to be sure, but pronounced her to be uncommon fine dressed, as indeed she was—with the finest of shawls, the finest of pelisses, the brilliantest of bonnets and wreaths, and a power of rings, cameos, brooches, chains, bangles, and other nameless gimcracks; and ribbons of every breadth and colour of the rainbow flaming on her person. Miss Amory appeared meek in dove colour, like a vestal virgin—while Master Francis was in the costume then prevalent of Rob Roy MacGregor, a celebrated Highland outlaw. The baronet was not more animated than ordinarily—there was a happy vacuity about him which enabled him to face a dinner, a death, a church, a marriage, with the same indifferent ease.

A pew for the Clavering servants was filled by these domestics, and the enraptured congregation saw the gentlemen from London with 'vlower on their heeds,'* and the miraculous coachman with his silver wig, take their places

in that pew so soon as his horses were put up at the 'Clavering Arms.'

In the course of the service, Master Francis began to make such a yelling in the pew, that Frederic, the tallest of the footmen, was beckoned by his master, and rose and went and carried out Master Francis, who roared and beat him on the head, so that the powder flew round about, like clouds of incense. Nor was he pacified until placed on the box of the carriage, where he played at horses with John's whip.

'You see, the little beggar's never been to church before, Miss Bell,' the baronet drawled out to a young lady who was visiting him ; 'no wonder he should make a row : I don't go in town neither, but I think it's right in the country to give a good example—and that sort of thing.'

Miss Bell laughed and said, 'The little boy had not given a particularly good example.'

'Gad, I don't know,' said the baronet. 'It ain't so bad neither. Whenever he wants a thing, Frank always cwies, and whenever he cwies he gets it.'

Here the child in question began to howl for a dish of sweetmeats on the luncheon-table, and making a lunge across the tablecloth, upset a glass of wine over the best waistcoat of one of the guests present, Mr. Arthur Pendennis, who was greatly annoyed at being made to look foolish ; and at having his spotless cambric shirt-front blotched with wine.

'We do spoil him so,' said Lady Clavering to Mrs. Pendennis, fondly gazing at the cherub, whose hands and face were now frothed over with the species of lather which is inserted in the confection called *meringues à la crême*.[4]

'Gad, I was quite wight,' said the baronet. 'He has cwied, and he has got it, you see. Go it, Fwank, old boy.'

'Sir Francis is a very judicious parent,' Miss Amory whispered. 'Don't you think so, Miss Bell ? I shan't call you Miss Bell—I shall call you Laura. I admired you so at church. Your robe was not well made, nor your bonnet very fresh. But you have such beautiful grey eyes, and such a lovely tint.'

'Thank you,' said Miss Bell, laughing.

'Your cousin is handsome, and thinks so. He is uneasy *de sa personne*. He has not seen the world yet. Has he genius ? Has he suffered ? A lady, a little woman in a

MASTER FRANCIS IN A STATE OF REVOLT

rumpled satin and velvet shoes—a Miss Pybus—came here, and said he has suffered. I, too, have suffered—and you, Laura, has your heart ever been touched ?'

Laura said 'No !' but perhaps blushed a little at the idea or the question, so that the other said—

'Ah, Laura ! I see it all. It is the *beau cousin.* Tell me everything. I already love you as a sister.'

'You are very kind,' said Miss Bell, smiling, 'and—and it must be owned that it is a very sudden attachment.'

'All attachments are so. It is electricity—spontaneity. It is instantaneous. I knew I should love you from the moment I saw you. Do you not feel it yourself ?'

'Not yet,' said Laura ; 'but I dare say I shall if I try.'

'Call me by my name, then.'

'But I don't know it,' Laura cried out.

'My name is Blanche—isn't it a pretty name ? Call me by it.'

'Blanche—it is very pretty, indeed.'

'And while mamma talks with that kind-looking lady—what relation is she to you ? She must have been pretty once, but is rather *passée ;* she is not well *gantée*, but she has a pretty hand—and while mamma talks to her, come with me to my own room—my own, own room. It's a darling room, though that horrid creature, Captain Strong, did arrange it. Are you *éprise* of him ? He says you are, but I know better ; it is the *beau cousin.* Yes—*il a de beaux yeux. Je n'aime pas les blonds, ordinairement. Car je suis blonde moi—je suis Blanche et blonde* '—and she looked at her face and made a *moue* in the glass ; and never stopped for Laura's answer to the questions which she had put.

Blanche was fair, and like a sylph. She had fair hair, with green reflections in it. But she had dark eyebrows. She had long black eyelashes, which veiled beautiful brown eyes. She had such a slim waist, that it was a wonder to behold ; and such slim little feet, that you would have thought the grass would hardly bend under them. Her lips were of the colour of faint rosebuds, and her voice warbled limpidly over a set of the sweetest little pearly teeth ever seen. She showed them very often, for they were very pretty. She was always smiling, and a smile not only showed her teeth wonderfully, but likewise exhibited two lovely little pink dimples, that nestled in either cheek.

She showed Laura her drawings, which the other thought charming. She played her some of her waltzes, with a rapid and brilliant finger, and Laura was still more charmed. And she then read her some poems, in French and English, likewise of her own composition, and which she kept locked in her own book—her own dear little book; it was bound in blue velvet, with a gilt lock, and on it was printed in gold the title of *Mes Larmes*.

'*Mes Larmes!*—isn't it a pretty name?' the young lady continued, who was pleased with everything that she did, and did everything very well. Laura owned that it was. She had never seen anything like it before; anything so lovely, so accomplished, so fragile and pretty; warbling so prettily, and tripping about such a pretty room, with such a number of pretty books, pictures, flowers, round about her. The honest and generous country girl forgot even jealousy in her admiration. 'Indeed, Blanche,' she said, 'everything in the room is pretty; and you are the prettiest of all.' The other smiled, looked in the glass, went up and took both of Laura's hands, and kissed them, and sat down to the piano, and shook out a little song.[5]

The intimacy between the young ladies sprang up like Jack's beanstalk to the skies in a single night. The large footmen were perpetually walking with little pink notes to Fairoaks; where there was a pretty housemaid in the kitchen, who might possibly tempt those gentlemen to so humble a place. Miss Amory sent music, or Miss Amory sent a new novel, or a picture from the *Journal des Modes*, to Laura; or my lady's compliments arrived with flowers and fruit; or Miss Amory begged and prayed Miss Bell to come to dinner; and dear Mrs. Pendennis, if she was strong enough; and Mr. Arthur, if a humdrum party were not too stupid for him; and would send a pony-carriage for Mrs. Pendennis; and would take no denial.

Neither Arthur nor Laura wished to refuse. And Helen, who was, indeed, somewhat ailing, was glad that the two should have their pleasure; and would look at them fondly as they set forth, and ask in her heart that she might not be called away until those two beings whom she loved best in the world should be joined together. As they went out and crossed over the bridge, she remembered summer evenings five-and-twenty years ago, when she, too, had bloomed in her brief prime of love and happiness. It was all over

MR. PEN BEGINS TO BE CONSOLED

now. The moon was looking from the purpling sky, and the stars glittering there, just as they used in the early well-remembered evenings. He was lying dead far away, with the billows rolling between them. Good God! how well she remembered the last look of his face as they parted. It looked out at her through the vista of long years, as sad and as clear as then.

So Mr. Pen and Miss Laura found the society at Clavering Park an uncommonly agreeable resort of summer evenings. Blanche vowed that she *raffolé*'d of Laura; and, very likely, Mr. Pen was pleased with Blanche. His spirits came back: he laughed and rattled till Laura wondered to hear him. It was not the same Pen, yawning in a shooting-jacket, in the Fairoaks parlour, who appeared alert and brisk, and smiling, and well dressed, in Lady Clavering's drawing-room. Sometimes they had music. Laura had a sweet contralto voice, and sang with Blanche, who had had the best Continental instruction, and was charmed to be her friend's mistress. Sometimes Mr. Pen joined in these concerts, or oftener looked sweet upon Miss Blanche as she sang. Sometimes they had glees, when Captain Strong's chest was of vast service, and he boomed out in a prodigious bass, of which he was not a little proud.

'Good fellow, Strong—ain't he, Miss Bell?' Sir Francis would say to her. 'Plays at écarté with Lady Clavering—plays anything, pitch-and-toss, pianaforty, cwibbage if you like. How long do you think he's been staying with me? He came for a week with a carpet-bag, and gad, he's been staying thwee years. Good fellow, ain't he? Don't know how he gets a shillin' though, by Jove I don't, Miss Laura.'

And yet the chevalier, if he lost his money to Lady Clavering, always paid it; and if he lived with his friend for three years, paid for that too—in good humour, in kindness and joviality, in a thousand little services by which he made himself agreeable. What gentleman could want a better friend than a man who was always in spirits, never in the way or out of it, and was ready to execute any commission for his patron, whether it was to sing a song or meet a lawyer, to fight a duel or to carve a capon?

Although Laura and Pen commonly went to Clavering Park together, yet sometimes Mr. Pen took walks there unattended by her, and about which he did not tell her. He took to fishing the Brawl, which runs through the Park,

and passes not very far from the garden-wall; and by the oddest coincidence, Miss Amory would walk out (having been to look at her flowers), and would be quite surprised to see Mr. Pendennis fishing.

I wonder what trout Pen caught while the young lady was looking on? or whether Miss Blanche was the pretty little fish which played round his fly, and which Mr. Pen was endeavouring to hook?[6]

As for Miss Blanche, she had a kind heart; and having, as she owned, herself 'suffered' a good deal in the course

of her brief life and experience—why, she could compassionate other susceptible beings like Pen, who had suffered too. Her love for Laura and that dear Mrs. Pendennis redoubled: if they were not at the Park, she was not easy unless she herself was at Fairoaks. She played with Laura; she read French and German with Laura; and Mr. Pen read French and German along with them. He turned sentimental ballads of Schiller and Goethe into English verse for the ladies, and Blanche unlocked *Mes Larmes* for him, and imparted to him some of the plaintive outpourings of her own tender Muse.

It appeared from these poems that the young creature had indeed suffered prodigiously. She was familiar with the idea of suicide. Death she repeatedly longed for. A faded rose inspired her with such grief that you would have thought she must die in pain of it. It was a wonder how a young creature[7] should have suffered so much—should have found the means of getting at such an ocean of despair and passion (as a runaway boy who *will* get to sea), and having embarked on it, should survive it. What a talent she must have had for weeping to be able to pour out so many of *Mes Larmes !*

They were not particularly briny, Miss Blanche's tears, that is the truth ; but Pen, who read her verses, thought them very well for a lady—and wrote some verses himself for her. His were very violent and passionate, very hot, sweet, and strong : and he not only wrote verses ; but—oh, the villain ! oh, the deceiver ! he altered and adapted former poems in his possession, and which had been composed for a certain Miss Emily Fotheringay, for the use and to the Christian name of Miss Blanche Amory.

CHAPTER XXIII

A LITTLE INNOCENT

'I[1] SAY, Strong,' one day the baronet said, as the pair were conversing after dinner over the billiard-table, and that great unbosomer of secrets, a cigar ; 'I say, Strong, I wish to the doose your wife was dead.'

'So do I. That's a cannon, by Jove ! But she won't ; she'll live for ever—you see if she don't. Why do you wish her off the hooks, Frank, my boy ?' asked Captain Strong.

'Because then you might marry Missy. She ain't bad-looking. She'll have ten thousand, and that's a good bit of money for such a poor old devil as you,' drawled out the other gentleman. 'And gad, Strong, I hate her worse and

worse every day. I can't stand her, Strong, by gad, I can't.'

'I wouldn't take her at twice the figure,' Captain Strong said, laughing. 'I never saw such a little devil in my life.'

'I should like to poison her,' said the sententious baronet; 'by Jove I should.'

'Why, what has she been at now?' asked his friend.

'Nothing particular,' answered Sir Francis; 'only her old tricks. That girl has such a knack of making everybody miserable that, hang me, it's quite surprising. Last night she sent the governess crying away from the dinner-table. Afterwards, as I was passing Frank's room, I heard the poor little beggar howling in the dark, and found his sister had been frightening his soul out of his body, by telling him stories about the ghost that's in the house. At lunch she gave my lady a turn; and though my wife's a fool, she's a good soul—I'm hanged if she ain't.'

'What did Missy do to her?' Strong asked.

'Why, hang me, if she didn't begin talking about the late Amory, my predecessor,' the baronet said, with a grin. 'She got some picture out of *The Keepsake*,* and said she was sure it was like her dear father. She wanted to know where her father's grave was. Hang her father! Whenever Miss Amory talks about him, Lady Clavering always bursts out crying: and the little devil will talk about him in order to spite her mother. To-day when she began, I got in a confounded rage, said I was her father, and—and that sort of thing, and then, sir, she took a shy at me.'

'And what did she say about you, Frank?' Mr. Strong, still laughing, inquired of his friend and patron.

'Gad, she said I wasn't her father; that I wasn't fit to comprehend her; that her father must have been a man of genius, and fine feelings, and that sort of thing; whereas I had married her mother for money.'

'Well, didn't you?' asked Strong.

'It don't make it any the pleasanter to hear because it's true, don't you know,' Sir Francis Clavering answered. 'I ain't a literary man and that; but I ain't such a fool as she makes me out. I don't know how it is, but she always manages to—to put me in the hole, don't you understand? She turns all the house round her in her quiet way, and with her confounded sentimental airs. I wish she was dead, Ned.'

'It was my wife whom you wanted dead just now,' Strong said, always in perfect good humour; upon which the baronet, with his accustomed candour, said, 'Well, when people bore my life out, I *do* wish they were dead, and I wish Missy were down a well with all my heart.'

Thus it will be seen from the above report of this candid conversation that our accomplished little friend had some peculiarities or defects of character which rendered her not very popular. She was a young lady of some genius, exquisite sympathies and considerable literary attainments, living, like many another genius, with relatives who could not comprehend her. Neither her mother nor her stepfather were persons of a literary turn. *Bell's Life* and the *Racing Calendar* were the extent of the baronet's reading, and Lady Clavering still wrote like a schoolgirl of thirteen, and with an extraordinary disregard to grammar and spelling. And as Miss Amory felt very keenly that she was not appreciated, and that she lived with persons who were not her equals in intellect or conversational power, she lost no opportunity to acquaint her family circle with their inferiority to herself, and not only was a martyr, but took care to let everybody know that she was so. If she suffered, as she said and thought she did, severely, are we to wonder that a young creature of such delicate sensibilities should shriek and cry out a good deal ?[2] If a poetess may not bemoan her lot, of what earthly use is her lyre ? Blanche struck hers only to the saddest of tunes ; and sang elegies over her dead hopes, dirges over her early frost-nipt buds of affection, as became such a melancholy fate and Muse.

Her actual distresses, as we have said, had not been up to the present time very considerable : but her griefs lay, like those of most of us, in her own soul—that being sad and habitually dissatisfied, what wonder that she should weep ? So *Mes Larmes* dribbled out of her eyes any day at command : she could furnish an unlimited supply of tears, and her faculty of shedding them increased by practice. For sentiment is like another complaint mentioned by Horace, as increasing by self-indulgence (I am sorry to say, ladies, that the complaint in question is called the dropsy);* and the more you cry, the more you will be able and desirous to do so.

Missy had begun to gush at a very early age. Lamartine

was her favourite bard from the period when she first could feel; and she had subsequently improved her mind by a sedulous study of novels of the great modern authors of the French language. There was not a romance of Balzac and George Sand which the indefatigable little creature had not devoured by the time she was sixteen: and, however little she sympathized with her relatives at home, she had friends, as she said, in the spirit-world, meaning the tender Indiana, the passionate and poetic Lelia, the amiable Trenmor, that high-souled convict, that angel of the galleys—the fiery Stenio—and the other numberless heroes of the French romances. She had been in love with Prince Rodolph and Prince Djalma while she was yet at school, and had settled the divorce question, and the rights of woman,* with Indiana, before she had left off pinafores. The impetuous little lady played at love with these imaginary worthies, as a little while before she had played at maternity with her doll. Pretty little poetical spirits! it is curious to watch them with those playthings. To-day the blue-eyed one is the favourite, and the black-eyed one is pushed behind the drawers. To-morrow blue-eyes may take its turn of neglect: and it may be an odious little wretch with a burnt nose, or torn head of hair, and no eyes at all, that takes the first place in Miss's affection, and is dandled and caressed in her arms.

As novelists are supposed to know everything, even the secrets of female hearts, which the owners themselves do not perhaps know, we may state that at eleven years of age Mademoiselle Betsi, as Miss Amory was then called, had felt tender emotions towards a young Savoyard organ-grinder at Paris, whom she persisted in believing to be a prince carried off from his parents; that at twelve an old and hideous drawing-master (but, ah, what age or personal defects are proof against woman's love?) had agitated her young heart; and that, at thirteen, being at Madame de Caramel's boarding-school, in the Champs Élysées, which, as everybody knows, is next door to Monsieur Rogron's (Chevalier of the Legion of Honour) *pension* for young gentlemen, a correspondence by letter took place between the *séduisante Miss Betsi* and two young gentlemen of the college of Charlemagne, who were pensioners of the Chevalier Rogron.

In the above paragraph our young friend has been called

by a Christian name, different to that under which we were lately presented to her. The fact is, that Miss Amory, called Missy at home, had really at the first been christened Betsy—but assumed the name of Blanche of her own will and fantasy, and crowned herself with it; and the weapon which the baronet, her stepfather, held in terror over her, was the threat to call her publicly by her name of Betsy, by which menace he sometimes managed to keep the young rebel in order.

Blanche[3] had had hosts of dear, dear, darling friends ere now, and had quite a little museum of locks of hair in her treasure-chest, which she had gathered in the course of her sentimental progress. Some dear friends had married: some had gone to other schools: one beloved sister she had lost from the *pension*, and found again, oh, horror! her darling, her Léocadie, keeping the books in her father's shop, a grocer in the Rue du Bac: in fact, she had met with a number of disappointments, estrangements, disillusionments, as she called them in her pretty French jargon, and had seen and suffered a great deal for so young a woman. But it is the lot of sensibility to suffer, and of confiding tenderness to be deceived, and she felt that she was only undergoing the penalties of genius in these pangs and disappointments of her young career.

Meanwhile, she managed to make the honest lady, her mother, as uncomfortable as circumstances would permit; and caused her worthy stepfather to wish she was dead. With the exception of Captain Strong, whose invincible good humour was proof against her sarcasms, the little lady ruled the whole house with her tongue. If Lady Clavering talked about sparrowgrass instead of asparagus, or called an object a hobject, as this unfortunate lady would sometimes do, Missy calmly corrected her, and frightened the good soul, her mother, into errors only the more frequent as she grew more nervous under her daughter's eye.

It is not to be supposed, considering the vast interest which the arrival of the family at Clavering Park inspired in the inhabitants of the little town, that Madame Fribsby alone, of all the folks in Clavering, should have remained unmoved and incurious. At the first appearance of the Park family in church, madame noted every article of toilette which the ladies wore, from their bonnets to their

brodequins, and took a survey of the attire of the ladies'-maids in the pew allotted to them. We fear that Dr. Portman's sermon, though it was one of his oldest and most valued compositions, had little effect upon Madame Fribsby on that day. In a very few days afterwards, she had managed for herself an interview with Lady Clavering's confidential attendant, in the housekeeper's room, at the Park; and her cards in French and English, stating that she received the newest fashions from Paris from her correspondent Madame Victorine, and that she was in the custom of making court and ball dresses for the nobility and gentry of the shire, were in the possession of Lady Clavering and Miss Amory, and favourably received, as she was happy to hear, by those ladies.

Mrs. Bonner, Lady Clavering's lady, became soon a great frequenter of Madame Fribsby's drawing-room, and partook of many entertainments at the milliner's expense. A meal of green tea, scandal, hot Sally-Lunn cakes,* and a little novel-reading, were always at the service of Mrs. Bonner, whenever she was free to pass an evening in the town. And she found much more time for these pleasures than her junior officer, Miss Amory's maid, who seldom could be spared for a holiday, and was worked as hard as any factory girl by that inexorable little Muse, her mistress.[4]

And there was another person connected with the Clavering establishment, who became a constant guest of our friend, the milliner. This was the chief of the kitchen, Monsieur Mirobolant, with whom Madame Fribsby soon formed an intimacy.

Not having been accustomed to the appearance or society of persons of the French nation, the rustic inhabitants of Clavering were not so favourably impressed by Monsieur Alcide's manners and appearance as that gentleman might have desired that they should be. He walked among them quite unsuspiciously upon the afternoon of a summer day, when his services were not required at the house, in his usual favourite costume, namely, his light green frock or paletot, his crimson velvet waistcoat, with blue glass buttons, his *pantalon Écossais*, of a very large and decided check pattern, his orange satin neckcloth, and his jean-boots, with tips of shiny leather—these, with a gold embroidered cap, and a richly-gilt cane, or other varieties of ornament of a similar tendency, formed his usual holiday

MIROBOLANT FASCINATES THE NATIVES

costume, in which he flattered himself there was nothing remarkable (unless, indeed, the beauty of his person should attract observation), and in which he considered that he exhibited the appearance of a gentleman of good Parisian *ton*.

He walked then down the street, grinning and ogling every woman he met with glances, which he meant should kill them outright, and peered over the railings, and in at the windows, where females were, in the tranquil summer evening. But Betsy, Mrs. Pybus's maid, shrank back with a 'Lor' bless us!' as Alcide ogled her over the laurel-bush; the Miss Bakers, and their mamma, stared with wonder; and presently a crowd began to follow the interesting foreigner, of ragged urchins and children, who left their dirt-pies in the street to pursue him.

For some time he thought that admiration was the cause which led these persons in his wake, and walked on, pleased himself that he could so easily confer on others so much harmless pleasure. But the little children and dirt-pie manufacturers were presently succeeded by followers of a larger growth, and a number of lads and girls from the factory being let loose at this hour, joined the mob, and began laughing, jeering, hooting, and calling opprobrious names at the Frenchman. Some cried out, 'Frenchy! Frenchy!' some exclaimed 'Frogs!' one asked for a lock of his hair, which was long and in richly-flowing ringlets; and at length the poor artist began to perceive that he was an object of derision rather than of respect to the rude grinning mob.

It was at this juncture that Madame Fribsby spied the unlucky gentleman with the train at his heels, and heard the scornful shouts with which they assailed him. She ran out of her room, and across the street to the persecuted foreigner; she held out her hand, and, addressing him in his own language, invited him into her abode; and when she had housed him fairly within her door, she stood bravely at the threshold before the gibing factory girls and boys, and said they were a pack of cowards to insult a poor man who could not speak their language, and was alone and without protection. The little crowd, with some ironical cheers and hootings, nevertheless felt the force of Madame Fribsby's vigorous allocution, and retreated before her; for the old lady was rather respected in the place, and her

oddity and her kindness had made her many friends there.

Poor Mirobolant was grateful indeed to hear the language of his country ever so ill spoken. Frenchmen pardon our faults in their language much more readily than we excuse their bad English; and will face our blunders throughout a long conversation, without the least propensity to grin. The rescued artist vowed that Madame Fribsby was his guardian angel, and that he had not as yet met with such suavity and politeness among *les Anglaises.* He was as courteous and complimentary to her as if it was the fairest and noblest of ladies whom he was addressing: for Alcide Mirobolant paid homage after his fashion to all womankind, and never dreamed of a distinction of ranks in the realms of beauty, as his phrase was.

A cream, flavoured with pineapple—a mayonnaise of lobster, which he flattered himself was not unworthy of his hand, or of her to whom he had the honour to offer it as an homage, and a box of preserved fruits of Provence, were brought by one of the chef's aides de camp, in a basket, the next day to the milliner's, and were accompanied with a gallant note to the amiable Madame Fribsby. 'Her kindness,' Alcide said, 'had made a green place in the desert of his existence—her suavity would ever contrast in memory with the *grossièreté* of the rustic population, who were not worthy to possess such a jewel. An intimacy of the most confidential nature thus sprang up between the milliner and the chief of the kitchen; but I do not know whether it was with pleasure or mortification that Madame received the declarations of friendship which the young Alcide proffered to her, for he persisted in calling her '*La respectable Fribsbi*,' '*La vertueuse Fribsbi*'—and in stating that he should consider her as his mother, while he hoped she would regard him as her son. Ah! it was not very long ago, Fribsby thought, that words had been addressed to her in that dear French language, indicating a different sort of attachment. And she sighed as she looked up at the picture of her Carabineer. For it is surprising how young some people's hearts remain when their heads have need of a front or a little hair-dye—and, at this moment, Madame Fribsby, as she told young Alcide, felt as romantic as a girl of eighteen.

When the conversation took this turn—and at their first

intimacy Madame Fribsby was rather inclined so to lead it —Alcide always politely diverged to another subject: it was as his mother that he persisted in considering the good milliner. He would recognize her in no other capacity, and with that relationship the gentle lady was forced to content herself, when she found how deeply the artist's heart was engaged elsewhere.

He was not long before he described to her the subject and origin of his passion.

'I declared myself to her,' said Alcide, laying his hand on his heart, 'in a manner which was as novel as I am charmed to think it was agreeable. Where cannot Love penetrate, respectable Madame Fribsbi? Cupid is the father of invention!—I inquired of the domestics what were the *plats* of which mademoiselle partook with most pleasure; and built up my little battery accordingly. On a day when her parents had gone to dine in the world (and I am grieved to say that a *grossier* dinner at a *restaurateur*, in the Boulevard, or in the Palais Royal, seemed to form the delights of these unrefined persons), the charming miss entertained some comrades of the *pension;* and I advised myself to send up a little repast suitable to so delicate young palates. Her lovely name is Blanche. The veil of the maiden is white; the wreath of roses which she wears is white. I determined that my dinner should be as spotless as the snow. At her accustomed hour, and instead of the rude *gigot à l'eau*, which was ordinarily served at her too simple table, I sent her up a little *potage à la Reine—à la Reine Blanche* I called it—as white as her own tint—and confectioned with the most fragrant cream and almonds. I then offered up at her shrine a *filet de merlan à l'Agnès*, and a delicate *plat*, which I have designated as *Éperlan à la Sainte-Thérèse*, and of which my charming miss partook with pleasure. I followed this by two little entrées of sweetbread and chicken; and the only brown thing which I permitted myself in the entertainment was a little roast of lamb, which I laid in a meadow of spinaches, surrounded with *croustillons*, representing sheep, and ornamented with daisies and other savage flowers. After this came my second service: a pudding *à la Reine Élisabeth* (who, Madame Fribsbi knows, was a maiden princess); a dish of opal-coloured plovers' eggs, which I called *Nid de tourtereaux à la Roucoule;* placing in the midst of them two of those

tender volatiles, billing each other, and confectioned with butter; a basket containing little *gâteaux* of apricots, which, I know, all young ladies adore; and a jelly of marasquin, bland, insinuating, intoxicating as the glance of beauty. This I designated *Ambroisie de Calypso à la Souveraine de mon Cœur*. And when the ice was brought in—an ice of *plombière* and cherries—how do you think I had shaped them, Madame Fribsbi? In the form of two hearts united with an arrow, on which I had laid, before it entered, a bridal veil in cut-paper, surmounted by a wreath of virginal orange-flowers. I stood at the door to watch the effect of this entry. It was but one cry of admiration. The three young ladies filled their glasses with the sparkling Aÿ, and carried me in a toast. I heard it—I heard miss speak of me—I heard her say, "Tell Monsieur Mirobolant that we thank him—we admire him—we love him!" My feet almost failed me as I spoke.

'Since that, can I have any reason to doubt that the young artist has made some progress in the heart of the English miss? I am modest, but my glass informs me that I am not ill-looking. Other victories have convinced me of the fact.'

'Dangerous man!' cried the milliner.

'The blonde misses of Albion see nothing in the dull inhabitants of their brumous isle, which can compare with the ardour and vivacity of the children of the South. We bring our sunshine with us; we are Frenchmen, and accustomed to conquer. Were it not for this affair of the heart, and my determination to marry an *Anglaise*, do you think I would stop in this island (which is not altogether ungrateful, since I have found here a tender mother in the respectable Madame Fribsbi), in this island, in this family? My genius would use itself in the company of these rustics—the poesy of my art cannot be understood by these carnivorous insularies. No—the men are odious, but the women—the women! I own, dear Fribsbi, are seducing! I have vowed to marry one; and as I cannot go into your markets and purchase, according to the custom of the country, I am resolved to adopt another custom, and fly with one to Gretna Green. The blonde miss will go. She is fascinated. Her eyes have told me so. The white dove wants but the signal to fly.'

'Have you any correspondence with her?' asked Fribsby,

in amazement, and not knowing whether the young lady or the lover might be labouring under a romantic delusion.

'I correspond with her by means of my art. She partakes of dishes which I make expressly for her. I insinuate to her thus a thousand hints, which, as she is perfectly spiritual, she receives. But I want other intelligences near her.'

'There is Pincott, her maid,' said Madame Fribsby, who, by aptitude or education, seemed to have some knowledge of affairs of the heart, but the great artist's brow darkened at this suggestion.

'Madame,' he said, 'there are points upon which a gallant man ought to silence himself; though, if he break the secret, he may do so with the least impropriety to his best friend—his adopted mother. Know then, that there is a cause why Miss Pincott should be hostile to me—a cause not uncommon with your sex—jealousy.'

'Perfidious monster!' said the confidante.

'Ah, no,' said the artist, with a deep bass voice, and a tragic accent worthy of the Porte St. Martin and his favourite *mélodrames*, 'not perfidious, but fatal. Yes, I am a fatal man, Madame Fribsbi. To inspire hopeless passion is my destiny. I cannot help it that women love me. Is it my fault that that young woman deperishes and languishes to the view of the eye, consumed by a flame which I cannot return? Listen! There are others in this family who are similarly unhappy. The governess of the young milor has encountered me in my walks, and looked at me in a way which can bear but one interpretation. And milady herself, who is of mature age, but who has Oriental blood,* has once or twice addressed compliments to the lonely artist which can admit of no mistake. I avoid the household, I seek solitude, I undergo my destiny. I can marry but one, and am resolved it shall be to a lady of your nation. And, if her fortune is sufficient, I think miss would be the person who would be most suitable. I wish to ascertain what her means are before I lead her to Gretna Grin.'

Whether Alcide was as irresistible a conqueror as his namesake, or whether he was simply crazy, is a point which must be left to the reader's judgement. But the latter, if he has had the benefit of much French acquaintance, has perhaps met with men amongst them who fancied

themselves almost as invincible ; and who, if you credit them, have made equal havoc in the hearts of *les Anglaises.*

CHAPTER XXIV

CONTAINS BOTH LOVE AND JEALOUSY

OUR readers have already heard Sir Francis Clavering's candid opinion of the lady who had given him her fortune and restored him to his native country and home, and it must be owned that the baronet was not far wrong in his estimate of his wife, and that Lady Clavering was not the wisest or the best educated of women. She had had a couple of years' education in Europe, in a suburb of London, which she persisted in calling Ackney to her dying day, whence she had been summoned to join her father at Calcutta at the age of fifteen. And it was on her voyage thither, on board the *Ramchunder* East Indiaman, Captain Bragg, in which ship she had two years previously made her journey to Europe, that she formed the acquaintance of her first husband, Mr. Amory, who was third mate of the vessel in question.

We are not going to enter into the early part of Lady Clavering's history, but Captain Bragg, under whose charge Miss Snell went out to her father, who was one of the captain's consignees, and part owner of the *Ramchunder* and many other vessels, found reason to put the rebellious rascal of a mate in irons, until they reached the Cape, where the captain left his officer behind : and finally delivered his ward to her father at Calcutta, after a stormy and perilous voyage in which the *Ramchunder* and the cargo and passengers incurred no small danger and damage.

Some months afterwards Amory made his appearance at Calcutta, having worked his way out before the mast from the Cape—married the rich attorney's daughter in spite of that old speculator—set up as indigo-planter and failed—set up as agent and failed again—set up as editor of the *Sunderbund Pilot* and failed again—quarrelling ceaselessly with his father-in-law and his wife during the progress of all these mercantile transactions and disasters, and ending his career finally with a crash which compelled him to leave Calcutta and go to New South Wales. It was in the course of these luckless proceedings, that Mr. Amory probably made the acquaintance of Sir Jasper Rogers, the respected Judge of the Supreme Court of Calcutta, who has been mentioned before : and, as the truth must out, it was by making an improper use of his father-in-law's name, who could write perfectly well, and had no need of an amanuensis, that fortune finally forsook Mr. Amory and caused him to abandon all further struggles with her.

Not being in the habit of reading the Calcutta law-reports very assiduously, the European public did not know of these facts as well as people did in Bengal, and Mrs. Amory and her father, finding her residence in India not a comfortable one, it was agreed that the lady should return to Europe, whither she came with her little daughter Betsy or Blanche, then four years old. They were accompanied by Betsy's nurse, who has been presented to the reader in the last chapter as the confidential maid of Lady Clavering, Mrs. Bonner : and Captain Bragg took a house for them in the near neighbourhood of his residence in Pocklington Street.

It was a very hard, bitter summer, and the rain it rained every day for some time after Mrs. Amory's arrival. Bragg was very pompous and disagreeable, perhaps ashamed, perhaps anxious, to get rid of the Indian lady. She believed that all the world in London was talking about her husband's disaster, and that the King and Queen and the Court of Directors* were aware of her unlucky history. She had a good allowance from her father ; she had no call to live in England ; and she determined to go abroad. Away she went, then, glad to escape the gloomy surveillance of the odious bully, Captain Bragg. People had no objection to receive her at the Continental towns where she stopped, and at the various boarding-houses, where she

royally paid her way. She called Hackney Ackney, to be sure (though otherwise she spoke English with a little foreign twang, very curious and not unpleasant); she dressed amazingly; she was conspicuous for her love of eating and drinking, and prepared curries and pilaws at every boarding-house which she frequented; but her singularities of language and behaviour only gave a zest to her society, and Mrs. Amory was deservedly popular. She was the most good-natured, jovial, and generous of women. She was up to any party of pleasure by whomsoever proposed. She brought three times more champagne and fowls and ham to the picnics than anyone else. She took endless boxes for the play, and tickets for the masked balls, and gave them away to everybody. She paid the boarding-house people months beforehand; she helped poor shabby moustachioed bucks and dowagers, whose remittances had not arrived, with constant supplies from her purse; and in this way she tramped through Europe, and appeared at Brussels, at Paris, at Milan, at Naples, at Rome, as her fancy led her. News of Amory's death reached her at the latter place,* where Captain Clavering was then staying, unable to pay his hotel bill, as, indeed, was his friend, the Chevalier Strong, and the good-natured widow married the descendant of the ancient house of Clavering—professing, indeed, no particular grief for the scapegrace of a husband whom she had lost: and thus we have brought her up[1] to the present time when she was mistress of Clavering Park.[2]

Missy followed her mamma in most of her peregrinations, and so learned a deal of life. She had a governess for some time; and after her mother's second marriage, the benefit of Madame de Caramel's select *pension* in the Champs Élysées. When the Claverings came to England, she of course came with them. It was only within a few years, after the death of her grandfather, and the birth of her little brother, that she began to understand that her position in life was altered, and that Miss Amory, nobody's daughter, was a very small personage in a house compared with Master Francis Clavering, heir to an ancient baronetcy and a noble estate. But for little Frank, she would have been an heiress, in spite of her father: and though she knew, and cared not much about money, of which she never had any stint, and though she was a romantic little Muse, as

we have seen, yet she could not reasonably be grateful to the persons who had so contributed to change her condition: nor, indeed, did she understand what the latter really was, until she had made some further progress, and acquired more accurate knowledge in the world.

But this was clear, that her stepfather was dull and weak: that mamma dropped her *h*'s, and was not refined in manners or appearance; and that little Frank was a spoiled, quarrelsome urchin, always having his way, always treading upon her feet, always upsetting his dinner on her dresses, and keeping her out of her inheritance. None of these, as she felt, could comprehend her: and her solitary heart naturally pined for other attachments, and she sought around her where to bestow the precious boon of her unoccupied affection.

This dear girl, then, from want of sympathy, or other cause, made herself so disagreeable at home, and frightened her mother, and bored her stepfather so much, that they were quite as anxious as she could be that she should settle for herself in life; and hence Sir Francis Clavering's desire expressed to his friend, in the last chapter, that Mrs. Strong should die, and that he would take Blanche to himself as a second Mrs. Strong.

But as this could not be, any other person was welcome to win her: and a smart young fellow, well-looking and well-educated, like our friend Arthur Pendennis, was quite free to propose for her if he had a mind, and would have been received with open arms by Lady Clavering as a son-in-law, had he had the courage to come forward as a competitor for Miss Amory's hand.

Mr. Pen, however, besides other drawbacks, chose to entertain an extreme diffidence about himself. He was ashamed of his late failures, of his idle and nameless condition, of the poverty which he had brought on his mother by his folly, and there was as much of vanity as remorse in his present state of doubt and distrust. How could he ever hope for such a prize as this brilliant Blanche Amory, who lived in a fine park and mansion, and was waited on by a score of grand domestics, whilst a maid-servant brought in their meagre meal at Fairoaks, and his mother was obliged to pinch and manage to make both ends meet? Obstacles seemed to him insurmountable, which would have vanished had he marched manfully upon them: and

he preferred despairing, or dallying with his wishes,—or perhaps he had not positively shaped them as yet,—to attempting to win gallantly the object of his desire. Many a young man fails by that species of vanity called shyness, who might, for the asking, have his will.

But we do not pretend to say that Pen had, as yet, ascertained his: or that he was doing much more than thinking about falling in love. Miss Amory was charming and lively. She fascinated and cajoled him by a thousand arts or natural graces or flatteries. But there were lurking reasons and doubts, besides shyness and vanity, withholding him. In spite of her cleverness, and her protestations, and her fascinations, Pen's mother had divined the girl, and did not trust her. Mrs. Pendennis saw Blanche light-minded and frivolous, detected many wants in her which offended the pure and pious-minded lady; a want of reverence for her parents, and for things more sacred, Helen thought: worldliness and selfishness couched under pretty words and tender expressions. Laura and Pen battled these points strongly at first with the widow—Laura being as yet enthusiastic about her new friend, and Pen not far-gone enough in love to attempt any concealment of his feelings. He would laugh at these objections of Helen's, and say, 'Psha, mother! you are jealous about Laura—all women are jealous.'

But when, in the course of a month or two, and by watching the pair with that anxiety with which brooding women watch over their sons' affections—and in acknowledging which, I have no doubt there is a sexual jealousy on the mother's part, and a secret pang—when Helen saw that the intimacy appeared to make progress, that the two young people were perpetually finding pretexts to meet, and that Miss Blanche was at Fairoaks or Mr. Pen at the Park every day, the poor widow's heart began to fail her—her darling project seemed to vanish before her; and, giving way to her weakness, she fairly told Pen one day what her views and longings were; that she felt herself breaking, and not long for this world, and that she hoped and prayed before she went, that she might see her two children one. The late events, Pen's life and career and former passion for the actress, had broken the spirit of this tender lady. She felt that he had escaped her, and was in the maternal nest no more; and she clung with a

sickening fondness to Laura, Laura who had been left to her by Francis in heaven.

Pen kissed and soothed her in his grand patronizing way. He had seen something of this, he had long thought his mother wanted to make this marriage—did Laura know anything of it ? (Not she,—Mrs. Pendennis said—not for worlds would she have breathed a word of it to Laura.) 'Well, well, there was time enough, his mother wouldn't die,' Pen said, laughingly : 'he wouldn't hear of any such thing, and as for the Muse, she is too grand a lady to think about poor little me—and as for Laura, who knows that she would have me ? She would do anything you told her, to be sure. But am I worthy of her ?'

'Oh, Pen, you might be !' was the widow's reply ; not that Mr. Pen ever doubted that he was ; and a feeling of indefinable pleasure and self-complacency came over him as he thought over this proposal, and imaged Laura to himself, as his memory remembered her for years past, always fair and open, kindly and pious, cheerful, tender, and true. He looked at her with brightening eyes as she came in from the garden at the end of this talk, her cheeks rather flushed, her looks frank and smiling—a basket of roses in her hand.

She took the finest of them and brought it to Mrs. Pendennis, who was refreshed by the odour and colour of these flowers ; and hung over her fondly and gave it to her.

'And I might have this prize for the asking !' Pen thought, with a thrill of triumph, as he looked at the kindly girl. 'Why, she is as beautiful and as generous as her roses.' The image of the two women remained for ever after in his mind, and he never recalled it but the tears came into his eyes.

Before very many weeks' intimacy with her new acquaintance, however, Miss Laura was obliged to give in to Helen's opinion, and own that the Muse was selfish, unkind, and inconstant.[3]

Little Frank, for instance, might be very provoking, and might have deprived Blanche of her mamma's affection, but this was no reason why Blanche should box the child's ears because he upset a glass of water over her drawing, and why she should call him many opprobrious names in the English and French language ; and the preference

accorded to little Frank was certainly no reason why Blanche should give herself imperial airs of command towards the boy's governess, and send that young lady upon messages through the house to bring her book, or to fetch her pocket-handkerchief. When a domestic performed an errand for honest Laura, she was always thankful and pleased ; whereas, she could not but perceive that the little Muse had not the slightest scruple in giving her

commands to all the world round about her, and in disturbing anybody's ease or comfort, in order to administer to her own. It was Laura's first experience in friendship ; and it pained the kind creature's heart to be obliged to give up as delusions, one by one, those charms and brilliant qualities in which her fancy had dressed her new friend, and to find that the fascinating little fairy was but a mortal, and not a very amiable mortal after all. What generous

person is there that has not been so deceived in his time ?—what person, perhaps, that has not so disappointed others in his turn ?

After the scene with little Frank, in which that refractory son and heir of the house of Clavering had received the compliments in French and English, and the accompanying box on the ear from his sister, Miss Laura, who had plenty of humour, could not help calling to mind some very touching and tender verses which the Muse had read to her out of *Mes Larmes*, and which began, 'My pretty baby brother, may angels guard thy rest,' in which the Muse, after complimenting the baby upon the station in life which it was about to occupy, and contrasting it with her own lonely condition, vowed nevertheless that the angel boy would never enjoy such affection as hers was, or find in the false world before him anything so constant and tender as a sister's heart. 'It may be,' the forlorn one said, 'it may be, you will slight it, my pretty baby sweet, You will spurn me from your bosom, I'll cling around your feet ! Oh, let me, let me love you ! the world will prove to you As false as 'tis to others, but *I* am ever true.' And behold the Muse was boxing the darling brother's ears instead of kneeling at his feet, and giving Miss Laura her first lesson in the Cynical philosophy—not quite her first, however,—something like this selfishness and waywardness, something like this contrast between practice and poetry, between grand versified aspirations and everyday life, she had witnessed at home in the person of our young friend Mr. Pen.

But then Pen was different. Pen was a man. It seemed natural, somehow, that he should be self-willed and should have his own way. And under his waywardness and selfishness, indeed, there was a kind and generous heart. Oh, it was hard that such a diamond should be changed away against such a false stone as this. In a word, Laura began to be tired of her admired Blanche. She had assayed her and found her not true ; and her former admiration and delight, which she had expressed with her accustomed generous artlessness, gave way to a feeling, which we shall not call contempt, but which was very near it ; and which caused Laura to adopt towards Miss Amory a grave and tranquil tone of superiority, which was at first by no means to the Muse's liking.

Nobody likes to be found out, or, having held a high place, to submit to step down.

The consciousness that this event was impending did not serve to increase Miss Blanche's good humour, and as it made her peevish and dissatisfied with herself, it probably rendered her even less agreeable to the persons round about her. So there arose, one fatal day, a battle-royal between dearest Blanche and dearest Laura, in which the friendship between them was all but slain outright. Dearest Blanche had been unusually capricious and wicked on this day. She had been insolent to her mother; savage with little Frank; odiously impertinent in her behaviour to the boy's governess; and intolerably cruel to Pincott, her attendant. Not venturing to attack her friend (for the little tyrant was of a timid feline nature, and only used her claws upon those who were weaker than herself), she maltreated all these, and especially poor Pincott, who was menial, confidante, companion (slave always), according to the caprice of her young mistress.

This girl, who had been sitting in the room with the young ladies, being driven thence in tears, occasioned by the cruelty of her mistress, and raked with a parting sarcasm as she went sobbing from the door, Laura fairly broke out into a loud and indignant invective—wondered how one so young could forget the deference owing to her elders as well as to her inferiors in station; and professing so much sensibility of her own, could torture the feelings of others so wantonly. Laura told her friend that her conduct was absolutely wicked, and that she ought to ask pardon of Heaven on her knees for it. And having delivered herself of a hot and voluble speech whereof the delivery astonished the speaker as much almost as her auditor, she ran to her bonnet and shawl, and went home across the park in a great flurry and perturbation, and to the surprise of Mrs. Pendennis, who had not expected her until night.

Alone with Helen, Laura gave an account of the scene, and gave up her friend henceforth. 'Oh, mamma,' she said, 'you were right; Blanche, who seems so soft and so kind, is, as you have said, selfish and cruel. She who is always speaking of her affections can have no heart. No honest girl would afflict a mother so, or torture a dependant; and—and, I give her up from this day, and I will have no other friend but you.'

On this the two ladies went through the osculatory ceremony which they were in the habit of performing, and Mrs. Pendennis got a great secret comfort from the little quarrel—for Laura's confession seemed to say, 'That girl can never be a wife for Pen, for she is light-minded and heartless, and quite unworthy of our noble hero. He will be sure to find out her unworthiness for his own part, and then he will be saved from this flighty creature, and awake out of his delusion.'

But Miss Laura did not tell Mrs. Pendennis, perhaps did not acknowledge to herself, what had been the real cause of the day's quarrel. Being in a very wicked mood, and bent upon mischief everywhere, the little wicked Muse of a Blanche had very soon begun her tricks. Her darling Laura had come to pass a long day; and as they were sitting in her own room together, had chosen to bring the conversation round to the subject of Mr. Pen.

'I am afraid he is sadly fickle,' Miss Blanche observed; 'Mrs. Pybus, and many more Clavering people, have told us all about the actress.'

'I was quite a child when it happened, and I don't know anything about it,' Laura answered, blushing very much.

'He used her very ill,' Blanche said, wagging her little head. 'He was false to her.'

'I am sure he was not,' Laura cried out; 'he acted most generously by her: he wanted to give up everything to marry her. It was she that was false to him. He nearly broke his heart about it: he——'

'I thought you didn't know anything about the story, dearest,' interposed Miss Blanche.

'Mamma has said so,' said Laura.

"Well, he is very clever,' continued the other little dear. 'What a sweet poet he is! Have you ever read his poems?'

'Only the *Fisherman and the Diver*, which he translated for us, and his prize poem, which didn't get the prize; and, indeed, I thought it very pompous and prosy,' Laura said, laughing.

'Has he never written *you* any poems, then, love?' asked Miss Amory.

'No, my dear,' said Miss Bell.

Blanche ran up to her friend, kissed her fondly, called her 'My dearest Laura' at least three times, looked her

archly in the face, nodded her head, and said, 'Promise to tell no-o-body, and I will show you something.'

And tripping across the room daintily to a little mother-of-pearl inlaid desk, she opened it with a silver key, and took out two or three papers crumpled and rather stained with green, which she submitted to her friend. Laura took them and read them. They were love verses sure enough—something about Undine—about a Naiad*—about a river. She looked at them for a long time; but in truth the lines were not very distinct before her eyes.

'And you have answered them, Blanche?' she asked, putting them back.

'Oh, no! not for worlds, dearest,' the other said: and when her dearest Laura had *quite* done with the verses, she tripped back, and popped them again into the pretty desk.

Then she went to her piano, and sang two or three songs of Rossini, whose flourishes of music her flexible little voice could execute to perfection, and Laura sat by, vaguely listening, as she performed these pieces. What was Miss Bell thinking about the while? She hardly knew; but sat there silent as the songs rolled by. After this concert the young ladies were summoned to the room where luncheon was served; and whither they of course went with their arms round each other's waists.

And it could not have been jealousy or anger on Laura's part which had made her silent; for, after they had tripped along the corridor and descended the steps, and were about to open the door which leads into the hall, Laura paused, and looking her friend kindly and frankly in the face, kissed her with a sisterly warmth.

Something occurred after this—Master Frank's manner of eating, probably, or mamma's blunders, or Sir Francis smelling of cigars—which vexed Miss Blanche, and she gave way to that series of naughtinesses whereof we have spoken, and which ended in the above little quarrel.

CHAPTER XXV

A HOUSE FULL OF VISITORS

THE difference between the girls did not last long. Laura was always too eager to forgive and be forgiven, and as for Miss Blanche, her hostilities, never very long or durable, had not been provoked by the above scene. Nobody cares about being accused of wickedness. No vanity is hurt by that sort of charge: Blanche was rather pleased than provoked by her friend's indignation, which never would have been raised but for a cause which both knew, though neither spoke of.

And so Laura, with a sigh, was obliged to confess that the romantic part of her first friendship was at an end, and that the object of it was only worthy of a very ordinary sort of regard.

As for Blanche, she instantly composed a copy of touching verses, setting forth her desertion and disenchantment. It was only the old story she wrote, of love meeting with coldness, and fidelity returned by neglect; and some new neighbours arriving from London about this time, in whose family there were daughters, Miss Amory had the advantage of selecting an eternal friend from one of these young ladies, and imparting her sorrows and disappointments to this new sister. The tall footmen came but seldom now with notes to the sweet Laura; the pony-carriage was but rarely dispatched to Fairoaks to be at the orders of the ladies there. Blanche adopted a sweet look of suffering martyrdom when Laura came to see her. The other laughed at her friend's sentimental mood, and treated it with a good humour that was by no means respectful.

But if Miss Blanche found new female friends to console her, the faithful historian is also bound to say that she discovered some acquaintances of the other sex

who seemed to give her consolation too. If ever this artless young creature met a young man, and had ten minutes' conversation with him in a garden walk, in a drawing-room window, or in the intervals of a waltz, she confided in him, so to speak—made play with her beautiful eyes—spoke in a tone of tender interest, and simple and touching appeal, and left him, to perform the same pretty little drama in behalf of his successor.

When the Claverings first came down to the Park, there were very few audiences before whom Miss Blanche could perform : hence Pen had all the benefits of her glances, and confidences, and the drawing-room window, or the garden walk all to himself. In the town of Clavering, it has been said, there were actually no young men : in the near surrounding country, only a curate or two, or a rustic young squire, with large feet and ill-made clothes. To the Dragoons quartered at Chatteris the baronet made no overtures : it was unluckily his own regiment : he had left it on bad terms with some officers of the corps—an ugly business about a horse bargain—a disputed play account at blind-hookey—a white feather—who need ask ? —it is not our business to inquire too closely into the bygones of our characters, except in so far as their previous history appertains to the development of this present story.

The autumn, and the end of the Parliamentary Session, and the London season, brought one or two country families down to their houses, and filled tolerably the neighbouring little watering-place of Baymouth, and opened our friend Mr. Bingley's Theatre Royal at Chatteris, and collected the usual company at the assizes and race-balls there. Up to this time, the old county families had been rather shy of our friends of Clavering Park. The Fogeys of Drummington ; the Squares of Dozely Park ; the Welbores of the Barrow, etc. All sorts of stories were current among these folks regarding the family at Clavering ;—indeed, nobody ought to say that people in the country have no imagination, who heard them talk about new neighbours. About Sir Francis and his lady, and her birth and parentage, about Miss Amory, about Captain Strong, there had been endless histories which need not be recapitulated ; and the family of the Park had been three months in the county before the great people around began to call.

But at the end of the season, the Earl of Trehawke,

Lord-Lieutenant of the county, coming to Eyrie Castle, and the Countess Dowager of Rockminster, whose son was also a magnate of the land, to occupy a mansion on the Marine Parade at Baymouth—these great folks came publicly, immediately, and in state, to call upon the family of Clavering Park ; and the carriages of the county families speedily followed in the track, which had been left in the avenue by their lordly wheels.

It was then that Mirobolant began to have an opportunity of exercising that skill which he possessed, and of forgetting, in the occupations of his art, the pangs of love. It was then that the large footmen were too much employed at Clavering Park to be able to bring messages, or dally over the cup of small beer with the poor little maids at Fairoaks. It was then that Blanche found other dear friends than Laura, and other places to walk in besides the river-side, where Pen was fishing. He came day after day, and whipped the stream, but the ‘ fish, fish !’ wouldn't do their duty, nor the Peri appear. And here, though in strict confidence, and with a request that the matter go no further, we may as well allude to a delicate business, of which previous hint has been given. Mention has been made, in a former page, of a certain hollow tree, at which Pen used to take his station when engaged in his passion for Miss Fotheringay, and the cavity of which he afterwards used for other purposes than to insert his baits and fishing-cans in. The truth is, he converted this tree into a post office. Under a piece of moss and a stone, he used to put little poems, or letters equally poetical, which were addressed to a certain Undine, or Naiad who frequented the stream, and which, once or twice, were replaced by a receipt in the shape of a flower, or by a modest little word or two of acknowledgement, written in a delicate hand, in French or English, and on pink scented paper. Certainly, Miss Amory used to walk by this stream, as we have seen ; and it is a fact that she used pink scented paper for her correspondence. But after the great folks had invaded Clavering Park, and the family coach passed out of the lodge-gates, evening after evening, on their way to the other great country houses, nobody came to fetch Pen's letters at the post office ; the white paper was not exchanged for the pink, but lay undisturbed under its stone and its moss, whilst the tree was reflected into the stream, and the

Brawl went rolling by. There was not much in the letters certainly: in the pink notes scarcely anything—merely a little word or two, half jocular, half sympathetic, such as might be written by any young lady. But oh, you silly Pendennis, if you wanted this one, why did you not speak? Perhaps neither party was in earnest. You were only playing at being in love, and the sportive little Undine was humouring you at the same play.

Nevertheless, if a man is balked at this game, he not unfrequently loses his temper; and when nobody came any more for Pen's poems, he began to look upon those compositions in a very serious light. He felt almost tragical and romantic again, as in his first affair of the heart:—at any rate, he was bent upon having an explanation. One day he went to the Hall, and there was a roomful of visitors: on another, Miss Amory was not to be seen; she was going to a ball that night, and was lying down to take a little sleep. Pen cursed balls, and the narrowness of his means, and the humility of his position in the county that caused him to be passed over by the givers of these entertainments. On a third occasion, Miss Amory was in the garden, and he ran thither; she was walking there in state with no less personages than the Bishop and Bishopess of Chatteris and the episcopal family, who scowled at him, and drew up in great dignity when he was presented to them, and they heard his name. The right reverend prelate had heard it before, and also of the little transaction in the dean's garden.

'The bishop says you're a sad young man,' good-natured Lady Clavering whispered to him. 'What have you been a-doing of? Nothink, I hope, to vex such a dear mar as yours? How is your dear mar? Why don't she come and see me? We an't seen her this ever such a time. We're a-goin' about a-gaddin', so that we don't see no neighbours now. Give my love to her and Laurar, and come all to dinner to-morrow.'

Mrs. Pendennis was too unwell to come out, but Laura and Pen came, and there was a great party, and Pen only got an opportunity of a hurried word with Miss Amory. 'You never come to the river now,' he said.

'I can't,' said Blanche, 'the house is full of people.'

'Undine has left the stream,' Mr. Pen went on, choosing to be poetical.

'She never ought to have gone there,' Miss Amory answered. 'She won't go again. It was very foolish, very wrong: it was only play. Besides, you have other consolations at home,' she added, looking him full in the face an instant, and dropping her eyes.

If he wanted her, why did he not speak then? She might have said 'Yes' even then. But as she spoke of other consolations at home, he thought of Laura, so affectionate and so pure, and of his mother at home, who had bent her fond heart upon uniting him with her adopted daughter. 'Blanche!' he began, in a vexed tone,—'Miss Amory!'

'Laura is looking at us, Mr. Pendennis,' the young lady said. 'I must go back to the company,' and she ran off, leaving Mr. Pendennis to bite his nails in perplexity, and to look out into the moonlight in the garden.

Laura indeed was looking at Pen. She was talking with, or appearing to listen to the talk of, Mr. Pynsent, Lord Rockminster's son, and grandson of the dowager lady, who was seated in state in the place of honour, gravely receiving Lady Clavering's bad grammar, and patronizing the vacuous Sir Francis, whose interest in the county she was desirous to secure. Pynsent and Pen had been at Oxbridge together, where the latter, during his heyday of good fortune and fashion, had been the superior of the young patrician, and perhaps rather supercilious towards him. They had met for the first time, since they parted at the University, at the table to-day, and given each other that exceedingly impertinent and amusing demi-nod of recognition which is practised in England only, and only to perfection by University men,—and which seems to say, 'Confound you—what do you do here?'

'I knew that man at Oxbridge,' Mr. Pynsent said to Miss Bell—'a Mr. Pendennis, I think.'

'Yes,' said Miss Bell.

'He seems rather sweet upon Miss Amory,' the gentleman went on. Laura looked at them, and perhaps thought so too, but said nothing.

'A man of large property in the county, ain't he? He used to talk about representing it. He used to speak at the Union. Whereabouts do his estates lie?'

Laura smiled. 'His estates lie on the other side of the

river, near the lodge-gate. He is my cousin, and I live there.'

'Where ?' asked Mr. Pynsent, with a laugh.

'Why, on the other side of the river, at Fairoaks,' answered Miss Bell.

'Many pheasants there ? Cover looks rather good,' said the simple gentleman.

Laura smiled again. 'We have nine hens and a cock, a pig, and an old pointer.'

'Pendennis don't preserve, then ?' continued Mr. Pynsent.

'You should come and see him,' the girl said, laughing, and greatly amused at the notion that her Pen was a great county gentleman, and perhaps had given himself out to be such.

'Indeed, I quite long to renew our acquaintance,' Mr. Pynsent said gallantly, and with a look which fairly said, 'It is you that I would like to come and see'—to which look and speech Miss Laura vouchsafed a smile, and made a little bow.

Here Blanche came stepping up with her most fascinating smile and ogle, and begged dear Laura to come and take the second in a song. Laura was ready to do anything good-natured, and went to the piano; by which Mr. Pynsent listened as long as the duet lasted, and until Miss Amory began for herself, when he strode away.

'What a nice, frank, amiable, well-bred girl that is, Wagg,' said Mr. Pynsent to a gentleman who had come over with him from Baymouth—'the tall one, I mean, with the ringlets and the red lips—monstrous red, ain't they ?'

'What do you think of the girl of the house ?' asked Mr. Wagg.

'I think she's a lean, scraggy humbug,' said Mr. Pynsent, with great candour. 'She drags her shoulders out of her dress: she never lets her eyes alone: and she goes simpering and ogling about like a French waiting-maid.'

'Pynsent, be civil,' cried the other; 'somebody can hear.'

'Oh, it's Pendennis of Boniface,' Mr. Pynsent said. 'Fine evening, Mr. Pendennis; we were just talking of your charming cousin.'

'Any relation to my old friend, Major Pendennis ?' asked Mr. Wagg.

'His nephew. Had the pleasure of meeting you at

Gaunt House,' Mr. Pen said, with his very best air—the acquaintance between the gentlemen was made in an instant.

In the afternoon of the next day, the two gentlemen who were staying at Clavering Park were found by Mr. Pen on his return from a fishing excursion, in which he had no sport, seated in his mother's drawing-room in comfortable conversation with the widow and her ward. Mr. Pynsent, tall and gaunt, with large red whiskers and an imposing tuft to his chin, was striding over a chair in the intimate neighbourhood of Miss Laura. She was amused by his talk, which was simple, straightforward, rather humorous, and keen, and interspersed with homely expressions of a style which is sometimes called slang. It was the first specimen of a young London dandy that Laura had seen or heard; for she had been but a chit at the time of Mr. Foker's introduction at Fairoaks, nor indeed was that ingenuous gentleman much more than a boy, and his refinement was only that of a school and college.

Mr. Wagg, as he entered the Fairoaks premises with his companion, eyed and noted everything. 'Old gardener,' he said, seeing Mr. John at the lodge—'old red livery waistcoat—clothes hanging out to dry on the gooseberry bushes—blue aprons, white ducks—gad, they must be young Pendennis's white ducks—nobody else wears 'em in the family. Rather a shy place for a sucking county member, ay, Pynsent?'

'Snug little crib,' said Mr. Pynsent, 'pretty cosy little lawn.'

'Mr. Pendennis at home, old gentleman?' Mr. Wagg said to the old domestic. John answered, 'No, Master Pendennis was a-gone out.'

'Are the ladies at home?' asked the younger visitor. Mr. John answered, 'Yes, they be'; and as the pair walked over the trim gravel, and by the neat shrubberies, up the steps to the hall-door, which old John opened, Mr. Wagg noted everything that he saw; the barometer and the letter-bag, the umbrellas and the ladies' clogs, Pen's hats and tartan wrapper, and old John opening the drawing-room door, to introduce the new-comers. Such minutiae attracted Wagg instinctively; he seized them in spite of himself.

'Old fellow does all the work,' he whispered to Pynsent.

'Caleb Balderstone.* Shouldn't wonder if he's the housemaid.' The next minute the pair were in the presence of the Fairoaks ladies; in whom Pynsent could not help recognizing two perfectly well-bred ladies, and to whom Mr. Wagg made his obeisance, with florid bows, and extra courtesy, accompanied with an occasional knowing leer at his companion. Mr. Pynsent did not choose to acknowledge these signals, except by extreme haughtiness towards Mr. Wagg, and particular deference to the ladies. If there was one thing laughable in Mr. Wagg's eyes, it was poverty. He had the soul of a butler who had been brought from his pantry to make fun in the drawing-room. His jokes were plenty, and his good nature thoroughly genuine, but he did not seem to understand that a gentleman could wear an old coat, or that a lady could be respectable unless she had her carriage or employed a French milliner.

'Charming place, ma'am,' said he, bowing to the widow; 'noble prospect—delightful to us Cockneys, who seldom see anything but Pall Mall.' The widow said, simply, she had never been in London but once in her life—before her son was born.

'Fine village, ma'am, fine village,' said Mr. Wagg, 'and increasing every day. It'll be quite a large town soon. It's not a bad place to live in for those who can't get the country, and will repay a visit when you honour it.'

'My brother, Major Pendennis, has often mentioned your name to us,' the widow said, 'and we have been—amused by some of your droll books, sir,' Helen continued, who never could be brought to like Mr. Wagg's books, and detested their tone most thoroughly.

'He is my very good friend,' Mr. Wagg said, with a low bow, 'and one of the best known men about town, and where known, ma'am, appreciated—I assure you appreciated. He is with our friend Steyne, at Aix-la-Chapelle. Steyne has a touch of the gout, and so, between ourselves, has your brother. I am going to Stillbrook for the pheasant-shooting, and afterwards to Bareacres, where Pendennis and I shall probably meet;' and he poured out a flood of fashionable talk, introducing the names of a score of peers, and rattling on with breathless spirits, whilst the simple widow listened in silent wonder. What a man, she thought; are all the men of fashion in London like this? I am sure Pen will never be like him.

Mr. Pynsent was in the meanwhile engaged with Miss Laura. He named some of the houses in the neighbourhood whither he was going, and hoped very much that he should see Miss Bell at some of them. He hoped that her aunt would give her a season in London. He said, that in the next Parliament it was probable he should canvass the county, and he hoped to get Pendennis's interest here. He spoke of Pen's triumph as an orator at Oxbridge, and asked was he coming into Parliament too? He talked on very pleasantly, and greatly to Laura's satisfaction, until Pen himself appeared, and, as has been said, found these gentlemen.

Pen behaved very courteously to the pair, now that they had found their way into his quarters; and though he recollected with some twinges a conversation at Oxbridge, when Pynsent was present, and in which, after a great debate at the Union, and in the midst of considerable excitement, produced by a supper and champagne-cup, he had announced his intention of coming in for his native county, and had absolutely returned thanks in a fine speech as the future member; yet Mr. Pynsent's manner was so frank and cordial, that Pen hoped Pynsent might have forgotten his little fanfaronade, and any other braggadocio speeches or actions which he might have made. He suited himself to the tone of the visitors then, and talked about Plinlimmon and Magnus Charters, and the old set at Oxbridge, with careless familiarity and high-bred ease, as if he lived with marquises every day, and a duke was no more to him than a village curate.

But at this juncture, and it being then six o'clock in the evening, Betsy, the maid, who did not know of the advent of strangers, walked into the room without any preliminary but that of flinging the door wide open before her, and bearing in her arms a tray, containing three teacups, a teapot, and a plate of thick bread-and-butter. All Pen's splendour and magnificence vanished away at this—and he faltered and became quite abashed. 'What will they think of us?' he thought: and, indeed, Wagg thrust his tongue in his cheek, thought the tea infinitely contemptible, and leered and winked at Pynsent to that effect.

But to Mr. Pynsent the transaction appeared perfectly simple—there was no reason present to his mind why people should not drink tea at six* if they were minded,

as well as at any other hour; and he asked of Mr. Wagg, when they went away, 'What the devil he was grinning and winking at, and what amused him?'

'Didn't you see how the cub was ashamed of the thick bread-and-butter? I dare say they are going to have treacle if they are good. I'll take an opportunity of telling old Pendennis when we get back to town,' Mr. Wagg chuckled out.

'Don't see the fun,' said Mr. Pynsent.

'Never thought you did,' growled Wagg between his teeth; and they walked home rather sulkily.

Wagg told the story at dinner very smartly, with wonderful accuracy of observation. He described old John, the clothes that were drying, the clogs in the hall, the drawing-room, and its furniture and pictures; 'Old man with a beak and bald head—*feu* Pendennis I bet two to one; sticking-plaster full-length of a youth in a cap and gown—the present Marquis of Fairoaks, of course; the widow when young in a miniature, Mrs. Mee;* she had the gown on when we came, or a dress made the year after, and the tips cut off the fingers of her gloves which she stitches her son's collars with; and then the sarving-maid came in with their teas; so we left the earl and the countess to their bread-and-butter.'

Blanche, near whom he sat as he told this story, and who adored *les hommes d'esprit*, burst out laughing, and called him such an odd, droll creature. But Pynsent, who began to be utterly disgusted with him, broke out in a loud voice, and said, 'I don't know, Mr. Wagg, what sort of ladies you are accustomed to meet in your own family, but by gad, as far as a first acquaintance can show, I never met two better-bred women in my life, and I hope, ma'am, you'll call upon 'em,' he added, addressing Lady Rockminster, who was seated at Sir Francis Clavering's right hand.

Sir Francis turned to the guest on his left, and whispered, 'That's what I call a sticker for Wagg.' And Lady Clavering, giving the young gentleman a delighted tap with her fan, winked her black eyes at him, and said, 'Mr. Pynsent, you're a good feller.'

After the affair with Blanche, a difference ever so slight, a tone of melancholy, perhaps a little bitter, might be perceived in Laura's converse with her cousin. She

A MORNING VISIT AT TEA-TIME

seemed to weigh him, and find him wanting too; the widow saw the girl's clear and honest eyes watching the young man at times, and a look of almost scorn pass over her face, as he lounged in the room with the women, or lazily sauntered smoking upon the lawn, or lolled under a tree there over a book which he was too listless to read.

'What has happened between you?' eager-sighted Helen asked of the girl. 'Something has happened. Has that wicked little Blanche been making mischief? Tell me, Laura.'

'Nothing has happened at all,' Laura said.

'Then why do you look at Pen so?' asked his mother quickly.

'Look at him, dear mother!' said the girl. 'We two women are no society for him: we don't interest him; we are not clever enough for such a genius as Pen. He wastes his life and energies away among us, tied to our apron-strings. He interests himself in nothing: he scarcely cares to go beyond the garden-gate. Even Captain Glanders and Captain Strong pall upon him,' she added, with a bitter laugh; 'and they are men, you know, and our superiors. He will never be happy while he is here. Why is he not facing the world, and without a profession?'

'We have got enough, with great economy,' said the widow, her heart beginning to beat violently. 'Pen has spent nothing for months. I'm sure he is very good. I am sure he might be very happy with us.'

'Don't agitate yourself so, dear mother,' the girl answered. 'I don't like to see you so. You should not be sad because Pen is unhappy here. All men are so. They must work. They must make themselves names and a place in the world. Look, the two captains have fought and seen battles: that Mr. Pynsent, who came here, and who will be very rich, is in a public office; he works very hard, he aspires to a name and a reputation. He says Pen was one of the best speakers at Oxbridge, and had as great a character for talent as any of the young gentlemen there. Pen himself laughs at Mr. Wagg's celebrity (and indeed he is a horrid person), and says he is a dunce, and that anybody could write his books.'

'I am sure they are odious,' interposed the widow.

'Yet he has a reputation.—You see the *County Chronicle* says, "The celebrated Mr. Wagg has been sojourning at Baymouth—let our fashionables and eccentrics look out

for something from his caustic pen." If Pen can write better than this gentleman, and speak better than Mr. Pynsent, why doesn't he? Mamma, he can't make speeches to us; or distinguish himself here. He ought to go away, indeed he ought.'

'Dear Laura,' said Helen, taking the girl's hand, 'is it kind of you to hurry him so? I have been waiting. I have been saving up money these many months—to—to pay back your advance to us.'

'Hush, mother!' Laura cried, embracing her friend hastily. 'It was your money, not mine. Never speak about that again. How much money have you saved?'

Helen said there were more than two hundred pounds at the bank, and that she would be enabled to pay off all Laura's money by the end of the next year.

'Give it him—let him have the two hundred pounds. Let him go to London and be a lawyer: be something, be worthy of his mother—and of mine, dearest mamma,' said the good girl; upon which, and with her usual tenderness and emotion, the fond widow declared that Laura was a blessing to her, and the best of girls—and I hope no one in this instance will be disposed to contradict her.

The widow and her daughter had more than one conversation on this subject: the elder gave way to the superior reason of the honest and stronger-minded girl; and, indeed, whenever there was a sacrifice to be made on her part, this kind lady was only too eager to make it. But she took her own way, and did not lose sight of the end she had in view, in imparting these new plans to Pen. One day she told him of these projects, and who it was that had formed them; how it was Laura who insisted upon his going to London and studying; how it was Laura who would not hear of the—the money arrangements when he came back from Oxbridge—being settled just then: how it was Laura whom he had to thank, if indeed he thought he ought to go.

At that news Pen's countenance blazed up with pleasure, and he hugged his mother to his heart with an ardour that I fear disappointed the fond lady; but she rallied when he said, 'By Heaven! she is a noble girl, and may God Almighty bless her! O mother! I have been wearing myself away for months here, longing to work, and not knowing how. I've been fretting over the thoughts of my

shame, and my debts, and my past cursed extravagance and follies. I've suffered infernally. My heart has been half broken—never mind about that. If I can get a chance to redeem the past, and to do my duty to myself and the best mother in the world, indeed, indeed, I will. I'll be worthy of you yet. Heaven bless you! God bless Laura! Why isn't she here, that I may go and thank her?' Pen went on with more incoherent phrases; paced up and down the room, drank glasses of water, jumped about his mother with a thousand embraces—began to laugh—began to sing—was happier than she had seen him since he was a boy—since he had tasted of the fruit of that awful Tree of Life which, from the beginning, has tempted all mankind.

Laura was not at home. Laura was on a visit to the stately Lady Rockminster, daughter to my Lord Bareacres, sister to the late Lady Pontypool, and by consequence a distant kinswoman of Helen's, as her ladyship, who was deeply versed in genealogy, was the first graciously to point out to the modest country lady. Mr. Pen was greatly delighted at the relationship being acknowledged, though perhaps not over well pleased that Lady Rockminster took Miss Bell home with her for a couple of days to Baymouth, and did not make the slightest invitation to Mr. Arthur Pendennis. There was to be a ball at Baymouth, and it was to be Miss Laura's first appearance. The dowager came to fetch her in her carriage, and she went off with a white dress in her box, happy and blushing, like the rose to which Pen compared her.

This was the night of the ball—a public entertainment at the Baymouth Hotel. 'By Jove!' said Pen, 'I'll ride over—no, I won't ride, but I'll go too.' His mother was charmed that he should do so; and, as he was debating about the conveyance in which he should start for Baymouth, Captain Strong called opportunely, said he was going himself, and that he would put his horse, the Butcher Boy, into the gig, and drive Pen over.

When the grand company began to fill the house at Clavering Park, the Chevalier Strong[1] seldom intruded himself upon its society, but went elsewhere to seek his relaxation. 'I've seen plenty of grand dinners in my time,' he said, 'and dined, by Jove, in a company where there

was a king and royal duke at top and bottom, and every man along the table had six stars on his coat; but dammy, Glanders, this finery don't suit me; and the English ladies with their confounded buckram airs, and the squires with their politics after dinner, send me to sleep—sink me dead if they don't. I like a place where I can blow my cigar when the cloth is removed, and when I'm thirsty, have my beer in its native pewter.' So on a gala day at Clavering Park, the chevalier would content himself with superintending the arrangements of the table, and drilling the major-domo and servants; and having looked over the bill of fare with Monsieur Mirobolant, would not care to take the least part in the banquet. 'Send me up a cutlet and a bottle of claret to my room,' this philosopher would say, and from the windows of that apartment, which commanded the terrace and avenue, he would survey the company as they arrived in their carriages, or take a peep at the ladies in the hall through an *œil-de-bœuf* which commanded it from his corridor. And the guests being seated, Strong would cross the park to Captain Glanders's cottage at Clavering, or to pay the landlady a visit at the 'Clavering Arms,' or to drop in upon Madame Fribsby over her novel and tea. Wherever the chevalier went he was welcome, and whenever he came away a smell of hot brandy-and-water lingered behind him.

The Butcher Boy—not the worst horse in Sir Francis's stable—was appropriated to Captain Strong's express use; and the old campaigner saddled him and brought him home at all hours of the day or night, and drove or rode him up and down the country. Where there was a public-house with a good tap of beer—where there was a tenant with a pretty daughter who played on the piano—to Chatteris, to the play, or the barracks—to Baymouth, if any fun was on foot there; to the rural fairs or races, the chevalier and his brown horse made their way continually; and this worthy gentleman lived at free quarters in a friendly country. The Butcher Boy soon took Pen and the chevalier to Baymouth. The latter was as familiar with the hotel and landlord there as with every other inn round about; and having been accommodated with a bedroom to dress, they entered the ball-room. The chevalier was splendid. He wore three little gold crosses in a brochette on the portly breast of his blue coat, and looked like a foreign field-marshal.

The ball was public and all sorts of persons were admitted and encouraged to come, young Pynsent having views upon the county, and Lady Rockminster being patroness of the ball. There was a quadrille for the aristocracy at one end, and select benches for the people of fashion. Towards this end the chevalier did not care to penetrate far (as he said he did not care for the nobs); but in the other part of the room he knew everybody—the wine-merchants', inn-keepers', tradesmen's, solicitors', squire-farmers' daughters, their sires and brothers, and plunged about shaking hands.

'Who is that man with the blue ribbon and the three-pointed star?' asked Pen. A gentleman in black with ringlets and a tuft stood gazing fiercely about him, with one hand in the arm-hole of his waistcoat and the other holding his claque.

'By Jupiter, it's Mirobolant!' cried Strong, bursting out laughing. '*Bon jour, chef!—Bon jour, chevalier!*'

'*De la croix de Juillet,* chevalier!*' said the *chef*, laying his hand on his decoration.

'By Jove, here's some more ribbon!' said Pen, amused.

A man with very black hair and whiskers, dyed evidently with the purple of Tyre, with twinkling eyes and white eyelashes, and a thousand wrinkles in his face, which was of a strange red colour, with two under-vests, and large gloves and hands, and a profusion of diamonds and jewels in his waistcoat and stock, with coarse feet crumpled into immense shiny boots, and a piece of parti-coloured ribbon in his button-hole, here came up and nodded familiarly to the chevalier.

The chevalier shook hands. 'My friend Mr. Pendennis,' Strong said. 'Colonel Altamont, of the bodyguard of His Highness the Nawaub of Lucknow.' That officer bowed to the salute of Pen; who was now looking out eagerly to see if the person he wanted had entered the room.

Not yet. But the band began presently performing 'See the Conquering Hero Comes,' and a host of fashionables—Dowager Countess of Rockminster, Mr. Pynsent and Miss Bell, Sir Francis Clavering, Bart., of Clavering Park, Lady Clavering and Miss Amory, Sir Horace Fogey, Bart., Lady Fogey, Colonel and Mrs. Higgs, —— Wagg, Esq. (as the county paper afterwards described them), entered the room.

Pen rushed by Blanche, ran up to Laura, and seized her hand. 'God bless you!' he said. 'I want to speak to you

—I must speak to you.—Let me dance with you.' 'Not for three dances, dear Pen,' she said, smiling: and he fell back, biting his nails with vexation, and forgetting to salute Pynsent.

After Lady Rockminster's party, Lady Clavering's followed in the procession.

Colonel Altamont eyed it hard, holding a most musky pocket-handkerchief up to his face, and bursting with laughter behind it.

'Who's the gal in green along with 'em, cap'n?' he asked of Strong.

'That's Miss Amory, Lady Clavering's daughter,' replied the chevalier.

The colonel could hardly contain himself for laughing.

CHAPTER XXVI

CONTAINS SOME BALL-PRACTISING

UNDER some calico draperies in the shady embrasure of a window, Arthur Pendennis chose to assume a very gloomy and frowning countenance, and to watch Miss Bell dance her first quadrille with Mr. Pynsent for a partner.[1] Miss Laura's face was beaming with pleasure and good nature. The lights and the crowd and music excited her. As she spread out her white robes, and performed her part of the dance, smiling and happy, her brown ringlets flowing back over her fair shoulders from her honest rosy face, more than one gentleman in the room admired and looked after her; and Lady Fogey, who had a house in London and gave herself no small airs of fashion when in the country, asked of Lady Rockminster who the young person was, mentioned a reigning beauty in London whom, in her ladyship's opinion, Laura was rather like, and pronounced that she would 'do.'

Lady Rockminster would have been very much surprised

if any protégée of hers would not 'do,' and wondered at Lady Fogey's impudence in judging upon the point at all. She surveyed Laura with majestic glances through her eye-glass. She was pleased with the girl's artless looks, and gay innocent manner. Her manner is very good, her ladyship thought. Her arms are rather red, but that is a defect of her youth. Her *ton* is far better than that of the little pert Miss Amory, who is dancing opposite to her.

Miss Blanche was, indeed, the *vis-à-vis* of Miss Laura, and smiled most killingly upon her dearest friend, and nodded to her, and talked to her, when they met during the quadrille evolutions, and patronized her a great deal. Her shoulders were the whitest in the whole room: and they were never easy in her frock for one single instant: nor were her eyes, which rolled about incessantly: nor was her little figure:—it seemed to say to all the people, 'Come and look at me—not at that pink, healthy, bouncing country lass, Miss Bell, who scarcely knew how to dance till I taught her. This is the true Parisian manner—this is the prettiest little foot in the room, and the prettiest little *chaussure,* too. Look at it, Mr. Pynsent. Look at it, Mr. Pendennis, you who are scowling behind the curtain—I know you are longing to dance with me.'

Laura went on dancing, and keeping an attentive eye upon Mr. Pen in the embrasure of the window. He did not quit that retirement during the first quadrille, nor until the second, when the good-natured Lady Clavering beckoned to him to come up to her to the dais or place of honour where the dowagers were, and whither Pen went blushing and exceedingly awkward, as most conceited young fellows are. He performed a haughty salutation to Lady Rockminster, who hardly acknowledged his bow, and then went and paid his respects to the widow of the late Amory, who was splendid in diamonds, velvet, lace, feathers, and all sorts of millinery and goldsmith's ware.

Young Mr. Fogey, then in the fifth form at Eton, and ardently expecting his beard and his commission in a Dragoon regiment, was the second partner who was honoured with Miss Bell's hand. He was rapt in admiration of that young lady. He thought he had never seen so charming a creature. 'I like you much better than the French girl' (for this young gentleman had been dancing with Miss Amory before), he candidly said to her. Laura laughed,

and looked more good-humoured than ever; and in the midst of her laughter caught a sight of Pen, and continued to laugh as he, on his side, continued to look absurdly pompous and sulky. The next dance was a waltz, and young Fogey thought, with a sigh, that he did not know how to waltz, and vowed he would have a master the next holidays.

Mr. Pynsent again claimed Miss Bell's hand for this dance; and Pen beheld her, in a fury, twirling round the room, her waist encircled by the arm of that gentleman. He never used to be angry before when, on summer evenings, the chairs and tables being removed, and the governess called downstairs to play the piano, he and the Chevalier Strong (who was a splendid performer, and could dance a British hornpipe, a German waltz, or a Spanish fandango, if need were), and the two young ladies, Blanche and Laura, improvised little balls at Clavering Park. Laura enjoyed this dancing so much, and was so animated, that she even animated Mr. Pynsent. Blanche, who could dance beautifully, had an unlucky partner, Captain Broadfoot, of the Dragoons, then stationed at Chatteris. For Captain Broadfoot, though devoting himself with great energy to the object in view, could not get round in time: and, not having the least ear for music, was unaware that his movements were too slow.

So, in the waltz as in the quadrille, Miss Blanche saw that her dear friend Laura had the honours of the dance, and was by no means pleased with the latter's success. After a couple of turns with the heavy Dragoon, she pleaded fatigue, and requested to be led back to her place, near her mamma, to whom Pen was talking: and she asked him why he had not asked her to waltz, and had left her to the mercies of that great odious man in spurs and a red coat?

'I thought spurs and scarlet were the most fascinating objects in the world to young ladies,' Pen answered. 'I never should have dared to put my black coat in competition with that splendid red jacket.'

'You are very unkind and cruel and sulky and naughty,' said Miss Amory, with another shrug of the shoulders. 'You had better go away. Your cousin is looking at us over Mr. Pynsent's shoulder.'

'Will you waltz with me?' said Pen.

'Not this waltz. I can't, having just sent away that great hot Captain Broadfoot. Look at Mr. Pynsent; did

you ever see such a creature ? But I will dance the next waltz with you, and the quadrille too. I am promised, but I will tell Mr. Poole that I had forgotten my engagement to you.'

'Women forget very readily,' Pendennis said.

'But they always come back, and are very repentant and sorry for what they've done,' Blanche said. 'See, here comes the Poker, and dear Laura leaning on him. How pretty she looks !'

Laura came up, and put out her hand to Pen, to whom Pynsent made a sort of bow, appearing to be not much more graceful than that domestic instrument to which Miss Amory compared him.

But Laura's face was full of kindness. 'I am so glad you have come, dear Pen,' she said. 'I can speak to you now. How is mamma ? The three dances are over, and I am engaged to you for the next, Pen.'

'I have just engaged myself to Miss Amory,' said Pen ; and Miss Amory nodded her head, and made her usual little curtsy. 'I don't intend to give him up, dearest Laura,' she said.

'Well, then, he'll waltz with me, dear Blanche,' said the other. 'Won't you, Pen ?'

'I promised to waltz with Miss Amory.'

'Provoking !' said Laura, and making a curtsy in her turn, she went and placed herself under the ample wing of Lady Rockminster.

Pen was delighted with his mischief. The two prettiest girls in the room were quarrelling about him. He flattered himself he had punished Miss Laura. He leaned in a dandified air, with his elbow over the wall, and talked to Blanche : he quizzed unmercifully all the men in the room —the heavy Dragoons in their tight jackets—the country dandies in their queer attire—the strange toilettes of the ladies. One seemed to have a bird's nest in her head ; another had six pounds of grapes in her hair, besides her false pearls. 'It's a *coiffure* of almonds and raisins,' said Pen, 'and might be served up for dessert.' In a word, he was exceedingly satirical and amusing.

During the quadrille he carried on this kind of conversation with unflinching bitterness and vivacity, and kept Blanche continually laughing, both at his wickedness and jokes, which were good, and also because Laura was again

their *vis-à-vis*, and could see and hear how merry and confidential they were.

'Arthur is charming to-night,' she whispered to Laura across Cornet Perch's shell jacket, as Pen was performing *cavalier seul* before them, drawling through that figure with a thumb in the pocket of each waistcoat.

'*Who?*' said Laura.

'Arthur,' answered Blanche, in French. 'Oh, it's such a pretty name!' And now the young ladies went over to Pen's side, and Cornet Perch performed a *pas seul* in his turn. He had no waistcoat pocket to put his hands into, and they looked large and swollen as they hung before him depending from the tight arms in the jacket.

During the interval between the quadrille and the succeeding waltz, Pen did not take any notice of Laura, except to ask her whether her partner, Cornet Perch, was an amusing youth, and whether she liked him so well as her other partner, Mr. Pynsent. Having planted which two daggers in Laura's[2] bosom, Mr. Pendennis proceeded to rattle on with Blanche Amory, and to make jokes good or bad, but which were always loud. Laura was at a loss to account for her cousin's sulky behaviour, and ignorant in what she had offended him; however, she was not angry in her turn at Pen's splenetic mood, for she was the most good-natured and forgiving of women, and besides, an exhibition of jealousy on a man's part is not always disagreeable to a lady.

As Pen could not dance with her, she was glad to take up with the active Chevalier Strong, who was a still better performer than Pen; and being very fond of dancing, as every brisk and innocent young girl should be, when the waltz music began she set off, and chose to enjoy herself with all her heart. Captain Broadfoot on this occasion occupied the floor in conjunction with a lady of proportions scarcely inferior to his own: Miss Roundle, a large young woman in a strawberry-ice-coloured crape dress, the daughter of the lady with the grapes in her head, whose bunches Pen had admired.

And now taking his time, and with his fair partner Blanche hanging lovingly on the arm which encircled her, Mr. Arthur Pendennis set out upon his waltzing career, and felt, as he whirled round to the music, that he and Blanche were performing very brilliantly indeed. Very likely he

looked to see if Miss Bell thought so too ; but she did not or would not see him, and was always engaged with her partner Captain Strong. But Pen's triumph was not destined to last long : and it was doomed that poor Blanche was to have yet another discomfiture on that unfortunate night. While she and Pen were whirling round as light and brisk as a couple of opera-dancers, honest Captain Broadfoot and the lady round whose large waist he was clinging, were twisting round very leisurely according to their natures, and indeed were in everybody's way. But they were more in Pendennis's way than in anybody's else, for he and Blanche, whilst executing their rapid gyrations, came bolt up against the heavy Dragoon and his lady, and with such force that the centre of gravity was lost by all four of the circumvolving bodies ; Captain Broadfoot and Miss Roundle were fairly upset, as was Pen himself, who was less lucky than his partner Miss Amory, who was only thrown upon a bench against a wall.

But Pendennis came fairly down upon the floor, sprawling in the general ruin with Broadfoot and Miss Roundle. The captain, though heavy, was good-natured, and was the first to burst out into a loud laugh at his own misfortune, which nobody therefore heeded. But Miss Amory was savage at her mishap ; Miss Roundle placed on her *séant*, and looking pitifully round, presented an object which very few people could see without laughing ; and Pen was furious when he heard the people giggling about him. He was one of those sarcastic young fellows that did not bear a laugh at his own expense, and of all things in the world feared ridicule most.

As he got up Laura and Strong were laughing at him ; everybody was laughing ; Pynsent and his partner were laughing ; and Pen boiled with wrath against the pair, and could have stabbed them both on the spot. He turned away in a fury from them, and began blundering out apologies to Miss Amory. It was the other couple's fault —the woman in pink had done it—Pen hoped Miss Amory was not hurt—would she not have the courage to take another turn ?

Miss Amory in a pet said she *was* very much hurt indeed, and she would not take another turn ; and she accepted with great thanks a glass of water which a cavalier, who wore a blue ribbon and a three-pointed star, rushed to

fetch for her when he had seen the deplorable accident, She drank the water, smiled upon the bringer gracefully, and turning her white shoulder at Mr. Pen in the most marked and haughty manner, besought the gentleman with the star to conduct her to her mamma ; and she held out her hand in order to take his arm.

The man with the star trembled with delight at this mark of her favour ; he bowed over her hand, pressed it to his coat fervidly, and looked round him with triumph.

It was no other than the happy Mirobolant whom Blanche had selected as an escort. But the truth is, that the young lady had never fairly looked in the artist's face since he had been employed in her mother's family, and had no idea but it was a foreign nobleman on whose arm she was leaning. As she went off, Pen forgot his humiliation in his surprise, and cried out, 'By Jove, it's the cook!'

The instant he had uttered the words, he was sorry for having spoken them—for it was Blanche who had herself invited Mirobolant to escort her, nor could the artist do otherwise than comply with a lady's command. Blanche in her flutter did not hear what Arthur said ; but Mirobolant heard him, and cast a furious glance at him over his shoulder, which rather amused Mr. Pen. He was in a mischievous and sulky humour ; wanting perhaps to pick a quarrel with somebody ; but the idea of having insulted a cook, or that such an individual should have any feeling of honour at all, did not much enter into the mind of this lofty young aristocrat, the apothecary's son.

It had never entered that poor artist's head, that he as a man was not equal to any other mortal, or that there was anything in his position so degrading as to prevent him from giving his arm to a lady who asked for it. He had seen in the fêtes in his own country fine ladies, not certainly demoiselles (but the *demoiselle Anglaise* he knew was a great deal more free than the spinster in France), join in the dance with Blaise or Pierre ; and he would have taken Blanche up to Lady Clavering, and possibly have asked her to dance too, but he heard Pen's exclamation, which struck him as if it had shot him, and cruelly humiliated and angered him. She did not know what caused him to start, and to grind a Gascon oath between his teeth.

But Strong, who was acquainted with the poor fellow's

state of mind, having had the interesting information from our friend Madame Fribsby, was luckily in the way when wanted, and saying something rapidly in Spanish, which the other understood, the chevalier begged Miss Amory to come and take an ice before she went back to Lady Clavering. Upon which the unhappy Mirobolant relinquished the arm which he had held for a minute, and with a most profound and piteous bow, fell back. 'Don't you know who it is?' Strong asked of Miss Amory, as he led her away. 'It is the *chef* Mirobolant.'

'How should I know?' asked Blanche. 'He has a *croix;* he is very *distingué;* he has beautiful eyes.'

'The poor fellow is mad for your *beaux yeux*, I believe,' Strong said. 'He is a very good cook, but he is not quite right in the head.'

'What did you say to him in the unknown tongue?' asked Miss Blanche.

'He is a Gascon, and comes from the borders of Spain,' Strong answered. 'I told him he would lose his place if he walked with you.'

'Poor Monsieur Mirobolant!' said Blanche.

'Did you see the look he gave Pendennis?'—Strong asked, enjoying the idea of the mischief—'I think he would like to run little Pen through with one of his spits.'

'He is an odious, conceited, clumsy creature, that Mr. Pen,' said Blanche.

'Broadfoot looked as if he would like to kill him too, so did Pynsent,' Strong said. 'What ice will you have—water ice or cream ice?'

'Water ice. Who is that odd man staring at me—he is *decoré* too.'

'That is my friend Colonel Altamont, a very queer character, in the service of the Nawaub of Lucknow. Hullo! what's that noise? I'll be back in an instant,' said the chevalier, and sprang out of the room to the ballroom, where a scuffle and a noise of high voices was heard.

The refreshment-room, in which Miss Amory now found herself, was a room set apart for the purposes of supper, which Mr. Rincer, the landlord, had provided for those who chose to partake, at the rate of five shillings per head. Also, refreshments of a superior class were here ready for the ladies and gentlemen of the county families who came to the ball; but the commoner sort of persons were kept

out of the room by a waiter who stood at the portal, and who said that was a select room for Lady Clavering and Lady Rockminster's parties, and not to be opened to the public till supper-time, which was not to be until past midnight. Pynsent, who danced with the constituents' daughters, took them and their mammas in for their refreshment there. Strong, who was manager and master of the revels wherever he went, had of course the entrée—and the only person who was now occupying the room was the gentleman with the black wig and the orders in his button-hole; the officer in the service of His Highness the Nawaub of Lucknow.

This gentleman had established himself very early in the evening in this apartment, where, saying he was confoundedly thirsty, he called for a bottle of champagne. At this order, the waiter instantly supposed that he had to do with a grandee, and the colonel sat down and began to eat his supper and absorb his drink, and enter affably into conversation with anybody who entered the room.

Sir Francis Clavering and Mr. Wagg found him there; when they left the ball-room, which they did pretty early—Sir Francis to go and smoke a cigar, and look at the people gathered outside the ball-room on the shore, which he declared was much better fun than to remain within; Mr. Wagg to hang on to a baronet's arm, as he was always pleased to do on the arm of the greatest man in the company. Colonel Altamont had stared at these gentlemen in so odd a manner, as they passed through the 'select' room, that Clavering made inquiries of the landlord who he was, and hinted a strong opinion that the officer of the Nawaub's service was drunk.

Mr. Pynsent, too, had had the honour of a conversation with the servant of the Indian potentate. It was Pynsent's cue to speak to everybody (which he did, to do him justice, in the most ungracious manner); and he took the gentleman in the black wig for some constituent, some merchant captain, or other outlandish man of the place. Mr. Pynsent, then, coming into the refreshment-room with a lady, the wife of a constituent, on his arm, the colonel asked him if he would try a glass of sham? Pynsent took it with great gravity, bowed, tasted the wine, and pronounced it excellent, and with the utmost politeness retreated before Colonel Altamont. This gravity and

decorum routed and surprised the colonel more than any other kind of behaviour probably would: he stared after Pynsent stupidly, and pronounced to the landlord over the counter that he was a rum one. Mr. Rincer blushed, and hardly knew what to say. Mr. Pynsent was a county earl's grandson, going to set up as a Parliament man. Colonel Altamont, on the other hand, wore orders and diamonds, jingled sovereigns constantly in his pocket, and

paid his way like a man; so not knowing what to say, Mr. Rincer said, 'Yes, colonel—yes, ma'am, did you say tea? Cup a tea for Mr. Jones, Mrs. R.,' and so got off that discussion regarding Mr. Pynsent's qualities, into which the Nizam's officer appeared inclined to enter.

In fact, if the truth must be told, Mr. Altamont, having remained at the buffet almost all night, and employed himself very actively whilst there, had considerably flushed

his brain by drinking, and he was still going on drinking when Mr. Strong and Miss Amory entered the room.

When the chevalier ran out of the apartment, attracted by the noise in the dancing-room, the colonel rose from his chair with his little red eyes glowing like coals, and, with rather an unsteady gait, advanced towards Blanche, who was sipping her ice. She was absorbed in absorbing it, for it was very fresh and good ; or she was not curious to know what was going on in the adjoining room, although the waiters were, who ran after Chevalier Strong. So that when she looked up from her glass, she beheld this strange man staring at her out of his little red eyes. 'Who was he ? It was quite exciting.'

'And so you're Betsy Amory,' said he, after gazing at her. 'Betsy Amory, by Jove !'

'Who—who speaks to me ?' said Betsy, *alias* Blanche.

But the noise in the ball-room is really becoming so loud, that we must rush back thither, and see what is the cause of the disturbance.

CHAPTER XXVII

WHICH IS BOTH QUARRELSOME AND SENTIMENTAL

CIVIL war was raging, high words passing, people pushing and squeezing together in an unseemly manner, round a window in the corner of the ball-room, close by the door through which the Chevalier Strong shouldered his way. Through the opened window the crowd in the street below was sending up sarcastic remarks, such as 'Pitch into him !' 'Where's the police ?' and the like ; and a ring of individuals, among whom Madame Fribsby was conspicuous, was gathered round Monsieur Alcide Mirobolant on the one side ; whilst several gentlemen and ladies surrounded our friend Arthur Pendennis on the other. Strong penetrated into this

assembly, elbowing by Madame Fribsby, who was charmed at the chevalier's appearance, and cried, 'Save him, save him!' in frantic and pathetic accents.

The cause of the disturbance, it appeared, was the angry little *chef* of Sir Francis Clavering's culinary establishment. Shortly after Strong had quitted the room, and whilst Mr. Pen, greatly irate at his downfall in the waltz, which had made him look ridiculous in the eyes of the nation, and by Miss Amory's behaviour to him, which had still further insulted his dignity, was endeavouring to get some coolness of body and temper, by looking out of window towards the sea, which was sparkling in the distance, and murmuring in a wonderful calm—whilst he was really trying to compose himself, and owning to himself, perhaps, that he had acted in a very absurd and peevish manner during the night—he felt a hand upon his shoulder; and, on looking round, beheld, to his utter surprise and horror, that the hand in question belonged to Monsieur Mirobolant, whose eyes were glaring out of his pale face and ringlets at Mr. Pen. To be tapped on the shoulder by a French cook was a piece of familiarity which made the blood of the Pendennises to boil up in the veins of their descendant, and he was astounded, almost more than enraged, at such an indignity.

'You speak French?' Mirobolant said, in his own language, to Pen.

'What is that to you, pray?' said Pen, in English.

'At any rate, you understand it?' continued the other, with a bow.

'Yes, sir,' said Pen, with a stamp of his foot; 'I understand it pretty well.'

'*Vous me comprendrez alors, Monsieur Pendennis,*' replied the other, rolling out his *r* with Gascon force, '*quand je vous dis que vous êtes un lâche. Monsieur Pendennis—un lâche, entendez-vous?*'

'What?' said Pen, starting round on him.

'You understand the meaning of the word and its consequences among men of honour?' the artist said, putting his hand on his hip, and staring at Pen.

'The consequences are, that I will fling you out of window, you—impudent scoundrel!' bawled out Mr. Pen; and darting upon the Frenchman, he would very likely have put his threat into execution, for the window was at

hand, and the artist by no means a match for the young gentleman—had not Captain Broadfoot and another heavy officer flung themselves between the combatants—had not the ladies begun to scream—had not the fiddles stopped—had not the crowd of people come running in that direction—had not Laura, with a face of great alarm, looked over their heads and asked for Heaven's sake what was wrong—had not the opportune Strong made his appearance from the refreshment-room, and found Alcides grinding his teeth and jabbering oaths in his Gascon French, and Pen looking uncommonly wicked, although trying to appear as calm as possible, when the ladies and the crowd came up.

'What has happened ?' Strong asked of the *chef*, in Spanish.

'I am Chevalier de Juillet,' said the other, slapping his breast, 'and he has insulted me.'

'What has he said to you ?' asked Strong.

'*Il m'a appelé—cuisinier*,' hissed out the little Frenchman.

Strong could hardly help laughing. 'Come away with me, my poor chevalier,' he said. 'We must not quarrel before ladies. Come away; I will carry your message to Mr. Pendennis.—The poor fellow is not right in his head,' he whispered to one or two people about him ;—and others, and anxious Laura's face visible amongst these, gathered round Pen and asked the cause of the disturbance.

Pen did not know. 'The man was going to give his arm to a young lady, on which I said that he was a cook, and the man called me a coward and challenged me to fight. I own I was so surprised and indignant, that if you gentlemen had not stopped me, I should have thrown him out of window,' Pen said.

'D—— him, serve him right, too, the d—— impudent foreign scoundrel !' the gentlemen said.

'I—I'm very sorry if I hurt his feelings, though,' Pen added : and Laura was glad to hear him say that ; although some of the young bucks said, 'No, hang the fellow—hang those impudent foreigners—little thrashing would do them good.'

'You will go and shake hands with him before you go to sleep—won't you, Pen ?' said Laura, coming up to him. 'Foreigners may be more susceptible than we are, and have different manners. If you hurt a poor man's feelings, I am

sure you would be the first to ask his pardon. Wouldn't you, dear Pen ?'

She looked all forgiveness and gentleness, like an angel, as she spoke, and Pen took both her hands, and looked into her kind face, and said indeed he would.

'How fond that girl is of me !' he thought, as she stood gazing at him. 'Shall I speak to her now ? No—not now. I must have this absurd business with the Frenchman over.'

Laura asked—Wouldn't he stop and dance with her ? She was as anxious to keep him in the room, as he to quit it. 'Won't you stop and waltz with me, Pen ? I'm not afraid to waltz with you.'

This was an affectionate, but an unlucky speech. Pen saw himself prostrate on the ground, having tumbled over Miss Roundle and the Dragoon, and flung Blanche up against the wall—saw himself on the ground, and all the people laughing at him, Laura and Pynsent amongst them.

'I shall never dance again,' he replied, with a dark and determined face. 'Never. I'm surprised you should ask me.'

'Is it because you can't get Blanche for a partner ?' asked Laura, with a wicked, unlucky captiousness.

'Because I don't wish to make a fool of myself, for other people to laugh at me,' Pen answered—'for *you* to laugh at me, Laura. I saw you and Pynsent. By Jove ! no man shall laugh at me.'

'Pen, Pen, don't be so wicked !' cried out the poor girl, hurt at the morbid perverseness and savage vanity of Pen. He was glaring round in the direction of Mr. Pynsent as if he would have liked to engage that gentleman as he had done the cook. 'Who thinks the worse of you for stumbling in a waltz ?' If Blanche does, we don't. 'Why are you so sensitive, and ready to think evil ?'

Here again, by ill-luck, Mr. Pynsent came up to Laura, and said, 'I have it in command from Lady Rockminster to ask whether I may take you in to supper ?'

'I—I was going in with my cousin,' Laura said.

'Oh—pray, no !' said Pen. 'You are in such good hands, that I can't do better than leave you : and I'm going home.'

'Good night, Mr. Pendennis,' Pynsent said dryly—to which speech (which, in fact, meant, 'Go to the deuce for an insolent, jealous, impertinent jackanapes, whose ears I should like to box') Mr. Pendennis did not vouchsafe any

reply, except a bow: and, in spite of Laura's imploring looks, he left the room.

'How beautifully calm and bright the night outside is!' said Mr. Pynsent; 'and what a murmur the sea is making! It would be pleasanter to be walking on the beach, than in this hot room.'

'Very,' said Laura.

'What a strange congregation of people,' continued Pynsent. 'I have had to go up and perform the agreeable to most of them*—the attorney's daughters—the apothecary's wife—I scarcely know whom. There was a man in the refreshment-room, who insisted upon treating me to champagne—a seafaring-looking man—extraordinarily dressed, and seeming half tipsy. As a public man, one is bound to conciliate all these people, but it is a hard task—especially when one would so very much like to be elsewhere'—and he blushed rather as he spoke.

'I beg your pardon,' said Laura—'I—I was not listening. Indeed—I was frightened about that quarrel between my cousin and that—that—French person.'

'Your cousin has been rather unlucky to-night,' Pynsent said. 'There are three or four persons whom he has not succeeded in pleasing—Captain Broadwood; what is his name—the officer—and the young lady in red with whom he danced—and Miss Blanche—and the poor *chef*—and I don't think he seemed to be particularly pleased with me.'

'Didn't he leave me in charge to you?' Laura said, looking up into Mr. Pynsent's face, and dropping her eyes instantly, like a guilty little story-telling coquette.

'Indeed, I can forgive him a good deal for that,' Pynsent eagerly cried out; and she took his arm, and he led off his little prize in the direction of the supper-room.

She had no great desire for that repast, though it was served in Rincer's well-known style, as the county paper said, giving an account of the entertainment afterwards; indeed, she was very *distraite;* and exceedingly pained and unhappy about Pen. Captious and quarrelsome; jealous and selfish; fickle and violent and unjust when his anger led him astray; how could her mother (as indeed Helen had by a thousand words and hints) ask her to give her heart to such a man? and suppose she were to do so, would it make him happy?

But she got some relief at length, when, at the end of

half an hour—a long half-hour it had seemed to her—a waiter brought her a little note in pencil from Pen, who said, 'I met Cooky below ready to fight me; and I asked his pardon. I'm glad I did it. I wanted to speak to you to-night, but will keep what I had to say till you come home. God bless you. Dance away all night with Pynsent, and be very happy. PEN.'—Laura was very thankful for this letter, and to think that there was goodness and forgiveness still in her mother's boy.

Pen went downstairs, his heart reproaching him for his absurd behaviour to Laura, whose gentle and imploring looks followed and rebuked him; and he was scarcely out of the ball-room door but he longed to turn back and ask her pardon. But he remembered that he had left her with that confounded Pynsent. He could not apologize before *him*. He would compromise and forget his wrath, and make his peace with the Frenchman.

The chevalier was pacing down below in the hall of the inn when Pen descended from the ball-room; and he came up to Pen, with all sorts of fun and mischief lighting up his jolly face.

'I have got him in the coffee-room,' he said, 'with a brace of pistols and a candle. Or would you like swords on the beach? Mirobolant is a dead hand with the foils, and killed four *gardes du corps* with his own point in the barricades of July.'

'Confound it,' said Pen, in a fury, 'I can't fight a cook!'

'He is a chevalier of July,' replied the other. 'They present arms to him in his own country.'

'And do you ask me, Captain Strong, to go out with a servant?' Pen asked fiercely; 'I'll call a policeman for *him*; but—but——'

'You'll invite me to hair triggers?' cried Strong, with a laugh. 'Thank you for nothing; I was but joking. I came to settle quarrels, not to fight them. I have been soothing down Mirobolant; I have told him that you did not apply the word "cook" to him in an offensive sense: that it was contrary to all the customs of the country that a hired officer of a household, as I called it, should give his arm to the daughter of the house.' And then he told Pen the grand secret which he had had from Madame Fribsby,

of the violent passion under which the poor artist was labouring.

When Arthur heard this tale, he broke out into a hearty laugh, in which Strong joined, and his rage against the poor cook vanished at once. He had been absurdly jealous himself all the evening, and had longed for a pretext to insult Pynsent. He remembered how jealous he had been of Oaks in his first affair; he was ready to pardon anything to a man under a passion like that: and he went into the coffee-room where Mirobolant was waiting, with an outstretched hand, and made him a speech in French, in which he declared that he was '*Sincèrement fâché d'avoir usé une expression qui avait pu blesser Monsieur Mirobolant, et qu'il donnait sa parole comme un gentilhomme qu'il ne l'avait jamais, jamais—intendé*,' said Pen, who made a shot at a French word for 'intended,' and was secretly much pleased with his own fluency and correctness in speaking that language.

'Bravo, bravo!' cried Strong, as much amused with Pen's speech as pleased by his kind manner. And the Chevalier Mirobolant of course withdraws, and sincerely regrets the expression of which he made use.

'Monsieur Pendennis has disproved my words himself,' said Alcide, with great politeness; 'he has shown that he is a *galant homme*.'

And so they shook hands and parted, Arthur in the first place dispatching his note to Laura before he and Strong committed themselves to the Butcher Boy.

As they drove along, Strong complimented Pen upon his behaviour, as well as upon his skill in French. 'You're a good fellow, Pendennis, and you speak French like Chateaubriand,* by Jove.'

'I've been accustomed to it from my youth upwards,' said Pen; and Strong had the grace not to laugh for five minutes, when he exploded into fits of hilarity which Pendennis has never, perhaps, understood up to this day.

It was daybreak when they got to the Brawl, where they separated. By that time the ball at Baymouth was over too. Madame Fribsby and Mirobolant were on their way home in the Clavering fly; Laura was in bed with an easy heart and asleep at Lady Rockminster's; and the Claverings at rest at the inn at Baymouth, where they had quarters for the night. A short time after the disturbance between Pen

and the *chef*, Blanche had come out of the refreshment-room, looking as pale as a lemon-ice. She told her maid, having no other confidante at hand, that she had met with the most romantic adventure—the most singular man—one who had known the author of her being—her persecuted—her unhappy—her heroic—her murdered father ; and she began a sonnet to his manes before she went to sleep.

So Pen returned to Fairoaks, in company with his friend the chevalier, without having uttered a word of the message which he had been so anxious to deliver to Laura at Baymouth. He could wait, however, until her return home, which was to take place on the succeeding day. He was not seriously jealous of the progress made by Mr. Pynsent in her favour ; and he felt pretty certain that in this, as in any other family arrangement, he had but to ask and have, and Laura, like his mother, could refuse him nothing.

When Helen's anxious looks inquired of him what had happened at Baymouth, and whether her darling project was fulfilled, Pen, in a gay tone, told of the calamity which had befallen ; laughingly said, that no man could think about declarations under such a mishap, and made light of the matter. 'There will be plenty of time for sentiment, dear mother, when Laura comes back,' he said, and he looked in the glass with a killing air, and his mother put his hair off his forehead and kissed him, and of course thought, for her part, that no woman could resist him ; and was exceedingly happy that day.

When he was not with her, Mr. Pen occupied himself in packing books and portmanteaus, burning and arranging papers, cleaning his gun and putting it into its case : in fact, in making dispositions for departure. For though he was ready to marry, this gentleman was eager to go to London too, rightly considering that at three-and-twenty it was quite time for him to begin upon the serious business of life, and to set about making a fortune as quickly as possible.

The means to this end he had already shaped out for himself. 'I shall take chambers,' he said, 'and enter myself at an Inn of Court. With a couple of hundred pounds I shall be able to carry through the first year very well: after that I have little doubt my pen will support me, as it is doing with several Oxbridge men now in town. I

have a tragedy, a comedy, and a novel, all nearly finished, and for which I can't fail to get a price. And so I shall be able to live pretty well, without drawing upon my poor mother, until I have made my way at the Bar. Then, some day I will come back and make her dear soul happy by marrying Laura. She is as good and as sweet-tempered a girl as ever lived, besides being really very good-looking, and the engagement will serve to steady me—won't it, Ponto ?' Thus, smoking his pipe, and talking to his dog as he sauntered through the gardens and orchards of the little domain of Fairoaks, this young day-dreamer built castles in the air for himself : 'Yes, she'll steady me, won't she ? And you'll miss me when I've gone, won't you, old boy ?' he asked of Ponto, who quivered his tail and thrust his brown nose into his master's fist. Ponto licked his hand and shoe, as they all did in that house, and Mr. Pen received their homage as other folks do the flattery which they get.

Laura came home rather late in the evening of the second day ; and Mr. Pynsent, as ill-luck would have it, drove her from Clavering. The poor girl could not refuse his offer, but his appearance brought a dark cloud upon the brow of Arthur Pendennis. Laura saw this, and was pained by it : the eager widow, however, was aware of nothing, and being anxious, doubtless, that the delicate question should be asked at once, was for going to bed very soon after Laura's arrival, and rose for that purpose to leave the sofa where she now generally lay, and where Laura would come and sit and work or read by her. But when Helen rose, Laura said, with a blush and rather an alarmed voice, that she was also very tired and wanted to go to bed : so that the widow was disappointed in her scheme for that night at least, and Mr. Pen was left another day in suspense regarding his fate.

His dignity was offended at being thus obliged to remain in the antechamber when he wanted an audience. Such a sultan as he could not afford to be kept waiting. However, he went to bed and slept upon his disappointment pretty comfortably, and did not wake until the early morning, when he looked up and saw his mother standing in his room.

'Dear Pen, rouse up,' said this lady. 'Do not be lazy. It is the most beautiful morning in the world. I have not

been able to sleep since daybreak; and Laura has been out for an hour. She is in the garden. Everybody ought to be in the garden and out on such a morning as this.'

Pen laughed. He saw what thoughts were uppermost in the simple woman's heart. His good-natured laughter cheered the widow. 'O you profound dissembler,' he said, kissing his mother. 'O you artful creature! Can nobody escape from your wicked tricks? and will you make your only son your victim?' Helen too laughed, she blushed, she fluttered, and was agitated. She was as happy as she could be—a good, tender, match-making woman, the dearest project of whose heart was about to be accomplished.

So, after exchanging some knowing looks and hasty words, Helen left Arthur; and this young hero, rising from his bed, proceeded to decorate his beautiful person, and shave his ambrosial chin; and in half an hour he issued out from his apartment into the garden in quest of Laura. His reflections as he made his toilette were rather dismal. 'I am going to tie myself for life,' he thought, 'to please my mother. Laura is the best of women, and—and she has given me her money. I wish to Heaven I had not received it; I wish I had not this duty to perform just yet. But as both the women have set their hearts on the match, why, I suppose I must satisfy them—and now for it. A man may do worse than make happy two of the best creatures in the world.' So Pen, now he was actually come to the point, felt very grave, and by no means elated, and, indeed, thought it was a great sacrifice he was going to perform.

It was Miss Laura's custom, upon her garden excursions, to wear a sort of uniform, which, though homely, was thought by many people to be not unbecoming. She had a large straw hat, with a streamer of broad ribbon, which was useless probably, but the hat sufficiently protected the owner's pretty face from the sun. Over her accustomed gown she wore a blouse or pinafore, which, being fastened round her little waist by a smart belt, looked extremely well, and her hands were guaranteed from the thorns of her favourite rose-bushes by a pair of gauntlets, which gave this young lady a military and resolute air.

Somehow she had the very same smile with which she had laughed at him on the night previous, and the recollection

of his disaster again offended Pen. But Laura, though she saw him coming down the walk looking so gloomy and full of care, accorded to him a smile of the most perfect and provoking good humour, and went to meet him, holding one of the gauntlets to him, so that he might shake it if he liked—and Mr. Pen condescended to do so. His face, however, did not lose its tragic expression in consequence of this favour, and he continued to regard her with a dismal and solemn air.

'Excuse my glove,' said Laura, with a laugh, pressing Pen's hand kindly with it. 'We are not angry again, are we, Pen?'

'Why do you laugh at me?' said Pen. 'You did the other night, and made a fool of me to the people at Baymouth.'

'My dear Arthur, I meant you no wrong,' the girl answered. 'You and Miss Roundle looked so droll as you—as you met with your little accident, that I could not make a tragedy of it. Dear Pen, it wasn't a serious fall.

And, besides, it was Miss Roundle who was the most unfortunate.'

'Confound Miss Roundle!' bellowed out Pen.

'I'm sure she looked so,' said Laura archly. 'You were up in an instant; but that poor lady sitting on the ground in her red crape dress, and looking about her with that piteous face—can I ever forget her?'—and Laura began to make a face in imitation of Miss Roundle's under the disaster, but she checked herself repentantly, saying, 'Well, we must not laugh at her, but I am sure we ought to laugh at you, Pen, if you were angry about such a trifle.'

'*You* should not laugh at me, Laura,' said Pen, with some bitterness; 'not you, of all people.'

'And why not? Are you such a great man?' asked Laura.

'Ah no, Laura, I'm such a poor one,' Pen answered. 'Haven't you baited me enough already?'

'My dear Pen, and how?' cried Laura. 'Indeed, indeed, I didn't think to vex you by such a trifle. I thought such a clever man as you could bear a harmless little joke from his sister,' she said, holding her hand out again. 'Dear Arthur, if I have hurt you, I beg your pardon.'

'It is your kindness that humiliates me more even than your laughter, Laura,' Pen said. 'You are always my superior.'

'What! superior to the great Arthur Pendennis? How can it be possible?' said Miss Laura, who may have had a little wickedness as well as a great deal of kindness in her composition. 'You can't mean that any woman is your equal?'

'Those who confer benefits should not sneer,' said Pen. 'I don't like my benefactor to laugh at me, Laura; it makes the obligation very hard to bear. You scorn me because I have taken your money, and I am worthy to be scorned; but the blow is hard, coming from you.'

'Money! Obligation! For shame, Pen; this is ungenerous,' Laura said, flushing red. 'May not our mother claim everything that belongs to us? Don't I owe her all my happiness in this world, Arthur? What matters about a few paltry guineas, if we can set her tender heart at rest, and ease her mind regarding you? I would dig in

the fields, I would go out and be a servant—I would die for her. You know I would,' said Miss Laura, kindling up; 'and you call this paltry money an obligation? Oh, Pen, it's cruel—it's unworthy of you to take it so! If my brother may not share with me my superfluity, who may?—Mine?—I tell you it was not mine; it was all mamma's to do with as she chose, and so is everything I have,' said Laura; 'my life is hers.' And the enthusiastic girl looked towards the windows of the widow's room, and blessed in her heart the kind creature within.

Helen was looking, unseen, out of that window towards which Laura's eyes and heart were turned as she spoke, and was watching her two children with the deepest interest and emotion, longing and hoping that the prayer of her life might be fulfilled; and if Laura had spoken as Helen hoped, who knows what temptations Arthur Pendennis might have been spared, or what different trials he would have had to undergo? He might have remained at Fairoaks all his days, and died a country gentleman. But would he have escaped then? Temptation is an obsequious servant that has no objection to the country, and we know that it takes up its lodging in hermitages as well as in cities; and that in the most remote and inaccessible desert it keeps company with the fugitive solitary.

'*Is* your life my mother's?' said Pen, beginning to tremble, and speak in a very agitated manner. 'You know, Laura, what the great object of hers is?' And he took her hand once more.

'What, Arthur?' she said, dropping it, and looking at him, at the window again, and then dropping her eyes to the ground, so that they avoided Pen's gaze. She, too, trembled, for she felt that the crisis for which she had been secretly preparing was come.

'Our mother has one wish above all others in the world, Laura,' Pen said; 'and I think you know it. I own to you that she has spoken to me of it; and if you will fulfil it, dear sister, I am ready. I am but very young as yet; but I have had so many pains and disappointments, that I am old and weary. I think I have hardly got a heart to offer. Before I have almost begun the race in life, I am a tired man. My career has been a failure; I have been protected by those whom I by right should have

protected. I own that your nobleness and generosity, dear Laura, shame me, whilst they render me grateful. When I heard from our mother what you had done for me : that it was you who armed me and bade me go out for one struggle more ; I longed to go and throw myself at your feet, and say, " Laura, will you come and share the contest with me ? Your sympathy will cheer me while it lasts. I shall have one of the tenderest and most generous creatures under heaven to aid and bear me company." Will you take me, dear Laura, and make our mother happy ?'

'Do you think mamma would be happy if you were otherwise, Arthur ?' Laura said in a low sad voice.

'And why should I not be,' asked Pen eagerly, 'with so dear a creature as you by my side ? I have not my first love to give you. I am a broken man. But indeed I would love you fondly and truly. I have lost many an illusion and ambition, but I am not without hope still. Talents I know I have, wretchedly as I have misapplied them : they may serve me yet : they would, had I a motive for action. Let me go away and think that I am pledged to return to you. Let me go and work, and hope that you will share my success if I gain it. You have given me so much, dear Laura, will you take from me nothing ?'

'What have you got to give, Arthur ?' Laura said, with a grave sadness of tone, which made Pen start, and see that his words had committed him. Indeed, his declaration had not been such as he would have made it two days earlier, when, full of hope and gratitude, he had run over to Laura, his liberatress, to thank her for his recovered freedom. Had he been permitted to speak then, he had spoken, and she, perhaps, had listened differently. It would have been a grateful heart asking for hers ; not a weary one offered to her, to take or to leave. Laura was offended with the terms in which Pen offered himself to her. He had, in fact, said that he had no love, and yet would take no denial. 'I give myself to you to please my mother,' he had said : 'take me, as she wishes that I should make this sacrifice.' The girl's spirit would brook a husband under no such conditions : she was not minded to run forward because Pen chose to hold out the handkerchief, and her tone, in reply to Arthur, showed her determination to be independent.

'No, Arthur,' she said, 'our marriage would not make mamma happy, as she fancies; for it would not content you very long. I, too, have known what her wishes were; for she is too open to conceal anything she has at heart: and once, perhaps, I thought—but that is over now—that I could have made you—that it might have been as she wished.'

'You have seen somebody else,' said Pen, angry at her tone, and recalling the incidents of the past days.

'That allusion might have been spared,' Laura replied, flinging up her head. 'A heart which has worn out love at three-and-twenty,* as yours has, you say, should have survived jealousy too. I do not condescend to say whether I have seen or encouraged any other person. I shall neither admit the charge, nor deny it: and beg you also to allude to it no more.'

'I ask your pardon, Laura, if I have offended you: but if I am jealous, does it not prove that I have a heart?'

'Not for me, Arthur. Perhaps you think you love me now: but it is only for an instant, and because you are foiled. Were there no obstacle, you would feel no ardour to overcome it. No, Arthur, you don't love me. You would weary of me in three months, as—as you do of most things; and mamma, seeing you tired of me, would be more unhappy than at my refusal to be yours. Let us be brother and sister, Arthur, as heretofore—but no more. You will get over this little disappointment.'

'I will try,' said Arthur, in a great indignation.

'Have you not tried before?' Laura said, with some anger, for she had been angry with Arthur for a very long time, and was now determined, I suppose, to speak her mind. 'And the next time, Arthur, when you offer yourself to a woman, do not say as you have done to me, "I have no heart—I do not love you; but I am ready to marry you because my mother wishes for the match." We require more than this in return for our love—that is, I think so. I have had no experience hitherto, and have not had the—the practice which you supposed me to have, when you spoke but now of my having seen somebody else. Did you tell your first love that you had no heart, Arthur? or your second that you did not love her, but that she might have you if she liked?'

'What—what do you mean?' asked Arthur, blushing, and still in great wrath.

'I mean Blanche Amory, Arthur Pendennis,' Laura said proudly. 'It is but two months since you were sighing at her feet—making poems to her—placing them in hollow trees by the river-side. I knew all. I watched you—that is, she showed them to me. Neither one nor the other were in earnest perhaps; but it is too soon now, Arthur, to begin a new attachment. Go through the time of your—your widowhood at least, and do not think of marrying until you are out of mourning.'—(Here the girl's eyes filled with tears, and she passed her hand across them.) 'I am angry and hurt, and I have no right to be so, and I ask your pardon in my turn now, dear Arthur. You had a right to love Blanche. She was a thousand times prettier and more accomplished than—than any girl near us here; and you could not know that she had no heart; and so you were right to leave her too. I ought not to rebuke you about Blanche Amory, and because she deceived you. Pardon me, Pen,'—and she held the kind hand out to Pen once more.

'We were both jealous,' said Pen. 'Dear Laura, let us both forgive'—and he seized her hand and would have drawn her towards him. He thought that she was relenting, and already assumed the airs of a victor.

But she shrank back, and her tears passed away; and she fixed on him a look so melancholy and severe, that the young man in his turn shrank before it. 'Do not mistake me, Arthur,' she said, 'it cannot be. You do not know what you ask, and do not be too angry with me for saying that I think you do not deserve it. What do you offer in exchange to a woman for her love, honour, and obedience? If ever I say these words, dear Pen, I hope to say them in earnest, and by the blessing of God to keep my vow. But you—what tie binds you? You do not care about many things which we poor women hold sacred. I do not like to think or ask how far your incredulity leads you. You offer to marry to please our mother, and own that you have no heart to give away? Oh, Arthur, what is it you offer me? What a rash compact would you enter into so lightly? A month ago, and you would have given yourself to another. I pray you do not trifle with your own or others' hearts so recklessly. Go and work; go and

mend, dear Arthur, for I see your faults, and dare speak of them now: go and get fame, as you say that you can, and I will pray for my brother, and watch our dearest mother at home.'

'Is that your final decision, Laura?' Arthur cried.

'Yes,' said Laura, bowing her head; and once more giving him her hand, she went away. He saw her pass under the creepers of the little porch, and disappear into the house. The curtains of his mother's window fell at the same minute, but he did not mark that, or suspect that Helen had been witnessing the scene.

Was he pleased, or was he angry at its termination? He had asked her, and a secret triumph filled his heart to think that he was still free. She had refused him, but did she not love him? That avowal of jealousy made him still think that her heart was his own, whatever her lips might utter.

And now we ought, perhaps, to describe another scene which took place at Fairoaks, between the widow and Laura, when the latter had to tell Helen that she had refused Arthur Pendennis. Perhaps it was the hardest task of all which Laura had to go through in this matter: and the one which gave her the most pain. But as we do not like to see a good woman unjust, we shall not say a word more of the quarrel which now befell between Helen and her adopted daughter, or of the bitter tears which the poor girl was made to shed. It was the only difference which she and the widow had ever had as yet, and the more cruel from this cause. Pen left home whilst it was as yet pending—and Helen, who could pardon almost everything, could not pardon an act of justice in Laura.

CHAPTER XXVIII

BABYLON*

UR reader must now please to quit the woods and seashore of the West, and the gossip of Clavering, and the humdrum life of poor little Fairoaks, and transport himself with Arthur Pendennis, on the 'Alacrity' coach, to London, whither he goes once for all to face the world and to make his fortune. As the coach whirls through the night away from the friendly gates of home, many a plan does the young man cast in his mind of future life and conduct, prudence, and peradventure success and fame. He knows he is a better man than many who have hitherto been ahead of him in the race: his first failure has caused him remorse, and brought with it reflection; it has not taken away his courage, or, let us add, his good opinion of himself. A hundred eager fancies and busy hopes keep him awake. How much older his mishaps and a year's thought and self-communion have made him, than when, twelve months since, he passed on this road on his way to and from Oxbridge! His thoughts turn in the night with inexpressible fondness and tenderness towards the fond mother, who blessed him when parting, and who, in spite of all his past faults and follies, trusts him and loves him still. Blessings be on her! he prays, as he looks up to the stars overhead. O Heaven, give him strength to work, to endure, to be honest, to avoid temptation, to be worthy of the loving soul who loves him so entirely! Very likely she is awake, too, at that moment, and sending up to the same Father purer prayers than his for the welfare of her boy. That woman's love is a talisman by which he holds and hopes to get his safety. And Laura's—he would have fain carried her affection with him too, but she has denied it, as he is not worthy of it. He owns as much with

shame and remorse; confesses how much better and loftier her nature is than his own—confesses it, and yet is glad to be free. 'I am not good enough for such a creature,' he owns to himself. He draws back before her spotless beauty and innocence, as from something that scares him. He feels he is not fit for such a mate as that; as many a wild prodigal who has been pious and guiltless in early days keeps away from a church which he used to frequent once—shunning it, but not hostile to it—only feeling that he has no right in that pure place.

With these thoughts to occupy him, Pen did not fall asleep until the nipping dawn of an October morning, and woke considerably refreshed when the coach stopped at the old breakfasting place at B——, where he had had a score of merry meals on his way to and from school and college many times since he was a boy. As they left that place, the sun broke out brightly, the pace was rapid, the horn blew, the milestones flew by, Pen smoked and joked with guard and fellow-passengers and people along the familiar road; it grew more busy and animated at every instant; the last team of greys came out at H——, and the coach drove into London. What young fellow has not felt a thrill as he entered the vast place? Hundreds of other carriages, crowded with their thousands of men, were hastening to the great city. 'Here is my place,' thought Pen; 'here is my battle beginning, in which I must fight and conquer, or fall. I have been a boy and a dawdler as yet. Oh, I long, I long to show that I can be a man.' And from his place on the coach-roof the eager young fellow looked down upon the city, with the sort of longing desire which young soldiers feel on the eve of a campaign.

As they came along the road, Pen had formed acquaintance with a cheery fellow-passenger in a shabby cloak, who talked a great deal about men of letters with whom he was very familiar, and who was, in fact, the reporter of a London newspaper, as whose representative he had been to attend a great wrestling match in the West. This gentleman knew intimately, as it appeared, all the leading men of letters of his day, and talked about Tom Campbell, and Tom Hood, and Sydney Smith, and this and the other, as if he had been their most intimate friend. As they passed by Brompton, this gentleman pointed out to Pen Mr. Hurtle, the reviewer, walking with his umbrella. Pen

craned over the coach to have a long look at the great Hurtle. He was a Boniface man, said Pen. And Mr. Doolan, of the *Star* newspaper (for such was the gentleman's name and address upon the card which he handed to Pen), said 'Faith he was, and he knew him very well.' Pen thought it was quite an honour to have seen the great Mr. Hurtle, whose works he admired. He believed fondly, as yet, in authors, reviewers, and editors of newspapers. Even Wagg, whose books did not appear to him to be masterpieces of human intellect, he yet secretly revered as a successful writer. He mentioned that he had met Wagg in the country, and Doolan told him how that famous novelist received three hundther pounds a volume for every one of his novels. Pen began to calculate instantly whether he might not make five thousand a year.

The very first acquaintance of his own whom Arthur met, as the coach pulled up at the 'Gloster' Coffee-house, was his old friend Harry Foker, who came prancing down Arlington Street behind an enormous cab-horse. He had white kid gloves and white reins, and nature had by this time decorated him with a considerable tuft on the chin. A very small cab-boy, *vice* Stoopid retired, swung on behind Foker's vehicle; knock-kneed and in the tightest leather breeches. Foker looked at the dusty coach, and the smoking horses of the 'Alacrity,' by which he had made journeys in former times.—'What, Foker!' cried out Pendennis.—'Hallo, Pen, my boy!' said the other, and he waved his whip by way of amity and salute to Arthur, who was very glad to see his queer friend's kind old face. Mr. Doolan had a great respect for Pen, who had an acquaintance in such a grand cab; and Pen was greatly excited and pleased to be at liberty and in London. He asked Doolan to come and dine with him at the Covent Garden Coffee-house, where he put up: he called a cab and rattled away thither in the highest spirits. He was glad to see the bustling waiter and polite bowing landlord again; and asked for the landlady, and missed the old Boots, and would have liked to shake hands with everybody. He had a hundred pounds in his pocket. He dressed himself in his very best; dined in the coffee-room with a modest pint of sherry (for he was determined to be very economical), and went to the theatre adjoining.

The lights and the music, the crowd and the gaiety,

charmed and exhilarated Pen, as those sights will do young fellows from college and the country, to whom they are tolerably new. He laughed at the jokes; he applauded the songs, to the delight of some of the dreary old *habitués* of the boxes, who had ceased long ago to find the least excitement in their place of nightly resort, and were pleased to see anyone so fresh, and so much amused. At the end of the first piece, he went and strutted about the lobbies of the theatre, as if he was in a resort of the highest fashion. What tired frequenter of the London *pavé* is there that cannot remember having had similar early delusions, and would not call them back again? Here was young Foker again, like an ardent votary of pleasure as he was. He was walking with Granby Tiptoff, of the Household Brigade, Lord Tiptoff's brother, and Lord Colchicum, Captain Tiptoff's uncle, a venerable peer, who had been a man of pleasure since the first French Revolution. Foker rushed upon Pen with eagerness, and insisted that the latter should come into his private box, where a lady with the longest ringlets, and the fairest shoulders, was seated. This was Miss Blenkinsop, the eminent actress of high comedy; and in the back of the box snoozing in a wig, sat old Blenkinsop, her papa. He was described in the theatrical prints as the 'veteran Blenkinsop'—'the useful Blenkinsop'—'that old favourite of the public, Blenkinsop': those parts in the drama, which are called the heavy fathers, were usually assigned to this veteran, who, indeed, acted the heavy father in public, as in private life.

At this time, it being about eleven o'clock, Mrs. Pendennis was gone to bed at Fairoaks, and wondering whether her dearest Arthur was at rest after his journey. At this time Laura, too, was awake. And at this time yesterday night, as the coach rolled over silent commons, where cottage windows twinkled, and by darkling woods under calm starlit skies, Pen was vowing to reform and to resist temptation, and his heart was at home. . . . Meanwhile the farce was going on very successfully, and Mrs. Leary, in a hussar jacket and braided pantaloons, was enchanting the audience with her archness, her lovely figure, and her delightful ballads.

Pen, being new to the town, would have liked to listen to Mrs. Leary; but the other people in the box did not care about her song or her pantaloons, and kept up an

incessant chattering. Tiptoff knew where her *maillots* came from. Colchicum saw her when she came out in '14. Miss Blenkinsop said she sang out of all tune, to the pain and astonishment of Pen, who thought that she was as beautiful as an angel, and that she sang like a nightingale; and when Hoppus came on as Sir Harcourt Featherby, the young man of the piece, the gentlemen in the box declared that Hoppus was getting too stale, and Tiptoff was for flinging Miss Blenkinsop's bouquet to him.

'Not for the world,' cried the daughter of the veteran Blenkinsop; 'Lord Colchicum gave it to me.'

Pen remembered that nobleman's name, and with a bow and a blush said he believed he had to thank Lord Colchicum for having proposed him at the Polyanthus[1]* Club, at the request of his uncle, Major Pendennis.

'What, you're Wigsby's nephew, are you?' said the peer. 'I beg your pardon, we always call him Wigsby.' Pen blushed to hear his venerable uncle called by such a familiar name. 'We balloted you in last week, didn't we? Yes, last Wednesday night. Your uncle wasn't there.'

Here was delightful news for Pen! He professed himself very much obliged indeed to Lord Colchicum, and made him a handsome speech of thanks, to which the other listened, with his double opera-glass up to his eyes. Pen was full of excitement at the idea of being a member of this polite club.

'Don't be always looking at that box, you naughty creature,' cried Miss Blenkinsop.

'She's a dev'lish fine woman, that Mirabel,' said Tiptoff; 'though Mirabel was a d——d fool to marry her.'

'A stupid old spooney,' said the peer.

'Mirabel!' cried out Pendennis.

'Ha! ha!' laughed out Harry Foker. 'We've heard of her before, haven't we, Pen?'

It was Pen's first love. It was Miss Fotheringay. The year before she had been led to the altar by Sir Charles Mirabel, G.C.B., and formerly envoy to the Court of Pumpernickel, who had taken so active a part in the negotiations before the Congress of Swammerdam, and signed, on behalf of H.B.M., the Peace of Pultusk.*

'Emily was always as stupid as an owl,' said Miss Blenkinsop.

'Eh! eh! *Pas si bête*,' the old peer said.

'Oh, for shame!' cried the actress, who did not in the least know what he meant.

And Pen looked out and beheld his first love once again —and wondered how he ever could have loved her.

Thus, on the very first night of his arrival in London, Mr. Arthur Pendennis found himself introduced to a club, to an actress of genteel comedy and a heavy father of the Stage, and to a dashing society of jovial blades, old and young; for my Lord Colchicum, though stricken in years, bald of head, and enfeebled in person, was still indefatigable in the pursuit of enjoyment, and it was the venerable Viscount's boast that he could drink as much claret as the youngest member of the society which he frequented. He lived with the youth about town: he gave them countless dinners at Richmond and Greenwich: an enlightened patron of the drama in all languages and of the Terpsichorean art, he received dramatic professors of all nations at his banquets —English from the Covent Garden and Strand houses, Italians from the Haymarket, French from their own pretty little theatre, or the boards of the Opera where they danced. And at his villa on the Thames, this pillar of the State gave sumptuous entertainments to scores of young men of fashion, who very affably consorted with the ladies and gentlemen of the green-room—with the former chiefly, for Viscount Colchicum preferred their society as more polished and gay than that of their male brethren.

Pen went the next day and paid his entrance-money at the club, which operation carried off exactly one-third of his hundred pounds: and took possession of the edifice, and ate his luncheon there with immense satisfaction. He plunged into an easy chair in the library, and tried to read all the magazines. He wondered whether the members were looking at him, and that they could dare to keep on their hats in such fine rooms. He sat down and wrote a letter to Fairoaks on the club paper, and said, what a comfort this place would be to him after his day's work was over. He went over to his uncle's lodgings in Bury Street with some considerable tremor, and in compliance with his mother's earnest desire, that he should instantly call on Major Pendennis; and was not a little relieved to find that the major had not yet returned to town. His apartments were blank. Brown hollands covered his library-table, and

bills and letters lay on the mantelpiece, grimly awaiting the return of their owner. The major was on the Continent, the landlady of the house said, at Badnbadn, with the Marcus of Steyne. Pen left his card upon the shelf with the rest. Fairoaks was written on it still.

When the major returned to London, which he did in time for the fogs of November, after enjoying which he proposed to spend Christmas with some friends in the country, he found another card of Arthur's, on which Lamb Court, Temple, was engraved, and a note from that young gentleman and from his mother, stating that he was come to town, was entered a member of the Upper Temple, and was reading hard for the Bar.

Lamb Court, Temple :—where was it ?* Major Pendennis remembered that some ladies of fashion used to talk of dining with Mr. Ayliffe, the barrister, who was 'in society,' and who lived there in the King's Bench, of which prison there was probably a branch in the Temple, and Ayliffe was very likely an officer. Mr. Deuceace, Lord Crab's son,* had also lived there, he recollected. He dispatched Morgan to find out where Lamb Court was, and to report upon the lodging selected by Mr. Arthur. That alert messenger had little difficulty in discovering Mr. Pen's abode. Discreet Morgan had in his time traced people far more difficult to find than Arthur.

'What sort of a place is it, Morgan ?' asked the major, out of the bed-curtains in Bury Street the next morning, as the valet was arranging his toilette in the deep yellow London fog.*

'I should say raythera shy place,' said Mr. Morgan. 'The lawyers lives there, and has their names on the doors. Mr. Harthur lives three pair high, sir. Mr. Warrington live there too, sir.'

'Suffolk Warringtons ! I shouldn't wonder : a good family,' thought the major. 'The cadets of many of our good families follow the robe as a profession. Comfortable rooms, eh ?'

'Honly saw the outside of the door, sir, with Mr. Warrington's name and Mr. Arthur's painted up, and a piece of paper with "Back at six"; but I couldn't see no servant, sir.'

'Economical, at any rate,' said the major.

'Very, sir. Three pair, sir. Nasty black staircase as

ever I see. Wonder how a gentleman can live in such a place.'

'Pray, who taught you where gentlemen should or should not live, Morgan? Mr. Arthur, sir, is going to study for the Bar, sir,' the major said, with much dignity; and closed the conversation and began to array himself in the yellow fog.

'Boys will be boys,' the mollified uncle thought to himself. 'He has written to me a devilish good letter. Colchicum says he has had him to dine, and thinks him a gentlemanlike lad. His mother is one of the best creatures in the world. If he has sown his wild oats, and will stick to his business, he may do well yet. Think of Charley Mirabel, the old fool, marrying that flame of his! that Fotheringay! He doesn't like to come here until I give him leave, and puts it in a very manly, nice way. I was deuced angry with him, after his Oxbridge escapades—and showed it, too, when he was here before—Gad, I'll go and see him, hang me if I don't.'

And having ascertained from Morgan that he could reach the Temple without much difficulty, and that a City omnibus* would put him down at the gate, the major one day after breakfast at his club—not the Polyanthus, whereof Mr. Pen was just elected a member, but another club: for the major was too wise to have a nephew as a constant inmate of any house where he was in the habit of passing his time—the major one day entered one of those public vehicles, and bade the conductor to put him down at the gate of the Upper Temple.

When Major Pendennis reached that dingy portal it was about twelve o'clock in the day; and he was directed by a civil personage with a badge and a white apron, through some dark alleys, and under various melancholy archways into courts each more dismal than the other, until finally he reached Lamb Court. If it was dark in Pall Mall, what was it in Lamb Court? Candles were burning in many of the rooms there—in the pupil-room of Mr. Hodgeman, the special pleader, where six pupils were scribbling declarations under the tallow; in Sir Hokey Walker's clerk's room, where the clerk, a person far more gentlemanlike and cheerful in appearance than the celebrated counsel, his master, was conversing in a patronizing manner with the managing clerk of an attorney at the door; and in Curling, the wigmaker's melancholy shop, where, from behind the feeble

PEN PURSUING HIS LAW STUDIES

glimmer of a couple of lights, large serjeants' and judges' wigs were looming drearily, with the blank blocks looking at the lamp-post in the court. Two little clerks were playing at toss-halfpenny under that lamp. A laundress in pattens passed in at one door, a newspaper-boy issued from another. A porter, whose white apron was faintly visible, paced up and down. It would be impossible to conceive a place more dismal, and the major shuddered to think that anyone should select such a residence. 'Good Ged!' he said, 'the poor boy mustn't live on here.'

The feeble and filthy oil-lamps, with which the staircases of the Upper Temple are lighted of nights, were of course not illuminating the stairs by day, and Major Pendennis, having read with difficulty his nephew's name under Mr. Warrington's on the wall of No. 6, found still greater difficulty in climbing the abominable black stairs, up the banisters of which, which contributed their damp exudations to his gloves, he groped painfully until he came to the third story. A candle was in the passage of one of the two sets of rooms; the doors were open, and the names of Mr. Warrington and Mr. A. Pendennis were very clearly visible to the major as he went in. An Irish charwoman, with a pail and broom, opened the door for the major.

'Is that the beer?' cried out a great voice: 'give us hold of it.'

The gentleman who was speaking was seated on a table, unshorn and smoking a short pipe; in a farther chair sat Pen, with a cigar, and his legs near the fire. A little boy, who acted as the clerk of these gentlemen, was grinning in the major's face, at the idea of his being mistaken for beer. Here, upon the third floor, the rooms were somewhat lighter, and the major could see the place.

'Pen, my boy, it's I—it's your uncle,' he said, choking with the smoke. But as most young men of fashion used the weed, he pardoned the practice easily enough.

Mr. Warrington got up from the table, and Pen, in a very perturbed manner, from his chair. 'Beg your pardon for mistaking you,' said Warrington, in a frank, loud voice. 'Will you take a cigar, sir? Clear those things off the chair, Pidgeon, and pull it round to the fire.'

Pen flung his cigar into the grate; and was pleased with the cordiality with which his uncle shook him by the hand. As soon as he could speak for the stairs and the smoke, the

major began to ask Pen very kindly about himself and about his mother; for blood is blood, and he was pleased once more to see the boy.

Pen gave his news, and then introduced Mr. Warrington —an old Boniface man—whose chambers he shared.

The major was quite satisfied when he heard that Mr. Warrington was a younger son of Sir Miles Warrington of Suffolk. He had served with an uncle of his in India and in New South Wales, years ago.

'Took a sheep-farm there, sir, made a fortune—better thing than law or soldiering,' Warrington said. 'Think I shall go there, too.' And here, the expected beer coming in, in a tankard with a glass bottom, Mr. Warrington, with a laugh, said he supposed the major would not have any, and took a long, deep draught himself, after which he wiped his wrist across his beard with great satisfaction. The young man was perfectly easy and unembarrassed. He was dressed in a ragged old shooting-jacket, and had a bristly blue beard. He was drinking beer like a coal-heaver, and yet you couldn't but perceive that he was a gentleman.

When he had sat for a minute or two after his draught he went out of the room, leaving it to Pen and his uncle, that they might talk over family affairs were they so inclined.

'Rough and ready, your chum seems,' the major said. 'Somewhat different from your dandy friends at Oxbridge.'

'Times are altered,' Arthur replied, with a blush. 'Warrington is only just called, and has no business, but he knows law pretty well; and until I can afford to read with a pleader, I use his books and get his help.'

'Is that one of the books?' the major asked, with a smile. A French novel was lying at the foot of Pen's chair.

'This is not a working-day, sir,' the lad said. 'We were out very late at a party last night—at Lady Whiston's,' Pen added, knowing his uncle's weakness. 'Everybody in town was there, except you, sir; counts, ambassadors, Turks, Stars and Garters—I don't know who—it's all in the paper—and my name, too,' said Pen, with great glee. 'I met an old flame of mine there, sir,' he added, with a laugh. 'You know whom I mean, sir—Lady Mirabel—to whom I was introduced over again. She shook hands, and was gracious enough. I may thank you for being out of that scrape, sir. She presented me to the husband, too— an old beau in a star and a blonde wig. He does not seem

ARTHUR MEETS WITH AN OLD ACQUAINTANCE

very wise. She has asked me to call on her, sir : and I may go now without any fear of losing my heart.'

'What, we have had some new loves, have we ?' the major asked, in high good humour.

'Some two or three,' Mr. Pen said, laughing. 'But I don't put on my *grand sérieux* any more, sir. That goes off after the first flame.'

'Very right, my dear boy. Flames and darts and passion, and that sort of thing, do very well for a lad : and you were but a lad when that affair with the Fotheringill —Fotheringay (what's her name ?)—came off. But a man of the world gives up those follies. You still may do very well. You have been hit, but you may recover. You are heir to a little independence, which everybody fancies is a doosid deal more. You have a good name, good wits, good manners, and a good person—and, begad ! I don't see why you shouldn't marry a woman with money—get into Parliament—distinguish yourself, and—and, in fact, that sort of thing. Remember, it's as easy to marry a rich woman as a poor woman : and a devilish deal pleasanter to sit down to a good dinner than to a scrag of mutton in lodgings. Make up your mind to that. A woman with a good jointure is a doosid deal easier a profession than the law, let me tell you. Look out ; *I* shall be on the watch for you : and I shall die content, my boy, if I can see you with a good ladylike wife, and a good carriage, and a good pair of horses, living in society, and seeing your friends, like a gentleman.[2]' It was thus this affectionate uncle spoke, and expounded to Pen his simple philosophy.

'What would my mother and Laura say to this, I wonder ?' thought the lad. Indeed, old Pendennis's morals were not their morals, nor was his wisdom theirs.

This affecting conversation between uncle and nephew had scarcely concluded, when Warrington came out of his bedroom, no longer in rags, but dressed like a gentleman, straight and tall, and perfectly frank and good-humoured. He did the honours of his ragged sitting-room with as much ease as if it had been the finest apartment in London. And queer rooms they were in which the major found his nephew. The carpet was full of holes—the table stained with many circles of Warrington's previous ale-pots. There was a small library of law-books, books of poetry, and of mathematics, of which he was very fond. (He had been one of

the hardest livers and hardest readers of his time at Oxbridge, where the name of Stunning Warrington was yet famous for beating bargemen, pulling matches, winning prizes, and drinking milk-punch.) A print of the old college hung up over the mantelpiece, and some battered volumes of Plato, bearing its well-known arms, were on the bookshelves. There were two easy chairs; a standing reading-desk piled with bills; a couple of very meagre briefs on a broken-legged study-table. Indeed, there was scarcely any article of furniture that had not been in the wars, and was not wounded. 'Look here, sir, here is Pen's room. He is a dandy, and has got curtains to his bed, and wears shiny boots, and a silver dressing-case.' Indeed, Pen's room was rather coquettishly arranged, and a couple of neat prints of opera-dancers, besides a drawing of Fairoaks, hung on the walls. In Warrington's room there was scarcely any article of furniture, save a great shower-bath, and a heap of books by the bedside; where he lay upon straw like Margery Daw,* and smoked his pipe, and read half through the night his favourite poetry or mathematics.

When he had completed his simple toilette, Mr. Warrington came out of this room, and proceeded to the cupboard to search for his breakfast.

'Might I offer you a mutton-chop, sir? We cook 'em ourselves, hot and hot; and I am teaching Pen the first principles of law, cooking, and morality at the same time. He's a lazy beggar, sir, and too much of a dandy.'

And so saying, Mr. Warrington wiped a gridiron with a piece of paper, put it on the fire, and on it two mutton-chops, and took from the cupboard a couple of plates and some knives and silver forks, and castors.

'Say but a word, Major Pendennis,' he said; 'there's another chop in the cupboard, or Pidgeon shall go out and get you anything you like.'

Major Pendennis sat in wonder and amusement, but he said he had just breakfasted, and wouldn't have any lunch. So Warrington cooked the chops, and popped them hissing hot upon the plates.

Pen fell to at his chop with a good appetite, after looking up at his uncle, and seeing that gentleman was still in good humour.

'You see, sir,' Warrington said, 'Mrs. Flanagan isn't here to do 'em, and we can't employ the boy, for the little

beggar is all day occupied cleaning Pen's boots. And now for another swig at the beer. Pen drinks tea ; it's only fit for old women.'

'And so you were at Lady Whiston's last night,' the major said, not in truth knowing what observation to make to this rough diamond.

'I at Lady Whiston's ! not such a flat, sir. I don't care for female society. In fact, it bores me. I spent my evening philosophically at the Back Kitchen.'

'The Back Kitchen ? indeed !' said the major.

'I see you don't know what it means,' Warrington said. 'Ask Pen. He was there after Lady Whiston's. Tell Major Pendennis about the Back Kitchen, Pen—don't be ashamed of yourself.'

So Pen said it was a little eccentric society of men of letters, and men about town, to which he had been presented ; and the major began to think that the young fellow had seen a good deal of the world since his arrival in London.

CHAPTER XXIX

THE KNIGHTS OF THE TEMPLE*

COLLEGES, schools, and inns of court, still have some respect for antiquity, and maintain a great number of the customs and institutions of our ancestors with which those persons who do not particularly regard their forefathers, or perhaps are not very well acquainted with them, have long since done away. A well-ordained workhouse or prison is much better provided with the appliances of health, comfort, and cleanliness, than a respectable Foundation School, a venerable College, or a learned Inn. In the latter place of residence men are contented to sleep in dingy closets, and to pay for the sitting-room and the cupboard, which is their dormitory, the price of a good villa and garden in the suburbs, or of a roomy house in the neglected squares of the town. The poorest mechanic in Spitalfields has a

cistern and an unbounded supply of water at his command; but the gentlemen of the inns of court, and the gentlemen of the universities, have their supply of this cosmetic fetched in jugs by laundresses and bedmakers, and live in abodes which were erected long before the custom of cleanliness and decency obtained among us. There are individuals still alive who sneer at the people and speak of them with epithets of scorn. Gentlemen, there can be but little doubt that your ancestors were the Great Unwashed: and in the Temple especially, it is pretty certain, that, only under the greatest difficulties and restrictions, the virtue which has been pronounced to be next to godliness could have been practised at all.

Old Grump, of the Norfolk Circuit, who had lived for more than thirty years in the chambers under those occupied by Warrington and Pendennis, and who used to be awakened by the roaring of the shower-baths* which those gentlemen had erected in their apartments—a part of the contents of which occasionally trickled through the roof into Mr. Grump's room—declared that the practice was an absurd, new-fangled, dandified folly, and daily cursed the laundress who slopped the staircase by which he had to pass. Grump, now much more than half a century old, had indeed never used the luxury in question. He had done without water very well, and so had our fathers before him. Of all those knights and baronets, lords and gentlemen, bearing arms, whose escutcheons are painted upon the walls of the famous hall of the Upper Temple, was there no philanthropist good-natured enough to devise a set of Hummums for the benefit of the lawyers, his fellows and successors? The Temple historian makes no mention of such a scheme. There is Pump Court and Fountain Court, with their hydraulic apparatus, but one never heard of a bencher disporting in the fountain; and can't but think how many a counsel learned in the law of old days might have benefited by the pump.

Nevertheless, those venerable Inns which have the Lamb and Flag and the Winged Horse for their ensigns, have attractions for persons who inhabit them, and a share of rough comforts and freedom, which men always remember with pleasure. I don't know whether the student of law permits himself the refreshment of enthusiasm, or indulges in poetical reminiscences as he passes by historical chambers

and says, 'Yonder Eldon lived—upon this site Coke mused upon Lyttleton—here Chitty toiled—here Barnwell and Alderson joined in their famous labours—here Byles composed his great work upon bills, and Smith compiled his immortal leading cases—here Gustavus still toils, with Solomon to aid him':* but the man of letters can't but love the place which has been inhabited by so many of his brethren, or peopled by their creations as real to us at this day as the authors whose children they were—and Sir Roger de Coverley walking in the Temple Garden, and discoursing with Mr. Spectator about the beauties in hoops and patches who are sauntering over the grass, is just as lively a figure to me as old Samuel Johnson rolling through the fog with the Scotch gentleman at his heels on their way to Dr. Goldsmith's chambers in Brick Court; or Harry Fielding, with inked ruffles and a wet towel round his head, dashing off articles at midnight for the *Covent Garden Journal*, while the printer's boy is asleep in the passage.

If we could but get the history of a single day* as it passed in any one of those four-storied houses in the dingy court where our friends Pen and Warrington dwelt, some Temple Asmodeus might furnish us with a queer volume. There may be a great Parliamentary counsel on the ground-floor, who drives off to Belgravia at dinner-time, when his clerk, too, becomes a gentleman, and goes away to entertain his friends, and to take his pleasure. But a short time since he was hungry and briefless in some garret of the Inn; lived by stealthy literature; hoped, and waited, and sickened, and no clients came; exhausted his own means and his friends' kindness; had to remonstrate humbly with duns, and to implore the patience of poor creditors. Ruin seemed to be staring him in the face, when, behold, a turn of the wheel of fortune, and the lucky wretch in possession of one of those prodigious prizes which are sometimes drawn in the great lottery of the Bar. Many a better lawyer than himself does not make a fifth part of the income of his clerk, who, a few months since, could scarcely get credit for blacking for his master's unpaid boots. On the first floor, perhaps, you will have a venerable man whose name is famous, who has lived for half a century in the Inn, whose brains are full of books, and whose shelves are stored with classical and legal lore. He has lived alone all these fifty years, alone and for himself, amassing learning, and compiling a fortune. He comes

home now at night only from the club, where he has been dining freely, to the lonely chambers where he lives a godless old recluse. When he dies, his Inn will erect a tablet to his honour, and his heirs burn a part of his library. Would you like to have such a prospect for your old age, to store up learning and money, and end so? But we must not linger too long by Mr. Doomsday's door. Worthy Mr. Grump lives over him, who is also an ancient inhabitant of the Inn, and who, when Doomsday comes home to read Catullus, is sitting down with three steady seniors of his standing, to a steady rubber at whist, after a dinner at which they have consumed their three steady bottles of port. You may see the old boys asleep at the Temple Church of a Sunday. Attorneys seldom trouble them, and they have small fortunes of their own. On the other side of the third landing, where Pen and Warrington live, till long after midnight, sits Mr. Paley, who took the highest honours, and who is a fellow of his college, who will sit and read and note cases until two o'clock in the morning; who will rise at seven and be at the pleader's chambers as soon as they are open, where he will work until an hour before dinner-time; who will come home from Hall and read and note cases again until dawn next day, when perhaps Mr. Arthur Pendennis and his friend Mr. Warrington are returning from some of their wild expeditions. How differently employed Mr. Paley has been! He has not been throwing himself away: he has only been bringing a great intellect laboriously down to the comprehension of a mean subject, and in his fierce grasp of that, resolutely excluding from his mind all higher thoughts, all better things, all the wisdom of philosophers and historians, all the thoughts of poets; all wit, fancy, reflection, art, love, truth altogether—so that he may master that enormous legend of the law, which he proposes to gain his livelihood by expounding. Warrington and Paley had been competitors for University honours in former days, and had run each other hard; and everybody said now that the former was wasting his time and energies, whilst all people praised Paley for his industry. There may be doubts, however, as to which was using his time best. The one could afford time to think, and the other never could. The one could have sympathies and do kindnesses; and the other must needs be always selfish. He could not cultivate a friendship or do a charity, or

admire a work of genius, or kindle at the sight of beauty or the sound of a sweet song—he had no time, and no eyes for anything but his law-books. All was dark outside his reading-lamp. Love, and Nature, and Art (which is the expression of our praise and sense of the beautiful world of God), were shut out from him. And as he turned off his lonely lamp at night, he never thought but that he had spent the day profitably, and went to sleep alike thankless and remorseless. But he shuddered when he met his old companion Warrington on the stairs, and shunned him as one that was doomed to perdition.

It may have been the sight of that cadaverous ambition and self-complacent meanness, which showed itself in Paley's yellow face, and twinkled in his narrow eyes, or it may have been a natural appetite for pleasure and joviality, of which it must be confessed Mr. Pen was exceedingly fond, which deterred that luckless youth from pursuing his designs upon the Bench or the Woolsack with the ardour, or rather steadiness, which is requisite in gentlemen who would climb to those seats of honour. He enjoyed the Temple life with a great deal of relish : his worthy relatives thought he was reading as became a regular student : and his uncle wrote home congratulatory letters to the kind widow at Fairoaks, announcing that the lad had sown his wild oats, and was becoming quite steady. The truth is, that it was a new sort of excitement to Pen, the life in which he was now engaged, and having given up some of the dandified pretensions, and fine-gentleman airs which he had contracted among his aristocratic college acquaintances, of whom he now saw but little, the rough pleasures and amusements of a London bachelor were very novel and agreeable to him, and he enjoyed them all. Time was he would have envied the dandies their fine horses in Rotten Row, but he was contented now to walk in the Park and look at them. He was too young to succeed in London society without a better name and a larger fortune than he had, and too lazy to get on without these adjuncts. Old Pendennis fondly thought he was busied with law because he neglected the social advantages presented to him, and, having been at half a dozen balls and evening parties, retreated before their dullness and sameness; and whenever anybody made inquiries of the worthy major about his nephew, the old gentleman said the young rascal was reformed, and

could not be got away from his books. But the major would have been almost as much horrified as Mr. Paley was, had he known what was Mr. Pen's real course of life, and how much pleasure entered into his law studies.

A long morning's reading, a walk in the Park, a pull on the river, a stretch up the hill to Hampstead, and a modest tavern dinner; a bachelor night passed here or there, in

joviality, not vice (for Arthur Pendennis admired women so heartily that he could never bear the society of any of them that were not, in his fancy at least, good and pure); a quiet evening at home, alone with a friend and a pipe or two, and a humble potation of British spirits, whereof Mrs. Flanagan, the laundress, invariably tested the quality;—these were our young gentleman's pursuits, and it must be

owned that his life was not unpleasant. In term-time, Mr. Pen showed a most praiseworthy regularity in performing one part of the law-student's course of duty, and eating his dinners in Hall. Indeed, that Hall of the Upper Temple is a sight not uninteresting, and with the exception of some trifling improvements and anachronisms which have been introduced into the practice there, a man may sit down and fancy that he joins in a meal of the seventeenth century. The Bar have their messes, the students their tables apart; the benchers sit at the high table on the raised platform, surrounded by pictures of judges of the law and portraits of royal personages who have honoured its festivities with their presence and patronage. Pen looked about, on his first introduction, not a little amused with the scene which he witnessed. Among his comrades of the student class there were gentlemen of all ages, from sixty to seventeen; stout grey-headed attorneys who were proceeding to take the superior dignity—dandies and men-about-town who wished for some reason to be barristers of seven years' standing—swarthy, black-eyed natives of the Colonies, who came to be called here before they practised in their own islands—and many gentlemen of the Irish nation, who make a sojourn in Middle Temple Lane before they return to the green country of their birth. There were little squads of reading students who talked law all dinner-time; there were rowing men, whose discourse was of sculling matches, the Red House, Vauxhall, and the Opera;* there were others great in politics, and orators of the students' debating clubs; with all of which sets, except the first, whose talk was an almost unknown and a quite uninteresting language to him, Mr. Pen made a gradual acquaintance, and had many points of sympathy.

The ancient and liberal Inn of the Upper Temple* provides in its Hall, and for a most moderate price, an excellent wholesome dinner of soup, meat, tarts, and port wine or sherry, for the barristers and students who attend that place of refection. The parties are arranged in messes of four, each of which quartets has its piece of beef or leg of mutton, its sufficient apple-pie and its bottle of wine. But the honest *habitués* of the Hall, amongst the lower rank of students, who have a taste for good living, have many harmless arts by which they improve their banquet, and innocent 'dodges' (if we may be permitted to use an excellent

phrase that has become vernacular since the appearance of the last dictionaries) by which they strive to attain for themselves more delicate food than the common everyday roast meat of the students' tables.

'Wait a bit,' said Mr. Lowton, one of these Temple gourmands. 'Wait a bit,' said Mr. Lowton, tugging at Pen's gown—'the tables are very full, and there's only three benchers to eat ten side dishes—if we wait, perhaps we shall get something from their table.' And Pen looked with some amusement, as did Mr. Lowton with eyes of fond desire, towards the benchers' high table, where three old gentlemen were standing up before a dozen silver dish-covers, while the clerk was quavering out a grace.

Lowton was great in the conduct of the dinner. His aim was to manage so as to be the first, or captain of the mess, and to secure for himself the thirteenth glass of the bottle of port wine. Thus he would have the command of the joint on which he operated his favourite cuts, and made rapid dexterous appropriations of gravy, which amused Pen infinitely. Poor Jack Lowton! thy pleasures in life were very harmless; an eager epicure, thy desires did not go beyond eighteenpence.

Pen was somewhat older than many of his fellow-students, and there was that about his style and appearance which, as we have said, was rather haughty and impertinent, that stamped him as a man of *ton*—very unlike those pale students who were talking law to one another, and those ferocious dandies, in rowing shirts and astonishing pins and waistcoats, who represented the idle part of the little community. The humble and good-natured Lowton had felt attracted by Pen's superior looks and presence—and had made acquaintance with him at the mess by opening the conversation.

'This is boiled-beef day, I believe, sir,' said Lowton to Pen.

'Upon my word, sir, I'm not aware,' said Pen, hardly able to contain his laughter, but added, 'I'm a stranger; this is my first term;' on which Lowton began to point out to him the notabilities in the Hall.

'That's Boosey the bencher, the bald one sitting under the picture and 'aving soup; I wonder whether it's turtle? They often 'ave turtle. Next is Balls, the King's Counsel, and Swettenham—Hodge and Swettenham, you know.

That's old Grump, the senior of the Bar; they say he's dined here forty years. They often send 'em down their fish from the benchers to the senior table. Do you see those four fellows seated opposite us? They are regular swells—tip-top fellows, I can tell you—Mr. Trail, the Bishop of Ealing's son, Honourable Fred Ringwood, Lord Cinqbar's brother, you know. *He'll* have a good place, I bet any money: and Bob Suckling, who's always with him—a high fellow, too. Ha! ha!' Here Lowton burst into a laugh.

'What is it?' said Pen, still amused.

'I say, I'd like to mess with those chaps,' Lowton said, winking his eye knowingly, and pouring out his glass of wine.

'And why?' asked Pen.

'Why! they don't come down here to dine, you know; they only make believe to dine. *They* dine here, Law bless you! They go to some of the swell clubs, or else to some grand dinner-party. You see their names in the *Morning Post* at all the fine parties in London. Why, I bet anything that Ringwood has his cab, or Trail his brougham (he's a devil of a fellow, and makes the bishop's money spin, I can tell you) at the corner of Essex Street at this minute. They dine! They won't dine these two hours, I dare say.'

'But why should you like to mess with them, if they don't eat any dinner?' Pen asked, still puzzled. 'There's plenty, isn't there?'

'How green you are,' said Lowton. 'Excuse me, but you *are* green. They don't drink any wine, don't you see, and a fellow gets the bottle to himself if he likes it when he messes with those three chaps. That's why Corkoran got in with 'em.'

'Ah, Mr. Lowton, I see you are a sly fellow,' Pen said, delighted with his acquaintance: on which the other modestly replied, that he had lived in London the better part of his life, and of course had his eyes about him; and went on with his catalogue to Pen.

'There's a lot of Irish here,' he said; 'that Corkoran's one, and I can't say I like him. You see that handsome chap with the blue neckcloth, and pink shirt, and yellow waistcoat, that's another: that's Molloy Maloney, of Ballymaloney, and nephew to Major-General Sir Hector O'Dowd, he, he,' Lowton said, trying to imitate the Hibernian accent. 'He's always bragging about his uncle; and came into Hall

in silver-striped trousers the day he had been presented. That other near him, with the long black hair, is a tremendous rebel. By Jove, sir, to hear him at the Forum it makes your blood freeze ; and the next is an Irishman, too, Jack Finucane, reporter of a newspaper. They all stick together, those Irish. It's your turn to fill your glass. What ? you won't have any port ? Don't like port with your dinner ? Here's your health." And this worthy man found himself not the less attached to Pendennis because the latter disliked port wine at dinner.

It was while Pen was taking his share of one of these dinners with his acquaintance Lowton as the captain of his mess, that there came to join them a gentleman in a barrister's gown, who could not find a seat, as it appeared, amongst the persons of his own degree, and who strode over the table and took his place on the bench where Pen sat. He was dressed in old clothes and a faded gown, which hung behind him, and he wore a shirt which, though clean, was extremely ragged, and very different to the magnificent pink raiment of Mr. Molloy Maloney, who occupied a commanding position in the next mess. In order to notify their appearance at dinner, it is the custom of the gentlemen who eat in the Upper Temple Hall to write down their names upon slips of paper, which are provided for that purpose, with a pencil for each mess. Lowton wrote his name first, then came Arthur Pendennis, and the next was that of the gentleman in the old clothes. He smiled when he saw Pen's name, and looked at him. 'We ought to know each other,' he said. 'We're both Boniface men ; my name's Warrington."

'Are you St—— Warrington ?' Pen said, delighted to see this hero.

Warrington laughed—'Stunning Warrington—yes,' he said. 'I recollect you in your freshman's term. But you appear to have quite cut me out.'

'The college talks about you still,' said Pen, who had a generous admiration for talent and pluck. 'The bargeman you thrashed, Bill Simes, don't you remember, wants you up again at Oxbridge. The Miss Notleys, the haberdashers——'

'Hush !' said Warrington—'glad to make your acquaintance, Pendennis. Heard a good deal about you.'

The young men were friends immediately, and at once

deep in college-talk. And Pen, who had been acting rather the fine gentleman on a previous day, when he pretended to Lowton that he could not drink port wine at dinner, seeing Warrington take his share with a great deal of gusto, did not scruple about helping himself any more, rather to the disappointment of honest Lowton. When the dinner was over, Warrington asked Arthur where he was going.

'I thought of going home to dress, and hear Grisi in *Norma*,* Pen said.

'Are you going to meet anybody there?' he asked.

Pen said, 'No—only to hear the music, of which he was very fond.'

'You had much better come home and smoke a pipe with me,' said Warrington, '—a very short one. Come, I live close by in Lamb Court, and we'll talk over Boniface and old times.'

They went away; Lowton sighed after them. He knew that Warrington was a baronet's son, and he looked up with simple reverence to all the aristocracy. Pen and Warrington became sworn friends from that night. Warrington's cheerfulness and jovial temper, his good sense, his rough welcome, and his never-failing pipe of tobacco, charmed Pen, who found it more pleasant to dive into shilling taverns with him, than to dine in solitary state amongst the silent and polite frequenters of the Polyanthus.

Ere long Pen gave up his lodgings in St. James's, to which he had migrated on quitting his hotel, and found it was much more economical to take up his abode with Warrington in Lamb Court, and furnish and occupy his friend's vacant room there. For it must be said of Pen, that no man was more easily led than he to do a thing, when it was a novelty, or when he had a mind to it. And Pidgeon, the youth, and Flanagan, the laundress, divided their allegiance now between Warrington and Pen.

CHAPTER XXX

OLD AND NEW ACQUAINTANCES

ELATED with the idea of seeing life, Pen went into a hundred queer London haunts. He liked to think he was consorting with all sorts of men—so he beheld coal-heavers in their taprooms; boxers in their inn-parlours; honest citizens disporting in the suburbs or on the river; and he would have liked to hob and nob with celebrated pickpockets, or drink a pot of ale with a company of burglars and cracksmen, had chance afforded him an opportunity of making the acquaintance of this class of society. It was good to see the gravity with which Warrington listened to the Tutbury Pet or the Brighton Stunner at the 'Champion's Arms,' and behold the interest which he took in the coal-heaving company assembled at the 'Fox-under-the-Hill.' His acquaintance with the public-houses of the metropolis and its neighbourhood, and with the frequenters of their various parlours, was prodigious. He was the personal friend of the landlord and landlady, and welcome to the bar as to the club-room. He liked their society, he said, better than that of his own class, whose manners annoyed him, and whose conversation bored him. 'In society,' he used to say, 'everybody is the same, wears the same dress, eats and drinks, and says the same things; one young dandy at the club talks and looks just like another, one miss at a ball exactly resembles another, whereas there's character here. I like to talk with the strongest man in England, or the man who can drink the most beer in England, or with that tremendous republican of a hatter, who thinks Thistlewood* was the greatest character in history. I like gin-and-water better than claret. I like a sanded floor in Carnaby Market better than a chalked one in May Fair. I prefer Snobs, I own it.' Indeed, this gentleman was a social

republican; and it never entered his head while conversing with Jack and Tom that he was in any respect their better; although, perhaps, the deference which they paid him might secretly please him.

Pen followed him then to these various resorts of men with great glee and assiduity. But he was considerably younger, and therefore much more pompous and stately than Warrington; in fact, a young prince in disguise, visiting the poor of his father's kingdom. They respected him as a high chap, a fine fellow, a regular young swell. He had somehow about him an air of imperious good humour, and a royal frankness and majesty, although he was only heir-apparent to twopence-halfpenny, and but one in descent from a gallipot. If these positions are made for us, we acquiesce in them very easily; and are always pretty ready to assume a superiority over those who are as good as ourselves. Pen's condescension at this time of his life was a fine thing to witness. Amongst men of ability this assumption and impertinence passes off with extreme youth: but it is curious to watch the conceit of a generous and clever lad—there is something almost touching in that early exhibition of simplicity and folly.

So, after reading pretty hard of a morning, and, I fear, not law merely, but politics and general history and literature, which were as necessary for the advancement and instruction of a young man as mere dry law, after applying with tolerable assiduity to letters, to reviews, to elemental books of law, and, above all, to the newspaper, until the hour of dinner was drawing nigh, these young gentlemen would sally out upon the town with great spirits and appetite, and bent upon enjoying a merry night as they had passed a pleasant forenoon. It was a jovial time, that of four-and-twenty, when every muscle of mind and body was in healthy action, when the world was new as yet, and one moved over it spurred onwards by good spirits and the delightful capability to enjoy. If ever we feel young afterwards, it is with the comrades of that time: the tunes we hum in our old age are those we learned then. Sometimes, perhaps, the festivity of that period revives in our memory; but how dingy the pleasure-garden has grown, how tattered the garlands look, how scant and old the company, and what a number of the lights have gone out since that day! Grey hairs have come on like daylight streaming in—daylight

and a headache with it. Pleasure has gone to bed with the rouge on her cheeks. Well, friend, let us walk through the day, sober and sad, but friendly.

I wonder what Laura and Helen would have said, could they have seen, as they might not unfrequently have done had they been up and in London, in the very early morning when the bridges began to blush in the sunrise, and the tranquil streets of the city to shine in the dawn, Mr. Pen and Mr. Warrington rattling over the echoing flags towards the Temple, after one of their wild nights of carouse—nights wild, but not so wicked as such nights sometimes are, for Warrington was a woman-hater ; and Pen, as we have said, too lofty to stoop to a vulgar intrigue. Our young Prince of Fairoaks never could speak to one of the sex but with respectful courtesy, and shrank from a coarse word or gesture with instinctive delicacy—for though we have seen him fall in love with a fool, as his betters and inferiors have done, and as it is probable that he did more than once in his life, yet for the time of the delusion it was always as a goddess that he considered her, and chose to wait upon her. Men serve women kneeling—when they get on their feet, they go away.

That was what an acquaintance of Pen's said to him in his hard homely way ;—an old friend with whom he had fallen in again in London—no other than honest Mr. Bows of the Chatteris Theatre, who was now employed as pianoforte player, to accompany the eminent lyrical talent which nightly delighted the public at the 'Fielding's Head' in Covent Garden : and where was held the little club called the Back Kitchen.

Numbers of Pen's friends frequented this very merry meeting. The 'Fielding's Head' had been a house of entertainment, almost since the time when the famous author of *Tom Jones* presided as magistrate in the neighbouring Bow Street ; his place was pointed out, and the chair said to have been his, still occupied by the president of the night's entertainment. The worthy Cutts, the landlord of the 'Fielding's Head,' generally occupied this post when not disabled by gout or other illness. His jolly appearance and fine voice may be remembered by some of my male readers ; he used to sing profusely in the course of the harmonic meeting, and his songs were of what may be called the British Brandy-and-Water School of Song—such

AN OLD ACQUAINTANCE

as 'The Good Old English Gentleman,' 'Dear Tom, this Brown Jug,' and so forth—songs in which pathos and hospitality are blended, and the praises of good liquor and the social affections are chanted in a baritone voice. The charms of our women, the heroic deeds of our naval and military commanders, are often sung in the ballads of this school, and many a time in my youth have I admired how Cutts the singer, after he had worked us all up to patriotic enthusiasm, by describing the way in which the brave Abercrombie received his death-wound, or made us join him in tears, which he shed liberally himself, as in faltering accents he told how 'autumn's falling leaf proclaimed the old man he must die'—how Cutts the singer became at once Cutts the landlord, and, before the applause which we were making with our fists on his table, in compliment to his heart-stirring melody, had died away, was calling, 'Now, gentlemen, give your orders; the waiter's in the room—John, a champagne cup for Mr. Green. I think, sir, you said sausages and mashed potatoes? John, attend on the gentleman.'

'And I'll thank ye give me a glass of punch too, John, and take care the wather boils,' a voice would cry not unfrequently, a well-known voice to Pen, which made the lad blush and start when he heard it first—that of the venerable Captain Costigan; who was now established in London, and one of the great pillars of the harmonic meetings at the 'Fielding's Head.'

The captain's manners and conversation brought very many young men to the place. He was a character, and his fame had begun to spread soon after his arrival in the metropolis, and especially after his daughter's marriage. He was great in his conversation to the friend for the time being (who was the neighbour drinking by his side) about 'me daughter.' He told of her marriage, and of the events previous and subsequent to that ceremony; of the carriages she kept; of Mirabel's adoration for her and for him; of the hundther pounds which he was at perfect liberty to draw from his son-in-law, whenever necessity urged him. And having stated that it was his firm intention to 'dthraw next Sathurday, I give ye me secred word and honour next Sathurday, the fourteenth, when ye'll see the money will be handed over to me at Coutts's, the very instant I present the cheque,' the captain would not unfrequently propose

to borrow a half-crown of his friend until the arrival of that day of Greek Calends,* when, on the honour of an officer and a gentleman, he would repee the thrifling obligetion.

Sir Charles Mirabel had not that enthusiastic attachment to his father-in-law, of which the latter sometimes boasted (although in other stages of emotion Cos would inveigh, with tears in his eyes, against the ingratitude of the child of his bosom, and the stinginess of the wealthy old man who had married her); but the pair had acted not unkindly towards Costigan; had settled a small pension on him, which was paid regularly, and forestalled with even more regularity by poor Cos; and the period of the payments were always well known by his friend at the 'Fielding's Head,' whither the honest captain took care to repair, bank-notes in hand, calling loudly for change in the midst of the full harmonic meeting. 'I think ye'll find *that* note won't be refused at the Bank of England, Cutts, my boy,' Captain Costigan would say. 'Bows, have a glass? Ye needn't stint yourself to-night, anyhow; and a glass of punch will make ye play *con spirito*.' For he was lavishly free with his money when it came to him, and was scarcely known to button his breeches pocket, except when the coin was gone, or sometimes, indeed, when a creditor came by.

It was in one of these moments of exultation that Pen found his old friend swaggering at the singers' table at the Back Kitchen of the 'Fielding's Head,' and ordering glasses of brandy-and-water for any of his acquaintances who made their appearance in the apartment. Warrington, who was on confidential terms with the bass singer, made his way up to this quarter of the room, and Pen walked at his friend's heels.

Pen started and blushed to see Costigan. He had just come from Lady Whiston's party, where he had met and spoken with the captain's daughter again for the first time after very old, old days. He came up with outstretched hand, very kindly and warmly to greet the old man; still retaining a strong remembrance of the time when Costigan's daughter had been everything in the world to him. For though this young gentleman may have been somewhat capricious in his attachments, and occasionally have transferred his affections from one woman to another, yet he always respected the place where Love had dwelt, and,

like the Sultan of Turkey, desired that honours should be paid to the lady towards whom he had once thrown the royal pocket-handkerchief.

The tipsy captain returned the clasp of Pen's hand with all the strength of a palm which had become very shaky by the constant lifting up of weights of brandy-and-water, looked hard in Pen's face, and said 'Grecious Heavens, is it possible ? Me dear boy, me dear fellow, me dear friend '; and then with a look of muddled curiosity, fairly broke down with 'I know your face, me dear, dear friend, but, bedad, I've forgot your name.' Five years of constant punch had passed since Pen and Costigan met. Arthur was a good deal changed, and the captain may surely be excused for forgetting him ; when a man at the actual moment sees things double, we may expect that his view of the past will be rather muzzy.

Pen saw his condition and laughed, although, perhaps, he was somewhat mortified. 'Don't you remember me, captain ?' he said. 'I am Pendennis—Arthur Pendennis, of Chatteris.'

The sound of the young man's friendly voice recalled and steadied Cos's tipsy remembrance, and he saluted Arthur, as soon as he knew him, with a loud volley of friendly greetings. Pen was his dearest boy, his gallant young friend, his noble collagian, whom he had held in his inmost heart ever since they had parted—how was his fawther, no, his mother, and his guardian, the general, the major ? 'I preshoom, from your appearance, that you've come into your prawpertee ; and, bedad, yee'll spend it like a man of spirit—I'll go bail for *that*. No ! not yet come into your estete ? If ye want any thrifle, hark ye, there's poor old Jack Costigan has got a guinea or two in his pocket—and, be heavens ! *you* shall never want, Awthur, me dear boy. What'll ye have ? John, come hither, and look aloive ; give this gentleman a glass of punch, and I'll pay for't.—Your friend ? I've seen him before. Permit me to have the honour of making meself known to ye, sir, and requesting ye'll take a glass of punch.'

'I don't envy Sir Charles Mirabel his father-in-law,' thought Pendennis. 'And how is my old friend, Mr. Bows, captain ? Have you any news of him, and do you see him still ?'

'No doubt he's very well,' said the captain, jingling his

money, and whistling the air of a song—'The Little Doodeen'—for the singing of which he was celebrated at the 'Fielding's Head.' 'Me dear boy—I've forgot your name again—but me name's Costigan, Jack Costigan, and I'd loike ye to take as many tumblers of punch in me name as ever ye loike. Ye know me name; I'm not ashamed of it.' And so the captain went maundering on.

'It's pay-day with the general,' said Mr. Hodgen, the bass singer, with whom Warrington was in deep conversation: 'and he's a precious deal more than half-seas over. He has already tried that "Little Doodeen" of his, and broke it, too, just before I sang "King Death." Have you heard my new song, "The Body-Snatcher," Mr. Warrington?—angcored at St. Bartholomew's the other night—composed expressly for me. Per'aps you or your friend would like a copy of the song, sir? John, just 'ave the kindness to 'and over a "Body-Snatcher" 'ere, will yer?—There's a portrait of me, sir, as I sing it—as the Snatcher—considered rather like.'

'Thank you,' said Warrington; 'heard it nine times—know it by heart, Hodgen.'

Here the gentleman who presided at the pianoforte began to play upon his instrument, and Pen, looking in the direction of the music, beheld that very Mr. Bows, for whom he had been asking but now, and whose existence Costigan had momentarily forgotten. The little old man sat before the battered piano (which had injured its constitution woefully by sitting up so many nights, and spoke with a voice, as it were, at once hoarse and faint), and accompanied the singers, or played with taste and grace in the intervals of the songs.

Bows had seen and recollected Pen at once when the latter came into the room, and had remarked the eager warmth of the young man's recognition of Costigan. He now began to play an air, which Pen instantly remembered as one which used to be sung by the chorus of villagers in *The Stranger*, just before Mrs. Haller came in. It shook Pen as he heard it. He remembered how his heart used to beat as that air was played, and before the divine Emily made her entry. Nobody, save Arthur, took any notice of old Bows's playing: it was scarcely heard amidst the clatter of knives and forks, the calls for poached eggs and kidneys, and the tramp of guests and waiters.

Pen went up and kindly shook the player by the hand at the end of his performance; and Bows greeted Arthur with great respect and cordiality. 'What, you haven't forgot the old tune, Mr. Pendennis?' he said; 'I thought you'd remember it. I take it, it was the first tune of that sort you ever heard played—wasn't it, sir? You were quite a young chap then. I fear the captain's very bad to-night. He breaks out on a pay-day; and I shall have the deuce's own trouble in getting home. We live together. We still hang on, sir, in partnership, though Miss Em—though my Lady Mirabel has left the firm.—And so you remember old times, do you? Wasn't she a beauty, sir?—Your health and my service to you,'—and he took a sip at the pewter measure of porter which stood by his side as he played.

Pen had many opportunities of seeing his early acquaintances afterwards, and of renewing his relations with Costigan and the old musician.

As they sat thus in friendly colloquy, men of all sorts and conditions entered and quitted the house of entertainment; and Pen had the pleasure of seeing as many different persons of his race, as the most eager observer need desire to inspect. Healthy country tradesmen and farmers, in London for their business, came and recreated themselves with the jolly singing and suppers of the Back Kitchen,—squads of young apprentices and assistants, the shutters being closed over the scene of their labours, came hither, for fresh air doubtless,—rakish young medical students, gallant, dashing, what is called 'loudly' dressed, and (must it be owned?) somewhat dirty,—were here smoking and drinking, and vociferously applauding the songs;—young university bucks were to be found here, too, with that indescribable genteel simper which is only learned at the knees of Alma Mater;—and handsome young guardsmen, and florid bucks from the St. James's Street clubs;—nay, senators English and Irish: and even members of the House of Peers.

The bass singer had made an immense hit with his song of 'The Body-Snatcher,'* and the town rushed to listen to it. A curtain drew aside, and Mr. Hodgen appeared in the character of the Snatcher, sitting on a coffin, with a flask of gin before him, with a spade, and a candle stuck in a

skull. The song was sung with a really admirable terrific humour. The singer's voice went down so low, that its grumbles rumbled into the hearer's awe-stricken soul; and in the chorus he clamped with his spade, and gave a demoniac 'Ha! ha!' which caused the very glasses to quiver on the table, as with terror. None of the other singers, not even Cutts himself, as that high-minded man owned, could stand up before the Snatcher, and he commonly used to retire to Mrs. Cutts's private apartments, or into the bar, before that fatal song extinguished him. Poor Cos's ditty, 'The Little Doodeen,' which Bows accompanied charmingly on the piano, was sung but to a few admirers, who might choose to remain after the tremendous resurrectionist chant. The room was commonly emptied after that, or only left in possession of a very few and persevering votaries of pleasure.

Whilst Pen and his friend were sitting here together one night, or rather morning, two *habitués* of the house entered almost together. 'Mr. Hoolan and Mr. Doolan,' whispered Warrington to Pen, saluting these gentlemen, and in the latter Pen recognized his friend of the 'Alacrity' coach, who could not dine with Pen on the day on which the latter had invited him, being compelled by his professional duties to decline dinner-engagements on Fridays, he had stated, with his compliments to Mr. Pendennis.

Doolan's paper, the *Dawn*, was lying on the table much bestained by porter, and cheek by jowl with Hoolan's paper, which we shall call the *Day*; the *Dawn* was Liberal—the *Day* was ultra-Conservative. Many of our journals are officered by Irish gentlemen, and their gallant brigade does the penning among us, as their ancestors used to transact the fighting in Europe; and engage under many a flag, to be good friends when the battle is over.

'Kidneys, John, and a glass of stout,' says Hoolan. 'How are you, Morgan? how's Mrs. Doolan?'

'Doing pretty well, thank ye, Mick, my boy—faith, she's accustomed to it,' said Doolan. 'How's the lady that owns ye? Maybe I'll step down Sunday, and have a glass of punch, Kilburn way.'

'Don't bring Patsey with you, Mick, for our Georgy's got the measles,' said the friendly Morgan, and they straightway fell to talk about matters connected with their trade—about the foreign mails—about who was correspondent at

Paris, and who wrote from Madrid—about the expense the *Morning Journal* was at in sending couriers, about the circulation of the *Evening Star*, and so forth.

Warrington, laughing, took the *Dawn* which was lying before him, and pointed to one of the leading articles in that journal, which commenced thus :—

As rogues of note in former days who had some wicked work to perform,—an enemy to put out of the way, a quantity of false coin to be passed, a lie to be told, or a murder to be done,—employed a professional perjurer or assassin to do the work, which they were themselves too notorious or too cowardly to execute ; our notorious contemporary, the *Day*, engages smashers out of doors to utter forgeries against individuals, and calls in auxiliary cut-throats to murder the reputation of those who offend him. A black-vizarded ruffian (whom we will unmask), who signs the forged name of Trefoil, is at present one of the chief bravoes and bullies in our contemporary's establishment. He is the eunuch who brings the bowstring, and strangles at the order of the *Day*. We can convict this cowardly slave, and propose to do so. The charge which he has brought against Lord Bangbanagher, because he is a Liberal Irish peer, and against the Board of Poor Law Guardians of the Bangbanagher Union, is, etc.

'How did they like the article at your place, Mick ?' asked Morgan ; 'when the captain puts his hand to it he's a tremendous hand at a smasher. He wrote the article in two hours—in—whew—you know where, while the boy was waiting.'

'Our governor thinks the public don't mind a straw about these newspaper rows, and has told the docthor to stop answering,' said the other. 'Them two talked it out together in my room. The docthor would have liked a turn, for he says it's such easy writing, and requires no reading up of a subject : but the governor put a stopper on him.'

'The taste for eloquence is going out, Mick,' said Morgan.

''Deed then it is, Morgan,' said Mick. 'That was fine writing when the docthor wrote in the *Phaynix*, and he and Condy Roony blazed away at each other day after day.'

'And with powder and shot, too,* as well as paper,' says Morgan. 'Faith, the docthor was out twice, and Condy Roony winged his man.'

'They are talking about Dr. Boyne and Captain Shandon,' Warrington said, 'who are the two Irish controversialists of the *Dawn* and the *Day*, Dr. Boyne being the

Protestant champion, and Captain Shandon the Liberal orator. They are the best friends in the world, I believe, in spite of their newspaper controversies; and though they cry out against the English for abusing their country, by Jove they abuse it themselves more in a single article than we should take the pains to do in a dozen volumes. How are you, Doolan?'

'Your servant, Mr. Warrington—Mr. Pendennis, I am delighted to have the honour of seeing ye again. The night's journey on the top of the "Alacrity" was one of the most agreeable I ever enjoyed in my life, and it was your liveliness and urbanity that made the trip so charming. I have often thought over that happy night, sir, and talked over it to Mrs. Doolan. I have seen your elegant young friend, Mr. Foker, too, here, sir, not unfrequently. He is an occasional frequenter of this hostelry, and a right good one it is. Mr. Pendennis, when I saw you I was on the *Tom and Jerry* weekly paper; I have now the honour to be sub-editor of the *Dawn*, one of the best-written papers of the empire'—and he bowed very slightly to Mr. Warrington. His speech was unctuous and measured, his courtesy Oriental, his tone, when talking with the two Englishmen, quite different to that with which he spoke to his comrade.

'Why the devil will the fellow compliment so?' growled Warrington, with a sneer which he hardly took the pains to suppress. 'Psha—who comes here?—all Parnassus is abroad to-night: here's Archer.* We shall have some fun. Well, Archer, House up?'

'Haven't been there. I have been,' said Archer, with an air of mystery, 'where I was wanted. Get me some supper, John—something substantial. I hate your grandees who give you nothing to eat. If it had been at Apsley House, it would have been quite different. The Duke knows what I like, and says to the Groom of the Chambers, 'Martin, you will have some cold beef, not too much done, and a pint bottle of pale ale, and some brown sherry, ready in my study as usual; Archer is coming here this evening.' The duke doesn't eat supper himself, but he likes to see a man enjoy a hearty meal, and he knows that I dine early. A man can't live upon air, be hanged to him.'

'Let me introduce you to my friend, Mr. Pendennis,' Warrington said, with great gravity. 'Pen, this is Mr. Archer, whom you have heard me talk about. You must

know Pen's uncle, the major, Archer, you who know everybody ?'

'Dined with him the day before yesterday at Gaunt House,' Archer said. 'We were four—the French Ambassador, Steyne, and we two commoners.'

'Why, my uncle is in Scot——" Pen was going to break out, but Warrington pressed his foot under the table as a signal for him to be quiet.

'It was about the same business that I have been to the palace to-night,' Archer went on simply, 'and where I've been kept four hours, in an ante-room, with nothing but yesterday's *Times*, which I knew by heart, as I wrote three of the leading articles myself ; and though the Lord Chamberlain came in four times, and once holding the royal teacup and saucer in his hand, he did not so much as say to me, 'Archer, will you have a cup of tea ?'

'Indeed ! what is in the wind now ?' asked Warrington—and turning to Pen, added, 'You know, I suppose, that when there is anything wrong at Court they always send for Archer.'

'There is something wrong,' said Mr. Archer, 'and as the story will be all over the town in a day or two I don't mind telling it. At the last Chantilly races, where I rode Brian Boru for my old friend the Duke de Saint-Cloud—the old king said to me, " Archer, I'm uneasy about Saint-Cloud. I have arranged his marriage with the Princess Marie Cunégonde ; the peace of Europe depends upon it—for Russia will declare war if the marriage does not take place, and the young fool is so mad about Madame Massena, Marshal Massena's wife, that he actually refuses to be a party to the marriage.' Well, sir, I spoke to Saint-Cloud, and having got him into a pretty good humour by winning the race, and a good bit of money into the bargain, he said to me, " Archer, tell the governor I'll think of it." '

'How do you say governor in French ?' asked Pen, who piqued himself on knowing that language.

'Oh, we speak in English—I taught him when we were boys, and I saved his life at Twickenham, when he fell out of a punt,' Archer said. 'I shall never forget the queen's looks as I brought him out of the water. She gave me this diamond ring, and always calls me Charles to this day.'

'Madame Massena must be rather an old woman, Archer,' Warrington said.

'Dev'lish old—old enough to be his grandmother; I told him so,' Archer answered at once. 'But those attachments for old women are the deuce and all. That's what the king feels: that's what shocks the poor queen so much. They went away from Paris last Tuesday night, and are living at this present moment at Jaunay's hotel.'

'Has there been a private marriage, Archer?' asked Warrington.

'Whether there has or not I don't know,' Mr. Archer replied; 'all I know is that I was kept waiting four hours at the palace; that I never saw a man in such a state of agitation as the King of Belgium when he came out to speak to me, and that I'm devilish hungry—and here comes some supper.'

'He has been pretty well to-night,' said Warrington, as the pair went home together: 'but I have known him in much greater force, and keeping a whole room in a state of wonder. Put aside his archery practice, that man is both able and honest—a good man of business, an excellent friend, admirable to his family as husband, father, and son.'

'What is it makes him pull the long bow in that wonderful manner?'

'An amiable insanity,' answered Warrington. 'He never did anybody harm by his talk, or said evil of anybody. He is a stout politician too, and would never write a word or do an act against his party, as many of us do.'

'Of *us?* Who are *we?*' asked Pen. 'Of what profession is Mr. Archer?'

'Of the Corporation of the Goosequill—of the press, my boy,' said Warrington; 'of the fourth estate.'

'Are you, too, of the craft, then?' Pendennis said.

'We will talk about that another time,' answered the other. They were passing through the Strand as they talked, and by a newspaper office, which was all lighted up and bright. Reporters were coming out of the place, or rushing up to it in cabs; there were lamps burning in the editors' rooms, and above where the compositors were at work: the windows of the building were in a blaze of gas.

'Look at that, Pen,' Warrington said. 'There she is—the great engine—she never sleeps. She has her ambassadors in every quarter of the world—her couriers upon every road. Her officers march along with armies, and her envoys walk into statesmen's cabinets. They are ubiqui-

tous. Yonder journal has an agent, at this minute, giving bribes at Madrid ; and another inspecting the price of potatoes in Covent Garden. Look ! here comes the Foreign Express galloping in. They will be able to give news to Downing Street to-morrow : funds will rise or fall, fortunes be made or lost ; Lord B. will get up, and, holding the paper in his hand, and seeing the noble marquis in his place, will make a great speech ; and—and Mr. Doolan will be called away from his supper at the Back Kitchen ; for he is foreign sub-editor, and sees the mail on the newspaper sheet before he goes to his own.'*

And so talking, the friends turned into their chambers, as the dawn was beginning to peep.

CHAPTER XXXI

IN WHICH THE PRINTER'S DEVIL COMES TO THE DOOR

PEN, in the midst of his revels and enjoyments, humble as they were, and moderate in cost if not in kind, saw an awful swcrd hanging over him which must drop down before long and put an end to his frolics and feasting. His money was very nearly spent. His club subscription had carried away a third part of it. He had paid for the chief articles of furniture with which he had supplied his little bedroom : in fine, he was come to the last five-pound note in his pocket-book, and could think of no method of providing a successor : for our friend had been bred up like a young prince as yet, or as a child in arms whom his mother feeds when it cries out.

Warrington did not know what his comrade's means were. An only child, with a mother at her country house, and an old dandy of an uncle who dined with a great man every day, Pen might have a large bank at his command for anything that the other knew. He had gold chains and a dressing-case fit for a lord. His habits were those of an

aristocrat,—not that he was expensive upon any particular point, for he dined and laughed over the pint of porter and the plate of beef from the cook's shop with perfect content and good appetite,—but he could not adopt the penny-wise precautions of life. He could not give twopence to a waiter; he could not refrain from taking a cab if he had a mind to do so, or if it rained, and as surely as he took the cab he overpaid the driver. He had a scorn for cleaned gloves and minor economies. Had he been bred to ten thousand a year he could scarcely have been more free-handed; and for a beggar, with a sad story, or a couple of pretty piteous-faced children, he never could resist putting his hand into his pocket. It was a sumptuous nature, perhaps, that could not be brought to regard money; a natural generosity and kindness; and possibly a petty vanity that was pleased with praise, even with the praise of waiters and cabmen. I doubt whether the wisest of us know what our own motives are, and whether some of the actions of which we are the very proudest will not surprise us when we trace them, as we shall one day, to their source.

Warrington then did not know, and Pen had not thought proper to confide to his friend, his pecuniary history. That Pen had been wild and wickedly extravagant at college, the other was aware; everybody at college was extravagant and wild; but how great the son's expenses had been, and how small the mother's means, were points which had not been as yet submitted to Mr. Warrington's examination.

At last the story came out, while Pen was grimly surveying the change for the last five-pound note, as it lay upon the tray from the public-house by Mr. Warrington's pot of ale.

'It is the last rose of summer,' said Pen; 'its blooming companions have gone long ago; and behold, the last one of the garland has shed its leaves;' and he told Warrington the whole story which we know of his mother's means, of his own follies, of Laura's generosity; during which time Warrington smoked his pipe and listened intent.

'Impecuniosity will do you good,' Pen's friend said, knocking out the ashes at the end of the narration; 'I don't know anything more wholesome for a man—for an honest man, mind you—for another, the medicine loses its effect—than a state of tick. It is an alterative and a

tonic; it keeps your moral man in a perpetual state of excitement: as a man who is riding at a fence, or has his opponent's single-stick before him, is forced to look his obstacle steadily in the face, and braces himself to repulse or overcome it; a little necessity brings out your pluck if you have any, and nerves you to grapple with fortune. You will discover what a number of things you can do without when you have no money to buy them. You won't want new gloves and varnished boots, eau-de-Cologne, and cabs to ride in. You have been bred up as a molly-coddle, Pen, and spoilt by the women. A single man who has health and brains, and can't find a livelihood in the world, doesn't deserve to stay there. Let him pay his last halfpenny and jump over Waterloo Bridge. Let him steal a leg of mutton and be transported and get out of the country—he is not fit to live in it. *Dixi;* I have spoken. Give us another pull at the pale ale.'

'You have certainly spoken; but how is one to live?' said Pen. 'There is beef and bread in plenty in England, but you must pay for it with work or money. And who will take my work? and what work can I do?'

Warrington burst out laughing. 'Suppose we advertise in the *Times*,' he said, 'for an usher's place at a classical and commercial academy:—A gentleman, B.A. of St. Boniface College, Oxbridge, and who was plucked for his degree—'

'Confound you,' cried Pen.

'—Wishes to give lessons in classics and mathematics, and the rudiments of the French language; he can cut hair, attend to the younger pupils, and play a second on the piano with the daughters of the principal. Address A. P., Lamb Court, Temple.'

'Go on,' said Pen, growling.

'Men take to all sorts of professions. Why, there is your friend Bloundell—Bloundell is a professional blackleg, and travels the Continent, where he picks up young gentlemen of fashion and fleeces them. There is Bob O'Toole, with whom I was at school, who drives the Ballynafad mail now, and carries honest Jack Finucane's own correspondence to that city. I know a man, sir, a doctor's son, like—well, don't be angry, I meant nothing offensive—a doctor's son, I say, who was walking the hospitals here, and quarrelled with his governor on questions of finance, and what did he

do when he came to his last five-pound note ? he let his moustachios grow, went into a provincial town, where he announced himself as Professor Spineto, chiropodist to the Emperor of All the Russias, and by a happy operation on the editor of the country newspaper, established himself in practice, and lived reputably for three years. He has been reconciled to his family, and has now succeeded to his father's gallipots.'

'Hang gallipots,' cried Pen. 'I can't drive a coach, cut corns, or cheat at cards. There's nothing else you propose.'

'Yes ; there's our own correspondent,' Warrington said. 'Every man has his secrets, look you. Before you told me the story of your money-matters, I had no idea but that you were a gentleman of fortune, for, with your confounded airs and appearance, anybody would suppose you to be so. From what you tell me about your mother's income, it is clear that you must not lay any more hands on it. You can't go on spunging upon the women. You must pay off that trump of a girl. Laura is her name ?—here is your health, Laura !—and carry a hod rather than ask for a shilling from home.'

'But how earn one ?' asked Pen.

'How do I live, think you ?' said the other. 'On my younger brother's allowance, Pendennis ? I have secrets of my own, my boy ;' and here Warrington's countenance fell. 'I made away with that allowance five years ago : if I had made away with myself a little time before, it would have been better. I have played off my own bat, ever since. I don't want much money. When my purse is out, I go to work and fill it, and then lie idle like a serpent or an Indian, until I have digested the mass. Look, I begin to feel empty,' Warrington said, and showed Pen a long lean purse, with but a few sovereigns at one end of it.

'But how do you fill it ?' said Pen.

'I write,' said Warrington. 'I don't tell the world that I do so,' he added, with a blush. 'I do not choose that questions should be asked : or, perhaps, I am an ass, and don't wish it to be said that George Warrington writes for bread. But I write in the Law Reviews : look here, these articles are mine.' And he turned over some sheets. 'I write in a newspaper now and then, of which a friend of mine is editor.' And Warrington, going with Pendennis to the club one day, called for a file of the *Dawn*, and pointed

with his finger silently to one or two articles, which Pen read with delight. He had no difficulty in recognizing the style afterwards—the strong thoughts and curt periods, the sense, the satire, and the scholarship.

'I am not up to this,' said Pen, with a genuine admiration of his friend's powers. 'I know very little about politics or history, Warrington; and have but a smattering of letters. I can't fly upon such a wing as yours.'

'But you can on your own, my boy, which is lighter, and soars higher, perhaps,' the other said good-naturedly. 'Those little scraps and verses which I have seen of yours show me, what is rare in these days, a natural gift, sir. You needn't blush, you conceited young jackanapes. You have thought so yourself any time these ten years. You have got the sacred flame—a little of the real poetical fire, sir, I think; and all our oil-lamps are nothing, compared to that, though ever so well trimmed. You are a poet, Pen, my boy,' and so speaking, Warrington stretched out his broad hand, and clapped Pen on the shoulder.

Arthur was so delighted that the tears came into his eyes. 'How kind you are to me, Warrington!' he said.

'I like you, old boy,' said the other. 'I was dev'lish lonely in chambers and wanted somebody, and the sight of your honest face somehow pleased me. I liked the way you laughed at Lowton—that poor good little snob. And, in fine, the reason why I cannot tell—but so it is, young 'un. I'm alone in the world, sir; and I wanted someone to keep me company:' and a glance of extreme kindness and melancholy passed out of Warrington's dark eyes.

Pen was too much pleased with his own thoughts to perceive the sadness of the friend who was complimenting him. 'Thank you, Warrington,' he said, 'thank you for your friendship to me, and—and what you say about me. I *have* often thought I was a poet. I will be one—I think I am one, as you say so, though the world mayn't. Is it —is it the "Ariadne in Naxos" which you liked (I was only eighteen when I wrote it), or the Prize Poem?'

Warrington burst into a roar of laughter. 'Why, you young goose,' he yelled out—'of all the miserable weak rubbish I ever tried, "Ariadne in Naxos" is the most mawkish and disgusting. The Prize Poem is so pompous and feeble, that I'm positively surprised, sir, it didn't get the medal. You don't suppose that you are a serious poet,

do you, and are going to cut out Milton and Aeschylus? Are you setting up to be a Pindar, you absurd little tomtit, and fancy you have the strength and pinion which the Theban eagle bear, sailing with supreme dominion through the azure fields of air?* No, my boy, I think you can write a magazine article, and turn out a pretty copy of verses; that's what I think of you.'

'By Jove!' said Pen, bouncing up and stamping his foot, 'I'll show you that I am a better man than you think for.'

Warrington only laughed the more, and blew twenty-four puffs rapidly out of his pipe by way of reply to Pen.

An opportunity for showing his skill presented itself before very long. That eminent publisher, Mr. Bacon (formerly Bacon and Bungay)* of Paternoster Row, besides being the proprietor of the *Legal Review*, in which Mr. Warrington wrote, and of other periodicals of note and gravity, used to present to the world every year a beautiful gilt volume called the *Spring Annual*, edited by the Lady Violet Lebas, and numbering amongst its contributors not only the most eminent, but the most fashionable, poets of our time. Young Lord Dodo's poems first appeared in this miscellany—the Honourable Percy Popjoy, whose chivalrous ballads have obtained him such a reputation—Bedwin Sands's *Eastern Ghazuls*,* and many more of the works of our young nobles were first given to the world in the *Spring Annual*, which has since shared the fate of other vernal blossoms, and perished out of the world. The book was daintily illustrated with pictures of reigning beauties, or other prints of a tender and voluptuous character; and, as these plates were prepared long beforehand, requiring much time in engraving, it was the eminent poets who had to write to the plates, and not the painters who illustrated the poems.

One day, just when this volume was on the eve of publication, it chanced that Mr. Warrington called in Paternoster Row to talk with Mr. Hack, Mr. Bacon's reader and general manager of publications—for Mr. Bacon, not having the least taste in poetry or in literature of any kind, wisely employed the services of a professional gentleman. Warrington, then, going into Mr. Hack's room on business of his own, found that gentleman with a bundle of proof plates and sheets of the *Spring Annual* before him, and glanced at some of them.

Percy Popjoy had written some verses to illustrate one of the pictures, which was called 'The Church Porch.' A Spanish damsel was hastening to church with a large Prayer Book; a youth in a cloak was hidden in a niche watching this young woman. The picture was pretty: but the great genius of Percy Popjoy had deserted him, for he had made the most execrable verses which ever were perpetrated by a young nobleman.

Warrington burst out laughing as he read the poem: and Mr. Hack laughed too, but with rather a rueful face. 'It

won't do,' he said, 'the public won't stand it. Bungay's people are going to bring out a very good book, and have set up Miss Bunyan against Lady Violet.* We have most titles to be sure—but the verses are too bad. Lady Violet herself owns it; she's busy with her own poem; what's to be done? We can't lose the plate. The governor gave sixty pounds for it.'

'I know a fellow who would do some verses, I think,' said Warrington. 'Let me take the plate home in my pocket: and send to my chambers in the morning for the verses. You'll pay well, of course.'

'Of course,' says Mr. Hack; and Warrington, having dispatched his own business, went home to Mr. Pen, plate in hand.

'Now, boy, here's a chance for you. Turn me off a copy of verses to this.'

'What's this? A Church Porch—A lady entering it, and a youth out of a wine-shop window ogling her.—What the deuce am I to do with it?'

'Try,' said Warrington. 'Earn your livelihood for once, you who long so to do it.'

'Well, I will try,' said Pen.

'And I'll go out to dinner,' said Warrington, and left Mr. Pen in a brown study.

When Warrington came home that night, at a very late hour, the verses were done. 'There they are,' said Pen. 'I've screwed 'em out at last. I think they'll do.'

'I think they will,' said Warrington, after reading them; they ran as follows:

THE CHURCH PORCH.

Although I enter not,
Yet round about the spot
  Sometimes I hover,
And at the sacred gate,
With longing eyes I wait,
  Expectant of her.

The minster bell tolls out
Above the city's rout
  And noise and humming:
They've stopp'd the chiming bell,
I hear the organ's swell—
  She's coming, she's coming!

My lady comes at last,
Timid and stepping fast,
  And hastening hither,
With modest eyes downcast
She comes—she's here—she's past.
  May Heaven go with her!

Kneel undisturb'd, fair saint,
Pour out your praise or plaint
  Meekly and duly.
I will not enter there,
To sully your pure prayer
  With thoughts unruly.

But suffer me to pace
Round the forbidden place,
 Lingering a minute,
Like outcast spirits, who wait
And see through Heaven's gate
 Angels within it.

'Have you got any more, young fellow?' asked Warrington. 'We must make them give you a couple of guineas a page; and if the verses are liked, why, you'll get an entrée into Bacon's magazines, and may turn a decent penny.'

Pen examined his portfolio and found another ballad which he thought might figure with advantage in the *Spring Annual*, and consigning these two precious documents to Warrington, the pair walked from the Temple to the famous haunt of the Muses and their masters, Paternoster Row. Bacon's shop was an ancient low-browed building, with a few of the books published by the firm displayed in the windows, under a bust of my Lord of Verulam,* and the name of Mr. Bacon in brass on the private door. Exactly opposite to Bacon's house was that of Mr. Bungay, which was newly painted and elaborately decorated in the style of the seventeenth century, so that you might have fancied stately Mr. Evelyn passing over the threshold, or curious Mr. Pepys examining the books in the window. Warrington went into the shop of Mr. Bacon, but Pen stayed without. It was agreed that his ambassador should act for him entirely; and the young fellow paced up and down the street in a very nervous condition, until he should learn the result of the negotiation. Many a poor devil before him has trodden those flags, with similar cares and anxieties at his heels, his bread and his fame dependent upon the sentence of his magnanimous patrons of the Row. Pen looked at all the wonders of all the shops; and the strange variety of literature which they exhibit. In this were displayed black-letter volumes and books in the clear pale types of Aldus and Elzevir: in the next, you might see the *Penny Horrific Register*, the *Halfpenny Annals of Crime*, and *History of the Most Celebrated Murderers of all Countries*, *The Raff's Magazine*, *The Larky Swell*,* and other publications of the penny press; whilst at the next window, portraits of ill-favoured individuals, with facsimiles of the venerated signatures of the Reverend Grimes Wapshot, the

Reverend Elias Howle,* and the works written and the sermons preached by them, showed the British Dissenter where he could find mental pabulum. Hard by would be a little casement hung with emblems, with medals and rosaries, with little paltry prints of saints gilt and painted, and books of controversial theology, by which the faithful of the Roman opinion might learn a short way to deal with Protestants, at a penny a-piece, or ninepence the dozen for distribution; whilst in the very next window you might see 'Come out of Rome,' a sermon preached at the opening of the Shepherd's Bush College, by John Thomas, Lord Bishop of Ealing. Scarce an opinion but has its expositor and its place of exhibition in this peaceful old Paternoster Row, under the toll of the bells of St. Paul.

Pen looked in at all the windows and shops, as a gentleman who is going to have an interview with the dentist examines the books on the waiting-room table. He remembered them afterwards. It seemed to him that Warrington would never come out; and indeed the latter was engaged for some time in pleading his friend's cause.

Pen's natural conceit would have swollen immensely if he could but have heard the report which Warrington gave of him. It happened that Mr. Bacon himself had occasion to descend to Mr. Hack's room whilst Warrington was talking there, and Warrington, knowing Bacon's weaknesses, acted upon them with great adroitness in his friend's behalf. In the first place, he put on his hat to speak to Bacon, and addressed him from the table on which he seated himself. Bacon liked to be treated with rudeness by a gentleman, and used to pass it on to his inferiors as boys pass the mark. 'What! not know Mr. Pendennis, Mr. Bacon?' Warrington said. 'You can't live much in the world, or you would know him. A man of property in the West, of one of the most ancient families in England, related to half the nobility in the empire—he's cousin to Lord Pontypool—he was one of the most distinguished men at Oxbridge; he dines at Gaunt House every week.'

'Law bless me, you don't say so, sir. Well—really—Law bless me now,' said Mr. Bacon.

'I have just been showing Mr. Hack some of his verses, which he sat up last night, at my request, to write; and Hack talks about giving him a copy of the book—the what-d'you-call-'em.'

'Law bless me now, does he? The what-d'you-call-'em. Indeed!'

'The *Spring Annual* is its name—as payment for these verses. You don't suppose that such a man as Mr. Arthur Pendennis gives up a dinner at Gaunt House for nothing? You know, as well as anybody, that the men of fashion want to be paid.'

'That they do, Mr. Warrington, sir,' said the publisher.

'I tell you he's a star; he'll make a name, sir. He's a new man, sir.'

'They've said that of so many of those young swells, Mr. Warrington,' the publisher interposed, with a sigh. 'There was Lord Viscount Dodo, now; I gave his lordship a good bit of money for his poems, and only sold eighty copies. Mr. Popjoy's "Hadgincourt," sir, fell dead.'

'Well, then, I'll take my man over to Bungay,' Warrington said, and rose from the table. This threat was too much for Mr. Bacon, who was instantly ready to accede to any reasonable proposal of Mr. Warrington's, and finally asked his manager what those proposals were? When he heard that the negotiation only related as yet to a couple of ballads, which Mr. Warrington offered for the *Spring Annual*, Mr. Bacon said, 'Law bless you, give him a cheque directly;' and with this paper Warrington went out to his friend, and placed it, grinning, in Pen's hands. Pen was as elated as if somebody had left him a fortune. He offered Warrington a dinner at Richmond instantly. 'What should he go and buy for Laura and his mother? He must buy something for them.'

'They'll like the book better than anything else,' said Warrington, 'with the young one's name to the verses, printed among the swells.'

'Thank God! thank God!' cried Arthur, 'I needn't be a charge upon the old mother. I can pay off Laura now. I can get my own living. I can make my own way.'

'I can marry the grand vizier's daughter: I can purchase a house in Belgrave Square; I can build a fine castle in the air,' said Warrington, pleased with the other's exultation. 'Well, you may get bread and cheese, Pen: and I own it tastes well, the bread which you earn yourself.'

They had a magnum of claret at dinner at the club that day, at Pen's charges. It was long since he had indulged in

such a luxury, but Warrington would not balk him: and they drank together to the health of the *Spring Annual*.

It never rains but it pours, according to the proverb; so very speedily another chance occurred, by which Mr. Pen was to be helped in his scheme of making a livelihood. Warrington one day threw him a letter across the table, which was brought by a printer's boy, 'from Captain Shandon, sir'—the little emissary said: and then went and fell asleep on his accustomed bench in the passage. He paid many a subsequent visit there, and brought many a message to Pen.

F. P. Tuesday Morning.

MY DEAR SIR,—Bungay will be here to-day, about the *Pall Mall Gazette*.* You will be the very man to help us *with a genuine West End article*,—you understand—dashing, trenchant, and d—— aristocratic. Lady Hipshaw will write: but she's not much, you know; and we've two lords; but the less they do the better. We must have you. We'll give you your own terms, and we'll make a hit with the *Gazette*.

Shall B. come and see you, or can you look in upon me here?

Ever yours,—C. S.

'Some more opposition,' Warrington said, when Pen had read the note. 'Bungay and Bacon are at daggers drawn; each married the sister of the other, and they were for some time the closest friends and partners. Hack says it was Mrs. Bungay who caused all the mischief between the two; whereas Shandon, who reads for Bungay a good deal, says Mrs. Bacon did the business; but I don't know which is right, Peachum or Lockit. Since they have separated, it is a furious war between the two publishers; and no sooner does one bring out a book of travels, or poems, a magazine or periodical, quarterly, or monthly, or weekly, or annual, but the rival is in the field with something similar. I have heard poor Shandon tell with great glee how he made Bungay give a grand dinner at Blackwall to all his writers, by saying that Bacon had invited his corps to an entertainment at Greenwich. When Bungay engaged your celebrated friend Mr. Wagg to edit the *Londoner*, Bacon straightway rushed off and secured Mr. Grindle to give his name to the *Westminster Magazine*. When Bacon brought out his comic Irish novel of *Barney Brallaghan*, off went Bungay to Dublin, and produced his rollicking Hibernian

story of *Looney MacTwolter.** When Doctor Hicks brought out his *Wanderings in Mesopotamia* under Bacon's auspices, Bungay produced Professor Sandiman's *Researches in Zahara ;* and Bungay is publishing his *Pall Mall Gazette* as a counterpoise to Bacon's *Whitehall Review.* Let us go and hear about the *Gazette.* There may be a place for you in it, Pen, my boy. We will go and see Shandon. We are sure to find him at home.'

'Where does he live ?' asked Pen.

'In the Fleet Prison,' Warrington said. 'And very much at home he is there, too. He is the king of the place.'

Pen had never seen this scene of London life, and walked with no small interest in at the grim gate of that dismal edifice. They went through the ante-room, where the officers and janitors of the place were seated, and passing in at the wicket, entered the prison. The noise and the crowd, the life and the shouting, the shabby bustle of the place, struck and excited Pen. People moved about ceaselessly and restless, like caged animals in a menagerie. Men were playing at fives. Others pacing and tramping : this one in colloquy with his lawyer in dingy black—that one walking sadly, with his wife by his side, and a child on his arm. Some were arrayed in tattered dressing-gowns, and had a look of rakish fashion. Everybody seemed to be busy, humming, and on the move. Pen felt as if he choked in the place, and as if the door being locked upon him they never would let him out.

They went through a court up a stone staircase, and through passages full of people, and noise, and cross lights, and black doors clapping and banging ;—Pen feeling as one does in a feverish morning-dream. At last the same little runner who had brought Shandon's note, and had followed them down Fleet Street munching apples, and who showed the way to the two gentlemen through the prison, said, 'This is the captain's door,' and Mr. Shandon's voice from within bade them enter.

The room, though bare, was not uncheerful. The sun was shining in at the window—near which sat a lady at work, who had been gay and beautiful once, but in whose faded face kindness and tenderness still beamed. Through all his errors and reckless mishaps and misfortunes, this faithful creature adored her husband, and thought him the best and cleverest, as indeed he was one of the kindest of men.

Nothing ever seemed to disturb the sweetness of his temper; not debts: not duns: not misery: not the bottle: not his wife's unhappy position, or his children's ruined chances. He was perfectly fond of wife and children after his fashion: he always had the kindest words and smiles for them, and ruined them with the utmost sweetness of temper. He never could refuse himself or any man any enjoyment which his money could purchase; he would share his last guinea with Jack and Tom, and we may be sure he had a score of such retainers. He would sign his name at the back of any man's bill, and never pay any debt of his own. He would write on any side, and attack himself or another man with equal indifference. He was one of the wittiest, the most amiable, and the most incorrigible of Irishmen. Nobody could help liking Charley Shandon who saw him once, and those whom he ruined could scarcely be angry with him.

When Pen and Warrington arrived, the captain (he had been in an Irish militia regiment once, and the title remained with him) was sitting on his bed in a torn dressing-gown, with a desk on his knees, at which he was scribbling as fast as his rapid pen could write. Slip after slip of paper fell off the desk wet on to the ground. A picture of his children was hung up over his bed, and the youngest of them was pattering about the room.

Opposite the captain sat Mr. Bungay, a portly man of stolid countenance, with whom the little child had been trying a conversation.

'Papa's a very clever man,' said she; 'mamma says so.'

'Oh, very,' said Mr. Bungay.

'And you're a very rich man, Mr. Bundy,' cried the child, who could hardly speak plain.

'Mary!' said mamma, from her work.

'Oh, never mind,' Bungay roared out, with a great laugh; 'no harm in saying I'm rich—he, he—I am pretty well off, my little dear.'

'If you're rich, why don't you take papa out of piz'n?' asked the child.

Mamma at this began to wipe her eyes with the work on which she was employed. (The poor lady had hung curtains up in the room, had brought the children's picture and placed it there, and had made one or two attempts to ornament it.) Mamma began to cry; Mr. Bungay turned red, and looked fiercely out of his bloodshot little eyes;

THE 'PALL MALL GAZETTE'

Shandon's pen went on, and Pen and Warrington arrived with their knock.

Captain Shandon looked up from his work. 'How do you do, Mr. Warrington?' he said. 'I'll speak to you in a minute. Please sit down, gentlemen, if you can find places,' and away went the pen again.

Warrington pulled forward an old portmanteau—the only available seat—and sat down on it with a bow to Mrs. Shandon, and a nod to Bungay; the child came and looked at Pen solemnly; and in a couple of minutes the swift scribbling ceased; and Shandon, turning the desk over on the bed, stopped and picked up the papers.

'I think this will do,' said he. 'It's the prospectus for the *Pall Mall Gazette*.'

'And here's the money for it,' Mr. Bungay said, laying down a five-pound note. 'I'm as good as my word, I am. When I say I'll pay, I pay.'

'Faith, that's more than some of us can say,' said Shandon, and he eagerly clapped the note into his pocket.

CHAPTER XXXII

WHICH IS PASSED IN THE NEIGHBOURHOOD OF LUDGATE HILL

UR imprisoned captain announced, in smart and emphatic language in his prospectus, that the time had come at last when it was necessary for the gentlemen of England to band together in defence of their common rights and their glorious order, menaced on all sides by foreign revolutions, by intestine radicalism, by the artful calumnies of mill-owners and cotton-lords, and the stupid hostility of the masses whom they gulled and led. 'The ancient monarchy was insulted,' the captain said, 'by a ferocious republican rabble. The Church was deserted by envious Dissent, and undermined

by stealthy infidelity. The good institutions, which had made our country glorious, and the name of English gentlemen the proudest in the world, were left without defence, and exposed to assault and contumely from men to whom no sanctuary was sacred, for they believed in nothing holy; no history venerable, for they were too ignorant to have heard of the past; and no law was binding which they were strong enough to break, when their leaders gave the signal for plunder. It was because the kings of France mistrusted their gentlemen,' Mr. Shandon remarked, 'that the monarchy of St. Louis went down: it was because the people of England still believed in their gentlemen, that this country encountered and overcame the greatest enemy a nation ever met: it was because we were headed by gentlemen that the Eagles retreated before us from the Douro to the Garonne: it was a gentleman who broke the line at Trafalgar, and swept the plain of Waterloo.'

Bungay nodded his head in a knowing manner, and winked his eyes when the captain came to the Waterloo passage: and Warrington burst out laughing.

'You see how our venerable friend Bungay is affected,' Shandon said, slyly looking up from his papers—'that's your true sort of test. I have used the Duke of Wellington and the Battle of Waterloo a hundred times: and I never knew the duke to fail.'

The captain then went on to confess, with much candour, that up to the present time the gentlemen of England, confident of their right, and careless of those who questioned it, had left the political interest of their order as they did the management of their estates, or the settlement of their legal affairs, to persons affected to each peculiar service, and had permitted their interests to be represented in the press by professional proctors and advocates. That time Shandon professed to consider was now gone by: the gentlemen of England must be their own champions: the declared enemies of their order were brave, strong, numerous, and uncompromising. They must meet their foes in the field: they must not be belied and misrepresented by hireling advocates: they must not have Grub Street publishing *Gazettes* from Whitehall; 'that's a dig at Bacon's people, Mr. Bungay,' said Shandon, turning round to the publisher.

Bungay clapped his stick on the floor. 'Hang him, pitch into him, capting,' he said, with exultation: and turning to

Warrington, wagged his dull head more vehemently than ever, and said, 'For a slashing article, sir, there's nobody like the capting—no-obody like him.'

The prospectus-writer went on to say that some gentlemen, whose names were, for obvious reasons, not brought before the public (at which Mr. Warrington began to laugh again), had determined to bring forward a journal, of which the principles were so and so. 'These men are proud of their order, and anxious to uphold it,' cried out Captain Shandon, flourishing his paper with a grin. 'They are loyal to their sovereign, by faithful conviction and ancestral allegiance; they love their Church, where they would have their children worship, and for which their forefathers bled; they love their country, and would keep it what the gentlemen of England—yes, *the gentlemen of England* (we'll have that in large caps., Bungay, my boy) have made it—the greatest and freest in the world: and as the names of some of them are appended to the deed which secured our liberties at Runnymede—'

'What's that?' asked Mr. Bungay.

'An ancestor of mine sealed it with his sword-hilt——' Pen said, with great gravity.

'It's the Habeas Corpus, Mr. Bungay,'*Warrington said, on which the publisher answered, 'All right, I dare say,' and yawned, though he said, 'Go on, capting.'

'—At Runnymede; they are ready to defend that freedom to-day with sword and pen, and now, as then, to rally round the old laws and liberties of England.'

'Brayvo!' cried Warrington. The little child stood wondering; the lady was working silently, and looking with fond admiration. 'Come here, little Mary,' said Warrington, and patted the child's fair curls with his large hand. But she shrank back from his rough caress, and preferred to go and take refuge at Pen's knee, and play with his fine watch-chain: and Pen was very much pleased that she came to him; for he was very soft-hearted and simple, though he concealed his gentleness under a shy and pompous demeanour. So she clambered up on his lap, whilst her father continued to read his programme.

'You were laughing,' the captain said to Warrington, 'about "the obvious reasons" which I mentioned. Now, I'll show ye what they are, ye unbelieving heathen. "We have said,"' he went on, '"that we cannot give the names

of the parties engaged in this undertaking, and that there were obvious reasons for that concealment. We number influential friends in both Houses of the Senate, and have secured allies in every diplomatic circle in Europe. Our sources of intelligence are such as cannot, by any possibility, be made public—and, indeed, such as no other London or European journal could, by any chance, acquire. But this we are free to say, that the very earliest information connected with the movement of English and Continental politics, will be found ONLY in the columns of the *Pall Mall Gazette*. The statesman and the capitalist, the country gentleman and the divine, will be amongst our readers, because our writers are amongst them. We address ourselves to the higher circles of society : we care not to disown it—the *Pall Mall Gazette* is written by gentlemen for gentlemen ; its conductors speak to the classes in which they live and were born. The field-preacher has his journal, the Radical freethinker has his journal : why should the gentlemen of England be unrepresented in the Press ?'

Mr. Shandon then went on with much modesty to descant upon the literary and fashionable departments of the *Pall Mall Gazette*, which were to be conducted by gentlemen of acknowledged reputation ; men famous at the universities (at which Mr. Pendennis could scarcely help laughing and blushing), known at the clubs and of the society which they described. He pointed out delicately to advertisers that there would be no such medium as the *Pall Mall Gazette* for giving publicity to their sales ; and he eloquently called upon the nobility of England, the baronetage of England, the revered clergy of England, the Bar of England, the matrons, the daughters, the homes and hearths of England, to rally round the good old cause ; and Bungay at the conclusion of the reading woke up from a second snooze in which he had indulged himself, and again said it was all right.

The reading of the prospectus concluded, the gentlemen present entered into some details regarding the political and literary management of the paper, and Mr. Bungay sat by listening and nodding his head, as if he understood what was the subject of their conversation, and approved of their opinions. Bungay's opinions, in truth, were pretty simple. He thought the captain could write the best smashing

article in England. He wanted the opposition house of Bacon smashed, and it was his opinion that the captain could do that business. If the captain had written a Letter of Junius on a sheet of paper, or copied a part of the Church Catechism, Mr. Bungay would have been perfectly contented, and have considered that the article was a smashing article. And he pocketed the papers with the greatest satisfaction: and he not only paid for the manuscript, as we have seen, but he called little Mary to him, and gave her a penny as he went away.

The reading of the manuscript over, the party engaged in general conversation, Shandon leading with a jaunty fashionable air in compliment to the two guests who sat with him, and who, by their appearance and manner, he presumed to be persons of the *beau monde*. He knew very little indeed of the great world, but he had seen it, and made the most of what he had seen. He spoke of the characters of the day, and great personages of the fashion, with easy familiarity and jocular allusions, as if it was his habit to live amongst them. He told anecdotes of their private life, and of conversations he had had, and entertainments at which he had been present, and at which such and such a thing occurred. Pen was amused to hear the shabby prisoner in a tattered dressing-gown talking glibly about the great of the land. Mrs. Shandon was always delighted when her husband told these tales, and believed in them fondly every one. She did not want to mingle in the fashionable world herself, she was not clever enough; but the great society was the very place for her Charles: he shone in it: he was respected in it. Indeed, Shandon had once been asked to dinner by the Earl of X.; his wife treasured the invitation-card in her work-box at that very day.

Mr. Bungay presently had enough of this talk and got up to take leave, whereupon Warrington and Pen rose to depart with the publisher, though the latter would have liked to stay to make a further acquaintance with this family, who interested him and touched him. He said something about hoping for permission to repeat his visit, upon which Shandon, with a rueful grin, said he was always to be found at home, and should be delighted to see Mr. Pennington.

'I'll see you to my park-gate, gentlemen,' said Captain

Shandon, seizing his hat, in spite of a deprecatory look, and a faint cry of 'Charles!' from Mrs. Shandon. And the captain, in shabby slippers, shuffled out before his guests, leading the way through the dismal passages of the prison. His hand was already fiddling with his waistcoat pocket, where Bungay's five-pound note was, as he took leave of the three gentlemen at the wicket; one of them, Mr. Arthur Pendennis, being greatly relieved when he was out of the

horrid place, and again freely treading the flags of Farringdon Street.

Mrs. Shandon sadly went on with her work at the window looking into the court. She saw Shandon with a couple of men at his heels run rapidly in the direction of the prison tavern. She had hoped to have had him to dinner herself that day: there was a piece of meat, and some salad in a basin, on the ledge outside of the window of their room,

which she had expected that she and little Mary were to share with the child's father. But there was no chance of that now. He would be in that tavern until the hours for closing it; then he would go and play at cards or drink in some other man's room, and come back silent, with glazed eyes, reeling a little on his walk, that his wife might nurse him. Oh, what varieties of pain do we not make our women suffer!

So Mrs. Shandon went to the cupboard, and, in lieu of a dinner, made herself some tea. And in those varieties of pain of which we spoke anon, what a part of confidante has that poor teapot played ever since the kindly plant was introduced among us! What myriads of women have cried over it, to be sure! What sick-beds it has smoked by! What fevered lips have received refreshment from out of it! Nature meant very gently by women when she made that tea-plant. With a little thought what a series of pictures and groups the fancy may conjure up and assemble round the teapot and cup. Melissa and Sacharissa are talking love-secrets over it. Poor Polly has it and her lover's letters upon the table; his letters who was her lover yesterday, and when it was with pleasure, not despair, she wept over them. Mary comes tripping noiselessly into her mother's bedroom, bearing a cup of the consoler to the widow who will take no other food. Ruth is busy concocting it for her husband, who is coming home from the harvest-field—one could fill a page with hints for such pictures;—finally, Mrs. Shandon and little Mary sit down and drink their tea together, while the captain goes out and takes his pleasure. She cares for nothing else but that, when her husband is away.

A gentleman with whom we are already slightly acquainted, Mr. Jack Finucane, a townsman of Captain Shandon's, found the captain's wife and little Mary (for whom Jack always brought a sweetmeat in his pocket) over this meal. Jack thought Shandon the greatest of created geniuses, had had one or two helps from the good-natured prodigal, who had always a kind word, and sometimes a guinea for any friend in need; and never missed a day in seeing his patron. He was ready to run Shandon's errands and transact his money-business with publishers and newspaper editors, duns, creditors, holders of Shandon's acceptances, gentlemen disposed to speculate in those

securities, and to transact the thousand little affairs of an embarrassed Irish gentleman. I never knew an embarrassed Irish gentleman yet, but he had an aide de camp of his own nation, likewise in circumstances of pecuniary discomfort. That aide de camp has subordinates of his own, who again may have other insolvent dependents—all through his life our captain marched at the head of a ragged staff, who shared in the rough fortunes of their chieftain.

'He won't have that five-pound note very long, I bet a guinea,' Mr. Bungay said of the captain, as he and his two companions walked away from the prison; and the publisher judged rightly, for when Mrs. Shandon came to empty her husband's pockets, she found but a couple of shillings and a few halfpence out of the morning's remittance. Shandon had given a pound to one follower; had sent a leg of mutton and potatoes and beer to an acquaintance in the poor side of the prison; had paid an outstanding bill at the tavern where he had changed his five-pound note; had had a dinner with two friends there, to whom he lost sundry half-crowns at cards afterwards; so that the night left him as poor as the morning had found him.

The publisher and the two gentlemen had had some talk together after quitting Shandon, and Warrington reiterated to Bungay what he had said to his rival, Bacon, viz., that Pen was a high fellow, of great genius, and what was more, well with the great world, and related to 'no end' of the peerage. Bungay replied that he should be happy to have dealings with Mr. Pendennis, and hoped to have the pleasure of seeing both gents to cut mutton with him before long, and so, with mutual politeness and protestations, they parted.

'It is hard to see such a man as Shandon,' Pen said, musing, and talking that night over the sight which he had witnessed, 'of accomplishments so multifarious, and of such an undoubted talent and humour, an inmate of a jail for half his time, and a bookseller's hanger-on when out of prison.'

'I am a bookseller's hanger-on—you are going to try your paces as a hack,' Warrington said, with a laugh. 'We are all hacks upon some road or other. I would rather be myself, than Paley our neighbour in chambers: who has as much enjoyment of his life as a mole. A deuced deal

of undeserved compassion has been thrown away upon what you call your bookseller's drudge.'

'Much solitary pipes and ale make a cynic of you,' Pen said. 'You are a Diogenes by a beer-barrel, Warrington. No man shall tell me that a man of genius, as Shandon is, ought to be driven by such a vulgar slave-driver, as yonder Mr. Bungay, whom we have just left, who fattens on the profits of the other's brains, and enriches himself out of his journeyman's labour. It makes me indignant to see a gentleman the serf of such a creature as that, of a man who can't speak the language that he lives by, who is not fit to black Shandon's boots.'

'So you have begun already to gird at the publishers, and to take your side amongst our order. Bravo, Pen, my boy!' Warrington answered, laughing still. 'What have you got to say against Bungay's relations with Shandon? Was it the publisher, think you, who sent the author to prison? Is it Bungay who is tippling away the five-pound note which we saw just now, or Shandon?'

'Misfortune drives a man into bad company,' Pen said. 'It is easy to cry "Fie!" against a poor fellow who has no society but such as he finds in a prison; and no resource except forgetfulness and the bottle. We must deal kindly with the eccentricities of genius, and remember that the very ardour and enthusiasm of temperament which makes the author delightful often leads the man astray.'

'A fiddlestick about men of genius!' Warrington cried out, who was a very severe moralist upon some points, though possibly a very bad practitioner. 'I deny that there are so many geniuses as people who whimper about the fate of men of letters assert there are. There are thousands of clever fellows in the world who could, if they would, turn verses, write articles, read books, and deliver a judgement upon them; the talk of professional critics and writers is not a whit more brilliant, or profound, or amusing, than that of any other society of educated people. If a lawyer, or a soldier, or a parson, outruns his income, and does not pay his bills, he must go to jail;* and an author must go, too. If an author fuddles himself, I don't know why he should be let off a headache the next morning,—if he orders a coat from the tailor's, why he shouldn't pay for it.'

'I would give him more money to buy coats,' said Pen, smiling. 'I suppose I should like to belong to a well-

dressed profession. I protest against that wretch of a middle-man whom I see between Genius and his great landlord, the Public, and who stops more than half of the labourer's earnings and fame.'

'I am a prose labourer,' Warrington said: 'you, my boy, are a poet in a small way, and so, I suppose, consider you are authorized to be flighty. What is it you want? Do you want a body of capitalists that shall be forced to purchase the works of all authors, who may present themselves, manuscript in hand? Everybody who writes his epic, every driveller who can or can't spell, and produces his novel or his tragedy,—are they all to come and find a bag of sovereigns in exchange for their worthless reams of paper? Who is to settle what is good or bad, saleable or otherwise? Will you give the buyer leave, in fine, to purchase or not? Why, sir, when Johnson sat behind the screen at St. John's Gate, and took his dinner apart, because he was too shabby and poor to join the literary bigwigs who were regaling themselves round Mr. Cave's best tablecloth,* the tradesman was doing him no wrong. You couldn't force the publisher to recognize the man of genius in the young man who presented himself before him, ragged, gaunt, and hungry. Rags are not a proof of genius; whereas capital is absolute, as times go, and is perforce the bargain-master. It has a right to deal with the literary inventor as with any other;—if I produce a novelty in the book trade, I must do the best I can with it; but I can no more force Mr. Murray to purchase my book of travels or sermons, than I can compel Mr. Tattersall* to give me a hundred guineas for my horse. I may have my own ideas of the value of my Pegasus, and think him the most wonderful of animals; but the dealer has a right to his opinion, too, and may want a lady's horse, or a cob for a heavy, timid rider, or a sound hack for the road, and my beast won't suit him.'

'You deal in metaphors, Warrington,' Pen said; 'but you rightly say that you are very prosaic. Poor Shandon! There is something about the kindness of that man, and the gentleness of that sweet creature of a wife, which touches me profoundly. I like him, I am afraid, better than a better man.'

'And so do I,' Warrington said. 'Let us give him the benefit of our sympathy, and the pity that is due to his

weakness: though I fear that sort of kindness would be resented as contempt by a more high-minded man. You see he takes his consolation along with his misfortune, and one generates the other or balances it, as is the way of the world. He is a prisoner, but he is not unhappy.'

'His genius sings within his prison bars,' Pen said.

'Yes,' Warrington said bitterly; 'Shandon accommodates himself to a cage pretty well. He ought to be wretched, but he has Jack and Tom to drink with, and that consoles him: he might have a high place, but, as he can't, why, he can drink with Tom and Jack;—he might be providing for his wife and children, but Thomas and John have got a bottle of brandy which they want him to taste;—he might pay poor Snip, the tailor, the twenty pounds which the poor devil wants for his landlord, but John and Thomas lay their hands upon his purse;—and so he drinks whilst his tradesman goes to jail and his family to ruin. Let us pity the misfortunes of genius, and conspire against the publishing tyrants who oppress men of letters.'

'What! are you going to have another glass of brandy-and-water?' Pen said, with a humorous look. It was at the Back Kitchen that the above philosophical conversation took place between the two young men.

Warrington began to laugh as usual. '*Video meliora proboque**—I mean, bring it me hot, with sugar, John,' he said to the waiter.

'I would have some more, too, only I don't want it,' said Pen. 'It does not seem to me, Warrington, that we are much better than our neighbours.' And Warrington's last glass having been dispatched, the pair returned to their chambers.

They found a couple of notes in the letter-box, on their return, which had been sent by their acquaintance of the morning, Mr. Bungay. That hospitable gentleman presented his compliments to each of the gentlemen, and requested the pleasure of their company at dinner on an early day, to meet a few literary friends.

'We shall have a grand spread,' said Warrington. 'We shall meet all Bungay's corps.'

'All except poor Shandon,' said Pen, nodding a good-night to his friend, and he went into his own little room. The events and acquaintances of the day had excited him

a good deal, and he lay for some time awake thinking over them, as Warrington's vigorous and regular snore from the neighbouring apartment pronounced that that gentleman was engaged in deep slumber.

Is it true, thought Pendennis, lying on his bed and gazing at a bright moon without, that lighted up a corner of his dressing-table, and the frame of a little sketch of Fairoaks drawn by Laura, that hung over his drawers—is it true that I am going to earn my bread at last, and with my pen? that I shall impoverish the dear mother no longer; and that I may gain a name and reputation in the world, perhaps? These are welcome if they come, thought the young visionary, laughing and blushing to himself, though alone and in the night, as he thought how dearly he would relish honour and fame if they could be his. If fortune favours me, I laud her; if she frowns, I resign her. I pray Heaven I may be honest if I fail, or if I succeed. I pray Heaven I may tell the truth as far as I know it: that I mayn't swerve from it through flattery, or interest, or personal enmity, or party prejudice. Dearest old mother, what a pride will you have, if I can do anything worthy of our name! and you, Laura, you won't scorn me as the worthless idler and spendthrift, when you see that I—when I have achieved a—psha! what an Alnaschar* I am because I have made five pounds by my poems, and am engaged to write half a dozen articles for a newspaper. He went on with these musings, more happy and hopeful, and in a humbler frame of mind, than he had felt to be for many a day. He thought over the errors and idleness, the passions, extravagances, disappointments, of his wayward youth: he got up from the bed: threw open the window, and looked out into the night: and then, by some impulse, which we hope was a good one, he went up and kissed the picture of Fairoaks, and flinging himself down on his knees by the bed, remained for some time in that posture of hope and submission. When he rose, it was with streaming eyes. He had found himself repeating, mechanically, some little words which he had been accustomed to repeat as a child at his mother's side, after the saying of which she would softly take him to his bed and close the curtains round him, hushing him with a benediction.

The next day, Mr. Pidgeon, their attendant, brought in a large brown-paper parcel, directed to G. Warrington, Esq., with Mr. Trotter's compliments, and a note which Warrington read.

'Pen, you beggar!' roared Warrington to Pen, who was in his own room.

'Hullo!' sung out Pen.

'Come here, you're wanted,' cried the other, and Pen came out.

'What is it?' said he.

'*Catch!*' cried Warrington, and flung the parcel at Pen's head, who would have been knocked down had he not caught it.

'It's books for review for the *Pall Mall Gazette;* pitch into 'em,' Warrington said. As for Pen, he never had been so delighted in his life: his hand trembled as he cut the string of the packet, and beheld within a smart set of new neat calico-bound books, travels, and novels, and poems.

'Sport the oak, Pidgeon,' said he. 'I'm not at home to anybody to-day.' And he flung into his easy chair, and hardly gave himself time to drink his tea, so eager was he to begin to read and to review.

CHAPTER XXXIII

IN WHICH THE HISTORY STILL HOVERS ABOUT FLEET STREET

CAPTAIN SHANDON, urged on by his wife, who seldom meddled in business matters, had stipulated that John Finucane, Esq., of the Upper Temple, should be appointed sub-editor of the forthcoming *Pall Mall Gazette*, and this post was accordingly conferred upon Mr. Finucane by the spirited proprietor of the journal. Indeed he deserved any kindness at the hands of Shandon, so fondly attached was he, as we have said, to the captain and his family, and so eager to do him a service. It was in Finucane's chambers that Shandon used in former days to hide when danger was near and bailiffs abroad . until at length his hiding-place was known, and the sheriff's officers came as regularly to wait for the captain on Finucane's staircase as at his own door. It was to Finucane's chambers

that poor Mrs. Shandon came often and often to explain her troubles and griefs, and devise means of rescue for her adored captain. Many a meal did Finucane furnish for her and the child there. It was an honour to his little rooms to be visited by such a lady; and as she went down the staircase with her veil over her face, Fin would lean over the balustrade looking after her, to see that no Temple Lovelace assailed her upon the road, perhaps hoping that some rogue might be induced to waylay her, so that he, Fin, might have the pleasure of rushing to her rescue, and breaking the rascal's bones. It was a sincere pleasure to Mrs. Shandon when the arrangements were made by which her kind honest champion was appointed her husband's aide de camp in the newspaper.

He would have sat with Mrs. Shandon as late as the prison hours permitted, and had indeed many a time witnessed the putting to bed of little Mary, who occupied a crib in the room; and to whose evening prayers that God might bless papa, Finucane, although of the Romish faith himself, had said Amen with a great deal of sympathy—but he had an appointment with Mr. Bungay regarding the affairs of the paper which they were to discuss over a quiet dinner. So he went away at six o'clock from Mrs. Shandon, but made his accustomed appearance at the Fleet Prison next morning, having arrayed himself in his best clothes and ornaments, which, though cheap as to cost, were very brilliant as to colour and appearance, and having in his pocket four pounds two shillings, being the amount of his week's salary at the *Daily Journal*, minus two shillings expended by him in the purchase of a pair of gloves on his way to the prison.

He had cut his mutton with Mr. Bungay, as the latter gentleman phrased it, and Mr. Trotter, Bungay's reader and literary man of business, at Dick's Coffee-house on the previous day, and entered at large into his views respecting the conduct of the *Pall Mall Gazette*. In a masterly manner he had pointed out what should be the sub-editorial arrangements of the paper: what should be the type for the various articles: who should report the markets; who the turf and ring; who the Church intelligence; and who the fashionable chit-chat. He was acquainted with gentlemen engaged in cultivating these various departments of knowledge, and in communicating

them afterwards to the public—in fine, Jack Finucane was, as Shandon had said of him, and as he proudly owned himself to be, one of the best sub-editors of a paper in London. He knew the weekly earnings of every man connected with the Press, and was up to a thousand dodges, or ingenious economic contrivances, by which money could be saved to spirited capitalists, who were going to set up a paper. He at once dazzled and mystified Mr. Bungay, who was slow of comprehension, by the rapidity of the calculations which he exhibited on paper, as they sat in the box. And Bungay afterwards owned to his subordinate, Mr. Trotter, that that Irishman seemed a clever fellow.

And now having succeeded in making this impression upon Mr. Bungay, the faithful fellow worked round to the point which he had very near at heart, viz., the liberation from prison of his admired friend and chief, Captain Shandon. He knew to a shilling the amount of the detainers which were against the captain at the porter's lodge of the Fleet; and, indeed, professed to know all his debts, though this was impossible, for no man in England, certainly not the captain himself, was acquainted with them. He pointed out what Shandon's engagements already were; and how much better he would work if removed from confinement (though this Mr. Bungay denied, for, 'when the captain's locked up,' he said, 'we are sure to find him at home; whereas, when he's free, you can never catch hold of him'); finally, he so worked on Mr. Bungay's feelings, by describing Mrs. Shandon pining away in the prison, and the child sickening there, that the publisher was induced to promise that, if Mrs. Shandon would come to him in the morning, he would see what could be done. And the colloquy ending at this time with the second round of brandy-and-water, although Finucane, who had four guineas in his pocket, would have discharged the tavern reckoning with delight, Bungay said, 'No, sir,—this is my affair, sir, if you please. James, take the bill, and eighteenpence for yourself,' and he handed over the necessary funds to the waiter. Thus it was that Finucane, who went to bed at the Temple after the dinner at Dick's, found himself actually with his week's salary intact upon Saturday morning.

He gave Mrs. Shandon a wink so knowing and joyful, that that kind creature knew some good news was in store

for her, and hastened to get her bonnet and shawl, when Fin asked if he might have the honour of taking her a walk, and giving her a little fresh air. And little Mary jumped for joy at the idea of this holiday, for Finucane never neglected to give her a toy, or to take her to a show, and brought newspaper orders in his pocket for all sorts of London diversions to amuse the child. Indeed, he loved them with all his heart, and would cheerfully have dashed out his rambling brains to do them, or his adored captain, a service.

'May I go, Charley? or shall I stay with you, for you're poorly, dear, this morning? He's got a headache, Mr. Finucane. He suffers from headaches, and I persuaded him to stay in bed,' Mrs. Shandon said.

'Go along with you, and Polly. Jack, take care of 'em. Hand me over the Burton's *Anatomy*, and leave me to my abominable devices,' Shandon said, with perfect good-humour. He was writing, and not uncommonly took his Greek and Latin quotations (of which he knew the use as a public writer) from that wonderful repertory of learning.

So Fin gave his arm to Mrs. Shandon, and Mary went skipping down the passages of the prison, and through the gate into the free air. From Fleet Street to Paternoster Row is not very far. As the three reached Mr. Bungay's shop, Mrs. Bungay was also entering at the private door, holding in her hand a paper parcel and a manuscript volume bound in red, and, indeed, containing an account of her transactions with the butcher in the neighbouring market. Mrs. Bungay was in a gorgeous shot-silk dress, which flamed with red and purple; she wore a yellow shawl, and had red flowers inside her bonnet, and a brilliant light blue parasol. Mrs. Shandon was in an old black watered silk; her bonnet had never seen very brilliant days of prosperity any more than its owner, but she could not help looking like a lady whatever her attire was. The two women curtsied to each other, each according to her fashion.

'I hope you're pretty well, mum?' said Mrs. Bungay.

'It's a very fine day,' said Mrs. Shandon.

'Won't you step in, mum?' said Mrs. Bungay, looking so hard at the child as almost to frighten her.

'I—I came about business with Mr. Bungay—I—I hope he's pretty well?' said timid Mrs. Shandon.

'If you go to see him in the counting-house, couldn't

MRS. BUNGAY MOLLIFIED

you—couldn't you leave your little *gurl* with me?' said Mrs. Bungay, in a deep voice, and with a tragic look, as she held out one finger towards the child.

'I want to stay with mamma,' cried little Mary, burying her face in her mother's dress.

'Go with this lady, Mary, my dear,' said the mother.

'I'll show you some pretty pictures,' said Mrs. Bungay, with the voice of an ogress, 'and some nice things besides; look here'—and opening her brown-paper parcel, Mrs. Bungay displayed some choice sweet biscuits, such as her Bungay loved after his wine. Little Mary followed after this attraction, the whole party entering at the private entrance, from which a side door led into Mr. Bungay's commercial apartments. Here, however, as the child was about to part from her mother, her courage again failed her, and again she ran to the maternal petticoat; upon which the kind and gentle Mrs. Shandon, seeing the look of disappointment in Mrs. Bungay's face, good-naturedly said, 'If you will let me, I will come up too, and sit for a few minutes,' and so the three females ascended the stairs together. A second biscuit charmed little Mary into perfect confidence, and in a minute or two she prattled away without the least restraint.

Faithful Finucane meanwhile found Mr. Bungay in a severer mood than he had been on the night previous, when two-thirds of a bottle of port, and two large glasses of brandy-and-water, had warmed his soul into enthusiasm, and made him generous in his promises towards Captain Shandon. His impetuous wife had rebuked him on his return home. She had ordered that he should give no relief to the captain; he was a good-for-nothing fellow, whom no money would help; she disapproved of the plan of the *Pall Mall Gazette*, and expected that Bungay would only lose his money in it as they were losing over the way (she always called her brother's establishment 'over the way') by the *Whitehall Journal*. Let Shandon stop in prison and do his work; it was the best place for him. In vain Finucane pleaded and promised and implored, for his friend Bungay had had an hour's lecture in the morning and was inexorable.

But what honest Jack failed to do below stairs in the counting-house, the pretty faces and manners of the mother and child were effecting in the drawing-room, where they

were melting the fierce but really soft Mrs. Bungay. There was an artless sweetness in Mrs. Shandon's voice, and a winning frankness of manner, which made most people fond of her, and pity her : and taking courage by the rugged kindness with which her hostess received her, the captain's lady told her story, and describing her husband's goodness and virtues, and her child's failing health (she

was obliged to part with two of them, she said, and send them to school, for she could not have them in that horrid place)—that Mrs. Bungay, though as grim as Lady Macbeth, melted under the influence of the simple tale, and said she would go down and speak to Bungay. Now in this household to speak was to command, with Mrs. Bungay ; and with Bungay, to hear was to obey.

It was just when poor Finucane was in despair about his

negotiation, that the majestic Mrs. Bungay descended upon her spouse, politely requested Mr. Finucane to step up to his friends in her drawing-room, while she held a few minutes' conversation with Mr. B., and when the pair were alone the publisher's better half informed him of her intentions towards the captain's lady.

'What's in the wind now, my dear?' Maecenas asked, surprised at his wife's altered tone. 'You wouldn't hear of my doing anything for the captain this morning: I wonder what has been a-changing of you.'

'The capting is an Irishman,' Mrs. Bungay replied; 'and those Irish I have always said I couldn't abide. But his wife is a lady, as anyone can see; and a good woman, and a clergyman's daughter, and a West of England woman, B., which I am myself, by my mother's side—and, O Marmaduke! didn't you remark her little gurl?'

'Yes, Mrs. B., I saw the little girl.'

'And didn't you see how like she was to our angel, Bessy, Mr. B.?'—and Mrs. Bungay's thoughts flew back to a period eighteen years back, when Bacon and Bungay had just set up in business as small booksellers in a country town, and when she had had a child, named Bessy, something like the little Mary who had just moved her compassion.

'Well, well, my dear,' Mr. Bungay said, seeing the little eyes of his wife begin to twinkle and grow red; 'the captain ain't in for much. There's only a hundred and thirty pound against him. Half the money will take him out of the Fleet, Finucane says, and we'll pay him half salaries till he has made the account square. When the little un said, "Why don't you take par out of pizn?" I did feel it, Elizabeth, upon my honour I did, now.' And the upshot of this conversation was, that Mr. and Mrs. Bungay both ascended to the drawing-room, and Mr. Bungay made a heavy and clumsy speech, in which he announced to Mrs. Shandon, that, hearing sixty-five pounds would set her husband free, he was ready to advance that sum of money, deducting it from the captain's salary, and that he would give it to her on condition that she would personally settle with the creditors regarding her husband's liberation.

I think this was the happiest day that Mrs. Shandon and Mr. Finucane had had for a long time. 'Bedad, Bungay, you're a trump!' roared out Fin, in an overpowering brogue and emotion. 'Give us your fist, old boy: and won't we

send the *Pall Mall Gazette* up to ten thousand a week, that's all!' and he jumped about the room, and tossed up little Mary, with a hundred frantic antics.

'If I could drive you anywhere in my carriage, Mrs. Shandon—I'm sure it's quite at your service,' Mrs. Bungay said, looking out at a one-horsed vehicle which had just driven up, and in which this lady took the air considerably—and the two ladies, with little Mary between them (whose tiny hand Maecenas's wife kept fixed in her great grasp), with the delighted Mr. Finucane on the back seat, drove away from Paternoster Row, as the owner of the vehicle threw triumphant glances at the opposite windows at Bacon's.

'It won't do the captain any good,' thought Bungay, going back to his desk and accounts, 'but Mrs. B. becomes regular upset when she thinks about her misfortune. The child would have been of age yesterday, if she'd lived. Bessy told me so': and he wondered how women did remember things.

We are happy to say that Mrs. Shandon sped with very good success upon her errand. She who had had to mollify creditors when she had no money at all, and only tears and entreaties wherewith to soothe them, found no difficulty in making them relent by means of a bribe of ten shillings in the pound; and the next Sunday was the last, for some time at least, which the captain spent in prison.

CHAPTER XXXIV

A DINNER IN THE ROW*

PON the appointed day our two friends made their appearance at Mr. Bungay's door in Paternoster Row; not the public entrance through which booksellers' boys issued with their sacks full of Bungay's volumes, and around which timid aspirants lingered with their virgin manuscripts ready for sale to Sultan Bungay, but at the private door of the house, whence the splendid Mrs. Bungay would come forth to step into her chaise and take her drive, settling herself on the cushions,

and casting looks of defiance at Mrs. Bacon's opposite windows—at Mrs. Bacon, who was as yet a chaiseless woman.

On such occasions, when very much wroth at her sister-in-law's splendour, Mrs. Bacon would fling up the sash of her drawing-room window, and look out with her four children at the chaise, as much as to say, 'Look at these four darlings, Flora Bungay! This is why I can't drive in my carriage; you would give a coach-and-four to have the same reason.' And it was with these arrows out of her quiver that Emma Bacon shot Flora Bungay as she sat in her chariot envious and childless.

As Pen and Warrington came to Bungay's door, a carriage and a cab drove up to Bacon's. Old Dr. Slocum descended heavily from the first; the doctor's equipage was as ponderous as his style, but both had a fine sonorous effect upon the publishers in the Row. A couple of dazzling white waistcoats stepped out of the cab.

Warrington laughed. 'You see Bacon has his dinner-party too. That is Dr. Slocum, author of *Memoirs of the Poisoners*. You would hardly have recognized our friend Hoolan in that gallant white waistcoat. Doolan is one of Bungay's men, and, faith, here he comes.' Indeed Messrs. Hoolan and Doolan had come from the Strand in the same cab, tossing up by the way which should pay the shilling; and Mr. D. stepped from the other side of the way, arrayed in black, with a large pair of white gloves which were spread out on his hands, and which the owner could not help regarding with pleasure.

The house-porter in an evening coat, and gentlemen with gloves as large as Doolan's, but of the famous Berlin web, were on the passage of Mr. Bungay's house to receive the guests' hats and coats, and bawl their names up the stair. Some of the latter had arrived when the three new visitors made their appearance; but there was only Mrs. Bungay in red satin and a turban to represent her own charming sex. She made curtsies to each new-comer as he entered the drawing-room, but her mind was evidently preoccupied by extraneous thoughts. The fact is, Mrs. Bacon's dinner-party was disturbing her, and, as soon as she had received each individual of her own company, Flora Bungay flew back to the embrasure of the window, whence she could rake the carriages of Emma Bacon's friends as they came

rattling up the Row. The sight of Dr. Slocum's large carriage, with the gaunt job-horses, crushed Flora: none but hack cabs had driven up to her own door on that day.

They were all literary gentlemen, though unknown as yet to Pen. There was Mr. Bole, the real editor of the magazine, of which Mr. Wagg was the nominal chief;* Mr. Trotter, who, from having broken out on the world as a poet of a tragic and suicidal cast,* had now subsided into one of Mr. Bungay's back shops as reader for that gentleman; and Captain Sumph,* an ex-beau still about town, and related in some indistinct manner to Literature and the Peerage. He was said to have written a book once, to have been a friend of Lord Byron, to be related to Lord Sumphington; in fact, anecdotes of Byron formed his staple, and he seldom spoke but with the name of that poet or some of his contemporaries in his mouth, as thus: 'I remember poor Shelley at school being sent up for good for a copy of verses, every line of which I wrote, by Jove'; or, 'I recollect, when I was at Missolonghi with Byron, offering to bet Gamba,' and so forth. This gentleman, Pen remarked, was listened to with great attention by Mrs. Bungay; his anecdotes of the aristocracy, of which he was a middle-aged member, delighted the publisher's lady; and he was almost a greater man than the great Mr. Wagg himself in her eyes. Had he but come in his own carriage, Mrs. Bungay would have made her Bungay purchase any given volume from his pen.

Mr. Bungay went about to his guests as they arrived, and did the honours of his house with much cordiality. 'How are you, sir? Fine day, sir. Glad to see you year, sir. Flora, my love, let me 'ave the honour of introducing Mr. Warrington to you. Mr. Warrington, Mrs. Bungay; Mr. Pendennis, Mrs. Bungay. Hope you've brought good appetites with you, gentlemen. *You*, Doolan, I know 'ave, for you've always 'ad a deuce of a twist.'

'Lor, Bungay!' said Mrs. Bungay.

'Faith, a man must be hard to please, Bungay, who can't eat a good dinner in *this* house,' Doolan said, and he winked and stroked his lean chops with his large gloves; and made appeals of friendship to Mrs. Bungay, which that honest woman refused with scorn from the timid man. 'She couldn't abide that Doolan,' she said in confidence to her friends. Indeed, all his flatteries failed to win her.

As they talked, Mrs. Bungay surveying mankind from her window, a magnificent vision of an enormous grey cab-horse appeared, and neared rapidly. A pair of white reins, held by small white gloves, were visible behind it; a face pale, but richly decorated with a chin-tuft, the head of an exiguous groom bobbing over the cab-head—these bright things were revealed to the delighted Mrs. Bungay. 'The Honourable Percy Popjoy's quite punctual, I declare,' she said, and sailed to the door to be in waiting at the nobleman's arrival.

'It's Percy Popjoy,' said Pen, looking out of window, and seeing an individual, in extremely lacquered boots, descend from the swinging cab: and, in fact, it was that young nobleman—Lord Falconet's eldest son, as we all very well know, who was come to dine with the publisher—his publisher of the Row.

'He was my fag at Eton,' Warrington said. 'I ought to have licked him a little more.' He and Pen had had some bouts at the Oxbridge Union debates, in which Pen had had very much the better of Percy: who presently appeared, with his hat under his arm, and a look of indescribable good humour and fatuity in his round dimpled face: upon which Nature had burst out with a chin-tuft, but, exhausted with the effort, had left the rest of the countenance bare of hair.

The temporary groom of the chambers bawled out, 'The Honourable Percy Popjoy,' much to that gentleman's discomposure at hearing his titles announced.

'What did the man want to take away my hat for, Bungay?' he asked of the publisher. 'Can't do without my hat—want it to make my bow to Mrs. Bungay. How well you look, Mrs. Bungay, to-day. Haven't seen your carriage in the Park: why haven't you been there? I missed you; indeed, I did.'

'I'm afraid you're a sad quiz,' said Mrs. Bungay.

'Quiz! Never made a joke in my—hullo! who's here? How d'ye do, Pendennis? How d'ye do, Warrington? These are old friends of mine, Mrs. Bungay. I say, how the doose did *you* come here?' he asked of the two young men, turning his lacquered heels upon Mrs. Bungay, who respected her husband's two young guests, now that she found they were intimate with a lord's son.

'What! do *they* know him?' she asked rapidly of Mr. B.

'High fellers, I tell you—the young one related to all the nobility,' said the publisher; and both ran forward, smiling and bowing, to greet almost as great personages as the young lord—no less characters, indeed, than the great Mr. Wenham and the great Mr. Wagg, who were now announced.

Mr. Wenham entered, wearing the usual demure look and stealthy smile with which he commonly surveyed the tips of his neat little shining boots, and which he but seldom brought to bear upon the person who addressed him. Wagg's white waistcoat spread out, on the contrary, with profuse brilliancy; his burly, red face shone resplendent over it, lighted up with the thoughts of good jokes and a good dinner. He liked to make his entrée into a drawing-room with a laugh, and, when he went away at night, to leave a joke exploding behind him. No personal calamities or distresses (of which that humourist had his share in common with the unjocular part of mankind) could altogether keep his humour down. Whatever his griefs might be, the thought of a dinner rallied his great soul; and when he saw a lord, he saluted him with a pun.

Wenham went up, then, with a smug smile and whisper, to Mrs. Bungay, and looked at her from under his eyes, and showed her the tips of his shoes. Wagg said she looked charming, and pushed on straight at the young nobleman, whom he called Pop; and to whom he instantly related a funny story, seasoned with what the French call *gros sel*. He was delighted to see Pen, too, and shook hands with him, and slapped him on the back cordially; for he was full of spirits and good-humour. And he talked in a loud voice about their last place and occasion of meeting at Baymouth; and asked how their friends of Clavering Park were, and whether Sir Francis was not coming to London for the season; and whether Pen had been to see Lady Rockminster, who had arrived—fine old lady, Lady Rockminster! These remarks Wagg made not for Pen's ear so much as for the edification of the company, whom he was glad to inform that he paid visits to gentlemen's country seats, and was on intimate terms with the nobility.

Wenham also shook hands with our young friend—all of which scenes Mrs. Bungay remarked with respectful pleasure, and communicated her ideas to Bungay, afterwards, regarding the importance of Mr. Pendennis—ideas by which Pen profited much more than he was aware.

Pen, who had read, and rather admired some of her works (and expected to find in Miss Bunion a person somewhat resembling her own description of herself in the *Passion-Flower*, in which she stated that her youth resembled—

A violet, shrinking meanly
When blows the March wind keenly;
A timid fawn, on wild wood lawn,
Where oak-boughs rustle greenly,—

and that her maturer beauty was something very different, certainly, to the artless loveliness of her prime, but still exceedingly captivating and striking), beheld, rather to his surprise and amusement, a large and bony woman in a crumpled satin dress, who came creaking into the room with a step as heavy as a grenadier's. Wagg instantly noted the straw which she brought in at the rumpled skirt of her dress, and would have stooped to pick it up, but Miss Bunion disarmed all criticism by observing this ornament herself, and, putting down her own large foot upon it, so as to separate it from her robe, she stopped and picked up the straw, saying to Mrs. Bungay, that she was very sorry to be a little late, but that the omnibus was very slow, and what a comfort it was to get a ride all the way from Brompton for sixpence. Nobody laughed at the poetess's speech, it was uttered so simply. Indeed, the worthy woman had not the least notion of being ashamed of an action incidental upon her poverty.

'Is that *Passion-Flowers?*' Pen said to Wenham, by whom he was standing. 'Why, her picture in the volume represents her as a very well-looking young woman.'

'You know passion-flowers, like all others, will run to seed,' Wenham said; 'Miss Bunion's portrait was probably painted some years ago.'

'Well, I like her for not being ashamed of her poverty.'

'So do I,' said Mr. Wenham, who would have starved rather than have come to dinner in an omnibus; 'but I don't think that she need flourish the straw about, do you, Mr. Pendennis? My dear Miss Bunion, how do you do? I was in a great lady's drawing-room this morning, and everybody was charmed with your new volume. Those lines on the christening of Lady Fanny Fantail brought tears into the duchess's eyes. I said that I thought I should have the pleasure of meeting you to-day, and she

begged me to thank you, and say how greatly she was pleased.'

This history, told in a bland, smiling manner, of a duchess whom Wenham had met that very morning, too, quite put poor Wagg's dowager and baronet out of court, and placed Wenham beyond Wagg as a man of fashion. Wenham kept this inestimable advantage, and having the conversation to himself, ran on with a number of anecdotes regarding the aristocracy. He tried to bring Mr. Popjoy into the conversation by making appeals to him, and saying, 'I was telling your father this morning,' or, 'I think you were present at W. house the other night when the duke said so and so'; but Mr. Popjoy would not gratify him by joining in the talk, preferring to fall back into the window recess with Mrs. Bungay, and watch the cabs that drove up to the opposite door. At least, if he would not talk, the hostess hoped that those odious Bacons would see how she had secured the noble Percy Popjoy for her party.

And now the bell of St. Paul's tolled half an hour later than that for which Mr. Bungay had invited his party, and it was complete with the exception of two guests, who at last made their appearance, and in whom Pen was pleased to recognize Captain and Mrs. Shandon.

When these two had made their greetings to the master and mistress of the house, and exchanged nods of more or less recognition with most of the people present, Pen and Warrington went up and shook hands very warmly with Mrs. Shandon, who, perhaps, was affected to meet them, and think where it was she had seen them but a few days before. Shandon was brushed up, and looked pretty smart, in a red velvet waistcoat, and a frill, into which his wife had stuck her best brooch. In spite of Mrs. Bungay's kindness, perhaps in consequence of it, Mrs. Shandon felt great terror and timidity in approaching her: indeed, she was more awful than ever in her red satin and bird of paradise, and it was not until she had asked in her great voice about the dear little gurl, that the latter was somewhat encouraged, and ventured to speak.

'Nice-looking woman,' Popjoy whispered to Warrington. 'Do introduce me to Captain Shandon, Warrington. I'm told he's a tremendous clever fellow; and, dammy, I adore intellect, by Jove I do!' This was the truth: Heaven had not endowed young Mr. Popjoy with much intellect of his

own, but had given him a generous faculty for admiring, if not for appreciating, the intellect of others. 'And introduce me to Miss Bunion. I'm told she's very clever too. She's rum to look at, certainly, but that don't matter. Dammy, I consider myself a literary man, and I wish to know all the clever fellows.' So Mr. Popjoy and Mr. Shandon had the pleasure of becoming acquainted with one another; and now the doors of the adjoining dining-room being flung open, the party entered and took their seats at table. Pen found himself next to Bunion on one side, and to Mr. Wagg—the truth is, Wagg fled alarmed from the vacant place by the poetess, and Pen was compelled to take it.

The gifted being did not talk much during dinner, but Pen remarked that she ate with a vast appetite, and never refused any of the supplies of wine which were offered to her by the butler. Indeed, Miss Bunion having considered Mr. Pendennis for a minute, who gave himself rather grand airs, and who was attired in an extremely fashionable style, with his very best chains, shirt-studs, and cambric fronts, he was set down, and not without reason, as a prig by the poetess; who thought it was much better to attend to her dinner than to take any notice of him. She told him as much in after-days, with her usual candour. 'I took you for one of the little May Fair dandies,' she said to Pen. 'You looked as solemn as a little undertaker; and as I disliked, beyond measure, the odious creature who was on the other side of me, I thought it was best to eat my dinner and hold my tongue.'

'And you did both very well, my dear Miss Bunion,' Pen said, with a laugh.

'Well, so I do, but I intend to talk to you the next time a great deal: for you are neither so solemn, nor so stupid, nor so pert as you look.'

'Ah, Miss Bunion, how I pine for that "next time" to come,' Pen said, with an air of comical gallantry.—But we must return to the day, and the dinner at Paternoster Row.

The repast was of the richest description—'What I call of the florid Gothic style,' Wagg whispered to Pen, who sat beside the humourist, in his side-wing voice. The men in creaking shoes and Berlin gloves were numerous and solemn, carrying on rapid conversations behind the guests, as they moved to and fro with the dishes. Doolan called out,

'Waither,' to one of them, and blushed when he thought of his blunder. Mrs. Bungay's own footboy was lost amidst those large and black-coated attendants.

'Look at that *very* bow-windowed man,' Wagg said. 'He's an undertaker in Amen Corner, and attends funerals and dinners. Cold meat and hot, don't you perceive? He's the sham butler here, and I observe, my dear Mr. Pendennis, as you will through life, that wherever there is a sham butler at a London dinner there is sham wine—this sherry is filthy. Bungay, my boy, where did you get this delicious brown sherry?'

'I'm glad you like it, Mr. Wagg; glass with you,' said the publisher. 'It's some I got from Alderman Benning's store, and gave a good figure for it, I can tell you. Mr. Pendennis, will you join us? Your 'ealth, gentlemen.'

'The old rogue, where does he expect to go to? It came from the public-house,' Wagg said. 'It requires two men to carry off that sherry, 'tis so uncommonly strong. I wish I had a bottle of old Steyne's wine here, Pendennis: your uncle and I have had many a one. He sends it about to people where he is in the habit of dining. I remember at poor Rawdon Crawley's, Sir Pitt Crawley's brother—he was Governor of Coventry Island—Steyne's *chef* always came in the morning, and the butler arrived with the champagne from Gaunt House, in the ice-pails, ready.'

'How good this is!' said Popjoy good-naturedly. 'You must have a *cordon bleu* in your kitchen.'

'Oh yes,' Mrs. Bungay said, thinking he spoke of a jack-chain very likely.

'I mean a French *chef*,' said the polite guest.

'Oh yes, your lordship,' again said the lady.

'Does your artist say he's a Frenchman, Mrs. B.?' called out Wagg.

'Well, I'm sure I don't know,' answered the publisher's lady.

'Because, if he does, he's a *quizzin yer*,' cried Mr. Wagg; but nobody saw the pun, which disconcerted somewhat the bashful punster. 'The dinner is from Griggs, in St. Paul's Churchyard; so is Bacon's,' he whispered Pen. 'Bungay writes to give half-a-crown a head more than Bacon,—so does Bacon. They would poison each other's ices if they could get near them; and as for the made-dishes—they are poison. This—hum—ha—this *brimborion*

à la Sévigné is delicious, Mrs. B.,' he said, helping himself to a dish which the undertaker handed to him.

'Well, I'm glad you like it,' Mrs. Bungay answered, blushing, and not knowing whether the name of the dish was actually that which Wagg gave to it, but dimly conscious that that individual was quizzing her. Accordingly she hated Mr. Wagg with female ardour; and would have deposed him from his command over Mr. Bungay's periodical, but that his name was great in the trade, and his reputation in the land considerable.

By the displacement of persons, Warrington had found himself on the right hand of Mrs. Shandon, who sat in plain black silk and faded ornaments by the side of the florid publisher. The sad smile of the lady moved his rough heart to pity. Nobody seemed to interest himself about her: she sat looking at her husband, who himself seemed rather abashed in the presence of some of the company. Wenham and Wagg both knew him and his circumstances. He had worked with the latter, and was immeasurably his superior in wit, genius, and acquirement; but Wagg's star was brilliant in the world, and poor Shandon was unknown there. He could not speak before the noisy talk of the coarser and more successful man; but drank his wine in silence, and as much of it as the people would give him. He was under surveillance. Bungay had warned the undertaker not to fill the captain's glass too often or too full. It was a melancholy precaution that, and the more melancholy that it was necessary. Mrs. Shandon, too, cast alarmed glances across the table to see that her husband did not exceed.

Abashed by the failure of his first pun, for he was impudent and easily disconcerted, Wagg kept his conversation pretty much to Pen during the rest of dinner, and of course chiefly spoke about their neighbours. 'This is one of Bungay's grand field-days,' he said. 'We are all Bungavians here.—Did you read Popjoy's novel? It was an old magazine story written by poor Buzzard years ago, and forgotten here until Mr. Trotter (that is Trotter with the large shirt-collar) fished it out, and bethought him that it was applicable to the late elopement; so Bob wrote a few chapters à propos—Popjoy permitted the use of his name, and I dare say supplied a page here and there—and *Desperation, or the Fugitive Duchess*, made its appearance. The

great fun is to examine Popjoy about his own work, of which he doesn't know a word.*—I say, Popjoy, what a capital passage that is in volume three,—where the cardinal, in disguise, after being converted by the Bishop of London, proposes marriage to the duchess's daughter.'

'Glad you like it,' Popjoy answered; 'it's a favourite bit of my own.'

'There's no such thing in the whole book,' whispered Wagg to Pen. 'Invented it myself. Gad! it wouldn't be a bad plot for a High Church novel.'

'I remember poor Byron, Hobhouse, Trelawny, and myself, dining with Cardinal Mezzocaldo, at Rome,' Captain Sumph began, 'and we had some Orvieto wine for dinner, which Byron liked very much. And I remember how the cardinal regretted that he was a single man. We went to Civita Vecchia two days afterwards, where Byron's yacht was—and, by Jove, the cardinal died within three weeks; and Byron was very sorry, for he rather liked him.'

'A devilish interesting story, Sumph, indeed,' Wagg said.

'You should publish some of those stories, Captain Sumph, you really should. Such a volume would make our friend Bungay's fortune,' Shandon said.

'Why don't you ask Sumph to publish 'em in your new paper—the what-d'ye-call-'em—hey, Shandon?' bawled out Wagg.

'Why don't you ask him to publish 'em in your old magazine, the Thingumbob?' Shandon replied.

'Is there going to be a new paper?' asked Wenham, who knew perfectly well; but was ashamed of his connexion with the Press.

'Bungay going to bring out a paper?' cried Popjoy, who, on the contrary, was proud of his literary reputation and acquaintances. 'You must employ me. Mrs. Bungay, use your influence with him, and make him employ me. Prose or verse—what shall it be? Novels, poems, travels, or leading articles, begad. Anything or everything—only let Bungay pay me, and I'm ready—I am now, my dear Mrs. Bungay, begad now.'

'It's to be called the *Small-Beer Chronicle*,' growled Wagg, 'and little Popjoy is to be engaged for the infantine department.'

'It is to be called the *Pall Mall Gazette*, sir, and we shall be very happy to have you with us,' Shandon said.

'*Pall Mall Gazette*—why *Pall Mall Gazette?*' asked Wagg.

'Because the editor was born at Dublin, the sub-editor at Cork, because the proprietor lives in Paternoster Row, and the paper is published in Catherine Street, Strand. Won't that reason suffice you, Wagg?' Shandon said; he was getting rather angry. 'Everything must have a name. My dog Ponto has got a name. You've got a name, and a name which you deserve, more or less, bedad. Why d'ye grudge the name to our paper?'

'By any other name it would smell as sweet,' said Wagg.

'I'll have ye remember its name's not what-d'ye-call-'em, Mr. Wagg,' said Shandon. 'You know its name well enough, and—and you know mine.'

'And I know your address too,' said Wagg, but this was spoken in an undertone, and the good-natured Irishman was appeased almost in an instant after his ebullition of spleen, and asked Wagg to drink wine with him in a friendly voice.

When the ladies retired from the table, the talk grew louder still; and presently Wenham, in a courtly speech, proposed that everybody should drink to the health of the new journal, eulogizing highly the talents, wit, and learning, of its editor, Captain Shandon. It was his maxim never to lose the support of a newspaper man, and in the course of that evening, he went round and saluted every literary gentleman present with a privy compliment specially addressed to him; informing this one how great an impression had been made in Downing Street by his last article, and telling that one how profoundly his good friend, the Duke of So-and-So, had been struck by the ability of the late numbers.

The evening came to a close, and in spite of all the precautions to the contrary, poor Shandon reeled in his walk, and went home to his new lodgings, with his faithful wife by his side, and the cabman on his box jeering at him. Wenham had a chariot of his own, which he put at Popjoy's service; and the timid Miss Bunion seeing Mr. Wagg, who was her neighbour, about to depart, insisted upon a seat in his carriage, much to that gentleman's discomfiture.

Pen and Warrington walked home together in the moonlight. 'And now,' Warrington said, 'that you have seen the men of letters, tell me, was I far wrong in saying that there are thousands of people in this town, who don't write

books, who are, to the full, as clever and intellectual as people who do ?'

Pen was forced to confess that the literary personages with whom he had become acquainted had not said much, in the course of the night's conversation, that was worthy to be remembered or quoted. In fact, not one word about literature had been said during the whole course of the night :—and it may be whispered to those uninitiated people who are anxious to know the habits and make the acquaintance of men of letters, that there are no race of people who talk about books, or, perhaps, who read books, so little as literary men.*

CHAPTER XXXV

THE 'PALL MALL GAZETTE'

ONSIDERABLE success at first attended the new journal. It was generally stated, that an influential political party supported the paper ; and great names were cited amongst the contributors to its columns. Was there any foundation for these rumours ? We are not at liberty to say whether they were well or ill founded ; but this much we may divulge, that an article upon foreign policy, which was generally attributed to a noble lord, whose connexion with the Foreign Office is very well known, was in reality composed by Captain Shandon, in the parlour of the 'Bear and Staff' public-house near Whitehall Stairs, whither the printer's boy had tracked him, and where a literary ally of his, Mr. Bludyer, had a temporary residence ; and that a series of papers on finance questions, which were universally supposed to be written by a great statesman of the House of Commons, were in reality composed by Mr. George Warrington of the Upper Temple.

That there may have been some dealings between the *Pall Mall Gazette* and this influential party is very possible.

Percy Popjoy (whose father, Lord Falconet, was a member of the party) might be seen not unfrequently ascending the stairs to Warrington's chambers ; and some information appeared in the paper which gave it a character, and could only be got from very peculiar sources. Several poems, feeble in thought, but loud and vigorous in expression, appeared in the *Pall Mall Gazette*, with the signature of 'P. P.' ; and it must be owned that his novel was praised in the new journal in a very outrageous manner.

In the political department of the paper Mr. Pen did not take any share ; but he was a most active literary contributor. The *Pall Mall Gazette* had its offices, as we have heard, in Catherine Street, in the Strand, and hither Pen often came with his manuscripts in his pocket, and with a great deal of bustle and pleasure ; such as a man feels at the outset of his literary career, when to see himself in print is still a novel sensation, and he yet pleases himself to think that his writings are creating some noise in the world.

Here it was that Mr. Jack Finucane, the sub-editor, compiled with paste and scissors the journal of which he was supervisor. With an eagle eye he scanned all the paragraphs of all the newspapers which had anything to do with the world of fashion over which he presided. He didn't let a death or a dinner-party of the aristocracy pass without having the event recorded in the columns of his journal ; and from the most recondite provincial prints, and distant Scotch and Irish newspapers, he fished out astonishing paragraphs and intelligence regarding the upper classes of society. It was a grand, nay, a touching sight, for a philosopher, to see Jack Finucane, Esq., with a plate of meat from the cook-shop, and a glass of porter from the public-house, for his meal, recounting the feasts of the great, as if he had been present at them ; and in tattered trousers and dingy shirt-sleeves, cheerfully describing and arranging the most brilliant fêtes of the world of fashion. The incongruity of Finucane's avocation, and his manners and appearance, amused his new friend Pen. Since he left his own native village, where his rank probably was not very lofty, Jack had seldom seen any society but such as used the parlour of the taverns which he frequented, whereas from his writing you would have supposed that he dined with ambassadors, and that his common lounge

was the bow-window of White's. Errors of description, it is true, occasionally slipped from his pen; but the *Ballinafad Sentinel*, of which he was own correspondent, suffered by these, not the *Pall Mall Gazette*, in which Jack was not permitted to write much, his London chiefs thinking that

the scissors and the paste were better wielded by him than the pen.

Pen took a great deal of pains with the writing of his reviews, and having a pretty fair share of desultory reading, acquired in the early years of his life, an eager fancy and

a keen sense of fun, his articles pleased his chief and the public, and he was proud to think that he deserved the money which he earned. We may be sure that the *Pall Mall Gazette* was taken in regularly at Fairoaks, and read with delight by the two ladies there. It was received at Clavering Park, too, where we know there was a young lady of great literary tastes; and old Doctor Portman himself, to whom the widow sent her paper after she had got her son's articles by heart, signified his approval of Pen's productions, saying that the lad had spirit, taste, and fancy, and wrote, if not like a scholar, at any rate like a gentleman.

And what was the astonishment and delight of our friend Major Pendennis, on walking into one of his clubs, the Regent, where Wenham, Lord Falconet, and some other gentlemen of good reputation and fashion were assembled, to hear them one day talking over a number of the *Pall Mall Gazette*, and of an article which appeared in its columns, making some bitter fun of a book recently published by the wife of a celebrated member of the opposition party. The book in question was a book of travels in Spain and Italy, by the Countess of Muffborough,* in which it was difficult to say which was the most wonderful, the French or the English, in which languages her ladyship wrote indifferently, and upon the blunders of which the critic pounced with delighted mischief. The critic was no other than Pen: he jumped and danced round about his subject with the greatest jocularity and high spirits: he showed up the noble lady's faults with admirable mock gravity and decorum. There was not a word in the article which was not polite and gentlemanlike; and the unfortunate subject of the criticism was scarified and laughed at during the operation. Wenham's bilious countenance was puckered up with malign pleasure as he read the critique. Lady Muffborough had not asked him to her parties during the last year. Lord Falconet giggled and laughed with all his heart: Lord Muffborough and he had been rivals ever since they began life; and these complimented Major Pendennis, who until now had scarcely paid any attention to some hints which his Fairoaks correspondence threw out of 'dear Arthur's constant and severe literary occupations, which I fear may undermine the poor boy's health,' and had thought any notice of Mr. Pen and his newspaper connexions quite below his dignity as a major and a gentleman.

But when the oracular Wenham praised the boy's production; when Lord Falconet, who had had the news from Percy Popjoy, approved of the genius of young Pen; when the great Lord Steyne himself, to whom the major referred the article, laughed and sniggered over it, swore it was capital, and that the Muffborough would writhe under it, like a whale under a harpoon, the major, as in duty bound, began to admire his nephew very much, said, 'By gad, the young rascal had some stuff in him, and would do something; he had always said he would do something;' and with a hand quite tremulous with pleasure, the old gentleman sat down to write to the widow at Fairoaks all that the great folks had said in praise of Pen; and he wrote to the young rascal, too, asking when he would come and eat a chop with his old uncle, and saying that he was commissioned to take him to dinner at Gaunt House, for Lord Steyne liked anybody who could entertain him, whether by his folly, wit, or by his dullness, by his oddity, affectation, good spirits, or any other quality. Pen flung his letter across the table to Warrington; perhaps he was disappointed that the other did not seem to be much affected by it.

The courage of young critics is prodigious: they clamber up to the judgement-seat, and, with scarce a hesitation, give their opinion upon works the most intricate or profound. Had Macaulay's *History* or Herschel's *Astronomy* been put before Pen at this period, he would have looked through the volumes, meditated his opinion over a cigar, and signified his august approval of either author, as if the critic had been their born superior and indulgent master and patron. By the help of the *Biographie Universelle* or the British Museum, he would be able to take a rapid *résumé* of a historical period, and allude to names, dates, and facts, in such a masterly, easy way, as to astonish his mamma at home, who wondered where her boy could have acquired such a prodigious store of reading, and himself, too, when he came to read over his articles two or three months after they had been composed, and when he had forgotten the subject and the books which he had consulted. At that period of his life Mr. Pen owns that he would not have hesitated, at twenty-four hours' notice, to pass an opinion upon the greatest scholars, or to give a judgement upon the *Encyclopaedia*. Luckily he had Warrington to laugh at him and to keep down his impertinence by a constant and

wholesome ridicule, or he might have become conceited beyond all sufferance; for Shandon liked the dash and flippancy of his young aide de camp, and was, indeed, better pleased with Pen's light and brilliant flashes, than with the heavier metal which his elder coadjutor brought to bear.

But though he might justly be blamed on the score of impertinence and a certain prematurity of judgement, Mr. Pen was a perfectly honest critic; a great deal too candid for Mr. Bungay's purposes, indeed, who grumbled sadly at his impartiality. Pen and his chief, the captain, had a dispute upon this subject one day. 'In the name of common sense, Mr. Pendennis,' Shandon asked, 'what have you been doing—praising one of Mr. Bacon's books? Bungay has been with me in a fury this morning, at seeing a laudatory article upon one of the works of the odious firm over the way.'

Pen's eyes opened with wide astonishment. 'Do you mean to say,' he asked, 'that we are to praise no books that Bacon publishes; or that, if the books are good, we are to say they are bad?'

'My good young friend—for what do you suppose a benevolent publisher undertakes a critical journal, to benefit his rivai?' Shandon inquired.

'To benefit himself certainly, but to tell the truth too,' Pen said—'*ruat coelum*, to tell the truth.'

'And my prospectus,' said Shandon, with a laugh and a sneer; 'do you consider that was a work of mathematical accuracy of statement?'

'Pardon me, that is not the question,' Pen said; 'and I don't think you very much care to argue it. I had some qualms of conscience about that same prospectus, and debated the matter with my friend Warrington. We agreed, however,' Pen said, laughing, 'that because the prospectus was rather declamatory and poetical, and the giant was painted upon the show-board rather larger than the original who was inside the caravan, we need not be too scrupulous about this trifling inaccuracy, but might do our part of the show, without loss of character or remorse of conscience. We are the fiddlers, and play our tunes only; you are the showman.'

'And leader of the van,' said Shandon. 'Well, I am glad that your conscience gave you leave to play for us.'

'Yes, but,' said Pen, with a fine sense of the dignity of

his position, 'we are all party men in England, and I will stick to my party like a Briton. I will be as good-natured as you like to our own side; he is a fool who quarrels with his own nest; and I will hit the enemy as hard as you like —but with fair play, captain, if you please. One can't tell all the truth, I suppose; but one can tell nothing but the truth: and I would rather starve, by Jove, and never earn another penny by my pen' (this redoubted instrument had now been in use for some six weeks, and Pen spoke of it with vast enthusiasm and respect) 'than strike an opponent an unfair blow, or, if called upon to place him, rank him below his honest desert.'

'Well, Mr. Pendennis, when we want Bacon smashed, we must get some other hammer to do it,' Shandon said, with fatal good-nature; and very likely thought within himself, 'a few years hence perhaps the young gentleman won't be so squeamish.' The veteran *condottiere* himself was no longer so scrupulous. He had fought and killed on so many a side for many a year past, that remorse had long left him. 'Gad,' said he, 'you've a tender conscience, Mr. Pendennis. It's the luxury of all novices, and I may have had one once myself; but that sort of bloom wears off with the rubbing of the world, and I'm not going to the trouble myself of putting on an artificial complexion, like our pious friend Wenham, or our model of virtue, Wagg.'

'I don't know whether some people's hypocrisy is not better, captain, than other's cynicism.'

'It's more profitable, at any rate,' said the captain, biting his nails. 'That Wenham is as dull a quack as ever quacked: and you see the carriage in which he drove to dinner. Faith, it'll be a long time before Mrs. Shandon will take a drive in her own chariot. God help her, poor thing!' And Pen went away from his chief, after their little dispute and colloquy, pointing his own moral to the captain's tale, and thinking to himself, 'Behold this man, stored with genius, wit, learning, and a hundred good natural gifts: see how he has wrecked them, by paltering with his honesty, and forgetting to respect himself. Wilt thou remember thyself, O Pen? thou art conceited enough! Wilt thou sell thy honour for a bottle? No, by Heaven's grace, we will be honest, whatever befalls, and our mouths shall only speak the truth when they open.'

A punishment, or, at least, a trial, was in store for

PEN HEARS HIMSELF IN PRINT

Mr. Pen. In the very next number of the *Pall Mall Gazette*, Warrington read out, with roars of laughter, an article which by no means amused Arthur Pendennis, who was himself at work with a criticism for the next week's number of the same journal : and in which the *Spring Annual* was ferociously maltreated by some unknown writer. The person of all most cruelly mauled was Pen himself. His verses had not appeared with his own name in the *Spring Annual*, but under an assumed signature. As he had refused to review the book, Shandon had handed it over to Mr. Bludyer,* with directions to that author to dispose of it. And he had done so effectually. Mr. Bludyer, who was a man of very considerable talent, and of a race which, I believe, is quite extinct in the press of our time, had a certain notoriety in his profession, and reputation for savage humour. He smashed and trampled down the poor spring flowers with no more mercy than a bull would have on a parterre ; and having cut up the volume to his heart's content, went and sold it at a bookstall, and purchased a pint of brandy with the proceeds of the volume.

CHAPTER XXXVI

WHERE PEN APPEARS IN TOWN AND COUNTRY*

LET us be allowed to pass over a few months of the history of Mr. Arthur Pendennis's lifetime, during the which, many events may have occurred which were more interesting and exciting to himself, than they would be likely to prove to the reader of his present memoirs. We left him, in his last chapter, regularly entered upon his business as a professional writer, or literary hack, as Mr. Warrington chooses to style himself and his friend ; and we know how the life of any hack, legal or literary, in a curacy, or in a marching regiment, or at a merchant's desk, is dull of routine, and tedious of description. One day's labour

resembles another much too closely. A literary man has often to work for his bread against time, or against his will, or in spite of his health, or of his indolence, or of his repugnance to the subject on which he is called to exert himself, just like any other daily toiler. When you want to make money by Pegasus (as he must, perhaps, who has no other saleable property), farewell poetry and aerial flights: Pegasus only rises now like Mr. Green's balloon,* at periods advertised beforehand, and when the spectators' money has been paid. Pegasus trots in harness, over the stony pavement, and pulls a cart or a cab behind him. Often Pegasus does his work with panting sides and trembling knees, and not seldom gets a cut of the whip from his driver.

Do not let us, however, be too prodigal of our pity upon Pegasus. There is no reason why this animal should be exempt from labour, or illness, or decay, any more than any of the other creatures of God's world. If he gets the whip, Pegasus very often deserves it, and I for one am quite ready to protest with my friend, George Warrington, against the doctrine which some poetical sympathizers are inclined to put forward, viz., that men of letters, and what is called genius, are to be exempt from the prose duties of this daily, bread-wanting, tax-paying life, and are not to be made to work and pay like their neighbours.

Well then, the *Pall Mall Gazette* being duly established, and Arthur Pendennis's merits recognized as a flippant, witty, and amusing critic, he worked away hard every week, preparing reviews of such works as came into his department, and writing his reviews with flippancy certainly, but with honesty, and to the best of his power. It might be that a historian of threescore, who had spent a quarter of a century in composing a work of which our young gentleman disposed in the course of a couple of days' reading at the British Museum, was not altogether fairly treated by such a facile critic; or that a poet, who had been elaborating sublime sonnets and odes until he thought them fit for the public and for fame, was annoyed by two or three dozen pert lines in Mr. Pen's review, in which the poet's claims were settled by the critic, as if the latter were my lord on the bench, and the author a miserable little suitor trembling before him. The actors at the theatres complained of him wofully, too, and very likely he was too

hard upon them. But there was not much harm done after all. It is different now, as we know; but there were so few great historians, or great poets, or great actors, in Pen's time, that scarce any at all came up for judgement before his critical desk. Those who got a little whipping, got what in the main was good for them; not that the judge was any better or wiser than the persons whom he sentenced, or indeed, ever fancied himself so. Pen had a strong sense of humour and justice, and had not therefore an overweening respect for his own works; besides, he had his friend Warrington at his elbow—a terrible critic if the young man was disposed to be conceited, and more savage over Pen than ever he was to those whom he tried at his literary assize.

By these critical labours, and by occasional contributions to leading articles of the journal, when, without wounding his paper, this eminent publicist could conscientiously speak his mind, Mr. Arthur Pendennis gained the sum of four pounds four shillings weekly, and with no small pains and labour. Likewise he furnished magazines and reviews with articles of his composition, and is believed to have been (though on this score he never chooses to speak) London correspondent of the *Chatteris Champion*, which at that time contained some very brilliant and eloquent letters from the metropolis. By these labours the fortunate youth was enabled to earn a sum very nearly equal to four hundred pounds a year; and on the second Christmas after his arrival in London, he actually brought a hundred pounds to his mother, as a dividend upon the debt which he owed to Laura. That Mrs. Pendennis read every word of her son's works, and considered him to be the profoundest thinker, and most elegant writer of the day; that she thought his retribution of the hundred pounds an act of angelic virtue; that she feared he was ruining his health by his labours, and was delighted when he told her of the society which he met, and of the great men of letters and fashion whom he saw, will be imagined by all readers who have seen son-worship amongst mothers, and that charming simplicity of love with which women in the country watch the career of their darlings in London. If John has held such and such a brief; if Tom has been invited to such and such a ball; or George has met this or that great and famous man at dinner; what a delight there is in the hearts

of mothers and sisters at home in Somersetshire! How young Hopeful's letters are read and remembered! What a theme for village talk they give, and friendly congratulation! In the second winter, Pen came for a very brief space, and cheered the widow's heart, and lightened up the lonely house at Fairoaks. Helen had her son all to herself; Laura was away on a visit to old Lady Rockminster; the folks of Clavering Park were absent; the very few old friends of the house, Doctor Portman at their head, called upon Mr. Pen, and treated him with marked respect; between mother and son, it was all fondness, confidence, and affection. It was the happiest fortnight of the widow's whole life; perhaps in the lives of both of them. The holiday was gone only too quickly; and Pen was back in the busy world, and the gentle widow alone again. She sent Arthur's money to Laura: I don't know why this young lady took the opportunity of leaving home when Pen was coming thither, or whether he was the more piqued or relieved by her absence.

He was by this time, by his own merits and his uncle's introductions, pretty well introduced into London, and known both in literary and polite circles. Amongst the former, his fashionable reputation stood him in no little stead; he was considered to be a gentleman of good present means and better expectations, who wrote for his pleasure, than which there cannot be a greater recommendation to a young literary aspirant. Bacon, Bungay and Co. were proud to accept his articles; Mr. Wenham asked him to dinner; Mr. Wagg looked upon him with a favourable eye; and they reported how they met him at the houses of persons of fashion, amongst whom he was pretty welcome, as they did not trouble themselves about his means, present or future; as his appearance and address were good; and as he had got a character for being a clever fellow. Finally, he was asked to one house because he was seen at another house: and thus no small varieties of London life were presented to the young man: he was made familiar with all sorts of people from Paternoster Row to Pimlico, and was as much at home at May Fair dining-tables as at those tavern boards where some of his companions of the pen were accustomed to assemble.

Full of high spirits and curiosity, easily adapting himself to all whom he met, the young fellow pleased himself in

this strange variety and jumble of men, and made himself welcome, or at ease at least, wherever he went. He would breakfast, for instance, at Mr. Plover's of a morning, in company with a peer, a bishop, a parliamentary orator, two blue ladies of fashion, a popular preacher, the author of the last new novel, and the very latest lion imported from Egypt or from America ; and would quit this distinguished society for the back room at the newspaper office, where

pens and ink and the wet proof-sheets were awaiting him. Here would be Finucane, the sub-editor, with the last news from the Row : and Shandon would come in presently, and giving a nod to Pen, would begin scribbling his leading article at the other end of the table, flanked by the pint of sherry, which, when the attendant boy beheld him, was always silently brought for the captain : or Mr. Bludyer's roaring voice would be heard in the front room, where that

truculent critic would impound the books on the counter, in spite of the timid remonstrances of Mr. Midge, the publisher, and after looking through the volumes, would sell them at his accustomed bookstall, and having drunken and dined upon the produce of the sale in a tavern box, would call for ink and paper, and proceed to 'smash' the author of his dinner and the novel. Towards evening Mr. Pen would stroll in the direction of his club, and take up Warrington there for a constitutional walk. This exercise freed the lungs, and gave an appetite for dinner, after which Pen had the privilege to make his bow at some very pleasant houses which were opened to him; or the town before him for amusement. There was the Opera; or the 'Eagle Tavern'; or a ball to go to in May Fair; or a quiet night with a cigar and a book, and a long talk with Warrington; or a wonderful new song at the Back Kitchen;—at this time of his life Mr. Pen beheld all sorts of places and men; and very likely did not know how much he enjoyed himself until long after, when balls gave him no pleasure, neither did farces make him laugh; nor did the tavern joke produce the least excitement in him; nor did the loveliest dancer that ever showed her ankles, cause him to stir from his chair after dinner. At his present mature age, all these pleasures are over, and the times have passed away too. It is but a very, very few years since—but the time is gone, and most of the men. Bludyer will no more bully authors, or cheat landlords of their score. Shandon, the learned and thriftless, the witty and unwise, sleeps his last sleep. They buried honest Doolan the other day: never will he cringe or flatter, never pull long-bow or empty whisky-noggin any more.

The London season was now blooming in its full vigour, and the fashionable newspapers abounded with information regarding the grand banquets, routs, and balls which were enlivening the polite world. Our gracious Sovereign was holding Levées and Drawing-rooms at St. James's: the bow-windows of the clubs were crowded with the heads of respectable, red-faced, newspaper-reading gentlemen: along the Serpentine trailed thousands of carriages: squadrons of dandy horsemen trampled over Rotten Row: everybody was in town, in a word; and of course Major Arthur Pendennis, who was somebody, was not absent.

With his head tied up in a smart bandanna handkerchief, and his meagre carcass enveloped in a brilliant Turkish dressing-gown, the worthy gentleman sat on a certain morning by his fireside, letting his feet gently simmer in a bath, whilst he took his early cup of tea, and perused his *Morning Post*. He could not have faced the day without his two hours' toilette, without his early cup of tea, without his *Morning Post*. I suppose nobody in the world except Morgan, not even Morgan's master himself, knew how feeble and ancient the major was growing, and what numberless little comforts he required.

If men sneer, as our habit is, at the artifices of an old beauty, at her paint, perfumes, ringlets ; at those innumerable, and to us unknown, stratagems with which she is said to remedy the ravages of time and reconstruct the charms whereof years have bereft her ; the ladies, it is to be presumed, are not on their side altogether ignorant that men are vain as well as they, and that the toilettes of old bucks are to the full as elaborate as their own. How is it that old Blushington keeps that constant little rose-tint on his cheeks ; and where does old Blondel get the preparation which makes his silver hair pass for golden ? Have you ever seen Lord Hotspur get off his horse when he thinks nobody is looking ? Taken out of his stirrups, his shiny boots can hardly totter up the steps of Hotspur House. He is a dashing young nobleman still as you see the back of him in Rotten Row ; when you behold him on foot, what an old, old fellow ! Did you ever form to yourself any idea of Dick Lacy (Dick has been Dick these sixty years) in a natural state, and without his stays ? All these men are objects whom the observer of human life and manners may contemplate with as much profit as the most elderly Belgravian Venus, or inveterate May Fair Jezebel. An old reprobate daddy-long-legs, who has never said his prayers (except perhaps in public) these fifty years : an old buck who still clings to as many of the habits of youth as his feeble grasp of health can hold by : who has given up the bottle, but sits with young fellows over it, and tells naughty stories upon toast and water—who has given up beauty, but still talks about it as wickedly as the youngest roué in company—such an old fellow, I say, if any parson in Pimlico or St. James's were to order the beadles to bring him into the middle aisle, and there set him in an arm-chair,

and make a text of him, and preach about him to the congregation, could be turned to a wholesome use for once in his life, and might be surprised to find that some good thoughts came out of him. But we are wandering from our text, the honest major, who sits all this while with his feet cooling in the bath : Morgan takes them out of that place of purification, and dries them daintily, and proceeds to set the old gentleman on his legs, with waistband and wig, starched cravat, and spotless boots and gloves.

It was during these hours of the toilette that Morgan and his employer had their confidential conversations, for they did not meet much at other times of the day—the major abhorring the society of his own chairs and tables in his lodgings; and Morgan, his master's toilette over and letters delivered, had his time very much on his own hands.

This spare time the active and well-mannered gentleman bestowed among the valets and butlers of the nobility, his acquaintance ; and Morgan Pendennis, as he was styled—for by such compound names, gentlemen's gentlemen are called in their private circles—was a frequent and welcome guest at some of the very highest tables in this town. He was a member of two influential clubs in May Fair and Pimlico ; and he was thus enabled to know the whole gossip of the town, and entertain his master very agreeably during the two hours' toilette conversation. He knew a hundred tales and legends regarding persons of the very highest *ton*, whose valets canvass their august secrets, just, my dear madam, as our own parlour-maids and dependants in the kitchen discuss our characters, our stinginess and generosity, our pecuniary means or embarrassments, and our little domestic or connubial tiffs and quarrels. If I leave this manuscript open on my table, I have not the slightest doubt Betty will read it, and they will talk it over in the lower regions to-night ; and to-morrow she will bring in my breakfast with a face of such entire imperturbable innocence, that no mortal could suppose her guilty of playing the spy. If you and the captain have high words upon any subject, which is just possible, the circumstances of the quarrel, and the characters of both of you, will be discussed with impartial eloquence over the kitchen tea-table ; and if Mrs. Smith's maid should by chance be taking a dish of tea with yours, her presence will not undoubtedly act as a restraint upon the discussion in question ; her

opinion will be given with candour; and the next day her mistress will probably know that Captain and Mrs. Jones have been a-quarrelling as usual. Nothing is secret. Take it as a rule that John knows everything: and as in our humble world, so in the greatest: a duke is no more a hero to his valet de chambre than you or I; and his Grace's man at his club, in company doubtless with other men of equal social rank, talks over his master's character and affairs with the ingenuous truthfulness which befits gentlemen who are met together in confidence. Who is a niggard and screws up his money-boxes: who is in the hands of the moneylenders, and is putting his noble name on the back of bills of exchange: who is intimate with whose wife: who wants whom to marry her daughter, and which he won't, no, not at any price:—all these facts gentlemen's confidential gentlemen discuss confidentially, and are known and examined by every person who has any claim to rank in genteel society. In a word, if old Pendennis himself was said to know everything, and was at once admirably scandalous and delightfully discreet; it is but justice to Morgan to say, that a great deal of his master's information was supplied to that worthy man by his valet, who went out and foraged knowledge for him. Indeed, what more effectual plan is there to get a knowledge of London society, than to begin at the foundation—that is, at the kitchen-floor?

So Mr. Morgan and his employer conversed as the latter's toilette proceeded. There had been a Drawing-room on the day previous, and the major read among the presentations that of Lady Clavering by Lady Rockminster, and of Miss Amory by her mother, Lady Clavering,—and in a further part of the paper their dresses were described, with a precision and in a jargon which will puzzle and amuse the antiquary of future generations. The sight of these names carried Pendennis back to the country. 'How long have the Claverings been in London?' he asked; 'pray, Morgan, have you seen any of their people?'

'Sir Francis have sent away his foring man, sir,' Mr. Morgan replied; 'and have took a friend of mine as own man, sir. Indeed, he applied on my reckmendation. You may recklect Towler, sir,—tall red-aired man—but dyes his air. Was groom of the chambers in Lord Levant's famly till his lordship broke hup. It's a fall for Towler, sir;

but pore men can't be particklar,' said the valet, with a pathetic voice.

'Devilish hard on Towler, by gad!' said the major, amused, 'and not pleasant for Lord Levant—he, he!'

'Always knew it was coming, sir. I spoke to you of it Michaelmas was four years: when her ladyship put the diamonds in pawn. It was Towler, sir, took 'em in two cabs to Dobree's—and a good deal of the plate went the same way. Don't you remember seeing of it at Blackwall, with the Levant arms and coronick, and Lord Levant settn oppsit to it at the Marquis of Steyne's dinner? Beg your pardon; did I cut you, sir?'

Morgan was now operating upon the major's chin—he continued the theme while strapping the skilful razor. 'They've took a house in Grosvenor Place, and are coming out strong, sir. Her ladyship's going to give three parties, besides a dinner a week, sir. Her fortune won't stand it—can't stand it.'

'Gad, she had a devilish good cook when I was at Fairoaks,' the major said, with very little compassion for the widow Amory's fortune.

'Marobblan was his name, sir;—Marobblan's gone away, sir,' Morgan said,—and the major, this time with hearty sympathy, said, 'he was devilish sorry to lose him.'

'There's been a tremenjuous row about that Mosseer Mirobblan,' Morgan continued. 'At a ball at Baymouth, sir, bless his impadence, he challenged Mr. Harthur to fight a jewel, sir, which Mr. Arthur was very near knocking him down, and pitchin' him outawinder, and serve him right; but Chevalier Strong, sir, came up and stopped the shindy—I beg pardon, the holtercation, sir—them French cooks has as much pride and hinsolence as if they was real gentlemen.'

'I heard something of that quarrel,' said the major; 'but Mirobolant was not turned off for that?'

'No, sir—that affair, sir, which Mr. Harthur forgave it him and beaved most handsome, was hushed hup: it was about Miss Hamory, sir, that he ad is dismissial. Those French fellers, they fancy everybody is in love with 'em: and he climbed up the large grape-vine to her winder, sir, and was a trying to get in, when he was caught, sir; and Mr. Strong came out, and they got the garden-engine and played on him, and there was no end of a row, sir.'

'Confound his impudence! You don't mean to say Miss

Amory encouraged him,' cried the major, amazed at a peculiar expression in Mr. Morgan's countenance.

Morgan resumed his imperturbable demeanour. 'Know nothing about it, sir. Servants don't know them kind of things the least. Most probbly there was nothing in it—so many lies is told about families—Marobblan went away, bag and baggage, saucepans, and piano, and all—the feller ad a pianna, and wrote potry in French, and he took a

lodging at Clavering, and he hankered about the primises, and it was said that Madam Fribsby, the milliner, brought letters to Miss Hamory, though I don't believe a word about it; nor that he tried to pison hisself with charcoal, which it was all a humbug betwigst him and Madam Fribsby; and he was nearly shot by the keeper in the park.'

In the course of that very day, it chanced that the major had stationed himself in the great window of Bays's Club

in St. James's Street, at the hour in the afternoon when you see a half-score of respectable old bucks similarly recreating themselves (Bays's is rather an old-fashioned place of resort now, and many of its members more than middle-aged; but in the time of the Prince Regent, these old fellows occupied the same window, and were some of the very greatest dandies in this empire)—Major Pendennis was looking from the great window, and spied his nephew Arthur walking down the street in company with his friend Mr. Popjoy.

'Look!' said Popjoy to Pen, as they passed, 'did you ever pass Bays's at four o'clock, without seeing that collection of old fogies? It's a regular museum. They ought to be cast in wax, and set up at Madame Tussaud's—'

'—In a chamber of old horrors by themselves,' Pen said, laughing.

'—In the Chamber of Horrors; Gad, doosid good!' Pop cried. 'They *are* old rogues, most of 'em, and no mistake. There's old Blondel; there's my Uncle Colchicum, the most confounded old sinner in Europe; there's—hullo: there's somebody rapping the window and nodding at us.'

'It's my uncle, the major,' said Pen. 'Is he an old sinner too?'

'Notorious old rogue,' Pop said, wagging his head. '(Notowious old wogue,' he pronounced the words, thereby rendering them much more emphatic.) 'He's beckoning you in; he wants to speak to you.'

'Come in too,' Pen said.

'—Can't,' replied the other. 'Cut Uncle Col. two years ago, about Mademoiselle Frangipane—Ta, ta,' and the young sinner took leave of Pen, and the club of the elder criminals, and sauntered into Blacquière's, an adjacent establishment, frequented by reprobates of his own age.

Colchicum, Blondel, and the senior bucks had just been conversing about the Clavering family, whose appearance in London had formed the subject of Major Pendennis's morning conversation with his valet. Mr. Blondel's house was next to that of Sir Francis Clavering, in Grosvenor Place: giving very good dinners himself, he had remarked some activity in his neighbour's kitchen. Sir Francis, indeed, had a new *chef*, who had come in more than once and dressed Mr. Blondel's dinner for him; that gentleman

having only a remarkably expert female artist permanently engaged in his establishment, and employing such *chefs* of note as happened to be free on the occasion of his grand banquets. 'They go to a devilish expense and see devilish bad company as yet, I hear,' Mr. Blondel said,—'they scour the streets, by gad, to get people to dine with 'em. Champignon says it breaks his heart to serve up a dinner to their society. What a shame it is that those low people should have money at all,' cried Mr. Blondel, whose grandfather had been a reputable leather-breeches maker, and whose father had lent money to the Princes.

'I wish I had fallen in with the widow myself,' sighed Lord Colchicum, 'and not been laid up with that confounded gout at Leghorn.—I would have married the woman myself.—I'm told she has six hundred thousand pounds in the Threes.'*

'Not *quite* so much as that,—I knew her family in India,' —Major Pendennis said. 'I knew her family in India; her father was an enormously rich old indigo-planter,—know all about her,—Clavering has the next estate to ours in the country.—Ha: there's my nephew walking with——'

'With mine,—the infernal young scamp,' said Lord Colchicum, glowering at Popjoy out of his heavy eyebrows; and he turned away from the window as Major Pendennis tapped upon it.

The major was in high good-humour. The sun was bright, the air brisk and invigorating. He had determined upon a visit to Lady Clavering on that day, and bethought him that Arthur would be a good companion for the walk across the Green Park to her ladyship's door. Master Pen was not displeased to accompany his illustrious relative, who pointed out a dozen great men in their brief transit through St. James's Street, and got bows from a duke at a crossing, a bishop (on a cob), and a Cabinet Minister with an umbrella. The duke* gave the elder Pendennis a finger of a pipe-clayed glove to shake, which the major embraced with great veneration; and all Pen's blood tingled, as he found himself in actual communication, as it were, with this famous man (for Pen had possession of the major's left arm, whilst that gentleman's other wing was engaged with his Grace's right), and he wished all Grey Friars' School, all Oxbridge University, all Paternoster Row and the Temple, and Laura and his mother at Fairoaks, could be

standing on each side of the street, to see the meeting between him and his uncle, and the most famous duke in Christendom.

'How do, Pendennis ?—fine day,' were his Grace's remarkable words, and with a nod of his august head he passed on—in a blue frock-coat and spotless white duck trousers, in a white stock, with a shining buckle behind.

Old Pendennis, whose likeness to his Grace has been remarked, began to imitate him unconsciously, after they had parted, speaking with curt sentences, after the manner of the great man. We have all of us, no doubt, met with more than one military officer who has so imitated the manner of a certain great captain of the age; and has, perhaps, changed his own natural character and disposition, because Fate had endowed him with an aquiline nose. In like manner have we not seen many another man pride himself on having a tall forehead and a supposed likeness to Mr. Canning ? many another go through life swelling with self-gratification on account of an imagined resemblance (we say 'imagined,' because that anybody should be *really* like that most beautiful and perfect of men is impossible) to the great and revered George IV.: many third parties, who wore low necks to their dresses because they fancied that Lord Byron and themselves were similar in appearance: and has not the grave closed but lately upon poor Tom Bickerstaff, who having no more imagination than Mr. Joseph Hume,* looked in the glass and fancied himself like Shakespeare ? shaved his forehead so as farther to resemble the immortal bard, wrote tragedies incessantly, and died perfectly crazy—actually perished of his forehead ? These or similar freaks of vanity most people who have frequented the world must have seen in their experience. Pen laughed in his roguish sleeve at the manner in which his uncle began to imitate the great man from whom they had just parted: but Mr. Pen was as vain in his own way, perhaps, as the elder gentleman, and strutted, with a very consequential air of his own, by the major's side.

'Yes, my dear boy,' said the old bachelor, as they sauntered through the Green Park, where many poor children were disporting happily, and errand-boys were playing at toss-halfpenny, and black sheep were grazing in the sunshine, and an actor was learning his part on a bench, and nursery-maids and their charges sauntered here

and there, and several couples were walking in a leisurely manner; 'yes, depend on it, my boy; for a poor man, there is nothing like having good acquaintances. Who were those men with whom you saw me in the bow-window at Bays's? Two were peers of the realm. Hobananob *will* be a peer, as soon as his grand-uncle dies, and he has had his third seizure; and of the other four, not one has less than his seven thousand a year. Did you see that dark blue brougham, with that tremendous stepping horse, waiting at the door of the club? You'll know it again. It is Sir Hugh Trumpington's; he was never known to walk in his life; never appears in the streets on foot—never: and if he is going two doors off, to see his mother, the old dowager (to whom I shall certainly introduce you, for she receives some of the best company in London), gad, sir, he mounts his horse at No. 23, and dismounts again at No. 25A. He is now upstairs, at Bays's, playing picquet with Count Punter: he is the second-best player in England—as well he may be; for he plays every day of his life, except Sundays (for Sir Hugh is an uncommonly religious man), from half-past three till half-past seven, when he dresses for dinner.'

'A very pious manner of spending his time,' Pen said, laughing, and thinking that his uncle was falling into the twaddling state.

'Gad, sir, that is not the question. A man of his estate may employ his time as he chooses. When you are a baronet, a county member, with ten thousand acres of the best land in Cheshire, and such a place as Trumpington (though he never goes there), you may do as you like.'

'And so that was his brougham, sir, was it?' the nephew said, with almost a sneer.

'His brougham—oh aye, yes:—and that brings me back to my point—*revenons à nos moutons*. Yes, begad! *revenons à nos moutons*. Well, that brougham is mine if I choose, between four and seven. Just as much mine as if I jobbed it from Tilbury's,* begad, for thirty pound a month. Sir Hugh is the best-natured fellow in the world; and if it hadn't been so fine an afternoon as it is, you and I would have been in that brougham at this very minute, on our way to Grosvenor Place. That is the benefit of knowing rich men;—I dine for nothing, sir;—I go into the country, and I'm mounted for nothing. Other fellows keep hounds and gamekeepers for me. *Sic vos non vobis*, as we

used to say at Grey Friars, hey? I'm of the opinion of my old friend Leech, of the Forty-fourth; and a devilish good shrewd fellow he was, as most Scotchmen are. Gad, sir, Leech used to say, "He was so poor that he couldn't afford to know a poor man."'

'You don't act up to your principles, uncle,' Pen said, good-naturedly.

'Up to my principles; how, sir?' the major asked, rather testily.

'You would have cut me in St. James's Street, sir,' Pen said, 'were your practice not more benevolent than your theory; you who live with dukes and magnates of the land would take no notice of a poor devil like me.' By which speech we may see that Mr. Pen was getting on in the world, and could flatter as well as laugh in his sleeve.

Major Pendennis was appeased instantly, and very much pleased. He tapped affectionately his nephew's arm on which he was leaning, and said,—'You, sir, you are my flesh and blood! Hang it, sir, I've been very proud of you and very fond of you, but for your confounded follies and extravagances—and wild oats, sir, which I hope you've sown. Yes, begad! I hope you've sown 'em; I hope you've sown 'em, begad! My object, Arthur, is to make a man of you—to see you well placed in the world, as becomes one of your name and my own, sir. You have got yourself a little reputation by your literary talents, which I am very far from undervaluing, though in my time, begad, poetry and genius and that sort of thing were devilish disreputable. There was poor Byron, for instance, who ruined himself, and contracted the worst habits by living with poets and newspaper writers, and people of that kind. But the times are changed now—there's a run upon literature—clever fellows get into the best houses in town, begad! *Tempora mutantur*, sir, and, by Jove, I suppose whatever is is right, as Shakespeare says.'*

Pen did not think fit to tell his uncle who was the author who had made use of that remarkable phrase, and here descending from the Green Park, the pair made their way into Grosvenor Place, and to the door of the mansion occupied there by Sir Francis and Lady Clavering.

The dining-room shutters of this handsome mansion were freshly gilded; the knockers shone gorgeous upon the newly painted door; the balcony before the drawing-room bloomed

with a portable garden of the most beautiful plants, and with flowers, white, and pink, and scarlet; the windows of the upper room (the sacred chamber and dressing-room of my lady, doubtless), and even a pretty little casement of the third story, which keen-sighted Mr. Pen presumed to belong to the virgin bedroom of Miss Blanche Amory, were similarly adorned with floral ornaments, and the whole exterior face of the house presented the most brilliant aspect which fresh new paint, shining plate-glass, newly cleaned bricks, and spotless mortar, could offer to the beholder.

'How Strong must have rejoiced in organizing all this splendour,' thought Pen. He recognized the chevalier's genius in the magnificence before him.

'Lady Clavering is going out for her drive,' the major said. 'We shall only have to leave our pasteboards, Arthur.' He used the word 'pasteboards,' having heard it from some of the ingenuous youth of the nobility about town, and as a modern phrase suited to Pen's tender years. Indeed, as the two gentlemen reached the door, a landau drove up, a magnificent yellow carriage, lined with brocade or satin of a faint cream colour, drawn by wonderful grey horses, with flaming ribbons, and harness blazing all over with crests: no less than three of these heraldic emblems surmounted the coats of arms on the panels, and these shields contained a prodigious number of quarterings, betokening the antiquity and splendour of the house of Clavering and Snell. A coachman in a tight silver wig surmounted the magnificent hammer-cloth (whereon the same arms were worked in bullion), and controlled the prancing greys—a young man still, but of a solemn countenance, with a laced waistcoat, and buckles in his shoes—little buckles, unlike those which John and Jeames, the footmen, wear, and which we know are large, and spread elegantly over the foot.

One of the leaves of the hall door was opened, and John—one of the largest of his race—was leaning against the door pillar, with his ambrosial hair powdered, his legs crossed; beautiful, silk-stockinged; in his hand his cane, gold-headed, *dolichoskion*.* Jeames was invisible, but near at hand, waiting in the hall, with the gentleman who does not wear livery, and ready to fling down the roll of hair-cloth over which her ladyship was to step to her carriage.

These things and men, the which to tell of demands time, are seen in the glance of a practised eye ; and, in fact, the major and Pen had scarcely crossed the street, when the second *battant* of the door flew open ; the horse-hair carpet tumbled down the doorsteps to those of the carriage ; John was opening it on one side of the emblazoned door, and Jeames on the other, and two ladies, attired in the highest style of fashion, and accompanied by a third, who carried a Blenheim spaniel, yelping in a light blue ribbon, came forth to ascend the carriage.

Miss Amory was the first to enter, which she did with aerial lightness, and took the place which she liked best. Lady Clavering next followed, but her ladyship was more mature of age and heavy of foot, and one of those feet, attired in a green satin boot, with some part of a stocking, which was very fine, whatever the ankle might be which it encircled, might be seen swaying on the carriage-step, as her ladyship leaned for support on the arm of the unbending Jeames, by the enraptured observer of female beauty who happened to be passing at the time of this imposing ceremonial.

The Pendennises senior and junior beheld those charms as they came up to the door—the major looking grave and courtly, and Pen somewhat abashed at the carriage and its owners ; for he thought of sundry little passages at Clavering, which made his heart beat rather quick.

At that moment Lady Clavering, looking round, saw the pair—she was on the first carriage-step, and would have been in the vehicle in another second, but she gave a start backwards (which caused some of the powder to fly from the hair of ambrosial Jeames), and crying out, 'Lor, if it isn't Arthur Pendennis and the old major !' jumped back to terra firma directly, and holding out two fat hands, encased in tight orange-coloured gloves, the good-natured woman warmly greeted the major and his nephew.

'Come in, both of you.—Why haven't you been before ? —Get out, Blanche, and come and see your old friends.— Oh, I'm *so* glad to see you. We've been waitin' and waitin' for you ever so long. Come in, luncheon ain't gone down,' cried out this hospitable lady, squeezing Pen's hand in both hers (she had dropped the major's after a brief wrench of recognition), and Blanche, casting up her eyes towards the chimneys, descended from the carriage presently, with a

timid, blushing, appealing look, and gave a little hand to Major Pendennis.

The companion with the spaniel looked about irresolute, and doubting whether she should not take Fido his airing; but she too turned right about face and entered the house, after Lady Clavering, her daughter, and the two gentlemen. And the carriage, with the prancing greys, was left unoccupied, save by the coachman in the silver wig.

CHAPTER XXXVII

IN WHICH THE SYLPH REAPPEARS

BETTER folks than Morgan, the valet, were not so well instructed as that gentleman regarding the amount of Lady Clavering's riches; and the legend in London, upon her ladyship's arrival in the polite metropolis, was, that her fortune was enormous. Indigo factories, opium clippers, banks overflowing with rupees, diamonds and jewels of native princes, and vast sums of interest paid by them for loans contracted by themselves or their predecessors to Lady Clavering's father, were mentioned as sources of her wealth. Her account at her London banker's was positively known, and the sum embraced so many ciphers as to create as many oh's of admiration in the wondering hearer. It was a known fact that an envoy from an Indian prince, a Colonel Altamont, the Nawaub of Lucknow's prime favourite, an extraordinary man, who had, it was said, embraced Mahometanism, and undergone a thousand wild and perilous adventures, was at present in this country, trying to negotiate with the Begum Clavering, the sale of the Nawaub's celebrated nose-ring diamond, 'the light of the Dewan.'

Under the title of the Begum, Lady Clavering's fame

began to spread in London before she herself descended upon the capital, and as it has been the boast of Delolme, and Blackstone, and all panegyrists of the British Constitution, that we admit into our aristocracy merit of every kind, and that the lowliest-born man, if he but deserve it, may wear the robes of a peer, and sit alongside of a Cavendish or a Stanley : so it ought to be the boast of our good society, that haughty though it be, naturally jealous of its privileges, and careful who shall be admitted into its circle, yet, if an individual be but rich enough, all barriers are instantly removed, and he or she is welcomed, as from her wealth he merits to be. This fact shows our British independence and honest feeling—our higher orders are not such mere haughty aristocrats as the ignorant represent them : on the contrary, if a man have money, they will hold out their hands to him, eat his dinners, dance at his balls, marry his daughters, or give their own lovely girls to his sons, as affably as your commonest *roturier* would do.

As he had superintended the arrangements of the country mansion, our friend, the Chevalier Strong, gave the benefit of his taste and advice to the fashionable London upholsterers, who prepared the town house for the reception of the Clavering family. In the decoration of this elegant abode, honest Strong's soul rejoiced as much as if he had been himself its proprietor. He hung and rehung the pictures, he studied the positions of sofas, he had interviews with wine-merchants and purveyors who were to supply the new establishment ; and at the same time the baronet's factotum and confidential friend took the opportunity of furnishing his own chambers, and stocking his snug little cellar : his friends complimented him upon the neatness of the former ; and the select guests who came in to share Strong's cutlet now found a bottle of excellent claret to accompany the meal. The chevalier was now, as he said, ' in clover ': he had a very comfortable set of rooms in Shepherd's Inn. He was waited on by a former Spanish Legionary and comrade of his whom he had left at a breach of a Spanish fort, and found at a crossing in Tottenham Court Road, and whom he had elevated to the rank of body-servant to himself and to the chum who, at present, shared his lodgings. This was no other than the favourite of the Nawaub of Lucknow, the valiant Colonel Altamont.

No man was less curious, or at any rate more discreet,

than Ned Strong, and he did not care to inquire into the mysterious connexion which, very soon after their first meeting at Baymouth, was established between Sir Francis Clavering and the envoy of the Nawaub. The latter knew some secret regarding the former, which put Clavering into his power, somehow; and Strong, who knew that his patron's early life had been rather irregular, and that his career with his regiment in India had not been brilliant, supposed that the colonel, who swore he knew Clavering well at Calcutta, had some hold upon Sir Francis, to which the latter was forced to yield. In truth, Strong had long understood Sir Francis Clavering's character, as that of a man utterly weak in purpose, in principle, and intellect, a moral and physical trifler and poltroon.

With poor Clavering, his excellency had had one or two interviews after their Baymouth meeting, the nature of which conversations the baronet did not confide to Strong: although he sent letters to Altamont by that gentleman, who was his ambassador in all sorts of affairs. On one of these occasions the Nawaub's envoy must have been in an exceeding ill-humour; for he crushed Clavering's letter in his hand, and said with his own particular manner and emphasis:—'A hundred be hanged! I'll have no more letters nor no more shilly-shally. Tell Clavering I'll have a thousand, or by Jove I'll split, and burst him all to atoms. Let him give me a thousand and I'll go abroad, and I give you my honour as a gentleman, I'll not ask him for no more for a year. Give him that message from me, Strong, my boy; and tell him if the money ain't here next Friday at twelve o'clock, as sure as my name's what it is, I'll have a paragraph in the newspaper on Saturday, and next week I'll blow up the whole concern.'

Strong carried back these words to his principal, on whom their effect was such that actually on the day and hour appointed, the chevalier made his appearance once more at Altamont's hotel at Baymouth, with the sum of money required. Altamont was a gentleman, he said, and behaved as such; he paid his bill at the inn, and the Baymouth paper announced his departure on a foreign tour. Strong saw him embark at Dover. 'It must be forgery at the very least,' he thought, 'that has put Clavering into this fellow's power, and the colonel has got the bill.'

Before the year was out, however, this happy country

saw the colonel once more upon its shores. A confounded run on the red had finished him, he said, at Baden-Baden: no gentleman could stand against a colour coming up fourteen times. He had been obliged to draw upon Sir Francis Clavering for means of returning home: and Clavering, though pressed for money (for he had election expenses, had set up his establishment in the country, and was engaged in furnishing his London house), yet found means to accept Colonel Altamont's bill, though evidently very much against his will; for in Strong's hearing, Sir Francis wished to Heaven, with many curses, that the colonel could have been locked up in a debtor's jail in Germany for life, so that he might never be troubled again.

These sums for the colonel Sir Francis was obliged to raise without the knowledge of his wife; for though perfectly liberal, nay, sumptuous in her expenditure, the good lady had inherited a tolerable aptitude for business along with the large fortune of her father, Snell, and gave to her husband only such a handsome allowance as she thought befitted a gentleman of his rank. Now and again she would give him a present, or pay an outstanding gambling debt; but she always exacted a pretty accurate account of the moneys so required; and respecting the subsidies to the colonel, Clavering fairly told Strong that he *couldn't* speak to his wife.

Part of Mr. Strong's business in life was to procure this money and other sums for his patron. And in the chevalier's apartments, in Shepherd's Inn, many negotiations took place between gentlemen of the moneyed world and Sir Francis Clavering; and many valuable bank-notes and pieces of stamped paper were passed between them. When a man has been in the habit of getting in debt from his early youth, and of exchanging his promises to pay at twelve months against present sums of money, it would seem as if no piece of good fortune ever permanently benefited him: a little while after the advent of prosperity, the money-lender is pretty certain to be in the house again, and the bills with the old signature in the market. Clavering found it more convenient to see these gentry at Strong's lodgings than at his own; and such was the chevalier's friendship for the baronet, that although he did not possess a shilling of his own, his name might be seen as the drawer of almost all the bills of exchange which Sir Francis Claver-

ing accepted. Having drawn Clavering's bills, he got them discounted 'in the City.' When they became due he parleyed with the bill-holders, and gave them instalments of their debt, or got time in exchange for fresh acceptances. Regularly or irregularly, gentlemen must live somehow: and as we read how, the other day, at Comorn,* the troops forming that garrison were gay and lively, acted plays, danced at balls, and consumed their rations; though menaced with an assault from the enemy without the walls, and with a gallows if the Austrians were successful, —so there are hundreds of gallant spirits in this town, walking about in good spirits, dining every day in tolerable gaiety and plenty, and going to sleep comfortably; with a bailiff always more or less near, and a rope of debt round their necks—the which trifling inconveniences, Ned Strong, the old soldier, bore very easily.

But we shall have another opportunity of making acquaintance with these and some other interesting inhabitants of Shepherd's Inn, and in the meanwhile are keeping Lady Clavering and her friends too long waiting on the doorsteps of Grosvenor Place.

First they went into the gorgeous dining-room, fitted up, Lady Clavering couldn't for goodness gracious tell why, in the middle-aged style, 'unless,' said her good-natured ladyship, laughing, 'because me and Clavering are middle-aged people;'—and here they were offered the copious remains of the luncheon of which Lady Clavering and Blanche had just partaken. When nobody was near, our little Sylphide, who scarcely ate at dinner more than the six grains of rice of Amina, the friend of the Ghouls in the *Arabian Nights*, was most active with her knife and fork, and consumed a very substantial portion of mutton cutlets: in which piece of hypocrisy it is believed she resembled other young ladies of fashion. Pen and his uncle declined the refection, but they admired the dining-room with fitting compliments, and pronounced it 'very chaste,' that being the proper phrase. There were, indeed, high-backed Dutch chairs of the seventeenth century; there was a sculptured carved buffet of the sixteenth; there was a sideboard robbed out of the carved work of a church in the Low Countries, and a large brass cathedral lamp over the round oak table; there were old family portraits from Wardour Street* and tapestry from France, bits of armour, double-handed swords

and battle-axes made of *carton-pierre*, looking-glasses, statuettes of saints, and Dresden china—nothing, in a word, could be chaster. Behind the dining-room was the library, fitted with busts and books all of a size, and wonderful easy-chairs, and solemn bronzes in the severe classic style. Here it was that, guarded by double doors, Sir Francis smoked cigars, and read *Bell's Life in London*, and went to sleep after dinner, when he was not smoking over the billiard-table at his clubs, or punting at the gambling-houses in St. James's.

But what could equal the chaste splendour of the drawing-rooms ?—the carpets were so magnificently fluffy that your foot made no more noise on them than your shadow : on their white ground bloomed roses and tulips as big as warming-pans : about the room were high chairs and low chairs, bandy-legged chairs, chairs so attenuated that it was a wonder any but a sylph could sit upon them, marqueterie-tables covered with marvellous gimcracks, china ornaments of all ages and countries, bronzes, gilt daggers, Books of Beauty, yataghans, Turkish papooshes, and boxes of Parisian bonbons. Wherever you sat down there were Dresden shepherds and shepherdesses convenient at your elbow ; there were, moreover, light blue poodles and ducks and cocks and hens in porcelain ; there were nymphs by Boucher, and shepherdesses by Greuze, very chaste indeed ; there were muslin curtains and brocade curtains, gilt cages with parroquets and love-birds, two squealing cockatoos, each out-squealing and out-chattering the other ; a clock singing tunes on a console-table, and another booming the hours like Great Tom, on the mantelpiece—there was, in a word, everything that comfort could desire, and the most elegant taste devise. A London drawing-room, fitted up without regard to expense, is surely one of the noblest and most curious sights of the present day. The Romans of the Lower Empire, the dear marchionesses and countesses of Louis XV., could scarcely have had a finer taste than our modern folks exhibit ; and everybody who saw Lady Clavering's reception-rooms was forced to confess that they were most elegant ; and that the prettiest rooms in London —Lady Harley Quin's, Lady Hanway Wardour's, or Mrs. Hodge-Podgson's own, the great Railroad Croesus's wife*—were not fitted up with a more consummate 'chastity.'

Poor Lady Clavering, meanwhile, knew little regarding

these things, and had a sad want of respect for the splendours around her. 'I only know they cost a precious deal of money, major,' she said to her guest, 'and that I don't advise you to try one of them gossamer gilt chairs : *I* came down on one the night we gave our second dinner-party. Why didn't you come and see us before ? We'd have asked you to it.'

'You would have liked to see mamma break a chair, wouldn't you, Mr. Pendennis ?' dear Blanche said, with a sneer. She was angry because Pen was talking and laughing with mamma, because mamma had made a number of blunders in describing the house—for a hundred other good reasons.

'I should like to have been by to give Lady Clavering my arm if she had need of it,' Pen answered, with a bow and a blush.

'*Quel preux chevalier !*' cried the Sylphide, tossing up her little head.

'I have a fellow-feeling with those who fall, remember,' Pen said. 'I suffered myself very much from doing so once.'

'And you went home to Laura to console you,' said Miss Amory. Pen winced. He did not like the remembrance of the consolation which Laura had given to him, nor was he very well pleased to find that his rebuff in that quarter was known to the world : so as he had nothing to say in reply, he began to be immensely interested in the furniture round about him, and to praise Lady Clavering's taste with all his might.

'Me, don't praise me,' said honest Lady Clavering, 'it's all the upholsterer's doings, and Captain Strong's ; they did it all while we was at the Park—and—and—Lady Rockminster has been here, and says the salongs are very well,' said Lady Clavering, with an air and tone of great deference.

'My cousin Laura has been staying with her,' Pen said. 'It's not the dowager : it is *the* Lady Rockminster.'

'Indeed !' cried Major Pendennis, when he heard this great name of fashion. 'If you have her ladyship's approval, Lady Clavering, you cannot be far wrong. No, no, you cannot be far wrong. Lady Rockminster, I should say, Arthur, is the very centre of the circle of fashion and taste. The rooms *are* beautiful indeed !' and the major's voice

hushed as he spoke of this great lady, and he looked round and surveyed the apartments awfully and respectfully, as if he had been at church.

'Yes, Lady Rockminster has took us up,' said Lady Clavering.

'Taken us up, mamma,' cried Blanche, in a shrill voice.

'Well, taken us up, then,' said my lady; 'it's very kind of her, and I dare say we shall like it when we git used to it, only at first one don't fancy being took—well, taken up, at all. She is going to give our balls for us; and wants to invite all our dinners. But I won't stand that. I will have my old friends, and I won't let her send all the cards out, and sit mum at the head of my own table. You must come to me, Arthur and major—come, let me see, on the 14th.—It ain't one of our grand dinners, Blanche,' she said, looking round at her daughter, who bit her lips and frowned very savagely for a sylphide.

The major, with a smile and a bow, said he would much rather come to a quiet meeting than to a grand dinner. He had had enough of those large entertainments, and preferred the simplicity of the home circle.

'I always think a dinner's the best the second day,' said Lady Clavering, thinking to mend her first speech. 'On the 14th we'll be quite a snug little party;' at which second blunder Miss Blanche clasped her hands in despair, and said, 'Oh, mamma, *vous êtes incorrigible*.' Major Pendennis vowed that he liked snug dinners of all things in the world, and confounded her ladyship's impudence for daring to ask such a man as *him* to a second day's dinner. But he was a man of an economical turn of mind, and bethinking himself that he could throw over these people if anything better should offer, he accepted with the blandest air. As for Pen, he was not a diner-out of thirty years' standing as yet, and the idea of a fine feast in a fine house was still perfectly welcome to him.

'What was that pretty little quarrel which engaged itself between your worship and Miss Amory?' the major asked of Pen, as they walked away together. 'I thought you used to be *au mieux* in that quarter.'

'Used to be,' answered Pen, with a dandified air, 'is a vague phrase regarding a woman. "Was" and "is" are two very different terms, sir, as regards women's hearts, especially.'

'Egad, they change as we do,' cried the elder. 'When we took the Cape of Good Hope,* I recollect there was a lady who talked of poisoning herself for your humble servant; and, begad, in three months, she ran away from her husband with somebody else. Don't get yourself entangled with that Miss Amory. She is forward, affected, and underbred; and her character is somewhat—never mind what. But don't think of her; ten thousand pound won't do for you. What, my good fellow, is ten thousand pound? I would scarcely pay that girl's milliner's bill with the interest of the money.'

'You seem to be a connoisseur in millinery, uncle,' Pen said.

'I was, sir, I was,' replied the senior; 'and the old war-horse, you know, never hears the sound of a trumpet but he begins to he, he!—you understand,'—and he gave a killing though somewhat superannuated leer and bow to a carriage that passed them and entered the Park.

'Lady Catherine Martingale's carriage,' he said, 'mon-s'ous fine girls the daughters, though, gad, I remember their mother a thousand times handsomer. No, Arthur, my dear fellow, with your person and expectations, you ought to make a good *coup* in marriage some day or other; and though I wouldn't have this repeated at Fairoaks, you rogue, ha! ha! a reputation for a little wickedness, and for being an *homme dangereux*, don't hurt a young fellow with the women. They like it, sir—they hate a milksop. . . . Young men must be young men, you know. But for marriage,' continued the veteran moralist, 'that is a very different matter. Marry a woman with money. I've told you before it is as easy to get a rich wife as a poor one; and a doosed deal more comfortable to sit down to a well-cooked dinner, with your little entrées nicely served, than to have nothing but a damned cold leg of mutton between you and your wife. We shall have a good dinner on the 14th, when we dine with Sir Francis Clavering: stick to that, my boy, in your relations with the family. Cultivate 'em, but keep 'em for dining. No more of your youthful follies and nonsense about love in a cottage.'

'It must be a cottage with a double coach-house, a cottage of gentility, sir,' said Pen, quoting the hackneyed ballad of the *Devil's Walk*:* but his uncle did not know that poem (though, perhaps, he might be leading Pen upon

the very promenade in question), and went on with his philosophical remarks, very much pleased with the aptness of the pupil to whom he addressed them. Indeed, Arthur Pendennis was a clever fellow, who took his colour very readily from his neighbour, and found the adaptation only too easy.

Warrington, the grumbler, growled out that Pen was becoming such a puppy that soon there would be no bearing him. But the truth is, the young man's success and dashing manners pleased his elder companion. He liked to see Pen gay and spirited, and brimful of health, and life, and hope; as a man who has long since left off being amused with clown and harlequin still gets a pleasure in watching a child at a pantomime. Mr. Pen's former sulkiness disappeared with his better fortune: and he bloomed as the sun began to shine upon him.

CHAPTER XXXVIII

IN WHICH COLONEL ALTAMONT APPEARS AND DISAPPEARS

N the day appointed, Major Pendennis, who had formed no better engagement, and Arthur, who desired none, arrived together to dine with Sir Francis Clavering. The only tenants of the drawing-room when Pen and his uncle reached it, were Sir Francis and his wife, and our friend Captain Strong, whom Arthur was very glad to see, though the major looked very sulkily at Strong, being by no means well pleased to sit down to dinner with Clavering's d—— house-steward, as he irreverently called Strong. But Mr. Welbore Welbore, Clavering's country neighbour and brother member of Parliament,

speedily arriving, Pendennis the elder was somewhat appeased, for Welbore, though perfectly dull, and taking no more part in the conversation at dinner than the footman behind his chair, was a respectable country gentleman of ancient family and seven thousand a year; and the major felt always at ease in such society. To these were added other persons of note: the Dowager Lady Rockminster, who had her reasons for being well with the Clavering family, and the Lady Agnes Foker, with her son Mr. Harry, our old acquaintance. Mr. Pynsent could not come, his parliamentary duties keeping him at the House, duties which sat upon the two other senators very lightly. Miss Blanche Amory was the last of the company who made her appearance. She was dressed in a killing white silk dress, which displayed her pearly shoulders to the utmost advantage. Foker whispered to Pen, who regarded her with eyes of evident admiration, that he considered her 'a stunner.' She chose to be very gracious to Arthur upon this day, and held out her hand most cordially, and talked about dear Fairoaks, and asked for dear Laura and his mother, and said she was longing to go back to the country, and in fact was entirely simple, affectionate, and artless.

Harry Foker thought he had never seen anybody so amiable and delightful. Not accustomed much to the society of ladies, and ordinarily being dumb in their presence, he found that he could speak before Miss Amory, and became uncommonly lively and talkative, even before the dinner was announced and the party descended to the lower rooms. He would have longed to give his arm to the fair Blanche, and conduct her down the broad carpeted stair; but she fell to the lot of Pen upon this occasion, Mr. Foker being appointed to escort Mrs. Welbore Welbore, in consequence of his superior rank as an earl's grandson.

But though he was separated from the object of his desire during the passage downstairs, the delighted Foker found himself by Miss Amory's side at the dinner-table, and flattered himself that he had manœuvred very well in securing that happy place. It may be that the move was not his, but that it was made by another person. Blanche had thus the two young men, one on each side of her, and each tried to render himself gallant and agreeable.

Foker's mamma, from her place, surveying her darling boy, was surprised at his vivacity. Harry talked con-

stantly to his fair neighbour about the topics of the day.

'Seen Taglioni in *The Sylphide*, Miss Amory ?* Bring me that soupreme of Volile again, if you please' (this was addressed to the attendant near him), 'very good: can't think where the soupremes come fıom; what becomes of the legs of the fowls, I wonder? She's clipping in *The Sylphide*, ain't she?' and he began very kindly to hum the pretty air which pervades that prettiest of all ballets, now faded into the past with that most beautiful and gracious of all dancers. Will the young folks ever see anything so charming, anything so classic, anything like Taglioni?

'Miss Amory is a sylph herself,' said Mr. Pen.

'What a delightful tenor voice you have, Mr. Foker!' said the young lady. 'I am sure you have been well taught. I sing a little myself. I should like to sing with you.'

Pen remembered that words very similar had been addressed to himself by the young lady, and that she had liked to sing with him in former days. And sneering within himself, he wondered with how many other gentlemen she had sung duets since his time? But he did not think fit to put this awkward question aloud: and only said, with the very tenderest air which he could assume, 'I should like to hear you sing again, Miss Blanche. I never heard a voice I liked so well as yours, I think.'

'I thought you liked Laura's,' said Miss Blanche.

'Laura's is a contralto: and that voice is very often out, you know,' Pen said bitterly. 'I have heard a great deal of music in London,' he continued. 'I'm tired of those professional people—they sing too loud—or I have grown too old or too blasé. One grows old very soon, in London, Miss Amory. And like all old fellows, I only care for the songs I heard in my youth.'

'I like English music best. I don't care for foreign songs much. Get me some saddle of mutton,' said Mr. Foker.

'I adore English ballads of all things,' said Miss Amory.

'Sing me one of the old songs after dinner, will you?' said Pen, with an imploring voice.

'Shall I sing you an English song after dinner?' asked the Sylphide, turning to Mr. Foker. 'I will, if you will promise to come up soon:' and she gave him a perfect broadside of her eyes.

'*I'll* come up after dinner, fast enough,' he said simply.

'I don't care about much wine afterwards—I take my whack at dinner—I mean my share, you know ; and when I have had as much as I want, I toddle up to tea. I'm a domestic character, Miss Amory—my habits are simple—and when I'm pleased I'm generally in a good humour, ain't I, Pen ?—that jelly, if you please—not that one, the other with the cherries inside. How the doose *do* they get those cherries inside the jellies ?' In this way the artless youth prattled on : and Miss Amory listened to him with inexhaustible good-humour. When the ladies took their departure for the upper regions, Blanche made the two young men promise faithfully to quit the table soon, and departed with kind glances to each. She dropped her gloves on Foker's side of the table, and her handkerchief on Pen's. Each had some little attention paid to him ; her politeness to Mr. Foker was perhaps a little more encouraging than her kindness to Arthur : but the benevolent little creature did her best to make both the gentlemen happy. Foker caught her last glance as she rushed out of the door ; that bright look passed over Mr. Strong's broad white waistcoat, and shot straight at Harry Foker's. The door closed on the charmer : he sat down with a sigh, and swallowed a bumper of claret.

As the dinner at which Pen and his uncle took their places was not one of our grand parties, it had been served at a considerably earlier hour than those ceremonial banquets of the London season, which custom has ordained shall scarcely take place before nine o'clock ; and the company being small, and Miss Blanche, anxious to betake herself to her piano in the drawing-room, giving constant hints to her mother to retreat,—Lady Clavering made that signal very speedily, so that it was quite daylight yet when the ladies reached the upper apartments, from the flower-embroidered balconies of which they could command a view of the two parks, of the poor couples and children still sauntering in the one, and of the equipages of ladies and the horses of dandies passing through the arch of the other. The sun, in a word, had not set behind the elms of Kensington Gardens, and was still gilding the statue erected by the ladies of England in honour of His Grace the Duke of Wellington, when Lady Clavering and her female friends left the gentlemen drinking wine.

The windows of the dining-room were opened to let in the fresh air, and afforded to the passers-by in the street a pleasant, or, perhaps, tantalizing view of six gentlemen in white waistcoats, with a quantity of decanters and a variety of fruits before them—little boys, as they passed and jumped up at the area-railings, and took a peep, said to one another, 'Mi hi, Jim, shouldn't you like to be there, and have a cut of that there pineapple ?'—the horses and carriages of the nobility and gentry passed by, conveying them to Belgravian toilettes : the policeman, with clamping feet, patrolled up and down before the mansion : the shades of evening began to fall : the gasman came and lighted the lamps before Sir Francis's door : the butler entered the dining-room, and illuminated the antique gothic chandelier over the antique carved oak dining-table : so that from outside the house you looked inwards upon a night scene of feasting and wax candles ; and from within you beheld a vision of a calm summer evening, and the wall of St. James's Park, and the sky above, in which a star or two was just beginning to twinkle.

Jeames, with folded legs, leaning against the door-pillar of his master's abode, looked forth musingly upon the latter tranquil sight : whilst a spectator, clinging to the railings, examined the former scene. Policeman X,* passing, gave his attention to neither, but fixed it upon the individual holding by the railings, and gazing into Sir Francis Clavering's dining-room, where Strong was laughing and talking away, making the conversation for the party.

The man at the railings was very gorgeously attired with chains, jewellery, and waistcoats, which the illumination from the house lighted up to great advantage ; his boots were shiny ; he had brass buttons to his coat, and large white wristbands over his knuckles ; and indeed looked so grand, that X imagined he beheld a member of Parliament, or a person of consideration, before him. Whatever his rank, however, the M.P., or person of consideration, was considerably excited by wine ; for he lurched and reeled somewhat in his gait, and his hat was cocked over his wild and bloodshot eyes in a manner which no sober hat ever could assume. His copious black hair was evidently surreptitious, and his whiskers of the Tyrian purple.

As Strong's laughter, following after one of his own *gros mots*, came ringing out of window, this gentleman without

laughed and sniggered in the queerest way likewise, and he slapped his thigh and winked at Jeames pensive in the portico, as much as to say, 'Plush, my boy, isn't that a good story ?'

Jeames's attention had been gradually drawn from the moon in the heavens to this sublunary scene ; and he was puzzled and alarmed by the appearance of the man in shiny boots. 'A holtercation,' he remarked, afterwards, in the servants'-hall—'a holtercation with a feller in the streets is never no good ; and indeed, he was not hired for any such purpose.' So, having surveyed the man for some time, who went on laughing, reeling, nodding his head with tipsy knowingness, Jeames looked out of the portico, and softly called 'Pleaceman,' and beckoned to that officer.

X marched up resolute, with one Berlin glove stuck in his belt-side, and Jeames simply pointed with his index-finger to the individual who was laughing against the railings. Not one single word more than 'Pleaceman' did he say, but stood there in the calm summer evening, pointing calmly : a grand sight.

X advanced to the individual and said, 'Now, sir, will you have the kindness to move hon ?'

The individual, who was in perfect good-humour, did not appear to hear one word which Policeman X uttered, but nodded and waggled his grinning head at Strong, until his hat almost fell from his head over the area railings.

'Now, sir, move on, do you hear?' cries X, in a much more peremptory tone, and he touched the stranger gently with one of the fingers enclosed in the gauntlets of the Berlin woof.

He of the many rings instantly started, or rather staggered back, into what is called an attitude of self-defence, and in that position began the operation which is entitled 'squaring,' at Policeman X, and showed himself brave and warlike, if unsteady. 'Hullo ! keep your hands off a gentleman,' he said, with an oath which need not be repeated.

'Move on out of this,' said X, 'and don't be a-blocking up the pavement, staring into gentlemen's dining-rooms.'

'Not stare—ho, ho,—not stare—that *is* a good one,' replied the other, with a satiric laugh and sneer,—'Who's to prevent me from staring, looking at my friends, if I like ? not you, old highlows.'

'Friends ! I dessay. Move on,' answered X.

'If you touch me, I'll pitch into you, I will,' roared the other. 'I tell you I know 'em all.—That's Sir Francis Clavering, Baronet, M.P.,—I know him, and he knows me—and that's Strong, and that's the young chap that made the row at the ball. I say, Strong, Strong!'

'It's that d—— Altamont,' cried Sir Francis within, with a start and a guilty look; and Strong also, with a look of annoyance, got up from the table, and ran out to the intruder.

A gentleman in a white waistcoat, running out from a dining-room bare-headed, a policeman, and an individual decently attired, engaged in almost fisticuffs on the pavement, were enough to make a crowd, even in that quiet neighbourhood, at half-past eight o'clock in the evening, and a small mob began to assemble before Sir Francis Clavering's door. 'For God's sake, come in,' Strong said, seizing his acquaintance's arm. 'Send for a cab, James, if you please,' he added in an under-voice to that domestic; and carrying the excited gentleman out of the street, the outer door was closed upon him, and the small crowd began to move away.

Mr. Strong had intended to convey the stranger into Sir Francis's private sitting-room, where the hats of the male guests were awaiting them, and having there soothed his friend by bland conversation, to have carried him off as soon as the cab arrived—but the new-comer was in a great state of wrath at the indignity which had been put upon him; and when Strong would have led him into the second door, said in a tipsy voice, '*That* ain't the door—that's the dining-room door—where the drink's going on—and I'll go and have some, by Jove; I'll go and have some.' At this audacity the butler stood aghast in the hall, and placed himself before the door: but it opened behind him, and the master of the house made his appearance, with anxious looks.

'I *will* have some,—by —— I will,' the intruder was roaring out, as Sir Francis came forward. 'Hullo! Clavering, I say I'm come to have some wine with you; hey! old boy—hey, old corkscrew? Get us a bottle of the yellow seal, you old thief—the very best—a hundred rupees a dozen, and no mistake.'

The host reflected a moment over his company. There is only Welbore, Pendennis, and those two lads, he thought—and with a forced laugh and piteous look, he said,—'Well, Altamont, come in. I am very glad to see you, I'm sure.'

COLONEL ALTAMONT REFUSES TO MOVE ON

Colonel Altamont, for the intelligent reader has doubtless long ere this discovered in the stranger His Excellency the Ambassador of the Nawaub of Lucknow, reeled into the dining-room, with a triumphant look towards Jeames, the footman, which seemed to say, 'There, sir, what do you think of that? *Now*, am I a gentleman or no?' and sank down into the first vacant chair. Sir Francis Clavering timidly stammered out the colonel's name to his guest Mr. Welbore Welbore, and His Excellency began drinking wine forthwith and gazing round upon the company, now with the most wonderful frowns, and anon with the blandest smiles, and hiccupped remarks encomiastic of the drink which he was imbibing.

'Very singular man. Has resided long in a native court in India,' Strong said, with great gravity, the Chevalier's presence of mind never deserting him—'in those Indian courts they get very singular habits.'

'Very,' said Major Pendennis dryly, and wondering what in goodness' name was the company into which he had got.

Mr. Foker was pleased with the new-comer. 'It's the man who would sing the Malay song at the Back Kitchen,' he whispered to Pen. 'Try this pine, sir,' he then said to Colonel Altamont, 'it's uncommonly fine.'

'Pines—I've seen 'em feed pigs on pines,' said the colonel.

'All the Nawaub of Lucknow's pigs are fed on pines,' Strong whispered to Major Pendennis.

'Oh, of course,' the major answered. Sir Francis Clavering was, in the meanwhile, endeavouring to make an excuse to his brother guest for the new-comer's condition, and muttered something regarding Altamont, that he was an extraordinary character, very eccentric, very—had Indian habits—didn't understand the rules of English society—to which old Welbore, a shrewd old gentleman, who drank his wine with great regularity, said, 'that seemed pretty clear.'

Then, the colonel seeing Pen's honest face, regarded it for a while with as much steadiness as became his condition; and said, 'I know you, too, young fellow. I remember you. Baymouth ball, by Jingo. Wanted to fight the Frenchman. *I* remember you;' and he laughed, and he squared with his fists, and seemed hugely amused in the drunken depths of his mind, as these recollections passed, or rather, reeled across it.

'Mr. Pendennis, you remember Colonel Altamont, at Baymouth?' Strong said: upon which Pen, bowing rather stiffly, said, 'he had the pleasure of remembering that circumstance perfectly.'

'*What's* his name?' cried the colonel. Strong named Mr. Pendennis again.

'Pendennis!—Pendennis be hanged!' Altamont roared out, to the surprise of everyone, and thumping with his fist on the table.

'My name is also Pendennis, sir,' said the major, whose dignity was exceedingly mortified by the evening's events—that he, Major Pendennis, should have been asked to such a party, and that a drunken man should have been introduced to it. 'My name is Pendennis, and I will be obliged to you not to curse it too loudly.'

The tipsy man turned round to look at him, and as he looked, it appeared as if Colonel Altamont suddenly grew sober. He put his hand across his forehead, and in doing so, displaced somewhat the black wig which he wore; and his eyes stared fiercely at the major, who, in his turn, like a resolute old warrior as he was, looked at his opponent very keenly and steadily. At the end of the mutual inspection, Altamont began to button up his brass-buttoned coat, and rising up from his chair, suddenly, and to the company's astonishment, reeled towards the door, and issued from it, followed by Strong: all that the latter heard him utter was —'Captain Beak!* Captain Beak, by jingo!'

There had not passed above a quarter of an hour from his strange appearance to his equally sudden departure. The two young men and the baronet's other guest wondered at the scene, and could find no explanation for it. Clavering seemed exceedingly pale and agitated, and turned with looks of almost terror towards Major Pendennis. The latter had been eyeing his host keenly for a minute or two. 'Do you know him?' asked Sir Francis of the major.

'I am sure I have seen the fellow,' the major replied, looking as if he, too, was puzzled. 'Yes, I have it. He was a deserter from the Horse Artillery, who got into the Nawaub's service. I remember his face quite well.'

'Oh!' said Clavering, with a sigh which indicated immense relief of mind, and the major looked at him with a twinkle of his sharp old eyes. The cab which Strong had

desired to be called, drove away with the chevalier and Colonel Altamont; coffee was brought to the remaining gentlemen, and they went upstairs to the ladies in the drawing-room, Foker declaring confidentially to Pen that 'this was the rummest go he ever saw,' which decision, Pen said, laughing, 'showed great discrimination on Mr. Foker's part.'

Then, according to her promise, Miss Amory made music for the young men. Foker was enraptured with her performance, and kindly joined in the airs which she sang, when he happened to be acquainted with them. Pen affected to talk aside with others of the party, but Blanche brought him quickly to the piano, by singing some of his own words—those which we have given in a previous number, indeed, and which the sylphide had herself, she said, set to music. I don't know whether the air was hers, or how much of it was arranged for her by Signor Twankidillo, from whom she took lessons: but good or bad, original or otherwise, it delighted Mr. Pen, who remained by her side, and turned the leaves now for her most assiduously—'Gad! how I wish I could write verses like you, Pen,' Foker sighed afterwards to his companion. 'If I could do 'em, wouldn't I, that's all? But I never was a dab at writing, you see, and I'm sorry I was so idle when I was at school.'

No mention was made before the ladies of the curious little scene which had been transacted below stairs; although Pen was just on the point of describing it to Miss Amory, when that young lady inquired for Captain Strong, who she wished should join her in a duet. But chancing to look up towards Sir Francis Clavering, Arthur saw a peculiar expression of alarm in the baronet's ordinarily vacuous face, and discreetly held his tongue. It was rather a dull evening. Welbore went to sleep, as he always did at music and after dinner: nor did Major Pendennis entertain the ladies with copious anecdotes and endless little scandalous stories, as his wont was, but sat silent for the most part, and appeared to be listening to the music, and watching the fair young performer.

The hour of departure having arrived, the major rose, regretting that so delightful an evening should have passed away so quickly, and addressed a particularly fine compliment to Miss Amory, upon her splendid talents as a singer.

'Your daughter, Lady Clavering,' he said to that lady, 'is a perfect nightingale—a perfect nightingale, begad! I have scarcely ever heard anything equal to her, and her pronunciation of every language—begad, of every language—seems to me to be perfect; and the best houses in London must open before a young lady who has such talents, and, allow an old fellow to say, Miss Amory, such a face.'

Blanche was as much astonished by these compliments as Pen was, to whom his uncle, a little time since, had been speaking in very disparaging terms of the sylph. The major and the two young men walked home together, after Mr. Foker had placed his mother in her carriage, and procured a light for an enormous cigar.

The young gentleman's company, or his tobacco, did not appear to be agreeable to Major Pendennis, who eyed him askance several times, and with a look which plainly indicated that he wished Mr. Foker would take his leave; but Foker hung on resolutely to the uncle and nephew, even until they came to the former's door in Bury Street, where the major wished the lads good-night.

'And I say, Pen,' he said, in a confidential whisper, calling his nephew back, 'mind you make a point of calling in Grosvenor Place to-morrow. They've been uncommonly civil; mons'ously civil and kind.'

Pen promised and wondered, and the major's door having been closed upon him by Morgan, Foker took Pen's arm, and walked with him for some time, silently puffing his cigar. At last, when they had reached Charing Cross on Arthur's way home to the Temple, Harry Foker relieved himself, and broke out with that eulogium upon poetry, and those regrets regarding a misspent youth, which have just been mentioned. And all the way along the Strand, and up to the door of Pen's very staircase, in Lamb Court, Temple, young Harry Foker did not cease to speak about singing and Blanche Amory.

CHAPTER XXXIX

RELATES TO MR. HARRY FOKER'S AFFAIRS

SINCE that fatal but delightful night in Grosvenor Place, Mr. Harry Foker's heart had been in such a state of agitation as you would hardly have thought so great a philosopher could endure. When we remember what good advice he had given to Pen in former days, how an early wisdom and knowledge of the world had manifested itself in the gifted youth; how a constant course of self-indulgence, such as becomes a gentleman of his means and expectations, ought by right to have increased his cynicism, and made him, with every succeeding day of his life, care less and less for every individual in the world, with the single exception of Mr. Harry Foker, one may wonder that he should fall into the mishap to which most of us are subject once or twice in our lives, and disquiet his great mind about a woman. But Foker, though early wise, was still a man. He could no more escape the common lot than Achilles, or Ajax, or Lord Nelson, or Adam our first father, and now, his time being come, young Harry became a victim to Love, the All-conqueror.

When he went to the Back Kitchen that night after quitting Arthur Pendennis at his staircase-door in Lamb Court, the gin-twist and devilled turkey had no charms for him, the jokes of his companions fell flatly on his ear; and when Mr. Hodgen, the singer of 'The Body-Snatcher,' had a new chant even more dreadful and humorous than that famous composition, Foker, although he appeared his

friend, and said, 'Bravo, Hodgen,' as common politeness and his position as one of the chiefs of the Back Kitchen bound him to do, yet never distinctly heard one word of the song, which, under its title of 'The Cat in the Cupboard,' Hodgen has since rendered so famous. Late and very tired, he slipped into his private apartments at home and sought the downy pillow, but his slumbers were disturbed by the fever of his soul,[1] and the image of Miss Amory.

Heavens, how stale and distasteful his former pursuits and friendships appeared to him! He had not been, up to the present time, much accustomed to the society of females of his own rank in life. When he spoke of such, he called them 'modest women.' That virtue which, let us hope, they possessed, had not hitherto compensated to Mr. Foker for the absence of more lively qualities which most of his own relatives did not enjoy, and which he found in mesdemoiselles the ladies of the theatre. His mother, though good and tender, did not amuse her boy; his cousins, the daughters of his maternal uncle, the respectable Earl of Rosherville, wearied him beyond measure. One was blue, and a geologist; one was a horsewoman, and smoked cigars; one was exceedingly Low Church, and had the most heterodox views on religious matters; at least, so the other said, who was herself of the very Highest Church faction, and made the cupboard in her room into an oratory, and fasted on every Friday in the year. Their paternal house of Drummington, Foker could very seldom be got to visit. He swore he had rather go the treadmill* than stay there. He was not much beloved by the inhabitants. Lord Erith, Lord Rosherville's heir, considered his cousin a low person, of deplorably vulgar habits and manners; while Foker, and with equal reason, voted Erith a prig and a dullard, the nightcap of the House of Commons, the Speaker's opprobrium, the dreariest of philanthropic spouters. Nor could George Robert, Earl of Gravesend and Rosherville, ever forget that on one evening when he condescended to play at billiards with his nephew, that young gentleman poked his lordship in his side with his cue, and said, 'Well, old cock, I've seen many a bad stroke in my life, but I never saw such a bad one as that there.' He played the game out with angelic sweetness of temper, for Harry was his guest as well as his nephew;

but he was nearly having a fit in the night ; and he kept to his own rooms until young Harry quitted Drummington on his return to Oxbridge, where the interesting youth was finishing his education at the time when the occurrence took place. It was an awful blow to the venerable earl ; the circumstance was never alluded to in the family ; he shunned Foker whenever he came to see them in London

or in the country, and could hardly be brought to gasp out a 'How d'ye do ?' to the young blasphemer. But he would not break his sister Agnes's heart, by banishing Harry from the family altogether ; nor, indeed, could he afford to break with Mr. Foker, senior, between whom and his lordship there had been many private transactions, producing an exchange of bank cheques from Mr. Foker,

and autographs from the earl himself, with the letters I O U written over his illustrious signature.

Besides the four daughters of Lord Gravesend whose various qualities have been enumerated in the former paragraph, his lordship was blessed with a fifth girl, the Lady Ann Milton, who, from her earliest years and nursery, had been destined to a peculiar position in life. It was ordained between her parents and her aunt, that when Mr. Harry Foker attained a proper age, Lady Ann should become his wife. The idea had been familiar to her mind when she yet wore pinafores, and when Harry, the dirtiest of little boys, used to come back with black eyes from school to Drummington, or to his father's house of Logwood, where Lady Ann lived much with her aunt. Both of the young people coincided with the arrangement proposed by the elders, without any protests or difficulty. It no more entered Lady Ann's mind to question the order of her father, than it would have entered Esther's to dispute the commands of Ahasuerus. The heir-apparent of the house of Foker was also obedient, for when the old gentleman said, 'Harry, your uncle and I have agreed that when you're of a proper age you'll marry Lady Ann. She won't have any money, but she's good blood, and a good one to look at, and I shall make you comfortable. If you refuse, you'll have your mother's jointure, and two hundred a year during my life'—Harry, who knew that his sire, though a man of few words, was yet implicitly to be trusted, acquiesced at once in the parental decree, and said, 'Well, sir, if Ann's agreeable, I say ditto. She's not a bad-looking girl.'

'And she has the best blood in England, sir. Your mother's blood, your own blood, sir,' said the brewer. 'There's nothing like it, sir.'

'Well, sir, as you like it,' Harry replied. 'When you want me, please ring the bell. Only there's no hurry, and I hope you'll give us a long day. I should like to have my fling out before I marry.'

'Fling away, Harry,' answered the benevolent father. 'Nobody prevents you, do they?' And so very little more was said upon this subject, and Mr. Harry pursued those amusements in life which suited him best; and hung up a little picture of his cousin in his sitting-room, amidst the French prints, the favourite actresses and dancers,

the racing and coaching works of art, which suited his taste and formed his gallery. It was an insignificant little picture, representing a simple round face with ringlets; and it made, as it must be confessed, a very poor figure by the side of Mademoiselle Petitot, dancing over a rainbow, or Mademoiselle Redowa, grinning in red boots and a lancer's cap.

Being engaged and disposed of, Lady Ann Milton did not go out so much in the world as her sisters: and often stayed at home in London at the family house in Gaunt Square, when her mamma with the other ladies went abroad. They talked and they danced with one man after another, and the men came and went, and the stories about them were various. But there was only this one story about Ann: she was engaged to Harry Foker: she never was to think about anybody else. It was not a very amusing story.

Well, the instant Foker awoke on the day after Lady Clavering's dinner, there was Blanche's image glaring upon him, with its clear grey eyes and winning smile. There was her tune ringing in his ears, 'Yet round about the spot, ofttimes I hover, ofttimes I hover,'* which poor Foker began piteously to hum, as he sat up in his bed under the crimson silken coverlet. Opposite him was a French print, of a Turkish lady and her Greek lover, surprised by a venerable Ottoman, the lady's husband; on the other wall was a French print of a gentleman and lady, riding and kissing each other at the full gallop; all round the chaste bedroom were more French prints, either portraits of gauzy nymphs of the Opera or lovely illustrations of the novels; or, mayhap, an English *chef-d'œuvre* or two, in which Miss Pinckney of T. R. E. O.* would be represented in tight pantaloons in her favourite page part; or Miss Rougemont as Venus; their value enhanced by the signature of these ladies, Maria Pinckney, or Frederica Rougemont, inscribed underneath the prints in an exquisite facsimile. Such were the pictures in which honest Harry delighted. He was no worse than many of his neighbours; he was an idle, jovial, kindly, fast man about town; and if his rooms were rather profusely decorated with works of French art, so that simple Lady Agnes, his mamma, on entering the apartments where her darling sat enveloped in fragrant clouds of Latakia, was often bewildered by the

novelties which she beheld there, why, it must be remembered, that he was richer than most young men, and could better afford to gratify his taste.

A letter from Miss Pinckney, written in a very *dégagé* style of spelling and handwriting, scrawling freely over the filigree paper, and commencing by calling Mr. Harry her dear Hokey-pokey-fokey, lay on his bed-table by his side, amidst keys, sovereigns, cigar-cases, and a bit of verbena, which Miss Amory had given him, and reminding him of the arrival of the day when he was 'to stand that dinner at the "Elefant and Castle," at Richmond, which he had promised;' a card for a private box at Miss Rougemont's approaching benefit, a bundle of tickets for 'Ben Budgeon's night, the North Lancashire Pippin, at Martin Faunce's, the "Three-cornered Hat," in St. Martin's Lane; where Conkey Sam, Dick the Nailor, the Deadman (the Worcestershire Nobber), would put on the gloves, and the lovers of the good old British sport were invited to attend' —these and sundry other memoirs of Mr. Foker's pursuits and pleasures lay on the table by his side when he woke.

Ah! how faint all these pleasures seemed now. What did he care for Conkey Sam or the Worcestershire Nobber? What for the French prints ogling him from all sides of the room; those regular stunning slap-up out-and-outers? And Pinckney spelling bad, and calling him Hokey-fokey, confound her impudence? The idea of being engaged to a dinner at the 'Elephant and Castle' at Richmond, with that old woman (who was seven-and-thirty years old, if she was a day), filled his mind with dreary disgust now, instead of that pleasure which he had only yesterday expected to find from the entertainment.

When his fond mamma beheld her boy that morning, she remarked on the pallor of his cheek, and the general gloom of his aspect. 'Why do you go on playing billiards at that wicked Spratt's?' Lady Agnes asked. 'My dearest child, those billiards will kill you, I'm sure they will.'

'It isn't the billiards,' Harry said gloomily.

'Then it's the dreadful Back Kitchen,' said the Lady Agnes. 'I've often thought, d'you know, Harry, of writing to the landlady, and begging that she would have the kindness to put only very little wine in the negus which you take, and see that you have your shawl on before you get into your brougham.'

'Do, ma'am. Mrs. Cutts is a most kind motherly woman,' Harry said. 'But it isn't the Back Kitchen, neither,' he added, with a ghastly sigh.

As Lady Agnes never denied her son anything, and fell into all his ways with the fondest acquiescence, she was rewarded by a perfect confidence on young Harry's part, who never thought to disguise from her a knowledge of the haunts which he frequented; and, on the contrary, brought her home choice anecdotes from the clubs and billiard-rooms, which the simple lady relished, if she did not understand. 'My son goes to Spratt's,' she would say to her confidential friends. 'All the young men go to Spratt's after their balls. It is *de rigueur*, my dear; and they play billiards as they used to play macao and hazard in Mr. Fox's time. Yes, my dear father often told me that they sat up *always* until nine o'clock the next morning with Mr. Fox at Brookes's, whom I remember at Drummington, when I was a little girl, in a buff waistcoat and black satin small-clothes. My brother Erith never played as a young man, nor sat up late—he had no health for it; but my boy must do as everybody does, you know. Yes, and then he often goes to a place called the Back Kitchen, frequented by all the wits and authors, you know, whom one does not see in society, but whom it is a great privilege and pleasure for Harry to meet, and there he hears the questions of the day discussed; and my dear father often said that it was our duty to encourage literature, and he had hoped to see the late Dr. Johnson at Drummington, only Dr. Johnson died. Yes, and Mr. Sheridan came over, and drank a great deal of wine,—everybody drank a great deal of wine in those days,—and papa's wine-merchant's bill was ten times as much as Erith's is, who gets it as he wants it from Fortnum and Mason's, and doesn't keep any stock at all.'

'That was an uncommon good dinner we had yesterday, ma'am,' the artful Harry broke out. 'Their clear soup's better than ours. Moufflet will put too much tarragon into everything. The *suprême de volaille* was very good—uncommon, and the sweets were better than Moufflet's sweets. Did you taste the plombière, ma'am, and the maraschino jelly? Stunningly good that maraschino jelly!'

Lady Agnes expressed her agreement in these, as in

almost all other sentiments of her son, who continued the artful conversation, saying :

'Very handsome house that of the Claverings. Furniture, I should say, got up regardless of expense. Magnificent display of plate, ma'am.' The lady assented to all these propositions.

'Very nice people the Claverings.'

'Hm !' said Lady Agnes.

'I know what you mean. Lady C. ain't distangy exactly, but she is very good-natured.'

'Oh, very,' mamma said, who was herself one of the most good-natured of women.

'And Sir Francis, he don't talk much before ladies ; but after dinner he comes out uncommon strong, ma'am—a highly agreeable, well-informed man. When will you ask them to dinner ? Look out for an early day, ma'am ;' and looking into Lady Agnes's pocket-book, he chose a day only a fortnight hence (an age that fortnight seemed to the young gentleman), when the Claverings were to be invited to Grosvenor Street.

The obedient Lady Agnes wrote the required invitation. She was accustomed to do so without consulting her husband, who had his own society and habits, and who left his wife to see her own friends alone. Harry looked at the card : but there was an omission in the invitation which did not please him.

'You have not asked Miss What-d'ye-call-'em—Miss Emery; Lady Clavering's daughter.'

'Oh, that little creature !' Lady Agnes cried. 'No, I think not, Harry.'

'We must ask Miss Amory,' Foker said. 'I—I want to ask Pendennis ; and—and he's very sweet upon her. Don't you think she sings very well, ma'am ?'

'I thought her rather forward, and didn't listen to her singing. She only sang at you and Mr. Pendennis, it seemed to me. But I will ask her if you wish, Harry,' and so Miss Amory's name was written on the card with her mother's.

This piece of diplomacy being triumphantly executed, Harry embraced his fond parent with the utmost affection, and retired to his own apartments, where he stretched himself on his ottoman, and lay brooding silently, sighing for the day which was to bring the fair Miss Amory under

his paternal roof, and devising a hundred wild schemes for meeting her.

On his return from making the grand tour, Mr. Foker, junior, had brought with him a polyglot valet, who took the place of Stoopid, and condescended to wait at dinner, attired in shirt-fronts of worked muslin, with many gold studs and chains.[2] This man, who was of no particular country, and spoke all languages indifferently ill, made himself useful to Mr. Harry in a variety of ways,—read all the artless youth's correspondence, knew his favourite haunts and the addresses of his acquaintance, and officiated at the private dinners which the young gentleman gave. As Harry lay upon his sofa after his interview with his mamma, robed in a wonderful dressing-gown, and puffing his pipe in gloomy silence, Anatole, too, must have remarked that something affected his master's spirits; though he did not betray any ill-bred sympathy with Harry's agitation of mind. When Harry began to dress himself in his out-of-door morning costume, he was very hard indeed to please, and particularly severe and snappish about his toilette: he tried, and cursed, pantaloons of many different stripes, checks, and colours: all the boots were villainously varnished; the shirts too 'loud' in pattern. He scented his linen and person with peculiar richness this day; and what must have been the valet's astonishment, when, after some blushing and hesitation on Harry's part, the young gentleman asked, 'I say, Anatole, when I engaged you, didn't you—hem—didn't you say that you could dress—hem—dress hair?'

The valet said, 'Yes, he could.'

'*Cherchy alors une paire de tongs—et—curly-moi un pew*,' Mr. Foker said, in an easy manner; and the valet, wondering whether his master was in love or was going masquerading, went in search of the articles,—first from the old butler who waited upon Mr. Foker, senior, on whose bald pate the tongs would have scarcely found a hundred hairs to seize, and finally of the lady who had the charge of the meek auburn fronts of the Lady Agnes. And the tongs being got, Monsieur Anatole twisted his young master's locks until he had made Harry's head as curly as a negro's; after which the youth dressed himself with the utmost care and splendour, and proceeded to sally out.

'At what dime sall I order de drag, sir, to be to Miss

Pingney's door, sir?' the attendant whispered as his master was going forth.

'Confound her!—Put the dinner off—I can't go!' said Foker. 'No, hang it—I must go. Poyntz and Rougemont, and ever so many more are coming. The drag at Pelham Corner at six o'clock, Anatole.'

The drag was not one of Mr. Foker's own equipages, but was hired from a livery stable for festive purposes; Foker, however, put his own carriage into requisition that morning, and for what purpose does the kind reader suppose? Why, to drive down to Lamb Court, Temple, taking Grosvenor Place by the way (which lies in the exact direction of the Temple from Grosvenor Street, as everybody knows), where he just had the pleasure of peeping upwards at Miss Amory's pink window curtains, having achieved which satisfactory feat, he drove off to Pen's chambers. Why did he want to see his dear friend Pen so much? Why did he yearn and long after him? and did it seem necessary to Foker's very existence that he should see Pen that morning, having parted with him in perfect health on the night previous? Pen had lived two years in London, and Foker had not paid half a dozen visits to his chambers. What sent him thither now in such a hurry?

What?—If any young ladies read this page, I have only to inform them that when the same mishap befalls them, which now had for more than twelve hours befallen Harry Foker, people will grow interesting to them for whom they did not care sixpence on the day before; as on the other hand persons of whom they fancied themselves fond will be found to have become insipid and disagreeable. Then your dearest Eliza or Maria of the other day, to whom you wrote letters and sent locks of hair yards long, will on a sudden be as indifferent to you as your stupidest relation; whilst, on the contrary, about *his* relations you will begin to feel such a warm interest! such a loving desire to ingratiate yourself with *his* mamma! such a liking for that dear kind old man *his* father! If He is in the habit of visiting at any house, what advances you will make in order to visit there too. If He has a married sister you will like to spend long mornings with her. You will fatigue your servant by sending notes to her, for which there will be the most pressing occasion, twice or thrice in a day. You will cry if your mamma objects to your going too

MR. FOKER PREPARING TO CONQUER

often to see His family. The only one of them you will dislike is perhaps his younger brother, who is at home for the holidays, and who will persist in staying in the room when you come to see your dear new-found friend, his darling second sister. Something like this will happen to you, young ladies, or at any rate, let us hope it may. Yes, you must go through the hot fits and the cold fits of that pretty fever. Your mothers, if they would acknowledge it, have passed through it before you were born, your dear papa being the object of the passion, of course,—who could it be but he? And as you suffer it, so will your brothers, in their way,—and after their kind. More selfish than you: more eager and headstrong than you: they will rush on their destiny when the doomed charmer makes her appearance. Or if they don't, and you don't, Heaven help you! As the gambler said of his dice, to love and win is the best thing, to love and lose is the next best.[3] Now, then, if you ask why Harry Foker, Esq., was in such a hurry to see Arthur Pendennis, and felt such a sudden value and esteem for him, there is no difficulty in saying it was because Pen had become really valuable in Mr. Foker's eyes: because if Pen was not the rose, he had yet been near that fragrant flower of love. Was not he in the habit of going to her house in London? Did he not live near her in the country?—know all about the enchantress? What, I wonder, would Lady Ann Milton, Mr. Foker's cousin and *prétendue*, have said, if her ladyship had known all that was going on in the bosom of that funny little gentleman?

Alas! when Foker reached Lamb Court, leaving his carriage for the admiration of the little clerks who were lounging in the archway that leads thence into Flag Court, which leads into Upper Temple Lane, Warrington was in the chambers, but Pen was absent. Pen was gone to the printing-office to see his proofs. 'Would Foker have a pipe, and should the laundress go to the Cock and get him some beer?'—Warrington asked, remarking with a pleased surprise the splendid toilet of this scented and shiny-booted young aristocrat: but Foker had not the slightest wish for beer or tobacco: he had very important business: he rushed away to the *Pall Mall Gazette* office, still bent upon finding Pen. Pen had quitted that place. Foker wanted him that they might go together to call upon Lady

Clavering. Foker went away disconsolate, and whiled away an hour or two vaguely at clubs; and when it was time to pay a visit, he thought it would be but decent and polite to drive to Grosvenor Place and leave a card upon Lady Clavering. He had not the courage to ask to see her when the door was opened; he only delivered two cards, with Mr. Henry Foker engraved upon them, to Jeames, in a speechless agony. Jeames received the tickets bowing his powdered head. The varnished doors closed upon him. The beloved object was as far as ever from him, though so near. He thought he heard the tones of a piano and of a siren singing, coming from the drawing-room and sweeping over the balcony-shubbery of geraniums. He would have liked to stop and listen, but it might not be. 'Drive to Tattersall's,' he said to the groom, in a voice smothered with emotion,—'and bring my pony round,' he added, as the man drove rapidly away.

As good luck would have it, that splendid barouche of Lady Clavering's, which has been inadequately described in a former chapter, drove up to her ladyship's door just as Foker mounted the pony which was in waiting for him. He bestrode the fiery animal, and dodged about the arch of the Green Park, keeping the carriage well in view, until he saw Lady Clavering enter, and with her—whose could be that angel form, but the enchantress's, clad in a sort of gossamer, with a pink bonnet and a light-blue parasol,—but Miss Amory?

The carriage took its fair owners to Madame Rigodon's cap and lace shop, to Mrs. Wolsey's berlin worsted shop,—who knows to what other resorts of female commerce? Then it went and took ices at Hunter's,* for Lady Clavering was somewhat florid in her tastes and amusements, and not only liked to go abroad in the most showy carriage in London, but that the public should see her in it too. And so, in a white bonnet with a yellow feather, she ate a large pink ice in the sunshine before Hunter's door, till Foker on his pony, and the red jacket who accompanied him, were almost tired of dodging.

Then at last she made her way into the Park, and the rapid Foker made his dash forward. What to do? Just to get a nod of recognition from Miss Amory and her mother; to cross them a half-dozen times in the drive; to watch and ogle them from the other side of the ditch,

where the horsemen assemble when the band plays in Kensington Gardens. What is the use of looking at a woman in a pink bonnet across a ditch? What is the earthly good to be got out of a nod of the head? Strange that men will be contented with such pleasures, or if not contented, at least that they will be so eager in seeking them. Not one word did Harry, he so fluent of conversation ordinarily, change with his charmer on that day. Mutely he beheld her return to her carriage, and drive away among rather ironical salutes from the young men in the Park. One said that the Indian widow was making the paternal rupees spin rapidly; another said that she ought to have burned herself alive, and left the money to her daughter. This one asked who Clavering was?—and old Tom Eales, who knew everybody, and never missed a day in the Park on his grey cob, kindly said that Clavering had come into an estate over head and heels in mortgage: that there were dev'lish ugly stories about him when he was a young man, and that it was reported of him that he had a share in a gambling-house, and had certainly shown the white feather in his regiment. 'He plays still; he is in a hell every night almost,' Mr. Eales added.

'I should think so, since his marriage,' said a wag.

'He gives devilish good dinners,' said Foker, striking up for the honour of his host of yesterday.

'I dare say, and I dare say he doesn't ask Eales,' the wag said. 'I say, Eales, do you dine at Clavering's,—at the Begum's?'

'*I* dine there?' said Mr. Eales, who would have dined with Beelzebub if sure of a good cook, and when he came away, would have painted his host blacker than fate had made him.

'You might, you know, although you *do* abuse him so,' continued the wag. 'They say it's very pleasant. Clavering goes to sleep after dinner; the Begum gets tipsy with cherry-brandy, and the young lady sings songs to the young gentlemen. She sings well, don't she, Fo?'

'Slap up,' said Fo. 'I tell you what, Poyntz, she sings like a—what-d'ye-call-'um—you know what I mean—like a mermaid, you know, but that's not their name.'

'I never heard a mermaid sing,' Mr. Poyntz the wag replied. 'Who ever heard a mermaid? Eales, you are an old fellow, did you?'

'Don't make a lark of me, hang it, Poyntz,' said Foker, turning red, and with tears almost in his eyes; 'you know what I mean: it's those what's-his-names—in Homer, you know. I never said I was a good scholar.'

'And nobody ever said it of you, my boy,' Mr. Poyntz remarked; and Foker, striking spurs into his pony, cantered away down Rotten Row, his mind agitated with various emotions, ambitions, mortifications. He *was* sorry that he had not been good at his books in early life—that he might have cut out all those chaps who were about her, and who talked the languages, and wrote poetry, and painted pictures in her album, and—and that.—'What am I,' thought little Foker, 'compared to her? She's all soul, she is, and can write poetry or compose music, as easy as I could drink a glass of beer. Beer?—damme, that's all I'm fit for, is beer. I am a poor, ignorant little beggar, good for nothing but Foker's Entire. I misspent my youth, and used to get the chaps to do my exercises. And what's the consequences now? Oh, Harry Foker, what a confounded little fool you have been!'

As he made this dreary soliloquy, he had cantered out of Rotten Row into the Park, and there was on the point of riding down a large old roomy family carriage, of which he took no heed, when a cheery voice cried out, 'Harry, Harry!' and looking up, he beheld his aunt, the Lady Rosherville, and two of her daughters, of whom the one who spoke was Harry's betrothed, the Lady Ann.

He started back with a pale, scared look, as a truth, about which he had not thought during the whole day, came across him. *There* was his fate, there, in the back seat of that carriage.

'What is the matter, Harry? why are you so pale? You have been raking and smoking too much, you wicked boy,' said Lady Ann.

Foker said, 'How do, aunt?' 'How do, Ann?' in a perturbed manner—muttered something about a pressing engagement,—indeed he saw by the Park clock that he must have been keeping his party in the drag waiting for nearly an hour—and waved a good-bye. The little man and the little pony were out of sight in an instant—the great carriage rolled away. Nobody inside was very much interested about his coming or going; the countess being occupied with her spaniel, the Lady Lucy's thoughts and

eyes being turned upon a volume of sermons, and those of Lady Ann upon a new novel, which the sisters had just procured from the library.

CHAPTER XL

CARRIES THE READER BOTH TO RICHMOND AND GREENWICH

OOR Foker found the dinner at Richmond to be the most dreary entertainment upon which ever mortal man wasted his guineas. 'I wonder how the deuce I could ever have liked these people,' he thought in his own mind. 'Why, I can see the crow's-feet under Rougemont's eyes, and the paint on her cheeks is laid on as thick as Clown's in a pantomime! The way in which that Pinckney talks slang is quite disgusting. I hate chaff in a woman. And old Colchicum! that old Col, coming down here in his brougham, with his coronet on it, and sitting bodkin between Mademoiselle Coralie and her mother! It's too bad. An English peer, and a horse-rider of Franconi's!—It won't do; by Jove, it won't do. I ain't proud; but it will *not* do!'

'Twopence-halfpenny for your thoughts, Fokey!' cried out Miss Rougemont, taking her cigar from her truly vermilion lips, as she beheld the young fellow lost in thought, seated at the head of his table, amidst melting ices, and cut pineapples, and bottles full and empty, and cigar-ashes scattered on fruit, and the ruins of a dessert which had no pleasure for him.

'*Does* Foker ever think?' drawled out Mr. Poyntz. 'Foker, here is a considerable sum of money offered by a fair capitalist at this end of the table for the present emanations of your valuable and acute intellect, old boy!'

'What the deuce is that Poyntz a-talking about?' Mrs. Pinckney asked of her neighbour. 'I hate him. He's a drawlin', sneerin' beast.'

'What a droll of a little man is that little Fokare, my lor',' Mademoiselle Coralie said, in her own language, and with

the rich twang of that sunny Gascony in which her swarthy cheeks and bright black eyes had got their fire. 'What a droll of a man! He does not look to have twenty years.'

'I wish I were of his age,' said the venerable Colchicum, with a sigh, as he inclined his purple face towards a large goblet of claret.

'*C'te jeunesse. Peuh! je m'en fiche,*' said Madame Brack, Coralie's mamma, taking a great pinch out of Lord Colchicum's delicate gold snuff-box. '*Je n'aime que les hommes faits, moi. Comme milor. Coralie! n'est-ce pas que tu n'aimes que les hommes faits, ma bichette?*'

My lord said, with a grin, 'You flatter me, Madame Brack.'

'*Taisez-vous, maman, vous n'êtes qu'une bête,*' Coralie cried, with a shrug of her robust shoulders; upon which, my lord said that *she* did not flatter at any rate; and pocketed his snuff-box, not desirous that Madame Brack's dubious fingers should plunge too frequently into his Mackabaw.

There is no need to give a prolonged detail of the animated conversation which ensued during the rest of the banquet; a conversation which would not much edify the reader. And it is scarcely necessary to say, that all ladies of the *corps de danse* are not like Miss Pinckney, any more than that all peers resemble that illustrious member of their order, the late lamented Viscount Colchicum.[1]

Mr. Foker drove his lovely guests home to Brompton in the drag that night; but he was quite thoughtful and gloomy during the whole of the little journey from Richmond; neither listening to the jokes of the friends behind him and on the box by his side, nor enlivening them, as was his wont, by his own facetious sallies. And when the ladies whom he had conveyed alighted at the door of their house, and asked their accomplished coachman whether he would not step in and take something to drink, he declined with so melancholy an air, that they supposed that the governor and he had had a difference, or that some calamity had befallen him; and he did not tell these people what the cause of his grief was, but left Mesdames Rougemont and Pinckney, unheeding the cries of the latter, who hung over her balcony like Jezebel, and called out to him to ask him to give another party soon.

He sent the drag home under the guidance of one of the

grooms, and went on foot himself; his hands in his pockets, plunged in thought. The stars and moon shining tranquilly overhead, looked down upon Mr. Foker that night, as he in his turn sentimentally regarded them. And he went and gazed upwards at the house in Grosvenor Place, and at the windows which he supposed to be those of the beloved object; and he moaned and he sighed in a way piteous and surprising to witness, which Policeman X did, who informed Sir Francis Clavering's people, as they took the refreshment of beer on the coach-box at the neighbouring public-house, after bringing home their lady from the French play, that there had been another chap hanging about the premises that evening—a little chap dressed like a swell.

And now with that perspicuity and ingenuity and enterprise which only belongs to a certain passion, Mr. Foker began to dodge Miss Amory through London, and to appear wherever he could meet her. If Lady Clavering went to the French play, where her ladyship had a box, Mr. Foker, whose knowledge of the language, as we have heard, was not conspicuous, appeared in a stall. He found out where her engagements were (it is possible that Anatole, his man, was acquainted with Sir Francis Clavering's gentleman, and so got a sight of her ladyship's engagement-book), and at many of these evening parties Mr. Foker made his appearance—to the surprise of the world, and of his mother especially, whom he ordered to apply for cards to these parties, for which until now he had shown a supreme contempt. He told the pleased and unsuspicious lady that he went to parties because it was right for him to see the world: he told her that he went to the French play because he wanted to perfect himself in the language, and there was no such good lesson as a comedy or vaudeville,—and when one night the astonished Lady Agnes saw him stand up and dance, and complimented him upon his elegance and activity, the mendacious little rogue asserted that he had learned to dance in Paris, whereas Anatole knew that his young master used to go off privily to an academy in Brewer Street, and study there for some hours in the morning. The casino of our modern days was not invented, or was in its infancy as yet; and gentlemen of Mr. Foker's time had not the facilities of acquiring the science of dancing which are enjoyed by our present youth.

Old Pendennis seldom missed going to church. He considered it to be his duty as a gentleman to patronize the institution of public worship, and that it was quite a correct thing to be seen at church of a Sunday. One day it chanced that he and Arthur went thither together: the latter, who was now in high favour, had been to breakfast with his uncle, from whose lodging they walked across the Park to a church not far from Belgrave Square. There was a charity sermon at St. James's, as the major knew by the bills posted on the pillars of his parish church, which probably caused him, for he was a thrifty man, to forsake it for that day: besides, he had other views for himself and Pen. 'We will go to church, sir, across the Park: and then, begad, we will go to the Claverings' house, and ask them for lunch in a friendly way. Lady Clavering likes to be asked for lunch, and is uncommonly kind, and monstrous hospitable.'

'I met them at dinner last week, at Lady Agnes Foker's, sir,' Pen said, 'and the Begum was very kind indeed. So she was in the country: so she is everywhere. But I share your opinion about Miss Amory; one of your opinions, that is, uncle, for you were changing the last time we spoke about her.'

'And what do you think of her now?' the elder said.

'I think her the most confounded little flirt in London,' Pen answered, laughing. 'She made a tremendous assault upon Harry Foker, who sat next to her; and to whom she gave all the talk, though I took her down.'

'Bah! Henry Foker is engaged to his cousin, all the world knows it: not a bad *coup* of Lady Rosherville's, that. I should say, that the young man at his father's death, and old Mr. Foker's life's devilish bad: you know he had a fit, at Arthur's, last year—I should say, that young Foker won't have less than fourteen thousand a year from the brewery, besides Logwood and the Norfolk property. I've no pride about *me*, Pen. I like a man of birth certainly, but dammy, I like a brewery which brings in a man fourteen thousand a year; hey, Pen? Ha, ha, that's the sort of man for me. And I recommend you now that you are *lancé*'d in the world, to stick to fellows of that sort; to fellows who have a stake in the country, begad.'

'Foker sticks to me, sir,' Arthur answered. 'He has

been at our chambers several times lately. He has asked me to dinner. We are almost as great friends as we used to be in our youth : and his talk is about Blanche Amory from morning till night. I'm sure he's sweet upon her.'

'I'm sure he is engaged to his cousin, and that they will keep the young man to his bargain,' said the major. 'The marriages in these families are affairs of state. Lady Agnes was made to marry old Foker by the late lord, although she was notoriously partial to her cousin who was killed at Albuera afterwards, and who saved her life out of the lake at Drummington. I remember Lady Agnes, sir, an exceedingly fine woman. But what did she do ?—of course she married her father's man. Why, Mr. Foker sat for Drummington till the Reform Bill, and paid dev'lish well for his seat, too. And you may depend upon this, sir, that Foker senior, who is a parvenu, and loves a great man, as all parvenus do, has ambitious views for his son as well as himself, and that your friend Harry must do as his father bids him. Lord bless you ! I've known a hundred cases of love in young men and women : hey, Master Arthur, do you take me ? They kick, sir, they resist, they make a deuce of a riot and that sort of thing, but they end by listening to reason, begad.'

'Blanche is a dangerous girl, sir,' Pen said. 'I was smitten with her myself once, and very far gone, too,' he added ; 'but that is years ago.'

'Were you ? How far did it go ? Did she return it ?' asked the major, looking hard at Pen.

Pen, with a laugh, said 'that at one time he did think he was pretty well in Miss Amory's good graces. But my mother did not like her, and the affair went off.' Pen did not think it fit to tell his uncle all the particulars of that courtship which had passed between himself and the young lady.

'A man might go farther and fare worse, Arthur,' the major said, still looking queerly at his nephew.

'Her birth, sir ; her father was the mate of a ship, they say : and she has not money enough,' objected Pen, in a dandified manner. 'What's ten thousand pound and a girl bred up like her ?'

'You use my own words, and it is all very well. But, I tell you in confidence, Pen,—in strict honour, mind,—that it's my belief she has a devilish deal more than ten thousand

pound : and from what I saw of her the other day, and—and have heard of her—I should say she was a devilish accomplished, clever girl : and would make a good wife with a sensible husband.'

'How do you know about her money ?' Pen asked, smiling. 'You seem to have information about everybody, and to know about all the town.'

'I do know a few things, sir, and I don't tell all I know. Mark that,' the uncle replied. 'And as for that charming Miss Amory,—for charming, begad ! she is,—if I saw her Mrs. Arthur Pendennis, I should neither be sorry nor surprised, begad ! and if you object to ten thousand pound, what would you say, sir, to thirty, or forty, or fifty ?' and the major looked still more knowingly, and still harder at Pen.

'Well, sir,' he said, to his godfather and namesake, 'make her Mrs. Arthur Pendennis. You can do it as well as I.'

'Psha ! you are laughing at me, sir,' the other replied, rather peevishly, 'and you ought not to laugh so near a church gate. Here we are at St. Benedict's. They say Mr. Oriel is a beautiful preacher.'*

Indeed, the bells were tolling, the people were trooping into the handsome church, the carriages of the inhabitants of the lordly quarter poured forth their pretty loads of devotees, in whose company Pen and his uncle, ending their edifying conversation, entered the fane. I do not know whether other people carry their worldly affairs to the church door. Arthur, who, from habitual reverence and feeling, was always more than respectful in a place of worship, thought of the incongruity of their talk, perhaps ; whilst the old gentleman at his side was utterly unconscious of any such contrast. His hat was brushed : his wig was trim : his neckcloth was perfectly tied. He looked at every soul in the congregation, it is true : the bald heads and the bonnets, the flowers and the feathers : but so demurely that he hardly lifted up his eyes from his book—from his book which he could not read without glasses. As for Pen's gravity, it was sorely put to the test when, upon looking by chance towards the seats where the servants were collected, he spied out, by the side of a demure gentleman in plush, Henry Foker, Esquire, who had discovered this place of devotion. Following the direction

of Harry's eye, which strayed a good deal from his book, Pen found that it alighted upon a yellow bonnet and a pink one: and that these bonnets were on the heads of Lady Clavering and Blanche Amory. If Pen's uncle is not the only man who has talked about his worldly affairs up to the church door, is poor Harry Foker the only one who has brought his worldly love into the aisle?

When the congregation issued forth at the conclusion of the service, Foker was out amongst the first, but Pen came up with him presently, as he was hankering about the entrance, which he was unwilling to leave, until my lady's barouche, with the bewigged coachman, had borne away its mistress and her daughter from their devotions.

When the two ladies came out, they found together the Pendennises, uncle and nephew, and Harry Foker, Esquire, sucking the crook of his stick, standing there in the sunshine. To see and to ask to eat were simultaneous with the good-natured Begum, and she invited the three gentlemen to luncheon straightway.

Blanche was, too, particularly gracious. 'Oh! do come,' she said to Arthur, 'if you are not too great a man. I want so to talk to you about—but we mustn't say what, *here*, you know. What would Mr. Oriel say?' And the young devotee jumped into the carriage after her mamma.—'I've read every word of it. It's *adorable*,' she added, still addressing herself to Pen.

'I know *who* is,' said Mr. Arthur, making rather a pert bow.

'What's the row about?' asked Mr. Foker, rather puzzled.

'I suppose Miss Amory means *Walter Lorraine*,' said the major, looking knowing, and nodding at Pen.

'I suppose so, sir. There was a famous review in the *Pall Mall* this morning. It was Warrington's doing though, and I must not be too proud.'

'A review in Pall Mall?—Walter Lorraine? What the doose do you mean?' Foker asked. 'Walter Lorraine died of the measles, poor little beggar, when we were at Grey Friars. I remember his mother coming up.'

'You are not a literary man, Foker,' Pen said, laughing, and hooking his arm into his friend's. 'You must know I have been writing a novel, and some of the papers have spoken very well of it. Perhaps you don't read the Sunday papers?'

'I read *Bell's Life* regular, old boy,' Mr. Foker answered: at which Pen laughed again, and the three gentlemen proceeded in great good-humour to Lady Clavering's house.

The subject of the novel was resumed after luncheon by Miss Amory, who indeed loved poets and men of letters if she loved anything, and was sincerely an artist in feeling. 'Some of the passages in the book made me cry, positively they did,' she said.

Pen said, with some fatuity, 'I am happy to think I have a part of *vos larmes*, Miss Blanche'—And the major (who had not read more than six pages of Pen's book) put on his sanctified look, saying, 'Yes, there are some passages quite affecting, mons'ous affecting: and,'—'Oh, if it

makes you cry,'—Lady Clavering declared she would not read it, 'that she wouldn't.'

'Don't, mamma,' Blanche said, with a French shrug of her shoulders; and then she fell into a rhapsody about the book, about the snatches of poetry interspersed in it, about the two heroines, Leonora and Neaera; about the two heroes, Walter Lorraine and his rival the young duke —'and what good company you introduce us to,' said the young lady archly, '*quel ton!* How much of your life have you passed at court, and are you a prime minister's son, Mr. Arthur?'

Pen began to laugh—'It is as cheap for a novelist to create a duke as to make a baronet,' he said. 'Shall I tell you a secret, Miss Amory? I promoted all my characters at the request of the publisher. The young duke was only a young baron when the novel was first written; his false friend the viscount was a simple commoner, and so on with all the characters of the story.'

'What a wicked, satirical, pert young man you have become! *Comme vous voilà formé!*' said the young lady. 'How different from Arthur Pendennis of the country! Ah! I think I like Arthur Pendennis of the country best, though!' and she gave him the full benefit of her eyes,—both of the fond appealing glance into his own, and of the modest look downwards towards the carpet, which showed off her dark eyelids and long fringed lashes.

Pen of course protested that he had not changed in the least, to which the young lady replied by a tender sigh; and thinking that she had done quite enough to make Arthur happy or miserable (as the case might be), she proceeded to cajole his companion, Mr. Harry Foker, who during the literary conversation had sat silently imbibing the head of his cane, and wishing he was a clever chap like that Pen.

If the major thought that by telling Miss Amory of Mr. Foker's engagement to his cousin, Lady Ann Milton (which information the old gentleman neatly conveyed to the girl as he sat by her side at luncheon below stairs),—if, we say, the major thought that the knowledge of this fact would prevent Blanche from paying any further attention to the young heir of Foker's Entire, he was entirely mistaken. She became only the more gracious to Foker: she praised him, and everything belonging to him; she praised his

mamma; she praised the pony which he rode in the Park; she praised the lovely breloques or gimcracks which the young gentleman wore at his watch-chain, and that dear little darling of a cane, and those dear little delicious monkeys' heads with ruby eyes, which ornamented Harry's shirt, and formed the buttons of his waistcoat. And then, having praised and coaxed the weak youth until he blushed and tingled with pleasure, and until Pen thought she really had gone quite far enough, she took another theme.

'I am afraid Mr. Foker is a very sad young man,' she said, turning round to Pen.

'He does not look so,' Pen answered, with a sneer.

'I mean we have heard sad stories about him. Haven't we, mamma? What was Mr. Poyntz saying here, the other day, about that party at Richmond? Oh, you naughty creature!' But here, seeing that Harry's countenance assumed a great expression of alarm, while Pen's wore a look of amusement, she turned to the latter and said, 'I believe you are just as bad: I believe you would have liked to have been there,—wouldn't you? I know you would: yes—and so should I.'

'Lor, Blanche!' mamma cried.

'Well, I would. I never saw an actress in my life. I would give anything to know one; for I adore talent. And I adore Richmond, that I do; and I adore Greenwich, and I say, I *should* like to go there.'

'Why should not we three bachelors,' the major here broke out gallantly, and to his nephew's special surprise, 'beg these ladies to honour us with their company at Greenwich? Is Lady Clavering to go on for ever being hospitable to us, and may we make no return? Speak for yourselves, young men,—eh, begad! Here is my nephew, with his pockets full of money—his pockets full, begad! and Mr. Henry Foker, who, as I have heard say, is pretty well to do in the world,—how is your lovely cousin, Lady Ann, Mr. Foker?—here are these two young ones,—and they allow an old fellow like me to speak. Lady Clavering, will you do me the favour to be my guest? and Miss Blanche shall be Arthur's, if she will be so good.'

'Oh, delightful!' cried Blanche.

'I like a bit of fun too,' said Lady Clavering; 'and we will take some day when Sir Francis——'

ALMOST PERFECT HAPPINESS

'When Sir Francis dines out,—yes, mamma,' the daughter said, 'it will be charming.'

And a charming day it was. The dinner was ordered at Greenwich, and Foker, though he did not invite Miss Amory, had some delicious opportunities of conversation with her during the repast, and afterwards on the balcony of their room at the hotel, and again during the drive home in her ladyship's barouche. Pen came down with his uncle, in Sir Hugh Trumpington's brougham, which the major borrowed for the occasion. 'I am an old soldier, begad,' he said, 'and I learned in early life to make myself comfortable.'

And, being an old soldier, he allowed the two young men to pay for the dinner between them, and all the way home in the brougham he rallied Pen about Miss Amory's evident partiality for him: praised her good looks, spirits, and wit: and again told Pen, in the strictest confidence, that she would be a devilish deal richer than people thought.

CHAPTER XLI

CONTAINS A NOVEL INCIDENT

SOME account has been given, in a former part of this story, how Mr. Pen, during his residence at home, after his defeat at Oxbridge, had occupied himself with various literary compositions, and, amongst other works, had written the greater part of a novel. This book, written under the influence of his youthful embarrassments, amatory and pecuniary, was of a very fierce, gloomy, and passionate sort,—the Byronic despair, the Wertherian despondency, the mocking bitterness of Mephistopheles of *Faust*, were all reproduced and developed in the character of the hero; for our youth had just been learning the German language, and imitated, as almost all clever lads do, his favourite poets and writers. Passages in the volumes once so loved, and now read so seldom, still bear

the mark of the pencil with which he noted them in those days. Tears fell upon the leaf of the book, perhaps, or blistered the pages of his manuscript as the passionate young man dashed his thoughts down. If he took up the books afterwards, he had no ability or wish to sprinkle the leaves with that early dew of former times : his pencil was no longer eager to score its marks of approval : but as he looked over the pages of his manuscript, he remembered what had been the overflowing feelings which had caused him to blot it, and the pain which had inspired the line. If the secret history of books could be written, and the author's private thoughts and meanings noted down along-side of his story, how many insipid volumes would become interesting, and dull tales excite the reader ! Many a bitter smile passed over Pen's face as he read his novel, and recalled the time and feelings which gave it birth. How pompous some of the grand passages appeared ; and how weak others were in which he thought he had expressed his full heart ! This page was imitated from a then favourite author, as he could now clearly see and confess, though he had believed himself to be writing originally then. As he mused over certain lines he recollected the place and hour where he wrote them : the ghost of the dead feeling came back as he mused, and he blushed to review the faint image. And what meant those blots on the page ? As you come in the desert to a ground where camels' hoofs are marked in the clay, and traces of withered herbage are yet visible, you know that water was there once ; so the place in Pen's mind was no longer green, and the *fons lacrymarum* was dried up.

He used this simile one morning to Warrington, as the latter sat over his pipe and book, and Pen, with much gesticulation, according to his wont when excited, and with a bitter laugh, thumped his manuscript down on the table, making the tea-things rattle, and the blue milk dance in the jug. On the previous night he had taken the manu-script out of a long-neglected chest, containing old shooting-jackets, old Oxbridge scribbling books, his old surplice, and battered cap and gown, and other memorials of youth, school, and home. He read in the volume in bed until he fell asleep, for the commencement of the tale was somewhat dull, and he had come home tired from a London evening party.

'By Jove!' said Pen, thumping down his papers, 'when I think that these were written only a very few years ago, I am ashamed of my memory. I wrote this when I believed myself to be eternally in love with that little coquette, Miss Amory. I used to carry down verses to her, and put them into the hollow of a tree, and dedicate them "Amori."'

'That was a sweet little play upon words,' Warrington remarked, with a puff. 'Amory—Amori. It showed profound scholarship. Let us hear a bit of the rubbish.' And he stretched over from his easy-chair, and caught hold of Pen's manuscript with the fire-tongs, which he was just using in order to put a coal into his pipe. Thus, in possession of the volume, he began to read out from the *Leaves from the Life-Book of Walter Lorraine.*

'"False as thou art beautiful! heartless as thou art fair! mockery of Passion!" Walter cried, addressing Leonora; "what evil spirit hath sent thee to torture me so? Oh, Leonora——"'

'Cut that part,' cried out Pen, making a dash at the book, which, however, his comrade would not release. 'Well! don't read it out at any rate. That's about my other flame, my first—Lady Mirabel that is now. I saw her last night at Lady Whiston's. She asked me to a party at her house, and said that, as old friends, we ought to meet oftener. She has been seeing me any time these two years in town, and never thought of inviting me before; but seeing Wenham talking to me, and Monsieur Dubois, the French literary man, who had a dozen orders on, and might have passed for a Marshal of France, she condescended to invite me. The Claverings are to be there on the same evening. Won't it be exciting to meet one's two flames at the same table?'

'Two flames!—two heaps of burnt-out cinders,' Warrington said. 'Are both the beauties in this book?'

'Both, or something like them,' Pen said. 'Leonora, who marries the duke, is the Fotheringay. I drew the duke from Magnus Charters, with whom I was at Ox[bridge][1]; it's a little like him; and Miss Amory is Neaera. By gad, Warrington, I did love that first woman! I thought of her as I walked home from Lady Whiston's in the moonlight; and the whole early scenes came back to me as if they had been yesterday. And when I got home,

I pulled out the story which I wrote about her and the other three years ago: do you know, outrageous as it is, it has some good stuff in it, and if Bungay won't publish it, I think Bacon will.'

'That's the way of poets,' said Warrington. 'They fall in love, jilt, or are jilted; they suffer and they cry out that they suffer more than any other mortals: and when they have experienced feelings enough they note them down in a book, and take the book to market. All poets are humbugs, all literary men are humbugs; directly a man begins to sell his feelings for money he's a humbug. If a poet gets a pain in his side from too good a dinner, he bellows "Ai, Ai," louder than Prometheus.'

'I suppose a poet has a greater sensibility than another man,' said Pen, with some spirit. 'That is what makes him a poet. I suppose that he sees and feels more keenly: it is that which makes him speak of what he feels and sees. You speak eagerly enough in your leading articles when you espy a false argument in an opponent, or detect a quack in the House. Paley, who does not care for anything else in the world, will talk for an hour about a question of law. Give another the privilege which you take yourself, and the free use of his faculty, and let him be what nature has made him. Why should not a man sell his sentimental thoughts as well as you your political ideas, or Paley his legal knowledge? Each alike is a matter of experience and practice. It is not money which causes you to perceive a fallacy, or Paley to argue a point; but a natural or acquired aptitude for that kind of truth: and a poet sets down his thoughts and experiences upon paper as a painter does a landscape or a face upon canvas, to the best of his ability, and according to his particular gift. If ever I think I have the stuff in me to write an epic, by Jove I will try. If I only feel that I am good enough to crack a joke or tell a story, I will do that.'

'Not a bad speech, young one,' Warrington said, 'but that does not prevent all poets from being humbugs.'

'What—Homer, Aeschylus, Shakespere and all?'

'Their names are not to be breathed in the same sentence with you pigmies,' Warrington said; 'there are men and men, sir.'

'Well, Shakespere was a man who wrote for money,* just as you and I do,' Pen answered, at which Warrington

confounded his impudence, and resumed his pipe and his manuscript.

There was not the slightest doubt, then, that this document contained a great deal of Pen's personal experiences, and that *Leaves from the Life-book of Walter Lorraine* would never have been written but for Arthur Pendennis's own private griefs, passions, and follies. As we have become acquainted with these in the earlier part of his biography, it will not be necessary to make large extracts from the novel of *Walter Lorraine*, in which the young gentleman had depicted such of them as he thought were likely to interest the reader, or were suitable for the purposes of his story.

Now, though he had kept it in his box for nearly half of the period during which, according to the Horatian maxim,* a work of art ought to lie ripening (a maxim the truth of which may, by the way, be questioned altogether), Mr. Pen had not buried his novel for this time, in order that the work might improve, but because he did not know where else to bestow it, or had no particular desire to see it. A man who thinks of putting away a composition for ten years before he shall give it to the world, or exercise his own maturer judgement upon it, had best be very sure of the original strength and durability of the work ; otherwise, on withdrawing it from its crypt he may find that, like small wine, it has lost what flavour it once had, and is only tasteless when opened. There are works of all tastes and smacks, the small and the strong, those that improve by age, and those that won't bear keeping at all, but are pleasant at the first draught, when they refresh and sparkle.

Now Pen had never any notion, even in the time of his youthful inexperience and fervour of imagination, that the story he was writing was a masterpiece of composition, or that he was the equal of the great authors whom he admired ; and when he now reviewed his little performance, he was keenly enough alive to its faults, and pretty modest regarding its merits. It was not very good, he thought ; but it was as good as most books of the kind that had the run of circulating libraries and the career of the season. He had critically examined more than one fashionable novel by the authors of the day then popular, and he thought that his intellect was as good as theirs, and that he could write the English language as well as those ladies or gentlemen ;

and as he now ran over his early performance, he was pleased to find here and there passages exhibiting both fancy and vigour, and traits, if not of genius, of genuine passion and feeling. This, too, was Warrington's verdict, when that severe critic, after half an hour's perusal of the manuscript, and the consumption of a couple of pipes of tobacco, laid Pen's book down, yawning portentously. 'I can't read any more of that balderdash now,' he said; 'but it seems to me there is some good stuff in it, Pen, my boy. There's a certain greenness and freshness in it which I like somehow. The bloom disappears off the face of poetry after you begin to shave. You can't get up that naturalness and artless rosy tint in after-days. Your cheeks are pale, and have got faded by exposure to evening parties, and you are obliged to take curling-irons, and macassar, and the deuce-knows-what, to your whiskers; they curl ambrosially, and you are very grand and genteel, and so forth; but, ah! Pen, the spring-time was the best.'

'What the deuce have my whiskers to do with the subject in hand?' Pen said (who, perhaps, may have been nettled by Warrington's allusion to those ornaments, which, to say the truth, the young man coaxed, and curled, and oiled, and perfumed, and petted, in rather an absurd manner). 'Do you think we can do anything with *Walter Lorraine?* Shall we take him to the publishers, or make an *auto-da-fé* of him?'

'I don't see what is the good of incremation,' Warrington said, 'though I have a great mind to put him into the fire, to punish your atrocious humbug and hypocrisy. Shall I burn him indeed? You have much too great a value for him to hurt a hair of his head.'

'Have I? Here goes,' said Pen, and *Walter Lorraine* went off the table, and was flung on to the coals. But the fire, having done its duty of boiling the young man's breakfast-kettle, had given up work for the day, and had gone out, as Pen knew very well; and Warrington, with a scornful smile, once more took up the manuscript with the tongs from out of the harmless cinders.

'Oh, Pen, what a humbug you are!' Warrington said; 'and, what is worst of all, sir, a clumsy humbug. I saw you look to see that the fire was out before you sent *Walter Lorraine* behind the bars. No, we won't burn him: we will carry him to the Egyptians, and sell him. We will

exchange him away for money—yea, for silver and gold, and for beef and for liquors, and for tobacco and for raiment. This youth will fetch some price in the market; for he is a comely lad, though not over strong; but we will fatten him up, and give him the bath, and curl his hair, and we will sell him for a hundred piastres to Bacon or to Bungay. The rubbish is saleable enough, sir; and my advice to you is this: the next time you go home for a

holiday, take *Walter Lorraine* in your carpet-bag—give him a more modern air, prune away, though sparingly, some of the green passages, and add a little comedy, and cheerfulness, and satire, and that sort of thing, and then we'll take him to market and sell him. The book is not a wonder of wonders, but it will do very well.'

'Do you think so, Warrington?' said Pen, delighted, for this was great praise from his cynical friend.

'You silly young fool! I think it is uncommonly clever,' Warrington said in a kind voice. 'So do you, sir.' And with the manuscript which he held in his hand, he playfully struck Pen on the cheek. That part of Pen's countenance turned as red as it had ever done in the earliest days of his blushes: he grasped the other's hand, and said, 'Thank you, Warrington,' with all his might; and then he retired to his own room with his book, and passed the greater part of the day upon his bed re-reading it: and he did as Warrington had advised, and altered not a little, and added a great deal, until at length he had fashioned *Walter Lorraine* pretty much into the shape in which, as the respected novel-reader knows, it subsequently appeared.

Whilst he was at work upon this performance, the good-natured Warrington artfully inspired the two gentlemen who 'read' for Messrs. Bacon and Bungay, with the greatest curiosity regarding *Walter Lorraine*, and pointed out the peculiar merits of its distinguished author. It was at the period when the novel called the 'fashionable' was in vogue* among us; and Warrington did not fail to point out, as before, how Pen was a man of the very first fashion himself, and received at the houses of some of the greatest personages in the land. The simple and kind-hearted Percy Popjoy was brought to bear upon Mrs. Bungay, whom he informed that his friend Pendennis was occupied upon a work of the most exciting nature; a work that the whole town would run after, full of wit, genius, satire, pathos, and every conceivable good quality. We have said before that Bungay knew no more about novels than he did about Hebrew or algebra, and neither read nor understood any of the books which he published and paid for; but he took his opinions from his professional advisers, and from Mrs. B., and, evidently with a view to a commercial transaction, asked Pendennis and Warrington to dinner again.

Bacon, when he found that Bungay was about to treat, of course, began to be anxious and curious, and desired to outbid his rival. Was anything settled between Mr. Pendennis and the odious house 'over the way,' about the new book? Mr. Hack, the confidential reader, was told to make inquiries, and see if anything was to be done, and the result of the inquiries of that diplomatist was that one morning Bacon himself toiled up the staircase of Lamb

Court, and to the door on which the names of Mr. Warrington and Mr. Pendennis were painted.

For a gentleman of fashion, as poor Pen was represented to be, it must be confessed that the apartments he and his friend occupied were not very suitable. The ragged carpet had grown only more ragged during the two years of joint occupancy : a constant odour of tobacco perfumed the sitting-room : Bacon tumbled over the laundress's buckets in the passage through which he had to pass ; Warrington's shooting-jacket was as tattered at the elbows as usual ; and the chair which Bacon was requested to take on entering broke down with the publisher. Warrington burst out laughing, said that Bacon had got the game chair, and bawled out to Pen to fetch a sound one from his bedroom. And seeing the publisher looking round the dingy room with an air of profound pity and wonder, asked him whether he didn't think the apartments were elegant, and if he would like, for Mrs. Bacon's drawing-room, any of the articles of furniture ? Mr. Warrington's character as a humourist was known to Mr. Bacon : 'I never can make that chap out,' the publisher was heard to say, 'or tell whether he is in earnest or only chaffing.'

It is very possible that Mr. Bacon would have set the two gentlemen down as impostors altogether, but that there chanced to be on the breakfast-table certain cards of invitation which the post of the morning had brought in for Pen, and which happened to come from some very exalted personage of the beau-monde, into which our young man had his introduction. Looking down upon these, Bacon saw that the Marchioness of Steyne would be at home to Mr. Arthur Pendennis upon a given day, and that another lady of distinction proposed to have dancing at her house upon a certain future evening. Warrington saw the admiring publisher eyeing these documents. 'Ah,' said he, with an air of simplicity, 'Pendennis is one of the most affable young men I ever knew, Mr. Bacon. Here is a young fellow that dines with all the great men in London, and yet he'll take his mutton-chop with you and me quite contentedly. There's nothing like the affability of the old English gentleman.'

'Oh no, nothing,' said Mr. Bacon.

'And you wonder why he should go on living up three pair of stairs with me, don't you, now ? Well, it *is* a queer

taste. But we are fond of each other; and as I can't afford to live in a grand house, he comes and stays in these rickety old chambers with me. He's a man that can afford to live anywhere.'

'I fancy it don't cost him much *here*,' thought Mr. Bacon; and the object of these praises presently entered the room from his adjacent sleeping apartment.

Then Mr. Bacon began to speak upon the subject of his visit; said he heard that Mr. Pendennis had a manuscript novel; professed himself anxious to have a sight of that work, and had no doubt that they could come to terms respecting it. What would be his price for it? Would he give Bacon the refusal of it? He would find our house a liberal house, and so forth. The delighted Pen assumed an air of indifference, and said that he was already in treaty with Bungay, and could give no definite answer. This piqued the other into such liberal, though vague offers, that Pen began to fancy El Dorado was opening to him, and that his fortune was made from that day.

I shall not mention what was the sum of money which Mr. Arthur Pendennis finally received for the first edition of his novel of *Walter Lorraine*, lest other young literary aspirants should expect to be as lucky as he was, and unprofessional persons forsake their own callings, whatever they may be, for the sake of supplying the world with novels, whereof there is already a sufficiency. Let no young people be misled and rush fatally into romance-writing: for one book which succeeds let them remember the many that fail, I do not say deservedly or otherwise, and wholesomely abstain: or, if they venture, at least let them do so at their own peril. As for those who have already written novels, this warning is not addressed, of course, to them. Let them take their wares to market; let them apply to Bacon and Bungay, and all the publishers in the Row, or the Metropolis, and may they be happy in their ventures. This world is so wide, and the tastes of mankind happily so various, that there is always a chance for every man, and he may win the prize by his genius or by his good fortune. But what is the chance of success or failure; of obtaining popularity, or of holding it when achieved? One man goes over the ice, which bears him, and a score who follow flounder in. In fine, Mr. Pendennis's was an exceptional case, and applies to

himself only; and I assert solemnly, and will to the last maintain, that it is one thing to write a novel, and another to get money for it.

By merit, then, or good fortune, or the skilful playing off of Bungay against Bacon which Warrington performed (and which an amateur novelist is quite welcome to try upon any two publishers in the trade), Pen's novel was actually sold for a certain sum of money to one of the two eminent patrons of letters whom we have introduced to our readers. The sum was so considerable that Pen thought of opening an account at a banker's or of keeping a cab and horse, or of descending into the first floor of Lamb Court into newly furnished apartments, or of migrating to the fashionable end of the town.

Major Pendennis advised the latter move strongly; he opened his eyes with wonder when he heard of the good luck that had befallen Pen; and which the latter, as soon as it occurred, hastened eagerly to communicate to his uncle. The major was almost angry that Pen should have earned so much money. 'Who the doose reads this kind of thing?' he thought to himself, when he heard of the bargain which Pen had made. '*I* never read your novels and rubbish. Except Paul de Kock, who certainly makes me laugh, I don't think I've looked into a book of the sort these thirty years. 'Gad! Pen's a lucky fellow. I should think he might write one of these in a month now—say, a month—that's twelve in a year. Dammy, he may go on spinning this nonsense for the next four or five years, and make a fortune. In the meantime, I should wish him to live properly, take respectable apartments, and keep a brougham.' [2]

Arthur, laughing, told Warrington what his uncle's advice had been; but he luckily had a much more reasonable counsellor than the old gentleman in the person of his friend, and in his own conscience, which said to him, 'Be grateful for this piece of good fortune; don't plunge into any extravagances. Pay back Laura!' And he wrote a letter to her, in which he told her his thanks and his regard; and enclosed to her such an instalment of his debt as nearly wiped it off. The widow and Laura herself might well be affected by the letter. It was written with genuine tenderness and modesty; and old Dr. Portman, when he read a passage in the letter, in which Pen, with an honest

heart full of gratitude, humbly thanked Heaven for his present prosperity, and for sending him such dear and kind friends to support him in his ill-fortune—when Doctor Portman read this portion of the letter, his voice faltered, and his eyes twinkled behind his spectacles. And when he had quite finished reading the same, and had taken his glasses off his nose, and had folded up the paper, and given it back to the widow, I am constrained to say that, after holding Mrs. Pendennis's hand for a minute, the doctor drew that lady towards him, and fairly kissed her: at which salute, of course, Helen burst out crying on the doctor's shoulder, for her heart was too full to give any other reply: and the doctor, blushing a great deal after his feat, led the lady, with a bow, to the sofa, on which he seated himself by her; and he mumbled out, in a low voice, some words of a Great Poet whom he loved very much, and who describes how in the days of his prosperity he had made 'the widow's heart to sing for joy.'*

'The letter does the boy very great honour, very great honour, my dear,' he said, patting it as it lay on Helen's knee—'and I think we have all reason to be thankful for it—very thankful. I need not tell you in what quarter, my dear, for you are a sainted woman—yes, Laura, my love, your mother is a sainted woman. And Mrs. Pendennis, ma'am, I shall order a copy of the book for myself, and another at the Book Club.'

We may be sure that the widow and Laura walked out to meet the mail which brought them their copy of Pen's precious novel, as soon as that work was printed and ready for delivery to the public, and that they read it to each other, and that they also read it privately and separately, for when the widow came out of her room in her dressing-gown at one o'clock in the morning with volume two, which she had finished, she found Laura devouring volume three in bed. Laura did not say much about the book, but Helen pronounced that it was a happy mixture of Shakespere, and Byron, and Walter Scott, and was quite certain that her son was the greatest genius, as he was the best son, in the world.

Did Laura not think about the book and the author, although she said so little? At least she thought about Arthur Pendennis. Kind as his tone was, it vexed her. She did not like his eagerness to repay that money. She

would rather that her brother had taken her gift as she intended it: and was pained that there should be money calculations between them. His letters from London, written with the good-natured wish to amuse his mother, were full of descriptions of the famous people and the entertainments, and magnificence of the great city. Everybody was flattering him and spoiling him she was sure. Was he not looking to some great marriage, with that cunning uncle for a mentor (between whom and Laura there was always an antipathy), that inveterate worldling, whose whole thoughts were bent upon pleasure and rank and fortune? He never alluded to—to old times, when he spoke of her. He had forgotten them and her, perhaps: had he not forgotten other things and people?

These thoughts may have passed in Miss Laura's mind, though she did not, she could not, confide them to Helen. She had one more secret, too, from that lady, which she could not divulge, perhaps, because she knew how the widow would have rejoiced to know it. This regarded an event which had occurred during that visit to Lady Rockminster, which Laura had paid in the last Christmas holidays: when Pen was at home with his mother, and when Mr. Pynsent, supposed to be so cold and so ambitious, had formally offered his hand to Miss Bell. No one except herself and her admirer knew of this proposal: or that Pynsent had been rejected by her, and probably the reasons she gave to the mortified young man himself were not those which actuated her refusal, or those which she chose to acknowledge to herself. 'I never,' she told Pynsent, 'can accept such an offer as that which you make me, which you own is unknown to your family, as I am sure it would be unwelcome to them. The difference of rank between us is too great. You are very kind to me here—too good and kind, dear Mr. Pynsent—but I am little better than a dependant.'

'A dependant? Who ever so thought of you? You are the equal of all the world,' Pynsent broke out.

'I am a dependant at home, too,' Laura said sweetly, 'and indeed I would not be otherwise. Left early a poor orphan, I have found the kindest and tenderest of mothers, and I have vowed never to leave her—never. Pray do not speak of this again—here, under your relative's roof, or elsewhere. It is impossible.'

'If Lady Rockminster asks you herself, will you listen to her ?' Pynsent cried eagerly.

'No,' Laura said. 'I beg you never to speak of this any more. I must go away if you do'—and with this she left him.

Pynsent never asked for Lady Rockminster's intercession : he knew how vain it was to look for that : and he never spoke again on that subject to Laura or to any person.

When at length the famous novel appeared, it not only met with applause from more impartial critics than Mrs. Pendennis, but, luckily for Pen, it suited the taste of the public, and obtained a quick and considerable popularity. Before two months were over, Pen had the satisfaction and surprise of seeing the second edition of *Walter Lorraine* advertised in the newspapers; and enjoyed the pleasure of reading and sending home the critiques of various literary journals and reviewers upon his book. Their censure did not much affect him; for the good-natured young man was disposed to accept with considerable humility the dispraise of others. Nor did their praise elate him over much; for, like most honest persons, he had his own opinion about his own performance, and when a critic praised him in the wrong place, he was hurt rather than pleased by the compliment. But if a review of his work was very laudatory, it was a great pleasure to him to send it home to his mother at Fairoaks, and to think of the joy which it would give there. There are some natures, and perhaps, as we have said, Pendennis's was one, which are improved and softened by prosperity and kindness, as there are men of other dispositions, who become arrogant and graceless under good fortune. Happy he who can endure one or the other with modesty and good humour ! Lucky he who has been educated to bear his fate, whatsoever it may be, by an early example of uprightness, and a childish training in honour !

CHAPTER XLII

ALSATIA*

Bred up, like a bailiff or a shabby attorney, about the purlieus of the Inns of Court, Shepherd's Inn is always to be found in the close neighbourhood of Lincoln's Inn Fields, and the Temple. Somewhere behind the black gables and smutty chimney-stacks of Wych Street, Holywell Street, Chancery Lane, the quadrangle lies, hidden from the outer world; and it is approached by curious passages and ambiguous smoky alleys, on which the sun has forgotten to shine. Slop-sellers, brandy-ball and hard-bake vendors, purveyors of theatrical prints for youth, dealers in dingy furniture, and bedding suggestive of anything but sleep, line the narrow walls and dark casements with their wares. The doors are many-belled: and crowds of dirty children form endless groups about the steps: or around the shell-fish dealers' trays in these courts; whereof the damp pavements resound with pattens, and are drabbled with a never-failing mud. Ballad-singers come and chant here, in deadly guttural tones, satirical songs against the Whig Administration, against the bishops and dignified clergy, against the German relatives of an august royal family: Punch sets up his theatre, sure of an audience, and occasionally of a halfpenny from the swarming occupants of the houses: women scream after their children for loitering in the gutter, or, worse still, against the husband who comes reeling from the gin-shop;—there is a ceaseless din and life in these courts, out of which you pass into the tranquil, old-fashioned quadrangle of Shepherd's Inn. In a mangy little grass-plat in the centre rises up the statue of Shepherd, defended by iron railings from the assaults of boys. The hall of the Inn, on which the founder's arms are painted, occupies one side of the square, the tall and ancient chambers are carried round other two sides, and over the central

archway, which leads into Oldcastle Street, and so into the great London thoroughfare.

The Inn may have been occupied by lawyers once: but the laity have long since been admitted into its precincts, and I do not know that any of the principal legal firms have their chambers here. The offices of the Polwheedle and Tredyddlum Copper Mines occupy one set of the ground-floor chambers; the Registry of Patent Inventions and Union of Genius and Capital Company, another;—the only gentleman whose name figures here, and in the *Law List*, is Mr. Campion, who wears moustachios, and who comes in his cab twice or thrice in a week; and whose West End offices are in Curzon Street, May Fair, where Mrs. Campion entertains the nobility and gentry to whom her husband lends money. There, and on his glazed cards, he is Mr. Somerset Campion; here he is Campion and Co.; and the same tuft which ornaments his chin, sprouts from the under-lip of the rest of the firm. It is splendid to see his cab-horse harness blazing with heraldic bearings, as the vehicle stops at the door leading to his chambers. The horse flings froth off his nostrils as he chafes and tosses under the shining bit. The reins and the breeches of the groom are glittering white,—the lustre of that equipage makes a sunshine in that shady place.

Our old friend, Captain Costigan, has examined Campion's cab and horse many an afternoon, as he trailed about the court in his carpet slippers and dressing-gown, with his old hat cocked over his eye. He suns himself there after his breakfast when the day is suitable; and goes and pays a visit to the porter's lodge, where he pats the heads of the children, and talks to Mrs. Bolton about the thayatres and me daughther Leedy Mirabel. Mrs. Bolton was herself in the profession once, and danced at the Wells in early days as the thirteenth of Mr. Serle's forty pupils.*

Costigan lives in the third floor at No. 4, in the rooms which were Mr. Podmore's, and whose name is still on the door (somebody else's name, by the way, is on almost all the doors in Shepherd's Inn). When Charley Podmore (the pleasing tenor singer, T.R.D.L.,* and at the Back Kitchen Concert Rooms) married, and went to live at Lambeth, he ceded his chambers to Mr. Bows and Captain Costigan, who occupy them in common now, and you may often hear the tones of Mr. Bows's piano of fine days when

THE CAPTAIN IN THE PORTER'S LODGE

the windows are open, and when he is practising for amusement, or for the instruction of a theatrical pupil, of whom he has one or two. Fanny Bolton is one, the portress's daughter, who has heard tell of her mother's theatrical glories, which she longs to emulate. She has a good voice and a pretty face and figure for the stage; and she prepares the rooms and makes the beds and breakfasts for Messrs. Costigan and Bows, in return for which the latter instructs her in music and singing. But for his unfortunate propensity to liquor (and in that excess she supposes that all men of fashion indulge), she thinks the captain the finest gentleman in the world, and believes in all the versions of all his stories; and she is very fond of Mr. Bows too, and very grateful to him, and this shy queer old gentleman has a fatherly fondness for her too, for in truth his heart is full of kindness, and he is never easy unless he loves somebody.

Costigan has had the carriages of visitors of distinction before his humble door in Shepherd's Inn: and to hear him talk of a morning (for his evening song is of a much more melancholy nature) you would fancy that Sir Charles and Lady Mirabel were in the constant habit of calling at his chambers, and bringing with them the select nobility to visit the 'old man, the honest old half-pay captain, poor old Jack Costigan,' as Cos calls himself.

The truth is, that Lady Mirabel has left her husband's card (which has been stuck in the little looking-glass over the mantelpiece of the sitting-room at No. 4, for these many months past), and has come in person to see her father, but not of late days. A kind person, disposed to discharge her duties gravely, upon her marriage with Sir Charles, she settled a little pension upon her father, who occasionally was admitted to the table of his daughter and son-in-law. At first poor Cos's behaviour 'in the hoight of poloit societee,' as he denominated Lady Mirabel's drawing-room table, was harmless, if it was absurd. As he clothed his person in his best attire, so he selected the longest and richest words in his vocabulary to deck his conversation, and adopted a solemnity of demeanour which struck with astonishment all those persons in whose company he happened to be.—'Was your leedyship in the Pork to-dee?' he would demand of his daughter. 'I looked for your equipage in veen:—the poor old man was not gratified by the soight of his daughther's choriot.

Sir Chorlus, I saw your neem at the Levee; many's the Levee at the Castle at Dublin that poor old Jack Costigan has attended in his time. Did the Juke look pretty well? Bedad, I'll call at Apsley House* and lave me cyard upon 'um. I thank ye, James, a little dthrop more champeane.' Indeed, he was magnificent in his courtesy to all, and addressed his observations not only to the master and the guests, but to the domestics who waited at the table, and who had some difficulty in maintaining their professional gravity while they waited on Captain Costigan.

On the first two or three visits to his son-in-law, Costigan maintained a strict sobriety, content to make up for his lost time when he got to the Back Kitchen, where he bragged about his son-in-law's clart and burgundee, until his own utterance began to fail him, over his sixth tumbler of whisky-punch. But with familiarity his caution vanished, and poor Cos lamentably disgraced himself at Sir Charles Mirabel's table, by premature inebriation. A carriage was called for him: the hospitable door was shut upon him. Often and sadly did he speak to his friends at the Kitchen of his resemblance to King Lear in the plee—of his having a thankless choild, bedad—of his being a pore worn-out lonely old man, dthriven to dthrinking by ingratitude, and seeking to dthrown his sorrows in punch.

It is painful to be obliged to record the weaknesses of fathers, but it must be furthermore told of Costigan, that when his credit was exhausted and his money gone, he would not unfrequently beg money from his daughter, and make statements to her not altogether consistent with strict truth. On one day a bailiff was about to lead him to prison, he wrote, 'unless the—to you insignificant—sum of three pound five can be forthcoming to liberate a poor man's grey hairs from jail.' And the good-natured Lady Mirabel dispatched the money necessary for her father's liberation, with a caution to him to be more economical for the future. On a second occasion the captain met with a frightful accident, and broke a plate-glass window in the Strand, for which the proprietor of the shop held him liable. The money was forthcoming on this time too, to repair her papa's disaster, and was carried down by Lady Mirabel's servant to the slip-shod messenger and aide-de-camp of the captain, who brought the letter announcing his mishap. If the servant had followed the captain's aide-de-

camp who carried the remittance, he would have seen that gentleman, a person of Costigan's country too (for have we not said that, however poor an Irish gentleman is, he always has a poorer Irish gentleman to run on his errands and transact his pecuniary affairs ?), call a cab from the nearest stand, and rattle down to the Roscius's Head, Harlequin Yard, Drury Lane, where the captain was indeed in pawn, and for several glasses containing rum and

water, or other spirituous refreshment, of which he and his staff had partaken. On a third melancholy occasion he wrote that he was attacked by illness, and wanted money to pay the physician whom he was compelled to call in; and this time Lady Mirabel, alarmed about her father's safety, and perhaps reproaching herself that she had of late lost sight of him, called for her carriage and drove to Shepherd's Inn, at the gate of which she alighted, whence

she found the way to her father's chambers, 'No. 4, third floor, name of Podmore over the door,' the portress said, with many curtsies, pointing towards the door of the house into which the affectionate daughter entered and mounted the dingy stair. Alas ! the door, surmounted by the name of Podmore, was opened to her by poor Cos in his shirt-sleeves, and prepared with the gridiron to receive the mutton-chops, which Mrs. Bolton had gone to purchase.

Also, it was not pleasant for Sir Charles Mirabel to have letters constantly addressed to him at Brookes's, with the information that Captain Costigan was in the hall, waiting for an answer ; or when he went to play his rubber at the Travellers', to be obliged to shoot out of his brougham and run up the steps rapidly, lest his father-in-law should seize upon him ; and to think that while he read his paper or played his whist, the captain was walking on the opposite side of Pall Mall, with that dreadful cocked hat, and the eye beneath it fixed steadily upon the windows of the club. Sir Charles was a weak man ; he was old, and had many infirmities : he cried about his father-in-law to his wife, whom he adored with senile infatuation : he said he must go abroad,—he must go and live in the country,—he should die, or have another fit if he saw that man again—he knew he should. And it was only by paying a second visit to Captain Costigan, and representing to him, that if he plagued Sir Charles by letters, or addressed him in the street, or made any further applications for loans, his allowance would be withdrawn altogether, that Lady Mirabel was enabled to keep her papa in order, and to restore tranquillity to her husband. And on occasion of this visit, she sternly rebuked Bows for not keeping a better watch over the captain ; desired that he should not be allowed to drink in that shameful way ; and that the people at the horrid taverns which he frequented should be told upon no account to give him credit. 'Papa's conduct is bringing me to the grave,' she said (though she looked perfectly healthy), 'and you, as an old man, Mr. Bows, and one that pretended to have a regard for us, ought to be ashamed of abetting him in it.' These were the thanks which honest Bows got for his friendship and his life's devotion. And I do not suppose that the old philosopher was much worse off than many other men, or had greater reason to grumble.

HER LADYSHIP'S VISIT

On the second floor of the next house to Bows's, in Shepherd's Inn, at No. 3, live two other acquaintances of ours. Colonel Altamont, agent to the Nawaub of Lucknow, and Captain the Chevalier Edward Strong. No name at all is over their door. The captain does not choose to let all the world know where he lives, and his cards bear the address of a Jermyn Street hotel; and as for the Ambassador Plenipotentiary of the Indian potentate, he is not an envoy accredited to the courts of St. James's or Leadenhall Street, but is here on a confidential mission, quite independent of the East India Company or the Board of Control. 'In fact,' as Strong says, 'Colonel Altamont's object being financial, and to effectuate a sale of some of the principal diamonds and rubies of the Lucknow crown, his wish is *not* to report himself at the India House or in Cannon Row, but rather to negotiate with private capitalists—with whom he has had important transactions both in this country and on the Continent.'

We have said that these anonymous chambers of Strong's had been very comfortably furnished since the arrival of Sir Francis Clavering in London, and the Chevalier might boast with reason to the friends who visited him, that few retired captains were more snugly quartered than he, in his crib in Shepherd's Inn. There were three rooms below: the office where Strong transacted his business—whatever that might be—and where still remained the desk and railings of the departed officials who had preceded him, and the chevalier's own bedroom and sitting-room; and a private stair led out of the office to two upper apartments, the one occupied by Colonel Altamont, and the other serving as the kitchen of the establishment, and the bedroom of Mr. Grady, the attendant. These rooms were on a level with the apartments of our friends Bows and Costigan next door at No. 4; and by reaching over the communicating leads, Grady could command the mignonette-box which bloomed in Bows's window.

From Grady's kitchen casement often came odours still more fragrant. The three old soldiers who formed the garrison of No. 4 were all skilled in the culinary art. Grady was great at an Irish stew; the colonel was famous for pilaws and curries; and as for Strong, he could cook anything. He made French dishes, and Spanish dishes, stews, fricassees, and omelettes, to perfection; nor was there any

man in England more hospitable than he when his purse was full, or his credit was good. At those happy periods, he could give a friend, as he said, a good dinner, a good glass of wine, and a good song afterwards; and poor Cos often heard with envy the roar of Strong's choruses, and the musical clinking of the glasses, as he sat in his own room, so far removed and yet so near to those festivities. It was not expedient to invite Mr. Costigan always: his practice of inebriation was lamentable; and he bored Strong's guests with his stories when sober, and with his maudlin tears when drunk.

A strange and motley set they were, these friends of the chevalier; and though Major Pendennis would not much have relished their company, Arthur and Warrington liked it not a little.[1] There was a history about every man of the set: they seemed all to have had their tides of luck and bad fortune. Most of them had wonderful schemes and speculations in their pockets, and plenty for making rapid and extraordinary fortunes. Jack Holt had been in Queen Christina's[2] army,* when Ned Strong had fought on the other side; and was now organizing a little scheme for smuggling tobacco into London, which must bring thirty thousand a year to any man who would advance fifteen hundred, just to bribe the last officer of the Excise who held out, and had wind of the scheme. Tom Diver, who had been in the Mexican navy, knew of a specie-ship which had been sunk in the first year of the war, with three hundred and eighty thousand dollars on board, and a hundred and eighty thousand pounds in bars and doubloons. 'Give me eighteen hundred pounds,' Tom said, 'and I'm off to-morrow. I take out four men, and a diving-bell with me; and I return in ten months to take my seat in Parliament, by Jove! and to buy back my family estate.' Keightley, the manager of the Tredyddlum and Polwheedle Copper Mines (which were as yet under water), besides singing as good a second as any professional man, and besides the Tredyddlum Office, had a Smyrna Sponge Company, and a little quicksilver operation in view, which would set him straight with the world yet. Filby had been everything: a corporal of dragoons, a field-preacher, and missionary-agent for converting the Irish; an actor at a Greenwich fair-booth, in front of which his father's attorney found him when the old gentleman died and left him that

famous property, from which he got no rents now, and of which nobody exactly knew the situation. Added to these was Sir Francis Clavering, Bart., who liked their society, though he did not much add to its amusements by his convivial powers. But he was made much of by the company now, on account of his wealth and position in the world. He told his little story and sang his little song or two with great affability; and he had had his own history, too, before his accession to good fortune; and had seen the inside of more prisons than one, and written his name on many a stamped paper.

When Altamont first returned from Paris, and after he had communicated with Sir Francis Clavering from the hotel at which he had taken up his quarters (and which he had reached in a very denuded state, considering the wealth of diamonds and rubies with which this honest man was entrusted), Strong was sent to him by his patron the baronet; paid his little bill at the inn, and invited him to come and sleep for a night or two at the chambers, where he subsequently took up his residence. To negotiate with this man was very well, but to have such a person settled in his rooms, and to be constantly burthened with such society, did not suit the chevalier's taste much; and he grumbled not a little to his principal.

'I wish you would put this bear into somebody else's cage,' he said to Clavering. 'The fellow's no gentleman. I don't like walking with him. He dresses himself like a nigger on a holiday. I took him to the play the other night; and, by Jove, sir, he abused the actor who was doing the part of villain in the play, and swore at him so, that the people in the boxes wanted to turn him out. The afterpiece was *The Brigand*, where Wallack* comes in wounded, you know, and dies. When he died, Altamont began to cry like a child, and said it was a d——d shame, and cried and swore so, that there was another row, and everybody laughing. Then I had to take him away, because he wanted to take his coat off to one fellow who laughed at him: and bellowed to him to stand up like a man.—Who is he? Where the deuce does he come from? You had best tell me the whole story, Frank: you must one day. You and he have robbed a church together, that's my belief. You had better get it off your mind at once, Clavering, and tell me what this Altamont is, and what hold he has over you.'

'Hang him! I wish he was dead!' was the Baronet's only reply; and his countenance became so gloomy, that Strong did not think fit to question his patron any further at that time; but resolved, if need were, to try and discover for himself what was the secret tie between Altamont and Clavering.

CHAPTER XLIII

IN WHICH THE COLONEL NARRATES SOME OF HIS ADVENTURES

EARLY in the forenoon of the day after the dinner in Grosvenor Place, at which Colonel Altamont had chosen to appear, the colonel emerged from his chamber in the upper story at Shepherd's Inn, and entered into Strong's sitting-room, where the chevalier sat in his easy-chair with the newspaper and his cigar. He was a man who made his tent comfortable wherever he pitched it, and long before Altamont's arrival, had done justice to a copious breakfast of fried eggs and broiled rashers, which Mr. Grady had prepared *secundum artem*.* Good-humoured and talkative, he preferred any company rather than none; and though he had not the least liking for his fellow-lodger, and would not have grieved to hear that the accident had befallen him which Sir Francis Clavering desired so fervently, yet kept on fair terms with him. He had seen Altamont to bed with great friendliness on the night previous, and taken away his candle for fear of accidents; and finding a spirit-bottle empty, upon which he had counted for his nocturnal refreshment, had drunk a glass of water with perfect contentment over his pipe, before he turned into his own crib and to sleep. That enjoyment never failed him: he had always an easy temper, a faultless digestion, and a rosy cheek; and whether he was going into action the next morning or to prison (and both had been his lot), in the camp or the Fleet, the worthy captain snored healthfully

through the night, and woke with a good heart and appetite, for the struggles or difficulties or pleasures of the day.

The first act of Colonel Altamont was to bellow to Grady for a pint of pale ale, the which he first poured into a pewter flagon, whence he transferred it to his own lips. He put down the tankard empty, drew a great breath, wiped his mouth in his dressing-gown (the difference of the colour of his beard from his dyed whiskers had long struck Captain Strong, who had seen too that his hair was fair under his black wig, but made no remarks upon these circumstances)—the colonel drew a great breath, and professed himself immensely refreshed by his draught. 'Nothing like that beer,' he remarked, 'when the coppers are hot. Many a day I've drunk a dozen of Bass at Calcutta, and—and——'

'And at Lucknow, I suppose,' Strong said, with a laugh. 'I got the beer for you on purpose: knew you'd want it after last night.' And the colonel began to talk about his adventures of the preceding evening.

'I cannot help myself,' the colonel said, beating his head with his big hand. 'I'm a madman when I get the liquor on board me; and ain't fit to be trusted with a spirit-bottle. When I once begin I can't stop till I've emptied it; and when I've swallowed it, Lord knows what I say or what I don't say. I dined at home here quite quiet. Grady gave me just my two tumblers, and I intended to pass the evening at the Black and Red as sober as a parson. Why did you leave that confounded sample-bottle of hollands out of the cupboard, Strong? Grady must go out too, and leave me the kettle a-boiling for tea. It was of no use, I couldn't keep away from it. Washed it all down, sir, by jingo. And it's my belief I had some more too, afterwards, at that infernal little thieves' den.'

'What, were you there too?' Strong asked, 'and before you came to Grosvenor Place? That was beginning betimes.'

'Early hours to be drunk and cleared out before nine o'clock, eh? But so it was. Yes, like a great big fool, I must go there; and found the fellows dining, Blackland and young Moss, and two or three more of the thieves. If we'd gone to Rouge et Noir, I must have won. But we didn't try the black and red. No, hang 'em, they know'd I'd have beat 'em at that—I must have beat 'em—I can't help beating 'em, I tell you. But they was too cunning

for me. That rascal Blackland got the bones out, and we played hazard on the dining-table. And I dropped all the money I had from you in the morning, be hanged to my luck. It was that that set me wild, and I suppose I must have been very hot about the head, for I went off thinking to get some more money from Clavering, I recollect; and then—and then I don't much remember what happened till I woke this morning, and heard old Bows at No. 3 playing on his pianner.'

Strong mused for a while as he lighted his cigar with a coal. 'I should like to know how you always draw money from Clavering, colonel,' he said.

The colonel burst out with a laugh—'Ha, ha! he owes it me,' he said.

'I don't know that that's a reason with Frank for paying,' Strong answered. 'He owes plenty besides you.'

'Well, he gives it me because he is so fond of me,' the other said, with the same grinning sneer. 'He loves me like a brother; you know he does, captain.—No?—He don't?—Well, perhaps he don't; and if you ask me no questions, perhaps I'll tell you no lies, Captain Strong—put that in your pipe and smoke it, my boy.

'But I'll give up that confounded brandy-bottle,' the colonel continued, after a pause. 'I must give it up, or it'll be the ruin of me.'

'It makes you say queer things,' said the captain, looking Altamont hard in the face. 'Remember what you said last night, at Clavering's table.'

'Say? What *did* I say?' asked the other hastily. 'Did I split anything? Dammy, Strong, did I split anything?'

'Ask me no questions, and I will tell you no lies,' the chevalier replied on his part. Strong thought of the words Mr. Altamont had used, and his abrupt departure from the baronet's dining-table and house as soon as he recognized Major Pendennis, or Captain Beak, as he called the major. But Strong resolved to seek an explanation of these words otherwise than from Colonel Altamont, and did not choose to recall them to the other's memory. 'No,' he said then, 'you didn't split as you call it, colonel; it was only a trap of mine to see if I could make you speak; but you didn't say a word that anybody could comprehend—you were too far gone for that.'

So much the better, Altamont thought; and heaved a

great sigh, as if relieved. Strong remarked the emotion, but took no notice, and the other being in a communicative mood, went on speaking.

'Yes, I own to my faults,' continued the colonel. 'There is some things I can't, do what I will, resist: a bottle of brandy, a box of dice, and a beautiful woman. No man of pluck and spirit, no man as was worth his salt, ever could, as I knows of. There's hardly p'raps a country in the world in which them three ain't got me into trouble.'

'Indeed?' said Strong.

'Yes, from the age of fifteen, when I ran away from home, and went cabin-boy on board an Indiaman, till now, when I'm fifty years old, pretty nigh, them women have always been my ruin. Why, it was one of 'em, and with such black eyes, and jewels on her neck, and sattens and ermine like a duchess, I tell you—it was one of 'em at Paris that swept off the best part of the thousand pound as I went off. Didn't I ever tell you of it? Well, I don't mind. At first I was very cautious, and having such a lot of money kep it close and lived like a gentleman—Colonel Altamont, Meurice's hotel, and that sort of thing—never played, except at the public tables, and won more than I lost. Well, sir, there was a chap that I saw at the hotel and the Palace Royal too, a regular swell fellow, with white kid gloves and a tuft to his chin, Bloundell-Bloundell his name was, as I made acquaintance with somehow, and he asked me to dinner, and took me to Madame the Countess de Foljambe's soirées—such a woman, Strong!—such an eye!—such a hand at the pianner! Lor bless you, she'd sit down and sing to you, and gaze at you, until she warbled your soul out of your body a'most. She asked me to go to her evening parties every Toosday; and didn't I take opera-boxes and give her dinners at the restaurateur's, that's all? But I had a run of luck at the tables, and it was not in the dinners and opera-boxes that poor Clavering's money went. No, be hanged to it, it was swep off in another way. One night, at the countess's, there was several of us at supper—Mr. Bloundell-Bloundell, the Honourable Deuceace, the Marky de la Tour de Force—all tip-top nobs, sir, and the height of fashion, when we had supper, and champagne you may be sure in plenty, and then some of that confounded brandy. I would have it—I would go on at it—the countess mixed the tumblers of

punch for me, and we had cards as well as grog after supper, and I played and drank until I don't know what I did. I was like I was last night. I was taken away and put to bed somehow, and never woke until the next day, to a roaring headache, and to see my servant, who said the Honourable Deuceace wanted to see me, and was waiting in the sitting-room. "How are you, colonel?" says he, a-coming into my bedroom. "How long did you stay last night after I went away? The play was getting too high for me, and I'd lost enough to you for one night."

'"To me," says I: "how's that, my dear feller?" (for though he was an earl's son, we was as familiar as you and me). "How's that, my dear feller?" says I, and he tells me, that he had borrowed thirty louis of me at *vingt-et-un*, that he gave me an IOU for it the night before, which I put into my pocket-book before he left the room. I takes out my card-case—it was the countess as worked it for me—and there was the IOU sure enough, and he paid me thirty louis in gold down upon the table at my bedside. So I said he was a gentleman, and asked him if he would like to take anything, when my servant should get it for him; but the Honourable Deuceace don't drink of a morning, and he went away to some business which he said he had.

'Presently there's another ring at my outer door; and this time it's Bloundell-Bloundell and the marky that comes in. "Bong jour, marky," says I. "Good-morning—no headache," says he. So I said I had one; and how I must have been uncommon queer the night afore; but they both declared I didn't show no signs of having had too much, but took my liquor as grave as a judge.

'"So," says the marky, "Deuceace has been with you; we met him in the Palais Royal as we were coming from breakfast. Has he settled with you? Get it while you can: he's a slippery card; and as he won three ponies of Bloundell, I recommend you to get your money while he has some."

'"He has paid me," says I; "but I knew no more than the dead that he owed me anything, and don't remember a bit about lending him thirty louis."

'The marky and Bloundell looks and smiles at each other at this; and Bloundell says, "Colonel, you are a queer feller. No man could have supposed, from your manners,

that you had tasted anything stronger than tea all night, and yet you forget things in the morning. Come, come,—tell that to the marines, my friend,—we won't have it at any price."

'"*En effet*," says the marky, twiddling his little black moustachios in the chimney-glass, and making a lunge or two as he used to do at the fencing-school. (He was a wonder at the fencing-school, and I've seen him knock down the image fourteen times running, at Lepage's.) "Let us speak of affairs. Colonel, you understand that affairs of honour are best settled at once: perhaps it won't be inconvenient to you to arrange our little matters of last night."

'"What little matters?" says I. "Do you owe me any money, marky?"

'"Bah!" says he; "do not let us have any more jesting. I have your note of hand for three hundred and forty louis. *Là voici!*" says he, taking out a paper from his pocket-book.

'"And mine for two hundred and ten," says Bloundell-Bloundell, and he pulls out *his* bit of paper.

'I was in such a rage of wonder at this, that I sprang out of bed, and wrapped my dressing-gown round me. "Are you come here to make a fool of me?" says I. "I don't owe you two hundred, or two thousand, or two louis; and I won't pay you a farthing. Do you suppose you can catch me with your notes of hand? I laugh at 'em and at you; and I believe you to be a couple——"

'"A couple of what?" says Mr. Bloundell. "You, of course, are aware that we are a couple of men of honour, Colonel Altamont, and not come here to trifle or to listen to abuse from you. You will either pay us or we will expose you as a cheat, and chastise you as a cheat, too," says Bloundell.

'"Oui, parbleu," says the marky,—but I didn't mind him, for I could have thrown the little fellow out of the window; but it was different with Bloundell,—he was a large man, that weighs three stone more than me, and stands six inches higher, and I think he could have done for me.

'"Monsieur will pay, or monsieur will give me the reason why. I believe you're little better than a *polisson*,* Colonel Altamont,"—that was the phrase he used,'

Altamont said with a grin—' and I got plenty more of this language from the two fellows, and was in the thick of the row with them, when another of our party came in. This was a friend of mine—a gent I had met at Boulogne, and had taken to the countess's myself. And as he hadn't played at all on the previous night, and had actually warned me against Bloundell and the others, I told the story to him, and so did the other two.

' "I am very sorry," says he. "You would go on playing : the countess entreated you to discontinue. These gentlemen offered repeatedly to stop. It was you that insisted on the large stakes, not they." In fact he charged dead against me : and when the two others went away, he told me how the marky would shoot me as sure as my name was—was what it is. "I left the countess crying, too," said he. "She hates these two men ; she has warned you repeatedly against them" (which she actually had done, and often told me never to play with them), "and now, colonel, I have left her in hysterics almost, lest there should be any quarrel between you, and that confounded marky should put a bullet through your head. It's my belief," says my friend, "that that woman is distractedly in love with you."

' "Do you think so ?" says I ; upon which my friend told me how she had actually gone down on her knees to him and said, "Save Colonel Altamont !"

'As soon as I was dressed, I went and called upon that lovely woman. She gave a shriek and pretty near fainted when she saw me. She called me Ferdinand,—I'm blest if she didn't.'

'I thought your name was Jack,' said Strong, with a laugh ; at which the colonel blushed very much behind his dyed whiskers.

'A man may have more names than one, mayn't he, Strong ?' Altamont asked. 'When I'm with a lady, I like to take a good one. She called me by my Christian name. She cried fit to break your heart. I can't stand seeing a woman cry—never could—not whilst I'm fond of her. She said she could not bear to think of my losing so much money in her house. Wouldn't I take her diamonds and necklaces, and pay part ?

'I swore I wouldn't touch a farthing's worth of her jewellery, which perhaps I did not think was worth a great

deal,—but what can a woman do more than give you her all ? That's the sort I like, and I know there's plenty of 'em. And I told her to be easy about the money, for I would not pay one single farthing.'

'"Then they'll shoot you," says she ; "they'll kill my Ferdinand."'

'"They'll kill my Jack" wouldn't have sounded well in French,' Strong said, laughing.

'Never mind about names,' said the other sulkily : 'a man of honour may take any name he chooses, I suppose.'

'Well, go on with your story,' said Strong. 'She said they would kill you.'

'"No," says I, "they won't : for I will not let that scamp of a marquis send me out of the world ; and if he lays a hand on me, I'll brain him, marquis as he is."

'At this the countess shrank back from me as if I had said something very shocking. "Do I understand Colonel Altamont aright ?" says she ; "and that a British officer refuses to meet any person who provokes him to the field of honour ?"

'"Field of honour be hanged, countess !" says I. "You would not have me be a target for that little scoundrel's pistol practice."

'"Colonel Altamont," says the countess, "I thought you were a man of honour—I thought, I—but no matter. Good-bye, sir."—And she was sweeping out of the room, her voice regular choking in her pocket-handkerchief.

'"Countess !" says I, rushing after her and seizing her hand.

'"Leave me, monsieur le colonel," says she, shaking me off, "my father was a general of the Grand Army. A soldier should know how to pay *all* his debts of honour."

'What could I do ? Everybody was against me. Caroline said I had lost the money : though I didn't remember a syllable about the business. I had taken Deuceace's money, too ; but then it was because he offered it to me, you know, and that's a different thing. Every one of these chaps was a man of fashion and honour ; and the marky and the countess of the first families in France. And by Jove, sir, rather than offend her, I paid the money up : five hundred and sixty gold napoleons, by Jove : besides three hundred which I lost when I had my revenge.

'And I can't tell you at this minute whether I was done

or not,' concluded the colonel, musing. 'Sometimes I think I was: but then Caroline was so fond of me. That woman would never have seen me done: never, I'm sure she wouldn't: at least, if she would, I'm deceived in woman.'

Any further revelations of his past life which Altamont might have been disposed to confide to his honest comrade the chevalier were interrupted by a knocking at the outer door of their chambers; which, when opened by Grady the servant, admitted no less a person than Sir Francis Clavering into the presence of the two worthies.

'The governor, by Jove,' cried Strong, regarding the arrival of his patron with surprise. 'What's brought you here?' growled Altamont, looking sternly from under his heavy eyebrows at the baronet. 'It's no good, I warrant.' And indeed good very seldom brought Sir Francis Clavering into that or any other place.

Whenever he came into Shepherd's Inn, it was money that brought the unlucky baronet into those precincts; and there was commonly a gentleman of the money-dealing world in waiting for him at Strong's chambers, or at Campion's below; and a question of bills to negotiate or to renew. Clavering was a man who had never looked his debts fairly in the face, familiar as he had been with them all his life; as long as he could renew a bill, his mind was easy regarding it; and he would sign almost anything for to-morrow, provided to-day could be left unmolested. He was a man whom scarcely any amount of fortune could have benefited permanently, and who was made to be ruined; to cheat small tradesmen, to be the victim of astuter sharpers: to be niggardly and reckless, and as destitute of honesty as the people who cheated him, and a dupe, chiefly because he was too mean to be a successful knave. He had told more lies in his time, and undergone more baseness of stratagem in order to stave off a small debt, or to swindle a poor creditor, than would have sufficed to make a fortune for a braver rogue. He was abject and a shuffler in the very height of his prosperity. Had he been a Crown Prince—he could not have been more weak, useless, dissolute or ungrateful. He could not move through life except leaning on the arm of somebody; and yet he never had an agent but he mistrusted him; and marred any plans which might be arranged for his benefit, by secretly acting against the people whom he employed. Strong knew Clavering,

and judged him quite correctly. It was not as friends that this pair met; but the chevalier worked for his principal, as he would when in the army have pursued a harassing march, or undergone his part in the danger and privations of a siege; because it was his duty, and because he had agreed to it. 'What is it he wants?' thought the two officers of the Shepherd's Inn garrison, when the baronet came among them.

His pale face expressed extreme anger and irritation. 'So, sir,' he said, addressing Altamont, 'you've been at your old tricks.'

'Which of um?' asked Altamont, with a sneer.

'You have been at the Rouge et Noir: you were there last night,' cried the baronet.

'How do you know,—were you there?' the other said. 'I was at the club: but it wasn't on the colours I played,—ask the captain,—I've been telling him of it. It was with the bones. It was at hazard, Sir Francis, upon my word and honour it was:' and he looked at the baronet with a knowing humorous mock humility, which only seemed to make the other more angry.

'What the deuce do I care, sir, how a man like you loses his money, and whether it is at hazard or roulette?' screamed the baronet, with a multiplicity of oaths, and at the top of his voice. 'What I will not have, sir, is that you should use my name, or couple it with yours.—Damn him, Strong, why don't you keep him in better order? I tell you he has gone and used my name again, sir,—drawn a bill upon me, and lost the money on the table—I can't stand it—I won't stand it. Flesh and blood won't bear it—Do you know how much I have paid for you, sir?'

'This was only a very little 'un, Sir Francis—only fifteen pound, Captain Strong; they wouldn't stand another: and it oughtn't to anger you, governor. Why, it's so trifling I did not even mention it to Strong,—did I now, captain? I protest it had quite slipped my memory, and all on account of that confounded liquor I took.'

'Liquor or no liquor, sir, it is no business of mine. I don't care what you drink, or where you drink it—only it shan't be in my house. And I will not have you breaking into my house of a night, and a fellow like you intruding himself on my company: how dared you show yourself in Grosvenor Place last night, sir,—and—and what do you

suppose my friends must think of me when they see a man of your sort walking into my dining-room uninvited, and drunk, and calling for liquor as if you were master of the house?'

'They'll think you know some very queer sort of people, I dare say,' Altamont said, with impenetrable good-humour. 'Look here, baronet, I apologize; on my honour I do, and ain't an apology enough between two gentlemen? It was a strong measure, I own, walking into your cuddy,* and calling for drink as if I was the captain: but I had had too much before, you see, that's why I wanted some more; nothing can be more simple—and it was because they wouldn't give me no more money upon your name at the Black and Red, that I thought I would come down and speak to you about it. To refuse me was nothing: but to refuse a bill drawn on you that have been such a friend to the shop, and are a baronet and a Member of Parliament, and a gentleman and no mistake—Damme, it's ungrateful.'

'By heavens, if ever you do it again—if ever you dare to show yourself in my house; or give my name at a gambling house or at any other house, by Jove—at any other house—or give any reference at all to me, or speak to me in the street, by Gad, or anywhere else until I speak to you—I disclaim you altogether—I won't give you another shilling.'

'Governor, don't be provoking,' Altamont said surlily. 'Don't talk to me about daring to do this thing or t'other, or when my dander is up it's the very thing to urge me on. I oughtn't to have come last night, I know I oughtn't: but I told you I was drunk, and that ought to be sufficient between gentleman and gentleman.'

'You a gentleman! dammy, sir,' said the baronet, 'how dares a fellow like you to call himself a gentleman?'

'I ain't a baronet, I know,' growled the other; 'and I've forgotten how to be a gentleman almost now, but—but I was one once, and my father was one, and I'll not have this sort of talk from you, Sir F. Clavering, that's flat. I want to go abroad again. Why don't you come down with the money, and let me go? Why the devil are you to be rolling in riches, and me to have none? Why should you have a house and a table covered with plate, and me be in a garret here in this beggarly Shepherd's Inn? We're partners, ain't we? I've as good a right to be rich

as you have, haven't I ? Tell the story to Strong here, if you like ; and ask him to be umpire between us. I don't mind letting my secret out to a man that won't split. Look here, Strong—perhaps you guess the story already—the fact is, me and the governor——'

'D——, hold your tongue,' shrieked out the baronet in a fury. 'You shall have the money as soon as I can get it. I ain't made of money. I'm so pressed and badgered, I don't know where to turn. I shall go mad ; by Jove, I shall. I wish I was dead, for I'm the most miserable brute alive. I say, Mr. Altamont, don't mind me. When I'm out of health—and I'm devilish bilious this morning—hang me, I abuse everybody, and don't know what I say. Excuse me if I've offended you. I—I'll try and get that little business done. Strong shall try. Upon my word he shall. And I say, Strong, my boy, I want to speak to you. Come into the office for a minute.'

Almost all Clavering's assaults ended in this ignominious way, and in a shameful retreat. Altamont sneered after the baronet as he left the room, and entered into the office, to talk privately with his factotum.

'What is the matter now ?' the latter asked of him. 'It's the old story, I suppose.'

'D—— it, yes,' the baronet said. 'I dropped two hundred in ready money at the Little Coventry last night, and gave a cheque for three hundred more. On her ladyship's bankers too, for to-morrow ; and I must meet it, for there'll be the deuce to pay else. The last time she paid my play-debts, I swore I would not touch a dice-box again, and she'll keep her word, Strong, and dissolve partnership, if I go on. I wish I had three hundred a year, and was away. At a German watering-place you can do devilish well with three hundred a year. But my habits are so d—— reckless : I wish I was in the Serpentine.* I wish I was dead, by Gad I wish I was. I wish I had never touched those confounded bones. I had such a run of luck last night, with five for the main, and seven to five all night, until those ruffians wanted to pay me with Altamont's bill upon me. The luck turned from that minute. Never held the box again for three mains, and came away cleared out, leaving that infernal cheque behind me. How shall I pay it ? Blackland won't hold it over. Hulker and Bullock will write about it directly to her ladyship.

By Jove, Ned, I'm the most miserable brute in all England.'

It was necessary for Ned to devise some plan to console the baronet under this pressure of grief; and no doubt he found the means of procuring a loan for his patron, for he was closeted at Mr. Campion's offices that day for some time. Altamont had once more a guinea or two in his pocket, with the promise of a further settlement; and the baronet had no need to wish himself dead for the next two or three months at least. And Strong, putting together what he had learned from the colonel and Sir Francis, began to form in his own mind a pretty accurate opinion as to the nature of the tie which bound the two men together.

CHAPTER XLIV

A CHAPTER OF CONVERSATIONS

EVERY day, after the entertainments at Grosvenor Place and Greenwich, of which we have seen Major Pendennis partake, the worthy gentleman's friendship and cordiality for the Clavering family seemed to increase. His calls were frequent; his attentions to the lady of the house unremitting. An old man about town, he had the good fortune to be received in many houses, at which a lady of Lady Clavering's distinction ought also to be seen. Would her ladyship not like to be present at the grand entertainment at Gaunt House? There was to be a very pretty breakfast ball at Viscount Marrowfat's at Fulham. Everybody was to be there (including august personages of the highest rank), and there was to be a Watteau quadrille,* in which Miss Amory would surely look charming. To these and other amusements the obsequious old gentleman kindly offered to conduct Lady Clavering,

and was also ready to make himself useful to the baronet in any way agreeable to the latter.

In spite of his present station and fortune, the world persisted in looking rather coldly upon Clavering, and strange suspicious rumours followed him about. He was blackballed at two clubs in succession. In the House of Commons, he only conversed with a few of the most disreputable members of that famous body, having a happy knack of choosing bad society, and adapting himself naturally to it, as other people do to the company of their betters. To name all the senators with whom Clavering consorted would be invidious. We may mention only a few. There was Captain Raff, the honourable member for Epsom, who retired after the last Goodwood races, having accepted, as Mr. Hotspur, the whip of the party, said, a mission to the Levant: there was Hustingson, the patriotic member for Islington, whose voice is never heard now denunciating corruption, since his appointment to the Governorship of Coventry Island; there was Bob Freeny, of the Booterstown Freenys, who is a dead shot, and of whom we therefore wish to speak with every respect; and of all these gentlemen, with whom in the course of his professional duty Mr. Hotspur had to confer, there was none for whom he had a more thorough contempt and dislike than for Sir Francis Clavering, the representative of an ancient race, who had sat for their own borough of Clavering time out of mind in the House. 'If that man is wanted for a division,' Hotspur said, 'ten to one he is to be found in a hell. He was educated in the Fleet, and he has not heard the end of Newgate yet, take my word for it. He'll muddle away the Begum's fortune at thimblerig, be caught picking pockets, and finish on board the hulks.'* And if the high-born Hotspur, with such an opinion of Clavering, could yet from professional reasons be civil to him, why should not Major Pendennis also have reasons of his own for being attentive to this unlucky gentleman?

'He has a very good cellar, and a very good cook,' the major said: 'as long as he is silent he is not offensive, and he very seldom speaks. If he chooses to frequent gambling-tables, and lose his money to blacklegs, what matters to me? Don't look too curiously into any man's affairs, Pen, my boy; every fellow has some cupboard in his house,

begad, which he would not like you and me to peep into. Why should we try, when the rest of the house is open to us? And a devilish good house, too, as you and I know. And if the man of the family is not all one could wish, the women are excellent. The Begum is not over-refined, but as kind a woman as ever lived, and devilish clever too; and as for the little Blanche, you know my opinion about her, you rogue; you know my belief is that she is sweet on you, and would have you for the asking. But you are growing such a great man, that I suppose you won't be content under a duke's daughter—hey, sir? I recommend you to ask one of them and try.'

Perhaps Pen was somewhat intoxicated by his success in the world; and it may also have entered into the young man's mind (his uncle's perpetual hints serving not a little to encourage the notion) that Miss Amory was tolerably well disposed to renew the little flirtation which had been carried on in the early days of both of them by the banks of the rural Brawl. But he was little disposed to marriage, he said, at that moment, and, adopting some of his uncle's worldly tone, spoke rather contemptuously of the institution, and in favour of a bachelor life.

'You are very happy, sir,' said he, 'and you get on very well alone, and so do I. With a wife at my side, I should lose my place in society; and I don't, for my part, much fancy retiring into the country with a Mrs. Pendennis; or taking my wife into lodgings to be waited upon by the servant-of-all-work. The period of my little illusions is over. You cured me of my first love, who certainly was a fool, and would have had a fool for her husband, and a very sulky discontented husband too, if she had taken me. We young fellows live fast, sir; and I feel as old at five-and-twenty as many of the old fo—the old bachelors—whom I see in the bow-window at Bays's. Don't look offended, I only mean that I am blasé about love matters, and that I could no more fan myself into a flame for Miss Amory now, than I could adore Lady Mirabel over again. I wish I could; I rather like old Mirabel for his infatuation about her, and think his passion is the most respectable part of his life.'

'Sir Charles Mirabel was always a theatrical man, sir,' the major said, annoyed that his nephew should speak flippantly of any person of Sir Charles's rank and station.

'He has been occupied with theatricals since his early days. He acted at Carlton House when he was page to the prince;*—he has been mixed up with that sort of thing: he could afford to marry whom he chooses; and Lady Mirabel is a most respectable woman, received everywhere—everywhere, mind. The Duchess of Connaught receives her, Lady Rockminster receives her—it doesn't become young fellows to speak lightly of people in that station. There's not a more respectable woman in England than Lady Mirabel:—and the old fogies, as you call them at Bays's, are some of the first gentlemen in England, of whom you youngsters had best learn a little manners, and a little breeding, and a little modesty.' And the major began to think that Pen was growing exceedingly pert and conceited, and that the world made a great deal too much of him.

The major's anger amused Pen. He studied his uncle's peculiarities with a constant relish, and was always in a good humour with his worldly old mentor. 'I am a youngster of fifteen years' standing, sir,' he said adroitly, 'and if you think that *we* are disrespectful, you should see those of the present generation. A protégé of yours came to breakfast with me the other day. You told me to ask him, and I did it to please you. We had a day's sights together, and dined at the club, and went to the play. He said the wine at the Polyanthus was not so good as Ellis's wine at Richmond, smoked Warrington's cavendish after breakfast, and when I gave him a sovereign as a farewell token, said he had plenty of them, but would take it to show he wasn't proud.'

'Did he?—did you ask young Clavering?' cried the major, appeased at once—'fine boy, rather wild, but a fine boy—parents like that sort of attention, and you can't do better than pay it to our worthy friends of Grosvenor Place. And so you took him to the play and tipped him? That was right, sir, that was right:' with which Mentor quitted Telemachus, thinking that the young men were not so very bad, and that he should make something of that fellow yet.

As Master Clavering grew into years and stature, he became too strong for the authority of his fond parents and governess; and rather governed them than permitted himself to be led by their orders. With his papa he was

silent and sulky, seldom making his appearance, however, in the neighbourhood of that gentleman; with his mamma he roared and fought when any contest between them arose as to the gratification of his appetite, or other wish of his heart; and in his disputes with his governess over his book, he kicked that quiet creature's shins so fiercely, that she was entirely overmastered and subdued by him. And he would have so treated his sister Blanche, too, and did on one or two occasions attempt to prevail over her; but she showed an immense resolution and spirit on her part, and boxed his ears so soundly, that he forebore from molesting Miss Amory, as he did the governess and his mamma, and his mamma's maid.

At length, when the family came to London, Sir Francis gave forth his opinion, that 'the little beggar had best be sent to school.' Accordingly the young son and heir of the house of Clavering was dispatched to the Rev. Otto Rose's establishment at Twickenham, where young noblemen and gentlemen were received preparatory to their introduction to the great English public schools.

It is not our intention to follow Master Clavering in his scholastic career; the paths to the Temple of Learning were made more easy to him than they were to some of us of earlier generations. He advanced towards that fane in a carriage-and-four, so to speak, and might halt and take refreshment almost whenever he pleased. He wore varnished boots from the earliest period of youth, and had cambric handkerchiefs and lemon-coloured kid gloves, of the smallest size ever manufactured by Privat. They dressed regularly at Mr. Rose's to come down to dinner: the young gentlemen had shawl dressing-gowns, fires in their bedrooms, horse and carriage exercise occasionally, and oil for their hair. Corporal punishment was altogether dispensed with by the Principal, who thought that moral discipline was entirely sufficient to lead youth; and the boys were so rapidly advanced in many branches of learning, that they acquired the art of drinking spirits and smoking cigars, even before they were old enough to enter a public school. Young Frank Clavering stole his father's havannahs, and conveyed them to school, or smoked them in the stables, at a surprisingly early period of life, and at ten years old drank his champagne* almost as stoutly as any whiskered cornet of Dragoons could do.

When this interesting youth came home for his vacations, Major Pendennis was as laboriously civil and gracious to him as he was to the rest of the family; although the boy had rather a contempt for old Wigsby, as the major was denominated,—mimicked him behind his back, as the polite major bowed and smirked with Lady Clavering or Miss Amory; and drew rude caricatures, such as are designed by ingenious youths, in which the major's wig, his nose, his tie, etc., were represented with artless exaggeration. Untiring in his efforts to be agreeable, the major wished that Pen, too, should take particular notice of this child; incited Arthur to invite him to his chambers, to give him a dinner at the club, to take him to Madame Tussaud's, the Tower, the play, and so forth, and to tip him, as the phrase is, at the end of the day's pleasures. Arthur, who was good-natured and fond of children, went through all these ceremonies one day; had the boy to breakfast at the Temple, where he made the most contemptuous remarks regarding the furniture, the crockery, and the tattered state of Warrington's dressing-gown; and smoked a short pipe, and recounted the history of a fight between Tuffy and Long Biggings, at Rose's, greatly to the edification of the two gentlemen his hosts.

As the major rightly predicted, Lady Clavering was very grateful for Arthur's attention to the boy; more grateful than the lad himself, who took attentions as a matter of course, and very likely had more sovereigns in his pocket than poor Pen, who generously gave him one of his own slender stock of those coins.

The major, with the sharp eyes with which nature endowed him, and with the glasses of age and experience, watched this boy, and surveyed his position in the family without seeming to be rudely curious about their affairs. But, as a country neighbour, one who had many family obligations to the Claverings, an old man of the world, he took occasion to find out what Lady Clavering's means were, how her capital was disposed, and what the boy was to inherit. And setting himself to work,—for what purposes will appear, no doubt, ulteriorly,—he soon had got a pretty accurate knowledge of Lady Clavering's affairs and fortune, and of the prospects of her daughter and son. The daughter was to have but a slender provision; the bulk of the property was, as before has been said, to go to the son,—

his father did not care for him or anybody else,—his mother was dotingly fond of him as the child of her latter days,—his sister disliked him. Such may be stated, in round numbers, to be the result of the information which Major Pendennis got. 'Ah! my dear madam,' he would say, patting the head of the boy, 'this boy may wear a baron's coronet on his head on some future coronation, if matters are but managed rightly, and if Sir Francis Clavering would but play his cards well.'

At this the widow Amory heaved a deep sigh. 'He plays only too much of his cards, major, I'm afraid,' she said. The major owned that he knew as much; did not disguise that he had heard of Sir Francis Clavering's unfortunate propensity to play; pitied Lady Clavering sincerely; but spoke with such genuine sentiment and sense, that her ladyship, glad to find a person of experience to whom she could confide her grief and her condition, talked about them pretty unreservedly to Major Pendennis, and was

eager to have his advice and consolation. Major Pendennis became the Begum's confidant and house-friend, and as a mother, a wife, and a capitalist, she consulted him.

He gave her to understand (showing at the same time a great deal of respectful sympathy) that he was acquainted with some of the circumstances of her first unfortunate marriage, and with even the person of her late husband, whom he remembered in Calcutta—when she was living in seclusion with her father. The poor lady, with tears of shame more than of grief in her eyes, told her version of her story. Going back a child to India after two years at a European school, she had met Amory, and foolishly married him. 'Oh, you don't know how miserable that man made me,' she said, 'or what a life I passed betwixt him and my father. Before I saw him I had never seen a man except my father's clerks and native servants. You know we didn't go into society in India on account of——' ('I know,' said Major Pendennis, with a bow). 'I was a wild, romantic child, my head was full of novels which I'd read at school—I listened to his wild stories and adventures, for he was a daring fellow, and I thought he talked beautifully of those calm nights on the passage out, when he used to—— Well, I married him, and I was wretched from that day—wretched with my father, whose character you know, Major Pendennis, and I won't speak of: but he wasn't a good man, sir,—neither to my poor mother, nor to me, except that he left me his money,—nor to no one else that I ever heard of: and he didn't do many kind actions in his lifetime, I'm afraid. And as for Amory, he was almost worse; he was a spendthrift when my father was close: he drank dreadfully, and was furious when in that way. He wasn't in any way a good or a faithful husband to me, Major Pendennis; and if he'd died in the jail before his trial, instead of afterwards, he would have saved me a deal of shame and of unhappiness since, sir.' Lady Clavering added: 'For perhaps I should not have married at all if I had not been so anxious to change his horrid name, and I have not been happy in my second husband, as I suppose you know, sir. Ah, Major Pendennis, I've got money to be sure, and I'm a lady, and people fancy I'm very happy, but I ain't. We all have our cares, and griefs, and troubles: and many's the day that I sit down to one of my grand dinners with an aching heart, and many a

night do I lay awake on my fine bed, a great deal more unhappy than the maid that makes it. For I'm not a happy woman, major, for all the world says; and envies the Begum her diamonds, and carriages, and the great company that comes to my house. I'm not happy in my husband; I'm not happy in my daughter. She ain't a good girl like that dear Laura Bell at Fairoaks. She's cost me many a tear, though you don't see 'em; and she sneers at her mother because I haven't had learning and that. How should I? I was brought up amongst natives till I was twelve, and went back to India when I was fourteen. Ah, major, I should have been a good woman if I had had a good husband. And now I must go upstairs and wipe my eyes, for they're red with cryin'. And Lady Rockminster's a-comin', and we're goin' to 'ave a drive in the Park.' And when Lady Rockminster made her appearance, there was not a trace of tears or vexation on Lady Clavering's face, but she was full of spirits, and bounced out with her blunders and talk, and murdered the king's English with the utmost liveliness and good-humour.

'Begad, she is not such a bad woman!' the major thought within himself. 'She is not refined, certainly, and calls "Apollo" "Apoller"; but she has some heart, and I like that sort of thing, and a devilish deal of money, too. Three stars* in India Stock to her name, begad! which that young cub is to have—is he?' And he thought how he should like to see a little of the money transferred to Miss Blanche, and, better still, one of those stars shining in the name of Mr. Arthur Pendennis.

Still bent upon pursuing his schemes, whatsoever they might be, the old negotiator took the privilege of his intimacy and age, to talk in a kindly and fatherly manner to Miss Blanche, when he found occasion to see her alone. He came in so frequently at luncheon-time, and became so familiar with the ladies, that they did not even hesitate to quarrel before him; and Lady Clavering, whose tongue was loud, and temper brusque, had many a battle with the Sylphide in the family friend's presence. Blanche's wit seldom failed to have the mastery in these encounters, and the keen barbs of her arrows drove her adversary discomfited away. 'I am an old fellow,' the major said; 'I have nothing to do in life. I have my eyes open. I keep good counsel. I am the friend of both of you; and

if you choose to quarrel before me, why, I shan't tell anyone. But you are two good people, and I intend to make it up between you. I have between lots of people—husbands and wives, fathers and sons, daughters and mammas, before this. I like it ; I've nothing else to do.'

One day, then, the old diplomatist entered Lady Clavering's drawing-room, just as the latter quitted it, evidently in a high state of indignation, and ran past him up the stairs to her own apartments. 'She couldn't speak to him now,' she said ; 'she was a great deal too angry with that—that—that little, wicked——' anger choked the rest of the words, or prevented their utterance until Lady Clavering had passed out of hearing.

'My dear, good Miss Amory,' the major said, entering the drawing-room, 'I see what is happening. You and mamma have been disagreeing. Mothers and daughters disagree in the best families. It was but last week that I healed up a quarrel between Lady Clapperton and her daughter Lady Claudia. Lady Lear and her eldest daughter have not spoken for fourteen years. Kinder and more worthy people than these I never knew in the whole course of my life ; for everybody but each other admirable. But they can't live together : they oughtn't to live together : and I wish, my dear creature, with all my soul, that I could see you with an establishment of your own—for there is no woman in London who could conduct one better—with your own establishment, making your own home happy.'

'I am not very happy in this one,' said the Sylphide ; 'and the stupidity of mamma is enough to provoke a saint.'

'Precisely so ; you are not suited to one another. Your mother committed one fault in early life—or was it Nature, my dear, in your case ?—she ought not to have educated you. You ought not to have been bred up to become the refined and intellectual being you are, surrounded, as I own you are, by those who have not your genius or your refinement. Your place would be to lead in the most brilliant circles, not to follow, and take a second place in any society. I have watched you, Miss Amory : you are ambitious ; and your proper sphere is command. You ought to shine ; and you never can in this house, I know it. I hope I shall see you in another and a happier one, some day, and the mistress of it.'

The Sylphide shrugged her lily shoulders with a look of scorn. 'Where is the prince, and where is the palace, Major Pendennis?' she said. 'I am ready. But there is no romance in the world now, no real affection.'

'No, indeed,' said the major, with the most sentimental and simple air which he could muster.

'Not that I know anything about it,' said Blanche, casting her eyes down, 'except what I have read in novels.'

'Of course not,' Major Pendennis cried; 'how should you, my dear young lady? and novels ain't true, as you remark admirably, and there is no romance left in the world. Begad, I wish I was a young fellow like my nephew.'

'And what,' continued Miss Amory, musing, 'what are the men whom we see about at the balls every night—dancing guardsmen, penniless Treasury clerks—boobies! If I had my brother's fortune, I might have such an establishment as you promise me—but with my name, and with my little means, what am I to look to? A country parson, or a barrister in a street near Russell Square, or a captain in a Dragoon regiment, who will take lodgings for me, and come home from the mess tipsy and smelling of smoke like Sir Francis Clavering. That is how we girls are destined to end life. Oh, Major Pendennis, I am sick of London, and of balls, and of young dandies, with their chin-tips, and of the insolent great ladies who know us one day and cut us the next—and of the world altogether. I should like to leave it and go into a convent, that I should. I shall never find anybody to understand me. And I live here as much alone in my family and in the world, as if I were in a cell locked up for ever. I wish there were Sisters of Charity here, and that I could be one and catch the plague, and die of it—I wish to quit the world. I am not very old: but I am tired, I have suffered so much—I've been so disillusionated—I'm weary, I'm weary—oh that the Angel of Death would come and beckon me away!'

This speech may be interpreted as follows. A few nights since a great lady, Lady Flamingo, had cut Miss Amory and Lady Clavering. She was quite mad because she could not get an invitation to Lady Drum's ball: it was the end of the season and nobody had proposed to her: she had made no sensation at all, she who was so much cleverer than any girl of the year, and of the young ladies forming her special circle. Dora who had but five thousand pounds, Flora

who had nothing, and Leonora who had red hair, were going to be married, and nobody had come for Blanche Amory!

'You judge wisely about the world, and about your position, my dear Miss Blanche,' the major said. 'The prince don't marry nowadays, as you say: unless the princess has a doosid deal of money in the funds, or is a lady of his own rank.—The young folks of the great families marry into the great families: if they haven't fortune they have each other's shoulders, to push on in the world, which is pretty nearly as good.—A girl with your fortune can scarcely hope for a great match: but a girl with your genius and your admirable tact and fine manners, with a clever husband by her side, may make *any* place for herself in the world.—We are grown doosidly republican. Talent ranks with birth and wealth now, begad: and a clever man with a clever wife may take any place they please.'

Miss Amory did not of course in the least understand what Major Pendennis meant.—Perhaps she thought over circumstances in her mind, and asked herself could he be a negotiator for a former suitor of hers, and could he mean Pen? No, it was impossible.—He had been civil, but nothing more.—So she said, laughing, 'Who is the clever man, and when will you bring him to me, Major Pendennis? I am dying to see him.'

At this moment a servant threw open the door, and announced Mr. Henry Foker: at which name, and the appearance of our friend, both the lady and the gentleman burst out laughing.

'That is not the man,' Major Pendennis said. 'He is engaged to his cousin, Lord Gravesend's daughter.—Good-bye, my dear Miss Amory.'

Was Pen growing worldly, and should a man not get the experience of the world and lay it to his account? 'He felt, for his part,' as he said, 'that he was growing very old very soon. How this town forms and changes us,' he said once to Warrington. Each had come in from his night's amusement; and Pen was smoking his pipe, and recounting, as his habit was, to his friend the observations and adventures of the evening just past. 'How I am changed,' he said, 'from the simpleton boy at Fairoaks, who was fit to break his heart about his first love! Lady Mirabel had a reception to-night, and was as grave and collected as

if she had been born a duchess, and had never seen a trapdoor in her life. She gave me the honour of a conversation, and patronized me about *Walter Lorraine*, quite kindly.'

'What condescension!' broke in Warrington.

'Wasn't it?' Pen said simply—at which the other burst out laughing, according to his wont. 'Is it possible,' he

said, 'that anybody should think of patronizing the eminent author of *Walter Lorraine*?'

'You laugh at both of us,' Pen said, blushing a little—'I was coming to that myself. She told me that she had not read the book (as indeed I believe she never read a book in her life), but that Lady Rockminster had, and that the Duchess of Connaught pronounced it to be very clever. In that case, I said I should die happy, for that to please those two ladies was in fact the great aim of my existence,

and having their approbation, of course I need look for no other. Lady Mirabel looked at me solemnly out of her fine eyes, and said, "Oh, indeed," as if she understood me ; and then she asked me whether I went to the duchess's Thursdays, and when I said No, hoped she should see me there, and that I must try and get there, everybody went there—everybody who was in society : and then we talked of the new ambassador from Timbuctoo, and how he was better than the old one ; and how Lady Mary Billington was going to marry a clergyman quite below her in rank ; and how Lord and Lady Ringdove had fallen out three months after their marriage about Tom Pouter of the Blues, Lady Ringdove's cousin—and so forth. From the gravity of that woman you would have fancied she had been born in a palace, and lived all the seasons of her life in Belgrave Square.'

'And you, I suppose you took your part in the conversation pretty well, as the descendant of the earl your father, and the heir of Fairoaks Castle ?' Warrington said. 'Yes, I remember reading of the festivities which occurred when you came of age. The countess gave a brilliant tea soirée to the neighbouring nobility ; and the tenantry were regaled in the kitchen with a leg of mutton and a quart of ale. The remains of the banquet were distributed amongst the poor of the village, and the entrance to the park was illuminated until old John put the candle out on retiring to rest at his usual hour.'

'My mother is not a countess,' said Pen, 'though she has very good blood in her veins too—but commoner as she is, I have never met a peeress who was more than her peer, Mr. George ; and if you will come to Fairoaks Castle you shall judge for yourself of her and of my cousin too. They are not so witty as the London women, but they certainly are as well bred. The thoughts of women in the country are turned to other objects than those which occupy your London ladies. In the country a woman has her household and her poor, her long calm days and long calm evenings.'

'Devilish long,' Warrington said, 'and a great deal too calm ; I've tried 'em.'

'The monotony of that existence must be to a certain degree melancholy—like the tune of a long ballad ; and its harmony grave and gentle, sad and tender : it would be

unendurable else. The loneliness of women in the country makes them of necessity soft and sentimental. Leading a life of calm duty, constant routine, mystic reverie,—a sort of nuns at large—too much gaiety or laughter would jar upon their almost sacred quiet, and would be as out of place there as in a church.'

'Where you go to sleep over the sermon,' Warrington said.

'You are a professed misogynist, and hate the sex because, I suspect, you know very little about them,' Mr. Pen continued, with an air of considerable self-complacency. 'If you dislike the women in the country for being too slow, surely the London women ought to be fast enough for you. The pace of London life is enormous: how do people last at it, I wonder,—male and female? Take a woman of the world: follow her course through the season; one asks how she can survive it? or if she tumbles into a sleep at the end of August, and lies torpid until the spring? She goes into the world every night, and sits watching her marriageable daughters dancing till long after dawn. She has a nursery of little ones, very likely, at home, to whom she administers example and affection; having an eye likewise to bread-and-milk, catechism, music and French, and roast leg of mutton at one o'clock; she has to call upon ladies of her own station, either domestically or in her public character, in which she sits upon Charity Committees, or Ball Committees, or Emigration Committees, or Queen's College Committees, and discharges I don't know what more duties of British stateswomanship. She very likely keeps a poor-visiting list; has conversations with the clergyman about soup or flannel, or proper religious teaching for the parish; and (if she lives in certain districts) probably attends early church. She has the newspapers to read, and at least, must know what her husband's party is about, so as to be able to talk to her neighbour at dinner; and it is a fact that she reads every new book that comes out; for she can talk, and very smartly and well, about them all, and you see them all upon her drawing-room table. She has the cares of her household besides:—to make both ends meet; to make the girls' milliner's bills appear not too dreadful to the father and paymaster of the family; to snip off, in secret, a little extra article of expenditure here and there, and convey it, in the shape of a

bank-note, to the boys at college or at sea; to check the encroachments of tradesmen and housekeepers' financial fallacies; to keep upper and lower servants from jangling with one another, and the household in order. Add to this, that she has a secret taste for some art or science, models in clay, makes experiments in chemistry, or plays in private on the violoncello,—and I say, without exaggeration, many London ladies are doing this,—and you have a character before you such as our ancestors never heard of, and such as belongs entirely to our era and period of civilization. Ye gods! how rapidly we live and grow! In nine months, Mr. Paxton grows you a pineapple* as large as a portmanteau, whereas a little one, no bigger than a Dutch cheese, took three years to attain his majority in old times; and as the race of pineapples, so is the race of man. Hoiaper*—what's the Greek for a pineapple, Warrington?'

'Stop, for mercy's sake, stop with the English and before you come to the Greek,' Warrington cried out, laughing. 'I never heard you make such a long speech, or was aware that you had penetrated so deeply into the female mysteries. Who taught you all this, and into whose boudoirs and nurseries have you been peeping, whilst I was smoking my pipe, and reading my book, lying on my straw bed?'

'You are on the bank, old boy, content to watch the waves tossing in the winds, and the struggles of others at sea,' Pen said. 'I am in the stream now, and by Jove I like it. How rapidly we go down it, hey?—strong and feeble, old and young—the metal pitchers and the earthen pitchers—the pretty little china boat swims gaily till the big bruised brazen one bumps him and sends him down—eh, *vogue la galère!*—you see a man sink in the race, and say good-bye to him—look, he has only dived under the other fellow's legs, and comes up shaking his poll, and striking out ever so far ahead. Eh, *vogue la galère*, I say. It's good sport, Warrington—not winning merely, but playing.'

'Well, go in and win, young 'un. I'll sit and mark the game,' Warrington said, surveying the ardent young fellow with an almost fatherly pleasure. 'A generous fellow plays for the play, a sordid one for the stake; an old fogy sits by and smokes the pipe of tranquillity, while Jack and Tom are pommelling each other in the ring.'

'Why don't you come in, George, and have a turn with

the gloves? You are big enough and strong enough,' Pen said. 'Dear old boy, you are worth ten of me.'

'You are not quite as tall as Goliath, certainly,' the other answered, with a laugh that was rough and yet tender. 'And as for me, I am disabled. I had a fatal hit in early life. I will tell you about it some day. You may, too, meet with your master. Don't be too eager, or too confident, or too worldly, my boy.'

Was Pendennis becoming worldly, or only seeing the world, or both? and is a man very wrong for being after all only a man? Which is the most reasonable, and does his duty best: he who stands aloof from the struggle of life, calmly contemplating it, or he who descends to the ground, and takes his part in the contest? 'That philosopher,' Pen said, 'had held a great place amongst the leaders of the world, and enjoyed to the full what it had to give of rank and riches, renown and pleasure, who came, weary-hearted, out of it, and said that all was vanity and vexation of spirit. Many a teacher of those whom we reverence, and who steps out of his carriage up to his carved cathedral place, shakes his lawn ruffles over the velvet cushion, and cries out, that the whole struggle is an accursed one, and the works of the world are evil. Many a conscience-stricken mystic flies from it altogether, and shuts himself out from it within convent walls (real or spiritual), whence he can only look up to the sky, and contemplate the heaven out of which there is no rest, and no good.

'But the earth, where our feet are, is the work of the same Power as the immeasurable blue yonder, in which the future lies into which we would peer. Who ordered toil as the condition of life, ordered weariness, ordered sickness, ordered poverty, failure, success—to this man a foremost place, to the other a nameless struggle with the crowd—to that a shameful fall, or paralysed limb, or sudden accident—to each some work upon the ground he stands on, until he is laid beneath it.' While they were talking, the dawn came shining through the windows of the room, and Pen threw them open to receive the fresh morning air. 'Look, George,' said he; 'look and see the sun rise: he sees the labourer on his way a-field; the work-girl plying her poor needle; the lawyer at his desk, perhaps;

the beauty smiling asleep upon her pillow of down; or the jaded reveller reeling to bed; or the fevered patient tossing on it; or the doctor watching by it, over the throes of the mother for the child that is to be born into the world;—to be born and to take his part in the suffering and struggling, the tears and laughter, the crime, remorse, love, folly, sorrow, rest.'

CHAPTER XLV

MISS AMORY'S PARTNERS

The noble Henry Foker, of whom we have lost sight for a few pages, has been in the meanwhile occupied, as we might suppose a man of his constancy would be, in the pursuit and indulgence of his all-absorbing passion of love.[1]

He longed after her, and cursed the fate which separated him from her. When Lord Gravesend's family retired to the country (his lordship leaving his proxy with the venerable Lord Bagwig), Harry still remained lingering on in London, certainly not much to the sorrow of Lady Ann, to whom he was affianced, and who did not in the least miss him. Wherever Miss Amory went, this infatuated young fellow continued to follow her; and being aware that his engagement to his cousin was known in the world, he was forced to make a mystery of his passion, and confine it to his own breast, so that it was so pent in there and pressed down, that it is a wonder he did not explode some day with the stormy secret, and perish collapsed after the outburst.

There had been a grand entertainment at Gaunt House on one beautiful evening in June, and the next day's journals contained almost two columns of the names of the most closely-printed nobility and gentry who had been honoured with invitations to the ball. Among the guests were Sir Francis and Lady Clavering and Miss Amory, for

whom the indefatigable Major Pendennis had procured an invitation, and our two young friends Arthur and Harry. Each exerted himself, and danced a great deal with Miss Blanche. As for the worthy major, he assumed the charge of Lady Clavering, and took care to introduce her to that department of the mansion where her ladyship specially distinguished herself, namely, the refreshment-room, where, amongst pictures of Titian and Giorgione, and regal portraits of Vandyke and Reynolds, and enormous salvers of gold and silver, and pyramids of large flowers, and constellations of wax candles—in a manner perfectly regardless of expense, in a word—a supper was going on all night. Of how many creams, jellies, salads, peaches, white soups, grapes, patés, galantines, cups of tea, champagne, and so forth, Lady Clavering partook, it does not become us to say. How much the major suffered as he followed the honest woman about, calling to the solemn male attendants and lovely servant-maids, and administering to Lady Clavering's various wants with admirable patience, nobody knows ;—he never confessed. He never allowed his agony to appear on his countenance in the least ; but with a constant kindness brought plate after plate to the Begum.

Mr. Wagg counted up all the dishes of which Lady Clavering partook as long as he could count (but as he partook very freely himself of champagne during the evening, his powers of calculation were not to be trusted at the close of the entertainment), and he recommended Mr. Honeyman, Lady Steyne's medical man, to look carefully after the Begum, and to call and get news of her ladyship the next day.

Sir Francis Clavering made his appearance, and skulked for a while about the magnificent rooms ; but the company and the splendour which he met there were not to the baronet's taste, and after tossing off a tumbler of wine or two at the buffet, he quitted Gaunt House for the neighbourhood of Jermyn Street, where his friends Loder, Punter, little Moss Abrams, and Captain Skewball were assembled at the familiar green table. In the rattle of the box, and of their agreeable conversation, Sir Francis's spirits rose to their accustomed point of feeble hilarity.

Mr. Pynsent, who had asked Miss Amory to dance, came up on one occasion to claim her hand, but scowls of recogni-

tion having already passed between him and Mr. Arthur Pendennis in the dancing-room, Arthur suddenly rose up and claimed Miss Amory as his partner for the present dance, on which Mr. Pynsent, biting his lips and scowling yet more savagely, withdrew with a profound bow, saying that he gave up his claim. There are some men who are always falling in one's way in life. Pynsent and Pen had this view of each other; and regarded each other accordingly.

'What a confounded conceited provincial fool that is!' thought the one. 'Because he has written a twopenny novel, his absurd head is turned, and a kicking would take his conceit out of him.'

'What an impertinent idiot that man is!' remarked the other to his partner. 'His soul is in Downing Street; his neckcloth is foolscap; his hair is sand; his legs are rulers; his vitals are tape and sealing-wax; he was a prig in his cradle; and never laughed since he was born, except three times at the same joke of his chief. I have the same liking for that man, Miss Amory, that I have for cold boiled veal.' Upon which Blanche of course remarked, that Mr. Pendennis was wicked, *méchant*, perfectly abominable, and wondered what he would say when *her* back was turned.

'Say!—Say that you have the most beautiful figure, and the slimmest waist in the world, Blanche—Miss Amory, I mean. I beg your pardon. Another turn; this music would make an alderman dance.'

'And you have left off tumbling, when you waltz now?' Blanche asked, archly looking up at her partner's face.

'One falls and one gets up again in life, Blanche; you know I used to call you so in old times, and it is the prettiest name in the world: besides, I have practised since then.'

'And with a great number of partners, I'm afraid,' Blanche said, with a little sham sigh, and a shrug of the shoulders. And so in truth Mr. Pen had practised a good deal in his life; and had undoubtedly arrived at being able to dance better.

If Pendennis was impertinent in his talk, Foker, on the other hand, so bland and communicative on most occasions, was entirely mum and melancholy when he danced with Miss Amory. To clasp her slender waist was a rapture, to whirl round the room with her was a delirium; but to

speak to her, what could he say that was worthy of her? What pearl of conversation could he bring that was fit for the acceptance of such a queen of love and wit as Blanche? It was she who made the talk when she was in the company of this love-stricken partner. It was she who asked him how that dear little pony was, and looked at him and thanked him with such a tender kindness and regret, and refused the dear little pony with such a delicate sigh when he offered it. 'I have nobody to ride with in London,' she said. 'Mamma is timid, and her figure is not pretty on horseback. Sir Francis never goes out with me. He loves me like—like a step-daughter. Oh, how delightful it must be to have a father—a father, Mr. Foker!'

'Oh, uncommon,' said Mr. Harry, who enjoyed that blessing very calmly, upon which, and forgetting the sentimental air which she had just before assumed, Blanche's grey eyes gazed at Foker with such an arch twinkle, that both of them burst out laughing, and Harry enraptured and at his ease began to entertain her with a variety of innocent prattle—good, kind, simple Foker talk, flavoured with many expressions by no means to be discovered in dictionaries, and relating to the personal history of himself or horses, or other things dear and important to him, or to persons in the ball-room then passing before them, and about whose appearance or character Mr. Harry spoke with artless freedom and a considerable dash of humour.

And it was Blanche who, when the conversation flagged, and the youth's modesty came rushing back and overpowering him, knew how to reanimate her companion: asked him questions about Logwood, and whether it was a pretty place? Whether he was a hunting-man, and whether he liked women to hunt? (in which case she was prepared to say that she adored hunting)—but Mr. Foker expressing his opinion against sporting females, and pointing out Lady Bullfinch, who happened to pass by, as a horse-godmother, whom he had seen at cover with a cigar in her face, Blanche too expressed her detestation of the sports of the field, and said it would make her shudder to think of a dear, sweet little fox being killed, on which Foker laughed and waltzed with renewed vigour and grace.

And at the end of the waltz,—the last waltz they had on

that night,—Blanche asked him about Drummington, and whether it was a fine house. His cousins, she had heard, were very accomplished: Lord Erith she had met, and which of his cousins was his favourite? Was it not Lady Ann? Yes, she was sure it was she: sure by his looks and his blushes. She was tired of dancing; it was getting very late; she must go to mamma;—and, without another word, she sprang away from Harry Foker's arm, and seized upon Pen's, who was swaggering about the dancing-room, and again said, 'Mamma, mamma!—take me to mamma, dear Mr. Pendennis!' transfixing Harry with a Parthian shot as she fled from him.

My Lord Steyne, with garter and ribbon, with a bald head and shining eyes, and a collar of red whiskers round his face, always looked grand upon an occasion of state: and made a great effect upon Lady Clavering, when he introduced himself to her at the request of the obsequious Major Pendennis. With his own white and royal hand he handed to her ladyship a glass of wine, said he had heard of her charming daughter, and begged to be presented to her; and, at this very juncture, Mr. Arthur Pendennis came up with the young lady on his arm.

The peer made a profound bow, and Blanche the deepest curtsy that ever was seen. His lordship gave Mr. Arthur Pendennis his hand to shake; said he had read his book, which was very wicked and clever; asked Miss Blanche if she had read it,—at which Pen blushed and winced. Why, Blanche was one of the heroines of the novel. Blanche, in black ringlets and a little altered, was the Neaera of *Walter Lorraine*.

Blanche had read it: the language of the eyes expressed her admiration and rapture at the performance. This little play being achieved, the Marquis of Steyne made other two profound bows to Lady Clavering and her daughter, and passed on to some other of his guests at the splendid entertainment.

Mamma and daughter were loud in their expressions of admiration of the noble marquis so soon as his broad back was turned upon them. 'He said they make a very nice couple,' whispered Major Pendennis to Lady Clavering. Did he now, really? Mamma thought they would; Mamma was so flustered with the honour which had just been shown to her, and with other intoxicating events of

the evening, that her good-humour knew no bounds. She laughed, she winked, and nodded knowingly at Pen; she tapped him on the arm with her fan; she tapped Blanche; she tapped the major;—her contentment was boundless, and her method of showing her joy equally expansive.

As the party went down the great staircase of Gaunt House, the morning had risen stark and clear over the black trees of the square; the skies were tinged with pink: and the cheeks of some of the people at the ball,—ah, how ghastly they looked! That admirable and devoted major, above all,—who had been for hours by Lady Clavering's side, ministering to her and feeding her body with everything that was nice, and her ear with everything that was sweet and flattering,—oh! what an object he was! The rings round his eyes were of the colour of bistre;* those orbs themselves were like the plovers' eggs whereof Lady Clavering and Blanche had each tasted; the wrinkles in his old face were furrowed in deep gashes; and a silver stubble, like an elderly morning dew, was glittering on his chin, and alongside the dyed whiskers, now limp and out of curl.

There he stood, with admirable patience, enduring, uncomplaining, a silent agony; knowing that people could see the state of his face (for could he not himself perceive the condition of others, males and females, of his own age?)—longing to go to rest for hours past; aware that suppers disagreed with him, and yet having eaten a little so as to keep his friend, Lady Clavering, in good humour; with twinges of rheumatism in the back and knees; with weary feet burning in his varnished boots,—so tired, oh, so tired

and longing for bed! If a man, struggling with hardship and bravely overcoming it, is an object of admiration for the gods, that Power in whose chapels the old major was a faithful worshipper must have looked upwards approvingly upon the constancy of Pendennis's martyrdom. There are sufferers in that cause as in the other: the negroes in the service of Mumbo Jumbo tattoo and drill themselves with burning skewers with great fortitude; and we read that the priests in the service of Baal gashed themselves and bled freely. You who can smash the idols, do so with a good courage; but do not be too fierce with the idolaters,—they worship the best thing they know.

The Pendennises, the elder and the younger, waited with Lady Clavering and her daughter until her ladyship's carriage was announced, when the elder's martyrdom may be said to have come to an end, for the good-natured Begum insisted upon leaving him at his door in Bury Street; so he took the back seat of the carriage, after a feeble bow or two, and speech of thanks, polite to the last, and resolute in doing his duty. The Begum waved her dumpy little hand by way of farewell to Arthur and Foker, and Blanche smiled languidly out upon the young men, thinking whether she looked very wan and green under her rose-coloured hood, and whether it was the mirrors at Gaunt House, or the fatigue and fever of her own eyes, which made her fancy herself so pale.

Arthur, perhaps, saw quite well how yellow Blanche looked, but did not attribute that peculiarity of her complexion to the effect of the looking-glasses, or to any error in his sight or her own. Our young man of the world could use his eyes very keenly, and could see Blanche's face pretty much as nature had made it. But for poor Foker it had a radiance which dazzled and blinded him: he could see no more faults in it than in the sun, which was now flaring over the house-tops.

Amongst other wicked London habits which Pen had acquired, the moralist will remark that he had got to keep very bad hours; and often was going to bed at the time when sober country people were thinking of leaving it. Men get used to one hour as to another. Editors of newspapers, Covent Garden market-people, night cabmen and coffee-sellers, chimney-sweeps, and gentlemen and ladies of fashion who frequent balls, are often quite lively at three

or four o'clock of a morning, when ordinary mortals are snoring. We have shown in the last chapter how Pen was in a brisk condition of mind at this period, inclined to smoke his cigar at ease, and to speak freely.

Foker and Pen walked away from Gaunt House, then, indulging in both the above amusements: or rather Pen talked, and Foker looked as if he wanted to say something. Pen was sarcastic and dandified when he had been in the company of great folks; he could not help imitating some of their airs and tones, and having a most lively imagination, mistook himself for a person of importance very easily. He rattled away, and attacked this person and that; sneered at Lady John Turnbull's bad French, which her ladyship will introduce into all conversations in spite of the sneers of everybody; at Mrs. Slack Rover's extraordinary costume and sham jewels; at the old dandies and the young ones;—at whom didn't he sneer and laugh?

'You fire at everybody, Pen—you're grown awful, that you are,' Foker said. 'Now, you've pulled about Blondel's yellow wig, and Colchicum's black one, why don't you have a shy at a brown one, hey? you know whose I mean. It got into Lady Clavering's carriage.'

'Under my uncle's hat? My uncle is a martyr, Foker, my boy. My uncle has been doing excruciating duties all night. He likes to go to bed rather early. He has a dreadful headache if he sits up and touches supper. He always has the gout if he walks or stands much at a ball. He has been sitting up, and standing up, and supping. He has gone home to the gout and the headache, and for my sake. Shall I make fun of the old boy? no, not for Venice!'*

'How do you mean that he has been doing it for your sake?' Foker asked, looking rather alarmed.

'Boy! canst thou keep a secret if I impart it to thee?' Pen cried out, in high spirits. 'Art thou of good counsel? Wilt thou swear? Wilt thou be mum, or wilt thou peach? Wilt thou be silent and hear, or wilt thou speak and die?' And as he spoke, flinging himself into an absurd theatrical attitude, the men in the cab-stand in Piccadilly wondered and grinned at the antics of the two young swells.

'What the doose are you driving at?' Foker asked, looking very much agitated.

Pen, however, did not remark this agitation much, but continued in the same bantering and excited vein. 'Henry,

friend of my youth,' he said, 'and witness of my early follies, though dull at thy books, yet thou art not altogether deprived of sense,—nay, blush not, Henrico, thou hast a good portion of that, and of courage and kindness too, at the service of thy friends. Were I in a strait of poverty, I would come to my Foker's purse. Were I in grief, I would discharge my grief upon his sympathizing bosom——'

'Gammon, Pen—go on,' Foker said.

'I would, Henrico, upon thy studs, and upon thy cambric worked by the hands of beauty, to adorn the breast of valour! Know then, friend of my boyhood's days, that Arthur Pendennis, of the Upper Temple, student-at-law, feels that he is growing lonely, and old Care is furrowing his temples, and Baldness is busy with his crown. Shall we stop and have a drop of coffee at this stall, it looks very hot and nice? Look how that cabman is blowing at his saucer. No, you won't? Aristocrat! I resume my tale. I am getting on in life. I have got devilish little money. I want some. I am thinking of getting some, and settling in life. I'm thinking of settling. I'm thinking of marrying, old boy. I'm thinking of becoming a moral man; a steady port and sherry character: with a good reputation in my *quartier*, and a moderate establishment of two maids and a man—with an occasional brougham to drive out Mrs. Pendennis, and a house near the Parks for the accommodation of the children. Ha! what sayest thou? Answer thy friend, thou worthy child of beer. Speak, I adjure thee by all thy vats.'

'But you ain't got any money, Pen,' said the other, still looking alarmed.

'I ain't? No, but *she* 'ave. I tell thee there is gold in store for me—not what *you* call money, nursed in the lap of luxury, and cradled on grains, and drinking in wealth from a thousand mash-tubs. What do you know about money? What is poverty to you is splendour to the hardy son of the humble apothecary. You can't live without an establishment, and your houses in town and country. A snug little house somewhere off Belgravia, a brougham for my wife, a decent cook, and a fair bottle of wine for my friends at home sometimes; these simple necessaries suffice for me, my Foker.' And here Pendennis began to look more serious. Without bantering further, Pen continued, 'I've rather serious thoughts of settling

and marrying. No man can get on in the world without some money at his back. You must have a certain stake to begin with, before you can go in and play the great game. Who knows that I'm not going to try, old fellow? Worse men than I have won at it. And as I have not got enough capital from my fathers, I must get some by my wife—that's all.'

They were walking down Grosvenor Street, as they talked, or rather as Pen talked, in the selfish fullness of his heart; and Mr. Pen must have been too much occupied with his own affairs to remark the concern and agitation of his neighbour, for he continued—'We are no longer children, you know, you and I, Harry. Bah! the time of our romance has passed away. We don't marry for passion, but for prudence and for establishment. What do you take your cousin for? Because she is a nice girl, and an earl's daughter, and the old folks wish it, and that sort of thing.

'And you, Pendennis,' asked Foker, 'you ain't very fond of the girl—you're going to marry?'

Pen shrugged his shoulders. '*Comme ça*,' said he; 'I like her well enough. She's pretty enough; she's clever enough. I think she'll do very well. And she has got money enough—that's the great point. Psha! you know who she is, don't you? I thought you were sweet on her yourself one night when we dined with her mamma. It's little Amory.'

'I—I thought so,' Foker said: 'and has she accepted you?'

'Not quite,' Arthur replied, with a confident smile, which seemed to say, I have but to ask, and she comes to me that instant.

'Oh, not quite,' said Foker; and he broke out with such a dreadful laugh, that Pen, for the first time, turned his thoughts from himself towards his companion, and was struck by the other's ghastly pale face.

'My dear fellow, Fo! what's the matter? You're ill,' Pen said, in a tone of real concern.

'You think it was the champagne at Gaunt House, don't you? It ain't that. Come in; let me talk to you for a minute. I'll tell you what it is. D—— it, let me tell somebody,' Foker said.

They were at Mr. Foker's door by this time, and, opening it, Harry walked with his friend into his apartments, which

were situated in the back part of the house, and behind the family dining-room, where the elder Foker received his guests, surrounded by pictures of himself, his wife, his infant son on a donkey, and the late Earl of Gravesend in his robes as a peer. Foker and Pen passed by this chamber, now closed with death-like shutters, and entered into the young man's own quarters. Dusky streams of sunbeams were playing into that room, and lighting up poor Harry's gallery of dancing girls and Opera nymphs with flickering illuminations.

'Look here! I can't help telling you, Pen,' he said. 'Ever since the night we dined there, I'm so fond of that girl, that I think I shall die if I don't get her. I feel as if I should go mad sometimes. I can't stand it, Pen. I couldn't bear to hear you talking about her, just now, about marrying her only because she's money. Ah, Pen! *that* ain't the question in marrying. I'd bet anything it ain't. Talking about money and such a girl as that, it's—it's—what-d'ye-call-'em—*you* know what I mean—I ain't good at talking—sacrilege, then. If she'd have me, I'd take and sweep a crossing, that I would!'

'Poor Fo! I don't think that would tempt her,' Pen said, eyeing his friend with a great deal of real good nature and pity. 'She is not a girl for love and a cottage.'

'She ought to be a duchess, I know that very well, and I know she wouldn't take me unless I could make her a great place in the world—for I ain't good for anything myself much—I ain't clever and that sort of thing,' Foker said sadly. 'If I had all the diamonds that all the duchesses and marchionesses had on to-night, wouldn't I put 'em in her lap? But what's the use of talking? I'm booked for another race. It's that kills me, Pen. I can't get out of it; though I die, I can't get out of it. And though my cousin's a nice girl, and I like her very well, and that, yet I hadn't seen this one when our governors settled that matter between us. And when you talked, just now, about her doing very well, and about her having money enough for both of you, I thought to myself it isn't money or mere liking a girl, that ought to be enough to make a fellow marry. He may marry, and find he likes somebody else better. All the money in the world won't make you happy then. Look at me; I've plenty of money, or shall have, out of the mash-tubs, as you call 'em. My governor thought

he'd made it all right for me in settling my marriage with my cousin. I tell you it won't do; and when Lady Ann has got her husband, it won't be happy for either of us, and she'll have the most miserable beggar in town.'

'Poor old fellow!' Pen said, with rather a cheap magnanimity, 'I wish I could help you. I had no idea of this, and that you were so wild about the girl. Do you think she would have you without your money? No. Do you think your father would agree to break off your engagement with your cousin? You know him very well, and that he would cast you off rather than do so.'

The unhappy Foker only groaned a reply, flinging himself prostrate on the sofa, face forwards, his head in his hands.

'As for my affair,' Pen went on—'my dear fellow, if I had thought matters were so critical with you, at least I would not have pained you by choosing you as my confidant. And my business is not serious, at least not as yet. I have not spoken a word about it to Miss Amory. Very likely she would not have me if I asked her. Only I have had a great deal of talk about it with my uncle, who says that the match might be an eligible one for me. I'm ambitious and I'm poor. And it appears Lady Clavering will give her a good deal of money, and Sir Francis might be got to—never mind the rest. Nothing is settled, Harry. They are going out of town directly. I promise you I won't ask her before she goes. There's no hurry: there's time for everybody. But, suppose you got her, Foker. Remember what you said about marriages just now, and the misery of a man who doesn't care for his wife; and what sort of a wife would you have who didn't care for her husband?'

'But she would care for me,' said Foker, from his sofa—'that is, I think she would. Last night only, as we were dancing, she said——'

'What did she say?' Pen cried, starting up in great wrath. But he saw his own meaning more clearly than Foker, and broke off with a laugh—'Well, never mind what she said, Harry. Miss Amory is a clever girl, and says numbers of civil things—to you—to me, perhaps—and who the deuce knows to whom besides? Nothing's settled, old boy. At least, *my* heart won't break if I don't get her. Win her if you can, and I wish you joy of her. Good-bye! Don't think about what I said to you. I was excited, and confoundedly thirsty in those hot rooms, and

didn't, I suppose, put enough seltzer-water into the champagne. Good-night! I'll keep your counsel too. "Mum" is the word between us; and "let there be a fair fight, and let the best man win," as Peter Crawley says.'

So saying, Mr. Arthur Pendennis, giving a very queer and rather dangerous look at his companion, shook him by the hand, with something of that sort of cordiality which befitted his just repeated simile of the boxing-match, and which Mr. Bendigo displays when he shakes hands with Mr. Caunt* before they fight each other for the champion's belt and two hundred pounds a side. Foker returned his friend's salute with an imploring look, and a piteous squeeze of the hand, sank back on his cushions again, and Pen, putting on his hat, strode forth into the air, and almost over the body of the matutinal housemaid, who was rubbing the steps at the door.

'And so he wants her too? does he?' thought Pen as he marched along—and noted within himself with a fatal keenness of perception, and almost an infernal mischief, that the very pains and tortures which that honest heart of Foker's was suffering gave a zest and an impetus to his own pursuit of Blanche: if pursuit that might be called which had been no pursuit as yet, but mere sport and idle dallying. 'She said something to him, did she? perhaps she gave him the fellow flower to this;' and he took out of his coat and twiddled in his thumb and finger a poor little shrivelled, crumpled bud that had faded and blackened with the heat and flare of the night.—'I wonder to how many more she has given her artless tokens of affection—the little flirt!' and he flung his into the gutter, where the water may have refreshed it, and where any amateur of rosebuds may have picked it up. And then bethinking him that the day was quite bright, and that the passers-by might be staring at his beard and white neckcloth, our modest young gentleman took a cab and drove to the Temple.

Ah! is this the boy that prayed at his mother's knee but a few years since, and for whom very likely at this hour of morning she is praying? Is this jaded and selfish worldling the lad who, a short while back, was ready to fling away his worldly all, his hope, his ambition, his chance of life, for his love? This is the man you are proud of, old Pendennis. You boast of having formed him: and of having

reasoned him out of his absurd romance and folly—and groaning in your bed over your pains and rheumatisms, satisfy yourself still by thinking, that, at last, that lad will do something to better himself in life, and that the Pendennises will take a good place in the world. And is he the only one, who in his progress through this dark life goes wilfully or fatally astray, whilst the natural truth and love which should illumine him grow dim in the poisoned air, and suffice to light him no more?

When Pen was gone away, poor Harry Foker got up from the sofa, and taking out from his waistcoat—the splendidly buttoned, the gorgeously embroidered, the work of his mamma—a little white rosebud, he drew from his dressing-case, also the maternal present, a pair of scissors, with which he nipped carefully the stalk of the flower, and placing it in a glass of water opposite his bed, he sought refuge there from care and bitter remembrances.

It is to be presumed that Miss Blanche Amory had more than one rose in her bouquet, and why should not the kind young creature give out of her superfluity, and make as many partners as possible happy?

CHAPTER XLVI

MONSEIGNEUR S'AMUSE

THE exertions of that last night at Gaunt House had proved almost too much for Major Pendennis; and as soon as he could move his weary old body with safety, he transported himself groaning to Buxton, and sought relief in the healing waters of that place. Parliament broke up. Sir Francis Clavering and family left town, and the affairs which we have just mentioned to the reader were not advanced, in the brief interval of a few days or weeks which have occurred between this and the last chapter. The town was, however, emptied since then.

The season was now come to a conclusion : Pen's neighbours, the lawyers, were gone upon circuit : and his more fashionable friends had taken their passports for the Continent, or had fled for health or excitement to the Scotch moors. Scarce a man was to be seen in the bow-windows of the clubs, or on the solitary Pall-Mall pavement. The red jackets had disappeared from before the palace gate : the tradesmen of St. James's were abroad taking their pleasure : the tailors had grown moustachios and were gone up the Rhine : the bootmakers were at Ems or Baden, blushing when they met their customers at those places of recreation, or punting beside their creditors at the gambling tables : the clergymen of St. James's only preached to half a congregation, in which there was not a single sinner of distinction : the band in Kensington Gardens had shut up their instruments of brass and trumpets of silver : only two or three old flys and chaises crawled by the banks of the Serpentine, and Clarence Bulbul, who was retained in town by his arduous duties as a Treasury clerk, when he took his afternoon ride in Rotten Row, compared its loneliness to the vastness of the Arabian desert, and himself to a Bedouin wending his way through that dusty solitude. Warrington stowed away a quantity of Cavendish tobacco in his carpet-bag, and betook himself, as his custom was in the vacation, to his brother's house in Norfolk. Pen was left alone in chambers for a while, for this man of fashion could not quit the metropolis when he chose always : and was at present detained by the affairs of his newspaper, the *Pall Mall Gazette*, of which he acted as the editor and chargé d'affaires during the temporary absence of the chief, Captain Shandon, who was with his family at the salutary watering-place of Boulogne-sur-Mer.*

Although, as we have seen, Mr. Pen had pronounced himself for years past to be a man perfectly blasé and wearied of life, yet the truth is that he was an exceedingly healthy young fellow still ; with a fine appetite, which he satisfied with the greatest relish and satisfaction at least once a day ; and a constant desire for society, which showed him to be anything but misanthropical. If he could not get a good dinner, he sat down to a bad one with entire contentment ; if he could not procure the company of witty, or great, or beautiful persons, he put up with any society that came to hand ; and was perfectly satisfied in a tavern

parlour, or on board a Greenwich steamboat, or in a jaunt to Hampstead with Mr. Finucane, his colleague at the *Pall Mall Gazette;* or in a visit to the summer theatres across the river: or to the Royal Gardens of Vauxhall, where he was on terms of friendship with the great Simpson,* and where he shook the principal comic singer or the lovely equestrian of the arena by the hand. And while he could watch the grimaces or the graces of these with a satiric humour that was not deprived of sympathy, he could look on with an eye of kindness at the lookers-on too; at the roystering youth bent upon enjoyment, and here taking it: at the honest parents, with their delighted children laughing and clapping their hands at the show: at the poor outcasts, whose laughter was less innocent though perhaps louder, and who brought their shame and their youth here, to dance and be merry till the dawn at least; and to get bread and drown care. Of this sympathy with all conditions of men, Arthur often boasted: he was pleased to possess it: and said that he hoped thus to the last he should retain it. As another man has an ardour for art or music, or natural science, Mr. Pen said that anthropology was his favourite pursuit; and had his eyes always eagerly open to its infinite varieties and beauties: contemplating with an unfailing delight all specimens of it in all places to which he resorted, whether it was the coquetting of a wrinkled dowager in a ball-room, or a high-bred young beauty blushing in her prime there; whether it was a hulking guardsman coaxing a servant-girl in the Park—or innocent little Tommy that was feeding the ducks whilst the nurse listened. And, indeed, a man whose heart is pretty clean can indulge in this pursuit with an enjoyment that never ceases, and is only perhaps the more keen because it is secret and has a touch of sadness in it; because he is of his mood and humour lonely, and apart although not alone.

Yes, Pen used to brag and talk in his impetuous way to Warrington. 'I was in love so fiercely in my youth, that I have burned out that flame for ever, I think; and if ever I marry, it will be a marriage of reason that I will make, with a well-bred, good-tempered, good-looking person who has a little money, and so forth, that will cushion our carriage in its course through life. As for romance, it is all done; I have spent that out, and am old before my time—I'm proud of it.'

'Stuff!' growled the other, 'you fancied you were getting bald the other day, and bragged about it as you do about everything. But you began to use the bear's-grease pot directly the hairdresser told you; and are scented like a barber ever since.'

'You are Diogenes,' the other answered, 'and you want every man to live in a tub like yourself. Violets smell better than stale tobacco, you grisly old cynic.' But Mr. Pen was blushing whilst he made this reply to his unromantical friend, and indeed cared a great deal more about himself still than such a philosopher perhaps should have done. Indeed, considering that he was careless about the world, Mr. Pen ornamented his person with no small pains in order to make himself agreeable to it, and for a weary pilgrim as he was, wore very tight boots and bright varnish.

It was in this dull season of the year then, of a shining Friday night in autumn, that Mr. Pendennis, having completed at his newspaper office a brilliant leading article—such as Captain Shandon himself might have written, had the captain been in good humour, and inclined to work, which he never would do except under compulsion—that Mr. Arthur Pendennis, having written his article, and reviewed it approvingly as it lay before him in its wet proof-sheet at the office of the paper, bethought him that he would cross the water, and regale himself with the fireworks and other amusements of Vauxhall. So he affably put in his pocket the order which admitted 'Editor of *Pall Mall Gazette* and friend' to that place of recreation, and paid with the coin of the realm a sufficient sum to enable him to cross Waterloo Bridge. The walk thence to the Gardens was pleasant, the stars were shining in the skies above, looking down upon the royal property, whence the rockets and Roman candles had not yet ascended to outshine the stars.

Before you enter the enchanted ground, where twenty thousand additional lamps are burned every night as usual, most of us have passed through the black and dreary passage and wickets which hide the splendours of Vauxhall from uninitiated men. In the walls of this passage are two holes strongly illuminated, in the midst of which you see two gentlemen at desks, where they will take either your money as a private individual, or your order of admission if you are provided with that passport to the

Gardens. Pen went to exhibit his ticket at the last-named orifice, where, however, a gentleman and two ladies were already in parley before him.

The gentleman, whose hat was very much on one side, and who wore a short and shabby cloak in an excessively smart manner, was crying out in a voice which Pen at once recognized—

'Bedad, sir, if ye doubt me honour, will ye obleege me by stipping out of that box, and——'

'Lor, Capting!' cried the elder lady.

'Don't bother me,' said the man in the box.

'And ask Mr. Hodgen himself, who's in the gyardens, to let these leedies pass. Don't be froightened, me dear madam, I'm not going to quarl with this gintleman, at anyreet before leedies. Will ye go, sir, and desoire Mr. Hodgen (whose orther I keem in with, and he's me most intemate friend, and I know he's goan to sing the "Body-Snatcher" here to-noight), with Captain Costigan's compliments, to stip out and let in the leedies—for meself, sir, oi've seen Vauxhall, and I scawrun any interfayrance on moi account: but for these leedies, one of them has never been there, and oi should think ye'd harly take advantage of me misfartune in losing the tickut, to deproive her of her pleasure.'

'It ain't no use, captain. I can't go about your business,' the checktaker said: on which the captain swore an oath, and the elder lady said, 'Lor, 'ow provokin'!'

As for the young one, she looked up at the captain and said, 'Never mind, Captain Costigan, I'm sure I don't want to go at all. Come away, mamma.' And with this, although she did not want to go at all, her feelings overcame her, and she began to cry.

'Me poor child!' the captain said. 'Can ye see that, sir, and will ye not let this innocent creature in?"

'It ain't my business,' cried the doorkeeper peevishly, out of the illuminated box. And at this minute Arthur came up, and recognizing Costigan, said, 'Don't you know me, captain? Pendennis!' And he took off his hat, and made a bow to the two ladies. 'Me dear boy! Me dear friend!' cried the captain, extending towards Pendennis the grasp of friendship; and he rapidly explained to the other what he called a 'most unluckee conthratong.' He had an order for Vauxhall, admitting two, from Mr. Hodgen, then

CAPTAIN COSTIGAN IN PERPLEXITY

within the Gardens, and singing (as he did at the Back Kitchen and the nobility's concerts, the 'Body-Snatcher,' the 'Death of General Wolfe,' the 'Banner of Blood,' and other favourite melodies); and, having this order for the admission of two persons, he thought that it would admit three, and had come accordingly to the Gardens with his friends. But on his way Captain Costigan had lost the paper of admission—it was not forthcoming at all; and the leedies must go back again, to the great disappointment of one of them, as Pendennis saw.

Arthur had a great deal of good nature for everybody,[1] and how could he refuse his sympathy in such a case as this? He had seen the innocent face as it looked up to the captain, the appealing look of the girl, the piteous quiver of the mouth, and the final outburst of tears. If it had been his last guinea in the world, he must have paid it to have given the poor little thing pleasure. She turned the sad imploring eyes away—they lighted upon a stranger—and began to wipe them with her handkerchief. Arthur looked very handsome and kind as he stood before the women, with his hat off, blushing, bowing, generous, a gentleman. 'Who are they?' he asked of himself. He thought he had seen the elder lady before.

'If I can be of any service to you, Captain Costigan,' the young man said, 'I hope you will command me. Is there any difficulty about taking these ladies into the garden? Will you kindly make use of my purse? And—and I have a ticket myself which will admit two—I hope, ma'am, you will permit me?'

The first impulse of the Prince of Fairoaks was to pay for the whole party, and to make away with his newspaper order as poor Costigan had done with his own ticket. But his instinct, and the appearance of the two women, told him that they would be better pleased if he did not give himself the airs of a *grand seigneur*, and he handed his purse to Costigan, and laughingly pulled out his ticket with one hand, as he offered the other to the elder of the ladies—ladies was not the word—they had bonnets and shawls, and collars and ribbons, and the youngest showed a pretty little foot and boot under her modest grey gown, but His Highness of Fairoaks was courteous to every person who wore a petticoat, whatever its texture was, and the humbler the wearer, only the more stately and polite in his demeanour.

'Fanny, take the gentleman's arm,' the elder said; 'since you will be so very kind—I've seen you often come in at our gate, sir, and go in to Captain Strong's at No. 4.'

Fanny made a little curtsy, and put her hand under Arthur's arm. It had on a shabby little glove, but it was pretty and small. She was not a child, but she was scarcely a woman as yet; her tears had dried up, her cheek mantled with youthful blushes, and her eyes glistened with pleasure and gratitude, as she looked up into Arthur's kind face.

Arthur, in a protecting way, put his other hand upon the little one resting on his arm. 'Fanny's a very pretty little name,' he said, 'and so you know me, do you?'

'We keep the lodge, sir, at Shepherd's Inn,' Fanny said, with a curtsy; 'and I've never been at Vauxhall, sir, and pa didn't like me to go—and—and—oh—oh—law, how beautiful!' She shrank back as she spoke, starting with wonder and delight as she saw the Royal Gardens blaze before her with a hundred million of lamps, with a splendour such as the finest fairy tale, the finest pantomime-she had ever witnessed at the theatre, had never realized. Pen was pleased with her pleasure, and pressed to his side the little hand which clung so kindly to him. 'What would I not give for a little of this pleasure?' said the blasé young man.

'Your purse, Pendennis, me dear boy,' said the captain's voice behind him. 'Will ye count it? it's all roight—no—ye thrust in old Jack Costigan (he thrusts me, ye see, madam). Ye've been me preserver, Pen (I've known um since choildhood, Mrs. Bolton; he's the proproietor of Fair-oaks Castle, and many's the cooper of clart I've dthrunk there with the first nobilitee of his neetive countee)—Mr. Pendennis, ye've been me preserver, and oi thank ye; me daughtther will thank ye;—Mr. Simpson, your humble servant, sir.'

If Pen was magnificent in his courtesy to the ladies, what was his splendour in comparison to Captain Costigan's bowing here and there, and crying bravo to the singers?

A man, descended like Costigan from a long line of Hibernian kings, chieftains, and other magnates and sheriffs of the county, had of course too much dignity and self-respect to walk arrum-in-arrum (as the Captain phrased it) with a lady who occasionally swept his room out, and cooked his mutton-chops. In the course of their journey from Shepherd's Inn to Vauxhall Gardens, Captain Costigan had

walked by the side of the two ladies in a patronizing and affable manner, pointing out to them the edifices worthy of note, and discoorsing, according to his wont, about other cities and countries which he had visited, and the people of rank and fashion with whom he had the honour of an acquaintance. Nor could it be expected that, arrived in the Royal property, and strongly illuminated by the flare of the twenty thousand additional lamps,* the captain could relax from his dignity, and give an arm to a lady who was, in fact, little better than a housekeeper or charwoman.

But Pen, on his part, had no such scruples. Miss Fanny Bolton did not make his bed nor sweep his chambers; and he did not choose to let go his pretty little partner. As for Fanny, her colour heightened, and her bright eyes shone the brighter with pleasure, as she leaned for protection on the arm of such a fine gentleman as Mr. Pen. And she looked at numbers of other ladies in the place, and at scores of other gentlemen under whose protection they were walking here and there; and she thought that her gentleman was handsomer and grander-looking than any other gent there. Of course there were votaries of pleasure of all ranks in the garden—rakish young surgeons, fast young clerks and commercialists, occasional dandies of the Guard regiments, and the rest. Old Lord Colchicum was there in attendance upon Mademoiselle Caracoline, who had been riding in the ring; and who talked her native French very loud, and used idiomatic expressions of exceeding strength as she walked about, leaning on the arm of his lordship.

Colchicum was in attendance upon Mademoiselle Caracoline, little Tom Tufthunt was in attendance upon Lord Colchicum; and rather pleased, too, with his position. When Don Juan scales the wall, there's never a want of a Leporello to hold the ladder. Tom Tufthunt was quite happy to act as friend to the elderly viscount, and to carve the fowl, and to make the salad at supper. When Pen and his young lady met the viscount's party, that noble peer only gave Arthur a passing leer of recognition as his lordship's eyes passed from Pen's face under the bonnet of Pen's companion. But Tom Tufthunt wagged his head very good-naturedly at Mr. Arthur, and said, 'How are you, old boy?' and looked extremely knowing at the godfather of this history.

'That is the great rider at Astley's; I have seen her there,'

Miss Bolton said, looking after Mademoiselle Caracoline;* 'and who is that old man ? is it not the gentleman in the ring ?'

'That is Lord Viscount Colchicum, Miss Fanny,' said Pen, with an air of protection. He meant no harm; he was pleased to patronize the young girl, and he was not displeased that she should be so pretty, and that she should be hanging upon his arm, and that yonder elderly Don Juan should have seen her there.

Fanny was very pretty; her eyes were dark and brilliant; her teeth were like little pearls; her mouth was almost as red as Mademoiselle Caracoline's, when the latter had put on her vermilion. And what a difference there was between the one's voice and the other's, between the girl's laugh and the woman's! It was only very lately, indeed, that Fanny, when looking in the little glass over the Bows-Costigan mantelpiece as she was dusting it, had begun to suspect that she was a beauty. But a year ago she was a clumsy, gawky girl, at whom her father sneered, and of whom the girls at the day-school (Miss Minifer's, Newcastle Street, Strand; Miss M., the younger sister, took the leading business at the Norwich circuit in 182–; and she herself had played for two seasons with some credit T. R. E. O., T. R. S. W.,* until she fell down a trap-door and broke her leg)—the girls at Fanny's school, we say, took no account of her, and thought her a dowdy little creature as long as she remained under Miss Minifer's instruction. And it was unremarked and almost unseen in the dark porter's lodge of Shepherd's Inn, that this little flower bloomed into beauty.

So this young person hung upon Mr. Pen's arm, and they paced the gardens together. Empty as London was, there were still some two millions of people left lingering about it; and amongst them, one or two of the acquaintances of Mr. Arthur Pendennis.

Amongst them, silent and alone, pale, with his hands in his pockets, and a rueful nod of the head to Arthur as they met, passed Henry Foker, Esq. Young Henry was trying to ease his mind by moving from place to place, and from excitement to excitement. But he thought about Blanche as he sauntered in the dark walks; he thought about Blanche as he looked at the devices of the lamps. He consulted the fortune-teller about her, and was disappointed when that gipsy told him that he was in love with a dark lady who

would make him happy; and at the concert, though Mr. Momus sang his most stunning comic songs, and asked his most astonishing riddles, never did a kind smile come to visit Foker's lips. In fact, he never heard Mr. Momus at all.

Pen and Miss Bolton were hard by listening to the same concert, and the latter remarked, and Pen laughed at, Mr. Foker's woebegone face.

Fanny asked what it was that made that odd-looking little man so dismal? 'I think he is crossed in love!' Pen said. 'Isn't that enough to make any man dismal, Fanny?' And he looked down at her, splendidly protecting her, like Egmont at Clara in Goethe's play, or Leicester at Amy* in Scott's novel.

'Crossed in love, is he? poor gentleman,' said Fanny, with a sigh, and her eyes turned round towards him with no little kindness and pity—but Harry did not see the beautiful dark eyes.

'How dy do, Mr. Pendennis?'—a voice broke in here—it was that of a young man in a large white coat with a red neckcloth, over which a dingy short collar was turned so as to exhibit a dubious neck—with a large pin of bullion or other metal, and an imaginative waistcoat with exceedingly fanciful glass buttons, and trousers that cried with a loud voice, 'Come look at me and see how cheap and tawdry I am: my master, what a dirty buck!' and a little stick in one pocket of his coat, and a lady in pink satin on the other arm —'How dy do?—Forget me, I dare say? Huxter,—Clavering.'

'How do you do, Mr. Huxter?' the Prince of Fairoaks said, in his most princely manner—'I hope you are very well.'

'Pretty bobbish, thanky.'—And Mr. Huxter wagged his head. 'I say, Pendennis, you've been coming it uncommon strong since we had the row at Wapshot's, don't you remember. Great author, hey? Go about with the swells. Saw your name in the *Morning Post*. I suppose you're too much of a swell to come and have a bit of supper with an old friend?—Charterhouse Lane to-morrow night,—some devilish good fellows from Bartholomew's,* and some stunning gin punch. Here's my card.' And with this Mr. Huxter released his hand from the pocket where his cane was, and pulling off the top of his card-case with his teeth produced thence a visiting-ticket, which he handed to Pen.

'You are exceedingly kind, I am sure,' said Pen: 'but I

regret that I have an engagement which will take me out of town to-morrow night.' And the Marquis of Fairoaks, wondering that such a creature as this could have the audacity to give him a card, put Mr. Huxter's card into his waistcoat pocket with a lofty courtesy. Possibly Mr. Samuel Huxter was not aware that there was any great social difference between Mr. Arthur Pendennis and himself. Mr.

Huxter's father was a surgeon and apothecary at Clavering, just as Mr. Pendennis's papa had been a surgeon and apothecary at Bath. But the impudence of some men is beyond all calculation.

'Well, old fellow, never mind,' said Mr. Huxter, who, always frank and familiar, was from vinous excitement even more affable than usual. 'If ever you are passing, look up at our place,—I'm mostly at home Saturdays; and there's

generally a cheese in the cupboard. Ta, ta.—There's the bell for the fireworks ringing. Come along, Mary.' And he set off running with the rest of the crowd in the direction of the fireworks.

So did Pen presently, when this agreeable youth was out of sight, begin to run with his little companion ; Mrs. Bolton following after them, with Captain Costigan at her side. But the captain was too majestic and dignified in his movements to run for friend or enemy, and he pursued his course with the usual jaunty swagger which distinguished his steps, so that he and his companion were speedily distanced by Pen and Miss Fanny.

Perhaps Arthur forgot, or perhaps he did not choose to remember, that the elder couple had no money in their pockets, as had been proved by their adventure at the entrance of the Gardens ; howbeit, Pen paid a couple of shillings for himself and his partner, and with her hanging close on his arm, scaled the staircase which leads to the firework gallery. The captain and mamma might have followed them if they liked, but Arthur and Fanny were too busy to look back. People were pushing and squeezing there beside and behind them. One eager individual rushed by Fanny, and elbowed her so, that she fell back with a little cry, upon which, of course, Arthur caught her adroitly in his arms, and, just for protection, kept her so defended, until they mounted the stair, and took their places.

Poor Foker sat alone on one of the highest benches, his face illuminated by the fireworks, or in their absence by the moon. Arthur saw him, and laughed, but did not occupy himself about his friend much. He was engaged with Fanny. How she wondered ! how happy she was ! how she cried 'Oh, oh, oh !' as the rockets soared into the air, and showered down in azure, and emerald, and vermilion. As these wonders blazed and disappeared before her, the little girl thrilled and trembled with delight at Arthur's side—her hand was under his arm still, he felt it pressing him as she looked up delighted.

'How beautiful they are, sir !' she cried.

'Don't call me sir, Fanny,' Arthur said.

A quick blush rushed up into the girl's face. 'What shall I call you ?' she said, in a low voice, sweet and tremulous. 'What would you wish me to say, sir ?'

'Again, Fanny ! Well, I forgot ; it is best so, my dear,'

Pendennis said, very kindly and gently. 'I may call you Fanny?'

'Oh yes!' she said, and the little hand pressed his arm once more very eagerly, and the girl clung to him so that he could feel her heart beating on his shoulder.

'I may call you Fanny, because you are a young girl, and a good girl, Fanny, and I am an old gentleman. But you mustn't call me anything but sir, or Mr. Pendennis, if you like; for we live in very different stations, Fanny; and don't think I speak unkindly; and—and why do you take your hand away, Fanny? Are you afraid of me? Do you think I would hurt you? Not for all the world, my dear little girl. And—and look how beautiful the moon and stars are, and how calmly they shine when the rockets have gone out, and the noisy wheels have done hissing and blazing. When I came here to-night I did not think I should have had such a pretty little companion to sit by my side and see these fine fireworks. You must know I live by myself, and work very hard. I write in books and newspapers, Fanny;

and I was quite tired out, and expected to sit alone all night; and—don't cry, my dear, dear, little girl.' Here Pen broke out, rapidly putting an end to the calm oration which he had begun to deliver; for the sight of a woman's tears always put his nerves in a quiver, and he began forthwith to coax her and soothe her, and to utter a hundred-and-twenty little ejaculations of pity and sympathy, which need not be repeated here, because they would be absurd in print. So would a mother's talk to a child be absurd in print; so would a lover's to his bride. That sweet artless poetry bears no translation; and is too subtle for

grammarians' clumsy definitions. You have but the same four letters to describe the salute which you perform on your grandmother's forehead, and that which you bestow on the sacred cheek of your mistress ; but the same four letters, and not one of them a labial. Do we mean to hint that Mr. Arthur Pendennis made any use of the monosyllable in question ? Not so. In the first place, it was dark : the fireworks were over, and nobody could see him ; secondly, he was not a man to have this kind of secret, and tell it ; thirdly and lastly, let the honest fellow who has kissed a pretty girl say what would have been his own conduct in such a delicate juncture.

Well, the truth is, that however you may suspect him, and whatever you would have done under the circumstances, or Mr. Pen would have liked to do, he behaved honestly, and like a man. 'I will not play with this little girl's heart,' he said within himself, 'and forget my own or her honour. She seems to have a great deal of dangerous and rather contagious sensibility, and I am very glad the fireworks are over, and that I can take her back to her mother. Come along, Fanny ; mind the steps, and lean on me. Don't stumble, you heedless little thing ; this is the way, and there is your mamma at the door.'

And there, indeed, Mrs. Bolton was, unquiet in spirit, and grasping her umbrella. She seized Fanny with maternal fierceness and eagerness, and uttered some rapid abuse to the girl in an undertone. The expression in Captain Costigan's eye—standing behind the matron and winking at Pendennis from under his hat—was, I am bound to say, indefinably humorous.

It was so much so, that Pen could not refrain from bursting into a laugh. 'You should have taken my arm, Mrs. Bolton,' he said, offering it. 'I am very glad to bring Miss Fanny back quite safe to you. We thought you would have followed us up into the gallery. We enjoyed the fireworks, didn't we ?'

'Oh yes !' said Miss Fanny, with rather a demure look.

'And the bouquet* was magnificent,' said Pen. 'And it is ten hours since I had anything to eat, ladies ; and I wish you would permit me to invite you to supper.'

'Dad,' said Costigan, 'I'd loike a snack tu ; only I forgawt me purse, or I should have invoited these leedies to a colleetion.'

Mrs. Bolton, with considerable asperity, said, She 'ad an 'eadache, and would much rather go 'ome.

'A lobster salad is the best thing in the world for a headache,' Pen said gallantly, 'and a glass of wine I'm sure will do you good. Come, Mrs. Bolton, be kind to me and oblige me. I shan't have the heart to sup without you, and upon my word I have had no dinner. Give me your arm: give me the umbrella. Costigan, I'm sure you'll take care of Miss Fanny; and I shall think Mrs. Bolton angry with me, unless she will favour me with her society. And we will all sup quietly, and go back in a cab together.'

The cab, the lobster salad, the frank and good-humoured look of Pendennis, as he smilingly invited the worthy matron, subdued her suspicions and her anger. Since he *would* be so obliging, she thought she could take a little bit of lobster, and so they all marched away to a box; and Costigan called for a waither with such a loud and belligerent voice, as caused one of those officials instantly to run to him.

The carte was examined on the wall, and Fanny was asked to choose her favourite dish; upon which the young creature said she was fond of lobster, too, but also owned to a partiality for raspberry-tart. This delicacy was provided by Pen, and a bottle of the most frisky champagne was moreover ordered for the delight of the ladies. Little Fanny drank this;—what other sweet intoxication had she not drunk in the course of the night?

When the supper, which was very brisk and gay, was over, and Captain Costigan and Mrs. Bolton had partaken of some of the rack punch* that is so fragrant at Vauxhall, the bill was called and discharged by Pen with great generosity,—'loike a foin young English gentleman of th' olden toime, be Jove,' Costigan enthusiastically remarked. And as, when they went out of the box, he stepped forward and gave Mrs. Bolton his arm, Fanny fell to Pen's lot, and the young people walked away in high good-humour together, in the wake of their seniors.

The champagne and the rack punch, though taken in moderation by all persons, except perhaps poor Cos, who lurched ever so little in his gait, had set them in high spirits and good-humour, so that Fanny began to skip and move her brisk little feet in time to the band, which was playing waltzes and galops for the dancers. As they came up to

the dancing, the music and Fanny's feet seemed to go quicker together—she seemed to spring, as if naturally, from the ground, and as if she required repression to keep her there.

'Shouldn't you like a turn?' said the Prince of Fairoaks. 'What fun it would be! Mrs. Bolton, ma'am, do let me take her once round.' Upon which Mr. Costigan said, 'Off wid you!' and Mrs. Bolton not refusing (indeed, she was an old war-horse, and would have liked, at the trumpet's sound, to have entered the arena herself), Fanny's shawl was off her back in a minute, and she and Arthur were whirling round in a waltz in the midst of a great deal of queer, but exceedingly joyful company.

Pen had no mishap this time with little Fanny, as he had with Miss Blanche in old days,—at least, there was no mishap of his making. The pair danced away with great agility and contentment,—first a waltz, then a galop, then a waltz again, until, in the second waltz, they were bumped by another couple who had joined the Terpsichorean choir. This was Mr. Huxter and his pink satin young friend, of whom we have already had a glimpse.

Mr. Huxter very probably had been also partaking of supper, for he was even more excited now than at the time when he had previously claimed Pen's acquaintance; and, having run against Arthur and his partner, and nearly knocked them down, this amiable gentleman of course began to abuse the people whom he had injured, and broke out into a volley of slang against the unoffending couple. 'Now then, stoopid! Don't keep the ground if you can't dance, old Slow Coach!' the young surgeon roared out (using, at the same time, other expressions far more emphatic), and was joined in his abuse by the shrill language and laughter of his partner;—to the interruption of the ball, the terror of poor little Fanny, and the immense indignation of Pen.

Arthur was furious; and not so angry at the quarrel as at the shame attending it. A battle with a fellow like that! A row in a public garden, and with a porter's daughter on his arm! What a position for Arthur Pendennis! He drew poor little Fanny hastily away from the dancers to her mother, and wished that lady, and Costigan, and poor Fanny underground, rather than there, in his companionship, and under his protection.

When Huxter commenced his attack, that free-spoken young gentleman had not seen who was his opponent; and directly he was aware that it was Arthur whom he had insulted, he began to make apologies. 'Hold your stoopid tongue, Mary,' he said to his partner. 'It's an old friend and crony at home. I beg pardon, Pendennis; wasn't aware it was you, old boy.' Mr. Huxter had been one of the boys of the Clavering School, who had been present at a combat which has been mentioned in the early part of this story, when young Pen knocked down the biggest champion of the academy, and Huxter knew that it was dangerous to quarrel with Arthur.

His apologies were as odious to the other as his abuse had been. Pen stopped his tipsy remonstrances by telling him to hold his tongue, and desiring him not to use his (Pendennis's) name in that place or any other; and he walked out of the gardens with a titter behind him from the crowd, every one of whom he would have liked to massacre for having been witness to the degrading broil. He walked out of the gardens quite forgetting poor little Fanny, who came trembling behind him with her mother and the stately Costigan.

He was brought back to himself by a word from the captain, who touched him on the shoulder just as they were passing the inner gate.

'There's no ray-admittance except ye pay again,' the captain said. 'Hadn't I better go back and take the fellow your message?'

Pen burst out laughing. 'Take him a message! Do you think I would fight with such a fellow as that?' he asked.

'No, no! Don't, don't!' cried out little Fanny. 'How can you be so wicked, Captain Costigan?' The captain muttered something about honour, and winked knowingly at Pen, but Arthur said gallantly, 'No, Fanny, don't be frightened. It was my fault to have danced in such a place. I beg your pardon, to have asked you to dance there.' And he gave her his arm once more, and called a cab, and put his three friends into it.

He was about to pay the driver, and to take another carriage for himself, when little Fanny, still alarmed, put her little hand out, and caught him by the coat, and implored him and besought him to come in.

'Will nothing satisfy you,' said Pen, in great good-humour, 'that I am not going back to fight him? Well, I will come home with you. Drive to Shepherd's Inn, Cab.' The cab drove to its destination. Arthur was immensely pleased by the girl's solicitude about him: her tender terrors quite made him forget his previous annoyance.

Pen put the ladies into their lodge, having shaken hands kindly with both of them; and the captain again whispered to him that he would see um in the morning if he was inclined, and take his message to that 'scounthrel.' But the captain was in his usual condition when he made the proposal; and Pen was perfectly sure that neither he nor Mr. Huxter, when they awoke, would remember anything about the dispute.

CHAPTER XLVII

A VISIT OF POLITENESS

COSTIGAN never roused Pen from his slumbers; there was no hostile message from Mr. Huxter to disturb him; and when Pen woke it was with a brisker and more lively feeling than ordinarily attends that moment in the day of the tired and blasé London man. A City man wakes up to care and Consols, and the thoughts of 'Change and the counting-house take possession of him as soon as sleep flies from under his nightcap; a lawyer rouses himself with the early morning to think of the case that will take him all his day to work upon, and the inevitable attorney to whom he has promised his papers ere night. Which of us has not his anxiety instantly present when his eyes are opened, to it and to the world, after his night's sleep? Kind strengthener that enables us to face the day's task with renewed heart! Beautiful ordinance of Providence that creates rest as it awards labour!

Mr. Pendennis's labour, or rather his disposition, was of that sort that his daily occupations did not much interest him, for the excitement of literary composition pretty soon subsides with the hired labourer, and the delight of seeing oneself in print only extends to the first two or three appearances in the magazine or newspaper page. Pegasus put into harness, and obliged to run a stage every day, is as prosaic as any other hack, and won't work without his whip or his feed of corn. So, indeed, Mr. Arthur performed his work at the *Pall Mall Gazette* (and since his success as a novelist with an increased salary), but without the least enthusiasm, doing his best or pretty nearly, and sometimes writing ill and sometimes well. He was a literary hack, naturally fast in pace, and brilliant in action.

Neither did society, or that portion which he saw, excite or amuse him overmuch. In spite of his brag and boast to the contrary, he was too young as yet for women's society, which probably can only be had in perfection when a man has ceased to think about his own person, and has given up all designs of being a conqueror of ladies ; he was too young to be admitted as an equal amongst men who had made their mark in the world, and of whose conversation he could scarcely as yet expect to be more than a listener. And he was too old for the men of pleasure of his own age ; too much a man of pleasure for the men of business ; destined, in a word, to be a good deal alone. Fate awards this lot of solitude to many a man ; and many like it from taste as many without difficulty bear it. Pendennis, in reality, suffered it very equanimously ; but in words, and according to his wont, grumbled over it not a little.

'What a nice little artless creature that was,' Mr. Pen thought at the very instant of waking after the Vauxhall affair : 'what a pretty natural manner she has ; how much pleasanter than the minauderies of the young ladies in the ball-rooms' (and here he recalled to himself some instances, of what he could not help seeing, was the artful simplicity of Miss Blanche, and some of the stupid graces of other young ladies in the polite world) ; 'who could have thought that such a pretty rose could grow in a porter's lodge, or bloom in that dismal old flower-pot of a Shepherd's Inn ? So she learns to sing from old Bows ? If her singing voice is as sweet as her speaking voice, it must be pretty. I like those low *voilées* voices. "What would you like me to

call you?" indeed. Poor little Fanny! It went to my heart to adopt the grand air with her, and tell her to call me, "sir." But we'll have no nonsense of that sort—no Faust and Margaret business*for me. That old Bows! So he teaches her to sing, does he? He's a dear old fellow, old Bows: a gentleman in those old clothes: a philosopher, and with a kind heart, too. How good he was to me in the Fotheringay business. He, too, has had his griefs and his sorrows. I must cultivate old Bows. A man ought to see people of all sorts. I am getting tired of genteel society. Besides, there's nobody in town. Yes, I'll go and see Bows, and Costigan too: what a rich character! begad, I'll study him, and put him into a book.' In this way our young anthropologist talked with himself: and as Saturday was the holiday of the week, the *Pall Mall Gazette* making its appearance upon that day, and the contributors to that journal having no further calls upon their brains or ink-bottles, Mr. Pendennis determined he would take advantage of his leisure, and pay a visit to Shepherd's Inn—of course to see old Bows.

The truth is, that if Arthur had been the most determined roué and artful Lovelace* who ever set about deceiving a young girl, he could hardly have adopted better means for fascinating and overcoming poor little Fanny Bolton than those which he had employed on the previous night. His dandified protecting air, his conceit, generosity, and good-humour, the very sense of good and honesty which had enabled him to check the tremulous advances of the young creature, and not to take advantage of that little fluttering sensibility,—his faults and his virtues at once contributed to make her admire him; and if we could peep into Fanny's bed (which she shared in a cupboard, along with those two little sisters to whom we have seen Mr. Costigan administering gingerbread and apples), we should find the poor little maid tossing upon her mattress, to the great disturbance of its other two occupants, and thinking over all the delights and events of that delightful, eventful night, and all the words, looks, and actions of Arthur, its splendid hero. Many novels had Fanny read, in secret and at home, in three volumes and in numbers. Periodical literature had not reached the height which it has attained subsequently, and the girls of Fanny's generation were not enabled to purchase sixteen pages of excitement*for a penny, rich with

histories of crime, murder, oppressed virtue, and the heartless seductions of the aristocracy ; but she had had the benefit of the circulating library which, in conjunction with her school and a small brandy-ball and millinery business, Miss Minifer kept,—and Arthur appeared to her at once as the type and realization of all the heroes of all those darling greasy volumes which the young girl had devoured. Mr. Pen, we have seen, was rather a dandy about shirts and haberdashery in general. Fanny had looked with delight at the fineness of his linen, at the brilliancy of his shirt-studs, at his elegant cambric pocket-handkerchief and white gloves, and at the jetty brightness of his charming boots. The Prince had appeared and subjugated the poor little handmaid. His image traversed constantly her restless slumbers ; the tone of his voice, the blue light of his eyes, the generous look, half love, half pity,—the manly protecting smile, the frank, winning laughter,—all these were repeated in the girl's fond memory. She felt still his arm encircling her, and saw him smiling so grand as he filled up that delicious glass of champagne. And then she thought of the girls, her friends, who used to sneer at her—of Emma Baker, who was so proud, forsooth, because she was engaged to a cheesemonger, in a white apron, near Clare Market ; and of Betsy Rodgers, who made such a to-do about *her* young man —an attorney's clerk, indeed, that went about with a bag !

So that, at about two o'clock in the afternoon—the Bolton family having concluded their dinner (and Mr. B., who besides his place of porter of the Inn, was in the employ of Messrs. Tressler, the eminent undertakers of the Strand, being absent in the country with the Countess of Estrich's hearse)—when a gentleman in a white hat and white trousers made his appearance under the Inn archway, and stopped at the porter's wicket, Fanny was not in the least surprised, only delighted, only happy, and blushing beyond all measure. She knew it could be no other than He. She knew He'd come. There He was ; there was His Royal Highness beaming upon her from the gate. She called to her mother, who was busy in the upper apartment, 'Mamma, mamma,' and ran to the wicket at once, and opened it, pushing aside the other children. How she blushed as she gave her hand to him ! How affably he took off his white hat as he came in : the children staring up at him ! He asked Mrs. Bolton if she had slept well, after the

A VISITOR AT SHEPHERD'S INN

fatigues of the night, and hoped she had no headache; and he said that as he was going that way, he could not pass the door without asking news of his little partner.

Mrs. Bolton was perhaps rather shy and suspicious about these advances; but Mr. Pen's good-humour was inexhaustible; he could not see that he was unwelcome. He looked about the premises for a seat, and none being disengaged, for a dish-cover was on one, a work-box on the other, and so forth, he took one of the children's chairs, and perched himself upon that uncomfortable eminence. At this, the children began laughing, the child Fanny louder than all—at least, she was more amused than any of them, and amazed at His Royal Highness's condescension. *He* to sit down in that chair—that little child's chair!—Many and many a time after, she regarded it: haven't we almost all such furniture in our rooms, that our fancy peoples with dear figures, that our memory fills with sweet smiling faces, which may never look on us more?

So Pen sat down and talked away with great volubility to Mrs. Bolton. He asked about the undertaking business, and how many mutes went down with Lady Estrich's remains; and about the Inn, and who lived there. He seemed very much interested about Mr. Campion's cab and horse, and had met that gentleman in society. He thought he should like shares in the Polwheedle and Pontydiddlum: did Mrs. Bolton do for those chambers? Were there any chambers to let in the Inn? It was better than the Temple: he should like to come to live in Shepherd's Inn. As for Captain Strong, and—Colonel Altamont was his name?—he was deeply interested in them too. The captain was an old friend at home. He had dined with him at chambers here, before the colonel came to live with him. What sort of man was the colonel? Wasn't he a stout man, with a large quantity of jewellery, and a wig and large black whiskers—*very* black (here Pen was immensely waggish, and caused hysteric giggles of delight from the ladies)—very black indeed; in fact, blue-black; that is to say, a rich greenish purple? That was the man; he had met him, too, at Sir Fr—— in society.

'Oh, we know,' said the ladies, 'Sir F—— is Sir F. Clavering: he's often here: two or three times a week with the captain. My little boy has been out for bill-stamps for him. Oh Lor! I beg pardon, I shouldn't have mentioned

no secrets,' Mrs. Bolton blurted out, being talked perfectly into good nature by this time. 'But we know you to be a gentleman, Mr. Pendennis, for I'm sure you have shown that you can *beayve* as such. Hasn't Mr. Pendennis, Fanny ?'

Fanny loved her mother for that speech. She cast up her dark eyes to the low ceiling and said, 'Oh, that he has, I'm sure, ma,' with a voice full of feeling.

Pen was rather curious about the bill-stamps, and concerning the transactions in Strong's chambers. And he asked, when Altamont came and joined the chevalier, whether he too sent out for bill-stamps, who he was, whether he saw many people, and so forth. These questions, put with considerable adroitness by Pen, who was interested about Sir Francis Clavering's doings from private motives of his own, were artlessly answered by Mrs. Bolton, and to the utmost of her knowledge and ability, which, in truth, were not very great.

These questions answered, and Pen being at a loss for more, luckily recollected his privilege as a member of the Press, and asked the ladies whether they would like any orders for the play ? The play was their delight, as it is almost always the delight of every theatrical person. When Bolton was away professionally (it appeared that of late the porter of Shepherd's Inn had taken a serious turn, drank a good deal, and otherwise made himself unpleasant to the ladies of his family), they would like of all things to slip out and go to the theatre—little Barney, their son, keeping the lodge ; and Mr. Pendennis's most generous and most genteel compliment of orders was received with boundless gratitude by both mother and daughter.

Fanny clapped her hands with pleasure : her face beamed with it. She looked and nodded, and laughed at her mamma, who nodded and laughed in her turn. Mrs. Bolton was not superannuated for pleasure yet, or by any means too old for admiration, she thought. And very likely Mr. Pendennis, in his conversation with her, had insinuated some compliments, or shaped his talk so as to please her. At first, against Pen, and suspicious of him, she was his partisan now, and almost as enthusiastic about him as her daughter. When two women get together to like a man, they help each other on—each pushes the other forward—and the second, out of sheer sympathy, becomes as eager as

the principal;—at least, so it is said by philosophers who have examined this science.

So the offer of the play-tickets, and other pleasantries, put all parties into perfect good-humour, except for one brief moment, when one of the younger children, hearing the name of 'Astley's' pronounced, came forward and stated that she should like very much to go, too; on which Fanny said, 'Don't bother!' rather sharply; and mamma said, 'Git 'long, Betsy-Jane, do now, and play in the court:' so that the two little ones, namely, Betsy-Jane and Ameliar-Ann, went away in their little innocent pinafores, and disported in the courtyard on the smooth gravel, round about the statue of Shepherd the Great.

And here, as they were playing, they very possibly communicated with an old friend of theirs and dweller in the Inn; for while Pen was making himself agreeable to the ladies at the lodge, who were laughing delighted at his sallies, an old gentleman passed under the archway from the Inn-square, and came and looked in at the door of the lodge.

He made a very blank and rueful face when he saw Mr. Arthur seated upon a table, like Macheath in the play, in easy discourse with Mrs. Bolton and her daughter.

'What! Mr. Bows? How d'you do, Bows?' cried out Pen, in a cheery, loud voice. 'I was coming to see you, and was asking your address of these ladies.'

'You were coming to see *me*, were you, sir?' Bows said, and came in with a sad face, and shook hands with Arthur. 'Plague on that old man!' somebody thought in the room: and so, perhaps, someone else besides her.

CHAPTER XLVIII

IN SHEPHERD'S INN

OUR friend Pen said: 'How d'ye do, Mr. Bows?' in a loud, cheery voice on perceiving that gentleman, and saluted him in a dashing offhand manner, yet you could have seen a blush upon Arthur's face (answered by Fanny, whose cheek straightway threw out a similar fluttering red signal); and after Bows and Arthur had shaken hands, and the former had ironically accepted the other's assertion that he was about to pay Mr. Costigan's chambers a visit, there was a gloomy and rather guilty silence in the company, which Pen presently tried to dispel by making a great rattling and noise. The silence of course departed at Mr. Arthur's noise, but the gloom remained and deepened, as the darkness does in a vault if you light up a single taper in it. Pendennis tried to describe, in a jocular manner, the transactions of the night previous, and attempted to give an imitation of Costigan vainly expostulating with the checktaker at Vauxhall. It was not a good imitation. What stranger can imitate that perfection? Nobody laughed. Mrs. Bolton did not in the least understand what part Mr. Pendennis was performing, and whether it was the checktaker or the captain he was taking off. Fanny wore an alarmed face, and tried a timid giggle; old Mr. Bows looked as glum as when he fiddled in the orchestra, or played a difficult piece upon the old piano at the Back Kitchen. Pen felt that his story was a failure; his voice sank and dwindled away dismally at the end of it—flickered, and went out; and it was all dark again. You could hear the ticket-porter,* who lolls about Shepherd's Inn, as he passed on the flags under the archway: the clink of his boot-heels was noted by everybody.

'You were coming to see me, sir,' Mr. Bows said. 'Won't you have the kindness to walk up to my chambers with me? You do them a great honour, I am sure. They are rather high up; but——'

'Oh! I live in a garret myself, and Shepherd's Inn is twice as cheerful as Lamb Court,' Mr. Pendennis broke in.

'I knew that you had third-floor apartments,' Mr. Bows said; 'and was going to say—you will please not take my remark as discourteous—that the air up three pair of stairs is wholesomer for gentlemen, than the air of a porter's lodge.'

'Sir!' said Pen, whose candle flamed up again in his wrath, and who was disposed to be as quarrelsome as men are when they are in the wrong. 'Will you permit me to choose my society without——'

'You were so polite as to say that you were about to honour my 'umble domicile with a visit,' Mr. Bows said, with his sad voice. 'Shall I show you the way? Mr. Pendennis and I are old friends, Mrs. Bolton—very old acquaintances; and at the earliest dawn of his life we crossed each other.'

The old man pointed towards the door with a trembling finger, and a hat in the other hand, and in an attitude slightly theatrical; so were his words when he spoke somewhat artificial, and chosen from the vocabulary which he had heard all his life from the painted lips of the orators before the stage-lamps. But he was not acting or masquerading, as Pen knew very well, though he was disposed to pooh-pooh the old fellow's melodramatic airs. 'Come along, sir,' he said, 'as you are so very pressing. Mrs. Bolton, I wish you a good-day. Good-bye, Miss Fanny; I shall always think of our night at Vauxhall with pleasure; and be sure I will remember the theatre-tickets.' And he took her hand, pressed it, was pressed by it, and was gone.

'What a nice young man, to be sure!' cried Mrs. Bolton.

'D'you think so, ma?' said Fanny.

'I was a-thinkin' who he was like. When I was at the Wells with Mrs. Serle,' Mrs. Bolton continued, looking through the window-curtain after Pen, as he went up the court with Bows, 'there was a young gentleman from the city, that used to come in a tilbry, in a white 'at, the very

image of him, ony his whiskers was black, and Mr. P.'s is red.'

'Law, ma! they are a most beautiful hawburn,' Fanny said.

'He used to come for Emly Budd, who danced Columbine in "Arleykin Ornpipe, or the Battle of Navarino," when Miss De la Bosky was took ill—a pretty dancer, and a fine stage figure of a woman—and he was a great sugar-baker in the city, with a country ouse at Omerton; and he used to drive her in the tilbry down Goswell Street Road; and one day they drove and was married at St. Bartholomew's Church, Smithfield, where they 'ad their bands read quite private; and she now keeps her carriage, and I sor her name in the paper as patroness of the Manshing-House Ball for the Washywomen's Asylum. And look at Lady Mirabel—Capting Costigan's daughter—she was profeshnl, as all very well know.' Thus, and more to this purpose, Mrs. Bolton spoke, now peeping through the window-curtain, now cleaning the mugs and plates, and consigning them to their place in the corner cupboard; and finishing her speech as she and Fanny shook out and folded up the dinner-cloth between them, and restored it to its drawer in the table.

Although Costigan had once before been made pretty accurately to understand what Pen's pecuniary means and expectations were, I suppose Cos had forgotten the information acquired at Chatteris years ago, or had been induced by his natural enthusiasm to exaggerate his friend's income. He had described Fairoaks Park in the most glowing terms to Mrs. Bolton, on the preceding evening, as he was walking about with her during Pen's little escapade with Fanny, had dilated upon the enormous wealth of Pen's famous uncle, the major, and shown an intimate acquaintance with Arthur's funded and landed property. Very likely Mrs. Bolton, in her wisdom, had speculated upon these matters during the night; and had had visions of Fanny driving in her carriage, like Mrs. Bolton's old comrade, the dancer of Sadler's Wells.

In the last operation of table-cloth folding, these two foolish women, of necessity, came close together; and as Fanny took the cloth and gave it the last fold, her mother put her finger under the young girl's chin, and kissed her. Again the red signal flew out, and fluttered on Fanny's

cheek. What did it mean? It was not alarm this time. It was pleasure which caused poor little Fanny to blush so. Poor little Fanny! What? is love sin, that it is so pleasant at the beginning, and so bitter at the end?

After the embrace, Mrs. Bolton thought proper to say that she was a-going out upon business, and that Fanny must keep the lodge; which Fanny, after a very faint objection indeed, consented to do. So Mrs. Bolton took her bonnet and market-basket, and departed; and the instant she was gone, Fanny went and sat by the window which commanded Bows's door, and never once took her eyes away from that quarter of Shepherd's Inn.

Betsy-Jane and Ameliar-Ann were buzzing in one corner of the place, and making believe to read out of a picture-book, which one of them held topsy-turvy. It was a grave and dreadful tract, of Mr. Bolton's collection. Fanny did not hear her sisters prattling over it. She noticed nothing but Bows's door.

At last she gave a little shake, and her eyes lighted up. He had come out. He would pass the door again. But her poor little countenance fell in an instant more. Pendennis, indeed, came out; but Bows followed after him. They passed under the archway together. He only took off his hat, and bowed as he looked in. He did not stop to speak.

In three or four minutes—Fanny did not know how long, but she looked furiously at him when he came into the lodge—Bows returned alone, and entered into the porter's room.

'Where's your ma, dear?' he said to Fanny.

'I don't know,' Fanny said, with an angry toss. 'I don't follow ma's steps wherever she goes, I suppose, Mr. Bows.'

'Am I my mother's keeper?' Bows said, with his usual melancholy bitterness. 'Come here, Betsy-Jane and Amelia-Ann; I've brought a cake for the one who can read her letters best, and a cake for the other who can read them the next best.'

When the young ladies had undergone the examination through which Bows put them, they were rewarded with their gingerbread medals, and went off to discuss them in the court. Meanwhile Fanny took out some work, and pretended to busy herself with it, her mind being in great

excitement and anger, as she plied her needle. Bows sat so that he could command the entrance from the lodge to the street. But the person whom, perhaps, he expected to see never made his appearance again. And Mrs. Bolton came in from market, and found Mr. Bows in place of the person whom *she* had expected to see. The reader perhaps can guess what was his name ?

The interview between Bows and his guest, when those two mounted to the apartment occupied by the former in common with the descendant of the Milesian kings, was not particularly satisfactory to either party. Pen was sulky. If Bows had anything on his mind, he did not care to deliver himself of his thoughts in the presence of Captain Costigan, who remained in the apartment during the whole of Pen's visit ; having quitted his bedchamber, indeed, but a very few minutes before the arrival of that gentleman. We have witnessed the deshabille of Major Pendennis : will any man wish to be valet de chambre to our other hero, Costigan ? It would seem that the captain, before issuing from his bedroom, scented himself with otto of whisky. A rich odour of that delicious perfume breathed from out him, as he held out the grasp of cordiality to his visitor. The hand which performed that grasp shook wofully : it was a wonder how it could hold the razor with which the poor gentleman daily operated on his chin.

Bows's room was as neat, on the other hand, as his comrade's was disorderly. His humble wardrobe hung behind a curtain. His books and manuscript music were trimly arranged upon shelves. A lithographed portrait of Miss Fotheringay, as Mrs. Haller, with the actress's sprawling signature at the corner, hung faithfully over the old gentleman's bed. Lady Mirabel wrote much better than Miss Fotheringay had been able to do. Her ladyship had laboured assiduously to acquire the art of penmanship since her marriage ; and, in a common note of invitation or acceptance, acquitted herself very genteelly. Bows loved the old handwriting best, though ; the fair artist's earlier manner. He had but one specimen of the new style, a note in reply to a song composed and dedicated to Lady Mirabel, by her most humble servant Robert Bows ; and which document was treasured in his desk amongst his other state papers. He was teaching Fanny Bolton now to sing and to write, as he had taught Emily in former

ON THE LOOK-OUT

days. It was the nature of the man to attach himself to something. When Emily was torn from him he took a substitute: as a man looks out for a crutch when he loses a leg, or lashes himself to a raft when he has suffered shipwreck. Latude* had given his heart to a woman, no doubt, before he grew to be so fond of a mouse in the Bastille. There are people who in their youth have felt and inspired an heroic passion, and end by being happy in the caresses, or agitated by the illness, of a poodle. But it was hard upon Bows, and grating to his feelings as a man and a sentimentalist, that he should find Pen again upon his track, and in pursuit of this little Fanny.

Meanwhile, Costigan had not the least idea but that his company was perfectly welcome to Messrs. Pendennis and Bows, and that the visit of the former was intended for himself. He expressed himself greatly pleased with that mark of poloightness, and promised, in his own mind, that he would repay that obligation at least—which was not the only debt which the captain owed in life—by several visits to his young friend. He entertained him affably with news of the day, or rather of ten days previous; for Pen, in his quality of journalist, remembered to have seen some of the captain's opinions in the *Sporting and Theatrical Newspaper*, which was Costigan's oracle. He stated that Sir Charles and Lady Mirabel were gone to Baden-Baden, and were most pressing in their invitations that he should join them there. Pen replied with great gravity, that he had heard that Baden was very pleasant, and the grand duke exceedingly hospitable to English. Costigan answered, that the laws of hospitalitee bekeam a grand juke; that he sariously would think about visiting him; and made some remarks upon the splendid festivities at Dublin Castle, when his Excellency the Earl of Portansherry held the Viceraygal Coort there, and of which he, Costigan, had been a humble but pleased spectator. And Pen—as he heard these oft-told well-remembered legends—recollected the time when he had given a sort of credence to them, and had a certain respect for the captain. Emily and first love, and the little room at Chatteris, and the kind talk with Bows on the bridge came back to him. He felt quite kindly disposed towards his two old friends; and cordially shook the hands of both of them when he rose to go away.

He had quite forgotten about little Fanny Bolton whilst

the captain was talking, and Pen himself was absorbed in other selfish meditations. He only remembered her again as Bows came hobbling down the stairs after him, bent evidently upon following him out of Shepherd's Inn.

Mr. Bows's precaution was not a lucky one. The wrath of Mr. Arthur Pendennis rose at the poor old fellow's feeble persecution. Confound him, what does he mean by dogging me ? thought Pen. And he burst out laughing when he was in the Strand and by himself, as he thought of the elder's stratagem. It was not an honest laugh, Arthur Pendennis. Perhaps the thought struck Arthur himself, and he blushed at his own sense of humour.

He went off to endeavour to banish the thoughts which occupied him, whatever those thoughts might be, and tried various places of amusement with but indifferent success. He struggled up the highest stairs of the Panorama ;* but when he had arrived, panting, at the height of the eminence, Care had come up with him, and was bearing him company. He went to the club, and wrote a long letter home, exceedingly witty and sarcastic, and in which, if he did not say a single word about Vauxhall and Fanny Bolton, it was because he thought that subject, however interesting to himself, would not be very interesting to his mother and Laura. Nor could the novels or the library table fix his attention, nor the grave and respectable Jawkins (the only man in town), who wished to engage him in conversation ; nor any of the amusements which he tried, after flying from Jawkins. He passed a comic theatre on his way home, and saw 'Stunning Farce,' 'Roars of Laughter,' 'Good Old English Fun and Frolic,' placarded in vermilion letters on the gate. He went into the pit, and saw the lovely Mrs. Leary, as usual, in a man's attire ; and that eminent buffo actor, Tom Horseman, dressed as a woman. Horseman's travestie seemed to him a horrid and hideous degradation ; Mrs. Leary's glances and ankles had not the least effect. He laughed again, and bitterly, to himself, as he thought of the effect which she had produced upon him, on the first night of his arrival in London, a short time—what a long, long time ago.

CHAPTER XLIX

IN OR NEAR THE TEMPLE GARDEN

FASHION has long deserted the green and pretty Temple Garden, in which Shakespere makes York and Lancaster to pluck the innocent white and red roses which became the badges of their bloody wars; and the learned and pleasant writer of the *Handbook of London* tells us that 'the commonest and hardiest kind of rose has long ceased to put forth a bud'* in that smoky air. Not many of the present occupiers of the buildings round about the quarter know or care, very likely, whether or not roses grow there, or pass the old gate, except on their way to chambers. The attorney's clerks don't carry flowers in their bags, or posies under their arms, as they run to the counsel's chambers—the few lawyers who take constitutional walks think very little about York and Lancaster, especially since the railroad business is over.* Only antiquarians and literary amateurs care to look at the gardens with much interest, and fancy good Sir Roger de Coverley and Mr. Spectator with his short face pacing up and down the road; or dear Oliver Goldsmith in the summer-house, perhaps meditating about the next *Citizen of the World*, or the new suit that Mr. Filby, the tailor, is fashioning for him, or the dunning letter that Mr. Newbery has sent. Treading heavily on the gravel, and rolling majestically along in a snuff-coloured suit, and a wig that sadly wants the barber's powder and irons, one sees the Great Doctor step up to him (his Scotch lackey* following at the lexicographer's heels, a little the worse for port wine that they have been taking at the 'Mitre'), and Mr. Johnson asks Mr. Goldsmith to come home and take a dish of tea with Miss Williams. Kind faith of

Fancy! Sir Roger and Mr. Spectator are as real to us now as the two doctors and the boozy and faithful Scotchman. The poetical figures live in our memory just as much as the real personages,—and as Mr. Arthur Pendennis was of a romantic and literary turn, by no means addicted to the legal pursuits common in the neighbourhood of the place, we may presume that he was cherishing some such poetical reflections as these, when, upon the evening after the events recorded in the last chapter, the young gentleman chose the Temple Gardens as a place for exercise and meditation.

On the Sunday evening the Temple is commonly calm. The chambers are for the most part vacant: the great lawyers are giving grand dinner-parties at their houses in the Belgravian or Tyburnian districts; the agreeable young barristers are absent, attending those parties, and paying their respects to Mr. Kewsy's excellent claret, or Mr. Justice Ermine's accomplished daughters: the uninvited are partaking of the economic joint, and the modest half-pint of wine at the club, entertaining themselves, and the rest of the company in the club-room, with circuit jokes and points of wit and law. Nobody is in chambers at all, except poor Mr. Cockle, who is ill, and whose laundress is making him gruel; or Mr. Toodle, who is an amateur of the flute, and whom you may hear piping solitary from his chambers in the second floor; or young Tiger, the student, from whose open windows comes a great gush of cigar smoke, and at whose door are a quantity of dishes and covers, bearing the insignia of Dick's or the Cock. But stop! Wither does Fancy lead us? It is vacation-time; and with the exception of Pendennis, nobody is in chambers at all.

Perhaps it was solitude, then, which drove Pen into the garden; for although he had never before passed the gate, and had looked rather carelessly at the pretty flower-beds, and the groups of pleased citizens sauntering over the trim lawn and the broad gravel-walks by the river, on this evening it happened, as we have said, that the young gentleman, who had dined alone at a tavern in the neighbourhood of the Temple, took a fancy, as he was returning home to his chambers, to take a little walk in the gardens, and enjoy the fresh evening air, and the sight of the shining Thames. After walking for a brief space, and looking at

the many peaceful and happy groups round about him, he grew tired of the exercise, and betook himself to one of the summer-houses which flank either end of the main walk, and there modestly seated himself. What were his cogitations? The evening was delightfully bright and calm; the sky was cloudless; the chimneys on the opposite bank were not smoking; the wharfs and warehouses looked rosy in the sunshine, and as clear as if they, too, had washed for the holiday. The steamers rushed rapidly up and down the stream, laden with holiday passengers. The bells of the multitudinous city churches were ringing to evening prayers,—such peaceful Sabbath evenings as this Pen may have remembered in his early days, as he paced, with his arm round his mother's waist, on the terrace before the lawn at home. The sun was lighting up the little Brawl, too, as well as the broad Thames, and sinking downwards majestically behind the Clavering elms, and the tower of the familiar village church. Was it thoughts of these, or the sunset merely, that caused the blush in the young man's face? He beat time on the bench, to the chorus of the bells without; flicked the dust off his shining boots with his pocket-handkerchief, and starting up, stamped with his foot and said, 'No, by Jove, I'll go home.' And with this resolution, which indicated that some struggle as to the propriety of remaining where he was, or of quitting the garden, had been going on in his mind, he stepped out of the summer-house.

He nearly knocked down two little children, who did not indeed reach much higher than his knee, and were trotting along the gravel-walk, with their long blue shadows slanting towards the east.

One cried out 'Oh!' the other began to laugh; and with a knowing little infantine chuckle, said, 'Missa Pen-dennis!' And Arthur, looking down, saw his two little friends of the day before, Mesdemoiselles Ameliar-Ann and Betsy-Jane. He blushed more than ever at seeing them, and seizing the one whom he had nearly upset, jumped her up into the air, and kissed her: at which sudden assault Ameliar-Ann began to cry in great alarm.

This cry brought up instantly two ladies in clean collars and new ribbons, and grand shawls, namely: Mrs. Bolton in a rich scarlet Caledonian Cashmere, and a black silk dress, and Miss F. Bolton with a yellow scarf and a sweet

sprigged muslin, and a parasol—quite the lady. Fanny did not say one single word: though her eyes flashed a welcome, and shone as bright—as bright as the most blazing windows in Paper Buildings. But Mrs. Bolton, after admonishing Betsy-Jane, said, 'Lor, sir—how *very* odd that we should meet *you* year? I 'ope you 'ave your 'ealth well, sir.—Ain't it odd, Fanny, that we should meet Mr. Pendennis?' What do you mean by sniggering, Mesdames? When young Croesus has been staying at a country-house, have you never, by any singular coincidence, been walking with your Fanny in the shrubberies? Have you and your Fanny never happened to be listening to the band of the Heavies at Brighton, when young De Boots and Captain Padmore came clinking down the pier? Have you and your darling Frances never chanced to be visiting old widow Wheezy at the cottage on the common, when the young curate has stepped in with a tract adapted to the rheumatism? Do you suppose that, if singular coincidences occur at the hall, they don't also happen at the lodge?

It *was* a coincidence, no doubt: that was all. In the course of the conversation on the day previous, Mr. Pendennis had merely said, in the simplest way imaginable, and in reply to a question of Miss Bolton, that although some of the courts were gloomy, parts of the Temple were very cheerful and agreeable, especially the chambers looking on the river and around the gardens, and that the gardens were a very pleasant walk on Sunday evenings and frequented by a great number of people—and here, by the merest chance, all our acquaintances met together, just like so many people in genteel life. What could be more artless, good-natured, or natural?

Pen looked very grave, pompous, and dandified. He was unusually smart and brilliant in his costume. His white duck trousers and white hat, his neckcloth of many colours, his light waistcoat, gold chains, and shirt-studs, gave him the air of a prince of the blood at least. How his splendour became his figure! Was anybody ever like him? someone thought. He blushed—how his blushes became him! the same individual said to herself. The children, on seeing him the day before, had been so struck with him, that after he had gone away they had been playing at him. And Ameliar-Ann, sticking her little chubby

fingers into the arm-holes of her pinafore, as Pen was wont to do with his waistcoat, had said, 'Now, Bessy-Jane, I'll be Missa Pendennis.' Fanny had laughed till she cried, and smothered her sister with kisses for that feat. How happy, too, she was to see Arthur embracing the child!

If Arthur was red, Fanny, on the contrary, was very

worn and pale. Arthur remarked it, and asked kindly why she looked so fatigued.

'I was awake all night,' said Fanny, and began to blush a little.

'I put out her candle, and *hordered* her to go to sleep and leave off readin',' interposed the fond mother.

'You were reading! And what was it that interested you so?' asked Pen, amused.

'Oh, it's *so* beautiful!' said Fanny.

'What ?'

'*Walter Lorraine*,' Fanny sighed out. 'How I do *hate* that Neara—Naera—I don't know the pronounciation. And how I love Leonora ; and Walter, oh, how dear he is !'

How had Fanny discovered the novel of *Walter Lorraine*, and that Pen was the author ? This little person remembered every single word which Mr. Pendennis had spoken on the night previous, and how he wrote in books and newspapers. What books ? She was so eager to know, that she had almost a mind to be civil to old Bows, who was suffering under her displeasure since yesterday, but she determined first to make application to Costigan. She began by coaxing the captain and smiling upon him in her most winning way, as she helped to arrange his dinner and set his humble apartment in order. She was sure his linen wanted mending (and indeed the captain's linen-closet contained some curious specimens of manufactured flax and cotton). She would mend his shirts—*all* his shirts. What horrid holes—what funny holes ! She put her little face through one of them, and laughed at the old warrior in the most winning manner. She would have made a funny little picture looking through the holes. Then she daintily removed Costigan's dinner things, tripping about the room as she had seen the dancers do at the play ; and she danced to the captain's cupboard, and produced his whisky-bottle, and mixed him a tumbler, and must taste a drop of it—a little drop ; and the captain must sing her one of his songs, his dear songs, and teach it to her. And when he had sung an Irish melody in his rich quavering voice, fancying it was he who was fascinating the little siren, she put her little question about Arthur Pendennis and his novel, and having got an answer, cared for nothing more, but left the captain at the piano about to sing her another song, and the dinner-tray on the passage, and the shirts on the chair, and ran downstairs, quickening her pace as she sped.

Captain Costigan, as he said, was not a litherary cyarkter, nor had he as yet found time to peruse his young friend's ellygant perfaurumance, though he intended to teak an early opporchunitee of purchasing a cawpee of his work. But he knew the name of Pen's novel from the fact that Messrs. Finucane, Bludyer, and other frequenters of the Back Kitchen, spoke of Mr. Pendennis (and not all of them

with great friendship ; for Bludyer called him a confounded coxcomb, and Hoolan wondered that Doolan did not kick him, etc.) by the sobriquet of Walter Lorraine,—and was hence enabled to give Fanny the information which she required.

'And she went and ast for it at the libery,' Mrs. Bolton said,—'several liberies—and some 'ad it and it was hout, and some 'adn't it. And one of the liberies as 'ad it wouldn't let 'er 'ave it without a sovering : and she 'adn't one, and she came back a-cryin' to me—didn't you, Fanny ?—and I gave her a sovering.'

'And, oh, I was in such a fright lest anyone should have come to the libery and took it while I was away,' Fanny said, her cheeks and eyes glowing. 'And, oh, I do like it so !'

Arthur was touched by this artless sympathy, immensely flattered and moved by it. 'Do you like it ?' he said. 'If you will come up to my chambers I will—no, I will bring you one—no, I will send you one. Good-night. Thank you, Fanny. God bless you. I mustn't stay with you. Good-bye, good-bye.' And, pressing her hand once, and nodding to her mother and the other children, he strode out of the gardens.

He quickened his pace as he went from them, and ran out of the gate talking to himself. 'Dear, dear little thing,' he said—'darling little Fanny ! You are worth them all. I wish to Heaven Shandon was back. I'd go home to my mother. I mustn't see her. I won't. I won't, so help me——'

As he was talking thus, and running, the passers-by turning to look at him, he ran against a little old man, and perceived it was Mr. Bows.

'Your very 'umble servant, sir,' said Mr. Bows, making a sarcastic bow, and lifting his old hat from his forehead.

'I wish you a good-day,' Arthur answered sulkily. 'Don't let me detain you, or give you the trouble to follow me again. I am in a hurry, sir. Good-evening.'

Bows thought Pen had some reason for hurrying to his rooms. 'Where are they ?' exclaimed the old gentleman. 'You know whom I mean. They're not in your rooms, sir, are they ? They told Bolton they were going to church at the Temple : they weren't there. They are in your

chambers: they mustn't stay in your chambers, Mr. Pendennis.'

'Damn it, sir!' cried out Pendennis fiercely. 'Come and see if they are in my chambers: here's the court and the door—come in and see.' And Bows, taking off his hat and bowing first, followed the young man.

They were not in Pen's chambers, as we know. But when the gardens were closed, the two women, who had had but a melancholy evening's amusement, walked away sadly with the children, and they entered into Lamb Court, and stood under the lamp-post which cheerfully ornaments the centre of that quadrangle, and looked up to the third floor of the house where Pendennis's chambers were, and where they saw a light presently kindled. Then this couple of fools went away, the children dragging wearily after them, and returned to Mr. Bolton, who was immersed in rum-and-water at his lodge in Shepherd's Inn.

Mr. Bows looked round the blank room which the young man occupied, and which had received but very few ornaments or additions since the last time we saw them. Warrington's old bookcase and battered library, Pen's writing-table with its litter of papers, presented an aspect cheerless enough. 'Will you like to look in the bedrooms, Mr. Bows, and see if my victims are there?' he said bitterly; 'or whether I have made away with the little girls, and hid them in the coal-hole?'

'Your word is sufficient, Mr. Pendennis,' the other said in his sad tone. 'You say they are not here, and I know they are not. And I hope they never have been here, and never will come.'

'Upon my word, sir, you are very good, to choose my acquaintances for me,' Arthur said, in a haughty tone; 'and to suppose that anybody would be the worse for my society. I remember you, and owe you kindness from old times, Mr. Bows; or I should speak more angrily than I do, about a very intolerable sort of persecution to which you seem inclined to subject me. You followed me out of your inn yesterday, as if you wanted to watch that I shouldn't steal something.' Here Pen stammered and turned red, directly he had said the words; he felt he had given the other an opening, which Bows instantly took.

'I do think you came to steal something, as you say the

words, sir,' Bows said. 'Do you mean to say that you came to pay a visit to poor old Bows, the fiddler; or to Mrs. Bolton, at the Porter's Lodge? Oh, fie! Such a fine gentleman as Arthur Pendennis, Esquire, doesn't condescend to walk up to my garret, or to sit in a laundress's kitchen, but for reasons of his own. And my belief is that you came to steal a pretty girl's heart away, and to ruin it, and to spurn it afterwards, Mr. Arthur Pendennis. That's what the world makes of you young dandies, you gentlemen of fashion, you high and mighty aristocrats that trample upon the people. It's sport to you, but what is it to the poor, think you; the toys of your pleasures, whom you play with and whom you fling into the streets when you are tired? I know your order, sir. I know your selfishness, and your arrogance, and your pride. What does it matter to my lord, that the poor man's daughter is made miserable, and her family brought to shame? You must have your pleasures, and the people of course must pay for them. What are we made for, but for that? It's the way with you all—the way with you all, sir.'

Bows was speaking beside the question, and Pen had his advantage here, which he was not sorry to take—not sorry to put off the debate from the point upon which his adversary had first engaged it. Arthur broke out with a sort of laugh, for which he asked Bows's pardon. 'Yes, I am an aristocrat,' he said, 'in a palace up three pair of stairs, with a carpet nearly as handsome as yours, Mr. Bows. My life is passed in grinding the people, is it?—in ruining virgins and robbing the poor? My good sir, this is very well in a comedy, where Job Thornberry* slaps his breast, and asks my lord how dare he trample on an honest man and poke out an Englishman's fireside? but in real life, Mr. Bows, to a man who has to work for his bread as much as you do—how can you talk about aristocrats tyrannizing over the people? Have I ever done you a wrong? or assumed airs of superiority over you? Did you not have an early regard for me—in days when we were both of us romantic young fellows, Mr. Bows? Come, don't be angry with me now, and let us be as good friends as we were before.'

'Those days were very different,' Mr. Bows answered; 'and Mr. Arthur Pendennis was an honest, impetuous young fellow then; rather selfish and conceited, perhaps,

but honest. And I liked you then, because you were ready to ruin yourself for a woman.'

'And now, sir?' Arthur asked.

'And now times are changed, and you want a woman to ruin herself for you,' Bows answered. 'I know this child, sir. I've always said this lot was hanging over her. She has heated her little brain with novels, until her whole thoughts are about love and lovers, and she scarcely sees that she treads on a kitchen floor. I have taught the little thing. She is full of many talents and winning ways, I grant you. I am fond of the girl, sir. I'm a lonely old man; I lead a life that I don't like, among boon companions, who make me melancholy. I have but this child that I care for. Have pity upon me, and don't take her away from me, Mr. Pendennis—don't take her away.'

The old man's voice broke as he spoke. Its accents touched Pen, much more than the menacing or sarcastic tone which Bows had commenced by adopting.

'Indeed,' said he kindly, 'you do me a wrong if you fancy I intend one to poor little Fanny. I never saw her till Friday night. It was the merest chance that our friend Costigan threw her into my way. I have no intentions regarding her—that is——'

'That is, you know very well that she is a foolish girl, and her mother a foolish woman,—that is, you meet her in the Temple Gardens, and of course, without previous concert,—that is, that when I found her yesterday, reading the book you've wrote, she scorned me,' Bows said. 'What am I good for but to be laughed at? a deformed old fellow like me; an old fiddler, that wears a threadbare coat, and gets his bread by playing tunes at an alehouse? You are a fine gentleman, you are. You wear scent in your handkerchief, and a ring on your finger. You go to dine with great people. Who ever gives a crust to old Bows? And yet I might have been as good a man as the best of you. I might have been a man of genius, if I had had the chance; aye, and have lived with the master-spirits of the land. But everything has failed with me. I'd ambition once, and wrote plays, poems, music — nobody would give me a hearing. I never loved a woman but she laughed at me; and here I am in my old age alone—alone! Don't take this girl from me, Mr. Pendennis, I say again. Leave her with me a little longer. She was like a child to me till

yesterday. Why did you step in, and make her mock my deformity and old age ?'

'I am guiltless of that, at least,' Arthur said, with something of a sigh. 'Upon my word of honour, I wish I had never seen the girl. My calling is not seduction, Mr. Bows. I did not imagine that I had made an impression on poor Fanny, until—until to-night. And then, sir, I was sorry, and was flying from my temptation, as you came upon me. And,' he added, with a glow upon his cheek, which, in the gathering darkness, his companion could not see, and with an audible tremor in his voice, 'I do not mind telling you, sir, that on this Sabbath evening, as the church bells were ringing, I thought of my own home, and of women angelically pure and good, who dwell there ; and I was running hither, as I met you, that I might avoid the danger which beset me, and ask strength of God Almighty to do my duty.'

After these words from Arthur a silence ensued, and when the conversation was resumed by his guest, the latter spoke in a tone which was much more gentle and friendly. And on taking farewell of Pen, Bows asked leave to shake hands with him, and with a very warm and affectionate greeting on both sides, apologized to Arthur for having mistaken him, and paid him some compliments which caused the young man to squeeze his old friend's hand heartily again. And as they parted at Pen's door, Arthur said he had given a promise, and he hoped and trusted that Mr. Bows might rely on it.

'Amen to that prayer,' said Mr. Bows, and went slowly down the stair.

CHAPTER L

THE HAPPY VILLAGE AGAIN

EARLY in this history, we have had occasion to speak of the little town of Clavering, near which Pen's paternal home of Fairoaks stood, and of some of the people who inhabited the place; and as the society there was by no means amusing or pleasant, our reports concerning it were not carried to any very great length. Mr. Samuel Huxter, the gentleman whose acquaintance we lately made at Vauxhall, was one of the choice spirits of the little town, when he visited it during his vacations, and enlivened the tables of his friends there, by the wit of Bartholomew's and the gossip of the fashionable London circles which he frequented.

Mr. Hobnell, the young gentleman whom Pen had thrashed, in consequence of the quarrel in the Fotheringay affair, was, whilst a pupil at the Grammar School at Clavering, made very welcome at the tea-table of Mrs. Huxter, Samuel's mother, and was free of the Surgery, where he knew the way to the tamarind-pots, and could scent his pocket-handkerchief with rose-water. And it was at this period of his life that he formed an attachment for Miss Sophy Huxter, whom, on his father's demise, he married, and took home to his house of the Warren, at a few miles from Clavering.

The family had possessed and cultivated an estate there for many years, as yeomen and farmers. Mr. Hobnell's father pulled down the old farmhouse; built a flaring new whitewashed mansion, with capacious stables; and a piano in the drawing-room; kept a pack of harriers; and assumed the title of Squire Hobnell. When he died, and his son reigned in his stead, the family might be fairly considered to be established as county gentry. And Sam Huxter, at London, did no great wrong in boasting about his brother-in-law's place, his hounds, horses, and hospitality, to his admiring comrades at Bartholomew's. Every year, at the time commonly when Mrs. Hobnell

could not leave the increasing duties of her nursery, Hobnell came up to London for a lark, had rooms at the Tavistock, and he and Sam[1] indulged in the pleasures of the town together. Ascot, the theatres, Vauxhall, and the convivial taverns in the joyous neighbourhood of Covent Garden, were visited by the vivacious squire, in company with his learned brother. When he was in London, as he said, he liked to do as London does, and to 'go it a bit,' and when he returned to the west, he took a new bonnet and shawl to Mrs. Hobnell, and relinquished, for country sports and occupations during the next eleven months, the elegant amusements of London life.

Sam Huxter kept up a correspondence with his relative, and supplied him with choice news of the metropolis, in return for the baskets of hares, partridges, and clouted cream which the squire and his good-natured wife forwarded to Sam. A youth more brilliant and distinguished they did not know. He was the life and soul of their house, when he made his appearance in his native place. His songs, jokes, and fun kept the Warren in a roar. He had saved their eldest darling's life, by taking a fish-bone out of her throat : in fine, he was the delight of their circle.

As ill-luck would have it, Pen again fell in with Mr. Huxter, only three days after the rencontre at Vauxhall. Faithful to his vow, he had not been to see little Fanny. He was trying to drive her from his mind by occupation, or other mental excitement. He laboured, though not to much profit, incessantly in his rooms ; and, in his capacity of critic for the *Pall Mall Gazette*, made woful and savage onslaught on a poem and a romance which came before him for judgement. These authors slain, he went to dine alone at the lonely club of the Polyanthus, where the vast solitudes frightened him, and made him only the more moody. He had been to more theatres for relaxation. The whole house was roaring with laughter and applause, and he saw only an ignoble farce that made him sad. It would have damped the spirits of the buffoon on the stage to have seen Pen's dismal face. He hardly knew what was happening ; the scene and the drama passed before him like a dream or a fever. Then he thought he would go to the Back Kitchen, his old haunt with Warrington—he was not a bit sleepy yet. The day before he had walked twenty miles in search after rest, over Hampstead Common

and Hendon lanes, and had got no sleep at night. He would go to the Back Kitchen. It was a sort of comfort to him to think he should see Bows. Bows was there, very calm, presiding at the old piano. Some tremendous comic songs were sung, which made the room crack with laughter. How strange they seemed to Pen! He could only see Bows. In an extinct volcano, such as he boasted that his breast was, it was wonderful how he should feel such a flame! Two days' indulgence had kindled it; two days' abstinence had set it burning in fury. So, musing upon this, and drinking down one glass after another, as ill-luck would have it, Arthur's eyes lighted upon Mr. Huxter, who had been to the theatre, like himself, and, with two or three comrades, now entered the room. Huxter whispered to his companions, greatly to Pen's annoyance. Arthur felt that the other was talking about him. Huxter then worked through the room, followed by his friends, and came and took a place opposite to Pen, nodding familiarly to him, and holding him out a dirty hand to shake.

Pen shook hands with his fellow townsman. He thought he had been needlessly savage to him on the last night when they had met. As for Huxter, perfectly at good-humour with himself and the world, it never entered his mind that he could be disagreeable to anybody; and the little dispute, or 'chaff,' as he styled it, of Vauxhall, was a trifle which he did not in the least regard.

The disciple of Galen having called for 'four stouts,' with which he and his party refreshed themselves, began to think what would be the most amusing topic of conversation with Pen, and hit upon that precise one which was most painful to our young gentleman.

'Jolly night at Vauxhall—wasn't it?' he said, and winked in a very knowing way.

'I'm glad you liked it,' poor Pen said, groaning in spirit.

'I was dev'lish cut—uncommon—been dining with some chaps at Greenwich. That was a pretty bit of muslin hanging on your arm—who was she?' asked the fascinating student.

The question was too much for Arthur. 'Have I asked you any questions about yourself, Mr. Huxter?' he said.

'I didn't mean any offence—beg pardon—hang it, you cut up quite savage,' said Pen's astonished interlocutor.

'Do you remember what took place between us the

other night ?' Pen asked, with gathering wrath. 'You forget ? Very probably. You were tipsy, as you observed just now, and very rude.'

'Hang it, sir, I asked your pardon,' Huxter said, looking red.

'You did certainly, and it was granted with all my heart, I am sure. But if you recollect, I begged that you would have the goodness to omit me from the list of your acquaintance for the future ; and when we met in public, that you would not take the trouble to recognize me. Will you please to remember this hereafter ; and as the song is beginning, permit me to leave you to the unrestrained enjoyment of the music.'

He took his hat, and making a bow to the amazed Mr. Huxter, left the table, as Huxter's comrades, after a pause of wonder, set up such a roar of laughter at Huxter, as called for the intervention of the president of the room ; who bawled out, 'Silence, gentlemen ; *do* have silence for the "Body-Snatcher" !' which popular song began as Pen left the Back Kitchen. He flattered himself that he had commanded his temper perfectly. He rather wished that Huxter had been pugnacious. He would have liked to fight him or somebody. He went home. The day's work, the dinner, the play, the whisky-and-water, the quarrel—nothing soothed him. He slept no better than on the previous night.

A few days afterwards, Mr. Sam Huxter wrote home a letter to Mr. Hobnell in the country, of which Mr. Arthur Pendennis formed the principal subject. Sam described Arthur's pursuits in London, and his confounded insolence of behaviour to his old friends from home. He said he was an abandoned criminal, a regular Don Juan, a fellow who, when he *did* come into the country, ought to be kept out of *honest people's houses*. He had seen him at Vauxhall, dancing with an innocent girl in the lower ranks of life, of whom he was making a victim. He had found out from an Irish gentleman (formerly in the army), who frequented a club of which he, Huxter, was member, who the girl was, on whom this *conceited humbug* was practising his infernal arts ; and he thought he should warn her father, etc., etc., —the letter then touched on general news, conveyed the writer's thanks for the last parcel and the rabbits, and hinted his extreme readiness for further favours.

About once a year, as we have stated, there was occasion for a christening at the Warren, and it happened that this ceremony took place a day after Hobnell had received the letter of his brother-in-law in town. The infant (a darling little girl) was christened Myra-Lucretia, after its two godmothers, Miss Portman, and Mrs. Pybus, of Clavering, and as of course Hobnell had communicated Sam's letter to his wife, Mrs. Hobnell imparted its horrid contents to her two gossips. A pretty story it was, and prettily it was told throughout Clavering in the course of that day.

Myra did not—she was too much shocked to do so—speak on the matter to her mamma, but Mrs. Pybus had no such feelings of reserve. She talked over the matter not only with Mrs. Portman, but with Mr. and the Honourable Mrs. Simcoe, with Mrs. Glanders, her daughters being to that end ordered out of the room, with Madame Fribsby, and, in a word, with the whole of the Clavering society. Madame Fribsby, looking furtively up at her picture of the Dragoon, and inwards into her own wounded memory, said that men would be men, and as long as they were men would be deceivers; and she pensively quoted some lines from *Marmion*,* requesting to know where deceiving lovers should rest? Mrs. Pybus had no words of hatred, horror, contempt, strong enough for a villain who could be capable of conduct so base. This was what came of early indulgence, and insolence, and extravagance, and aristocratic airs (it is certain that Pen had refused to drink tea with Mrs. Pybus), and attending the corrupt and horrid parties in the dreadful modern Babylon! Mrs. Portman was afraid that she must acknowledge that the mother's fatal partiality had spoiled this boy, that his literary successes had turned his head, and his horrid passions had made him forget the principles which Doctor Portman had instilled into him in early life. Glanders, the atrocious captain of Dragoons, when informed of the occurrence by Mrs. Glanders, whistled and made jocular allusions to it at dinner-time; on which Mrs. Glanders called him a brute, and ordered the girls again out of the room, as the horrid captain burst out laughing. Mr. Simcoe was calm under the intelligence; but rather pleased than otherwise; it only served to confirm the opinion which he had always had of that wretched young man: not that he knew anything about him—not that he had read one line of his

dangerous and poisonous works; Heaven forbid that he should: but what could be expected from such a youth, and such frightful, such lamentable, such deplorable want of seriousness? Pen formed the subject for a second sermon at the Clavering chapel of ease: where the dangers of London, and the crime of reading or writing novels, were pointed out on a Sunday evening, to a large and warm congregation. They did not wait to hear whether he was guilty or not. They took his wickedness for granted: and with these admirable moralists, it was who should fling the stone at poor Pen.

The next day Mrs. Pendennis, alone and almost fainting with emotion and fatigue, walked or rather ran to Dr. Portman's house, to consult the good doctor. She had had an anonymous letter;—some Christian had thought it his or her duty to stab the good soul who had never done mortal a wrong—an anonymous letter, with references to Scripture, pointing out the doom of such sinners, and a detailed account of Pen's crime. She was in a state of terror and excitement pitiable to witness. Two or three hours of this pain had aged her already. In her first moment of agitation she had dropped the letter, and Laura had read it. Laura blushed when she read it; her whole frame trembled, but it was with anger. 'The cowards,' she said.—'It isn't true.—No, mother, it isn't true.'

'It *is* true, and you've done it, Laura,' cried out Helen fiercely. 'Why did you refuse him when he asked you? Why did you break my heart and refuse him? It is you who led him into crime. It is you who flung him into the arms of this—this woman.—Don't speak to me.—Don't answer me. I will never forgive you, never. Martha, bring me my bonnet and shawl. I'll go out. I won't have you come with me. Go away. Leave me, cruel girl; why have you brought this shame on me?' And bidding her daughter and her servants keep away from her, she ran down the road to Clavering.

Doctor Portman, glancing over the letter, thought he knew the handwriting, and, of course, was already acquainted with the charge made against poor Pen. Against his own conscience, perhaps (for the worthy doctor, like most of us, had a considerable natural aptitude for receiving any report unfavourable to his neighbours), he strove to

console Helen ; he pointed out that the slander came from an anonymous quarter, and therefore must be the work of a rascal ; that the charge might not be true—was not true, most likely—at least, that Pen must be heard before he was condemned ; that the son of such a mother was not likely to commit such a crime, etc., etc.

Helen at once saw through his feint of objection and denial. 'You think he has done it,' she said,—'you know you think he has done it. Oh, why did I ever leave him, Doctor Portman, or suffer him away from me ? But he can't be dishonest—pray God, not dishonest—you don't think that, do you ? Remember his conduct about that other —person—how madly he was attached to her. He was an honest boy then—he is now. And I thank God—yes, I fall down on my knees and thank God he paid Laura. You said he was good—you did yourself. And now—if this woman loves him—and you know they must—if he has taken her from her home, or she tempted him, which is most likely—why still, she must be his wife and my daughter. And he must leave the dreadful world and come back to me—to his mother, Doctor Portman. Let us go away and bring him back—yes—bring him back—and there shall be joy for the—the sinner that repenteth. Let us go now, directly, dear friend—this very——'

Helen could say no more. She fell back and fainted. She was carried to a bed in the house of the pitying doctor, and the surgeon was called to attend her. She lay all night in an alarming state. Laura came to her, or to the Rectory rather ; for she would not see Laura. And Dr. Portman, still beseeching her to be tranquil, and growing bolder and more confident of Arthur's innocence as he witnessed the terrible grief of the poor mother, wrote a letter to Pen warning him of the rumours that were against him, and earnestly praying that he would break off and repent of a connection so fatal to his best interests and his soul's welfare.

And Laura ?—was her heart not wrung by the thought of Arthur's crime and Helen's estrangement ? Was it not a bitter blow for the innocent girl to think that at one stroke she should lose *all* the love which she cared for in the world ?

CHAPTER LI

WHICH HAD VERY NEARLY BEEN THE LAST OF THE STORY

Doctor Portman's letter was sent off to its destination in London, and the worthy clergyman endeavoured to soothe down Mrs. Pendennis into some state of composure until an answer should arrive, which the doctor tried to think, or at any rate persisted in saying, would be satisfactory as regarded the morality of Mr. Pen. At least Helen's wish of moving upon London and appearing in person to warn her son of his wickedness, was impracticable for a day or two. The apothecary forbade her moving even so far as Fairoaks for the first day, and it was not until the subsequent morning that she found herself again back on her sofa at home, with the faithful, though silent Laura, nursing at her side.

Unluckily for himself and all parties, Pen never read that homily which Doctor Portman addressed to him, until many weeks after the epistle had been composed ; and day after day the widow waited for her son's reply to the charges against him ; her own illness increasing with every day's delay. It was a hard task for Laura to bear the anxiety ; to witness her dearest friend's suffering ; worst of all, to support Helen's estrangement, and the pain caused to her by that averted affection. But it was the custom of this young lady to the utmost of her power, and by means of that gracious assistance which Heaven awarded to her pure and constant prayers, to do her duty. And, as that duty was performed quite noiselessly,—while the supplications, which endowed her with the requisite strength for fulfilling it, also took place in her own chamber, away from all mortal sight,—we, too, must be perforce silent about these virtues of hers, which no more bear public talking about than a flower will bear to bloom in a ball-room. This only we will say—that a good woman is the loveliest flower that blooms under heaven ; and that

we look with love and wonder upon its silent grace, its pure fragrance, its delicate bloom of beauty. Sweet and beautiful!—the fairest and the most spotless!—is it not pity to see them bowed down or devoured by Grief or Death inexorable—wasting in disease—pining with long pain—or cut off by sudden fate in their prime? *We* may deserve grief—but why should these be unhappy?—except that we know that Heaven chastens those whom it loves best; being pleased, by repeated trials, to make these pure spirits more pure.

So Pen never got the letter, although it was duly posted and faithfully discharged by the postman into his letter-box in Lamb Court, and thence carried by the laundress to his writing-table, with the rest of his lordship's correspondence.[1]

Those kind readers who have watched Mr. Arthur's career hitherto, and have made, as they naturally would do, observations upon the moral character and peculiarities of their acquaintance, have probably discovered by this time what was the prevailing fault in Mr. Pen's disposition, and who was that greatest enemy, artfully indicated in the title-page, with whom he had to contend. Not a few of us, my beloved public, have the very same rascal to contend with: a scoundrel who takes every opportunity of bringing us into mischief, of plunging us into quarrels, of leading us into idleness and unprofitable company, and what not. In a word, Pen's greatest enemy was himself: and as he had been pampering, and coaxing, and indulging that individual all his life, the rogue grew insolent, as all spoiled servants will be; and at the slightest attempt to coerce him, or make him do that which was unpleasant to him, became frantically rude and unruly. A person who is used to making sacrifices—Laura, for instance, who had got such a habit of giving up her own pleasure for others—can do the business quite easily; but Pen, unaccustomed as he was to any sort of self-denial, suffered woundily when called on to pay his share, and savagely grumbled at being obliged to forgo anything he liked.

He had resolved in his mighty mind, then, that he would not see Fanny; and he wouldn't. He tried to drive the thoughts of that fascinating little person out of his head, by constant occupation, by exercise, by dissipation

and society. He worked then too much; he walked and rode too much; he ate, drank, and smoked too much: nor could all the cigars and the punch of which he partook drive little Fanny's image out of his inflamed brain, and at the end of a week of this discipline and self-denial our young gentleman was in bed with a fever. Let the reader who has never had a fever in chambers pity the wretch who is bound to undergo that calamity.

A committee of marriageable ladies, or of any Christian persons interested in the propagation of the domestic virtues, should employ a Cruikshank or a Leech,* or some other kindly expositor of the follies of the day, to make a series of designs representing the horrors of a bachelor's life in chambers, and leading the beholder to think of better things, and a more wholesome condition. What can be more uncomfortable than the bachelor's lonely breakfast?—with the black kettle in the dreary fire in midsummer; or, worse still, with the fire gone out at Christmas, half an hour after the laundress has quitted the sitting-room? Into this solitude the owner enters shivering, and has to commence his day by hunting for coals and wood; and before he begins the work of a student, has to discharge the duties of a housemaid, vice Mrs. Flanagan, who is absent without leave. Or, again, what can form a finer subject for the classical designer than the bachelor's shirt—that garment which he wants to assume just at dinner-time, and which he finds without any buttons to fasten it? Then there is the bachelor's return to chambers, after a merry Christmas holiday, spent in a cosy country-house, full of pretty faces, and kind welcomes and regrets. He leaves his portmanteau at the barber's in the Court: he lights his dismal old candle at the sputtering little lamp on the stair: he enters the blank familiar room, where the only tokens to greet him, that show any interest in his personal welfare, are the Christmas bills, which are lying in wait for him, amiably spread out on his reading-table. Add to these scenes an appalling picture of bachelor's illness, and the rents in the Temple will begin to fall from the day of the publication of the dismal diorama.* To be well in chambers is melancholy, and lonely and selfish enough; but to be ill in chambers—to pass nights of pain and watchfulness—to long for the morning and the laundress—to serve yourself your own

medicine by your own watch—to have no other companion for long hours but your own sickening fancies and fevered thoughts: no kind hand to give you drink if you are thirsty, or to smooth the hot pillow that crumples under you,—this, indeed, is a fate so dismal and tragic, that we shall not enlarge upon its horrors; and shall only heartily pity those bachelors in the Temple who brave it every day.

This lot befell Arthur Pendennis after the various excesses which we have mentioned, and to which he had subjected his unfortunate brains. One night he went to bed ill, and the next day awoke worse. His only visitor that day, besides the laundress, was the printer's devil, from the *Pall Mall Gazette* office, whom the writer endeavoured, as best he could, to satisfy. His exertions to complete his work rendered his fever the greater: he could only furnish a part of the quantity of 'copy' usually supplied by him; and Shandon being absent, and Warrington not in London to give a help, the political and editorial columns of the *Gazette* looked very blank indeed; nor did the sub-editor know how to fill them.

Mr. Finucane rushed up to Pen's chambers, and found that gentleman so exceedingly unwell, that the good-natured Irishman set to work to supply his place, if possible, and produced a series of political and critical compositions, such as no doubt greatly edified the readers of the periodical in which he and Pen were concerned. Allusions to the greatness of Ireland, and the genius and virtue of the inhabitants of that injured country, flowed magnificently from Finucane's pen; and Shandon, the chief of the paper, who was enjoying himself placidly at Boulogne-sur-Mer, looking over the columns of the journal, which was forwarded to him, instantly recognized the hand of the great sub-editor, and said, laughing, as he flung over the paper to his wife, 'Look here, Mary, my dear, here is Jack at work again.' Indeed, Jack was a warm friend, and a gallant partisan, and when he had the pen in hand, seldom let slip an opportunity of letting the world know that Rafferty was the greatest painter in Europe, and wondering at the petty jealousy of the Academy, which refused to make him an R.A.: of stating that it was generally reported at the West End, that Mr. Rooney, M.P., was appointed Governor of Barataria; or of introducing into the subject in hand, whatever it might be, a compli-

ment to the Round Towers, or the Giant's Causeway. And besides doing Pen's work for him, to the best of his ability, his kind-hearted comrade offered to forgo his Saturday's and Sunday's holiday, and pass those days of holiday and rest as nurse-tender to Arthur, who, however, insisted that the other should not forgo his pleasure, and thankfully assured him that he could bear best his malady alone.

Taking his supper at the Back Kitchen on the Friday night, after having achieved the work of the paper, Finucane informed Captain Costigan of the illness of their young friend in the Temple ; and remembering the fact two days afterwards, the captain went to Lamb Court and paid a visit to the invalid on Sunday afternoon. He found Mrs. Flanagan, the laundress, in tears in the sitting-room, and got a bad report of the poor dear young gentleman within. Pen's condition had so much alarmed her, that she was obliged to have recourse to the stimulus of brandy to enable her to support the grief which his illness occasioned. As she hung about his bed, and endeavoured to minister to him, her attentions became intolerable to the invalid, and he begged her peevishly not to come near him. Hence the laundress's tears and redoubled grief, and renewed application to the bottle, which she was accustomed to use as an anodyne. The captain rated the woman soundly for her intemperance, and pointed out to her the fatal consequences which must ensue if she persisted in her imprudent courses.

Pen, who was by this time in a very fevered state, was yet greatly pleased to receive Costigan's visit. He heard the well-known voice in his sitting-room, as he lay in the bedroom within, and called the captain eagerly to him, and thanked him for coming, and begged him to take a chair and talk to him. The captain felt the young man's pulse with great gravity—(his own tremulous and clammy hand growing steady for the instant while his finger pressed Arthur's throbbing vein)—the pulse was beating very fiercely —Pen's face was haggard and hot—his eyes were bloodshot and gloomy ; his 'bird,' as the captain pronounced the word, afterwards giving a description of his condition, had not been shaved for nearly a week. Pen made his visitor sit down, and, tossing and turning in his comfortless bed, began to try and talk to the captain in a lively

manner, about the Back Kitchen, about Vauxhall and when they should go again, and about Fanny—how was little Fanny ?

Indeed how was she ? We know how she went home very sadly on the previous Sunday evening, after she had seen Arthur light his lamp in his chambers, whilst he was having his interview with Bows. Bows came back to his own rooms presently, passing by the lodge door, and looking into Mrs. Bolton's, according to his word, as he passed, but with a very melancholy face. She had another

weary night that night. Her restlessness wakened her little bedfellows more than once. She daren't read more of *Walter Lorraine :* father was at home, and would suffer no light. She kept the book under her pillow, and felt for it in the night. She had only just got to sleep, when the children began to stir with the morning, almost as early as the birds. Though she was very angry with Bows, she went to his room at her accustomed hour in the day, and there the good-hearted musician began to talk to her.

'I saw Mr. Pendennis last night, Fanny,' he said.

'Did you ? I thought you did,' Fanny answered, looking fiercely at the melancholy old gentleman.

'I've been fond of you ever since we came to live in this place,' he continued. 'You were a child when I came; and you used to like me, Fanny, until three or four days ago: until you saw this gentleman.'

'And now, I suppose, you are going to say ill of him,' said Fanny. 'Do, Mr. Bows—that will make me like you better.'

'Indeed I shall do no such thing,' Bows answered; 'I think he is a very good and honest young man.'

'Indeed! you know that if you said a word against him, I would never speak a word to you again—never!' cried Miss Fanny; and clenched her little hand, and paced up and down the room. Bows noted, watched, and followed the ardent little creature with admiration and gloomy sympathy. Her cheeks flushed, her frame trembled; her eyes beamed love, anger, defiance. 'You would like to speak ill of him,' she said; 'but you daren't—you know you daren't!'

'I knew him many years since,' Bows continued, 'when he was almost as young as you are, and he had a romantic attachment for our friend the captain's daughter—Lady Mirabel that is now.'

Fanny laughed. 'I suppose there was other people, too, that had romantic attachments for Miss Costigan,' she said: 'I don't want to hear about 'em.'

'He wanted to marry her; but their ages were quite disproportionate: and their rank in life. She would not have him because he had no money. She acted very wisely in refusing him; for the two would have been very unhappy, and she wasn't a fit person to go and live with his family, or to make his home comfortable. Mr. Pendennis has his way to make in the world, and must marry a lady of his own rank. A woman who loves a man will not ruin his prospects, cause him to quarrel with his family, and lead him into poverty and misery for her gratification. An honest girl won't do that, for her own sake, or for the man's.'

Fanny's emotion, which but now had been that of defiance and anger, here turned to dismay and supplication. 'What do I know about marrying, Bows?' she

said. ‘When was there any talk of it? What has there been between this young gentleman and me that's to make people speak so cruel? It was not my doing; nor Arthur's—Mr. Pendennis's—that I met him at Vauxhall. It was the captain took me and ma there. We never thought of nothing wrong, I'm sure. He came and rescued us, and was so very kind. Then he came to call and ask after us: and very, very good it was of such a grand gentleman to be so polite to humble folks like us! And yesterday ma and me just went to walk in the Temple Gardens, and—and——’ Here she broke out with that usual, unanswerable female argument of tears—and cried, ‘Oh! I wish I was dead! I wish I was laid in my grave; and had never, never seen him!’

‘He said as much himself, Fanny,’ Bows said; and Fanny asked through her sobs, ‘Why, why should he wish he had never seen her? Had she ever done him any harm? Oh, she would perish rather than do him any harm.’ Whereupon the musician informed her of the conversation of the day previous, showed her that Pen could not and must not think of her as a wife fitting for him, and that she, as she valued her honest reputation, must strive too to forget him. And Fanny, leaving the musician, convinced but still of the same mind, and promising that she would avoid the danger which menaced her, went back to the porter's lodge, and told her mother all. She talked of her love for Arthur, and bewailed, in her artless manner, the inequality of their condition, that set barriers between them. ‘There's the *Lady of Lyons*,’ Fanny said; ‘oh, ma! how I did love Mr. Macready*when I sor him do it; and Pauline, for being faithful to poor Claude, and always thinking of him; and he coming back to her, an officer, through all his dangers! And if everybody admires Pauline—and I'm sure everybody does, for being so true to a poor man—why should a gentleman be ashamed of loving a poor girl? Not that Mr. Arthur loves me—oh, no, no! I ain't worthy of him; only a princess is worthy of such a gentleman as him. Such a poet!—writing so beautifully, and looking so grand! I'm sure he's a nobleman, and of ancient famly, and kep out of his estate. Perhaps his uncle has it. Ah, if I might, oh, how I'd serve him, and work for him, and slave for him, that I would. I wouldn't ask for more than that, ma,—just to

be allowed to see him of a morning: and sometimes he'd say, "How d'you do, Fanny?" or "God bless you, Fanny!" as he said on Sunday. And I'd work, and work; and I'd set up all night, and read, and learn, and make myself worthy of him. The captain says his mother lives in the country, and is a grand lady there. Oh, how I wish I might go and be her servant, ma! I can do plenty of things, and work very neat; and—and sometimes he'd come home, and I should see him!'

The girl's head fell on her mother's shoulder, as she spoke, and she gave way to a plentiful outpouring of girlish tears, to which the matron, of course, joined her own. 'You mustn't think no more of him, Fanny,' she said. 'If he don't come to you, he's a horrid, wicked man.'

'Don't call him so, mother,' Fanny replied. 'He's the best of men, the best and the kindest. Bows says he thinks he is unhappy at leaving poor little Fanny. It wasn't his fault, was it, that we met?—and it ain't his that I mustn't see him again. He says I mustn't—and I mustn't, mother. He'll forget me, but I shall never forget him. No! I'll pray for him, and love him always —until I die—and I shall die, I know I shall—and then my spirit will always go and be with him.'

'You forget your poor mother, Fanny, and you'll break my heart by goin' on so,' Mrs. Bolton said. 'Perhaps you will see him. I'm sure you'll see him. I'm sure he'll come to-day. If ever I saw a man in love, that man is him. When Emily Budd's young man first came about her, he was sent away by old Budd, a most respectable man, and violoncello in the orchestra at the Wells; and his own family wouldn't hear of it neither. But he came back. We all knew he would. Emily always said so; and he married her; and this one will come back too; and you mark a mother's words, and see if he don't, dear.'

At this point of the conversation Mr. Bolton entered the lodge for his evening meal. At the father's appearance, the talk between mother and daughter ceased instantly. Mrs. Bolton caressed and cajoled the surly undertaker's aide-de-camp, and said, 'Lor, Mr. B., who'd have thought to see *you* away from the club of a Saturday night. Fanny dear, get your pa some supper. What will you have, B.? The poor gurl's got a gathering in her eye, or somethink in it—I was lookin' at it just now as you

came in.' And she squeezed her daughter's hand as a signal of prudence and secrecy; and Fanny's tears were dried up likewise; and by that wondrous hypocrisy and power of disguise which women practise, and with which weapons of defence nature endows them, the traces of her emotion disappeared; and she went and took her work, and sat in the corner so demure and quiet, that the careless male parent never suspected that anything ailed her.

Thus, as if fate seemed determined to inflame and increase the poor child's malady and passion, all circumstances and all parties round about her urged it on. Her mother encouraged and applauded it; and the very words which Bows used in endeavouring to repress her flame only augmented this unlucky fever. Pen was not wicked and a seducer: Pen was high-minded in wishing to avoid her. Pen loved her: the good and the great, the magnificent youth, with the chains of gold and the scented auburn hair! And so he did: or so he would have loved her five years back perhaps, before the world had hardened the ardent and reckless boy—before he was ashamed of a foolish and imprudent passion, and strangled it as poor women do their illicit children, not on account of the crime, but of the shame, and from dread that the finger of the world should point to them.

What respectable person in the world will not say he was quite right to avoid a marriage with an ill-educated person of low degree, whose relations a gentleman could not well acknowledge, and whose manners would not become her new station?—and what philosopher would not tell him that the best thing to do with these little passions if they spring up, is to get rid of them, and let them pass over and cure them: that no man dies about a woman, or vice versa: and that one or the other having found the impossibility of gratifying his or her desire in the particular instance, must make the best of matters, forget each other, look out elsewhere, and choose again? And yet, perhaps, there may be something said on the other side. Perhaps Bows was right in admiring that passion of Pen's, blind and unreasoning as it was, that made him ready to stake his all for his love; perhaps, if self-sacrifice is a laudable virtue, mere worldly self-sacrifice is not very much to be praised;—in fine, let this be a reserved point to be settled by the individual moralist who chooses to debate it.

So much is certain, that with the experience of the world which Mr. Pen now had, he would have laughed at and scouted the idea of marrying a penniless girl out of a kitchen. And this point being fixed in his mind, he was but doing his duty as an honest man, in crushing any unlucky fondness which he might feel towards poor little Fanny.

So she waited and waited in hopes that Arthur would come. She waited for a whole week, and it was at the end of that time that the poor little creature heard from Costigan of the illness under which Arthur was suffering.

It chanced on that very evening after Costigan had visited Pen, that Arthur's uncle the excellent major arrived in town from Buxton, where his health had been mended, and sent his valet Morgan to make inquiries for Arthur, and to request that gentleman to breakfast with the major the next morning. The major was merely passing through London on his way to the Marquis of Steyne's house of Stillbrook, where he was engaged to shoot partridges.

Morgan came back to his master with a very long face. He had seen Mr. Arthur ; Mr. Arthur was very bad indeed ; Mr. Arthur was in bed with a fever. A doctor ought to be sent to him ; and Morgan thought his case most alarming.

Gracious goodness ! this was sad news indeed. He had hoped that Arthur could come down to Stillbrook : he had arranged that he should go, and procured an invitation for his nephew from Lord Steyne. He must go himself : he couldn't throw Lord Steyne over : the fever might be catching : it might be measles : he had never himself had the measles ; they were dangerous when contracted at his age. Was anybody with Mr. Arthur ?

Morgan said there was somebody a nussing of Mr. Arthur.

The major then asked, had his nephew taken any advice ? Morgan said he had asked that question, and had been told that Mr. Pendennis had had no doctor.

Morgan's master was sincerely vexed at hearing of Arthur's calamity. He would have gone to him, but what good could it do Arthur that he (the major) should catch a fever ? His own ailments rendered it absolutely impossible that he should attend to anybody but himself. But the young man must have advice—the best advice ; and Morgan was straightway dispatched with a note from

Major Pendennis to his friend Doctor Goodenough, who by good luck happened to be in London and at home, and who quitted his dinner instantly, and whose carriage was in half an hour in Upper Temple Lane, near Pen's chambers.

The major had asked the kind-hearted physician to bring him news of his nephew at the club where he himself was dining, and in the course of the night the doctor made his appearance. The affair was very serious : the patient was in a high fever : he had had Pen bled instantly : and would see him the first thing in the morning. The major went disconsolate to bed with this unfortunate news. When Goodenough came to see him according to his promise the next day, the doctor had to listen for a quarter of an hour to an account of the major's own maladies, before the latter had leisure to hear about Arthur.

He had had a very bad night—his—his nurse said : at one hour he had been delirious. It might end badly : his mother had better be sent for immediately. The major wrote the letter to Mrs. Pendennis with the greatest alacrity, and at the same time with the most polite precautions. As for going himself to the lad, in his state it was impossible. 'Could I be of any use to him, my dear doctor ?' he asked.

The doctor, with a peculiar laugh, said, No : he didn't think the major could be of any use : that his own precious health required the most delicate treatment, and that he had best go into the country and stay : that he himself would take care to see the patient twice a day, and do all in his power for him.

The major declared upon his honour, that if he could be of any use he would rush to Pen's chambers. As it was, Morgan should go and see that everything was right. The doctor must write to him by every post to Stillbrook : it was but forty miles distant from London, and if anything happened he would come up at any sacrifice.

Major Pendennis transacted his benevolence by deputy and by post. 'What else could he do ?' as he said. 'Gad, you know, in these cases, it's best not disturbing a fellow. If a poor fellow goes to the bad, why, Gad, you know he's disposed of. But in order to get well (and in this, my dear doctor, I'm sure that you will agree with me), the best way is to keep him quiet—perfectly quiet.'

Thus it was the old gentleman tried to satisfy his

PEN'S NURSE

conscience: and he went his way that day to Stillbrook by railway (for railways have sprung up in the course of this narrative, though they have not quite penetrated* into Pen's country yet), and made his appearance in his usual trim order and curly wig, at the dinner-table of the Marquis of Steyne. But we must do the major the justice to say that he was very unhappy and gloomy in demeanour. Wagg and Wenham rallied him about his low spirits; asked whether he was crossed in love? and otherwise diverted themselves at his expense. He lost his money at whist after dinner, and actually trumped his partner's highest spade. And the thoughts of the suffering boy, of whom he was proud, and whom he loved after his manner, kept the old fellow awake half through the night, and made him feverish and uneasy.

On the morrow he received a note in a handwriting which he did not know: it was that of Mr. Bows, indeed, saying that Mr. Arthur Pendennis had had a tolerable night; and that as Dr. Goodenough had stated that the major desired to be informed of his nephew's health, he, R. B., had sent him the news per rail.

The next day he was going out shooting, about noon, with some of the gentlemen staying at Lord Steyne's house; and the company, waiting for the carriages, were assembled on the terrace in front of the house, when a fly drove up from the neighbouring station, and a grey-headed, rather shabby old gentleman jumped out, and asked for Major Pendennis. It was Mr. Bows. He took the major aside and spoke to him; most of the gentlemen round about saw that something serious had happened, from the alarmed look of the major's face.

Wagg said, 'It's a bailiff come down to nab the major;' but nobody laughed at the pleasantry.

'Hullo! What's the matter, Pendennis?' cried Lord Steyne, with his strident voice;—'anything wrong?'

'It's—it's—my boy that's *dead*,' said the major, and burst into a sob—the old man was quite overcome.

'Not dead, my lord; but very ill when I left London,' Mr. Bows said, in a low voice.

A britzka came up at this moment as the three men were speaking. The peer looked at his watch. 'You've twenty minutes to catch the mail-train. Jump in, Pendennis; and drive like h—, sir, do you hear?'

The carriage drove off swiftly with Pendennis and his companions, and let us trust that the oath will be pardoned to the Marquis of Steyne.

The major drove rapidly from the station to the Temple, and found a travelling carriage already before him, and blocking up the narrow Temple Lane. Two ladies got out of it, and were asking their way of the porters; the major looked by chance at the panel of the carriage, and saw the worn-out crest of the Eagle looking at the Sun, and the motto, *Nec tenui penna*, painted beneath. It was his brother's old carriage, built many, many years ago. It was Helen and Laura that were asking their way to poor Pen's room.

He ran up to them; hastily clasped his sister's arm and kissed her hand; and the three entered into Lamb Court, and mounted the long gloomy stair.

They knocked very gently at the door, on which Arthur's name was written, and it was opened by Fanny Bolton.

CHAPTER LII

A CRITICAL CHAPTER

As Fanny saw the two ladies and the anxious countenance of the elder, who regarded her with a look of inscrutable alarm and terror, the poor girl at once knew that Pen's mother was before her; there was a resemblance between the widow's haggard eyes and Arthur's as he tossed in his bed in fever. Fanny looked wistfully at Mrs. Pendennis and at Laura afterwards; there was no more expression in the latter's face than if it had been a mass of stone. Hard-heartedness and gloom dwelt on the figures of both the new-comers: neither showed any the faintest gleam of mercy or sym-

pathy for Fanny. She looked desperately from them to the major behind them. Old Pendennis dropped his eyelids, looking up ever so stealthily from under them at Arthur's poor little nurse.

'I—I wrote to you yesterday, if you please, ma'am,' Fanny said, trembling in every limb as she spoke; and as pale as Laura, whose sad, menacing face looked over Mrs. Pendennis's shoulder.

'Did you, madam?' Mrs. Pendennis said. 'I suppose I may now relieve you from nursing my son. I am his mother, you understand.'

'Yes, ma'am. I—this is the way to his—oh, wait a minute,' cried out Fanny. 'I must prepare you for his——'

The widow, whose face had been hopelessly cruel and ruthless, here started back with a gasp and a little cry, which she speedily stifled.

'He's been so since yesterday,' Fanny said, trembling very much, and with chattering teeth.

A horrid shriek of laughter came out of Pen's room, whereof the door was open; and, after several shouts, the poor wretch began to sing a college drinking song, and then to hurray and to shout as if he was in the midst of a wine-party, and to thump with his fist against the wainscot. He was quite delirious.

'He does not know me, ma'am,' Fanny said.

'Indeed. Perhaps he will know his mother; let me pass, if you please, and go in to him.' And the widow hastily pushed by little Fanny, and through the dark passage which led into Pen's sitting-room. Laura sailed by Fanny, too, without a word; and Major Pendennis followed them. Fanny sat down on a bench in the passage, and cried, and prayed as well as she could. She would have died for him; and they hated her. They had not a word of thanks or kindness for her, the fine ladies. She sat there in the passage, she did not know how long. They never came out to speak to her. She sat there until Doctor Goodenough came to pay his second visit that day; he found the poor little thing at the door.

'What, nurse? How's your patient?' asked the good-natured doctor. 'Has he had any rest?'

'Go and ask them. They're inside,' Fanny answered.

'Who? his mother?'

Fanny nodded her head and didn't speak.

'You must go to bed yourself, my poor little maid,' said the doctor. 'You will be ill, too, if you don't.'

'Oh, mayn't I come and see him: mayn't I come and see him? I—I—love him so,' the little girl said; and as she spoke she fell down on her knees and clasped hold of the doctor's hand in such an agony that to see her melted the kind physician's heart, and caused a mist to come over his spectacles.

'Pooh, pooh! Nonsense! Nurse, has he taken his draught? Has he had any rest? Of course you must come and see him. So must I.'

'They'll let me sit here, won't they, sir? I'll never make no noise. I only ask to stop here,' Fanny said. On which the doctor called her a stupid little thing: put her down upon the bench where Pen's printer's devil used to sit so many hours; tapped her pale cheek with his finger, and bustled into the further room.

Mrs. Pendennis was ensconced pale and solemn in a great chair by Pen's bedside. Her watch was on the bed-table by Pen's medicines. Her bonnet and cloaks were laid in the window. She had her Bible in her lap, without which she never travelled. Her first movement, after seeing her son, had been to take Fanny's shawl and bonnet which were on his drawers, and bring them out and drop them down upon his study-table. She had closed the door upon Major Pendennis, and Laura, too; and taken possession of her son.

She had had a great doubt and terror lest Arthur should not know her; but that pang was spared to her in part at least. Pen knew his mother quite well, and familiarly smiled and nodded at her. When she came in he instantly fancied that they were at home at Fairoaks; and began to talk and chatter and laugh in a rambling wild way. Laura could hear him outside. His laughter shot shafts of poison into her heart. It was true then. He had been guilty—and with *that* creature!—an intrigue with a servant-maid; and she had loved him—and he was dying most likely—raving and unrepentant. The major now and then hummed out a word of remark or consolation, which Laura scarce heard. A dismal sitting it was for all parties; and when Goodenough appeared, he came like an angel into the room.

It is not only for the sick man, it is for the sick man's friends that the doctor comes. His presence is often as

VICE FANNY CASHIERED

good for them as for the patient, and they long for him yet more eagerly. How we have all watched after him! what an emotion the thrill of his carriage-wheels in the street, and at length at the door, has made us feel! how we hang upon his words, and what a comfort we get from a smile or two, if he can vouchsafe that sunshine to lighten our darkness! Who hasn't seen the mother praying into his face, to know if there is hope for the sick infant that cannot speak, and that lies yonder, its little frame battling with fever? Ah, how she looks into his eyes! What thanks if there is light there; what grief and pain if he casts them down, and dares not say 'hope'! Or it is the house-father who is stricken. The terrified wife looks on, while the physician feels his patient's wrist, smothering her agonies, as the children have been called upon to stay their plays and their talk. Over the patient in the fever, the wife expectant, the children unconscious, the doctor stands as if he were Fate, the dispenser of life and death: he *must* let the patient off this time: the woman prays so for his respite! One can fancy how awful the responsibility must be to a conscientious man: how cruel the feeling that he has given the wrong remedy, or that it might have been possible to do better: how harassing the sympathy with survivors, if the case is unfortunate—how immense the delight of victory!

Having passed through a hasty ceremony of introduction to the new comers, of whose arrival he had been made aware by the heart-broken little nurse in waiting without, the doctor proceeded to examine the patient, about whose condition of high fever there could be no mistake, and on whom he thought it necessary to exercise the strongest antiphlogistic remedies in his power. He consoled the unfortunate mother as best he might; and giving her the most comfortable assurances on which he could venture, that there was no reason to despair yet, that everything might still be hoped from his youth, the strength of his constitution, and so forth: and having done his utmost to allay the horrors of the alarmed matron, he took the elder Pendennis aside into the vacant room (Warrington's bedroom), for the purpose of holding a little consultation.

The case was very critical. The fever, if not stopped, might and would carry off the young fellow: he must be bled forthwith: the mother must be informed of this

necessity. Why was that other young lady brought with her? She was out of place in a sick-room.

'And there was another woman still, be hanged to it!' the major said, 'the—the little person who opened the door.' His sister-in-law had brought the poor little devil's bonnet and shawl out, and flung them upon the study-table. Did Goodenough know anything about the—the little person? 'I just caught a glimpse of her as we passed

in,' the major said, 'and begad she was uncommonly nice-looking.' The doctor looked queer: the doctor smiled—in the very gravest moments, with life and death pending, such strange contrasts and occasions of humour will arise, and such smiles will pass, to satirize the gloom, as it were, and to make it more gloomy.

'I have it,' at last he said, re-entering the study; and he wrote a couple of notes hastily at the table there, and sealed one of them. Then, taking up poor Fanny's shawl

and bonnet, and the notes, he went out in the passage to that poor little messenger, and said, 'Quick, nurse; you must carry this to the surgeon, and bid him come instantly: and then go to my house, and ask for my servant, Harbottle, and tell him to get this prescription prepared; and wait until I—until it is ready. It may take a little time in preparation.'

So poor Fanny trudged away with her two notes, and found the apothecary, who lived in the Strand hard by, and who came straightway, his lancet in his pocket, to operate on his patient; and then Fanny made for the doctor's house, in Hanover Square.

The doctor was at home again before the prescription was made up, which took Harbottle, his servant, such a long time in compounding; and, during the remainder of Arthur's illness, poor Fanny never made her appearance in the quality of nurse at his chambers any more. But for that day and the next, a little figure might be seen lurking about Pen's staircase,—a sad, sad little face looked at and interrogated the apothecary, and the apothecary's boy, and the laundress, and the kind physician himself, as they passed out of the chambers of the sick man. And on the third day, the kind doctor's chariot stopped at Shepherd's Inn, and the good, and honest, and benevolent man went into the Porter's Lodge, and tended a little patient he had there, for whom the best remedy he found was on the day when he was enabled to tell Fanny Bolton that the crisis was over, and that there was at length every hope for Arthur Pendennis.

J. Costigan, Esq., late of Her Majesty's service, saw the doctor's carriage, and criticized its horses and appointments. 'Green liveries, bedad!' the general said, 'and as foin a pair of high-stepping bee horses as ever a gentleman need sit behoind, let alone a docthor. There's no ind to the proide and ar'gance of them docthors, nowadays—not but that is a good one, and a scoientific cyarkter, and a roight good fellow, bedad; and he's brought the poor little girl well troo her faver, Bows, me boy;' and so pleased was Mr. Costigan with the doctor's behaviour and skill, that, whenever he met Dr. Goodenough's carriage in future, he made a point of saluting it and the physician inside, in as courteous and magnificent a manner as if Dr. Goodenough* had been the Lord-Liftenant himself,

and Captain Costigan had been in his glory in Phaynix Park.

The widow's gratitude to the physician knew no bounds —or scarcely any bounds, at least. The kind gentleman laughed at the idea of taking a fee from a literary man, or the widow of a brother practitioner; and she determined when she got back to Fairoaks that she would send Goodenough the silver-gilt vase, the jewel of the house, and the glory of the late John Pendennis, preserved in green baize, and presented to him at Bath by the Lady Elizabeth Firebrace, on the recovery of her son, the late Sir Anthony Firebrace, from the scarlet fever. Hippocrates, Hygeia, King Bladud, and a wreath of serpents surmount the cup to this day; which was executed, in their finest manner, by Messrs. Abednego, of Milsom Street; and the inscription was by Mr. Birch, tutor to the young baronet.

This priceless gem of art the widow determined to devote to Goodenough, the preserver of her son; and there was scarcely any other favour which her gratitude would not have conferred upon him, except one, which he desired most, and which was that she should think a little charitably and kindly of poor Fanny, of whose artless, sad story, he had got something during his interviews with her, and of whom he was induced to think very kindly,—not being disposed, indeed, to give much credit to Pen for his conduct in the affair, or not knowing what that conduct had been. He knew enough, however, to be aware that the poor infatuated little girl was without stain as yet; that while she had been in Pen's room it was to see the last of him, as she thought, and that Arthur was scarcely aware of her presence; and that she suffered under the deepest and most pitiful grief, at the idea of losing him, dead or living.

But on the one or two occasions when Goodenough alluded to Fanny, the widow's countenance, always soft and gentle, assumed an expression so cruel and inexorable that the doctor saw it was in vain to ask her for justice or pity, and he broke off all entreaties, and ceased making any further allusions regarding his little client. There is a complaint which neither poppy, nor mandragora, nor all the drowsy syrups of the East could allay, in the men in his time, as we are informed by a popular poet of the days of Elizabeth; and which, when exhibited in women, no

medical discoveries or practice subsequent — neither homœopathy, nor hydropathy, nor mesmerism, nor Dr. Simpson, nor Dr. Locock* can cure, and that is—we won't call it jealousy, but rather gently denominate it, rivalry and emulation in ladies.

Some of those mischievous and prosaic people who carp and calculate at every detail of the romancer, and want to know, for instance, how, when the characters in the *Critic* are at a dead-lock with their daggers at each other's throats,* they are to be got out of that murderous complication of circumstances, may be induced to ask how it was possible in a set of chambers in the Temple, consisting of three rooms, two cupboards, a passage, and a coal-box, Arthur a sick gentleman, Helen his mother, Laura her adopted daughter, Martha their country attendant, Mrs. Wheezer a nurse from St. Bartholomew's Hospital, Mrs. Flanagan an Irish laundress, Major Pendennis a retired military officer, Morgan his valet, Pidgeon Mr. Arthur Pendennis's boy, and others could be accommodated—the answer is given at once, that almost everybody in the Temple was out of town, and that there was scarcely a single occupant of Pen's house in Lamb Court, except those who were engaged round the bed of the sick gentleman, about whose fever we have not given a lengthy account, neither shall we enlarge very much upon the more cheerful theme of his recovery.

Everybody, we have said, was out of town, and of course such a fashionable man as young Mr. Sibwright, who had chambers on the second floor in Pen's staircase, could not be supposed to remain in London. Mrs. Flanagan, Mr. Pendennis's laundress, was acquainted with Mrs. Rouncy, who did for Mr. Sibwright, and that gentleman's bedroom was got ready for Miss Bell, or Mrs. Pendennis, when the latter should be inclined to leave her son's sick-room, to try and seek for a little rest for herself.

If that young buck and flower of Baker Street, Percy Sibwright, could have known who was the occupant of his bedroom, how proud he would have been of that apartment :—what poems he would have written about Laura! (several of his things have appeared in the annuals, and in manuscript in the nobility's albums)—he was a Camford man, and very nearly got the English Prize Poem, it was said—Sibwright, however, was absent, and his bed given

up to Miss Bell. It was the prettiest little brass bed in the world, with chintz curtains lined with pink—he had a mignonette box* in his bedroom window, and the mere sight of his little exhibition of shiny boots, arranged in trim rows over his wardrobe, was a gratification to the beholder. He had a museum of scent, pomatum, and bear's grease pots, quite curious to examine, too; and a choice selection of portraits of females almost always in sadness, and generally in disguise or deshabille, glittered round the neat walls of his elegant little bower of repose. Medora with dishevelled hair was consoling herself over her banjo for the absence of her Conrad—the Princesse Fleur de Marie (of *Rudolstein* and the *Mystères de Paris*)* was sadly ogling out of the bars of her convent cage, in which, poor prisoned bird, she was moulting away,—Dorothea of *Don Quixote* was washing her eternal feet:—in fine, it was such an elegant gallery as became a gallant lover of the sex. And in Sibwright's sitting-room, while there was quite an infantine law library clad in skins of fresh new-born calf, there was a tolerably large collection of classical books which he could not read, and of English and French works of poetry and fiction which he read a great deal too much. His invitation cards of the past season still decorated his looking-glass: and scarce anything told of the lawyer but the wig-box beside the Venus upon the middle shelf of the book-case, on which the name of P. Sibwright, Esquire, was gilded.

With Sibwright in chambers was Mr. Bangham. Mr. Bangham was a sporting man, married to a rich widow. Mr. Bangham had no practice—did not come to chambers thrice in a term: went a circuit for those mysterious reasons which make men go circuit,—and his room served as a great convenience to Sibwright when that young gentleman gave his little dinners. It must be confessed that these two gentlemen have nothing to do with our history, will never appear in it again probably, but we cannot help glancing through their doors as they happen to be open to us, and as we pass to Pen's rooms; as in the pursuit of our own business in life through the Strand, at the club, nay, at church itself, we cannot help peeping at the shops on the way, or at our neighbour's dinner, or at the faces under the bonnets in the next pew.

Very many years after the circumstances about which

we are at present occupied, Laura, with a blush and a laugh showing much humour, owned to having read a French novel once much in vogue, and when her husband asked her, wondering where on earth she could have got such a volume, she owned that it was in the Temple, when she lived in Mr. Percy Sibwright's chambers.

'And, also, I never confessed,' she said, 'on that same occasion, what I must now own to: that I opened the japanned box, and took out that strange-looking wig inside it, and put it on and looked at myself in the glass in it.'

Suppose Percy Sibwright had come in at such a moment as that? What would he have said,—the enraptured rogue? What would have been all the pictures of disguised beauties in his room compared to that living one? Ah, we are speaking of old times, when Sibwright was a bachelor, and before he got a county court,—when people were young—when *most* people were young. Other people are young now; but we no more.

When Miss Laura played this prank with the wig, you can't suppose that Pen could have been very ill upstairs; otherwise, though she had grown to care for him ever so little, common sense of feeling and decorum would have prevented her from performing any tricks or trying any disguises.

But all sorts of events had occurred in the course of the last few days which had contributed to increase or account for her gaiety, and a little colony of the reader's old friends and acquaintances was by this time established in Lamb Court, Temple, and round Pen's sick bed there. First, Martha, Mrs. Pendennis's servant, had arrived from Fair-oaks, being summoned thence by the major, who justly thought her presence would be comfortable and useful to her mistress and her young master, for neither of whom the constant neighbourhood of Mrs. Flanagan (who during Pen's illness required more spirituous consolation than ever to support her) could be pleasant. Martha then made her appearance in due season to wait upon Mrs. Pendennis, nor did that lady go once to bed until the faithful servant had reached her, when, with a heart full of maternal thankfulness, she went and lay down upon Warrington's straw mattress, and among his mathematical books, as has been already described.

It is true that ere that day a great and delightful alteration in Pen's condition had taken place. The fever, subjugated by Dr. Goodenough's blisters, potions, and lancet, had left the young man, or only returned at intervals of feeble intermittence; his wandering senses had settled in his weakened brain: he had had time to kiss and bless his mother for coming to him, and calling for Laura and his uncle (who were both affected according to their different natures by his wan appearance, his lean shrunken hands, his hollow eyes and voice, his thin bearded face) to press their hands and thank them affectionately; and after this greeting, and after they had been turned out of the room by his affectionate nurse, he had sunk into a fine sleep which had lasted for about sixteen hours, at the end of which period he awoke, calling out that he was very hungry. If it is hard to be ill and to loathe food, oh, how pleasant to be getting well and to be feeling hungry—*how* hungry! Alas, the joys of convalescence become feebler with increasing years, as other joys do—and then—and then comes that illness when one does not convalesce at all.

On the day of this happy event, too, came another arrival in Lamb Court. This was introduced into the Pen-Warrington sitting-room by large puffs of tobacco smoke—the puffs of smoke were followed by an individual with a cigar in his mouth, and a carpet-bag under his arm—this was Warrington, who had run back from Norfolk, when Mr. Bows thoughtfully wrote to inform him of his friend's calamity. But he had been from home when Bows's letter had reached his brother's house—the Eastern Counties did not then boast of a railway (for we beg the reader to understand that we only commit anachronisms when we choose, and when by a daring violation of those natural laws some great ethical truth is to be advanced)—in fine, Warrington only appeared with the rest of the good luck upon the lucky day after Pen's convalescence may have been said to have begun.

His surprise was, after all, not very great when he found the chambers of his sick friend occupied, and his old acquaintance the major seated demurely in an easy-chair (Warrington had let himself into the rooms with his own pass-key), listening, or pretending to listen, to a young lady who was reading to him a play of Shakespere in a low sweet voice. The lady stopped and started, and laid

down her book, at the apparition of the tall traveller with the cigar and the carpet-bag. He blushed, he flung the cigar into the passage : he took off his hat, and dropped that too, and going up to the major, seized that old gentleman's hand, and asked questions about Arthur.

The major answered in a tremulous, though cheery voice—it was curious how emotion seemed to olden him —and returning Warrington's pressure with a shaking hand, told him the news—of Arthur's happy crisis, of his mother's arrival—with her young charge—with Miss——

'You need not tell me her name,' Mr. Warrington said, with great animation, for he was affected and elated with the thought of his friend's recovery—'you need not tell me your name. I knew at once it was Laura.' And he held out his hand and took hers. Immense kindness and tenderness gleamed from under his rough eyebrows, and shook his voice as he gazed at her and spoke to her. 'And this is Laura!' his looks seemed to say. 'And this is Warrington,' the generous girl's heart beat back. 'Arthur's hero—the brave and the kind—he has come hundreds of miles to succour him, when he heard of his friend's misfortune!'

'Thank you, Mr. Warrington,' was all that Laura said, however; and as she returned the pressure of his kind hand, she blushed so, that she was glad the lamp was behind her to conceal her flushing face.

As these two were standing in this attitude, the door of Pen's bed-chamber was opened stealthily as his mother was wont to open it, and Warrington saw another lady, who looked first at him, and then turning round towards the bed, said, 'Hsh!' and put up her hand.

It was to Pen Helen was turning, and giving caution. He called out with a feeble, tremulous, but cheery voice, 'Come in, Stunner—come in, Warrington. I knew it was you—by the—by the smoke, old boy,' he said, as holding his worn hand out, and with tears at once of weakness and pleasure in his eyes, he greeted his friend.

'I—I beg pardon, ma'am, for smoking,' Warrington said, who now almost for the first time blushed for his wicked propensity.

Helen only said, 'God bless you, Mr. Warrington.' She was so happy, she would have liked to kiss George. Then, and after the friends had had a brief, very brief interview,

the delighted and inexorable mother, giving her hand to Warrington, sent him out of the room too, back to Laura and the major, who had not resumed their play of *Cymbeline*[*] where they had left it off at the arrival of the rightful owner of Pen's chambers.

CHAPTER LIII

CONVALESCENCE

OUR duty now is to record a fact concerning Pendennis, which, however shameful and disgraceful, when told regarding the chief personage and godfather of a novel, must, nevertheless, be made known to the public who reads his veritable memoirs. Having gone to bed ill with fever, and suffering to a certain degree under the passion of love, after he had gone through his physical malady, and had been bled and had been blistered, and had had his head shaved, and had been treated and medicamented as the doctor ordained: —it is a fact, that, when he rallied up from his bodily ailment, his mental malady had likewise quitted him, and he was no more in love with Fanny Bolton than you or I, who are much too wise, or too moral, to allow our hearts to go gadding after porters' daughters.

He laughed at himself as he lay on his pillow, thinking of this second cure which had been effected upon him. He did not care the least about Fanny now: he wondered how he ever should have cared: and according to his custom made an autopsy of that dead passion, and anatomized his own defunct sensation for his poor little nurse. What could have made him so hot and eager about her but a few weeks back? Not her wit, not her breeding, not her beauty —there were hundreds of women better looking than she. It was out of himself that the passion had gone: it did not reside in her. She was the same; but the eyes which saw

her were changed ; and alas, that it should be so ! were not particularly eager to see her any more. He felt very well disposed towards the little thing, and so forth, but as for violent personal regard, such as he had but a few weeks ago, it had fled under the influence of the pill and lancet, which had destroyed the fever in his frame. And an immense source of comfort and gratitude it was to Pendennis (though there was something selfish in that feeling, as in most others of our young man), that he had been enabled to resist temptation at the time when the danger was greatest, and had no particular cause of self-reproach as he remembered his conduct towards the young girl. As from a precipice down which he might have fallen, so from the fever from which he had recovered, he reviewed the Fanny Bolton snare, now that he had escaped out of it, but I'm not sure that he was not ashamed of the very satisfaction which he experienced. It is pleasant, perhaps, but it is humiliating to own that you love no more.

Meanwhile the kind smiles and tender watchfulness of the mother at his bedside filled the young man with peace and security. To see that health was returning was all the unwearied nurse demanded : to execute any caprice or order of her patient's, her chiefest joy and reward. He felt himself environed by her love, and thought himself almost as grateful for it as he had been when weak and helpless in childhood.

Some misty notions regarding the first part of his illness, and that Fanny had nursed him, Pen may have had, but they were so dim that he could not realize them with accuracy, or distinguish them from what he knew to be delusions which had occurred and were remembered during the delirium of his fever. So as he had not thought proper on former occasions to make any allusions about Fanny Bolton to his mother, of course he could not now confide to her his sentiments regarding Fanny, or make this worthy lady a confidante. It was on both sides an unlucky precaution and want of confidence ; and a word or two in time might have spared the good lady, and those connected with her, a deal of pain and anguish.

Seeing Miss Bolton installed as nurse and tender to Pen, I am sorry to say Mrs. Pendennis had put the worst construction on the fact of the intimacy of these two unlucky young persons, and had settled in her own mind that the

accusations against Arthur were true. Why not have stopped to inquire ?—There are stories to a man's disadvantage that the women who are fondest of him are always the most eager to believe. Isn't a man's wife often the first to be jealous of him ? Poor Pen got a good stock of this suspicious kind of love from the nurse who was now watching over him ; and the kind and pure creature thought that her boy had gone through a malady much more awful and debasing than the mere physical fever, and was stained by crime as well as weakened by illness. The consciousness of this she had to bear perforce silently, and to try to put a mask of cheerfulness and confidence over her inward doubt and despair and horror.

When Captain Shandon, at Boulogne, read the next number of the *Pall Mall Gazette*, it was to remark to Mrs. Shandon that Jack Finucane's hand was no longer visible in the leading articles, and that Mr. Warrington must be at work there again. 'I know the crack of his whip in a hundred, and the cut which the fellow's thong leaves. There's Jack Bludyer, goes to work like a butcher, and mangles a subject. Mr. Warrington finishes a man, and lays his cuts neat and regular, straight down the back, and drawing blood every line ;' at which dreadful metaphor, Mrs. Shandon said, 'Law, Charles, how can you talk so ! I always thought Mr. Warrington very high, but a kind gentleman ; and I'm sure he was most kind to the children.' Upon which Shandon said, 'Yes ; he's kind to the children ; but he's savage to the men ; and to be sure, my dear, you don't understand a word about what I'm saying ; and it's best you shouldn't ; for it's little good comes out of writing for newspapers ; and it's better here, living easy at Boulogne, where the wine's plenty, and the brandy costs but two francs a bottle. Mix us another tumbler, Mary my dear ; we'll go back into harness soon. "*Cras ingens iterabimus aequor*"*—bad luck to it.'

In a word, Warrington went to work with all his might, in place of his prostrate friend, and did Pen's portion of the *Pall Mall Gazette* 'with a vengeance,' as the saying is. He wrote occasional articles and literary criticisms ; he attended theatres and musical performances, and discoursed about them with his usual savage energy. His hand was too strong for such small subjects, and it pleased him to tell Arthur's mother, and uncle, and Laura, that there was no

HELEN INSTALLED

hand in all the band of penmen more graceful and light, more pleasant and more elegant, than Arthur's. 'The people in this country, ma'am, don't understand what style is, or they would see the merits of our young one,' he said to Mrs. Pendennis. 'I call him ours, ma'am, for I bred him; and I am as proud of him as you are; and, bating a little wilfulness, and a little selfishness, and a little dandification, I don't know a more honest, or loyal, or gentle creature. His pen is wicked sometimes, but he is as kind as a young lady—as Miss Laura here—and I believe he would not do any living mortal harm.'

At this, Helen, though she heaved a deep, deep sigh, and Laura, though she, too, was sadly wounded, nevertheless were most thankful for Warrington's good opinion of Arthur, and loved him for being so attached to their Pen. And Major Pendennis was loud in his praises of Mr. Warrington,—more loud and enthusiastic than it was the major's wont to be. 'He is a gentleman, my dear creature,' he said to Helen, 'every inch a gentleman, my good madam—the Suffolk Warringtons—Charles the First's baronets:—what could he be but a gentleman, come out of that family?—father,—Sir Miles Warrington; ran away with—beg your pardon, Miss Bell. Sir Miles was a very well-known man in London, and a friend of the Prince of Wales. This gentleman is a man of the greatest talents, the very highest accomplishments,—sure to get on, if he had a motive to put his energies to work.'

Laura blushed for herself whilst the major was talking and praising Arthur's hero. As she looked at Warrington's manly face, and dark, melancholy eyes, this young person had been speculating about him, and had settled in her mind that he must have been the victim of an unhappy attachment; and as she caught herself so speculating, why, Miss Bell blushed.

Warrington got chambers hard by,—Grenier's chambers in Flag Court; and having executed Pen's task with great energy in the morning, his delight and pleasure of an afternoon was to come and sit with the sick man's company in the sunny autumn evenings; and he had the honour more than once of giving Miss Bell his arm for a walk in the Temple Gardens; to take which pastime, when the frank Laura asked of Helen permission, the major eagerly said, 'Yes, yes, begad—of course you go out with him—it's like

the country, you know: everybody goes out with everybody in the Gardens, and there are beadles, you know, and that sort of thing—everybody walks in the Temple Gardens.' If the great arbiter of morals did not object, why should simple Helen? She was glad that her girl should have such fresh air as the river could give, and to see her return with heightened colour and spirits from these harmless excursions.

Laura and Helen had come, you must know, to a little explanation. When the news arrived of Pen's alarming illness, Laura insisted upon accompanying the terrified mother to London, would not hear of the refusal which the still angry Helen gave her, and, when refused a second time yet more sternly, and when it seemed that the poor lost lad's life was despaired of, and when it was known that his conduct was such as to render all thoughts of union hopeless, Laura had, with many tears, told her mother a secret with which every observant person who reads this story is acquainted already. Now she never could marry him, was she to be denied the consolation of owning how fondly, how truly, how entirely she had loved him? The mingling tears of the women appeased the agony of their grief somewhat, and the sorrows and terrors of their journey were at least in so far mitigated that they shared them together.

What could Fanny expect when suddenly brought up for sentence before a couple of such judges? Nothing but swift condemnation, awful punishment, merciless dismissal! Women are cruel critics in cases such as that in which poor Fanny was implicated; and we like them to be so; for, besides the guard which a man places round his own harem, and the defences which a woman has in her heart, her faith, and honour, hasn't she all her own friends of her own sex to keep watch that she does not go astray, and to tear her to pieces if she is found erring? When our Mahmouds or Selims of Baker Street or Belgrave Square visit their Fatimas with condign punishment, their mothers sew up Fatima's sack for her, and her sisters and sisters-in-law see her well under water. And this present writer does not say nay. He protests most solemnly he is a Turk, too. He wears a turban and a beard like another, and is all for the sack practice, Bismillah! But oh, you spotless, who have the right of capital punishment vested in you, at least be very cautious that you make away with the proper

(if so she may be called) person. Be very sure of the fact before you order the barge out: and don't pop your subject into the Bosphorus, until you are quite certain that she deserves it. This is all I would urge in poor Fatima's behalf—absolutely all—not a word more, by the beard of the Prophet. If she's guilty, down with her—heave over the sack, away with it into the Golden Horn bubble and squeak, and justice being done, give way, men, and let us pull back to supper.

So the major did not in any way object to Warrington's continued promenades with Miss Laura, but, like a benevolent old gentleman, encouraged in every way the intimacy of that couple. Were there any exhibitions in town? he was for Warrington conducting her to them. If Warrington had proposed to take her to Vauxhall itself, this most complaisant of men would have seen no harm,—nor would Helen, if Pendennis the elder had so ruled it,—nor would there have been any harm between two persons whose honour was entirely spotless,—between Warrington, who saw in intimacy a pure, and high-minded, and artless woman for the first time in his life,—and Laura, who too for the first time was thrown into the constant society of a gentleman of great natural parts and powers of pleasing; who possessed varied acquirements, enthusiasm, simplicity, humour, and that freshness of mind which his simple life and habits gave him, and which contrasted so much with Pen's dandy indifference of manner and faded sneer. In Warrington's very uncouthness there was a refinement, which the other's finery lacked. In his energy, his respect, his desire to please, his hearty laughter, or simple, confiding pathos, what a difference to Sultan Pen's yawning sovereignty and languid acceptance of homage! What had made Pen at home such a dandy and such a despot? The women had spoiled him, as we like them and as they like to do. They had cloyed him with obedience, and surfeited him with sweet respect and submission, until he grew weary of the slaves who waited upon him, and their caresses and cajoleries excited him no more. Abroad, he was brisk and lively, and eager and impassioned enough—most men are, so constituted and so nurtured. Does this, like the former sentence, run a chance of being misinterpreted, and does anyone dare to suppose that the writer would incite the women to revolt? Never, by the whiskers of the Prophet,

again he says. He wears a beard, and he likes his women to be slaves. What man doesn't? What man would be henpecked, I say? We will cut off all the heads in Christendom or Turkeydom rather than that.

Well then, Arthur being so languid, and indifferent, and careless about the favours bestowed upon him, how came it that Laura should have such a love and rapturous regard for him, that a mere inadequate expression of it should have kept the girl talking all the way from Fairoaks to London, as she and Helen travelled in the post-chaise? As soon as Helen had finished one story about the dear fellow, and narrated, with a hundred sobs and ejaculations, and looks up to heaven, some thrilling incidents which occurred about the period when the hero was breeched, Laura began another, equally interesting and equally ornamented with tears, and told how heroically he had a tooth out or wouldn't have it out, or how daringly he robbed a bird's nest, or how magnanimously he spared it; or how he gave a shilling to the old woman on the common, or went without his bread-and-butter for the beggar-boy who came into the yard—and so on. One to another the sobbing women sang laments upon their hero, who, my worthy reader has long since perceived, is no more a hero than either one of us. Being as he was, why should a sensible girl be so fond of him?

This point has been argued before in a previous unfortunate sentence* (which lately drew down all the wrath of Ireland upon the writer's head), and which said that the greatest rascal cut-throats have had somebody to be fond of them, and if those monsters, why not ordinary mortals? And with whom shall a young lady fall in love but with the person she sees? She is not supposed to lose her heart in a dream, like a princess in the *Arabian Nights*; or to plight her young affections to the portrait of a gentleman in the Exhibition, or a sketch in the *Illustrated London News*. You have an instinct within you which inclines you to attach yourself to someone: you meet Somebody: you hear Somebody constantly praised: you walk, or ride, or waltz, or talk, or sit in the same pew at church with Somebody: you meet again, and again, and—'Marriages are made in heaven,' your dear mamma says, pinning your orange-flowers wreath on, with her blessed eyes dimmed with tears—and there is a wedding-breakfast, and you take

off your white satin and retire to your coacn-and-four, and you and he are a happy pair.—Or, the affair is broken off, and then, poor dear wounded heart! why then you meet Somebody Else, and twine your young affections round number two. It is your nature so to do. Do you suppose it is all for the man's sake that you love, and not a bit for your own? Do you suppose you would drink if you were not thirsty, or eat if you were not hungry?

So then Laura liked Pen because she saw scarcely anybody else at Fairoaks except Doctor Portman and Captain Glanders, and because his mother constantly praised her Arthur, and because he was gentleman-like, tolerably good-looking and witty, and because, above all, it was of her nature to like somebody. And having once received this image into her heart, she there tenderly nursed it and clasped it—she there, in his long absences and her constant solitudes, silently brooded over it and fondled it—and when after this she came to London, and had an opportunity of becoming rather intimate with Mr. George Warrington, what on earth was to prevent her from thinking him a most odd, original, agreeable, and pleasing person?

A long time afterwards, when these days were over, and Fate in its own way had disposed of the various persons now assembled in the dingy building in Lamb Court, perhaps some of them looked back and thought how happy the time was, and how pleasant had been their evening talks and little walks and simple recreations round the sofa of Pen the convalescent. The major had a favourable opinion of September in London from that time forward, and declared at his clubs and in society that the dead season in town was often pleasant, doosid pleasant, begad. He used to go home to his lodgings in Bury Street of a night, wondering that it was already so late, and that the evening had passed away so quietly. He made his appearance at the Temple pretty constantly in the afternoon, and tugged up the long black staircase with quite a benevolent activity and perseverance. And he made interest with the *chef* at Bays's (that renowned cook, the superintendence of whose work upon Gastronomy compelled the gifted author to stay in the metropolis), to prepare little jellies, delicate clear soups, aspics, and other trifles good for invalids, which Morgan the valet constantly brought down to the little Lamb Court colony. And the permission to drink a glass

or two of pure sherry being accorded to Pen by Doctor Goodenough, the major told with almost tears in his eyes how his noble friend the Marquis of Steyne, passing through London on his way to the Continent, had ordered any quantity of his precious, his priceless Amontillado, that had been a present from King Ferdinand to the noble marquis, to be placed at the disposal of Mr. Arthur Pendennis. The widow and Laura tasted it with respect (though they didn't in the least like the bitter flavour), but the invalid was greatly invigorated by it, and Warrington pronounced it superlatively good, and proposed the major's health in a mock speech after dinner on the first day when the wine was served, and that of Lord Steyne and the aristocracy in general.

Major Pendennis returned thanks with the utmost gravity, and in a speech in which he used the words 'the present occasion,' at least the proper number of times. Pen cheered with his feeble voice from his arm-chair. Warrington taught Miss Laura to cry 'Hear! hear!' and tapped the table with his knuckles. Pidgeon the attendant grinned, and honest Doctor Goodenough found the party so merrily engaged, when he came in to pay his faithful gratuitous visit.

Warrington knew Sibwright, who lived below, and that gallant gentleman, in reply to a letter informing him of the use to which his apartments had been put, wrote back the most polite and flowery letter of acquiescence. He placed his chambers at the service of their fair occupants, his bed at their disposal, his carpets at their feet. Everybody was kindly disposed towards the sick man and his family. His heart (and his mother's too, as we may fancy) melted within him at the thought of so much good feeling and good nature. Let Pen's biographer be pardoned for alluding to a time not far distant when a somewhat similar mishap brought him a providential friend, a kind physician, and a thousand proofs of a most touching and surprising kindness and sympathy.

There was a piano in Mr. Sibwright's chamber (indeed this gentleman, a lover of all the arts, performed himself—and exceedingly ill too—upon the instrument; and had had a song dedicated to him—the words by himself, the air by his devoted friend Leopoldo Twankidillo), and at this music-box, as Mr. Warrington called it, Laura, at first

with a great deal of tremor and blushing (which became her very much), played and sang, sometimes of an evening, simple airs, and old songs of home. Her voice was a rich contralto, and Warrington, who scarcely knew one tune from another, and who had but one tune or bray in his *répertoire*,—a most discordant imitation of 'God Save the King,'—sat rapt in delight listening to these songs. He could follow their rhythm if not their harmony; and he could watch, with a constant and daily growing enthusiasm, the pure and tender and generous creature who made the music.

I wonder how that poor pale little girl in the black bonnet, who used to stand at the lamp-post in Lamb Court sometimes of an evening, looking up to the open windows from which the music came, liked to hear it? When Pen's bed-time came the songs were hushed. Lights appeared in the upper room: *his* room, whither the widow used to conduct him; and then the major and Mr. Warrington, and sometimes Miss Laura, would have a game at écarté or backgammon; or she would sit by working a pair of slippers in worsted—a pair of gentleman's slippers—they might have been for Arthur, or for George, or for Major Pendennis: one of those three would have given anything for the slippers.

Whilst such business as this was going on within, a rather shabby old gentleman would come and lead away the pale girl in the black bonnet, who had no right to be abroad in the night air; and the Temple porters, the few laundresses, and other amateurs who had been listening to the concert, would also disappear.

Just before ten o'clock there was another musical performance, namely that of the chimes of St. Clement's clock in the Strand, which played the clear, cheerful notes of a psalm, before it proceeded to ring its ten fatal strokes. As they were ringing, Laura began to fold up the slippers; Martha from Fairoaks appeared with a bed-candle, and a constant smile on her face; the major said, 'God bless my soul, is it so late?' Warrington and he left their unfinished game, and got up and shook hands with Miss Bell. Martha from Fairoaks lighted them out of the passage and down the stair, and, as they descended, they could hear her bolting and locking 'the sporting door' after them, upon her young mistress and herself. If there had been any

danger, grinning Martha said she would have got down 'that thar hooky soord which hung up in gantleman's room,'—meaning the Damascus scimitar with the names of the Prophet engraved on the blade and the red-velvet scabbard, which Percy Sibwright, Esquire, brought back from his tour in the Levant, along with an Albanian dress, and which he wore with such elegant effect at Lady Mullinger's fancy ball, Gloucester Square, Hyde Park. It entangled itself in Miss Kewsey's train, who appeared in the dress in which she, with her mamma, had been presented to their sovereign (the latter by the L—d Ch–nc–ll–r's lady), and led to events which have nothing to do with this history. Is not Miss Kewsey now Mrs. Sibwright? Has Sibwright not got a county court?—Good-night, Laura and Fairoaks Martha. Sleep well and wake happy, pure and gentle lady.

Sometimes after these evenings Warrington would walk a little way with Major Pendennis—just a little way—just as far as the Temple gate—as the Strand—as Charing Cross—as the club—he was not going into the club? Well, as far as Bury Street, where he would laughingly shake hands on the major's own door-step. They had been talking about Laura all the way. It was wonderful how enthusiastic the major, who, as we know, used to dislike her, had grown to be regarding the young lady.—'Dev'lish fine girl, begad. Dev'lish well-mannered girl—my sister-in-law has the manners of a duchess and would bring up any girl well. Miss Bell's a *little* countrified. But the smell of the hawthorn is pleasant, demmy. How she blushes! Your London girls would give many a guinea for a bouquet like that—natural flowers, begad! And she's a little money too—nothing to speak of—but a pooty little bit of money.' In all which opinions no doubt Mr. Warrington agreed; and though he laughed as he shook hands with the major, his face fell as he left his veteran companion; and he strode back to chambers, and smoked pipe after pipe long into the night, and wrote article upon article, more and more savage, in lieu of friend Pen disabled.

Well, it was a happy time for almost all parties concerned. Pen mended daily. Sleeping and eating were his constant occupations. His appetite was something frightful. He was ashamed of exhibiting it before Laura, and almost before his mother, who laughed and applauded him.

As the roast chicken of his dinner went away he eyed the departing friend with sad longing, and began to long for jelly, or tea, or what not. He was like an ogre in devouring. The doctor cried stop, but Pen would not. Nature called out to him more loudly than the doctor, and that kind and friendly physician handed him over with a very good grace to the other healer.

And here let us speak very tenderly and in the strictest confidence of an event which befell him, and to which he never liked an allusion. During his delirium the ruthless Goodenough ordered ice to be put to his head, and all his lovely hair to be cut. It was done in the time of—of the other nurse, who left every single hair, of course, in a paper for the widow to count and treasure up. She never believed but that the girl had taken away some of it, but then women are so suspicious upon these matters.

When this direful loss was made visible to Major Pendennis, as of course it was the first time the older saw the poor young man's shorn pate, and when Pen was quite out of danger, and gaining daily vigour, the major, with something like blushes and a queer wink of his eyes, said he knew of a—a person—a coiffeur, in fact—a good man, whom he would send down to the Temple, and who would —a—apply—a—a temporary remedy to that misfortune.

Laura looked at Warrington with the archest sparkle in her eyes—Warrington fairly burst out into a boohoo of laughter : even the widow was obliged to laugh : and the major erubescent confounded the impudence of the young folks, and said when he had his hair cut he would keep a lock of it for Miss Laura.

Warrington voted that Pen should wear a barrister's wig. There was Sibwright's down below, which would become him hugely. Pen said ' Stuff,' and seemed as confused as his uncle ; and the end was that a gentleman from Burlington Arcade waited next day upon Mr. Pendennis, and had a private interview with him in his bedroom ; and a week afterwards the same individual appeared with a box under his arm, and an ineffable grin of politeness on his face, and announced that he had brought 'ome Mr. Pendennis's 'ead of 'air.

It must have been a grand but melancholy sight to see Pen in the recesses of his apartment, sadly contemplating his ravaged beauty, and the artificial means of hiding its

ruin. He appeared at length in the 'ead of 'air; but Warrington laughed so that Pen grew sulky, and went back for his velvet cap, a neat turban which the fondest of mammas had worked for him. Then Mr. Warrington and Miss Bell got some flowers off the ladies' bonnets and made a wreath, with which they decorated the wig and brought it out in procession, and did homage before it. In fact they indulged in a hundred sports, jocularities, waggeries and *petits jeux innocents*: so that the second and third floors of Number 6, Lamb Court, Temple, rang with more cheerfulness and laughter than had been known in those precincts for many a long day.

At last, after about ten days of this life, one evening when the little spy of the court came out to take her usual post of observation at the lamp, there was no music from the second floor window, there were no lights in the third story chambers, the windows of each were open, and the occupants were gone. Mrs. Flanagan, the laundress, told Fanny what had happened. The ladies and all the party had gone to Richmond for change of air. The antique travelling chariot was brought out again and cushioned with many pillows for Pen and his mother; and Miss Laura went in the most affable manner in the omnibus under the guardianship of Mr. George Warrington. He came back and took possession of his old bed that night in the vacant and cheerless chambers, and to his old books and his old pipes, but not perhaps to his old sleep.

The widow had left a jar full of flowers upon his table, prettily arranged, and when he entered they filled the solitary room with odour. They were memorials of the kind, gentle souls who had gone away, and who had decorated for a little while that lonely, cheerless place. He had had the happiest days of his whole life, George felt—he knew it now they were just gone: he went and

took up the flowers and put his face to them, smelt them —perhaps kissed them. As he put them down, he rubbed his rough hand across his eyes with a bitter word and laugh. He would have given his whole life and soul to win that prize which Arthur rejected. Did she want fame ? he would have won it for her :—devotion ?—a great heart full of pent-up tenderness and manly love and gentleness was there for her, if she might take it. But it might not be. Fate had ruled otherwise. 'Even if I could, she would not have me,' George thought. 'What has an ugly, rough old fellow like me, to make any woman like him ? I'm getting old, and I've made no mark in life. I've neither good looks, nor youth, nor money, nor reputation. A man must be able to do something besides stare at her and offer on his knees his uncouth devotion, to make a woman like him. What can I do ? Lots of young fellows have passed me in the race—what they call the prizes of life didn't seem to me worth the trouble of the struggle. But for *her*. If she had been mine and liked a diamond—ah ! shouldn't she have worn it ! Psha, what a fool I am to brag of what I would have done ! We are the slaves of destiny. Our lots are shaped for us, and mine is ordained long ago. Come, let us have a pipe, and put the smell of these flowers out of court. Poor little silent flowers ! you'll be dead to-morrow. What business had you to show your red cheeks in this dingy place ?'

By his bedside George found a new Bible which the widow had placed there, with a note inside saying that she had not seen the book amongst his collection in a room where she had spent a number of hours, and where God had vouchsafed to her prayers the life of her son, and that she gave to Arthur's friend the best thing she could, and besought him to read in the volume sometimes, and to keep it as a token of a grateful mother's regard and affection. Poor George mournfully kissed the book as he had done the flowers ; and the morning found him still reading in its awful pages, in which so many stricken hearts, in which so many tender and faithful souls, have found comfort under calamity, and refuge and hope in affliction.

CHAPTER LIV

FANNY'S OCCUPATION GONE

GOOD Helen, ever since her son's illness, had taken, as we have seen, entire possession of the young man, of his drawers and closets, and all which they contained: whether shirts that wanted buttons, or stockings that required mending, or, must it be owned? letters that lay amongst those articles of raiment, and which of course it was necessary that somebody should answer during Arthur's weakened and incapable condition. Perhaps Mrs. Pendennis was laudably desirous to have some explanations about the dreadful Fanny Bolton mystery, regarding which she had never breathed a word to her son, though it was present in her mind always, and occasioned her inexpressible anxiety and disquiet. She had caused the brass knocker to be screwed off the inner door of the chambers, whereupon the postman's startling double rap would, as she justly argued, disturb the rest of her patient, and she did not allow him to see any letter which arrived, whether from bootmakers who importuned him, or hatters who had a heavy account to make up against next Saturday, and would be very much obliged if Mr. Arthur Pendennis would have the kindness to settle, etc. Of these documents, Pen, who was always freehanded and careless, of course had his share, and though no great one, one quite enough to alarm his scrupulous and conscientious mother. She had some savings; Pen's magnificent self-denial, and her own economy amounting from her great simplicity and avoidance of show to parsimony almost, had enabled her to put by a little sum of money, a part of which she delightedly consecrated to the paying off the young gentleman's obligations. At this price, many a worthy youth and respected reader would hand over his correspondence to his parents; and perhaps there is no greater test of a man's regularity

and easiness of conscience, than his readiness to face the postman. Blessed is he who is made happy by the sound of a rat-tat! The good are eager for it: but the naughty tremble at the sound thereof. So it was very kind of Mrs. Pendennis doubly to spare Pen the trouble of hearing or answering letters during his illness.

There could have been nothing in the young man's chests of drawers and wardrobes which could be considered as inculpating him in any way, nor any satisfactory documents regarding the Fanny Bolton affair found there, for the widow had to ask her brother-in-law if he knew anything about the odious transaction, and the dreadful intrigue in which her son was engaged. When they were at Richmond one day, and Pen with Warrington had taken a seat on a bench on the terrace, the widow kept Major Pendennis in consultation, and laid her terrors and perplexities before him, such of them at least (for as is the wont of men and women, she did not make *quite* a clean confession, and I suppose no spendthrift asked for a schedule of his debts, no lady of fashion asked by her husband for her dressmaker's bills ever sent in the whole of them yet)—such, we say, of her perplexities, at least, as she chose to confide to her director for the time being.

When, then, she asked the major what course she ought to pursue, about this dreadful—this horrid affair, and whether he knew anything regarding it, the old gentleman puckered up his face, so that you could not tell whether he was smiling or not; gave the widow one queer look with his little eyes; cast them down to the carpet again, and said, 'My dear, good creature, I don't know anything about it; and I don't wish to know anything about it; and, as you ask me my opinion, I think you had best know nothing about it too. Young men will be young men; and, begad, my good ma'am, if you think our boy is a Jo——'*

'Pray, spare me this,' Helen broke in, looking very stately.

'My dear creature, I did not commence the conversation, permit me to say,' the major said, bowing very blandly.

'I can't bear to hear such a sin—such a dreadful sin—spoken of in such a way,' the widow said, with tears of annoyance starting from her eyes. 'I can't bear to think

that my boy should commit such a crime. I wish he had died, almost, before he had done it. I don't know how I survive it myself: for it is breaking my heart, Major Pendennis, to think that his father's son—my child—whom I remember so good—oh, so good, and full of honour!—should be fallen so dreadfully low, as to—as to——'

'As to flirt with a little *grisette*,* my dear creature?' said the major. 'Egad, if all the mothers in England were to break their hearts because—Nay, nay; upon my word and honour now, don't agitate yourself—don't cry. I can't bear to see a woman's tears—I never could—never. But how do we know that anything serious has happened? Has Arthur said anything?'

'His silence confirms it,' sobbed Mrs. Pendennis, behind her pocket-handkerchief.

'Not at all. There are subjects, my dear, about which a young fellow cannot surely talk to his mamma,' insinuated the brother-in-law.

'She has written to him,' cried the lady, behind the cambric.

'What, before he was ill? Nothing more likely.'

'No, since,' the mourner with the batiste mask gasped out; 'not before; that is, I don't think so—that is, I——'

'Only since; and you have—yes, I understand. I suppose when he was too ill to read his own correspondence, you took charge of it, did you?'

'I am the most unhappy mother in the world,' cried out the unfortunate Helen.

'The most unhappy mother in the world, because your son is a man and not a hermit! Have a care, my dear sister. If you have suppressed any letters to him, you may have done yourself a great injury; and, if I know anything of Arthur's spirit, may cause a difference between him and you, which you'll rue all your life—a difference that's a dev'lish deal more important, my good madam, than the little—little—trumpery cause which originated it.'

'There was only one letter,' broke out Helen,—'only a very little one—only a few words. Here it is—oh, how can you, how can you speak so?'

When the good soul said only 'a very little one,' the major could not speak at all, so inclined was he to laugh, in spite of the agonies of the poor soul before him, and for

whom he had a hearty pity and liking too. But each was looking at the matter with his or her peculiar eyes and view of morals, and the major's morals, as the reader knows, were not those of an ascetic.

'I recommend you,' he gravely continued, 'if you can, to seal it up—those letters ain't unfrequently sealed with wafers—and to put it amongst Pen's other letters, and let him have them when he calls for them. Or, if we can't seal it, we mistook it for a bill.'

'I can't tell my son a lie,' said the widow. It had been put silently into the letter-box two days previous to their departure from the Temple, and had been brought to Mrs. Pendennis by Martha. She had never seen Fanny's hand-writing, of course; but when the letter was put into her hands, she knew the author at once. She had been on the watch for that letter every day since Pen had been ill. She had opened some of his other letters because she wanted to get at that one. She had the horrid paper poisoning her bag at that moment. She took it out and offered it to her brother-in-law.

'*Arther Pendennis, Esq.*,' he read in a timid little, sprawling hand-writing, and with a sneer on his face. 'No, my dear, I won't read any more. But you, who have read it, may tell me what the letter contains—only prayers for his health in bad spelling, you say—and a desire to see him? Well—there's no harm in that. And as you ask me—' here the major began to look a little queer for his own part, and put on his demure look—'as you ask me, my dear, for information, why, I don't mind telling you that—ah—that—Morgan, my man, has made some inquiries regarding this affair, and that—my friend Doctor Goodenough also looked into it—and it appears that this person was greatly smitten with Arthur; that he paid for her and took her to Vauxhall Gardens, as Morgan heard from an old acquaintance of Pen's and ours, an Irish gentleman, who was very nearly once having the honour of being the—from an Irishman, in fact;—that the girl's father, a violent man of intoxicated habits, has beaten her mother, who persists in declaring her daughter's entire innocence to her husband on the one hand, while on the other she told Goodenough that Arthur had acted like a brute to her child. And so you see the story remains in a mystery. Will you have it cleared up? I have but to

ask Pen, and he will tell me at once—he is as honourable a man as ever lived.'

'Honourable!' said the widow, with bitter scorn. 'Oh, brother, what is this you call honour? If my boy has been guilty, he must marry her. I would go down on my knees and pray him to do so.'

'Good God! are you mad?' screamed out the major: and remembering former passages in Arthur's history and Helen's, the truth came across his mind that, were Helen to make this prayer to her son, he *would* marry the girl: he was wild enough and obstinate enough to commit any folly when a woman he loved was in the case. 'My dear sister, have you lost your senses?' he continued (after an agitated pause, during which the above dreary reflection crossed him), and in a softened tone. 'What right have we to suppose that anything has passed between this girl and him? Let's see the letter. Her heart is breaking; pray, pray write to me—home unhappy—unkind father—your nurse—poor little Fanny—spelt, as you say, in a manner to outrage all sense of decorum. But, good heavens! my dear, what is there in this? only that the little devil is making love to him still. Why, she didn't come into his chambers until he was so delirious that he didn't know her. What-d'you-call-'em, Flanagan, the laundress, told Morgan, my man, so. She came in company of an old fellow, an old Mr. Bows, who came most kindly down to Stillbrook and brought me away—by the way, I left him in the cab, and never paid the fare: and devilish kind it was of him. No, there's nothing in the story.'

'Do you think so? Thank Heaven,—thank God!' Helen cried. 'I'll take the letter to Arthur and ask him now. Look at him there. He's on the terrace with Mr. Warrington. They are talking to some children. My boy was always fond of children. He's innocent, thank God—thank God! Let me go to him.'

Old Pendennis had his own opinion. When he briskly took the not guilty side of the case, but a moment before, very likely the old gentleman had a different view from that which he chose to advocate, and judged of Arthur by what he himself would have done. If she goes to Arthur, and he speaks the truth, as the rascal will, it spoils all, he thought. And he tried one more effort.

'My dear, good soul,' he said, taking Helen's hand and kissing it, 'as your son has not acquainted you with this affair, think if you have any right to examine it. As you believe him to be a man of honour, what right have you to doubt his honour in this instance? Who is his accuser? An anonymous scoundrel who has brought no specific charge against him. If there were any such, wouldn't the girl's parents have come forward? He is not called upon to rebut, nor you to entertain, an anonymous accusation; and as for believing him guilty because a girl of that rank happened to be in his rooms acting as nurse to him, begad you might as well insist upon his marrying that dem'd old Irish gin-drinking laundress, Mrs. Flanagan.'

The widow burst out laughing through her tears—the victory was gained by the old general.

'Marry Mrs. Flanagan, by Ged,' he continued, tapping her slender hand. 'No. The boy has told you nothing about it, and you know nothing about it. The boy is innocent—of course. And what, my good soul, is the course for us to pursoo? Suppose he is attached to this girl—don't look sad again, it's merely a supposition—and begad a young fellow may have an attachment, mayn't he?—Directly he gets well he will be at her again.'

'He must come home! We must go off directly to Fairoaks,' the widow cried out.

'My good creature, he'll bore himself to death at Fairoaks. He'll have nothing to do but to think about his passion there. There's no place in the world for making a little passion into a big one, and where a fellow feeds on his own thoughts, like a[1] lonely country-house, where there's nothing to do. We must occupy him: amuse him: we must take him abroad: he's never been abroad except to Paris for a lark. We must travel a little. He must have a nurse with him, to take great care of him, for Goodenough says he had a dev'lish narrow squeak of it (don't look frightened), and so you must come and watch: and I suppose you'll take Miss Bell, and I should like to ask Warrington to come. Arthur's dev'lish fond of Warrington. He can't do without Warrington. Warrington's family is one of the oldest in England, and he is one of the best young fellows I ever met in my life. I like him exceedingly.'

'Does Mr. Warrington know anything about this—this

affair ?' asked Helen. 'He had been away, I know, for two months before it happened: Pen wrote me so.'

'Not a word—I—I've asked him about it. I've pumped him. He never heard of the transaction, never; I pledge you my word,' cried out the major, in some alarm. 'And, my dear, I think you had much best not talk to him about it—much best not—of course not: the subject is most delicate and painful.'

The simple widow took her brother's hand and pressed it. 'Thank you, brother,' she said. 'You have been very, very kind to me. You have given me a great deal of comfort. I'll go to my room, and think of what you have said. This illness and these—these emotions—have agitated me a great deal; and I'm not very strong, you know. But I'll go and thank God that my boy is innocent. He *is* innocent. Isn't he, sir ?'

'Yes, my dearest creature, yes,' said the old fellow, kissing her affectionately, and quite overcome by her tenderness. He looked after her as she retreated, with a fondness which was rendered more piquant, as it were, by the mixture of a certain scorn which accompanied it. 'Innocent !' he said; 'I'd swear, till I was black in the face, he was innocent, rather than give that good soul pain.'

Having achieved this victory, the fatigued and happy warrior laid himself down on the sofa, and put his yellow silk pocket-handkerchief over his face, and indulged in a snug little nap, of which the dreams, no doubt, were very pleasant, as he snored with refreshing regularity. The young men sat, meanwhile, dawdling away the sunshiny hours on the terrace, very happy, and Pen, at least, very talkative. He was narrating to Warrington a plan for a new novel, and a new tragedy. Warrington laughed at the idea of his writing a tragedy. By Jove, he would show that he could; and he began to spout some of the lines of his play.

The little solo on the wind instrument which the major was performing was interrupted by the entrance of Miss Bell. She had been on a visit to her old friend, Lady Rockminster, who had taken a summer villa in the neighbourhood; and who, hearing of Arthur's illness, and his mother's arrival at Richmond, had visited the latter; and, for the benefit of the former, whom she didn't like, had

been prodigal of grapes, partridges, and other attentions. For Laura the old lady had a great fondness, and longed that she should come and stay with her ; but Laura could not leave her mother at this juncture. Worn out by constant watching over Arthur's health, Helen's own had suffered very considerably ; and Doctor Goodenough had had reason to prescribe for her as well as for his younger patient.

Old Pendennis started up on the entrance of the young lady. His slumbers were easily broken. He made her a gallant speech—he had been full of gallantry towards her of late. Where had she been gathering those roses which she wore on her cheeks ? How happy he was to be disturbed out of his dreams by such a charming reality ! Laura had plenty of humour and honesty; and these two caused her to have on her side something very like a contempt for the old gentleman. It delighted her to draw out his worldlinesses, and to make the old *habitué* of clubs and drawing-rooms tell his twaddling tales about great folks, and expound his views of morals.

Not in this instance, however, was she disposed to be satirical. She had been to drive with Lady Rockminster in the Park, she said ; and she had brought home game for Pen, and flowers for mamma. She looked very grave about mamma. She had just been with Mrs. Pendennis. Helen was very much worn, and she feared she was very, very ill. Her large eyes filled with tender marks of the sympathy which she felt in her beloved friend's condition. She was alarmed about her. Could not that good—that dear Dr. Goodenough cure her ?

'Arthur's illness, and *other* mental anxieties,' the major slowly said, 'had, no doubt, shaken Helen.' A burning blush upon the girl's face showed that she understood the old man's allusions. But she looked him full in the face and made no reply. 'He might have spared me that,' she thought. 'What is he aiming at in recalling that shame to me ?'

That he had an aim in view is very possible. The old diplomatist seldom spoke without some such end. Doctor Goodenough had talked to him, he said, about their dear friend's health, and she wanted rest and change of scene —yes, change of scene. Painful circumstances which had occurred must be forgotten and never alluded to ; he

begged pardon for ever hinting at them to Miss Bell—he never should do so again—nor, he was sure, would she. Everything must be done to soothe and comfort their friend, and his proposal was that they should go abroad for the autumn to a watering-place in the Rhine neighbourhood, where Helen might rally her exhausted spirits, and Arthur try and become a new man. Of course, Laura would not forsake her mother ?

Of course not. It was about Helen, and Helen only—that is, about Arthur too for her sake—that Laura was anxious. She would go abroad or anywhere with Helen.

And Helen having thought the matter over for an hour in her room, had by that time grown to be as anxious for the tour as any schoolboy, who has been reading a book of voyages, is eager to go to sea. Whither should they go ? the farther the better—to some place so remote that even recollection could not follow them thither : so delightful that Pen should never want to leave it—anywhere so that he could be happy. She opened her desk with trembling fingers and took out her banker's book, and counted up her little savings. If more was wanted, she had the diamond cross. She would borrow from Laura again. 'Let us go—let us go,' she thought ; 'directly he can bear the journey let us go away. Come, kind Doctor Goodenough—come quick, and give us leave to quit England.'

The good doctor drove over to dine with them that very day. 'If you agitate yourself so,' he said to her, 'and if your heart beats so, and if you persist in being so anxious about a young gentleman who is getting well as fast as he can, we shall have you laid up, and Miss Laura to watch you ; and then it will be her turn to be ill, and I should like to know how the deuce a doctor is to live who is obliged to come and attend you all for nothing ? Mrs. Goodenough is already jealous of you, and says, with perfect justice, that I fall in love with my patients. And you must please to get out of the country as soon as ever you can, that I may have a little peace in my family.'

When the plan of going abroad was proposed to Arthur, it was received by that gentleman with the greatest alacrity and enthusiasm. He longed to be off at once. He let his moustachios grow from that very moment, in order, I suppose, that he might get his mouth into training for a perfect French and German pronunciation ; and he was

seriously disquieted in his mind because the moustachios, when they came, were of a decidedly red colour. He had looked forward to an autumn at Fairoaks; and perhaps the idea of passing two or three months there did not amuse the young man. 'There is not a soul to speak to in the place,' he said to Warrington. 'I can't stand old Portman's sermons, and pompous after-dinner conversation. I know all old Glanders's stories about the Peninsular War. The Claverings are the only Christian people in the neighbourhood, and they are not to be at home before Christmas, my uncle says: besides, Warrington, I want to get out of the country. Whilst you were away, confound it, I had a temptation, from which I am very thankful to have escaped, and which I count that even my illness came very luckily to put an end to.' And here he narrated to his friend the circumstances of the Vauxhall affair, with which the reader is already acquainted.

Warrington looked very grave when he heard this story. Putting the moral delinquency out of the question, he was extremely glad for Arthur's sake that the latter had escaped from a danger which might have made his whole life wretched; 'which certainly,' said Warrington, 'would have occasioned the wretchedness and ruin of the other party. And your mother, and—and your friends—what a pain it would have been to them!' urged Pen's companion, little knowing what grief and annoyance these good people had already suffered.

'Not a word to my mother!' Pen cried out, in a state of great alarm. 'She would never get over it. An *esclandre* of that sort would kill her, I do believe. And,' he added, with a knowing air, and as if, like a young rascal of a Lovelace, he had been engaged in what are called *affaires de cœur* all his life; 'the best way, when a danger of that sort menaces, is not to face it, but to turn one's back on it and run.'

'And were you very much smitten?' Warrington asked.

'H'm!' said Lovelace. 'She dropped her h's, but she was a dear little girl.'

O Clarissas of this life, O you poor little ignorant vain foolish maidens! if you did but know the way in which the Lovelaces speak of you: if you could but hear Jack talking to Tom across the coffee-room of a club; or see Ned taking your poor little letters out of his cigar-case,

and handing them over to Charley, and Billy, and Harry across the mess-room table, you would not be so eager to write, or so ready to listen! There's a sort of crime which is not complete unless the lucky rogue boasts of it afterwards; and the man who betrays your honour in the first place, is pretty sure, remember that, to betray your secret too.

'It's hard to fight, and it's easy to fall,' Warrington said gloomily. 'And as you say, Pendennis, when a danger like this is imminent, the best way is to turn your back on it and run.'

After this little discourse upon a subject about which Pen would have talked a great deal more eloquently a month back, the conversation reverted to the plans for going abroad, and Arthur eagerly pressed his friend to be of the party. Warrington was a part of the family—a part of the cure. Arthur said he should not have half the pleasure without Warrington.

But George said no, he couldn't go. He must stop at home and take Pen's place. The other remarked that that was needless, for Shandon was now come back to London, and Arthur was entitled to a holiday.

'Don't press me,' Warrington said; 'I can't go. I've particular engagements. I'm best at home. I've not got the money to travel, that's the long and short of it—for travelling costs money, you know.'

This little obstacle seemed fatal to Pen. He mentioned it to his mother: Mrs. Pendennis was very sorry; Mr. Warrington had been exceedingly kind; but she supposed he knew best about his affairs. And then, no doubt, she reproached herself for selfishness in wishing to carry the boy off and have him to herself altogether.

'What is this I hear from Pen, my dear Mr. Warrington?' the major asked one day, when the pair were alone and after Warrington's objection had been stated to him. 'Not go with us? We can't hear of such a thing—Pen won't get well without you. I promise you, I'm not going to be his nurse. He must have somebody with him that's stronger and gayer and better able to amuse him than a rheumatic old fogy like me. I shall go to Carlsbad very likely, when I've seen you people settle down. Travelling costs nothing nowadays—or so little! And—and pray,

Warrington, remember that I was your father's very old friend, and if you and your brother are not on such terms as to enable you to—to anticipate your younger brother's allowance, I beg you to make me your banker, for hasn't Pen been getting into your debt these three weeks past, during which you have been doing what he informs me is his work, with such exemplary talent and genius, begad ?'

Still, in spite of this kind offer and unheard-of generosity on the part of the major, George Warrington refused, and said he would stay at home. But it was with a faltering voice and an irresolute accent which showed how much he would like to go, though his tongue persisted in saying nay.

But the major's persevering benevolence was not to be balked in this way. At the tea-table that evening, Helen happening to be absent from the room for the moment, looking for Pen who had gone to roost, old Pendennis returned to the charge and rated Warrington for refusing to join in their excursion. 'Isn't it ungallant, Miss Bell ?' he said, turning to that young lady. 'Isn't it unfriendly ? Here we have been the happiest party in the world, and this odious selfish creature breaks it up !'

Miss Bell's long eyelashes looked down towards her tea-cup : and Warrington blushed hugely but did not speak. Neither did Miss Bell speak : but when he blushed she blushed too.

'*You* ask him to come, my dear,' said the benevolent old gentleman, 'and then perhaps he will listen to you——'

'Why should Mr. Warrington listen to me ?' asked the young lady, putting the query to her teaspoon seemingly and not to the major.

'Ask him ; you have not asked him,' said Pen's artless uncle.

'I should be very glad indeed if Mr. Warrington would come,' remarked Laura to the teaspoon.

'Would you ?' said George.

She looked up and said, 'Yes.' Their eyes met. 'I will go anywhere you ask me, or do anything,' said George slowly, and forcing out the words as if they gave him pain.

Old Pendennis was delighted ; the affectionate old creature clapped his hands and cried, 'Bravo ! bravo ! It's a bargain—a bargain, begad ! Shake hands on it, young people !' And Laura, with a look full of tender brightness,

put out her hand to Warrington. He took hers; his face indicated a strange agitation. He seemed to be about to speak, when from Pen's neighbouring room Helen entered, looking at them as the candle which she held lighted her pale frightened face.

Laura blushed more red than ever and withdrew her hand.

'What is it?' Helen asked.

'It's a bargain we have been making, my dear creature,' said the major in his most caressing voice. 'We have just bound over Mr. Warrington in a promise to come abroad with us.'

'Indeed!' Helen said.

CHAPTER LV

IN WHICH FANNY ENGAGES A NEW MEDICAL MAN

COULD Helen have suspected that, with Pen's returning strength, his unhappy partiality for little Fanny would also reawaken? Though she never spoke a word regarding that young person, after her conversation with the major, and though, to all appearance, she utterly ignored Fanny's existence, yet Mrs. Pendennis kept a particularly close watch upon all Master Arthur's actions; on the plea of ill-health, would scarcely let him out of her sight; and was especially anxious that he should be spared the trouble of all correspondence for the present at least. Very likely Arthur looked at his own letters with some tremor; very likely, as he received them at the family table, feeling his mother's watch upon him (though the good soul's eye seemed fixed upon her tea-cup or her book), he expected daily to see a little handwriting, which he would have known, though he had never seen it yet, and his heart beat as he received the letters to his address. Was he more pleased or annoyed, that, day after day, his expectations were not realized; and was his

mind relieved, that there came no letter from Fanny? Though, no doubt, in these matters, when Lovelace is tired of Clarissa (or the contrary), it is best for both parties to break at once, and each, after the failure of the attempt at union, to go his own way, and pursue his course through life solitary; yet our self-love, or our pity, or our sense of decency, does not like that sudden bankruptcy. Before we announce to the world that our firm of Lovelace and Co. can't meet its engagements, we try to make compromises: we have mournful meetings of partners: we delay the putting up of the shutters, and the dreary announcement of the failure. It must come: but we pawn our jewels to keep things going a little longer. On the whole, I dare say, Pen was rather annoyed that he had no remonstrances from Fanny. What! could she part from him, and never so much as once look round? could she sink, and never once hold a little hand out, or cry, 'Help, Arthur'? Well, well: they don't all go down who venture on that voyage. Some few drown when the vessel founders; but most are only ducked, and scramble to shore. And the reader's experience of A. Pendennis, Esquire, of the Upper Temple, will enable him to state whether that gentleman belonged to the class of persons who were likely to sink or to swim.

Though Pen was as yet too weak to walk half a mile; and might not, on account of his precious health, be trusted to take a drive in a carriage by himself, and without a nurse in attendance; yet Helen could not keep watch over Mr. Warrington too, and had no authority to prevent that gentleman from going to London if business called him thither. Indeed, if he had gone and stayed, perhaps the widow, from reasons of her own, would have been glad; but she checked these selfish wishes as soon as she ascertained or owned them; and, remembering Warrington's great regard and services, and constant friendship for her boy, received him as a member of her family almost, with her usual melancholy kindness and submissive acquiescence. Yet somehow, one morning when his affairs called him to town, she divined what Warrington's errand was, and that he was gone to London to get news about Fanny for Pen.

Indeed, Arthur had had some talk with his friend, and told him more at large what his adventures had been with Fanny (adventures which the reader knows already), and

what were his feelings respecting her. He was very thankful that he had escaped the great danger, to which Warrington said Amen heartily: that he had no great fault wherewith to reproach himself in regard of his behaviour to her, but that if they parted, as they must, he would be glad to say a God bless her, and to hope that she would remember him kindly. In his discourse with Warrington he spoke upon these matters with so much gravity, and so much emotion, that George, who had pronounced himself most strongly for the separation too, began to fear that his friend was not so well cured as he boasted of being; and that, if the two were to come together again, all the danger and the temptation might have to be fought once more. And with what result? 'It is hard to struggle, Arthur, and it is easy to fall,' Warrington said: 'and the best courage for us poor wretches is to fly from danger. I would not have been what I am now, had I practised what I preach.'

'And what did you practise, George?' Pen asked eagerly. 'I knew there was something. Tell us about it, Warrington.'

'There was something that can't be mended, and that shattered my whole fortunes early,' Warrington answered. 'I said I would tell you about it some day, Pen: and will, but not now. Take the moral without the fable now, Pen, my boy; and if you want to see a man whose whole life has been wrecked, by an unlucky rock against which he struck as a boy—here he is, Arthur: and so I warn you.'

We have shown how Mr. Huxter, in writing home to his Clavering friends, mentioned that there was a fashionable club in London of which he was an attendant, and that he was there in the habit of meeting an Irish officer of distinction, who, amongst other news, had given that intelligence regarding Pendennis which the young surgeon had transmitted to Clavering. This club was no other than the Back Kitchen, where the disciple of St. Bartholomew was accustomed to meet the general, the peculiarities of whose brogue, appearance, disposition, and general conversation, greatly diverted many young gentlemen who used the Back Kitchen as a place of nightly entertainment and refreshment. Huxter, who had a fine natural genius for mimicking everything, whether it was a favourite tragic or comic

actor, a cock on a dunghill, a corkscrew going into a bottle and a cork issuing thence, or an Irish officer of genteel connexions who offered himself as an object of imitation with only too much readiness, talked his talk, and twanged his poor old long-bow whenever drink, a hearer, and an opportunity occurred, studied our friend the general with peculiar gusto, and drew the honest fellow out many a night. A bait, consisting of sixpennyworth of brandy-and-water, the worthy old man was sure to swallow : and under the influence of this liquor, who was more happy than he to tell his stories of his daughter's triumphs and his own, in love, war, drink, and polite society ? Thus Huxter was enabled to present to his friends many pictures of Costigan : of Costigan fighting a jewel in the Phaynix—of Costigan and his interview with the Juke of York—of Costigan at his sonunlaw's teeble, surrounded by the nobilitee of his countree—of Costigan, when crying drunk, at which time he was in the habit of confidentially lamenting his daughter's ingratichewd, and stating that his grey hairs were hastening to a praymachure greeve. And thus our friend was the means of bringing a number of young fellows to the Back Kitchen, who consumed the landlord's liquors whilst they relished the general's peculiarities, so that mine host pardoned many of the latter's foibles, in consideration of the good which they brought to his house. Not the highest position in life was this certainly, or one which, if we had a reverence for an old man, we would be anxious that he should occupy : but of this aged buffoon it may be mentioned that he had no particular idea that his condition of life was not a high one, and that in his whiskied blood there was not a black drop, nor in his muddled brains a bitter feeling, against any mortal being. Even his child, his cruel Emily, he would have taken to his heart and forgiven with tears ; and what more can one say of the Christian charity of a man than that he is actually ready to forgive those who have done him every kindness, and with whom he is wrong in a dispute ?

There was some idea amongst the young men who frequented the Back Kitchen, and made themselves merry with the society of Captain Costigan, that the captain made a mystery regarding his lodgings for fear of duns, or from a desire of privacy, and lived in some wonderful place. Nor would the landlord of the premises, when questioned upon

this subject, answer any inquiries ; his maxim being that he only knew gentlemen who frequented that room, *in* that room ; that when they quitted that room, having paid their scores as gentlemen, and behaved as gentlemen, his communication with them ceased ; and that, as a gentleman himself, he thought it was only impertinent curiosity to ask where any other gentleman lived. Costigan, in his most intoxicated and confidential moments, also evaded any replies to questions or hints addressed to him on this subject : there was no particular secret about it, as we have seen, who have had more than once the honour of entering his apartments, but in the vicissitudes of a long life he had been pretty often in the habit of residing in houses where privacy was necessary to his comfort, and where the appearance of some visitors would have brought him anything but pleasure. Hence all sorts of legends were formed by wags or credulous persons respecting his place of abode. It was stated that he slept habitually in a watch-box in the city : in a cab at a mews, where a cab-proprietor gave him a shelter : in the Duke of York's Column, etc., the wildest of these theories being put abroad by the facetious and imaginative Huxter. For Huxey, when not silenced by the company of ' swells,' and when in the society of his own friends, was a very different fellow to the youth whom we have seen cowed by Pen's impertinent airs, and, adored by his family at home, was the life and soul of the circle whom he met, either round the festive board or the dissecting-table.

On one brilliant September morning, as Huxter was regaling himself with a cup of coffee at a stall in Covent Garden, having spent a delicious night dancing at Vauxhall, he spied the general reeling down Henrietta Street, with a crowd of hooting blackguard boys at his heels, who had left their beds under the arches of the river betimes, and were prowling about already for breakfast, and the strange livelihood of the day. The poor old general was not in that condition when the sneers and jokes of these young beggars had much effect upon him : the cabmen and watermen at the cabstand knew him, and passed their comments upon him : the policemen gazed after him, and warned the boys off him, with looks of scorn and pity ; what did the scorn and pity of men, the jokes of ribald children, matter to the general ? He reeled along the

THE CAPTAIN WON'T GO HOME TILL MORNING

street with glazed eyes, having just sense enough to know whither he was bound, and to pursue his accustomed beat homewards. He went to bed not knowing how he had reached it, as often as any man in London. He woke and found himself there, and asked no questions, and he was tacking about on this daily though perilous voyage, when, from his station at the coffee-stall, Huxter spied him. To note his friend, to pay his twopence (indeed, he had but eightpence left, or he would have had a cab from Vauxhall to take him home), was with the eager Huxter the work of an instant—Costigan dived down the alleys by Drury Lane

Theatre, where gin-shops, oyster-shops, and theatrical wardrobes abound, the proprietors of which were now asleep behind their shutters, as the pink morning lighted up their chimneys; and through these courts Huxter followed the general, until he reached Oldcastle Street, in which is the gate of Shepherd's Inn.

Here, just as he was within sight of home, a luckless slice of orange-peel came between the general's heel and the pavement, and caused the poor old fellow to fall backwards.

Huxter ran up to him instantly, and after a pause, during which the veteran, giddy with his fall and his

previous whisky, gathered, as he best might, his dizzy brains together, the young surgeon lifted up the limping general, and very kindly and good-naturedly offered to conduct him to his home. For some time, and in reply to the queries which the student of medicine put to him, the muzzy general refused to say where his lodgings were, and declared that they were hard by, and that he could reach them without difficulty; and he disengaged himself from Huxter's arm, and made a rush, as if to get to his own home unattended: but he reeled and lurched so, that the young surgeon insisted upon accompanying him, and, with many soothing expressions and cheering and consolatory phrases, succeeded in getting the general's dirty old hand under what he called his own fin, and led the old fellow, moaning piteously, across the street. He stopped when he came to the ancient gate, ornamented with the armorial bearings of the venerable Shepherd. 'Here 'tis,' said he, drawing up at the portal, and he made a successful pull at the gate-bell, which presently brought out old Mr. Bolton, the porter, scowling fiercely, and grumbling as he was used to do every morning when it became his turn to let in that early bird.

Costigan tried to hold Bolton for a moment in genteel conversation, but the other surlily would not. 'Don't bother me,' he said; 'go to your hown bed, capting, and don't keep honest men out of theirs.' So the captain tacked across the square, and reached his own staircase, up which he stumbled with the worthy Huxter at his heels. Costigan had a key of his own, which Huxter inserted into the keyhole for him, so that there was no need to call up little Mr. Bows from the sleep into which the old musician had not long since fallen, and Huxter having aided to disrobe his tipsy patient, and ascertained that no bones were broken, helped him to bed, and applied compresses and water to one of his knees and shins, which, with the pair of trousers which encased them, Costigan had severely torn in his fall. At the general's age, and with his habit of body, such wounds as he had inflicted on himself are slow to heal: a good deal of inflammation ensued, and the old fellow lay ill for some days suffering both pain and fever.

Mr. Huxter undertook the case of his interesting patient with great confidence and alacrity, and conducted it with becoming skill. He visited his friend day after day, and consoled him with lively rattle and conversation for the

absence of the society which Costigan needed, and of which he was an ornament: and he gave special instructions to the invalid's nurse about the quantity of whisky which the patient was to take—instructions which, as the poor old fellow could not for many days get out of his bed or sofa himself, he could not by any means infringe. Bows, Mrs. Bolton, and our little friend Fanny, when able to do so, officiated at the general's bedside, and the old warrior was made as comfortable as possible under his calamity.

Thus Huxter, whose affable manners and social turn made him quickly intimate with persons in whose society he fell,[1] became pretty soon intimate in Shepherd's Inn, both with our acquaintances in the garrets and those in the porter's lodge. He thought he had seen Fanny somewhere: he felt certain that he had; but it is no wonder that he should not accurately remember her, for the poor little thing never chose to tell him where she had met him; he himself had seen her at a period when his own views both of persons and of right and wrong were clouded by the excitement of drinking and dancing, and also little Fanny was very much changed and worn by the fever and agitation, and passion and despair, which the past three weeks had poured upon the head of that little victim. Borne down was the head now, and very pale and wan the face: and many and many a time the sad eyes had looked into the postman's, as he came to the Inn, and the sickened heart had sunk as he passed away. When Mr. Costigan's accident occurred, Fanny was rather glad to have an opportunity of being useful and doing something kind—something that would make her forget her own little sorrows perhaps: she felt she bore them better whilst she did her duty, though I dare say many a tear dropped into the old Irishman's gruel. Ah, me! stir the gruel well, and have courage, little Fanny! If everybody who has suffered from your complaint were to die of it straightway, what a fine year the undertakers would have!

Whether from compassion for his only patient, or delight in his society, Mr. Huxter found now occasion to visit Costigan two or three times in the day at least, and if any of the members of the porter's lodge family were not in attendance on the general, the young doctor was sure to have some particular directions to address to those at their own place of habitation. He was a kind fellow; he made

or purchased toys for the children ; he brought them apples and brandy-balls ; he brought a mask and frightened them with it, and caused a smile upon the face of pale Fanny. He called Mrs. Bolton Mrs. B., and was very intimate, familiar, and facetious with that lady, quite different from that ' 'aughty 'artless beast,' as Mrs. Bolton now denominated a certain young gentleman of our acquaintance, and whom she now vowed she never could abear.

It was from this lady, who was very free in her conversation, that Huxter presently learnt what was the illness which was evidently preying upon little Fan, and what had been Pen's behaviour regarding her. Mrs. Bolton's account of the transaction was not, it may be imagined, entirely an impartial narrative. One would have thought from her story that the young gentleman had employed a course of the most persevering and flagitious artifices to win the girl's heart, had broken the most solemn promises made to her, and was a wretch to be hated and chastised by every champion of woman. Huxter, in his present frame of mind respecting Arthur, and suffering under the latter's contumely, was ready, of course, to take all for granted that was said in the disfavour of this unfortunate convalescent. But why did he not write home to Clavering, as he had done previously, giving an account of Pen's misconduct, and of the particulars regarding it, which had now come to his knowledge ? He once, in a letter to his brother-in-law, announced that that *nice young man*, Mr. Pendennis, had escaped narrowly from a fever, and that no doubt all Clavering, *where he was so popular*, would be pleased at his recovery ; and he mentioned that he had an interesting case of compound fracture, an officer of distinction, which kept him in town ; but as for Fanny Bolton, he made no more mention of her in his letters—no more than Pen himself had made mention of her. O you mothers at home, how much do you think you know about your lads ? How much do you think you know ?

But with Bows there was no reason why Huxter should not speak his mind, and so, a very short time after his conversation with Mrs. Bolton, Mr. Sam talked to the musician about his early acquaintance with Pendennis ; described him as a confounded conceited blackguard, and expressed a determination to punch his impudent head as

soon as ever he should be well enough to stand up like a man.

Then it was that Bows on his part spoke, and told *his* version of the story, whereof Arthur and little Fan were the hero and heroine ; how they had met by no contrivance of the former, but by a blunder of the old Irishman, now in bed with a broken shin—how Pen had acted with manliness and self-control in the business—how Mrs. Bolton was an idiot ; and he related the conversation which he, Bows, had had with Pen, and the sentiments uttered by the young man. Perhaps Bows's story caused some twinges of conscience in the breast of Pen's accuser, and that gentleman frankly owned that he had been wrong with regard to Arthur, and withdrew his project for punching Mr. Pendennis's head.

But the cessation of his hostility for Pen did not diminish Huxter's attentions to Fanny, which unlucky Mr. Bows marked with his usual jealousy and bitterness of spirit. 'I have but to like anybody,' the old fellow thought, 'and somebody is sure to be preferred to me. It has been the same ill-luck with me since I was a lad, until now that I am sixty years old. What can I expect better than to be laughed at ? It is for the young to succeed, and to be happy, and not for old fools like me. I've played a second fiddle all through life,' he said, with a bitter laugh ; 'how can I suppose the luck is to change after it has gone against me so long ?' This was the selfish way in which Bows looked at the state of affairs : though few persons would have thought there was any cause for his jealousy, who looked at the pale and grief-stricken countenance of the hapless little girl, its object. Fanny received Huxter's good-natured efforts at consolation and kind attentions kindly. She laughed now and again at his jokes and games with her little sisters, but relapsed quickly into a dejection which ought to have satisfied Mr. Bows that the new-comer had no place in her heart as yet, had jealous Mr. Bows been enabled to see with clear eyes.

But Bows did not. Fanny attributed Pen's silence somehow to Bows's interference. Fanny hated him. Fanny treated Bows with constant cruelty and injustice. She turned from him when he spoke—she loathed his attempts at consolation. A hard life had Mr. Bows, and a cruel return for his regard.

When Warrington came to Shepherd's Inn as Pen's ambassador, it was for Mr. Bows's apartments he inquired (no doubt upon a previous agreement with the principal for whom he acted in this delicate negotiation), and he did not so much as catch a glimpse of Miss Fanny when he stopped at the Inn-gate and made his inquiry. Warrington was, of course, directed to the musician's chambers, and found him tending the patient there, from whose chamber he came out to wait upon his guest. We have said that they had been previously known to one another, and the pair shook hands with sufficient cordiality. After a little preliminary talk, Warrington said that he had come from his friend Arthur Pendennis, and from his family, to thank Bows for his attention at the commencement of Pen's illness, and for his kindness in hastening into the country to fetch the major.

Bows replied that it was but his duty: he had never thought to have seen the young gentleman alive again when he went in search of Pen's relatives, and he was very glad of Mr. Pendennis's recovery, and that he had his friends with him. 'Lucky are they who have friends, Mr. Warrington,' said the musician. 'I might be up in this garret and nobody would care for me, or mind whether I was alive or dead.'

'What! not the general, Mr. Bows?' Warrington asked.

'The general likes his whisky-bottle more than anything in life,' the other answered: 'we live together from habit and convenience, and he cares for me no more than you do. What is it you want to ask me, Mr. Warrington? You ain't come to visit *me*, I know very well. Nobody comes to visit me. It is about Fanny, the porter's daughter, you are come—I see that very well. Is Mr. Pendennis, now he has got well, anxious to see her again? Does his lordship the Sultan propose to throw his 'andkerchief to her? She has been very ill, sir, ever since the day when Mrs. Pendennis turned her out of doors—kind of a lady, wasn't it? The poor girl and myself found the young gentleman raving in a fever, knowing nobody, with nobody to tend him but his drunken laundress—she watched day and night by him. I set off to fetch his uncle. Mamma comes and turns Fanny to the right about. Uncle comes and leaves me to pay the cab. Carry my compliments to the ladies and gentlemen, and say we are both very thank-

ful—very. Why, a countess couldn't have behaved better, and for an apothecary's lady—as I'm given to understand Mrs. Pendennis was—I'm sure her behaviour is most uncommon aristocratic and genteel. She ought to have a double-gilt pestle and mortar to her coach.'

It was from Mr. Huxter that Bows had learned Pen's parentage, no doubt, and if he took Pen's part against the young surgeon, and Fanny's against Mr. Pendennis, it was because the old gentleman was in so savage a mood, that his humour was to contradict everybody.

Warrington was curious, and not ill-pleased at the musician's taunts and irascibility. 'I never heard of these transactions,' he said, 'or got but a very imperfect account of them from Major Pendennis. What was a lady to do? I think (I have never spoken with her on the subject) she had some notion that the young woman and my friend Pen were on—on terms of—of an intimacy which Mrs. Pendennis could not, of course, recognize——'

'Oh, of course not, sir. Speak out, sir; say what you mean at once, that the young gentleman of the Temple had made a victim of the girl of Shepherd's Inn, eh? And so she was to be turned out of doors—or brayed alive in the double-gilt pestle and mortar, by Jove! No, Mr. Warrington, there was no such thing: there was no victimizing, or if there was, Mr. Arthur was the victim, not the girl. He is an honest fellow, he is, though he is conceited, and a puppy sometimes. He can feel like a man, and run away from temptation like a man. I own it, though I suffer by it, I own it. He has a heart, he has: but the girl hasn't, sir. That girl will do anything to win a man, and fling him away without a pang, sir. If she's flung away herself, sir, she'll feel it and cry. She had a fever when Mrs. Pendennis turned her out of doors; and she made love to the doctor, Doctor Goodenough, who came to cure her. Now she has taken on with another chap—another sawbones, ha, ha! d—— it, sir, she likes the pestle and mortar, and hangs round the pill-boxes, she's so fond of 'em, and she has got a fellow from St. Bartholomew's, who grins through a horse-collar for her sisters, and charms away her melancholy. Go and see, sir: very likely he's in the lodge now. If you want news about Miss Fanny, you must ask at the doctor's shop, sir, not of an old fiddler like me. Good-bye, sir. There's my patient calling.'

And a voice was heard from the captain's bedroom, a well-known voice, which said, 'I'd loike a dthrop of dthrink, Bows, I'm thirstee.' And not sorry, perhaps, to hear that such was the state of things, and that Pen's forsaken was consoling herself, Warrington took his leave of the irascible musician.

As luck would have it, he passed the lodge door just as Mr. Huxter was in the act of frightening the children with the mask whereof we have spoken, and Fanny was smiling languidly at his farces. Warrington laughed bitterly. 'Are all women like that?' he thought. 'I think there's one that's not,' he added, with a sigh.

At Piccadilly, waiting for the Richmond omnibus, George fell in with Major Pendennis, bound in the same direction, and he told the old gentleman of what he had seen and heard respecting Fanny.

Major Pendennis was highly delighted: and as might be expected of such a philosopher, made precisely the same observation as that which had escaped from Warrington. 'All women are the same,' he said. '*La petite se console.* Daymy, when I used to read *Télémaque* at school, *Calypso ne pouvait se consoler*,*—you know the rest, Warrington,—I used to say it was absard. Absard, by Gad,* and so it is. And so she's got a new *soupirant*, has she, the little porteress? Dayvlish nice little girl. How mad Pen will be—eh, Warrington? But we must break it to him gently, or he'll be in such a rage that he will be going after her again. We must *ménager* the young fellow.'

'I think Mrs. Pendennis ought to know that Pen acted very well in the business. She evidently thinks him guilty, and according to Mr. Bows, Arthur behaved like a good fellow,' Warrington said.

'My dear Warrington,' said the major, with a look of some alarm. 'In Mrs. Pendennis's agitated state of health and that sort of thing, the best way, I think, is not to say a single word about the subject—or, stay, leave it to me: and I'll talk to her—break it to her gently, you know, and that sort of thing. I give you my word I will. And so Calypso's consoled, is she?' And he sniggered over this gratifying truth, happy in the corner of the omnibus during the rest of the journey.

Pen was very anxious to hear from his envoy what had been the result of the latter's mission: and as soon as the

FANNY'S NEW PHYSICIAN

two young men could be alone, the ambassador spoke in reply to Arthur's eager queries.

'You remember your poem, Pen, of *Ariadne in Naxos*,' Warrington said; 'devilish bad poetry it was, to be sure.'

'*Après?*' asked Pen, in a great state of excitement.

'When Theseus left Ariadne, do you remember what happened to her, young fellow?'*

'It's a lie, it's a lie! You don't mean that!' cried out Pen, starting up, his face turning red.

'Sit down, stoopid,' Warrington said, and with two fingers pushed Pen back into his seat again. 'It's better for you as it is, young one,' he said sadly, in reply to the savage flush in Arthur's face.

CHAPTER LVI

FOREIGN GROUND

[1]Major Pendennis fulfilled his promise to Warrington so far as to satisfy his own conscience, and in so far to ease poor Helen with regard to her son, as to make her understand that all connection between Arthur and the odious little gatekeeper was at an end, and that she need have no further anxiety with respect to an imprudent attachment or a degrading marriage on Pen's part. And that young fellow's mind was also relieved (after he had recovered the shock to his vanity) by thinking that Miss Fanny was not going to die of love for him, and that no unpleasant consequences were to be apprehended from the luckless and brief connection.

So the whole party were free to carry into effect their projected Continental trip, and Arthur Pendennis, *rentier, voyageant avec* Madame Pendennis and Mademoiselle Bell, and George Warrington, *particulier, âge de 32 ans, taille 6 pieds (Anglais), figure ordinaire, cheveux noirs, barbe idem*, etc., procured passports from the consul of H.M. the King of the Belgians at Dover, and passed over from that

port to Ostend, whence the party took their way leisurely, visiting Bruges and Ghent on their way to Brussels and the Rhine. It is not our purpose to describe this oft-travelled tour, or Laura's delight at the tranquil and ancient cities which she saw for the first time, or Helen's wonder and interest at the Béguine convents* which they visited, or the almost terror with which she saw the black-veiled nuns with outstretched arms kneeling before the illuminated altars, and beheld the strange pomps and ceremonials of the Catholic worship. Bare-footed friars in the streets, crowned images of Saints and Virgins in the churches before which people were bowing down and worshipping, in direct defiance, as she held, of the written law; priests in gorgeous robes, or lurking in dark confessionals, theatres opened, and people dancing on Sundays;—all these new sights and manners shocked and bewildered the simple country lady; and when the young men after their evening drive or walk returned to the widow and her adopted daughter, they found their books of devotion on the table, and at their entrance Laura would commonly cease reading some of the psalms or the sacred pages which, of all others, Helen loved. The late events connected with her son had cruelly shaken her; Laura watched with intense, though hidden anxiety, every movement of her dearest friend; and poor Pen was most constant and affectionate in waiting upon his mother, whose wounded bosom yearned with love towards him, though there was a secret between them, and an anguish or rage almost on the mother's part, to think that she was dispossessed somehow of her son's heart, or that there were recesses in it which she must not or dared not enter. She sickened as she thought of the sacred days of boyhood when it had not been so—when her Arthur's heart had no secrets, and she was his all in all: when he poured his hopes and pleasures, his childish griefs, vanities, triumphs into her willing and tender embrace; when her home was his nest still; and before fate, selfishness, nature, had driven him forth on wayward wings—to range on his own flight—to sing his own song—and to seek his own home and his own mate. Watching this devouring care and racking disappointment in her friend, Laura once said to Helen, 'If Pen had loved me as you wished, I should have gained him, but I should have lost you, mamma, I know I should; and I like you to love me best. Men do

not know what it is to love as we do, I think,'—and Helen, sighing, agreed to this portion of the young lady's speech, though she protested against the former part. For my part I suppose Miss Laura was right in both statements, and with regard to the latter assertion especially, that it is an old and received truism—love is an hour with us : it is all night and all day with a woman. Damon has taxes, sermon, parade, tailor's bills, parliamentary duties, and the deuce knows what to think of ; Delia has to think about Damon—Damon is the oak (or the post), and stands up, and Delia is the ivy or the honeysuckle whose arms twine about him. Is it not so, Delia ? Is it not your nature to creep about his feet and kiss them, to twine round his trunk and hang there ; and Damon's to stand like a British man with his hands in his breeches pocket, while the pretty fond parasite clings round him ?

Old Pendennis had only accompanied our friends to the water's edge, and left them on board the boat, giving the chief charge of the little expedition to Warrington. He himself was bound on a brief visit to the house of a great man, a friend of his, after which sojourn he proposed to join his sister-in-law at the German watering-place, whither the party was bound. The major himself thought that his long attentions to his sick family had earned for him a little relaxation—and though the best of the partridges were thinned off, the pheasants were still to be shot at Stillbrook, where the noble owner still was ; old Pendennis betook himself to that hospitable mansion and disported there with great comfort to himself. A royal duke, some foreigners of note, some illustrious statesmen, and some pleasant people visited it : it did the old fellow's heart good to see his name in the *Morning Post* amongst the list of the distinguished company which the Marquis of Steyne was entertaining at his country house at Stillbrook. He was a very useful and pleasant personage in a country-house. He entertained the young men with queer little anecdotes and *grivoises** stories on their shooting-parties or in their smoking-room, where they laughed at him and with him. He was obsequious with the ladies of a morning, in the rooms dedicated to them. He walked the new arrivals about the park and gardens, and showed them the *carte du pays*, and where there was the best view of the mansion,

and where the most favourable point to look at the lake: he showed where the timber was to be felled, and where the old road went before the new bridge was built, and the hill cut down; and where the place in the wood was where old Lord Lynx discovered Sir Phelim O'Neal on his knees before her ladyship, etc., etc.; he called the lodge-keepers and gardeners by their names: he knew the number of domestics that sat down in the housekeeper's room, and how many dined in the servants' hall; he had a word for everybody, and about everybody, and a little against everybody. He was invaluable in a country-house, in a word: and richly merited and enjoyed his vacation after his labours. And perhaps whilst he was thus deservedly enjoying himself with his country friends, the major was not ill-pleased at transferring to Warrington the command of the family expedition to the Continent, and thus perforce keeping him in the service of the ladies,—a servitude which George was only too willing to undergo, for his friend's sake, and for that of a society which he found daily more delightful. Warrington was a good German scholar, and was willing to give Miss Laura lessons in the language, who was very glad to improve herself, though Pen, for his part, was too weak or lazy now to resume his German studies. Warrington acted as courier and interpreter: Warrington saw the baggage in and out of ships, inns, and carriages, managed the money matters, and put the little troop into marching order. Warrington found out where the English church was, and, if Mrs. Pendennis and Miss Laura were inclined to go thither, walked with great decorum along with them. Warrington walked by Mrs. Pendennis's donkey, when that lady went out on her evening excursions; or took carriages for her; or got *Galignani** for her, or devised comfortable seats under the lime-trees for her, when the guests paraded after dinner, and the Kursaal band at the bath, where our tired friends stopped, performed their pleasant music under the trees. Many a fine whiskered Prussian or French dandy, come to the bath for the *trente-et-quarante*, cast glances of longing towards the pretty fresh-coloured English girl who accompanied the pale widow, and would have longed to take a turn with her at the galop or the waltz. But Laura did not appear in the ball-room, except once or twice, when Pen vouchsafed to walk with her; and as for Warrington, that rough

diamond had not had the polish of a dancing-master, and he did not know how to waltz,—though he would have liked to learn, if he could have had such a partner as Laura. —Such a partner! psha, what had a stiff bachelor to do with partners and waltzing? What was he about, dancing attendance here? drinking in sweet pleasure at a risk he knows not of what after-sadness, and regret, and lonely

longing? But yet he stayed on. You would have said he was the widow's son, to watch his constant care and watchfulness of her; or that he was an adventurer, and wanted to marry her fortune, or, at any rate, that he wanted some very great treasure or benefit from her,—and very likely he did,—for ours, as the reader has possibly already discovered, is a Selfish Story, and almost every person, according to his nature, more or less generous than

George, and according to the way of the world as it seems to us, is occupied about Number One. So Warrington selfishly devoted himself to Helen, who selfishly devoted herself to Pen, who selfishly devoted himself to himself at this present period, having no other personage or object to occupy him, except, indeed, his mother's health, which gave him a serious and real disquiet; but though they sat together, they did not talk much, and the cloud was always between them.

Every day Laura looked for Warrington, and received him with more frank and eager welcome. He found himself talking to her as he didn't know himself that he could talk. He found himself performing acts of gallantry which astounded him after the performance: he found himself looking blankly in the glass at the crow's-feet round his eyes, and at some streaks of white in his hair, and some intrusive silver bristles in his grim blue beard. He found himself looking at the young bucks at the bath—at the blond, tight-waisted Germans—at the capering Frenchmen, with their lacquered moustachios and trim varnished boots—at the English dandies, Pen amongst them, with their calm, domineering air, and insolent languor: and envied each one of these some excellence or quality of youth, or good looks, which he possessed, and of which Warrington felt the need. And every night, as the night came, he quitted the little circle with greater reluctance; and, retiring to his own lodging in their neighbourhood, felt himself the more lonely and unhappy. The widow could not help seeing his attachment. She understood, now, why Major Pendennis (always a tacit enemy of her darling project) had been so eager that Warrington should be of their party. Laura frankly owned her great, her enthusiastic, regard for him: and Arthur would make no movement. Arthur did not choose to see what was going on; or did not care to prevent, or actually encouraged it. She remembered his often having said that he could not understand how a man proposed to a woman twice. She was in torture; at secret feud with her son, of all objects in the world the dearest to her; in doubt, which she dared not express to herself, about Laura; averse to Warrington, the good and generous. No wonder that the healing waters of Rosenbad did not do her good, or that Dr. von Glauber, the bath physician, when he came to visit her, found that

the poor lady made no progress to recovery. Meanwhile Pen got well rapidly; slept with immense perseverance twelve hours out of the twenty-four; ate huge meals; and, at the end of a couple of months, had almost got back the bodily strength and weight which he had possessed before his illness.

After they had passed some fifteen days at their place of rest and refreshment, a letter came from Major Pendennis announcing his speedy arrival at Rosenbad, and, soon after the letter, the major himself made his appearance, accompanied by Morgan, his faithful valet, without whom the old gentleman could not move. When the major travelled he wore a jaunty and juvenile travelling costume; to see his back still you would have taken him for one of the young fellows whose slim waist and youthful appearance Warrington was beginning to envy. It was not until the worthy man began to move, that the observer remarked that Time had weakened his ancient knees, and had unkindly interfered to impede the action of the natty little varnished boots in which the gay old traveller still pinched his toes. There were magnates both of our own country and of foreign nations present that autumn at Rosenbad. The elder Pendennis read over the strangers' list with great gratification on the night of his arrival, was pleased to find several of his acquaintances among the great folks, and would have the honour of presenting his nephew to a German grand duchess, a Russian princess, and an English marquis, before many days were over: nor was Pen by any means averse to making the acquaintance of these great personages, having a liking for polite life, and all the splendours and amenities belonging to it. That very evening the resolute old gentleman, leaning on his nephew's arm, made his appearance in the halls of the Kursaal, and lost or won a napoleon or two at the table of *trente-et-quarante*. He did not play to lose, he said, or to win, but he did as other folks did, and betted his napoleon, and took his luck as it came. He pointed out the Russians and Spaniards gambling for heaps of gold, and denounced their eagerness as something sordid and barbarous; an English gentleman should play where the fashion is play, but should not elate or depress himself at the sport; and he told how he had seen his friend the Marquis of Steyne, when Lord Gaunt, lose eighteen thousand at a sitting, and break the

bank three nights running at Paris, without ever showing the least emotion at his defeat or victory—'And that's what I call being an English gentleman, Pen, my dear boy,' the old gentleman said, warming as he prattled about his recollections—'what I call the great manner only remains with us and with a few families in France.' And as Russian princesses passed him, whose reputation had long ceased to be doubtful, and damaged English ladies, who are constantly seen in company of their faithful attendant for the time being in these gay haunts of dissipation, the old major, with eager garrulity and mischievous relish, told his nephew wonderful particulars regarding the lives of these

heroines; and diverted the young man with a thousand scandals. Egad, he felt himself quite young again, he remarked to Pen, as, rouged and grinning, her enormous *chasseur* behind her bearing her shawl, the Princess Obstropski smiled and recognized and accosted him. He remembered her in '14, when she was an actress of the Paris Boulevard, and the Emperor Alexander's aide-de-camp Obstropski (a man of great talents, who knew a good deal about the Emperor Paul's death, and was a devil to play) married her. He most courteously and respectfully asked leave to call upon the princess, and to present to her his nephew, Mr. Arthur Pendennis; and he pointed out to

the latter a half-dozen of other personages whose names were as famous, and whose histories were as edifying. What would poor Helen have thought, could she have heard those tales, or known to what kind of people her brother-in-law was presenting her son? Only once, leaning on Arthur's arm, she had passed through the room where the green tables were prepared for play, and the croaking croupiers were calling out their fatal words of '*Rouge gagne*' and '*Couleur perd.*' She had shrunk terrified out of the pandemonium, imploring Pen, extorting from him a promise, on his word of honour, that he would never play at those tables; and the scene which so frightened the simple widow, only amused the worldly old veteran, and made him young again! He could breathe the air cheerfully which stifled her. Her right was not his right: his food was her poison. Human creatures are constituted thus differently, and with this variety the marvellous world is peopled. To the credit of Mr. Pen, let it be said, that he kept honestly the promise made to his mother, and stoutly told his uncle of his intention to abide by it.

When the major arrived, his presence somehow cast a damp upon at least three of the persons of our little party—upon Laura, who had anything but respect for him; upon Warrington, whose manner towards him showed an involuntary haughtiness and contempt; and upon the timid and alarmed widow, who dreaded lest he should interfere with her darling, though almost desperate, projects for her boy. And, indeed, the major, unknown to himself, was the bearer of tidings which were to bring about a catastrophe in the affairs of all our friends.

Pen, with his two ladies, had apartments in the town of Rosenbad; honest Warrington had lodgings hard by; the major, on arrival at Rosenbad, had, as befitted his dignity, taken up his quarters at one of the great hotels, at the 'Roman Emperor' or the 'Four Seasons,' where two or three hundred gamblers, pleasure-seekers, or invalids, sat down and over-ate themselves daily at the enormous table d'hôte. To this hotel Pen went on the morning after the major's arrival, dutifully to pay his respects to his uncle, and found the latter's sitting-room duly prepared and arranged by Mr. Morgan, with the major's hats brushed, and his coats laid out: his dispatch-boxes and umbrella-cases; his guide-books, passports, maps, and other elaborate necessaries of

the English traveller, all as trim and ready as they could be in their master's own room in Jermyn Street. Everything was ready, from the medicine-bottle fresh filled from the pharmacien's, down to the old fellow's Prayer-book, without which he never travelled, for he made a point of appearing at the English church at every place which he honoured with a stay. 'Everybody did it,' he said; 'every English gentleman did it,' and this pious man would as soon have thought of not calling upon the English ambassador in a Continental town, as of not showing himself at the national place of worship.

The old gentleman had been to take one of the baths for which Rosenbad is famous, and which everybody takes, and his after-bath toilet was not yet completed when Pen arrived. The elder called out to Arthur in a cheery voice from the inner apartment, in which he and Morgan were engaged, and the valet presently came in, bearing a little packet to Pen's address—Mr. Arthur's letters and papers, Morgan said, which he had brought from Mr. Arthur's chambers in London, and which consisted chiefly of numbers of the *Pall Mall Gazette*, which our friend Mr. Finucane thought his *collaborateur* would like to see. The papers were tied together: the letters in an envelope, addressed to Pen, in the last-named gentleman's handwriting.

Amongst the letters there was a little note addressed, as a former letter we have heard of had been, to 'Arthur Pendennis, Esq.,' which Arthur opened with a start and a blush, and read with a very keen pang of interest, and sorrow, and regard. She had come to Arthur's house, Fanny Bolton said—and found that he was gone—gone away to Germany without ever leaving a word for her—or answer to her last letter, in which she prayed but for one word of kindness—or the books which he had promised her in happier times, before he was ill, and which she should like to keep in remembrance of him. She said she would not reproach those who had found her at his bedside when he was in the fever, and knew nobody, and who had turned the poor girl away without a word. She thought she should have died, she said, of that, but Dr. Goodenough had kindly tended her, and kep her life, when, perhaps, the keeping of it was of no good, and she forgave everybody: and as for Arthur, she would pray for him for ever. And when he was so ill, and they cut off his hair, she had made so

free as to keep one little lock for herself,* and that she owned. And might she still keep it, or would his mamma order that that should be gave up too? She was willing to obey him in all things, and couldn't but remember that once he was so kind, oh! so good and kind! to his poor Fanny.

When Major Pendennis, fresh and smirking from his toilette, came out of his bedroom to his sitting-room, he found Arthur, with this note before him, and an expression of savage anger on his face, which surprised the elder gentleman. 'What news from London, my boy?' he rather faintly asked; 'are the duns at you that you look so glum?'

'Do you know anything about this letter, sir?' Arthur asked.

'What letter, my good sir?' said the other dryly, at once perceiving what had happened.

'You know what I mean—about, about Miss—about Fanny Bolton—the poor dear little girl,' Arthur broke out. 'When was she in my room? Was she there when I was delirious—I fancied she was—was she? Who sent her out of my chambers? Who intercepted her letters to me? Who dared to do it? Did you do it, uncle?'

'It's not my practice to tamper with gentlemen's letters, or to answer damned impertinent questions,' Major Pendennis cried out, in a great tremor of emotion and indignation. 'There was a girl in your rooms when I came up at great personal inconvenience, daymy—and to meet with a return of this kind for my affection to you, is not pleasant, by Gad, sir—not at all pleasant.'

'That's not the question, sir,' Arthur said hotly—'and —and, I beg your pardon, uncle. You were, you always have been, most kind to me: but I say again, did you say anything harsh to this poor girl? Did you send her away from me?'

'I never spoke a word to the girl,' the uncle said, 'and I never sent her away from you, and know no more about her, and wish to know no more about her, than about the man in the moon.'

'Then it's my mother that did it,' Arthur broke out. 'Did my mother send that poor child away?'

'I repeat I know nothing about it, sir,' the elder said testily. 'Let's change the subject, if you please.'

'I'll never forgive the person who did it,' said Arthur, bouncing up and seizing his hat.

The major cried out, 'Stop, Arthur, for God's sake, stop;' but before he had uttered his sentence Arthur had rushed out of the room, and at the next minute the major saw him striding rapidly down the street that led towards his home.

'Get breakfast!' said the old fellow to Morgan, and he wagged his head and sighed as he looked out of the window. 'Poor Helen—poor soul! There'll be a row. I knew there would: and begad, all the fat's in the fire.'

When Pen reached home he only found Warrington in the ladies' drawing-room, waiting their arrival in order to conduct them to the room where the little English colony at Rosenbad held their Sunday church. Helen and Laura had not appeared as yet; the former was ailing, and her daughter was with her. Pen's wrath was so great that he could not defer expressing it. He flung Fanny's letter across the table to his friend. 'Look there, Warrington,' he said; 'she tended me in my illness, she rescued me out of the jaws of death, and this is the way they have treated the dear little creature. They have kept her letters from me; they have treated me like a child, and her like a dog, poor thing! My mother has done this.'

'If she has, you must remember it is your mother,' Warrington interposed.

'It only makes the crime the greater because it is she who has done it,' Pen answered. 'She ought to have been the poor girl's defender, not her enemy: she ought to go down on her knees and ask pardon of her. I ought! I will! I am shocked at the cruelty which has been shown her. What? She gave me her all, and this is her return! She sacrifices everything for me, and they spurn her.'

'Hush!' said Warrington, 'they can hear you from the next room.'

'Hear; let them hear!' Pen cried out, only so much the louder. 'Those may overhear my talk who intercept my letters. I say this poor girl has been shamefully used, and I will do my best to right her; I will.'

The door of the neighbouring room opened, and Laura came forth with pale and stern face. She looked at Pen with glances from which beamed pride, defiance, aversion. 'Arthur, your mother is very ill,' she said;

'it is a pity that you should speak so loud as to disturb her.'

'It is a pity that I should have been obliged to speak at all,' Pen answered. 'And I have more to say before I have done.'

'I should think what you have to say will hardly be fit for me to hear,' Laura said haughtily.

'You are welcome to hear it or not, as you like,' said Mr. Pen. 'I shall go in now and speak to my mother.'

Laura came rapidly forward, so that she should not be overheard by her friend within. 'Not now, sir,' she said to Pen. 'You may kill her if you do. Your conduct has gone far enough to make her wretched.'

'What conduct?' cried out Pen, in a fury. 'Who dares impugn it? Who dares meddle with me? Is it you who are the instigator of this persecution?'

'I said before it was a subject of which it did not become me to hear or to speak,' Laura said. 'But as for mamma, if she had acted otherwise than she did with regard to—to the person about whom you seem to take such an interest, it would have been I that must have quitted your house, and not that—that person.'

'By heavens! this is too much,' Pen cried out, with a violent execration.

'Perhaps that is what you wished,' Laura said, tossing her head up. 'No more of this, if you please; I am not accustomed to hear such subjects spoken of in such language;' and with a stately curtsy the young lady passed to her friend's room, looking her adversary full in the face as she retreated and closed the door upon him.

Pen was bewildered with wonder, perplexity, fury, at this monstrous and unreasonable persecution. He burst out into a loud and bitter laugh as Laura quitted him, and with sneers and revilings, as a man who jeers under an operation, ridiculed at once his own pain and his persecutor's anger. The laugh, which was one of bitter humour, and no unmanly or unkindly expression of suffering under most cruel and unmerited torture, was heard in the next apartment, as some of his unlucky previous expressions had been, and, like them, entirely misinterpreted by the hearers. It struck like a dagger into the wounded and tender heart of Helen; it pierced Laura, and inflamed the high-spirited girl with scorn and anger. 'And it was

to this hardened libertine,' she thought—' to this boaster of low intrigues, that I had given my heart away.' 'He breaks the most sacred laws,' thought Helen. 'He prefers the creature of his passion to his own mother; and when he is upbraided, he laughs, and glories in his crime. "She gave me her all," I heard him say it,' argued the poor widow; 'and he boasts of it, and laughs, and breaks his mother's heart.' The emotion, the shame, the grief, the mortification almost killed her. She felt she should die of his unkindness.

Warrington thought of Laura's speech—' Perhaps that is what you wished.' 'She loves Pen still,' he said. 'It was jealousy made her speak.—Come away, Pen. Come away, and let us go to church and get calm. You must explain this matter to your mother. She does not appear to know the truth: nor do you quite, my good fellow. Come away, and let us talk about it.' And again he muttered to himself, '"Perhaps that is what you wished." Yes, she loves him. Why shouldn't she love him? Whom else would I have her love? What can she be to me but the dearest and the fairest and the best of women?'

So, leaving the women similarly engaged within, the two gentlemen walked away, each occupied with his own thoughts, and silent for a considerable space. 'I must set this matter right,' thought honest George, 'as she loves him still—I must set his mother's mind right about the other woman.' And with this charitable thought, the good fellow began to tell more at large what Bows had said to him regarding Miss Bolton's behaviour and fickleness, and he described how the girl was no better than a little light-minded flirt; and, perhaps, he exaggerated the good-humour and contentedness which he had himself, as he thought, witnessed in her behaviour in the scene with Mr. Huxter.

Now, all Bows's statements had been coloured by an insane jealousy and rage on that old man's part; and instead of allaying Pen's renascent desire to see his little conquest again, Warrington's accounts inflamed and angered Pendennis, and made him more anxious than before to set himself right, as he persisted in phrasing it, with Fanny. They arrived at the church-door presently; but scarce one word of the service, and not a syllable of Mr. Shamble's sermon, did either of them comprehend,

probably—so much was each engaged with his own private speculations. The major came up to them after the service, with his well-brushed hat and wig, and his jauntiest, most cheerful, air. He complimented them upon being seen at church ; again he said that every *comme-il-faut* person made a point of attending the English service abroad ; and he walked back with the young men, prattling to them in garrulous good-humour, and making bows to his acquaintances as they passed ; and thinking innocently that Pen and George were both highly delighted by his anecdotes, which they suffered to run on in a scornful and silent acquiescence.

At the time of Mr. Shamble's sermon (an erratic Anglican divine, hired for the season at places of English resort, and addicted to debts, drinking, and even to roulette, it was said), Pen, chafing under the persecution which his womankind inflicted upon him, had been meditating a great act of revolt and of justice, as he had worked himself up to believe ; and Warrington on his part had been thinking that a crisis in his affairs had likewise come, and that it was necessary for him to break away from a connection which every day made more and more wretched and dear to him. Yes, the time was come. He took those fatal words, 'Perhaps that is what you wished,' as a text for a gloomy homily, which he preached to himself, in the dark crypt[2] of his own heart, whilst Mr. Shamble was feebly giving utterance to his sermon.

CHAPTER LVII

'FAIROAKS TO LET'

UR poor widow (with the assistance of her faithful Martha of Fairoaks, who laughed and wondered at the German ways, and superintended the affairs of the simple household) had made a little feast in honour of Major Pendennis's arrival, of which, however, only the major and his two younger friends partook, for Helen sent to say that she was too unwell to dine at their table, and Laura bore her company. The major talked for the

party, and did not perceive, or choose to perceive, what a gloom and silence pervaded the other two sharers of the modest dinner. It was evening before Helen and Laura came into the sitting-room to join the company there. She came in leaning on Laura, with her back to the waning light, so that Arthur could not see how pallid and woe-stricken her face was, and as she went up to Pen, whom she had not seen during the day, and placed her fond arms on his shoulder and kissed him tenderly, Laura left her, and moved away to another part of the room. Pen remarked that his mother's voice and her whole frame trembled, her hand was clammy cold as she put it up to his forehead, piteously embracing him. The spectacle of her misery only added, somehow, to the wrath and testiness of the young man. He scarcely returned the kiss which the suffering lady gave him: and the countenance with which he met the appeal of her look was hard and cruel. 'She persecutes me,' he thought within himself, 'and she comes to me with the air of a martyr.' 'You look very ill, my child,' she said. 'I don't like to see you look in that way.' And she tottered to a sofa, still holding one of his passive hands in her thin, cold, clinging fingers.

'I have had much to annoy me, mother,' Pen said, with a throbbing breast: and as he spoke Helen's heart began to beat so, that she sat almost dead and speechless with terror.

Warrington, Laura, and Major Pendennis, all remained breathless, aware that the storm was about to break.

'I have had letters from London,' Arthur continued, 'and one that has given me more pain than I ever had in my life. It tells me that former letters of mine have been intercepted and purloined away from me;—that—that a young creature who has shown the greatest love and care for me, has been most cruelly used by—by you, mother.'

'For God's sake, stop,' cried out Warrington. 'She's ill—don't you see she is ill?'

'Let him go on,' said the widow faintly.

'Let him go on and kill her,' said Laura, rushing up to her mother's side. 'Speak on, sir, and see her die.'

'It is you who are cruel,' cried Pen, more exasperated and more savage, because his own heart, naturally soft and weak, revolted indignantly at the injustice of the very suffering which was laid at his door. 'It is you that are

cruel, who attribute all this pain to me: it is you who are cruel with your wicked reproaches, your wicked doubts of me, your wicked persecutions of those who love me,—yes, those who love me, and who brave everything for me, and whom you despise and trample upon because they are of lower degree than you. Shall I tell you what I will do,—what I am resolved to do, now that I know what your conduct has been?—I will go back to this poor girl whom you turned out of my doors, and ask her to come back and share my home with me. I'll defy the pride which persecutes her, and the pitiless suspicion which insults her and me.'

'Do you mean, Pen, that you——' here the widow, with eager eyes and outstretched hands, was breaking out, but Laura stopped her: 'Silence, hush, dear mother,' she cried, and the widow hushed. Savagely as Pen spoke, she was only too eager to hear what more he had to say. 'Go on, Arthur; go on, Arthur,' was all she said, almost swooning away as she spoke.

'By Gad, I say he shan't go on, or I won't hear him, by Gad,' the major said, trembling too in his wrath. 'If you choose, sir, after all we've done for you, after all I've done for you myself, to insult your mother, and disgrace your name, by allying yourself with a low-born kitchen-girl, go and do it, by Gad,—but let us, ma'am, have no more to do with him. I wash my hands of you, sir,—I wash my hands of you. I'm an old fellow,—I ain't long for this world. I come of as ancient and honourable a family as any in England, and I did hope, before I went off the hooks, by Gad, that the fellow that I'd liked, and brought up, and nursed through life, by Jove, would do something to show me that our name—yes, the name of Pendennis, was left undishonoured behind us, but if he won't, dammy, I say, amen. By G—, both my father and my brother Jack were the proudest men in England, and I never would have thought that there would come this disgrace to my name,—never—and—and I'm ashamed that it's Arthur Pendennis.' The old fellow's voice here broke off into a sob: it was a second time that Arthur had brought tears from those wrinkled lids.

The sound of his breaking voice stayed Pen's anger instantly, and he stopped pacing the room, as he had been doing until that moment. Laura was by Helen's sofa; and Warrington had remained hitherto an almost silent, but

not uninterested spectator of the family storm. As the parties were talking, it had grown almost dark; and after the lull which succeeded the passionate outbreak of the major, George's deep voice, as it here broke trembling into the twilight room, was heard with no small emotion by all.

'Will you let me tell you something about myself, my kind friends?' he said; 'you have been so good to me, ma'am—you have been so kind to me, Laura—I hope I may call you so sometimes—my dear Pen and I have been such friends that—that I have long wanted to tell you my story such as it is, and would have told it to you earlier but that it is a sad one and contains another's secret. However, it may do good for Arthur to know it; it is right that every one here should. It will divert you from thinking about a subject which, out of a fatal misconception, has caused a great deal of pain to all of you. May I please tell you, Mrs. Pendennis?'

'Pray speak,' was all Helen said; and indeed she was not much heeding; her mind was full of another idea with which Pen's words had supplied her, and she was in a terror of hope that what he had hinted might be as she wished.

George filled himself a bumper of wine and emptied it, and began to speak. 'You all of you know how you see me,' he said, 'a man without a desire to make an advance in the world: careless about reputation; and living in a garret and from hand to mouth, though I have friends and a name, and I dare say capabilities of my own that would serve me if I had a mind. But mind I have none. I shall die in that garret, most likely, and alone. I nailed myself to that doom in early life. Shall I tell you what it was that interested me about Arthur years ago, and made me inclined towards him when first I saw him? The men from our college at Oxbridge brought up accounts of that early affair with the Chatteris actress, about whom Pen has often talked to me since; and who, but for the major's generalship, might have been your daughter-in-law, ma'am. I can't see Pen in the dark, but he blushes, I'm sure; and I dare say Miss Bell does; and my friend, Major Pendennis, I dare say, laughs as he ought to do—for he won. What would have been Arthur's lot now, had he been tied at nineteen to an illiterate woman older than himself, with no qualities in common between them to make one a companion for the other, no equality, no confidence, and no

love speedily? What could he have been but most miserable? And when he spoke just now, and threatened a similar union, be sure it was but a threat occasioned by anger, which you must give me leave to say, ma'am, was very natural on his part, for after a generous and manly conduct—let me say, who know the circumstances well—most generous and manly and self-denying (which is rare with him),—he has met from some friends of his with a most unkind suspicion, and has had to complain of the unfair treatment of another innocent person, towards whom he and you all are under much obligation.'

The widow was going to get up here, and Warrington, seeing her attempt to rise, said, 'Do I tire you, ma'am?'

'Oh no—go on—go on,' said Helen, delighted, and he continued.

'I liked him, you see, because of that early history of his, which had come to my ears in college gossip, and because I like a man, if you will pardon me for saying so, Miss Laura, who shows that he can have a great unreasonable attachment for a woman. That was why we became friends—and all are friends here—for always, aren't we?' he added, in a lower voice, leaning over to her, 'and Pen has been a great comfort and companion to a lonely and unfortunate man.

'I am not complaining of my lot, you see; for no man's is what he would have it; and up in my garret, where you left the flowers, and with my old books and my pipe for a wife, I am pretty contented, and only occasionally envy other men, whose careers in life are more brilliant, or who can solace their ill-fortune by what Fate and my own fault has deprived me of—the affection of a woman or a child.' Here there came a sigh from somewhere near Warrington in the dark, and a hand was held out in his direction, which, however, was instantly withdrawn, for the prudery of our females is such, that before all expression of feeling, or natural kindness and regard, a woman is taught to think of herself and the proprieties, and to be ready to blush at the very slightest notice; and checking, as, of course, it ought, this spontaneous motion, modesty drew up again, kindly friendship shrank back ashamed of itself, and Warrington resumed his history. 'My fate is such as I made it, and not lucky for me or for others involved in it.

'I, too, had an adventure before I went to college; and

there was no one to save me as Major Pendennis saved Pen. Pardon me, Miss Laura, if I tell this story before you. It it as well that you all of you should hear my confession. Before I went to college, as a boy of eighteen, I was at a private tutor's, and there, like Arthur, I became attached, or fancied I was attached, to a woman of a much lower degree and a greater age than my own. You shrink from me——'

'No, I don't,' Laura said, and here the hand went out resolutely, and laid itself in Warrington's. She had divined his story from some previous hints let fall by him, and his first words at its commencement.

'She was a yeoman's daughter in the neighbourhood,' Warrington said, with rather a faltering voice, 'and I fancied—what all young men fancy. Her parents knew who my father was, and encouraged me, with all sorts of coarse artifices and scoundrel flatteries, which I see now, about their house. To do her justice, I own she never cared for me, but was forced into what happened by the threats and compulsion of her family. Would to God that I had not been deceived: but in these matters we are deceived because we wish to be so, and I thought I loved that poor woman.

'What could come of such a marriage? I found, before long, that I was married to a boor. She could not comprehend one subject that interested me. Her dullness palled upon me till I grew to loathe it. And after some time of a wretched, furtive union—I must tell you all—I found letters somewhere (and such letters they were!) which showed me that her heart, such as it was, had never been mine, but had always belonged to a person of her own degree.

'At my father's death, I paid what debts I had contracted at college, and settled every shilling which remained to me in an annuity, upon—upon those who bore my name, on condition that they should hide themselves away, and not assume it. They have kept that condition, as they would break it, for more money. If I had earned fame or reputation, that woman would have come to claim it: if I had made a name for myself, those who had no right to it would have borne it; and I entered life at twenty, God help me—hopeless and ruined beyond remission. I was the boyish victim of vulgar cheats, and, perhaps, it is only

of late I have found out how hard—ah, how hard—it is to forgive them. I told you the moral before, Pen ; and now I have told you the fable. Beware how you marry out of your degree. I was made for a better lot than this, I think : but God has awarded me this one—and so, you see, it is for me to look on, and see others successful and others happy, with a heart that shall be as little bitter as possible.'

'By Gad, sir,' cried the major, in high good-humour, 'I intended you to marry Miss Laura here.'

'And, by Gad, Master Shallow, I owe you a thousand pound,' Warrington said.

'How d'ye mean a thousand ? It was only a pony, sir,' replied the major simply, at which the other laughed.

As for Helen, she was so delighted, that she started up, and said, 'God bless you—God for ever bless you, Mr. Warrington ;' and kissed both his hands, and ran up to Pen, and fell into his arms.

'Yes, dearest mother,' he said, as he held her to him, and with a noble tenderness and emotion embraced and forgave her. 'I am innocent, and my dear, dear mother has done me a wrong.'

'Oh yes, my child, I have wronged you, thank God, I have wronged you !' Helen whispered. 'Come away, Arthur—not here—I want to ask my child to forgive me —and—and my God, to forgive me ; and to bless you, and love you, my son.'

He led her, tottering, into her room, and closed the door, as the three touched spectators of the reconciliation looked on in pleased silence. Ever after, ever after, the tender accents of that voice faltering sweetly at his ear—the look of the sacred eyes beaming with an affection unutterable —the quiver of the fond lips smiling mournfully—were remembered by the young man. And at his best moments, and at his hours of trial and grief, and at his times of success or well-doing, the mother's face looked down upon him, and blessed him with its gaze of pity and purity, as he saw it in that night when she yet lingered with him ; and when she seemed, ere she quite left him, an angel, transfigured and glorified with love—for which love, as for the greatest of the bounties and wonders of God's provision for us, let us kneel and thank Our Father.

The moon had risen by this time ; Arthur recollected well

afterwards how it lighted up his mother's sweet pale face. Their talk, or his rather, for she scarcely could speak, was more tender and confidential than it had been for years before. He was the frank and generous boy of her early days and love. He told her the story, the mistake regarding which had caused her so much pain—his struggles to fly from temptation, and his thankfulness that he had been able to overcome it. He never would do the girl wrong, never; or wound his own honour or his mother's pure heart. The threat that he would return was uttered in a moment of exasperation, of which he repented. He never would see her again. But his mother said yes, he should; and it was she who had been proud and culpable—and she would like to give Fanny Bolton something—and she begged her dear boy's pardon for opening the letter—and she would write to the young girl, if,—if she had time. Poor thing! was it not natural that she should love her Arthur? And again she kissed him, and she blessed him.

As they were talking the clock struck nine, and Helen reminded him how, when he was a little boy, she used to go up to his bedroom at that hour, and hear him say 'Our Father.' And once more, oh, once more, the young man fell down at his mother's sacred knees, and sobbed out the prayer which the Divine Tenderness uttered for us, and which has been echoed for twenty ages since by millions of sinful and humbled men. And as he spoke the last words of the supplication, the mother's head fell down on her boy's, and her arms closed round him, and together they repeated the words 'for ever and ever,' and 'Amen.'

A little time after, it might have been a quarter of an hour, Laura heard Arthur's voice calling from within, 'Laura! Laura!' She rushed into the room instantly, and found the young man still on his knees, and holding his mother's hand. Helen's head had sunk back and was quite pale in the moon. Pen looked round, scared with a ghastly terror. 'Help, Laura, help!' he said—'she's fainted—she's——'

Laura screamed, and fell by the side of Helen. The shriek brought Warrington and Major Pendennis and the servants to the room. The sainted woman was dead. The last emotion of her soul here was joy, to be henceforth unchequered and eternal. The tender heart beat no more;

it was to have no more pangs, no more doubts, no more griefs and trials. Its last throb was love: and Helen's last breath was a benediction.

The melancholy party bent their way speedily homewards, and Helen was laid by her husband's side at Clavering, in the old church where she had prayed so often. For awhile Laura went to stay with Dr. Portman, who read the service over his dear sister departed, amidst his own sobs and those of the little congregation which assembled round Helen's tomb. There were not many who cared for her, or who spoke of her when gone. Scarcely more than of a nun in a cloister did people know of that pious and gentle lady. A few words among the cottagers whom her bounty was accustomed to relieve, a little talk from house to house at Clavering, where this lady told how their neighbour died of a complaint in the heart; whilst that speculated upon the amount of property which the widow had left; and a third wondered whether Arthur would let Fairoaks or live in it, and expected that he would not be long getting through his property,—this was all, and, except with one or two who cherished her, the kind soul was forgotten by the next market-day. Would you desire that grief for you should last for a few more weeks? and does after-life seem less solitary, provided that our names, when we 'go down into silence,' are echoing on this side of the grave yet for a little while, and human voices are still talking about us? She was gone, the pure soul, whom only two or three loved and knew. The great blank she left was in Laura's heart, to whom her love had been everything, and who had now but to worship her memory. 'I am glad that she gave me her blessing before she went away,' Warrington said to Pen; and as for Arthur, with a humble acknowledgement and wonder at so much affection, he hardly dared to ask of Heaven to make him worthy of it, though he felt that a saint there was interceding for him.

All the lady's affairs were found in perfect order, and her little property ready for transmission to her son, in trust for whom she held it. Papers in her desk showed that she had long been aware of the complaint, one of the heart, under which she laboured, and knew that it would suddenly remove her: and a prayer was found in her hand-

writing, asking that her end might be, as it was, in the arms of her son.

Laura and Arthur talked over her sayings, all of which the former most fondly remembered, to the young man's shame somewhat, who thought how much greater her love had been for Helen than his own. He referred himself entirely to Laura to know what Helen would have wished should be done; what poor persons she would have liked to relieve; what legacies or remembrances she would have wished to transmit. They packed up the vase which Helen in her gratitude had destined to Dr. Goodenough, and duly sent it to the kind doctor: a silver coffee-pot, which she used, was sent off to Portman: a diamond ring, with her hair, was given with affectionate greeting to Warrington.

It must have been a hard day for poor Laura when she went over to Fairoaks first, and to the little room which she had occupied, and which was hers no more, and to the widow's own blank chamber in which those two had passed so many beloved hours. There, of course, were the clothes in the wardrobe, the cushion on which she prayed, the chair at the toilette, the glass that was no more to reflect her dear sad face. After she had been here awhile, Pen knocked and led her downstairs to the parlour again, and made her drink a little wine, and said, 'God bless you,' as she touched the glass. 'Nothing shall ever be changed in your room,' he said—'it is always your room—it is always my sister's room. Shall it not be so, Laura?' and Laura said, 'Yes!'

Among the widow's papers was found a packet, marked by the widow 'Letters from Laura's father,' and which Arthur gave to her. They were the letters which had passed between the cousins in the early days before the marriage of either of them.* The ink was faded in which they were written: the tears dried out that both perhaps had shed over them: the grief healed now whose bitterness they chronicled: the friends doubtless united whose parting on earth had caused to both pangs so cruel. And Laura learned fully now for the first time what the tie was which had bound her so tenderly to Helen: how faithfully her more than mother had cherished her father's memory, how truly she had loved him, how meekly resigned him.

One legacy of his mother's Pen remembered, of which Laura could have no cognizance. It was that wish of Helen's to make some present to Fanny Bolton; and Pen

wrote to her, putting his letter under an envelope to Mr. Bows, and requesting that gentleman to read it before he delivered it to Fanny. 'Dear Fanny,' Pen said, 'I have to acknowledge two letters from you, one of which was delayed in my illness' (Pen found the first letter in his mother's desk after her decease, and the reading it gave him a strange pang), 'and to thank you, my kind nurse and friend, who watched me so tenderly during my fever. And I have to tell you that the last words of my dear mother, who is no more, were words of goodwill and gratitude to you for nursing me: and she said she would have written to you, had she had time—that she would like to ask your pardon if she had harshly treated you—and that she would beg you to show your forgiveness by accepting some token of friendship and regard from her.' Pen concluded by saying that his friend, George Warrington, Esq., of Lamb Court, Temple, was trustee of a little sum of money, of which the interest would be paid to her until she became of age, or changed her name, which would always be affectionately remembered by her grateful friend, A. Pendennis. The sum was in truth but small, although enough to make a little heiress of Fanny Bolton, whose parents were appeased, and whose father said Mr. P. had acted quite as the gentleman—though Bows growled out that to plaster a wounded heart with a bank-note was an easy kind of sympathy; and poor Fanny felt only too clearly that Pen's letter was one of farewell.

'Sending hundred-pound notes to porters' daughters is all dev'lish well,' old Major Pendennis said to his nephew (whom, as the proprietor of Fairoaks and the head of the family, he now treated with marked deference and civility), 'and as there was a little ready money at the bank, and your poor mother wished it, there's perhaps no harm done. But, my good lad, I'd have you to remember that you've not above five hundred a year, though, thanks to me, the world gives you credit for being a doosid deal better off; and, on my knees, I beg you, my boy, don't break into your capital. Stick to it, sir; don't speculate with it, sir; keep your land, and don't borrow on it. Tatham tells me that the Chatteris branch of the railway may—will, almost certainly, pass through Clavering, and if it can be brought on this side of the Brawl, sir, and through your fields, they'll be worth a dev'lish deal of money, and your five hundred

a year will jump up to eight or nine. Whatever it is, keep it, I implore you, keep it. And I say, Pen, I think you should give up living in those dirty chambers in the Temple and get a decent lodging. And I should have a man, sir, to wait upon me ; and a horse or two in town in the season. All this will pretty well swallow up your income, and I know you must live close. But remember you have a certain place in society, and you can't afford to cut a poor figure in the world. What are you going to do in the winter ? You don't intend to stay down here, or, I suppose, to go on writing for that—what-d'ye-call'em—that newspaper ?'

'Warrington and I are going abroad again, sir, for a little, and then we shall see what is to be done,' Arthur replied.

'And you'll let Fairoaks, of course ? Good school in the neighbourhood : cheap country : dev'lish nice place for East India colonels,* or families wanting to retire. I'll speak about it at the club ; there are lots of fellows at the club want a place of that sort.'

'I hope Laura will live in it for the winter, at least, and will make it her home,' Arthur replied : at which the major pish'd, and psha'd, and said that there ought to be convents, begad, for English ladies, and wished that Miss Bell had not been there to interfere with the arrangements of the family, and that she would mope herself to death alone in that place.

Indeed, it would have been a very dismal abode for poor Laura, who was not too happy either in Dr. Portman's household, and in the town where too many things reminded her of the dear parent whom she had lost. But old Lady Rockminster, who adored her young friend Laura, as soon as she read in the paper of her loss, and of her presence in the country, rushed over from Baymouth, where the old lady was staying, and insisted that Laura should remain six months, twelve months, all her life with her ; and to her ladyship's house, Martha from Fairoaks, as *femme de chambre*, accompanied her young mistress.

Pen and Warrington saw her depart. It was difficult to say which of the young men seemed to regard her the most tenderly. 'Your cousin is pert and rather vulgar, my dear, but he seems to have a good heart,' little Lady Rockminster said, who said her say about everybody—'but I like Bluebeard best. Tell me, is he *touché au cœur* ?'

'Mr. Warrington has been long—engaged,' Laura said, dropping her eyes.

'Nonsense, child! And good heavens, my dear! that's a pretty diamond cross. What do you mean by wearing it in the morning?'

'Arthur—my brother, gave it me just now. It was—it was——' She could not finish the sentence. The carriage passed over the bridge, and by the dear, dear gate of Fairoaks—home no more.

CHAPTER LVIII

OLD FRIENDS

It chanced at that great English festival, at which all London takes a holiday upon Epsom Downs, that a great number of the personages to whom we have been introduced in the course of this history were assembled to see the Derby. In a comfortable open carriage, which had been brought to the ground by a pair of horses, might be seen Mrs. Bungay, of Paternoster Row, attired like Solomon in all his glory, and having by her side modest Mrs. Shandon, for whom, since the commencement of their acquaintance, the worthy publisher's lady had maintained a steady friendship. Bungay, having recreated himself with a copious luncheon, was madly shying at the sticks hard by, till the perspiration ran off his bald pate. Shandon was shambling about among the drinking-tents and gipsies: Finucane constant in attendance on the two ladies, to whom gentlemen of their acquaintance, and connected with the publishing-house, came up to pay a visit.

Among others, Mr. Archer came up to make her his bow, and told Mrs. Bungay who was on the course. Yonder was the Prime Minister: his lordship had just told him to back Borax for the race; but Archer thought Muffineer the better horse. He pointed out countless dukes and grandees to the delighted Mrs. Bungay. 'Look yonder in the Grand Stand,' he said. 'There sits the Chinese ambassador with

the mandarins of his suite. Fou-choo-foo brought me over letters of introduction from the Governor-General of India, my most intimate friend, and I was for some time very kind to him, and he had his chopsticks laid for him at my table whenever he chose to come and dine. But he brought his own cook with him, and—would you believe it, Mrs. Bungay ?—one day, when I was out, and the ambassador was with Mrs. Archer in our garden eating gooseberries, of which the Chinese are passionately fond, the beast of a cook, seeing my wife's dear little Blenheim spaniel (that we had from the Duke of Marlborough himself, whose ancestor's life Mrs. Archer's great-great-grandfather saved at the battle of Malplaquet), seized upon the poor little devil, cut his throat, and skinned him, and served him up stuffed with forced meat in the second course.'

'Law !' said Mrs. Bungay.

'You may fancy my wife's agony when she knew what had happened ! The cook came screaming upstairs, and told us that she had found poor Fido's skin in the area, just after we had all of us tasted of the dish ! She never would speak to the ambassador again—never ; and, upon my word, he has never been to dine with us since. The Lord Mayor, who did me the honour to dine, liked the dish very much ; and, eaten with green peas, it tastes rather like duck.'

'You don't say so, now !' cried the astonished publisher's lady.

'Fact, upon my word. Look at that lady in blue, seated by the ambassador : that is Lady Flamingo, and they say she is going to be married to him, and return to Pekin with his Excellency. She is getting her feet squeezed down on purpose. But she'll only cripple herself, and will never be able to do it—never. My wife has the smallest foot in England, and wears shoes for a six-years-old child ; but what is that to a Chinese lady's foot, Mrs. Bungay ?'

'Who is that carriage as Mr. Pendennis is with, Mr. Archer ?' Mrs. Bungay presently asked. 'He and Mr. Warrington was here jest now. He's 'aughty in his manners, that Mr. Pendennis, and well he may be, for I'm told he keeps tip-top company. 'As he 'ad a large fortune left him, Mr. Archer ? He's in black still, I see.'

'Eighteen hundred a year in land, and twenty-two thousand five hundred in the Three-and-a-Half per Cents ; that's about it,' said Mr. Archer.

'Law! why you know everything, Mr. A.!' cried the lady of Paternoster Row.

'I happen to know, because I was called in about poor Mrs. Pendennis's will,' Mr. Archer replied. 'Pendennis's uncle, the major, seldom does anything without me; and as he's likely to be extravagant we've tied up the property, so that he can't make ducks and drakes with it.—How do you do, my lord?—Do you know that gentleman, ladies? You have read his speeches in the House; it is Lord Rochester.'

'Lord Fiddlestick,' cried out Finucane, from the box. 'Sure it's Tom Staples, of the *Morning Advertiser*, Archer.'

'Is it?' Archer said simply. 'Well, I'm very short-sighted, and upon my word I thought it was Rochester. That gentleman with the double opera-glass' (another nod) 'is Lord John; and the tall man with him—don't you know him?—is Sir James.'*

'You know 'em because you see 'em in the House,' growled Finucane.

'I know them because they are kind enough to allow me to call them my most intimate friends,' Archer continued. 'Look at the Duke of Hampshire; what a pattern of a fine old English gentleman! He never misses "the Derby." "Archer," he said to me only yesterday, "I have been at sixty-five Derbys! appeared on the field for the first time on a piebald pony when I was seven years old, with my father, the Prince of Wales, and Colonel Hanger; and only missing two races—one when I had the measles at Eton, and one in the Waterloo year, when I was with my friend Wellington in Flanders."'

'And who is that yellow carriage, with the pink and yellow parasols, that Mr. Pendennis is talking to, and ever so many gentlemen?' asked Mrs. Bungay.

'That is Lady Clavering, of Clavering Park, next estate to my friend Pendennis. That is the young son and heir upon the box; he's awfully tipsy, the little scamp! and the young lady is Miss Amory, Lady Clavering's daughter by a first marriage, and uncommonly sweet upon my friend Pendennis; but I've reason to think he has his heart fixed elsewhere. You have heard of young Mr. Foker—the great brewer, Foker, you know—he was going to hang himself in consequence of a fatal passion for Miss Amory, who refused

him, but was cut down just in time by his valet, and is now abroad, under a keeper.'

'How happy that young fellow is!' sighed Mrs. Bungay. 'Who'd have thought when he came so quiet and demure to dine with us, three or four years ago, he would turn out such a grand character! Why, I saw his name at Court the other day, and presented by the Marquis of Steyne and all; and in every party of the nobility his name's down as sure as a gun.'

'I introduced him a good deal when he first came up to

town,' Mr. Archer said, 'and his uncle, Major Pendennis, did the rest. Hallo! There's Cobden here, of all men in the world! I must go and speak to him. Good-bye, Mrs. Bungay. Good-morning, Mrs. Shandon.'

An hour previous to this time, and at a different part of the course, there might have been seen an old stage-coach, on the battered roof of which a crowd of shabby raffs were stamping and hallooing, as the great event of the day—the Derby race—rushed over the greensward, and by the shouting millions of people assembled to view that magnificent scene. This was Wheeler's (the 'Harlequin's Head') drag,

which had brought down a company of choice spirits from Bow Street, with a slap-up luncheon in the ‘ boot.’ As the whirling race flashed by, each of the choice spirits bellowed out the name of the horse or the colours which he thought or he hoped might be foremost. ‘ The Cornet !’ ‘ It’s Muffineer !’ ‘ It’s blue sleeves !’ ‘ Yallow cap ! yallow cap ! yallow cap !’ and so forth, yelled the gentlemen sportsmen during that delicious and thrilling minute before the contest was decided ; and as the fluttering signal blew out, showing the number of the famous horse Podasokus* as winner of the race, one of the gentlemen on the ‘ Harlequin’s Head ’ drag sprang up off the roof, as if he was a pigeon and about to fly away to London or York with the news.

But his elation did not lift him many inches from his standing-place, to which he came down again on the instant, causing the boards of the crazy old coach-roof to crack with the weight of his joy. ‘ Hurray, hurray !’ he bawled out, ‘ Podasokus is the horse ! Supper for ten, Wheeler, my boy. Ask you all round of course, and damn the expense.’

And the gentlemen on the carriage, the shabby swaggerers, the dubious bucks, said, ‘ Thank you—congratulate you, colonel : sup with you with pleasure !’ and whispered to one another, ‘ The colonel stands to win fifteen hundred, and he got the odds from a good man, too.’

And each of the shabby bucks and dusky dandies began to eye his neighbour with suspicion, lest that neighbour, taking his advantage, should get the colonel into a lonely place and borrow money of him. And the winner on Podasokus could not be alone during the whole of that afternoon, so closely did his friends watch him and each other.

At another part of the course you might have seen a vehicle, certainly more modest, if not more shabby than that battered coach which had brought down the choice spirits from the ‘ Harlequin’s Head ’; this was cab No. 2,002, which had conveyed a gentleman and two ladies from the cab-stand in the Strand : whereof one of the ladies, as she sat on the box of the cab enjoying with her mamma and their companion a repast of lobster salad and bitter ale, looked so fresh and pretty that many of the splendid young dandies who were strolling about the course, and enjoying themselves at the noble diversion of sticks, and talking to the beautifully-dressed ladies in the beautiful carriages on

the hill, forsook these fascinations to have a glance at the smiling and rosy-cheeked lass on the cab. The blushes of youth and good-humour mantled on the girl's cheeks, and played over that fair countenance like the pretty shining cloudlets on the serene sky overhead ; the elder lady's cheek was red too ; but that was a permanent mottled rose, deepening only as it received fresh draughts of pale ale and brandy-and-water, until her face emulated the rich shell of the lobster which she devoured.

The gentleman who escorted these two ladies was most active in attendance upon them : here on the course, as he had been during the previous journey. During the whole of that animated and delightful drive from London, his jokes had never ceased. He spoke up undauntedly to the most awful drags full of the biggest and most solemn guardsmen, as to the humblest donkey-chaise in which Bob the dustman was driving Molly to the race. He had fired astonishing volleys of what is called 'chaff' into endless windows as he passed ; into lines of grinning girls' schools ; into little regiments of shouting urchins hurraying behind the railings of their classical and commercial academies ; into casements whence smiling maidservants, and nurses tossing babies, or demure old maiden ladies with dissenting countenances, were looking. And the pretty girl in the straw bonnet with pink ribbon, and her mamma the devourer of lobsters, had both agreed that when he was in 'spirits' there was nothing like that Mr. Sam. He had crammed the cab with trophies won from the bankrupt proprietors of the sticks hard by, and with countless pincushions, wooden apples, backy-boxes, Jack-in-the-boxes, and little soldiers. He had brought up a gipsy with a tawny child in her arms to tell the fortunes of the ladies ; and the only cloud which momentarily obscured the sunshine of that happy party, was when the teller of fate informed the young lady that she had had reason to beware of a fair man, who was false to her : that she had had a bad illness, and that she would find that a dark man would prove true.

The girl looked very much abashed at this news : her mother and the young man interchanged signs of wonder and intelligence. Perhaps the conjurer had used the same words to a hundred different carriages on that day.

Making his way solitary amongst the crowd and the car-

riages, and noting, according to his wont, the various circumstances and characters which the animated scene presented, a young friend of ours came suddenly upon cab 2,002, and the little group of persons assembled on the outside of the vehicle. As he caught sight of the young lady on the box, she started and turned pale: her mother became redder than ever: the heretofore gay and triumphant Mr. Sam immediately assumed a fierce and suspicious look, and his eyes turned savagely from Fanny Bolton (whom the reader, no doubt, has recognized in the young lady of the cab) to Arthur Pendennis, advancing to meet her.

Arthur, too, looked dark and suspicious on perceiving Mr. Samuel Huxter in company with his old acquaintances: but his suspicion was that of alarmed morality, and, I dare say, highly creditable to Mr. Arthur: like the suspicion of Mrs. Lynx, when she sees Mr. Brown and Mrs. Jones talking together, or when she remarks Mrs. Lamb twice or thrice in a handsome Opera-box. There *may* be no harm in the conversation of Mr. B. and Mrs. J.: and Mrs. Lamb's Opera-box (though she notoriously can't afford one) may be honestly come by: but yet a moralist like Mrs. Lynx has a right to the little precautionary fright: and Arthur was no doubt justified in adopting that severe demeanour of his.

Fanny's heart began to patter violently: Huxter's fists, plunged into the pockets of his paletot, clenched themselves involuntarily, and armed themselves, as it were, in ambush: Mrs. Bolton began to talk with all her might, and with a wonderful volubility: and Lor! she was so 'appy to see Mr. Pendennis, and how well he was a-lookin', and we'd been talkin' about Mr. P. only jest before; hadn't we, Fanny? and if this was the famous Hepsom races that they talked so much about, she didn't care, for her part, if she never saw them again. And how was Major Pendennis, and that kind Mr. Warrington, who brought Mr. P.'s great kindness to Fanny; and she never would forget it, never: and Mr. Warrington was so tall, he almost broke his 'ead up against their lodge door. You recollect Mr. Warrington a-knockin' of his 'ead—don't you, Fanny?

Whilst Mrs. Bolton was so discoursing, I wonder how many thousands of thoughts passed through Fanny's mind, and what dear times, sad struggles, lonely griefs, and subsequent shamefaced consolations were recalled to her?

What pangs had the poor little thing, as she thought how much she had loved him, and that she loved him no more ? There he stood, about whom she was going to die ten months since, dandified, supercilious, with a black crape to his white hat, and jet buttons in his shirt-front : and a pink in his coat, that someone else had probably given him : with the tightest lavender-coloured gloves sewn with black : and the smallest of canes. And Mr. Huxter wore no gloves, and great Blucher boots, and smelt very much of tobacco certainly ; and looked, oh, it must be owned, he looked as if a bucket of water would do him a great deal of good ! All these thoughts, and a myriad of others, rushed through Fanny's mind as her mamma was delivering herself of her speech, and as the girl, from under her eyes, surveyed Pendennis—surveyed him entirely from head to foot, the circle on his white forehead that his hat left when he lifted it (his beautiful, beautiful hair had grown again), the trinkets at his watch-chain, the ring on his hand under his glove, the neat shining boot, so, so unlike Sam's highlow !—and after her hand had given a little twittering pressure to the lavender-coloured kid grasp which was held out to it, and after her mother had delivered herself of her speech, all Fanny could find to say was : 'This is Mr. Samuel Huxter, whom you knew formerly, I believe, sir ; Mr. Samuel, you know you knew Mr. Pendennis formerly—and—and, will you take a little refreshment ?'

These little words, tremulous and uncoloured as they were, yet were understood by Pendennis in such a manner as to take a great load of suspicion from off his mind—of remorse, perhaps, from his heart. The frown on the countenance of the prince of Fairoaks disappeared, and a good-natured smile and a knowing twinkle of the eyes illuminated his highness's countenance. 'I am very thirsty,' he said, 'and I will be glad to drink your health, Fanny ; and I hope Mr. Huxter will pardon me for having been very rude to him the last time we met, and when I was so ill and out of spirits, that indeed I scarcely knew what I said.' And herewith the lavender-coloured dexter kid glove was handed out, in token of amity, to Huxter.

The dirty fist in the young surgeon's pocket was obliged to undouble itself, and come out of its ambush disarmed. The poor fellow himself felt, as he laid it in Pen's hand, how hot his own was, and how black—it left black marks on

MR. ARTHUR AND MR. SAMUEL

Pen's gloves ; he saw them,—he would have liked to have clenched it again and dashed it into the other's good-humoured face ; and have seen, there upon that ground, with Fanny, with all England looking on, which was the best man—he Sam Huxter of Bartholomew's, or that grinning dandy.

Pen, with ineffable good-humour, took a glass—he didn't mind what it was—he was content to drink after the ladies ; and he filled it with frothing lukewarm beer, which he pronounced to be delicious, and which he drank cordially to the health of the party.

As he was drinking and talking on in an engaging manner, a young lady in a shot dove-coloured dress, with a white parasol lined with pink, and the prettiest dove-coloured boots that ever stepped, passed by Pen, leaning on the arm of a stalwart gentleman with a military moustache.

The young lady clenched her little fist, and gave a mischievous side-look as she passed Pen. He of the moustachios burst out into a jolly laugh. He had taken off his hat to the ladies of cab No. 2,002. You should have seen Fanny Bolton's eyes watching after the dove-coloured young lady. Immediately Huxter perceived the direction which they took, they ceased looking after the dove-coloured nymph, and they turned and looked into Sam Huxter's orbs with the most artless good-humoured expression.

'What a beautiful creature !' Fanny said. 'What a lovely dress ! Did you remark, Mr. Sam, such little, little hands ?'

'It was Capting Strong,' said Mrs. Bolton : 'and who was the young woman, I wonder ?'

'A neighbour of mine in the country—Miss Amory,' Arthur said,—'Lady Clavering's daughter. You've seen Sir Francis often in Shepherd's Inn, Mrs. Bolton.'

As he spoke, Fanny built up a perfect romance in three volumes—love—faithlessness—splendid marriage at St. George's, Hanover Square—broken-hearted maid—and Sam Huxter was not the hero of that story—poor Sam, who by this time had got out an exceedingly rank Cuba cigar, and was smoking it under Fanny's little nose.

After that confounded prig Pendennis joined and left the party, the sun was less bright to Sam Huxter, the sky less blue—the sticks had no attraction for him—the bitter beer was hot and undrinkable—the world was changed. He had

a quantity of peas and a tin pea-shooter in the pocket of the cab for amusement on the homeward route. He didn't take them out, and forgot their existence until some other wag, on their return from the races, fired a volley into Sam's sad face; upon which salute, after a few oaths indicative of surprise, he burst into a savage and sardonic laugh.

But Fanny was charming all the way home. She coaxed, and snuggled, and smiled. She laughed pretty laughs; she admired everything; she took out the darling little Jack-in-the-boxes, and was *so* obliged to Sam. And when they got home, and Mr. Huxter, still with darkness on his countenance, was taking a frigid leave of her—she burst into tears, and said he was a naughty, unkind thing.

Upon which, with a burst of emotion almost as emphatic as hers, the young surgeon held the girl in his arms—swore that she was an angel, and that he was a jealous brute; owned that he was unworthy of her, and that he had no right to hate Pendennis; and asked her, implored her, to say once more that she——

That she what ?—The end of the question and Fanny's answer were pronounced by lips that were so near each other, that no bystander could hear the words. Mrs. Bolton only said, 'Come, come, Mr. H.—no nonsense, if you please; and I think you've acted like a wicked wretch, and been most uncommon cruel to Fanny, that I do.'

When Arthur left No. 2,002, he went to pay his respects to the carriage to which, and to the side of her mamma, the dove-coloured author of *Mes Larmes* had by this time returned. Indefatigable old Major Pendennis was in waiting upon Lady Clavering, and had occupied the back seat in her carriage; the box being in possession of young Hopeful, under the care of Captain Strong.

A number of dandies, and men of a certain fashion—of military bucks, of young rakes of the public offices, of those who may be styled men's men rather than ladies'—had come about the carriage during its station on the hill—and had exchanged a word or two with Lady Clavering, and a little talk (a little 'chaff' some of the most elegant of the men styled their conversation) with Miss Amory. They had offered her sportive bets, and exchanged with her all sorts of free-talk and knowing innuendoes. They pointed

MR. SAMUEL ASKS A QUESTION

out to her who was on the course : and the 'who' was not always the person a young lady should know.

When Pen came up to Lady Clavering's carriage, he had to push his way through a crowd of these young bucks who were paying their court to Miss Amory, in order to arrive as near that young lady, who beckoned him by many pretty signals to her side.

'*Je l'ai vue,*' she said ; '*elle a de bien beaux yeux ; vous êtes un monstre !*'

'Why monster ?' said Pen, with a laugh ; '*Honi soit qui mal y pense.* My young friend, yonder, is as well protected as any young lady in Christendom. She has her mamma on one side, her *prétendu* on the other. Could any harm happen to a girl between those two ?'

'One does not know what may or may not arrive,' said Miss Blanche, in French, 'when a girl has the mind, and when she is pursued by a wicked monster like you. Figure to yourself, major, that I come to find monsieur, your nephew, near to a cab, by two ladies and a man, oh, such a man ! and who ate lobsters, and who laughed, who laughed !'

'It did not strike me that the man laughed,' Pen said. 'And as for lobsters, I thought he would have liked to eat me after the lobsters. He shook hands with me, and gripped me so, that he bruised my glove black and blue. He is a young surgeon. He comes from Clavering. Don't you remember the gilt pestle and mortar in High Street ?'

'If he attends you when you are sick,' continued Miss Amory, 'he will kill you. He will serve you right ; for you are a monster.'

The perpetual recurrence to the word 'monster' jarred upon Pen. 'She speaks about these matters a great deal too lightly,' he thought. 'If I had been a monster, as she calls it, she would have received me just the same. This is not the way in which an English lady should speak or think. Laura would not speak in that way, thank God ;' and as he thought so, his own countenance fell.

'Of what are you thinking ? Are you going to *bouder* me* at present ?' Blanche asked. 'Major, scold your *méchant* nephew. He does not amuse me at all. He is as *bête* as Captain Crackenbury.'

'What are you saying about me, Miss Amory ?' said the Guardsman, with a grin. 'If it's anything good, say it in

English, for I don't understand French when it's spoke so devilish quick.'

'It *ain't* anything good, Crack,' said Crackenbury's fellow, Captain Clinker. 'Let's come away, and don't spoil sport. They say Pendennis is sweet upon her.'

'I'm told he's a devilish clever fellow,' sighed Crackenbury. 'Lady Violet Lebas says he's a devilish clever fellow. He wrote a work, or a poem, or something; and he writes those devilish clever things in the—in the papers, you know. Dammy, I wish *I* was a clever fellow, Clinker.'

'That's past wishing for, Crack, my boy,' the other said. 'I can't write a good book, but I think I can make a pretty good one on the Derby. What a flat Clavering is! And the Begum! I like that old Begum. She's worth ten of her daughter. How pleased the old girl was at winning the lottery!'

'Clavering's safe to pay up, ain't he?' asked Captain Crackenbury.

'I hope so,' said his friend; and they disappeared, to enjoy themselves among the sticks.

Before the end of the day's amusements, many more gentlemen of Lady Clavering's acquaintance came up to her carriage, and chatted with the party which it contained. The worthy lady was in high spirits and good-humour, laughing and talking according to her wont, and offering refreshments to all her friends, until her ample baskets and bottles were emptied, and her servants and postillions were in such a royal state of excitement as servants and postillions commonly are upon the Derby Day.

The major remarked that some of the visitors to the carriage appeared to look with rather queer and meaning glances towards its owner. 'How easily she takes it!' one man whispered to another. 'The Begum's made of money,' the friend replied. 'How easily she takes what?' thought old Pendennis. 'Has anybody lost any money?' Lady Clavering said she was happy in the morning because Sir Francis had promised her not to bet.

Mr. Welbore, the country neighbour of the Claverings, was passing the carriage, when he was called back by the Begum, who rallied him for wishing to cut her. 'Why didn't he come before? Why didn't he come to lunch?' Her ladyship was in great delight, she told him—she told everybody, that she had won five pounds in a lottery. As

she conveyed this piece of intelligence to him, Mr. Welbore looked so particularly knowing, and withal melancholy, that a dismal apprehension seized upon Major Pendennis. 'He would go and look after the horses and those rascals of postillions, who were so long in coming round.' When he came back to the carriage, his usually benign and smirking countenance was obscured by some sorrow. 'What is the matter with you now ?' the good-natured Begum asked. The major pretended a headache from the fatigue and sunshine of the day. The carriage wheeled off the course and took its way Londonwards, not the least brilliant equipage in that vast and picturesque procession. The tipsy drivers dashed gallantly over the turf, amidst the admiration of foot-passengers, the ironical cheers of the little donkey-carriages and spring-vans, and the loud objurgations of horse-and-chaise men, with whom the reckless post-boys came in contact. The jolly Begum looked the picture of good-humour as she reclined on her splendid cushions ; the lovely Sylphide smiled with languid elegance. Many an honest holiday-maker, with his family wadded into a tax-cart, many a cheap dandy working his way home on his weary hack, admired that brilliant turn-out, and thought, no doubt, how happy those 'swells' must be. Strong sat on the box still, with a lordly voice calling to the post-boys and the crowd. Master Frank had been put inside of the carriage and was asleep there by the side of the major, dozing away the effects of the constant luncheon and champagne of which he had freely partaken.

The major was revolving in his mind meanwhile the news the receipt of which had made him so grave. 'If Sir Francis Clavering goes on in this way,' Pendennis the elder thought, 'this little tipsy rascal will be as bankrupt as his father and grandfather before him. The Begum's fortune can't stand such drains upon it : no fortune can stand them : she has paid his debts half a dozen times already. A few years more of the turf, and a few *coups* like this will ruin her.'

'Don't you think we could get up races at Clavering, mamma ?' Miss Amory asked. 'Yes, we must have them there again. There were races there in the old times, the good old times. It's a national amusement, you know : and we could have a Clavering ball : and we might have dances for the tenantry, and rustic sports in the park.—Oh, it would be charming.'

'Capital fun,' said mamma. 'Wouldn't it, major?'

'The turf is a very expensive amusement, my dear lady,' Major Pendennis answered, with such a rueful face, that the Begum rallied him, and asked laughingly whether he had lost money on the race?

After a slumber of about an hour and a half, the heir of the house began to exhibit symptoms of wakefulness, stretching his youthful arms over the major's face, and kicking his sister's knees as she sat opposite to him. When the amiable youth was quite restored to consciousness, he began a sprightly conversation.

'I say, ma,' he said, 'I've gone and done it this time, I have.'

'What have you gone and done, Franky dear?' asked mamma.

'How much is seventeen half-crowns? Two pound and half a crown, ain't it? I drew Borax in our lottery, but I bought Podasokus and Man-milliner of Leggat minor for two open tarts and a bottle of ginger-beer.'

'You little wicked gambling creature, how dare you begin so soon?' cried Miss Amory.

'Hold *your* tongue, if you please. Whoever asked *your* leave, miss?' the brother said. 'And I say, ma——'

'Well, Franky dear?'

'You'll tip me all the same, you know, when I go back——' And here he broke out into a laugh. 'I say, ma, shall I tell you something?'

The Begum expressed her desire to hear this something, and her son and heir continued:—

'When me and Strong was down at the grand stand after the race, and I was talking to Leggat minor, who was there with his governor, I saw pa look as savage as a bear. And I say, ma, Leggat minor told me that he heard his governor say that pa had lost seven thousand backing the favourite. I'll never back the favourite when I'm of age. No, no—hang me if I do: leave me alone, Strong, will you?'

'Captain Strong! Captain Strong! is this true?' cried out the unfortunate Begum. 'Has Sir Francis been betting again? He promised me he wouldn't. He gave me his word of honour he wouldn't.'

Strong, from his place on the box, had overheard the end of young Clavering's communication, and was trying in vain to stop his unlucky tongue.

'I'm afraid it's true, ma'am,' he said, turning round. 'I deplore the loss as much as you can. He promised me as he promised you; but the play is too strong for him! he can't refrain from it.'

Lady Clavering at this sad news burst into a fit of tears. She deplored her wretched fate as the most miserable of women. She declared she would separate, and pay no more debts for this ungrateful man. She narrated with tearful volubility a score of stories only too authentic, which showed how her husband had deceived, and how constantly she had befriended him: and in this melancholy condition, whilst young Hopeful was thinking about the two guineas which he himself had won; and the major revolving, in his darkened mind, whether certain plans which he had been forming had better not be abandoned; the splendid carriage drove up at length to the Begum's house in Grosvenor Place; the idlers and boys lingering about the place to witness, according to public wont, the close of the Derby Day, cheering the carriage as it drew up, and envying the happy folks who descended from it.

'And it's for the son of this man that I am made a beggar!' Blanche said, quivering with anger, as she walked upstairs leaning on the major's arm—'for this cheat—for this black-leg—for this liar—for this robber of women.'

'Calm yourself, my dear Miss Blanche,' the old gentleman said; 'I pray, calm yourself. You have been hardly treated, most unjustly. But remember that you have always a friend in me; and trust to an old fellow who will try and serve you.'

And the young lady, and the heir of the hopeful house of Clavering, having retired to their beds, the remaining three of the Epsom party remained for some time in deep consultation.

CHAPTER LIX

EXPLANATIONS

ALMOST a year, as the reader will perceive, has passed since an event described a few pages back. Arthur's black coat is about to be exchanged for a blue one. His person has undergone other more pleasing and remarkable changes. His wig has been laid aside, and his hair, though somewhat thinner, has returned to public view. And he has had the honour of appearing at Court in the uniform of a cornet of the Clavering troop of the ——shire Yeomanry Cavalry, being presented to the Sovereign by the Marquis of Steyne.

This was a measure strongly and pathetically urged by Arthur's uncle. The major would not hear of a year passing before this ceremony of gentlemanhood was gone through. The old gentleman thought that his nephew should belong to some rather more select club than the Polyanthus[1]; and has announced everywhere in the world his disappointment that the young man's property has turned out not by any means as well as he could have hoped, and is under fifteen hundred a-year.

That is the amount at which Pendennis's property is set down in the world—where his publishers begin to respect him much more than formerly, and where even mammas are by no means uncivil to him. For if the pretty daughters are, naturally, to marry people of very different expectations—at any rate, he will be eligible for the plain ones: and if the brilliant and fascinating Myra is to hook an earl, poor little Beatrice, who has one shoulder higher than the other, must hang on to some boor through life, and why should not Mr. Pendennis be her support? In the very first winter after the accession to his mother's fortune, Mrs. Hawxby in a country-house caused her Beatrice to learn billiards from Mr. Pendennis, and would be driven by

nobody but him in the pony-carriage, because he was literary and her Beatrice was literary too, and declared that the young man, under the instigation of his horrid old uncle, had behaved most infamously in trifling with Beatrice's feelings. The truth is the old gentleman, who knew Mrs. Hawxby's character, and how desperately that lady would practise upon unwary young men, had come to the country-house in question and carried Arthur out of the danger of her immediate claws, though not out of the reach of her tongue. The elder Pendennis would have had his nephew pass a part of the Christmas at Clavering, whither the family had returned; but Arthur had not the heart for that. Clavering was too near poor old Fairoaks; and that was too full of sad recollections for the young man.

We have lost sight of the Claverings, too, until their re-appearance upon the Epsom race-ground, and must give a brief account of them in the interval. During the past year, the world has not treated any member of the Clavering family very kindly. Lady Clavering, one of the best-natured women that ever enjoyed a good dinner, or made a slip in grammar, has had her appetite and good-nature sadly tried by constant family grievances, and disputes such as make the efforts of the best French cook unpalatable, and the most delicately-stuffed sofa-cushions hard to lie on. 'I'd rather have a turnip, Strong, for dessert, than that pineapple, and all them Muscatel grapes, from Clavering,' says poor Lady Clavering, looking at her dinner-table, and confiding her griefs to her faithful friend, 'if I could but have a little quiet to eat it with. Oh, how much happier I was when I was a widow, and before all this money fell in to me!'

The Clavering family had indeed made a false start in life, and had got neither comfort nor position, nor thanks for the hospitalities which they administered, nor a return of kindness from the people whom they entertained. The success of their first London season was doubtful; and their failure afterwards notorious. 'Human patience was not great enough to put up with Sir Francis Clavering,' people said. 'He was too hopelessly low, dull, and disreputable. You could not say what, but there was a taint about the house and its *entourages*. Who was the Begum, with her money, and without her *h*'s, and where did she come from? What an extraordinary little piece of conceit the daughter

was, with her Gallicized graces, and daring affectations, not fit for well-bred English girls to associate with! What strange people were those they assembled round about them! Sir Francis Clavering was a gambler, living notoriously in the society of black-legs and profligates. Hely Clinker, who was in his regiment, said that he not only cheated at cards, but showed the white feather. What could Lady Rockminster have meant by taking her up?' After the first season, indeed, Lady Rockminster, who had taken up Lady Clavering, put her down; the great ladies would not take their daughters to her parties: the young men who attended them behaved with the most odious freedom and scornful familiarity; and poor Lady Clavering herself avowed that she was obliged to take what she called 'the canal'* into her parlour, because the tiptops wouldn't come.

She had not the slightest ill-will towards 'the canal,' the poor dear lady, or any pride about herself, or idea that she was better than her neighbour; but she had taken implicitly the orders which on her entry into the world her social godmother had given her: she had been willing to know whom they knew, and ask whom they asked. The 'canal,' in fact, was much pleasanter than what is called 'society'; but, as we said before, that to leave a mistress is easy, while, on the contrary, to be left by her is cruel; so you may give up society without any great pang, or anything but a sensation of relief at the parting; but severe are the mortifications and pains you have if society gives up you.

One young man of fashion we have mentioned, who at least it might have been expected would have been found faithful amongst the faithless, and Harry Foker, Esq., was indeed that young man. But he had not managed matters with prudence, and the unhappy passion at first confided to Pen, became notorious and ridiculous to the town, was carried to the ears of his weak and fond mother, and finally brought under the cognizance of the bald-headed and inflexible Foker senior.

When Mr. Foker learned this disagreeable news, there took place between him and his son a violent and painful scene, which ended in the poor little gentleman's banishment from England for a year, with a positive order to return at the expiration of that time and complete his marriage with his cousin, or to retire into private life and

three hundred a year altogether, and never see parent or brewery more. Mr. Henry Foker went away then, carrying with him that grief and care which passes free at the strictest Custom-houses, and which proverbially accompanies the exile; and with this crape over his eyes, even the Parisian Boulevard looked melancholy to him, and the sky of Italy black.

To Sir Francis Clavering, that year was a most unfortunate one. The events described in the last chapter came to complete the ruin of the year. It was that year of grace in which, as our sporting readers may remember, Lord Harrowhill's horse (he was a classical young nobleman, and named his stud out of the *Iliad*)—when Podasokus won the Derby, to the dismay of the knowing ones, who pronounced the winning horse's name in various extraordinary ways, and who backed Borax, who was nowhere in the race. Sir Francis Clavering, who was intimate with some of the most rascally characters of the turf, and, of course, had valuable 'information,' had laid heavy odds against the winning horse, and backed the favourite freely, and the result of his dealings was, as his son correctly stated to poor Lady Clavering, a loss of seven thousand pounds.

Indeed, it was a cruel blow upon the lady, who had discharged her husband's debts many times over: who had received as many times his oaths and promises of amendment; who had paid his money-lenders and horse-dealers; who had furnished his town and country houses; and who was called upon now instantly to meet this enormous sum, the penalty of her cowardly husband's extravagance.

It has been described in former pages how the elder Pendennis had become the adviser of the Clavering family, and, in his quality of intimate friend of the house, had gone over every room of it, and even seen that ugly closet which we all of us have, and in which, according to the proverb, the family skeleton is locked up. About the baronet's pecuniary matters, if the major did not know, it was because Clavering himself did not know them, and hid them from himself and others in such a hopeless entanglement of lies that it was impossible for adviser or attorney or principal to get an accurate knowledge of his affairs. But, concerning Lady Clavering, the major was much better informed; and when the unlucky mishap of the Derby arose, he took upon himself to become

completely and thoroughly acquainted with all her means, whatsoever they were; and was now accurately informed of the vast and repeated sacrifices which the widow Amory had made in behalf of her present husband.

He did not conceal—and he had won no small favour from Miss Blanche by avowing it—his opinion, that Lady Clavering's daughter had been hardly treated at the expense of her son, by her second marriage: and in his conversations with Lady Clavering had fairly hinted that he thought Miss Blanche ought to have a better provision. We have said that he had already given the widow to understand that he knew *all* the particulars of her early and unfortunate history, having been in India at the time when—when the painful circumstances occurred which had ended in her parting from her first husband. He could tell her where to find the Calcutta newspaper which contained the account of Amory's trial, and he showed, and the Begum was not a little grateful to him for his forbearance, how, being aware all along of this mishap which had befallen her, he had kept all knowledge of it to himself, and been constantly the friend of her family.

'Interested motives, my dear Lady Clavering,' he said, 'of course I may have had. We all have interested motives, and mine, I don't conceal from you, was to make a marriage between my nephew and your daughter.' To which Lady Clavering, perhaps with some surprise that the major should choose her family for a union with his own, said she was quite willing to consent.

But frankly he said, 'My dear lady, my boy has but five hundred a year, and a wife with ten thousand pounds to her fortune would scarcely better him. We could do better for him than that, permit me to say, and he is a shrewd cautious young fellow who has sown his wild oats now—who has very good parts and plenty of ambition—and whose object in marrying is to better himself. If you and Sir Francis chose—and Sir Francis, take my word for it, will refuse you nothing—you could put Arthur in a way to advance very considerably in the world, and show the stuff which he has in him. Of what use is that seat in Parliament to Clavering, who scarcely ever shows his face in the House, or speaks a word there? I'm told by gentlemen who heard my boy at Oxbridge, that he was famous as an orator, begad!—and once put his foot into the stirrup

and mount him, I've no doubt he won't be the last of the field, ma'am. I've tested the chap, and know him pretty well, I think. He is much too lazy, and careless, and flighty a fellow, to make a jog-trot journey, and arrive, as your lawyers do, at the end of their lives ! but give him a start and good friends, and an opportunity, and take my word for it, he'll make himself a name that his sons shall be proud of. I don't see any way for a fellow like him to *parvenir*, but by making a prudent marriage—not with a beggarly heiress—to sit down for life upon a miserable fifteen hundred a year—but with somebody whom he can help, and who can help him forward in the world, and whom he can give a good name and a station in the country, begad, in return for the advantages which she brings him. It would be better for you to have a distinguished son-in-law, than to keep your husband on in Parliament, who's of no good to himself or to anybody else there, and that's, I say, why I've been interested about you, and offer you what I think a good bargain for both.'

'You know I look upon Arthur as one of the family almost now,' said the good-natured Begum ; 'he comes and goes when he likes ; and the more I think of his dear mother, the more I see there's few people so good—none so good to me. And I'm sure I cried when I heard of her death, and would have gone into mourning for her myself, only black don't become me. And I know who his mother wanted him to marry—Laura, I mean—whom old Lady Rockminster has taken such a fancy to, and no wonder. She's a better girl than my girl. I know both. And my Betsy —Blanche, I mean—ain't been a comfort to me, major. It's Laura Pen ought to marry.'

'Marry on five hundred a year ! My dear good soul, you are mad !' Major Pendennis said. 'Think over what I have said to you. Do nothing in your affairs with that unhappy husband of yours without consulting me ; and remember that old Pendennis is always your friend.'

For some time previous, Pen's uncle had held similar language to Miss Amory. He had pointed out to her the convenience of the match which he had at heart, and was bound to say, that mutual convenience was of all things the very best in the world to marry upon—the only thing. 'Look at your love-marriages, my dear young creature. The love-match people are the most notorious of all for

quarrelling afterwards; and a girl who runs away with Jack to Gretna Green, constantly runs away with Tom to Switzerland afterwards. The great point in marriage is for people to agree to be useful to one another. The lady brings the means, and the gentleman avails himself of them. My boy's wife brings the horse, and begad Pen goes in and wins the plate. That's what I call a sensible union. A couple like that have something to talk to each other about when they come together. If you had Cupid himself to talk to—if Blanche and Pen were Cupid and Psyche, begad —they'd begin to yawn after a few evenings, if they had nothing but sentiment to speak on.'

As for Miss Amory, she was contented enough with Pen as long as there was nobody better. And how many other young ladies are like her ?—and how many love-marriages carry on well to the last ?—and how many sentimental firms do not finish in bankruptcy ?—and how many heroic passions don't dwindle down into despicable indifference, or end in shameful defeat ?

These views of life and philosophy the major was constantly, according to his custom, inculcating to Pen, whose mind was such that he could see the right on both sides of many questions, and, comprehending the sentimental life which was quite out of the reach of the honest major's intelligence, could understand the practical life too, and accommodate himself, or think he could accommodate himself, to it. So it came to pass that during the spring succeeding his mother's death he was a good deal under the influence of his uncle's advice, and domesticated in Lady Clavering's house; and in a measure was accepted by Miss Amory without being a suitor, and was received without being engaged. The young people were extremely familiar, without being particularly sentimental, and met and parted with each other in perfect good-humour. 'And I,' thought Pendennis, 'am the fellow who eight years ago had a grand passion, and last year was raging in a fever about Briseis !'*

Yes, it was the same Pendennis, and time had brought to him, as to the rest of us, its ordinary consequences, consolations, developments. We alter very little. When we talk of this man or that woman being no longer the same person whom we remember in youth, and remark (of course

to deplore) changes in our friends, we don't, perhaps, calculate that circumstance only brings out the latent defect or quality, and does not create it. The selfish languor and indifference of to-day's possession is the consequence of the selfish ardour of yesterday's pursuit : the scorn and weariness which cries *vanitas vanitatum* is but the lassitude of the sick appetite palled with pleasure : the insolence of the successful *parvenu* is only the necessary continuance of the career of the needy struggler : our mental changes are like our grey hairs or our wrinkles—but the fulfilment of the plan of mortal growth and decay : that which is snow-white now was glossy black once ; that which is sluggish obesity to-day was boisterous rosy health a few years back ; that calm weariness, benevolent, resigned, and disappointed, was ambition, fierce, and violent, but a few years since, and has only settled into submissive repose after many a battle and defeat. Lucky he who can bear his failure so generously, and give up his broken sword to Fate the Conqueror with a manly and humble heart ! Are you not awe-stricken, you, friendly reader, who, taking the page up for a moment's light reading, lay it down, perchance, for a graver reflection,—to think how you,—who have consummated your success or your disaster, may be holding marked station, or a hopeless and nameless place in the crowd—who have passed through how many struggles of defeat, success, crime, remorse, to yourself only known !—who may have loved and grown cold, wept and laughed again, how often ! —to think how you are the same *You*, whom in childhood you remember, before the voyage of life began ? It has been prosperous, and you are riding into port, the people huzzaing and the guns saluting,—and the lucky captain bows from the ship's side, and there is a care under the star on his breast which nobody knows of : or you are wrecked, and lashed, hopeless, to a solitary spar out at sea :—the sinking man and the successful one are thinking each about home, very likely, and remembering the time when they were children ; alone on the hopeless spar, drowning out of sight ; alone in the midst of the crowd applauding you.

CHAPTER LX

CONVERSATIONS

OUR good-natured Begum was at first so much enraged at this last instance of her husband's duplicity and folly, that she refused to give Sir Francis Clavering any aid in order to meet his debts of honour, and declared that she would separate from him, and leave him to the consequences of his incorrigible weakness and waste. After that fatal day's transactions at the Derby, the unlucky gambler was in such a condition of mind that he was disposed to avoid everybody ; alike his turf-associates with whom he had made debts which he trembled lest he should not have the means of paying, and his wife, his long-suffering banker, on whom he reasonably doubted whether he should be allowed any longer to draw. When Lady Clavering asked the next morning whether Sir Francis was in the house, she received answer that he had not returned that night, but had sent a messenger to his valet, ordering him to forward clothes and letters by the bearer. Strong knew that he should have a visit or a message from him in the course of that or the subsequent day, and accordingly got a note beseeching him to call upon his distracted friend F. C. at Short's Hotel, Blackfriars, and ask for Mr. Francis there. For the baronet was a gentleman of that peculiarity of mind that he would rather tell a lie than not, and always began a contest with fortune by running away and hiding himself. The boots of Mr. Short's establishment, who carried Clavering's message to Grosvenor Place, and brought back his carpet-bag, was instantly aware who was the owner of the bag, and he imparted his information to the footman who was laying the breakfast-table, who carried down the news to the servants' hall, who took it to Mrs. Bonner, my lady's housekeeper and confidential maid, who carried it to my lady. And thus every single person in the Grosvenor Place establishment knew that Sir Francis was

in hiding, under the name of Francis, at an inn in the Blackfriars Road. And Sir Francis's coachman told the news to other gentlemen's coachmen, who carried it to their masters, and to the neighbouring Tattersall's, where very gloomy anticipations were formed that Sir Francis Clavering was about to make a tour in the Levant.

In the course of that day the number of letters addressed to Sir Francis Clavering, Bart., which found their way to his hall-table was quite remarkable. The French cook sent in his account to my lady; the tradesmen who supplied her ladyship's table, and Messrs. Finer and Gimcrack, the mercers and ornamental dealers, and Madame Crinoline, the eminent milliner, also forwarded their little bills to her ladyship, in company with Miss Amory's private, and by no means inconsiderable, account at each establishment.

In the afternoon of the day after the Derby, when Strong (after a colloquy with his principal at Short's Hotel, whom he found crying and drinking curaçao) called to transact business according to his custom at Grosvenor Place, he found all these suspicious documents ranged in the baronet's study; and began to open them and examine them with a rueful countenance.

Mrs. Bonner, my lady's maid and housekeeper, came down upon him whilst engaged in this occupation. Mrs. Bonner, a part of the family and as necessary to her mistress as the Chevalier was to Sir Francis, was of course on Lady Clavering's side in the dispute between her and her husband, and as by duty bound even more angry than her ladyship herself.

'She won't pay, if she takes my advice,' Mrs. Bonner said. 'You'll please to go back to Sir Francis, captain— and he lurking about in a low public-house and don't dare to face his wife like a man!—and say that we won't pay his debts no longer. We made a man of him, we took him out of jail (and other folks too perhaps), we've paid his debts over and over again—we set him up in Parliament and gave him a house in town and country, and where he don't dare show his face, the shabby sneak! We've given him the horse he rides and the dinner he eats and the very clothes he has on his back; and we will give him no more. Our fortune, such as is left of it, is left to ourselves, and we won't waste any more of it on this ungrateful man. We'll give him enough to live upon and leave him, that's

what we'll do: and that's what you may tell him from Susan Bonner.'

Susan Bonner's mistress hearing of Strong's arrival, sent for him at this juncture, and the Chevalier went up to her ladyship not without hopes that he should find her more tractable than her factotum Mrs. Bonner. Many a time before had he pleaded his client's cause with Lady Clavering and caused her good-nature to relent. He tried again once more. He painted in dismal colours the situation in which he had found Sir Francis: and would not answer for any consequences which might ensue if he could not find means of meeting his engagements.

'Kill hisself,' laughed Mrs. Bonner, 'kill hisself, will he? Dying's the best thing he could do.' Strong vowed that he had found him with the razors on the table; but at this, in her turn, Lady Clavering laughed bitterly. 'He'll do himself no harm, as long as there's a shilling left of which he can rob a poor woman. His life's quite safe, captain: you may depend upon that. Ah! it was a bad day that ever I set eyes on him.'

'He's worse than the first man,' cried out my lady's aide-de-camp. 'He was a man, he was—a wild devil, but he had the courage of a man—whereas this fellow—what's the use of my lady paying his bills, and selling her diamonds, and forgiving him? He'll be as bad again next year. The very next chance he has he'll be a-cheating of her, and robbing of her; and her money will go to keep a pack of rogues and swindlers—I don't mean you, captain—you've been a good friend to us enough, bating we wish we'd never set eyes on you.'

The Chevalier saw from the words which Mrs. Bonner had let slip regarding the diamonds, that the kind Begum was disposed to relent once more at least, and that there were hopes still for his principal.

'Upon my word, ma'am,' he said, with a real feeling of sympathy for Lady Clavering's troubles, and admiration for her untiring good-nature, and with a show of enthusiasm which advanced not a little his graceless patron's cause—'anything you say against Clavering, or Mrs. Bonner here cries out against me, is no better than we deserve, both of us, and it was an unlucky day for you when you saw either. He has behaved cruelly to you: and if you were not the most generous and forgiving woman in the world, I know

there would be no chance for him. But you can't let the father of your son be a disgraced man, and send little Frank into the world with such a stain upon him. Tie him down; bind him by any promises you like: I vouch for him that he will subscribe them.'

'And break 'em,' said Mrs. Bonner.

'And keep 'em this time,' cried out Strong. 'He must keep them. If you could have seen how he wept, ma'am! "Oh, Strong," he said to me, "it's not for myself I feel now: it's for my boy—it's for the best woman in England, whom I have treated basely—I know I have." He didn't intend to bet upon this race, ma'am—indeed he didn't. He was cheated into it: all the ring was taken in.* He thought he might make the bet quite safely, without the least risk. And it will be a lesson to him for all his life long. To see a man cry—oh, it's dreadful.'

'He don't think much of making my dear missus cry,' said Mrs. Bonner—'poor dear soul!—look if he does, captain.'

'If you've the soul of a man, Clavering,' Strong said to his principal, when he recounted this scene to him, 'you'll keep your promise this time: and, so help me Heaven! if you break word with her, I'll turn against you, and tell all.'

'What, all?' cried Mr. Francis, to whom his ambassador brought the news back at Short's Hotel, where Strong found the baronet crying and drinking curaçao.

'Psha! Do you suppose I am a fool?' burst out Strong. 'Do you suppose I could have lived so long in the world, Frank Clavering, without having my eyes about me? You know I have but to speak and you are a beggar to-morrow. And I am not the only man who knows your secret.'

'Who else does?' gasped Clavering.

'Old Pendennis does, or I am very much mistaken. He recognized the man the first night he saw him, when he came drunk into your house.'

'He knows it, does he?' shrieked out Clavering. 'Damn him—kill him!'

'You'd like to kill us all, wouldn't you, old boy?' said Strong, with a sneer, puffing his cigar.

The baronet dashed his weak hand against his forehead; perhaps the other had interpreted his wish rightly. 'Oh, Strong!' he cried, 'if I dared, I'd put an end to myself, for

I'm the d——est miserable dog in all England. It's that that makes me so wild and reckless. It's that which makes me take to drink (and he drank, with a trembling hand, a bumper of his fortifier—the curaçao), and to live about with these thieves. I know they're thieves, every one of 'em, d——d thieves. And—and how can I help it?—and I didn't know it, you know—and, by Gad, I'm innocent—and until I saw the d——d scoundrel first, I knew no more about it than the dead—and I'll fly, and I'll go abroad out of the reach of the confounded hells, and I'll bury myself in a forest, by Gad! and hang myself up to a tree—and, oh—I'm the most miserable beggar in all England!' And so with more tears, shrieks, and curses, the impotent wretch vented his grief and deplored his unhappy fate; and, in the midst of groans and despair and blasphemy, vowed his miserable repentance.

The honoured proverb which declares that to be an ill wind which blows good to nobody, was verified in the case of Sir Francis Clavering, and another of the occupants of Mr. Strong's chambers in Shepherd's Inn. The man was 'good,' by a lucky hap, with whom Colonel Altamont made his bet; and on the settling day of the Derby—as Captain Clinker, who was appointed to settle Sir Francis Clavering's book for him (for Lady Clavering, by the advice of Major Pendennis, would not allow the baronet to liquidate his own money transactions), paid over the notes to the baronet's many creditors—Colonel Altamont had the satisfaction of receiving the odds of thirty to one in fifties, which he had taken against the winning horse of the day.

Numbers of the colonel's friends were present on the occasion to congratulate him on his luck—all Altamont's own set, and the gents who met in the private parlour of the convivial Wheeler, my host of the 'Harlequin's Head,' came to witness their comrade's good fortune, and would have liked, with a generous sympathy for success, to share in it. 'Now was the time,' Tom Driver had suggested to the colonel, 'to have up the specie ship that was sunk in the Gulf of Mexico, with the three hundred and eighty thousand dollars on board, besides bars and doubloons.' 'The Tredyddlums were very low—to be bought for an old song—never was such an opportunity for buying shares,' Mr. Keightley insinuated: and Jack Holt pressed forward his tobacco-smuggling scheme, the audacity of which

pleased the colonel more than any other of the speculations proposed to him. Then of the 'Harlequin's Head' boys: there was Jack Rackstraw, who knew of a pair of horses which the colonel must buy; Tom Fleet, whose satirical paper, *The Swell*, wanted but two hundred pounds of capital to be worth a thousand a year to any man—'with such a power and influence, colonel, you rogue, and the entrée of all the green-rooms in London,' Tom urged; whilst little Moss Abrams entreated the colonel not to listen to these absurd fellows with their humbugging speculations, but to invest his money in some good bills which Moss could get for him, and which would return him fifty per cent. as safe as the Bank of England.

Each and all of these worthies came round the colonel with their various blandishments; but he had courage enough to resist them, and to button up his notes in the pocket of his coat, and go home to Strong, and 'sport' the outer door of the chambers. Honest Strong had given his fellow-lodger good advice about all his acquaintances; and though, when pressed, he did not mind frankly taking twenty pounds himself out of the colonel's winnings, Strong was a great deal too upright to let others cheat him.

He was not a bad fellow when in good fortune, this Altamont. He ordered a smart livery for Grady, and made poor old Costigan shed tears of quickly dried gratitude by giving him a five-pound note after a snug dinner at the Back Kitchen, and he bought a green shawl for Mrs. Bolton, and a yellow one for Fanny: the most brilliant 'sacrifices' of a Regent Street haberdasher's window. And a short time after this, upon her birthday, which happened in the month of June, Miss Amory received from 'a friend' a parcel containing an enormous brass-inlaid writing-desk, in which there was a set of amethysts—the most hideous eyes ever looked upon,—a musical snuff-box, and two *Keepsakes* of the year before last, and accompanied with a couple of gown-pieces of the most astounding colours, the receipt of which goods made the Sylphide laugh and wonder immoderately. Now it is a fact that Colonel Altamont had made a purchase of cigars and French silks from some duffers in Fleet Street about this period; and he was found by Strong in the open auction-room in Cheapside, having invested some money in two desks, several pairs of richly-plated candlesticks, a dinner epergne, and a bagatelle-board. The

dinner epergne remained at chambers, and figured at the banquets there, which the colonel gave pretty freely. It seemed beautiful in his eyes, until Jack Holt said it looked as if it had been taken 'in a bill.' And Jack Holt certainly knew.

The dinners were pretty frequent at chambers, and Sir Francis Clavering condescended to partake of them constantly. His own house was shut up: the successor of Mirobolant, who had sent in his bills so prematurely, was dismissed by the indignant Lady Clavering: the luxuriance of the establishment was greatly pruned and reduced. One of the large footmen was cashiered, upon which the other gave warning, not liking to serve without his mate, or in a family where only one footman was kep'. General and severe economical reforms were practised by the Begum in her whole household, in consequence of the extravagance of which her graceless husband had been guilty. The major, as her ladyship's friend; Strong, on the part of poor Clavering; her ladyship's lawyer, and the honest Begum herself, executed these reforms with promptitude and severity. After paying the baronet's debts, the settlement of which occasioned considerable public scandal, and caused the baronet to sink even lower in the world's estimation than he had been before, Lady Clavering quitted London for Tunbridge Wells in high dudgeon, refusing to see her reprobate husband, whom nobody pitied. Clavering remained in London patiently, by no means anxious to meet his wife's just indignation, and sneaked in and out of the House of Commons, whence he and Captain Raff and Mr. Marker would go to have a game at billiards and a cigar: or showed in the sporting public-houses; or he might be seen lurking about Lincoln's Inn and his lawyers', where the principals kept him for hours waiting, and the clerks winked at each other as he sat in their office. No wonder that he relished the dinners at Shepherd's Inn, and was perfectly resigned there: resigned? he was so happy nowhere else; he was wretched amongst his equals, who scorned him—but here he was the chief guest at the table, where they continually addressed him with 'Yes, Sir Francis,' and 'No, Sir Francis,' where he told his wretched jokes, and where he quavered his dreary little French song, after Strong had sung his jovial chorus, and honest Costigan had piped his Irish ditties. Such a jolly *ménage* as Strong's with Grady's Irish stew, and

the Chevalier's brew of punch after dinner, would have been welcome to many a better man than Clavering, the solitude of whose great house at home frightened him, where he was attended only by the old woman who kept the house, and his valet, who sneered at him.

'Yes, dammit,' said he, to his friends in Shepherd's Inn. 'That fellow of mine, I must turn him away, only I owe him two years' wages, curse him, and can't ask my lady. He brings me my tea cold of a morning, with a dem'd leaden teaspoon, and he says my lady's sent all the plate to the banker's, because it ain't safe.—Now, ain't it hard that she won't trust me with a single teaspoon; ain't it ungentlemanlike, Altamont? You know my lady's of low birth—that is—I beg your pardon—hem—that is, it's most cruel of her not to show more confidence in me. And the very servants begin to laugh—the dam scoundrels! I'll break every bone in their great hulking bodies, curse 'em, I will.—They don't answer my bell: and—and my man was at Vauxhall last night, with one of my dress shirts and my velvet waistcoat on, I know it was mine—the confounded impudent blackguard!—and he went on dancing before my eyes, confound him! I'm sure he'll live to be hanged—he deserves to be hanged—all those infernal rascals of valets!'

He was very kind to Altamont now: he listened to the colonel's loud stories when Altamont described how—when he was working his way home once from New Zealand, where he had been on a whaling expedition—he and his comrades had been obliged to shirk on board at night, to escape from their wives,* by Jove—and how the poor devils put out in their canoes when they saw the ship under sail, and paddled madly after her: how he had been lost in the Bush once for three months in New South Wales, when he was there once on a trading speculation: how he had seen Boney at Saint Helena,* and been presented to him with the rest of the officers of the Indiaman of which he was a mate—to all these tales (and over his cups Altamont told many of them; and, it must be owned, lied and bragged a great deal) Sir Francis now listened with great attention; making a point of drinking wine with Altamont at dinner, and of treating him with every distinction.

'Leave him alone, I know what he's a-coming to,' Altamont said, laughing, to Strong, who remonstrated

with him, 'and leave me alone; I know what I'm a-telling, very well. I was officer on board an Indiaman, so I was; I traded to New South Wales, so I did, in a ship of my own, and lost her. I became officer to the Nawaub, so I did; only me and my royal master have had a difference, Strong—that's it. Who's the better or the worse for what I tell? or knows anything about me? The other chap is dead—shot in the Bush, and his body reckonized at Sydney. If I thought anybody would split, do you think I wouldn't wring his neck? I've done as good before now, Strong—I told you how I did for the overseer before I took leave—but in fair fight, I mean—in fair fight; or, raythe, he had the best of it. He had his gun and bay'net, and I had only an axe. Fifty of 'em saw it—aye, and cheered me when I did it—and I'd do it again, —— him, wouldn't I? I ain't afraid of anybody; and I'd have the life of the man who split upon me. That's my maxim, and pass me the liquor—*You* wouldn't turn on a man. I know you. You're an honest feller, and will stand by a feller, and have looked death in the face like a man. But as for that lily-livered sneak—that poor lyin' swindlin' cringin' cur of a Clavering—who stands in my shoes—stands in my shoes, hang him! I'll make him pull my boots off and clean 'em, I will. Ha, ha!' Here he burst out into a wild laugh, at which Strong got up and put away the brandy-bottle. The other still laughed good-humouredly. 'You're right, old boy,' he said; 'you always keep your head cool, you do—and when I begin to talk too much—I say, when I begin to *pitch*, I authorize you, and order you, and command you, to put away the rum-bottle.'[1]

The event for which, with cynical enjoyment, Altamont had been on the look-out, came very speedily. One day, Strong being absent upon an errand for his principal, Sir Francis made his appearance in the chambers, and found the envoy of the Nawaub alone. He abused the world in general for being heartless and unkind to him; he abused his wife for being ungenerous to him: he abused Strong for being ungrateful—hundreds of pounds had he given Ned Strong—been his friend for life and kept him out of jail, by Jove,—and now Ned was taking her ladyship's side against him, and abetting her in her infernal unkind treatment of him. 'They've entered into a conspiracy to keep me penniless, Altamont,' the baronet said: 'they

don't give me as much pocket-money as Frank has at school.'

'Why don't you go down to Richmond and borrow of him, Clavering?' Altamont broke out with a savage laugh. 'He wouldn't see his poor old beggar of a father without pocket-money, would he?'

'I tell you, I've been obliged to humiliate myself cruelly,' Clavering said. 'Look here, sir—look here, at these pawn-tickets! Fancy a Member of Parliament and an old English baronet, by Gad! obliged to put a drawing-room clock and a Buhl inkstand up the spout; and a gold duck's-head paper-holder, that I dare say cost my wife five pounds, for which they'd only give me fifteen and six! Oh, it's a humiliating thing, sir, poverty to a man of my habits; and it's made me shed tears, sir—tears; and that d——d valet of mine—curse him, I wish he was hanged!—has had the confounded impudence to threaten to tell my lady: as if the things in my own house weren't my own, to sell or to keep, or to fling out of window if I chose—by Gad! the confounded scoundrel.'

'Cry a little; don't mind cryin' before me—it'll relieve you, Clavering,' the other said. 'Why, I say, old feller, what a happy feller I once thought you, and what a miserable son of a gun you really are!'

'It's a shame that they treat me so, ain't it?' Clavering went on,—for, though ordinarily silent and apathetic, about his own griefs the baronet could whine for an hour at a time. 'And—and, by Gad, sir, I haven't got the money to pay the very cab that's waiting for me at the door; and the porteress, that Mrs. Bolton, lent me three shillin's, and I don't like to ask her for any more: and I asked that d——d old Costigan, the confounded old penniless Irish miscreant, and he hadn't got a shillin', the beggar; and Campion's out of town, or else he'd do a little bill for me, I know he would.'

'I thought you swore on your honour to your wife that you wouldn't put your name to paper,' said Mr. Altamont, puffing at his cigar.

'Why does she leave me without pocket-money, then? Damme, I must have money,' cried out the baronet. 'Oh, Am——, oh, Altamont, I'm the most miserable beggar alive.'

'You'd like a chap to lend you a twenty-pound note, wouldn't you now?' the other asked.

'If you would, I'd be grateful to you for ever—for ever, my dearest friend,' cried Clavering.

'How much would you give? Will you give a fifty-pound bill, at six months, for half down and half in plate,' asked Altamont.

'Yes, I would, so help me ——, and pay it on the day,'

screamed Clavering. 'I'll make it payable at my bankers': I'll do anything you like.'

'Well, I was only chaffing you. I'll *give* you twenty pound.'

'You said a pony,' interposed Clavering; 'my dear fellow, you said a pony, and I'll be eternally obliged to you; and I'll not take it as a gift—only as a loan, and pay you back in six months. I take my oath I will.'

'Well—well—there's the money, Sir Francis Clavering.

I ain't a bad fellow. When I've money in my pocket, dammy, I spend it like a man. Here's five-and-twenty for you. Don't be losing it at the hells now. Don't be making a fool of yourself. Go down to Clavering Park, and it'll keep you ever so long. You needn't 'ave butchers' meat: there's pigs, I dare say, on the premises: and you can shoot rabbits for dinner, you know, every day till the game comes in. Besides, the neighbours will ask you about to dinner, you know, sometimes: for you *are* a baronet, though you have outrun the constable. And you've got this comfort, that *I'm* off your shoulders for a good bit to come—p'raps this two years—if I don't play; and I don't intend to touch the confounded black and red: and by that time, my lady as you call her—Jimmy, I used to say—will have come round again; and you'll be ready for me, you know, and come down handsomely to yours truly.'

At this juncture of their conversation Strong returned, nor did the baronet care much about prolonging the talk, having got the money: and he made his way from Shepherd's Inn, and went home and bullied his servant in a manner so unusually brisk and insolent, that the man concluded his master must have pawned some more of the house furniture, or, at any rate, have come into possession of some ready money.

'And yet I've looked over the house, Morgan, and I don't think he has took any more of the things,' Sir Francis's valet said to Major Pendennis's man, as they met at their club soon after. 'My lady locked up a'most all the bejewtary* afore she went away, and he couldn't take away the picters and looking-glasses in a cab: and he wouldn't spout the fenders and fire-irons—he ain't so bad as that. But he's got money somehow. He's so dam'd imperent when he have. A few nights ago I sor him at Vauxhall, where I was a-polkin* with Lady Hemly Babewood's gals—a werry pleasant room that is, and an uncommon good lot in it, hall except the 'ousekeeper, and she's methodisticle—I was a-polkin—you're too old a cove to polk, Mr. Morgan—and 'ere's your 'ealth—and I happened to 'ave on some of Clavering's *abberdashery*, and he sor it too: and he didn't dare so much as speak a word.'

'How about the house in St. John's Wood?'* Mr. Morgan asked.

'Execution in it.—Sold up hevery thing: ponies, and pianna, and brougham, and all. Mrs. Montague Rivers hoff to Boulogne,—non est inwentus, Mr. Morgan. It's my belief she put the execution in herself: and was tired of him.'

'Play much?' asked Morgan.

'Not since the smash. When your governor, and the lawyers, and my lady and him had that tremendous scene: he went down on his knees, my lady told Mrs. Bonner, as told me,—and swoar as he never more would touch a card or a dice, or put his name to a bit of paper; and my lady was a-goin' to give him the notes down to pay his liabilities after the race: only your governor said (which he wrote it on a piece of paper, and passed it across the table to the lawyer and my lady) that some one else had better book up for him, for he'd have kep' some of the money. He's a sly old cove, your gov'nor.'

The expression of 'old cove,' thus flippantly applied by the younger gentleman to himself and his master, displeased Mr. Morgan exceedingly. On the first occasion, when Mr. Lightfoot used the obnoxious expression, his comrade's anger was only indicated by a silent frown; but on the second offence, Morgan, who was smoking his cigar elegantly, and holding it on the tip of his penknife, withdrew the cigar from his lips, and took his young friend to task.

'Don't call Major Pendennis an old cove, if you'll 'ave the goodness, Lightfoot, and don't call *me* an old cove, nether. Such words ain't used in society; and we have lived in the fust society, both at 'ome and foring. We've been intimate with the fust statesmen of Europe. When we go abroad we dine with Prince Metternitch and Louy Philup reg'lar. We go here to the best houses, the tip-tops, I tell you. We ride with Lord John and the noble Whycount at the edd of Foring Affairs.* We dine with the Hearl of Burgrave, and are consulted by the Marquis of Steyne in everythink. We *ought* to know a thing or two, Mr. Lightfoot. You're a young man, I'm an old cove, as you say. We've both seen the world, and we both know that it ain't money, nor bein' a baronet, nor 'avin' a town and country 'ouse, nor a paltry five or six thousand a year.'

'It's ten, Mr. Morgan,' cried Mr. Lightfoot, with great animation.

'It *may* have been, sir,' Morgan said, with calm severity;

'it may have been, Mr. Lightfoot, but it ain't six now, nor five, sir. It's been doosedly dipped and cut into, sir, by the confounded extravygance of your master, with his helbow shakin', and his bill discountin', and his cottage in the Regency Park, and his many wickednesses. He's a bad un, Mr. Lightfoot,—a bad lot, sir, and that you know. And it ain't money, sir—not such money as that, at any rate, come from a Calcuttar attorney, and I dussay wrung out of the pore starving blacks—that will give a pusson position in society, as you know very well. We've no money, but we go everywhere; there's not a housekeeper's room, sir, in this town of any consiquince, where James Morgan ain't welcome. And it was me who got you into this Club, Lightfoot, as you very well know, though I am an old cove, and they would have blackballed you without me as sure as your name is Frederic.'

'I know they would, Mr. Morgan,' said the other with much humility.

'Well, then, don't call me an old cove, sir. It ain't gentlemanlike, Frederic Lightfoot, which I knew you when you was a cab-boy, and when your father was in trouble, and got you the place you have now when the Frenchman went away. And if you think, sir, that because you're making up to Mrs. Bonner, who may have saved her two thousand pound—and I dare say she has in five-and-twenty years as she have lived confidential maid to Lady Clavering —yet, sir, you must remember who put you into that service, and who knows what you were before, sir, and it don't become you, Frederic Lightfoot, to call me an old cove.'

'I beg your pardon, Mr. Morgan—I can't do more than make an apology—will you have a glass, sir, and let me drink your 'ealth.'

'You know I don't take sperrits, Lightfoot,' replied Morgan, appeased. 'And so you and Mrs. Bonner is going to put up together, are you?'

'She's old, but two thousand pound's a good bit, you see, Mr. Morgan. And we'll get the "Clavering Arms" for a very little; and that'll be no bad thing when the railroad runs through Clavering. And when we are there, I hope you'll come and see us, Mr. Morgan.'

'It's a stoopid place, and no society,' said Mr. Morgan. 'I know it well. In Mrs. Pendennis's time we used to

go down reg'lar, and the hair refreshed me after the London racket.'

'The railroad will improve Mr. Arthur's property,' remarked Lightfoot. 'What's about the figure of it, should you say, sir ?'

'Under fifteen hundred, sir,' answered Morgan ; at which the other, who knew the extent of poor Arthur's acres, thrust his tongue in his cheek, but remained wisely silent.

'Is his man any good, Mr. Morgan ?' Lightfoot resumed.

'Pigeon ain't used to society as yet ; but he's young and has good talents, and has read a good deal, and I dessay he will do very well,' replied Morgan. 'He wouldn't quite do for *this* kind of thing, Lightfoot, for he ain't seen the world yet.'

When the pint of sherry for which Mr. Lightfoot called, upon Mr. Morgan's announcement that he declined to drink spirits, had been discussed by the two gentlemen, who held the wine up to the light, and smacked their lips, and winked their eyes at it, and rallied the landlord as to the vintage, in the most approved manner of connoisseurs, Morgan's ruffled equanimity was quite restored, and he was prepared to treat his young friend with perfect good-humour.

'What d'you think about Miss Amory, Lightfoot—tell us in confidence, now—Do you think we should do well—you understand—if we make Miss A. into Mrs. A. P., *comprendy-vous ?*'

'She and her ma's always quarrellin',' said Mr. Lightfoot. 'Bonner is more than a match for the old lady, and treats Sir Francis like that—like this year spill, which I fling into the grate. But she daren't say a word to Miss Amory. No more dare none of us. When a visitor comes in, she smiles and languishes, you'd think that butter wouldn't melt in her mouth : and the minute he is gone, very likely, she flares up like a little demon, and says things fit to send you wild. If Mr. Arthur comes, it's "Do let's sing that there delightful song !" or, "Come and write me them pooty verses in this halbum !" and very likely she's been a rilin' her mother, or sticking pins into her maid, a minute before. She do stick pins into her, and pinch her. Mary Hann showed me one of her arms quite black and blue ; and I recklect Mrs. Bonner, who's as jealous of me as a old cat, boxed her ears for showing me. And then you should should see Miss at luncheon, when there's nobody but the

family! She makes b'leave she never heats, and my! you should only jest see her. She has Mary Hann to bring her up plum-cakes and creams into her bedroom; and the cook's the only man in the house she's civil to. Bonner says, how, the second season in London, Mr. Soppington was a-going to propose for her, and actially came one day, and sor her fling a book into the fire, and scold her mother so, that he went down softly by the back droring-room door, which he came in by; and next thing we heard of him was, he was married to Miss Rider. Oh, she's a devil, that little Blanche, and that's my candig apinium, Mr. Morgan.'

'Apinion, not apinium, Lightfoot, my good fellow,' Mr. Morgan said, with parental kindness, and then asked of his own bosom with a sigh, why the deuce does my governor want Master Arthur to marry such a girl as this? and the *tête-à-tête* of the two gentlemen was broken up by the entry of other gentlemen, members of the Club—when fashionable town-talk, politics, cribbage, and other amusements ensued, and the conversation became general.

The Gentleman's Club was held in the parlour of the 'Wheel of Fortune' public-house, in a snug little by-lane, leading out of one of the great streets of May Fair, and frequented by some of the most select gentlemen about town. Their masters' affairs, debts, intrigues, adventures; their ladies' good and bad qualities and quarrels with their husbands; all the family secrets were here discussed with perfect freedom and confidence, and here, when about to enter into a new situation, a gentleman was enabled to get every requisite information regarding the family of which he proposed to become a member. Liveries, it may be imagined, were excluded from this select precinct; and the powdered heads of the largest metropolitan footman might bow down in vain entreating admission into the Gentleman's Club. These outcast giants in plush took their beer in an outer apartment of the 'Wheel of Fortune,' and could no more get an entry into the Club room than a Pall Mall tradesman or a Lincoln's Inn attorney could get admission into Bays's or Spratt's. And it is because the conversation which we have been permitted to overhear here, in some measure explains the characters and bearings of our story, that we have ventured to introduce the reader into a society so exclusive.

CHAPTER LXI

THE WAY OF THE WORLD

A SHORT time after the piece of good fortune which befell Colonel Altamont at Epsom, that gentleman put into execution his projected foreign tour, and the chronicler of the polite world who goes down to London Bridge for the purpose of taking leave of the people of fashion who quit this country, announced that among the company on board the *Soho* to Antwerp last Saturday were 'Sir Robert, Lady, and the Misses Hodge; Mr. Serjeant Kewsy, and Mrs. and Miss Kewsy; Colonel Altamont, Major Coddy,' etc. The colonel travelled in state, and as became a gentleman: he appeared in a rich travelling costume; he drank brandy-and-water freely during the passage, and was not sick, as some of the other passengers were; and he was attended by his body servant, the faithful Irish legionary who had been for some time in waiting upon himself and Captain Strong in their chambers of Shepherd's Inn.

The Chevalier partook of a copious dinner at Blackwall with his departing friend the colonel, and one or two others, who drank many healths to Altamont at that liberal gentleman's expense. 'Strong, old boy,' the Chevalier's worthy chum said, 'if you want a little money, now's your time. I'm your man. You're a good feller, and have been a good feller to me, and a twenty-pound note, more or less, will make no odds to me.' But Strong said, No, he didn't want any money; he was flush, quite flush—'that is, not flush enough to pay you back your last loan, Altamont, but quite able to carry on for some time to come'—and so, with a not uncordial greeting between them, the two parted. Had the possession of money really made Altamont more honest and amiable than he had hitherto been, or only caused him to seem more amiable in Strong's eyes? Perhaps he really was better, and money improved him.

Perhaps it was the beauty of wealth Strong saw and respected. But he argued within himself, 'This poor devil, this unlucky outcast of a returned convict, is ten times as good a fellow as my friend Sir Francis Clavering, Bart. He has pluck and honesty in his way. He will stick to a friend, and face an enemy. The other never had courage to do either. And what is it that has put the poor devil under a cloud ? He was only a little wild, and signed his father-in-law's name. Many a man has done worse, and come to no wrong, and holds his head up. Clavering does. No, he don't hold his head up : he never did in his best days.' And Strong, perhaps, repented him of the falsehood which he had told to the free-handed colonel, that he was not in want of money : but it was a falsehood on the side of honesty, and the Chevalier could not bring down his stomach to borrow a second time from his outlawed friend. Besides, he could get on. Clavering had promised him some : not that Clavering's promises were much to be believed, but the Chevalier was of a hopeful turn, and trusted in many chances of catching his patron, and waylaying some of those stray remittances and supplies, in the procuring of which for his principal lay Mr. Strong's chief business.

He had grumbled about Altamont's companionship in the Shepherd's Inn chambers ; but he found those lodgings more glum now without his partner than with him. The solitary life was not agreeable to his social soul ; and he had got into extravagant and luxurious habits, too, having a servant at his command to run his errands, to arrange his toilettes, and to cook his meal. It was rather a grand and touching sight now to see the portly and handsome gentleman painting his own bocts, and broiling his own mutton-chop. It has been before stated that the Chevalier had a wife, a Spanish lady of Vittoria, who had gone back to her friends, after a few months' union with the captain, whose head she broke with a dish. He began to think whether he should not go back and see his Juanita. The Chevalier was growing melancholy after the departure of his friend the colonel ; or, to use his own picturesque expression, was 'down on his luck.' These moments of depression and intervals of ill-fortune occur constantly in the lives of heroes. Marius at Minturnae, Charles Edward in the Highlands, Napoleon before Elba :—what great man has not been called upon to face evil fortune ?

From Clavering no supplies were to be had for some time. The five-and-twenty pounds, or 'pony,' which the exemplary baronet had received from Mr. Altamont, had fled out of Clavering's keeping as swiftly as many previous ponies. He had been down the river with a choice party of sporting gents, who dodged the police and landed in Essex, where they put up Billy Bluck to fight Dick the cabman, whom the baronet backed, and who had it all his own way for thirteen rounds, when, by an unlucky blow in the windpipe, Billy killed him. 'It's always my luck, Strong,' Sir Francis said ; 'the betting was three to one on the cabman, and I thought myself as sure of thirty pounds, as if I had it in my pocket. And dammy, I owe my man Lightfoot fourteen pound now which he's lent and paid for me : and he duns me—the confounded impudent blackguard : and I wish to Heaven I knew any way of getting a bill done, or of screwing a little out of my lady ! I'll give you half, Ned, upon my soul and honour, I'll give you half if you can get anybody to do us a little fifty.'

But Ned said sternly that he had given his word of honour, as a gentleman, that he would be no party to any future bill transactions in which her husband might engage (who had given his word of honour too), and the Chevalier said that he, at least, would keep his word, and would black his own boots all his life rather than break his promise. And what is more, he vowed he would advise Lady Clavering that Sir Francis was about to break his faith towards her upon the very first hint which he could get that such was Clavering's intention.

Upon this information Sir Francis Clavering, according to his custom, cried and cursed very volubly. He spoke of death as his only resource. He besought and implored his dear Strong, his best friend, his dear old Ned, not to throw him over : and when he quitted his dearest Ned, as he went down the stairs of Shepherd's Inn, swore and blasphemed at Ned as the most infernal villain, and traitor, and blackguard, and coward under the sun, and wished Ned was in his grave, and in a worse place, only he would like the confounded ruffian to live, until Frank Clavering had had his revenge out of him.

In Strong's chambers the baronet met a gentleman whose visits were now, as it has been shown, very frequent in Shepherd's Inn, Mr. Samuel Huxter, of Clavering. That

young fellow, who had poached the walnuts in Clavering Park in his youth, and had seen the baronet drive through the street at home with four horses, and prance up to church with powdered footmen, had an immense respect for his member, and a prodigious delight in making his acquaintance. He introduced himself with much blushing and trepidation, as a Clavering man—son of Mr. Huxter, of the Market Place—father attended Sir Francis's keeper, Coxwood, when his gun burst and took off three fingers—

proud to make Sir Francis's acquaintance. All of which introductions Sir Francis received affably. And honest Huxter talked about Sir Francis to the chaps at Bartholomew's; and told Fanny, in the lodge, that, after all, there was nothing like a thoroughbred un, a regular good old English gentleman, one of the olden time! To which Fanny replied, that she thought Sir Francis was an ojous creature—she didn't know why—but she couldn't abear him—she was sure he was wicked and low and mean—she knew he was; and when Sam to this replied that Sir Francis

was very affable, and had borrowed half a sov' of him quite kindly, Fanny burst into a laugh, pulled Sam's long hair (which was not yet of irreproachable cleanliness), patted his chin, and called him a stoopid, stoopid, old foolish stoopid, and said that Sir Francis was always borrering money of everybody, and that mar had actially refused him twice, and had had to wait three months to get seven shillings which he had borrered of 'er.

'Don't say 'er but her, borrer but borrow, actially but actually, Fanny,' Mr. Huxter replied—not to a fault in her argument, but to grammatical errors in her statement.

'Well then, her, and borrow, and hactually—there, then, you stoopid,' said the other; and the scholar made such a pretty face that the grammar-master was quickly appeased, and would have willingly given her a hundred more lessons on the spot at the price which he took for that one.

Of course Mrs. Bolton was by, and I suppose that Fanny and Mr. Sam were on exceedingly familiar and confidential terms by this time, and that time had brought to the former certain consolations, and soothed certain regrets, which are deucedly bitter when they occur, but which are, no more than tooth-pulling, or any other pang, eternal.

As you sit, surrounded by respect and affection; happy, honoured, and flattered in your old age; your foibles gently indulged; your least words kindly cherished; your garrulous old stories received for the hundredth time with dutiful forbearance, and never-failing hypocritical smiles; the women of your house constant in their flatteries; the young men hushed and attentive when you begin to speak; the servants awe-stricken; the tenants cap in hand, and ready to act in the place of your worship's horses when your honour takes a drive—it has often struck you, O thoughtful Dives! that this respect and these glories are for the main part transferred, with your fee-simple, to your successor—that the servants will bow, and the tenants shout, for your son as for you; that the butler will fetch him the wine (improved by a little keeping) that's now in your cellar; and that, when your night is come, and the light of your life is gone down, as sure as the morning rises after you and without you, the sun of prosperity and flattery shines on your heir. Men come and bask in the halo of Consols and acres that beams round about him: the reverence is

MR. HUXTER LIKES TO BE CALLED A GOOSE

transferred with the estate; of which, with all its advantages, pleasures, respect, and goodwill, he in turn becomes the life-tenant. How long do you wish or expect that your people will regret you? How much time does a man devote to grief before he begins to enjoy? A great man must keep his heir at his feast like a living *memento mori*. If he holds very much by life, the presence of the other must be a constant sting and warning. 'Make ready to go,' says the successor to your honour; 'I am waiting: and I could hold it as well as you.'

What has this reference to the possible reader to do with any of the characters of this history? Do we wish to apologize for Pen because he has got a white hat, and because his mourning for his mother is fainter? All the lapse of years, all the career of fortune, all the events of life, however strongly they may move or eagerly excite him, never can remove that sainted image from his heart, or banish that blessed love from its sanctuary. If he yields to wrong, the dear eyes will look sadly upon him when he dares to meet them; if he does well, endures pain, or conquers temptation, the ever-present love will greet him, he knows, with approval and pity; if he falls, plead for him; if he suffers, cheer him;—be with him and accompany him always until death is past, and sorrow and sin are no more. Is this mere dreaming, or, on the part of an idle story-teller, useless moralizing? May not the man of the world take his moment, too, to be grave and thoughtful? Ask of your own hearts and memories, brother and sister, if we do not live in the dead; and (to speak reverently) prove God by love?

Of these matters Pen and Warrington often spoke in many a solemn and friendly converse in after-days; and Pendennis's mother was worshipped in his memory, and canonized there, as such a saint ought to be. Lucky he in life who knows a few such women! A kind provision of Heaven it was that sent us such; and gave us to admire that touching and wonderful spectacle of innocence, and love, and beauty.

But as it is certain that if, in the course of these sentimental conversations, any outer stranger, Major Pendennis for instance, had walked into Pen's chambers, Arthur and Warrington would have stopped their talk, and chosen another subject, and discoursed about the Opera, or the

last debate in Parliament, or Miss Jones's marriage with Captain Smith, or what not,—so, let us imagine that the public steps in at this juncture, and stops the confidential talk between author and reader, and begs us to resume our remarks about this world, with which both are certainly better acquainted than with that other one into which we have just been peeping.

On coming into his property, Arthur Pendennis at first comported himself with a modesty and equanimity which obtained his friend Warrington's praises, though Arthur's uncle was a little inclined to quarrel with his nephew's meanness of spirit, for not assuming greater state and pretensions now that he had entered on the enjoyment of his kingdom. He would have had Arthur installed in handsome quarters, and riding on showy park hacks, or in well-built cabriolets, every day. 'I am too absent,' Arthur said, with a laugh, 'to drive a cab in London; the omnibuses would cut me in two, or I should send my horse's head into the ladies' carriage windows; and you wouldn't have me driven about by my servant like an apothecary, uncle?' No, Major Pendennis would on no account have his nephew appear like an apothecary; the august representative of the house of Pendennis must not so demean himself. And when Arthur, pursuing his banter, said 'And yet I dare say, sir, my father was proud enough when he first set up his gig,' the old major hemmed and ha'd, and his wrinkled face reddened with a blush as he answered, 'You know what Bonaparte said, sir, "*Il faut laver son linge sale en famille.*" There is no need, sir, for you to brag that your father was a—a medical man. He came of a most ancient but fallen house, and was obliged to reconstruct the family fortunes as many a man of good family has done before him. You are like the fellow in Sterne, sir—the marquis who came to demand his sword again.* Your father got back yours for you. You are a man of landed estate, by Gad, sir, and a gentleman—never forget you are a gentleman.'

Then Arthur slyly turned on his uncle the argument which he had heard the old gentleman often use regarding himself. 'In the society which I have the honour of frequenting through your introduction, who cares to ask about my paltry means or my humble gentility, uncle?' he asked. 'It would be absurd of me to attempt to compete with the

great folks; and all that they can ask from us is, that we should have a decent address and good manners.'

'But for all that, sir, I should belong to a better club or two,' the uncle answered: 'I should give an occasional dinner, and select my society well; and I should come out of that horrible garret in the Temple, sir.' And so Arthur compromised by descending to the second floor in Lamb Court: Warrington still occupying his old quarters, and the two friends being determined not to part one from the other. Cultivate kindly, reader, those friendships of your youth: it is only in that generous time that they are formed. How different the intimacies of after-days are, and how much weaker the grasp of your own hand after it has been shaken about in twenty years' commerce with the world, and has squeezed and dropped a thousand equally careless palms! As you can seldom fashion your tongue to speak a new language after twenty, the heart refuses to receive friendship pretty soon: it gets too hard to yield to the impression.

So Pen had many acquaintances, and being of a jovial and easy turn, got more daily: but no friend like Warrington; and the two men continued to live almost as much in common as the Knights of the Temple, riding upon one horse (for Pen's was at Warrington's service), and having their chambers and their servitor in common.

Mr. Warrington had made the acquaintance of Pen's friends of Grosvenor Place during their last unlucky season in London, and had expressed himself no better satisfied with Sir Francis and Lady Clavering and her ladyship's daughter than was the public in general. 'The world is right,' George said, 'about those people. The young men laugh and talk freely before those ladies, and about them. The girl sees people whom she has no right to know, and talks to men with whom no girl should have an intimacy. Did you see those two reprobates leaning over Lady Clavering's carriage in the park the other day, and leering under Miss Blanche's bonnet? No good mother would let her daughter know those men, or admit them within her doors.'

'The Begum is the most innocent and good-natured soul alive,' interposed Pen. 'She never heard any harm of Captain Blackball, or read that trial in which Charley Lovelace figures. Do you suppose that honest ladies read and

remember the *Chronique Scandaleuse* as well as you, you old grumbler?'

'Would you like Laura Bell to know those fellows?' Warrington asked, his face turning rather red. 'Would you let any woman you loved be contaminated by their company? I have no doubt that the poor Begum is ignorant of their histories. It seems to me she is ignorant of a great number of better things. It seems to me that your honest Begum is not a lady, Pen. It is not her fault, doubtless, that she has not had the education, or learned the refinements of a lady.'

'She is as moral as Lady Portsea, who has all the world at her balls, and as refined as Mrs. Bull, who breaks the king's English, and has half a dozen dukes at her table,' Pen answered rather sulkily. 'Why should you and I be more squeamish than the rest of the world? Why are we to visit the sins of her fathers on this harmless, kind creature? She never did anything but kindness to you or any mortal soul. As far as she knows she does her best. She does not set up to be more than she is. She gives you the best dinners she can buy, and the best company she can get. She pays the debts of that scamp of a husband of hers. She spoils her boy like the most virtuous mother in England. Her opinion about literary matters, to be sure, is not much; and I dare say she never read a line of Wordsworth, or heard of Tennyson in her life.'

'No more has Mrs. Flanagan the laundress,' growled out Pen's Mentor; 'no more has Betty the housemaid; and I have no word of blame against them. But a high-souled man doesn't make friends of these. A gentleman doesn't choose these for his companions, or bitterly rues it afterwards if he do. Are you, who are setting up to be a man of the world and a philosopher, to tell me that the aim of life is to guttle three courses and dine off silver? Do you dare to own to yourself that your ambition in life is good claret, and that you'll dine with any, provided you get a stalled ox to feed on? You call me a cynic—why, what a monstrous cynicism it is, which you and the rest of you men of the world admit. I'd rather live upon raw turnips and sleep in a hollow tree, or turn backwoodsman or savage, than degrade myself to this civilization, and own that a French cook was the thing in life best worth living for.'

Because you like a raw beefsteak and a pipe afterwards,'

broke out Pen, 'you give yourself airs of superiority over people whose tastes are more dainty, and are not ashamed of the world they live in. Who goes about professing particular admiration, or esteem, or friendship, or gratitude even, for the people one meets every day? If A. asks me to his house, and gives me his best, I take his good things for what they are worth and no more. I do not profess to pay him back in friendship, but in the convention's money of society. When we part, we part without any grief. When we meet, we are tolerably glad to see one another. If I were only to live with my friends, your black muzzle, old George, is the only face I should see.'

'You are your uncle's pupil,' said Warrington, rather sadly; 'and you speak like a worldling.'

'And why not?' asked Pendennis; 'why not acknowledge the world I stand upon, and submit to the conditions of the society which we live in and live by? I am older than you, George, in spite of your grizzled whiskers, and have seen much more of the world than you have in your garret here, shut up with your books and your reveries and your ideas of one-and-twenty. I say, I take the world as it is, and being of it, will not be ashamed of it. If the time is out of joint, have I any calling or strength to set it right?'

'Indeed, I don't think you have much of either,' growled Pen's interlocutor.

'If I doubt whether I am better than my neighbour,' Arthur continued,—'if I concede that I am no better,—I also doubt whether he is better than I. I see men who begin with ideas of universal reform, and who, before their beards are grown, propound their loud plans for the regeneration of mankind, give up their schemes after a few years of bootless talking and vainglorious attempts to lead their fellows; and after they have found that men will no longer hear them, as indeed they never were in the least worthy to be heard, sink quietly into the rank and file,—acknowledging their aims impracticable, or thankful that they were never put into practice. The fiercest reformers grow calm, and are fain to put up with things as they are: the loudest Radical orators become dumb, quiescent placemen: the most fervent Liberals, when out of power, become humdrum Conservatives, or downright tyrants, or despots in office. Look at Thiers, look at Guizot, in opposition

and in place !* Look at the Whigs appealing to the country, and the Whigs in power! Would you say that the conduct of these men is an act of treason, as the Radicals bawl,—who would give way in their turn, were their turn ever to come? No, only that they submit to circumstances which are stronger than they,—march as the world marches towards reform, but at the world's pace (and the movements of the vast body of mankind must needs be slow),—forgo this scheme as impracticable, on account of opposition,—that, as immature, because against the sense of the majority,—are forced to calculate drawbacks and difficulties as well as to think of reforms and advances,—and compelled finally to submit, and to wait, and to compromise.'

'The Right Honourable Arthur Pendennis could not speak better, or be more satisfied with himself, if he was First Lord of the Treasury and Chancellor of the Exchequer,' Warrington said.

'Self-satisfied? Why self-satisfied?' continued Pen. 'It seems to me that my scepticism is more respectful and more modest than the revolutionary ardour of other folks. Many a patriot of eighteen, many a Spouting Club orator, would turn the bishops out of the House of Lords to-morrow, and throw the lords out after the bishops, and throw the throne into the Thames after the peers and the bench. Is that man more modest than I, who take these institutions as I find them, and wait for time and truth to develop, or fortify, or (if you like) destroy them? A college tutor, or a nobleman's toady, who appears one fine day as my right reverend lord, in a silk apron and a shovel-hat, and assumes benedictory airs over me, is still the same man we remember at Oxbridge, when he was truckling to the tufts, and bullying the poor undergraduates in the lecture-room. An hereditary legislator, who passes his time with jockeys and blacklegs and ballet-girls, and who is called to rule over me and his other betters because his grandfather made a lucky speculation in the funds, or found a coal or tin mine on his property, or because his stupid ancestor happened to be in command of ten thousand men as brave as himself, who overcame twelve thousand Frenchmen, or fifty thousand Indians—such a man, I say, inspires me with no more respect than the bitterest democrat can feel towards him. But, such as he is, he is a part of the old society to which we belong; and I submit to his lordship with acquiescence;

and he takes his place above the best of us at all dinner-parties, and there bides his time. I don't want to chop his head off with a guillotine, or to fling mud at him in the streets. When they call such a man a disgrace to his order; and such another, who is good and gentle, refined and generous, who employs his great means in promoting every kindness and charity, and art and grace of life, in the kindest and most gracious manner, an ornament to his rank—the question as to the use and propriety of the order is not in the least affected one way or other. There it is, extant among us, a part of our habits, the creed of many of us, the growth of centuries, the symbol of a most complicated tradition—there stand my lord the bishop and my lord the hereditary legislator—what the French call *transactions* both of them,—representing in their present shape mail-clad barons and double-sworded chiefs (from whom their lordships the hereditaries, for the most part, *don't* descend), and priests, professing to hold an absolute truth and a divinely inherited power, the which truth absolute our ancestors burned at the stake, and denied there; the which divine transmissible power still exists in print—to be believed, or not, pretty much at choice; and of these, I say, I acquiesce that they exist, and no more. If you say that these schemes, devised before printing was known, or steam was born; when thought was an infant, scared and whipped; and truth under its guardians was gagged, and swathed, and blindfolded, and not allowed to lift its voice, or to look out or to walk under the sun; before men were permitted to meet, or to trade, or to speak with each other—if anyone says (as some faithful souls do) that these schemes are for ever, and having been changed and modified constantly are to be subject to no further development or decay, I laugh, and let the man speak. But I would have toleration for these, as I would ask it for my own opinions; and if they are to die, I would rather they had a decent and natural than an abrupt and violent death.'

'You would have sacrificed to Jove,' Warrington said, 'had you lived in the time of the Christian persecutions.'

'Perhaps I would,' said Pen, with some sadness. 'Perhaps I am a coward,—perhaps my faith is unsteady; but this is my own reserve. What I argue here is that I will not persecute. Make a faith or a dogma absolute, and persecution becomes a logical consequence; and Dominic burns

a Jew, or Calvin an Arian, or Nero a Christian, or Elizabeth or Mary a Papist or Protestant; or their father both or either, according to his humour; and acting without any pangs of remorse,—but, on the contrary, with strict notions of duty fulfilled. Make dogma absolute, and to inflict or to suffer death becomes easy and necessary; and Mahomet's soldiers shouting "Paradise! Paradise!" and dying on the Christian spears, are not more or less praiseworthy than the same men slaughtering a townful of Jews, or cutting off the heads of all prisoners who would not acknowledge that there was but one Prophet of God.'

'A little while since, young one,' Warrington said, who had been listening to his friend's confessions neither without sympathy nor scorn, for his mood led him to indulge in both, 'you asked me why I remained out of the strife of the world, and looked on at the great labour of my neighbour without taking any part in the struggle? Why, what a mere dilettante you own yourself to be, in this confession of general scepticism, and what a listless spectator yourself! You are six-and-twenty years old, and as blasé as a rake of sixty. You neither hope much, nor care much, nor believe much. You doubt about other men as much as about yourself. Were it made of such *pococuranti* as you, the world would be intolerable; and I had rather live in a wilderness of monkeys, and listen to their chatter, than in a company of men who denied everything.'

'Were the world composed of Saint Bernards or Saint Dominics, it would be equally odious,' said Pen; 'and at the end of a few score years would cease to exist altogether. Would you have every man with his head shaved, and every woman in a cloister,—carrying out to the full the ascetic principle? Would you have conventicle hymns twanging from every lane in every city of the world? Would you have all the birds of the forest sing one note and fly with one feather? You call me a sceptic because I acknowledge what *is;* and in acknowledging that, be it linnet or lark, or priest or parson; be it, I mean, any single one of the infinite varieties of the creatures of God (whose very name I would be understood to pronounce with reverence, and never to approach but with distant awe), I say that the study and acknowledgement of that variety amongst men especially increases our respect and wonder for the Creator, Commander, and Ordainer of all these minds, so different and yet so

united,—meeting in a common adoration, and offering up, each according to his degree and means of approaching the Divine centre, his acknowledgement of praise and worship, each singing (to recur to the bird simile) his natural song.'

'And so, Arthur, the hymn of a saint, or the ode of a poet, or the chant of a Newgate thief, are all pretty much the same in your philosophy,' said George.

'Even that sneer could be answered were it to the point,' Pendennis replied; 'but it is not; and it could be replied to you, that even to the wretched outcry of the thief on the tree, the wisest and the best of all teachers we know of, the untiring Comforter and Consoler, promised a pitiful hearing and a certain hope. Hymns of saints! Odes of poets! who are we to measure the chances and opportunities, the means of doing, or even judging, right and wrong awarded to men; and to establish the rule for meting out their punishments and rewards? We are as insolent and unthinking in judging of men's morals as of their intellects. We admire this man as being a great philosopher, and set down the other as a dullard, not knowing either, or the amount of truth in either, or being certain of the truth anywhere. We sing *Te Deum* for this hero who has won a battle, and *De Profundis* for that other one who has broken out of prison, and has been caught afterwards by the policemen. Our measure of rewards and punishments is most partial and incomplete, absurdly inadequate, utterly worldly, and we wish to continue it into the next world. Into that next and awful world we strive to pursue men, and send after them our impotent party verdicts of condemnation or acquittal. We set up our paltry little rods to measure heaven immeasurable, as if, in comparison to that, Newton's mind, or Pascal's, or Shakespeare's, was any loftier than mine; as if the ray which travels from the sun would reach me sooner than the man who blacks my boots. Measured by that altitude, the tallest and the smallest among us are so alike diminutive and pitifully base, that I say we should take no count of the calculation, and it is a meanness to reckon the difference.'

'Your figure fails there, Arthur,' said the other, better pleased; 'if even by common arithmetic we can multiply as we can reduce almost infinitely, the Great Reckoner must take count of all; and the small is not small, or the great great, to His infinity.'

'I don't call those calculations in question,' Arthur said; 'I only say that yours are incomplete and premature; false in consequence, and, by every operation, multiplying into wider error. I do not condemn the men who killed Socrates and damned Galileo. I say that they damned Galileo and killed Socrates.'

'And yet but a moment since you admitted the propriety of acquiescence in the present, and, I suppose, all other tyrannies?'

'No: but that if an opponent menaces me, of whom and without cost of blood and violence I can get rid, I would rather wait him out, and starve him out, than fight him out. Fabius fought Hannibal sceptically. Who was his Roman coadjutor,* whom we read of in Plutarch when we were boys, who scoffed at the other's procrastination and doubted his courage, and engaged the enemy, and was beaten for his pains?'

In these speculations and confessions of Arthur, the reader may perhaps see allusions to questions which, no doubt, have occupied and discomposed himself, and which he may have answered by very different solutions to those come to by our friend. We are not pledging ourselves for the correctness of his opinions, which readers will please to consider are delivered dramatically, the writer being no more answerable for them, than for the sentiments uttered by any other character of the story: our endeavour is merely to follow out, in its progress, the development of the mind of a worldly and selfish, but not ungenerous or unkind or truth-avoiding man. And it will be seen that the lamentable stage to which his logic at present has brought him, is one of general scepticism and sneering acquiescence in the world as it is; or if you like so to call it, a belief qualified with scorn in all things extant. The tastes and habits of such a man prevent him from being a boisterous demagogue, and his love of truth and dislike of cant keep him from advancing crude propositions, such as many loud reformers are constantly ready with; much more of uttering downright falsehoods in arguing questions or abusing opponents, which he would die or starve rather than use. It was not in our friend's nature to be able to utter certain lies; nor was he strong enough to protest against others, except with a polite sneer; his maxim being, that he owed

obedience to all Acts of Parliament, as long as they were not repealed.

And to what does this easy and sceptical life lead a man? Friend Arthur was a Sadducee, and the Baptist might be in the wilderness shouting to the poor, who were listening with all their might and faith to the preacher's awful accents and denunciations of wrath or woe or salvation; and our friend the Sadducee would turn his sleek mule with a shrug and a smile from the crowd, and go home to the shade of his terrace, and muse over preacher and audience, and turn to his roll of Plato, or his pleasant Greek song-book babbling of honey and Hybla, and nymphs and fountains and love. To what, we say, does this scepticism lead? It leads a man to a shameful loneliness and selfishness, so to speak—the more shameful, because it is so good-humoured and conscienceless and serene. Conscience! What is conscience? Why accept remorse? What is public or private faith? Mythuses alike enveloped in enormous tradition. If seeing and acknowledging the lies of the world, Arthur, as see them you can with only too fatal a clearness, you submit to them without any protest further than a laugh: if, plunged yourself in easy sensuality, you allow the whole wretched world to pass groaning by you unmoved: if the fight for the truth is taking place, and all men of honour are on the ground armed on the one side or the other, and you alone are to lie on your balcony and smoke your pipe out of the noise and the danger, you had better have died, or never have been at all, than such a sensual coward.

'The truth, friend!' Arthur said imperturbably; 'where is the truth? Show it me. That is the question between us. I see it on both sides. I see it in the Conservative side of the House, and amongst the Radicals, and even on the ministerial benches.* I see it in this man who worships by Act of Parliament, and is rewarded with a silk apron and five thousand a year; in that man, who, driven fatally by the remorseless logic of his creed, gives up everything, friends, fame, dearest ties, closest vanities, the respect of an army of Churchmen, the recognized position of a leader, and passes over, truth-impelled, to the enemy, in whose ranks he is ready to serve henceforth as a nameless private soldier:—I see the truth in that man, as I do in his brother, whose logic drives him to quite a different

conclusion, and who, after having passed a life in vain endeavours to reconcile an irreconcilable book, flings it at last down in despair, and declares, with tearful eyes, and hands up to heaven, his revolt and recantation.* If the truth is with all these, why should I take side with any one of them? Some are called upon to preach: let them preach. Of these preachers there are somewhat too many, methinks, who fancy they have the gift. But we cannot all be parsons in church, that is clear. Some must sit silent, and listen, or go to sleep mayhap. Have we not all our duties? The head charity-boy blows the bellows; the master canes the other boys in the organ-loft; the clerk sings out Amen from the desk; and the beadle with the staff opens the door for his reverence, who rustles in silk up to the cushion. I won't cane the boys, nay, or say Amen always, or act as the church's champion or warrior, in the shape of the beadle with the staff; but I will take off my hat in the place, and say my prayers there too, and shake hands with the clergyman as he steps on the grass outside. Don't I know that his being there is a compromise, and that he stands before me an Act of Parliament? That the church he occupies was built for other worship? That the Methodist chapel is next door; and that Bunyan the tinker is bawling out the tidings of damnation on the common hard by? Yes, I am a Sadducee; and I take things as I find them, and the world, and the Acts of Parliament of the world, as they are; and as I intend to take a wife, if I find one—not to be madly in love and prostrate at her feet like a fool—not to worship her as an angel, or to expect to find her as such—but to be good-natured to her, and courteous, expecting good-nature and pleasant society from her in turn. And so, George, if ever you hear of my marrying, depend upon it, it won't be a romantic attachment on my side: and if you hear of any good place under Government, I have no particular scruples that I know of, which would prevent me from accepting your offer.'

'O Pen, you scoundrel! I know what you mean,' here Warrington broke out. 'This is the meaning of your scepticism, of your quietism, of your atheism, my poor fellow. You're going to sell yourself, and Heaven help you! You are going to make a bargain which will degrade you and make you miserable for life, and there's no use talking of it. If you are once bent on it, the devil won't prevent you.'

'On the contrary, he's on my side, isn't he, George?' said Pen, with a laugh. 'What good cigars these are! Come down and have a little dinner at the club; the *chef's* in town, and he'll cook a good one for me. No, you won't? Don't be sulky, old boy; I'm going down to—to the country to-morrow.'

CHAPTER LXII

WHICH ACCOUNTS PERHAPS FOR CHAPTER LXI

THE information regarding the affairs of the Clavering family, which Major Pendennis had acquired through Strong, and by his own personal interference as the friend of the house, was such as almost made the old gentleman pause in any plans which he might have once entertained for his nephew's benefit. To bestow upon Arthur a wife with two such fathers-in-law, as the two worthies whom the guileless and unfortunate Lady Clavering had drawn in her marriage ventures, was to benefit no man. And though the one, in a manner, neutralized the other, and the appearance of Amory or Altamont in public would be the signal for his instantaneous withdrawal and condign punishment,—for the fugitive convict had cut down the officer in charge of him,—and a rope would be inevitably his end, if he came again under British authorities, yet no guardian would like to secure for his ward a wife whose parent was to be got rid of in such a way; and the old gentleman's notions always had been that Altamont, with the gallows before his eyes, would assuredly avoid recognition; while, at the same time, by holding the threat of his discovery over Clavering, the latter, who would lose everything by Amory's appearance, would be a slave in the hands of a person who knew so fatal a secret.

But if the Begum paid Clavering's debts many times more, her wealth would be expended altogether upon this irreclaimable reprobate; and her heirs, whoever they might be, would succeed but to an emptied treasury; and Miss

Amory, instead of bringing her husband a good income and a seat in Parliament, would bring to that individual her person only, and her pedigree, with that lamentable note of *sus. per coll.* at the name of the last male of her line.

There was, however, to the old schemer revolving these things in his mind, another course yet open ; the which will appear to the reader who may take the trouble to peruse a conversation, which presently ensued, between Major Pendennis and the honourable baronet, the member for Clavering.

When a man, under pecuniary difficulties, disappears from among his usual friends and equals,—dives out of sight, as it were, from the flock of birds in which he is accustomed to sail, it is wonderful at what strange and distant nooks he comes up again for breath. I have known a Pall Mall lounger and Rotten Row buck, of no inconsiderable fashion, vanish from amongst his comrades of the Clubs and the Park, and be discovered, very happy and affable, at an eighteenpenny ordinary in Billingsgate : another gentleman, of great learning and wit, when outrunning the constables (were I to say he was a literary man, some critics would vow that I intended to insult the literary profession),* once sent me his address at a little public-house called 'The Fox under the Hill,' down a most darksome and cavernous archway in the Strand. Such a man, under such misfortunes, may have a house, but he is never in his house ; and has an address where letters may be left ; but only simpletons go with the hopes of seeing him. Only a few of the faithful know where he is to be found, and have the clue to his hiding-place. So, after disputes with his wife, and the misfortunes consequent thereon, to find Sir Francis Clavering at home was impossible. 'Ever since I hast him for my book, which is fourteen pound, he don't come home till three o'clock, and purtends to be asleep when I bring his water of a mornin', and dodges hout when I'm downstairs,' Mr. Lightfoot remarked to his friend Morgan ; and announced that he should go down to my lady, and be butler there, and marry his old woman. In like manner, after his altercations with Strong, the baronet did not come near him, and fled to other haunts, out of the reach of the Chevalier's reproaches ;—out of reach of conscience, if possible, which many of us try to dodge and leave behind us by changes of scenes and other fugitive stratagems.

So, though the elder Pendennis, having his own ulterior object, was bent upon seeing Pen's country neighbour and representative in Parliament, it took the major no inconsiderable trouble and time before he could get him into such a confidential state and conversation, as were necessary for the ends which the major had in view. For since the major had been called in as family friend, and had cognizance of Clavering's affairs, conjugal and pecuniary, the baronet avoided him : as he always avoided all his lawyers and agents when there was an account to be rendered, or an affair of business to be discussed between them ; and never kept any appointment but when its object was the raising of money. Thus, previous to catching this most shy and timorous bird, the major made more than one futile attempt to hold him ;—on one day it was a most innocent-looking invitation to dinner at Greenwich, to meet a few friends : the baronet accepted, suspected something, and did not come ; leaving the major (who indeed proposed to represent in himself the body of friends) to eat his whitebait alone :—on another occasion the major wrote and asked for ten minutes' talk, and the baronet instantly acknowledged the note, and made the appointment at four o'clock the next day at Bays's *precisely* (he carefully underlined the 'precisely') ; but though four o'clock came, as in the course of time and destiny it could not do otherwise, no Clavering made his appearance. Indeed, if he had borrowed twenty pounds of Pendennis he could not have been more timid, or desirous of avoiding the major ; and the latter found that it was one thing to seek a man, and another to find him.

Before the close of that day in which Strong's patron had given the Chevalier the benefit of so many blessings before his face and curses behind his back, Sir Francis Clavering, who had pledged his word and his oath to his wife's advisers to draw or accept no more bills of exchange, and to be content with the allowance which his victimized wife still awarded him, had managed to sign his respectable name to a piece of stamped paper, which the baronet's friend, Mr. Moss Abrams, had carried off, promising to have the bill 'done' by a party with whose intimacy Mr. Abrams was favoured. And it chanced that Strong heard of this transaction at the place where the writings had been drawn, —in the back parlour, namely, of Mr. Santiago's cigar-shop,

where the Chevalier was constantly in the habit of spending an hour in the evening.

'He is at his old work again,' Mr. Santiago told his customer. 'He and Moss Abrams were in my parlour. Moss sent out my boy for a stamp. It must have been a bill for fifty pound. I heard the baronet tell Moss to date it two months back. He will pretend that it is an old bill, and that he forgot it when he came to a settlement with his wife the other day. I dare say they will give him some more money now he is clear.' A man who has the habit of putting his unlucky name to 'promises to pay' at six months, has the satisfaction of knowing, too, that his affairs are known and canvassed, and his signature handed round, among the very worst knaves and rogues of London.

Mr. Santiago's shop was close by St. James's Street and Bury Street, where we have had the honour of visiting our friend Major Pendennis in his lodgings. The major was walking daintily towards his apartment, as Strong, burning with wrath and redolent of Havana, strode along the same pavement opposite to him.

'Confound these young men: how they poison everything with their smoke,' thought the major. 'Here comes a fellow with moustachios and a cigar. Every fellow who smokes and wears moustachios is a low fellow. Oh! it's Mr. Strong.—I hope you are well, Mr. Strong?' and the old gentleman, making a dignified bow to the Chevalier, was about to pass into his house; directing towards the lock of the door, with trembling hand, the polished door-key.

We have said that, at the long and weary disputes and conferences regarding the payment of Sir Francis Clavering's last debts, Strong and Pendennis had both been present as friends and advisers of the baronet's unlucky family. Strong stopped and held out his hand to his brother negotiator, and old Pendennis put out towards him a couple of ungracious fingers.

'What is your good news?' said Major Pendennis, patronizing the other still further, and condescending to address him an observation, for old Pendennis had kept such good company all his life, that he vaguely imagined he honoured common men by speaking to them. 'Still in town, Mr. Strong? I hope I see you well.'

'My news is bad news, sir,' Strong answered; 'it concerns

our friends at Tunbridge Wells, and I should like to talk to you about it. Clavering is at his old tricks again, Major Pendennis.'

'Indeed! Pray do me the favour to come into my lodging,' cried the major with awakened interest; and the pair entered and took possession of his drawing-room. Here seated, Strong unburthened himself of his indignation to the major, and spoke at large of Clavering's recklessness and treachery. 'No promises will bind him, sir,' he said. 'You remember when we met, sir, with my lady's lawyer, how he wouldn't be satisfied with giving his honour, but wanted to take his oath on his knees to his wife, and rang the bell for a Bible, and swore perdition on his soul if he ever would give another bill. He has been signing one this very day, sir: and will sign as many more as you please for ready money: he will deceive anybody, his wife or his child, or his old friend, who has backed him a hundred times. Why, there's a bill of his and mine will be due next week——'

'I thought we had paid all——'

'Not that one,' Strong said, blushing. 'He asked me not to mention it, and—and—I had half the money for that, major. And they will be down on me. But I don't care for it; I'm used to it. It's Lady Clavering that riles me. It's a shame that that good-natured woman, who has paid him out of jail a score of times, should be ruined by his heartlessness. A parcel of bill-stealers, boxers, any rascals, get his money; and he don't scruple to throw an honest fellow over. Would you believe it, sir, he took money of Altamont—you know whom I mean.'

'Indeed? of that singular man, who I think came tipsy once to Sir Francis's house?' Major Pendennis said, with impenetrable countenance. 'Who is Altamont, Mr. Strong?'

'I am sure I don't know, if you don't know,' the Chevalier answered, with a look of surprise and suspicion.

'To tell you frankly,' said the major, 'I have my suspicions. I suppose—mind, I only suppose—that in our friend Clavering's life—who, between you and me, Captain Strong, we must own is about as loose a fish as any in my acquaintance—there are, no doubt, some queer secrets and stories which he would not like to have known: none of us would. And very likely this fellow, who calls himself

Altamont, knows some story against Clavering, and has some hold on him, and gets money out of him on the strength of his information. I know some of the best men of the best families in England who are paying through the nose in that way. But their private affairs are no business of mine, Mr. Strong ; and it is not to be supposed that because I go and dine with a man, I pry into his secrets, or am answerable for all his past life. And so with our friend Clavering, I am most interested for his wife's sake, and her daughter's, who is a most charming creature : and when her ladyship asked me, I looked into her affairs, and tried to set them straight ; and shall do so again, you understand, to the best of my humble power and ability, if I can make myself useful. And if I am called upon—you understand, if I am called upon—and—by the way, this Mr. Altamont, Mr. Strong ? How is this Mr. Altamont ? I believe you are acquainted with him. Is he in town ?'

'I don't know that I am called upon to know where he is, Major Pendennis,' said Strong, rising and taking up his hat in dudgeon, for the major's patronizing manner and impertinence of caution offended the honest gentleman not a little.

Pendennis's manner altered at once from a tone of hauteur to one of knowing good-humour. 'Ah, Captain Strong, you are cautious too, I see ; and quite right, my good sir, quite right. We don't know what ears walls may have, sir, or to whom we may be talking ; and as a man of the world, and an old soldier,—an old and distinguished soldier, I have been told, Captain Strong,—you know very well that there is no use in throwing away your fire ; you may have your ideas, and I may put two and two together and have mine. But there are things which don't concern him that many a man had better not know, eh, captain ? and which I, for one, won't know until I have reason for knowing them : and that I believe is your maxim too. With regard to our friend the baronet, I think with you, it would be most advisable that he should be checked in his imprudent courses ; and most strongly reprehend any man's departure from his word, or any conduct of his which can give any pain to his family, or cause them annoyance in any way. That is my full and frank opinion, and I am sure it is yours.'

'Certainly,' said Mr. Strong dryly.

'I am delighted to hear it; delighted, that an old brother soldier should agree with me so fully. And I am exceedingly glad of the lucky meeting which has procured me the good fortune of your visit. Good-evening. Thank you. Morgan, show the door to Captain Strong.'

And Strong, preceded by Morgan, took his leave of Major Pendennis; the Chevalier not a little puzzled at the old fellow's prudence; and the valet, to say the truth, to the full as much perplexed at his master's reticence. For Mr. Morgan, in his capacity of accomplished valet, moved here and there in a house as silent as a shadow; and, as it so happened, during the latter part of his master's conversation with his visitor, had been standing very close to the door, and had overheard not a little of the talk between the two gentlemen, and a great deal more than he could understand.

'Who is that Altamont? know anything about him and Strong?' Mr. Morgan asked of Mr. Lightfoot, on the next convenient occasion when they met at the club.

'Strong's his man of business, draws the governor's bills, and indosses 'em, and does his odd jobs and that; and I suppose Altamont's in it too,' Mr. Lightfoot replied. 'That kite-flying, you know, Mr. M., always takes two or three on 'em to set the paper going. Altamont put the pot on at the Derby, and won a good bit of money. I wish the governor could get some somewhere, and I could get my book paid up.'

'Do you think my lady would pay his debts again?' Morgan asked. 'Find out that for me, Lightfoot, and I'll make it worth your while, my boy.'

Major Pendennis had often said, with a laugh, that his valet Morgan was a much richer man than himself: and, indeed, by a long course of careful speculation, this wary and silent attendant had been amassing a considerable sum of money, during the years which he had passed in the major's service, where he had made the acquaintance of many other valets of distinction, from whom he had learned the affairs of their principals. When Mr. Arthur came into his property, but not until then, Morgan had surprised the young gentleman, by saying that he had a little sum of money, some fifty or a hundred pound, which he wanted to lay out to advantage; perhaps the gentlemen in the

Temple, knowing about affairs and business and that, could help a poor fellow to a good investment ? Morgan would be very much obliged to Mr. Arthur, most grateful and obliged indeed, if Arthur could tell him of one. When Arthur laughingly replied, that he knew nothing about money matters, and knew no earthly way of helping Morgan, the latter, with the utmost simplicity, was very grateful, very grateful indeed, to Mr. Arthur, and if Mr. Arthur *should* want a little money before his rents was paid, perhaps he would kindly remember that his uncle's old and faithful servant had some as he would like to put out : and be most proud if he could be useful anyways to any of the family.

The Prince of Fairoaks, who was tolerably prudent and had no need of ready money, would as soon have thought of borrowing from his uncle's servant as of stealing the valet's pocket-handkerchief, and was on the point of making some haughty reply to Morgan's offer, but was checked by the humour of the transaction. Morgan a capitalist ! Morgan offering to lend to him ! The joke was excellent. On the other hand, the man might be quite innocent, and the proposal of money a simple offer of goodwill. So Arthur withheld the sarcasm that was rising to his lips, and contented himself by declining Mr. Morgan's kind proposal. He mentioned the matter to his uncle, however, and congratulated the latter on having such a treasure in his service.

It was then that the major said that he believed Morgan had been getting devilish rich for a devilish long time ; in fact he had bought the house in Bury Street, in which his master was a lodger ; and had actually made a considerable sum of money, from his acquaintance with the Clavering family and the knowledge obtained through his master that the Begum would pay all her husband's debts, by buying up as many of the baronet's acceptances as he could raise money to purchase. Of these transactions the major, however, knew no more than most gentlemen do of their servants, who live with us all our days and are strangers to us, so strong custom is, and so pitiless the distinction between class and class.

'So he offered to lend you money, did he ?' the elder Pendennis remarked to his nephew. 'He's a dev'lish sly fellow, and a dev'lish rich fellow ; and there's many a nobleman would like to have such a valet in his service, and

borrow from him too. And he ain't a bit changed, Monsieur Morgan. He does his work just as well as ever—he's always ready to my bell—steals about the room like a cat—he's so dev'lishly attached to me, Morgan !'

On the day of Strong's visit, the major bethought him of Pen's story, and that Morgan might help him, and rallied the valet regarding his wealth with that free and insolent way which so high-placed a gentleman might be disposed to adopt towards so unfortunate a creature.

'I hear that you have got some money to invest, Morgan,' said the major.

It's Mr. Arthur has been telling, hang him, thought the valet.

'I'm glad my place is such a good one.'

'Thank you, sir—I've no reason to complain of my place, nor of my master,' replied Morgan demurely.

'You're a good fellow : and I believe you are attached to me ; and I'm glad you get on well. And I hope you'll be prudent, and not be taking a public-house or that kind of thing.'

A public-house, thought Morgan—me in a public-house ! —the old fool !—Dammy, if I was ten years younger I'd set in Parlyment before I died, that I would.—'No, thank you kindly, sir. I don't think of the public line, sir. And I've got my little savings pretty well put out, sir.'

'You do a little in the discounting way, eh, Morgan ?'

'Yes, sir, a very little—I—I beg your pardon, sir—might I be so free as to ask a question ?'

'Speak on, my good fellow,' the elder said graciously.

'About Sir Francis Clavering's paper, sir ? Do you think he's any longer any good, sir ? Will my lady pay on 'em any more, sir ?'

'What, you've done something in that business already ?'

'Yes, sir, a little,' replied Morgan, dropping down his eyes. 'And I don't mind owning, sir, and I hope I may take the liberty of saying, sir, that a little more would make me very comfortable if it turned out as well as the last.'

'Why, how much have you netted by him, in Gad's name ?' asked the major.

'I've done a good bit, sir, at it : that I own, sir. Having some information, and made acquaintance with the fam'ly through your kindness, I put on the pot, sir.'

'You did what ?'

'I laid my money on, sir—I got all I could, and borrowed, and bought Sir Francis's bills ; many of 'em had his name, and the gentleman as is just gone out, Edward Strong, Esq., sir : and of course I know of the blow up and shindy as is took place in Grosvenor Place, sir : and as I may as well make my money as another, I'd be *very* much obleeged to you if you'd tell me whether my lady will come down any more.'

Although Major Pendennis was as much surprised at this intelligence regarding his servant, as if he had heard that Morgan was a disguised marquis, about to throw off his mask and assume his seat in the House of Peers ; and although he was of course indignant at the audacity of the fellow who had dared to grow rich under his nose, and without his cognizance ; yet he had a natural admiration for every man who represented money and success, and found himself respecting Morgan, and being rather afraid of that worthy, as the truth began to dawn upon him.

'Well, Morgan,' said he, 'I mustn't ask how rich you are ; and the richer the better for your sake, I'm sure. And if I could give you any information that could serve you, I would speedily help you. But frankly, if Lady Clavering asks me whether she shall pay any more of Sir Francis's debts I shall advise and hope she won't, though I fear she will—and that is all I know. And so you are aware that Sir Francis is beginning again in his—eh—reckless and imprudent course ?'

'At his old games, sir—can't prevent that gentleman. He will do it.'

'Mr. Strong was saying that a Mr. Moss Abrams was the holder of one of Sir Francis Clavering's notes. Do you know anything of this Mr. Abrams, or the amount of the bill ?'

'Don't know the bill, know Abrams quite well, sir.'

'I wish you would find out about it for me. And I wish you would find out where I can see Sir Francis Clavering, Morgan.'

And Morgan said, 'Thank you, sir, yes, sir, I will, sir' ; and retired from the room, as he had entered it, with his usual stealthy respect and quiet humility ; leaving the major to muse and wonder over what he had just heard.

The next morning the valet informed Major Pendennis that he had seen Mr. Abrams ; what was the amount of the

bill that gentleman was desirous to negotiate ; and that the baronet would be sure to be in the back parlour of the 'Wheel of Fortune Tavern' that day at one o'clock.

To this appointment Sir Francis Clavering was punctual, and as at one o'clock he sat in the parlour of the tavern in question, surrounded by spittoons, Windsor chairs, cheerful prints of boxers, trotting horses, and pedestrians, and the lingering of last night's tobacco fumes—as the descendant of an ancient line sat in this delectable place, accommodated with an old copy of *Bell's Life in London*, much blotted with beer, the polite Major Pendennis walked into the apartment.

'So it's you, old boy ?' asked the baronet, thinking that Mr. Moss Abrams had arrived with the money.

'How do you do, Sir Francis Clavering ? I wanted to see you, and followed you here,' said the major, at sight of whom the other's countenance fell.

Now that he had his opponent before him, the major was determined to make a brisk and sudden attack upon him, and went into action at once. 'I know,' he continued, 'who is the exceedingly disreputable person for whom you took me, Clavering ; and the errand which brought you here.'

'It ain't your business, is it ?' asked the baronet, with a sulky and deprecatory look. 'Why are you following me about and taking the command, and meddling in my affairs, Major Pendennis ? I've never done *you* any harm, have I ? I've never had *your* money. And I don't choose to be dodged about in this way, and domineered over. I don't choose it, and I won't have it. If Lady Clavering has any proposal to make to me, let it be done in the regular way, and through the lawyers. I'd rather not have you.'

'I am not come from Lady Clavering,' the major said, 'but of my own accord, to try and remonstrate with you, Clavering, and see if you can be kept from ruin. It is but a month ago that you swore on your honour, and wanted to get a Bible to strengthen the oath, that you would accept no more bills, but content yourself with the allowance which Lady Clavering gives you. All your debts were paid with that proviso, and you have broken it ; this Mr. Abrams has a bill of yours for sixty pounds.'

'It's an old bill. I take my solemn oath it's an old bill,' shrieked out the baronet.

'You drew it yesterday, and you dated it three months back purposely. By Gad, Clavering, you sicken me with lies, I can't help telling you so. I've no patience with you, by Gad. You cheat everybody, yourself included. I've seen a deal of the world, but I never met your equal at humbugging. It's my belief you had rather lie than not.'

'Have you come here, you old, old beast, to tempt me to—to pitch into you, and—knock your old head off?' said the baronet, with a poisonous look of hatred at the major.

'What, sir?' shouted out the old major, rising to his feet and clasping his cane, and looking so fiercely, that the baronet's tone instantly changed towards him.

'No, no,' said Clavering piteously, 'I beg your pardon. I didn't mean to be angry, or say anything unkind, only you're so damned harsh to me, Major Pendennis. What is it you want of me? Why have you been hunting me so? Do *you* want money out of me too? By Jove, you know I've not got a shilling,'—and so Clavering, according to custom, passed from a curse into a whimper.

Major Pendennis saw from the other's tone, that Clavering knew his secret was in the major's hands.

'I've no errand from anybody, or no design upon you,' Pendennis said, 'but an endeavour, if it's not too late, to save you and your family from utter ruin, through the infernal recklessness of your courses. I knew your secret——'

"I didn't know it when I married her: upon my oath I didn't know it till the d——d scoundrel came back and told me, himself; and it's the misery about that which makes me so reckless, Pendennis; indeed it is!" the baronet cried, clasping his hands.

'I knew your secret from the very first day when I saw Amory come drunk into your dining-room in Grosvenor Place. I never forget faces. I remember that fellow in Sydney a convict, and he remembers me. I know his trial, the date of his marriage, and his reported death in the Bush. I could swear to him. And I know you are no more married to Lady Clavering than I am. I've kept your secret well enough, for I've not told a single soul that I know it, not your wife, not yourself till now.'

'Poor Lady C., it would cut her up dreadfully,' whimpered Sir Francis; 'and it wasn't my fault, major, you know it wasn't.'

'Rather than allow you to go on ruining her as you do, I *will* tell her, Clavering, and tell all the world too; that is what I swear I will do, unless I can come to some terms with you, and put some curb on your infernal folly. By play, debt, and extravagance of all kind, you've got through half your wife's fortune, and that of her legitimate heirs, mind, her legitimate heirs. Here it must stop. You can't live together. You're not fit to live in a great house like Clavering; and before three years more were over, would not leave a shilling to carry on. I've settled what must be done. You shall have six hundred a year; you shall go abroad and live on that. You must give up Parliament, and get on as well as you can. If you refuse, I give you my word I'll make the real state of things known to-morrow; I'll swear to Amory, who, when identified, will go back to the country from whence he came, and will rid the widow of you and himself together. And so that boy of yours loses at once all title to old Snell's property, and it goes to your wife's daughter. Ain't I making myself pretty clearly understood?'

'You wouldn't be so cruel to that poor boy, would you, Pendennis?' asked his father, pleading piteously; 'hang it, think about him. He's a nice boy; though he's dev'lish wild, I own—he's dev'lish wild.'

'It's you who are cruel to him,' said the old moralist. 'Why, sir, you'll ruin him yourself inevitably in three years.'

'Yes, but perhaps I won't have such dev'lish bad luck, you know; the luck must turn; and I'll reform, by Gad, I'll reform. And if you were to split on me, it would cut up my wife so; you know it would, most infernally.'

'To be parted from *you*,' said the old major, with a sneer; 'you know she won't live with you again.'

'But why can't Lady C. live abroad, or at Bath, or at Tunbridge, or at the doose, and I go on here?' Clavering continued. 'I like being here better than abroad, and I like being in Parliament. It's dev'lish convenient, being in Parliament.* There's very few seats like mine left; and if I gave it 'em I should not wonder the Ministry would give me an island to govern, or some dev'lish good thing; for you know I'm a gentleman of dev'lish good family, and have

a handle to my name, and—and that sort of thing, Major Pendennis. Eh, don't you see ? Don't you think they'd give me something dev'lish good if I was to play my cards well ? And then, you know, I'd save money, and be kept out of the way of the confounded hells and *rouge et noir*—and—and so I'd rather not give up Parliament, please.' For at one instant to hate and defy a man, at the next to weep before him, and at the next to be perfectly confidential and friendly with him, was not an unusual process with our versatile-minded baronet.

'As for your seat in Parliament,' the major said, with something of a blush on his cheek, and a certain tremor, which the other did not see, 'you must part with that, Sir Francis Clavering, to—to me.'

'What ! are you going into the House, Major Pendennis ?'

'No—not I ; but my nephew, Arthur, is a very clever fellow, and would make a figure there ; and when Clavering had two members,* his father might very likely have been one ; and—and I should like Arthur to be there,' the major said.

'Dammy, does *he* know it, too ?' cried out Clavering.

'Nobody knows anything out of this room,' Pendennis answered ; 'and if you do this favour for me, I hold my tongue. If not, I'm a man of my word, and will do what I have said.'

'I say, major,' said Sir Francis, with a peculiarly humble smile, 'you—you couldn't get me my first quarter in advance, could you, like the best of fellows ? You can do anything with Lady Clavering ; and, upon my oath, I'll take up that bill of Abrams. The little dam scoundrel, I know he'll do me in the business—he always does ; and if you could do this for me, we'd see, major.'

'And I think your best plan would be to go down in September to Clavering to shoot, and take my nephew with you, and introduce him. Yes, that will be the best time. And we will try and manage about the advance.' (Arthur may lend him that, thought old Pendennis. Confound him, a seat in Parliament is worth a hundred and fifty pounds.) 'And, Clavering, you understand, of course, my nephew knows nothing about this business. You have a mind to retire : he is a Clavering man, and a good representative for the borough ; you introduce him, and your people vote for him—you see.'

'When can you get me the hundred and fifty, major? When shall I come and see you? Will you be at home this evening or to-morrow morning? Will you have anything here? They've got some dev'lish good bitters in the bar. I often have a glass of bitters, it sets one up so.'

The old major would take no refreshment; but rose and took his leave of the baronet, who walked with him to the door of the 'Wheel of Fortune,' and then strolled into the bar, where he took a glass of gin and bitters with the landlady there: and a gentleman connected with the ring (who boarded at the 'Wheel of F.') coming in, he and Sir Francis Clavering and the landlord talked about the fights and the news of the sporting world in general; and at length Mr. Moss Abrams arrived with the proceeds of the baronet's bill, from which his own handsome commission was deducted and out of the remainder Sir Francis 'stood' a dinner at Greenwich to his distinguished friend, and passed the evening gaily at Vauxhall.

Meanwhile Major Pendennis, calling a cab in Piccadilly, drove to Lamb Court, Temple, where he speedily was closeted with his nephew in deep conversation.

After their talk they parted on very good terms, and it was in consequence of that unreported conversation, whereof the reader nevertheless can pretty well guess the bearing, that Arthur expressed himself as we have heard in the colloquy with Warrington, which is reported in the last chapter.

When a man is tempted to do a tempting thing, he can find a hundred ingenious reasons for gratifying his liking; and Arthur thought very much that he would like to be in Parliament, and that he would like to distinguish himself there, and that he need not care much what side he took, as there was falsehood and truth on every side. And on this and on other matters he thought he would compromise with his conscience, and that Sadduceeism was a very convenient and good-humoured profession of faith.

CHAPTER LXIII

PHILLIS AND CORYDON

N a picturesque common in the neighbourhood of Tunbridge Wells, Lady Clavering had found a pretty villa, whither she retired after her conjugal disputes at the end of that unlucky London season. Miss Amory, of course, accompanied her mother, and Master Clavering came home for the holidays, with whom Blanche's chief occupation was to fight and quarrel. But this was only a home pastime, and the young schoolboy was not fond of home sports. He found cricket, and horses, and plenty of friends at Tunbridge. The good-natured Begum's house was filled with a constant society of young gentlemen of thirteen, who ate and drank much too copiously of tarts and champagne; who rode races on the lawn, and frightened the fond mother; who smoked and made themselves sick, and the dining-room unbearable to Miss Blanche. She did not like the society of young gentlemen of thirteen.

As for that fair young creature, any change as long as it was change was pleasant to her; and for a week or two she would have liked poverty and a cottage, and bread and cheese; and, for a night, perhaps, a dungeon and bread and water; and so the move to Tunbridge was by no means unwelcome to her. She wandered in the woods, and sketched trees and farm-houses; she read French novels habitually; she drove into Tunbridge Wells pretty often, and to any play, or ball, or conjurer, or musician who might happen to appear in the place; she slept a great deal; she quarrelled with mamma and Frank during the morning; she found the little village school and attended it, and first fondled the girls and thwarted the mistress, then scolded the girls and laughed at the teacher; she was constant at church, of course. It was a pretty little church, of immense antiquity—a little Anglo-Norman *bijou*,* built

the day before yesterday, and decorated with all sorts of painted windows, carved saints' heads, gilt Scripture texts, and open pews. Blanche began forthwith to work a most correct High-Church altar-cover for the church. She passed for a saint with the clergyman for a while, whom she quite took in, and whom she coaxed, and wheedled, and fondled so artfully, that poor Mrs. Smirke, who at first was charmed with her, then bored with her, then would hardly speak to her, was almost mad with jealousy. Mrs. Smirke was the wife of our old friend Smirke, Pen's tutor and poor Helen's suitor. He had consoled himself for her refusal with a young lady from Clapham whom his mamma provided. When the latter died, our friend's views became every day more and more pronounced. He cut off his coat collar, and let his hair grow over his back. He rigorously gave up the curl which he used to sport on his forehead, and the tie of his neckcloth of which he was rather proud. He went without any tie at all. He went without dinner on Fridays. He read the Roman Hours, and intimated that he was ready to receive confessions in the vestry. The most harmless creature in the world, he was denounced as a black and most dangerous Jesuit and Papist, by Muffin of the Dissenting chapel, and Mr. Simeon Knight at the old church. Mr. Smirke had built his chapel of ease with the money left him by his mother at Clapham. Lord! lord! what would she have said to hear a table called an altar! to see candlesticks on it! to get letters signed on the Feast of Saint So-and-so, or the Vigil of Saint What-do-you-call-'em! All these things did the boy of Clapham practise; his faithful wife following him. But when Blanche had a conference of near two hours in the vestry with Mr. Smirke, Belinda paced up and down on the grass, where there were only two little gravestones as yet; she wished that she had a third there: only, only he would offer very likely to that creature, who had infatuated him in a fortnight. No, she would retire; she would go into a convent, and profess, and leave him. Such bad thoughts had Smirke's wife and his neighbours regarding him; these, thinking him in direct correspondence with the Bishop of Rome; that, bewailing errors to her even more odious and fatal; and yet our friend meant no earthly harm. The post-office never brought him any letters from the Pope; he thought Blanche, to be sure, at first, the most pious, gifted, right-

thinking, fascinating person he had ever met; and her manner of singing the chants delighted him—but after a while he began to grow rather tired of Miss Amory, her ways and graces grew stale somehow; then he was doubtful about Miss Amory; then she made a disturbance in his school, lost her temper, and rapped the children's fingers. Blanche inspired this admiration and satiety, somehow, in many men. She tried to please them, and flung out all her graces at once; came down to them with all her jewels on; all her smiles, and cajoleries, and coaxings, and ogles. Then she grew tired of them and of trying to please them, and never having cared about them, dropped them: and the men grew tired of her, and dropped her too. It was a happy night for Belinda when Blanche went away; and her husband, with rather a blush and a sigh, said 'he had been deceived in her; he had thought her endowed with many precious gifts, he feared they were mere tinsel: he thought she had been a right-thinking person, he feared she had merely made religion an amusement—she certainly had quite lost her temper to the schoolmistress, and beat Polly Rucker's knuckles cruelly.' Belinda flew to his arms, there was no question about the grave or the veil any more. He tenderly embraced her on the forehead. 'There is none like thee, my Belinda,' he said, throwing his fine eyes up to the ceiling, 'precious among women!' As for Blanche, from the instant she lost sight of him and Belinda, she never thought or cared about either any more.

But when Arthur went down to pass a few days at Tunbridge Wells with the Begum, this stage of indifference had not arrived on Miss Blanche's part or on that of the simple clergyman. Smirke believed her to be an angel and wonder of a woman. Such a perfection he had never seen, and sat listening to her music in the summer evenings, open-mouthed, rapt in wonder, tealess, and bread-and-butterless. Fascinating as he had heard the music of the Opera to be—he had never but once attended an exhibition of that nature (which he mentioned with a blush and a sigh—it was on that day when he had accompanied Helen and her son to the play at Chatteris)—he could not conceive anything more delicious, more celestial, he had almost said, than Miss Amory's music. She was a most gifted being: she had a precious soul: she had the most remarkable talents—to all outward seeming, the most heavenly dis-

position, etc., etc. It was in this way that, being then at the height of his own fever and bewitchment for Blanche, Smirke discoursed to Arthur about her.

The meeting between the two old acquaintances had been very cordial. Arthur loved anybody who loved his mother; Smirke could speak on that theme with genuine feeling and emotion. They had a hundred things to tell each other of what had occurred in their lives. 'Arthur would perceive,' Smirke said, 'that his—his views on Church matters had developed themselves since their acquaintance.' Mrs. Smirke, a most exemplary person, seconded them with all her endeavours. He had built this little church on his mother's demise, who had left him provided with a sufficiency of worldly means. Though in the cloister himself, he had heard of Arthur's reputation. He spoke in the kindest and most saddened tone; he held his eyelids down, and bowed his fair head on one side. Arthur was immensely amused with him; with his airs; with his follies and simplicity; with his blank stock and long hair; with his real goodness, kindness, friendliness of feeling. And his praises of Blanche pleased and surprised our friend not a little, and made him regard her with eyes of particular favour.

The truth is, Blanche was very glad to see Arthur; as one is glad to see an agreeable man in the country, who brings down the last news and stories from the great city; who can talk better than most country folks, at least can talk that darling London jargon, so dear and indispensable to London people, so little understood by persons out of the world. The first day Pen came down, he kept Blanche laughing for hours after dinner. She sang her songs with redoubled spirit. She did not scold her mother; she fondled and kissed her, to the honest Begum's surprise. When it came to be bedtime, she said '*Déjà!*' with the prettiest air of regret possible; and was really quite sorry to go to bed, and squeezed Arthur's hand quite fondly. He on his side gave her pretty palm a very cordial pressure. Our young gentleman was of that turn, that eyes very moderately bright dazzled him.

'She is very much improved,' thought Pen, looking out into the night, 'very much. I suppose the Begum won't mind my smoking with the window open. She's a jolly good old woman, and Blanche is immensely improved. I liked her manner with her mother to-night. I liked her

laughing way with that stupid young cub of a boy, whom they oughtn't to allow to get tipsy. She sang those little verses very prettily; they were devilish pretty verses too, though I say it who shouldn't say it.' And he hummed a tune which Blanche had put to some verses of his own. 'Ah! what a fine night! How jolly a cigar is at night! How pretty that little Saxon church looks in the moonlight! I wonder what old Warrington's doing? Yes, she's a dayvlish nice little thing, as my uncle says.'

'Oh, heavenly!' Here broke out a voice from a clematis-covered casement near—a girl's voice: it was the voice of the author of *Mes Larmes*.

Pen burst into a laugh. 'Don't tell about my smoking,' he said, leaning out of his own window.

'Oh! go on! I adore it,' cried the lady of *Mes Larmes*. 'Heavenly night! Heavenly, heavenly moon! but I must shut my window, and not talk to you on account of *les mœurs*. How droll they are, *les mœurs!* Adieu.' And Pen began to sing the good-night to Don Basilio.*

The next day they were walking in the fields together, laughing and chattering—the gayest pair of friends. They talked about the days of their youth, and Blanche was prettily sentimental. They talked about Laura, dearest Laura—Blanche had loved her as a sister: was she happy with that odd Lady Rockminster? Wouldn't she come and stay with them at Tunbridge? Oh, what walks they would take together! What songs they would sing—the old, old songs. Laura's voice was splendid. Did Arthur—she must call him Arthur—remember the songs they sang in the happy old days, now he was grown such a great man, and had such a *succès*? etc., etc.

And the day after, which was enlivened with a happy ramble through the woods to Penshurst, and a sight of that pleasant park and hall, came the conversation with the curate which we have narrated, and which made our young friend think more and more.

'Is she all this perfection?' he asked himself. 'Has she become serious and religious? Does she tend schools, and visit the poor? Is she kind to her mother and brother? Yes, I am sure of that, I have seen her.' And walking with his old tutor over his little parish, and going to visit his school, it was with inexpressible delight that Pen found Blanche seated instructing the children, and fancied to

MISS AMORY'S INTERESTING EMPLOYMENT

himself how patient she must be, how good-natured, how ingenuous, how really simple in her tastes, and unspoiled by the world.

'And do you really like the country ?' he asked her, as they walked together.

'I should like never to see that odious city again. Oh, Arthur — that is, Mr.—well, Arthur, then—one's good thoughts grow up in these sweet woods and calm solitudes,

like those flowers which won't bloom in London, you know. The gardener comes and changes our balconies once a week. I don't think I shall bear to look London in the face again—its odious, smoky, brazen face ! But, heigho !'

'Why that sigh, Blanche ?'

'Never mind why.'

'Yes, I do mind why. Tell me, tell me everything.'

'I wish you hadn't come down ;' and a second edition of *Mes Soupirs* came out.

'You don't want me, Blanche ?'

'I don't want you to go away. I don't think this house will be very happy without you, and that's why I wish that you never had come.'

Mes Soupirs were here laid aside, and *Mes Larmes* had begun.

Ah ! What answer is given to those in the eyes of a young woman ? What is the method employed for drying them ? What took place ? O ringdoves and roses, O dews and wildflowers, O waving greenwoods and balmy airs of summer ! Here were two battered London rakes, taking themselves in for a moment, and fancying that they were in love with each other, like Phillis and Corydon !

When one thinks of country houses and country walks, one wonders that any man is left unmarried.

CHAPTER LXIV

TEMPTATION

EASY and frank-spoken as Pendennis commonly was with Warrington, how came it that Arthur did not inform the friend and depository of all his secrets, of the little circumstances which had taken place at the villa near Tunbridge Wells ? He talked about the discovery of his old tutor Smirke, freely enough, and of his wife, and of his Anglo-Norman church, and of his departure from Clapham to Rome ; but, when asked about Blanche, his answers were evasive or general ; he said she was a good-natured clever little thing, that rightly guided she might make no such bad wife after all, but that he had for the moment no intention of marriage, that his days of romance were over, that he was contented with his present lot, and so forth.

In the meantime there came occasionally to Lamb Court, Temple, pretty little satin envelopes, superscribed in the neatest handwriting, and sealed with one of those admirable

ciphers, which, if Warrington had been curious enough to watch his friend's letters, or indeed if the cipher had been decipherable, would have shown George that Mr. Arthur was in correspondence with a young lady whose initials were B. A. To these pretty little compositions Mr. Pen replied in his best and gallantest manner; with jokes, with news of the town, with points of wit, nay, with pretty little verses very likely, in reply to the versicles of the muse of *Mes Larmes*. Blanche we know rhymes with 'branch,' and 'stanch,' and 'launch,' and no doubt a gentleman of Pen's ingenuity would not forgo these advantages of position, and would ring the pretty little changes upon these pleasing notes. Indeed we believe that those love-verses of Mr. Pen's, which had such a pleasing success in the *Roseleaves*, that charming annual edited by Lady Violet Lebas,* and illustrated by portraits of the female nobility by the famous artist Pinkney, were composed at this period of our hero's life; and were first addressed to Blanche, per post, before they figured in print, *cornets* as it were to Pinkney's pictorial garland.

'Verses are all very well,' the elder Pendennis said, who found Pen scratching down one of these artless effusions at the club as he was waiting for his dinner; 'and letter-writing if mamma allows it, and between such old country friends of course there may be a correspondence, and that sort of thing—but mind, Pen, and don't commit yourself, my boy. For who knows what the doose may happen? The best way is to make your letters safe. I never wrote a letter in all my life that would commit me, and demmy, sir, I have had some experience of women.' And the worthy gentleman, growing more garrulous and confidential with his nephew as he grew older, told many affecting instances of the evil results consequent upon this want of caution to many persons in 'society';—how from using too ardent expressions in some poetical notes to the widow Naylor, young Spoony had subjected himself to a visit of remonstrance from the widow's brother, Colonel Flint; and thus had been forced into a marriage with a woman old enough to be his mother: how when Louisa Salter had at length succeeded in securing young Sir John Bird, Hopwood, of the Blues, produced some letters which Miss S. had written to him, and caused a withdrawal on Bird's part, who afterwards was united to Miss Stickney, of Lyme Regis, etc.

The major, if he had not reading, had plenty of observation, and could back his wise saws with a multitude of modern instances, which he had acquired in a long and careful perusal of the great book of the world.

Pen laughed at the examples, and blushing a little at his uncle's remonstrances, said that he would bear them in mind and be cautious. He blushed, perhaps, because he *had* borne them in mind ; because he *was* cautious : because in his letter to Miss Blanche he had from instinct, or honesty perhaps, refrained from any avowals which might compromise him. 'Don't you remember the lesson I had, sir, in Lady Mirabel's—Miss Fotheringay's affair ? I am not to be caught again, uncle,' Arthur said with mock frankness and humility. Old Pendennis congratulated himself and his nephew heartily on the latter's prudence and progress, and was pleased at the position which Arthur was taking as a man of the world.

No doubt, if Warrington had been consulted, his opinion would have been different : and he would have told Pen that the boy's foolish letters were better than the man's adroit compliments and slippery gallantries ; that to win the woman he loves, only a knave or a coward advances under cover, with subterfuges, and a retreat secured behind him : but Pen spoke not on this matter to Mr. Warrington, knowing pretty well that he was guilty, and what his friend's verdict would be.

Colonel Altamont had not been for many weeks absent on his foreign tour, Sir Francis Clavering having retired meanwhile into the country pursuant to his agreement with Major Pendennis, when the ills of fate began to fall rather suddenly and heavily upon the sole remaining partner of the little firm of Shepherd's Inn. When Strong, at parting with Altamont, refused the loan proffered by the latter in the fullness of his purse and the generosity of his heart, he made such a sacrifice to conscience and delicacy as caused him many an after-twinge and pang ; and he felt—it was not very many hours in his life he had experienced the feeling—that in this juncture of his affairs he had been too delicate and too scrupulous. Why should a fellow in want refuse a kind offer kindly made ? Why should a thirsty man decline a pitcher of water from a friendly hand, because it was a little soiled ? Strong's conscience smote him for refusing what the other had fairly come by, and gener-

ously proffered: and he thought ruefully, now it was too late, that Altamont's cash would have been as well in his pocket as in that of the gambling-house proprietor at Baden or Ems, with whom his excellency would infallibly leave his Derby winnings. It was whispered among the tradesmen, bill-discounters, and others who had commercial dealings with Captain Strong, that he and the baronet had parted company, and that the captain's 'paper' was henceforth of no value. The tradesmen, who had put a wonderful confidence in him hitherto,—for who could resist Strong's jolly face and frank and honest demeanour?—now began

to pour in their bills with a cowardly mistrust and unanimity. The knocks at the Shepherd's Inn chambers door were constant, and tailors, bootmakers, pastrycooks who had furnished dinners, in their own persons, or by the boys their representatives, held levées on Strong's stairs. To these were added one or two persons of a less clamorous but far more sly and dangerous sort,—the young clerks of lawyers, namely, who lurked about the Inn, or concerted with Mr. Campion's young man in the chambers hard by, having in their dismal pocket-books copies of writs to be served on Edward Strong, requiring him to appear on an

early day next term before our sovereign lady the Queen, and answer to, etc., etc.

From this invasion of creditors, poor Strong, who had not a guinea in his pocket, had, of course, no refuge but that of the Englishman's castle, into which he retired, shutting the outer and inner door upon the enemy, and not quitting his stronghold until after nightfall. Against this outer barrier the foe used to come and knock and curse in vain, whilst the Chevalier peeped at them from behind the little curtain which he had put over the orifice of his letter-box ; and had the dismal satisfaction of seeing the faces of furious clerk and fiery dun, as they dashed up against the door and retreated from it. But as they could not be always at his gate, or sleep on his staircase, the enemies of the Chevalier sometimes left him free.

Strong, when so pressed by his commercial antagonists, was not quite alone in his defence against them, but had secured for himself an ally or two. His friends were instructed to communicate with him by a system of private signals : and they thus kept the garrison from starving by bringing in necessary supplies, and kept up Strong's heart and prevented him from surrendering by visiting him and cheering him in his retreat. Two of Ned's most faithful allies were Huxter and Miss Fanny Bolton : when hostile visitors were prowling about the Inn, Fanny's litttle sisters were taught a particular cry or *jödel*, which they innocently whooped in the court : when Fanny and Huxter came up to visit Strong, they archly sang this same note at his door ; when that barrier was straightway opened, the honest garrison came out smiling, the provisions and the pot of porter were brought in, and in the society of his faithful friends the beleaguered one passed a comfortable night. There are some men who could not live under this excitement, but Strong was a brave man, as we have said, who had seen service and never lost heart in peril.

But besides allies, our general had secured for himself, under difficulties, that still more necessary aid,—a retreat. It has been mentioned in a former part of this history, how Messrs. Costigan and Bows lived in the house next door to Captain Strong, and that the window of one of their rooms was not very far off the kitchen window which was situated in the upper story of Strong's chambers. A leaden water-pipe and gutter served for the two ; and

Strong, looking out from his kitchen one day, saw that he could spring with great ease up to the sill of his neighbour's window, and clamber up the pipe which communicated from one to the other. He had laughingly shown this refuge to his chum, Altamont; and he had agreed that it would be as well not to mention the circumstance to Captain Costigan, whose duns were numerous, and who would be constantly flying down the pipe into their apartments if this way of escape were shown to him.

But now that the evil days were come, Strong made use of the passage, and one afternoon burst in upon Bows and Costigan with his jolly face, and explained that the enemy was in waiting on his staircase, and that he had taken this means of giving them the slip. So while Mr. Marks's aides-de-camp were in waiting in the passage of No. 3 Strong walked down the steps of No. 4, dined at the 'Albion,' went to the play, and returned home at midnight, to the astonishment of Mrs. Bolton and Fanny, who had not seen him quit his chambers and could not conceive how he could have passed the line of sentries.

Strong bore this siege for some weeks with admirable spirit and resolution, and as only such an old and brave soldier would, for the pains and privations which he had to endure were enough to depress any man of ordinary courage; and what vexed and 'riled' him (to use his own expression) was the infernal indifference and cowardly ingratitude of Clavering, to whom he wrote letter after letter, which the baronet never acknowledged by a single word, or by the smallest remittance, though a five-pound note, as Strong said, at that time would have been a fortune to him.

But better days were in store for the Chevalier, and in the midst of his despondency and perplexities there came to him a most welcome aid. 'Yes, if it hadn't been for this good fellow here,' said Strong; 'for a good fellow you are, Altamont, my boy, and hang me if I don't stand by you as long as I live; I think, Pendennis, it would have been all up with Ned Strong. It was the fifth week of my being kept a prisoner, for I couldn't always be risking my neck across that water-pipe, and taking my walks abroad through poor old Cos's window, and my spirit was quite broken, sir—dammy, quite beat, and I was thinking of putting an end

to myself, and should have done it in another week, when who should drop down from heaven but Altamont!'

'Heaven ain't exactly the place, Ned,' said Altamont. 'I came from Baden-Baden,' said he, 'and I had a deuced lucky month there, that's all.'

'Well, sir, he took up Marks's bill, and he paid the other fellows that were upon me, like a man, sir, that he did,' said Strong, enthusiastically.

'And I shall be very happy to stand a bottle of claret for this company, and as many more as the company chooses,' said Mr. Altamont, with a blush. 'Hallo! waiter, bring us a magnum of the right sort, do you hear? And we'll drink our healths all round, sir—and may every good fellow like Strong find another good fellow to stand by him at a pinch. That's *my* sentiment, Mr. Pendennis, though I don't like your name.'

'No! And why?' asked Arthur.

Strong pressed the colonel's foot under the table here; and Altamont, rather excited, filled up another bumper, nodded to Pen, drank off his wine, and said, '*He* was a gentleman, and that was sufficient, and they were all gentlemen.'

The meeting between these 'all gentlemen' took place at Richmond, whither Pendennis had gone to dinner, and where he found the Chevalier and his friend at table in the coffee-room. Both of the latter were exceedingly hilarious, talkative, and excited by wine; and Strong, who was an admirable story-teller, told the story of his own siege, and adventures, and escapes with great liveliness and humour, and described the talk of the sheriff's officers at his door, the pretty little signals of Fanny, the grotesque exclamations of Costigan when the Chevalier burst in at the window, and his final rescue by Altamont, in a most graphic manner, and so as greatly to interest his hearers.

'As for me, it's nothing,' Altamont said. 'When a ship's paid off, a chap spends his money, you know. And it's the fellers at the black and red at Baden-Baden that did it. I won a good bit of money there, and intend to win a good bit more, don't I, Strong? I'm going to take him with me. I've got a system. I'll make his fortune, I tell you. I'll make your fortune, if you like—dammy, everybody's fortune. But what I'll do, and no mistake, boys, I promise you. I'll put in for that little Fanny.

Dammy, sir, what do you think she did? She had two pound, and I'm blest if she didn't go and lend it to Ned Strong! Didn't she, Ned? Let's drink her health.'

'With all my heart,' said Arthur, and pledged this toast with the greatest cordiality.

Mr. Altamont then began, with the greatest volubility, and at great length, to describe his system. He said that it was infallible, if played with coolness; that he had it from a chap at Baden, who had lost by it, it was true, but because he had not capital enough; if he could have stood one more turn of the wheel, he would have all his money back; that he and several more chaps were going to make a bank, and try it; and that he would put every shilling he was worth into it, and had come back to this country for the express purpose of fetching away his money, and Captain Strong; that Strong should play for him; that he could trust Strong and his temper much better than he could his own, and much better than Bloundell-Bloundell or the Italian that 'stood in.' As he emptied his bottle, the colonel described at full length all his plans and prospects to Pen, who was interested in listening to his story, and the confessions of his daring and lawless good-humour.

'I met that queer fellow Altamont the other day,' Pen said to his uncle, a day or two afterwards.

'Altamont? What Altamont? There's Lord Westport's son,' said the major.

'No, no; the fellow who came tipsy into Clavering's dining-room one day when we were there,' said the nephew, laughing; 'and he said he did not like the name of Pendennis, though he did me the honour to think that I was a good fellow.'

'I don't know any man of the name of Altamont, I give you my honour,' said the impenetrable major; 'and as for your acquaintance, I think the less you have to do with him the better, Arthur.'

Arthur laughed again. 'He is going to quit the country, and make his fortune by a gambling system. He and my amiable college acquaintance, Bloundell, are partners, and the colonel takes out Strong with him as aide-de-camp. What is it that binds the Chevalier and Clavering, I wonder?'

'I should think—mind you, Pen, I should think, but of course I have only the idea—that there has been something

in Clavering's previous life which gives these fellows and some others a certain power over him ; and if there should be such a secret, which is no affair of ours, my boy, dammy, I say, it ought to be a lesson to a man to keep himself straight in life, and not to give any man a chance over him.'

'Why, I think *you* have some means of persuasion over Clavering, uncle, or why should he give me that seat in Parliament ?'

'Clavering thinks he ain't fit for Parliament,' the major answered. 'No more he is. What's to prevent him from putting you or anybody else into his place if he likes ? Do you think that the Government or the Opposition would make any bones about accepting the seat if he offered it to them ? Why should you be more squeamish than the first men, and the most honourable men, and men of the highest birth and position in the country, begad ?' The major had an answer of this kind to most of Pen's objections, and Pen accepted his uncle's replies, not so much because he believed them, but because he wished to believe them. We do a thing—which of us has not ?—not because 'everybody does it,' but because we like it ; and our acquiescence, alas ! proves not that everybody is right, but that we and the rest of the world are poor creatures alike.

At his next visit to Tunbridge, Mr. Pen did not forget to amuse Miss Blanche with the history which he had learned at Richmond of the Chevalier's imprisonment, and of Altamont's gallant rescue. And after he had told his tale in his usual satirical way, he mentioned with praise and emotion little Fanny's generous behaviour to the Chevalier, and Altamont's enthusiasm in her behalf.

Miss Blanche was somewhat jealous, and a good deal piqued and curious about Fanny. Among the many confidential little communications which Arthur made to Miss Amory in the course of their delightful rural drives and their sweet evening walks, it may be supposed that our hero would not forget a story so interesting to himself and so likely to be interesting to her, as that of the passion and care of the poor little Ariadne of Shepherd's Inn. His own part in that drama he described, to do him justice, with becoming modesty ; the moral which he wished to draw from the tale being one in accordance with his usual

satirical mood, viz., that women get over their first loves quite as easily as men do (for the fair Blanche, in their *intimes* conversations, did not cease to twit Mr. Pen about his notorious failure in his own virgin attachment to the Fotheringay), and, number one being withdrawn, transfer themselves to number two without much difficulty. And poor little Fanny was offered up in sacrifice as an instance to prove this theory. What griefs she had endured and surmounted, what bitter pangs of hopeless attachment she had gone through, what time it had taken to heal those wounds of the tender little bleeding heart, Mr. Pen did not know, or perhaps did not choose to know; for he was at once modest and doubtful about his capabilities as a conqueror of hearts, and averse to believe that he had executed any dangerous ravages on that particular one, though his own instance and argument told against himself in this case; for if, as he said, Miss Fanny was by this time in love with her surgical adorer, who had neither good looks, nor good manners, nor wit, nor anything but ardour and fidelity to recommend him, must she not, in her first sickness of the love-complaint, have had a serious attack, and suffered keenly for a man who had certainly a number of the showy qualities which Mr. Huxter wanted?

'You wicked, odious creature,' Miss Blanche said, 'I believe that you are enraged with Fanny for being so impudent as to forget you, and that you are actually jealous of Mr. Huxter.' Perhaps Miss Amory was right, as the blush which came in spite of himself and tingled upon Pendennis's cheek (one of those blows with which a man's vanity is constantly slapping his face) proved to Pen that he was angry to think he had been superseded by such a rival. By such a fellow as that! without any conceivable good quality! Oh, Mr. Pendennis! (although this remark does not apply to such a smart fellow as you) if Nature had not made that provision for each sex in the credulity of the other, which sees good qualities where none exist, good looks in donkeys' ears, wit in their numskulls, and music in their bray, there would not have been near so much marrying and giving in marriage as now obtains, and as is necessary for the due propagation and continuance of the noble race to which we belong!

'Jealous or not,' Pen said, 'and, Blanche, I don't say no, I should have liked Fanny to come to a better end than

that. I don't like histories that end in that cynical way; and when we arrive at the conclusion of the story of a pretty girl's passion, to find such a figure as Huxter's at the last page of the tale. Is all life a compromise, my lady fair, and the end of the battle of love an ignoble surrender? Is the search for the Cupid which my poor little Psyche pursued in the darkness—the god of her soul's longing—the god of the blooming cheek and rainbow pinions,—to result in Huxter, smelling of tobacco and gallipots? I wish, though I don't see it in life, that people could be like Jenny and Jessamy, or my lord and lady Clementina, in the story-books and fashionable novels, and at once under the ceremony, and, as it were, at the parson's benediction, become perfectly handsome and good and happy ever after.'

'And don't you intend to be good and happy, pray, *monsieur le misanthrope*—and are you very discontented with your lot—and will your marriage be a compromise—' asked the author of *Mes Larmes*, with a charming *moue*—'and is your Psyche an odious vulgar wretch? You wicked satirical creature, I can't abide you! You take the hearts of young things, play with them, and fling them away with scorn. You ask for love and trample on it. You—you make me cry, that you do, Arthur, and—and don't—and I *won't* be consoled in that way—and I think Fanny was quite right in leaving such a heartless creature.'

'Again, I don't say no,' said Pen, looking very gloomily at Blanche, and not offering by any means to repeat the attempt at consolation, which had elicited that sweet monosyllable 'don't' from the young lady. 'I don't think I have much of what people call heart; but I don't profess it. I made my venture when I was eighteen, and lighted my lamp and went in search of Cupid. And what was my discovery of love!—a vulgar dancing woman. I failed, as everybody does, almost everybody; only it is luckier to fail before marriage than after.'

'*Merci du choix, monsieur*,' said the Sylphide, making a curtsy.

'Look, my little Blanche,' said Pen, taking her hand, and with his voice of sad good-humour; 'at least I stoop to no flatteries.'

'Quite the contrary,' said Miss Blanche.

'And tell you no foolish lies, as vulgar men do. Why

should you and I, with our experience, ape romance and dissemble passion ? I do not believe Miss Blanche Amory to be peerless among the beautiful, nor the greatest poetess, nor the most surpassing musician, any more than I believe you to be the tallest woman in the whole world—like the giantess whose picture we saw as we rode through the fair yesterday. But if I don't set you up as a heroine, neither do I offer you your very humble servant as a hero. But I think you are—well, there, I think you are very sufficiently good-looking.'

'*Merci*,' Miss Blanche said, with another curtsy.

'I think you sing charmingly. I'm sure you're clever. I hope and believe that you are good-natured, and that you will be companionable."

'And so, provided I bring you a certain sum of money and a seat in Parliament, you condescend to fling to me your royal pocket-handkerchief,' said Blanche. '*Que d'honneur !* We used to call your Highness the Prince of Fairoaks. What an honour to think that I am to be elevated to the throne, and to bring the seat in Parliament as backsheesh to the Sultan ! I am glad I am clever, and that I can play and sing to your liking ; my songs will amuse my lord's leisure.'

'And if thieves are about the house,' said Pen, grimly pursuing the simile, 'forty besetting thieves in the shape of lurking cares and enemies in ambush and passions in arms, my Morgiana will dance round me with a tambourine,* and kill all my rogues and thieves with a smile. Won't she ?' But Pen looked as if he did not believe that she would. 'Ah, Blanche,' he continued, after a pause, 'don't be angry ; don't be hurt at my truth-telling. Don't you see that I always take you at your word ? You say you will be a slave and dance—I say, dance. You say, "I take you with what you bring :" I say, "I take you with what you bring." To the necessary deceits and hypocrisies of our life, why add any that are useless and unnecessary ? If I offer myself to you because I think we have a fair chance of being happy together, and because by your help I may get for both of us a good place and a not undistinguished name, why ask me to feign raptures and counterfeit romance, in which neither of us believe ? Do you want me to come wooing in a Prince Prettyman's dress, from the masquerade warehouse, and to pay you compliments like Sir Charles

Grandison? Do you want me to make you verses as in the days when we were—when we were children? I will if you like, and sell them to Bacon and Bungay afterwards. Shall I feed my pretty princess with *bonbons?*'

'*Mais j'adore les bonbons, moi,*' said the little Sylphide, with a queer, piteous look.

'I can buy a hatful at Fortnum and Mason's for a guinea. And it shall have its bonbons, its pooty little sugar-plums, that it shall,' Pen said, with a bitter smile. 'Nay, my dear, nay, my dearest little Blanche, don't cry. Dry the pretty eyes, I can't bear that;' and he proceeded to offer that consolation which the circumstance required, and which the tears, the genuine tears of vexation, which now sprang from the angry eyes of the author of *Mes Larmes* demanded.

The scornful and sarcastic tone of Pendennis quite frightened and overcame the girl. 'I—I don't want your consolation. I—I never was—so—spoken to bef—by any of my—my—by anybody'—she sobbed out, with much simplicity.

'*Anybody!*' shouted out Pen, with a savage burst of laughter, and Blanche blushed one of the most genuine blushes which her cheek had ever exhibited, and she cried out, 'O Arthur, *vous êtes un homme terrible!*' She felt bewildered, frightened, oppressed, the worldly little flirt who had been playing at love for the last dozen years of her life, and yet not displeased at meeting a master.

'Tell me, Arthur,' she said, after a pause in this strange love-making. 'Why does Sir Francis Clavering give up his seat in Parliament?'

'*Au fait,* why does he give it to me?' asked Arthur, now blushing in his turn.

'You always mock me, sir,' she said. 'If it is good to be in Parliament, why does Sir Francis go out?'

'My uncle has talked him over. He always said that you were not sufficiently provided for. In the—the family disputes, when your mamma paid his debts so liberally, it was stipulated, I suppose, that you—that is, that I—that is, upon my word, I don't know why he goes out of Parliament,' Pen said, with rather a forced laugh. 'You see, Blanche, that you and I are two good little children, and that this marriage has been arranged for us by our

mammas and uncles, and that we must be obedient, like a good little boy and girl.'

So, when Pen went to London, he sent Blanche a box of bonbons, each sugar-plum of which was wrapped up in ready-made French verses, of the most tender kind; and, besides, dispatched to her some poems of his own manufacture, quite as artless and authentic: and it was no wonder that he did not tell Warrington what his conversations with Miss Amory had been, of so delicate a sentiment were they, and of a nature so necessarily private.

And if, like many a worse and better man, Arthur Pendennis, the widow's son, was meditating an apostasy, and going to sell himself to—we all know whom,—at least the renegade did not pretend to be a believer in the creed to which he was ready to swear. And if every woman and man in this kingdom, who has sold her or himself for money or position, as Mr. Pendennis was about to do, would but purchase a copy of his memoirs, what tons of volumes Messrs. Bradbury and Evans would sell!

CHAPTER LXV

IN WHICH PEN BEGINS HIS CANVASS

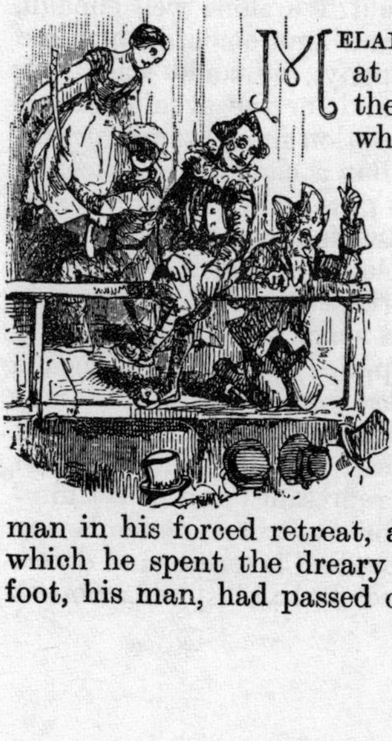

MELANCHOLY as the great house at Clavering Park had been in the days before his marriage, when its bankrupt proprietor was a refugee in foreign lands, it was not much more cheerful now when Sir Francis Clavering came to inhabit it. The greater part of the mansion was shut up, and the baronet only occupied a few of the rooms on the ground floor, where his housekeeper and her assistant from the lodge-gate waited upon the luckless gentleman in his forced retreat, and cooked a part of the game which he spent the dreary mornings in shooting. Lightfoot, his man, had passed over to my lady's service; and,

as Pen was informed in a letter from Mr. Smirke, who performed the ceremony, had executed his prudent intention of marrying Mrs. Bonner, my lady's woman, who, in her mature years, was stricken with the charms of the youth, and endowed him with her savings and her elderly person. To be landlord and landlady of the 'Clavering Arms' was the ambition of both of them; and it was agreed that they were to remain in Lady Clavering's service until quarter-day arrived, when they were to take possession of their hotel. Pen graciously promised that he would give his election dinner there, when the baronet should vacate his seat in the young man's favour; and, as it had been agreed by his uncle, to whom Clavering seemed to be able to refuse nothing, Arthur came down in September on a visit to Clavering Park, the owner of which was very glad to have a companion who would relieve his loneliness, and perhaps would lend him a little ready money.

Pen furnished his host with these desirable supplies a couple of days after he had made his appearance at Clavering: and no sooner were these small funds in Sir Francis's pocket, than the latter found he had business at Chatteris and at the neighbouring watering-places, of which ——shire boasts many, and went off to see to his affairs, which were transacted, as might be supposed, at the county race-grounds and billiard-rooms. Arthur could live alone well enough, having many mental resources and amusements which did not require other persons' company; he could walk with the gamekeeper of a morning, and for the evenings there was a plenty of books and occupation for a literary genius like Mr. Arthur, who required but a cigar and a sheet of paper or two to make the night pass away pleasantly. In truth, in two or three days he had found the society of Sir Francis Clavering perfectly intolerable; and it was with a mischievous eagerness and satisfaction that he offered Clavering the little pecuniary aid which the latter according to his custom solicited; and supplied him with the means of taking flight from his own house.

Besides, our ingenious friend had to ingratiate himself with the townspeople of Clavering, and with the voters of the borough which he hoped to represent; and he set himself to this task with only the more eagerness, remembering how unpopular he had before been in Clavering, and determined to vanquish the odium which he had inspired amongst

the simple people there. His sense of humour made him delight in this task. Naturally rather reserved and silent in public, he became on a sudden as frank, easy, and jovial, as Captain Strong. He laughed with everybody who would exchange a laugh with him, shook hands right and left, with what may be certainly called a dexterous cordiality; made his appearance at the market-day and the farmers' ordinary; and, in fine, acted like a consummate hypocrite, and as gentlemen of the highest birth and most spotless integrity act when they wish to make themselves agreeable to their constituents, and have some end to gain of the country folks. How is it that we allow ourselves, not to be deceived, but to be ingratiated so readily by a glib tongue, a ready laugh, and a frank manner? We know, for the most part, that it is false coin, and we take it: we know that it is flattery, which it costs nothing to distribute to everybody, and we had rather have it than be without it. Friend Pen went about at Clavering, laboriously simple and adroitly pleased, and quite a different being from the scornful and rather sulky young dandy whom the inhabitants remembered ten years ago.

The Rectory was shut up. Dr. Portman was gone, with his gout and his family, to Harrogate; an event which Pen deplored very much in a letter to the doctor, in which, in a few kind and simple words, he expressed his regret at not seeing his old friend, whose advice he wanted, and whose aid he might require some day: but Pen consoled himself for the doctor's absence by making acquaintance with Mr. Simcoe, the opposition preacher, and with the two partners of the cloth-factory at Chatteris, and with the Independent preacher there, all of whom he met at the Clavering Athenaeum, which the Liberal party had set up in accordance with the advanced spirit of the age, and perhaps in opposition to the aristocratic old reading-room, into which the *Edinburgh Review* had once scarcely got an admission,[*] and where no tradesmen were allowed an entrance. He propitiated the younger partner of the cloth-factory, by asking him to dine in a friendly way at the park; he complimented the Honourable Mrs. Simcoe with hares and partridges from the same quarter, and a request to read her husband's last sermon; and being a little unwell one day, the rascal took advantage of the circumstance to show his tongue to Mr. Huxter, who sent him medicines,

and called the next morning. How delighted old Pendennis would have been with his pupil! Pen himself was amused with the sport in which he was engaged, and his success inspired him with a wicked good-humour.

And yet, as he walked out of Clavering of a night, after 'presiding' at a meeting of the Athenaeum, or working through an evening with Mrs. Simcoe, who, with her hus-

band, was awed by the young Londoner's reputation, and had heard of his social successes; as he passed over the old familiar bridge of the rushing Brawl, and heard that well-remembered sound of waters beneath, and saw his own cottage of Fairoaks among the trees, their darkening outlines clear against the starlit sky, different thoughts no doubt came to the young man's mind, and awakened pangs of grief and shame there. There still used to be a light in the

windows of the room which he remembered so well, and in which the saint who loved him had passed so many hours of care and yearning and prayer. He turned away his gaze from the faint light which seemed to pursue him with its wan, reproachful gaze, as though it was his mother's spirit watching and warning. How clear the night was! how keen the stars shone; how ceaseless the rush of the flowing waters; the old home trees whispered, and waved gently their dark heads and branches over the cottage roof. Yonder, in the faint starlight glimmer, was the terrace where, as a boy, he walked of summer evenings, ardent and trustful, unspotted, untried, ignorant of doubts or passions; sheltered as yet from the world's contamination in the pure and anxious bosom of love. . . . The clock of the near town tolling midnight, with a clang, disturbs our wanderer's reverie, and sends him onwards towards his night's resting-place, through the lodge into Clavering avenue, and under the dark arcades of the rustling limes.

When he sees the cottage the next time, it is smiling in sunset: those bedroom windows are open where the light was burning the night before: and Pen's tenant, Captain Stokes, of the Bombay Artillery (whose mother, old Mrs. Stokes, lives in Clavering), receives his landlord's visit with great cordiality: shows him over the grounds and the new pond he has made in the back-garden from the stables; talks to him confidentially about the roof and chimneys, and begs Mr. Pendennis to name a day when he will do himself and Mrs. Stokes the pleasure to, etc. Pen, who has been a fortnight in the country, excuses himself for not having called sooner upon the captain by frankly owning that he had not the heart to do it. 'I understand you, sir,' the captain says; and Mrs. Stokes, who had slipped away at the ring of the bell (how odd it seemed to Pen to ring the bell!), comes down in her best gown, surrounded by her children. The young ones clamber about Stokes: the boy jumps into an arm-chair. It was Pen's father's arm-chair; and Arthur remembers the days when he would as soon have thought of mounting the king's throne as of seating himself in that arm-chair. He asks if Miss Stokes—she is the very image of her mamma—if she can play? He should like to hear a tune on that piano. She plays. He hears the notes of the old piano once more, enfeebled by age, but he does not listen to the player. He is listening

to Laura singing as in the days of their youth, and sees his mother bending and beating time over the shoulder of the girl.

The dinner at Fairoaks given in Pen's honour by his tenant, and at which old Mrs. Stokes, Captain Glanders, Squire Hobnell, and the clergyman and his lady, from Tinckleton, were present, was very stupid and melancholy for Pen, until the waiter from Clavering (who aided the captain's stable-boy and Mrs. Stokes's butler), whom Pen remembered as a street boy, and who was now indeed barber in that place, dropped a plate over Pen's shoulder, on which Mr. Hobnell (who also employed him) remarked, 'I suppose, Hodson, your hands are slippery with bear's-grease. He's always dropping the crockery about, that Hodson is—haw, haw!' On which Hodson blushed, and looked so disconcerted, that Pen burst out laughing; and good-humour and hilarity were the order of the evening. For the second course, there was a hare and partridges top and bottom, and when, after the withdrawal of the servants, Pen said to the vicar of Tinckleton, 'I think, Mr. Stooks, you should have asked Hodson to *cut the hare*,' the joke was taken instantly by the clergyman, who was followed in the course of a few minutes by Captain Stokes and Glanders, and by Mr. Hobnell, who arrived rather late, with an immense guffaw.

While Mr. Pen was engaged in the country in the above schemes, it happened that the lady of his choice, if not of his affections, came up to London from the Tunbridge villa bound upon shopping expeditions or important business, and in company of old Mrs. Bonner, her mother's maid, who had lived and quarrelled with Blanche many times since she was an infant, and who now being about to quit Lady Clavering's service for the hymeneal state, was anxious like a good soul to bestow some token of respectful kindness upon her old and young mistress before she quitted them altogether, to take her post as the wife of Lightfoot, and landlady of the 'Clavering Arms.'

The honest woman took the benefit of Miss Amory's taste to make the purchase which she intended to offer her ladyship; and requested the fair Blanche to choose something for herself that should be to her liking, and remind her of her old nurse who had attended her through many

a wakeful night, and eventful teething, and childish fever, and who loved her like a child of her own a'most. These purchases were made, and as the nurse insisted on buying an immense Bible for Blanche, the young lady suggested that Bonner should purchase a large Johnson's Dictionary for her mamma. Each of the two women might certainly profit by the present made to her.

Then Mrs. Bonner invested money in some bargains in

linendrapery, which might be useful at the 'Clavering Arms,' and bought a red and yellow neck-handkerchief, which Blanche could see at once was intended for Mr. Lightfoot. Younger than herself by at least five-and-twenty years, Mrs. Bonner regarded that youth with a fondness at once parental and conjugal, and loved to lavish ornaments on his person, which already glittered with pins, rings, shirt-studs, and chains and seals, purchased at the good creature's expense.

It was in the Strand that Mrs. Bonner made her purchases, aided by Miss Blanche, who liked the fun very well, and when the old lady had bought everything that she desired, and was leaving the shop, Blanche, with a smiling face, and a sweet bow to one of the shop, said, 'Pray, sir, will you have the kindness to show us the way to Shepherd's Inn ?'

Shepherd's Inn was but a few score of yards off ; Old Castle Street was close by ; the elegant young shopman pointed out the turning which the young lady was to take, and she and her companion walked off together.

'Shepherd's Inn ! What can you want in Shepherd's Inn, Miss Blanche ?' Bonner inquired. 'Mr. Strong lives there. Do you want to go and see the captain ?'

'I should like to see the captain very well. I like the captain ; but it is not him I want. I want to see a dear little good girl, who was very kind to—to Mr. Arthur when he was so ill last year, and saved his life almost ; and I want to thank her, and ask her if she would like anything. I looked out several of my dresses on purpose this morning, Bonner !' and she looked at Bonner as if she had a right to admiration, and had performed an act of remarkable virtue. Blanche, indeed, was very fond of sugar-plums ; she would have fed the poor upon them, when she had had enough, and given a country girl a ball-dress when she had worn it and was tired of it.

'Pretty girl—pretty young woman !' mumbled Mrs. Bonner. 'I know *I* want no pretty young women come about Lightfoot ;' and in imagination she peopled the 'Clavering Arms' with a harem of the most hideous chamber-maids and barmaids.

Blanche, with pink and blue, and feathers, and flowers, and trinkets,[1] and a shot-silk dress, and a wonderful mantle, and a charming parasol, presented a vision of elegance and beauty such as bewildered the eyes of Mrs. Bolton, who was scrubbing the lodge-floor of Shepherd's Inn, and caused Betsy-Jane and Ameliar-Ann to look with delight.

Blanche looked on them with a smile of ineffable sweetness and protection ; like Rowena going to see Ivanhoe ;* like Marie Antoinette visiting the poor in the famine ; like the Marchioness of Carabas alighting from her carriage and four at a pauper-tenant's door, and taking from John No. II the packet of Epsom salts for the invalid's benefit, carrying it with her own imperial hand into the sick-room—Blanche

ROWENA'S VISIT TO REBECCA

felt a queen stepping down from her throne to visit a subject, and enjoyed all the bland consciousness of doing a good action.

'My good woman! I want to see Fanny—Fanny Bolton; is she here?'

Mrs. Bolton had a sudden suspicion, from the splendour of Blanche's appearance, that it must be a play-actor, or something worse.

'What do you want with Fanny, pray?' she asked.

'I am Lady Clavering's daughter—you have heard of Sir Francis Clavering? And I wish very much indeed to see Fanny Bolton.'

'Pray step in, Miss—Betsy-Jane, where's Fanny?'

Betsy-Jane said Fanny had gone into No. 3 staircase, on which Mrs. Bolton said she was probably in Strong's rooms, and bade the child go and see if she was there.

'In Captain Strong's rooms! Oh, let us go to Captain Strong's rooms,' cried out Miss Blanche. 'I know him very well. You dearest little girl, show us the way to Captain Strong!' cried out Miss Blanche, for the floor reeked with the recent scrubbing, and the goddess did not like the smell of brown soap.

And as they passed up the stairs, a gentleman by the name of Costigan, who happened to be swaggering about the court, and gave a very knowing look with his 'oi' under Blanche's bonnet, remarked to himself, 'That's a devilish foine gyurll, bedad, goan up to Sthrong and Altamont: they're always having foine gyurlls up their stairs.'

'Hallo—hwhat's that?' he presently said, looking up at the windows: from which some piercing shrieks issued.

At the sound of the voice of a distressed female the intrepid Cos rushed up the stairs as fast as his old legs would carry him, being nearly overthrown by Strong's servant, who was descending the stair. Cos found the outer door of Strong's chambers open, and began to thunder at the knocker. After many and fierce knocks, the inner door was partially unclosed, and Strong's head appeared.

'It's oi, me boy. Hwhat's that noise, Sthrong?' asked Costigan.

'Go to the d——' was the only answer, and the door was shut on Cos's venerable red nose: and he went downstairs muttering threats at the indignity offered to him, and vowing that he would have satisfaction. In the meanwhile the

reader, more lucky than Captain Costigan, will have the privilege of being made acquainted with the secret which was withheld from that officer.

It has been said of how generous a disposition Mr. Altamont was, and when he was well supplied with funds, how liberally he spent them. Of a hospitable turn, he had no greater pleasure than drinking in company with other people; so that there was no man more welcome at Greenwich and Richmond than the emissary of the Nawaub of Lucknow.

Now it chanced that on the day when Blanche and Mrs. Bonner ascended the staircase to Strong's room in Shepherd's Inn, the colonel had invited Miss Delaval of the —— Theatre Royal, and her mother, Mrs. Hodge, to a little party down the river, and it had been agreed that they were to meet at chambers, and thence walk down to a port in the neighbouring Strand to take water. So that when Mrs. Bonner and *Mes Larmes* came to the door, where Grady, Altamont's servant, was standing, the domestic said, 'Walk in, ladies,' with the utmost affability, and led them into the room, which was arranged as if they had been expected there. Indeed, two bouquets of flowers, bought at Covent Garden that morning, and instances of the tender gallantry of Altamont, were awaiting his guests upon the table. Blanche smelt at the bouquet, and put her pretty little dainty nose into it, and tripped about the room, and looked behind the curtains, and at the books and prints, and at the plan of Clavering estate, hanging up on the wall; and had asked the servant for Captain Strong, and had almost forgotten his existence and the errand about which she had come, namely, to visit Fanny Bolton; so pleased was she with the new adventure, and the odd, strange, delightful, droll little idea of being in a bachelor's chambers in a queer old place in the city!

Grady meanwhile, with a pair of ample varnished boots, had disappeared into his master's room. Blanche had hardly the leisure to remark how big the boots were, and how unlike Mr. Strong's.

'The women 's come,' said Grady, helping his master to the boots.

'Did you ask 'em if they would take a glass of anything?' asked Altamont.

Grady came out—'He says, will you take anything to drink?' the domestic asked of them; at which Blanche,

amused with the artless question, broke out into a pretty little laugh, and asked of Mrs. Bonner, 'Shall we take anything to drink ?'

'Well, you may take it or lave it,' said Mr. Grady, who thought his offer slighted, and did not like the contemptuous manners of the new-comers, and so left them.

'Will we take anything to drink ?' Blanche asked again : and again began to laugh.

'Grady !' bawled out a voice from the chamber within :— a voice that made Mrs. Bonner start.

Grady did not answer : his song was heard from afar off, from the kitchen, his upper room, where Grady was singing at his work.

'Grady, my coat !' again roared the voice from within.

'Why, that is not Mr. Strong's voice,' said the Sylphide, still half laughing. 'Grady, my coat !—Bonner, who is Grady, my coat ? We ought to go away.'

Bonner still looked quite puzzled at the sound of the voice which she had heard.

The bedroom door here opened, and the individual who had called out 'Grady, my coat,' appeared without the garment in question.

He nodded to the women, and walked across the room. 'I beg your pardon, ladies. Grady, bring my coat down, sir ! Well, my dears, it's a fine day, and we'll have a jolly lark at——'

He said no more ; for here Mrs. Bonner, who had been looking at him with scared eyes, suddenly shrieked out, 'Amory ! Amory !' and fell back screaming and fainting in her chair.

The man, so apostrophized, looked at the woman an instant, and, rushing up to Blanche, seized her and kissed her. 'Yes, Betsy,' he said, 'by G— it is me. Mary Bonner knew me. What a fine gal we've grown ! But it's a secret, mind ! I'm dead, though I'm your father. Your poor mother don't know it. What a pretty gal we've grown ! Kiss me—kiss me close, my Betsy ! D— it, I love you : I'm your old father.'

Betsy or Blanche looked quite bewildered, and began to scream too—once, twice, thrice ; and it was her piercing shrieks which Captain Costigan heard as he walked the court below.

At the sound of those shrieks the perplexed parent clasped his hands (his wristbands were open, and on one brawny arm you could see letters tattooed in blue), and, rushing to his

apartment, came back with an eau-de-Cologne bottle from his grand silver dressing-case, with the fragrant contents of which he began liberally to sprinkle Bonner and Blanche.

The screams of these women brought the other occupants of the chamber into the room—Grady from his kitchen, and Strong from his apartment in the upper story. The latter at once saw from the aspect of the two women what had occurred.

'Grady, go and wait in the court,' he said, 'and if anybody comes—you understand me.'

'Is it the play-actress and her mother?' said Grady.

'Yes—confound you—say that there's nobody in chambers, and the party's off for to-day.'

'Shall I say that, sir? and after I bought them bokays?' asked Grady of his master.

'Yes,' said Amory, with a stamp of his foot: and Strong going to the door, too, reached it just in time to prevent the entrance of Captain Costigan, who had mounted the stair.

The ladies from the theatre did not have their treat to Greenwich, nor did Blanche pay her visit to Fanny Bolton on that day. And Cos, who took occasion majestically to inquire of Grady what the mischief was, and who was crying?—had for answer that 'twas a woman, another of them, and that they were, in Grady's opinion, the cause of 'most all the mischief in the world.

A RECOGNITION

CHAPTER LXVI

IN WHICH PEN BEGINS TO DOUBT HIS ELECTION

WHILST Pen, in his own county, was thus carrying on his selfish plans and Parliamentary schemes, news came to him that Lady Rockminster had arrived at Baymouth, and had brought with her our friend Laura. At the announcement that Laura his sister was near him, Pen felt rather guilty. His wish was to stand higher in her esteem, perhaps, than in that of any other person in the world. She was his mother's legacy to him. He was to be her patron and protector in some sort. How would she brave the news which he had to tell her; and how should he explain the plans which he was meditating? He felt as if neither he nor Blanche could bear Laura's dazzling glance of calm scrutiny, and as if he would not care to disclose his worldly hopes and ambitions to that spotless judge. At her arrival at Baymouth, he wrote a letter thither which contained a great number of fine phrases and protests of affection, and a great deal of easy satire and raillery; in the midst of all which Mr. Pen could not help feeling that he was in a panic, and that he was acting like a rogue and hypocrite.

How was it that a simple country-girl should be the object of fear and trembling to such an accomplished gentleman as Mr. Pen? His worldly tactics and diplomacy, his satire and knowledge of the world, could not bear the test of her purity, he felt somehow. And he had to own to himself that his affairs were in such a position, that he could not tell the truth to that honest soul. As he rode from Clavering to Baymouth, he felt as guilty as a school-boy who doesn't know his lesson and is about to face the awful master. For is not Truth the master always, and does she not have the power and hold the book?

Under the charge of her kind, though somewhat wayward and absolute, patroness, Lady Rockminster, Laura had seen somewhat of the world in the last year, had gathered some accomplishments, and profited by the lessons of society.

Many a girl who had been accustomed to that too great tenderness in which Laura's early life had been passed, would have been unfitted for the changed existence which she now had to lead. Helen worshipped her two children, and thought, as homebred women will, that all the world was made for them, or to be considered after them. She tended Laura with a watchfulness of affection which never left her. If she had a headache, the widow was as alarmed as if there had never been an aching head before in the world. She slept and woke, read and moved under her mother's fond superintendence, which was now withdrawn from her, along with the tender creature whose anxious heart would beat no more. And painful moments of grief and depression no doubt Laura had, when she stood in the great careless world alone. Nobody heeded her griefs or her solitude. She was not quite the equal, in social rank, of the lady whose companion she was, or of the friends and relatives of the imperious, but kind old dowager. Some very likely bore her no goodwill—some, perhaps, slighted her: it might have been that servants were occasionally rude; their mistress certainly was, often. Laura not seldom found herself in family meetings, the confidence and familiarity of which she felt were interrupted by her intrusion; and her sensitiveness of course was wounded at the idea that she should give or feel this annoyance. How many governesses are there in the world, thought cheerful Laura,—how many ladies, whose necessities make them slaves and companions by profession! What bad tempers and coarse unkindness have not these to encounter! How infinitely better my lot is with these really kind and affectionate people than that of thousands of unprotected girls! It was with this cordial spirit that our young lady adapted herself to her new position; and went in advance of her fortune with a trustful smile.

Did you ever know a person who met Fortune in that way, whom the goddess did not regard kindly? Are not even bad people won by a constant cheerfulness and a pure and affectionate heart? When the Babes in the Wood, in the ballad, looked up fondly and trustfully at those notorious rogues whom their uncle had set to make away with the little folks, we all know how one of the rascals relented, and made away with the other—not having the heart to be cruel to so much innocence and beauty. Oh, happy they who have that virgin loving trust and sweet smiling confidence in the world,

and fear no evil because they think none! Miss Laura Bell was one of these fortunate persons; and besides the gentle widow's little cross, which, as we have seen, Pen gave her, had such a sparkling and brilliant Koh-i-noor* in her bosom, as is even more precious than that famous jewel; for it not only fetches a price, and is retained by its owner in another world where diamonds are stated to be of no value, but here, too, is of inestimable worth to its possesser; is a talisman against evil, and lightens up the darkness of life, like Cogia Hassan's famous stone.

So that before Miss Bell had been a year in Lady Rockminster's house, there was not a single person in it whose love she had not won by the use of this talisman. From the old lady to the lowest dependant of her bounty, Laura had secured the goodwill of everybody. With a mistress of such a temper, my lady's woman (who had endured her mistress for forty years, and had been clawed and scolded and jibed every day and night in that space of time) could not be expected to have a good temper of her own; and was at first angry against Miss Laura, as she had been against her ladyship's fifteen preceding companions. But when Laura was ill at Paris, this old woman nursed her in spite of her mistress, who was afraid of catching the fever, and absolutely fought for her medicine with Martha from Fairoaks, now advanced to be Miss Laura's own maid. As she was recovering, Grandjean the chef wanted to kill her by the numbers of delicacies which he dressed for her, and wept when she ate her first slice of chicken. The Swiss major-domo of the house celebrated Miss Bell's praises in almost every European language, which he spoke with indifferent incorrectness; the coachman was happy to drive her out; the page cried when he heard she was ill; and Calverley and Coldstream (those two footmen, so large, so calm ordinarily, and so difficult to move) broke out into extraordinary hilarity at the news of her convalescence, and intoxicated the page at a wine-shop, to *fête* Laura's recovery. Even Lady Diana Pynsent (our former acquaintance Mr. Pynsent had married by this time), Lady Diana, who had had a considerable dislike to Laura for some time, was so enthusiastic as to say that she thought Miss Bell was a very agreeable person, and that grandmamma had a great *trouvaille* in her. All this kindness Laura had acquired, not by any arts, not by any flattery, but by the simple force of good-nature, and by the blessed gift of pleasing and being pleased.

On the one or two occasions when he had seen Lady Rockminster, the old lady, who did not admire him, had been very pitiless and abrupt with our young friend, and perhaps Pen expected, when he came to Baymouth, to find Laura installed in her house in the quality of humble companion, and treated no better than himself. When she heard of his arrival she came running downstairs, and I am not sure that she did not embrace him in the presence of Calverley and Coldstream: not that those gentlemen ever told: if the *fractus orbis** had come to a smash, if Laura, instead of kissing Pen, had taken her scissors and snipped off his head—Calverley and Coldstream would have looked on impavidly, without allowing a grain of powder to be disturbed by the calamity.

Laura had so much improved in health and looks that Pen could not but admire her. The frank eyes which met his, beamed with good health; the cheek which he kissed blushed with beauty. As he looked at her, artless and graceful, pure and candid, he thought he had never seen her so beautiful. Why should he remark her beauty now so much, and remark too to himself that he had not remarked it sooner? He took her fair trustful hand and kissed it fondly: he looked in her bright clear eyes, and read in them that kindling welcome which he was always sure to find there. He was affected and touched by the tender tone, and the pure sparkling glance; their innocence smote him somehow and moved him.

'How good you are to me, Laura—sister!' said Pen. 'I don't deserve that you should—that you should be so kind to me.'

'Mamma left you to me,' she said, stooping down and brushing his forehead with her lips hastily. 'You know you were to come to me when you were in trouble, or to tell me when you were very happy: that was our compact, Arthur, last year, before we parted. Are you very happy now, or are you in trouble, which is it?' and she looked at him with an arch glance. 'Do you like going into Parliament? Do you intend to distinguish yourself there? How I shall tremble for your first speech!'

'Do you know about the Parliament plan, then?' Pen asked.

'Know?—all the world knows! I have heard it talked about many times. Lady Rockminster's doctor talked about it to-day. I dare say it will be in the Chatteris paper tomorrow. It is all over the county that Sir Francis Clavering, of Clavering, is going to retire, in behalf of Mr. Arthur Pen-

dennis, of Fairoaks; and that the young and beautiful Miss Blanche Amory is——'

'What! that too?' asked Pendennis.

'That, too, dear Arthur. *Tout se sait,* as somebody would say, whom I intend to be very fond of; and who, I am sure, is very clever and pretty. I have had a letter from Blanche. The kindest of letters. She speaks so warmly of you, Arthur! I hope—I know she feels what she writes.—When is it to be, Arthur? Why did you not tell me? I may come and live with you then, mayn't I?'

'My home is yours, dear Laura, and everything I have,' Pen said. 'If I did not tell you, it was because—because—I do not know: nothing is decided yet. No words have passed between us. But you think Blanche could be happy with me—don't you? Not a romantic fondness, you know. I have no heart, I think; I've told her so: only a sober-sided attachment:—and want my wife on one side of the fire and my sister on the other,—Parliament in the session, and Fairoaks in the holidays, and my Laura never to leave me until somebody who has a right comes to take her away.'

Somebody who has a right—somebody with a right! Why did Pen, as he looked at the girl and slowly uttered the words, begin to feel angry and jealous of the invisible somebody with the right to take her away? Anxious, but a minute ago, how she would take the news regarding his probable arrangements with Blanche, Pen was hurt somehow that she received the intelligence so easily, and took his happiness for granted.

'Until somebody comes,' Laura said, with a laugh, 'I will stay at home and be Aunt Laura, and take care of the children when Blanche is in the world. I have arranged it all. I am an excellent housekeeper. Do you know I have been to market at Paris with Mrs. Beck, and have taken some lessons from M. Grandjean? And I have had some lessons in Paris in singing too, with the money which you sent me, you kind boy: and I can sing much better now: and I have learned to dance, though not so well as Blanche, and when you become a Minister of State, Blanche shall present me:' and with this, and with a provoking good-humour, she performed for him the last Parisian curtsy.

Lady Rockminster came in whilst this curtsy was being performed, and gave to Arthur one finger to shake; which he took, and over which he bowed as well as he could, which, in truth, was very clumsily.

'So you are going to be married, sir,' said the old lady.

'Scold him, Lady Rockminster, for not telling us,' Laura said, going away : which, in truth, the old lady began instantly to do.

'So you are going to marry, and to go into Parliament in place of that good-for-nothing Sir Francis Clavering. I wanted him to give my grandson his seat—why did he not give my grandson his seat ? I hope you are to have a great deal of money with Miss Amory. *I* wouldn't take her without a great deal.'

'Sir Francis Clavering is tired of Parliament,' Pen said, wincing, 'and—and I rather wish to attempt that career. The rest of the story is at least premature.'

'I wonder, when you had Laura at home, you could take up with such an affected little creature as that,' the old lady continued.

'I am very sorry Miss Amory does not please your ladyship,' said Pen, smiling.

'You mean—that it is no affair of mine, and that I am not going to marry her. Well, I'm not ; and I'm very glad I am not—a little odious thing—when I think that a man could prefer her to my Laura, I've no patience with him, and so I tell you, Mr. Arthur Pendennis.'

'I am very glad you see Laura with such favourable eyes,' Pen said.

'You are very glad, and you are very sorry. What does it matter, sir, whether you are very glad or very sorry ? A young man who prefers Miss Amory to Miss Bell has no business to be sorry or glad. A young man who takes up with such a crooked lump of affectation as that little Amory,—for she is crooked, I tell you she is,—after seeing my Laura, has no right to hold up his head again. Where is your friend Bluebeard ? The tall young man, I mean,—Warrington, isn't his name ? Why does he not come down and marry Laura ? What do the young men mean by not marrying such a girl as that ? They all marry for money now. You are all selfish and cowards. We ran away with each other, and made foolish matches in my time. I have no patience with the young men ! When I was at Paris in the winter, I asked all the three attachés at the Embassy why they did not fall in love with Miss Bell ? They laughed—they said they wanted money. You are all selfish—you are all cowards.'

'I hope before you offered Miss Bell to the attachés,' said Pen, with some heat, 'you did her the favour to consult her?'

'Miss Bell has only a little money. Miss Bell must marry soon. Somebody must make a match for her, sir; and a girl can't offer herself,' said the old dowager, with great state. 'Laura, my dear, I've been telling your cousin that all the young men are selfish; and that there is not a pennyworth of romance left among them. He is as bad as the rest.'

'Have you been asking Arthur why he won't marry me?' said Laura, with a smile, coming back and taking her cousin's hand. (She had been away, perhaps, to hide some traces of emotion, which she did not wish others to see.) 'He is going to marry somebody else; and I intend to be very fond of her, and to go and live with them, provided he then does not ask every bachelor who comes to his house, why he does not marry me?'

The terrors of Pen's conscience being thus appeased, and his examination before Laura over without any reproaches on the part of the latter, Pen began to find that his duty and inclination led him constantly to Baymouth, where Lady Rockminster informed him that a place was always reserved for him at her table. 'And I recommend you to come often,' the old lady said, 'for Grandjean is an excellent cook, and to be with Laura and me will do your manners good. It is easy to see that you are always thinking about yourself. Don't blush and stammer—almost all young men are always thinking about themselves. My sons and grandsons always were until I cured them. Come here, and let us teach you to behave properly; you will not have to carve, that is done at the side-table. Hecker will give you as much wine as is good for you; and on days when you are very good and amusing you shall have some champagne. Hecker, mind what I say. Mr. Pendennis is Miss Laura's brother; and you will make him comfortable, and see that he does not have too much wine, or disturb me whilst I am taking my nap after dinner. You are selfish: I intend to cure you of being selfish. You will dine here when you have no other engagements; and if it rains you had better put up at the hotel.' As long as the good lady could order everybody round about her, she was not hard to please; and all the slaves and subjects of her little dowager court trembled before her, but loved her.

She did not receive a very numerous or brilliant society. The doctor, of course, was admitted as a constant and faithful visitor; the vicar and his curate; and on public days the vicar's wife and daughters, and some of the season visitors at Baymouth were received at the old lady's entertainments: but generally the company was a small one, and Mr. Arthur drank his wine by himself, when Lady Rockminster retired to take her doze, and to be played and sung to sleep by Laura after dinner.

'If my music can give her a nap,' said the good-natured girl, 'ought I not to be very glad that I can do so much good? Lady Rockminster sleeps very little of night: and I used to read to her, until I fell ill at Paris, since when she will not hear of my sitting up.'

'Why did you not write to me when you were ill?' asked Pen, with a blush.

'What good could you do me? I had Martha to nurse me; and the doctor every day. You are too busy to write to women or to think about them. You have your books and your newspapers, and your politics and your railroads to occupy you. I wrote when I was well.'

And Pen looked at her, and blushed again, as he remembered that, during all the time of her illness, he had never written to her, and had scarcely thought about her.

In consequence of his relationship, Pen was free to walk and ride with his cousin constantly, and in the course of those walks and rides, could appreciate the sweet frankness of her disposition, and the truth, simplicity, and kindliness, of her fair and spotless heart. In their mother's life-time, she had never spoken so openly or so cordially as now. The desire of poor Helen to make a union between her two children, had caused a reserve on Laura's part towards Pen; for which, under the altered circumstances of Arthur's life, there was now no necessity. He was engaged to another woman; and Laura became his sister at once,—hiding, or banishing from herself, any doubts which she might have as to his choice; striving to look cheerfully forward, and hope for his prosperity; promising herself to do all that affection might do to make her mother's darling happy.

Their talk was often about the departed mother. And it was from a thousand stories which Laura told him that Arthur was made aware how constant and absorbing that silent maternal devotion had been; which had accompanied

him present and absent through life, and had only ended with the fond widow's last breath. One day the people in Clavering saw a lad in charge of a couple of horses at the churchyard-gate : and it was told over the place that Pen and Laura had visited Helen's grave together. Since Arthur had come down into the country, he had been there once or twice : but the sight of the sacred stone had brought no consolation to him. A guilty man doing a guilty deed : a mere speculator, content to lay down his faith and honour for a fortune and a worldly career ; and owning that his life was but a contemptible surrender—what right had he in the holy place ?—what booted it to him that others in the world he lived in, were no better than himself ? Arthur and Laura rode by the gates of Fairoaks ; and he shook hands with his tenant's children, playing on the lawn and terrace—Laura looked steadily at the cottage wall, at the creeper on the porch and the magnolia growing up to her window. 'Mr. Pendennis rode by to-day,' one of the boys told his mother, 'with a lady, and he stopped and talked to us, and he asked for a bit of honeysuckle off the porch, and gave it to the lady. I couldn't see if she was pretty ; she had her veil down. She was riding one of Cramp's horses, out of Baymouth.'

As they rode over the downs between home and Baymouth, Pen did not speak much, though they rode very close together. He was thinking what a mockery life was, and how men refuse happiness when they may have it ; or, having it, kick it down ; or barter it, with their eyes open, for a little worthless money or beggarly honour. And then the thought came, what does it matter for the little space ? The lives of the best and purest of us are consumed in a vain desire, and end in a disappointment : as the dear soul's who sleeps in her grave yonder. She had her selfish ambition, as much as Caesar had ; and died, balked of her life's longing. The stone covers over our hopes and our memories. Our place knows us not. 'Other people's children are playing on the grass,' he broke out, in a hard voice, 'where you and I used to play, Laura. And you see how the magnolia we planted has grown up since our time. I have been round to one or two of the cottages where my mother used to visit. It is scarcely more than a year that she is gone, and the people whom she used to benefit care no more for her death than for Queen Anne's. We are all selfish : the world is selfish : there are but a few exceptions,

like you, my dear, to shine like good deeds in a naughty world, and make the blackness more dismal.'

'I wish you would not speak in that way, Arthur,' said Laura, looking down and bending her head to the honeysuckle on her breast. 'When you told the little boy to give me this, you were not selfish.'

'A pretty sacrifice I made to get it for you!' said the sneerer.

'But your heart was kind and full of love when you did so. One cannot ask for more than love and kindness; and if you think humbly of yourself, Arthur, the love and kindness are not diminished—are they? I often thought our dearest mother spoiled you at home, by worshipping you; and that if you are—I hate the word—what you say, her too great fondness helped to make you so. And as for the world, when men go out into it, I suppose they cannot be otherwise than selfish. You have to fight for yourself, and to get on for yourself, and to make a name for yourself. Mamma and your uncle both encouraged you in this ambition. If it is a vain thing, why pursue it? I suppose such a clever man as you intend to do a great deal of good to the country, by going into Parliament, or you would not wish to be there. What are you going to do when you are in the House of Commons?'

'Women don't understand about politics, my dear,' Pen said, sneering at himself as he spoke.

'But why don't you make us understand? I could never tell about Mr. Pynsent why he should like to be there so much. He is not a clever man——'

'He certainly is not a genius, Pynsent,' said Pen.

'Lady Diana says that he attends Committees all day; that then again he is at the House all night; that he always votes as he is told; that he never speaks; that he will never get on beyond a subordinate place, and as his grandmother tells him, he is choked with red-tape. Are you going to follow the same career, Arthur? What is there in it so brilliant that you should be so eager for it? I would rather that you should stop at home, and write books—good books, kind books, with gentle kind thoughts, such as you have, dear Arthur, and such as might do people good to read. And if you do not win fame, what then? You own it is vanity, and you can live very happily without it. I must not pretend to advise; but I take you at your own word about the world; and as you own it is wicked, and that it tires you, ask you why you don't leave it?'

'And what would you have me do?' asked Arthur.

'I would have you bring your wife to Fairoaks to live there, and study, and do good round about you. I would like to see your own children playing on the lawn, Arthur, and that we might pray in our mother's church again once more, dear brother. If the world is a temptation, are we not told to pray that we may not be led into it?'

'Do you think Blanche would make a good wife for a petty country gentleman? Do you think I should become the character very well, Laura?' Pen asked. 'Remember temptation walks about the hedgerows as well as the city streets: and idleness is the greatest tempter of all.'

'What does—does Mr. Warrington say?' said Laura, as a blush mounted up to her cheek, and of which Pen saw the fervour, though Laura's veil fell over her face to hide it.

Pen rode on by Laura's side silently for a while. George's name so mentioned brought back the past to him, and the thoughts which he had once had regarding George and Laura. Why should the recurrence of the thought agitate him, now that he knew the union was impossible? Why should he be curious to know if, during the months of their intimacy, Laura had felt a regard for Warrington? From that day until the present time George had never alluded to his story, and Arthur remembered now that since then George had scarcely ever mentioned Laura's name.

At last he came close to her. 'Tell me something, Laura,' he said.

She put back her veil and looked at him. 'What is it, Arthur?' she asked—though from the tremor of her voice she guessed very well.

'Tell me—but for George's misfortune—I never knew him speak of it before or since that day—would you—would you have given him—what you refused me?'

'Yes, Pen,' she said, bursting into tears.

'He deserved you better than I did,' poor Arthur groaned forth, with an indescribable pang at his heart. 'I am but a selfish wretch, and George is better, nobler, truer, than I am. God bless him!'

'Yes, Pen,' said Laura, reaching out her hand to her cousin, and he put his arm round her, and for a moment she sobbed on his shoulder.

The gentle girl had had her secret, and told it. In the widow's last journey from Fairoaks, when hastening with her

mother to Arthur's sick bed, Laura had made a different confession; and it was only when Warrington told his own story, and described the hopeless condition of his life, that she discovered how much her feelings had changed, and with what tender sympathy, with what great respect, delight, and admiration she had grown to regard her cousin's friend. Until she knew that some plans she might have dreamed of were impossible, and that Warrington, reading in her heart, perhaps, had told his melancholy story to warn her, she had not asked herself whether it was possible that her affections could change; and had been shocked and scared by the discovery of the truth. How should she have told it to Helen, and confessed her shame? Poor Laura felt guilty before her friend, with the secret which she dared not confide to her; felt as if she had been ungrateful for Helen's love and regard; felt as if she had been wickedly faithless to Pen in withdrawing that love from him which he did not even care to accept; humbled even and repentant before Warrington, lest she should have encouraged him by undue sympathy, or shown the preference which she began to feel.

The catastrophe which broke up Laura's home, and the grief and anguish which she felt for her mother's death, gave her little leisure for thoughts more selfish; and by the time she rallied from that grief, the minor one was also almost cured. It was but for a moment that she had indulged a hope about Warrington. Her admiration and respect for him remained as strong as ever. But the tender feeling with which she knew she had regarded him, was schooled into such calmness, that it may be said to have been dead and passed away. The pang which it left behind was one of humility and remorse. 'Oh, how wicked and proud I was about Arthur,' she thought, 'how self-confident and unforgiving! I never forgave from my heart this poor girl, who was fond of him, or him for encouraging her love; and I have been more guilty than she, poor, little, artless creature! I, professing to love one man, could listen to another only too eagerly; and would not pardon the change of feelings in Arthur, whilst I myself was changing and unfaithful.' And so humiliating herself, and acknowledging her weakness, the poor girl sought for strength and refuge in the manner in which she had been accustomed to look for them.

She had done no wrong: but there are some folks who suffer for a fault ever so trifling as much as others whose

stout consciences can walk under crimes of almost any weight; and poor Laura chose to fancy that she had acted in this delicate juncture of her life as a very great criminal. She determined that she had done Pen a great injury by withdrawing that love which, privately in her mother's hearing, she had bestowed upon him; that she had been ungrateful to her dead benefactress by ever allowing herself to think of another, or of violating her promise; and that, considering her own enormous crimes, she ought to be very gentle in judging those of others, whose temptations were much greater, very likely; and whose motives she could not understand.

A year back Laura would have been indignant at the idea that Arthur should marry Blanche: and her high spirit would have risen, as she thought that from worldly motives he should stoop to one so unworthy. Now when the news was brought to her of such a chance (the intelligence was given to her by old Lady Rockminster, whose speeches were as direct and rapid as a slap on the face), the humbled girl winced a little at the blow, but bore it meekly, and with a desperate acquiescence. 'He has a right to marry, he knows a great deal more of the world than I do,' she argued with herself. 'Blanche may not be so light-minded as she seemed, and who am I to be her judge? I dare say it is very good that Arthur should go into Parliament and distinguish himself, and my duty is to do everything that lies in my power to aid him and Blanche, and to make his home happy. I dare say I shall live with them. If I am godmother to one of their children, I will leave her my three thousand pounds!' And forthwith she began to think what she could give Blanche out of her small treasures, and how best to conciliate her affection. She wrote her forthwith a kind letter, in which, of course, no mention was made of the plans in contemplation, but in which Laura recalled old times, and spoke her good-will, and in reply to this, she received an eager answer from Blanche: in which not a word about marriage was said, to be sure, but Mr. Pendennis was mentioned two or three times in the letter, and they were to be henceforth, dearest Laura, and dearest Blanche, and loving sisters, and so forth.

When Pen and Laura reached home, after Laura's confession (Pen's noble acknowledgement of his own inferiority, and generous expression of love for Warrington, causing the girl's heart to throb, and rendering doubly keen those tears

which she sobbed on his shoulder), a little slim letter was awaiting Miss Bell in the hall, which she trembled rather guiltily as she unsealed, and which Pen blushed as he recognized : for he saw instantly that it was from Blanche.

Laura opened it hastily, and cast her eyes quickly over it, as Pen kept his fixed on her, blushing.

'She dates from London,' Laura said. 'She has been with old Bonner, Lady Clavering's maid. Bonner is going to marry Lightfoot the butler. Where do you think Blanche has been ?' she cried out eagerly.

'To Paris, to Scotland, to the Casino ?'

'To Shepherd's Inn, to see Fanny ; but Fanny wasn't there, and Blanche is going to leave a present for her. Isn't it kind of her and thoughtful ?' And she handed the letter to Pen, who read—

I saw *Madame Mère*, who was scrubbing the room, and looked at me with very *scrubby* looks ; but *la belle* Fanny was not *au logis ;* and as I heard that she was in Captain Strong's apartments, Bonner and I mounted *au troisième* to see this famous beauty. Another disappointment—only the Chevalier Strong and a friend of his in the room : so we came away after all without seeing the enchanting Fanny.

Je t'envoie mille et mille baisers. When will that horrid canvassing be over ? Sleeves are worn, &c. &c. &c.

After dinner the doctor was reading the *Times*. 'A young gentleman I attended when he was here some eight or nine years ago has come into a fine fortune,' the doctor said. 'I see here announced the death of John Henry Foker, Esq., of Logwood Hall, at Pau, in the Pyrenees, on the 15th ult.'

CHAPTER LXVII

IN WHICH THE MAJOR IS BIDDEN TO STAND AND DELIVER

ANY gentleman who has frequented the 'Wheel of Fortune' public-house, where it may be remembered that Mr. James Morgan's club was held, and where Sir Francis Clavering had an interview with Major Pendennis, is aware that there are three rooms for guests upon the ground floor, besides the bar where the landlady sits. One is a parlour frequented by the public at large; to another room gentlemen in livery resort; and the third apartment, on the door of which 'Private' is painted, is that hired by the club of 'The Confidentials,' of which Messrs. Morgan and Lightfoot were members.

The noiseless Morgan had listened to the conversation between Strong and Major Pendennis at the latter's own lodgings, and had carried away from it matter for much private speculation; and a desire of knowledge had led him to follow his master when the major came to the 'Wheel of Fortune,' and to take his place quietly in the Confidential room, whilst Pendennis and Clavering had their discourse in the parlour. There was a particular corner in the Confidential room from which you could hear almost all that passed in the next apartment; and as the conversation between the two gentlemen there was rather angry, and carried on in a high key, Morgan had the benefit of overhearing almost the whole of it: and what he heard, strengthened the conclusions which his mind had previously formed.

'He knew Altamont at once, did he, when he saw him in Sydney? Clavering ain't no more married to my lady than I am! Altamont's the man: Altamont's a convict; young Harthur comes into Parlyment, and the gov'nor promises not to split. By Jove, what a sly old rogue it is, that old gov'nor! No wonder he's anxious to make the match between Blanche and Harthur: why, she'll have a hundred thousand if she's a penny, and bring her man a seat in Parlyment into the bargain.' Nobody saw, but a physiognomist

would nave liked to behold, the expression of Mr. Morgan's countenance, when this astounding intelligence was made clear to him. 'But for my hage, and the confounded prejudices of society,' he said, surveying himself in the glass, 'dammy, James Morgan, you might marry her yourself.' But if he could not marry Miss Blanche and her fortune, Morgan thought he could mend his own by the possession of this information, and that it might be productive of benefit to him from very many sources. Of all the persons whom the secret affected, the greater number would not like to have it known. For instance, Sir Francis Clavering, whose fortune it involved, would wish to keep it quiet; Colonel Altamont, whose neck it implicated, would naturally be desirous to hush it; and that young upstart beast, Mr. Harthur, who was for gettin' into Parlyment on the strenth of it, and was as proud as if he was a duke with half a millium a year (such, we grieve to say, was Morgan's opinion of his employer's nephew), would pay anythink sooner than let the world know that he was married to a convick's daughter, and had got his seat in Parlyment by trafficking with this secret. As for Lady C., Morgan thought, if she's tired of Clavering, and wants to get rid of him, she'll pay: if she's frightened about her son, and fond of the little beggar, she'll pay all the same: and Miss Blanche will certainly come down handsome to the man who will put her into her rights, which she was unjustly defrauded of them, and no mistake. 'Dammy,' concluded the valet, reflecting upon this wonderful hand which luck had given him to play, 'with such cards as these, James Morgan, you are a made man. It may be a reg'lar enewity to me. Every one of 'em must susscribe. And with what I've made already, I may cut business, give my old gov'nor warning, turn gentleman, and have a servant of my own, begad.' Entertaining himself with calculations such as these, that were not a little likely to perturb a man's spirit, Mr. Morgan showed a very great degree of self-command by appearing and being calm, and by not allowing his future prospects in any way to interfere with his present duties.

One of the persons whom the story chiefly concerned, Colonel Altamont, was absent from London, when Morgan was thus made acquainted with his history. The valet knew of Sir Francis Clavering's Shepherd's Inn haunt, and walked thither an hour or two after the baronet and Pendennis had had their conversation together. But that bird was flown;

Colonel Altamont had received his Derby winnings, and was gone to the Continent. The fact of his absence was exceedingly vexatious to Mr. Morgan. 'He'll drop all that money at the gambling-shops on the Rhind,' thought Morgan, 'and I might have had a good bit of it. It's confounded annoying to think he's gone and couldn't have waited a few days longer.' Hope, triumphant or deferred, ambition or disappointment, victory or patient ambush, Morgan bore all alike, with similar equable countenance. Until the proper day came, the major's boots were varnished and his hair was curled, his early cup of tea was brought to his bedside, his oaths, rebukes, and senile satire borne, with silent, obsequious fidelity. Who would think, to see him waiting upon his master, packing and shouldering his trunks, and occasionally assisting at table, at the country-houses where he might be staying, that Morgan was richer than his employer, and knew his secrets and other people's? In the profession Mr. Morgan was greatly respected and admired, and his reputation for wealth and wisdom got him much renown at most supper-tables: the younger gentlemen voted him stoopid, a feller of no ideas, and a fogey, in a word: but not one of them would not say amen to the heartfelt prayer which some of the most serious-minded among the gentlemen uttered, 'When I die may I cut up as well as Morgan Pendennis!'

As became a man of fashion, Major Pendennis spent the autumn passing from house to house of such country friends as were at home to receive him, and if the duke happened to be abroad, or the marquis in Scotland, condescending to sojourn with Sir John or the plain squire. To say the truth, the old gentleman's reputation was somewhat on the wane: many of the men of his time had died out, and the occupants of their halls and the present wearers of their titles knew not Major Pendennis; and little cared for his traditions 'of the wild Prince and Poyns,' and of the heroes of fashion passed away. It must have struck the good man with melancholy as he walked by many a London door, to think how seldom it was now opened for him, and how often he used to knock at it—to what banquets and welcome he used to pass through it—a score of years back. He began to own that he was no longer of the present age, and dimly to apprehend that the young men laughed at him. Such melancholy musings must come across many a Pall Mall philosopher. The men, thinks he,

are not such as they used to be in his time: the old grand manner and courtly grace of life are gone: what is Castlewood House* and the present Castlewood, compared to the magnificence of the old mansion and owner? The late lord came to London with four postchaises and sixteen horses: all the West Road hurried out to look at his cavalcade: the people in London streets even stopped as his procession passed them. The present lord travels with five bagmen* in a railway carriage, and sneaks away from the stations, smoking a cigar in a brougham. The late lord in autumn filled Castlewood with company, who drank claret till midnight: the present man buries himself in a hut on a Scotch mountain, and passes November in two or three closets in an entresol at Paris, where his amusements are a dinner at a café and a box at a little theatre. What a contrast there is between *his* Lady Lorraine, the Regent's Lady Lorraine, and her little ladyship of the present era! He figures to himself the first, beautiful, gorgeous, magnificent in diamonds and velvets, daring in rouge, the wits of the world (the old wits, the old polished gentlemen—not the *canaille* of to-day with their language of the cab-stand, and their coats smelling of smoke) bowing at her feet; and then thinks of to-day's Lady Lorraine—a little woman in a black silk gown, like a governess, who talks astronomy, and labouring classes, and emigration, and the deuce knows what, and lurks to church at eight o'clock in the morning. Abbots-Lorraine, that used to be the noblest house in the county, is turned into a monastery—a regular La Trappe. They don't drink two glasses of wine after dinner, and every other man at table is a country curate, with a white neckcloth, whose talk is about Polly Higson's progress at school, or widow Watkins's lumbago. 'And the other young men, those lounging guardsmen and great lazy dandies—sprawling over sofas and billiard-tables, and stealing off to smoke pipes in each other's bedrooms, caring for nothing, reverencing nothing, not even an old gentleman who has known their fathers and their betters, not even a pretty woman—what a difference there is between these men, who poison the very turnips and stubble-fields with their tobacco, and the gentlemen of our time!' thinks the major; 'the breed is gone—there's no use for 'em; they're replaced by a parcel of damned cotton-spinners and utilitarians, and young sprigs of parsons with their hair combed down their backs. I'm getting old: they're getting past me: they laugh

at us old boys, thought old Pendennis. And he was not far wrong; the times and manners which he admired were pretty nearly gone—the gay young men 'larked' him irreverently, whilst the serious youth had a grave pity and wonder at him, which would have been even more painful to bear had the old gentleman been aware of its extent. But he was rather simple: his examination of moral questions had never been very deep; it had never struck him, perhaps, until very lately, that he was otherwise than a most respectable and rather fortunate man. Is there no old age but his without reverence? Did youthful folly never jeer at other bald pates? For the past two or three years, he had begun to perceive that his day was wellnigh over, and that the men of the new time had begun to reign.

After a rather unsuccessful autumn season, then, during which he was faithfully followed by Mr. Morgan, his nephew Arthur being engaged, as we have seen, at Clavering, it happened that Major Pendennis came back for a while to London, at the dismal end of October, when the fogs and the lawyers come to town. Who has not looked with interest at those loaded cabs, piled boxes, and crowded children, rattling through the streets on the dun October evenings; stopping at the dark houses, where they discharge nurse and infant, girls, matron and father, whose holidays are over? Yesterday it was France and sunshine, or Broadstairs and liberty; to-day comes work and a yellow fog; and, ye gods! what a heap of bills there lies in master's study. And the clerk has brought the lawyer's papers from chambers; and in half an hour the literary man knows that the printer's boy will be in the passage; and Mr. Smith with that little account (that particular little account) has called presentient of your arrival, and has left word that he will call to-morrow morning at ten. Who amongst us has not said good-bye to his holiday; returned to dun London and his fate; surveyed his labours and liabilities laid out before him, and been aware of that inevitable little account to settle? Smith and his little account, in the morning, symbolize duty, difficulty, struggle, which you will meet, let us hope, friend, with a manly and honest heart.—And you think of him, as the children are slumbering once more in their own beds, and the watchful housewife tenderly pretends to sleep.

Old Pendennis had no special labours or bills to encounter

on the morrow, as he had no affection at home to soothe him. He had always money in his desk sufficient for his wants ; and being by nature and habit tolerably indifferent to the wants of other people, these latter were not likely to disturb him. But a gentleman may be out of temper though he does not owe a shilling : and though he may be ever so selfish, he must occasionally feel dispirited and lonely. He had had two or three twinges of gout in the country-house where he had been staying : the birds were wild and shy, and the walking over the ploughed fields had fatigued him deucedly : the young men had laughed at him, and he had been peevish at table once or twice : he had not been able to get his whist of an evening : and, in fine, was glad to come away. In all his dealings with Morgan, his valet, he had been exceedingly sulky and discontented. He had sworn at him and abused him for many days past. He had scalded his mouth with bad soup at Swindon. He had left his umbrella in the railroad carriage : at which piece of forgetfulness, he was in such a rage, that he cursed Morgan more freely than ever. Both the chimneys smoked furiously in his lodgings ; and when he caused the windows to be flung open, he swore so acrimoniously, that Morgan was inclined to fling him out of window, too, through that opened casement. The valet swore after his master, as Pendennis went down the street on his way to the club.

Bays's was not at all pleasant. The house had been new painted, and smelt of varnish and turpentine, and a large streak of white paint inflicted itself on the back of the old boy's fur-collared surtout. The dinner was not good : and the three most odious men in all London—old Hawkshaw, whose cough and accompaniments are fit to make any man uncomfortable ; old Colonel Gripley, who seizes on all the newspapers ; and that irreclaimable old bore Jawkins, who would come and dine at the next table to Pendennis, and describe to him every inn-bill which he had paid in his foreign tour : each and all of these disagreeable personages and incidents had contributed to make Major Pendennis miserable ; and the club waiter trod on his toe as he brought him his coffee. Never alone appear the Immortals. The Furies always hunt in company : they pursued Pendennis from home to the club, and from his club home.

Whilst the major was absent from his lodgings, Morgan

MR. MORGAN AT HIS EASE

had been seated in the landlady's parlour, drinking freely of hot brandy-and-water, and pouring out on Mrs. Brixham some of the abuse which he had received from his master upstairs. Mrs. Brixham was Morgan's slave. He was his landlady's landlord. He had bought the lease of the house which she rented ; he had got her name and her son's to acceptances, and a bill of sale which made him master of the luckless widow's furniture. The young Brixham was a clerk in an insurance office, and Morgan could put him into what he called quod any day. Mrs. Brixham was a clergyman's widow, and Mr. Morgan, after performing his duties on the first floor, had a pleasure in making the old lady fetch him his boot-jack and his slippers. She was his slave. The little black profiles of her son and daughter ; the very picture of Tiddlecot Church, where she was married, and her poor dear Brixham lived and died, was now Morgan's property, as it hung there over the mantelpiece of his back-parlour. Morgan sat in the widow's back room, in the ex-curate's old horsehair study-chair, making Mrs. Brixham bring supper for him, and fill his glass again and again.

The liquor was bought with the poor woman's own coin, and hence Morgan indulged in it only the more freely ; and he had eaten his supper and was drinking a third tumbler, when old Pendennis returned from the club, and went upstairs to his rooms. Mr. Morgan swore very savagely at him and his bell, when he heard the latter, and finished his tumbler of brandy before he went up to answer the summons.

He received the abuse consequent on this delay in silence, nor did the major condescend to read in the flushed face and glaring eyes of the man, the anger under which he was labouring. The old gentleman's foot-bath was at the fire ; his gown and slippers awaiting him there. Morgan knelt down to take his boots off with due subordination : and as the major abused him from above, kept up a growl of maledictions below at his feet. Thus, when Pendennis was crying, 'Confound you, sir, mind that strap—curse you, don't wrench my foot off,' Morgan *sotto voce* below was expressing a wish to strangle him, drown him, and punch his head off.

The boots removed, it became necessary to divest Mr. Pendennis of his coat : and for this purpose the valet had necessarily to approach very near to his employer ; so near

that Pendennis could not but perceive what Mr. Morgan's late occupation had been; to which he adverted in that simple and forcible phraseology which men are sometimes in the habit of using to their domestics; informing Morgan that he was a drunken beast, and that he smelt of brandy.

At this the man broke out, losing patience, and flinging up all subordination, 'I'm drunk, am I? I'm a beast, am I? I'm d——d, am I? you infernal old miscreant. Shall I wring your old head off, and drownd yer in that pail of water? Do you think I'm a-goin' to bear your confounded old harrogance, you old Wigsby! Chatter your old hivories at me, do you, you grinning old baboon? Come on, if you are a man, and can stand to a man. Ha! you coward, knives, knives!'

'If you advance a step, I'll send it into you,' said the major, seizing up a knife that was on the table near him. 'Go downstairs, you drunken brute, and leave the house; send for your book and your wages in the morning, and never let me see your insolent face again. This d——d impertinence of yours has been growing for some months past. You have been growing too rich. You are not fit for service. Get out of it, and out of the house.'

'And where would you wish me to go, pray, out of the 'ouse?' asked the man, 'and won't it be equal convenient to-morrow mornin'?—tootyfay mame shose, sivvaplay, munseer?'

'Silence, you beast, and go!' cried out the major.

Morgan began to laugh, with rather a sinister laugh. 'Look yere, Pendennis,' he said, seating himself; 'since I've been in this room you've called me a beast, brute, dog: and d——d me, haven't you? How do you suppose one man likes that sort of talk from another? How many years have I waited on you, and how many damns and cusses have you given me, along with my wages? Do you think a man's a dog, that you can talk to him in this

way? If I choose to drink a little, why shouldn't I? I've seen many a gentleman drunk formly, and peraps have the 'abit from them. I ain't a-goin' to leave this house, old feller, and shall I tell you why? The house is my house; every stick of furnitur' in it is mine, excep' *your* old traps, and your shower-bath, and your wig-box. I've bought the place, I tell you, with my own industry and perseverance. I can show a hundred pound, where you can show a fifty, or your damned supersellious nephew either. I've served you honourable, done everythink for you these dozen years, and I'm a dog, am I? I'm a beast, am I? That's the language for gentlemen, not for our rank. But I'll bear it no more. I throw up your service: I'm tired on it; I've combed your old wig and buckled your old girths and waistbands long enough, I tell you. Don't look savage at me. I'm sitting in my own chair, in my own room, a-telling the truth to you. I'll be your beast, and your brute, and your dog, no more, Major Pendennis 'Alf Pay.'

The fury of the old gentleman, met by the servant's abrupt revolt, had been shocked and cooled by the concussion, as much as if a sudden shower-bath or a pail of cold water had been flung upon him. That effect produced, and his anger calmed, Morgan's speech had interested him, and he rather respected his adversary, and his courage in facing him, as of old days, in the fencing-room, he would have admired the opponent who hit him.

'You are no longer my servant,' the major said, 'and the house may be yours; but the lodgings are mine, and you will have the goodness to leave them. To-morrow morning, when we have settled our accounts, I shall remove into other quarters. In the meantime, I desire to go to bed, and have not the slightest wish for your further company.'

'*We'll* have a settlement, don't you be afraid,' Morgan said, getting up from his chair. 'I ain't done with you yet; nor with your family, nor with the Clavering family, Major Pendennis; and that you shall know.'

'Have the goodness to leave the room, sir;—I'm tired,' said the major.

'Hah! you'll be more tired of me afore you've done,' answered the man, with a sneer, and walked out of the room; leaving the major to compose himself, as best he might, after the agitation of this extraordinary scene.

He sat and mused by his fireside over the past events, and the confounded impudence and ingratitude of servants; and thought how he should get a new man: how devilish unpleasant it was for a man of his age, and with his habits, to part with a fellow to whom he had been accustomed: how Morgan had a receipt for boot-varnish, which was incomparably better and more comfortable to the feet than any he had ever tried: how very well he made mutton-broth, and tended him when he was unwell. 'Gad, it's a hard thing to lose a fellow of that sort: but he must go,' thought the major. 'He has grown rich, and impudent since he has grown rich. He was horribly tipsy and abusive to-night. We must part, and I must go out of the lodgings. Dammy, I like the lodgings; I'm used to 'em. It's very unpleasant, at my time of life, to change my quarters.' And so on, mused the old gentleman. The shower-bath had done him good: the testiness was gone: the loss of the umbrella, the smell of paint at the club, were forgotten under the superior excitement. 'Confound the insolent villain!' thought the old gentleman. 'He understood my wants to a nicety; he was the best servant in England.' He thought about his servant as a man thinks of a horse that has carried him long and well, and that has come down with him, and is safe no longer. How the deuce to replace him? Where can he get such another animal?

In these melancholy cogitations the major, who had donned his own dressing-gown and replaced his head of hair (a little grey had been introduced into the coiffure of late by Mr. Truefitt,* which had given the major's head the most artless and respectable appearance); in these cogitations, we say, the major, who had taken off his wig and put on his night-handkerchief, sat absorbed by the fireside, when a feeble knock came at his door, which was presently opened by the landlady of the lodgings.

'God bless my soul, Mrs. Brixham!' cried out the major, startled that a lady should behold him in the *simple appareil* of his night-toilette. 'It—it's very late, Mrs. Brixham.'

'I wish I might speak to you, sir,' said the landlady very piteously.

'About Morgan, I suppose? He has cooled himself at the pump. Can't take him back, Mrs. Brixham. Impos-

sible. I'd determined to part with him before, when I heard of his dealings in the discount business—I suppose you've heard of them, Mrs. Brixham? My servant's a capitalist, begad.'

'Oh, sir,' said Mrs. Brixham, 'I know it to my cost. I borrowed from him a little money five years ago; and though I have paid him many times over, I am entirely in his power. I am ruined by him, sir. Everything I had is his. He's a dreadful man.'

'Eh, Mrs. Brixham? *tant pis*—dev'lish sorry for you, and that I must quit your house after lodging here so long: there's no help for it. I must go.'

'He says we must all go, sir,' sobbed out the luckless widow. 'He came downstairs from you just now—he had been drinking, and it always makes him very wicked—and he said that you had insulted him, sir, and treated him like a dog, and spoken to him unkindly; and he swore he would be revenged, and—and I owe him a hundred and twenty pounds, sir,—and he has a bill of sale of all my

furniture—and says he will turn me out of my house, and send my poor George to prison. He has been the ruin of my family, that man.'

'Dev'lish sorry, Mrs. Brixham; pray take a chair. What can I do?'

'Could you not intercede with him for us? George will give half his allowance; my daughter can send something. If you will but stay on, sir, and pay a quarter's rent in advance——'

'My good madam, I would as soon give you a quarter in advance as not, if I were going to stay in the lodgings. But I can't; and I can't afford to fling away twenty pounds, my good madam. I'm a poor half-pay officer, and want every shilling I have, begad. As far as a few pounds goes—say five pounds—I don't say—and shall be most happy, and that sort of thing: and I'll give it to you in the morning with pleasure: but—but it's getting late, and I have made a railroad journey.'

'God's will be done, sir,' said the poor woman, drying her tears. 'I must bear my fate.'

'And a dev'lish hard one it is, and most sincerely I pity you, Mrs. Brixham. I—I'll say ten pounds, if you will permit me. Good-night.'

'Mr. Morgan, sir, when he came downstairs, and when—when I besought him to have pity on me, and told him he had been the ruin of my family, said something which I did not well understand—that he would ruin every family in the house—that he knew something would bring you down too—and that you should pay him for your—your insolence to him. I—I must own to you, that I went down on my knees to him, sir; and he said, with a dreadful oath against you, that he would have you on your knees.'

'Me?—by Gad, that is too pleasant! Where is the confounded fellow?'

'He went away, sir. He said he should see you in the morning. Oh, pray try and pacify him, and save me and my poor boy.' And the widow went away with this prayer, to pass her night as she might, and look for the dreadful morrow.

The last words about himself excited Major Pendennis so much, that his compassion for Mrs. Brixham's misfortunes was quite forgotten in the consideration of his own case.

'Me on my knees?' thought he, as he got into bed: 'confound his impudence. Who ever saw me on my knees? What the devil does the fellow know? Gad, I've not had an affair these twenty years. I defy him.' And the old campaigner turned round and slept pretty sound, being rather excited and amused by the events of the day—the last day in Bury Street he was determined it should be. 'For it's impossible to stay on with a valet over me, and a bankrupt landlady. What good can I do this poor devil of a woman? I'll give her twenty pound—there's Warrington's twenty pound, which he has just paid—but what's the use? She'll want more, and more, and more, and that cormorant Morgan will swallow all. No, dammy, I can't afford to know poor people; and to-morrow I'll say good-bye—to Mrs. Brixham and Mr. Morgan.'

CHAPTER LXVIII

IN WHICH THE MAJOR NEITHER YIELDS HIS MONEY NOR HIS LIFE

EARLY next morning Pendennis's shutters were opened by Morgan, who appeared as usual, with a face perfectly grave and respectful, bearing with him the old gentleman's clothes, cans of water, and elaborate toilette requisites.

'It's you, is it?' said the old fellow, from the bed. 'I shan't take you back again, you understand.'

'I 'ave not the least wish to be took back agin, Major Pendennis,' Mr. Morgan said, with grave dignity, 'nor to serve you nor hany man. But as I wish you to be comf'table as long as you stay in my house, I came up to do what's nessary.' And once more, and for the last time, Mr. James Morgan laid out the silver dressing-case, and strapped the shining razor.

These offices concluded, he addressed himself to the major with an indescribable solemnity, and said: 'Thinkin' that you would most likely be in want of a respectable

pusson, until you suited yourself, I spoke to a young man last night, who is 'ere.'

'Indeed,' said the warrior in the tent-bed.

'He 'ave lived in the fust famlies, and I can wouch for his respectability.'

'You are monstrous polite,' grinned the old major. And the truth is, that after the occurrences of the previous evening, Morgan had gone out to his own club at the 'Wheel of Fortune,' and there finding Frosch, a courier and valet just returned from a foreign tour with young Lord Cubley, and for the present disposable, had represented to Mr. Frosch, that he, Morgan, had 'a devil of a blow hup with his own gov'nor, and was goin' to retire from the business haltogether, and that if Frosch wanted a tempory job, he might probbly have it by applying in Bury Street.'

'You are very polite,' said the major, 'and your recommendation, I am sure, will have every weight.'

Morgan blushed: he felt his master was 'a-chaffin' of him.' 'The man have awaited on you before, sir,' he said, with great dignity. 'Lord De la Pole, sir, gave him to his nephew, young Lord Cubley, and he have been with him on his foring tour, and not wishing to go to Fitzurse Castle, which Frosch's chest is delicate, and he cannot bear the cold in Scotland, he is free to serve you or not, as you choose.'

'I repeat, sir, that you are exceedingly polite,' said the major. 'Come in, Frosch—you will do very well—Mr. Morgan, will you have the great kindness to——'

'I shall show him what is nessary, sir, and what is customry for you to wish to 'ave done. Will you please to take breakfast 'ere or at the club, Major Pendennis?'

'With your kind permission, I will breakfast here, and afterwards we will make our little arrangements.'

'If you please, sir.'

'Will you now oblige me by leaving the room?'

Morgan withdrew; the excessive politeness of his ex-employer made him almost as angry as the major's bitterest words. And whilst the old gentleman is making his mysterious toilette, we will also modestly retire.

After breakfast, Major Pendennis and his new aide-de-camp occupied themselves in preparing for their departure. The establishment of the old bachelor was not very complicated. He encumbered himself with no useless wardrobe.

A Bible (his mother's), a road-book, Pen's novel (calf elegant), and the Duke of Wellington's Dispatches, with a few prints, maps, and portraits of that illustrious general, and of various sovereigns and consorts of this country, and of the general under whom Major Pendennis had served in India, formed his literary and artistical collection : he was always ready to march at a few hours' notice, and the cases in which he had brought his property into his lodgings some fifteen years before were still in the lofts, amply sufficient to receive all his goods. These, the young woman who did the work of the house, and who was known by the name of Betty to her mistress, and of 'Slavey' to Mr. Morgan, brought down from their resting-place, and obediently dusted and cleaned under the eyes of the terrible Morgan. His demeanour was guarded and solemn ; he had spoken no word as yet to Mrs. Brixham respecting his threats of the past night, but he looked as if he would execute them, and the poor widow tremblingly awaited her fate.

Old Pendennis, armed with his cane, superintended the package of his goods and chattels, under the hands of Mr. Frosch, and the slavey burned such of his papers as he did not care to keep : flung open doors and closets until they were all empty ; and now all boxes and chests were closed, except his desk, which was ready to receive the final accounts of Mr. Morgan.

That individual now made his appearance, and brought his books. 'As I wish to speak to you in privick, peraps you will 'ave the kindness to request Frosch to step downstairs,' he said, on entering.

'Bring a couple of cabs, Frosch, if you please—and wait downstairs until I ring for you,' said the major. Morgan saw Frosch downstairs, watched him go along the street upon his errand, and produced his books and accounts, which were simple and very easily settled.

'And now, sir,' said he, having pocketed the cheque, which his ex-employer gave him, and signed his name to his book with a flourish, 'and now that accounts is closed between us, sir,' he said, 'I porpose to speak to you as one man to another' (Morgan liked the sound of his own voice ; and, as an individual, indulged in public speaking whenever he could get an opportunity, at the club, or the housekeeper's room), 'and I must tell you, that I'm in *possussion of certing infamation.*'

'And may I inquire of what nature, pray?' asked the major.

'It's valuble information, Major Pendennis, as you know very well. I know of a marriage as is no marriage—of a honourable baronet as is no more married than I am; and which his wife is married to somebody else, as you know too, sir.'

Pendennis at once understood all. 'Ha! this accounts for your behaviour. You have been listening at the door, sir, I suppose,' said the major, looking very haughty; 'I forgot to look at the key-hole when I went to that public-house, or I might have suspected what sort of a person was behind it.'

'I may have my schemes as you may have yours, I suppose,' answered Morgan. 'I may get my information, and I may act on that information, and I may find that information valuble as anybody else may. A poor servant may have a bit of luck as well as a gentleman, mayn't he? Don't you be putting on your 'aughty looks, sir, and comin' the aristocrat over me. That's all gammon with me. I'm an Englishman, I am, and as good as you.'

'To what the devil does this tend, sir? and how does the secret which you have surprised concern me, I should like to know?' asked Major Pendennis, with great majesty.

'How does it concern me, indeed? how grand we are! How does it concern my nephew, I wonder? How does it concern my nephew's seat in Parlyment: and to subornation of bigamy? How does it concern that? What, are you to be the only man to have a secret, and to trade on it? Why shouldn't I go halves, Major Pendennis? I've found it out too. Look here! I ain't goin' to be unreasonable with you. Make it worth my while, and I'll keep the thing close. Let Mr. Arthur take his seat, and his rich wife, if you like; I don't want to marry her. But I will have my share, as sure as my name's James Morgan. And if I don't——'

'And if you don't, sir—what?' Pendennis asked.

'If I don't, I'll split, and tell all. I smash Clavering, and have him and his wife up for bigamy—so help me, I will! I smash young Hopeful's marriage, and I show up you and him as makin' use of this secret, in order to squeeze a seat in Parlyment out of Sir Francis, and a fortune out of his wife.'

'Mr. Pendennis knows no more of this business than the babe unborn, sir,' cried the major, aghast. 'No more than Lady Clavering, than Miss Amory does.'

'Tell that to the marines, major,' replied the valet; 'that cock won't fight with me.'

'Do you doubt my word, you villain?'

'No bad language. I don't care one twopence 'a'p'ny whether your word's true or not. I tell you, I intend this to be a nice little annuity to me, major: for I have every one of you; and I ain't such a fool as to let you go. I should say that you might make it five hundred a year to me among you, easy. Pay me down the first quarter now, and I'm as mum as a mouse. Just give me a note for one twenty-five. There's your cheque-book on your desk.'

'And there's this too, you villain,' cried the old gentleman. In the desk to which the valet pointed was a little double-barrelled pistol, which had belonged to Pendennis's old patron, the Indian commander-in-chief,* and which had accompanied him in many a campaign. 'One more word, you scoundrel, and I'll shoot you, like a mad dog. Stop—by Jove, I'll do it now. You'll assault me, will you? You'll strike at an old man, will you, you lying coward? Kneel down and say your prayers, sir, for by the Lord you shall die.'

The major's face glared with rage at his adversary, who looked terrified before him for a moment, and at the next, with a shriek of 'Murder,' sprang towards the open window, under which a policeman happened to be on his beat. 'Murder! Police!' bellowed Mr. Morgan.

To his surprise, Major Pendennis wheeled away the table and walked to the other window, which was also open. He beckoned the policeman. 'Come up here, policeman,' he said, and then went and placed himself against the door.

'You miserable sneak,' he said to Morgan; 'the pistol hasn't been loaded these fifteen years: as you would have known very well, if you had not been such a coward. That policeman is coming, and I will have him up, and have your trunks searched; I have reason to believe that you are a thief, sir. I know you are. I'll swear to the things.'

'You gave 'em to me—you gave 'em to me!' cried Morgan.

The major laughed. 'We'll see,' he said; and the

guilty valet remembered some fine lawn-fronted shirts—a certain gold-headed cane—an opera-glass, which he had forgotten to bring down, and of which he had assumed the use along with certain articles of his master's clothes, which the old dandy neither wore nor asked for.

Policeman X entered; followed by the scared Mrs. Brixham and her maid-of-all-work, who had been at the door and found some difficulty in closing it against the street amateurs, who wished to see the row. The major began instantly to speak.

'I have had occasion to discharge this drunken scoundrel,' he said. 'Both last night and this morning he insulted and assaulted me. I am an old man and took up a pistol. You see it is not loaded, and this coward cried out before he was hurt. I am glad you are come. I was charging him with taking my property, and desired to examine his trunks and his room.'

'The velvet cloak you ain't worn these three years, nor the weskits, and I thought I might take the shirts, and I—I take my hoath I intended to put back the hopera-glass,' roared Morgan, writhing with rage and terror.

'The man acknowledges that he is a thief,' the major said, calmly. 'He has been in my service for years, and I have treated him with every kindness and confidence. We will go upstairs and examine his trunks.'

In those trunks Mr. Morgan had things which he would fain keep from public eyes. Mr. Morgan, the bill discounter, gave goods as well as money to his customers. He provided young spendthrifts with snuff-boxes and pins and jewels and pictures and cigars, and of a very doubtful quality those cigars and jewels and pictures were. Their display at a police-office, the discovery of his occult profession, and the exposure of the major's property, which he had appropriated, indeed, rather than stolen,—would not have added to the reputation of Mr. Morgan. He looked a piteous image of terror and discomfiture.

'He'll smash me, will he?' thought the major. 'I'll crush him now, and finish with him.'

But he paused. He looked at poor Mrs. Brixham's scared face; and he thought for a moment to himself that the man brought to bay and in prison might make disclosures which had best be kept secret, and that it was best not to deal too fiercely with a desperate man.

A GOOD SHOT

'Stop,' he said, 'policeman. I'll speak with this man by himself.'

'Do you give Mr. Morgan in charge?' said the policeman.

'I have brought no charge as yet,' the major said, with a significant look at his man.

'Thank you, sir,' whispered Morgan, very low.

'Go outside the door, and wait there, policeman, if you please.—Now, Morgan, you have played one game with me, and you have not had the best of it, my good man. No, begad, you've not had the best of it, though you had the best hand; and you've got to pay, too, now, you scoundrel.'

'Yes, sir,' said the man.

'I've only found out, within the last week, the game which you have been driving, you villain. Young De Boots, of the Blues, recognized you as the man who came to barracks, and did business one-third in money, one-third in eau-de-Cologne, and one-third in French prints, you confounded demure old sinner! I didn't miss anything, or care a straw what you'd taken, you booby; but I took the shot, and it hit—hit the bull's-eye, begad. Dammy, sir, I'm an old campaigner.'

'What do you want with me, sir?'

'I'll tell you. Your bills, I suppose, you keep about you in that dem'd great leather pocket-book, don't you? You'll burn Mrs. Brixham's bills?'

'Sir, I ain't a-goin' to part with my property,' growled the man.

'You lent her sixty pounds five years ago. She and that poor devil of an insurance clerk, her son, have paid you fifty pounds a year ever since; and you have got a bill of sale of her furniture, and her note of hand for a hundred and fifty pounds. She told me so last night. By Jove, sir, you've bled that poor woman enough.'

'I won't give it up,' said Morgan; 'If I do I'm——'

'Policeman!' cried the major.

'You shall have the bill,' said Morgan. 'You're not going to take money of me, and you a gentleman?'

'I shall want you directly,' said the major to X, who here entered, and who again withdrew.

'No, my good sir,' the old gentleman continued; 'I have not any desire to have further pecuniary transactions with you; but we will draw out a little paper, which you will have

the kindness to sign. No, stop!—you shall write it: you have improved immensely in writing of late, and have now a very good hand. You shall sit down and write, if you please—there, at that table—so—let me see—we may as well have the date. Write "Bury Street, St. James's, October 21, 18—."'

And Morgan wrote as he was instructed, and as the pitiless old major continued:—

'"I, James Morgan, having come in extreme poverty into the service of Arthur Pendennis, Esquire, of Bury Street, St. James's, a major in her Majesty's service, acknowledge that I received liberal wages and board wages from my employer, during fifteen years."—You can't object to that, I'm sure,' said the major.

'During fifteen years,' wrote Morgan.

'"In which time, by my own care and prudence,"' the dictator resumed, '"I have managed to amass sufficient money to purchase the house in which my master resides, and, besides, to effect other savings. Amongst other persons from whom I have had money, I may mention my present tenant, Mrs. Brixham, who, in consideration of sixty pounds advanced by me five years since, has paid back to me the sum of two hundred and fifty pounds sterling, besides giving me a note of hand for one hundred and twenty pounds, which I restore to her at the desire of my late master, Major Arthur Pendennis, and therewith free her furniture, of which I had a bill of sale."—Have you written?'

'I think if this pistol was loaded, I'd blow your brains out,' said Morgan.

'No, you wouldn't. You have too great a respect for your valuable life, my good man,' the major answered. 'Let us go on and begin a new sentence.'

'"And having, in return for my master's kindness, stolen his property from him, which I acknowledge to be now upstairs in my trunks; and having uttered falsehoods regarding his and other honourable families, I do hereby, in consideration of his clemency to me, express my regret for uttering these falsehoods, and for stealing his property; and declare that I am not worthy of belief, and that I hope —yes, begad—that I hope to amend for the future. Signed, James Morgan."'

'I'm d——d if I sign it,' said Morgan.

'My good man, it will happen to you, whether you sign

or no, begad,' said the old fellow, chuckling at his own wit. 'There, I shall not use this, you understand, unless—unless I am compelled to do so. Mrs. Brixham, and our friend the policeman, will witness it, I dare say, without reading it : and I will give the old lady back her note of hand, and say, which you will confirm, that she and you are quits. I see there is Frosch come back with the cab for my trunks ; I shall go to an hotel.—You may come in now, policeman ; Mr. Morgan and I have arranged our little dispute. If Mrs. Brixham will sign this paper, and you, policeman, will do so, I shall be very much obliged to you both. Mrs. Brixham, you and your worthy landlord, Mr. Morgan, are quits. I wish you joy of him. Let Frosch come and pack the rest of the things.'

Frosch, aided by the slavey, under the calm superintendence of Mr. Morgan, carried Major Pendennis's boxes to the cabs in waiting ; and Mrs. Brixham, when her persecutor was not by, came and asked a Heaven's blessing upon the major, her preserver, and the best and quietest and kindest of lodgers. And having given her a finger to shake, which the humble lady received with a curtsy, and over which she was ready to make a speech full of tears, the major cut short that valedictory oration, and walked out of the house to the hotel in Jermyn Street, which was not many steps from Morgan's door.

That individual, looking forth from the parlour window, discharged anything but blessings at his parting guest ; but the stout old boy could afford not to be frightened at Mr. Morgan, and flung him a look of great contempt and humour as he strutted away with his cane.

Major Pendennis had not quitted his house of Bury Street many hours, and Mr. Morgan was enjoying his *otium* in a dignified manner, surveying the evening fog, and smoking a cigar, on the doorsteps, when Arthur Pendennis, Esq., the hero of this history, made his appearance at the well-known door.

'My uncle out, I suppose, Morgan ?' he said to the functionary ; knowing full well that to smoke was treason, in the presence of the major.

'Major Pendennis *is* hout, sir,' said Morgan, with gravity, bowing, but not touching the elegant cap which he wore. 'Major Pendennis have left this 'ouse to-day, sir, and I

have no longer the honour of being in his service, sir.'

'Indeed, and where is he?'

'I believe he 'ave taken tempory lodgings at Cox's 'Otel, in Jummin Street,' said Mr. Morgan; and added, after a pause, 'Are you in town for some time, pray, sir? Are you in chambers? I should like to have the honour of waiting on you there: and would be thankful if you would favour me with a quarter of an hour.'

'Do you want my uncle to take you back?' asked Arthur, insolent and good-natured.

'I want no such thing; I'd see him——' The man glared at him for a minute, but he stopped. 'No, sir, thank you,' he said in a softer voice; 'it's only with you that I wish to speak, on some business which concerns you; and perhaps you would favour me by walking into my house.'

'If it is but for a minute or two, I will listen to you, Morgan,' said Arthur; and thought to himself, 'I suppose the fellow wants me to patronize him;' and he entered the house. A card was already in the front windows, proclaiming that apartments were to be let, and having introduced Mr. Pendennis into the dining-room, and offered him a chair, Mr. Morgan took one himself, and proceeded to convey some information to him, with which the reader has already had ognizance.

CHAPTER LXIX

IN WHICH PENDENNIS COUNTS HIS EGGS

OUR friend had arrived in London on that day only, though but for a brief visit, and having left some fellow-travellers at an hotel to which he had convoyed them from the West, he hastened to the chambers in Lamb Court, which were basking in as much sun as chose to visit that dreary but not altogether comfortless building. Freedom stands in lieu of sunshine in chambers; and Templars grumble, but take their ease in their Inn. Pen's domestic announced to him that Warrington was in chambers too, and, of course, Arthur ran up to his friend's room straightway, and found it as of old, perfumed with the pipe, and George once more at work at his newspapers and reviews. The pair greeted each other with the rough cordiality which young Englishmen use one to another: and which carries a great deal of warmth and kindness under its rude exterior. Warrington smiled and took his pipe out of his mouth, and said, 'Well, young one!' Pen advanced and held out his hand, and said, 'How are you, old boy?' And so this greeting passed between two friends who had not seen each other for months. Alphonse and Frédéric would have rushed into each other's arms and shrieked, 'Ce bon cœur! ce cher Alphonse!' over each other's shoulders. Max and Wilhelm would have bestowed half a dozen kisses, scented with Havannah, upon each other's moustachios. 'Well, young one!' 'How are you, old boy?' is what two Britons say: after saving each other's lives, possibly, the day before. To-morrow they will leave off shaking hands, and only wag their heads at one another as they come to breakfast. Each has for the other the very warmest confidence and regard: each would share his purse with the other: and hearing him attacked would break out in the loudest and most enthusiastic praise of his friend; but they part with a mere 'Good-bye,' they meet

with a mere ' How-d'you-do '; and they don't write to each other in the interval. Curious modesty, strange stoical decorum of English friendship! ' Yes, we are not demonstrative like those confounded foreigners,' says Hardman;* who not only shows no friendship, but never felt any all his life long.

' Been in Switzerland?' says Pen. ' Yes,' says Warrington. ' Couldn't find a bit of tobacco fit to smoke till we came to Strasburg, where I got some caporal.' The man's mind is full, very likely, of the great sights which he has seen, of the great emotions with which the vast works of Nature have inspired it. But his enthusiasm is too coy to show itself, even to his closest friend, and he veils it with a cloud of tobacco. He will speak more fully of confidential evenings, however, and write ardently and frankly about that which he is shy of saying. The thoughts and experience of his travel will come forth in his writings; as the learning, which he never displays in talk, enriches his style with pregnant allusion and brilliant illustration, colours his generous eloquence, and points his wit.

The elder gives a rapid account of the places which he has visited in his tour. He has seen Switzerland, North Italy, and the Tyrol—he has come home by Vienna, and Dresden, and the Rhine. He speaks about these places in a shy sulky voice, as if he had rather not mention them at all, and as if the sight of them had rendered him very unhappy. The outline of the elder man's tour thus gloomily sketched out, the young one begins to speak. He has been in the country—very much bored—canvassing—uncommonly slow—he is here for a day or two, and going on to—to the neighbourhood of Tunbridge Wells, to some friends—that will be uncommonly slow, too. How hard it is to make an Englishman acknowledge that he is happy!

' And the seat in Parliament, Pen? Have you made it all right?' asks Warrington.

' All right,—as soon as Parliament meets and a new writ can be issued, Clavering retires, and I step into his shoes,' says Pen.

' And under which king does Bezonian* speak or die?' asked Warrington. ' Do we come out as Liberal Conservative, or as Government man, or on our own hook?'

' Hem! There are no politics now; every man's politics, at least, are pretty much the same. I have not got acres

enough to make me a Protectionist; nor could I be one, I think, if I had all the land in the county. I shall go pretty much with Government, and in advance of them upon some social questions which I have been getting up during the vacation;—don't grin, you old cynic, I *have* been getting up the Blue Books, and intend to come out rather strong on the Sanitary and Colonization questions.'

'We reserve to ourselves the liberty of voting against Government, though we are generally friendly. We are, however, friends of the people *avant tout*. We give lectures at the Clavering Institute, and shake hands with the intelligent mechanics. We think the franchise ought to be very considerably enlarged; at the same time we are free to accept office some day, when the House has listened to a few crack speeches from us, and the Administration perceives our merit.'

'I am not Moses,' said Pen, with, as usual, somewhat of melancholy in his voice. 'I have no laws from Heaven to bring down to the people from the mountain. I don't belong to the mountain at all, or set up to be a leader and reformer of mankind. My faith is not strong enough for that; nor my vanity, nor my hypocrisy, great enough. I will tell no lies, George, that I promise you; and do no more than coincide in those which are necessary and pass current, and can't be got in without recalling the whole circulation. Give a man at least the advantage of his sceptical turn. If I find a good thing to say in the House, I will say it; a good measure, I will support it; a fair place, I will take it, and be glad of my luck. But I would no more flatter a great man than a mob; and now you know as much about my politics as I do. What call have I to be a Whig? Whiggism is not a divine institution. Why not vote with the Liberal Conservatives? They have done for the nation what the Whigs would never have done without them. Who converted both?—the Radicals and the country outside. I think the *Morning Post* is often right, and *Punch** is often wrong. I don't profess a call, but take advantage of a chance. *Parlons d'autre chose*.'

'The next thing at your heart, after ambition, is love, I suppose?' Warrington said. 'How have our young loves prospered? Are we going to change our condition, and give up our chambers? Are you going to divorce me, Arthur, and take unto yourself a wife?'

'I suppose so. She is very good-natured and lively. She sings, and she don't mind smoking. She'll have a fair fortune—I don't know how much—but my uncle augurs everything from the Begum's generosity, and says that she will come down very handsomely. And I think Blanche is dev'lish fond of me,' said Arthur, with a sigh.

'That means that we accept her caresses and her money.'

'Haven't we said before that life was a transaction?' Pendennis said. 'I don't pretend to break my heart about her. I have told her pretty fairly what my feelings are—and—and have engaged myself to her. And since I saw her last, and for the last two months especially, whilst I have been in the country, I think she has been growing fonder and fonder of me; and her letters to me, and especially to Laura, seem to show it. Mine have been simple enough—no raptures nor vows, you understand—but looking upon the thing as an *affaire faite*; and not desirous to hasten or defer the completion.'

'And Laura? how is she?' Warrington asked frankly.

'Laura, George,' said Pen, looking his friend hard in the face—'by Heaven, Laura is the best, and noblest, and dearest girl the sun ever shone upon.' His own voice fell as he spoke: it seemed as if he could hardly utter the words: he stretched out his hand to his comrade, who took it and nodded his head.

'Have you only found out that now, young un?' Warrington said, after a pause.

'Who has not learned things too late, George?' cried Arthur, in his impetuous way, gathering words and emotion as he went on. 'Whose life is not a disappointment? Who carries his heart entire to the grave without a mutilation? I never knew anybody who was happy quite: or who has not had to ransom himself out of the hands of Fate with the payment of some dearest treasure or other. Lucky if we are left alone afterwards, when we have paid our fine, and if the tyrant visits us no more. Suppose I have found out that I have lost the greatest prize in the world, now that it can't be mine—that for years I had an angel under my tent, and let her go?—am I the only one—ah, dear old boy, am I the only one? And do you think my lot is easier to bear because I own that I deserve it? She's gone from us. God's blessing be with her! She might have stayed, and I lost her; it's like Undine:* isn't it, George?'

'She was in this room once,' said George.

He saw her there—he heard the sweet low voice—he saw the sweet smile and eyes shining so kindly—the face remembered so fondly—thought of in what night-watches—blest and loved always—gone now! A glass that had held a nosegay—a Bible with Helen's handwriting—were all that were left him of that brief flower of his life. Say it is a dream: say it passes: better the recollection of a dream than an aimless waking from a blank stupor.

The two friends sat in silence awhile, each occupied with his own thoughts and aware of the other's. Pen broke it presently, by saying that he must go and seek for his uncle, and report progress to the old gentleman. The major had written in a very bad humour; the major was getting old. 'I should like to see you in Parliament, and snugly settled with a comfortable house and an heir to the name before I make my bow. Show me these,' the major wrote, 'and then, let old Arthur Pendennis make room for the younger fellows; he has walked the Pall Mall *pavé* long enough.'

'There is kindness about the old heathen,' said Warrington. 'He cares for somebody besides himself, at least for some other part of himself besides that which is buttoned into his own coat;—for you and your race. He would like to see the progeny of the Pendennises multiplying and increasing, and hopes that they may inherit the land. The old patriarch blesses you from the club window of Bays's, and is carried off and buried under the flags of St. James's Church, in sight of Piccadilly, and the cab-stand, and the carriages going to the levee. It is an edifying ending.'

'The new blood I bring into the family,' mused Pen, 'is rather tainted. If I had chosen, I think my father-in-law Amory would not have been the progenitor I should have desired for my race; nor my grandfather-in-law Snell; nor our oriental ancestors. By the way, who was Amory? Amory was lieutenant of an Indiaman. Blanche wrote some verses about him, about the storm, the mountain wave, the seaman's grave, the gallant father, and that sort of thing. Amory was drowned commanding a country ship between Calcutta and Sydney; Amory and the Begum weren't happy together. She has been unlucky in her selection of husbands, the good old lady, for, between ourselves, a more despicable creature than Sir Francis

Clavering, of Clavering Park, baronet, never——' 'Never legislated for his country,' broke in Warrington; at which Pen blushed rather.

'By the way, at Baden,' said Warrington, 'I found our friend the Chevalier Strong in great state, and wearing his orders. He told me that he had quarrelled with Clavering, of whom he seemed to have almost as bad an opinion as you have, and in fact, I think, though I will not be certain, confided to me his opinion, that Clavering was an utter scoundrel. That fellow Bloundell, who taught you card-playing at Oxbridge, was with Strong; and time, I think, has brought out his valuable qualities, and rendered him a more accomplished rascal than he was during your undergraduateship. But the king of the place was the famous Colonel Altamont, who was carrying all before him, giving fêtes to the whole society, and breaking the bank, it was said.'

'My uncle knows something about that fellow—Clavering knows something about him. There's something *louche* regarding him. But come! I must go to Bury Street, like a dutiful nephew.' And, taking his hat, Pen prepared to go.

'I will walk, too,' said Warrington. And they descended the stairs, stopping, however, at Pen's chambers, which, as the reader has been informed, were now on the lower story.

Here Pen began sprinkling himself with eau-de-Cologne, and carefully scenting his hair and whiskers with that odoriferous water.

'What is the matter? You've not been smoking. Is it my pipe that has poisoned you?' growled Warrington.

'I am going to call upon some women,' said Pen. 'I'm —I'm going to dine with 'em. They are passing through town, and are at an hotel in Jermyn Street.'

Warrington looked with good-natured interest at the young fellow dandifying himself up to a pitch of completeness; and appearing at length in a gorgeous shirt-front and neckcloth, fresh gloves, and glistening boots. George had a pair of thick high-lows, and his old shirt was torn about the breast, and ragged at the collar, where his blue beard had worn it.

'Well, young un,' said he simply, 'I like you to be a buck, somehow. When I walk about with you, it is as if

I had a rose in my button-hole. And you are still affable. I don't think there is any young fellow in the Temple turns out like you; and I don't believe you were ever ashamed of walking with me yet.'

'Don't laugh at me, George,' said Pen.

'I say, Pen,' continued the other sadly, 'if you write—if you write to Laura, I wish you would say "God bless her," from me.'

Pen blushed; and then looked at Warrington; and then—and then burst into an uncontrollable fit of laughing.

'I'm going to dine with her,' he said. 'I brought her and Lady Rockminster up from the country to-day—made two days of it—slept last night at Bath—I say, George, come and dine, too. I may ask anyone I please, and the old lady is constantly talking about you.'

George refused. George had an article to write. George hesitated; and oh, strange to say! at last he agreed to go. It was agreed that they should go and call upon the ladies; and they marched away in high spirits to the hotel in Jermyn Street. Once more the dear face shone upon him; once more the sweet voice spoke to him, and the tender hand pressed a welcome.

There still wanted half an hour to dinner. 'You will go and see your uncle now, Mr. Pendennis,' old Lady Rockminster said. 'You will not bring him to dinner—no—his old stories are intolerable; and I want to talk to Mr. Warrington; I dare say he will amuse us. I think we have heard all your stories. We have been together for two whole days, and I think we are getting tired of each other.'

So, obeying her ladyship's orders, Arthur went downstairs and walked to his uncle's lodgings.

CHAPTER LXX

FIAT JUSTITIA

THE dinner was served when Arthur returned, and Lady Rockminster began to scold him for arriving late. But Laura, looking at her cousin, saw that his face was so pale and scared, that she interrupted her imperious patroness; and asked, with tender alarm, what had happened? Was Arthur ill?

Arthur drank a large bumper of sherry. 'I have heard the most extraordinary news; I will tell you afterwards,' he said, looking at the servants. He was very nervous and agitated during the dinner. 'Don't tramp and beat so with your feet under the table,' Lady Rockminster said. 'You have trodden on Fido, and upset his saucer. You see Mr. Warrington keeps his boots quiet.'

At the dessert—it seemed as if the unlucky dinner would never be over—Lady Rockminster said, 'This dinner has been exceedingly stupid. I suppose something has happened, and that you want to speak to Laura. I will go and have my nap. I am not sure that I shall have any tea—no. Good-night, Mr. Warrington. You must come again, and when there is no business to talk about.' And the old lady, tossing up her head, walked away from the room with great dignity.

George and the others had risen with her, and Warrington was about to go away, and was saying 'Good-night' to Laura, who, of course, was looking much alarmed about her cousin, when Arthur said, 'Pray, stay, George. You should hear my news too, and give me your counsel in this case. I hardly know how to act in it.'

'It's something about Blanche, Arthur,' said Laura, her heart beating, and her cheek blushing, as she thought it had never blushed in her life.

'Yes—and the most extraordinary story,' said Pen. 'When I left you to go to my uncle's lodgings, I found his servant, Morgan, who has been with him so long, at the door, and

he said that he and his master had parted that morning; that my uncle had quitted the house, and had gone to an hotel—this hotel. I asked for him when I came in; but he was gone out to dinner. Morgan then said that he had something of a most important nature to communicate to me, and begged me to step into the house; his house it is now. It appears the scoundrel has saved a great deal of money whilst in my uncle's service, and is now a capitalist and a millionaire, for what I know. Well, I went into the house, and what do you think he told me? This must be a secret between us all—at least if we can keep it, now that it is in possession of that villain. Blanche's father is not dead. He has come to life again. The marriage between Clavering and the Begum is no marriage.'

'And Blanche, I suppose, is her grandfather's heir,' said Warrington.

'Perhaps: but the child of what a father! Amory is an escaped convict—Clavering knows it; my uncle knows it—and it was with this piece of information held over Clavering *in terrorem* that the wretched old man got him to give up his borough to me.'

'Blanche doesn't know it,' said Laura, 'nor poor Lady Clavering.'

'No,' said Pen; 'Blanche does not even know the history of her father. She knew that he and her mother had separated, and had heard as a child, from Bonner, her nurse, that Mr. Amory was drowned in New South Wales. He was there as a convict, not as a ship's captain, as the poor girl thought. Lady Clavering has told me that they were not happy, and that her husband was a bad character. She would tell me all, she said, some day: and I remember her saying to me, with tears in her eyes, that it was hard for a woman to be forced to own that she was glad to hear her husband was dead: and that twice in her life she should have chosen so badly. What is to be done now? The man can't show and claim his wife: death is probably over him if he discovers himself: return to transportation certainly. But the rascal has held the threat of discovery over Clavering for some time past, and has extorted money from him time after time.'

'It is our friend Colonel Altamont, of course,' said Warrington: 'I see all now.'

'If the rascal comes back,' continued Arthur, 'Morgan,

who knows his secret, will use it over him—and having it in his possession, proposes to extort money from us all. The d——d rascal supposed I was cognizant of it,' said Pen, white with anger; 'asked me if I would give him an annuity to keep it quiet; threatened me, *me*, as if I was trafficking with this wretched old Begum's misfortune; and would extort a seat in Parliament out of that miserable Clavering. Good heavens! was my uncle mad, to tamper in such a conspiracy? Fancy our mother's son, Laura, trading on such a treason!'

'I can't fancy it, dear Arthur,' said Laura, seizing Arthur's hand, and kissing it.

'No!' broke out Warrington's deep voice, with a tremor; he surveyed the two generous and loving young people with a pang of indescribable love and pain. 'No. Our boy can't meddle with such a wretched intrigue as that. Arthur Pendennis can't marry a convict's daughter; and sit in Parliament as member for the hulks. You must wash your hands of the whole affair, Pen. You must break off. You must give no explanations of why and wherefore, but state that family reasons render a match impossible. It is better that those poor women should fancy you false to your word than that they should know the truth. Besides, you can get from that dog Clavering—I can fetch that for you easily enough—an acknowledgement that the reasons which you have given to him as the head of the family are amply sufficient for breaking off the union. Don't you think with me, Laura?' He scarcely dared to look her in the face as he spoke. Any lingering hope that he might have—any feeble hold that he might feel upon the last spar of his wrecked fortune, he knew he was casting away; and he let the wave of his calamity close over him. Pen had started up whilst he was speaking, looking eagerly at him. He turned his head away. He saw Laura rise up also and go to Pen, and once more take his hand and kiss it. 'She thinks so too—God bless her!' said George.

'Her father's shame is not Blanche's fault, dear Arthur, is it?' Laura said, very pale, and speaking very quickly. 'Suppose you had been married, would you desert her because she had done no wrong? Are you not pledged to her? Would you leave her because she is in misfortune? And if she is unhappy, wouldn't you console her? Our mother would, had she been here.' And, as she spoke,

the kind girl folded her arms round him, and buried her face upon his heart.

'Our mother is an angel with God,' Pen sobbed out. 'And you are the dearest and best of women—the dearest, the dearest and the best. Teach me my duty. Pray for me that I may do it—pure heart. God bless you—God bless you, my sister.'

'Amen,' groaned out Warrington, with his head in his hands. 'She is right,' he murmured to himself. 'She can't do any wrong, I think—that girl.' Indeed, she looked and smiled like an angel. Many a day after he saw that smile—saw her radiant face as she looked up at Pen—saw her putting back her curls, blushing and smiling, and still looking fondly towards him.

She leaned for a moment her little fair hand on the table, playing on it. 'And now, and now,' she said, looking at the two gentlemen—

'And what now ?' asked George.

'And now we will have some tea,' said Miss Laura, with her smile.

But before this unromantic conclusion to a rather sentimental scene could be suffered to take place, a servant brought word that Major Pendennis had returned to the hotel, and was waiting to see his nephew. Upon this announcement, Laura, not without some alarm, and an appealing look to Pen, which said, 'Behave yourself well—hold to the right, and do your duty—be gentle, but firm with your uncle '—Laura, we say, with these warnings written in her face, took leave of the two gentlemen, and retreated to her dormitory. Warrington, who was not generally fond of tea, yet grudged that expected cup very much. Why could not old Pendennis have come in an hour later ? Well, an hour sooner or later, what matter ? The hour strikes at last. The inevitable moment comes to say 'Farewell.' The hand is shaken, the door closed, and the friend gone ; and, the brief joy over, you are alone. 'In which of those many windows of the hotel does *her* light beam ?' perhaps he asks himself as he passes down the street. He strides away to the smoking-room of a neighbouring club, and there applies himself to his usual solace of a cigar. Men are brawling and talking loud about politics, opera-girls, horse-racing, the atrocious tyranny of

the committee ;—bearing this sacred secret about him, he enters into this brawl. Talk away, each louder than the other. Rattle and crack jokes. Laugh and tell your wild stories. It is strange to take one's place and part in the midst of the smoke and din, and think every man here has his secret ego most likely, which is sitting lonely and apart, away in the private chamber, from the loud game in which the rest of us is joining !

Arthur, as he traversed the passages of the hotel, felt his anger rousing up within him. He was indignant to think that yonder old gentleman whom he was about to meet, should have made him such a tool and puppet, and so compromised his honour and good name. The old fellow's hand was very cold and shaky when Arthur took it. He was coughing ; he was grumbling over the fire ; Frosch could not bring his dressing-gown or arrange his papers as that d——d confounded impudent scoundrel of a Morgan. The old gentleman bemoaned himself, and cursed Morgan's ingratitude with peevish pathos.

'The confounded impudent scoundrel ! He was drunk last night, and challenged me to fight him, Pen ; and, begad, at one time I was so excited that I thought I should have driven a knife into him ; and the infernal rascal has made ten thousand pound, I believe—and deserves to be hanged, and will be ; but, curse him, I wish he could have lasted out my time. He knew all my ways, and, dammy, when I rang the bell, the confounded thief brought the thing I wanted—not like that stupid German lout. And what sort of time have you had in the country ? Been a good deal with Lady Rockminster ? You can't do better. She is one of the old school—*vieille école, bonne école*, hey ? Dammy, they don't make gentlemen and ladies now ; and in fifty years you'll hardly know one man from another. But they'll last my time. I ain't long for this business : I am getting very old, Pen, my boy ; and, gad, I was thinking to-day, as I was packing up my little library, there's a Bible amongst the books that belonged to my poor mother ; I would like you to keep that, Pen. I was thinking, sir, that you would most likely open the box when it was your property, and the old fellow was laid under the sod, sir,' and the major coughed and wagged his old head over the fire.

His age—his kindness, disarmed Pen's anger somewhat,

and made Arthur feel no little compunction for the deed which he was about to do. He knew that the announcement which he was about to make would destroy the darling hope of the old gentleman's life, and create in his breast a woful anger and commotion.

'Hey—hey—I'm off, sir,' nodded the Elder; 'but I'd like to read a speech of yours in the *Times* before I go—"Mr. Pendennis said, Unaccustomed as I am to public speaking"—hey, sir? hey, Arthur? Begad, you look dev'lish well and healthy, sir. I always said my brother Jack would bring the family right. You must go down into the west, and buy the old estate, sir. *Nec tenui pennâ*, hey? We'll rise again, sir—rise again on the wing—and, begad, I shouldn't be surprised that you will be a baronet before you die.'

His words smote Pen. 'And it is I,' he thought, 'that am going to fling down the poor old fellow's air-castle. Well, it must be. Here goes.—I—I went into your lodgings at Bury Street, though I did not find you,' Pen slowly began—'and I talked with Morgan, uncle.'

'Indeed!' The old gentleman's cheek began to flush involuntarily, and he muttered, 'The cat's out of the bag now, begad!'

'He told me a story, sir, which gave me the deepest surprise and pain,' said Pen.

The major tried to look unconcerned. 'What—that story about—about—What-d'you-call-'em, hey?'

'About Miss Amory's father—about Lady Clavering's first husband, and who he is, and what.'

'Hem—a devilish awkward affair!' said the old man, rubbing his nose. 'I—I've been aware of that—eh—confounded circumstance for some time.'

'I wish I had known it sooner, or not at all,' said Arthur gloomily.

'He is all safe,' thought the senior, greatly relieved. 'Gad! I should have liked to keep it from you altogether—and from those two poor women, who are as innocent as unborn babes in the transaction.'

'You are right. There is no reason why the two women should hear it; and I shall never tell them—though that villain, Morgan, perhaps, may,' Arthur said gloomily. 'He seems disposed to trade upon his secret, and has already proposed terms of ransom to me. I wish I had known of

the matter earlier, sir. It is not a very pleasant thought to me that I am engaged to a convict's daughter.'

'The very reason why I kept it from you—my dear boy. But Miss Amory is not a convict's daughter, don't you see? Miss Amory is the daughter of Lady Clavering, with fifty or sixty thousand pounds for a fortune; and her father-in-law, a baronet and country gentleman, of high reputation, approves of the match, and gives up his seat in Parliament to his son-in-law. What can be more simple?'

'Is it true, sir?'

'Begad, yes, it is true, of course it's true. Amory's dead. I tell you he *is* dead. The first sign of life he shows, he is dead. He can't appear. We have him at a dead-lock, like the fellow in the play—*The Critic*, hey?—devilish amusing play that *Critic*. Monstrous witty man Sheridan; and so was his son. By Gad, sir, when I was at the Cape, I remember——'

The old gentleman's garrulity, and wish to conduct Arthur to the Cape, perhaps arose from a desire to avoid the subject which was nearest his nephew's heart; but Arthur broke out, interrupting him—'If you had told me this tale sooner, I believe you would have spared me and yourself a great deal of pain and disappointment; and I should not have found myself tied to an engagement from which I can't, in honour, recede.'

'No, begad, we've fixed you—and a man who's fixed to a seat in Parliament, and a pretty girl, with a couple of thousand a year, is fixed to no bad thing, let me tell you,' said the old man.

'Great Heavens, sir!' said Arthur; 'are you blind? Can't you see?'

'See what, young gentleman?' asked the other.

'See, that rather than trade upon this secret of Amory's,' Arthur cried out, 'I would go and join my father-in-law at the hulks! See, that rather than take a seat in Parliament as a bribe from Clavering for silence, I would take the spoons off the table! See, that you have given me a felon's daughter for a wife; doomed me to poverty and shame; cursed my career when it might have been—when it might have been so different but for you! Don't you see that we have been playing a guilty game, and have been over-reached;—that in offering to marry this poor girl, for the sake of her money, and the advancement she would

bring, I was degrading myself, and prostituting my honour?'

'What in Heaven's name do you mean, sir?' cried the old man.

'I mean to say that there is a measure of baseness which I can't pass,' Arthur said. 'I have no other words for it, and am sorry if they hurt you. I have felt, for months past, that my conduct in this affair has been wicked, sordid, and worldly. I am rightly punished by the event, and having sold myself for money and a seat in Parliament, by losing both.'

'How do you mean that you lose either?' shrieked the old gentleman. 'Who the devil's to take your fortune or your seat away from you? By G—, Clavering *shall* give 'em to you. You shall have every shilling of eighty thousand pounds.'

'I'll keep my promise to Miss Amory, sir,' said Arthur.

'And, begad, her parents shall keep theirs to you.'

'Not so, please God,' Arthur answered. 'I have sinned, but, Heaven help me, I will sin no more. I will let Clavering off from that bargain which was made without my knowledge. I will take no money with Blanche but that which was originally settled upon her; and I will try to make her happy. You have done it. You have brought this on me, sir. But you knew no better: and I forgive——'

'Arthur—in God's name—in your father's, who, by Heavens, was the proudest man alive, and had the honour of the family always at heart—in mine—for the sake of a poor broken-down old fellow, who has always been dev'lish fond of you—don't fling this chance away—I pray you, I beg you, I implore you, my dear, dear boy, don't fling this chance away. It's the making of you. You're sure to get on. You'll be a baronet; it's three thousand a year: dammy, on my knees, there, I beg of you, don't do this.'

And the old man actually sank down on his knees, and seizing one of Arthur's hands, looked up piteously at him. It was cruel to remark the shaking hands, the wrinkled and quivering face, the old eyes weeping and winking, the broken voice. 'Ah, sir,' said Arthur, with a groan, 'you have brought pain enough on me, spare me this. You have wished me to marry Blanche. I marry her. For God's sake, sir, rise, I can't bear it.'

'You—you mean to say that you will take her as a

beggar, and be one yourself ?' said the old gentleman, rising up and coughing violently.

'I look at her as a person to whom a great calamity has befallen, and to whom I am promised. She cannot help the misfortune ; and as she had my word when she was prosperous, I shall not withdraw it now she is poor. I will not take Clavering's seat, unless afterwards it should be given of his free will. I will not have a shilling more than her original fortune.'

'Have the kindness to ring the bell,' said the old gentleman. 'I have done my best, and said my say ; and I'm a dev'lish old fellow. And—and—it don't matter. And—and Shakespere was right—and Cardinal Wolsey—begad—"and had I but served my God as I've served you"*—yes, on my knees, by Jove, to my own nephew—I mightn't have been—— Good-night, sir ; you needn't trouble yourself to call again.'

Arthur took his hand, which the old man left to him ; it was quite passive and clammy. He looked very much oldened ; and it seemed as if the contest and defeat had quite broken him.

On the next day he kept his bed, and refused to see his nephew.

CHAPTER LXXI

IN WHICH THE DECKS BEGIN TO CLEAR

When, arrayed in his dressing-gown, Pen walked up, according to custom, to Warrington's chambers next morning, to inform his friend of the issue of the last night's interview with his uncle, and to ask, as usual, for George's advice and opinion, Mrs. Flanagan, the laundress, was the only person whom Arthur found in the dear old chambers. George had taken a carpet-bag, and was gone. His address was to his brother's house, in Suffolk. Packages addressed to the

newspaper and review for which he wrote lay on the table, awaiting delivery.

'I found him at the table, when I came, the dear gentleman!' Mrs. Flanagan said, 'writing at his papers, and one of the candles was burned out; and hard as his bed is, he wasn't in it all night, sir.'

Indeed, having sat at the club until the brawl there became intolerable to him, George had walked home, and had passed the night finishing some work on which he was employed, and to the completion of which he bent himself with all his might. The labour was done, and the night was worn away somehow, and the tardy November dawn came and looked in on the young man as he sat over his desk. In the next day's paper, or quarter's review, many of us very likely admired the work of his genius, the variety of his illustration, the fierce vigour of his satire, the depth of his reason. There was no hint in his writing of the other thoughts which occupied him, and always accompanied him in his work: a tone more melancholy than was customary, a satire more bitter and impatient than that which he afterwards showed, may have marked the writings of this period of his life to the very few persons who knew his style or his name. We have said before, could we know the man's feelings as well as the author's thoughts—how interesting most books would be!—more interesting than merry. I suppose harlequin's face behind his mask is always grave, if not melancholy—certainly each man who lives by the pen, and happens to read this, must remember, if he will, his own experiences, and recall many solemn hours of solitude and labour. What a constant care sat at the side of the desk and accompanied him! Fever or sickness were lying possibly in the next room: a sick child might be there, with a wife watching over it terrified and in prayer; or grief might be bearing him down, and the cruel mist before the eyes rendering the paper scarce visible as he wrote on it, and the inexorable necessity drove on the pen. What man among us has not had nights and hours like these? But to the manly heart—severe as these pangs are, they are endurable: long as the night seems, the dawn comes at last, and the wounds heal, and the fever abates, and rest comes, and you can afford to look back on the past misery with feelings that are anything but bitter.

Two or three books for reference, fragments of torn-up

manuscript, drawers open, pens in inkstands, lines half visible on the blotting-paper, a bit of sealing-wax twisted and bitten and broken into sundry pieces—such relics as these were about the table, and Pen flung himself down in George's empty chair—noting things according to his wont, or in spite of himself. There was a gap in the book-case (next to the old college Plato, with the Boniface Arms), where Helen's Bible used to be. He has taken that with him, thought Pen. He knew why his friend was gone. Dear, dear old George!

Pen rubbed his hand over his eyes. Oh, how much wiser, how much better, how much nobler he is than I, he thought. Where was such a friend, or such a brave heart? Where shall I ever hear such a frank voice, and kind laughter? Where shall I ever see such a true gentleman? No wonder she loved him. God bless him. What was I compared to him? What could she do else but love him? To the end of our days we will be her brothers, as fate wills that we can be no more. We'll be her knights, and wait on her: and when we're old, we'll say how we loved her. Dear, dear old George!

When Pen descended to his own chambers, his eye fell on the letter-box of his outer door, which he had previously overlooked, and there was a little note to A. P., Esq., in George's well-known handwriting, George had put into Pen's box probably as he was going away.

D^r. Pen,

I shall be half way home when you breakfast, and intend to stay over Christmas, in Suff^k, or elsewhere.

I have my own opinion of the issue of matters about which we talked in J—— St. yesterday; and think my presence *de trop*.

Vale. G. W.

Give my very best regards and adieux to your cousin.

And so George was gone, and Mrs. Flanagan, the laundress, ruled over his empty chambers.

Pen of course had to go and see his uncle on the day after their colloquy, and not being admitted, he naturally went to Lady Rockminster's apartments, where the old lady instantly asked for Bluebeard, and insisted that he should come to dinner.

'Bluebeard is gone,' Pen said, and he took out poor George's scrap of paper, and handed it to Laura, who looked at it—did not look at Pen in return, but passed the paper

back to him, and walked away. Pen rushed into an eloquent eulogium upon his dear old George to Lady Rockminster, who was astonished at his enthusiasm. She had never heard him so warm in praise of anybody; and told him, with her usual frankness, that she didn't think it had been in his nature to care so much about any other person.

As Mr. Pendennis was passing through Waterloo Place, in one of his many walks to the hotel where Laura lived, and whither duty to his uncle carried Arthur every day, Arthur saw issuing from Messrs. Gimcrack's celebrated shop an old friend, who was followed to his brougham by an ob-

sequious shopman bearing parcels. The gentleman was in the deepest mourning: the brougham, the driver, and the horse, were in mourning. Grief in easy circumstances, and supported by the comfortablest springs and cushions, was typified in the equipage, and the little gentleman, its proprietor.

'What, Foker! Hail, Foker!' cried out Pen—the reader, no doubt, has likewise recognized Arthur's old schoolfellow—and he held out his hand to the heir of the late lamented John Henry Foker, Esq., the master of Logwood and other houses, the principal partner in the great brewery

of Foker and Co.: the greater portion of Foker's Entire.

A little hand, covered with a glove of the deepest ebony, and set off by three inches of a snowy wristband, was put forth to meet Arthur's salutation. The other little hand held a little morocco case, containing, no doubt, something precious, of which Mr. Foker had just become proprietor in Messrs. Gimcrack's shop. Pen's keen eyes and satiric turn showed him at once upon what errand Mr. Foker had been employed; and he thought of the heir in Horace pouring forth the gathered wine of his father's vats;* and that human nature is pretty much the same in Regent Street as in the Via Sacra.

'*Le Roi est mort. Vive le Roi!*' said Arthur.

'Ah!' said the other. 'Yes. Thank you—very much obliged. How do you do, Pen?—very busy—good-bye!' and he jumped into the black brougham, and sat like a little black Care behind the black coachman. He had blushed on seeing Pen, and shown other signs of guilt and perturbation, which Pen attributed to the novelty of his situation; and on which he began to speculate in his usual sardonic manner.

'Yes: so wags the world,' thought Pen. 'The stone closes over Harry the Fourth, and Harry the Fifth reigns in his stead. The old ministers at the brewery come and kneel before him with their books; the draymen, his subjects, fling up their red caps, and shout for him. What a grave deference and sympathy the bankers and the lawyers show! There was too great a stake at issue between those two that they should ever love each other very cordially. As long as one man keeps another out of twenty thousand a year, the younger must be always hankering after the crown, and the wish must be the father to the thought of possession. Thank Heaven, there was no thought of money between me and our dear mother, Laura.'

'There never could have been. You would have spurned it!' cried Laura. 'Why make yourself more selfish than you are, Pen; and allow your mind to own for an instant that it would have entertained such—such dreadful meanness? You make me blush for you, Arthur: you make me——' Her eyes finished the sentence, and she passed her handkerchief across them.

'There are some truths which women will never acknow-

ledge,' Pen said, 'and from which your modesty always turns away. I do not say that I never knew the feeling, only that I am glad I had not the temptation. Is there any harm in that confession of weakness ?'

'We are all taught to ask to be delivered from evil, Arthur,' said Laura, in a low voice. 'I am glad if you were spared from that great crime ; and only sorry to think that you could by any possibility have been led into it. But you never could ; and you don't think you could. Your acts are generous and kind : you disdain mean actions. You take Blanche without money, and without a bribe. Yes, thanks be to Heaven, dear brother. You could not have sold yourself away ; I knew you could not when it came to the day, and you did not. Praise be—be where praise is due. Why does this horrid scepticism pursue you, my Arthur ? Why doubt and sneer at your own heart—at every one's ? Oh, if you knew the pain you give me—how I lie awake and think of those hard sentences, dear brother, and wish them unspoken, unthought !'

'Do I cause you many thoughts and many tears, Laura ?' asked Arthur. The fullness of innocent love beamed from her in reply. A smile heavenly pure, a glance of unutterable tenderness, sympathy, pity, shone in her face—all which indications of love and purity Arthur beheld and worshipped in her, as you would watch them in a child, as one fancies one might regard them in an angel.

'I—I don't know what I have done,' he said simply, 'to have merited such regard from two such women. It is like undeserved praise, Laura—or too much good fortune, which frightens one—or a great post, when a man feels that he is not fit for it. Ah, sister, how weak and wicked we are ; how spotless, and full of love and truth, Heaven made you ! I think for some of you there has been no fall,' he said, looking at the charming girl with an almost paternal glance of admiration. 'You can't help having sweet thoughts, and doing good actions. Dear creature ! they are the flowers which you bear.'

'And what else, sir ?' asked Laura. 'I see a sneer coming over your face. What is it ? Why does it come to drive all the good thoughts away ?'

'A sneer, is there ? I was thinking, my dear, that nature in making you so good and loving did very well : but——'

'But what? What is that wicked but? and why are you always calling it up?'

'But will come in spite of us. But is reflection. But is the sceptic's familiar, with whom he has made a compact; and if he forgets it, and indulges in happy day-dreams, or building of air-castles, or listens to sweet music, let us say, or to the bells ringing to church, But taps at the door, and says, "Master, I am here. You are my master; but I am yours. Go where you will you can't travel without me. I will whisper to you when you are on your knees at church. I will be at your marriage pillow. I will sit down at your table with your children. I will be behind your death-bed curtain." That is what But is,' Pen said.

'Pen, you frighten me,' cried Laura.

'Do you know what But came and said to me just now, when I was looking at you? But said, "If that girl had reason as well as love, she would love you no more. If she knew you as you are—the sullied, selfish being which *you* know—she must part from you, and could give you no love and no sympathy." Didn't I say,' he added fondly, 'that some of you seem exempt from the fall? Love you know; but the knowledge of evil is kept from you.'

'What is this you young folks are talking about?' asked Lady Rockminster, who at this moment made her appearance in the room, having performed, in the mystic retirement of her own apartments, and under the hands of her attendant, those elaborate toilette-rites without which the worthy old lady never presented herself to public view. 'Mr. Pendennis, you are always coming here.'

'It is very pleasant to be here,' Arthur said: 'and we were talking, when you came in, about my friend Foker, whom I met just now; and who, as your ladyship knows, has succeeded to his father's kingdom.'

'He has a very fine property, he has fifteen thousand a year. He is my cousin. He is a very worthy young man. He must come and see me,' said Lady Rockminster, with a look at Laura.

'He has been engaged for many years past to his cousin, Lady——'

'Lady Ann is a foolish little chit,' Lady Rockminster said, with much dignity: 'and I have no patience with her. She has outraged every feeling of society. She has broken her father's heart and thrown away fifteen thousand a year.'

'Thrown away? What has happened?' asked Pen.

'It will be the talk of the town in a day or two; and there is no need why I should keep the secret any longer,' said Lady Rockminster, who had written and received a dozen letters on the subject. 'I had a letter yesterday from my daughter, who was staying at Drummington until all the world was obliged to go away on account of the frightful catastrophe which happened there. When Mr. Foker came home from Nice, and after the funeral, Lady Ann went down on her knees to her father, said that she never could marry her cousin, that she had contracted another attachment, and that she must die rather than fulfil her contract. Poor Lord Rosherville, who is dreadfully embarrassed, showed his daughter what the state of his affairs was, and that it was necessary that the arrangements should take place; and in fine, we all supposed that she had listened to reason, and intended to comply with the desires of her family. But what has happened?—last Thursday she went out after breakfast with her maid, and was married in the very church in Drummington Park to Mr. Hobson, her father's own chaplain and her brother's tutor; a red-haired widower with two children. Poor dear Rosherville is in a dreadful way: he wishes Henry Foker should marry Alice or Barbara; but Alice is marked with the small-pox, and Barbara is ten years older than he is. And, of course, now the young man is his own master, he will think of choosing for himself. The blow on Lady Agnes is very cruel. She is inconsolable. She has the house in Grosvenor Street for her life, and her settlement, which was very handsome. Have you not met her? Yes, she dined one day at Lady Clavering's—the first day I saw you, and a very disagreeable young man I thought you were. But I have formed you. We have formed him, haven't we, Laura? Where is Bluebeard? let him come. That horrid Grindley, the dentist, will keep me in town another week.'

To the latter part of her ladyship's speech Arthur gave no ear. He was thinking for whom could Foker be purchasing those trinkets which he was carrying away from the jeweller's? Why did Harry seem anxious to avoid him? Could he be still faithful to the attachment which had agitated him so much, and sent him abroad eighteen months back? Psha! The bracelets and presents were

for some of Harry's old friends of the Opera or the French theatre. Rumours from Naples and Paris, rumours such as are borne to Club smoking-rooms, had announced that the young man had found distractions ; or, precluded from his virtuous attachment, the poor fellow had flung himself back upon his old companions and amusements—not the only man or woman whom society forces into evil, or debars from good : not the only victim of the world's selfish and wicked laws.

As a good thing when it is to be done cannot be done too quickly, Laura was anxious that Pen's marriage intentions should be put into execution as speedily as possible, and pressed on his arrangements with rather a feverish anxiety. Why could she not wait ? Pen could afford to do so with perfect equanimity, but Laura would hear of no delay. She wrote to Pen : she implored Pen : she used every means to urge expedition. It seemed, as if she could have no rest until Arthur's happiness was complete.

She offered herself to dearest Blanche to come and stay at Tunbridge with her, when Lady Rockminster should go on her intended visit to the reigning house of Rockminster ; and although the old dowager scolded, and ordered, and commanded, Laura was deaf and disobedient ; she must go to Tunbridge, she would go to Tunbridge ; she who ordinarily had no will of her own, and complied smilingly with anybody's whim and caprices, showed the most selfish and obstinate determination in this instance. The dowager lady must nurse herself in her rheumatism, she must read herself to sleep, if she would not hear her maid, whose voice croaked, and who made sad work of the sentimental passages in the novels—Laura must go, and be with her new sister. In another week, she proposed, with many loves and regards to dear Lady Clavering, to pass some time with dearest Blanche.

Dearest Blanche wrote instantly in reply to dearest Laura's No. 1, to say with what extreme delight she should welcome her sister : how charming it would be to practise their old duets together, to wander o'er the grassy sward, and amidst the yellowing woods of Penshurst and Southborough ! Blanche counted the hours till she should embrace her dearest friend.

Laura, No. 2, expressed her delight at dearest Blanche's

affectionate reply. She hoped that their friendship would never diminish ; that the confidence between them would grow in after years ; that they should have no secrets from each other ; that the aim of the life of each would be to make one person happy.

Blanche, No. 2, followed in two days. ‘ How provoking ! Their house was very small, the two spare bedrooms were occupied by that horrid Mrs. Planter and her daughter, who had thought proper to fall ill (she always fell ill in country-houses), and she could not or would not be moved for some days.’

Laura, No. 3. ‘ It was indeed very provoking. L. had hoped to hear one of dearest B.’s dear songs on Friday : but she was the more consoled to wait, because Lady R. was not very well, and liked to be nursed by her. Poor Major Pendennis was very unwell, too, in the same hotel—too unwell even to see Arthur, who was constant in his calls on his uncle. Arthur’s heart was full of tenderness and affection. She had known Arthur all her life. She would answer,’—yes, even in italics she would answer—‘ for his kindness, his goodness, and his gentleness.’

Blanche, No. 3. ‘ What is this most surprising, most extraordinary letter from A. P. ? What does dearest Laura know about it ? What has happened ? What, what mystery is enveloped under his frightful reserve ?’

Blanche, No. 3, requires an explanation ; and it cannot be better given than in the surprising and mysterious letter of Arthur Pendennis.

CHAPTER LXXII

MR. AND MRS. SAM HUXTER

‘Dear Blanche,’ Arthur wrote, ‘you are always reading and dreaming pretty dramas, and exciting romances in real life, are you now prepared to enact a part of one? And not the pleasantest part, dear Blanche, that in which the heroine takes possession of her father's palace and wealth, and introducing her husband to the loyal retainers and faithful vassals, greets her happy bridegroom with “All of this is mine and thine,”—but the other character, that of the luckless lady, who suddenly discovers that she is not the Prince's wife, but Claude Melnotte's the beggar's:* that of Alnaschar's wife, who comes in just as her husband has kicked over the tray of porcelain which was to be the making of his fortune—But stay; Alnaschar, who kicked down the china, was not a married man; he had cast his eye on the Vizier's daughter, and his hopes of her went to the ground with the shattered bowls and tea-cups.

‘Will you be the Vizier's daughter, and refuse and laugh to scorn Alnaschar, or will you be the Lady of Lyons, and love the penniless Claude Melnotte? I will act that part if you like. I will love you my best in return. I will do my all to make your humble life happy: for humble it will be: at least the odds are against any other conclusion; we shall live and die in a poor prosy humdrum way. There will be no stars and epaulettes for the hero of our story. I shall write one or two more stories which will presently be forgotten. I shall be called to the Bar, and try to get on in my profession: perhaps some day, if I am very lucky, and work very hard (which is absurd), I may get a colonial appointment, and you may be an Indian Judge's lady. Meanwhile I shall buy back the *Pall Mall Gazette;* the publishers are tired of it since the death of poor Shandon,*

and will sell it for a small sum. Warrington will be my right hand, and write it up to a respectable sale. I will introduce you to Mr. Finucane the sub-editor, and I know who in the end will be Mrs. Finucane,—a very nice, gentle creature, who has lived sweetly through a sad life—and we will jog on, I say, and look out for better times, and earn our living decently. You shall have the opera-boxes, and superintend the fashionable intelligence, and break your little heart in the poet's corner. Shall we live over the offices ?—there are four very good rooms, a kitchen, and a garret for Laura, in Catherine Street in the Strand ; or would you like a house in the Waterloo Road ?—it would be very pleasant, only there is that halfpenny toll at the Bridge. The boys may go to King's College, mayn't they ? Does all this read to you like a joke ?

'Ah, dear Blanche, it is no joke, and I am sober and telling the truth. Our fine day-dreams are gone. Our carriage has whirled out of sight like Cinderella's : our house in Belgravia has been whisked away into the air by a malevolent Genius, and I am no more a member of Parliament than I am a Bishop on his bench in the House of Lords, or a duke with a garter at his knee. You know pretty well what my property is, and your own little fortune : we may have enough with those two to live in decent comfort : to take a cab sometimes when we go out to see our friends, and not to deny ourselves an omnibus when we are tired. But that is all : is that enough for you, my little dainty lady ? I doubt sometimes whether you can bear the life I offer you—at least, it is fair that you should know what it will be. If you say, "Yes, Arthur, I will follow your fate whatever it may be, and be a loyal and loving wife to aid and cheer you"—come to me, dear Blanche, and may God help me so that I may do my duty to you. If not, and you look to a higher station, I must not bar Blanche's fortune—I will stand in the crowd, and see your ladyship go to Court when you are presented, and you shall give me a smile from your chariot window. I saw Lady Mirabel going to the Drawing-room last season : the happy husband at her side glittered with stars and cordons. All the flowers in the garden bloomed in the coachman's bosom. Will you have these and the chariot, or walk on foot and mend your husband's stockings ?

'I cannot tell you now—afterwards I might, should the

day come when we may have no secrets from one another —what has happened within the last few hours which has changed all my prospects in life: but so it is, that I have learned something which forces me to give up the plans which I had formed, and many vain and ambitious hopes in which I had been indulging. I have written and dispatched a letter to Sir Francis Clavering, saying that I cannot accept his seat in Parliament until after my marriage; in like manner I cannot and will not accept any larger fortune with you than that which has always belonged to you since your grandfather's death, and the birth of your half-brother. Your good mother is not in the least aware —I hope she never may be—of the reasons which force me to this very strange decision. They arise from a painful circumstance, which is attributable to none of our faults; but, having once befallen, they are as fatal and irreparable as that shock which overset honest Alnaschar's porcelain, and shattered all his hopes beyond the power of mending. I write gaily enough, for there is no use in bewailing such a hopeless mischance. We have not drawn the great prize in the lottery, dear Blanche: but I shall be contented enough without it, if you can be so; and I repeat, with all my heart, that I will do my best to make you happy.

'And now, what news shall I give you? My uncle is very unwell, and takes my refusal of the seat in Parliament in sad dudgeon: the scheme was his, poor old gentleman, and he naturally bemoans its failure. But Warrington, Laura, and I had a council of war: they know this awful secret, and back me in my decision. You must love George as you love what is generous and upright and noble; and as for Laura—she must be our Sister, Blanche, our Saint, our good Angel. With two such friends at home, what need we care for the world without, or who is member for Clavering, or who is asked or not asked to the great balls of the season?'

To this frank communication came back the letter from Blanche to Laura, and one to Pen himself, which perhaps his own letter justified.

'You are spoiled by the world,' Blanche wrote; 'you do not love your poor Blanche as she would be loved, or you would not offer thus lightly to take her or to leave her. No,

Arthur, you love me not—a man of the world, you have given me your plighted troth, and are ready to redeem it ; but that entire affection, that love whole and abiding, where—where is that vision of my youth ? I am but a pastime of your life, and I would be its all :—but a fleeting thought, and I would be your whole soul. I would have our two hearts one ; but ah, my Arthur, how lonely yours is ! how little you give me of it ! You speak of our parting with a smile on your lip ; of our meeting, and you care not to hasten it ! Is life but a disillusion, then, and are the flowers of our garden faded away ? I have wept—I have prayed—I have passed sleepless hours—I have shed bitter, bitter tears over your letter ! To you I bring the gushing poesy of my being—the yearnings of the soul that longs to be loved—that pines for love, love, love, beyond all !—that flings itself at your feet, and cries, Love me, Arthur ! Your heart beats no quicker at the kneeling appeal of my love !—your proud eye is dimmed by no tear of sympathy !—you accept my soul's treasure as though 'twere dross ! not the pearls from the unfathomable deeps of affection ! not the diamonds from the caverns of the heart. You treat me like a slave, and bid me bow to my master ! Is this the guerdon of a free maiden—is this the price of a life's passion ? Ah me ! when was it otherwise ? when did love meet with aught but disappointment ? Could I hope (fond fool !) to be the exception to the lot of my race ; and lay my fevered brow on a heart that comprehended my own ? Foolish girl that I was ! One by one, all the flowers of my young life have faded away ; and this, the last, the sweetest, the dearest, the fondly, the madly loved, the wildly cherished—where is it ? But no more of this. Heed not my bleeding heart.—Bless you, bless you always, Arthur !

'I will write more when I am more collected. My racking brain renders thought almost impossible. I long to see Laura ! She will come to us directly we return from the country, will she not ? And you, cold one ! 'B.'

The words of this letter were perfectly clear, and written in Blanche's neatest hand upon her scented paper ; and yet the meaning of the composition not a little puzzled Pen. Did Blanche mean to accept or refuse his polite offer ? Her phrases either meant that Pen did not love her, and

she declined him, or that she took him, and sacrificed herself to him, cold as he was. He laughed sardonically over the letter, and over the transaction which occasioned it. He laughed to think how Fortune had jilted him, and how he deserved his slippery fortune. He turned over and over the musky gilt-edged riddle. It amused his humour : he enjoyed it as if it had been a funny story.

He was thus seated, twiddling the queer manuscript in his hand, joking grimly to himself, when his servant came in with a card from a gentleman, who wished to speak to him very particularly. And if Pen had gone out into the passage, he would have seen, sucking his stick, rolling his eyes, and showing great marks of anxiety, his old acquaintance, Mr. Samuel Huxter.

'Mr. Huxter on particular business! Pray, beg Mr. Huxter to come in,' said Pen, amused rather ; and not the less so when poor Samuel appeared before him.

'Pray take a chair, Mr. Huxter,' said Pen, in his most superb manner. 'In what way can I be of service to you ?'

'I had rather not speak before the flunk—before the man, Mr. Pendennis." On which Mr. Arthur's attendant quitted the room.

'I'm in a fix,' said Mr. Huxter gloomily.

'Indeed.'

'*She* sent me to you,' continued the young surgeon.

'What, Fanny ? Is she well ? I was coming to see her, but I have had a great deal of business since my return to London.'

'I heard of you through my governor and Jack Hobnell,' broke in Huxter. 'I wish you joy, Mr. Pendennis, both of the borough and the lady, sir. Fanny wishes you joy, too,' he added, with something of a blush.

'There's many a slip between the cup and the lip ! Who knows what may happen, Mr. Huxter, or who will sit in Parliament for Clavering next session ?'

'You can do anything with my governor,' continued Mr. Huxter. 'You got him Clavering Park. The old boy was very much pleased, sir, at your calling him in. Hobnell wrote me so. Do you think you could speak to the governor for me, Mr. Pendennis ?'

'And tell him what ?'

'I've gone and done it, sir,' said Huxter, with a particular look.

'You—you don't mean to say you have—you have done any wrong to that dear little creature, sir,' said Pen, starting up in a great fury.

'I hope not,' said Huxter, with a hang-dog look: 'but I've married her. And I know there will be an awful shindy at home. It was agreed that I should be taken into partnership when I had passed the college, and it was to have been Huxter and Son. But I *would* have it, confound it. It's all over now, and the old boy's wrote me that he's coming up to town for drugs: he will be here to-morrow, and then it must all come out.'

'And when did this event happen?' asked Pen, not over well pleased, most likely, that a person who had once attracted some portion of his royal good graces should have transferred her allegiance, and consoled herself for his loss.

'Last Thursday was five weeks—it was two days after Miss Amory came to Shepherd's Inn,' Huxter answered.

Pen remembered that Blanche had written and mentioned her visit. 'I was called in,' Huxter said. 'I was in the inn looking after old Cos's leg;*and about something else too, very likely: and I met Strong, who told me there was a woman taken ill in chambers, and went up to give her my professional services. It was the old lady who attends Miss Amory—her housekeeper, or some such thing. She was taken with strong hysterics: I found her kicking and scratching like a good one—in Strong's chamber, along with him and Colonel Altamont, and Miss Amory crying and as pale as a sheet; and Altamont fuming about—a regular kick-up. They were two hours in the chambers; and the old woman went whooping off in a cab. She was much worse than the young one. I called in Grosvenor Place next day to see if I could be of any service, but they were gone without so much as thanking me: and the day after I had business of my own to attend to—a bad business too,' said Mr. Huxter gloomily. 'But it's done, and can't be undone; and we must make the best of it.'

She has known the story for a month, thought Pen, with a sharp pang of grief, and a gloomy sympathy—this accounts for her letter of to-day. She will not implicate her father, or divulge his secret; she wishes to let me off from the marriage—and finds a pretext—the generous girl!

'Do you know who Altamont is, sir?' asked Huxter, after the pause during which Pen had been thinking of his

own affairs. 'Fanny and I have talked him over, and we can't help fancying that it's Mrs. Lightfoot's first husband come to life again, and she who has just married a second. Perhaps Lightfoot won't be very sorry for it,' sighed Huxter, looking savagely at Arthur, for the demon of jealousy was still in possession of his soul; and now, and more than ever since his marriage, the poor fellow fancied that Fanny's heart belonged to his rival.

'Let us talk about your affairs,' said Pen. 'Show me how I can be of any service to you, Huxter. Let me congratulate you on your marriage. I am thankful that

Fanny, who is so good, so fascinating, so kind a creature, has found an honest man, and a gentleman who will make her happy. Show me what I can do to help you.'

'She thinks you can, sir,' said Huxter, accepting Pen's proffered hand, 'and I'm very much obliged to you, I'm sure; and that you might talk over my father, and break the business to him, and my mother, who always has her back up about being a clergyman's daughter. Fanny ain't of a good family, I know, and not up to us in breeding and that—but she's a Huxter now.'

'The wife takes the husband's rank, of course,' said Pen.

'And with a little practice in society,' continued Huxter,

imbibing his stick, 'she'll be as good as any girl in Clavering. You should hear her sing and play on the piano. Did you ever ? Old Bows taught her. And she'll do on the stage, if the governor was to throw me over ; but I'd rather not have her there. She can't help being a coquette, Mr. Pendennis, she can't help it. Dammy, sir ! I'll be bound to say, that two or three of the Bartholomew chaps, that I've brought into my place, are sitting with her now : even Jack Linton, that I took down as my best man, is as bad as the rest, and she will go on singing and making eyes at him. It's what Bows says, if there were twenty men in a room, and one not taking notice of her, she wouldn't be satisfied until the twentieth was at her elbow.'

'You should have her mother with her,' said Pen, laughing.

'She must keep the lodge. She can't see so much of her family as she used. I can't, you know, sir, go on with that lot. Consider my rank in life,' said Huxter, putting a very dirty hand up to his chin.

'*Au fait*,' said Mr. Pen, who was infinitely amused, and concerning whom *mutato nomine* (and of course concerning nobody else in the world) the fable might have been narrated.

As the two gentlemen were in the midst of this colloquy, another knock came to Pen's door, and his servant presently announced Mr. Bows. The old man followed slowly, his pale face blushing, and his hand trembling somewhat as he took Pen's. He coughed, and wiped his face in his checked cotton pocket-handkerchief, and sat down with his hands on his knees, the sun shining on his bald head. Pen looked at the homely figure with no small sympathy and kindness. This man, too, has had his griefs, and his wounds, Arthur thought. This man, too, has brought his genius and his heart, and laid them at a woman's feet ; where she spurned them. The chance of life has gone against him, and the prize is with that creature yonder. Fanny's bridegroom, thus mutely apostrophized, had winked meanwhile with one eye at old Bows, and was driving holes in the floor with the cane which he loved.

'So we have lost, Mr. Bows, and here is the lucky winner,' Pen said, looking hard at the old man.

'Here is the lucky winner, sir, as you say.'

'I suppose you have come from my place ?' asked Huxter,

who, having winked at Bows with one eye, now favoured Pen with a wink of the other—a wink which seemed to say, 'Infatuated old boy—you understand—over head and ears in love with her—poor old fool.'

'Yes, I have been there ever since you went away. It was Mrs. Sam who sent me after you: who said that she thought you might be doing something stupid—something like yourself, Huxter.'

'There's as big fools as I am,' growled the young surgeon.

'A few, p'raps,' said the old man; 'not many, let us trust. Yes, she sent me after you for fear you should offend Mr. Pendennis; and I dare say because she thought you wouldn't give her message to him, and beg him to go and see her; and she knew *I* would take her errand. Did he tell you that, sir?'

Huxter blushed scarlet, and covered his confusion with an imprecation. Pen laughed; the scene suited his bitter humour more and more.

'I have no doubt Mr. Huxter was going to tell me,' Arthur said, 'and very much flattered I am sure I shall be to pay my respects to his wife.'

'It's in Charterhouse Lane, over the baker's, on the right-hand side as you go from St. John's Street,' continued Bows, without any pity. 'You know Smithfield, Mr. Pendennis? St. John's Street leads into Smithfield. Dr. Johnson has been down the street many a time with ragged shoes, and a bundle of penny-a-lining for the *Gent's Magazine.** You literary gents are better off now—eh? You ride in your cabs, and wear yellow kid gloves now.'

'I have known so many brave and good men fail, and so many quacks and impostors succeed, that you mistake me if you think I am puffed up by my own personal good luck, old friend,' Arthur said sadly. 'Do *you* think the prizes of life are carried by the most deserving? and set up that mean test of prosperity for merit? You must feel that you are as good as I. I have never questioned it. It is you that are peevish against the freaks of fortune, and grudge the good luck that befalls others. It's not the first time you have unjustly accused me, Bows.'

'Perhaps you are not far wrong, sir,' said the old fellow, wiping his bald forehead. 'I am thinking about myself and grumbling; most men do when they get on that sub-

ject. Here's the fellow that's got the prize in the lottery; here's the fortunate youth.'

'I don't know what you are driving at,' Huxter said, who had been much puzzled as the above remarks passed between his two companions.

'Perhaps not,' said Bows dryly. 'Mrs. H. sent me here to look after you, and to see that you brought that little message to Mr. Pendennis, which you didn't, you see, and so she was right. Women always are; they have always a reason for everything. Why, sir,' he said, turning round to Pen with a sneer, 'she had a reason even for giving me that message. I was sitting with her after you left us, very quiet and comfortable; I was talking away, and she was mending your shirts, when your two young friends, Jack Linton and Bob Blades, looked in from Bartholomew's; and then it was she found out that she had this message to send. You needn't hurry yourself, she don't want you back again; they'll stay these two hours, I dare say.'

Huxter arose with great perturbation at this news, and plunged his stick into the pocket of his paletot, and seized his hat.

'You'll come and see us, sir, won't you?' he said to Pen. 'You'll talk over the governor, won't you, sir, if I can get out of this place and down to Clavering?'

'You will promise to attend me gratis if ever I fall ill at Fairoaks, will you, Huxter?' Pen said good-naturedly. 'I will do anything I can for you. I will come and see Mrs. Huxter immediately, and we will conspire together about what is to be done.'

'I thought that would send him out, sir,' Bows said, dropping into his chair again as soon as the young surgeon had quitted the room. 'And it's all true, sir—every word of it. She wants you back again, and sends her husband after you. She cajoles everybody, the little devil. She tries it on you, on me, on poor Costigan, on the young chaps from Bartholomew's. She's got a little court of 'em already. And if there's nobody there, she practises on the old German baker in the shop or coaxes the black sweeper at the crossing.'

'Is she fond of that fellow?' asked Pen.

'There is no accounting for likes and dislikes,' Bows answered. 'Yes, she is fond of him; and having taken the thing into her head, she would not rest until she married

him. They had their banns published at St. Clement's, and nobody heard it or knew any just cause or impediment. And one day she slips out of the porter's lodge and has the business done, and goes off to Gravesend with Lothario; and leaves a note for me to go and explain all things to her ma. Bless you! the old woman knew it as well as I did, though she pretended ignorance. And so she goes, and I'm alone again. I miss her, sir, tripping along that court, and coming for her singing lesson; and I've no heart to look into the porter's lodge now, which looks very empty without her, the little flirting thing. And I go and sit and dangle about her lodgings, like an old fool. She makes 'em very trim and nice, though; gets up all Huxter's shirts and clothes: cooks his little dinner, and sings at her business like a little lark. What's the use of being angry? I lent 'em three pound to go on with: for they haven't got a shilling till the reconciliation, and pa comes down.'

When Bows had taken his leave, Pen carried his letter from Blanche, and the news which he had just received, to his usual adviser, Laura. It was wonderful upon how many points Mr. Arthur, who generally followed his own opinion, now wanted another person's counsel. He could hardly so much as choose a waistcoat without referring to Miss Bell: if he wanted to buy a horse he must have Miss Bell's opinion; all which marks of deference tended greatly to the amusement of the shrewd old lady with whom Miss Bell lived, and whose plans regarding her protégée we have indicated.

Arthur produced Blanche's letter then to Laura, and asked her to interpret it. Laura was very much agitated, and puzzled by the contents of the note.

'It seems to me,' she said, 'as if Blanche is acting very artfully.'

'And wishes so to place matters that she may take me or leave me? Is it not so?'

'It is, I am afraid, a kind of duplicity which does not augur well for your future happiness: and is a bad reply to your own candour and honesty, Arthur. Do you know, I think, I think—I scarcely like to say what I think,' said Laura, with a deep blush; but of course the blushing young lady yielded to her cousin's persuasion, and expressed what her thoughts were. 'It looks to me, Arthur, as if there

might be—there might be somebody else,' said Laura, with a repetition of the blush.

'And if there is,' broke in Arthur, 'and if I am free once again, will the best and dearest of all women——'

'You are not free, dear brother,' Laura said calmly. 'You belong to another; of whom I own it grieves me to think ill. But I can't do otherwise. It is very odd that in this letter she does not urge you to tell her the reason why you have broken arrangements which would have been so advantageous to you; and avoids speaking on the subject. She somehow seems to write as if she knows her father's secret.'

Pen said, 'Yes, she must know it;' and told the story, which he had just heard from Huxter, of the interview at Shepherd's Inn.

'It was not so that she described the meeting,' said Laura; and going to her desk, produced from it that letter of Blanche's which mentioned her visit to Shepherd's Inn. 'Another disappointment—only the Chevalier Strong and a friend of his in the room.' This was all that Blanche had said. 'But she was bound to keep her father's secret, Pen,' Laura added. 'And yet, and yet—it is very puzzling.'

The puzzle was this, that for three weeks after this eventful discovery Blanche had been only too eager about her dearest Arthur; was urging, as strongly as so much modesty could urge, the completion of the happy arrangements which were to make her Arthur's for ever; and now it seemed as if something had interfered to mar these happy arrangements—as if Arthur poor was not quite so agreeable to Blanche as Arthur rich and a member of Parliament—as if there was some mystery. At last she said—'Tunbridge Wells is not very far off, is it, Arthur? Hadn't you better go and see her?'

They had been in town a week, and neither had thought of that simple plan before!

CHAPTER LXXIII

SHOWS HOW ARTHUR HAD BETTER HAVE TAKEN A RETURN TICKET

THE train carried Arthur only too quickly to Tunbridge, though he had time to review all the circumstances of his life as he made the brief journey; and to acknowledge to what sad conclusions his selfishness and waywardness had led him. 'Here is the end of hopes and aspirations,' thought he, 'of romance and ambitions! Where I yield or where I am obstinate, I am alike unfortunate; my mother implores me, and I refuse an angel! Say I had taken her; forced on me as she was, Laura would never have been an angel to me. I could not have given her my heart at another's instigation; I could never have known her as she is had I been obliged to ask another to interpret her qualities and point out her virtues. I yield to my uncle's solicitations, and accept on his guarantee Blanche, and a seat in Parliament, and wealth, and ambition, and a career; and see!—fortune comes and leaves me the wife without the dowry, which I had taken in compensation of a heart. Why was I not more honest, or am I not less so? It would have cost my poor old uncle no pangs to accept Blanche's fortune whencesoever it came; he can't even understand, he is bitterly indignant, heart-stricken, almost, at the scruples which actuate me in refusing it. I dissatisfy everybody. A maimed, weak, imperfect wretch, it seems as if I am unequal to any fortune. I neither make myself nor anyone connected with me happy. What prospect is there for this poor little frivolous girl, who is to take my obscure name and share my fortune? I have not even ambition to excite me, or self-esteem enough to console myself, much more her, for my failure. If I were to write a book that should go through twenty editions, why, I should be the very first to sneer at my reputation. Say I could succeed at the Bar, and achieve a fortune by bullying witnesses and twisting evidence; is that a fame which would

satisfy my longings, or a calling in which my life would be well spent? How I wish I could be that priest opposite, who never has lifted his eyes from his breviary, except when we were in Reigate tunnel, when he could not see; or that old gentleman next him, who scowls at him with eyes of hatred over his newspaper. The priest shuts his eyes to the world, but has his thoughts on the book, which is his directory to the world to come. His neighbour hates him as a monster, tyrant, persecutor, and fancies burning martyrs, and that pale countenance looking on, and lighted up by the flame. These have no doubts; these march on trustfully, bearing their load of logic.'

'Would you like to look at the paper, sir?' here interposed the stout gentleman (it had a flaming article against the order of the black-coated gentleman who was travelling with them in the carriage); and Pen thanked him and took it, and pursued his reverie, without reading two sentences of the journal.

'And yet, would you take either of those men's creeds, with its consequences?' he thought. 'Ah me! you must bear your own burthen, fashion your own faith, think your own thoughts, and pray your own prayer. To what mortal ear could I tell all, if I had a mind? or who could understand all? Who can tell another's shortcomings, lost opportunities, weigh the passions which overpower, the defects which incapacitate reason?—what extent of truth and right his neighbour's mind is organized to perceive and to do?—what invisible and forgotten accident, terror of youth, chance or mischance of fortune, may have altered the current of life? A grain of sand may alter it, as the flinging of a pebble may end it. Who can weigh circumstances, passions, temptations, that go to our good and evil account, save One, before whose awful wisdom we kneel, and at whose mercy we ask absolution? Here it ends,' thought Pen; 'this day or to-morrow will wind up the account of my youth; a weary retrospect, alas! a sad history with many a page I would fain not look back on! But who has not been tired or fallen, and who has escaped without scars from that struggle?' And his head fell on his breast, and the young man's heart prostrated itself humbly and sadly before that Throne where sits wisdom, and love, and pity for all, and made its confession. 'What matters about fame or poverty?' he thought. 'If I marry this woman I have

chosen, may I have strength and will to be true to her, and to make her happy. If I have children, pray God teach me to speak and to do the truth among them, and to leave them an honest name. There are no splendours for my marriage. Does my life deserve any ? I begin a new phase of it ; a better than the last may it be, I pray Heaven !'

The train stopped at Tunbridge as Pen was making these reflections ; and he handed over the newspaper to his neighbour, of whom he took leave, while the foreign clergyman in the opposite corner still sat with his eyes on his book. Pen jumped out of the carriage then, his carpet-bag in hand, and briskly determined to face his fortune.

A fly carried him rapidly to Lady Clavering's house from the station ; and, as he was transported thither, Arthur composed a little speech, which he intended to address to Blanche, and which was really as virtuous, honest, and well-minded an oration as any man of his turn of mind, and under his circumstances, could have uttered. The purport of it was—'Blanche, I cannot understand from your last letter what your meaning is, or whether my fair and frank proposal to you is acceptable or no. I think you know the reason which induces me to forgo the worldly advantages which a union with you offered, and which I could not accept without, as I fancy, being dishonoured. If you doubt of my affection, here I am ready to prove it. Let Smirke be called in, and let us be married out of hand ; and with all my heart I purpose to keep my vow, and to cherish you through life, and to be a true and a loving husband to you.'

From the fly Arthur sprang out then to the hall-door, where he was met by a domestic whom he did not know. The man seemed to be surprised at the approach of the gentleman with the carpet-bag, which he made no attempt to take from Arthur's hands. 'Her ladyship's not at home, sir,' the man remarked.

'I am Mr. Pendennis,' Arthur said. 'Where is Lightfoot ?'

'Lightfoot is gone,' answered the man. 'My lady is out, and my orders was——'

'I hear Miss Amory's voice in the drawing-room,' said Arthur. 'Take the bag to a dressing-room, if you please ;' and, passing by the porter, he walked straight towards that apartment, from which, as the door opened, a warble of melodious notes issued.

Our little Siren was at her piano singing with all her might and fascinations. Master Clavering was asleep on the sofa, indifferent to the music; but near Blanche sat a gentleman who was perfectly enraptured with her strain, which was of a passionate and melancholy nature.

As the door opened, the gentleman started up with a Hullo: the music stopped, with a little shriek from the singer; Frank Clavering woke up from the sofa, and Arthur came forward and said, 'What, Foker! how do you do,

Foker?' He looked at the piano, and there, by Miss Amory's side, was just such another purple leather box as he had seen in Harry's hand three days before, when the heir of Logwood was coming out of a jeweller's shop in Waterloo Place. It was opened, and curled round the white satin cushion within was, oh, such a magnificent serpentine bracelet, with such a blazing ruby head and diamond tail!

'How de-do, Pendennis?' said Foker. Blanche made

many motions of the shoulders, and gave signs of interest and agitation. And she put her handkerchief over the bracelet, and then she advanced, with a hand which trembled very much, to greet Pen.

'How is dearest Laura?' she said. The face of Foker looking up from his profound mourning—that face, so piteous and puzzled, was one that the reader's imagination must depict for himself; also that of Master Frank Clavering, who, looking at the three interesting individuals with an expression of the utmost knowingness, had only time to ejaculate the words, 'Here's a jolly go!' and to disappear sniggering.

Pen, too, had restrained himself up to that minute; but looking still at Foker, whose ears and cheeks tingled with blushes, Arthur burst out into a fit of laughter, so wild and loud, that it frightened Blanche much more than any the most serious exhibition.

'And this was the secret, was it? Don't blush and turn away, Foker, my boy. Why, man, you are a pattern of fidelity. Could I stand between Blanche and such constancy—could I stand between Miss Amory and fifteen thousand a year?'

'It is not that, Mr. Pendennis,' Blanche said, with great dignity. 'It is not money, it is not rank, it is not gold that moves *me*; but it *is* constancy, it is fidelity, it is a whole, trustful, loving heart offered to me, that I treasure—yes, that I treasure!' And she made for her handkerchief, but, reflecting what was underneath it, she paused. 'I do not disown, I do not disguise—my life is above disguise—to him on whom it is bestowed, my heart must be for ever bare—that I once thought I loved you,—yes, thought I was beloved by you! I own. How I clung to that faith! How I strove, I prayed, I longed to believe it! But your conduct, always—your own words so cold, so heartless, so unkind, have undeceived me. You trifled with the heart of the poor maiden! You flung me back with scorn the troth which I had plighted! I have explained all—all to Mr. Foker.'

'That you have,' said Foker, with devotion, and conviction in his looks.

'What, all?' said Pen, with a meaning look at Blanche. 'It is I am in fault, is it? Well, well, Blanche, be it so. I won't appeal against your sentence, and bear it in silence.

I came down here looking to very different things, Heaven knows, and with a heart most truly and kindly disposed towards you. I hope you may be happy with another, as, on my word, it was my wish to make you so; and I hope my honest old friend here will have a wife worthy of his loyalty, his constancy, and affection. Indeed, they deserve the regard of any woman—even Miss Blanche Amory. Shake hands, Harry; don't look askance at me. Has anybody told you that I was a false and heartless character?'

'I think you're a——' Foker was beginning, in his wrath, when Blanche interposed.

'Henry, not a word!—I pray you let there be forgiveness!'

'You're an angel, by Jove, you're an angel!' said Foker, at which Blanche looked seraphically up to the chandelier.

'In spite of what has passed, for the sake of what has passed, I must always regard Arthur as a brother,' the Seraph continued; 'we have known each other years, we have trodden the same fields, and plucked the same flowers together. Arthur! Henry! I beseech you to take hands and to be friends! Forgive you!—*I* forgive you, Arthur, with my heart I do. Should I not do so for making me so happy?'

'There is only one person of us three whom I pity, Blanche,' Arthur said gravely, 'and I say to you again, that I hope you will make this good fellow, this honest and loyal creature, happy.'

'Happy! O Heavens!' said Harry. He could not speak. His happiness gushed out at his eyes. 'She don't know—she can't know how fond I am of her, and—and who am I? a poor little beggar, and she takes me up and says she'll try and l—l—love me. I ain't worthy of so much happiness. Give us your hand, old boy, since she forgives you after your heartless conduct, and says she loves you. I'll make you welcome. I tell you I'll love everybody who loves her. By——if she tells me to kiss the ground I'll kiss it. Tell me to kiss the ground! I say, tell me. I love you so. You see I love you so.'

Blanche looked up seraphically again. Her gentle bosom heaved. She held out one hand as if to bless Harry, and then royally permitted him to kiss it. She took up the pocket-handkerchief and hid her own eyes, as the other fair hand was abandoned to poor Harry's tearful embrace.

'I swear that is a villain who deceives such a loving creature as that,' said Pen.

Blanche laid down the handkerchief, and put hand No. 2 softly on Foker's head, which was bent down kissing and weeping over hand No. 1. 'Foolish boy!' she said, 'it shall be loved as it deserves: who could help loving such a silly creature?'

And at this moment Frank Clavering broke in upon the sentimental trio.

'I say, Pendennis!' he said.

'Well, Frank!'

'The man wants to be paid, and go back. He's had some beer.'

'I'll go back with him,' cried Pen. 'Good-bye, Blanche. God bless you, Foker, old friend. You know, neither of you want me here.' He longed to be off that instant.

'Stay—I must say one word to you. One word in private, if you please,' Blanche said. 'You can trust us together, can't you,—Henry?' The tone in which the word 'Henry' was spoken, and the appeal, ravished Foker with delight. 'Trust you!' said he; 'oh, who wouldn't trust you! Come along, Franky, my boy.'

'Let's have a cigar,' said Frank, as they went into the hall.

'She don't like it,' said Foker gently.

'Law bless you—*she* don't mind. Pendennis used to smoke regular,' said the candid youth.

'It was but a short word I had to say,' said Blanche to Pen, with great calm, when they were alone. 'You never loved me, Mr. Pendennis.'

'I told you how much,' said Arthur. 'I never deceived you.'

'I suppose you will go back and marry Laura,' continued Blanche.

'Was that what you had to say?' said Pen.

'You are going to her this very night, I am sure of it. There is no denying it. You never cared for me.'

'*Et vous?*'

'*Et moi c'est différent.* I have been spoilt early. I cannot live out of the world, out of excitement. I could have done so, but it is too late. If I cannot have emotions, I must have the world. You would offer me neither one

nor the other. You are blasé in everything, even in ambition. You had a career before you, and you would not take it. You give it up !—for what ?—for a *bêtise*, for an absurd scruple. Why would you not have that seat, and be such a *puritain ?* Why should you refuse what is mine by right, by right, *entendez-vous ?*'

'You know all then ?' said Pen.

'Only within a month. But I have suspected ever since Baymouth—*n'importe* since when. It is not too late. He is as if he had never been ; and there is a position in the world before you yet. Why not sit in Parliament, exert your talent, and give a place in the world to yourself, to your wife ? I take *celui-là. Il est bon. Il est riche. Il est—vous le connaissez autant que moi enfin.* Think you that I would not prefer *un homme qui fera parler de moi ?* If the secret appears I am rich *à millions.* How does it affect me ? It is not my fault. It will never appear.'

'You will tell Harry everything, won't you ?'

'*Je comprends. Vous refusez,*' said Blanche savagely. 'I will tell Harry at my own time, when we are married. You will not betray me, will you ? You, having a defenceless girl's secret, will not turn upon her and use it ? *S'il me plaît de le cacher, mon secret ; pourquoi le donnerai-je ? Je l'aime, mon pauvre père, voyez-vous ?* I would rather live with that man than with you *fades* intriguers of the world. I must have emotions—*il m'en donne. Il m'écrit. Il écrit très-bien, voyez-vous—comme un pirate—comme un Bohémien—comme un homme.* But for this I would have said to my mother—*Ma mère ! quittons ce lâche mari, cette lâche société—retournons à mon père.*'

'The pirate would have wearied you like the rest,' said Pen.

'*Eh ! Il me faut des émotions,*' said Blanche. Pen had never seen her or known so much about her in all the years of their intimacy as he saw and knew now : though he saw more than existed in reality. For this young lady was not able to carry out any emotion to the full ; but had a sham enthusiasm, a sham hatred, a sham love, a sham taste, a sham grief, each of which flared and shone very vehemently for an instant, but subsided and gave place to the next sham emotion.

CHAPTER LXXIV

A CHAPTER OF MATCH-MAKING

PON the platform at Tunbridge, Pen fumed and fretted until the arrival of the evening train to London, a full half-hour,—six hours it seemed to him; but even this immense interval was passed, the train arrived, the train sped on, the London lights came in view—a gentleman who forgot his carpet-bag in the train rushed at a cab, and said to the man, 'Drive as hard as you can go to Jermyn Street.' The cabman, although a hansom cabman, said 'Thank you' for the gratuity which was put into his hand, and Pen ran up the stairs of the hotel to Lady Rockminster's apartments. Laura was alone in the drawing-room, reading, with a pale face, by the lamp. The pale face looked up when Pen opened the door. May we follow him? The great moments of life are but moments like the others. Your doom is spoken in a word or two. A single look from the eyes; a mere pressure of the hand may decide it; or of the lips, though they cannot speak.

When Lady Rockminster, who has had her after-dinner nap, gets up and goes into her sitting-room, we may enter with her ladyship.

'Upon my word, young people!' are the first words she says, and her attendant makes wondering eyes over her shoulder. And well may she say so; and well may the attendant cast wondering eyes; for the young people are in an attitude; and Pen in such a position as every young lady who reads this has heard tell of, or has seen, or hopes, or at any rate deserves to see.

In a word, directly he entered the room, Pen went up to Laura of the pale face, who had not time even to say, 'What, back so soon?' and seizing her outstretched and trembling hand just as she was rising from her chair, fell

down on his knees before her, and said quickly, 'I have seen her. She has engaged herself to Harry Foker—and—and NOW, Laura?'

The hand gives a pressure—the eyes beam a reply—the quivering lips answer, though speechless. Pen's head sinks down in the girl's lap, as he sobs out, 'Come and bless us, dear mother,' and arms as tender as Helen's once more enfold him.

In this juncture it is that Lady Rockminster comes in and says, 'Upon my word, young people! Beck! leave the room. What do *you* want poking your nose in here?'

Pen starts up with looks of triumph, still holding Laura's hand. 'She is consoling me for my misfortune, ma'am,' he says.

'What do you mean by kissing her hand? I don't know what you will be next doing.'

Pen kissed her ladyship's. '*I* have been to Tunbridge,' he says, 'and seen Miss Amory; and find on my arrival that—that a villain has transplanted me in her affections,' he says with a tragedy air.

'Is that all? Is that what you are whimpering on your knees about?' says the old lady, growing angry. 'You might have kept the news till to-morrow.'

'Yes—another has superseded me,' goes on Pen; 'but why call him villain? He is brave, he is constant, he is young, he is wealthy, he is beautiful.'

'What stuff are you talking, sir?' cried the old lady. 'What has happened?'

'Miss Amory has jilted me, and accepted Henry Foker, Esq. I found her warbling ditties to him as he lay at her feet; presents had been accepted, vows exchanged, these ten days. Harry was old Mrs. Planter's rheumatism, which kept dearest Laura out of the house. He is the most constant and generous of men. He has promised the living of Logwood to Lady Ann's husband, and given her a splendid present on her marriage; and he rushed to fling himself at Blanche's feet the instant he found he was free.'

'And so, as you can't get Blanche, you put up with Laura: is that it, sir?' asked the old lady.

'He acted nobly,' Laura said.

'I acted as she bade me,' said Pen. 'Never mind how, Lady Rockminster; but to the best of my knowledge and

power. And if you mean that I am not worthy of Laura, I know it, and pray Heaven to better me; and if the love and company of the best and purest creature in the world can do so, at least I shall have these to help me.'

'Hm, hm,' replied the old lady to this, looking with rather an appeased air at the young people. 'It is all very well; but I should have preferred Bluebeard.'

And now Pen, to divert the conversation from a theme which was growing painful to some parties present, bethought him of his interview with Huxter in the morning, and of Fanny Bolton's affairs, which he had forgotten under the immediate pressure and excitement of his own. And he told the ladies how Huxter had elevated Fanny to the rank of wife, and what terrors he was in respecting the arrival of his father. He described the scene with considerable humour, taking care to dwell especially upon that part of it which concerned Fanny's coquetry and irrepressible desire of captivating mankind; his meaning being, 'You see, Laura, I was not so guilty in that little affair; it was the girl who made love to me, and I who resisted. As I am no longer present, the little Siren practises her arts and fascinations upon others. Let that transaction be forgotten in your mind, if you please; or visit me with a very gentle punishment for my error.'

Laura understood his meaning under the eagerness of his explanations. 'If you did any wrong, you repented, dear Pen,' she said, 'and you know,' she added, with meaning eyes and blushes, 'that *I* have no right to reproach you.'

'Hm!' grumbled the old lady; 'I should have preferred Bluebeard.'

'The past is broken away. The morrow is before us. I will do my best to make your morrow happy, dear Laura,' Pen said. His heart was humbled by the prospect of his happiness: it stood awe-stricken in the contemplation of her sweet goodness and purity. He liked his wife better that she had owned to that passing feeling for Warrington, and laid bare her generous heart to him. And she—very likely she was thinking, 'How strange it is that I ever should have cared for another; I am vexed almost to think I care for him so little, am so little sorry that he is gone away. Oh, in these past two months how I have learned to love Arthur. I care about nothing but Arthur; my waking and sleeping thoughts are about him; he is never absent

from me. And to think that he is to be mine, mine! and that I am to marry him, and not to be his servant as I expected to be only this morning; for I would have gone down on my knees to Blanche to beg her to let me live with him. And now—oh, it is too much. Oh, mother! mother, that you were here!' Indeed, she felt as if Helen were there—by her actually, though invisibly. A halo of happiness beamed from her. She moved with a different step, and bloomed with a new beauty. Arthur saw the change; and the old Lady Rockminster remarked it with her shrewd eyes.

'What a sly demure little wretch you have been,' she whispered to Laura—while Pen, in great spirits, was laughing, and telling his story about Huxter—'and how you have kept your secret!'

'How are we to help the young couple?' said Laura. Of course Miss Laura felt an interest in all young couples, as generous lovers always love other lovers.

'We must go and see them,' said Pen.

'Of course we must go and see them,' said Laura. 'I intend to be very fond of Fanny. Let us go this instant. Lady Rockminster, may I have the carriage?'

'Go now!—why, you stupid creature, it is eleven o'clock at night. Mr. and Mrs. Huxter have got their night-caps on, I dare say. And it is time for you to go now. Good-night, Mr. Pendennis.'

Arthur and Laura begged for ten minutes more.

'We will go to-morrow morning, then. I will come and fetch you with Martha.'

'An earl's coronet,' said Pen, who, no doubt, was pleased himself, 'will have a great effect in Lamb Court and Smithfield. Stay—Lady Rockminster, will you join us in a little conspiracy?'

'How do you mean conspiracy, young man?'

'Will you please to be a little ill to-morrow; and when old Mr. Huxter arrives, will you let me call him in? If he is put into a good humour at the notion of attending a baronet in the country, what influence won't a countess have on him? When he is softened—when he is quite ripe, we will break the secret upon him; bring in the young people, extort the paternal benediction, and finish the comedy.'

'A parcel of stuff,' said the old lady. 'Take your hat, sir. Come away, miss. There—my head is turned another

way. Good-night, young people.' And who knows but the old lady thought of her own early days as she went away on Laura's arm, nodding her head and humming to herself?

With the early morning came Laura and Martha, according to appointment; and the desired sensation was, let us hope, effected in Lamb Court, whence the three proceeded to wait upon Mr. and Mrs. Samuel Huxter, at their residence in Charterhouse Lane.

The two ladies looked at each other with great interest, and not a little emotion on Fanny's part. She had not seen her 'guardian,' as she was pleased to call Pen in consequence of his bequest, since the event had occurred which had united her to Mr. Huxter.

'Samuel told me how kind you had been,' she said. 'You were always very kind, Mr. Pendennis. And—and I hope your friend is better, who was took ill in Shepherd's Inn, ma'am.'*

'My name is Laura,' said the other, with a blush. 'I am—that is, I was—that is, I am Arthur's sister: and we shall always love you for being so good to him when he was ill. And when we live in the country, I hope we shall see each other. And I shall be always happy to hear of your happiness, Fanny.'

'We are going to do what you and Huxter have done, Fanny.—Where is Huxter? What nice, snug lodgings you've got! What a pretty cat!'

While Fanny is answering these questions in reply to Pen, Laura says to herself—'Well, now really! is *this* the creature about whom we were all so frightened? What *could* he see in her? She's a homely little thing, but such manners! Well, she was very kind to him—bless her for that.'

Mr. Samuel had gone out to meet his pa. Mrs. Huxter said that the old gentleman was to arrive that day at the Somerset Coffee House, in the Strand; and Fanny confessed that she was in a sad tremor about the meeting. 'If his parents cast him off, what are we to do?' she said. 'I shall never pardon myself for bringing ruing on my 'usband's 'ead. You must intercede for us, Mr. Arthur. If mortal man can, you can bend and influence Mr. Uxter senior.' Fanny still regarded Pen in the light of a superior being, that was evident. No doubt Arthur thought of the past, as he marked the solemn little tragedy-airs and looks,

the little ways, the little trepidations, vanities, of the little bride. As soon as the interview was over, entered Messrs. Linton and Blades, who came, of course, to visit Huxter, and brought with them a fine fragrance of tobacco. They had watched the carriage at the baker's door, and remarked the coronet with awe. They asked of Fanny who was that uncommonly heavy swell who had just driven off ? and pronounced the countess was of the right sort. And when they heard that it was Mr. Pendennis and his sister, they remarked that Pen's father was only a sawbones ; and that he gave himself confounded airs ; they had been in Huxter's company on the night of his little altercation with Pen in the Back Kitchen.

Returning homewards through Fleet Street, and as Laura was just stating to Pen's infinite amusement that Fanny was very well, but that really there was no beauty in her,—there might be, but *she* could not see it,—as they were locked near Temple Bar, they saw young Huxter returning to his bride. 'The governor had arrived ; was at the Somerset Coffee House—was in tolerable good-humour—something about the railway : but he had been afraid to speak about—about that business. Would Mr. Pendennis try it on ?'

Pen said he would go and call at that moment upon Mr. Huxter, and see what might be done. Huxter junior would lurk outside whilst that awful interview took place. The coronet on the carriage inspired his soul also with wonder ; and old Mr. Huxter himself beheld it with delight, as he looked from the coffee-house window on that Strand which it was always a treat to him to survey.

'And I can afford to give myself a lark, sir,' said Mr. Huxter, shaking hands with Pen. 'Of course you know the news ? We have got our bill, sir.* We shall have our branch line—our shares are up, sir—and we buy your three fields along the Brawl, and put a pretty penny into *your* pocket, Mr. Pendennis.'

'Indeed !—that was good news.' Pen remembered that there was a letter from Mr. Tatham, at Chambers, these three days ; but he had not opened the communication, being interested with other affairs.

'I hope you don't intend to grow rich, and give up practice,' said Pen. 'We can't lose you at Clavering, Mr. Huxter ; though I hear very good accounts of your son.

My friend, Dr. Goodenough, speaks most highly of his talents. It is hard that a man of your eminence, though, should be kept in a country town.'

'The metropolis would have been my sphere of action, sir,' said Mr. Huxter, surveying the Strand. 'But a man takes his business where he finds it; and I succeeded to that of my father.'

'It was my father's, too,' said Pen. 'I sometimes wish I had followed it.'

'You, sir, have taken a more lofty career,' said the old gentleman. 'You aspire to the senate: and to literary honours. You wield the poet's pen, sir, and move in the circles of fashion. We keep an eye upon you at Clavering. We read your name in the lists of the select parties of the nobility. Why, it was only the other day that my wife was remarking how odd it was that at a party at the Earl of Kidderminster's your name was *not* mentioned. To what member of the aristocracy may I ask does that equipage belong from which I saw you descend? The Countess Dowager of Rockminster? How is her ladyship?'

'Her ladyship is not very well; and when I heard that you were coming to town, I strongly urged her to see you, Mr. Huxter,' Pen said. Old Huxter felt, if he had a hundred votes for Clavering, he would give them all to Pen.

'There is an old friend of yours in the carriage—a Clavering lady, too—will you come out and speak to her?' asked Pen. The old surgeon was delighted to speak to a coroneted carriage in the midst of the full Strand: he ran out bowing and smiling. Huxter junior, dodging about the district, beheld the meeting between his father and Laura, saw the latter put out her hand, and presently, after a little colloquy with Pen, beheld his father actually jump into the carriage, and drive away with Miss Bell.

There was no room for Arthur, who came back, laughing, to the young surgeon, and told him whither his parent was bound. During the whole of the journey, that artful Laura coaxed, and wheedled, and cajoled him so adroitly, that the old gentleman would have granted her anything; and Lady Rockminster achieved the victory over him by complimenting him on his skill, and professing her anxiety to consult him. What were her ladyship's symptoms? Should he meet her ladyship's usual medical attendant? Mr. Jones was called out of town? He should be delighted to devote

his very best energies and experience to her ladyship's service.

He was so charmed with his patient, that he wrote home about her to his wife and family; he talked of nothing but Lady Rockminster to Samuel, when that youth came to partake of beef-steak and oyster-sauce and accompany his parent to the play. There was a simple grandeur, a polite urbanity, a high-bred grace about her ladyship, which he had never witnessed in any woman. Her symptoms did not seem alarming: he had prescribed—Spir: Ammon: Aromat: with a little Spir: Menth: Pip: and orange-flower, which would be all that was necessary.

'Miss Bell seemed to be on the most confidential and affectionate footing with her ladyship. She was about to form a matrimonial connection. All young people ought to marry. Such were her ladyship's words; and the countess condescended to ask respecting my own family, and I mentioned you by name to her ladyship, Sam, my boy. I shall look in to-morrow, when, if the remedies which I have prescribed for her ladyship have had the effect which I anticipate, I shall probably follow them up by a little Spir: Lavend: Comp:—and so set my noble patient up. What is the theatre which is most frequented by the—by the higher classes in town, hey, Sam? and to what amusement will you take an old country doctor to-night, hey, sir?'

On the next day, when Mr. Huxter called in Jermyn Street at twelve o'clock, Lady Rockminster had not yet left her room, but Miss Bell and Mr. Pendennis were in waiting to receive him. Lady Rockminster had had a most comfortable night, and was getting on as well as possible. How had Mr. Huxter amused himself? at the theatre? with his son? What a capital piece it was, and how charmingly Mrs. O'Leary looked and sang it! and what a good fellow young Huxter was! liked by everybody, an honour to his profession. He has not his father's manners, I grant you, or that old-world tone which is passing away from us, but a more excellent, sterling fellow never lived. 'He ought to practise in the country whatever you do, sir,' said Arthur—'he ought to marry—other people are going to do so—and settle.'

'The very words that her ladyship used yesterday, Mr. Pendennis. He ought to marry. Sam should marry, sir.'

'The town is full of temptations, sir,' continued Pen. The old gentleman thought of that *houri*, Mrs. O'Leary.

'There is no better safeguard for a young man than an early marriage with an honest, affectionate creature.'

'No better, sir, no better.'

'And love is better than money, isn't it ?'

'Indeed it is,' said Miss Bell.

'I agree with so fair an authority,' said the old gentleman, with a bow.

'And—and suppose, sir,' Pen said, 'that I had a piece of news to communicate to you.'

'God bless my soul, Mr. Pendennis ! what do you mean ?' asked the old gentleman.

'Suppose I had to tell you that a young man, carried away by an irresistible passion for an admirable and most virtuous young creature—whom everybody falls in love with—had consulted the dictates of reason and his heart, and had married. Suppose I were to tell you that that man is my friend ; that our excellent, our truly noble friend the Countess Dowager of Rockminster is truly interested about him (and you may fancy what a young man can do in life when THAT family is interested for him) ; suppose I were to tell you that you know him—that he is here—that he is——'

'Sam married ! God bless my soul, sir, you don't mean that !'

'And to such a nice creature, dear Mr. Huxter.'

'His lordship is charmed with her,' said Pen, telling almost the first fib which he has told in the course of this story.

'Married ! the rascal, is he ?' thought the old gentleman.

'They will do it, sir,' said Pen ; and went and opened the door.

Mr. and Mrs. Samuel Huxter issued thence, and both came and knelt down before the old gentleman. The kneeling little Fanny found favour in his sight. There *must* have been something attractive about her, in spite of Laura's opinion.

'Will never do so any more, sir,' said Sam.

'Get up, sir,' said Mr. Huxter. And they got up, and Fanny came a little nearer, and a little nearer still, and looked so pretty and pitiful, that somehow Mr. Huxter

MR HUXTER ASKS PARDON

found himself kissing the little crying-laughing thing, and feeling as if he liked it.

'What's your name, my dear ?' he said, after a minute of this sport.

'Fanny, papa,' said Mrs. Samuel.

CHAPTER LXXV

EXEUNT OMNES

UR characters are all a month older than they were when the last-described adventures and conversations occurred, and a great number of the personages of our story have chanced to reassemble at the little country town where we were first introduced to them. Frederic Lightfoot, formerly *maître d'hôtel* in the service of Sir Francis Clavering, of Clavering Park, Bart., has begged leave to inform the nobility and gentry of ——shire that he has taken that well-known and comfortable hotel, the 'Clavering Arms,' in Clavering, where he hopes for the continued patronage of the gentlemen and families of the county. 'This ancient and well-established house,' Mr. Lightfoot's manifesto states, 'has been repaired and decorated in a style of the greatest comfort. Gentlemen hunting with the Dumplingbeare hounds will find excellent stabling and loose-boxes for horses at the Clavering Arms. A commodious billiard-room has been attached to the hotel, and the cellars have been furnished with the choicest wines and spirits, selected, without regard to expense, by C. L. Commercial gentlemen will find the Clavering Arms a most comfortable place of resort : and the scale of charges has been regulated for all, so as to meet the economical spirit of the present times.'

Indeed, there is a considerable air of liveliness about the old inn. The Clavering arms have been splendidly re-painted over the gateway. The coffee-room windows are bright and fresh, and decorated with Christmas holly ; the magistrates have met in petty sessions in the card-room of

the old Assembly. The farmers' ordinary is held as of old, and frequented by increased numbers, who are pleased with Mrs. Lightfoot's cuisine. Her Indian curries and Mulligatawny soup are especially popular: Major Stokes, the respected tenant of Fairoaks Cottage, Captain Glanders, H.P., and other resident gentry, have pronounced in their favour, and have partaken of them more than once both in private and at the dinner of the Clavering Institute, attendant on the incorporation of the reading-room, and when the chief inhabitants of that flourishing little town met together and did justice to the hostess's excellent cheer. The chair was taken by Sir Francis Clavering, Bart., supported by the esteemed rector, Dr. Portman; the vice-chair being ably filled by — Barker, Esq. (supported by the Rev. J. Simcoe and the Rev. S. Jowls), the enterprising head of the ribbon factory in Clavering, and chief director of the Clavering and Chatteris Branch of the Great Western Railway, which will be opened in another year, and upon the works of which the engineers and workmen are now busily engaged.

An interesting event, which is likely to take place in the life of our talented townsman, Arthur Pendennis, Esq., has, we understand, caused him to relinquish the intentions which he had of offering himself as a candidate for our borough: and rumour whispers (says the *Chatteris Champion, Clavering Agriculturist,* and *Baymouth Fisherman,*—that independent county paper, so distinguished for its unswerving principles and loyalty to the British oak, and so eligible a medium for advertisements)—rumour states, says the *C. C., C. A.* and *B. F.*, that should Sir Francis Clavering's failing health oblige him to relinquish his seat in Parliament, he will vacate it in favour of a young gentleman of colossal fortune, and related to the highest aristocracy of the empire, who is about to contract a matrimonial alliance with an accomplished and lovely lady, connected by the nearest ties with the respected family at Clavering Park. Lady Clavering and Miss Amory have arrived at the Park for the Christmas holidays; and we understand that a large number of the aristocracy are expected, and that festivities of a peculiarly interesting nature will take place there at the commencement of the new year.

The ingenious reader will be enabled, by the help of the above announcement, to understand what has taken place during the little break which has occurred in our narrative. Although Lady Rockminster grumbled a little at Laura's preference for Pendennis over Bluebeard, those who are

aware of the latter's secret will understand that the young girl could make no other choice, and the kind old lady who had constituted herself Miss Bell's guardian was not ill-pleased that she was to fulfil the great purpose in life of young ladies and marry. She informed her maid of the interesting event that very night, and of course Mrs. Beck, who was perfectly aware of every single circumstance, and kept by Martha, of Fairoaks, in the fullest knowledge of what was passing, was immensely surprised and delighted. 'Mr. Pendennis's income is so much; the railroad will give him so much more, he states: Miss Bell has so much, and may probably have a little more one day. For persons in their degree, they will be able to manage very well. And I shall speak to my nephew Pynsent, who I suspect was once rather attached to her,—but of course that was out of the question' ('Oh! of course, my lady; I should think so indeed!')—'not that you know anything whatever about it, or have any business to think at all on the subject,—I shall speak to George Pynsent, who is now chief secretary of the Tape and Sealing-Wax Office, and have Mr. Pendennis made something. And, Beck, in the morning you will carry down my compliments to Major Pendennis, and say that I shall pay him a visit at one o'clock. Yes,' muttered the old lady, 'the major must be reconciled, and he must leave his fortune to Laura's children.'

Accordingly, at one o'clock, the Dowager Lady Rockminster appeared at Major Pendennis's, who was delighted, as may be imagined, to receive so noble a visitor. The major had been prepared, if not for the news which her ladyship was about to give him, at least with the intelligence that Pen's marriage with Miss Amory was broken off. The young gentleman bethinking him of his uncle, for the first time that day it must be owned, and meeting his new servant in the hall of the hotel, asked after the major's health from Mr. Frosch; and then went into the coffee-room of the hotel, where he wrote a half-dozen lines to acquaint his guardian with what had occurred.

Dear Uncle (he said), if there has been any question between us, it is over now. I went to Tunbridge Wells yesterday, and found that somebody else had carried off the prize about which we were hesitating. Miss A., without any compunction for me, has bestowed herself upon Harry Foker, with his fifteen thousand a-year. I came in suddenly upon their loves, and found and left him in possession.

And you'll be glad to hear, Tatham writes me that he has sold three of my fields at Fairoaks to the Railroad Company, at a great figure. I will tell you this, and more when we meet; and am always your affectionate—A. P.

'I think I am aware of what you were about to tell me,' the major said, with a most courtly smile and bow to Pen's ambassadress. 'It was a very great kindness of your ladyship to think of bringing me the news. How well you look! How very good you are! How very kind you have always been to that young man!'

'It was for the sake of his uncle,' said Lady Rockminster, most politely.

'He has informed me of the state of affairs, and written me a nice note,—yes, a nice note,' continued the old gentleman; 'and I find he has had an increase to his fortune,—yes; and, all things considered, I don't much regret that this affair with Miss Amory is *manquée*, though I wished for it once,—in fact, all things considered, I am very glad of it.'

'We must console him, Major Pendennis,' continued the lady; 'we must get him a wife.' The truth then came across the major's mind, and he saw for what purpose Lady Rockminster had chosen to assume the office of ambassadress.

It is not necessary to enter into the conversation which ensued, or to tell at any length how her ladyship concluded a negotiation, which, in truth, was tolerably easy. There could be no reason why Pen should not marry according to his own and his mother's wish: and as for Lady Rockminster, she supported the marriage by intimations which had very great weight with the major, but of which we shall say nothing, as her ladyship (now, of course, much advanced in years) is still alive, and the family might be angry; and, in fine, the old gentleman was quite overcome by the determined graciousness of the lady, and her fondness for Laura. Nothing, indeed, could be more bland and kind than Lady Rockminster's whole demeanour, except for one moment when the major talked about his boy throwing himself away, at which her ladyship broke out into a little speech, in which she made the major understand, what poor Pen and his friends acknowledge very humbly, that Laura was a thousand times too good for him. Laura was fit to be the wife of a king,—Laura was a paragon of

virtue and excellence. And it must be said, that when Major Pendennis found that a lady of the rank of the Countess of Rockminster seriously admired Miss Bell, he instantly began to admire her himself.

So that when Herr Frosch was requested to walk upstairs to Lady Rockminster's apartments, and inform Miss Bell and Mr. Arthur Pendennis that the major would receive them, and Laura appeared blushing and happy as she hung on Pen's arm, the major gave a shaky hand to one and the other, with an unaffected emotion and cordiality, and then went through another salutation to Laura, which caused her to blush still more. Happy blushes ! bright eyes beaming with the light of love ! The story-teller turns from this group to his young audience, and hopes that one day their eyes may all shine so.

Pen having retreated in the most friendly manner, and the lovely Blanche having bestowed her young affections upon a blushing bridegroom, with fifteen thousand a year, there was such an outbreak of happiness in Lady Clavering's heart and family as the good Begum had not known for many a year, and she and Blanche were on the most delightful terms of cordiality and affection. The ardent Foker pressed onwards the happy day, and was as anxious as might be expected to abridge the period of mourning which should put him in possession of so many charms and amiable qualities, of which he had been only, as it were, the heir apparent, not the actual owner, until then. The gentle Blanche, everything that her affianced lord could desire, was not averse to gratify the wishes of her fond Henry. Lady Clavering came up from Tunbridge. Milliners and jewellers were set to work and engaged to prepare the delightful paraphernalia of Hymen. Lady Clavering was in such a good humour, that Sir Francis even benefited by it, and such a reconciliation was effected between this pair, that Sir Francis came to London, sat at the head of his own table once more, and appeared tolerably flush of money at his billiard-rooms and gambling-houses again. One day, when Major Pendennis and Arthur went to dine in Grosvenor Place, they found an old acquaintance established in the quality of major-domo, and the gentleman in black, who, with perfect politeness and gravity, offered them their choice of sweet or dry champagne, was no other

than Mr. James Morgan. The Chevalier Strong was one of the party; he was in high spirits and condition, and entertained the company with accounts of his amusements abroad.

'It was my lady who invited me,' said Strong to Arthur, under his voice—'that fellow Morgan looked as black as thunder when I came in. He is about no good here. I will go away first, and wait for you and Major Pendennis at Hyde Park Gate.'

Mr. Morgan helped Major Pendennis to his great-coat when he was quitting the house; and muttered something about having accepted a temporary engagement with the Clavering family.

'I have got a paper of yours, Mr. Morgan,' said the old gentleman.

'Which you can show, if you please, to Sir Francis, sir, and perfectly welcome,' said Mr. Morgan, with downcast eyes. 'I'm very much obliged to you, Major Pendennis, and if I can pay you for all your kindness, I will.'

Arthur overheard the sentence, and saw the look of hatred which accompanied it, suddenly cried out that he had forgotten his handkerchief, and ran upstairs to the drawing-room again. Foker was still there; still lingering about his siren. Pen gave the siren a look full of meaning, and we suppose that the siren understood meaning looks, for when, after finding the veracious handkerchief of which he came in quest, he once more went out, the siren, with a laughing voice, said, 'Oh, Arthur—Mr. Pendennis—I want you to tell dear Laura something!' and she came out to the door.

'What is it?' she asked, shutting the door.

'Have you told Harry? Do you know that villain Morgan knows all?'

'I know it,' she said.

'Have you told Harry?'

'No, no,' she said. 'You won't betray me?'

'Morgan will,' said Pen.

'No, he won't,' said Blanche. 'I have promised him—*n'importe*. Wait until after our marriage—oh, until after our marriage—oh, how wretched I am,' said the girl, who had been all smiles, and grace, and gaiety during the evening.

Arthur said, 'I beg and implore you to tell Harry. Tell

him now. It is no fault of yours. He will pardon you anything. Tell him to-night.'

'And give her this—*il est là*—with my love, please; and I beg your pardon for calling you back; and if she will be at Madame Crinoline's at half-past three, and if Lady Rockminster can spare her, I should *so* like to drive with her in the Park;' and she went in, singing and kissing her little hand, as Morgan the velvet-footed came up the carpeted stair.

Pen heard Blanche's piano breaking out into brilliant music as he went down to join his uncle; and they walked away together. Arthur briefly told him what he had done. 'What was to be done?' he asked.

'What is to be done, begad?' said the old gentleman. 'What is to be done but to leave it alone? Begad, let us be thankful,' said the old fellow, with a shudder, 'that we are out of the business, and leave it to those it concerns.'

'I hope to Heaven she'll tell him,' said Pen.

'Begad, she'll take her own course,' said the old man. 'Miss Amory is a dev'lish wide-awake girl, sir, and must play her own cards; and I'm doosid glad you are out of it—doosid glad, begad. Who's this smoking? Oh, it's Mr. Strong again. He wants to put in *his* oar, I suppose. I tell you, don't meddle in the business, Arthur.'

Strong began once or twice, as if to converse upon the subject, but the major would not hear a word. He remarked on the moonlight on Apsley House, the weather, the cab-stands—anything but that subject. He bowed stiffly to Strong, and clung to his nephew's arm, as he turned down St. James's Street, and again cautioned Pen to leave the affair alone. 'It had like to have cost you so much, sir, that you may take my advice,' he said.

When Arthur came out of the hotel, Strong's cloak and cigar were visible a few doors off. The jolly chevalier laughed as they met. 'I'm an old soldier, too,' he said. 'I wanted to talk to you, Pendennis. I have heard of all that has happened, and all the chops and changes that have taken place during my absence. I congratulate you on your marriage, and I congratulate you on your escape, too,—you understand me. It was not my business to speak, but I know this, that a certain party is as arrant a little—well—well, never mind what. You acted like a man, and a trump, and are well out of it.'

'I have no reason to complain,' said Pen. 'I went back to beg and entreat poor Blanche to tell Foker all : I hope, for her sake, she will ; but I fear not. There is but one policy, Strong, there is but one.'

'And lucky he that can stick to it,' said the chevalier. 'That rascal Morgan means mischief. He has been lurking about our chambers for the last two months : he has found out that poor mad devil Amory's secret. He has been trying to discover where he was : he has been pumping Mr. Bolton, and making old Costigan drunk several times. He bribed the Inn porter to tell him when we came back : and he has got into Clavering's service on the strength of his information. He will get very good pay for it, mark my words, the villain.'

'Where is Amory ?' asked Pen.

'At Boulogne, I believe. I left him there, and warned him not to come back. I have broken with him, after a desperate quarrel, such as one might have expected with such a madman. And I'm glad to think that he is in my debt now, and that I have been the means of keeping him out of more harms than one.'

'He has lost all his winnings, I suppose,' said Pen.

'No : he is rather better than when he went away, or was a fortnight ago. He had extraordinary luck at Baden : broke the bank several nights, and was the fable of the place. He *liéd* himself there, with a fellow by the name of Bloundell, who gathered about him a society of all sorts of sharpers, male and female, Russians, Germans, French, English. Amory got so insolent, that I was obliged to thrash him one day within an inch of his life. I couldn't help myself ; the fellow has plenty of pluck, and I had nothing for it but to hit out.'

'And did he call you out ?' said Pen.

'You think if I had shot him I should have done nobody any harm ? No, sir ; I waited for his challenge, but it never came : and the next time I met him he begged my pardon, and said, "Strong, I beg your pardon ; you whopped me, and you served me right." I shook hands : but I couldn't live with him after that. I paid him what I owed him, the night before,' said Strong, with a blush. 'I pawned everything to pay him, and then I went with my last ten florins, and had a shy at the roulette. If I had lost, I should have let him shoot me in the morning. I

was weary of my life. By Jove, sir, isn't it a shame that a man like me, who may have had a few bills out, but who never deserted a friend, or did an unfair action, shouldn't be able to turn his hand to anything to get bread? I made a good night, sir, at roulette, and I've done with *that.* I'm going into the wine business. My wife's relations live at Cadiz. I intend to bring over Spanish wine and hams; there's a fortune to be made by it, sir,—a fortune—here's my card. If you want any sherry or hams, recollect Ned Strong is your man.' And the chevalier pulled out a handsome card, stating that Strong and Company, Shepherd's Inn, were sole agents of the celebrated Diamond Manzanilla of the Duke of Garbanzos, Grandee of Spain of the First Class; and of the famous Toboso hams, fed on acorns only in the country of Don Quixote. 'Come and taste 'em, sir,—come and try 'em at my chambers. You see, I've an eye to business, and by Jove this time I'll succeed.'

Pen laughed as he took the card. 'I don't know whether I shall be allowed to go to bachelors' parties,' he said. 'You know I'm going to——'

'But you *must* have sherry, sir. You must have sherry.'

'I will have it from you, depend on it,' said the other. 'And I think you are well out of your other partnership. That worthy Altamont and his daughter correspond, I hear,' Pen added after a pause.

'Yes; she wrote him the longest rigmarole letters that I used to read: the sly little devil; and he answered under cover to Mrs. Bonner. He was for carrying her off the first day or two, and nothing would content him but having back his child. But she didn't want to come, as you may fancy; and he was not very eager about it.' Here the chevalier burst out in a laugh. 'Why, sir, do you know what was the cause of our quarrel and boxing-match? There was a certain widow at Baden, a Madame la Baronne de la Cruche-cassée, who was not much better than himself, and whom the scoundrel wanted to marry; and would, but that I told her he was married already. I don't think that she was much better than he was. I saw her on the pier at Boulogne the day I came to England.'

And now we have brought up our narrative to the point whither the announcement in the *Chatteris Champion* had already conducted us.

It wanted but very, very few days before that blissful one when Foker should call Blanche his own; the Clavering folks had all pressed to see the most splendid new carriage in the whole world, which was standing in the coach-house at the 'Clavering Arms'; and shown, in grateful return for drink, commonly, by Mr. Foker's head coachman. Madame Fribsby was occupied in making some lovely dresses for the tenants' daughters, who were to figure as a sort of bridesmaids' chorus at the breakfast and marriage ceremony. And immense festivities were to take place at the Park upon this delightful occasion.

'Yes, Mr. Huxter, yes; a happy tenantry, its country's pride, will assemble in the baronial hall, where the beards will wag all. The ox shall be slain, and the cup they'll drain; and the bells shall peal quite genteel; and my father-in-law, with the tear of sensibility bedewing his eye, shall bless us at his baronial porch. That shall be the order of proceedings, I think, Mr. Huxter; and I hope we shall see you and *your* lovely bride by her husband's side; and what will you please to drink, sir? Mrs. Lightfoot, madam, you will give to my excellent friend and body surgeon, Mr. Huxter, Mr. Samuel Huxter, M.R.C.S., every refreshment that your hostel affords, and place the festive amount to my account; and Mr. Lightfoot, sir, what will *you* take? though you've had enough already, I think; yes, ha.'

So spoke Harry Foker in the bar of the 'Clavering Arms.' He had apartments at that hotel, and had gathered a circle of friends round him there. He treated all to drink who came. He was hail-fellow with every man. He was so happy! He danced round Madame Fribsby, Mrs. Lightfoot's great ally, as she sat pensive in the bar. He consoled Mrs. Lightfoot, who had already begun to have causes of matrimonial disquiet; for the truth must be told, that young Lightfoot, having now the full command of the cellar, had none over his own unbridled desires, and was tippling and tipsy from morning till night. And a piteous sight it was for his fond wife to behold the big youth reeling about the yard and coffee-room, or drinking with the farmers and tradesmen his own neat wines and carefully-selected stock of spirits.

When he could find time, Mr. Morgan the butler came from the Park, and took a glass at the expense of the land-

lord of the 'Clavering Arms.' He watched poor Lightfoot's tipsy vagaries with savage sneers. Mrs. Lightfoot felt always doubly uncomfortable when her unhappy spouse was under his comrade's eye. But a few months married, and to think he had got to this. Madame Fribsby could feel for her. Madame Fribsby could tell her stories of men every bit as bad. She had had her own woes too, and her sad experience of men. So it is that nobody seems happy altogether ; and that there's bitters, as Mr. Foker remarked, in the cup of every man's life. And yet there did not seem to be any in his, the honest young fellow ! It was brimming over with happiness and good-humour.

Mr. Morgan was constant in his attentions to Foker. 'And yet I don't like him somehow,' said the candid young man to Mrs. Lightfoot. 'He always seems as if he was measuring me for my coffin somehow. Pa-in-law's afraid of him ; pa-in-law's, ahem ! never mind, but ma-in-law's a trump, Mrs. Lightfoot.'

'Indeed my lady was ;' and Mrs. Lightfoot owned, with a sigh, that perhaps it had been better for her had she never left her mistress.

'No, I do not like thee, Dr. Fell ; the reason why I cannot tell,' continued Mr. Foker ; 'and he wants to be taken as my head man. Blanche wants me to take him. Why does Miss Amory like him so ?'

'Did Miss Blanche like him so ?' The notion seemed to disturb Mrs. Lightfoot very much ; and there came to this worthy landlady another cause for disturbance. A letter bearing the Boulogne post-mark was brought to her one morning, and she and her husband were quarrelling over it as Foker passed down the stairs by the bar, on his way to the Park. His custom was to breakfast there, and bask awhile in the presence of Armida ;* then, as the company of Clavering tired him exceedingly, and he did not care for sporting, he would return for an hour or two to billiards and the society of the 'Clavering Arms '; then it would be time to ride with Miss Amory, and, after dining with her, he left her and returned modestly to his inn.

Lightfoot and his wife were quarrelling over the letter. What was that letter from abroad ? Why was she always having letters from abroad ? Who wrote 'em ?—he would know. He didn't believe it was her brother. It was no business of his ? It *was* a business of his ; and, with a

curse, he seized hold of his wife, and dashed at her pocket for the letter.

The poor woman gave a scream ; and said, 'Well, take it.' Just as her husband seized on the letter, and Mr. Foker entered at the door, she gave another scream at seeing him, and once more tried to seize the paper. Lightfoot opened it, shaking her away, and an enclosure dropped down on the breakfast table.

'Hands off, man alive !' cried little Harry, springing in. 'Don't lay hands on a woman, sir. The man that lays his hand upon a woman, save in the way of kindness, is a— hallo ! it's a letter for Miss Amory. What's this, Mrs. Lightfoot ?'

Mrs. Lightfoot began, in piteous tones of reproach to her husband,—'You unmanly ! to treat a woman so who took you off the street. O you coward, to lay your hand upon your wife ! Why did I marry you ? Why did I leave my lady for you ? Why did I spend eight hundred pound in fitting up this house that you might drink and guzzle ?'

'She gets letters, and she won't tell me who writes letters,' said Mr. Lightfoot, with a muzzy voice; 'it's a family affair, sir. Will you take anything, sir ?'

'I will take this letter to Miss Amory, as I am going to the Park,' said Foker, turning very pale ; and taking it up from the table, which was arranged for the poor landlady's breakfast, he went away.

'He's comin'—dammy, who's a-comin' ? Who's J. A., Mrs. Lightfoot—curse me, who's J. A. ?' cried the husband.

Mrs. Lightfoot cried out, 'Be quiet, you tipsy brute, do,'—and running to her bonnet and shawl, threw them on, saw Mr. Foker walking down the street, took the by-lane which skirts it, and ran as quickly as she could to the lodge-gate, Clavering Park. Foker saw a running figure before him, but it was lost when he got to the lodge-gate. He stopped and asked, 'Who was that who had just come in ? Mrs. Bonner was it ?' He reeled almost in his walk : the trees swam before him. He rested once or twice against the trunks of the naked limes.

Lady Clavering was in the breakfast-room with her son, and her husband yawning over his paper. 'Good-morning, Harry,' said the Begum. 'Here's letters, lots of letters ;

Lady Rockminster will be here on Tuesday instead of Monday, and Arthur and the major come to-day; and Laura is to go to Dr. Portman's, and come to church from there: and—what's the matter, my dear? What makes you so pale, Harry?'

'Where is Blanche?' asked Harry, in a sickening voice—'not down yet?'

'Blanche is always the last,' said the boy, eating muffins; 'she's a regular dawdle, she is. When you're not here, she lays in bed till lunch-time.'

'Be quiet, Frank,' said the mother.

Blanche came down presently, looking pale, and with rather an eager look towards Foker; then she advanced and kissed her mother, and had a face beaming with her very best smiles on when she greeted Harry.

'How do you do, sir?' she said, and put out both her hands.

'I'm ill,' answered Harry. 'I—I've brought a letter for you, Blanche.'

'A letter, and from whom is it, pray? *Voyons*,' she said.

'I don't know—I should like to know,' said Foker.

'How can I tell until I see it?' asked Blanche.

'Has Mrs. Bonner not told you?' he said, with a shaking voice; 'there's some secret. *You* give her the letter, Lady Clavering.'

Lady Clavering, wondering, took the letter from poor Foker's shaking hand, and looked at the superscription. As she looked at it, she too began to shake in every limb, and with a scared face she dropped the letter, and running up to Frank, clutched the boy to her, and burst out with a sob—'Take that away—it's impossible, it's impossible.'

'What is the matter?' cried Blanche, with rather a ghastly smile; 'the letter is only from—from a poor pensioner and relative of ours.'

'It's not true, it's not true,' screamed Lady Clavering. 'No, my Frank—is it, Clavering?'

Blanche had taken up the letter, and was moving with it towards the fire, but Foker ran to her and clutched her arm—'I must see that letter,' he said; 'give it me. You shan't burn it.'

'You—you shall not treat Miss Amory so in my house,' cried the baronet; 'give back the letter, by Jove!'

'Read it—and look at her,' Blanche cried, pointing to her

mother; 'it—it was for her I kept the secret! Read it, cruel man!'

And Foker opened, and read the letter:—

I have not wrote, my darling Bessy, this three weeks: but this is to give her a *father's blessing*, and I shall come down pretty soon as quick as my note, and intend to see *the ceremony, and my son-in-law*. I shall put up at Bonner's. I have had a pleasant autumn, and am staying here at an hotel where there *is good company*, and which is kep' *in good style*. I don't know whether I quite approve of your throwing over Mr. P. for Mr. F., and don't think Foker's *such a pretty name*, and from your account of him he seems a *muff*, and *not a beauty*. But he has got *the rowdy*, which is the thing. So no more, my dear little Betsy, till we meet, from your affectionate father,—J. Amory Altamont.

'Read it, Lady Clavering; it is too late to keep it from you now,' said poor Foker; and the distracted woman, having cast her eyes over it, again broke out into hysterical screams, and convulsively grasped her son.

'They have made an outcast of you, my boy,' she said. 'They've dishonoured your old mother; but I'm innocent, Frank; before God, I'm innocent. I didn't know this, Mr. Foker; indeed, indeed, I didn't.'

'I'm sure you didn't,' said Foker, going up and kissing her hand.

'Generous, generous Harry,' cried out Blanche, in an ecstasy. But he withdrew his hand, which was upon *her* side, and turned from her with a quivering lip. 'That's different,' he says.

'It was for her sake—for her sake, Harry.' Again Miss Amory is in an attitude.

'There was something to be done for mine,' said Foker. 'I would have taken you, whatever you were. Everything's talked about in London. I knew that your father had come to—to grief. You don't think it was—it was for your connection I married you? D— it all! I've loved you with all my heart and soul for two years, and you've been playing with me, and cheating me,' broke out the young man with a cry. 'Oh, Blanche, Blanche, it's a hard thing, a hard thing!' and he covered his face with his hands, and sobbed behind them.

Blanche thought, 'Why didn't I tell him that night when Arthur warned me?'

'Don't refuse her, Harry,' cried out Lady Clavering.

'Take her, take everything I have. It's all hers, you know, at my death. This boy's disinherited.' (Master Frank, who had been looking as scared at the strange scene, here burst into a loud cry.) '—Take every shilling. Give me just enough to live, and to go and hide my head with this child, and to fly from both. Oh, they've both been bad, bad men. Perhaps he's here now. Don't let me see him. Clavering, you coward, defend me from him.'

Clavering started up at this proposal. 'You ain't serious, Jemima? You don't mean that?' he said. 'You won't throw me and Frank over? I didn't know it, so help me ——. Foker, I'd no more idea of it than the dead—until the fellow came and found me out, the d—d escaped convict scoundrel.'

'The what?' said Foker. Blanche gave a scream.

'Yes,' screamed out the baronet in his turn, 'yes, a d—d runaway convict—a fellow that forged his father-in-law's name—a d—d attorney, and killed a fellow in Botany Bay, hang him—and ran into the Bush, curse him; I wish he'd died there. And he came to me, a good six years ago, and robbed me; and I've been ruining myself to keep him, the infernal scoundrel! And Pendennis knows it, and Strong knows it, and that d—d Morgan knows it, and she knows it, ever so long; and I never would tell it, never: and I kept it from my wife.'

'And you saw him, and you didn't kill him, Clavering, you coward?' said the wife of Amory. 'Come away, Frank; your father's a coward. I am dishonoured, but I'm your old mother, and you'll—you'll love me, won't you?'

Blanche, *éplorée*, went up to her mother; but Lady Clavering shrank from her with a sort of terror. 'Don't touch me,' she said; 'you've no heart; you never had. I see all now. I see why that coward was going to give up his place in Parliament to Arthur; yes, that coward! and why you threatened that you would make me give you half Frank's fortune. And when Arthur offered to marry you without a shilling, because he wouldn't rob my boy, you left him, and you took poor Harry. Have nothing to do with her, Harry. You're good, you are. Don't marry that—that convict's daughter. Come away, Frank, my darling; come to your poor old mother. We'll hide ourselves; but we're honest, yes, we are honest.'

All this while a strange feeling of exultation had taken possession of Blanche's mind. That month with poor Harry had been a weary month to her. All his fortune and splendour scarcely sufficed to make the idea of himself supportable. She was wearied of his simple ways, and sick of coaxing and cajoling him.

'Stay, mamma; stay, madam!' she cried out, with a gesture, which was always appropriate, though rather theatrical; 'I have no heart, have I? I keep the secret of my mother's shame. I give up my rights to my half-brother and my bastard brother—yes, my rights and my fortune. I don't betray my father, and for this I have no heart. I'll have my rights now, and the laws of my country shall give them to me. I appeal to my country's laws—yes, my country's laws! The persecuted one returns this day. I desire to go to my father.' And the little lady swept round her hand, and thought that she was a heroine.

'You will, will you?' cried out Clavering, with one of his usual oaths. 'I'm a magistrate, and dammy, I'll commit him. Here's a chaise coming; perhaps it's him. Let him come.'

A chaise was indeed coming up the avenue; and the two women shrieked each their loudest, expecting at that moment to see Altamont arrive.

The door opened, and Mr. Morgan announced Major Pendennis and Mr. Pendennis, who entered, and found all parties engaged in this fierce quarrel. A large screen fenced the breakfast-room from the hall; and it is probable that, according to his custom, Mr. Morgan had taken advantage of the screen to make himself acquainted with all that occurred.

It had been arranged on the previous day that the young people should ride; and at the appointed hour in the afternoon, Mr. Foker's horses arrived from the 'Clavering Arms.' But Miss Blanche did not accompany him on this occasion. Pen came out and shook hands with him on the doorsteps; and Harry Foker rode away, followed by his groom in mourning. The whole transactions which have occupied the most active part of our history were debated by the parties concerned during those two or three hours. Many counsels had been given, stories told, and compromises suggested; and at the end, Harry Foker rode away, with a sad 'God bless you!' from Pen. There was a dreary

dinner at Clavering Park, at which the lately installed butler did not attend; and the ladies were both absent. After dinner, Pen said, 'I will walk down to Clavering and see if he is come.' And he walked through the dark avenue, across the bridge and road by his own cottage,—the once quiet and familiar fields of which were flaming with the kilns and forges of the artificers employed on the new railroad works; and so he entered the town, and made for the 'Clavering Arms.'

It was past midnight when he returned to Clavering Park. He was exceedingly pale and agitated. 'Is Lady Clavering up yet?' he asked. Yes, she was in her own sitting-room. He went up to her, and there found the poor lady in a piteous state of tears and agitation.

'It is I,—Arthur,' he said, looking in; and entering, he took her hand very affectionately and kissed it. 'You were always the kindest of friends to me, dear Lady Clavering,' he said. 'I love you very much. I have got some news for you.'

'Don't call me by that name,' she said, pressing his hand. 'You were always a good boy, Arthur; and it's kind of you to come now,—very kind. You sometimes look very like your ma, my dear.'

'Dear, good *Lady Clavering*,' Arthur repeated, with particular emphasis, 'something very strange has happened.'

'Has anything happened to him?' gasped Lady Clavering. 'Oh, it's horrid to think I should be glad of it—horrid!'

'He is well. He has been and is gone, my dear lady. Don't alarm yourself,—he is gone, and you are Lady Clavering still.'

'Is it true what he sometimes said to me?' she screamed out,—'that he——'

'He was married before he married you,' said Pen. 'He has confessed it to-night. He will never come back.' There came another shriek from Lady Clavering, as she flung her arms round Pen, and kissed him, and burst into tears on his shoulder.

What Pen had to tell, through a multiplicity of sobs and interruptions, must be compressed briefly, for behold our prescribed limit is reached, and our tale is coming to its end. With the Branch Coach from the railroad, which had

succeeded the old 'Alacrity' and 'Perseverance,' Amory arrived, and was set down at the 'Clavering Arms.' He ordered his dinner at the place under his assumed name of Altamont; and, being of a jovial turn, he welcomed the landlord, who was nothing loath, to a share of his wine. Having extracted from Mr. Lightfoot all the news regarding the family at the Park, and found, from examining his host, that Mrs. Lightfoot, as she said, had kept his counsel, he called for more wine of Mr. Lightfoot, and at the end of this symposium, both, being greatly excited, went into Mrs. Lightfoot's bar.

She was there taking tea with her friend, Madame Fribsby; and Lightfoot was by this time in such a happy state as not to be surprised at anything which might occur, so that, when Altamont shook hands with Mrs. Lightfoot as an old acquaintance, the recognition did not appear to him to be in the least strange, but only a reasonable cause for further drinking. The gentlemen partook then of brandy-and-water, which they offered to the ladies, not heeding the terrified looks of one or the other.

Whilst they were so engaged, at about six o'clock in the evening, Mr. Morgan, Sir Francis Clavering's new man, came in, and was requested to drink. He selected his favourite beverage, and the parties engaged in general conversation.

After awhile Mr. Lightfoot began to doze. Mr. Morgan had repeatedly given hints to Mrs. Fribsby to quit the premises; but that lady, strangely fascinated, and terrified it would seem, or persuaded by Mrs. Lightfoot not to go, kept her place. Her persistence occasioned much annoyance to Mr. Morgan, who vented his displeasure in such language as gave pain to Mrs. Lightfoot, and caused Mr. Altamont to say that he was a rum customer, and not polite to the sex.

The altercation between the two gentlemen became very painful to the women, especially to Mrs. Lightfoot, who did everything to soothe Mr. Morgan: and, under pretence of giving a pipe-light to the stranger, she handed him a paper on which she had privily written the words, 'He knows you. Go.' There may have been something suspicious in her manner of handing, or in her guest's of reading, the paper: for when he got up a short time afterwards, and said he would go to bed, Morgan rose too, with a laugh, and said it was too early to go to bed.

A DISCOVERY

The stranger then said he would go to his bedroom. Morgan said he would show him the way.

At this the guest said, 'Come up. I've got a brace of pistols up there to blow out the brains of any traitor or skulking spy,' and glared so fiercely upon Morgan, that the latter, seizing hold of Lightfoot by the collar, and waking him, said, 'John Amory, I arrest you in the Queen's name. Stand by me, Lightfoot. This capture is worth a thousand pounds.'

He put forward his hand as if to seize his prisoner, but the other, doubling his fist, gave Morgan with his left hand so fierce a blow on the chest, that it knocked him back behind Mr. Lightfoot. That gentleman, who was athletic and courageous, said he would knock his guest's head off, and prepared to do so, as the stranger, tearing off his coat, and cursing both of his opponents, roared to them to come on.

But with a piercing scream Mrs. Lightfoot flung herself before her husband, whilst with another and louder shriek Madame Fribsby ran to the stranger, and calling out 'Armstrong, Johnny Armstrong!' seized hold of his naked arm, on which a blue tattooing of a heart and M. F. were visible.

The ejaculation of Madame Fribsby seemed to astound and sober the stranger. He looked down upon her, and cried out, 'It's Polly, by Jove.'

Mrs. Fribsby continued to exclaim, 'This is not Amory. This is Johnny Armstrong, my wicked—wicked husband, married to me in St. Martin's Church, mate on board an Indiaman, and he left me two months after, the wicked wretch. This is John Armstrong—here's the mark on his arm which he made for me.'

The stranger said, 'I am John Armstrong, sure enough, Polly. I'm John Armstrong, Amory, Altamont,—and let 'em all come on, and try what they can do against a British sailor. Hurray, who's for it!'

Morgan still called out, 'Arrest him!' But Mrs. Lightfoot said, 'Arrest him! arrest you, you mean spy! What! stop the marriage and ruin my lady, and take away the "Clavering Arms" from us?'

'*Did* he say he'd take away the "Clavering Arms" from us?' asked Mr. Lightfoot, turning round. 'Hang him, I'll throttle him.'

'Keep him, darling, till the coach passes to the up-train. It'll be here now directly.'

'D— him, I'll choke him if he stirs,' said Lightfoot. And so they kept Morgan until the coach came, and Mr. Amory or Armstrong went away back to London.

Morgan had followed him : but of this event Arthur Pendennis did not inform Lady Clavering, and left her invoking blessings upon him at her son's door, going to kiss him as he was asleep. It had been a busy day.

We have to chronicle the events of but one day more, and that was a day when Mr. Arthur, attired in a new hat, a new blue frock-coat and blue handkerchief, in a new fancy waistcoat, new boots, and new shirt-studs (presented by the Right Honourable the Countess Dowager of Rockminster), made his appearance at a solitary breakfast-table, in Clavering Park, where he could scarce eat a single morsel of food. Two letters were laid by his worship's plate ; and he chose to open the first, which was in a round clerk-like hand, in preference to the second more familiar superscription.

Note 1 ran as follows :—

GARBANZOS WINE COMPANY, SHEPHERD'S INN.—Monday.

MY DEAR PENDENNIS,—In congratulating you heartily upon the event which is to make you happy for life, I send my very kindest remembrances to Mrs. Pendennis, whom I hope to know even longer than I have already known her. And when I call her attention to the fact, that one of the most necessary articles to her husband's comfort is *pure sherry*, I know I shall have her for a customer for your worship's sake.

But I have to speak to you of other than my own concerns. Yesterday afternoon, a certain J. A. arrived at my chambers from Clavering, which he had left under circumstances of which you are doubtless now aware. In spite of our difference I could not but give him food and shelter (and he partook freely both of the Garbanzos Amontillado and the Toboso ham), and he told me what had happened to him, and many other surprising adventures. The rascal married at sixteen, and has repeatedly since performed that ceremony—in Sydney, in New Zealand, in South America, in Newcastle, he says, first, before he knew our poor friend the milliner. He is a perfect Don Juan.

And it seemed as if the commendatore* had at last overtaken him, for, as we were at our meal, there came three heavy knocks at my outer door, which made our friend start. I have sustained a siege or two here, and went to my usual place to reconnoitre. Thank my

AN ESCAPE

stars I have not a bill out in the world, and besides, *those* gentry do not come in that way. I found that it was your uncle's late valet, Morgan, and a policeman (I think a sham policeman), and they said they had a warrant to take the person of John Armstrong, alias Amory, alias Altamont, a runaway convict, and threatened to break in the oak.

Now, sir, in my own days of captivity I had discovered a little passage along the gutter into Bows and Costigan's window, and I sent Jack Alias along this covered way, not without terror of his life, for it had grown very cranky; and then, after a parley, let in Mons. Morgan and friend.

The rascal had been instructed about that covered way, for he made for the room instantly, telling the policeman to go downstairs and keep the gate; and he charged up my little staircase as if he had known the premises. As he was going out of the window we heard a voice that you know, from Bows's garret, saying, 'Who are ye, and hwhat the divvle are ye at? You'd betther leave the gutther; bedad there's a man killed himself already.'

And as Morgan, crossing over and looking into the darkness, was trying to see whether this awful news was true, he took a broomstick and with a vigorous dash broke down the pipe of communication—and told me this morning, with great glee, that he was reminded of that 'aisy sthratagem by remembering his dorling Emilie, when she acted the pawrt of Cora in the Plee—and by the bridge in Pezawro,* bedad. I wish that scoundrel Morgan had been on the bridge when the General tried his 'sthratagem.'

If I hear more of Jack Alias I will tell you. He has got plenty of money still, and I wanted him to send some to our poor friend the milliner; but the scoundrel laughed and said, he had no more than he wanted, but offered to give anybody a lock of his hair. Farewell—be happy! and believe me always truly yours,—E. STRONG.

'And now for the other letter,' said Pen. 'Dear old fellow!' and he kissed the seal before he broke it.

WARRINGTON, Tuesday.

I must not let the day pass over without saying a 'God bless you,' to both of you. May Heaven make you happy, dear Arthur, and dear Laura. I think, Pen, that you have got the best wife in the world; and pray that, as such, you will cherish her and tend her. The chambers will be lonely without you, dear Pen; but if I am tired, I shall have a new home to go to in the house of my brother and sister. I am practising in the nursery here, in order to prepare for the part of Uncle George. Farewell! make your wedding tour, and come back to your affectionate—G. W.

Pendennis and his wife read this letter together after Dr. Portman's breakfast was over, and the guests were gone: and when the carriage was waiting amidst the crowd at

the doctor's outer gate. But the wicket led into the churchyard of St. Mary's, where the bells were pealing with all their might, and it was here, over Helen's green grass, that Arthur showed his wife George's letter. For which of those two—for grief was it or for happiness, that Laura's tears abundantly fell on the paper? And once more, in the presence of the sacred dust, she kissed and blessed her Arthur.

There was only one marriage on that day at Clavering Church: for in spite of Blanche's sacrifices for her dearest mother, honest Harry Foker could not pardon the woman who had deceived her husband, and justly argued that she would deceive him again. He went to the Pyramids and Syria, and there left his malady behind him, and returned with a fine beard, and a supply of tarbooshes and narghiles, with which he regales all his friends. He lives splendidly, and, through Pen's mediation, gets his wine from the celebrated vintages of the Duke of Garbanzos.

As for poor Cos, his fate has been mentioned in an early part of this story. No very glorious end could be expected to such a career. Morgan is one of the most respectable men in the parish of St. James's, and in the present political movement has pronounced himself like a man and a Briton. And Bows,—on the demise of Mr. Piper, who played the organ at Clavering, little Mrs. Sam Huxter, who has the entire command of Dr. Portman, brought Bows down from London to contest the organ-loft, and her candidate carried the chair. When Sir Francis Clavering quitted this worthless life, the same little indefatigable canvasser took the borough by storm, and it is now represented by Arthur Pendennis, Esq. Blanche Amory, it is well known, married at Paris, and the saloons of Madame la Comtesse de Montmorenci de Valentinois were amongst the most *suivis* of that capital. The duel between the count and the young and fiery Representative of the Mountain, Alcide de Mirobo,* arose solely from the latter questioning at the Club the titles borne by the former nobleman. Madame de Montmorenci de Valentinois travelled after the adventure: and Bungay bought her poems, and published them, with the countess's coronet emblazoned on the countess's work.

Major Pendennis became very serious in his last days, and was never so happy as when Laura was reading to him

with her sweet voice, or listening to his stories. For this sweet lady is the friend of the young and the old : and her life is always passed in making other lives happy.

'And what sort of a husband would this Pendennis be ?' many a reader will ask, doubting the happiness of such a marriage and the fortune of Laura. The querists, if they meet her, are referred to that lady herself, who, seeing his faults and wayward moods—seeing and owning that there are men better than he—loves him always with the most constant affection. His children or their mother have never heard a harsh word from him ; and when his fits of moodiness and solitude are over, welcome him back with a never-failing regard and confidence. His friend is his friend still,—entirely heart-whole. That malady is never fatal to a sound organ. And George goes through his part of godpapa perfectly, and lives alone. If Mr. Pen's works have procured him more reputation than has been acquired by his abler friend, whom no one knows, George lives contented without the fame. If the best men do not draw the great prizes in life, we know it has been so settled by the Ordainer of the lottery. We own, and see daily, how the false and worthless live and prosper, while the good are called away, and the dear and young perish untimely,—we perceive in every man's life the maimed happiness, the frequent falling, the bootless endeavour, the struggle of Right and Wrong, in which the strong often succumb and the swift fail : we see flowers of good blooming in foul places, as, in the most lofty and splendid fortunes, flaws of vice and meanness, and stains of evil ; and, knowing how mean the best of us is, let us give a hand of charity to Arthur Pendennis, with all his faults and shortcomings, who does not claim to be a hero, but only a man and a brother.*

APPENDIX

The text of *Pendennis* in this book is that of the 1864 edition, the last revised by Thackeray himself. The illustrations are from the first edition, published in 1849-50; they were omitted from the later issue. In this Appendix all the more important differences between the 1850 and 1864 texts are noted, the portions suppressed in the latter edition being subjoined.

Chapter I

1. p. 1. *The first edition inserts* As he was one of the finest judges of wine in England, and a man of active, dominating, and inquiring spirit, he had been very properly chosen to be a member of the Committee of this Club, and indeed was almost the manager of the institution; and the stewards and waiters bowed before him as reverentially as to a Duke or a Field-Marshal.

2. p. 2. *After* in former days *the first edition reads* and in freak or bravado, endeavoured twice or thrice to deprive, etc.

3. p. 2. *Insert* He carried it so gaily, you would hardly have known it was spectacles in disguise.

4. p. 2. *Insert* and speak French, which language the major possessed very perfectly;

5. p. 3. *Insert* with a strong dash of anxiety under the word,

6. p. 5. *Insert* It was Miss C.'s own delicacy which suggested that the difference of age, which I never felt, might operate as a bar to our union. But having loved,

7. p. 6. *Insert at beginning of next paragraph* And he must not only give up this but all other engagements for some time to come. Who knows how long the business might detain him?

Chapter II

1. p. 6. *Insert* For these facts a few folks at Clavering could vouch, where people's memories were more tenacious, perhaps, than they are in a great bustling metropolis.

2. p. 7. *Insert* and its gilt ornaments

3. p. 7. *Insert* as unworthy of a gentleman of an ancient lineage.

4. p. 8. *For* a shelter *read* a comfortable shelter as far as boarding and lodging went, but suffered under such an infernal tyranny as only women can inflict on, or bear from, one another;

5. p. 10. *Insert* who got up stories, as he sent in draughts, for his patient's amusement and his own profit:

6. p. 11. *Insert* Words cannot describe, nor did he himself ever care to confess to anyone, his pride when he found himself a real landed proprietor, and could walk over acres of which he was the master.

7. p. 12. *Insert* You could see by his wife's looks that she disbelieved in these genealogical legends, for she generally endeavoured to turn the conversation when he commenced them. But

8. p. 14. *Insert* was in the constant habit of dining with lords and great folks. He

9. p. 17. *For* declined *read* refused this negotiation, advantageous as it might seem to most persons.

10. p. 17. *Insert* was a great favourite with almost all the little establishment of Fairoaks. He was as good-natured as he was well-bred, and

11. p. 17. *Insert* and an honour to the family

12. p. 19. *Insert* He did, in fact, just as much as was required of him, and no more. If he was distinguished for anything, it was for verse-writing : but was his enthusiasm ever so great, it stopped when he had composed the number of lines demanded by the regulations (unlike young Swettenham, for instance, who, with no more of poetry in his composition than Mr. Wakley,* yet would bring up a hundred dreary hexameters to the master after a half-holiday ; or young Fluxmore, who not only did his own verses, but all the fifth form's besides).

13. p. 20. *Insert* and while his mother fancied him an angel of candour

14. p. 21. *After* which *read* when he was called upon to construe in school set the master

15. p. 25. *Insert as a new paragraph*—

So it was with this, in a word, that Mrs. Pendennis comforted herself on the death of her husband, whom, however, she always reverenced as the best, the most upright, wise, high-minded, accomplished, and awful of men. If the women did not make idols of us, and if they saw us as we see each other, would life be bearable, or could society go on ? Let a man pray that none of his womankind should form a just estimation of him. If your wife knew you as you are, neighbour, she would not grieve much about being your widow, and would let your grave-lamp go out very soon, or perhaps not even take the trouble to light it. Whereas Helen Pendennis put up the handsomest of memorials to her husband, and constantly renewed it with the most precious oil.

Chapter III

1. p. 27. *Insert* (when those facial ornaments for which he sighed so ardently were awarded to him by nature)

2. p. 28. *Insert* wear such epaulettes and

3. p. 28. *Insert* and his ardour for military glory

4. p. 29. *Insert at beginning of next paragraph* In order to keep Mr. Pen from indulging in that idleness of which his friend the doctor of the Cistercians had prophesied such awful consequences,

5. p. 30. *For* Smirke and his pupil *read* Smirke confided to his pupil his poems both Latin and English; and presented to Mrs. Pendennis a volume of the latter, printed at Clapham, his native place. The two

6. p. 30. *Insert* Our people are the most prosaic in the world, but the most faithful; and with curious reverence we keep up and transmit, from generation to generation, the superstition of what we call the education of a gentleman.

7. p. 32. *Insert* and this young fellow's heart was so ardent, and his imagination so eager, that it is not to be expected he should long escape the passion to which we allude,

8. p. 35. *Insert* from Gloucester Place, where they passed the season, and looked down upon Pen as a chit.

9. p. 35. *Insert* You are faultless; but it does not follow that everybody in your family is to think exactly like yourself.

10. p. 38. *Insert* 'it's recommended to me by the faculty as a what-do-you-call-'em—a stomatic, old boy.

11. p. 39. *Insert* , to whom he paid compliments similar to those before addressed to the bar at the 'George.'

12. p. 39. *Insert* and who are uncommonly pretty at Chatteris.

Chapter IV

1. p. 43. *Insert* Mr. Foker attacked the turtle and venison with as much gusto as he had shown the year before, when he used to make feasts off ginger-beer and smuggled polonies.

2. p. 44. *Insert* Anybody who has ever seen one of our great light comedians, X., in a chintz dressing-gown, such as nobody ever wore, and representing himself to the public as a young nobleman in his apartments, and whiling away the time with light literature until his friend Sir Harry shall arrive, or his father shall come down to breakfast—anybody, I say, who has seen the great X* over a sham book has indeed had a great pleasure and an abiding matter for thought.

3. p. 45. *Insert* When he was about to do a good action, and sent off Francis with his book, so that that domestic should not witness the deed of benevolence which he meditated, Bingley marked the page carefully, so that he might continue the perusal of the volume off the stage if he liked. But all was done in the direct face of Pendennis, whom the manager was bent upon subjugating.

4. p. 46. *Insert* (that beauties of late days have tried to imitate with the help of the crimping-irons)

5. p. 47. *Insert* In fact, if a man were to say it was a stupid play, he would not be far wrong.

Chapter V

1. p. 54. *For* Pen galloped, etc., *read* Without slackening her pace Rebecca the mare galloped on to Baymouth, where Pen put her up

2. p. 58. *Insert* The captain was perfumed with the recollections of the last night's cigars, and pulled and twisted the tuft on his chin as jauntily as any young dandy.

3. p. 60. *Insert* And he straightway poured out to Pen a series of stories regarding the claret drunk, the bets made, the races ridden by the garrison there, with which he kept the young gentleman amused until the arrival of their host and his breakfast.

4. p. 61. *Insert* ,—in not one word of which speech did the captain accurately believe.

5. p. 62. *Insert* down which you went into the passage of the house

6. p. 62. *For* As Pen *read* Pen tumbled down the step, and as he

7. p. 62. *Insert* , like ladies of honour round a throne, and she looked like an empress.

8. p. 64. *For* gave her lessons *read* who saw her capabilities, and is an uncommon 'cute man, gave her lessons in the dramatic art.

9. p. 65. *For* Pen tried to engage her *read* During dinner, when the captain, whom his daughter treated most respectfully, ceased prattling about himself and his adventures, Pen tried to engage the Fotheringay

10. p. 67. *Insert* She has married, and taken her position in the world as the most spotless and irreproachable lady since, and I have had the pleasure of making her acquaintance: and must certainly own, against my friend Pen's opinion, that his adored Emily is not a clever woman. The truth is, she had not only never heard of Kotzebue, but she had never heard of Farquhar, or Congreve, or any dramatist in whose plays she had not a part: and of these dramas she only knew that part which concerned herself. A wag once told her that Dante was born at Algiers: and asked her,—which Dr. Johnson wrote first, *Irene*, or *Every Man in his Humour*. But she had the best of the joke, for she had never heard of *Irene* or *Every Man in his Humour*, or Dante, or perhaps Algiers. It was all one to her. She acted what little Bows told her—where he told her to sob, she sobbed—where he told her to laugh, she laughed. She gave the tirade or the repartee without the slightest notion of its meaning. She went to church and goes every Sunday, with a reputation perfectly intact, and was (and is) as guiltless of sense as of any other crime.

Chapter VI

1. p. 69. *For* For some time after this *read* Cicero and Euripides did not occupy Mr. Pen much for some time after this, and

2. p. 69. *Insert* It is good sport (if you are not yourself engaged in the conversation) to hear two men in love talk.

3. p. 71. *Insert* (a difficult matter, for the young fellow blurted out no small quantity of nonsense)

4. p. 71. *Insert* —and delighted perhaps and wondering at his own eloquence, the lad would go on for twenty minutes at a time—

5. p. 72. *Insert* Pen would have been very much pleased if he had heard that phrase—he was galloping home wild with pleasure, and shouting out her name as he rode.

6. p. 78. *After* rhapsody *read* through which, as we have perfect command over our own feelings, we have no reason to follow the lad.

Of course, love, truth, and eternity were produced: and words were tried but found impossible to plumb the tremendous depth of his affection. This speech, we say, is no business of ours. It was most likely not very wise, but what right have we to overhear?

CHAPTER VII

1. p. 84. *For* Night and morning passed and *read* and were merry too. Next the widow, and by the side of the major's servant on the roof, were a couple of schoolboys going home for the midsummer holidays, and Major Pendennis wondered to see them sup at the inn at Bagshot, where they took in a cargo of ham, eggs, pie, pickles, tea, coffee, and boiled beef, which surprised the poor major, sipping a cup of very feeble tea, and thinking with a tender dejection that Lord Steyne's dinner was coming off at that very moment. The ingenuous ardour of the boys, however, amused the major, who was very good-natured, and he became the more interested when he found that the one who travelled inside with him was a lord's son, whose noble father Pendennis, of course, had met in the world of fashion which he frequented. The little lord slept all night through, in spite of the squeezing, and the horn-blowing, and the widow; and he looked as fresh as paint (and, indeed, pronounced himself to be so) when

2. p. 86. *Insert as a new paragraph—*

For as in the old allegory of the gold and silver shield, about which the two knights quarrelled, each is right according to the point from which he looks: so about marriage; the question whether it is foolish or good, wise or otherwise, depends upon the point of view from which you regard it. If it means a snug house in Belgravia, and pretty little dinner-parties, and a pretty little brougham to drive in the Park, and a decent provision not only for the young people, but for the little Belgravians to come; and if these are the necessaries of life (and they are with many honest people), to talk of any other arrangement is an absurdity: of love in lodgings—a babyish folly of affection: that can't pay coach-hire or afford a decent milliner—as mere wicked balderdash and childish romance. If on the other hand your opinion is that people, not with an assured subsistence, but with a fair chance to obtain it, and with the stimulus of hope, health, and strong affection, may take the chance of Fortune for better or worse, and share its good or its evil together, the polite theory then becomes an absurdity in its turn: worse than an absurdity, a blasphemy almost, and doubt of Providence; and a man who waits to make his chosen woman happy, until he can drive her to church in a neat little carriage with a pair of horses, is no better than a coward or a trifler, who is neither worthy of love nor of fortune.

I don't say that the town folks are not right, but

3. p. 86. *Insert* Like most soft and sentimental women, matchmaking, in general, formed a great part of her thoughts, and I dare

say she had begun to speculate about her son's falling in love and marrying long before the subject had ever entered into the brains of the young gentleman.

CHAPTER IX

1. p. 107. *For* All persons who have the blessed *read* Let those who have a real and heartfelt relish for London society and the, *and omit* must *before* admit.

2. p. 108. *Insert* with unfailing eloquence.

3. p. 110. *Insert* took his uncle's counsels to heart. He

4. p. 111. *Add* and he thought of a character in Pope to whom he had often involuntarily compared her.

5. p. 112. *Add* Morgan heard at the 'George' of Pen's acquaintance with Mr. Foker, and he went over to Baymouth to enter into relations with that gentleman's man; but the young student was gone to a coast regatta, and his servant, of course, travelled in charge of the dressing-case.

6. p. 113. *Insert* and threatened her with the terrors of the Church one day after afternoon service.

7. p. 113. *Add* which maintained his ardour as it excited his anger.

CHAPTER X

1. p. 115. *Before* Major Pendennis *insert* Sauntering slowly homewards,

2. p. 115. *Insert* He was rubbing his eyes, and sat before a table decorated with empty decanters and relics of dessert.

3. p. 117. *Insert* for he was in that state of absence, candour, and fearlessness which a man sometimes possesses after drinking a couple of bottles of wine

4. 117. *For* 'We went to the play one night' *read* 'He went to the play one night—for you see I'm down here readin' for my Little-go during the Long,* only I come over from Baymouth pretty often in my drag—well, sir, we went to the play,

5. p. 118. *Insert* though in truth he did not quite understand what Mr. Foker's meaning was

6. p. 119. *Before* Miss *insert* Perhaps I oughtn't to have said as much as I have.

7. p. 119. *Before* you *insert* and I can't tell you how delighted I am to have had the good fortune of making your acquaintance

CHAPTER XI

1. p. 125. *Insert* and whether he had no other knowledge of the captain than what he had thus gained, or whether he actually remembered him, we cannot say. But Major Pendennis was a person of honour and undoubted veracity,

2. p. 131. *Insert* as he recognized a shaft out of his own bow. It was he who had set Pen upon the idea of sitting in Parliament for the neighbouring borough—and the poor lad had evidently been bragging on the subject to Costigan and the lady of his affections.

3. p. 132. *Before* Have *insert* Have you yourself been working

upon the feelings of the young man's susceptible nature to injuice him to break off an engagement, and with it me adored Emily's heart ?

Chapter XII

1. p. 134. *After* in fine *read*: although Mr. Garbetts seldom called at Costigan's house, being disliked by Miss Fotheringay, of whom in her turn Mrs. Garbetts was considerably jealous. The truth is, that Garbetts had paid his court to Miss Fotheringay and been refused by her, before he offered his hand to Mrs. G. Their history, however, forms no part of our present scheme—suffice it, Mr. Garbetts was called in

Chapter XIII

1. p. 143. *Insert, to commence the chapter—*

Meanwhile they were wondering at Fairoaks that the major had not returned. Dr. Portman and his lady, on their way home to Clavering, stopped at Helen's lodge-gate, with a brief note for her from Major Pendennis, in which he said he should remain at Chatteris another day, being anxious to have some talk with Messrs. Tatham, the lawyers, whom he would meet that afternoon ; but no mention was made of the transaction in which the writer had been engaged during the morning. Indeed the note was written at the pause after the first part of the engagement, and when the major had decidedly had the worst of the battle.

Pen did not care somehow to go into the town whilst his uncle was there. He did not like to have to fancy that his guardian might be spying at him from that abominable Dean's grass-plat, whilst he was making love in Miss Costigan's drawing-room ; and the pleasures of a walk (a delight which he was very rarely permitted to enjoy) would have been spoiled if he had met the man of the polished boots on that occasion. His modest love could not show in public by any outward signs, except the eyes (with which the poor fellow ogled and gazed violently, to be sure), but it was dumb in the presence of third parties ; and so much the better, for of all the talk which takes place in this world, that of love-makers is surely, to the uninitiated, the most silly. It is the vocabulary without the key ; it is the lamp without the flame. Let the respected reader look or think over some old love-letters that he (or she) has had and forgotten, and try them over again. How blank and meaningless they seem ! What glamour of infatuation was it which made that nonsense beautiful ? One wonders that such puling and trash could ever have made one happy. And yet there were days when you kissed those silly letters with rapture—lived upon six absurd lines for a week, and until the reactionary period came, when you were restless and miserable until you got a fresh supply of folly.

That is why we decline to publish any of the letters and verses which Mr. Pen wrote at this period of his life, out of mere regard for the young fellow's character. They are too spoony and wild. Young ladies ought not to be called upon to read them in cold blood.

Bide your time, young women; perhaps you will get and write them on your own account soon. Meanwhile we will respect Mr. Pen's first outpourings, and keep them tied up in the newspapers with Miss Fotheringay's string, and sealed with Captain Costigan's great silver seal.

2. p. 143. *Insert* whither he contented himself with dispatching the note we have before mentioned.

3. p. 145. *Insert* —Mr. Tatham, who never entered the walls of a theatre, had heard nothing

Chapter XV

1. p. 166. *Add* After this period it was remarked that he was fond of bringing round the conversation to the American war, the massacre of Wyoming, and the brilliant actions of Saint-Lucie,* the fact being that he had a couple of volumes of the *Annual Register* in his bedroom, which he sedulously studied. It is thus a well-regulated man will accommodate himself to circumstances, and show himself calmly superior to fortune.

Chapter XVI

[The first part of this chapter is entitled 'More Storms in the Puddle' in the first edition.]

1. p. 179. *Insert* that he himself was very sorry for the affair; that the insult had come upon him without the slightest provocation on his part;

2. p. 179. *Insert* with great dignity to his uncle

3. p. 182. *Insert* —for he could not speak to his mother of his loves and disappointments—his uncle treated them in a scornful and worldly tone, which, though carefully guarded and polite, yet jarred greatly on the feelings of Mr. Pen—and Foker was much too coarse to appreciate those refined sentimental secrets—

4. p. 182. *Insert as a new paragraph—*

Pen's affection gushed out in a multitude of sonnets to the friend of his heart, as he styled the curate, which the latter received with great sympathy. He plied Smirke with Latin Sapphics and Alcaics. The love-songs multiplied under his fluent pen; and Smirke declared and believed that they were beautiful. On the other hand, Pen expressed a boundless gratitude to think that Heaven should have sent him such a friend at such a moment. He presented his tutor with his best-bound books, and his gold guard-chain, and wanted him to take his double-barrelled gun. He went into Chatteris and got a gold pencil-case on credit (for he had no money, and indeed was still in debt to Smirke for some of the Fotheringay presents), which he presented to Smirke, with an inscription indicative of his unalterable and eternal regard for the curate; who of course was pleased with every mark of the boy's attachment.

5. p. 188. *Insert* thus it was, that

6. p. 188. *Insert, to commence a new paragraph—*

Madame Fribsby had, of course, taken the strongest interest in the progress of Mr. Pen's love affair with Miss Fotheringay. She had been over to Chatteris, and having seen that actress perform, had pronounced that she was old and overrated: and had talked over Master Pen's passion in her shop many and many a time to the half-dozen old maids, and old women in male clothes, who are to be found in little country towns, and who formed the genteel population of Clavering. Captain Glanders, H.P., had pronounced that Pen was going to be a devil of a fellow, and had begun early: Mrs. Glanders had told him to check his horrid observations, and to respect his own wife, if he pleased. She said it would be a lesson to Helen for her pride and absurd infatuation about that boy. Mrs. Pybus said many people were proud of very small things, and for her part, she didn't know why an apothecary's wife should give herself such airs. Mrs. Wapshot called her daughters away from that side of the street, one day when Pen, on Rebecca, was stopping at the saddler's, to get a new lash to his whip—one and all of these people had made visits of curiosity to Fairoaks, and had tried to condole with the widow, or bring the subject of the Fotheringay affair on the tapis, and had been severally checked by the haughty reserve of Mrs. Pendennis, supported by the frigid politeness of the major her brother.

These rebuffs, however, did not put an end to the gossip, and slander went on increasing about the unlucky Fairoaks family. Glanders (H.P.), a retired cavalry officer, whose half-pay and large family compelled him to fuddle himself with brandy-and-water instead of claret after he quitted the Dragoons, had the occasional entrée at Fairoaks, and kept his friend the major there informed of all the stories which were current at Clavering. Mrs. Pybus had taken an inside place by the coach to Chatteris, and gone to the 'George' on purpose to get the particulars. Mrs. Speers's man had treated Mr. Foker's servant to drink at Baymouth for a similar purpose. It was said that Pen had hanged himself for despair in the orchard, and that his uncle had cut him down; that, on the contrary, it was Miss Costigan who was jilted, and not young Arthur; and that the affair had only been hushed up by the payment of a large sum of money, the exact amount of which there were several people in Clavering could testify—the sum of course varying according to the calculation of the individual narrator of the story.

Pen shook his mane and raged like a furious lion when these scandals, affecting Miss Costigan's honour and his own, came to his ears. Why was not Pybus a man (she had whiskers enough), that he might call her out and shoot her? Seeing Simcoe pass by, Pen glared at him so from his saddle on Rebecca, and clutched his whip in a manner so menacing, that that clergyman went home and wrote a sermon, or thought over a sermon (for he delivered oral testimony at great length), in which he spoke of Jezebel, theatrical entertainments (a double cut this—for Doctor Portman, the Rector of the old church, was known to frequent such), and of youth going to perdition, in a manner which made it clear to every capacity that Pen was the

individual meant, and on the road alluded to. What stories more were there not against young Pendennis, whilst he sat sulking, Achilles-like in his tent, for the loss of his ravished Briseis?

After the affair with Hobnell, Pen was pronounced to be a murderer as well as a profligate, and his name became a name of terror and a byword in Clavering. But this was not all; he was not the only one of the family about whom the village began to chatter, and his unlucky mother was the next to become a victim to their gossip.

'It is all settled,' said Mrs. Pybus to Mrs. Speers: 'the boy is to go to college, and then the widow is to console herself.'

'He's been there every day, in the most open manner, my dear,' continued Mrs. Speers.

'Enough to make poor Mr. Pendennis turn in his grave,' said Mrs. Wapshot.

'She never liked him, that we know,' says No. 1.

'Married him for his money. Everybody knows that: was a penniless hanger-on of Lady Pontypool's,' says No. 2.

'It's rather too open, though, to encourage a lover under pretence of having a tutor for your son,' cried No. 3.

'Hush! here comes Mrs. Portman,' someone said; as the good rector's wife entered Madame Fribsby's shop, to inspect her monthly book of fashions just arrived from London. And the fact is that Madame Fribsby had been able to hold out no longer; and one day, after she and her lodger had been talking of Pen's approaching departure, and the curate had gone off to give one of his last lessons to that gentleman, Madame Fribsby had communicated to Mrs. Pybus, who happened to step in with Mrs. Speers, her strong suspicion, her certainty almost, that there was an attachment between a certain clerical gentleman and a certain lady, whose naughty son was growing quite unmanageable, and that a certain marriage would take place pretty soon.

Mrs. Portman saw it all, of course, when the matter was mentioned. What a sly fox that curate was! He was Low Church, and she never liked him. And to think of Mrs. Pendennis taking a fancy to him after she had been married to such a man as Mr. Pendennis! She could hardly stay five minutes at Madame Fribsby's, so eager was she to run to the Rectory and give Dr. Portman the news.

When Dr. Portman heard this piece of intelligence, he was in such a rage with his curate, that his first movement was to break with Mr. Smirke, and to beg him to transfer his services to some other parish. 'That milksop of a creature pretend to be worthy of such a woman as Mrs. Pendennis,' broke out the doctor; 'where will impudence stop next?'

'She is much too old for Mr. Smirke,' Mrs. Portman remarked: 'why, poor dear Mrs. Pendennis might be his mother almost.'

'You always choose the most charitable reason, Betsy,' cried the rector. 'A matron with a son grown up—she would never think of marrying again.'

'You only think *men* should marry again, Dr. Portman,' answered his lady, bridling up.

'You stupid old woman,' said the doctor, 'when I am gone, you shall marry whomsoever you like. I will leave orders in my will, my dear, to that effect: and I'll bequeath a ring to my successor, and my ghost shall come and dance at your wedding.'

'It is cruel for a clergyman to talk so,' the lady answered, with a ready whimper: but these little breezes used to pass very rapidly over the surface of the doctor's domestic bliss; and were followed by a great calm and sunshine. The doctor adopted a plan for soothing Mrs. Portman's ruffled countenance, which has a great effect when it is tried between a worthy couple who are sincerely fond of one another; and which, I think, becomes 'John Anderson' at three-score, just as much as it used to do when he was a black-haired young Jo of five-and-twenty.

'Hadn't you better speak to Mr. Smirke, John?' Mrs. Portman asked.

'When Pen goes to college, *cadit quaestio*,' replied the rector, 'Smirke's visits at Fairoaks will cease of themselves, and there will be no need to bother the widow. She has trouble enough on her hands, with the affairs of that silly young scapegrace, without being pestered by the tittle-tattle of this place. It is all an invention of that fool, Fribsby.'

'Against whom I always warned you,—you know I did, my dear John,' interposed Mrs. Portman.

'That you did; you very often do, my love,' the doctor answered, with a laugh. 'It is not for want of warning on your part, I am sure, that I have formed my opinion of most women with whom we are acquainted. Madame Fribsby is a fool, and fond of gossip, and so are some other folks. But she is good to the poor: she takes care of her mother, and she comes to church twice every Sunday. And as for Smirke, my dear——' here the doctor's face assumed for one moment a comical expression, which Mrs. Portman did not perceive (for she was looking out of the drawing-room window, and wondering what Mrs. Pybus could want cheapening fowls again in the market, when she had had poultry from Livermore's two days before)—'and as for Mr. Smirke, my dear Betsy, will you promise me that you will never breathe to any mortal what I am going to tell you as a profound secret?'

'What is it, my dear John?—of course I won't,' answered the rector's lady.

'Well then—I cannot say it is a fact, mind—but if you find that Smirke is at this moment—aye, and has been for years—engaged to a young lady, a Miss—a Miss Thompson, if you will have the name, who lives on Clapham Common,—yes, on Clapham Common, not far from Mrs. Smirke's house, what becomes of your story then about Smirke and Mrs. Pendennis?'

'Why did you not tell me this before?' asked the doctor's wife.—'How long have you known it?—How we all of us have been deceived in that man!'

'Why should I meddle in other folks' business, my dear?' the doctor answered. 'I know how to keep a secret—and perhaps this

is only an invention like that other absurd story ; at least Madame Portman, I should never have told you this but for the other, which I beg you to contradict whenever you hear it.' And so saying the doctor went away to his study, and Mrs. Portman seeing that the day was a remarkably fine one, thought she would take advantage of the weather and pay a few visits.

The doctor looking out of his study window saw the wife of his bosom presently issue forth, attired in her best. She crossed the

market-place, saluting the market-women right and left, and giving a glance at the grocery and general emporium at the corner : then entering London Street (formerly Hog Lane), she stopped for a minute at Madame Fribsby's window, and looking at the fashions which hung up there, seemed hesitating whether she should enter ; but she passed on and never stopped again until she came to Mrs. Pybus's little green gate and garden, through which she went to that lady's cottage.

There, of course, her husband lost sight of Mrs. Portman. 'Oh, what a long bow I have pulled,' he said inwardly—'Goodness forgive me! and shot my own flesh and blood. There must be no more tattling and scandal about that house. I must stop it, and speak to Smirke. I'll ask him to dinner this very day.'

Having a sermon to compose, the doctor sat down to that work, and was so engaged in the composition, that he had not concluded it until near five o'clock in the afternoon: when he stepped over to Mr. Smirke's lodgings, to put his hospitable intentions, regarding that gentleman, into effect. He reached Madame Fribsby's door, just as the curate issued from it.

Mr. Smirke was magnificently dressed, and as he turned out his toes, he showed a pair of elegant open-worked silk stockings and glossy pumps. His white cravat was arranged in a splendid stiff tie, and his gold shirt studs shone on his spotless linen. His hair was curled round his fair temples. Had he borrowed Madame Fribsby's irons to give that curly grace? His white cambric pocket-handkerchief was scented with the most delicious eau-de-Cologne.

'*O gracilis puer*,'—cried the doctor.—'Whither are you bound? I wanted you to come home to dinner.'

'I am engaged to dine at—at Fairoaks,' said Mr. Smirke, blushing faintly and whisking the scented pocket-handkerchief, and his pony being in waiting, he mounted and rode away simpering down the street. No accident befell him that day, and he arrived with his tie in the very best order at Mrs. Pendennis's house.

Chapter XVII

WHICH CONCLUDES THE FIRST PART OF THIS HISTORY

THE curate had gone on his daily errand to Fairoaks, and was upstairs in Pen's study pretending to read with his pupil, in the early part of that very afternoon when Mrs. Portman, after transacting business with Mrs. Pybus, had found the weather so exceedingly fine that she pursued her walk as far as Fairoaks, in order to pay a visit to her dear friend there. In the course of their conversation, the rector's lady told Mrs. Pendennis and the major a very great secret about the curate, Mr. Smirke, which was no less than that he had an attachment, a very old attachment, which he had long kept quite private.

'And on whom is it that Mr. Smirke has bestowed his heart?' asked Mrs. Pendennis, with a superb air but rather an inward alarm.

'Why, my dear,' the other lady answered, 'when he first came and used to dine at the Rectory, people said we wanted him for Myra,

and we were forced to give up asking him. Then they used to say he was smitten in another quarter ; but I always contradicted it for my part, and said that you——'

'That *I*,' cried Mrs. Pendennis ; 'people are very impertinent, I am sure. Mr. Smirke came here as Arthur's tutor, and I am surprised that anybody should dare to speak so——'

''Pon my soul, it is a *little* too much,' the major said, laying down the newspaper and the double eyeglass.

'I've no patience with that Mrs. Pybus,' Helen continued indignantly.

'I told her there was no truth in it,' Mrs. Portman said. 'I always said so, my dear : and now it comes out that my demure gentleman has been engaged to a young lady—Miss Thompson, of Clapham Common, ever so long : and I am delighted for my part, and on Myra's account, too, for an unmarried curate is always objectionable about one's house : and of course it is strictly private, but I thought I would tell you, as it might remove unpleasantnesses. But mind : not one word, if you please, about the story.'

Mrs. Pendennis said, with perfect sincerity, that she was exceedingly glad to hear the news : and hoped Mr. Smirke, who was a very kind and amiable man, would have a deserving wife : and when her visitor went away, Helen and her brother talked of the matter with great satisfaction, the kind lady rebuking herself for her haughty behaviour to Mr. Smirke, whom she had avoided of late, instead of being grateful to him for his constant attention to Arthur.

'Gratitude to this kind of people,' the major said, 'is very well ; but familiarity is out of the question. This gentleman gives his lessons and receives his money like any other master. You are too humble, my good soul. There must be distinctions in ranks, and that sort of thing. I told you before, you were too kind to Mr. Smirke.'

But Helen did not think so

7. p. 188. *Insert* and *and omit* Helen's heart was rather softened towards the curate, from whom, perhaps divining his intentions, she had shrunk hitherto,

8. p. 188. *Before* Helen *insert* Eased, by the above report, of all her former doubts and misgivings regarding the curate,

9. p. 189. *Insert* 'What an unsufferable bore that man is, and how he did talk !' the major said.

'He has been very good to Arthur, who is very fond of him,' Mrs. Pendennis said,—'I wonder who the Miss Thompson is whom he is going to marry ?'

'I always thought the fellow was looking in another direction,' said the major.

'And in what ?' asked Mrs. Pendennis quite innocently,—'towards Myra Portman ?'

'Towards Helen Pendennis, if you must know,' answered her brother-in-law.

'Towards me! impossible!' Helen said, who knew perfectly well that such had been the case. 'His marriage will be a very happy thing. I hope Arthur will not take too much wine.'

10. p. 196. *Insert* (and, I need not say, as worthy a fellow as ever stood behind a bar),

CHAPTER XVII

1. p. 206. *Insert* (his son took the highest honours in the other University of Camford)

2. p. 207. *Insert* So they parted until dinner-time, which was very near at hand, and Major Pendennis pronounced Mr. Buck to be uncommonly civil indeed. Indeed

3. p. 207. *Add* The major smiled as he saw the boy dandifying himself in the glass: the old gentleman was not displeased with the appearance of the comely lad.

4. p. 209. *Add* But these circumstances, it must be remembered, took place some years back, when William the Fourth was king. Young men are much better behaved now, and besides, St. Boniface was rather a fast college.

5. p. 210. *Add* Pen had another Alma Mater now. But it is not all children who take to her kindly.

CHAPTER XVIII

1. p. 211. *For* Let us give the major due credit for his conduct *read* Say, worthy reader, if thou hast peradventure a beard, wouldst thou do as much? I will not say that a woman will not. They are used to it: we take care to accustom them to sacrifices: but, my good sir, the amount of self-denial which you have probably exerted through life, when put down to your account elsewhere, will not probably swell the balance on the credit side much. Well, well, there is no use in speaking of such ugly matters, and you are too polite to use a vulgar *tu quoque.* But I wish to state once for all that I greatly admire the major for his conduct

2. p. 211. *Insert at the beginning of the next paragraph*—
A quarter of the space which custom has awarded to works styled the Serial Nature, has been assigned to the account of one passage in Pen's career, and it is manifest that the whole of his adventures cannot be treated at a similar length, unless some descendant of the chronicler of Pen's history should take up the pen at his decease, and continue the narrative for the successors of the present generation of readers.

3. p. 211. *Read* the young fellow's academical career with, by any means, a similar minuteness.

4. p. 219. *For* Dilley *read* Dillon

5. p. 221. *Insert* and whose dinners are so good

6. p. 221. *Insert* and even disarmed the tutors who cried out at his idleness, and murmured about his extravagant way of life.

7. p. 223. *Insert* and drinking his stupid old port wine.'

Chapter XIX

1. p. 226. *Insert, to begin the chapter—*
Some short time before Mr. Foker's departure from Oxbridge, there had come up to Boniface a gentleman who had once, as it turned out, belonged to the other University of Camford, which he had quitted on account of some differences with the tutors and authorities there. This gentleman, whose name was Horace Bloundell, was of the ancient Suffolk family of Bloundell-Bloundell, of Bloundell-Bloundell Hall, Bloundell-Bloundellshire, as the young wags used to call it; and no doubt it was on account of his descent, and because Dr. Donne, the Master of Boniface, was a Suffolk man, and related perhaps to the family, that Mr. Horace Bloundell was taken in at Boniface, after St. George's and one or two other colleges bad refused to receive him. There was a living in the family, which it was important for Mr. Bloundell to hold; and, being in a Dragoon regiment at the time when his third brother, for whom the living was originally intended, sickened and died, Mr. Bloundell determined upon quitting crimson pantaloons and sable shakos, for the black coat and white neckcloth of the English divine. The misfortunes which occurred at Camford, occasioned some slight disturbance to Mr. Bloundell's plans; but although defeated upon one occasion, the resolute ex-Dragoon was not dismayed, and set to work to win a victory elsewhere.

2. p. 227. *For* and Bloundell-Bloundell, whom Mr. Pen entertained at a dinner whereof his uncle was the chief guest *read* Mr. Bloundell-Bloundell finally, who had at once taken his place among the select of the University.

Major Pendennis, though he did not understand Harland's Greek quotations, or quite appreciate Broadbent's thick shoes and dingy hands, was nevertheless delighted with the company assembled round his nephew, and highly approved of all the young men with the exception of that one who gave himself the greatest airs in the society, and affected most to have the manners of a man of the world.

As he and Pen sat at breakfast on the morning after the party in the rooms of the latter, the major gave his opinions regarding the young men, with whom he was in the greatest good-humour. He had regaled them with some of his stories, which, though not quite so fresh in London (where people have a diseased appetite for novelty in the way of anecdotes), were entirely new at Oxbridge, and the lads heard them with that honest sympathy, that eager pleasure, that boisterous laughter, or that profound respect, so rare in the metropolis, and which must be so delightful to the professed raconteur. Only once or twice during the telling of the anecdotes, Mr. Bloundell's face wore a look of scorn, or betrayed by its expression that he was acquainted with the tales narrated. Once he had the audacity to question the accuracy of one of the particulars of a tale as given by Major Pendennis, and gave his own version of the anecdote, about which he knew he was right, for he heard it openly talked of at the club by So-and-so and T'other, who were present at the business. The youngsters present looked up with wonder at their associate,

who dared to interrupt the major—few of them could appreciate that melancholy grace and politeness with which Major Pendennis at once acceded to Mr. Bloundell's version of the story, and thanked him for correcting his own error. They stared on the next occasion of meeting, when Bloundell spoke in contemptuous terms of old Pen, said everybody knew old Pen, regular old trencherman at Gaunt House, notorious old bore, regular old fogy.

Major Pendennis on his side liked Mr. Bloundell not a whit. These sympathies are pretty sure to be mutual amongst men and women, and if, for my part, some kind friend tells me that such-and-such a man has been abusing me, I am almost sure, on my own side, that I have a misliking to such-and-such a man. We like or dislike each other, as folks like or dislike the odour of certain flowers, or the taste of certain dishes or wines, or certain books. We can't tell why—but as a general rule, all the reasons in the world will not make us love Dr. Fell, and as sure as we dislike him, we may be sure that he dislikes us.

So the major said,

3. p. 227. *Omit* He was in the —— Dragoons before he came up.

4. p. 228. *Insert* than that (so long to learn, so difficult to acquire, so impossible and beyond the means of many unhappy people !)

5. p. 228. *Insert* I like to see them wink at a glass of claret, as if they had an intimate acquaintance with it, and discuss a *salmi*—poor boys—it is only when they grow old that they know they know nothing of the science, when perhaps their conscience whispers them that the science is in itself little worth, and that a leg of mutton and content is as good as the dinners of pontiffs. But little

6. p. 228. *Insert* What young men like in their companions is, what had got Pen a great part of his own repute and popularity, a real or supposed knowledge of life. A man who has seen the world, or can speak of it with a knowing air—a roué, or Lovelace, who has his adventures to relate, is sure of an admiring audience among boys. It is hard to confess, but so it is. We respect that sort of prowess. From our schooldays we have been taught to admire it. Are there five in the hundred, out of the hundreds and hundreds of English schoolboys, brought up at our great schools and colleges, that must not own at one time of their lives to having read and liked *Don Juan?* Awful propagation of evil !—The idea of it should make the man tremble who holds the pen, lest untruth, or impurity, or unjust anger, or unjust praise escape it.

One such diseased creature as this is enough to infect a whole colony, and the tutors of Boniface began to find the moral tone of their college lowered, and their young men growing unruly, and almost ungentleman-like, soon after Mr. Bloundell's arrival at Oxbridge.

7. p. 231. *Insert* (an amusement much pleasanter to men in their second and third year than the boisterous custom of singing songs

which bring the proctors about the rooms, and which have grown quite stale by this time, every man having expended his budget),

8. p. 232. *Insert—*

Captain Macheath had other accomplishments which he exercised for Pen's benefit. The captain's stories had a great and unfortunate charm for Arthur, who was never tired of hearing Bloundell's histories of garrison conquests, and of his feats in country quarters. He had been at Paris, and had plenty of legends about the Palais Royal, and the Salon, and Frascati's. He had gone to the Salon one night, after a dinner at the Café de Paris, 'when we were all devilishly cut, by Jove; and on waking in the morning in my own rooms, I found myself with twelve thousand francs under my pillow, and a hundred and forty-nine Napoleons in one of my boots. Wasn't that a *coup*, hey?' the captain said. Pen's eyes glistened with excitement as he heard this story. He respected the man who could win such a sum of money. He sighed, and said it would set him all right. Macheath laughed, and told him to drink another drop of maraschino. 'I could tell you stories much more wonderful than that,' he added; and so indeed the captain could have done, without any further trouble than that of invention, with which portion of the poetic faculty Nature had copiously endowed him.

He laughed to scorn Pen's love for Miss Fotheringay, when he came to hear of that amour from Arthur, as he pretty soon did, for, we have said, Pen was not averse to telling the story now to his confidential friends, and he and they were rather proud of the transaction. But Macheath took away all Pen's conceit on this head, not by demonstrating the folly of the lad's passion for an uneducated woman much his senior in years, but by exposing his absurd desire of gratifying his passion in a legitimate way. 'Marry *her*,' said he, 'you might as well marry ——,' and he named one of the most notorious actresses on the stage. 'She hadn't a shred of a character.' He knew twenty men who were openly admirers of her, and named them, and the sums each had spent upon her. I know no kind of calumny more frightful or frequent than this which takes away the character of women, no men more reckless and mischievous than those who lightly use it, and no kind of cowards more despicable than the people who invent these slanders.

Is it, or not, a misfortune that a man, himself of a candid disposition, and disposed, like our friend Pen, to blurt out the truth on all occasions, begins life by believing all that is said to him? Would it be better for a lad to be less trustful, and so less honest? It requires no small experience of the world to know that a man, who has no especial reason thereto, is telling you lies. I am not sure whether it is not best to go on being duped for a certain time. At all events, our honest Pen had a natural credulity, which enabled him to accept all statements which were made to him, and he took every one of Captain Macheath's figments as if they had been the most unquestioned facts of history.

So Bloundell's account about Miss Fotheringay pained and morti-

fied Pen exceedingly. If he had been ashamed of his passion before,—what were his feelings regarding it now, when the object of so much pure flame and adoration turned out to be only a worthless impostor, an impostor detected by all but him? It never occurred to Pen to doubt the fact, or to question whether the stories of a man who, like his new friend, never spoke well of any woman, were likely to be true.

9. p. 234. *For* we have *read* has been

Chapter XX

1. p. 239. *Before* During *insert*—

Everybody who has the least knowledge of heraldry and the peerage must be aware that the noble family of which, as we know, Helen Pendennis was a member bears for a crest, a nest full of little pelicans pecking at the ensanguined bosom of a big maternal bird, which plentifully supplies the little wretches with the nutriment on which, according to the heraldic legend, they are supposed to be brought up. Very likely female pelicans like so to bleed under the selfish little beaks of their young ones: it is certain that women do. There must be some sort of pleasure, which we men don't understand, which accompanies the pain of being scarified, and indeed I believe some women would rather actually so suffer than not. They like sacrificing themselves in behalf of the object which their instinct teaches them to love. Be it for a reckless husband, a dissipated son, a darling scapegrace of a brother, how ready their hearts are to pour out their best treasures for the benefit of the cherished person; and what a deal of this sort of enjoyment are we, on our side, ready to give the soft creatures! There is scarce a man that reads this, but has administered pleasure in this fashion to his womankind, and has treated them to the luxury of forgiving him. They don't mind how they live themselves; but when the prodigal comes home they make a rejoicing, and kill the fatted calf for him: and at the very first hint that the sinner is returning, the kind angels prepare their festival, and Mercy and Forgiveness go smiling out to welcome him. I hope it may be so always for us all: if we have only Justice to look to, Heaven help us!

Chapter XXII

1. p. 267. *Insert* —the Queen's Muleteros
2. p. 270. *Insert* that
3. p. 270. *Insert* with his little maid.
4. p. 272. *Insert, to commence a new paragraph*—

'It is very wrong,' said Mrs. Pendennis, as if she had never done such a thing herself as spoil a child.

'Mamma says she spoils my brother,—do you think anything could, Miss Bell? Look at him,—isn't he like a little angel?'

5. p. 276. *Insert* as if she had been a nightingale.

This was the first visit paid by Fairoaks to Clavering Park, in return for Clavering Park's visit to Fairoaks, in reply to Fairoaks's cards left a few days after the arrival of Sir Francis's family.

6. p. 280. *Add* It must be owned, he became very fond of that healthful and invigorating pursuit of angling, and was whipping the Brawl continually with his fly.

7. p. 281. *Insert* (who had had a snug home, or been at a comfortable boarding-school, and had no outward grief or hardship to complain of)

Chapter XXIII

1. p. 281. *Insert, to begin the chapter—*
Every house has its skeleton in it somewhere, and it may be a comfort to some unhappy folks to think that the luckiest and most wealthy of their neighbours have their miseries and causes of disquiet. Our little innocent Muse of a Blanche, who sang so nicely and talked so sweetly, you would have thought she must have made sunshine wherever she went, was the skeleton, or the misery, or the bore, or the Nemesis of Clavering House, and of most of the inhabitants thereof. As one little stone in your own shoe or your horse's, suffices to put either to torture and to make your journey miserable, so in life a little obstacle is sufficient to obstruct your entire progress, and subject you to endless annoyance and disquiet. Who would have guessed that such a smiling little fairy as Blanche Amory could be the cause of discord in any family?

2. p. 283. *Insert* Without sympathy, life is nothing; and would it not have been a want of candour on her part to affect a cheerfulness which she did not feel, or pretend a respect for those towards whom it was quite impossible she should entertain any reverence?

3. p. 285. *For* Blanche *read* We have spoken just now of children's dolls, and of the manner in which those little people take up and neglect their darling toys, and very likely this history will show that Miss Blanche assumed and put away her live dolls with a similar girlish inconstancy. She

4. p. 286. *Insert—*
The Muse loved to be dressed becomingly, and, having a lively fancy and a poetic desire for change, was for altering her attire every day. Her maid having a taste in dressmaking—to which art she had been an apprentice at Paris, before she entered into Miss Blanche's service there—was kept from morning till night altering and remodelling Miss Amory's habiliments; and rose very early and went to bed very late, in obedience to the untiring caprices of her little task-mistress. The girl was of respectable English parents. There are many of our people, colonists of Paris, who have seen better days, who are not quite ruined, who do not quite live upon charity, and yet cannot get on without it; and as her father was a cripple incapable of work, and her return home would only increase the burthen and add to the misery of the family, poor Pincott was fain to stay where she could maintain herself, and spare a little relief to her parents.

Our Muse, with the candour which distinguished her, never failed to remind her attendant of the real state of matters. 'I should send

you away, Pincott, for you are a great deal too weak, and your eyes are failing you, and you are always crying and snivelling and wanting the doctor; but I wish that your parents at home should be supported, and I go on enduring you for their sake, mind,' the dear Blanche would say to her timid little attendant. Or, 'Pincott, your wretched appearance and slavish manner, and red eyes, positively give me the migraine; and I think I shall make you wear rouge, so that you may look a little cheerful;' or, 'Pincott, I can't bear, even for the sake of your starving parents, that you should tear my hair out of my head in that manner; and I will thank you to write to them and say that I dispense with your services.' After which sort of speeches, and after keeping her for an hour trembling over her hair, which the young lady loved to have combed, as she perused one of her favourite French novels, she would go to bed at one o'clock, and say, 'Pincott, you may kiss me. Good-night. I should like you to have the pink-dress ready for the morning.' And so with a blessing upon her attendant, she would turn round and go to sleep.

The Muse might lie in bed as long as she chose of a morning, and availed herself of that privilege; but Pincott had to rise very early indeed to get her mistress's task done; and had to appear next day with the same red eyes and the same wan face, which displeased Miss Amory by their want of gaiety, and caused the mistress to be so angry, because the servant persisted in being and looking unwell and unhappy. Not that Blanche ever thought she was a hard mistress. Indeed, she made quite a friend of Pincott, at times, and wrote some very pretty verses about the lonely little tiring-maid, whose heart was far away. Our beloved Blanche was a superior being, and expected to be waited upon as such. And I do not know whether there are any other ladies in this world who treat their servants or dependents so, but it may be that there are such, and that the tyranny which they exercise over their subordinates, and the pangs which they can manage to inflict with a soft voice and a well-bred simper, are as cruel as those which a slave-driver administers with an oath and a whip.

But Blanche was a Muse—a delicate little creature, quite tremulous with excitability, whose eyes filled with tears at the smallest emotion; and who knows but that it was the very fineness of her feelings which caused them to be *froissé*'d so easily? You crush a butterfly by merely touching it. Vulgar people have no idea of the sensibility of a Muse.

So little Pincott, being occupied all day and night in stitching, hemming, ripping, combing, ironing, crimping, for her mistress; in reading to her when in bed,—for the girl was mistress of the two languages, and had a sweet voice and manner—could take no share in Madame Fribsby's soirées, nor indeed was she much missed, or considered of sufficient consequence to appear at their entertainments.

But there was

Chapter XXIV

1. p. 296. *Read* We have brought her thus up

2. p. 296. *Add* in the midst of which Mr. Pinckney, the celebrated painter, portrayed her with her little boy by her side.

3. p. 299. *Add* Of course Blanche confided to her bosom friend all the little griefs and domestic annoyances; how the family could not comprehend her, and she moved among them an isolated being; how her poor mamma's education had been neglected, and she was forced to blush for her blunders; how Sir Francis was a weak person deplorably unintellectual, and only happy when smoking his odious cigars; how, since the birth of her little brother, she had seen her mother's precious affection, which she valued more than anything in life, estranged from her once darling daughter; how she was alone, alone, alone in the world.

But these griefs, real and heart-rending though they might be to a young lady of exquisite sensibility, did not convince Laura of the propriety of Blanche's conduct in many small incidents of life.

Chapter XXV

1. p. 319. *Insert* who, as his patron said, was never in the way or out of it,

Chapter XXVI

1. p. 322. *Insert* That gentleman was as solemn and severe as Englishmen are upon such occasions, and walked through the dance as he would have walked up to his pew in church, without a smile upon his face, or allowing any outward circumstance to interfere with his attention to the grave duty in which he was engaged. But

2. p. 326. *Insert* gentle

Chapter XXVIII

1. p. 353. *For* Polyanthus *read* Megatherium

2. p. 363. *Insert* Would you like to vegetate, like your dear good mother at Fairoaks ? Dammy, sir ! life without money and the best society isn't worth having.

Chapter XXXIX

1. p. 490. *After* the fever of his soul *read* and the very instant that he woke from his agitated sleep, the image of Miss Amory presented itself to him, and said, 'Here I am ; I am your princess and beauty ; you have discovered me and shall care for nothing else hereafter.'

2. p. 497. *Insert* upon his master and the elders of the family.

3. p. 501. *Insert* You don't die of the complaint : or very few do. The generous wounded heart suffers and survives it. And he is not a man, or she a woman, who is not conquered by it, or who does not conquer it in his time. . . .

Chapter XL

1. p. 506. *Insert* But there have been such in our memories who have loved the society of riotous youth better than the company of men of their own age and rank, and have given the young ones the precious benefit of their experience and example ; and there have been very respectable men too who have not objected so much to the kind of entertainment as to the publicity of it. I am sure, for instance, that our friend Major Pendennis would have made no sort of objection to join a party of pleasure, provided that it were *en petit comité* and that such men as my Lord Steyne and my Lord Colchicum were of the society. 'Give the young men their pleasures,' this worthy guardian said to Pen more than once. 'I'm not one of your straitlaced moralists, but an old man of the world, begad ; and I know that as long as it lasts, young men will be young men.' And there were some young men to whom this estimable philosopher accorded about seventy years as the proper period for sowing their wild oats : but they were men of fashion.

Chapter XLI

1. p. 519. "Oxford" was retained for many years here.

2. p. 527. *Add* and on this simple calculation it was that the major counselled Pen.

Chapter XLII

1. p. 542. *Insert* and Pen thought it as amusing as the society of the finest gentlemen in the finest houses which he had the honour to frequent.

2. p. 542. *For* Queen Christina's *read* Don Carlos's.

Chapter XLV

1. p. 573. *Insert—*

I wish that a few of my youthful readers who are inclined to that

amusement would take the trouble to calculate the time which is spent in the pursuit, when they would find it to be one of the most costly occupations in which a man can possibly indulge. What don't you sacrifice to it, indeed, young gentlemen and young ladies of ill-regulated minds? Many hours of your precious sleep in the first place, in which you lie tossing and thinking about the adored object, whence you come down late to breakfast, when noon is advancing and all the family is long since away to its daily occupations. Then when you at length get to these occupations you pay no attention to them, and engage in them with no ardour—all your thoughts and powers of mind being fixed elsewhere. Then the day's work being slurred over, you neglect your friends and relatives, your natural companions and usual associates in life, that you may go and have a glance at the dear personage, or a look up at her windows, or a peep at her carriage in the Park. Then at night the artless blandishments of home bore you; mamma's conversation palls upon you; the dishes which that good soul prepares for the dinner of her favourite are sent away untasted,—the whole meal of life, indeed, except one particular *plat*, has no relish. Life, business, family ties, home, all things useful and dear once, become intolerable, and you are never easy except when you are in pursuit of your flame.

Such I believe to be not unfrequently the state of mind amongst ill-regulated young gentlemen, and such indeed was Mr. H. Foker's condition, who, having been bred up to indulge in every propensity towards which he was inclined, abandoned himself to this one with his usual sefish enthusiasm. Nor because he had given his friend Arthur Pendennis a great deal of good advice on a former occasion, need men of the world wonder that Mr. Foker became passion's slave in his turn. Who among us has not given a plenty of the very best advice to his friends? Who has not preached, and who has practised? To be sure, you, madam, are perhaps a perfect being, and never had a wrong thought in the whole course of your frigid and irreproachable existence: or you, sir, are a great deal too strong-minded to allow any foolish passion to interfere with your equanimity in chambers or your attendance on 'Change; you are so strong that you don't want any sympathy. We don't give you any, then; we keep ours for the humble and weak, that struggle and stumble and get up again, and so march with the rest of mortals. What need have *you* of a hand who never fall? Your serene virtue is never shaded by passion, or ruffled by temptation, or darkened by remorse; compassion would be impertinence for such an angel: but then with such a one companionship becomes intolerable; you are, from the very elevation of your virtue and high attributes, of necessity lonely; we can't reach up and talk familiarly with such potentates. Good-bye, then; our way lies with humble folks, and not with serene highnesses like you; and we give notice that there are no perfect characters in this history, except, perhaps, one little one, and that one is not perfect either, for she never knows to this day that she is perfect, and, with a deplorable misapprehension and perverseness of humility, believes herself to be as a great a sinner as need be.

This young person does not happen to be in London at the present period of our story, and it is by no means for the like of her that Mr. Henry Foker's mind is agitated. But what matters a few failings ? Need we be angels, male or female, in order to be worshipped as such ? Let us admire the diversity of the tastes of mankind ; and the oldest, the ugliest, the stupidest and most pompous, the silliest and most vapid, the greatest criminal, tyrant, booby, Bluebeard, Catherine Hayes,* George Barnwell, amongst us, we need never despair. I have read of the passion of a transported pickpocket for a female convict (each of them being advanced in age, repulsive in person, ignorant, quarrelsome, and given to drink), that was as magnificent as the loves of Cleopatra and Antony, or Lancelot and Guinevere. The passion which Count Borulawski, the Polish dwarf, inspired in the bosom of the most beautiful Baroness at the Court of Dresden, is a matter with which we are all of us acquainted : the flame which burned in the heart of young Cornet Tozer but the other day, and caused him to run off and espouse Mrs. Battersby, who was old enough to be his mamma,—all these instances are told in the page of history or the newspaper column. Are we to be ashamed or pleased to think that our hearts are formed so that the biggest and highest-placed Ajax among us may some day find himself prostrate before the pattens of his kitchen-maid ; as that there is no poverty or shame or crime, which will not be supported, hugged even with delight, and cherished more closely than virtue would be, by the perverse fidelity and admirable constant folly of a woman ?

So then Henry Foker, Esq.

Chapter XLVI

1. p. 593. *Insert* and sympathized with the misfortunes of all sorts of people :

Chapter L

1. p. 635. *Omit* he and Sam.

Chapter LI

1. p. 642. *Add* ; into which room, have we not seen a picture of him entering from his little bedroom adjoining, as Mrs. Flanagan, his laundress, was in the act of drinking his gin ?

Chapter LIV

1. p. 691. *Insert* dem'd

Chapter LV

1. p. 707. *Insert* and whose over-refinement did not lead them to repulse the familiarities of this young gentleman,

Chapter LVI

1. p. 715. *Insert* worthy.
2. p. 729. *For* crypt *read* pew

Chapter LIX

1. p. 760. *For* Polyanthus *read* Megatherium

Chapter LX

1. p. 776. *Add as a new paragraph*—

'Take my counsel, Altamont,' Strong said gravely, 'and mind how you deal with that man. Don't make it too much his interest to get rid of you; or who knows what he may do?'

Chapter LXV

1. p. 846. *Insert* (that wondrous invention, a châtelaine,* was not extant yet, or she would have had one, we may be sure)

EXPLANATORY NOTES

THERE is an exhaustive set of annotations to *Pendennis*, by Edgar Harden (see 'Select Bibliography' for details). Designed primarily for the American college reader, Professor Harden's notes range from the basic ('*The Times*: famous London newspaper') to expertly researched information. In a number of places I gratefully draw on this valuable volume. Donald Hawes has also prepared a more selective set of notes for his 'Penguin English Library' edition of *Pendennis*, which I have also occasionally drawn on. Two volumes particularly useful for historical background are J. W. Dodds, *The Age of Paradox* (1953), and R. D. Altick, *The Presence of the Present* (1991). Joan Stevens's essay on 'Thackeray's Pictorial Capitals' in *Costerus*, 2 (1974) I have found very instructive.

The following abbreviations are used in the Explanatory Notes:

AP John W. Dodds, *The Age of Paradox* (London, 1953)
AW Gordon N. Ray, *Thackeray: The Age of Wisdom* (London, 1958)
BL Gordon N. Ray, *The Buried Life* (Cambridge, Mass., 1952)
PP Richard D. Altick, *The Presence of the Present* (Columbus, Ohio, 1991)
UA Gordon N. Ray, *Thackeray: The Uses of Adversity* (London, 1955)

(1) *General Note on Thackeray's Illustrations*

Since this is unusual (and as I write unique) in being an affordable illustrated edition of the novel, close attention is paid to Thackeray's artwork. During the composition, Thackeray found drawing pictures a welcome distraction and called them 'a great relief to my mind' (*AW* 16). Thackeray's illustrations fall into three categories. Most demanding were the two etchings on steel for which he had to do the designs early in the month, before he had written the text. In strict aesthetic terms, these tend to be Thackeray's least effective artwork. None the less, the standard is much higher than in *Vanity Fair* and some of the plates (such as the matched pair of the scene outside Pen's Oxbridge lodgings in number 6) are among the best work of this kind Thackeray achieved.

Secondly, Thackeray provided a number of naturalistic wood-

cuts, to be dropped into the text. He gave thought to placing these sketches strategically (see, for instance, p. 331, where the sentence describing Altamont jingling sovereigns in his pocket is interrupted by a picture of the act). Again Thackeray had to provide his work early for the artisan who would engrave the woodblock. Sometimes there are discrepancies between the pictures and the written text (see note to p. 442) and sometimes discrepancies between adjoining pictures (see, for instance, pp. 703 and 705, where consecutive steel engraving and woodcut of the same scene show Costigan with entirely different clothing). But in general this category of artwork is highly successful in *Pendennis*. Nicholas Pickwoad ascribes the high quality of the woodcuts in *Pendennis* to Thackeray's working with highly talented French engravers (one of whom, François Pierdon, visibly signs his work). Living with Thackeray while he wrote *Pendennis* was a gifted French artist, Louis Marvy (a refugee from the 1848 Revolution) who may also have helped raise the quality of the novel's plates and wood-engravings. It is conjectured that Marvy supplied the delicacy of design in, for instance, 'Poor Pen' (p. 89) and inspired the fine depiction of domestic interiors in many of the drawings.

The third kind of illustration which Thackeray supplied were the pictorial initials, or vignettes, which begin every chapter. Here he drew on his formidable skills as a cartoonist in *Punch*. The vignettes range from the allegorical or exaggeratedly caricaturish to the naturalistic. They are often densely allusive. Typically the vignettes supply an ironic commentary on the action and invariably repay close attention (unlike the other kinds of illustration, Thackeray seems to have done the designs simultaneously with composition). There are frequent references to contemporary events (see note to p. 531) and the recurrent eighteenth-century motif shows Thackeray thinking ahead to his next major enterprises (the lectures on the English humorists and *Esmond*).

(2) *General Note on Thackeray's Chronology and the Topical Background in* Pendennis

In general, Thackeray took a relaxed view on chronological consistency. He jokes on the subject on p. 668: 'we beg the reader to understand that we only commit anachronisms when we choose, and when by a daring violation of those natural laws some great ethical truth is to be advanced'. The chronology of *Pendennis* is not consistent, looked at pedantically—although the

novel's loose structure discourages any such pedantry. The opening section—comprising Pen's family background, his infatuation with Emily Fotheringay, up to his departure to 'Oxbridge'—can be dated precisely. The reference on p. 27 to the Duke of York (who died in 1827) and to Keble's *The Christian Year* (published in 1827) confirm that Pen (16 at this point) was born in the same year as Thackeray, 1811. His early years at Grey Friars (Charterhouse) and at Fairoaks (Larkbeare) fit in with dates in Thackeray's own youth. Both young men go up to university in 1829.

Thackeray's writing became notably looser around the sixth and seventh numbers. The novel has minor repetitions and small narrative illogicalities. From internal evidence, he seems to have been under some pressure at this period (April–May 1849). Chronology suffers. Laura gains three years, and is suddenly a nubile 16, when she should, by earlier references, be a prepubescent 12 (see note to p. 346). The historical frame of the novel becomes similarly contradictory. It is, for instance, 1830 (if one reckons by Pen's college career) in Chapter 22, but by Strong's military career it must be at least 1839. Even more startlingly, in the next chapter (23) we are told that Blanche 'had been in love with Prince Rodoloph and Prince Djalma' (figures in novels by Eugène Sue which were not published until 1842–5) while she was 'yet at school' (p. 284).

These are not local anachronisms. The whole 'world' of Thackeray's novel is slipping through history, and is unstuck in time. By the last numbers of the novel, Pen is 26 (which gives a historical date of 1837) but he and Warrington are habitually discussing quite identifiable events of 1850. (Their tobacco, whiskers, and manly taciturnity also give a mid-century cultural date.) In the course of the novel, some characters age fast. Laura, for instance, gains four to five years to make her a sexual object for Pen and Pynsent. Warrington, who was a near contemporary of Pen's at Oxbridge mysteriously becomes ten years older. Other characters (such as young Frank Clavering) either do not age at all, or actually become younger over the course of the novel. I annotate some (though not all) of these anomalies. The point is not to catch Thackeray out but to note how skilfully he uses his artistic freedom to write, at the same time, a historical and a contemporary narrative.

One other aspect of these notes requires prefatory comment. *Pendennis* was the most interrupted of Thackeray's serial novels. Interrupted, that is, by illness (which led to a three month

suspension, October 1849–January 1850) and by angry readers. Four controversies stand out: (1) the 'Elias Howle' row with the Irish novelist Charles Lever (see note to p. 400); (2) the furore provoked by Thackeray's racist slur, 'No Irish Need Apply' (see note to p. 118); (3) his entirely accidental insult to the Irish people with his comment on Catherine Hayes (see note to p. 678); and (4) the so-called 'Dignity of Literature' controversy, sparked by the narrator's jaundiced comments on the writing profession at the end of Chapter 34. Rather than clutter this edition with appendices, I have compressed accounts of these disputes and put them where I think they are most relevant, in the explanatory notes.

DEDICATION: Dr John Elliotson (1791–1868) intervened (at the urgent request of John Forster, Dickens's friend) when Thackeray fell dangerously ill with cholera (probably) in September 1849. This dedication was included in the novel's first book form, hence the 'Thirteen months ago' reference. Elliotson, who is portrayed in *Pendennis* as 'Dr Goodenough', is best known for his advocacy and practice of 'mesmerism', particularly as an anaesthetizing technique.

lvi *the lovers of 'excitement' . . . St. Giles's . . . a young lady from Belgravia*: Thackeray here alludes broadly to the 'Newgate' novel (i.e. fiction glamorizing crime, associated particularly with Bulwer-Lytton). The specific hit may be against Douglas Jerrold's *The History of St James and St Giles* (1847–8, reissued in 1851). Thackeray had a feud with Jerrold—a fellow contributor on *Punch*—going back to 1846.

competition with M. Eugène Sue: Sue's sensational novel of the Parisian underworld, *Mysteries of Paris*, had come out in France in 1842–3, and was promptly piratically translated by a number of British publishers. But Thackeray's remark about 'competition' suggests that he is thinking of *The Mysteries of London* by G. W. M. Reynolds, which was published 1845–7. It was succeeded by *The Mysteries of the Court of London* (8 vols., 1848–56). The lurid contents are described by J. W. Dodds: 'Here were murders, seductions, rapes, bordello experiences, gambling hells, boozing kens, dens of horrors, executions, body-snatchers, suicides galore' (*AP* 124). The ready availability of such material suggests that Thackeray's subsequent comment in the preface about the inhibitions laid on the Victorian novelist should be taken with a pinch of salt.

Since the author of Tom Jones was buried: Fielding died in 1754. This preface is, in fact, an afterword, composed four days before the publication of the novel's last serial part, at a period when Thackeray was going on to write his *Lectures on the English Humourists*. Fielding was the subject of one of the lectures.

1 VIGNETTE: Morgiana with her tambourine, in the pantomime version of *Ali Baba and the Forty Thieves*. The novel was launched during the pantomime season in London.

a certain club in Pall Mall: later in the text called 'Bays'—indicating White's a club famous for its bay window (see illustration, p. 459). It was not one of Thackeray's clubs. At the period of writing *Pendennis*, his most-used club was the Reform, from which he dated his letters in the 'Dignity of Literature' controversy.

Mr. Brummell: George Bryan Brummell (1778–1840), called 'Beau', the leader of Regency fashion and dandyism. Brummell was forced by debt to flee to Calais in 1816. The 'Mr.' indicates to the contemporary reader that Brummell was still alive at this point in the narrative (historically 1828).

the Wellington pattern: as the subsequent text makes clear, Major Pendennis models himself slavishly on the great soldier of the age (and the major's erstwhile patron in India) Arthur Wellesley, Field Marshal the Duke of Wellington (1769–1852)—still alive and revered as Thackeray wrote *Pendennis*.

2 *his Royal Highness the Duke of York*: Frederick Augustus (1763–1827). The Duke was only recently dead at this point in the narrative (in Ch. 3 we are told that the major has asked him to intercede on 16-year-old Pen's behalf). From later references in the text we gather that the major served under the Duke (as commander-in-chief of the army, 1798–1809) in the unsuccessful Walcheren campaign. The Duke was subsequently dismissed in 1809 for sexual delinquency. It may help at this stage to sketch in the major's military career, as it emerges in the later narrative. He was sent out to India as a 'penniless lieutenant' at some point in the 1790s and rose to be secretary to the Viceroy, 'Lord Buckley' (i.e. Wellesley). Around 1806, the major returned to England by the Cape of Good Hope. He served on the Walcheren campaign, 1809–10, and then retired on half

pay. According to Gordon Ray, Major Pendennis is based on Lt.-Colonel Merrick Shawe, Thackeray's uncle by marriage, whose military career exactly parallels that outlined above.

2 *the Marquis of Steyne*: the lecherous would-be seducer of Becky Sharp in *Vanity Fair*. Steyne was based on the third Marquis of Hertford (1777–1842).

4 *Theatres Royal Drury Lane and Crow Street*: Crow Street is in Dublin.

with Richard II. in Ireland: 1399. An unlucky campaign from which the King was brought back to try, unsuccessfully, to put down rebellion at home. Thackeray slyly associates both Major Pendennis and the Pendennis ancestors with inglorious military operations (such as the Walcheren expedition).

5 *qui mores . . . et urbes*: one of the many allusions to Horace in *Pendennis*. Here the tag is from the *Art of Poetry*, 142, and alludes to Odysseus having seen the ways of many peoples.

6 VIGNETTE: Harden points out that the design alludes to a picture by Francis Cotes of Queen Charlotte holding up a finger to protect the slumbers of the infant asleep in her lap, later to become George IV (one of Thackeray's *bêtes noires*). The barely visible picture in the background depicts the Good Samaritan.

George the Magnificent: Prince Regent from 1811 to 1820.

Windsor soap: a familiar brand of toilet soap which apparently came into general use in the mid-1820s. The allusion carries on the line of oblique allusion to George IV (who built the modern Windsor Castle) and stresses John Pendennis's inherent snobbery.

7 *Oxbridge*: as the historian of slang Eric Partridge records, this term was 'coined by Thackeray in *Pendennis*, and revived by Virginia Woolf in the 1920s, but not popularised until the 1950s'.

8 *before the war was over; before George the Magnificent came to the throne*: the Napoleonic war finished in 1815 with Waterloo. George IV assumed the throne in 1820.

as Sterne's officer called for his sword: from 'The Sword' narrative in the 'Rennes' chapter of Sterne's *Sentimental Journey* (1768). It tells the touching story of a marquis who entrusts

his sword to the authorities while for twenty years he labours in commerce. Enriched, he is able to 'reclaim his nobility and to support it'. The fable touched Thackeray who was also obliged to go into trade (journalism) in order to re-establish himself as a gentleman.

Bareacres . . . Copenhagen: 'Bareacres' was one of Thackeray's favourite comic names for aristocrats with poor estates ('Thistlewood', Helen's maiden name, reiterates the point). Probably Thackeray does not want us to recall the extremely dislikeable Countess of Bareacres whom Becky Sharp bests in the horse-trading episode in Brussels in *Vanity Fair*. The Battle of Copenhagen continues the line of ignominious military campaigns. In 1801 the British, quite gratuitously, bombarded Copenhagen and destroyed its fleet.

10 *M.R.C.S.*: a member of the Royal College of Surgeons. By the Apothecaries Act of 1815, druggists (like 'Dr.' Pendennis) were no longer able to attend the sick without the assistance of a qualified surgeon. Having made his money, John Pendennis leaves the profession around 1817–18.

12 *Robinson Crusoe, or Peter Wilkins, or the Seven Champions of Christendom*: typical boy's reading matter of the period. *The Seven Champions* (1597) by Richard Johnson, was a chivalric romance which influenced Spenser. *Peter Wilkins* (1751), was an imitation of Defoe's *Robinson Crusoe*. It is noteworthy that Helen Pendennis has not yet developed her fanatic evangelicalism, to judge by the books she allows her son.

13 *Fairoaks*: taken to be Larkbeare, the house in Devon owned by Thackeray's parents from 1825. Clavering is taken to be the nearby village of Ottery St Mary. The church, based on Exeter Cathedral, figures in the background of a number of illustrations, notably 'Calm Summer Evenings'. But, as Nicholas Pickwoad points out, the landscape 'bears no resemblance to the actual geographical relationship between Larkbeare and Ottery St Mary'. Other local identifications which can be made are Clavering Park (Escot Park), Chatteris (Exeter), the Brawl (the River Otter).

thine this universal frame: from the morning hymn, uttered by Adam and Eve in Eden, Milton's *Paradise Lost*, v. 153–4.

19 *Grey Friars School*: elsewhere in Thackeray's writing 'Slaughter House' or 'Smiffle'—i.e. Charterhouse, where he was at school 1822–8 (rather longer than Pen). The site of

Charterhouse (by Smithfields slaughterhouse in London) was originally a Carthusian monastery, hence the name and the generic term 'Cistercians' for pupils. As G. N. Ray points out, the 'Doctor' whom we encounter on the next page was based on the school's classics master, Dr Russell. Thackeray believed Russell was brutal and singled him out unfairly ('on every possible occasion he shouts out reproaches against me', Thackeray told his mother in his last year at school).

19 (980) *than Mr. Wakley*: a *Punch* joke. Thomas Wakley, (1795–1862), was the coroner of West Middlesex, and a *Punch* butt on account what they took to be his insensitive judgements from the bench.

25 *storgè*: parental love (from the Greek).

26 *nec tenui penna*: an allusion to Horace, *Odes*, 2. 20. 1–2, 'on no ordinary wing shall I rise', pompous but expressive of the Pendennis desire to rise in the world.

27 VIGNETTE: Joan Stevens assumes this is a caricature of John Goldsworthy, a family servant. But as Gordon Ray points out, Goldsworthy died in 1845. It looks to me as if Thackeray has adapted a *Punch* cartoon of the Prime Minister Lord John Russell who was much cartooned in the magazine, 1848–9, sometimes as a servant.

reddish hue: Richard Altick points out how much the Victorians disliked red hair, and distrusted it as denoting moral ugliness (*PP* 321–9). Pen's reddish hair surrounds him with an aura of ambiguity. The Victorian prejudice against red hair comes up in a number of places in *Pendennis*.

30 *Pen's mare, Rebecca*: from Scott's *Ivanhoe* (1819), where the hero is torn between two opposite women, the fair Saxon Rowena and the dark Jewess Rebecca. The detail is predictive of the later plot of *Pendennis*. Thackeray often thought of *Ivanhoe* while writing this novel, and did a 'continuation' of Scott's tale for his 1849 Christmas Book.

Zuleika, I am not thy brother: a famous line from Byron's narrative poem, *The Bride of Abydos*, where the hero Selim reveals (in his grotto) that he is not the heroine's brother, but her cousin. He asks her to be his, but tragedy intervenes. The allusion is interesting both as a predictive detail, and as an early indication of the problems which will arise from the semi-incestous relationship of Pen and his 'sister'

Laura. 'Sworn fire worshipper and a Corsair' alludes to Thomas Moore's *Lalla Rookh* (1817) and Byron's *The Corsair* (1814). Pen's romanticism is already firmly established.

31 *Bishop Heber . . . Mrs. Hemans . . . The Christian Year*: Helen's reading is going in an ominously opposite direction to that of her Byron-mad son. Reginald Heber (1783–1826) and Mrs Felicia Hemans (1793–1835) wrote hymns and pious poetry, respectively. John Keble's (1792–1866) immensely popular collection of devotional verse, *The Living Year*, appeared in 1827.

Poet's Corner . . . emancipating the Roman Catholics: young Thackeray contributed poems to the local newspaper, *Flindell's Western Luminary*, in winter 1828 at the height of the furore over Catholic Emancipation. Like his parents, he was strongly opposed to the measure.

35 *St. Vincent's, or Fourth of June House*: an allusion to Nelson's victory at Cape St Vincent (14 Feb. 1797). 'Fourth of June House' commemorates the Royal Birthday of George III. It became the occasion for national rejoicing (particularly by Tories) on the King's fiftieth Jubilee, 1809. It will be evident to the reader how consistently witty the names of Thackeray's minor characters are (a practice that he honed in his comic writing for *Punch*). 'Backboards' were devices inflicted on young 19th-century ladies to train them in upright deportment (the unfortunate admiral evidently has no sons on whom to bestow his nautical discipline). Glanders (see the half-pay cavalry captain mentioned in the next sentence) is a horse disease.

36 *Mr. Foker*: usually taken to be based on Andrew Arcedeckne, a rather 'low' club associate of Thackeray's who has survived to posterity only through such jests as that directed to Thackeray after his debut as a lecturer, in May 1851: 'you ought to ha 'ad a pianner'. According to Lewis Melville, Arcedeckne's nickname among his club associates was 'Phoca' (i.e. seal) which would explain the vaguely indecent name Thackeray bestows on his character. Ray describes Arcedeckne as an 'indescribably grotesque personage . . . the son of a West Indian barrister, living as a country squire on a small Suffolk estate. An assiduous hanger-on of the theatres, he fancied himself as a low comedian' (*AW* 274–5). According to Ray, Arcedeckne did not resent the portraiture of himself as Foker. Other

accounts suggest that he blackballed the novelist at the Traveller's Club in 1856, and there is a record in Henry Silver's diary of Thackeray's snubbing Arcedeckne at a *Punch* dinner, 1862.

37 *fearful dreams*: Thackeray evidently experienced this dream himself, and refers to it elsewhere in his writing (see *Vanity Fair*, ch. 2). There is some reason to believe his schooldays were marred by the routine sadism of schoolmasters. This is reflected in the flagellatory names he gives schools in his writing: 'Slaughterhouse', or 'Dr Birch's Academy' located in 'Rodwell Regis'. Boys had also to put up with the violence and sexual predatoriness of fellow pupils. At Charterhouse Thackeray (who was remembered as 'a pretty, gentle, and rather timid boy') had his nose broken (and his looks disfigured for life) by George Stovin Venables (generally taken to be the original of Warrington in *Pendennis*). At the *Punch* table, Thackeray recalled that the first thing said to him on his arrival at the school was an instruction from another boy to come to the 'bog' and 'frig me'. It is a significant detail that in *Pendennis*, the young hero is rescued from school at a relatively early age—something that Thackeray may have wished had happened to him.

40 *The Stranger*: Benjamin Thompson's immensely popular English translation of August von Kotzebue's *Menschenhass und Reue* ('Misanthropy and Repentance', 1790). The play is set in the country (which is why it is high on Bingley's repertoire for Clavering). The heroine is Mrs Haller, a mysterious, beautiful, and charitable lady. There is an even more mysterious 'stranger' in the district. A Countess arrives with her brother, who falls in love with Mrs Haller. But it emerges that she is in fact the wife of the mysterious (and aristocratic) stranger, and a reconciliation is contrived.

43 VIGNETTE: the opening scene of Thompson's play, showing the Stranger and his servant Francis in conversation.

44 *Cooke . . . Mr. Quin*: Thackeray had a lifelong passion for the theatre which he cultivated in his youth not (like Pen) in the country but on his early visits to Paris and Germany. The allusion here is to: (1) Thomas Potter Cooke (1786–1864), a popular actor in melodrama, famous for his role as the hero William in Douglas Jerrold's *Black-eyed Susan* (1829); (2) James Quin (1693–1766), Garrick's Irish rival.

(981) *the great X.*: this vague and oddly spiteful allusion is probably to the Irish comic actor Charles Matthews, who in 1847 took over the Lyceum Theatre as the setting for his own starring performances. Thackeray was not fond of Matthews. He had written the greater part of a comedy for him in 1840 and was convinced that the actor did not even take the trouble to read the MS before rejecting it.

49 *The Bravo of the Battle-Axe*: the double or triple bill was normal practice in 19th-century theatre, frequently varying tragic melodrama with farce, or musical entertainment. Not all the audience would sit through the whole programme.

54 VIGNETTE: Canute, vainly attempting to turn back the waves. The same motif was used in *Punch* at this period, and the design strongly recalls the pictorial style of the magazine.

58 *the Siddons, sir, and the O'Nale*: (1) Sarah Siddons (1755–1831), who gave her farewell appearance as Lady Macbeth in 1812; (2) Eliza O'Neill (1791–1872) was an Irish actress, sometimes taken as the original for Emily. Having entranced him by her performances in tragedy, O'Neill married William Becher MP in 1819 and subsequently became Lady Eliza Becher.

60 *Duke of Kent*: the Duke, Queen Victoria's father (1767–1820), was Governor of Gibraltar, 1802–3.

63 *the Columbine*: one of many references in *Pendennis* to English pantomime adaptations of *commedia dell'arte*. Columbine is the daughter of Pantaloon and the lover of Harlequin. Costigan is, in his leanness and *braggadocio*, a version of Pantaloon. 'Falkland' and 'Julia' referred to a few sentences later are characters in the subplot of Sheridan's *The Rivals*.

65 *killed by Sand, too!*: Kotzebue was stabbed to death by Karl Ludwig Sand, a theology student, in 1819. Sand was infuriated by Kotzebue's anti-nationalist activities. The outrage led to repressive measures (the 'Karlsbad decrees') by Metternich. Emily does not even know that Kotzebue (not the English translator, Benjamin Thompson) was the author of the play in which she stars. Nor, of course, does she understand Pen's references to Goethe. Later in the chapter, the point is made that she does not know the difference between Dr Johnson (author of the tragedy *Irene*) and Ben Jonson.

69 VIGNETTE: Nicholas Pickwoad points to the fineness of the engraving (here signed by François Pierdon). The Watteauesque design is the first of many such 18th-century motifs in *Pendennis*.

73 *he began to teach her how to act*: *Pendennis* was a remarkably influential novel in terms of giving a younger generation of Victorian novelists inspiration. In this very minor underplot, Thackeray gave George Du Maurier the *donnée* for *Trilby* (1894)—although Bows is considerably more sympathetic than Svengali. Du Maurier knew Thackeray's work intimately, having been commissioned to illustrate his novels in the 1860s.

75 *Black-Eyed Susan*: see notes to pp. 44, 49.

79 *or is written in chapters*: a pun. One of the secondary meanings of 'chapter' is a gathering of Cathedral canons. Unlike Tom Hood, Theodore Hook ('Tom Wagg' in *Pendennis*), and Douglas Jerrold, Thackeray did not frequently employ puns in his comic writing (although 19th-century readers loved them). He may have thought them a rather low and primitive form of humour (see, for instance, the contemptuous description of Wagg's laboured punning in Ch. 34).

83 *Lord Hill's*: Rowland Hill, the first Viscount Hill (1772–1842). Hill was a general in the Peninsular campaign. Costigan presumably fought with him at Talavera. Major Pendennis's career was largely restricted to service in India—although we later learn that the two warriors' paths did cross at Walcheren.

87 *like Montrose*: James Graham (1612–50), the first Marquis of Montrose. A royalist general, Graham wrote the much anthologized 'My dear and only love' (said to be written on his prison window, the night before his execution) which contains the lines 'I'll make thee glorious by my pen, | And famous by my sword'.

88 *the Loves of the Angels . . . Béranger*: 'The Loves of the Angels' (1823), by Thomas Moore, tells of the loves of three fallen angels for mortal women. The poem provoked criticism of its irreligious themes. Thackeray had a particular affection for Pierre de Jean Béranger (1780–1857), and did a handful of imitations of the other poet's chansons including one of his best known poems, 'Le Roi d'Yvetot'.

92 *Lord Buckley, when commander-in-chief*: As Gordon Ray supposes (*BL* 58), Thackeray alludes to Arthur Wellesley (later the Duke of Wellington) who was commander of military forces in India (1797–1805), the period when Major Pendennis was a junior officer in the subcontinent. Although he was something of a protégé, the major did not follow his commander to the Peninsular campaign. As Ray plausibly surmises, Major Pendennis was closely drawn from Thackeray's relative, Lt.-Colonel Merrick Shawe, who was an aide-de-camp and secretary to Wellesley in India.

97 *Governor Crawley's time*: in *Vanity Fair*, after discovering his wife's misconduct with the Marquis of Steyne, Rawdon Crawley goes off to be Governor of Coventry Island—a plague spot in the Caribbean. The dates don't quite fit, since the episode in *Vanity Fair* occurs around 1830 and Bell takes up the island chaplaincy some ten years earlier. The oblique references to *Vanity Fair* with which *Pendennis* abounds reflect the fact that reprints of the novel (which came out in book form in July 1848) were still selling strongly.

98 *sending his little girl home to Helen Pendennis*: Thackeray is clearly thinking of the situation of his cousin (and adoptive sister) Mary Graham (1815–71), who was orphaned and left to the care of Mrs Carmichael-Smyth in 1826.

103 *Pumpernickel*: Weimar, an independent duchy, enjoying full diplomatic status. The climactic scenes of *Vanity Fair* are set in Pumpernickel, around 1830 (Thackeray spent a winter in Weimar, 1830–1).

105 *O Moses and Green Spectacles!*: an allusion to Goldsmith's *The Vicar of Wakefield* where Dr Primrose's son Moses sells the family's horse—their only asset—and promptly spends the money on a gross of green spectacles.

Mr. Stultz: London tailor, 10 Clifford Street, founded 1809. Stultz dominated London men's fashion and figures in much 19th-century fiction (notably, Bulwer's *Pelham*). With its echo of 'stolz' ('proud') it is, as Richard Altick notes, 'the sort of off-name that Thackeray so often licensed himself to invent' (*PP* 275).

106 *Ella Rosenberg*: by James Kenney, 1807. The action is set in Prussia and has as its main action the heroic resistance

of a virtuous wife against a ruthless seducer, Colonel Mountfort.

107 *his name in the Morning Post*: Thackeray had been in the forefront of a mid-1840s *Punch* campaign satirizing the *Morning Post*'s policy of listing (as 'news') the names of distinguished people attending London parties and entertainments. It reached a comic climax in 1847 when—in revenge—the paper omitted the now-famous Thackeray's name from their lists.

108 *ratting*: the verb had a particular political meaning in the 19th century, meaning to desert one's party (here, for ministerial bribes). As usual, there is meaningful undercurrent in Thackeray's names: Lord Hobanob wants to hobnob with political grandees, Mr Suckling is given to sucking up, and Admiral Bowser is fond of the bottle.

114 *Article XL*: the Thirty-nine Articles, or 'Articles of Belief' to which those taking orders in the Church of England must subscribe, were currently (in 1849) a burning religious issue. Newman's difficulties with Anglicanism began with his inability to subscribe to the Thirty-nine Articles and led to his famous *Tract XC* (1841) and his going across four years later to Rome.

117 (984) *readin' for my little-go during the Long*: i.e. he is cramming, or studying, for the first part of his degree examination during the Long (summer) Vacation.

ILLUSTRATION: Thackeray shows Sir Derby Oaks in a shell jacket, a narrow-fitting tunic. There was a huge controversy over this article of military dress in 1848–9, when it was reintroduced as compulsory. *Punch* had many jokes and cartoons about 'stout' warriors popping out of their jackets (we later learn that Derby Oaks 'rides sixteen stone', although he does not look so large in the illustrations). Foker is dressed here in a frock coat which is anachronistic for 1829. Sir Derby Oaks's name leaves little doubt as to how the fortune amassed by his physician father will be squandered.

118 *downy*: as Eric Partridge notes, 'an artful fellow'. The slang term became current in the 1820s.

No Irish need apply: this remark, which was routinely attached to newspaper advertisements for servants, landed Thackeray in considerable trouble. An Irishman having

Pendennis read out to him by one of his children was provoked by the remark (and the derogatory portrait of Captain Costigan) into writing a vituperative anonymous letter abusing Thackeray in grossly personal terms. Thackeray, in turn, was provoked into drafting a violent retort to be published in *Punch*. But evidently he cooled off, and never completed it. Thackeray's reply purported to be written to one of his correspondent's children ('my little friend'). 'As I do not know who he is,' Thackeray wrote, 'of course I cannot be angry with your dear Papa. If I had the happiness to know him (and I am sure he must be a most intelligent and refined person) I should say: Why my dear Sir should you take the trouble to write me your surmises as to whether I was or was not a gentleman?' In the MS of Thackeray's incomplete letter (held in the New York Public Library) there is much more of the same sarcasm. Following on the 'Elias Howle' attack by Lever in *Roland Cashel* a few weeks earlier (see note to p. 400) Thackeray felt threatened on all sides by the Irish. It must surely have soured his depiction of the Costigans (and the Irish generally) in the numbers that followed.

124 VIGNETTE: according to Harden an illustration of the Battle of Fontenoy (1745), 'where the English and the French politely offered each other the opportunity of opening fire'. According to Joan Stevens it shows George II at Dettingen.

125 *Sir Richard Strachan's table at Walcheren*: this detail fills in a little more of the major's military career. Sir Richard Strachan was the naval commander at the ill-fated Walcheren expedition, 1809, designed to blockade the enemy fleet off the coast of Belgium.

126 *Mrs. Jordan in her best time . . . Mars*: (1) Dorothy Jordan (1762–1816) was an Irish actress and a mistress of the Duke of Clarence, later William IV; (2) 'Mars' was the stage name of the French actress Anne-Françoise-Hippolyte Boutet (1779–1847). Thackeray saw and admired Mars on his first trip to Paris, 1829.

134 VIGNETTE: the major appears as a perverse Cupid, with a reverse bow (cunningly forming the initial 'e') destroying love. The balletic garb and posture suggest the nimbleness with which the major is carrying out his campaign.

136 *Bob Acres . . . Sir Lucius O'Trigger*: from Sheridan's *The Rivals*, v. iii. The Irish were traditionally notorious for their duelling propensities (the point is made that Costigan has actually killed men in Ireland). There was a successful campaign against the practice, led by Prince Albert, in the 1840s. Thackeray contributed to the anti-duelling movement with his depiction of the Irish bully, Barry Lyndon, in 1844.

143 VIGNETTE: a puzzling illustration, showing an Italian desperado assassinating an artist (the massive 'M' suggests 'murder'). Perhaps Sand's stabbing of Kotzebue is recalled. It may be also that Thackeray is alluding to some critical remarks about his illustrations in the reviews of the early numbers of the novel. The picture of the artist has some resemblance to Thackeray's appearance as a young man (spectacles were his trademark as an illustrator).

152 *Pizarro . . . Cora*: the allusion is to R. B. Sheridan's *Pizarro* (1799), taken from Kotzebue's *Die Spanier in Peru*. The play (which had a special significance for Irish dramatists like Sheridan, and Irish actors like the Costigans) deals with the conquistadores' genocide in Peru. Elvira, disgusted by Pizarro's bloody extermination of the natives, turns against him, and aids Alonzo (the saviour of Peru) and his wife Cora. In the scene illustrated on p. 157 (and alluded to again on p. 975) the faithful Rolla has rescued Alonzo and Cora's child by destroying a narrow bridge across a cataract. He expires in Alonzo's arms. Pizarro has been slain in combat by Alonzo.

159 *he should appear in the Gazette*: i.e. the bankruptcy lists. Mr Dolphin is usually taken to be a rather spiteful caricature of Alfred Bunn (1796–1860), the proprietor of Drury Lane and a favourite *Punch* butt (Thackeray derides him in the 'Before the Curtain' preface to *Vanity Fair*). Bunn had tried to mend his fortunes with spectacular stagings including live animals (see Herr Garbage's lions and tigers above—although that specific reference is clearly to Isaac Van Amburgh who, at Drury Lane in Jan. 1839, became the first lion-tamer to mix different species of cat; Amburgh was another favourite *Punch* butt). Bunn was declared bankrupt in 1840, and was forced out of theatrical business again in 1848. Dolphin also seems to take on something of Louis Jullien (1812–60) whose *concerts monstres* were a pro-

minent feature of the theatrical season in 1848–9. Jullien too was satirized in *Punch*. He pioneered the late 1840s fashion for 'burlettas' ('lyrical dramas') and in 1848 introduced, to huge success, the Italian tenor Sims Reeves, here 'Monsieur Poumons'.

Wenham . . . Wagg: generally taken to be (1) John Wilson Croker (1780–1857), Tory politician and factotum for the Marquis of Hertford ('Steyne') and (2) Theodore Hook (1788–1841), humorist and Tory journalist. Thackeray's dislike was in line with *Punch* political principles. Wenham and Wagg appear on the fringes of several of his novels.

161 *Georges in her best days*: Mlle George, stage name of Marguerite-Josephine Weimer (1787–1867). As Donald Hawes points out, she was famous for her tragic roles, and Thackeray mentions having seen her act many times in 'French Dramas and Melodramas' in the *Paris Sketch-Book* (1840). Steyne has a weakness for actresses, alluded to several times in *Vanity Fair*.

162 *swearing and cursing*: Bunn was notoriously violent, and was prosecuted by William Macready for assault in 1836.

165 VIGNETTE: the Bohemian-looking warrior on guard at the battlement alludes to the Austrian siege of the Hungarian town of Komarom, which lasted from Oct. 1848 until Sept. 1849.

166 (986) *the massacre of Wyoming, and the brilliant actions of Saint-Lucie*: the major evidently improved his shining hours by reading the *Annual Register* for 1778. In that year there occurred the massacre by American Indians of whites at Wyoming and the successful British action to recover the island of Santa Lucia from the French.

168 *Mr. Stanfield or Mr. Roberts, for their next tour*: (1) the artist Clarkson Stanfield (1793–1867) and (2) David Roberts (1796–1864). Both specialized in landscapes and Roberts was famous for his paintings recording his travels to Europe, Syria, and the Holy Land.

170 *the very Ebenezer*: a term used by Methodists and Baptists for their meeting houses.

184 *infinite isolations . . . some fellow-islands a little more or less near to us*: Saintsbury, in his (1908) introduction to *Pendennis*, notes that this phrase strikingly anticipates Matthew

Arnold's poem 'the second *Isolation*' ('Yes: in the sea of life enisl'd'). Analogues can be found elsewhere in the poetry of Clough. For a discussion of these connections, see Kathleen Tillotson's article on the subject in the *Review of English Studies* (Oct. 1952), 346–64.

187 *Madame Fribsby shook her Madonna front . . . more en Espang*: Harden explains the 'front' as hair drawn forward on each side of the face, after the madonna in Italian painting. One of the mysteries in the narrative, which is sustained until the last number, is how and when Madame Fribsby became attached to a 'French carbineer in a green coat'. Perhaps she served an apprenticeship as a milliner in Paris.

191 *Sheridan drink five bottles at Brookes's*: Richard Brinsley Sheridan (1751–1816), the dramatist and politician, was a famously convivial member of Brooks's (sic) Club in London.

Nunc vino: another Horatian quotation, *Odes*, 1. 7. 31–2: 'begone care, tomorrow we set out on the ocean'.

the drinking song out of Der Freischütz: Carl Weber's 1821 opera.

198 *in garrison, at Gibraltar, and at Malta, and had been at the taking of Flushing*: one can construct a sizeable section of the Captain's career. He served at Gibraltar 1799–1803 (when he formed his relationship with the Duke of Kent, who was Governor of the Rock), he served in the British recapture of Malta (1798–1800), and he served in raids from Walcheren on to Belgian soil in 1809. Other references in the text suggest he also served in the Peninsular campaign.

The Duke of York was a patron of the Drama: Frederick Augustus (1763–1827), the second son of George II, was indeed a lover of the drama—or at least of actresses. He was forced to resign as commander-in-chief of the British Army in 1809 because of the misconduct of his actress-mistress, Mary Anne Clarke.

The Shan Van Voght: a revolutionary song of 1798, revived in the Irish uprising of 1848. The refrain is, 'Yes, Ireland shall be free.' It casts Costigan in a slightly less amiable light.

199 *tracasseries*: small quarrels, spats.

200 *a brief visit to the old University of Oxbridge*: this is the first chapter of the Apr. number, written in late March.

Thackeray had made a trip to Cambridge on 12–13 Mar. 1849, presumably to research this number and refresh memories of his own university time, twenty years before. He had breakfast with some university blades and 'walked about in haunts once familiar', making himself 'bitterly melancholious' (*Letters*, ii. 509–10). It was not a happy experience. As he wrote to a relative, on 14 Mar., 'The young men would'nt talk to me, the Dons thought I had come to put them into a book, everybody suspected me: and I felt myself so miserable that I thought the best course was to fly. I rushed away in a perfect panic by the 2 o'clock train.' On this journey back he evidently met the 'young friend' mentioned here. The 'Oxbridge' chapters are something of a let down, and presumably reflect Thackeray's dispiriting visit. Thackeray had used 'St Boniface' as a pseudonym for his own college, Trinity, in *The Snobs of England*. But in *Pendennis* he masks Cambridge by the neologisms 'Oxbridge', 'Camford', etc.

201 *a hansom cab*: a precise historical (i.e. 1849) detail. There were no hansoms in Pen's day (he would have had to take a hackney cab when he came up to London). The hansom cab was introduced in 1834 by Joseph Aloysius Hansom (see *PP* 368). So too the carpet-bag is an 1840s detail, as is the commercial traveller's cigar.

202 *Foker's Entire*: 'entire' refers to unadulterated porter. The term came into use early in the century and was universal in advertisements for beer by the end of the 1840s. *Punch* punned on the term frequently.

206 *Roubilliac's statue*: as Harden points out, Trinity College Cambridge (Thackeray's old college) has two prominent works by this French sculptor. But Thackeray is careful to avoid too close an identification.

207 *a gentleman-pensioner's set*: i.e. an undergraduate paying his own way. 'Fellow-commoners' like Foker (see Ch. 5) enjoyed more privileges, 'servitors' less. Thackeray satirizes the class system among undergraduates in *The Snobs of England*.

209 *Doctor Donne*: not the metaphysical poet, but a play on 'don'.

the battle of whose life: a reference to Dickens's 1846 Christmas Book, *The Battle of Life*. The other novelist's new serial,

David Copperfield, was about to start next month, May 1849. Thackeray may have been slightly anxious.

211 VIGNETTE: a siren, or mermaid, profferring a wine goblet. This is the first of a complex series of water-spirit images in *Pendennis*.

212 *straps to their trousers*: dandies affected straps going under the soles of their shoes, so that the trouser came almost to the ground, covering the footwear. These unfashionable and hardworking undergraduates wear sensible 'highlows'. The curriculum in Pen's (Thackeray's) day is described by Gordon Ray: 'it consisted chiefly of mathematics, "the peculiar honour and glory of the university", though some attention was paid to classics and moral philosophy. Since the college measured the success of its instruction in terms of the positions attained by its students in the university's honours examination, principal emphasis was placed on the training of "reading men". If these industrious youths succeeded in the narrow but rigorous intellectual exercises set them, they gained prestige and substantial preferment. Most undergraduates, feeling themselves unequal to so exacting a routine, were content to take pass degrees' (*UA* 117). Ray's account of Thackeray's rather dismal undergraduate career should be read fully to appreciate the Oxbridge chapters of *Pendennis*.

214 *Fudson*: i.e. Joseph Hudson, tobacconist to the Royal family, 132 Oxford Street. Hudson specialized in 'Cubas' (i.e. Havanas). Byron's lines on the custom of smoking appear in *The Island* (1823), 'Sublime tobacco! which from east to west | Cheers the tar's labour or the Turkman's rest.' Smoking plays an important part in the cultural background to this and subsequent parts of the narrative. During the Victorian period, middle-class gentlemen despised the pipe as irredeemably working-class (it is a sign of his bohemianism that Pen's friend Warrington smokes a workman's pipe, later in the narrative). Cigars were introduced into England around the time of the Peninsular Wars (hence their Spanish character). In the 1830s, cigar-smoking was a practice associated with dandyish young men and vulgarians (it is significant that Major Pendennis, as a well-bred gentleman of an earlier vintage, cannot stand smoking). Cigarettes began to appear in the late 1850s, brought back from the Crimean war, after *Pendennis* had

run its course. For a thorough discussion of the 'Favourite Vice of the Nineteenth Century' see ch. 8 of Altick's *The Presence of the Present*.

215 *Paul de Kock*: a mildly indecent French novelist (1794–1871). According to the *Oxford Companion to French Literature* his works were written 'with an untiring comic vigour which made up for their complete lack of style, they were also good pictures of the life and amusements of the people in Paris and the country *c.*1825–48'.

217 *Stranges . . . Wilkies*: (1) Sir Robert Strange (1721–92) who made engravings from paintings by old masters; (2) Sir David Wilkie (1785–1845). As Harden points out, 'before the letter' means 'before lettering was added to entitle the etched images'.

219 *Raphael-Morghens, and Landseer proofs . . . Aldine editions . . . Missals of the sixteenth century*: Thackeray summarizes the cultivated tastes of a student like himself in the late 1820s. Raphael Morghen (1758–1833) was an Italian engraver. Edwin Landseer (1802–73) was a 'modern' artist, proofs of whose prints could still be had cheap.

Bell's Life: *Bell's Life in London* was the sporting paper of the age, concerned with the turf, regattas, prize fights, games of chance, etc. (*AP* 109).

220 *a few lustres*: a lustre, or *lustrum*, is a period of five years.

221 *with Tancred and Godfrey*: an allusion to Tasso's epic poem of the first crusade *Jerusalem Delivered* (1580). Godfrey is the crusaders' leader, Tancred the Norman, another hero. The text may have been put in Thackeray's mind by the last part of Disraeli's much-publicized 'Young England' trilogy, *Tancred or the New Crusade* (1847).

one of the brilliant orators of his day: wish fulfilment. As Gordon Ray records, Thackeray's attempts to 'spout at the union' (on the same republican–radical themes as Pen) were a wretched failure (see *UA* 118).

224 *Diversions of Purley*: a pun. To 'come a purler [or cropper]' is to crash. *The Diversions of Purley* (1786, 1798) was a philological treatise by John Horne Tooke that a well-read undergraduate like Pen (though not Foker) would have come across.

225 *two ponies*: a pony is racing slang for £25.

227 (994) *Horace Bloundell*: according to Gordon Ray, Bloundell was based on a well-known university rake of Thackeray's time, Harry Matthew. The son of a Somersetshire minister, Matthew went to Oxford (here 'Camford') and was obliged to leave in 1825. After a year at Trinity College, Cambridge, he was again obliged to shift colleges, to Sidney Sussex. There he remained, a perpetual student, until 1832 (see *UA* 135–7). Although his friends warned him against Matthew (as Foker warns Pen) Thackeray idolized him. It is possible that Matthew introduced Thackeray to the gambling addiction that was nearly to ruin him.

a more respectable man than my friend, Lord Martingale, never sat in a saddle: as Harden points out, a double-edged name. A martingale primarily indicates part of the reins used to control a horse, but a secondary meaning is a doubling system in gambling, sure to lead to ruin.

231 *Robert the Devil*: appropriate (see the chapter's opening vignette) but slightly anachronistic. The opera by Meyerbeer was first performed in 1831, but was not current in England until some time later.

233 *Don Giovanni and Taglioni*: (1) Mozart's opera; (2) Maria Taglioni, the opera dancer by whom Thackeray was entranced on his first visit to Paris, in July 1829. She was famous in the title part of *La Sylphide* which becomes a thematic allusion in *Pendennis*. Although later the narrator says that Pendennis has undertaken some 'larks' in Paris as a young man, it is not clear when his expeditions to France are supposed to have taken place.

239 VIGNETTE: a Roman flying the field of battle, where he has been defeated. The expression on the warrior's face suggests one of the many depictions of Cain fleeing from the body of Abel, although the implication is that Pen's flight from Oxbridge is unmanly and, as his uncle tells him, he is showing the white feather. Thackeray himself left Cambridge ignominiously, without a degree.

240 *like Joe Miller's friend*: a favourite jest of Thackeray's, from *Joe Miller's Jests* (1739) a much-reprinted anthology of jokes.

241 *Camisis*: like Camford and Oxbridge, a sandwich word combining the rivers (Cam and Isis) which run through the two university towns.

244 *Delcroix's shop*: as Harden and Hawes point out, an actual West End perfumier. Other shops and establishments mentioned in this chapter (e.g. Ackermann's print shop and the Bull and Mouth public house) are also actual. Thackeray's memory for peripheral detail seems so keen that one wonders whether he is recollecting his own unhappy return from Cambridge without a degree at the end of the Easter term 1830.

248 VIGNETTE: the little boy is wearing a dunce's cap.

249 *at the age of sixteen years*: Laura should be 13–14, given the comment on p. 36 that there is eight years difference between her and Pen. Thackeray is evidently reverting to the actual age difference between himself and Mary Graham.

257 *the Spanish legion*: during Thackeray's time at Trinity there was a strong sentiment in favour of the exiled Spanish Constitutionalists. Their leader, Jose Torrijos, visited the College in 1828. Thackeray's friend and near contemporary at Trinity, Alfred Tennyson, undertook (in company with Arthur Hallam) a daring mission to the Pyrenees in 1830 to deliver money to the Constitutionalists (for the rest of his life, Tennyson affected a Spanish cape and hat as his favourite garb).

258 VIGNETTE: the child is getting progressively younger, suggesting the cramping conditions of his home as Pen, now a young man, feels them.

260 *Barbarossa . . . Quashyboo . . . the poor persecuted Jesuits*: the passage is loaded with jokes. The monk's credibility is undermined by his red beard (see note to p. 27). 'Quashyboo' alludes to the philanthropic expedition in 1841 to abolish the slave-trade on the River Niger. Dickens wrote a satirical article on the subject in the *Examiner*, 19 Aug. 1848, and mocked the expedition as Mrs Jellyby's hobby-horse, 'Borrioboola Gha', in *Bleak House*. The Jesuits were, indeed, given a hard time after the July 1830 Revolution. But sympathy for the Society was scant in England in 1849, currently in the grip of an anti-Jesuit paranoia (see, for instance, Mrs Trollope's *Father Eustace; a Tale of the Jesuits*, 1847). The Revd J. Ramshorn's quixotic mission to convert the Pope of Rome to Anglicanism is the more absurd in view of Catholic aggression at the end of the 1840s and the

Vatican's expectation, following Newman's defection, that England might be about to return to the fold.

262 *the Castle of Otranto! the Mysteries of Udolpho*: gothic novels by Horace Walpole (1764) and Ann Radcliffe (1794).

Lely: Altick notes: 'Thackeray undoubtedly meant his readers to envision Lely's famous painting of Nell Gwyn as Venus, and her son, the Duke of St Albans, as Cupid' (*PP* 761). This episode, in which the servant gives a rote guide to a stately home, recycles a joke from *The Snobs of England*. Thackeray mingles real artists (such as Frans Snyders and Inigo Jones) with hilarious inventions such as 'Vanderputty'.

263 *twenty-thwee*: the baronet does not have a speech impediment. His lisp is affected; it was fashionable among dandies in the 1840s. *Punch* often satirizes the affectation.

capabilities: Strong (who is evidently a man of wide culture) quotes the famous saying of the landscape gardener, 'Capability' (Lancelot) Brown (1715–83).

266–7 *Missolonghi . . . Skrzynecki . . . Diebitsch's lines . . . Pedroites . . . Zumalacarreguy*: as Harden indicates, one can assemble the career of this soldier of fortune. He learnt his trade as a Hungarian irregular cavalryman. He was at Missolonghi, the town in Greece besieged by the Turks, where Byron died in 1824. Bozzaris attempted unsuccessfully to lift the siege with fireships in 1822. Jan Skrzynecki was a Polish general who was defeated by the Russians in 1831 (Strong seems always to fight for lost causes). Diebitsch was the opposing Russian general. Strong then fought for Dom Miguel in 1832–3, in the unsuccessful siege of Dom Pedro's forces ('the stock-jobbing Pedroites') at Oporto. Bourmont was the French general aiding Dom Miguel. Strong then drifted on to fight in the army of Zumalacarregui (1788–1835), the ruthless Spanish guerrilla commander, in the chaotic conflict over the Spanish succession. It will be noted that, even in this casually thrown-off conversational list, Thackeray carefully puts together a convincing career for his soldier of fortune. Since Zumalacarregui died in 1835 (at least four years after the present date in the narrative) some liberties have been taken with historical chronology (by reference to Pen's university career, it can only be 1831–2).

268 *Diana Vernon*: the dashing heroine of Scott's *Rob Roy* (1817). As Hawes notes, two originals have been suggested for Blanche Amory. Jane Carlyle was convinced that she was based on Theresa Reviss, the illegitimate daughter of Thackeray's friend, Charles Buller. Gordon Ray suggests Miss Reviss also inspired part of Becky Sharp's career (*UA* 502). The second candidate is 'the tarnished beauty' (as Ray calls her, *AW* 117) Miss Cecilia Gore (later Lady Thynne). As Thackeray notes in a letter to Jane Brookfield of 21 Aug. 1850, Miss Gore was proud of being thought Thackeray's dubious heroine. The name Blanche (which is self-bestowed) alludes primarily to her blonde hair, but the name was also given a recent glamour by the character of the false society beauty, Blanche Ingram, in *Jane Eyre*. Intellectually, Blanche is a disciple of George Sand and evoked in the middle-class English reader of the late 1840s the national contempt for the excesses of 'Sandism'.

270 *Monsieur Mirobolant*: Mirobolant is universally said to be a sketch of the French chef, Alexis Soyer (1809–58), who presided over the Reform Club kitchens. This identification is given authority by the *DNB*. Soyer's nationality, his culinary exoticism, and his personal dandyism make the identification plausible. But there remain some objections. Mirobolant is later shown as a hero of the Revolution of July 1830. Soyer, on his part, was forced to leave France by the Revolution. And Thackeray, to judge by a review he wrote of Soyer's *The Gastronomic Regenerator* in 1846, admired the cook. The Reform, moreover, was a club which Thackeray was regularly using at the period of writing *Pendennis*. (He addressed his 'Dignity of Literature' letter from there.) Someone as fond of his stomach as Thackeray would be unlikely to insult his own cook. Soyer, as Thackeray realized, was an admirably practical man (in 1847 he had supervised the feeding of the starving Irish population). It is hard to square this with the fantastic Mirobolant.

271 *vlower on their heeds*: i.e. floured wigs, to make them look fashionably white.

281 VIGNETTE: the dark threatening shadow should be noted.

282 *out of The Keepsake*: the *Keepsake* (1828–57) was the most famous and durable of the 'annuals'—gift-books, lavishly produced, containing a miscellany of light literary pieces

and artwork. As Hawes points out, Thackeray was a contributor to the *Keepsake* from 1849 to 1854, as a result of his friendship with its editor Lady Blessington.

283 *is called the dropsy*: Horace, *Odes*, 2. 2. 13.

283–4 *Lamartine . . . Balzac . . . George Sand . . . Indiana . . . Lelia . . . Trenmor . . . Stenio . . . Prince Rodolph and Prince Djalma . . . the rights of woman*: a catalogue which characterizes Blanche by her extravagantly romantic and 'modern' literary tastes. Lamartine (1790–1869) was a respectable poet prescribed in Blanche's early youth, the taste for whom led to less respectable reading. Balzac (1799–1850)—a novelist who clearly influenced Thackeray—would have been well embarked on his 91-strong *Comédie Humaine* (1827–47) at the supposed period of the Clavering family's arrival at Clavering Park (between 1830 and 1833, although the date is hard to fix precisely). George Sand (1804–76), the most influential figure in Blanche's literary firmament, wrote novels advocating the rights of women and the iniquities of bourgeois marriage (such as *Indiana*, 1831—which we are told Blanche read as a little girl). Lelia, Trenmor, Stenio are characters in Sand's *Lelia* (1833). The princes Rodolph and Djalma figure in Eugène Sue's *Mystères de Paris* (1842–3) and *Le Juif errant* (1844–5). The last of these literary allusions are, of course, anachronistic, if we measure the historical setting by Pen's college and subsequent career (born in 1811, he is between 22 and 23 at this point, although by strict calculation of events in his narrated life, it should be 1830). Thackeray had, for an Englishman of his background, an intimate knowledge of French literature (French critics conceive him a disciple of Balzac). He could read, write, and speak the language like a native and visited Paris regularly (several times during the course of writing *Pendennis*). But he had always distrusted the 'political' aims of much modern French literature, conceiving the novelist's role to be, instead, moral and (in a secular way) analogous to the Anglican minister's sermon. His anti-Gallicism was heightened by the Feb. 1848 Revolution which, like many cultivated Englishmen, he partly ascribed to the pernicious effect of ultra-romantic French writers (like Sand). It is noticeable that although *Pendennis* is a clearly autobiographical account of Thackeray's own youth, Pen does not travel to France, and speaks the

language poorly (although he is not aware of the fact). This ignorance is (in 1849) to his moral credit.

286 *hot Sally-Lunn cakes*: proprietary name for a traditional kind of tea cake. As John Carey points out, 'nothing mattered more to Thackeray than food—unless it was drink'. In the next few numbers of *Pendennis*, particularly, he seems even more than usually concerned with precise and mouth-watering references to comestibles.

293 *who has Oriental blood*: a significant detail which may be missed by the modern reader. Lady Clavering is the illegitimate daughter of her merchant father and a native Indian 'wife', or concubine. The novelist's own father, Richmond Thackeray, had maintained such a concubine before marrying. Thackeray had a 'black' (his term) half-sister, Sarah Redfield (Mrs James Blechynden) who died in 1841. The novelist had mixed feelings about his half-sister, and shame at the connection may explain the recurrent racism in his attitudes to Indian natives and half-castes. The taint inherited from her mother explains Blanche's (i.e. Betsy's) nervous insistence on every occasion of how 'blond' she is and the whiter than white name which she has chosen for herself.

294 VIGNETTE: Othello murdering Desdemona, put in mind, presumably, by the 'black' Lady Clavering.

295 *the Court of Directors*: of the East India Company.

296 *Rome . . . at the latter place*: earlier (see p. 259) said to be Lausanne.

304 *Undine . . . a Naiad*: *Undine* (1811) is a fairy-tale by the German, Friedrich de la Motte Fouqué. In the story Undine is a water sprite who falls in love with a knight, Huldbrand. They marry, but after his infidelity with Bertalda, Undine is forced to return to the waters of the Danube. She comes back from her element to kill Huldbrand (with a deadly kiss) as he is about to marry Bertalda. The story was made into an opera by E. T. A. Hoffmann in 1816 and by Albert Lortzing in 1848. Thackeray reviewed a Maclise picture on the Undine theme in 1844 which may have put it into his mind. The 'woman as water spirit' theme becomes very complex in *Pendennis*, as Blanche and Laura are variously conceived as dangerous sirens and mermaids, or benign

naiads or Undines. The motif is further complicated by the introduction of 'woman as air spirit', or sylph.

312 *Caleb Balderstone*: the tediously faithful butler in Scott's *The Bride of Lammermoor*. Thackeray was evidently steeping himself in the other novelist in preparation for his next Christmas Book, the continuation of *Ivanhoe*.

313 *drink tea at six*: the point here seems to be that the genteel upper classes in town (whose afternoons were unemployed) would take tea around three. In the country, and among the working classes, tea was taken later, when the day's work was done. For these hungry workers, tea would be accompanied by a substantial intake of food (for manual workers, tea and dinner would be one and the same thing). The episode here is complicated by the caption Thackeray devised for the full-plate illustration, 'A morning visit at tea-time'. Since these are the last pages in the last chapter of the number, and the illustration would have had to be done early in the month, before the episode was written up, it is conceivable that Thackeray originally had a more elaborate scene in mind. Otherwise, it is hard to make sense of the caption.

314 *Mrs. Mee*: i.e. by Anne Mee (1775–1851), a miniature painter.

321 *la croix de Juillet*: the Croix was awarded in 1830 to heroes of the 'Revolution' which forced the abdication of Charles X and made possible the accession of Louis Philippe. The mockery here would have had extra point for the reader of 1849 since, in 1848, Louis Philippe had been deposed and forced to flee ignominiously to refuge in England.

336 *and perform the agreeable to most of them*: this is, presumably, the first election after the Reform Act of 1832, which has enfranchised a large number of new petty-bourgeois voters. Pynsent is putting himself out to woo them. From later comments, it seems that Clavering—a rotten borough—had two members, both in the pocket of Sir Francis. It has lost one of those members to a new 'County' seat, which Pynsent is competing for. The fact that the old borough retains one of its seats (dominated by Clavering patronage) is important in the later narrative.

338 *Chateaubriand*: a romantic novelist (1768–1848), although Strong is thinking of his career as a French diplomatist here.

346 *A heart which has worn out love at three-and-twenty*: the point was made earlier (see p. 36) that there is an eight-year age difference between Pen and Laura, by which calculation she should be 15 here. but her moral assurance (and the illustrations) confirm that she is assumed to be 18 or more. It is unthinkable that both Pen and Pynsent would propose marriage to a 15-year-old.

349 BABYLON: London. The vignette depicts St George and the dragon or, conceivably, Spenser's Red Cross Knight outside the Cave of Error.

353 *the Polyanthus Club*: in the first edition called the Megatherium Club. Megatheria were a prehistoric genus of giant sloths. By the unflattering name, Thackeray indicated the most venerable of London clubs, the Athenaeum. During the writing of *Pendennis*, the novelist was having difficulty in being accepted for the Athenaeum (some of whose members resented the 'Club Snobs' depictions in *Punch*). He was blackballed in February 1850, and finally made a member in February 1851. In deference to his new club, Thackeray made the change to the neutral 'Polyanthus Club' in subsequent editions of *Pendennis*.

Swammerdam . . . Pultusk: the Congress of Swammerdam is an invention. The Peace of Pultusk, as preposterous sounding, was in fact an authentic treaty between the French and Russians in 1806.

355 *Lamb Court, Temple:—where was it?*: Lamb Court is fictional (as is the later-mentioned Shepherd's Inn). Hawes suggests that Clement's Inn or Lyon's Inn is intended. Lovers of *Pendennis* afterwards named premises in Middle Court, where Thackeray had chambers in 1831, 'Lamb Building'.

Mr. Deuceace, Lord Crab's son: the dissolute hero of 'The Amours of Mr Deuceace' in *The Yellowplush Correspondence* (1838). It is while in residence in 'Pump Court' in the Temple that Deuceace, a card-sharp, fleeces his innocent young neighbour, Thomas Dawkins, fresh from the university of Oxford. Thackeray based the story on experience of his own in which professional sharpers won £1,500 from him at cards (see *UA* 134). It took Thackeray longer to rid himself of his gambling addiction than it does Pen.

in the deep yellow London fog: there were huge fogs in London in the mid-1840s (see *AP* 286). Among other things, these

'pea-soupers' inspired the opening of Dickens's *Bleak House*, in 1852.

356 *a City omnibus*: as Richard Altick points out, the major's experiment belongs to the 1840s when omnibuses became fully respectable modes of transport among the genteel classes (*PP* 373–4).

364 *on straw like Margery Daw*: 'See saw, Margery Daw | Sold her bed, and lay upon straw.'

365 THE KNIGHTS OF THE TEMPLE: taken with the vignette, a pun. The Temple is the lawyers' quarter of London where the Inns of Court are. As inhabitants of this locality Pen and Warrington (the two figures on the horse) are alluded to. But the Knights Templar are also the chivalric society of crusaders who figure centrally in the plot of Scott's *Ivanhoe* (hence the medieval costume in the vignette).

366 *the roaring of the shower-baths*: there was a craze for shower baths in 1849 (partly inspired by sanitary panic about the cholera epidemic) and a number of *Punch* jokes on the subject. A constant theme of the jokes was that the showers only offered a douche of cold water, and required considerable nerve. (This is the point of the remark about 'a set of Hummums', lower in the paragraph. Hummums are Turkish baths and hot.)

367 *Eldon . . . with Solomon to aid him*: as the context suggests, a company of famous lawyers and legal authorities (as Harden points out, Gustavus and Solomon are invented). Thackeray spent a short period reading for the bar in 1831.

the history of single day: the challenge was taken up by G. A. Sala (1828–94) with his *Twice round the Clock* (1864). In tribute to this section of *Pendennis*, Sala also founded in 1860 a journal called *Temple Bar*. Sala was one of the new generation of bohemian journalist-authors inspired by *Pendennis*. So too was Edmund Yates (1831–94), who wrote in his memoirs: 'When in the course of Pen's fortunes he enters upon the literary career . . . when I came to this portion of the book my fate was sealed.'

371 *the Red House, Vauxhall, and the Opera*: 'rowing men' is a euphemism here. The Red House (a tavern) was a well-known gambling resort, the pleasure gardens at Vauxhall was a convenient place to pick up the cheaper class of whore, and the Opera was the place to find a classier kind of companion among the dancers and singers.

Upper Temple: there is an Inner and a Middle Temple (where the 20-year-old Thackeray had chambers) but no Upper Temple. The general Temple site lies just off Fleet Street; hence the fact that a journalist like Warrington lives in Lamb Court.

375 *Grisi in Norma*: Guilia Grisi (1811–69) was the most famous operatic soprano of her time, and sang in Bellini's *Norma* (1831). 'The presiding prima donna of Victorian fiction' (*PP* 473) Grisi features in the background of many novels. She made her London debut in 1834 and thereafter missed only one season until her retirement in 1861.

376 VIGNETTE: Pan teaches the young child the pleasures of the flesh. The cloven foot and horns hint at sexual licence.

Thistlewood: Arthur Thistlewood (1770–1820), one of the Cato Street conspirators who attempted to assassinate the whole English cabinet in 1820. He was executed. When Warrington uses 'snobs' a couple of sentences later, it is in the traditional sense of 'low fellows' or 'common people'.

382 *Greek Calends*: 'never'. Calends are a feature of the Roman calendar.

385 *an immense hit with his song of 'The Body-Snatcher'*: Thackeray is thinking of the huge success the singer Ross had with his song 'Sam Hall' (the monologue of a chimney sweep about to be hanged) at the Cider Cellars, Maiden Lane, in 1849. Ross appeared in make-up, and roared out the chorus, 'Damn Your Eyes'. Richard Doyle did a large cartoon with commentary by 'Mr Pips', *Punch*, 17 Mar. The Back Kitchen is generally taken to be an amalgam of several clubs: the Cider Cellars, the Coal Hole (in the Strand), and Evans's (in Covent Garden).

387 *with powder and shot, too*: William Maginn (1793–1842) is generally taken to be the original of 'Captain' Shandon. Maginn was a Protestant with a doctorate from Trinity College, Dublin. He drifted into the world of journalism, founding *Fraser's Magazine* in 1830. Thackeray became an intimate of Maginn's and a main contributor to the magazine in its first decade. He learnt much of his craft from the older man. Despite his gifts, scholarship, and earning power, Maginn was a byword for dissipation. In 1834 he was forced by debts to flee to Belgium. He made frequent visits to the sponging house and debtors' prison, from which he would, evidently, continue to run his journal-

istic business. (See Ch. 32, although the description of Shandon drawing up the prospectus for the *Pall Mall Gazette* evidently derives from Maginn's last spell in the Fleet Prison, in early 1842, a few months before his death from consumption.) From surviving extracts of Thackeray's diary of 1832, it seems that Maginn was a darker version of Pen's mentor, Warrington, conducting him into the London underworld. In June, for instance, Maginn took Thackeray to 'a common brothel where I left him, very much disgusted and sickened'. One of Maginn's fiercer reviews provoked a duel in 1836—see the comment about 'powder and shot'. But this bloodthirsty aspect of Shandon's character is not evident in the later development of the character in *Pendennis*. Thackeray seems, at this early stage, to be ascribing to Captain Shandon the character of the fire-eating Irish journalist, John ('Jack') Sheehan. I guess that at this preliminary stage he intended to use 'Doctor Boyne' as the 'Protestant champion' Dr Maginn and 'Captain Shandon' as the 'liberal orator' Sheehan (1809–82) but later decided to combine the two into one character. Since Shandon is so authoritatively identified as Maginn (in the *DNB*, for instance) it is worth pointing out a number of features which do not fit. Maginn unlike Shandon (who lifts his Latin and Greek tags from Burton's *Anatomy of Melancholy*) was a distinguished classical scholar; Maginn consistently attacked Colburn ('Bungay') who he is employed by in *Pendennis*; Shandon's flabby political views are quite different from Maginn's sharply worked out conservatism; Shandon is uxorious, Maginn was notoriously promiscuous. In *Rebellious Fraser's* (1934) Miriam Thrall goes so far as to say the identification of Maginn with Shandon is 'preposterous'. This is probably too extreme. What seems likely is that Thackeray attached legendary aspects of Maginn's career to an otherwise fictional character. None the less, Maginn's surviving friends were infuriated by this attack on a dead patron.

388 *here's Archer*: based, as Gordon Ray points out, on the book collector and society man Tom Hill (1760–1840). He has his name because of the 'long bow' he pulls in conversation. Thackeray vents most spite on characters like Hill and Maginn who were dead by 1849.

390–1 *the great engine . . . before he goes to his own*: this salute to Fleet Street belongs to late 1840s, not the early 1830s.

'Lord B.' is Lord Brougham (1778–1868)—then in opposition; the 'noble marquis' is the Marquis of Lansdowne (1780–1863) a senior cabinet minister. Thackeray is thinking of a specific exchange, on 6 Mar. 1849, when Brougham pressed Lansdowne about arms which the government had supplied to Sicily.

391 VIGNETTE: a printer's boy, or 'devil', by the door, waiting with his empty satchel for overdue copy (he has fallen asleep, it has been so long).

396 *the Theban eagle . . . through the azure fields of air?*: a loose quotation from Thomas Gray's *The Progress of Poetry* (1757). The allusion is ironic and it may have been in Thackeray's mind that in the preface to the 2nd edition of *Jane Eyre* (1848) Charlotte Brontë had compared the author of *Vanity Fair* to an eagle.

formerly Bacon and Bungay: another cluster of thinly pseudonymized figures from the 1830s–1840s literary world. Bacon and Bungay are generally taken to be the publishers Richard Bentley (1794–1871) and Henry Colburn (d. 1855). The two had a brief partnership 1829–32, but fell out badly and competed over the next two decades (mainly in their specialist areas of fashionable novels and magazine miscellanies).

Bedwin Sands's Eastern Ghazuls: James Morier (1780–1849), the popularizer of the oriental tale in England with *The Adventures of Hajji Baba* (1824). The delightfully named Sands also makes a brief appearance in the charade scenes at Gaunt House, in *Vanity Fair*.

397 *have set up Miss Bunyan against Lady Violet*: in his *Fraser's Magazine* (Dec. 1837) review, 'A Word on the Annuals', Thackeray identified three literary ladies as leading editresses in the field: 'L.E.L' (i.e. Letetia Elizabeth Landon, 1802–38), Lady Blessington (1789–1849), and Mary Mitford (1787–1855). Lady Violet Lebas (i.e. 'bluestocking') seems to combine the rank of Blessington and the intellectuality of Landon. Thackeray apparently depicted Miss Mitford as the homely 'Miss Bunyan' (sometimes spelt 'Bunion'—in recognition of her commonsensical habit of walking rather than taking a cab round London). Thackeray was a connoisseur of the genre, and himself contributed to Lady Blessington's *Keepsake* at the period of writing *Pendennis*.

399 *a bust of my Lord of Verulam*: i.e. Francis Bacon. Thackeray implies that Richard Bentley snobbishly claimed descent from his namesake, the great 18th-century scholar, to whom he was not, in fact, related.

The Raff's Magazine, The Larky Swell: Thackeray had an Orwellian interest in popular fiction, and wrote an article ('Half-a-Crown's Worth of Cheap Knowledge') on penny magazines like the *Larky Swell* for *Fraser's* (Feb. 1838).

400 *Elias Howle*: in Aug. 1847 Thackeray had hilariously parodied the Irish comic novelist Charles Lever in *Punch*, with a squib entitled 'Phil Fogarty, A Tale of the Fighting Onety-Oneth. By Harry Rollicker'. Thackeray, who liked Lever (and thought Lever liked him), was affectionate in his satire. But Lever was not amused. In the Nov. 1848 issue of *Roland Cashel* Lever included a gratuitously *ad hominem* caricature of Thackeray as 'Elias Howle': 'He was large and heavily built, but neither muscular nor athletic; his frame and all his gestures indicated weakness and uncertainty. His head was capacious, but not remarkable for what phrenologists call moral development, while the sinister expression of his eyes—half submissive, half satirical—suggested doubts of his sincerity. There was nothing honest about him but his mouth; this was large, full, thicklipped, and sensual.' Thackeray was deeply hurt by the 'personality' of this attack, and a formal complaint was made through Lever's publishers, Chapman & Hall (they also published Thackeray's Christmas Books). Lever made a disingenuous reply, claiming he had not intended to attack Thackeray personally, only a 'class of writers who have traded on Irish tour writing' (Thackeray had published an *Irish Sketch Book* in 1843, dedicated to Lever). Had he felt any grudges against Thackeray, Lever declared, he would rather pay them off in a different manner (i.e. by fighting a duel). Thackeray was already (in Nov. 1848) committed to giving Pen an Irish sweetheart and putative Irish in-laws, but Lever's attack can hardly have sweetened his conception of Emily Fotheringay's drunken, duelling, father.

402 *Pall Mall Gazette*: ironically, many young readers of the late 1840s took these literary-world sections of *Pendennis* (which Thackeray intended as sordid) as a romantically attractive depiction of the literary *vie bohème*. The publisher George

Smith (1824–1901) called his evening newspaper (which he began in 1865) the *Pall Mall Gazette*, in honour of *Pendennis*.

402–3 *Barney Brallaghan . . . Looney MacTwolter*: hits against Lever, who wrote such rollicking Irish works as *Harry Lorrequer* (1839), *Charles O'Malley* (1841), *Arthur O'Leary* (1844).

407 VIGNETTE: Captain Macheath in John Gay's *The Beggar's Opera* (1728). Thackeray obviously felt he could not directly allude to Maginn's womanizing (which led to him separating from his wife in 1838). It is hinted at here with the 'Captain' in gaol, seducing Polly Peachum.

409 *It's the Habeas Corpus, Mr. Bungay*: it should be the Magna Carta, of course. But habeas corpus is more appropriate to Shandon's plight. Since habeas corpus was suspended in Ireland in July 1848, this could be read as another anti-Hibernian slur.

412 ILLUSTRATION: this design seems not to fit the text. The two men (one of them carrying a fives racquet) are surely not Pen and Warrington (see, for instance, the down-at-heel footwear of the character on the right). Their raffish appearance suggests two other inmates of the prison. This presumably is an illustration which Thackeray did before writing his text, and which he could not smoothly integrate.

415 *and does not pay his bills, he must go to jail*: this is (or was taken as) a polemical hit against the benevolent campaigns mounted in the late 1840s by Dickens, John Forster, and Bulwer-Lytton, to assist distressed authors. Thackeray had staked out an uncompromisingly *laissez-faire* position in an essay (in *Fraser's*, Mar. 1846) on the suicide of the author Laman Blanchard. Thackeray refused to see Blanchard as a literary martyr, insisting that authors must take their chances in life like other professionals. Thackeray's disagreements with the Dickens camp exploded in the 'Dignity of Literature' controversy during the writing of *Pendennis* (see note to p. 440) and rumbled on in 1850–1, when Dickens set up his Guild of Literature and Art, as a kind of benevolent pension fund for authors.

416 *Johnson . . . round Mr. Cave's best table-cloth*: a favourite literary anecdote of Thackeray's illustrating the proud independence of the truly great writer. The episode took place early in Johnson's career, at the house of Edward Cave, publisher

of the *Gentleman's Magazine*. Thackeray played with the same allusion at length in one of his 'Roundabout Papers', 'On Screens in Dining-Rooms' (1860). In it Thackeray writes (still thinking of his differences with the Dickensians): 'As dear Sam Johnson sits behind the screen, too proud to show his threadbare coat and patches among the more prosperous brethren of his trade, there is no want of dignity in him.'

416 *Mr. Murray . . . Mr. Tattersall*: John Murray of Albemarle Street was one of the most venerable of London publishers, and specialized in travel guides. Tattersall's was the best known of London's horse auction rooms. Thackeray is, of course, making a tendentious point by equating bookish professions with horse-trading.

417 *Video melior proboque*: one of Thackeray's favourite quotations; from Ovid's *Metamorphoses*, 7. 20: 'I see and approve the better way [but follow the worse]'.

418 *Alnaschar*: a character in the *Arabian Nights* who, in dreaming of future prosperity, breaks the glassware on which his present well-being depends. A favourite term of Thackeray's for a day-dreamer.

419 VIGNETTE: Cupid with a letter attached to his arrow, signalling love interest. But the design is poor, by Thackeray's standards in *Pendennis*, and doesn't fit anything in the chapter (which is itself unsatisfactorily short and bitty). Thackeray wrote this number (published on 1 Sept. 1849) not long after hearing that Mrs Brookfield was pregnant and shortly before falling seriously ill himself. It may be that he wrote this section of the narrative under pressure. Shillingsburg has analysed some of the perplexing features of this chapter in 'Thackeray's *Pendennis*: A Rejected Page of Manuscript', *Huntington Library Quarterly* (Feb. 1975).

428 A DINNER IN THE ROW: i.e. Paternoster Row, the publishing centre of London.

430 *Mr. Bole, the real editor of the magazine, of which Mr. Wagg was the nominal chief*: 'Mr. Bole' hits at Frederic Shoberl (1775–1853) one of Bungay's office hacks. 'Mr. Wagg', as earlier, is Theodore Hook. In 1836, Colburn appointed Hook (who was failing fast) as editor of his revamped *New Monthly Magazine* to challenge Bentley's ('Bacon's') newly announced *Bentley's Miscellany*, starring Dickens.

Mr. Trotter . . . a poet of a tragic and suicidal cast: Thackeray apparently alludes to another of Colburn's hacks, Peter George Patmore (1786–1855), who edited the *New Monthly Magazine* after Hook's death in 1841. It is possible that Thackeray is also thinking of the once fashionable poet, Thomas Campbell (1777–1844), who edited the *New Monthly Magazine* in the 1820s.

Captain Sumph: a clear hit at another of Colburn's authors, Lord William (Pitt) Lennox (1799–1881). Lennox's godfather was William Pitt, and one of his cousins Charles James Fox. He was one of Wellington's aides-de-camp at Waterloo. (It was in his honour that his mother threw the ball which is immortalized in *Vanity Fair*.) After a brief period in Parliament Lennox became a man of letters, writing ultra-fashionable novels for Colburn and trading on his pedigree. By 1849 he was a broken-down figure willing to hire himself out for lectures on the theme of 'Celebrities I have known'. Lewis Melville suggests that Sumph and Percy Popjoy also draw on William Lennox's brother Henry and on 'a brother of the Duke of St Albans'.

438 *Popjoy about his own work, of which he doesn't know a word*: Thackeray alludes to a recent scandal concerning Colburn's cynical publishing practices. In 1843 Lord William Pitt Lennox produced a novel, called *The Tuft-Hunter*. Lennox's wretched novel was actually written by Colburn's hack, Frederick Shoberl, and largely consisted of plagiarisms. It was in disgust at this affair that Tom Hood (a figure for whom Thackeray had considerable affection) resigned from Colburn's service.

440 *so little as literary men*: it is clear that Thackeray was unusually bad-tempered in this chapter, which represents a return to his old, pre-*Vanity Fair*, 'savagery'. His mood may have been the result of the crisis of his relationship with Mrs Brookfield (whose pregnancy he had recently learnt about). He had a long-standing grudge against Colburn (i.e. Bungay, who is flayed in the first half of the chapter). The publisher had—humiliatingly—kept the MS of *Vanity Fair* for months and then declined to publish it. Thackeray was also irritated with Dickens and his followers, doubtless feeling that *David Copperfield* (now in its fifth month) was overshadowing *Pendennis*. Whatever his motives for uttering it, this remark (provokingly delivered by the nar-

rator) sparked off what is called the 'Dignity of Literature' controversy—effectively a flare-up of a dispute which had been going on for some years. This number came out on 1 Sept. 1849 and publication of *Pendennis* was suspended until 1 Jan. 1850, on account of Thackeray's life-threatening illness. Out of respect for his condition, Thackeray's opponents held their fire. But on 3 Jan. 1850 the *Morning Chronicle* published a leading article attacking Thackeray for fostering a 'baneful prejudice' against men of letters. It made the good point that Bungay/Colburn's dinner table hardly represented the cream of the literary profession. On 5 Jan., the theme was taken up by John Forster (Dickens's *alter ego*) in a leading article in the *Examiner*. While ostensibly discussing the question of pensions for writers, Forster stated that Thackeray 'too often' disparaged his 'literary fellow-workers'. On 8 Jan., Thackeray entered the fray with a letter to the *Morning Chronicle*. This letter (which has been frequently reprinted as one of the author's essays) aggressively maintains the accuracy of the satire in Ch. 34 of *Pendennis*: 'That I have a prejudice against running into debt, and drunkeness, and disorderly life, and against quackery and falsehood in my profession, I own.' In other words, he was attacking certain individuals not a class. On 19 Jan., Forster rejoined in the *Examiner*, ruthlessly quoting the offending passages from *Pendennis* (which are, as Thackeray later admitted, indefensible). 'The truth is,' Forster declared, 'Mr Thackeray is continually doing himself wrong by a tone of persiflage which is seldom in perfect good taste.' Perceptively (while applauding the power of his writing) Forster diagnosed an 'uneasy shame' in Thackeray's fiction. Thackeray, despite the eloquence of his 'Dignity of Literature' letter, did not get the better of the argument, and he returns to the theme parenthetically at many subsequent points of *Pendennis*'s narrative. (The above pieces are reprinted by Shillingsburg in his edition of *Pendennis*.)

440 VIGNETTE: an inkwell; the serpent indicates venom, and the fact that the pen is fledged like an arrow with a snake's head suggests that Thackeray is still in militant satirical mood.

442 ILLUSTRATION: as Shillingsburg points out, this illustration makes something of a mismatch with the text. It

alludes to a deleted description of Finucane fortifying himself with gin-and-water (rather than the beer and beefsteak of the published text). Shillingsburg also suggests that the illustration portrays a less friendly conception of the sub-editor of the *Pall Mall Gazette* as a feckless Irish hack. Thackeray seems to have based Finucane loosely on Maginn's faithful assistant, Edward Vaughan Kenealy (1819–80), who, unlike other friends, remained loyal to the end.

443 *a book of travels . . . by the Countess of Muffborough*: Thackeray is thinking of his own satirical attack in *Punch* (27 Jan. 1844) on Lady Londonderry's preposterously snobbish *Narrative of a Visit to the Courts of Vienna, Constantinople, Athens, and Naples*. Thackeray attacked the publication (a Colburn product) again in *The Snobs of England*, ch. 3.

449 *Mr. Bludyer*: Bludyer is a composite of the 'savage' *Fraser's* reviewer, combining features of John Abraham Heraud (1799–1887) and the young Thackeray himself. Bludgeoner that he is, in the context of the 1830s Bludyer's reviewing is admirably honest compared to the 'puffing' (or partisan reviewing) which *Fraser's* tirelessly campaigned against.

WHERE PEN APPEARS IN TOWN AND COUNTRY: this number (the twelfth) came out on 1 Jan. 1850, after a three-month delay caused by Thackeray's illness. During his convalescence Thackeray had time to lavish care on the vignette (the major *en déshabillé*) which is particularly fine.

450 *Mr. Green's balloon*: Charles Green (1785–1870) was famous for his hot-air balloon ascents from Vauxhall Gardens. In the 1840s, these would be accompanied by fireworks set off from the balloon in the upper air.

460 *Madame Tussaud's . . . Chamber of Horrors*: Madame Marie Tussaud (1760–1850) opened her exhibition of waxworks in 1833 in Baker Street. By 1849, her establishment was one of the main sights of London, and there were numerous *Punch* jokes. With reference to this passage, Richard Altick notes: 'setting aside two rooms formerly devoted to Napoleonic relics, whose topicality was beginning to fade, she developed what by 1843 came to be called the Chamber of Horrors, a gruesome and always well-patronized three-

dimensional supplement to the newspapers' crime coverage' (*PP* 514).

461 *in the Threes*: i.e. the Funds or 'Consols'—famously safe government investments that paid 3%.

the duke: the Duke of Wellington. He also makes a brief appearance in ch. 29 of *Vanity Fair*. Thackeray liked the effect of the greatest man of the age suddenly illuminating the edge of his narrative.

462 *Canning . . . Hume*: (1) George Canning (1770–1827), Tory politician; (2) Joseph Hume (1777–1855), Radical politician and a favourite butt of *Punch* for his dullness as a speaker.

463 *Tilbury's*: as Hawes points out, John Tilbury (based in Mount Street) hired out horses and carriages and gave his name to the vehicle called the 'Tilbury'.

464 *whatever is is right . . . as Shakespeare says*: Pope, of course, in the *Essay on Man*. At some points of the text the major is better read than in others.

465 *dolichoskion*: as Harden points out, a Homeric epithet for 'spear'.

467 VIGNETTE: a very fine design. It seems to show Laura carrying a martyr's palm, in the light of Pen's cynical marriage plans expressed later in the chapter.

471 *the other day, at Comorn*: the Hungarian town of Comorn was besieged by the Austrians from Oct. 1848 to Sept. 1849, when it capitulated. Thackeray wrote this during his convalescence (Nov. 1849–Jan. 1850) rendering 'the other day' slightly anachronistic.

from Wardour Street: where the main suppliers of theatrical props had their establishments.

472 *Mrs. Hodge-Podgson's own, the great Railroad Croesus's wife*: i.e. Mrs Hudson, the wife of George Hudson, the railway magnate who was ruined in 1849. Mrs Hudson was famous for the vulgarity of her furnishings, and for dropping her aitches. Richard Altick (*PP* 608–9) suggests that she may have inspired part of Lady Clavering's character.

475 *Cape of Good Hope*: the British took the Cape of Good Hope from the Dutch in 1806. It is one of the references by which we can fill in the major's career and which, as Gordon Ray

points out, tie him to the novelist's relative, Lt.-Colonel Merrick Shawe (see *BL* 66).

the hackneyed ballad of the Devil's Walk: by Coleridge and Southey, 1799.

476 VIGNETTE: the fall of Comorn (see note to p. 471).

478 *Seen Taglioni in The Sylphide, Miss Amory*: one of many allusions in *Pendennis* to the ballet, *La Sylphide* (1832), a favourite vehicle of Marie Taglioni's at the Paris Opera during her years as the star dancer there (1827–47). Thackeray had been entranced when he saw Taglioni for the first time in Paris in 1829 (see *Letters*, i. 85–6). His rueful remark at the end of the paragraph refers to her retirement in 1847.

480 *Policeman X*: standard journalistic description. Thackeray wrote a number of cockney-dialect 'Ballads of Policeman X' in the 1840s.

486 *Captain Beak*: as Gordon Ray points out (*BL* 58) the implication is that while in India the major came across Amory in his capacity as a military magistrate (although it could also refer to the major's Wellingtonian nose).

489 VIGNETTE: Either the Prince discovering Sleeping Beauty, or an illustration of Porphyro and Madeline in Keats's *The Eve of St Agnes*.

490 *the treadmill*: used to employ prisoners (worthlessly). The treadmill was associated with reforms brought in with Pentonville Prison, opened in 1842.

493 *ofttimes I hover*: Pen's anonymous song has become a hit (see Ch. 31).

T.R.E.O.: Theatre Royal English Opera.

502 *took ices at Hunter's*: i.e. Gunter's, purveyors of ices and pastries, Berkeley Square, founded 1757. The firm and its delicacies feature in much Victorian fiction but, as Richard Altick points out, 'it was in Thackeray's pages that Gunter reaped the most frequent publicity' (*PP* 222).

510 *Mr. Oriel is a beautiful preacher*: in this scene, and its illustration, Thackeray evokes William Brookfield's successes as a fashionable preacher at St James's, Piccadilly.

517 VIGNETTE: young gent, helped by his servant, skating on one of the frozen ponds in the London parks (suggestive of

Warrington helping Pen find his feet in the literary world). Thackeray invariably gets his seasons right. This is the number for Feb. 1850, written the month before.

520 *Shakespere was a man who wrote for money*: another seismic tremor from the 'Dignity of Literature' controversy.

521 *the Horatian maxim*: 'keep your piece (and peace) nine years', from the *Art of Poetry*. If it is four years since the affair with Blanche in the country the date should be 1834.

524 *the 'fashionable' was in vogue*: Colburn (Bungay) made fashionable, or 'silver fork', fiction the rage in the late 1820s. He and Bentley (Bacon) specialized in the genre throughout the 1830s. By the 1840s, the fashion was distinctly stale. Thackeray was largely responsible (with works like *Vanity Fair*) for extinguishing the fashionable novel's fashionability. None the less Matthew Rosa in *The Silver Fork School* (New York, 1936), points out how much Thackeray himself learnt from fashionable novelists like Mrs Gore and Disraeli.

528 *the widow's heart to sing for joy*: Job 29:13.

531 ALSATIA: another allusion to the wars still raging on the Continent. Alsatia is the disputed territory between France and Germany. In London, it was in the 17th century an area around Whitefriars where debtors and law-breakers could find sanctuary.

532 *Mr. Serle's forty pupils*: the dramatist and manager Thomas James Serle (1798–1889). As Hawes points out, Serle's wife, Cecilia, is mentioned on p. 615. Hawes thinks that 'Mrs' may be intended here, as well.

T.R.D.L.: Theatre Royal Drury Lane.

536 *Juke . . . Apsley House*: the Duke of Wellington and his London residence.

542 *Queen Christina's army*: Cristina was the Queen Regent of Spain, 1833–40. Her regency led to the so-called Carlist wars. In the 1st edition of *Pendennis*, Thackeray wrote 'Don Carlos's army', which would have put Jack Holt on the other side.

543 *The Brigand . . . Wallack*: as Harden notes, James William Wallack (?1791–1864) acted the role of Massaroni in *The Brigand* (1829), James Robinson Planché's adaptation of a play by Scribe. Thackeray saw Wallack act in Planché's

melodrama *The Compact* in 1832 (see *Letters*, i. 190). I guess he substituted *The Brigand* as more appropriate to Altamont's piratical character.

544 *secundum artem*: artfully.

549 *polisson*: rogue.

554 *cuddy*: cabin, a nautical term.

555 *the Serpentine*: the ornamental lake in Hyde Park. It was notorious at this period (1849–50) having been indicted by the *Lancet* as one of the main sources of London's cholera epidemic.

556 VIGNETTE: as Harden points out, Abraham's servant meeting Rebecca at the well (Genesis 24). The servant has been sent, with treasure, to find a wife for Abraham's son, Isaac. The allusion, in this chapter, is to the major's search for a suitable wife for Pen. The Abraham–Isaac–Rebecca story was a favourite with genre painters, and with the Italianate dress here Thackeray seems to be burlesquing a painting. The snake indicates sexual danger.

Watteau quadrille: the quadrille, introduced from France in 1816, was a complex dance which four partners walked through. Here the idea is that they dress in the style of the paintings of the French 18th-century artist Watteau.

557 *the hulks*: prison ships. They survived, to take the overflow of the British prison population, until 1856.

558–9 *Sir Charles Mirabel . . . page to the prince*: Richard Altick assumes from the description of Sir Charles that Thackeray must have Harriot Mellon in mind as Emily. Mellon, an actress, married the banker Thomas Coutts in 1815. He was some fifty years older than she, and died in 1822 leaving her one of the richest women in England. In 1825, she married the son of the Duke of St Albans.

560 *at ten years old drank his champagne*: there are some difficulties about Frank's age. As Pen says a little earlier to his uncle, he is 'five and twenty': that is, two years older than he was before leaving for London when he proposed to Laura. But at that period—two years ago—Frank was a baby. The seventh number has a picture ('Master Francis in a State of Revolt', p. 273) which shows him, literally a babe in arms, being carried out of church by a footman. How then can he now be 10 or more years old, smoking cigars and drinking

champagne? The problem is compounded by a later appearance of Frank in the novel (see p. 965) when, about a decade having passed, he is still 10 or younger.

564 *three stars*: that is, she has £6,000 worth of East India Company stock.

571 *Mr. Paxton grows you a pineapple*: Joseph Paxton (1801–65), in charge of the Duke of Devonshire's gardens, but in Thackeray's mind here as the appointed designer of the Crystal Palace.

Hoiaper: alluding to Homer's 'the race of men is as leaves', from the *Iliad*, 6. 146.

573 VIGNETTE: two soldiers playing cards, based on the numerous paintings on the same theme by the Dutch artist Gerard Ter Borch.

578 *bistre*: brown pigment prepared from soot.

580 *not for Venice*: Shylock, *The Merchant of Venice*, iv. i. 228: 'Shall I lay perjury upon my soul? . . . No, not for Venice'.

585 *Peter Crawley . . . Mr. Bendigo . . . Mr. Caunt*: boxing references. Peter Crawley (1799–1865) was a fight promoter. Bendigo (William Thompson) fought Benjamin Caunt three times for the English championship; Bendigo won in 1835 and 1845, and lost in 1838.

587 *Boulogne-sur-Mer*: the traditional refuge of British debtors.

588 *the Royal Gardens of Vauxhall . . . the great Simpson*: Vauxhall pleasure garden had first opened in 1729, and figures in much 18th-century literature. Thackeray introduced the gardens in their 19th-century heyday (1813) into ch. 6 of *Vanity Fair*. By the 1820s, 'Royal' Vauxhall (so called by permission of George IV in 1822) was in decline. In the 1830s the owners attempted to revive its fortunes with flashy displays of fireworks, balloon ascents, and panoramas. By the period assumed in the narrative here (the early 1840s) Vauxhall had become, as Richard Altick puts it, 'tacky' and 'sleazy'. Young men (and not so young men, like Sir Francis Clavering, as we later learn) went there to pick up girls with easy morals (it is, as Altick points out, an indication of Pen's precarious moral condition that he should be going there alone at night). Vauxhall finally expired in 1859. The reference to Simpson, the master of ceremonies, is somewhat anachronistic, as he retired in the mid-1830s.

595 *the twenty thousand additional lamps*: 8,000 lamps were added at a gala in honour of the Prince Regent's birthday in 1811. Thereafter the number was increased at each subsequent gala. 20,000 is probably extravagant.

595–6 *the great rider at Astley's . . . Mademoiselle Caracoline*: Astley's Royal Amphitheatre was one of the traditional shows of London, featuring equestrian entertainments. It moved to larger and more splendid premises in 1843, and in 1849 featured an item 'Corasco or the Warrior's Steed' which may have suggested Mademoiselle Caracoline (from the French, 'cavort').

596 *T.R.E.O., T.R.S.W.*: Theatre Royal English Opera and Theatre Royal Sadler's Wells.

597 *Egmont at Clara in Goethe's play, or Leicester at Amy*: both references are double-edged. In Goethe's tragedy, the hero is instrumental in driving the heroine to suicide. In Scott's novel *Kenilworth* (1821) Leicester betrays Amy, having taken sexual advantage of her.

Bartholomew's: Bart's Hospital; 'since we had the row at Wapshot's' suggests that Thackeray originally intended Sam to be the young man knocked into the grave in ch. 15 but momentarily forgot his name. It will be noted that, by the end of the chapter, Thackeray still cannot recall the name of 'the biggest champion at the academy' (Hobnell).

601 *the bouquet*: large flight of rockets.

602 *rack punch*: punch fortified with 'arrack'. Rack punch at Vauxhall changes the life-history of Becky Sharp in ch. 6 of *Vanity Fair*. Thackeray evidently wanted to partner that very successful episode with another, differently accented, Vauxhall adventure.

605 VIGNETTE: the picture seems to depict an event Thackeray did not get round to writing. It would seem to show Mrs Bolton sick in bed, and Fanny presumably free to go out unchaperoned (to Astley's?), dangerously prey to Pen's lusts.

607 *no Faust and Margaret business*: the allusion is to the first part of Goethe's *Faust* (1808), in which the hero seduces Margaret and drives her to her death.

Lovelace: the aristocratic seducer of the heroine in Richardson's *Clarissa Harlowe* (1747–8). Clarissa dies of shame; the omens are not good for Fanny.

607 *sixteen pages of excitement*: Thackeray is thinking of penny serials, specifically works like G. W. M. Reynolds's *Mysteries of the Court of London* (1848–56).

614 VIGNETTE: according to Joan Stevens this fine illustration depicts the Lady of Shalott. Tennyson's poem was first published in 1832, and reissued with extensive revision in 1842. Thackeray evidently alludes to part iii, 'A bow-shot from her bower-eaves, | He [Sir Lancelot] rode between the barley sheaves'. The narrative reference is to Fanny's hopeless longing for Pen—her impending death is insistently suggested by the string of literary allusions.

ticket-porter: a licensed porter. The character of the ticket-porter was immortalized by Dickens's Toby Veck, in *The Chimes* (1845).

621 *Latude*: John Henry Latude (1725–1805), imprisoned in the Bastille. The woman to whom he had foolishly given his heart was Madame de Pompadour.

622 *the Panorama*: one of most popular of London shows. Erected in Leicester Square, 1794, it remained until 1864. It specialized in visual displays—in 1845, for instance, it offered 'Naples by Moonlight'.

623 VIGNETTE: Sir Roger de Coverley and Mr Spectator (Addison) walking along Temple Garden with the Thames in the background.

put forth a bud: as Hawes points out the quotation comes from the article on the Temple in Peter Cunningham's *Hand-Book of London* (1849) which Thackeray must quite recently have acquired.

the railroad business is over: i.e. the 'mania' of 1845 which led to thousands of miles of railroad being built by private speculation. As J. W. Dodds points out, 'gambling shares became the pursuit of everyone from lord to lackey' (*AP* 223). Thackeray and many of his friends (including William Brookfield) lost money in the mania. The meaning of the sentence is not easy to grasp, unless Thackeray intends an elaborate pun between the red and white roses of York and Lancaster, and new rail-lines to those counties.

his Scotch lackey: James Boswell. Thackeray is anticipating much of his 'English Humourists' material here, with references to Addison, Goldsmith, and Dr Johnson. The Filby

and Newbery mentioned earlier were Goldsmith's tailor and publisher respectively. *The Citizen of the World* was published in 1762.

631 *Job Thornberry*: in George Colman's comedy *John Bull, or the Englishman's Fireside* (1803). The allusion is to the scene where the artisan Thornberry confronts the magistrate Sir Simon Rochdale with the complaint that his daughter Mary has been seduced. When Sir Simon says the seducer must be punished, Job reveals that the culprit is none other than the magistrate's son, Frank. The young people finally marry, Job declaring: 'I forgive you young man for what has passed; but no-one deserves forgiveness who refuses to make amends when he has destroyed the happiness of an English fireside'.

638 *some lines from Marmion*: 'Where shall the traitor rest, | He the deceiver, | Who could win Maiden's breast, | Ruin, and leave her?' (Walter Scott, *Marmion*, canto iii, stanza 10). The literary allusions continue ominous for Fanny. In Scott's poem, the hero Marmion seduces and abandons Constance to her death.

643 *a Cruikshank or a Leech*: Thackeray's favourite comic artists, George Cruikshank (1792–1878) and John Leech (1817–64).

the dismal diorama: an allusion to the London Diorama which opened in 1823 in Regent's Park and featured huge semi-transparent pictures accompanied by light and sound effects.

648 *the Lady of Lyons . . . Mr. Macready*: Bulwer-Lytton's hugely popular 1838 play which William Macready (1793–1873) produced and in which he played the lead at Covent Garden. The gardener's son, Claude Melnotte, succeeds in winning the rich merchant's daughter, Pauline Deschapelles (Fanny reverses the class positions of the lovers, since she is the poor partner).

655 *they have not quite penetrated*: as Richard Altick points out (*PP* 191) the construction of the Clavering (Ottery St Mary) and Chatteris branch of the Great Western Railway was completed in 1844, with a line from Paddington to Exeter. Thackeray would seem to indicate a date around 1842 here, although he is not consistent.

656 VIGNETTE: As Joan Stevens points out, Sarah casting out Hagar. The allusion is barbed since in Genesis it is made clear that Sarah (the older, legitimate wife) is jealous of the younger, more attractive concubine. At a number of points, Thackeray implies that Helen's solicitude for her son originates in naked sexual jealousy.

663 *Dr. Goodenough*: generally taken to be a grateful portrait of John Elliotson, who saved Thackeray's life by his prompt attention in Sept. 1849. Elliotson was brought to Thackeray's bedside by John Forster (Dickens's associate) who evidently played the part given to Bows in this section of *Pendennis*.

665 *neither homœopathy, nor hydropathy, nor mesmerism, nor Dr. Simpson, nor Dr. Locock*: an array of medical experiments and experimenters (in the form of the quotation from *Othello*, 3. 1. 331–2, 'neither poppy, etc.'). Thackeray's mother was addicted to homœopathy (had she reached him first, rather than Elliotson, she would have killed him, Thackeray believed). Some of Thackeray's friends—Tennyson for instance—were devoted to hydropathy. Thackeray had used it in the early days of his wife Isabella's illness, without success. Elliotson was a mesmerist and had, indeed, been dismissed from his position at the University of London in 1843 for advocating mesmerism as an anaesthetic technique. (He must, presumably, have mesmerized Thackeray in treating him in winter 1849.) The Edinburgh physician James Young Simpson (1811–70) pioneered the use of chloroform in 1847 to ease the pain of childbirth (one wonders if Jane Brookfield used it for the birth of her daughter in Feb., three months before this number). Sir Charles Locock (1799–1875), Queen Victoria's obstetrician from 1840, delivered all the royal children. Thackeray suffered from an agonizing obstruction of the urethra, and tried many forms of anaesthetic on himself over the years (he used chloroform in 1849, for instance).

when the characters in the Critic . . . daggers at each other's throats: from R. B. Sheridan's comedy *The Critic, or a Tragedy Rehearsed* (1779), ii. 1, where Puff has the characters playing his 'The Spanish Armada' all threaten each other.

666 *mignonette box*: a window box containg fragrant flowers.

Medora . . . the Princesse Fleur . . . Mystères de Paris: Medora is the heroine of Byron's 'The Corsair', the other reference

is to Eugène Sue's novel, 1842–3. For all his slighting references to Sibwright's pin-ups, Thackeray read Sue's sensational novel enthusiastically in Jan. 1843.

670 *Cymbeline*: as Harden points out, Shakespeare's play 'concludes with filial restoration to a parent'.

VIGNETTE: the design shows Costigan and the Mulligan of Ballymulligan (the belligerent and drunken Irishman from Thackeray's Christmas Book, *Mrs Perkins's Ball*, 1847) murderously attacking Thackeray over the 'Catherine Hayes' insult (the Irish bullies are hiding behind Hayes masks, a donkey—denoting the Irish newspapers which attacked Thackeray—is shown braying in the background). See note to p. 678.

672 *Cras ingens iterabimus aequor*: Horace, *Odes*, 1. 8. 32. '[Begone care,] tomorrow we embark on the great ocean.'

678 *a previous unfortunate sentence*: the offending sentence which originally came on p. 573 (see p. 1003 here) referred to 'Bluebeard, Catherine Hayes, and George Barnwell'. As Thackeray intended the reference these were three murderers of the most heinous kind, since they all killed relatives. Bluebeard is the wife-killer from Perrault's fairy story; Catherine Hayes is the 18th-century husband-killer Thackeray wrote about in *Catherine* (1839–40); George Barnwell is the uncle-murdering apprentice hero of George Lillo's play (1731), which Thackeray burlesqued in his parody of Bulwer-Lytton, 'George de Barnwell' (*Punch*, Apr. 1847). It was the Catherine Hayes reference which got Thackeray in hot water with his Irish readers, yet again. Catherine Hayes was also the name of a currently popular Dublin singer, and some of her admirers assumed, absurdly, that Thackeray's remark was aimed at their idol. The novelist's daughter, Anne Ritchie, tells the story in one of her biographical introductions: 'So high did feelings run in Dublin, that one evening my father received a letter signed by a Mr Briggs, announcing that a company of young Irishmen had determined to chastise him for this, and for various other supposed personal insults of an equally serious nature, and intended to come over one by one until their purpose was accomplished.' Thackeray handled the crisis with good-humoured diplomacy, and wrote an amusing ballad on the subject, 'Catherine Hayes'. The last stanza runs; 'Accursed let his memory be, | Who dares to

say aught in dispraise | Of Oireland, the land of the free, | And of beauty and janius and Hayes.'

687 *is a Jo—*: Hawes suggests that the major is going on to say 'a Joseph', i.e. a young man who remains chaste despite temptation. But it seems more likely that the major is about to say 'a John Pendennis'—that is, 'if you think Arthur is a plaster saint like your husband you are mistaken'.

688 *a little grisette*: a reference to French whores, named after their grey dresses. It is interesting that in this chapter, for the first time, we are told that Pen has 'never been abroad except to Paris for a lark'. The major has no doubt as to what the lark must have been.

712 *Calypso ne pouvait se consoler*: the first line of Fénelon's *Télémaque* (1699), which narrates the adventures of Odysseus's son. Calypso mourns at the departure of Odysseus at the beginning of the story, but later consoles herself with Telemachus.

Daymy . . . Absard, by Gad: with the passage of historical time the major's accent has begun to sound dated and mannered to the mid-1840s ear.

715 *what happened to her, young fellow*: at first distraught, she later consoled herself with Bacchus.

VIGNETTE: Pen (whose hair has not yet resumed its former luxuriance) as a shiny pated monk (studiously celibate), his mother's grave being dug in the background.

716 *Béguine convents*: Helen's wonder and interest is aroused because the nuns of this lay order can marry.

717 *grivoises*: loose, immoral.

718 *Galignani*: *Galignani's Messenger*, an English paper printed in Paris for expatriates and tourists. Thackeray worked for the paper for a while in 1838.

725 *to keep one little lock for herself*: either forgetful on Thackeray's part, or indicative of the duplicity of women (see p. 683, where it is specifically said that 'every single hair' is returned). Shillingsburg suggests it may be a 'complex irony' (p. 383).

738 *before the marriage of either of them*: this seems to contradict what is said on p. 97, namely that the letters were all returned to Laura's father.

740 *dev'lish nice place for East India colonels*: a family joke. Thackeray's stepfather, an East Indian major, bought Larkbeare (i.e. Fairoaks) after his retirement, in 1825.

743 *Lord John . . . Sir James*: Derby Day was a parliamentary holiday, and traditionally politicians attended the race. As Harden suggests, intended here are (1) Lord John Russell, the Prime Minister; (2) Sir James Graham, Russell's Whig ally. Later in his grandiloquent monologue Archer drops, among many other names, that of Richard Cobden, Russell's Radical opponent—who did not enter Parliament until 1847. These public figures place this as a contemporary Derby scene. (See also the comment on p. 743 by the Duke of Hampshire—a fictional personage—that he has 'been at sixty-five Derbies'. Since the race was founded in 1789, this gives a date no earlier than the mid-1840s for this scene.) Derby Day became a mania with the working classes of London in the 1840s (it remains one of the two races which interest the whole nation). Thackeray's Derby Day description clearly derives from a Richard Doyle panorama, in *Punch*, 26 May 1849 (three days after the race meeting). Frith later took the theme up in his celebrated painting.

745 *Podasokus*: named not after any Derby winner but, as Harden points out, one of the horses of Achilles in the *Iliad*. The owner, Lord Harrowhill, remembered his classics lessons at Harrow on the Hill (traditionally more scholarly than Eton).

755 *bouder me*: sulk with me.

762 *the canal*: canaille, riff-raff. She has picked the word up from Blanche.

766 *Briseis*: a prize won by Achilles during the Trojan war, she was taken from him (to his rage) by Agememnon.

768 VIGNETTE: the good fairy of pantomime.

771 *all the ring was taken in*: i.e. the betting ring, conspiring to fix the odds in their favour. In other words, Sir Francis was cheated by cleverer cheats than him.

775 *escape from their wives*: i.e. their concubines, tricked into fake marriages to make them more pliant. The practice was common in the South Seas (see R. L. Stevenson's *The Beach of Falesa*, 1892).

Boney at Saint Helena: Napoleon spent the final years of his exile after Waterloo and before his death in 1821 on the island of St Helena, in the Atlantic. He was a tourist

attraction for ocean-going passenger ships. Young William Thackeray saw the great tyrant on his journey from India to England in 1817.

779 *bejewtary*: bijouterie, jewellery.

I was a-polkin: the polka had been introduced into England from Bohemia, and by 1849 was a rage. As J. W. Dodds writes 'Ladies wore polka hats, polka jackets, and polka boots; men wore polka ties' (*AP* 153). As Richard Altick points out, Sir Francis is at Vauxhall to pick up the kind of women he prefers (*PP*. 436).

the house in St. John's Wood: traditionally the area in London where well-off men kept their mistresses—here 'Mrs Montague Rivers'. Morgan's 'non est inwentus' means that Sir Francis could not be found to answer for his debts, and the contents of the house were sold at auction.

780 *we dine with Prince Metternitch and Louy Philup reg'lar . . . Lord John and the noble Whycount at the edd of Foring Affairs*: precise dating references; Metternich departed office as Austrian chancellor of state in 1848. Louis Philippe was forced to fly to England in the French Revolution of Feb. 1848, so if Pendennis dined abroad with him it must have been before then. On the other hand, Lord John Russell became Prime Minister in 1846 and Viscount Palmerston Foreign Secretary in the same year. The date is therefore, presumably, 1846–7.

784 VIGNETTE: Laura, still drawing water from the well, having resisted the temptation of the bribes of Abraham's ambassador.

792 *the fellow in Sterne . . . demand his sword again*: see note to p. 8.

795–6 *Look at Thiers, look at Guizot, in opposition and in place*: Louis Adolphe Thiers (1797–1877), a liberal, and François Guillaume Guizot (1787–1874), a conservative. After the Revolution in 1848 Guizot followed Louis Philippe into exile in England. Thiers (previously in opposition) was currently, as Thackeray wrote, a powerful figure in the Second Republic. The Whigs (referred to in the next sentence) had come to power in 1846, under Russell. This conversation, of course, is supposed to be taking place contemporaneously with Thackeray's writing. But, on the next page, Warrington observes 'You [Pen] are six-and-twenty years old', which fits with the narrative (*Walter Lorraine* is still a relatively new

novel). Since Pen was born in 1811, this should give us a historical date of 1837, but Thackeray has deftly advanced the clock ten years.

800 *Who was his Roman coadjutor*: the less cautious Varro, who lost to Hannibal at Cannae.

801 *even on the ministerial benches*: Pen is thinking of the great Conservative U-turn over the Corn Laws, in 1846.

802 *his revolt and recantation*: Pen's references here are taken to refer to John Henry Newman (1801–90) and his brother Francis William Newman (1805–97). John went over to the Catholic Church in 1845. As Gordon Ray records, Thackeray attended John Henry's lectures on Anglican difficulties at the Oratory, King William Street, in summer 1850 (this number was published in Sept.). Francis, Professor of Latin at University College, London, 1846–69, published his reasons for being unable to accept traditional Christian arguments in the autobiographical *Phases of Faith* (1850). According to Ray (*AW* 122) Thackeray was much moved by the book. Clearly Pen's comments only make sense if we date them as being uttered in mid-1850, at the same period that this number was written.

803 VIGNETTE: the sign on the board presumably reads 'Danger! Keep Out!'

804 *were I to say he was a literary man . . . insult the literary profession*: another swipe in the 'Dignity of Literature' controversy.

815 *It's dev'lish convenient, being in Parliament*: because MPs cannot be arrested for debt, while the House is sitting.

816 *when Clavering had two members*: as a rotten borough Clavering lost one of its members in 1832. The major wants the one remaining safe seat for Pen, rather than have him compete with the sitting member Pynsent for the county seat that was set up after the Reform Bill.

818 *a little Anglo-Norman bijou*: Richard Altick points out the 'opportunism' with which Smirke and Blanche have thrown themselves into the High Church cult of Romanism of the late 1840s—the period between Newman's going over and the so-called Papal Aggression of 1851. On Smirke's part it is the more reprehensible since his orgins were in Clapham Sect evangelicalism.

822 *the good-night to Don Basilio*: 'Buona sera, mio signore' from Rossini's *The Barber of Seville* (1816).

826 VIGNETTE: Adam (sketchily visible at the side) about to pluck the forbidden fruit (according to Genesis, he received it from Eve).

827 *Roseleaves, that charming annual edited by Lady Violet Lebas*: 'L.E.L' (i.e. Letetia Elizabeth Landon, 1802–38), on whom Lady Violet Lebas seems to be based, brought out an annual called *Flowers of Loveliness* in 1838. Thackeray reviewed it for *Fraser's*.

837 *Morgiana . . . with a tambourine*: Morgiana is Ali Baba's helper. See the first vignette in the novel. As then, it is Oct. again and the pantomime season.

839 VIGNETTE: harlequinade—continuing the pantomime motif. As Joan Stevens points out, the design draws on Hogarth's 'Election' series of plates, hinting at developments in Pen's political career.

841 *the Edinburgh Review had once scarcely got an admission*: because it was a Whig organ. Founded in 1802, it was the tamest of journals by the 1830s.

846 (1004) *châtelaine*: a girdle worn by women, on which such household items as keys might hang. *Punch* had many châtelaine jokes in 1849, showing ladies, for instance, with saucepans and tea-kettles dangling from their waists.

Ivanhoe: Thackeray's comic continuation of Scott's *Ivanhoe* was published as a Christmas Book, *Rebecca and Rowena*, in Dec. 1850 (this number of *Pendennis* was published in Oct. 1850). Thackeray's Rowena (a blonde, in contrast to the dark beauty Rebecca) is portrayed in a very un-Scott way as a Blanche-like schemer—the implication of the passage here.

857 *Koh-i-noor*: as Harden points out, this fabulous diamond became a crown jewel on the annexation of the Punjab in 1849. 'Cogia Hassan's famous stone' is an allusion to the *Arabian Nights*, where the hero finds a jewel in a fish.

858 *the fractus orbis*: another Horatian allusion, 'if the heavens should crack', *Odes*, 3. 3. 7.

872 *Castlewood House*: the residence of Henry Esmond and his patrons. Thackeray is apparently stirring with ideas for his next novel (set principally in the Queen Anne period).

bagmen: not porters, but 'commercial travellers'.

880 *Mr. Truefitt*: wigmaker, hairdresser, and perfumier in Old Bond Street (see *PP* 216).

887 *the Indian commander-in-chief*: i.e. Wellington, the Great Duke himself.

896 *Hardman*: this sentence is odd. Thackeray seems up to this point in the paragraph to be applauding undemonstrative English manners. Now he apparently satirizes them. It may be that there was an explanatory continuation which Thackeray cut out for length reasons.

Bezonian: echoes Pistol in (*2 Henry IV*, v. iii. 113). Warrington's question is a good one. We are never told what Pen's politics are precisely. Blue Books, mentioned in Pen's reply, are official government reports.

897 *the Morning Post . . . Punch*: the one Conservative, the other Liberal. Thackeray had an influence in tempering the excesses of both journals—the newspaper by satirizing its snobbish deference to the nobility and the magazine by successfully opposing his fellow contributors' (notably Douglas Jerrold's) radicalism. When Thackeray stood for Parliament himself in 1857, it was as an Independent Liberal.

898 *it's like Undine*: as Hawes points out, the precise allusion here is the episode where Undine, having married Huldbrand, is snatched back into the waters of the Danube. The design which Thackeray has been playing with throughout the novel is now clear: Blanche is the dangerous 'siren'; Laura the good water sprite.

902 VIGNETTE: Taken together with the title 'Fiat Justitia' (from 'let justice be done, although the heavens fall') the implication of the design seems plain. But the figure of Justice (alluding to that perched on top of the Old Bailey) is not blindfolded as she should be, nor is her sword raised—justice will not be fully done, we apprehend.

910 *as I've served you*: Wolsey's accusation in *Henry VII*, II. ii. 455–6. As Hawes points out, it is slightly misquoted.

VIGNETTE: Thackeray pictures here his own writing desk and chair in Young Street (a photograph, taken after his death, indicates that he kept them the whole of his authorial career). The design is appropriate as this is the beginning of the last double number, and his work is done. The

design anticpates Luke Fildes's memorial to Dickens, 'The Empty Chair'.

914 *his father's vats*: *Odes*, 2. 14. 25–8.

920 VIGNETTE: as Joan Stevens reads the design it shows Harlequin-Pen and a masked Columbine-Blanche.

not the Prince's wife, but Claude Melnotte's the beggar's: as Harden points out, the allusion is to that part of Bulwer-Lytton's play *The Lady of Lyons* (earlier alluded to in the Fanny Bolton episode) where the heroine Pauline is disabused of the misconception that her husband Claude is a prince (he is, in fact, the gardener's son). Alnaschar, mentioned above, is the character in the *Arabian Nights* who builds castles in the air.

the death of poor Shandon: this has happened on the unnarrated edge of the novel. Maginn died in conditions of extreme destitution in 1842. Thackeray refused to contribute to a stone, saying he had provided enough bread during the editor's life.

925 *old Cos's leg*: as Shillingsburg points out, Sam is apparently not telling the strict truth here. Costigan in the episode alluded to (p. 849) has a completely mended leg and is able to rush up a flight of stairs. Shillingsburg suggests 'Huxter may still have needed Cos's leg as an excuse to visit Fanny' (pp. 383–4).

928 *penny-a-lining for the Gent's Magazine*: Thackeray's last hit in the 'Dignity of Literature' controversy. Early in his career Dr Johnson was a friend of Edward Cave, the editor of the *Gentleman's Magazine*, and a regular contributor during an impecunious period of his life.

932 VIGNETTE: refers back to the vignette of the preceding chapter. Now unmasked, Columbine (Blanche) gives herself to the clown (Foker) rather than Harlequin (Pen) who pines in the background.

944 *I hope your friend is better, who was took ill in Shepherd's Inn, ma'am*: who does Fanny mean? Helen?

945 *We have got our bill, sir*: the two great waves of railway expansion in the 1830s and 1840s were financed by private speculators. But companies required the permission of parliamentary committees to go ahead with the construction of a line. This permission is what Huxter refers to here.

951 VIGNETTE: the maid has a warming pan—it is the last chapter and bedtime. The design reflects that of Morgiana with her tambourine in Ch. 1.

961 *Armida*: a Circe-like sorceress in Tasso's *Jerusalem Delivered.*

964 *the rowdy*: slang, the cash.

965 *Master Frank . . . burst into a loud cry*: see note to p. 560.

972 *the commendatore*: the vengeful father who rises from the grave to carry Don Juan off to hell in Mozart's *Don Giovanni.*

975 *the bridge in Pezawro*: see p. 152. In Sheridan's play Rolla, to save Cora's child from Pizarro, tears from the rock the tree supporting a narrow bridge over a cataract. He then dies, returning the child to its grateful parents.

976 *Alcide de Mirobo*: the cook has risen in the world. The 'Mountain' in French politics indicates an ultra-revolutionary affiliation.

977 *a man and a brother*: a wry allusion to the Abolitionists' motto: 'Am I not a Man and a Brother?'